The Big Book of

ROGUES AND VILLAINS

ALSO EDITED BY OTTO PENZLER

The Big Book of Jack the Ripper

The Big Book of Sherlock Holmes Stories

The Black Lizard Big Book of Locked-Room Mysteries

The Big Book of Christmas Mysteries

The Big Book of Ghost Stories

Zombies! Zombies! Zombies!

The Big Book of Adventure Stories

The Vampire Archives

Agents of Treachery

Bloodsuckers

Fangs

Coffins

The Black Lizard Big Book of Black Mask *Stories*

The Black Lizard Big Book of Pulps

The Big Book of ROGUES *and* VILLAINS

Edited and with an Introduction by

Otto Penzler

Vintage Crime/Black Lizard
Vintage Books
A Division of Penguin Random House LLC
New York

A VINTAGE CRIME/BLACK LIZARD ORIGINAL, OCTOBER 2017

 Published in the United States by Vintage Books, a division of Penguin Random House LLC, New York, and distributed in Canada by Random House of Canada, a division of Penguin Random House Canada Limited, Toronto.

The Cataloging-in-Publication data is on file at the Library of Congress.

Vintage Crime/Black Lizard Trade Paperback ISBN: 978-0-525-43248-7
eBook ISBN: 978-0-525-43249-4

Book design by Anna B. Knighton

www.blacklizardcrime.com

Printed in the United States of America
10 9 8 7 6 5 4 3 2 1

For Andrew Klavan

My wise, hilarious, and trusted friend and confidant—

sometimes roguish but never villainous

CONTENTS

EARLY TWENTIETH-CENTURY AMERICANS

BETWEEN THE WORLD WARS

THE PULP ERA

POST-WORLD WAR II

THE MODERNS

INTRODUCTION

MYSTERY FICTION encompasses a broad spectrum of subgenres, although it is common for casual aficionados to focus on the detective story as the only "true" mystery. As I have often defined it (and, quite naturally, I regard it as a good and fair definition), a mystery is any work of prose fiction in which a crime or the threat of a crime is central to the theme or plot.

On a football field, the pure detective story may go from the end zone to the twenty-five-yard line. The crime story, in which the central figure is a criminal of some kind, whether rogue or villain (and I'll get to that shortly), may move the ball another twenty yards. The novel of suspense, which includes women or children in jeopardy, the everyday gone wrong, as well as tales of psychological unease and irrational behavior, whether of sociopathy or fear, will produce a long gain well past midfield, and espionage/international intrigue will cross the goal line. The killing of a large number of people is, of course, part of the same horrific game as the killing of an individual.

There are numerous sub-subgenres (historical mysteries, police procedurals, comedies, etc.) but they fall within the prime subgenres, many of which also overlap: all forms may (one might say *should*) create suspense, spies may work as detectives to catch moles, psychopaths tend to be criminals, and their actions may well create suspense and a detective is probably hunting them, so the lines blur.

The first legitimate mystery anthology, the anonymously edited *The Long Arm and Other Detective Tales*, was released in 1895. In the nearly century-and-a-quarter since, the preponderance of anthologies published have featured detectives as the central characters. This collection has reversed that common practice to focus on criminals. The title, *The Big Book of Rogues and Villains*, very specifically divides the protagonists into two groups, mostly quite different from each other, although those lines also blur from time to time.

Roguery must be distinguished from villainy. The latter is the creature of evil and malice, if not of outright pathology. It is bad behavior carried to an unpleasant extreme—generally murder. The former tends not to be vicious, prefers no serious physical injury to others, and defines itself as rascality soaked in humor or explained as the result of an unfortunate social environment. Again, the lines may blur from time to time, as a rogue may cause severe hardship or fear in others, while the villain may have a tender heart for a dog or a child, even if he has murdered someone.

While we may normally be able to easily perceive the distinction between roguery and villainy, the contrast may hinge less upon the venality or atrocity of the deed perpetrated than upon the character's and the author's point of view.

The typical crime of the rogue is theft, whether by burglary, swindle, forgery, blackmail, or other physically nonviolent transgressions. If his escapades lead to serious physical violence, that action will generally end his career as a rascal, and place him into the category of villain. Most rogues prefer to win by guile or dexterity that which others have earned by labor or inheritance. They may create a phony business with worthless stock, forge a will or a check, cheat at cards, scheme for marriage to an heiress, crack a safe in the dark of night, or replace a genuine Old Master with a fake. History and literature have shown there is no end to the nefarious schemes that the amoral mind is capable of devising.

The typical crime of the villain is murder, for which there is seldom an acceptable excuse. Although one of the protagonists in this book excuses his action by saying, "He needed killing," not everyone would agree. Still, there are myriad reasons to not only excuse killing but applaud it. Not all killing, it may be said, is murder. Self-defense is the easiest to justify; with other examples of taking a human life, there are often two sides vehemently opposed to each other. The most frequently posited challenge in such disagreements is: "Given the chance to go back in time, would you kill [pick your *real* villain—Hitler, Stalin, Mao, Idi Amin—it's a long list] given the opportunity?" And would it make you a villain if you did?

I'm in danger of asking next how many angels could dance around the head of a pin, while this large gathering of fictional rogues and villains is designed merely to give pleasure. It's a giant shelf-filler of what was once known as escapist fiction, before the term fell into disfavor. Is any fiction not escapist?

This big book is thoughtfully but impossibly divided into sections, though as I compiled the table of contents I realized that there are many stories that easily could fall into more than one category, so please don't take the divisions too seriously.

The heyday of the gentleman thief was the end of the Victorian era and the Edwardian era, and many of the stories have a similarity that's hard to avoid with a book of this kind. The crooks often have good standing in the community and they dress well. It's a game to them, even if a dangerous one, and they carry off their roles with insouciance and verve. Many of them are brilliant and have nerves of steel. They are seemingly infallible, rarely getting caught, but, if they do, they always find a way out through their wit, a bogus alibi, or a flummoxed witness.

As a grammatical aside, I've been using the pronoun "he" because "they" is just flat-out wrong and "he or she" is cumbersome, so no offense to anybody. But women have their roles here, too, and you will undoubtedly find them as charming as their "gangs" do. You will find Fidelity Dove and Four Square Jane very similar, but there was never a thought of omitting either. Almost all the female rogues (and villains) are young and beautiful—all the better to fool their victims as well as the police.

Other similarities of style and performance occur in the stories about the morally challenged lawyers Randolph Mason and Ehrengraf, the adventures of hit men Quarry and Keller, the modus operandi of con men Wallingford and Colonel Clay, the conscienceless actions of "Yellow Peril" monsters Quong Lung and Fu Manchu, and the rogues of Erle Stanley Gardner. Then again, there are not many differences between the methods of such iconic detectives as Philip Marlowe, Sam Spade, and Lew Archer.

What matters is how creatively and beautifully the authors tell the stories.

The genre has its rules and restrictions, just as symphonies and sonnets have theirs. One raspberry has its similarities to another, but the point is not to seek a major variation, merely to enjoy it. I hope you enjoy these stories and their variations.

And remember: Crime may pay in fiction but it's not a good choice in real life. Sherlock Holmes is still alive and will catch you!

—*Otto Penzler*

THE VICTORIANS

Villain: Madame Katherine Koluchy

At the Edge of the Crater

L. T. MEADE & ROBERT EUSTACE

ELIZABETH THOMASINA MEADE SMITH (1844–1914), nom de plume Lillie Thomas Meade, wrote numerous volumes of detective fiction, several of which are historically important. *Stories from the Diary of a Doctor* (1894; second series 1896), written in collaboration with Dr. Edgar Beaumont (pseudonym Dr. Clifford Halifax), is the first series of medical mysteries published in England. Other memorable books by Meade include *A Master of Mysteries* (1898), *The Gold Star Line* (1899), and *The Sanctuary Club* (1900), the last featuring an unusual health club in which a series of murders is committed by apparently supernatural means; all three were written in collaboration with Dr. Eustace Robert Barton (18??–1943), writing as Robert Eustace. Another notable work was *The Sorceress of the Strand* (1903), in which Madame Sara, an utterly sinister villainess, specializes in murder.

The Brotherhood of the Seven Kings (1899), also a collaborative effort with Eustace, is the first series of stories about a female crook. The thoroughly evil leader of an Italian criminal organization, the dazzlingly beautiful and brilliant Madame Koluchy matches wits with Norman Head, a reclusive philosopher who had once joined her gang. The volume was selected by Ellery Queen for *Queen's Quorum* as one of the one hundred and six most important collections of mystery short stories. Curiously, only Meade's name appears on the front cover and spine of the book, though Eustace is given credit as the cowriter on the title page.

Robert Eustace is known mainly for his collaborations with other writers. In addition to working with Meade, he cowrote several stories with Edgar Jepson; a novel with the once-popular mystery writer Gertrude Warden, *The Stolen Pearl: A Romance of London* (1903); and, most famously, a novel with Dorothy L. Sayers, *The Documents in the Case* (1930).

"At the Edge of the Crater" was first published in *The Brotherhood of the Seven Kings* (London, Ward, Lock, 1899).

AT THE EDGE OF THE CRATER

L. T. Meade & Robert Eustace

IT WAS IN THE YEAR 1894 that the first of the remarkable events which I am about to give to the world occurred. They found me something of a philosopher and a recluse, having, as I thought, lived my life and done with the active part of existence. It is true that I was young, not more than thirty-five years of age, but in the ghastly past I had committed a supreme error, and because of that paralyzing experience I had left the bustling world and found my solace in the scientist's laboratory and the philosopher's study.

Ten years before these stories begin, when in Naples studying biology, I fell a victim to the wiles and fascinations of a beautiful Italian. A scientist of no mean attainments herself, with beauty beyond that of ordinary mortals, she had appealed not only to my head, but also to my heart. Dazzled by her beauty and intellect, she led me where she would. Her aims and ambitions, which in the false glamour she threw over them I thought the loftiest in the world, became also mine. She introduced me to the men of her set—I was quickly in the toils, and on a night never to be forgotten, I took part in a grotesque and horrible ceremony, and became a member of her Brotherhood.

It was called the Brotherhood of the Seven Kings, and dated its origin from one of the secret societies of the Middle Ages. In my first enthusiasm it seemed to me to embrace all the principles of true liberty. Katherine was its chief and queen. Almost immediately after my initiation, however, I made an appalling discovery. Suspicion pointed to the beautiful Italian as the instigator, if not the author, of a most terrible crime. None of the details could be brought home to her, but there was little doubt that she was its moving spring. Loving her passionately as I then did, I tried to close my intellect against the all too conclusive evidence of her guilt. For a time I succeeded, but when I was ordered myself to take part in a transaction both dishonourable and treacherous, my eyes were opened. Horror seized me, and I fled to England to place myself under the protection of its laws.

Ten years went by, and the past was beginning to fade. It was destined to be recalled to me with startling vividness.

When a young man at Cambridge I had studied physiology, but never qualified myself as a doctor, having independent means; but in my laboratory in the vicinity of Regent's Park I worked at biology and physiology for the pure love of these absorbing sciences.

I was busily engaged on the afternoon of the 3rd of August, 1894, when Mrs. Kenyon, an old friend, called to see me. She was shown into my study, and I went to her there. Mrs. Kenyon was a widow, but her son, a lad of about twelve years of age, had, owing to the unexpected death of a relative, just come in for a large fortune and a title. She took the seat I offered her.

"It is too bad of you, Norman," she said; "it is months since you have been near me. Do you intend to forget your old friends?"

"I hope you will forgive me," I answered; "you know how busy I always am."

"You work too hard," she replied. "Why a man with your brains and opportunities for enjoying life wishes to shut himself up in the way you do, I cannot imagine."

"I am quite happy as I am, Mrs. Kenyon," I replied; "why, therefore, should I change? By the way, how is Cecil?"

"I have come here to speak about him. You know, of course, the wonderful change in his fortunes?"

"Yes," I answered.

"He has succeeded to the Kairn property, and is now Lord Kairn. There is a large rent-roll and considerable estates. You know, Norman, that Cecil has always been a most delicate boy."

"I hoped you were about to tell me that he was stronger," I replied.

"He is, and I will explain how in a moment. His life is a most important one. As Lord Kairn much is expected of him. He has not only, under the providence of God, to live, but by that one little life he has to keep a man of exceedingly bad character out of a great property. I allude to Hugh Doncaster. Were Cecil to die, Hugh would be Lord Kairn. You have already doubtless heard of his character?"

"I know the man well by repute," I said.

"I thought you did. His disappointment and rage at Cecil succeeding to the title are almost beyond bounds. Rumours of his malevolent feelings towards the child have already reached me. I am told that he is now in London, but his life, like yours, is more or less mysterious. I thought it just possible, Norman, that you, as an old friend, might be able to get me some particulars with regard to his whereabouts."

"Why do you want to know?" I asked.

"I feel a strange uneasiness about him; something which I cannot account for. Of course, in these enlightened days he would not attempt the child's life, but I should be more comfortable if I were assured that he were nowhere in Cecil's vicinity."

"But the man can do nothing to your boy!" I said. "Of course, I will find out what I can, but——"

Mrs. Kenyon interrupted me.

"Thank you. It is a relief to know that you will help me. Of course, there is no real danger; but I am a widow, and Cecil is only a child. Now, I must tell you about his health. He is almost quite well. The most marvellous resurrection has taken place. For the last two months he has been under the care of that extraordinary woman, Mme. Koluchy. She has worked miracles in his case, and now to complete the cure she is sending him to the Mediterranean. He sails tomorrow night under the care of Dr. Fietta. I cannot bear parting with him, but it is for his good, and Mme. Koluchy insists that a sea voyage is indispensable."

"But won't you accompany him?" I asked.

"I am sorry to say that is impossible. My eldest girl, Ethel, is about to be married, and I cannot leave her on the eve of her wedding; but Cecil will be in good hands. Dr. Fietta is a capital fellow—I have every faith in him."

"Where are they going?"

"To Cairo. They sail tomorrow night in the *Hydaspes*."

"Cairo is a fearfully hot place at this time of year. Are you quite sure that it is wise to send a delicate lad like Cecil there in August?"

"Oh, he will not stay. He sails for the sake of the voyage, and will come back by the return boat. The voyage is, according to Mme. Koluchy, to complete the cure. That marvellous woman has succeeded where the medical profession gave little hope. You have heard of her, of course?"

"I am sick of her very name," I replied; "one hears it everywhere. She has bewitched London with her impostures and quackery."

"There is no quackery about her, Norman. I believe her to be the cleverest woman in England. There are authentic accounts of her wonderful cures which cannot be contradicted. There are even rumours that she is able to restore youth and beauty by her arts. The whole of society is at her feet, and it is whispered that even Royalty are among her patients. Of course, her fees are enormous, but look at the results! Have you ever met her?"

"Never. Where does she come from? Who is she?"

"She is an Italian, but she speaks English perfectly. She has taken a house which is a perfect palace in Welbeck Street."

"And who is Dr. Fietta?"

"A medical man who assists Madame in her treatments. I have just seen him. He is charming, and devoted to Cecil. Five o'clock! I had no idea it was so late. I must be going. You will let me know when you hear any news of Mr. Doncaster? Come and see me soon."

I accompanied my visitor to the door, and then, returning to my study, sat down to resume the work I had been engaged in when I was interrupted.

But Mrs. Kenyon's visit had made me restless. I knew Hugh Doncaster's character well. Reports of his evil ways now and then agitated society, but the man had hitherto escaped the stern arm of justice. Of course, there could be no real foundation for Mrs. Kenyon's fears, but I felt that I could sympathize with her. The child was young and delicate; if Doncaster could injure him without discovery, he would not scruple to do so. As I thought over these things, a vague sensation of coming trouble possessed me. I hastily got into my evening dress, and having dined at my club, found myself at half-past ten in a drawing-room in Grosvenor Square. As I passed on into the reception-rooms, having exchanged a few words with my hostess, I came across Dufrayer, a lawyer, and a special friend of mine. We got into conversation. As we talked, and my eyes glanced idly round the groups of smartly dressed people, I noticed where a crowd of men were clustering round and paying homage to a stately woman at the farther end of the room. A diamond star flashed in her dusky hair. On her neck and arms diamonds also glittered. She had an upright bearing and a regal appearance. Her rosy lips were smiling. The marked intelligence and power of her face could not fail to arrest attention, even in the most casual observer. At the first glance I felt that I had seen her before, but could not tell when or where.

"Who is that woman?" I asked of my companion.

"My dear fellow," he replied, with an amused smile, "don't you know? That is the great Mme. Koluchy, the rage of the season, the great specialist, the great consultant. London is mad about her. She has only been here ten minutes, and look, she is going already. They say she has a dozen engagements every night."

Mme. Koluchy began to move towards the door, and, anxious to get a nearer view, I also passed rapidly through the throng. I reached the head of the stairs before she did, and as she went by looked her full in the face. Her eyes met mine. Their dark depths seemed to read me through. She half smiled, half paused as if to speak, changed her mind, made a stately inclination of her queenly head, and went slowly downstairs. For a moment I stood still, there was a ringing in my ears, and my heart was beating to suffocation. Then I hastily followed her. When I reached the pavement Mme. Koluchy's carriage stopped the way. She did not notice me, but I was able to observe her. She was bending out and talking eagerly to someone. The following words fell on my ear:

"It is all right. They sail tomorrow evening."

The man to whom she spoke made a reply which I could not catch, but I had seen his face. He was Hugh Doncaster.

Mme. Koluchy's carriage rolled away, and I

hailed a hansom. In supreme moments we think rapidly. I thought quickly then.

"Where to?" asked the driver.

"No. 140, Earl's Terrace, Kensington," I called out. I sat back as I spoke. The horror of past memories was almost paralyzing me, but I quickly pulled myself together. I knew that I must act, and act quickly. I had just seen the Head of the Brotherhood of the Seven Kings. Mme. Koluchy, changed in much since I last saw her, was the woman who had wrecked my heart and life ten years ago in Naples.

With my knowledge of the past, I was well aware that where this woman appeared victims fell. Her present victim was a child. I must save that child, even if my own life were the penalty. She had ordered the boy abroad. He was to sail tomorrow with an emissary of hers. She was in league with Doncaster. If she could get rid of the boy, Doncaster would doubtless pay her a fabulous sum. For the working of her she above all things wanted money. Yes, without doubt the lad's life was in the gravest danger, and I had not a moment to lose. The first thing was to communicate with the mother, and if possible put a stop to the intended voyage.

I arrived at the house, flung open the doors of the hansom, and ran up the steps. Here unexpected news awaited me. The servant who answered my summons said that Mrs. Kenyon had started for Scotland by the night mail—she had received a telegram announcing the serious illness of her eldest girl. On getting it she had started for the north, but would not reach her destination until the following evening.

"Is Lord Kairn in?" I asked.

"No, sir," was the reply. "My mistress did not like to leave him here alone, and he has been sent over to Mme. Koluchy's, 100, Welbeck Street. Perhaps you are not aware, sir, that his lordship sails tomorrow evening for Cairo?"

"Yes, I know all about that," I replied, "and now, if you will give me your mistress's address, I shall be much obliged to you."

The man supplied it. I entered my hansom again. For a moment it occurred to me that I would send a telegram to intercept Mrs. Kenyon on her rapid journey north, but I finally made up my mind not to do so. The boy was already in the enemy's hands, and I felt sure that I could now only rescue him by guile. I returned home, having already made up my mind how to act. I would accompany Cecil and Dr. Fietta to Cairo.

At eleven o'clock on the following morning I had taken my berth in the *Hydaspes*, and at nine that evening was on board. I caught a momentary glimpse of young Lord Kairn and his attendant, but in order to avoid explanations kept out of their way. It was not until the following morning, when the steamer was well down Channel, that I made my appearance on deck, where I at once saw the boy sitting at the stern in a chair. Beside him was a lean, middle-aged man wearing a pair of *pince-nez*. He looked every inch a foreigner, with his pointed beard, waxed moustache, and deep-set, beady eyes. As I sauntered across the deck to where they were sitting, Lord Kairn looked up and instantly recognised me.

"Mr. Head!" he exclaimed, jumping from his chair. "You here? I am very glad to see you."

"I am on my way to Cairo, on business," I said, shaking the boy warmly by the hand.

"To Cairo? Why, that is where we are going; but you never told mother you were coming, and she saw you the day before yesterday. It was such a pity that mother had to rush off to Scotland so suddenly; but last night, just before we sailed, there came a telegram telling us that Ethel was better. As mother had to go away, I went to Mme. Koluchy's for the night. I love going there. She has a lovely house, and she is so delightful herself. And this is Dr. Fietta, who has come with me." As the boy added these words Dr. Fietta came forward and peered at me through his *pince-nez*. I bowed, and he returned my salutation.

"This is an extraordinary coincidence, Dr. Fietta!" I exclaimed. "Cecil Kenyon happens to be the son of one of my greatest friends. I am glad to see him looking so well. Whatever Mme. Koluchy's treatment has been, it has had a marvellous effect. I am told that you are fortunate enough to be the participator in her wonderful secrets and cures."

"I have the honour of assisting Mme. Koluchy," he replied, with a strong foreign accent; "but may I take the liberty of inquiring who gave you the information about myself?"

"It was Mrs. Kenyon," I answered. "She told me all about you the other day."

"She knew, then, that you were going to be a fellow-passenger of her son's?"

"No, for I did not know myself. An urgent telegram calling me to Egypt arrived that evening, and I only booked my passage yesterday. I am fortunate in having the honour of meeting so distinguished a savant as yourself. I have heard much about Mme. Koluchy's marvellous occult powers, but I suppose the secrets of her success are very jealously guarded. The profession, of course, pooh-pooh her, I know, but if one may credit all one hears, she possesses remedies undreamt-of in their philosophy."

"It is quite true, Mr. Head. As a medical man myself, I can vouch for her capacity, and, unfettered by English professional scrupulousness, I appreciate it. Mme. Koluchy and I are proud of our young friend here, and hope that the voyage will complete his cure, and fit him for the high position he is destined to occupy."

The voyage flew by. Fietta was an intelligent man, and his scientific attainments were considerable. But for my knowledge of the terrible past my fears might have slumbered, but as it was they were always present with me, and the moment all too quickly arrived when suspicion was to be plunged into certainty.

On the day before we were due at Malta, the wind sprang up and we got into a choppy sea. When I had finished breakfast I went to Cecil's cabin to see how he was. He was just getting up, and looked pale and unwell.

"There is a nasty sea on," I said, "but the captain says we shall be out of it in an hour or so."

"I hope we shall," he answered, "for it makes me feel squeamish, but I daresay I shall be all right when I get on deck. Dr. Fietta has given me something to stop the sickness, but it has not had much effect."

"I do not know anything that really stops sea-sickness," I answered; "but what has he done?"

"Oh: a curious thing, Mr. Head. He pricked my arm with a needle on a syringe, and squirted something in. He says it is a certain cure for sea-sickness. Look," said the child, baring his arm, "that is where he did it."

I examined the mark closely. It had evidently been made with a hypodermic injection needle.

"Did Dr. Fietta tell you what he put into your arm?" I asked.

"Yes, he said it was morphia."

"Where does he keep his needle?"

"In his trunk there under his bunk. I shall be dressed directly, and will come on deck."

I left the cabin and went up the companion. The doctor was pacing to and fro on the hurricane-deck. I approached him.

"Your charge has not been well," I said, "I have just seen him. He tells me you have given him a hypodermic of morphia."

He turned round and gave me a quick glance of uneasy fear.

"Did Lord Kairn tell you so?"

"Yes."

"Well, Mr. Head, it is the very best cure for sea-sickness. I have found it most efficacious."

"Do you think it wise to give a child morphia?" I asked.

"I do not discuss my treatment with an unqualified man," he replied brusquely, turning away as he spoke. I looked after him, and as he disappeared down the deck my fears became certainties. I determined, come what would, to find out what he had given the boy. I knew only too well the infinite possibilities of that dangerous little instrument, a hypodermic syringe.

As the day wore on the sea moderated, and at five o'clock it was quite calm again, a welcome change to the passengers, who, with the permission of the captain, had arranged to give a dance that evening on deck. The occasion was one when ordinary scruples must fade out of sight. Honour in such a mission as I had set myself must give place to the watchful zeal of the detective. I was determined to take advantage of the dance to explore Dr. Fietta's cabin. The doctor was fond of dancing, and as soon as I saw that he and Lord Kairn were well engaged, I descended the companion, and went to their cabin. I switched on the electric light, and, dragging the trunk from beneath the bunk, hastily opened it. It was unlocked and only secured by straps. I ran my hand rapidly through the contents, which were chiefly clothes, but tucked in one corner I found a case, and, pulling it out, opened it. Inside lay the delicate little hypodermic syringe which I had come in search of.

I hurried up to the light and examined it. Smeared round the inside of the glass, and adhering to the bottom of the little plunger, was a whitish, gelatinous-looking substance. This was no ordinary hypodermic solution. It was half-liquefied gelatine such as I knew so well as the medium for the cultivation of micro-organisms. For a moment I felt half-stunned. What infernal culture might it not contain?

Time was flying, and at any moment I might be discovered. I hastily slipped the syringe into my pocket, and closing the trunk, replaced it, and, switching off the electric light, returned to the deck. My temples were throbbing, and it was with difficulty I could keep my self-control. I made up my mind quickly. Fietta would of course miss the syringe, but the chances were that he would not do so that night. As yet there was nothing apparently the matter with the boy, but might there not be flowing through his veins some poisonous germs of disease, which only required a period of incubation for their development?

At daybreak the boat would arrive at Malta. I would go on shore at once, call upon some medical man, and lay the case before him in confidence, in the hope of his having the things I should need in order to examine the contents of the syringe. If I found any organisms, I would take the law into my own hands, and carry the boy back to England by the next boat.

No sleep visited me that night, and I lay tossing to and fro in my bunk longing for daylight. At 6 A.M. I heard the engine-bell ring, and the screw suddenly slow down to half-speed. I leapt up and went on deck. I could see the outline of the rock-bound fortress and the lighthouse of St. Elmo looming more vividly every moment. As soon as we were at anchor and the gangway down, I hailed one of the little green boats and told the men to row me to the shore. I drove at once to the Grand Hotel in the Strada Reale, and asked the Italian guide the address of a medical man. He gave me the address of an English doctor who lived close by, and I went there at once to see him. It was now seven o'clock, and I found him up. I made my apologies for the early hour of my visit, put the whole matter before him, and produced the syringe. For a moment he was inclined to take my story with incredulity, but by degrees he became interested, and ended by inviting me to breakfast with him. After the meal we repaired to his consulting-room to make our investigations. He brought out his microscope, which I saw, to my delight, was of the latest design, and I set to work at once, while he watched me with evident interest. At last the crucial moment came, and I bent over the instrument and adjusted the focus on my preparation. My suspicions were only too well confirmed by which I had extracted what I saw. The substance from the syringe was a mass of micro-organisms, but of what nature I did not know. I had never seen any quite like them before. I drew back.

"I wish you would look at this," I said. "You tell me you have devoted considerable attention to bacteriology. Please tell me what you see."

Dr. Benson applied his eye to the instrument, regulating the focus for a few moments in silence, then he raised his head, and looked at me with a curious expression.

"Where did this culture come from?" he asked.

"From London, I presume," I answered.

"It is extraordinary," he said, with emphasis, "but there is no doubt whatever that these organisms are the specific germs of the very disease I have studied here so assiduously; they are the micrococci of Mediterranean fever, the minute round or oval bacteria. They are absolutely characteristic."

I jumped to my feet.

"Is that so?" I cried. The diabolical nature of the plot was only too plain. These germs injected into a patient would produce a fever which only occurs in the Mediterranean. The fact that the boy had been in the Mediterranean even for a short time would be a complete blind as to the way in which they obtained access to the body, as every one would think the disease occurred from natural causes.

"How long is the period of incubation?" I asked.

"About ten days," replied Dr. Benson.

I extended my hand.

"You have done me an invaluable service," I said.

"I may possibly be able to do you a still further service," was his reply. "I have made Mediterranean fever the study of my life, and have, I believe, discovered an antitoxin for it. I have tried my discovery on the patients of the naval hospital with excellent results. The local disturbance is slight, and I have never found bad symptoms follow the treatment. If you will bring the boy to me I will administer the antidote without delay."

I considered for a moment, then I said: "My position is a terrible one, and I am inclined to accept your proposition. Under the circumstances it is the only chance."

"It is," repeated Dr. Benson. "I shall be at your service whenever you need me."

I bade him good-bye and quickly left the house.

It was now ten o'clock. My first object was to find Dr. Fietta, to speak to him boldly, and take the boy away by main force if necessary. I rushed back to the Grand Hotel, where I learned that a boy and a man, answering to the description of Dr. Fietta and Cecil, had breakfasted there, but had gone out again immediately afterwards. The *Hydaspes* I knew was to coal, and would not leave Malta before one o'clock. My only chance, therefore, was to catch them as they came on board. Until then I could do nothing. At twelve o'clock I went down to the quay and took a boat to the *Hydaspes*. Seeing no sign of Fietta and the boy on deck, I made my way at once to Lord Kairn's cabin. The door was open and the place in confusion—every vestige of baggage had disappeared. Absolutely at a loss to divine the cause of this unexpected discovery, I pressed the electric bell. In a moment a steward appeared.

"Has Lord Kairn left the ship?" I asked, my heart beating fast.

"I believe so, sir," replied the man. "I had orders to pack the luggage and send it on shore. It went about an hour ago."

I waited to hear no more. Rushing to my cabin, I began flinging my things pell-mell into my portmanteau. I was full of apprehension at this sudden move of Dr. Fietta's. Calling a steward who was passing to help me, I got my things on deck, and in a few moments had them in a boat and was making rapidly for the shore. I drove back at once to the Grand Hotel in the Strada Reale.

"Did the gentleman who came here to-day from the *Hydaspes*, accompanied by a little boy, engage rooms for the night?" I asked of the proprietor in the bureau at the top of the stairs.

"No, sir," answered the man; "they breakfasted here, but did not return. I think they said they were going to the gardens of San Antonio."

For a minute or two I paced the hall in uncontrollable excitement. I was completely at a loss what step to take next. Then suddenly an idea struck me. I hurried down the steps and made my way to Cook's office.

"A gentleman of that description took two tickets for Naples by the *Spartivento*, a Rupertino boat, two hours ago," said the clerk, in answer to my inquiries. "She has started by now," he continued, glancing up at the clock.

"To Naples?" I cried. A sickening fear seized me. The very name of the hated place struck me like a poisoned weapon.

"Is it too late to catch her?" I cried.

"Yes, sir, she has gone."

"Then what is the quickest route by which I can reach Naples?"

"You can go by the *Gingra*, a P. & O. boat, tonight to Brindisi, and then overland. That is the quickest way now."

I at once took my passage and left the office. There was not the least doubt what had occurred. Dr. Fietta had missed his syringe, and in consequence had immediately altered his plans. He was now taking the lad to the very fountain-head of the Brotherhood, where other means if necessary would be employed to put an end to his life.

It was nine o'clock in the evening, three days later, when, from the window of the railway carriage, I caught my first glimpse of the glow on the summit of Vesuvius. During the journey I had decided on my line of action. Leaving my luggage in the cloak-room I entered a carriage and began to visit hotel after hotel. For a long time I had no success. It was past eleven o'clock that night when, weary and heart-sick, I drew up at the Hotel Londres. I went to the concierge with my usual question, expecting the invariable reply, but a glow of relief swept over me when the man said:

"Dr. Fietta is out, sir, but the young man is in. He is in bed—will you call tomorrow? What name shall I say?"

"I shall stay here," I answered; "let me have a room at once, and have my bag taken to it. What is the number of Lord Kairn's room?"

"Number forty-six. But he will be asleep, sir; you cannot see him now."

I made no answer, but going quickly upstairs, I found the boy's room. I knocked; there was no reply, I turned the handle and entered. All was dark. Striking a match I looked round. In a white bed at the farther end lay the child. I went up and bent softly over him. He was lying with one hand beneath his cheek. He looked worn and tired, and now and then moaned as if in trouble. When I touched him lightly on the shoulder he started up and opened his eyes. A dazed expression of surprise swept over his face; then with an eager cry he stretched out both his hands and clasped one of mine.

"I am so glad to see you," he said. "Dr. Fietta told me you were angry—that I had offended you. I very nearly cried when I missed you that morning at Malta, and Dr. Fietta said I should never see you anymore. I don't like him—I am afraid of him. Have you come to take me home?" As he spoke he glanced eagerly round in the direction of the door, clutching my hand still tighter as he did so.

"Yes, I shall take you home, Cecil. I have come for the purpose," I answered; "but are you quite well?"

"That's just it; I am not. I have awful dreams at night. Oh, I am so glad you have come back and you are not angry. Did you say you were really going to take me home?"

"Tomorrow, if you like."

"Please do. I am—stoop down, I want to whisper to you—I am dreadfully afraid of Dr. Fietta."

"What is your reason?" I asked.

"There is no reason," answered the child, "but somehow I dread him. I have done so ever since you left us at Malta. Once I woke in the middle of the night and he was bending over me—he had such a queer look on his face, and he used that syringe again. He was putting something into my arm—he told me it was morphia. I did not want him to do it, for I thought you would rather he didn't. I wish mother had sent me away with you. I am afraid of him; yes, I am afraid of him."

"Now that I have come, everything will be right," I said.

"And you will take me home tomorrow?"

"Certainly."

"But I should like to see Vesuvius first. Now that we are here it seems a pity that I should not see it. Can you take me to Vesuvius tomorrow morning, and home in the evening, and will you explain to Dr. Fietta?"

"I will explain everything. Now go to sleep. I am in the house, and you have nothing whatever to fear."

"I am very glad you have come," he said wearily. He flung himself back on his pillow; the exhausted look was very manifest on his small, childish face. I left the room, shutting the door softly.

To say that my blood boiled can express but little the emotions which ran through my frame—the child was in the hands of a monster. He was in the very clutch of the Brotherhood, whose intention was to destroy his life. I thought for a moment. There was nothing now for it but to see Fietta, tell him that I had discovered his machinations, claim the boy, and take him away by force. I knew that I was treading on dangerous ground. At any moment my own life might be the forfeit for my supposed treachery to the cause whose vows I had so madly taken. Still, if I saved the boy nothing else really mattered.

I went downstairs into the great central hall, interviewed the concierge, who told me that Fietta had returned, asked for the number of his private sitting-room, and, going there, opened the door without knocking. At a writing-table at the farther end sat the doctor. He turned as I entered, and, recognising me, started up with a sudden exclamation. I noticed that his face changed colour, and that his beady eyes flashed all ugly fire. Then, recovering himself, he advanced quietly towards me.

"This is another of your unexpected surprises, Mr. Head," he said with politeness. "You have not, then, gone on to Cairo? You change your plans rapidly."

"Not more so than you do, Dr. Fietta," I replied, watching him as I spoke.

"I was obliged to change my mind," he answered. "I heard in Malta that cholera had broken out in Cairo. I could not therefore take my patient there. May I inquire why I have the honour of this visit? You will excuse my saying so, but this action of yours forces me to suspect that you are following me. Have you a reason?"

He stood with his hands behind him, and a look of furtive vigilance crept into his small eyes.

"This is my reason," I replied. I boldly drew the hypodermic syringe from my pocket as I spoke.

With an inconceivably rapid movement he hurried past me, locked the door, and placed the key in his pocket. As he turned towards me again I saw the glint of a long, bright stiletto which he had drawn and was holding in his right hand, which he kept behind him.

"I see you are armed," I said quietly, "but do not be too hasty. I have a few words to say to you." As I spoke I looked him full in the face, then I dropped my voice.

"I am one of the Brotherhood of the Seven Kings!"

When I uttered these magical words he started back and looked at me with dilated eyes.

"Your proofs instantly, or you are a dead man," he cried hoarsely. Beads of sweat gleamed upon his forehead.

"Put that weapon on the table, give me your right hand, and you shall have the proofs you need," I answered.

He hesitated, then changed the stiletto to his left hand, and gave me his right. I grasped it in the peculiar manner which I had never forgotten, and bent my head close to his. The next moment I had uttered the password of the Brotherhood.

"La Regina," I whispered.

"*E la regina*," he replied, flinging the stiletto on the carpet.

"Ah!" he continued, with an expression of the strongest relief, while he wiped the moisture from his forehead. "This is too wonderful. And now tell me, my friend, what your mission is? I knew you had stolen my syringe, but why did you do it? Why did you not reveal yourself to me before? You are, of course, under the Queen's orders?"

"I am," I answered, "and her orders to me now are to take Lord Kairn home to England overland tomorrow morning."

"Very well. Everything is finished—he will die in one month."

"From Mediterranean fever? But it is not necessarily fatal," I continued.

"That is true. It is not always fatal acquired in the ordinary way, but by our methods it is so."

"Then you have administered more of the micro-organisms since Malta?"

"Yes; I had another syringe in my case, and now nothing can save him. The fever will commence in six days from now."

He paused for a moment or two.

"It is very odd," he went on, "that I should have had no communication. I cannot understand it." A sudden flash of suspicion shot across his dark face. My heart sank as I saw it. It passed, however, the next instant; the man's words were courteous and quiet.

"I of course accede to your proposition," he said: "everything is quite safe. This that I have done can never by any possibility be discovered. Madame is invincible. Have you yet seen Lord Kairn?"

"Yes, and I have told him to be prepared to accompany me home tomorrow."

"Very well."

Dr. Fietta walked across the room, unlocked the door and threw it open.

"Your plans will suit me admirably," he continued. "I shall stay on here for a few days more, as I have some private business to transact. Tonight I shall sleep in peace. Your shadow has been haunting me for the last three days."

I went from Fietta's room to the boy's. He was wide awake and started up when he saw me.

"I have arranged everything, Cecil," I said, "and you are my charge now. I mean to take you to my room to sleep."

"Oh," he answered, "I am glad. Perhaps I shall sleep better in your room. I am not afraid of you—I love you." His eyes, bright with affection, looked into mine. I lifted him into my arms, wrapped his dressing-gown over his shoulders, and conveyed him through the folding-doors, down the corridor, into the room I had secured for myself. There were two beds in the room, and I placed him in one.

"I am so happy," he said, "I love you so much. Will you take me to Vesuvius in the morning, and then home in the evening?"

"I will see about that. Now go to sleep," I answered.

He closed his eyes with a sigh of pleasure. In ten minutes he was sound asleep. I was standing by him when there came a knock at the door. I went to open it. A waiter stood without. He held a salver in his hand. It contained a letter, also a sheet of paper and an envelope stamped with the name of the hotel.

"From the doctor, to be delivered to the signor immediately," was the laconic remark.

Still standing in the doorway, I took the letter from the tray, opened it, and read the following words:

"You have removed the boy and that action arouses my mistrust. I doubt your having received any Communication from Madame. If you wish me to believe that you are a *bona fide* member of the Brotherhood, return the boy to his own sleeping-room, immediately."

I took a pencil out of my pocket and hastily wrote a few words on the sheet of paper, which had been sent for this purpose.

"I retain the boy. You are welcome to draw your own conclusions."

Folding up the paper I slipped it into the envelope, and wetting the gum with my tongue, fastened it together, and handed it to the waiter who withdrew. I re-entered my room and locked the door. To keep the boy was imperative, but there was little doubt that Fietta would now telegraph to Mme. Koluchy (the telegraphic office being open day and night) and find out the trick I was playing upon him. I considered whether I might not remove the boy there and then to another hotel, but decided that such a step would be useless. Once the emissaries of the Brotherhood were put upon my track the case for the child and myself would be all but hopeless.

There was likely to be little sleep for me that night. I paced up and down my lofty room. My thoughts were keen and busy. After a time, however, a strange confusion seized me. One moment I thought of the child, the next of Mme. Koluchy, and then again I found myself pondering some abstruse and comparatively unimportant point in science, which I was perfecting at home. I shook myself free of these thoughts, to walk about again, to pause by the bedside of the child, to listen to his quiet breathing.

Perfect peace reigned over his little face. He had resigned himself to me, his terrors were things of the past, and he was absolutely happy. Then once again that queer confusion of brain returned. I wondered what I was doing, and why I was anxious about the boy. Finally I sank upon the bed at the farther end of the room, for my limbs were tired and weighted with a heavy oppression. I would rest for a moment, but nothing would induce me to close my eyes. So I thought, and flung myself back on my pillow. But the next instant all present things were forgotten in dreamless and heavy slumber.

I awoke long hours afterwards, to find the sunshine flooding the room, the window which led on to the balcony wide open, and Cecil's bed empty. I sprang up with a cry; memory returned with a flash. What had happened? Had Fietta managed to get in by means of the window? I had noticed the balcony outside the window on the previous night. The balcony of the next room was but a few feet distant from mine. It would be easy for anyone to enter there, spring from one balcony to the other, and so obtain access to my room. Doubtless this had been done. Why had I slept? I had firmly resolved to stay awake all night. In an instant I had found the solution. Fietta's letter had been a trap. The envelope which he sent me contained poison on the gum. I had licked it, and so received the fatal soporific. My heart beat wildly. I knew I had not an instant to lose. With hasty strides I went into Fietta's sitting-room: there was no one there; into his bedroom, the door of which was open: it was also empty. I rushed into the hall.

"The gentleman and the little boy went out about half an hour ago," said the concierge, in answer to my inquiries. "They have gone to Vesuvius—a fine day for the trip." The man smiled as he spoke.

My heart almost stopped.

"How did they go?" I asked.

"A carriage, two horses—best way to go."

In a second I was out in the Piazza del Municipio. Hastily selecting a pair-horse carriage out of the group of importunate drivers, I jumped in.

"Vesuvius," I shouted, "as hard as you can go."

The man began to bargain. I thrust a roll of paper-money into his hand. On receiving it he waited no longer, and we were soon dashing at a furious speed along the crowded, ill-paved streets, scattering the pedestrians as we went. Down the Via Roma, and out on to the Santa Lucia Quay, away and away through endless labyrinths of noisome, narrow streets, till at length we got out into the more open country at the base of the burning mountain. Should I be in time to prevent the catastrophe which I dreaded? For I had been up that mountain before, and knew well the horrible danger at the crater's mouth—a slip, a push, and one would never be seen again.

The ascent began, and the exhausted horses were beginning to fail. I leapt out, and giving the driver a sum which I did not wait to count, ran up the winding road of cinders and pumice that curves round beneath the observatory. My breath had failed me, and my heart was beating so hard that I could scarcely speak when I reached the station where one takes ponies to go over the new, rough lava. In answer to my inquiries, Cook's agent told me that Fietta and Cecil had gone on not a quarter of an hour ago.

I shouted my orders, and flinging money right and left, I soon obtained a fleet pony, and was galloping recklessly over the broken lava. Throwing the reins over the pony's head I presently jumped off, and ran up the little, narrow path to the funicular wire-laid railway that takes passengers up the steep cone to the crater.

"Just gone on, sir," said a Cook's official, in answer to my question.

"But I must follow at once," I said excitedly, hurrying towards the little shed.

The man stopped me.

"We don't take single passengers," he answered.

"I will, and must, go alone," I said. "I'll buy

the car, and the railway, and you, and the mountain, if necessary, but go I will. How much do you want to take me alone?"

"One hundred francs," he answered impertinently, little thinking that I would agree to the bargain.

"Done!" I replied.

In astonishment he counted out the notes which I handed to him, and hurried at once into the shed. Here he rang an electric bell to have the car at the top started back, and getting into the empty car, I began to ascend—up, and up, and up. Soon I passed the empty car returning. How slowly we moved! My mouth was parched and dry, and I was in a fever of excitement. The smoke from the crater was close above me in great wreaths. At last we reached the top. I leapt out, and without waiting for a guide, made my way past, and rushed up the active cone, slipping in the shifting, loose, gritty soil. When I reached the top a gale was blowing, and the scenery below, with the Bay and Naples and Sorrento, lay before me, the most magnificent panorama in the world. I had no time to glance at it, but hurried forward past crags of hot rock, from which steam and sulphur were escaping. The wind was taking the huge volumes of smoke over to the farther side of the crater, and I could just catch sight of two figures as the smoke cleared for a moment. The figures were those of Fietta and the boy. They were evidently making a *détour* of the crater, and had just entered the smoke. I heard a guide behind shout something to me in Italian, but I took no notice, and plunged at once into the blinding, suffocating smoke that came belching forth from the crater.

I was now close behind Fietta and the boy. They held their handkerchiefs up to their faces to keep off the choking sulphurous fumes, and had evidently not seen me. Their guide was ahead of them. Fietta was walking slowly; he was farthest away from the crater's mouth. The boy's hand was within his; the boy was nearest to the yawning gulf. A hot and choking blast of smoke blinded me for a moment, and hid the pair from view; the next instant it passed. I saw Fietta suddenly turn, seize the boy, and push him towards the edge. Through the rumbling thunder that came from below I heard a sharp cry of terror, and bounding forward I just caught the lad as he reeled, and hurled him away into safety.

With a yell of baffled rage Fietta dashed through the smoke and flung himself upon me. I moved nimbly aside, and the doctor, carried on by the impetus of his rush, missed his footing in the crumbling ashes and fell headlong down through the reeking smoke and steam into the fathomless, seething cauldron below.

What followed may be told in a few words. That evening I sailed for Malta with the boy. Dr. Benson administered the antitoxin in time, and the child's life was saved. Within a fortnight I brought him back to his mother.

It was reported that Dr. Fietta had gone mad at the edge of the crater, and in an excess of maniacal fury had first tried to destroy the boy and then flung himself in. I kept my secret.

Rogue: Colonel Clay

The Episode of the Mexican Seer

GRANT ALLEN

CHARLES GRANT BLAIRFINDIE ALLEN (1848–1899) was responsible for two literary breakthroughs. The first was his novel *The Woman Who Did* (1895), which created a sensation in Victorian England because of its candid discussion of sex, especially featuring the titular character—who did exactly what you think she did.

The second book guaranteed Allen a lasting place in the annals of crime fiction. In *An African Millionaire: Episodes in the Life of the Illustrious Colonel Clay* (1897), Allen created the first important series of stories about a rogue, the adventures of Colonel Clay preceding the immortal Raffles by two years. The African millionaire of the title refers to Sir Charles Vandrift, the colonel's personal and repeated victim, who might have taken solace in the fact that he is the only character in the history of mystery fiction who gave his identity to a short story series as the victim. Vandrift is a fabulously wealthy man who made his fortune in Africa but is cheated, duped, robbed, bilked, and fooled again and again by Clay. Although Vandrift is wary of Clay, the colonel is such a master of disguise that he can almost instantly transform himself from a Mexican seer to a Scottish parson—neither of whom even slightly resembles Clay, whose fresh, clean face is the embodiment of innocence and honesty.

Allen wrote numerous books in various fields, ranging from science, philosophy, travel, and nature, to fiction, including ghost stories, science fiction, mystery novels, and short stories—more than fifty books in all, even though he died at only fifty-one. On his deathbed, he wanted to be sure that his last book, an episodic novel titled *Hilda Wade*, would be published, so he asked his friend Arthur Conan Doyle to write the final chapter; it was published posthumously in 1900.

"The Episode of the Mexican Seer" was originally published in the June 1896 issue of *The Strand Magazine*; it was first collected in *An African Millionaire: Episodes in the Life of the Illustrious Colonel Clay* (London, Grant Richards, 1897).

THE EPISODE OF THE MEXICAN SEER

Grant Allen

MY NAME IS Seymour Wilbraham Wentworth. I am brother-in-law and secretary to Sir Charles Vandrift, the South African millionaire and famous financier. Many years ago, when Charlie Vandrift was a small lawyer in Cape Town, I had the (qualified) good fortune to marry his sister. Much later, when the Vandrift estate and farm near Kimberley developed by degrees into the Cloetedorp Golcondas, Limited, my brother-in-law offered me the not unremunerative post of secretary; in which capacity I have ever since been his constant and attached companion.

He is not a man whom any common sharper can take in, is Charles Vandrift. Middle height, square build, firm mouth, keen eyes—the very picture of a sharp and successful business genius. I have only known one rogue impose upon Sir Charles, and that one rogue, as the Commissary of Police at Nice remarked, would doubtless have imposed upon a syndicate of Vidocq, Robert Houdin, and Cagliostro.

We had run across to the Riviera for a few weeks in the season. Our object being strictly rest and recreation from the arduous duties of financial combination, we did not think it necessary to take our wives out with us. Indeed, Lady Vandrift is absolutely wedded to the joys of London, and does not appreciate the rural delights of the Mediterranean littoral. But Sir Charles and I, though immersed in affairs when at home, both thoroughly enjoy the complete change from the City to the charming vegetation and pellucid air on the terrace at Monte Carlo. We *are* so fond of scenery. That delicious view over the rocks of Monaco, with the Maritime Alps in the rear, and the blue sea in front, not to mention the imposing Casino in the foreground, appeals to me as one of the most beautiful prospects in all Europe. Sir Charles has a sentimental attachment for the place. He finds it restores and freshens him, after the turmoil of London, to win a few hundreds at roulette in the course of an afternoon among the palms and cactuses and pure breezes of Monte Carlo. The country, say I, for a jaded intellect! However, we never on any account actually stop in the Principality itself. Sir Charles thinks Monte Carlo is not a sound address for a financier's letters. He prefers a comfortable hotel on the Promenade des Anglais at Nice, where he recovers health and renovates his nervous system by taking daily excursions along the coast to the Casino.

This particular season we were snugly

ensconced at the Hôtel des Anglais. We had capital quarters on the first floor—salon, study, and bedrooms—and found on the spot a most agreeable cosmopolitan society. All Nice, just then, was ringing with talk about a curious impostor, known to his followers as the Great Mexican Seer, and supposed to be gifted with second sight, as well as with endless other supernatural powers. Now, it is a peculiarity of my able brother-in-law's that, when he meets with a quack, he burns to expose him; he is so keen a man of business himself that it gives him, so to speak, a disinterested pleasure to unmask and detect imposture in others. Many ladies at the hotel, some of whom had met and conversed with the Mexican Seer, were constantly telling us strange stories of his doings. He had disclosed to one the present whereabouts of a runaway husband; he had pointed out to another the numbers that would win at roulette next evening; he had shown a third the image on a screen of the man she had for years adored without his knowledge. Of course, Sir Charles didn't believe a word of it; but his curiosity was roused; he wished to see and judge for himself of the wonderful thought-reader.

"What would be his terms, do you think, for a private séance?" he asked of Madame Picardet, the lady to whom the Seer had successfully predicted the winning numbers.

"He does not work for money," Madame Picardet answered, "but for the good of humanity. I'm sure he would gladly come and exhibit for nothing his miraculous faculties."

"Nonsense!" Sir Charles answered. "The man must live. I'd pay him five guineas, though, to see him alone. What hotel is he stopping at?"

"The Cosmopolitan, I think," the lady answered. "Oh no; I remember now, the Westminster."

Sir Charles turned to me quietly. "Look here, Seymour," he whispered. "Go round to this fellow's place immediately after dinner, and offer him five pounds to give a private séance at once in my rooms, without mentioning who I am to him; keep the name quite quiet. Bring him back with you, too, and come straight upstairs with him, so that there may be no collusion. We'll see just how much the fellow can tell us."

I went as directed. I found the Seer a very remarkable and interesting person. He stood about Sir Charles's own height, but was slimmer and straighter, with an aquiline nose, strangely piercing eyes, very large black pupils, and a finely chiselled close-shaven face, like the bust of Antinous in our hall in Mayfair. What gave him his most characteristic touch, however, was his odd head of hair, curly and wavy like Paderewski's, standing out in a halo round his high white forehead and his delicate profile. I could see at a glance why he succeeded so well in impressing women; he had the look of a poet, a singer, a prophet.

"I have come round," I said, "to ask whether you will consent to give a séance at once in a friend's rooms; and my principal wishes me to add that he is prepared to pay five pounds as the price of the entertainment."

Señor Antonio Herrera—that was what he called himself—bowed to me with impressive Spanish politeness. His dusky olive cheeks were wrinkled with a smile of gentle contempt as he answered gravely—

"I do not sell my gifts; I bestow them freely. If your friend—your anonymous friend—desires to behold the cosmic wonders that are wrought through my hands, I am glad to show them to him. Fortunately, as often happens when it is necessary to convince and confound a sceptic (for that your friend is a sceptic I feel instinctively), I chance to have no engagements at all this evening." He ran his hand through his fine, long hair reflectively. "Yes, I go," he continued, as if addressing some unknown presence that hovered about the ceiling; "I go; come with me!" Then he put on his broad sombrero, with its crimson ribbon, wrapped a cloak round his shoulders, lighted a cigarette, and strode forth by my side towards the Hôtel des Anglais.

He talked little by the way, and that little in curt sentences. He seemed buried in deep thought; indeed, when we reached the door and

I turned in, he walked a step or two farther on, as if not noticing to what place I had brought him. Then he drew himself up short, and gazed around him for a moment. "Ha, the Anglais," he said—and I may mention in passing that his English, in spite of a slight southern accent, was idiomatic and excellent. "It is here, then; it is here!" He was addressing once more the unseen presence.

I smiled to think that these childish devices were intended to deceive Sir Charles Vandrift. Not quite the sort of man (as the City of London knows) to be taken in by hocus-pocus. And all this, I saw, was the cheapest and most commonplace conjurer's patter.

We went upstairs to our rooms. Charles had gathered together a few friends to watch the performance. The Seer entered, wrapt in thought. He was in evening dress, but a red sash round his waist gave a touch of picturesqueness and a dash of colour. He paused for a moment in the middle of the salon, without letting his eyes rest on anybody or anything. Then he walked straight up to Charles, and held out his dark hand.

"Good-evening," he said. "You are the host. My soul's sight tells me so."

"Good shot," Sir Charles answered. "These fellows have to be quick-witted, you know, Mrs. Mackenzie, or they'd never get on at it."

The Seer gazed about him, and smiled blankly at a person or two whose faces he seemed to recognise from a previous existence. Then Charles began to ask him a few simple questions, not about himself, but about me, just to test him. He answered most of them with surprising correctness. "His name? His name begins with an S I think:—You call him Seymour." He paused long between each clause, as if the facts were revealed to him slowly. "Seymour—Wilbraham—Earl of Strafford. No, not Earl of Strafford! Seymour Wilbraham Wentworth. There seems to be some connection in somebody's mind now present between Wentworth and Strafford. I am not English. I do not know what it means. But they are somehow the same name, Wentworth and Strafford."

He gazed around, apparently for confirmation. A lady came to his rescue.

"Wentworth was the surname of the great Earl of Strafford," she murmured gently; "and I was wondering, as you spoke, whether Mr. Wentworth might possibly be descended from him."

"He is," the Seer replied instantly, with a flash of those dark eyes. And I thought this curious; for though my father always maintained the reality of the relationship, there was one link wanting to complete the pedigree. He could not make sure that the Hon. Thomas Wilbraham Wentworth was the father of Jonathan Wentworth, the Bristol horse-dealer, from whom we are descended.

"Where was I born?" Sir Charles interrupted, coming suddenly to his own case.

The Seer clapped his two hands to his forehead and held it between them, as if to prevent it from bursting. "Africa," he said slowly, as the facts narrowed down, so to speak. "South Africa; Cape of Good Hope; Jansenville; De Witt Street. 1840."

"By Jove, he's correct," Sir Charles muttered. "He seems really to do it. Still, he may have found me out. He may have known where he was coming."

"I never gave a hint," I answered; "till he reached the door, he didn't even know to what hotel I was piloting him."

The Seer stroked his chin softly. His eye appeared to me to have a furtive gleam in it. "Would you like me to tell you the number of a bank-note inclosed in an envelope?" he asked casually.

"Go out of the room," Sir Charles said, "while I pass it round the company."

Señor Herrera disappeared. Sir Charles passed it round cautiously, holding it all the time in his own hand, but letting his guests see the number. Then he placed it in an envelope and gummed it down firmly.

The Seer returned. His keen eyes swept the company with a comprehensive glance. He shook his shaggy mane. Then he took the envelope in his hands and gazed at it fixedly. "AF, 73549," he answered, in a slow tone. "A Bank of England note for fifty pounds—exchanged at the Casino for gold won yesterday at Monte Carlo."

"I see how he did that," Sir Charles said triumphantly. "He must have changed it there himself; and then I changed it back again. In point of fact, I remember seeing a fellow with long hair loafing about. Still, it's capital conjuring."

"He can see through matter," one of the ladies interposed. It was Madame Picardet. "He can see through a box." She drew a little gold vinaigrette, such as our grandmothers used, from her dress-pocket. "What is in this?" she inquired, holding it up to him.

Señor Herrera gazed through it. "Three gold coins," he replied, knitting his brows with the effort of seeing into the box: "one, an American five dollars; one, a French ten-franc piece; one, twenty marks, German, of the old Emperor William."

She opened the box and passed it round. Sir Charles smiled a quiet smile.

"Confederacy!" he muttered, half to himself. "Confederacy!"

The Seer turned to him with a sullen air. "You want a better sign?" he said, in a very impressive voice. "A sign that will convince you! Very well: you have a letter in your left waistcoat pocket—a crumpled-up letter. Do you wish me to read it out? I will, if you desire it."

It may seem to those who know Sir Charles incredible, but, I am bound to admit, my brother-in-law coloured. What that letter contained I cannot say; he only answered, very testily and evasively, "No, thank you; I won't trouble you. The exhibition you have already given us of your skill in this kind more than amply suffices." And his fingers strayed nervously to his waistcoat pocket, as if he was half afraid, even then, Señor Herrera would read it.

I fancied, too, he glanced somewhat anxiously towards Madame Picardet.

The Seer bowed courteously. "Your will, señor, is law," he said. "I make it a principle, though I can see through all things, invariably to respect the secrecies and sanctities. If it were not so, I might dissolve society. For which of us is there who could bear the whole truth being told about him?" He gazed around the room. An unpleasant thrill supervened. Most of us felt this uncanny Spanish American knew really too much. And some of us were engaged in financial operations.

"For example," the Seer continued blandly, "I happened a few weeks ago to travel down here from Paris by train with a very intelligent man, a company promoter. He had in his bag some documents—some confidential documents." He glanced at Sir Charles. "You know the kind of thing, my dear sir: reports from experts—from mining engineers. You may have seen some such; marked *strictly private*."

"They form an element in high finance," Sir Charles admitted coldly.

"Pre-cisely," the Seer murmured, his accent for a moment less Spanish than before. "And, as they were marked *strictly private*, I respect, of course, the seal of confidence. That's all I wish to say. I hold it a duty, being intrusted with such powers, not to use them in a manner which may annoy or incommode my fellow-creatures."

"Your feeling does you honour," Sir Charles answered, with some acerbity. Then he whispered in my ear: "Confounded clever scoundrel, Sey; rather wish we hadn't brought him here."

Señor Herrera seemed intuitively to divine this wish, for he interposed, in a lighter and gayer tone—

"I will now show you a different and more interesting embodiment of occult power, for which we shall need a somewhat subdued arrangement of surrounding lights. Would you mind, señor host—for I have purposely abstained from reading your name on the brain of any one present—would you mind my turning down this lamp just a little? . . . So! That will do. Now, this one; and this one. Exactly! that's right." He poured a few grains of powder out of a packet into a saucer. "Next, a match, if you please. Thank you!" It burnt with a strange green light. He drew from his pocket a card, and produced a little ink-bottle. "Have you a pen?" he asked.

I instantly brought one. He handed it to Sir Charles. "Oblige me," he said, "by writing your name there." And he indicated a place in the centre of the card, which had an embossed edge, with a small middle square of a different colour.

Sir Charles has a natural disinclination to signing his name without knowing why. "What do you want with it?" he asked. (A millionaire's signature has so many uses.)

"I want you to put the card in an envelope," the Seer replied, "and then to burn it. After that, I shall show you your own name written in letters of blood on my arm, in your own handwriting."

Sir Charles took the pen. If the signature was to be burned as soon as finished, he didn't mind giving it. He wrote his name in his usual firm clear style—the writing of a man who knows his worth and is not afraid of drawing a cheque for five thousand.

"Look at it long," the Seer said, from the other side of the room. He had not watched him write it.

Sir Charles stared at it fixedly. The Seer was really beginning to produce an impression.

"Now, put it in that envelope," the Seer exclaimed.

Sir Charles, like a lamb, placed it as directed.

The Seer strode forward. "Give me the envelope," he said. He took it in his hand, walked over towards the fireplace, and solemnly burnt it. "See—it crumbles into ashes," he cried. Then he came back to the middle of the room, close to the green light, rolled up his sleeve, and held his arm before Sir Charles. There, in blood-red letters, my brother-in-law read the name, "Charles Vandrift," in his own handwriting!

"I see how that's done," Sir Charles murmured, drawing back. "It's a clever delusion; but still, I see through it. It's like that ghost-book. Your ink was deep green; your light was green; you made me look at it long; and then I saw the same thing written on the skin of your arm in complementary colours."

"You think so?" the Seer replied, with a curious curl of the lip.

"I'm sure of it," Sir Charles answered.

Quick as lightning the Seer again rolled up his sleeve. "That's your name," he cried, in a very clear voice, "but not your whole name. What do you say, then, to my right? Is this one also a complementary colour?" He held his other arm out. There, in sea-green letters, I read the name, "Charles O'Sullivan Vandrift." It is my brother-in-law's full baptismal designation; but he has dropped the O'Sullivan for many years past, and, to say the truth, doesn't like it. He is a little bit ashamed of his mother's family.

Charles glanced at it hurriedly. "Quite right," he said, "quite right!" But his voice was hollow. I could guess he didn't care to continue the séance. He could see through the man, of course; but it was clear the fellow knew too much about us to be entirely pleasant.

"Turn up the lights," I said, and a servant turned them. "Shall I say coffee and benedictine?" I whispered to Vandrift.

"By all means," he answered. "Anything to keep this fellow from further impertinences! And, I say, don't you think you'd better suggest at the same time that the men should smoke? Even these ladies are not above a cigarette—some of them."

There was a sigh of relief. The lights burned brightly. The Seer for the moment retired from business, so to speak. He accepted a partaga with a very good grace, sipped his coffee in a corner, and chatted to the lady who had suggested Strafford with marked politeness. He was a polished gentleman.

Next morning, in the hall of the hotel, I saw Madame Picardet again, in a neat tailor-made travelling dress, evidently bound for the railway-station.

"What, off, Madame Picardet?" I cried.

She smiled, and held out her prettily-gloved hand. "Yes, I'm off," she answered archly. "Florence, or Rome, or somewhere. I've drained Nice dry—like a sucked orange. Got all the fun I can out of it. Now I'm away again to my beloved Italy."

But it struck me as odd that, if Italy was her

game, she went by the omnibus which takes down to the train de luxe for Paris. However, a man of the world accepts what a lady tells him, no matter how improbable; and I confess, for ten days or so, I thought no more about her, or the Seer either.

At the end of that time our fortnightly pass-book came in from the bank in London. It is part of my duty, as the millionaire's secretary, to make up this book once a fortnight, and to compare the cancelled cheques with Sir Charles's counterfoils. On this particular occasion I happened to observe what I can only describe as a very grave discrepancy—in fact, a discrepancy of 5000 pounds. On the wrong side, too. Sir Charles was debited with 5000 pounds more than the total amount that was shown on the counterfoils.

I examined the book with care. The source of the error was obvious. It lay in a cheque to Self or Bearer, for 5000 pounds, signed by Sir Charles, and evidently paid across the counter in London, as it bore on its face no stamp or indication of any other office.

I called in my brother-in-law from the salon to the study. "Look here, Charles," I said, "there's a cheque in the book which you haven't entered." And I handed it to him without comment, for I thought it might have been drawn to settle some little loss on the turf or at cards, or to make up some other affair he didn't desire to mention to me. These things will happen.

He looked at it and stared hard. Then he pursed up his mouth and gave a long low "Whew!" At last he turned it over and remarked, "I say, Sey, my boy, we've just been done jolly well brown, haven't we?"

I glanced at the cheque. "How do you mean?" I inquired.

"Why, the Seer," he replied, still staring at it ruefully. "I don't mind the five thou., but to think the fellow should have gammoned the pair of us like that—ignominious, I call it!"

"How do you know it's the Seer?" I asked.

"Look at the green ink," he answered. "Besides, I recollect the very shape of the last flourish. I flourished a bit like that in the excitement of the moment, which I don't always do with my regular signature."

"He's done us," I answered, recognising it. "But how the dickens did he manage to transfer it to the cheque? This looks like your own handwriting, Charles, not a clever forgery."

"It is," he said. "I admit it—I can't deny it. Only fancy his bamboozling me when I was most on my guard! I wasn't to be taken in by any of his silly occult tricks and catch-words; but it never occurred to me he was going to victimise me financially in this way. I expected attempts at a loan or an extortion; but to collar my signature to a blank cheque—atrocious!"

"How did he manage it?" I asked.

"I haven't the faintest conception. I only know those are the words I wrote. I could swear to them anywhere."

"Then you can't protest the cheque?"

"Unfortunately, no; it's my own true signature."

We went that afternoon without delay to see the Chief Commissary of Police at the office. He was a gentlemanly Frenchman, much less formal and red-tapey than usual, and he spoke excellent English with an American accent, having acted, in fact, as a detective in New York for about ten years in his early manhood.

"I guess," he said slowly, after hearing our story, "you've been victimised right here by Colonel Clay, gentlemen."

"Who is Colonel Clay?" Sir Charles asked.

"That's just what I want to know," the Commissary answered, in his curious American-French-English. "He is a Colonel, because he occasionally gives himself a commission; he is called Colonel Clay, because he appears to possess an india-rubber face, and he can mould it like clay in the hands of the potter. Real name, unknown. Nationality, equally French and English. Address, usually Europe. Profession, former maker of wax figures to the Musée Grévin. Age, what he chooses. Employs his knowledge to mould his own nose and cheeks, with wax additions, to the character he desires to personate. Aquiline this time, you say. Hein! Anything like these photographs?"

He rummaged in his desk and handed us two.

"Not in the least," Sir Charles answered. "Except, perhaps, as to the neck, everything here is quite unlike him."

"Then that's the Colonel!" the Commissary answered, with decision, rubbing his hands in glee. "Look here," and he took out a pencil and rapidly sketched the outline of one of the two faces—that of a bland-looking young man, with no expression worth mentioning. "There's the Colonel in his simple disguise. Very good. Now watch me: figure to yourself that he adds here a tiny patch of wax to his nose—an aquiline bridge—just so; well, you have him right there; and the chin, ah, one touch: now, for hair, a wig: for complexion, nothing easier: that's the profile of your rascal, isn't it?"

"Exactly," we both murmured. By two curves of the pencil, and a shock of false hair, the face was transmuted.

"He had very large eyes, with very big pupils, though," I objected, looking close; "and the man in the photograph here has them small and boiled-fishy."

"That's so," the Commissary answered. "A drop of belladonna expands—and produces the Seer; five grains of opium contract—and give a dead-alive, stupidly-innocent appearance. Well, you leave this affair to me, gentlemen. I'll see the fun out. I don't say I'll catch him for you; nobody ever yet has caught Colonel Clay; but I'll explain how he did the trick; and that ought to be consolation enough to a man of your means for a trifle of five thousand!"

"You are not the conventional French office-holder, M. le Commissaire," I ventured to interpose.

"You bet!" the Commissary replied, and drew himself up like a captain of infantry. "Messieurs," he continued, in French, with the utmost dignity, "I shall devote the resources of this office to tracing out the crime, and, if possible, to effectuating the arrest of the culpable."

We telegraphed to London, of course, and we wrote to the bank, with a full description of the suspected person. But I need hardly add that nothing came of it.

Three days later the Commissary called at our hotel. "Well, gentlemen," he said, "I am glad to say I have discovered everything!"

"What? Arrested the Seer?" Sir Charles cried.

The Commissary drew back, almost horrified at the suggestion.

"Arrested Colonel Clay?" he exclaimed. "Mais, monsieur, we are only human! Arrested him? No, not quite. But tracked out how he did it. That is already much—to unravel Colonel Clay, gentlemen!"

"Well, what do you make of it?" Sir Charles asked, crestfallen.

The Commissary sat down and gloated over his discovery. It was clear a well-planned crime amused him vastly. "In the first place, monsieur," he said, "disabuse your mind of the idea that when monsieur your secretary went out to fetch Señor Herrera that night, Señor Herrera didn't know to whose rooms he was coming. Quite otherwise, in point of fact. I do not doubt myself that Señor Herrera, or Colonel Clay (call him which you like), came to Nice this winter for no other purpose than just to rob you."

"But I sent for him," my brother-in-law interposed.

"Yes; he *meant* you to send for him. He forced a card, so to speak. If he couldn't do that I guess he would be a pretty poor conjurer. He had a lady of his own—his wife, let us say, or his sister—stopping here at this hotel; a certain Madame Picardet. Through her he induced several ladies of your circle to attend his séances. She and they spoke to you about him, and aroused your curiosity. You may bet your bottom dollar that when he came to this room he came ready primed and prepared with endless facts about both of you."

"What fools we have been, Sey," my brother-in-law exclaimed. "I see it all now. That designing woman sent round before dinner to say I wanted to meet him; and by the time you got there he was ready for bamboozling me."

"That's so," the Commissary answered. "He had your name ready painted on both his arms; and he had made other preparations of still greater importance."

"You mean the cheque. Well, how did he get it?"

The Commissary opened the door. "Come in," he said. And a young man entered whom we recognised at once as the chief clerk in the Foreign Department of the Crédit Marseillais, the principal bank all along the Riviera.

"State what you know of this cheque," the Commissary said, showing it to him, for we had handed it over to the police as a piece of evidence.

"About four weeks since—" the clerk began.

"Say ten days before your séance," the Commissary interposed.

"A gentleman with very long hair and an aquiline nose, dark, strange, and handsome, called in at my department and asked if I could tell him the name of Sir Charles Vandrift's London banker. He said he had a sum to pay in to your credit, and asked if we would forward it for him. I told him it was irregular for us to receive the money, as you had no account with us, but that your London bankers were Darby, Drummond, and Rothenberg, Limited."

"Quite right," Sir Charles murmured.

"Two days later a lady, Madame Picardet, who was a customer of ours, brought in a good cheque for three hundred pounds, signed by a first-rate name, and asked us to pay it in on her behalf to Darby, Drummond, and Rothenberg's, and to open a London account with them for her. We did so, and received in reply a cheque-book."

"From which this cheque was taken, as I learn from the number, by telegram from London," the Commissary put in. "Also, that on the same day on which your cheque was cashed, Madame Picardet, in London, withdrew her balance."

"But how did the fellow get me to sign the cheque?" Sir Charles cried. "How did he manage the card trick?"

The Commissary produced a similar card from his pocket. "Was that the sort of thing?" he asked.

"Precisely! A facsimile."

"I thought so. Well, our Colonel, I find, bought a packet of such cards, intended for admission to a religious function, at a shop in the Quai Massena. He cut out the centre, and, see here—" The Commissary turned it over, and showed a piece of paper pasted neatly over the back; this he tore off, and there, concealed behind it, lay a folded cheque, with only the place where the signature should be written showing through on the face which the Seer had presented to us. "I call that a neat trick," the Commissary remarked, with professional enjoyment of a really good deception.

"But he burnt the envelope before my eyes," Sir Charles exclaimed.

"Pooh!" the Commissary answered. "What would he be worth as a conjurer, anyway, if he couldn't substitute one envelope for another between the table and the fireplace without your noticing it? And Colonel Clay, you must remember, is a prince among conjurers."

"Well, it's a comfort to know we've identified our man, and the woman who was with him," Sir Charles said, with a slight sigh of relief. "The next thing will be, of course, you'll follow them up on these clues in England and arrest them?"

The Commissary shrugged his shoulders. "Arrest them!" he exclaimed, much amused. "Ah, monsieur, but you are sanguine! No officer of justice has ever succeeded in arresting le Colonel Caoutchouc, as we call him in French. He is as slippery as an eel, that man. He wriggles through our fingers. Suppose even we caught him, what could we prove? I ask you. Nobody who has seen him once can ever swear to him again in his next impersonation. He is impayable, this good Colonel. On the day when I arrest him, I assure you, monsieur, I shall consider myself the smartest police-officer in Europe."

"Well, I shall catch him yet," Sir Charles answered, and relapsed into silence.

Villain: Wolfe Macfarlane

The Body Snatcher

ROBERT LOUIS STEVENSON

ONE CAN ONLY CONTEMPLATE how much great literature was doomed to never having been written because of the early death of Robert Louis Stevenson (1850–1894). In addition to being one of the greatest adventure story authors of all time with such classics as *Treasure Island* (1881), *Prince Otto* (1885), *Kidnapped* (1886), and *The Black Arrow* (1888) to his credit, he also wrote the beloved volume of poems for young readers *A Child's Garden of Verses* (1885).

Stevenson frequently wrote of mystery and crime, most famously *The Strange Case of Dr. Jekyll and Mr. Hyde* (1886), a macabre allegory once described as the only crime story in which the solution is more terrifying than the problem. He wrote such classic crime stories as "The Suicide Club," "The Pavilion on the Links," "Markheim," and "The Dynamiter" (in collaboration with his wife, Fanny Van de Grift Osbourne), as well as the novel *The Wrong Box* (1889, in collaboration with his stepson, Lloyd Osbourne) that inspired the 1966 star-studded black comedy with John Mills, Ralph Richardson, Michael Caine, Peter Cook, Dudley Moore, and Peter Sellers.

Born in Edinburgh, Stevenson stopped studying engineering because of lack of interest and later passed his bar examination but never practiced law. He moved several times due to his chronic lung disease, winding up in Samoa in 1889, where he ended up living with his wife for the rest of his life.

The Body Snatcher was a successful RKO feature film when it was released in 1945, starring Boris Karloff, Henry Daniell, and Bela Lugosi. It was first published in the *Pall Mall* Christmas "Extra" for 1884, and again in the *Pall Mall Gazette* on January 31 and February 1, 1895. Its first book appearance was *The Body Snatcher* (New York, The Merriam Company, 1895).

THE BODY SNATCHER

Robert Louis Stevenson

EVERY NIGHT IN THE YEAR, four of us sat in the small parlour of the George at Debenham—the undertaker, and the landlord, and Fettes, and myself. Sometimes there would be more; but blow high, blow low, come rain or snow or frost, we four would be each planted in his own particular arm-chair. Fettes was an old drunken Scotchman, a man of education obviously, and a man of some property, since he lived in idleness. He had come to Debenham years ago, while still young, and by a mere continuance of living had grown to be an adopted townsman. His blue camlet cloak was a local antiquity, like the church-spire. His place in the parlour at the George, his absence from church, his old, crapulous, disreputable vices, were all things of course in Debenham. He had some vague Radical opinions and some fleeting infidelities, which he would now and again set forth and emphasise with tottering slaps upon the table. He drank rum—five glasses regularly every evening; and for the greater portion of his nightly visit to the George sat, with his glass in his right hand, in a state of melancholy alcoholic saturation. We called him the Doctor, for he was supposed to have some special knowledge of medicine, and had been known, upon a pinch, to set a fracture or reduce a dislocation; but beyond these slight particulars, we had no knowledge of his character and antecedents.

One dark winter night—it had struck nine some time before the landlord joined us—there was a sick man in the George, a great neighbouring proprietor suddenly struck down with apoplexy on his way to Parliament; and the great man's still greater London doctor had been telegraphed to his bedside. It was the first time that such a thing had happened in Debenham, for the railway was but newly open, and we were all proportionately moved by the occurrence.

"He's come," said the landlord, after he had filled and lighted his pipe.

"He?" said I. "Who?—not the doctor?"

"Himself," replied our host.

"What is his name?"

"Doctor Macfarlane," said the landlord.

Fettes was far through his third tumbler, stupidly fuddled, now nodding over, now staring mazily around him; but at the last word he seemed to awaken, and repeated the name "Macfarlane" twice, quietly enough the first time, but with sudden emotion at the second.

"Yes," said the landlord, "that's his name, Doctor Wolfe Macfarlane."

Fettes became instantly sober; his eyes awoke, his voice became clear, loud, and steady, his language forcible and earnest. We were all startled by the transformation, as if a man had risen from the dead.

"I beg your pardon," he said, "I am afraid I have not been paying much attention to your talk. Who is this Wolfe Macfarlane?" And then, when he had heard the landlord out, "It cannot be, it cannot be," he added; "and yet I would like well to see him face to face."

"Do you know him, Doctor?" asked the undertaker, with a gasp.

"God forbid!" was the reply. "And yet the name is a strange one; it were too much to fancy two. Tell me, landlord, is he old?"

"Well," said the host, "he's not a young man, to be sure, and his hair is white; but he looks younger than you."

"He is older, though; years older. But," with a slap upon the table, "it's the rum you see in my face—rum and sin. This man, perhaps, may have an easy conscience and a good digestion. Conscience! Hear me speak. You would think I was some good, old, decent Christian, would you not? But no, not I; I never canted. Voltaire might have canted if he'd stood in my shoes; but the brains"—with a rattling fillip on his bald head—"the brains were clear and active, and I saw and made no deductions."

"If you know this doctor," I ventured to remark, after a somewhat awful pause, "I should gather that you do not share the landlord's good opinion."

Fettes paid no regard to me.

"Yes," he said, with sudden decision, "I must see him face to face."

There was another pause, and then a door was closed rather sharply on the first floor, and a step was heard upon the stair.

"That's the doctor," cried the landlord. "Look sharp, and you can catch him."

It was but two steps from the small parlour to the door of the old George Inn; the wide oak staircase landed almost in the street; there was room for a Turkey rug and nothing more between the threshold and the last round of the descent; but this little space was every evening brilliantly lit up, not only by the light upon the stair and the great signal-lamp below the sign, but by the warm radiance of the bar-room window. The George thus brightly advertised itself to passers-by in the cold street. Fettes walked steadily to the spot, and we, who were hanging behind, beheld the two men meet, as one of them had phrased it, face to face. Dr. Macfarlane was alert and vigorous. His white hair set off his pale and placid, although energetic, countenance. He was richly dressed in the finest of broadcloth and the whitest of linen, with a great gold watch-chain, and studs and spectacles of the same precious material. He wore a broad-folded tie, white and speckled with lilac, and he carried on his arm a comfortable driving-coat of fur. There was no doubt but he became his years, breathing, as he did, of wealth and consideration; and it was a surprising contrast to see our parlour sot—bald, dirty, pimpled, and robed in his old camlet cloak—confront him at the bottom of the stairs.

"Macfarlane!" he said somewhat loudly, more like a herald than a friend.

The great doctor pulled up short on the fourth step, as though the familiarity of the address surprised and somewhat shocked his dignity.

"Toddy Macfarlane!" repeated Fettes.

The London man almost staggered. He stared for the swiftest of seconds at the man before him, glanced behind him with a sort of scare, and then in a startled whisper, "Fettes!" he said, "You!"

"Ay," said the other, "me! Did you think I was dead too? We are not so easy shut of our acquaintance."

"Hush, hush!" exclaimed the doctor. "Hush, hush! this meeting is so unexpected—I can see you are unmanned. I hardly knew you, I confess, at first; but I am overjoyed—overjoyed to have this opportunity. For the present it must be how-d'ye-do and good-bye in one, for my fly is waiting, and I must not fail the train; but you shall—let me see—yes—you shall give me your address, and you can count on early news of me. We must do something for you, Fettes. I fear you are out at elbows; but we must see to that for auld lang syne, as once we sang at suppers."

"Money!" cried Fettes; "money from you! The money that I had from you is lying where I cast it in the rain."

Dr. Macfarlane had talked himself into some measure of superiority and confidence, but the uncommon energy of this refusal cast him back into his first confusion.

A horrible, ugly look came and went across his almost venerable countenance. "My dear fellow," he said, "be it as you please; my last thought is to offend you. I would intrude on none. I will leave you my address, however—"

"I do not wish it—I do not wish to know the roof that shelters you," interrupted the other. "I heard your name; I feared it might be you; I wished to know if, after all, there were a God; I know now that there is none. Begone!"

He still stood in the middle of the rug, between the stair and doorway; and the great London physician, in order to escape, would be forced to step to one side. It was plain that he hesitated before the thought of this humiliation. White as he was, there was a dangerous glitter in his spectacles; but while he still paused uncertain, he became aware that the driver of his fly was peering in from the street at this unusual scene and caught a glimpse at the same time of our little body from the parlour, huddled by the corner of the bar. The presence of so many witnesses decided him at once to flee. He crouched together, brushing on the wainscot, and made a dart like a serpent, striking for the door. But his tribulation was not yet entirely at an end, for even as he was passing Fettes clutched him by the arm and these words came in a whisper, and yet painfully distinct, "Have you seen it again?"

The great rich London doctor cried out aloud with a sharp, throttling cry; he dashed his questioner across the open space, and, with his hands over his head, fled out of the door like a detected thief. Before it had occurred to one of us to make a movement the fly was already rattling toward the station. The scene was over like a dream, but the dream had left proofs and traces of its passage. Next day the servant found the fine gold spectacles broken on the threshold, and that very night we were all standing breathless by the bar-room window, and Fettes at our side, sober, pale, and resolute in look.

"God protect us, Mr. Fettes!" said the landlord, coming first into possession of his customary senses. "What in the universe is all this? These are strange things you have been saying."

Fettes turned toward us; he looked us each in succession in the face. "See if you can hold your tongues," said he. "That man Macfarlane is not safe to cross; those that have done so already have repented it too late."

And then, without so much as finishing his third glass, far less waiting for the other two, he bade us good-bye and went forth, under the lamp of the hotel, into the black night.

We three turned to our places in the parlour, with the big red fire and four clear candles; and as we recapitulated what had passed, the first chill of our surprise soon changed into a glow of curiosity. We sat late; it was the latest session I have known in the old George. Each man, before we parted, had his theory that he was bound to prove; and none of us had any nearer business in this world than to track out the past of our condemned companion, and surprise the secret that he shared with the great London doctor. It is no great boast, but I believe I was a better hand at worming out a story than either of my fellows at the George; and perhaps there is now no other man alive who could narrate to you the following foul and unnatural events.

In his young days Fettes studied medicine in the schools of Edinburgh. He had talent of a kind, the talent that picks up swiftly what it hears and readily retails it for its own. He worked little at home; but he was civil, attentive, and intelligent in the presence of his masters. They soon picked him out as a lad who listened closely and remembered well; nay, strange as it seemed to me when I first heard it, he was in those days well favoured, and pleased by his exterior. There was, at that period, a certain extramural teacher of anatomy, whom I shall here designate by the letter K. His name was subsequently too well known. The man who bore it skulked through the streets of Edinburgh in disguise, while the mob that applauded at the execution of Burke called loudly for the blood of his employer. But Mr. K—— was then at the top of his vogue; he enjoyed a popularity due partly to his own talent and address, partly to the incapacity of his rival, the university professor. The students, at least, swore by his name, and Fettes believed himself, and was believed by others, to have laid the foundations of success when he had acquired the favour of this meteorically famous man. Mr. K—— was a *bon vivant* as well as an accomplished teacher; he liked a sly illusion no less than a careful preparation. In both capacities Fettes enjoyed and deserved his notice, and by the second year of his attendance he held the half-regular position of second demonstrator or sub-assistant in his class.

In this capacity the charge of the theatre and lecture-room devolved in particular upon his shoulders. He had to answer for the cleanliness of the premises and the conduct of the other students, and it was a part of his duty to supply, receive, and divide the various subjects. It was with a view to this last—at that time very delicate—affair that he was lodged by Mr. K—— in the same wynd, and at last in the same building, with the dissecting-rooms. Here, after a night of turbulent pleasures, his hand still tottering, his sight still misty and confused, he would be called out of bed in the black hours before the winter dawn by the unclean and desperate interlopers who supplied the table. He would open the door to these men, since infamous throughout the land. He would help them with their tragic burden, pay them their sordid price, and remain alone, when they were gone, with the unfriendly relics of humanity. From such a scene he would return to snatch another hour or two of slumber, to repair the abuses of the night, and refresh himself for the labours of the day.

Few lads could have been more insensible to the impressions of a life thus passed among the ensigns of mortality. His mind was closed against all general considerations. He was incapable of interest in the fate and fortunes of another, the slave of his own desires and low ambitions. Cold, light, and selfish in the last resort, he had that modicum of prudence, miscalled morality, which keeps a man from inconvenient drunkenness or punishable theft. He coveted, besides, a measure of consideration from his masters and his fellow-pupils, and he had no desire to fail conspicuously in the external parts of life. Thus he made it his pleasure to gain some distinction in his studies, and day after day rendered unimpeachable eye-service to his employer, Mr. K——. For his day of work he indemnified himself by nights of roaring, blackguardly enjoyment; and when that balance had been struck, the organ that he called his conscience declared itself content.

The supply of subjects was a continual trouble to him as well as to his master. In that large and busy class, the raw material of the anatomists kept perpetually running out; and the business thus rendered necessary was not only unpleasant in itself, but threatened dangerous consequences to all who were concerned. It was the policy of Mr. K—— to ask no questions in his dealings with the trade. "They bring the body, and we pay the price," he used to say, dwelling on the alliteration—"*quid pro quo*." And, again, and somewhat profanely, "Ask no questions," he would tell his assistants, "for conscience's sake." There was no understanding that the subjects were provided by the crime of murder. Had that idea been broached to him in words, he would have recoiled in horror; but the lightness of his speech upon so grave a matter was, in itself, an offence against good manners, and a temptation to the men with whom he dealt. Fettes, for instance, had often remarked to himself upon the singular freshness of the bodies. He had been struck again and again by the hang-dog, abominable looks of the ruffians who came to him before the dawn; and putting things together clearly in his private thoughts, he perhaps attributed a meaning too immoral and too categorical to the unguarded counsels of his master. He understood his duty, in short, to have three branches: to take what was brought, to pay the price, and to avert the eye from any evidence of crime.

One November morning this policy of silence was put sharply to the test. He had been awake all night with a racking toothache—pacing his room like a caged beast or throwing himself in fury on his bed—and had fallen at last into that profound, uneasy slumber that so often follows on a night of pain, when he was awakened by the third or fourth angry repetition of the concerted signal. There was a thin, bright moonshine; it was bitter cold, windy, and frosty; the town had not yet awakened, but an indefinable stir already preluded the noise and business of the day. The ghouls had come later than usual, and they seemed more than usually eager to be gone. Fettes, sick with sleep, lighted them upstairs. He heard their grumbling Irish voices through a dream; and as they stripped the sack from their sad merchandise he leaned dozing, with his shoulder propped against the wall; he had to shake himself to find the men their money. As he did so his eyes lighted on the dead face. He started; he took two steps nearer, with the candle raised.

"God Almighty!" he cried. "That is Jane Galbraith!"

The men answered nothing, but they shuffled nearer the door.

"I know her, I tell you," he continued. "She was alive and hearty yesterday. It's impossible she can be dead; it's impossible you should have got this body fairly."

"Sure, sir, you're mistaken entirely," said one of the men.

But the other looked Fettes darkly in the eyes, and demanded the money on the spot.

It was impossible to misconceive the threat or to exaggerate the danger. The lad's heart failed him. He stammered some excuses, counted out the sum, and saw his hateful visitors depart. No sooner were they gone than he hastened to confirm his doubts. By a dozen unquestionable marks he identified the girl he had jested with the day before. He saw, with horror, marks upon her body that might well betoken violence. A panic seized him, and he took refuge in his room. There he reflected at length over the discovery that he had made; considered soberly the bearing of Mr. K——'s instructions and the danger to himself of interference in so serious a business, and at last, in sore perplexity, determined to wait for the advice of his immediate superior, the class assistant.

This was a young doctor, Wolfe Macfarlane, a high favourite among all the reckless students, clever, dissipated, and unscrupulous to the last degree. He had travelled and studied abroad. His manners were agreeable and a little forward. He was an authority on the stage, skilful on the ice or the links with skate or golf-club; he dressed with nice audacity, and, to put the finishing touch upon his glory, he kept a gig and a strong trotting-horse. With Fettes he was on terms of intimacy; indeed, their relative positions called for some community of life; and when subjects were scarce the pair would drive far into the country in Macfarlane's gig, visit and desecrate some lonely graveyard, and return before dawn with their booty to the door of the dissecting-room.

On that particular morning Macfarlane arrived somewhat earlier than his wont. Fettes heard him, and met him on the stairs, told him his story, and showed him the cause of his alarm. Macfarlane examined the marks on her body.

"Yes," he said with a nod, "it looks fishy."

"Well, what should I do?" asked Fettes.

"Do?" repeated the other. "Do you want to do anything? Least said soonest mended, I should say."

"Someone else might recognise her," objected Fettes. "She was as well-known as the Castle Rock."

"We'll hope not," said Macfarlane, "and

if anybody does—well, you didn't, don't you see, and there's an end. The fact is, this has been going on too long. Stir up the mud, and you'll get K—— into the most unholy trouble; you'll be in a shocking box yourself. So will I, if you come to that. I should like to know how any one of us would look, or what the devil we should have to say for ourselves, in any Christian witness-box. For me, you know there's one thing certain—that, practically speaking, all our subjects have been murdered."

"Macfarlane!" cried Fettes.

"Come now!" sneered the other. "As if you hadn't suspected it yourself!"

"Suspecting is one thing—"

"And proof another. Yes, I know; and I'm as sorry as you are this should have come here," tapping the body with his cane. "The next best thing for me is not to recognise it; and," he added coolly, "I don't. You may, if you please. I don't dictate, but I think a man of the world would do as I do; and I may add, I fancy that is what K—— would look for at our hands. The question is, Why did he choose us two for his assistants? And I answer, because he didn't want old wives."

This was the tone of all others to affect the mind of a lad like Fettes. He agreed to imitate Macfarlane. The body of the unfortunate girl was duly dissected, and no one remarked or appeared to recognise her.

One afternoon, when his day's work was over, Fettes dropped into a popular tavern and found Macfarlane sitting with a stranger. This was a small man, very pale and dark, with coal-black eyes. The cut of his features gave a promise of intellect and refinement which was but feebly realised in his manners, for he proved, upon a nearer acquaintance, coarse, vulgar, and stupid. He exercised, however, a very remarkable control over Macfarlane; issued orders like the Great Bashaw; became inflamed at the least discussion or delay, and commented rudely on the servility with which he was obeyed. This most offensive person took a fancy to Fettes on the spot, plied him with drinks, and honoured him with unusual confidences on his past career. If a tenth part of what he confessed were true, he was a very loathsome rogue; and the lad's vanity was tickled by the attention of so experienced a man.

"I'm a pretty bad fellow myself," the stranger remarked, "but Macfarlane is the boy—Toddy Macfarlane I call him. Toddy, order your friend another glass." Or it might be, "Toddy, you jump up and shut the door." "Toddy hates me," he said again. "Oh yes, Toddy, you do!"

"Don't you call me that confounded name," growled Macfarlane.

"Hear him! Did you ever see the lads play knife? He would like to do that all over my body," remarked the stranger.

"We medicals have a better way than that," said Fettes. "When we dislike a dead friend of ours, we dissect him."

Macfarlane looked up sharply, as though this jest were scarcely to his mind.

The afternoon passed. Gray, for that was the stranger's name, invited Fettes to join them at dinner, ordered a feast so sumptuous that the tavern was thrown into commotion, and when all was done commanded Macfarlane to settle the bill. It was late before they separated; the man Gray was incapably drunk. Macfarlane, sobered by his fury, chewed the cud of the money he had been forced to squander and the slights he had been obliged to swallow. Fettes, with various liquors singing in his head, returned home with devious footsteps and a mind entirely in abeyance. Next day Macfarlane was absent from the class, and Fettes smiled to himself as he imagined him still squiring the intolerable Gray from tavern to tavern. As soon as the hour of liberty had struck he posted from place to place in quest of his last night's companions. He could find them, however, nowhere; so returned early to his rooms, went early to bed, and slept the sleep of the just.

At four in the morning he was awakened by the well-known signal. Descending to the door, he was filled with astonishment to find Macfarlane with his gig, and in the gig one of those long and ghastly packages with which he was so well acquainted.

"What?" he cried. "Have you been out alone? How did you manage?"

But Macfarlane silenced him roughly, bidding him turn to business. When they had got the body upstairs and laid it on the table, Macfarlane made at first as if he were going away. Then he paused and seemed to hesitate; and then, "You had better look at the face," said he, in tones of some constraint. "You had better," he repeated, as Fettes only stared at him in wonder.

"But where, and how, and when did you come by it?" cried the other.

"Look at the face," was the only answer.

Fettes was staggered; strange doubts assailed him. He looked from the young doctor to the body, and then back again. At last, with a start, he did as he was bidden. He had almost expected the sight that met his eyes, and yet the shock was cruel. To see, fixed in the rigidity of death and naked on that coarse layer of sackcloth, the man whom he had left well clad and full of meat and sin upon the threshold of a tavern, awoke, even in the thoughtless Fettes, some of the terrors of the conscience. It was a *cras tibi* which re-echoed in his soul, that two whom he had known should have come to lie upon these icy tables. Yet these were only secondary thoughts. His first concern regarded Wolfe. Unprepared for a challenge so momentous, he knew not how to look his comrade in the face. He durst not meet his eye, and he had neither words nor voice at his command.

It was Macfarlane himself who made the first advance. He came up quietly behind and laid his hand gently but firmly on the other's shoulder.

"Richardson," said he, "may have the head."

Now Richardson was a student who had long been anxious for that portion of the human subject to dissect. There was no answer, and the murderer resumed: "Talking of business, you must pay me; your accounts, you see, must tally."

Fettes found a voice, the ghost of his own: "Pay you!" he cried. "Pay you for that?"

"Why, yes, of course you must. By all means and on every possible account, you must," returned the other. "I dare not give it for nothing, you dare not take it for nothing; it would compromise us both. This is another case like Jane Galbraith's. The more things are wrong the more we must act as if all were right. Where does old K—— keep his money?"

"There," answered Fettes hoarsely, pointing to a cupboard in the corner.

"Give me the key, then," said the other, calmly, holding out his hand.

There was an instant's hesitation, and the die was cast. Macfarlane could not suppress a nervous twitch, the infinitesimal mark of an immense relief, as he felt the key between his fingers. He opened the cupboard, brought out pen and ink and a paper-book that stood in one compartment, and separated from the funds in a drawer a sum suitable to the occasion.

"Now, look here," he said, "there is the payment made—first proof of your good faith: first step to your security. You have now to clinch it by a second. Enter the payment in your book, and then you for your part may defy the devil."

The next few seconds were for Fettes an agony of thought; but in balancing his terrors it was the most immediate that triumphed. Any future difficulty seemed almost welcome if he could avoid a present quarrel with Macfarlane. He set down the candle which he had been carrying all this time, and with a steady hand entered the date, the nature, and the amount of the transaction.

"And now," said Macfarlane, "it's only fair that you should pocket the lucre. I've had my share already. By the bye, when a man of the world falls into a bit of luck, has a few shillings extra in his pocket—I'm ashamed to speak of it, but there's a rule of conduct in the case. No treating, no purchase of expensive class-books, no squaring of old debts; borrow, don't lend."

"Macfarlane," began Fettes, still somewhat hoarsely, "I have put my neck in a halter to oblige you."

"To oblige me?" cried Wolfe. "Oh, come! You did, as near as I can see the matter, what you downright had to do in self-defence. Suppose I got into trouble, where would you be? This second little matter flows clearly from the first. Mr. Gray is the continuation of Miss Galbraith. You can't begin and then stop. If you begin, you must keep on beginning; that's the truth. No rest for the wicked."

A horrible sense of blackness and the treachery of fate seized hold upon the soul of the unhappy student.

"My God!" he cried, "but what have I done? and when did I begin? To be made a class assistant—in the name of reason, where's the harm in that? Service wanted the position; Service might have got it. Would *he* have been where I am now?"

"My dear fellow," said Macfarlane, "what a boy you are! What harm *has* come to you? What harm *can* come to you if you hold your tongue? Why, man, do you know what this life is? There are two squads of us—the lions and the lambs. If you're a lamb, you'll come to lie upon these tables like Gray or Jane Galbraith; if you're a lion, you'll live and drive a horse like me, like K——, like all the world with any wit or courage. You're staggered at the first. But look at K——! My dear fellow, you're clever, you have pluck. I like you, and K—— likes you. You were born to lead the hunt; and I tell you, on my honour and my experience of life, three days from now you'll laugh at all these scarecrows like a High School boy at a farce."

And with that Macfarlane took his departure and drove off up the wynd in his gig to get under cover before daylight. Fettes was thus left alone with his regrets. He saw the miserable peril in which he stood involved. He saw, with inexpressible dismay, that there was no limit to his weakness, and that, from concession to concession, he had fallen from the arbiter of Macfarlane's destiny to his paid and helpless accomplice. He would have given the world to have been a little braver at the time, but it did not occur to him that he might still be brave. The secret of Jane Galbraith and the cursed entry in the day-book closed his mouth.

Hours passed; the class began to arrive; the members of the unhappy Gray were dealt out to one and to another, and received without remark. Richardson was made happy with the head; and before the hour of freedom rang Fettes trembled with exultation to perceive how far they had already gone toward safety.

For two days he continued to watch, with increasing joy, the dreadful process of disguise.

On the third day Macfarlane made his appearance. He had been ill, he said; but he made up for lost time by the energy with which he directed the students. To Richardson in particular he extended the most valuable assistance and advice, and that student, encouraged by the praise of the demonstrator, burned high with ambitious hopes, and saw the medal already in his grasp.

Before the week was out Macfarlane's prophecy had been fulfilled. Fettes had outlived his terrors and had forgotten his baseness. He began to plume himself upon his courage, and had so arranged the story in his mind that he could look back on these events with an unhealthy pride. Of his accomplice he saw but little. They met, of course, in the business of the class; they received their orders together from Mr. K——. At times they had a word or two in private, and Macfarlane was from first to last particularly kind and jovial. But it was plain that he avoided any reference to their common secret; and even when Fettes whispered to him that he had cast in his lot with the lions and foresworn the lambs, he only signed to him smilingly to hold his peace.

At length an occasion arose which threw the pair once more into a closer union. Mr. K—— was again short of subjects; pupils were eager, and it was a part of this teacher's pretensions to be always well supplied. At the same time there came the news of a burial in the rustic graveyard of Glencorse. Time has little changed the place in question. It stood then, as now, upon a cross-road, out of call of human habitations, and buried fathom deep in the foliage of six cedar trees. The cries of the sheep upon the neighbouring hills, the streamlets upon either hand, one loudly singing among pebbles, the other dripping furtively from pond to pond, the stir of the wind in mountainous old flowering chestnuts, and once in seven days the voice of the bell and the old tunes of the precentor, were the only sounds that disturbed the silence around the rural church. The Resurrection Man—to use a byname of the period—was not to be deterred by any of the sanctities of customary piety. It was part of his trade to despise and desecrate the scrolls and trumpets of old tombs, the paths worn by the feet of worshippers and mourners, and the offerings and the inscriptions of bereaved affection. To rustic neighbourhoods, where love is more than commonly tenacious, and where some bonds of blood or fellowship unite the entire society of a parish, the body-snatcher, far from being repelled by natural respect, was attracted by the ease and safety of the task. To bodies that had been laid in earth, in joyful expectation of a far different awakening, there came that hasty, lamp-lit, terror-haunted resurrection of the spade and mattock. The coffin was forced, the cerements torn, and the melancholy relics, clad in sackcloth, after being rattled for hours on moonless byways, were at length exposed to uttermost indignities before a class of gaping boys.

Somewhat as two vultures may swoop upon a dying lamb, Fettes and Macfarlane were to be let loose upon a grave in that green and quiet resting-place. The wife of a farmer, a woman who had lived for sixty years, and been known for nothing but good butter and a godly conversation, was to be rooted from her grave at midnight and carried, dead and naked, to that far-away city that she had always honoured with her Sunday's best; the place beside her family was to be empty till the crack of doom; her innocent and almost venerable members to be exposed to that last curiosity of the anatomist.

Late one afternoon the pair set forth, well wrapped in cloaks and furnished with a formidable bottle. It rained without remission—a cold, dense, lashing rain. Now and again there blew a puff of wind, but these sheets of falling water kept it down. Bottle and all, it was a sad and silent drive as far as Penicuik, where they were to spend the evening. They stopped once, to hide their implements in a thick bush not far from the churchyard, and once again at the Fisher's Tryst, to have a toast before the kitchen fire and vary their nips of whisky with a glass of ale. When they reached their journey's end the gig was housed, the horse was fed and comforted, and the two young doctors in a private room sat down to the best dinner and the best wine the house afforded. The lights, the fire, the beating rain upon the window, the cold, incongruous work that lay before them, added zest to their enjoyment of the meal. With every glass their cordiality increased. Soon Macfarlane handed a little pile of gold to his companion.

"A compliment," he said. "Between friends these little d——d accommodations ought to fly like pipe-lights."

Fettes pocketed the money, and applauded the sentiment to the echo. "You are a philosopher," he cried. "I was an ass till I knew you. You and K—— between you, by the Lord Harry! but you'll make a man of me."

"Of course we shall," applauded Macfarlane. "A man? I tell you, it required a man to back me up the other morning. There are some big, brawling, forty-year-old cowards who would have turned sick at the look of the d——d thing; but not you—you kept your head. I watched you."

"Well, and why not?" Fettes thus vaunted himself. "It was no affair of mine. There was nothing to gain on the one side but disturbance, and on the other I could count on your gratitude, don't you see?" And he slapped his pocket till the gold pieces rang.

Macfarlane somehow felt a certain touch of alarm at these unpleasant words. He may have regretted that he had taught his young companion so successfully, but he had no time to interfere, for the other noisily continued in this boastful strain:—

"The great thing is not to be afraid. Now,

between you and me, I don't want to hang—that's practical; but for all cant, Macfarlane, I was born with a contempt. Hell, God, Devil, right, wrong, sin, crime, and all the old gallery of curiosities—they may frighten boys, but men of the world, like you and me, despise them. Here's to the memory of Gray!"

It was by this time growing somewhat late. The gig, according to order, was brought round to the door with both lamps brightly shining, and the young men had to pay their bill and take the road. They announced that they were bound for Peebles, and drove in that direction till they were clear of the last houses of the town; then, extinguishing the lamps, returned upon their course, and followed a by-road toward Glencorse. There was no sound but that of their own passage, and the incessant, strident pouring of the rain. It was pitch dark; here and there a white gate or a white stone in the wall guided them for a short space across the night; but for the most part it was at a foot pace, and almost groping, that they picked their way through that resonant blackness to their solemn and isolated destination. In the sunken woods that traverse the neighbourhood of the burying-ground the last glimmer failed them, and it became necessary to kindle a match and re-illumine one of the lanterns of the gig. Thus, under the dripping trees, and environed by huge and moving shadows, they reached the scene of their unhallowed labours.

They were both experienced in such affairs, and powerful with the spade; and they had scarce been twenty minutes at their task before they were rewarded by a dull rattle on the coffin lid. At the same moment Macfarlane, having hurt his hand upon a stone, flung it carelessly above his head. The grave, in which they now stood almost to the shoulders, was close to the edge of the plateau of the graveyard; and the gig lamp had been propped, the better to illuminate their labours, against a tree, and on the immediate verge of the steep bank descending to the stream. Chance had taken a sure aim with the stone. Then came a clang of broken glass; night fell upon them; sounds alternately dull and ringing announced the bounding of the lantern down the bank, and its occasional collision with the trees. A stone or two, which it had dislodged in its descent, rattled behind it into the profundities of the glen; and then silence, like night, resumed its sway; and they might bend their hearing to its utmost pitch, but naught was to be heard except the rain, now marching to the wind, now steadily falling over miles of open country.

They were so nearly at an end of their abhorred task that they judged it wisest to complete it in the dark. The coffin was exhumed and broken open; the body inserted in the dripping sack and carried between them to the gig; one mounted to keep it in its place, and the other, taking the horse by the mouth, groped along by wall and bush until they reached the wider road by the Fisher's Tryst. Here was a faint, diffused radiancy, which they hailed like daylight; by that they pushed the horse to a good pace and began to rattle along merrily in the direction of the town.

They had both been wetted to the skin during their operations, and now, as the gig jumped among the deep ruts, the thing that stood propped between them fell now upon one and now upon the other. At every repetition of the horrid contact each instinctively repelled it with the greater haste; and the process, natural although it was, began to tell upon the nerves of the companions. Macfarlane made some ill-favoured jest about the farmer's wife, but it came hollowly from his lips, and was allowed to drop in silence. Still their unnatural burden bumped from side to side; and now the head would be laid, as if in confidence, upon their shoulders, and now the drenching sack-cloth would flap icily about their faces. A creeping chill began to possess the soul of Fettes. He peered at the bundle, and it seemed somehow larger than at first. All over the country-side, and from every degree of distance, the farm dogs accompanied their passage with tragic ululations; and it grew and grew upon his mind that some unnatural miracle had been accomplished, that some nameless change had befallen the dead body, and that it was in fear of their unholy burden that the dogs were howling.

"For God's sake," said he, making a great effort to arrive at speech, "for God's sake, let's have a light!"

Seemingly Macfarlane was affected in the same direction; for, though he made no reply, he stopped the horse, passed the reins to his companion, got down, and proceeded to kindle the remaining lamp. They had by that time got no farther than the cross-road down to Auchenclinny. The rain still poured as though the deluge were returning, and it was no easy matter to make a light in such a world of wet and darkness. When at last the flickering blue flame had been transferred to the wick and began to expand and clarify, and shed a wide circle of misty brightness round the gig, it became possible for the two young men to see each other and the thing they had along with them. The rain had moulded the rough sacking to the outlines of the body underneath; the head was distinct from the trunk, the shoulders plainly modelled; something at once spectral and human riveted their eyes upon the ghastly comrade of their drive.

For some time Macfarlane stood motionless, holding up the lamp. A nameless dread was swathed, like a wet sheet, about the body, and tightened the white skin upon the face of Fettes; a fear that was meaningless, a horror of what could not be, kept mounting to his brain. Another beat of the watch, and he had spoken. But his comrade forestalled him.

"That is not a woman," said Macfarlane, in a hushed voice.

"It was a woman when we put her in," whispered Fettes.

"Hold that lamp," said the other. "I must see her face."

And as Fettes took the lamp his companion untied the fastenings of the sack and drew down the cover from the head. The light fell very clear upon the dark, well-moulded features and smooth-shaven cheeks of a too familiar countenance, often beheld in dreams of both of these young men. A wild yell rang up into the night; each leaped from his own side into the roadway: the lamp fell, broke, and was extinguished; and the horse, terrified by this unusual commotion, bounded and went off toward Edinburgh at a gallop, bearing along with it, sole occupant of the gig, the body of the dead and long-dissected Gray.

Villain: Count Dracula

Dracula's Guest

BRAM STOKER

DRACULA (1897) is the most famous horror novel of the nineteenth century, both a critical and popular success, reprinted countless times, yet Abraham (Bram) Stoker (1847–1912) never wrote another book or short story about the titular character; "Dracula's Guest" is a complete story originally written as a chapter of the novel but never used, finally seeing publication in a posthumous short story collection.

Stoker was born in a seaside suburb of Dublin. Extremely sickly as a child, his long bedridden hours were made bearable by his mother's stories of horror: fiction, folklore, and real life, including grisly tales of the 1832 cholera epidemic in Sligo. His health improved when he went to school at seven; he later became a star athlete at Trinity College in Dublin. He began writing short fiction as well as theater reviews for the *Dublin Evening Mail*, which was partly owned by the famous writer of horror and supernatural fiction, Sheridan Le Fanu, then took the job of manager to Henry Irving, the most popular and acclaimed actor of his generation, a position Stoker held for twenty-seven years, reportedly with eighteen-hour workdays.

In spite of the debilitating schedule, Stoker was able to write more than a dozen novels and other works during the years with Irving, most notably *Dracula*, the only one of his books still widely read today. Freudian elements may have been at work in Stoker's subconscious, as he named the tireless vampire hunter Abraham Van Helsing, using his own first name, while Irving had the attributes of a "psychic" vampire, draining the life out of the author with the relentless workload.

"Dracula's Guest" was originally published in *Dracula's Guest and Other Weird Stories* (London, Routledge, 1914).

DRACULA'S GUEST

Bram Stoker

WHEN WE STARTED for our drive the sun was shining brightly on Munich, and the air was full of the joyousness of early summer. Just as we were about to depart, Herr Delbrück (the maître d'hôtel of the Quatre Saisons, where I was staying) came down, bareheaded, to the carriage and, after wishing me a pleasant drive, said to the coachman, still holding his hand on the handle of the carriage door:

"Remember you are back by nightfall. The sky looks bright but there is a shiver in the north wind that says there may be a sudden storm. But I am sure you will not be late." Here he smiled, and added, "For you know what night it is."

Johann answered with an emphatic, "Ja, mein Herr," and, touching his hat, drove off quickly. When we had cleared the town, I said, after signalling to him to stop:

"Tell me, Johann, what is tonight?"

He crossed himself, as he answered laconically: "Walpurgisnacht." Then he took out his watch, a great, old-fashioned German silver thing as big as a turnip, and looked at it, with his eyebrows gathered together and a little impatient shrug of his shoulders. I realized that this was his way of respectfully protesting against the unnecessary delay, and sank back in the carriage, merely motioning him to proceed. He started off rapidly, as if to make up for lost time. Every now and then the horses seemed to throw up their heads and sniffed the air suspiciously. On such occasions I often looked round in alarm. The road was pretty bleak, for we were traversing a sort of high, windswept plateau. As we drove, I saw a road that looked but little used, and which seemed to dip through a little, winding valley. It looked so inviting that, even at the risk of offending him, I called Johann to stop—and when he had pulled up, I told him I would like to drive down that road. He made all sorts of excuses, and frequently crossed himself as he spoke. This somewhat piqued my curiosity, so I asked him various questions. He answered fencingly, and repeatedly looked at his watch in protest. Finally I said:

"Well, Johann, I want to go down this road. I shall not ask you to come unless you like; but tell me why you do not like to go, that is all I ask." For answer he seemed to throw himself off the box, so quickly did he reach the ground. Then he stretched out his hands appealingly to me, and implored me not to go. There was just enough of English mixed with the German for me to understand the drift of his talk. He seemed always just about to tell me something—the very idea of which evidently frightened him; but each time he pulled himself up, saying, as he crossed himself: "Walpurgisnacht!"

I tried to argue with him, but it was difficult to argue with a man when I did not know his language. The advantage certainly rested with him, for although he began to speak in English, of a very crude and broken kind, he always got excited and broke into his native tongue—and every time he did so, he looked at his watch. Then the horses became restless and sniffed the air. At this he grew very pale, and, looking around in a frightened way, he suddenly jumped forward, took them by the bridles, and led them on some twenty feet. I followed, and asked why he had done this. For answer he crossed himself, pointed to the spot we had left and drew his carriage in the direction of the other road, indicating a cross, and said, first in German, then in English: "Buried him—him what killed themselves."

I remembered the old custom of burying suicides at cross-roads: "Ah! I see, a suicide. How interesting!" But for the life of me I could not make out why the horses were frightened.

While we were talking, we heard a sort of sound between a yelp and a bark. It was far away; but the horses got very restless, and it took Johann all his time to quiet them. He was pale, and said: "It sounds like a wolf—but yet there are no wolves here now."

"No?" I said, questioning him. "Isn't it long since the wolves were so near the city?"

"Long, long," he answered, "in the spring and summer; but with the snow the wolves have been here not so long."

While he was petting the horses and trying to quiet them, dark clouds drifted rapidly across the sky. The sunshine passed away, and a breath of cold wind seemed to drift past us. It was only a breath, however, and more in the nature of a warning than a fact, for the sun came out brightly again. Johann looked under his lifted hand at the horizon and said:

"The storm of snow, he comes before long time." Then he looked at his watch again, and, straightway holding his reins firmly—for the horses were still pawing the ground restlessly and shaking their heads—he climbed to his box as though the time had come for proceeding on our journey.

I felt a little obstinate and did not at once get into the carriage.

"Tell me," I said, "about this place where the road leads," and I pointed down.

Again he crossed himself and mumbled a prayer, before he answered: "It is unholy."

"What is unholy?" I enquired.

"The village."

"Then there is a village?"

"No, no. No one lives there hundreds of years."

My curiosity was piqued: "But you said there was a village."

"There was."

"Where is it now?"

Whereupon he burst out into a long story in German and English, so mixed up that I could not quite understand exactly what he said, but roughly I gathered that long ago, hundreds of years, men had died there and been buried in their graves; and sounds were heard under the clay, and when the graves were opened, men and women were found rosy with life, and their mouths red with blood. And so, in haste to save their lives (aye, and their souls!—and here he crossed himself) those who were left fled away to other places, where the living died, and the dead were dead and not—not something. He was evidently afraid to speak the last words. As he proceeded with his narration, he grew more and more excited. It seemed as if his imagination had got hold of him, and he ended in a perfect paroxysm of fear—white-faced, perspiring, trembling, and looking round him, as if expecting that some dreadful presence would manifest itself there in the bright sunshine on the open plain. Finally, in an agony of desperation, he cried:

"Walpurgisnacht!" and pointed to the carriage for me to get in. All my English blood rose at this, and, standing back, I said:

"You are afraid, Johann—you are afraid. Go home; I shall return alone; the walk will do me good." The carriage door was open. I took from the seat my oak walking stick—which I always carry on my holiday excursions—and closed the door, pointing back to Munich, and said, "Go home, Johann—Walpurgisnacht doesn't concern Englishmen."

The horses were now more restive than ever, and Johann was trying to hold them in while excitedly imploring me not to do anything so foolish. I pitied the poor fellow, he was so deeply in earnest; but all the same I could not help laughing. His English was quite gone now. In his anxiety he had forgotten that his only means of making me understand was to talk my language, so he jabbered away in his native German. It began to be a little tedious. After giving the direction, "Home!" I turned to go down the cross-road into the valley.

With a despairing gesture, Johann turned his horses towards Munich. I leaned on my stick and looked after him. He went slowly along the road for a while; then there came over the crest of the hill a man tall and thin. I could see so much in the distance. When he drew near the horses, they began to jump and kick about, then to scream with terror. Johann could not hold them in; they bolted down the road, running away madly. I watched them out of sight, then looked for the stranger, but I found that he, too, was gone.

With a light heart I turned down the side road through the deepening valley to which Johann had objected. There was not the slightest reason, that I could see, for his objection; and I daresay I tramped for a couple of hours without thinking of time or distance, and certainly without seeing a person or a house. So far as the place was concerned, it was desolation itself. But I did not notice this particularly till, on turning a bend in the road, I came upon a scattered fringe of wood; then I recognized that I had been impressed unconsciously by the desolation of the region through which I had passed.

I sat down to rest myself, and began to look around. It struck me that it was considerably colder than it had been at the commencement of my walk—a sort of sighing sound seemed to be around me, with, now and then, high overhead, a sort of muffled roar. Looking upwards I noticed that great thick clouds were drifting rapidly across the sky from North to South at a great height. There were signs of a coming storm in some lofty stratum of the air. I was a little chilly, and, thinking that it was the sitting still after the exercise of walking, I resumed my journey.

The ground I passed over was now much more picturesque. There were no striking objects that the eye might single out; but in all there was a charm of beauty. I took little heed of time and it was only when the deepening twilight forced itself upon me that I began to think of how I should find my way home. The brightness of the day had gone. The air was cold, and the drifting of clouds high overhead was more marked. They were accompanied by a sort of far-away rushing sound, through which seemed to come at intervals that mysterious cry which the driver had said came from a wolf. For a while I hesitated. I had said I would see the deserted village, so on I went, and presently came on a wide stretch of open country, shut in by hills all around. Their sides were covered with trees which spread down to the plain, dotting, in clumps, the gentler slopes and hollows which showed here and there. I followed with my eye the winding of the road, and saw that it curved close to one of the densest of these clumps and was lost behind it.

As I looked there came a cold shiver in the air, and the snow began to fall. I thought of the miles and miles of bleak country I had passed, and then hurried on to seek the shelter of the wood in front. Darker and darker grew the sky, and faster and heavier fell the snow, till the earth before and around me was a glistening white carpet the further edge of which was lost in misty vagueness. The road was here but crude, and when on the level its boundaries were not so marked, as when it passed through the cuttings; and in a little while I found that I must have strayed from it, for I missed underfoot the hard surface, and my feet sank deeper in the grass and moss. Then the wind grew stronger and blew with ever increasing force, till I was fain to run before it. The air became icy cold, and in spite of my exercise I began to suffer. The snow was now falling so thickly and whirling around me in such rapid eddies that I could hardly keep my eyes open. Every now and then the heavens were torn asunder by vivid lightning, and in the flashes I could see ahead of me a great mass of trees, chiefly yew and cypress all heavily coated with snow.

I was soon amongst the shelter of the trees, and there in comparative silence, I could hear the rush of the wind high overhead. Presently the blackness of the storm had become merged in the darkness of the night. By-and-by the storm seemed to be passing away: it now only came in fierce puffs and blasts. At such moments the weird sound of the wolf appeared to be echoed by many similar sounds around me.

Now and again, through the black mass of drifting cloud, came a straggling ray of moonlight, which lit up the expanse, and showed me that I was at the edge of a dense mass of cypress and yew trees. As the snow had ceased to fall, I walked out from the shelter and began to investigate more closely. It appeared to me that, amongst so many old foundations as I had passed, there might be still standing a house in which, though in ruins, I could find some sort of shelter for a while. As I skirted the edge of the copse, I found that a low wall encircled it, and following this I presently found an opening. Here the cypresses formed an alley leading up to a square mass of some kind of building. Just as I caught sight of this, however, the drifting clouds obscured the moon, and I passed up the path in darkness. The wind must have grown colder, for I felt myself shiver as I walked; but there was hope of shelter, and I groped my way blindly on.

I stopped, for there was a sudden stillness. The storm had passed; and, perhaps in sympathy with nature's silence, my heart seemed to cease to beat. But this was only momentarily; for suddenly the moonlight broke through the clouds, showing me that I was in a graveyard, and that the square object before me was a great massive tomb of marble, as white as the snow that lay on and all around it. With the moonlight there came a fierce sigh of the storm, which appeared to resume its course with a long, low howl, as of many dogs or wolves. I was awed and shocked, and felt the cold perceptibly grow upon me till it seemed to grip me by the heart. Then while the flood of moonlight still fell on the marble tomb, the storm gave further evidence of renewing, as though it was returning on its track. Impelled by some sort of fascination, I approached the sepulchre to see what it was, and why such a thing stood alone in such a place. I walked around it, and read, over the Doric door, in German—

COUNTESS DOLINGEN OF GRATZ
IN STYRIA
SOUGHT AND FOUND DEATH,
1801

On the top of the tomb, seemingly driven through the solid marble—for the structure was composed of a few vast blocks of stone—was a great iron spike or stake. On going to the back I saw, graven in great Russian letters:

THE DEAD TRAVEL FAST

There was something so weird and uncanny about the whole thing that it gave me a turn and made me feel quite faint. I began to wish, for the first time, that I had taken Johann's advice. Here a thought struck me, which came under almost mysterious circumstances and with a terrible shock. This was Walpurgis Night!

Walpurgis Night, when, according to the belief of millions of people, the devil was abroad—when the graves were opened and the dead came forth and walked. When all evil things of earth and air and water held revel. This very place the driver had specially shunned. This was the depopulated village of centuries ago. This was where the suicide lay; and this was the place where I was alone—unmanned, shivering with cold in a shroud of snow with a wild storm gathering again upon me! It took all my philosophy, all the religion I had been taught, all my courage, not to collapse in a paroxysm of fright.

And now a perfect tornado burst upon me. The ground shook as though thousands of horses thundered across it; and this time the storm bore on its icy wings, not snow, but great hailstones which drove with such violence that they might have come from the thongs of Balearic slingers—hailstones that beat down leaf and branch and made the shelter of the cypresses of no more avail than though their stems were standing corn. At the first I had rushed to the nearest tree; but I was soon fain to leave it and seek the only spot that seemed to afford refuge, the deep Doric doorway of the marble tomb. There, crouching against the massive bronze door, I gained a certain amount of protection from the beating of the hailstones, for now they only drove against me as they ricocheted from the ground and the side of the marble.

As I leaned against the door, it moved slightly and opened inwards. The shelter of even a tomb was welcome in that pitiless tempest, and I was about to enter it when there came a flash of forked lightning that lit up the whole expanse of the heavens. In the instant, as I am a living man, I saw, as my eyes were turned into the darkness of the tomb, a beautiful woman, with rounded cheeks and red lips, seemingly sleeping on a bier. As the thunder broke overhead, I was grasped as by the hand of a giant and hurled out into the storm. The whole thing was so sudden that, before I could realize the shock, moral as well as physical, I found the hailstones beating me down. At the same time I had a strange, dominating feeling that I was not alone. I looked towards the tomb. Just then there came another blinding flash, which seemed to strike the iron stake that surmounted the tomb and to pour through to the earth, blasting and crumbling the marble, as in a burst of flame. The dead woman rose for a moment of agony, while she was lapped in the flame, and her bitter scream of pain was drowned in the thundercrash. The last thing I heard was this mingling of dreadful sound, as again I was seized in the giant grasp and dragged away, while the hailstones beat on me, and the air around seemed reverberant with the howling of wolves. The last sight that I remembered was a vague, white, moving mass, as if all the graves around me had sent out the phantoms of their sheeted dead, and that they were closing in on me through the white cloudiness of the driving hail.

Gradually there came a sort of vague beginning of consciousness; then a sense of weariness that was dreadful. For a time I remembered nothing; but slowly my senses returned. My feet seemed positively racked with pain, yet I could not move them. They seemed to be numbed. There was an icy feeling at the back of my neck and all down my spine, and my ears, like my feet, were dead, yet in torment; but there was in my breast a sense of warmth which was, by comparison, delicious. It was as a nightmare, if one may use such an expression; for some heavy weight on my chest made it difficult for me to breathe.

This period of semi-lethargy seemed to remain a long time, and as it faded away I must have slept or swooned. Then came a sort of loathing, like the first stage of sea-sickness, and a wild desire to be free from something—I knew not what. A vast stillness enveloped me, as though all the world were asleep or dead—only broken by the low panting as of some animal close to me. I felt a warm rasping at my throat, then came a consciousness of the awful truth, which chilled me to the heart and sent the blood surging up through my brain. Some great animal was lying on me and now licking my throat. I feared to stir, for some instinct of prudence bade me lie still; but the brute seemed to realize that there was now some change in me, for it raised its head. Through my eyelashes I saw above me the two great flaming eyes of a gigantic wolf. Its sharp white teeth gleamed in the gaping red mouth, and I could feel its hot breath fierce and acrid upon me.

For another spell of time I remembered no more. Then I became conscious of a low growl, followed by a yelp, renewed again and again. Then, seemingly very far away, I heard a "Holloa! Holloa!" as of many voices calling in unison. Cautiously I raised my head and looked in the direction whence the sound came; but the cemetery blocked my view. The wolf still continued to yelp in a strange way, and a red glare began to move round the grove of cypresses, as though following the sound. As the voices drew closer, the wolf yelped faster and louder. I feared to make either sound or motion. Nearer came the red glow, over the white pall which stretched into the darkness around me. Then all at once from beyond the trees there came at a trot a troop of horsemen bearing torches. The wolf rose from my breast and made for the cemetery. I saw one of the horsemen (soldiers by their caps and their long military cloaks) raise his carbine and take aim. A companion knocked up his arm, and I heard the ball whizz over my head. He had evidently taken my body for that of the wolf. Another sighted the animal as it slunk away, and a shot followed. Then, at a gallop, the troop rode forward—some towards me, others following the wolf as it disappeared amongst the snow-clad cypresses.

As they drew nearer I tried to move, but was powerless, although I could see and hear all that went on around me. Two or three of the soldiers jumped from their horses and knelt beside me. One of them raised my head, and placed his hand over my heart.

"Good news, comrades!" he cried. "His heart still beats!"

Then some brandy was poured down my throat; it put vigor into me, and I was able to open my eyes fully and look around. Lights and shadows were moving among the trees, and I heard men call to one another. They drew together, uttering frightened exclamations; and the lights flashed as the others came pouring out of the cemetery pell-mell, like men possessed. When the further ones came close to us, those who were around me asked them eagerly:

"Well, have you found him?"

The reply rang out hurriedly:

"No! No! Come away quick—quick! This is no place to stay, and on this of all nights!"

"What was it?" was the question, asked in all manner of keys. The answer came variously and all indefinitely as though the men were moved by some common impulse to speak, yet were restrained by some common fear from giving their thoughts.

"It—it—indeed!" gibbered one, whose wits had plainly given out for the moment.

"A wolf—and yet not a wolf!" another put in shudderingly.

"No use trying for him without the sacred bullet," a third remarked in a more ordinary manner.

"Serve us right for coming out on this night! Truly we have earned our thousand marks!" were the ejaculations of a fourth.

"There was blood on the broken marble," another said after a pause—"the lightning never brought that there. And for him—is he safe? Look at his throat! See, comrades, the wolf has been lying on him and keeping his blood warm."

The officer looked at my throat and replied:

"He is all right; the skin is not pierced. What does it all mean? We should never have found him but for the yelping of the wolf."

"What became of it?" asked the man who was holding up my head, and who seemed the least panic-stricken of the party, for his hands were steady and without tremor. On his sleeve was the chevron of a petty officer.

"It went to its home," answered the man, whose long face was pallid, and who actually shook with terror as he glanced around him fearfully. "There are graves enough there in which it may lie. Come, comrades—come quickly! Let us leave this cursed spot."

The officer raised me to a sitting posture, as he uttered a word of command; then several men placed me upon a horse. He sprang to the saddle behind me, took me in his arms, gave the word to advance; and, turning our faces away from the cypresses, we rode away in swift, military order.

As yet my tongue refused its office, and I was perforce silent. I must have fallen asleep; for the next thing I remembered was finding myself standing up, supported by a soldier on each side of me. It was almost broad daylight, and to the north a red streak of sunlight was reflected, like a path of blood, over the waste of snow. The officer was telling the men to say nothing of what they had seen, except that they found an English stranger, guarded by a large dog.

"Dog! That was no dog," cut in the man who had exhibited such fear. "I think I know a wolf when I see one."

The young officer answered calmly: "I said a dog."

"Dog!" reiterated the other ironically. It was evident that his courage was rising with the sun; and, pointing to me, he said, "Look at his throat. Is that the work of a dog, master?"

Instinctively I raised my hand to my throat, and as I touched it I cried out in pain. The men crowded round to look, some stooping down from their saddles; and again there came the calm voice of the young officer:

"A dog, as I said. If aught else were said we should only be laughed at."

I was then mounted behind a trooper, and we rode on into the suburbs of Munich. Here we came across a stray carriage, into which I was lifted, and it was driven off to the Quatre Saisons—the young officer accompanying me, while a trooper followed with his horse, and the others rode off to their barracks.

When we arrived, Herr Delbrück rushed so quickly down the steps to meet me, that it was apparent he had been watching within. Taking me by both hands he solicitously led me in. The officer saluted me and was turning to withdraw, when I recognized his purpose, and insisted that he should come to my rooms. Over a glass of wine I warmly thanked him and his brave comrades for saving me. He replied simply that he was more than glad, and that Herr Delbrück had at the first taken steps to make all the searching party pleased; at which ambiguous utterance the maître d'hôtel smiled, while the officer pleaded duty and withdrew.

"But Herr Delbrück," I inquired, "how and why was it that the soldiers searched for me?"

He shrugged his shoulders, as if in depreciation of his own deed, as he replied:

"I was so fortunate as to obtain leave from the commander of the regiment in which I served, to ask for volunteers."

"But how did you know I was lost?" I asked.

"The driver came hither with the remains of his carriage, which had been upset when the horses ran away."

"But surely you would not send a search-party of soldiers merely on this account?"

"Oh, no!" he answered. "But even before the coachman arrived, I had this telegram from the Boyar whose guest you are," and he took from his pocket a telegram which he handed to me, and I read:

> Bistritz
> Be careful of my guest—his safety is most precious to me. Should aught happen to him, or if he be missed, spare nothing to find him and ensure his safety. He is English and therefore adventurous. There are often dangers from snow and wolves and night. Lose not a moment if you suspect harm to him. I answer your zeal with my fortune.
>
> Dracula

As I held the telegram in my hand, the room seemed to whirl around me; and, if the attentive maître d'hôtel had not caught me, I think I should have fallen. There was something so strange in all this, something so weird and impossible to imagine, that there grew on me a sense of my being in some way the sport of opposite forces—the mere vague idea of which seemed in a way to paralyze me. I was certainly under some form of mysterious protection. From a distant country had come, in the very nick of time, a message that took me out of the danger of the snow-sleep and the jaws of the wolf.

Villain: Horace Dorrington

The Narrative of Mr. James Rigby

ARTHUR MORRISON

AFTER THE STAGGERING SUCCESS enjoyed by Arthur Conan Doyle with his Sherlock Holmes series, other authors, undoubtedly pressed by publishers who hoped to cash in on the new phenomenon of detective adventures, released a deluge of novels and short stories whose protagonists followed in the footsteps of Holmes. The most successful was Arthur Morrison's (1863–1945) Martin Hewitt, who made his debut in *Martin Hewitt: Investigator* (1894), followed by two more short story collections and a novel, *The Red Triangle* (1903).

Like Doyle, Morrison had little interest in or affection for his detective, convinced that his atmospheric tales of the London slums were far more significant. He may have been right, as they sold well in their time, show greater vitality, and are said to have been instrumental in initiating many important social reforms, particularly with regard to housing.

In addition to his naturalistic novels of crime and poverty in London's East End and the exploits of Hewitt, Morrison wrote other books connected to the mystery genre, including *Cunning Murrell* (1900), a fictionalized account of a witch doctor's activities in early nineteenth-century rural Essex; *The Hole in the Wall* (1902), a story of murder in a London slum; and, most significant, *The Dorrington Deed-Box* (1897), a collection of stories about the unscrupulous Horace Dorrington, a con man and thief who occasionally earns his money honestly—by working as a private detective!

"The Narrative of Mr. James Rigby" was originally published in *The Dorrington Deed-Box* (London, Ward, Lock & Co., 1897).

THE NARRATIVE OF MR. JAMES RIGBY

Arthur Morrison

I SHALL HERE SET DOWN in language as simple and straightforward as I can command, the events which followed my recent return to England; and I shall leave it to others to judge whether or not my conduct has been characterised by foolish fear and ill-considered credulity. At the same time I have my own opinion as to what would have been the behaviour of any other man of average intelligence and courage in the same circumstances; more especially a man of my exceptional upbringing and retired habits.

I was born in Australia, and I have lived there all my life till quite recently, save for a single trip to Europe as a boy, in company with my father and mother. It was then that I lost my father. I was less than nine years old at the time, but my memory of the events of that European trip is singularly vivid.

My father had emigrated to Australia at the time of his marriage, and had become a rich man by singularly fortunate speculations in land in and about Sydney. As a family we were most uncommonly self-centred and isolated. From my parents I never heard a word as to their relatives in England; indeed to this day I do not as much as know what was the Christian name of my grandfather. I have often supposed that some serious family quarrel or great misfortune must have preceded or accompanied my father's marriage. Be that as it may, I was never able to learn anything of my relatives, either on my mother's or my father's side. Both parents, however, were educated people, and indeed I fancy that their habit of seclusion must first have arisen from this circumstance, since the colonists about them in the early days, excellent people as they were, were not as a class distinguished for extreme intellectual culture. My father had his library stocked from England, and added to by fresh arrivals from time to time; and among his books he would pass most of his days, taking, however, now and again an excursion with a gun in search of some new specimen to add to his museum of natural history, which occupied three long rooms in our house by the Lane Cove river.

I was, as I have said, eight years of age when I started with my parents on a European tour, and it was in the year 1873. We stayed but a short while in England at first arrival, intending to make a longer stay on our return from the Continent. We made our tour, taking Italy last, and it was here that my father encountered a dangerous adventure.

We were at Naples, and my father had taken an odd fancy for a picturesque-looking ruffian who had attracted his attention by a complexion unusually fair for an Italian, and in whom he professed to recognise a likeness to Tasso the poet. This man became his guide in excursions about the neighbourhood of Naples, though he was not one of the regular corps of guides, and indeed seemed to have no regular occupation of a definite sort. "Tasso," as my father always called him, seemed a civil fellow enough, and was fairly intelligent; but my mother disliked him extremely from the first, without being able to offer any very distinct reason for her aversion. In the event her instinct was proved true.

"Tasso"—his correct name, by the way, was Tommaso Marino—persuaded my father that something interesting was to be seen at the Astroni crater, four miles west of the city, or thereabout; persuaded him, moreover, to make the journey on foot; and the two accordingly set out. All went well enough till the crater was reached, and then, in a lonely and broken part of the hill, the guide suddenly turned and attacked my father with a knife, his intention, without a doubt, being murder and the acquisition of the Englishman's valuables. Fortunately my father had a hip-pocket with a revolver in it, for he had been warned of the danger a stranger might at that time run wandering in the country about Naples. He received a wound in the flesh of his left arm in an attempt to ward off a stab, and fired, at wrestling distance, with the result that his assailant fell dead on the spot. He left the place with all speed, tying up his arm as he went, sought the British consul at Naples, and informed him of the whole circumstances. From the authorities there was no great difficulty. An examination or two, a few signatures, some particular exertions on the part of the consul, and my father was free, so far as the officers of the law were concerned. But while these formalities were in progress no less than three attempts were made on his life—two by the knife and one by shooting—and in each his escape was little short of miraculous. For the dead ruffian, Marino, had been a member of the dreaded Camorra, and the Camorristi were eager to avenge his death. To anybody acquainted with the internal history of Italy—more particularly the history of the old kingdom of Naples—the name of the Camorra will be familiar enough. It was one of the worst and most powerful of the many powerful and evil secret societies of Italy, and had none of the excuses for existence which have been from time to time put forward on behalf of the others. It was a gigantic club for the commission of crime and the extortion of money. So powerful was it that it actually imposed a regular tax on all food material entering Naples—a tax collected and paid with far more regularity than were any of the taxes due to the lawful Government of the country. The carrying of smuggled goods was a monopoly of the Camorra, a perfect organisation existing for the purpose throughout the kingdom. The whole population was terrorised by this detestable society, which had no less than twelve centres in the city of Naples alone. It contracted for the commission of crime just as systematically and calmly as a railway company contracts for the carriage of merchandise. A murder was so much, according to circumstances, with extras for disposing of the body; arson was dealt in profitably; maimings and kidnappings were carried out with promptitude and despatch; and any diabolical outrage imaginable was a mere matter of price. One of the staple vocations of the concern was of course brigandage. After the coming of Victor Emmanuel and the fusion of Italy into one kingdom the Camorra lost some of its power, but for a long time gave considerable trouble. I have heard that in the year after the matters I am describing two hundred Camorristi were banished from Italy.

As soon as the legal forms were complied with, my father received the broadest possible official hint that the sooner and the more secretly he left the country the better it would be for himself and his family. The British consul, too, impressed it upon him that the law would be entirely unable to protect him against the machinations of the Camorra; and indeed it needed but little persuasion to induce us to leave, for my poor mother was in a state of constant terror lest we were murdered together in our hotel; so that we lost no time in returning to England and bringing our European trip to a close.

In London we stayed at a well-known private hotel near Bond Street. We had been but three days here when my father came in one evening with a firm conviction that he had been followed for something like two hours, and followed very skilfully too. More than once he had doubled suddenly with a view to confront the pursuers, who he felt were at his heels, but he had met nobody of a suspicious appearance. The next afternoon I heard my mother telling my governess (who was travelling with us) of an unpleasant-looking man, who had been hanging about opposite the hotel door, and who, she felt sure, had afterwards been following her and my father as they were walking. My mother grew nervous, and communicated her fears to my father. He, however, pooh-poohed the thing, and took little thought of its meaning. Nevertheless the dogging continued, and my father, who was never able to fix upon the persons who caused the annoyance—indeed he rather felt their presence by instinct, as one does in such cases, than otherwise—grew extremely angry, and had some idea of consulting the police. Then one morning my mother discovered a little paper label stuck on the outside of the door of the bedroom occupied by herself and my father. It was a small thing, circular, and about the size of a sixpenny-piece, or even smaller, but my mother was quite certain that it had not been there when she last entered the door the night before, and she was much terrified. For the label carried a tiny device, drawn awkwardly in ink—a pair of knives of curious shape, crossed: the sign of the Camorra.

Nobody knew anything of this label, or how it came where it had been found. My mother urged my father to place himself under the protection of the police at once, but he delayed. Indeed, I fancy he had a suspicion that the label might be the production of some practical joker staying at the hotel who had heard of his Neapolitan adventure (it was reported in many newspapers) and designed to give him a fright. But that very evening my poor father was found dead, stabbed in a dozen places, in a short, quiet street not forty yards from the hotel. He had merely gone out to buy a few cigars of a particular brand which he fancied, at a shop two streets away, and in less than half an hour of his departure the police were at the hotel door with the news of his death, having got his address from letters in his pockets.

It is no part of my present design to enlarge on my mother's grief, or to describe in detail the incidents that followed my father's death, for I am going back to this early period of my life merely to make more clear the bearings of what has recently happened to myself. It will be sufficient therefore to say that at the inquest the jury returned a verdict of wilful murder against some person or persons unknown; that it was several times reported that the police had obtained a most important clue, and that being so, very naturally there was never any arrest. We returned to Sydney, and there I grew up.

I should perhaps have mentioned ere this that my profession—or I should rather say my hobby—is that of an artist. Fortunately or unfortunately, as you may please to consider it, I have no need to follow any profession as a means of livelihood, but since I was sixteen years of age my whole time has been engrossed in drawing and painting. Were it not for my mother's invincible objection to parting with me, even for the shortest space of time, I should long ago have come to Europe to work and to study in the regular schools. As it was I made shift to do my best in Australia, and wandered about pretty freely, struggling with the difficulties of moulding into artistic form the curious Australian landscape. There is an odd, desolate, uncanny note in characteristic Australian scenery, which most people are apt to regard as of little value for the purposes of the landscape painter, but with which I have always been convinced that an able painter could do great things. So I did my feeble best.

Two years ago my mother died. My age was then twenty-eight, and I was left without a friend in the world, and, so far as I know, without a relative. I soon found it impossible any longer to inhabit the large house by the Lane Cove river. It was beyond my simple needs, and the whole thing was an embarrassment, to say nothing of the associations of the house with my dead mother, which exercised a painful and depressing effect on me. So I sold the house, and cut myself adrift. For a year or more I pursued the life of a lonely vagabond in New South Wales, painting as well as I could its scattered forests of magnificent trees, with their curious upturned foliage. Then, miserably dissatisfied with my performance, and altogether filled with a restless spirit, I determined to quit the colony and live in England, or at any rate somewhere in Europe. I would paint at the Paris schools, I promised myself, and acquire that technical mastery of my material that I now felt the lack of.

The thing was no sooner resolved on than begun. I instructed my solicitors in Sydney to wind up my affairs and to communicate with their London correspondents in order that, on my arrival in England, I might deal with business matters through them. I had more than half resolved to transfer all my property to England, and to make the old country my permanent headquarters; and in three weeks from the date of my resolve I had started. I carried with me the necessary letters of introduction to the London solicitors, and the deeds appertaining to certain land in South Australia, which my father had bought just before his departure on the fatal European trip. There was workable copper in this land, it had since been ascertained, and I believed I might profitably dispose of the property to a company in London.

I found myself to some extent out of my element on board a great passenger steamer. It seemed no longer possible for me in the constant association of shipboard to maintain that reserve which had become with me a second nature. But so much had it become my nature that I shrank ridiculously from breaking it, for, grown man as I was, it must be confessed that I was absurdly shy, and indeed I fear little better than an overgrown schoolboy in my manner. But somehow I was scarce a day at sea before falling into a most pleasant acquaintanceship with another passenger, a man of thirty-eight or forty, whose name was Dorrington. He was a tall, well-built fellow, rather handsome, perhaps, except for a certain extreme roundness of face and fulness of feature; he had a dark military moustache, and carried himself erect, with a swing as of a cavalryman, and his eyes had, I think, the most penetrating quality I ever saw. His manners were extremely engaging, and he was the only good talker I had ever met. He knew everybody, and had been everywhere. His fund of illustration and anecdote was inexhaustible, and during all my acquaintance with him I never heard him tell the same story twice. Nothing could happen—not a bird could fly by the ship, not a dish could be put on the table, but Dorrington was ready with a pungent remark and the appropriate anecdote. And he never bored nor wearied one. With all his ready talk he never appeared unduly obtrusive nor in the least egotistic. Mr. Horace Dorrington was altogether the most charming person I had ever met. Moreover we discovered a community of taste in cigars.

"By the way," said Dorrington to me one magnificent evening as we leaned on the rail and smoked, "Rigby isn't a very common name in Australia, is it? I seem to remember a case, twenty years ago or more, of an Australian gentleman of that name being very badly treated in London—indeed, now I think of it, I'm not sure that he wasn't murdered. Ever hear anything of it?"

"Yes," I said, "I heard a great deal, unfortunately. He was my father, and he *was* murdered."

"Your father? There—I'm awfully sorry. Perhaps I shouldn't have mentioned it; but of course I didn't know."

"Oh," I replied, "that's all right. It's so far back now that I don't mind speaking about it. It was a very extraordinary thing altogether." And then, feeling that I owed Dorrington a story of some sort, after listening to the many he had been telling me, I described to him the whole circumstances of my father's death.

"Ah," said Dorrington when I had finished, "I have heard of the Camorra before this—I know a thing or two about it, indeed. As a matter of fact it still exists; not quite the widespread and open thing it once was, of course, and much smaller; but pretty active in a quiet way, and pretty mischievous. They were a mighty bad lot, those Camorristi. Personally I'm rather surprised that you heard no more of them. They were the sort of people who would rather any day murder three people than one, and their usual idea of revenge went a good way beyond the mere murder of the offending party; they had a way of including his wife and family, and as many relatives as possible. But at any rate *you* seem to have got off all right, though I'm inclined to call it rather a piece of luck than otherwise."

Then, as was his invariable habit, he launched into anecdote. He told me of the crimes of the Maffia, that Italian secret society, larger even and more powerful than the Camorra, and almost as criminal; tales of implacable revenge visited on father, son, and grandson in succession, till the race was extirpated. Then he talked of the methods; of the large funds at the disposal of the Camorra and the Maffia, and of the cunning patience with which their schemes were carried into execution; of the victims who had discovered too late that their most trusted servants were sworn to their destruction, and of those who had fled to remote parts of the earth and hoped to be lost and forgotten, but who had been shadowed and slain with barbarous ferocity in their most trusted hiding-places. Wherever Italians were, there was apt to be a branch of one of the societies, and one could never tell where they might or might not turn up. The two Italian forecastle hands on board at that moment might be members, and might or might not have some business in hand not included in their signed articles.

I asked if he had ever come into personal contact with either of these societies or their doings.

"With the Camorra, no, though I know things about them that would probably surprise some of them not a little. But I have had professional dealings with the Maffia—and that without coming off second best, too. But it was not so serious a case as your father's; one of a robbery of documents and blackmail."

"Professional dealings?" I queried.

Dorrington laughed. "Yes," he answered. "I find I've come very near to letting the cat out of the bag. I don't generally tell people who I am when I travel about, and indeed I don't always use my own name, as I am doing now. Surely you've heard the name at some time or another?"

I had to confess that I did not remember it. But I excused myself by citing my secluded life, and the fact that I had never left Australia since I was a child.

"Ah," he said, "of course we should be less heard of in Australia. But in England we're really pretty well known, my partner and I. But, come now, look me all over and consider, and I'll give you a dozen guesses and bet you a sovereign you can't tell me my trade. And it's not such an uncommon or unheard-of trade, neither."

Guessing would have been hopeless, and I said so. He did not seem the sort of man who would trouble himself about a trade at all. I gave it up.

"Well," he said, "I've no particular desire to have it known all over the ship, but I don't mind telling you—you'd find it out probably before long if you settle in the old country—that we are what is called private inquiry agents—detectives—secret service men—whatever you like to call it."

"Indeed!"

"Yes, indeed. And I think I may claim that we stand as high as any—if not a trifle higher. Of course I can't tell you, but you'd be rather astonished if you heard the names of some of our clients. We have had dealings with certain royalties, European and Asiatic, that would startle you a bit if I could tell them. Dorrington & Hicks is the name of the firm, and we are both pretty busy men, though we keep going a regiment of assistants and correspondents. I have been in Australia three months over a rather awkward and complicated matter, but I fancy I've pulled it through pretty well, and I mean to reward myself with a little holiday when I get back. There—now you know the worst of me. And D. & H. present their respectful compliments, and trust that by unfailing punctuality and a strict attention to business they may hope to receive your esteemed commands whenever you may be so unfortunate as to require their services. Family secrets extracted, cleaned, scaled, or stopped with gold. Special attention given to wholesale orders." He laughed and pulled out his cigar-case. "You haven't another cigar in your pocket," he said, "or you wouldn't smoke that stump so low. Try one of these."

I took the cigar and lit it at my remainder. "Ah, then," I said, "I take it that it is the practice of your profession that has given you such a command of curious and out-of-the-way information and anecdote. Plainly you must have been in the midst of many curious affairs."

"Yes, I believe you," Dorrington replied. "But, as it happens, the most curious of my experiences I am unable to relate, since they are matters of professional confidence. Such as I *can* tell I usually tell with altered names, dates, and places. One learns discretion in such a trade as mine."

"As to your adventure with the Maffia, now. Is there any secrecy about that?"

Dorrington shrugged his shoulders. "No," he said, "none in particular. But the case was not particularly interesting. It was in Florence. The documents were the property of a wealthy American, and some of the Maffia rascals managed to steal them. It doesn't matter what the documents were—that's a private matter—but their owner would have parted with a great deal to get them back, and the Maffia held them for ransom. But they had such a fearful notion of the American's wealth, and of what he ought to pay, that, badly as he wanted the papers back, he couldn't stand their demands, and employed us to negotiate and to do our best for him. I think I might have managed to get the things stolen back again—indeed I spent some time thinking a plan over—but I decided in the end that it wouldn't pay. If the Maffia were tricked in that way they might consider it appropriate to stick somebody with a knife, and that was not an easy thing to provide against. So I took a little time and went another way to work. The details don't matter—they're quite uninteresting, and to tell you them would be to talk mere professional 'shop'; there's a deal of dull and patient work to be done in my business. Anyhow, I contrived to find out exactly in whose hands the documents lay. He wasn't altogether a blameless creature, and there were two or three little things that, properly handled, might have brought him into awkward complications with the law. So I delayed the negotiations while I got my nets effectually round this gentleman, who was the president of that particular branch of the Maffia, and when all was ready I had a friendly interview with him, and just showed him my hand of cards. They served as no other argument would have done, and in the end we concluded quite an amicable arrangement on easy terms for both parties, and my client got his property back, including all expenses, at about a fifth of the price he expected to have to pay. That's all. I learnt a deal about the Maffia while the business lasted, and at that and other times I learnt a good deal about the Camorra too."

Dorrington and I grew more intimate every day of the voyage, till he knew every detail of my uneventful little history, and I knew many of his own most curious experiences. In truth he was a man with an irresistible fascination for a dull home-bird like myself. With all his gaiety he never forgot business, and at most of our stopping places he sent off messages by cable to his partner. As the voyage drew near its end he grew anxious and impatient lest he should not arrive in time to enable him to get to Scotland for grouse-shooting on the twelfth of August. His one amusement, it seemed, was shooting, and the holiday he had promised himself was to be spent on a grouse-moor which he rented in Perthshire. It would be a great nuisance to miss the twelfth, he said, but it would apparently be a near shave. He thought, however, that in any case it might be done by leaving the ship at Plymouth, and rushing up to London by the first train.

"Yes," he said, "I think I shall be able to do it that way, even if the boat is a couple of days late. By the way," he added suddenly, "why not come along to Scotland with me? You haven't any particular business in hand, and I can promise you a week or two of good fun."

The invitation pleased me. "It's very good of you," I said, "and as a matter of fact I haven't any very urgent business in London. I must see those solicitors I told you of, but that's not a matter of hurry; indeed an hour or two on my way through London would be enough. But as I don't know any of your party and——"

"Pooh, pooh, my dear fellow," answered Dorrington, with a snap of his fingers, "that's all right. I shan't have a party. There won't be time to get it together. One or two might come down a little later, but if they do they'll be capital fellows, delighted to make your acquaintance, I'm sure. Indeed you'll do me a great favour if you'll come, else I shall be all alone, without a soul to say a word to. Anyway, I *won't* miss the twelfth, if it's to be done by any possibility. You'll really have to come, you know—you've no excuse. I can lend you guns and anything you want, though I believe you've such things with you. Who is your London solicitor, by the way?"

"Mowbray, of Lincoln's Inn Fields."

"Oh, Mowbray? We know him well; his partner died last year. When I say *we* know him well, I mean as a firm. I have never met him personally, though my partner (who does the office work) has regular dealings with him. He's an excellent man, but his managing clerk's frightful; I wonder Mowbray keeps him. Don't you let him do anything for you on his own hook; he makes the most disastrous messes, and I rather fancy he drinks. Deal with Mowbray himself; there's nobody better in London. And by the way, now I think of it, it's lucky you've nothing urgent for him, for he's sure to be off out of town for the twelfth; he's a rare old gunner, and never misses a season. So that now you haven't a shade of an excuse for leaving me in the lurch, and we'll consider the thing settled."

Settled accordingly it was, and the voyage ended uneventfully. But the steamer was late, and we left it at Plymouth and rushed up to town on the tenth. We had three or four hours to prepare before leaving Euston by the night train. Dorrington's moor was a long drive from Crieff station, and he calculated that at best we could not arrive there before the early evening of the following day, which would, however, give us comfortable time for a good long night's rest before the morning's sport opened. Fortunately I had plenty of loose cash with me, so that there was nothing to delay us in that regard. We made ready in Dorrington's rooms (he was a bachelor) in Conduit Street, and got off comfortably by the ten o'clock train from Euston.

Then followed a most delightful eight days. The weather was fine, the birds were plentiful, and my first taste of grouse-shooting was a complete success. I resolved for the future to come out of my shell and mix in the world that contained such charming fellows as Dorrington, and such delightful sports as that I was then enjoying. But on the eighth day Dorrington received a telegram calling him instantly to London.

"It's a shocking nuisance," he said; "here's my holiday either knocked on the head altogether or cut in two, and I fear it's the first rather than the second. It's just the way in such an uncertain profession as mine. There's no possible help for it, however; I must go, as you'd understand at once if you knew the case. But what chiefly annoys me is leaving you all alone."

I reassured him on this point, and pointed out that I had for a long time been used to a good deal of my own company. Though indeed, with Dorrington away, life at the shooting-lodge threatened to be less pleasant than it had been.

"But you'll be bored to death here," Dorrington said, his thoughts jumping with my own. "But on the other hand it won't be much good going up to town yet. Everybody's out of town, and Mowbray among them. There's a little business of ours that's waiting for him at this moment—my partner mentioned it in his letter yesterday. Why not put in the time with a little tour round? Or you might work up to London by irregular stages, and look about you. As an artist you'd like to see a few of the old towns—probably Edinburgh, Chester, Warwick, and so on. It isn't a great programme, perhaps, but I hardly know what else to suggest. As for myself I must be off as I am by the first train I can get."

I begged him not to trouble about me, but to attend to his business. As a matter of fact, I was disposed to get to London and take chambers, at any rate for a little while. But Chester was a place I much wanted to see—a real old town, with walls round it—and I was not indisposed to take a day at Warwick. So in the end I resolved to pack up and make for Chester the following day, and from there to take a train for Warwick. And in half an hour Dorrington was gone.

Chester was all delight to me. My recollections of the trip to Europe in my childhood were vivid enough as to the misfortunes that followed my father, but of the ancient buildings we visited I remembered little. Now in Chester I found the mediæval town I had so often read of. I wandered for hours together in the quaint old "Rows," and walked on the city wall. The evening after my arrival was fine and moonlit, and I was tempted from my hotel. I took a stroll about the town and finished by a walk along the wall from the Watergate toward the cathedral. The moon, flecked over now and again by scraps of cloud, and at times obscured for half a minute together, lighted up all the Roodee in the intervals, and touched with silver the river beyond. But as I walked I presently grew aware of a quiet shuffling footstep some little way behind me. I took little heed of it at first, though I could see nobody near me from whom the sound might come. But soon I perceived that when I stopped, as I did from time to time to gaze over the parapet, the mysterious footsteps stopped also, and when I resumed my walk the quiet shuffling tread began again. At first I thought it might be an echo; but a moment's reflection dispelled that idea. Mine was an even, distinct walk, and this which followed was a soft, quick, shuffling step—a mere scuffle. Moreover, when, by way of test, I took a few silent steps on tip-toe, the shuffle still persisted. I was being followed.

Now I do not know whether or not it may sound like a childish fancy, but I confess I thought of my father. When last I had been in England, as a child, my father's violent death had been preceded by just such followings. And now after all these years, on my return, on the very first night I walked abroad alone, there were strange footsteps in my track. The walk was narrow, and nobody could possibly pass me unseen. I turned suddenly, therefore, and hastened back. At once I saw a dark figure rise from the shadow of the parapet and run. I ran too, but I could not gain on the figure, which receded farther and more indistinctly before me. One reason was that I felt doubtful of my footing on the unfamiliar track. I ceased my chase, and continued my stroll. It might easily have been some vagrant thief, I thought, who had a notion to rush, at a convenient opportunity, and snatch my watch. But ere I was far past the spot where I had turned there was the shuffling footstep behind me again. For a little while I feigned not to notice it; then, swinging round as swiftly as I could, I made a quick rush. Useless again, for there in the distance scuttled that same indistinct figure, more rapidly than I could run. What did it mean? I liked the affair so little that I left the walls and walked toward my hotel.

The streets were quiet. I had traversed two, and was about emerging into one of the two main streets, where the Rows are, when, from the farther part of the dark street behind me, there came once more the sound of the now unmistakable footstep. I stopped; the footsteps stopped also. I turned and walked back a few steps, and as I did it the sounds went scuffling away at the far end of the street.

It could not be fancy. It could not be chance. For a single incident perhaps such an explanation might serve, but not for this persistent recurrence. I hurried away to my hotel, resolved, since I could not come at my pursuer, to turn back no more. But before I reached the hotel there were the shuffling footsteps again, and not far behind.

It would not be true to say that I was alarmed at this stage of the adventure, but I was troubled to know what it all might mean, and altogether puzzled to account for it. I thought a great deal, but I went to bed and rose in the morning no wiser than ever.

Whether or not it was a mere fancy induced by the last night's experience I cannot say, but I went about that day with a haunting feeling that I was watched, and to me the impression was very real indeed. I listened often, but in the bustle of the day, even in quiet old Chester, the individual characters of different footsteps were not easily recognisable. Once, however, as I descended a flight of steps from the Rows, I fancied I heard the quick shuffle in the curious old gallery I had just quitted. I turned up the steps again and looked. There was a shabby sort of man looking in one of the windows, and leaning so far as to hide his head behind the heavy oaken pilaster that supported the building above. It might have been his footstep, or it might have been my fancy. At any rate I would have a look at him. I mounted the top stair, but as I turned in his direction the man ran off, with his face averted and his head ducked, and vanished down another stair. I made all speed after him, but when I reached the street he was nowhere to be seen.

What *could* it all mean? The man was rather above the middle height, and he wore one of those soft felt hats familiar on the head of the London organ-grinder. Also his hair was black and bushy, and protruded over the back of his coat-collar. Surely *this* was no delusion; surely I was not imagining an Italian aspect for this man simply because of the recollection of my father's fate?

Perhaps I was foolish, but I took no more pleasure in Chester. The embarrassment was a novel one for me, and I could not forget it. I went back to my hotel, paid my bill, sent my bag to the railway station, and took a train for Warwick by way of Crewe.

It was dark when I arrived, but the night was near as fine as last night had been at Chester. I took a very little late dinner at my hotel, and fell into a doubt what to do with myself. One rather fat and very sleepy commercial traveller was the only other customer visible, and the billiard room was empty. There seemed to be nothing to do but to light a cigar and take a walk.

I could just see enough of the old town to give me good hopes of tomorrow's sight-seeing. There was nothing visible of quite such an interesting character as one might meet in Chester, but there were a good few fine old sixteenth-century houses, and there were the two gates with the chapels above them. But of course the castle was the great show-place, and that I should visit on the morrow, if there were no difficulties as to permission. There were some very fine pictures there, if I remembered aright what I had read. I was walking down the incline from one of the gates, trying to remember who the painters of these pictures were, besides Van Dyck and Holbein, when—that shuffling step was behind me again!

I admit that it cost me an effort, this time, to turn on my pursuer. There was something uncanny in that persistent, elusive footstep, and indeed there was something alarming in my circumstances, dogged thus from place to place, and unable to shake off my enemy, or to understand his movements or his motive. Turn I did, however, and straightway the shuffling step went off at a hastened pace in the shadow of the gate. This time I made no more than half-a-dozen steps back. I turned again, and pushed my way to the hotel. And as I went the shuffling step came after.

The thing was serious. There must be some object in this unceasing watching, and the object could bode no good to me. Plainly some unseen eye had been on me the whole of that day, had noted my goings and comings and my journey from Chester. Again, and irresistibly, the watchings that preceded my father's death came to mind, and I could not forget them. I could have no doubt now that I had been closely watched from the moment I had set foot at Plymouth. But who could have been waiting to watch me at Plymouth, when indeed I had only decided to land at the last moment? Then I thought of the two Italian forecastle hands on the steamer—the very men whom Dorrington had used to illustrate in what unexpected quarters members of the terrible Italian secret societies might be found. And the Camorra was not satisfied with single revenge; it destroyed the son after the father, and it waited for many years, with infinite patience and cunning.

Dogged by the steps, I reached the hotel and went to bed. I slept but fitfully at first, though better rest came as the night wore on. In the early morning I woke with a sudden shock, and with an indefinite sense of being disturbed by somebody about me. The window was directly opposite the foot of the bed, and there, as I looked, was the face of a man, dark, evil, and grinning, with a bush of black hair about his uncovered head, and small rings in his ears.

It was but a flash, and the face vanished. I was struck by the terror that one so often feels on a sudden and violent awakening from sleep, and it was some seconds ere I could leave my bed and get to the window. My room was on the first floor, and the window looked down on a stable-yard. I had a momentary glimpse of a human figure leaving the gate of the yard, and it was the figure that had fled before me in the Rows, at Chester. A ladder belonging to the yard stood under the window, and that was all.

I rose and dressed; I could stand this sort of thing no longer. If it were only something tangible, if there were only somebody I could take hold of, and fight with if necessary, it would not have been so bad. But I was surrounded by some mysterious machination, persistent, unexplainable, that it was altogether impossible to tackle or to face. To complain to the police would have been absurd—they would take me for a lunatic. They are indeed just such complaints that lunatics so often make to the police—complaints of being followed by indefinite enemies, and of being besieged by faces that look in at windows. Even if they did not set me down a lunatic, what could the police of a provincial town do for me in a case like this? No, I must go and consult Dorrington.

I had my breakfast, and then decided that I would at any rate try the castle before leaving. Try it I did accordingly, and was allowed to go over it. But through the whole morning I was oppressed by the horrible sense of being watched by malignant eyes. Clearly there was no comfort for me while this lasted; so after lunch I caught a train which brought me to Euston soon after half-past six.

I took a cab straight to Dorrington's rooms, but he was out, and was not expected home till late. So I drove to a large hotel near Charing Cross—I avoid mentioning its name for reasons which will presently be understood—sent in my bag, and dined.

I had not the smallest doubt but that I was still under the observation of the man or the men who had so far pursued me; I had, indeed, no hope of eluding them, except by the contrivance of Dorrington's expert brain. So as I had no desire to hear that shuffling footstep again—indeed it had seemed, at Warwick, to have a physically painful effect on my nerves—I stayed within and got to bed early.

I had no fear of waking face to face with a grinning Italian here. My window was four floors up, out of reach of anything but a fire-escape. And, in fact, I woke comfortably and naturally, and saw nothing from my window but the bright sky, the buildings opposite, and the traffic below. But as I turned to close my door behind me as I emerged into the corridor, there, on the muntin of the frame, just below the bedroom number, was a little round paper label, perhaps a trifle smaller than a sixpence, and on the label, drawn awkwardly in ink, was a device of two crossed knives of curious, crooked shape. The sign of the Camorra!

I will not attempt to describe the effect of this sign upon me. It may best be imagined, in view of what I have said of the incidents preceding the murder of my father. It was the sign of an inexorable fate, creeping nearer step by step, implacable, inevitable, and mysterious. In little more than twelve hours after seeing that sign my father had been a mangled corpse. One of the hotel servants passed as I stood by the door, and I made shift to ask him if he knew anything of the label. He looked at the paper, and then, more curiously, at me, but he could offer no explanation. I spent little time over breakfast, and then went by cab to Conduit Street. I paid my bill and took my bag with me.

Dorrington had gone to his office, but he had left a message that if I called I was to follow him; and the office was in Bedford Street, Covent Garden. I turned the cab in that direction forthwith.

"Why," said Dorrington as we shook hands, "I believe you look a bit out of sorts! Doesn't England agree with you?"

"Well," I answered, "it has proved rather trying so far." And then I described, in exact detail, my adventures as I have set them down here.

Dorrington looked grave. "It's really extraordinary," he said, "most extraordinary; and it isn't often that I call a thing extraordinary neither, with my experience. But it's plain something must be done—something to gain time at any rate. We're in the dark at present, of course, and I expect I shall have to fish about a little before I get at anything to go on. In the meantime I think you must disappear as artfully as we can manage it." He sat silent for a little while, thoughtfully tapping his forehead with his finger-tips. "I wonder," he said presently, "whether or not those Italian fellows on the steamer *are* in it or not. I suppose you haven't made yourself known anywhere, have you?"

"Nowhere. As you know, you've been with me all the time till you left the moor, and since then I have been with nobody and called on nobody."

"Now there's no doubt it's the Camorra," Dorrington said—"that's pretty plain. I think I told you on the steamer that it was rather wonderful that you had heard nothing of them after your father's death. What has caused them all this delay there's no telling—they know best themselves; it's been lucky for you, anyway, so far. What I'd like to find out now is how they have identified you, and got on your track so promptly. There's no guessing where these fellows get their information—it's just wonderful; but if we can find out, then perhaps we can stop the supply, or turn on something that will lead them into a pit. If you had called anywhere on business and declared yourself—as you might have done, for instance, at Mowbray's—I might be inclined to suspect that they got the tip in some crooked way from there. But you haven't. Of course, if those Italian chaps on the steamer *are* in it, you're probably identified pretty certainly; but if they're not, they may only have made a guess. We two landed together, and kept together, till a day or two ago; as far as any outsider would know, I might be Rigby and you might be Dorrington. Come, we'll work on those lines. I think I smell a plan. Are you staying anywhere?"

"No. I paid my bill at the hotel and came along here with my bag."

"Very well. Now there's a house at Highgate kept by a very trustworthy man, whom I know very well, where a man might be pretty comfortable for a few days, or even for a week, if he doesn't mind staying indoors, and keeping himself out of sight. I expect your friends of the Camorra are watching in the street outside at this moment; but I think it will be fairly easy to get you away to Highgate without letting them into the secret, if you don't mind secluding yourself for a bit. In the circumstances, I take it you won't object at all?"

"Object? I should think not."

"Very well, that's settled. You can call yourself Dorrington or not, as you please, though perhaps it will be safest not to shout 'Rigby' too loud. But as for myself, for a day or two at least

I'm going to be Mr. James Rigby. Have you your card-case handy?"

"Yes, here it is. But then, as to taking my name, won't you run serious risk?"

Dorrington winked merrily. "I've run a risk or two before now," he said, "in course of my business. And if *I* don't mind the risk, you needn't grumble, for I warn you I shall charge for risk when I send you my bill. And I think I can take care of myself fairly well, even with the Camorra about. I shall take you to this place at Highgate, and then you won't see me for a few days. It won't do for me, in the character of Mr. James Rigby, to go dragging a trail up and down between this place and your retreat. You've got some other identifying papers, haven't you?"

"Yes, I have." I produced the letter from my Sydney lawyers to Mowbray, and the deeds of the South Australian property from my bag.

"Ah," said Dorrington, "I'll just give you a formal receipt for these, since they're valuable; it's a matter of business, and we'll do it in a business-like way. I may want something solid like this to support any bluff I may have to make. A mere case of cards won't always act, you know. It's a pity old Mowbray's out of town, for there's a way in which he might give a little help, I fancy. But never mind—leave it all to me. There's your receipt. Keep it snug away somewhere, where inquisitive people can't read it."

He handed me the receipt, and then took me to his partner's room and introduced me. Mr. Hicks was a small, wrinkled man, older than Dorrington, I should think, by fifteen or twenty years, and with all the aspect and manner of a quiet old professional man.

Dorrington left the room, and presently returned with his hat in his hand. "Yes," he said, "there's a charming dark gentleman with a head like a mop, and rings in his ears, skulking about at the next corner. If it was he who looked in at your window, I don't wonder you were startled. His dress suggests the organ-grinding interest, but he looks as though cutting a throat would be more in his line than grinding a tune; and no doubt he has friends as engaging as himself close at call. If you'll come with me now I think we shall give him the slip. I have a growler ready for you—a hansom's a bit too glassy and public. Pull down the blinds and sit back when you get inside."

He led me to a yard at the back of the building wherein the office stood, from which a short flight of steps led to a basement. We followed a passage in this basement till we reached another flight, and ascending these, we emerged into the corridor of another building. Out at the door at the end of this, and we passed a large block of model dwellings, and were in Bedfordbury. Here a four-wheeler was waiting, and I shut myself in it without delay.

I was to proceed as far as King's Cross in this cab, Dorrington had arranged, and there he would overtake me in a swift hansom. It fell out as he had settled, and, dismissing the hansom, he came the rest of the journey with me in the four-wheeler.

We stopped at length before one of a row of houses, apparently recently built—houses of the over-ornamented, gabled, and tiled sort that abound in the suburbs.

"Crofting is the man's name," Dorrington said, as we alighted. "He's rather an odd sort of customer, but quite decent in the main, and his wife makes coffee such as money won't buy in most places."

A woman answered Dorrington's ring—a woman of most extreme thinness. Dorrington greeted her as Mrs. Crofting, and we entered.

"We've just lost our servant again, Mr. Dorrington," the woman said in a shrill voice, "and Mr. Crofting ain't at home. But I'm expecting him before long."

"I don't think I need wait to see him, Mrs. Crofting," Dorrington answered. "I'm sure I can't leave my friend in better hands than yours. I hope you've a vacant room?"

"Well, for a friend of yours, Mr. Dorrington, no doubt we can find room."

"That's right. My friend Mr."—Dorrington gave me a meaning look—"Mr. Phelps, would like to stay here for a few days. He wants to be quite quiet for a little—do you understand?"

"Oh, yes, Mr. Dorrington, I understand."

"Very well, then, make him as comfortable as you can, and give him some of your very best coffee. I believe you've got quite a little library of books, and Mr. Phelps will be glad of them. Have you got any cigars?" Dorrington added, turning to me.

"Yes; there are some in my bag."

"Then I think you'll be pretty comfortable now. Goodbye. I expect you'll see me in a few days—or at any rate you'll get a message. Meantime be as happy as you can."

Dorrington left, and the woman showed me to a room upstairs, where I placed my bag. In front, on the same floor, was a sitting-room, with, I suppose, some two or three hundred books, mostly novels, on shelves. The furniture of the place was of the sort one expects to find in an ordinary lodging-house—horsehair sofas, loo tables, lustres, and so forth. Mrs. Crofting explained to me that the customary dinner hour was two, but that I might dine when I liked. I elected, however, to follow the custom of the house, and sat down to a cigar and a book.

At two o'clock the dinner came, and I was agreeably surprised to find it a very good one, much above what the appointments of the house had led me to expect. Plainly Mrs. Crofting was a capital cook. There was no soup, but there was a very excellent sole, and some well-done cutlets with peas, and an omelet; also a bottle of Bass. Come, I felt that I should not do so badly in this place after all. I trusted that Dorrington would be as comfortable in his half of the transaction, bearing my responsibilities and troubles. I had heard a heavy, blundering tread on the floor below, and judged from this that Mr. Crofting had returned.

After dinner I lit a cigar, and Mrs. Crofting brought her coffee. Truly it was excellent coffee, and brewed as I like it—strong and black, and plenty of it. It had a flavour of its own too, novel, but not unpleasing. I took one cupful, and brought another to my side as I lay on the sofa with my book. I had not read six lines before I was asleep.

I woke with a sensation of numbing cold in my right side, a terrible stiffness in my limbs, and a sound of loud splashing in my ears. All was pitch dark, and—what was this? Water! Water all about me. I was lying in six inches of cold water, and more was pouring down upon me from above. My head was afflicted with a splitting ache. But where was I? Why was it dark? And whence all the water? I staggered to my feet, and instantly struck my head against a hard roof above me. I raised my hand; there was the roof or whatever place it was, hard, smooth, and cold, and little more than five feet from the floor, so that I bent as I stood. I spread my hand to the side; that was hard, smooth, and cold too. And then the conviction struck me like a blow—I was in a covered iron tank, and the water was pouring in to drown me!

I dashed my hands frantically against the lid, and strove to raise it. It would not move. I shouted at the top of my voice, and turned about to feel the extent of my prison. One way I could touch the opposite sides at once easily with my hands, the other way it was wider—perhaps a little more than six feet altogether. What was this? Was this to be my fearful end, cooped in this tank while the water rose by inches to choke me? Already the water was a foot deep. I flung myself at the sides, I beat the pitiless iron with fists, face, and head, I screamed and implored. Then it struck me that I might at least stop the inlet of water. I put out my hand and felt the falling stream, then found the inlet and stopped it with my fingers. But water still poured in with a resounding splash; there was another opening at the opposite end, which I could not reach without releasing the one I now held! I was but prolonging my agony. Oh, the devilish cunning that had devised those two inlets, so far apart! Again I beat the sides, broke my nails with tearing at the corners, screamed and entreated in my agony. I was mad, but with no dulling of the senses, for the horrors of my awful, helpless state, overwhelmed my brain, keen and perceptive to every ripple of the unceasing water.

In the height of my frenzy I held my breath,

for I heard a sound from outside. I shouted again—implored some quicker death. Then there was a scraping on the lid above me, and it was raised at one edge, and let in the light of a candle. I sprang from my knees and forced the lid back, and the candle flame danced before me. The candle was held by a dusty man, a workman apparently, who stared at me with scared eyes, and said nothing but, "Goo' lor'!"

Overhead were the rafters of a gabled roof, and tilted against them was the thick beam which, jammed across from one sloping rafter to another, had held the tank-lid fast. "Help me!" I gasped. "Help me out!"

The man took me by the armpits and hauled me, dripping and half dead, over the edge of the tank, into which the water still poured, making a noise in the hollow iron that half drowned our voices. The man had been at work on the cistern of a neighbouring house, and hearing an uncommon noise, he had climbed through the spaces left in the party walls to give passage along under the roofs to the builders' men. Among the joists at our feet was the trap-door through which, drugged and insensible, I had been carried, to be flung into that horrible cistern.

With the help of my friend the workman I made shift to climb through by the way he had come. We got back to the house where he had been at work, and there the people gave me brandy and lent me dry clothes. I made haste to send for the police, but when they arrived Mrs. Crofting and her respectable spouse had gone. Some unusual noise in the roof must have warned them. And when the police, following my directions further, got to the offices of Dorrington and Hicks, those acute professional men had gone too, but in such haste that the contents of the office, papers and everything else, had been left just as they stood.

The plot was clear now. The followings, the footsteps, the face at the window, the label on the door—all were a mere humbug arranged by Dorrington for his own purpose, which was to drive me into his power and get my papers from me. Armed with these, and with his consummate address and knowledge of affairs, he could go to Mr. Mowbray in the character of Mr. James Rigby, sell my land in South Australia, and have the whole of my property transferred to himself from Sydney. The rest of my baggage was at his rooms; if any further proof were required it might be found there. He had taken good care that I should not meet Mr. Mowbray—who, by the way, I afterwards found had not left his office, and had never fired a gun in his life. At first I wondered that Dorrington had not made some murderous attempt on me at the shooting place in Scotland. But a little thought convinced me that that would have been bad policy for him. The disposal of the body would be difficult, and he would have to account somehow for my sudden disappearance. Whereas, by the use of his Italian assistant and his murder apparatus at Highgate I was made to efface my own trail, and could be got rid of in the end with little trouble; for my body, stripped of everything that might identify me, would be simply that of a drowned man unknown, whom nobody could identify. The whole plot was contrived upon the information I myself had afforded Dorrington during the voyage home. And it all sprang from his remembering the report of my father's death. When the papers in the office came to be examined, there each step in the operations was plainly revealed. There was a code telegram from Suez directing Hicks to hire a grouse-moor. There were telegrams and letters from Scotland giving directions as to the later movements; indeed the thing was displayed completely. The business of Dorrington and Hicks had really been that of private inquiry agents, and they had done much *bona fide* business; but many of their operations had been of a more than questionable sort. And among their papers were found complete sets, neatly arranged in dockets, each containing in skeleton a complete history of a case. Many of these cases were of a most interesting character, and I have been enabled to piece together, out of the material thus supplied, the narratives which will follow this. As to my own case, it only remains to say that as yet neither Dorrington, Hicks, nor the Croftings have been caught. They played in the end for a high stake (they might have made six figures of me if they had killed me, and the first figure would not have been a one) and they lost by a mere accident. But I have often wondered how many of the bodies which the coroners' juries of London have returned to be "Found Drowned" were drowned, not where they were picked up, but in that horrible tank at Highgate. What the drug was that gave Mrs. Crofting's coffee its value in Dorrington's eyes I do not know, but plainly it had not been sufficient in my case to keep me unconscious against the shock of cold water till I could be drowned altogether. Months have passed since my adventure, but even now I sweat at the sight of an iron tank.

Rogue: A. J. Raffles

The Ides of March

E. W. HORNUNG

JUST AS SHERLOCK HOLMES stands alone among Victorian- and Edwardian-era detectives, A. J. Raffles towers over the rogues of those eras just as indisputably. In fact, when Holmes was apparently killed by a plunge into the Reichenbach Falls in 1894, the figure who replaced him as the most popular character in mystery fiction was the gentleman jewel thief whose name has become part of the English language.

Ironically, Ernest William Hornung (1866–1921), the creator of Raffles, was the brother-in-law of Arthur Conan Doyle, who wrote the Holmes stories. The generally accepted family narrative is that Hornung created a thief, a definitive counterpoint to Doyle's detective, to tweak his somewhat stuffy relative.

Raffles was an internationally famous cricket player who found himself penniless while in Australia and, in desperation, decided to steal. He had intended the robbery to be a singular adventure, but, once he had "tasted blood," he found that he loved being a "gentleman thief" and continued his nighttime exploits when he returned to London. "Why settle down to some humdrum, uncongenial billet," he once said, "when excitement, romance, danger, and a decent living were all going begging together? Of course, it's very wrong, but we can't all be moralists, and the distribution of wealth is very wrong to begin with."

The stories are told in first person by Harry "Bunny" Manders, the devoted companion of the charming and handsome amateur cracksman who lives in luxury at the Albany. Bunny had served as Raffles's fag, or personal servant, as an underclassman when they were in public (i.e., private) school.

Hornung wrote three short story collections about the notorious jewel thief. The first, *The Amateur Cracksman* (1899), was selected for *Queen's Quorum*; it was followed by *The Black Mask*, 1901 (U.S. title: *Raffles: Further Adventures of the Amateur Cracksman*), and *A Thief in the Night* (1905). By the time of *Mr. Jus-*

tice Raffles (1909), Hornung's only novel about the character, Raffles had become a detective.

Philip Atkey, using the pseudonym Barry Perowne, began to write about Raffles in 1933 (*Raffles After Dark*) and produced nine books and numerous uncollected short stories about the character. Other writers have also written parodies and pastiches about Raffles, the most famous being Graham Greene's comic play *The Return of A. J. Raffles*, produced by the Royal Shakespeare Company, which opened in London in December 1975. Noted actors who portrayed Raffles include John Barrymore (in *Raffles, the Amateur Cracksman*, 1917), Ronald Colman (in *Raffles*, 1930), and David Niven (in *Raffles*, 1940).

"The Ides of March," the first Raffles story, was originally published in the June 1898 issue of *Cassell's Magazine*; it was first collected in *The Amateur Cracksman* (London, Methuen & Co., 1899). The dedication, to his brother-in-law, reads: "To A.C.D. This form of flattery."

THE IDES OF MARCH

E. W. Hornung

I

IT WAS HALF-PAST TWELVE when I returned to the Albany as a last desperate resort. The scene of my disaster was much as I had left it. The baccarat-counters still strewed the table, with the empty glasses and the loaded ash-trays. A window had been opened to let the smoke out, and was letting in the fog instead. Raffles himself had merely discarded his dining jacket for one of his innumerable blazers. Yet he arched his eyebrows as though I had dragged him from his bed.

"Forgotten something?" said he, when he saw me on his mat.

"No," said I, pushing past him without ceremony. And I led the way into his room with an impudence amazing to myself.

"Not come back for your revenge, have you? Because I'm afraid I can't give it to you single-handed. I was sorry myself that the others——"

We were face to face by his fireside, and I cut him short.

"Raffles," said I, "you may well be surprised at my coming back in this way and at this hour. I hardly know you. I was never in your rooms before tonight. But I fagged for you at school, and you said you remembered me. Of course that's no excuse; but will you listen to me—for two minutes?"

In my emotion I had at first to struggle for every word; but his face reassured me as I went on, and I was not mistaken in its expression.

"Certainly, my dear man," said he; "as many minutes as you like. Have a Sullivan and sit down." And he handed me his silver cigarette-case.

"No," said I, finding a full voice as I shook my head; "no, I won't smoke, and I won't sit down, thank you. Nor will you ask me to do either when you've heard what I have to say."

"Really?" said he, lighting his own cigarette with one clear blue eye upon me. "How do you know?"

"Because you'll probably show me the door," I cried bitterly; "and you will be justified in doing it! But it's no use beating about the bush. You know I dropped over two hundred just now?"

He nodded.

"I hadn't the money in my pocket."

"I remember."

"But I had my check-book, and I wrote each of you a check at that desk."

"Well?"

"Not one of them was worth the paper it was written on, Raffles. I am overdrawn already at my bank!"

"Surely only for the moment?"

"No. I have spent everything."

"But somebody told me you were so well off. I heard you had come in for money?"

"So I did. Three years ago. It has been my curse; now it's all gone—every penny! Yes, I've been a fool; there never was nor will be such a fool as I've been. . . . Isn't this enough for you? Why don't you turn me out?" He was walking up and down with a very long face instead.

"Couldn't your people do anything?" he asked at length.

"Thank God," I cried, "I have no people! I was an only child. I came in for everything there was. My one comfort is that they're gone, and will never know."

I cast myself into a chair and hid my face. Raffles continued to pace the rich carpet that was of a piece with everything else in his rooms. There was no variation in his soft and even footfalls.

"You used to be a literary little cuss," he said at length; "didn't you edit the mag. before you left? Anyway I recollect fagging you to do my verses; and literature of all sorts is the very thing nowadays; any fool can make a living at it."

I shook my head. "Any fool couldn't write off my debts," said I.

"Then you have a flat somewhere?" he went on.

"Yes, in Mount Street."

"Well, what about the furniture?"

I laughed aloud in my misery. "There's been a bill of sale on every stick for months!"

And at that Raffles stood still, with raised eyebrows and stern eyes that I could meet the better now that he knew the worst; then, with a shrug, he resumed his walk, and for some minutes neither of us spoke. But in his handsome, unmoved face I read my fate and death-warrant; and with every breath I cursed my folly and my cowardice in coming to him at all. Because he had been kind to me at school, when he was captain of the eleven, and I his fag, I had dared to look for kindness from him now; because I was ruined, and he rich enough to play cricket all the summer, and do nothing for the rest of the year, I had fatuously counted on his mercy, his sympathy, his help! Yes, I had relied on him in my heart, for all my outward diffidence and humility; and I was rightly served. There was as little of mercy as of sympathy in that curling nostril, that rigid jaw, that cold blue eye which never glanced my way. I caught up my hat. I blundered to my feet. I would have gone without a word; but Raffles stood between me and the door.

"Where are you going?" said he.

"That's my business," I replied. "I won't trouble *you* any more."

"Then how am I to help you?"

"I didn't ask your help."

"Then why come to me?"

"Why, indeed!" I echoed. "Will you let me pass?"

"Not until you tell me where you are going and what you mean to do."

"Can't you guess?" I cried. And for many seconds we stood staring in each other's eyes.

"Have you got the pluck?" said he, breaking the spell in a tone so cynical that it brought my last drop of blood to the boil.

"You shall see," said I, as I stepped back and whipped the pistol from my overcoat pocket. "Now, will you let me pass or shall I do it here?"

The barrel touched my temple, and my thumb the trigger. Mad with excitement as I was, ruined, dishonored, and now finally determined to make an end of my misspent life, my only surprise to this day is that I did not do so then and there. The despicable satisfaction of involving another in one's destruction added its miserable appeal to my baser egoism; and had fear or horror flown to my companion's face, I shudder to think I might have died diabolically happy with that look for my last impious consolation. It was the look that came instead which held my hand. Neither fear nor horror were in it; only wonder, admiration, and such a measure of pleased expectancy as caused me after all to pocket my revolver with an oath.

"You devil!" I said. "I believe you wanted me to do it!"

"Not quite," was the reply, made with a little start, and a change of color that came too late. "To tell you the truth, though, I half thought you meant it, and I was never more fascinated in my life. I never dreamt you had such stuff in you, Bunny! No, I'm hanged if I let you go now. And you'd better not try that game again, for you won't catch me stand and look on a second time. We must think of some way out of the mess. I had no idea you were a chap of that sort! There, let me have the gun."

One of his hands fell kindly on my shoulder, while the other slipped into my overcoat pocket, and I suffered him to deprive me of my weapon without a murmur. Nor was this simply because Raffles had the subtle power of making himself irresistible at will. He was beyond comparison the most masterful man whom I have ever known; yet my acquiescence was due to more than the mere subjection of the weaker nature to the stronger. The forlorn hope which had brought me to the Albany was turned as by magic into an almost staggering sense of safety. Raffles would help me after all! A. J. Raffles would be my friend! It was as though all the world had come round suddenly to my side; so far therefore from resisting his action, I caught and clasped his hand with a fervor as uncontrollable as the frenzy which had preceded it.

"God bless you!" I cried. "Forgive me for everything. I will tell you the truth. I *did* think you might help me in my extremity, though I well knew that I had no claim upon you. Still—for the old school's sake—the sake of old times—I thought you might give me another chance. If you wouldn't I meant to blow out my brains—and will still if you change your mind!"

In truth I feared that it was changing, with his expression, even as I spoke, and in spite of his kindly tone and kindlier use of my old school nickname. His next words showed me my mistake.

"What a boy it is for jumping to conclusions! I have my vices, Bunny, but backing and filling is not one of them. Sit down, my good fellow, and have a cigarette to soothe your nerves. I insist. Whiskey? The worst thing for you; here's some coffee that I was brewing when you came in. Now listen to me. You speak of 'another chance.' What do you mean? Another chance at baccarat? Not if I know it! You think the luck must turn; suppose it didn't? We should only have made bad worse. No, my dear chap, you've plunged enough. Do you put yourself in my hands or do you not? Very well, then you plunge no more, and I undertake not to present my check. Unfortunately there are the other men; and still more unfortunately, Bunny, I'm as hard up at this moment as you are yourself!"

It was my turn to stare at Raffles. "You?" I vociferated. "You hard up? How am I to sit here and believe that?"

"Did I refuse to believe it of you?" he returned, smiling. "And, with your own experience, do you think that because a fellow has rooms in this place, and belongs to a club or two, and plays a little cricket, he must necessarily have a balance at the bank? I tell you, my dear man, that at this moment I'm as hard up as you ever were. I have nothing but my wits to live on—absolutely nothing else. It was as necessary for me to win some money this evening as it was for you. We're in the same boat, Bunny; we'd better pull together."

"Together!" I jumped at it. "I'll do anything in this world for you, Raffles," I said, "if you really mean that you won't give me away. Think of anything you like, and I'll do it! I was a desperate man when I came here, and I'm just as desperate now. I don't mind what I do if only I can get out of this without a scandal."

Again I see him, leaning back in one of the luxurious chairs with which his room was furnished. I see his indolent, athletic figure; his pale, sharp, clean-shaven features; his curly black hair; his strong, unscrupulous mouth.

And again I feel the clear beam of his wonderful eye, cold and luminous as a star, shining into my brain—sifting the very secrets of my heart.

"I wonder if you mean all that!" he said at length. "You do in your present mood; but who can back his mood to last? Still, there's hope when a chap takes that tone. Now I think of it, too, you were a plucky little devil at school; you once did me rather a good turn, I recollect. Remember it, Bunny? Well, wait a bit, and perhaps I'll be able to do you a better one. Give me time to think."

He got up, lit a fresh cigarette, and fell to pacing the room once more, but with a slower and more thoughtful step, and for a much longer period than before. Twice he stopped at my chair as though on the point of speaking, but each time he checked himself and resumed his stride in silence. Once he threw up the window, which he had shut some time since, and stood for some moments leaning out into the fog which filled the Albany courtyard. Meanwhile a clock on the chimney-piece struck one, and one again for the half-hour, without a word between us.

Yet I not only kept my chair with patience, but I acquired an incongruous equanimity in that half-hour. Insensibly I had shifted my burden to the broad shoulders of this splendid friend, and my thoughts wandered with my eyes as the minutes passed. The room was the good-sized, square one, with the folding doors, the marble mantel-piece, and the gloomy, old-fashioned distinction peculiar to the Albany. It was charmingly furnished and arranged, with the right amount of negligence and the right amount of taste. What struck me most, however, was the absence of the usual insignia of a cricketer's den. Instead of the conventional rack of war-worn bats, a carved oak bookcase, with every shelf in a litter, filled the better part of one wall; and where I looked for cricketing groups, I found reproductions of such works as "Love and Death" and "The Blessed Damozel," in dusty frames and different parallels. The man might have been a minor poet instead of an athlete of the first water. But there had always been a fine streak of æstheticism in his complex composition; some of these very pictures I had myself dusted in his study at school; and they set me thinking of yet another of his many sides—and of the little incident to which he had just referred.

Everybody knows how largely the tone of a public school depends on that of the eleven, and on the character of the captain of cricket in particular; and I have never heard it denied that in A. J. Raffles's time our tone was good, or that such influence as he troubled to exert was on the side of the angels. Yet it was whispered in the school that he was in the habit of parading the town at night in loud checks and a false beard. It was whispered, and disbelieved. I alone knew it for a fact; for night after night had I pulled the rope up after him when the rest of the dormitory were asleep, and kept awake by the hour to let it down again on a given signal. Well, one night he was over-bold, and within an ace of ignominious expulsion in the hey-day of his fame. Consummate daring and extraordinary nerve on his part, aided, doubtless, by some little presence of mind on mine, averted the untoward result; and no more need be said of a discreditable incident. But I cannot pretend to have forgotten it in throwing myself on this man's mercy in my desperation. And I was wondering how much of his leniency was owing to the fact that Raffles had not forgotten it either, when he stopped and stood over my chair once more.

"I've been thinking of that night we had the narrow squeak," he began. "Why do you start?"

"I was thinking of it too."

He smiled, as though he had read my thoughts.

"Well, you were the right sort of little beggar then, Bunny; you didn't talk and you didn't flinch. You asked no questions and you told no tales. I wonder if you're like that now?"

"I don't know," said I, slightly puzzled by his tone. "I've made such a mess of my own affairs that I trust myself about as little as I'm likely to be trusted by anybody else. Yet I never in my life went back on a friend. I will say that, otherwise perhaps I mightn't be in such a hole tonight."

"Exactly," said Raffles, nodding to himself, as though in assent to some hidden train of thought; "exactly what I remember of you, and I'll bet it's as true now as it was ten years ago. We don't alter, Bunny. We only develop. I suppose neither you nor I are really altered since you used to let down that rope and I used to come up it hand over hand. You would stick at nothing for a pal—what?"

"At nothing in this world," I was pleased to cry.

"Not even at a crime?" said Raffles, smiling.

I stopped to think, for his tone had changed, and I felt sure he was chaffing me. Yet his eye seemed as much in earnest as ever, and for my part I was in no mood for reservations.

"No, not even at that," I declared; "name your crime, and I'm your man."

He looked at me one moment in wonder, and another moment in doubt; then turned the matter off with a shake of his head, and the little cynical laugh that was all his own.

"You're a nice chap, Bunny! A real desperate character—what? Suicide one moment, and any crime I like the next! What you want is a drag, my boy, and you did well to come to a decent law-abiding citizen with a reputation to lose. None the less we must have that money tonight—by hook or crook."

"Tonight, Raffles?"

"The sooner the better. Every hour after ten o'clock tomorrow morning is an hour of risk. Let one of those checks get round to your own bank, and you and it are dishonored together. No, we must raise the wind tonight and re-open your account first thing tomorrow. And I rather think I know where the wind can be raised."

"At two o'clock in the morning?"

"Yes."

"But how—but where—at such an hour?"

"From a friend of mine here in Bond Street."

"He must be a very intimate friend!"

"Intimate's not the word. I have the run of his place and a latch-key all to myself."

"You would knock him up at this hour of the night?"

"If he's in bed."

"And it's essential that I should go in with you?"

"Absolutely."

"Then I must; but I'm bound to say I don't like the idea, Raffles."

"Do you prefer the alternative?" asked my companion, with a sneer. "No, hang it, that's unfair!" he cried apologetically in the same breath. "I quite understand. It's a beastly ordeal. But it would never do for you to stay outside. I tell you what, you shall have a peg before we start—just one. There's the whiskey, here's a syphon, and I'll be putting on an overcoat while you help yourself."

Well, I daresay I did so with some freedom, for this plan of his was not the less distasteful to me from its apparent inevitability. I must own, however, that it possessed fewer terrors before my glass was empty. Meanwhile Raffles rejoined me, with a covert coat over his blazer, and a soft felt hat set carelessly on the curly head he shook with a smile as I passed him the decanter.

"When we come back," said he. "Work first, play afterward. Do you see what day it is?" he added, tearing a leaflet from a Shakespearian calendar, as I drained my glass. "March 15th. 'The Ides of March, the Ides of March, remember.' Eh, Bunny, my boy? You won't forget them, will you?"

And, with a laugh, he threw some coals on the fire before turning down the gas like a careful householder. So we went out together as the clock on the chimney-piece was striking two.

II

Piccadilly was a trench of raw white fog, rimmed with blurred street-lamps, and lined with a thin coating of adhesive mud. We met no other wayfarers on the deserted flagstones, and were ourselves favored with a very hard stare from the constable of the beat, who, however, touched his helmet on recognizing my companion.

"You see, I'm known to the police," laughed Raffles as we passed on. "Poor devils, they've got to keep their weather eye open on a night like this! A fog may be a bore to you and me, Bunny, but it's a perfect godsend to the criminal classes, especially so late in their season. Here we are, though—and I'm hanged if the beggar isn't in bed and asleep after all!"

We had turned into Bond Street, and had halted on the curb a few yards down on the right. Raffles was gazing up at some windows across the road, windows barely discernible through the mist, and without the glimmer of a light to throw them out. They were over a jeweller's shop, as I could see by the peep-hole in the shop door, and the bright light burning within. But the entire "upper part," with the private street-door next the shop, was black and blank as the sky itself.

"Better give it up for tonight," I urged. "Surely the morning will be time enough!"

"Not a bit of it," said Raffles. "I have his key. We'll surprise him. Come along."

And seizing my right arm, he hurried me across the road, opened the door with his latch-key, and in another moment had shut it swiftly but softly behind us. We stood together in the dark. Outside, a measured step was approaching; we had heard it through the fog as we crossed the street; now, as it drew nearer, my companion's fingers tightened on my arm.

"It may be the chap himself," he whispered. "He's the devil of a night-bird. Not a sound, Bunny! We'll startle the life out of him. Ah!"

The measured step had passed without a pause. Raffles drew a deep breath, and his singular grip of me slowly relaxed.

"But still, not a sound," he continued in the same whisper; "we'll take a rise out of him, wherever he is! Slip off your shoes and follow me."

Well, you may wonder at my doing so; but you can never have met A. J. Raffles. Half his power lay in a conciliating trick of sinking the commander in the leader. And it was impossible not to follow one who led with such a zest. You might question, but you followed first. So now, when I heard him kick off his own shoes, I did the same, and was on the stairs at his heels before I realized what an extraordinary way was this of approaching a stranger for money in the dead of night. But obviously Raffles and he were on exceptional terms of intimacy, and I could not but infer that they were in the habit of playing practical jokes upon each other.

We groped our way so slowly upstairs that I had time to make more than one note before we reached the top. The stair was uncarpeted. The spread fingers of my right hand encountered nothing on the damp wall; those of my left trailed through a dust that could be felt on the banisters. An eerie sensation had been upon me since we entered the house. It increased with every step we climbed. What hermit were we going to startle in his cell?

We came to a landing. The banisters led us to the left, and to the left again. Four steps more, and we were on another and a longer landing, and suddenly a match blazed from the black. I never heard it struck. Its flash was blinding. When my eyes became accustomed to the light, there was Raffles holding up the match with one hand, and shading it with the other, between bare boards, stripped walls, and the open doors of empty rooms.

"Where have you brought me?" I cried. "The house is unoccupied!"

"Hush! Wait!" he whispered, and he led the way into one of the empty rooms. His match went out as we crossed the threshold, and he struck another without the slightest noise. Then he stood with his back to me, fumbling with something that I could not see. But, when he threw the second match away, there was some other light in its stead, and a slight smell of oil. I stepped forward to look over his shoulder, but before I could do so he had turned and flashed a tiny lantern in my face.

"What's this?" I gasped. "What rotten trick are you going to play?"

"It's played," he answered, with his quiet laugh.

"On me?"

"I am afraid so, Bunny."

"Is there no one in the house, then?"

"No one but ourselves."

"So it was mere chaff about your friend in Bond Street, who could let us have that money?"

"Not altogether. It's quite true that Danby is a friend of mine."

"Danby?"

"The jeweller underneath."

"What do you mean?" I whispered, trembling like a leaf as his meaning dawned upon me. "Are we to get the money from the jeweller?"

"Well, not exactly."

"What, then?"

"The equivalent—from his shop."

There was no need for another question. I understood everything but my own density. He had given me a dozen hints, and I had taken none. And there I stood staring at him, in that empty room; and there he stood with his dark lantern, laughing at me.

"A burglar!" I gasped. "You—you!"

"I told you I lived by my wits."

"Why couldn't you tell me what you were going to do? Why couldn't you trust me? Why must you lie?" I demanded, piqued to the quick for all my horror.

"I wanted to tell you," said he. "I was on the point of telling you more than once. You may remember how I sounded you about crime, though you have probably forgotten what you said yourself. I didn't think you meant it at the time, but I thought I'd put you to the test. Now I see you didn't, and I don't blame you. I only am to blame. Get out of it, my dear boy, as quick as you can; leave it to me. You won't give me away, whatever else you do!"

Oh, his cleverness! His fiendish cleverness! Had he fallen back on threats, coercion, sneers, all might have been different even yet. But he set me free to leave him in the lurch. He would not blame me. He did not even bind me to secrecy; he trusted me. He knew my weakness and my strength, and was playing on both with his master's touch.

"Not so fast," said I. "Did I put this into your head, or were you going to do it in any case?"

"Not in any case," said Raffles. "It's true I've had the key for days, but when I won tonight I thought of chucking it; for, as a matter of fact, it's not a one-man job."

"That settles it. I'm your man."

"You mean it?"

"Yes—for tonight."

"Good old Bunny," he murmured, holding the lantern for one moment to my face; the next he was explaining his plans, and I was nodding, as though we had been fellow-cracksmen all our days.

"I know the shop," he whispered, "because I've got a few things there. I know this upper part too; it's been to let for a month, and I got an order to view, and took a cast of the key before using it. The one thing I don't know is how to make a connection between the two; at present there's none. We may make it up here, though I rather fancy the basement myself. If you wait a minute I'll tell you."

He set his lantern on the floor, crept to a back window, and opened it with scarcely a sound: only to return, shaking his head, after shutting the window with the same care.

"That was our one chance," said he; "a back window above a back window; but it's too dark to see anything, and we daren't show an outside light. Come down after me to the basement; and remember, though there's not a soul on the premises, you can't make too little noise. There—there—listen to that!"

It was the measured tread that we had heard before on the flagstones outside. Raffles darkened his lantern, and again we stood motionless till it had passed.

"Either a policeman," he muttered, "or a watchman that all these jewellers run between them. The watchman's the man for us to watch; he's simply paid to spot this kind of thing."

We crept very gingerly down the stairs, which creaked a bit in spite of us, and we picked up our shoes in the passage; then down some narrow stone steps, at the foot of which Raffles showed his light, and put on his shoes once more, bidding me do the same in a rather louder tone than he had permitted himself to employ overhead. We were now considerably below the level of the street, in a small space with as many doors as it had sides. Three were ajar, and we saw through them into empty cellars; but in the fourth a key was turned and a bolt drawn; and this one presently let us out into the bottom of a deep, square well of fog. A similar door faced it across this area, and Raffles had the lantern close against it, and was hiding the light with his body, when a short and sudden crash made my heart stand still. Next moment I saw the door wide open, and Raffles standing within and beckoning me with a jimmy.

"Door number one," he whispered. "Deuce knows how many more there'll be, but I know of two at least. We won't have to make much noise over them, either; down here there's less risk."

We were now at the bottom of the exact fellow to the narrow stone stair which we had just descended: the yard, or well, being the one part common to both the private and the business premises. But this flight led to no open passage; instead, a singularly solid mahogany door confronted us at the top.

"I thought so," muttered Raffles, handing me the lantern, and pocketing a bunch of skeleton keys, after tampering for a few minutes with the lock. "It'll be an hour's work to get through that!"

"Can't you pick it?"

"No. I know these locks. It's no use trying. We must cut it out, and it'll take us an hour."

It took us forty-seven minutes by my watch; or, rather, it took Raffles; and never in my life have I seen anything more deliberately done. My part was simply to stand by with the dark lantern in one hand, and a small bottle of rock-oil in the other. Raffles had produced a pretty embroidered case, intended obviously for his razors, but filled instead with the tools of his secret trade, including the rock-oil. From this case he selected a "bit," capable of drilling a hole an inch in diameter, and fitted it to a small but very strong steel "brace." Then he took off his covert-coat and his blazer, spread them neatly on the top step—knelt on them—turned up his shirt cuffs—and went to work with brace-and-bit near the key-hole. But first he oiled the bit to minimize the noise, and this he did invariably before beginning a fresh hole, and often in the middle of one. It took thirty-two separate borings to cut around that lock.

I noticed that through the first circular orifice Raffles thrust a forefinger; then, as the circle became an ever-lengthening oval, he got his hand through up to the thumb; and I heard him swear softly to himself.

"I was afraid so!"

"What is it?"

"An iron gate on the other side!"

"How on earth are we to get through that?" I asked in dismay.

"Pick the lock. But there may be two. In that case they'll be top and bottom, and we shall have two fresh holes to make, as the door opens inwards. It won't open two inches as it is."

I confess I did not feel sanguine about the lock-picking, seeing that one lock had baffled us already; and my disappointment and impatience must have been a revelation to me had I stopped to think. The truth is that I was entering into our nefarious undertaking with an involuntary zeal of which I was myself quite unconscious at the time. The romance and the peril of the whole proceeding held me spellbound and entranced. My moral sense and my sense of fear were stricken by a common paralysis. And there I stood, shining my light and holding my phial with a keener interest than I had ever brought to any honest avocation. And there knelt A. J. Raffles, with his black hair tumbled, and the same watchful, quiet, determined half-smile with which I have seen him send down over after over in a county match!

At last the chain of holes was complete, the lock wrenched out bodily, and a splendid bare arm plunged up to the shoulder through the aperture, and through the bars of the iron gate beyond.

"Now," whispered Raffles, "if there's only one lock it'll be in the middle. Joy! Here it is! Only let me pick it, and we're through at last."

He withdrew his arm, a skeleton key was selected from the bunch, and then back went his arm to the shoulder. It was a breathless moment. I heard the heart throbbing in my body, the very watch ticking in my pocket, and ever and anon the tinkle-tinkle of the skeleton key. Then—at last—there came a single unmistakable click. In another minute the mahogany door and the iron gate yawned behind us; and Raffles was sitting on an office table, wiping his face, with the lantern throwing a steady beam by his side.

We were now in a bare and roomy lobby behind the shop, but separated therefrom by an iron curtain, the very sight of which filled me with despair. Raffles, however, did not appear in the least depressed, but hung up his coat and hat on some pegs in the lobby before examining this curtain with his lantern.

"That's nothing," said he, after a minute's inspection; "we'll be through that in no time, but there's a door on the other side which may give us trouble."

"Another door!" I groaned. "And how do you mean to tackle this thing?"

"Prise it up with the jointed jimmy. The weak point of these iron curtains is the leverage you can get from below. But it makes a noise, and this is where you're coming in, Bunny; this is where I couldn't do without you. I must have you overhead to knock through when the street's clear. I'll come with you and show a light."

Well, you may imagine how little I liked the prospect of this lonely vigil; and yet there was something very stimulating in the vital responsibility which it involved. Hitherto I had been a mere spectator. Now I was to take part in the game. And the fresh excitement made me more than ever insensible to those considerations of conscience and of safety which were already as dead nerves in my breast.

So I took my post without a murmur in the front room above the shop. The fixtures had been left for the refusal of the incoming tenant, and fortunately for us they included Venetian blinds which were already down. It was the simplest matter in the world to stand peeping through the laths into the street, to beat twice with my foot when anybody was approaching, and once when all was clear again. The noises that even I could hear below, with the exception of one metallic crash at the beginning, were indeed incredibly slight; but they ceased altogether at each double rap from my toe; and a policeman passed quite half a dozen times beneath my eyes, and the man whom I took to be the jeweller's watchman oftener still, during the better part of an hour that I spent at the window. Once, indeed, my heart was in my mouth, but only once. It was when the watchman stopped and peered through the peep-hole into the lighted shop. I waited for his whistle—I waited for the gallows or the gaol! But my signals had been studiously obeyed, and the man passed on in undisturbed serenity. In the end I had a signal in my turn, and retraced my steps with lighted matches, down the broad stairs, down the narrow ones, across the area, and up into the lobby where Raffles awaited me with an outstretched hand.

"Well done, my boy!" said he. "You're the same good man in a pinch, and you shall have your reward. I've got a thousand pounds' worth if I've got a penn'oth. It's all in my pockets. And here's something else I found in this locker; very decent port and some cigars, meant for poor dear Danby's business friends. Take a pull, and you shall light up presently. I've found a lavatory, too, and we must have a wash-and-brush-up before we go, for I'm as black as your boot."

The iron curtain was down, but he insisted on raising it until I could peep through the glass door on the other side and see his handiwork in the shop beyond. Here two electric lights were left burning all night long, and in their cold white rays I could at first see nothing amiss. I looked along an orderly lane, an empty glass counter on my left, glass cupboards of untouched silver on my right, and facing me the filmy black eye of the peep-hole that shone like a stage moon on the street. The counter had not been emptied by Raffles; its contents were in the Chubb's safe, which he had given up at a glance; nor had he looked at the silver, except to choose a cigarette case for me. He had confined himself entirely to the shop window. This was in three compartments, each secured for the night by removable panels with separate locks. Raffles had removed them a few hours before their time, and the electric light shone on a corrugated shutter bare as the ribs of an empty carcase. Every article of value was gone from the one place which was invisible from the little window in the door; elsewhere all was as it had been left overnight. And but for a train of mangled doors behind the iron curtain, a bottle of wine and a cigar-box with which liberties had been taken, a rather black towel in the lavatory, a burnt match here and there, and our finger-marks on the dusty banisters, not a trace of our visit did we leave.

"Had it in my head for long?" said Raffles, as we strolled through the streets towards dawn, for all the world as though we were returning from a dance. "No, Bunny, I never thought of it till I saw that upper part empty about a month ago, and bought a few things in the shop to get the lie of the land. That reminds me that I never paid for them; but, by Jove, I will tomorrow, and if that isn't poetic justice, what is? One visit showed me the possibilities of the place, but a second convinced me of its impossibilities without a pal. So I had practically given up the idea, when you came along on the very night and in the very plight for it! But here we are at the Albany, and I hope there's some fire left; for I don't know how you feel, Bunny, but for my part I'm as cold as Keats's owl."

He could think of Keats on his way from a felony! He could hanker for his fireside like another! Floodgates were loosed within me, and the plain English of our adventure rushed over me as cold as ice. Raffles was a burglar. I had helped him to commit one burglary, therefore I was a burglar, too. Yet I could stand and warm myself by his fire, and watch him empty his pockets, as though we had done nothing wonderful or wicked!

My blood froze. My heart sickened. My brain whirled. How I had liked this villain! How I had admired him! Now my liking and admiration must turn to loathing and disgust. I waited for the change. I longed to feel it in my heart. But—I longed and I waited in vain!

I saw that he was emptying his pockets; the table sparkled with their hoard. Rings by the dozen, diamonds by the score; bracelets, pendants, aigrettes, necklaces, pearls, rubies, amethysts, sapphires; and diamonds always, diamonds in everything, flashing bayonets of light, dazzling me—blinding me—making me disbelieve because I could no longer forget. Last of all came no gem, indeed, but my own revolver from an inner pocket. And that struck a chord. I suppose I said something—my hand flew out. I can see Raffles now, as he looked at me once more with a high arch over each clear eye. I can see him pick out the cartridges with his quiet, cynical smile, before he would give me my pistol back again.

"You mayn't believe it, Bunny," said he, "but I never carried a loaded one before. On the whole I think it gives one confidence. Yet it would be very awkward if anything went wrong; one might use it, and that's not the game at all, though I have often thought that the murderer who has just done the trick must have great sensations before things get too hot for him. Don't look so distressed, my dear chap. I've never had those sensations, and I don't suppose I ever shall."

"But this much you have done before?" said I hoarsely.

"Before? My dear Bunny, you offend me! Did it look like a first attempt? Of course I have done it before."

"Often?"

"Well—no! Not often enough to destroy the charm, at all events; never, as a matter of fact, unless I'm cursedly hard up. Did you hear about the Thimbleby diamonds? Well, that was the last time—and a poor lot of paste they were.

Then there was the little business of the Dormer houseboat at Henley last year. That was mine also—such as it was. I've never brought off a really big coup yet; when I do I shall chuck it up."

Yes, I remembered both cases very well. To think that he was their author! It was incredible, outrageous, inconceivable. Then my eyes would fall upon the table, twinkling and glittering in a hundred places, and incredulity was at an end.

"How came you to begin?" I asked, as curiosity overcame mere wonder, and a fascination for his career gradually wove itself into my fascination for the man.

"Ah! that's a long story," said Raffles. "It was in the Colonies, when I was out there playing cricket. It's too long a story to tell you now, but I was in much the same fix that you were in tonight, and it was my only way out. I never meant it for anything more; but I'd tasted blood, and it was all over with me. Why should I work when I could steal? Why settle down to some humdrum uncongenial billet, when excitement, romance, danger, and a decent living were all going begging together? Of course it's very wrong, but we can't all be moralists, and the distribution of wealth is very wrong to begin with. Besides, you're not at it all the time. I'm sick of quoting Gilbert's lines to myself, but they're profoundly true. I only wonder if you'll like the life as much as I do!"

"Like it?" I cried out. "Not I! It's no life for me. Once is enough!"

"You wouldn't give me a hand another time?"

"Don't ask me, Raffles. Don't ask me, for God's sake!"

"Yet you said you would do anything for me! You asked me to name my crime! But I knew at the time you didn't mean it; you didn't go back on me tonight, and that ought to satisfy me, goodness knows! I suppose I'm ungrateful, and unreasonable, and all that. I ought to let it end at this. But you're the very man for me, Bunny, the—very—man! Just think how we got through tonight. Not a scratch—not a hitch! There's nothing very terrible in it, you see; there never would be, while we worked together."

He was standing in front of me with a hand on either shoulder; he was smiling as he knew so well how to smile. I turned on my heel, planted my elbows on the chimney-piece, and my burning head between my hands. Next instant a still heartier hand had fallen on my back.

"All right, my boy! You are quite right and I'm worse than wrong. I'll never ask it again. Go, if you want to, and come again about mid-day for the cash. There was no bargain; but, of course, I'll get you out of your scrape—especially after the way you've stood by me tonight."

I was round again with my blood on fire.

"I'll do it again," I said, through my teeth.

He shook his head. "Not you," he said, smiling quite good-humoredly on my insane enthusiasm.

"I will," I cried with an oath. "I'll lend you a hand as often as you like! What does it matter now? I've been in it once. I'll be in it again. I've gone to the devil anyhow. I can't go back, and wouldn't if I could. Nothing matters another rap! When you want me, I'm your man!"

And that is how Raffles and I joined felonious forces on the Ides of March.

NINETEENTH-CENTURY AMERICANS

Villain: The Captain

The Story of a Young Robber

WASHINGTON IRVING

AMONG THE LEAST LIKELY SUSPECTS for writing a story about a terrible villain is Washington Irving (1783–1859), whose sketches and full-length books earned him the title of "Father of American Literature," as he was the first author of significance to marry American literature with the literature of the world. His life abroad, spent mainly in Spain, Italy, and England, heavily influenced his own work in the formative years of nineteenth-century America.

The easy grace of his narratives and their gentle humor endeared him to the reading public and he enjoyed great success with such works as *A History of New-York* (under the byline Diedrich Knickerbocker, 1809), generally regarded as the first American work of humorous fiction, and, especially, *The Sketch Book of Geoffrey Crayon, Gent.* (1819–1820), which contained the immortal tales, known by all American schoolchildren, "Rip Van Winkle" and "The Legend of Sleepy Hollow."

In 1824 he wrote *Tales of a Traveller* under the Geoffrey Crayon byline, hoping to re-create the success of *The Sketch Book.* While his early stories were noted for their charm and sentimental, romantic views of life, many of the little sketches in *Tales of a Traveller* are downright shocking, especially "The Story of a Young Robber." Whereas Irving's many warm and kindly stories of love and marriage had portrayed charming young maidens and their suitors in syrupy, conventional terms of ethereal, pure devotion and bliss, the unfortunate heroine and the young man who loves her in this short tale appear to have been pulled from the pages of the most melodramatic examples of Gothic horror.

The titular character, one of the most horrific villains in American literature, narrates the story in the first person with a peculiar detachment that belies the violence and tragedy that it depicts. The chapter of *Tales of a Traveller* titled "The Story of a Young Robber" actually contains more than one tale, but this episode is complete as offered here. It is a crime story of such unusual brutality that it cannot be surprising to know that it, like so many of Irving's stories, influenced many American writers of the nineteenth century.

"The Story of a Young Robber" was first published in *Tales of a Traveller* (London, John Murray, 1824, two volumes); the first American edition was published later in 1824 in Philadelphia by H. C. Carey & I. Lea.

THE STORY OF A YOUNG ROBBER

Washington Irving

I WAS BORN at the little town of Frosinone, which lies at the skirts of the Abruzzi. My father had made a little property in trade, and gave me some education, as he intended me for the church, but I had kept gay company too much to relish the cowl, so I grew up a loiterer about the place. I was a heedless fellow, a little quarrelsome on occasions, but good-humored in the main, so I made my way very well for a time, until I fell in love. There lived in our town a surveyor, or land bailiff, of the prince's who had a young daughter, a beautiful girl of sixteen. She was looked upon as something better than the common run of our townsfolk, and kept almost entirely at home. I saw her occasionally, and became madly in love with her, she looked so fresh and tender, and so different to the sunburnt females to whom I had been accustomed.

As my father kept me in money, I always dressed well, and took all opportunities of showing myself to advantage in the eyes of the little beauty. I used to see her at church; and as I could play a little upon the guitar, I gave her a tune sometimes under her window of an evening; and I tried to have interviews with her in her father's vineyard, not far from the town, where she sometimes walked. She was evidently pleased with me, but she was young and shy, and her father kept a strict eye upon her, and took alarm at my attentions, for he had a bad opinion of me, and looked for a better match for his daughter. I became furious at the difficulties thrown in my way, having been accustomed always to easy success among the women, being considered one of the smartest young fellows of the place.

Her father brought home a suitor for her; a rich farmer from a neighboring town. The wedding-day was appointed, and preparations were making. I got sight of her at her window, and I thought she looked sadly at me. I determined the match should not take place, cost what it might. I met her intended bridegroom in the market-place, and could not restrain the expression of my rage. A few hot words passed between us, when I drew my stiletto, and stabbed him to the heart. I fled to a neighboring church for refuge; and with a little money I obtained absolution; but I did not dare to venture from my asylum.

At that time our captain was forming his troop. He had known me from boyhood, and hearing of my situation, came to me in secret, and made such offers that I agreed to enlist myself among his followers. Indeed, I had more than once thought of taking to this mode of life, having known several brave fellows of the mountains, who used to spend their money freely among us youngsters of the town. I accordingly left my asylum late one night, repaired to the appointed place of meeting, took the oaths prescribed, and became one of the troop. We were for some time in a distant part of the mountains, and our wild adventurous kind of life hit my fancy wonderfully, and diverted my thoughts. At length they returned with all their violence to the recollection of Rosetta. The solitude in which I often found myself gave me time to brood over her image, and as I have kept watch at night over our sleeping camp in the mountains, my feelings have been roused almost to a fever.

At length we shifted our ground, and determined to make a descent upon the road between Terracina and Naples. In the course of our expedition, we passed a day or two in the woody mountains which rise above Frosinone. I cannot tell you how I felt when I looked down upon the place, and distinguished the residence of Rosetta. I determined to have an interview with her; but to what purpose? I could not expect that she would quit her home, and accompany me in my hazardous life among the mountains. She had been brought up too tenderly for that; and when I looked upon the women who were associated with some of our troop, I could not have borne the thoughts of her being their companion. All return to my former life was likewise hopeless; for a price was set upon my head. Still I determined to see her; the very hazard and fruitlessness of the thing made me furious to accomplish it.

It is about three weeks since I persuaded our captain to draw down to the vicinity of Frosinone, in hopes of entrapping some of its principal inhabitants, and compelling them to a ransom. We were lying in ambush towards evening, not far from the vineyard of Rosetta's father. I stole quietly from my companions, and drew near to reconnoiter the place of her frequent walks.

How my heart beat when, among the vines, I beheld the gleaming of a white dress! I knew it must be Rosetta's; it being rare for any female of the place to dress in white. I advanced secretly and without noise, until putting aside the vines, I stood suddenly before her. She uttered a piercing shriek, but I seized her in my arms, put my hand upon her mouth and conjured her to be silent. I poured out all the frenzy of my passion; offered to renounce my mode of life, to put my fate in her hands, to fly with her where we might live in safety together. All that I could say, or do, would not pacify her. Instead of love, horror and affright seemed to have taken possession of her breast. She struggled partly from my grasp, and filled the air with her cries. In an instant the captain and the rest of my companions were around us. I would have given anything at that moment had she been safe out of our hands, and in her father's house. It was too late. The captain pronounced her a prize, and ordered that she should be borne to the mountains. I represented to him that she was my prize, that I had a previous claim to her; and I mentioned my former attachment. He sneered bitterly in reply; observed that brigands had no business with village intrigues, and that, according to the laws of the troop, all spoils of the kind were determined by lot. Love and jealousy were raging in my heart, but I had to choose between obedience and death. I surrendered her to the captain, and we made for the mountains.

She was overcome by affright, and her steps were so feeble and faltering, and it was necessary to support her. I could not endure the idea that my comrades should touch her, and assuming a forced tranquility, begged that she might be confided to me, as one to whom she was more accustomed. The captain regarded me for a moment with a searching look, but I bore it without flinching, and he consented, I took her in my arms: she was almost senseless. Her head rested on my shoulder, her mouth was near to mine. I felt her breath on my face, and it seemed to fan the flame which devoured me. Oh, God! to have this glowing treasure in my arms, and yet to think it was not mine!

We arrived at the foot of the mountain. I

ascended it with difficulty, particularly where the woods were thick; but I would not relinquish my delicious burthen. I reflected with rage, however, that I must soon do so. The thoughts that so delicate a creature must be abandoned to my rude companions maddened me. I felt tempted, the stiletto in my hand, to cut my way through them all, and bear her off in triumph. I scarcely conceived the idea, before I saw its rashness; but my brain was fevered with the thought that any but myself should enjoy her charms. I endeavored to outstrip my companions by the quickness of my movements; and to get a little distance ahead, in case any favorable opportunity of escape should present. Vain effort! The voice of the captain suddenly ordered a halt. I trembled, but had to obey. The poor girl partly opened a languid eye, but was without strength or motion. I laid her upon the grass. The captain darted on me a terrible look of suspicion, and ordered me to scour the woods with my companions, in search of some shepherd who might be sent to her father's to demand a ransom.

I saw at once the peril. To resist with violence was certain death; but to leave her alone, in the power of the captain!—I spoke out then with a fervor inspired by my passion and my despair. I reminded the captain that I was the first to seize her; that she was my prize, and that my previous attachment for her should make her sacred among my companions. I insisted, therefore, that he should pledge me his word to respect her; otherwise I should refuse obedience to his orders. His only reply was, to cock his carbine; and at the signal my comrades did the same. They laughed with cruelty at my impotent rage. What could I do? I felt the madness of resistance. I was menaced on all hands, and my companions obliged me to follow them. She remained alone with the chief—yes, alone and almost lifeless!—

Here the robber paused in his recital, overpowered by his emotions. Great drops of sweat stood on his forehead; he panted rather than breathed; his brawny bosom rose and fell like the waves of a troubled sea. When he had become a little calm, he continued his recital.

I was not long in finding a shepherd, said he. I ran with the rapidity of a deer, eager, if possible, to get back before what I dreaded might take place. I had left my companions far behind, and I rejoined them before they had reached one-half the distance I had made. I hurried them back to the place where we had left the captain. As we approached, I beheld him seated by the side of Rosetta. His triumphant look, and the desolate condition of the unfortunate girl, left me no doubt of her fate. I know not how I restrained my fury.

It was with extreme difficulty, and by guiding her hand, that she was made to trace a few characters, requesting her father to send three hundred dollars as her ransom. The letter was dispatched by the shepherd. When he was gone, the chief turned sternly to me: "You have set an example," said he, "of mutiny and self-will, which if indulged would be ruinous to the troop. Had I treated you as our laws require, this bullet would have been driven through your brain. But you are an old friend; I have borne patiently with your fury and your folly; I have even protected you from a foolish passion that would have unmanned you. As to this girl, the laws of our association must have their course." So saying, he gave his commands, lots were drawn, and the helpless girl was abandoned to the troop.

Here the robber paused again, panting with fury and it was some moments before he could resume his story.

Hell, said he, was raging in my heart. I beheld the impossibility of avenging myself, and I felt that, according to the articles in which we stood bound to one another, the captain was in the right. I rushed with frenzy from the place. I threw myself upon the earth; tore up the grass with my hands, and beat my head, and gnashed my teeth in agony and rage. When at length I returned, I beheld the wretched victim, pale, disheveled; her dress torn and disordered. An emotion of pity for a moment subdued my fiercer feelings. I bore her to the foot of a tree, and leaned her gently against it. I took my gourd, which was filled with wine, and applying it to her lips, endeavored to make her swallow a little. To what a condition was she recovered! She, whom I had once seen the pride of Frosinone, who but a short time before I had beheld sporting in her father's vineyard, so fresh and beautiful and happy! Her teeth were clenched; her eyes fixed on the ground; her form without motion, and in a state of absolute insensibility. I hung over her in an agony of recollection of all that she had been, and of anguish at what I now beheld her. I darted round a look of horror at my companions, who seemed like so many fiends exulting in the downfall of an angel, and I felt a horror at myself for being their accomplice.

The captain, always suspicious, saw with his usual penetration what was passing within me, and ordered me to go upon the ridge of woods to keep a look-out upon the neighborhood and await the return of the shepherd. I obeyed, of course, stifling the fury that raged within me, though I felt for the moment that he was my most deadly foe.

On my way, however, a ray of reflection came across my mind. I perceived that the captain was but following with strictness the terrible laws to which we had sworn fidelity. That the passion by which I had been blinded might with justice have been fatal to me but for his forbearance; that he had penetrated my soul, and had taken precautions, by sending me out of the way, to prevent my committing any excess in my anger. From that instant I felt that I was capable of pardoning him.

Occupied with these thoughts, I arrived at the foot of the mountain. The country was solitary and secure; and in a short time I beheld the shepherd at a distance crossing the plain. I hastened to meet him. He had obtained nothing. He had found the father plunged in the deepest distress. He had read the letter with violent emotion, and then calming himself with a sudden exertion, he had replied coldly, "My daughter has been dishonored by those wretches; let her be returned without ransom, or let her die!"

I shuddered at this reply. I knew, according to the laws of our troop, her death was inevitable. Our oaths required it. I felt, nevertheless, that, not having been able to have her to myself, I could become her executioner!

The robber again paused with agitation. I sat musing upon his last frightful words, which proved to what excess the passions may be carried when escaped from all moral restraint. There was a horrible verity in this story that reminded me of some of the tragic fictions of Dante.

We now came to a fatal moment, resumed the bandit. After the report of the shepherd, I returned with him, and the chieftain received from his lips the refusal of the father. At a signal, which we all understood, we followed him some distance from the victim. He there pronounced her sentence of death. Every one stood ready to execute his order; but I interfered. I observed that there was something due to pity, as well as to justice. That I was as ready as anyone to approve the implacable law which was to serve as a warning to all those who hesitated to pay the ransoms demanded for our prisoners, but that, though the sacrifice was proper, it ought to be made without cruelty. The night is approaching, continued I; she will soon be wrapped in sleep; let her then be dispatched. All that I now claim on the score of former fondness for her is, let me strike the blow. I will do it as surely, but more tenderly, than another.

Several raised their voices against my proposition, but the captain imposed silence on them. He told me I might conduct her into a thicket at some distance, and he relied upon my promise.

I hastened to seize my prey. There was a forlorn kind of triumph at having at length become her exclusive possessor. I bore her off into the thickness of the forest. She remained in the same state of insensibility and stupor. I was thankful that she did not recollect me; for had she once murmured my name, I should have been overcome. She slept at length in the arms of him who was to poniard her. Many were the conflicts I underwent before I could bring myself to strike the blow. My heart had become sore by the recent conflicts it had undergone, and I dreaded lest, by procrastination, some other should become her executioner. When her repose had continued for some time, I separated myself gently from her, that I might not disturb her sleep, and seizing suddenly my poniard, plunged it into her bosom. A painful and concentrated murmur, but without any convulsive movement, accompanied her last sigh. So perished this unfortunate.

Villain: Narrator

Moon-Face

JACK LONDON

BORN JOHN CHANEY, Jack London (1876–1916) was the illegitimate son of an itinerant astrologer. His mother married John London eight months after he was born. He grew up in poverty in California's Bay area, went on the road as a hobo, riding freight trains, and was thrown in jail for a month of hard labor, helping to give him both understanding of and sympathy for the working-class poor as well as distaste for the drudgery of that life. After reading the *Communist Manifesto*, he became enamored with socialism but was so eager to be rich that he joined the gold rush to the Klondike region in Yukon, Canada, in 1891. He returned to Oakland without having mined an ounce of gold, but with the background for the American classic novel *The Call of the Wild* (1903), which became one of the bestselling novels of the early twentieth century with more than one and a half million copies sold in his lifetime. He began to sell stories to *Overland Monthly*, *Black Cat*, and *Atlantic Monthly* in the 1890s. Books soon followed, and he was hired by Hearst to report on the Russo-Japanese War, became an international bestseller, earned more than a million dollars, and by 1913 was regarded as the highest-paid, best-known, and most popular author in the world. Among the books that remain read to this day are such adventure classics as *The Sea Wolf* (1904) and *White Fang* (1906), and the autobiographical *Martin Eden* (1909). London had become a heavy drinker while still a teenager, and alcoholism, illness, financial woes, and overworking probably induced him to commit suicide at the age of forty, though the official cause of death was listed as uremic poisoning.

"Moon-Face" was originally published in *The Argonaut* in 1902; it was first collected in *Moon-Face and Other Stories* (New York, Macmillan, 1906).

MOON-FACE

Jack London

JOHN CLAVERHOUSE was a moon-faced man. You know the kind, cheek-bones wide apart, chin and forehead melting into the cheeks to complete the perfect round, and the nose, broad and pudgy, equidistant from the circumference, flattened against the very centre of the face like a dough-ball upon the ceiling. Perhaps that is why I hated him, for truly he had become an offense to my eyes, and I believed the earth to be cumbered with his presence. Perhaps my mother may have been superstitious of the moon and looked upon it over the wrong shoulder at the wrong time.

Be that as it may, I hated John Claverhouse. Not that he had done me what society would consider a wrong or an ill turn. Far from it. The evil was of a deeper, subtler sort; so elusive, so intangible, as to defy clear, definite analysis in words. We all experience such things at some period in our lives. For the first time we see a certain individual, one who the very instant before we did not dream existed; and yet, at the first moment of meeting, we say: "I do not like that man." Why do we not like him? Ah, we do not know why; we know only that we do not. We have taken a dislike, that is all. And so I with John Claverhouse.

What right had such a man to be happy? Yet he was an optimist. He was always gleeful and laughing. All things were always all right, curse him! Ah I how it grated on my soul that he should be so happy! Other men could laugh, and it did not bother me. I even used to laugh myself—before I met John Claverhouse.

But his laugh! It irritated me, maddened me, as nothing else under the sun could irritate or madden me. It haunted me, gripped hold of me, and would not let me go. It was a huge, Gargantuan laugh. Waking or sleeping it was always with me, whirring and jarring across my heart-strings like an enormous rasp. At break of day it came whooping across the fields to spoil my pleasant morning revery. Under the aching noonday glare, when the green things drooped and the birds withdrew to the depths of the forest, and all nature drowsed, his great "Ha! ha!" and "Ho! ho!" rose up to the sky and challenged the sun. And at black midnight, from the lonely cross-roads where he turned from town into his own place, came his plaguey cachinnations to rouse me from my sleep and make me writhe and clench my nails into my palms.

I went forth privily in the night-time, and turned his cattle into his fields, and in the morning heard his whooping laugh as he drove them out again. "It is nothing," he said; "the poor, dumb beasties are not to be blamed for straying into fatter pastures."

He had a dog he called "Mars," a big, splendid brute, part deer-hound and part bloodhound, and resembling both. Mars was a great delight to him, and they were always together. But I bided my time, and one day, when opportunity was ripe, lured the animal away and settled for him with strychnine and beefsteak. It made positively no impression on John Claverhouse. His laugh was as hearty and frequent as ever, and his face as much like the full moon as it always had been.

Then I set fire to his haystacks and his barn. But the next morning, being Sunday, he went forth blithe and cheerful.

"Where are you going?" I asked him, as he went by the cross-roads.

"Trout," he said, and his face beamed like a full moon. "I just dote on trout."

Was there ever such an impossible man! His whole harvest had gone up in his haystacks and barn. It was uninsured, I knew. And yet, in the face of famine and the rigorous winter, he went out gayly in quest of a mess of trout, forsooth, because he "doted" on them! Had gloom but rested, no matter how lightly, on his brow, or had his bovine countenance grown long and serious and less like the moon, or had he removed that smile but once from off his face, I am sure I could have forgiven him for existing. But no. He grew only more cheerful under misfortune.

I insulted him. He looked at me in slow and smiling surprise.

"I fight you? Why?" he asked slowly. And then he laughed. "You are so funny! Ho! ho! You'll be the death of me! He! he! he! Oh! Ho! ho! ho!

What would you? It was past endurance. By the blood of Judas, how I hated him! Then there was that name—Claverhouse! What a name! Wasn't it absurd? Claverhouse! Merciful heaven, WHY Claverhouse? Again and again I asked myself that question. I should not have minded Smith, or Brown, or Jones—but CLAVERHOUSE! I leave it to you. Repeat it to yourself—Claverhouse. Just listen to the ridiculous sound of it—Claverhouse! Should a man live with such a name? I ask of you. "No," you say. And "No" said I.

But I bethought me of his mortgage. What of his crops and barn destroyed, I knew he would be unable to meet it. So I got a shrewd, close-mouthed, tight-fisted money-lender to get the mortgage transferred to him. I did not appear but through this agent I forced the foreclosure, and but few days (no more, believe me, than the law allowed) were given John Claverhouse to remove his goods and chattels from the premises. Then I strolled down to see how he took it, for he had lived there upward of twenty years. But he met me with his saucer-eyes twinkling, and the light glowing and spreading in his face till it was as a full-risen moon.

"Ha! ha! ha!" he laughed. "The funniest tike, that youngster of mine! Did you ever hear the like? Let me tell you. He was down playing by the edge of the river when a piece of the bank caved in and splashed him. 'O papa!' he cried; 'a great big puddle flewed up and hit me.' "

He stopped and waited for me to join him in his infernal glee.

"I don't see any laugh in it," I said shortly, and I know my face went sour.

He regarded me with wonderment, and then came the damnable light, glowing and spreading, as I have described it, till his face shone soft and warm, like the summer moon, and then the laugh—"Ha! ha! That's funny! You don't see it, eh? He! he! Ho! ho! ho! He doesn't see it! Why, look here. You know a puddle—"

But I turned on my heel and left him. That was the last. I could stand it no longer. The thing must end right there, I thought, curse him! The earth should be quit of him. And as I went over the hill, I could hear his monstrous laugh reverberating against the sky.

Now, I pride myself on doing things neatly, and when I resolved to kill John Claverhouse I had it in mind to do so in such fashion that I should not look back upon it and feel ashamed. I hate bungling, and I hate brutality. To me there is something repugnant in merely striking a man with one's naked fist—faugh! it is sickening! So, to shoot, or stab, or club John Claverhouse (oh, that name!) did not appeal to me. And not only was I impelled to do it neatly and artistically, but also in such manner that not the slightest possible suspicion could be directed against me.

To this end I bent my intellect, and, after a week of profound incubation, I hatched the scheme. Then I set to work. I bought a water spaniel bitch, five months old, and devoted my whole attention to her training. Had any one spied upon me, they would have remarked that this training consisted entirely of one thing—*retrieving*. I taught the dog, which I called "Bellona," to fetch sticks I threw into the water, and not only to fetch, but to fetch at once, without mouthing or playing with them. The point was that she was to stop for nothing, but to deliver the stick in all haste. I made a practice of running away and leaving her to chase me, with the stick in her mouth, till she caught me. She was a bright animal, and took to the game with such eagerness that I was soon content.

After that, at the first casual opportunity, I presented Bellona to John Claverhouse. I knew what I was about, for I was aware of a little weakness of his, and of a little private sinning of which he was regularly and inveterately guilty.

"No," he said, when I placed the end of the rope in his hand. "No, you don't mean it." And his mouth opened wide and he grinned all over his damnable moon-face.

"I—I kind of thought, somehow, you didn't like me," he explained. "Wasn't it funny for me to make such a mistake?" And at the thought he held his sides with laughter.

"What is her name?" he managed to ask between paroxysms.

"Bellona," I said.

"He! he!" he tittered. "What a funny name."

I gritted my teeth, for his mirth put them on edge, and snapped out between them, "She was the wife of Mars, you know."

Then the light of the full moon began to suffuse his face, until he exploded with: "That was my other dog. Well, I guess she's a widow now. Oh! Ho! ho! E! he! he! Ho!" he whooped after me, and I turned and fled swiftly over the hill.

The week passed by, and on Saturday evening I said to him, "You go away Monday, don't you?"

He nodded his head and grinned.

"Then you won't have another chance to get a mess of those trout you just 'dote' on."

But he did not notice the sneer. "Oh, I don't know," he chuckled. "I'm going up tomorrow to try pretty hard."

Thus was assurance made doubly sure, and I went back to my house hugging myself with rapture.

Early next morning I saw him go by with a dip-net and gunnysack, and Bellona trotting at his heels. I knew where he was bound, and cut out by the back pasture and climbed through the underbrush to the top of the mountain. Keeping carefully out of sight, I followed the crest along for a couple of miles to a natural amphitheatre in the hills, where the little river raced down out of a gorge and stopped for breath in a large and placid rock-bound pool. That was the spot! I sat down on the croup of the mountain, where I could see all that occurred, and lighted my pipe.

Ere many minutes had passed, John Claverhouse came plodding up the bed of the stream. Bellona was ambling about him, and they were in high feather, her short, snappy barks mingling with his deeper chest-notes. Arrived at the pool, he threw down the dip-net and sack, and drew from his hip-pocket what looked like a large, fat candle. But I knew it to be a stick of "giant"; for such was his method of catching trout. He dynamited them. He attached the fuse by wrapping the "giant" tightly in a piece of cotton. Then he ignited the fuse and tossed the explosive into the pool.

Like a flash, Bellona was into the pool after it. I could have shrieked aloud for joy. Claverhouse yelled at her, but without avail. He pelted her with clods and rocks, but she swam steadily on till she got the stick of "giant" in her mouth, when she whirled about and headed for shore. Then, for the first time, he realized his danger, and started to run. As foreseen and planned by me, she made the bank and took out after him. Oh, I tell you, it was great! As I have said, the pool lay in a sort of amphitheatre. Above and below, the stream could be crossed on stepping-stones. And around and around, up and down and across the stones, raced Claverhouse and Bellona. I could never have believed that such an ungainly man could run so fast. But run he did, Bellona hot-footed after him, and gaining. And then, just as she caught up, he in full stride, and she leaping with nose at his knee, there was a sudden flash, a burst of smoke, a terrific detonation, and where man and dog had been the instant before there was naught to be seen but a big hole in the ground.

"Death from accident while engaged in illegal fishing." That was the verdict of the coroner's jury; and that is why I pride myself on the neat and artistic way in which I finished off John Claverhouse. There was no bungling, no brutality; nothing of which to be ashamed in the whole transaction, as I am sure you will agree. No more does his infernal laugh go echoing among the hills, and no more does his fat moon-face rise up to vex me. My days are peaceful now, and my night's sleep deep.

The Shadow of Quong Lung

C. W. DOYLE

CHARLES WILLIAM DOYLE (1852–1903) was born in Landour, India, and studied at Calcutta University before moving to Great Britain to study medicine in London and Edinburgh, finally receiving his medical degree from the University of Aberdeen in 1875. He practiced in England until 1888, then emigrated to the United States to live in Santa Cruz, California, where he became a close friend of Ambrose Bierce.

His first book, *The Taming of the Jungle* (1899), was a series of sketches about the simple lives of the primitive Indian people who lived in Terai, the huge jungle that skirts the foothills of the Himalayas, depicting their superstitions and their love of the beauty of their surroundings. The book was (inevitably) compared with the works of Rudyard Kipling and more than one newspaper (Boston's *Saturday Evening Gazette*, Brooklyn's *Daily Eagle*, and *The Press*) rated his book a worthy rival.

Doyle wrote only one other book, *The Shadow of Quong Lung*, which appears to have been written mainly to show the inhumane condition of the slave girls of San Francisco's Chinatown. The five connected stories feature the evil Quong Lung who, unlike most "Oriental" villains of the time, was not intent on world conquest. He was merely a rich and powerful gangster with a band of thugs who would stop at nothing to guarantee his ongoing rule of the region, including his control of prostitution, slavery, kidnapping, and murder. Two of the stories won prominent prizes: "The Wings of Lee Toy" (*San Francisco Examiner*, December 19, 1897) for a Christmas story and "The Seats of Judgment" (*Argonaut*) for a short story written in 1898.

"The Shadow of Quong Lung" was originally published in *The Shadow of Quong Lung* (Philadelphia, J. B. Lippincott, 1900).

THE SHADOW OF QUONG LUNG

C. W. Doyle

I

A Tender Rhetorician

"THOU ART CHIN LEE, SCRIVENER?" asked a handsome young Chinaman of the professional letter-writer whose table, with his implements of writing, was set close to the wall at one of the crossings on Clay Street, San Francisco.

"Chin Lee, scrivener, am I; and thou art in good hap this fair morning to have come my way, instead of stopping at the station of Ah Moy (may the sea have his corpse!), who catcheth the unwary lower down the street."

"I am Ho Chung, and I am late come from Pekin, leaving behind me Moy Yen, my wife, who hath gone back to her kin, who are of the northern hills and speak not as we do. I am fain to send her a letter that can be read of her people, whereby they shall know that I am an honorable man, and that I am making preparation for her journey to this land. Thou art learned in the tongue of the hill people?"

"All the tongues of our great country have yielded me their secrets," said Chin Lee with the gravity becoming the lie that he uttered daily. (He had an agent in Chinatown who spoke the Manchu dialect, and translated the communications brought to him by Chin Lee.) "Thou art in great luck this propitious morning," he went on, "for Ah Moy is descended from striped swine."

"They say he hath a more tender pen, but that thou art more honest."

"They—mine enemies, doubtless!—tell the truth concerning my honesty, but they lie when they depreciate my qualities as a tender writer. Tenderness and Affection are of my household, and sup with me nightly. But how didst thou talk with Moy Yen, seeing that thy speech differs from hers?"

"I taught her a few words of my tongue, and she taught me a few of hers; and so——"

"Ay, ay!" interrupted Chin Lee; "love hath its own language, and is not in much need of mere words in any tongue. But what is your wish?"

"I would have you tell the young woman—Moy Yen, my wife—that when the man-child Ho Sung—or Moy Yep, if it be a girl (which the Gods forbid!)—hath arrived, I will send her moneys to bring her and the little one to San Francisco. And, Chin Lee," he hesitated a moment, "didst ever love a woman?"

"I have loved them in every province of

our Flowery Land—and in many tongues, Ho Chung."

"But hast thou knowledge of a *sam-yen* played under a balcony in a Lane of Death, where nothing is asked?"

"Behold the proof!" replied Chin Lee, rolling up his sleeve and displaying a scar on his arm.

"And did a little child come to thee thereafter?"

"Yea; and the songs I wrote to it are sung in the streets of Shanghai to this day—for I was overpowered with the marvel of its littleness. See, I will add one of those songs to the letter I shall write for thee for the consideration of a *ping-long* (betel leaf)."

They crossed the street to the reduced gentleman who sold the toothsome delicacy, which the Hindoos understand so much better. And as they discussed the spicy morsels they walked to and fro on the sunny side of Union Square, which is a sequestered retreat, as it were, in the teeming traffic of Chinatown.

"I will write thee two letters," began Chin Lee; "one to fit the case of a man-child, and the other if thy babe should be a girl. The price for two letters shall be the same as for one—and, my friend, where didst thou say Moy Yen, thy wife, lived?"

"In the lane Pin-yang, of the city Moukden, which is in the Manchu province Shing-king in the hill country. But, belike, thy letter will not reach her, for the lane is one of many small ones in a great city."

"His stubborn apprehension is clearly due to his much affection," thought Chin Lee; then he said aloud, "Never fear! Moy Yen, with a smiling babe at her breast, shall receive a letter that shall delight her greatly: my aged father, who looks after my affairs in China (Heaven soften his taking off!), hath an agent in Moukden, and will see to it that the letter doth not miscarry."

"But Moy Yen is——"

"She is very beautiful?" interrupted Chin Lee, guessing his thought with the aid of much practice.

"She is more beautiful than I can tell, and——"

"So it was in my case," again interrupted Chin Lee. "The woman that caused me the hurt I showed you—it was a dangerous hurt (he was talking in a confidential and friendly strain by this time—an old trick of his)—but the woman was worthy, by reason of her beauty and her tenderness, of the sudden taking off of even Chin Lee, who is the slave of a wakeful conscience, and the possessor of much experience in affairs of the heart; and it is an ointment to the hurt, which still twingeth shrewdly when the air nips, to clothe my so great experiences in the garments of my rhetoric for the benefit of my honorable patrons."

"Would it help thy rhetoric to see a presentment of Moy Yen?" asked Ho Chung, drawing an enamelled case from his pocket, and displaying a miniature of a young Chinese woman painted by a Chinese artist.

"The sight of Youth and Beauty are as spurs to the halting poet, or as the sun that waketh a sleeping valley whose charms are enhanced by his ardent rays"; and Chin Lee held the miniature at various distances from his bespectacled eyes, and examined it critically.

"To have looked on this once," he went on unctuously, "were sufficient inspiration to lay the foundation of a letter that should serve as a model for all lovers from Pekin to Yun-nan;—but to look at it in favored intervals till this hour tomorrow would result in the erection of such turrets and pinnacles of rhetoric as were never before built in our language."

He paused awhile in meditation, regarding the miniature with head aslant. "Wilt thou leave this with me till tomorrow at this hour, so that I may write that which befits thy affection, and is due to Moy Yen's beauty and worth?" Then, noticing Ho Chung's hesitation, he went on: "The picture hath no value to any one save thee—but who may appraise what is dear to the heart? Nevertheless, I will give thee twenty dollars to hold until the picture is restored to thee."

"It is my comfort in a strange land," said Ho Chung, eyeing it hungrily.

"And it is worthy of the rhetoric of Chin Lee," responded the other, loftily.

That settled it. The exchange of money and picture having been made, Ho Chung gave the scrivener many and full particulars to be transmitted to Moy Yen:—details of his own life and work in San Francisco; and hopes for her own welfare and that of the babe that had, doubtless, arrived.

"Write my heart into the letter, Chin Lee," he ended.

"I will enclose it in the amber of my rhetoric, and transmute the youth, and hope, and the wonders of this land of sunshine into words that shall ripple as pleasantly as the wavelets on the beach at Santa Cruz when the full moon lays its benediction on the sleeping sea and the winds are hushed!"

II

The Entertainment of a Mouse by a Cat

"Thou hast come, doubtless, to discharge thy debt to me, Chin Lee," said the stout, arrogant man behind the counter who had Destiny in his looks.

"Ay, Quong Lung," replied Chin Lee, with a newly acquired confidence. "I have that with me that shall not only free me from my indebtedness to thee, but which will put money in thy purse. But my words are privy, and to be spoken only in thy inner chamber."

Quong Lung bolted and locked his front door from within, and further fortified the passage with a fatefully contrived barricade;—for the wars of the *tongs* never cease, and there had been a standing reward for his life for many days. But the contending hatchetmen and highbinders agreed that Quong Lung had a charmed life, and that his enemies were short-lived.

And Chin Lee, professional letter-writer and past-master in the art of lying—and owing Quong Lung money, and a bitter debt of service!—stretched himself with easy negligence on the smoking mat in Quong Lung's inner apartment, whilst the latter took his place on the other side of the mat.

After they had smoked three or four pipes in silence, Chin Lee drew Moy Yen's miniature from his blouse and handed it to Quong Lung.

"Would she be worth while," he asked simply, for rhetoric was out of the question with *this* man.

"She would, if she were available."

"All things are available to the mighty. But the price I ask is a great one, Quong Lung, and the strong are ever merciful and generous, and it will not strain thy mercy and generosity to pay my dues."

"Name them."

"The remittance in full—to be given in writing—of the money I owe thee; and——" He paused a moment, and then went on in a trembling voice: "See, Quong Lung, the knowledge thou hast of that little happening in Ross Alley ten years ago, when a man was found dead with a certain writing in his hand, hath sat like lead on my soul, and frozen—time and again—the flow of words whereby I live."

"Yes?"

"Return the writing to me, and I will do thy bidding at all times."

"Thou *shalt* do my bidding at all times, in any case," said Quong Lung, carelessly. "See to it that the young woman is made 'available' without loss of time."

"Death hath no such bitterness as thy supremacy, Quong Lung!"

"Only fools kill themselves, Chin Lee; and 'twere pity," he went on, with a sneer, "'twere pity to put an end to the flow of thy 'rhetoric.'"

He turned his head slowly and looked insolently at the trembling Chin Lee, who had ceased smoking and was kneeling suppliantly before him with clasped hands. As a cat plays with a mouse only to enliven the little game of catching it again, he appeared to relent as he said, "Thy debt in money shall be remitted when the young woman is 'available'—to use thy phrase. But thy debt in service shall continue with growing interest: I have need of thy 'rhetoric.' Now, tell me about the young woman."

"Her name, Inexorable, is Moy Yen, and she is the wife of Ho Chung, who is a skilled goldsmith, and earneth high wage in the service of Quen Loy of Dupont Street."

"She is here?"

"Nay, Far Reacher; she is in Moukden, of the province of Shing-king, where the people use other speech than ours, as thou knowest. And Ho Chung, her husband, is saving money for her journey to this land with her babe, after it is born."

"Her babe?" asked Quong Lung, with a frown.

"Yes, Most Merciful."

"And what should *I* do with a babe? My shadow hath fallen on it. See to it that it withers."

"The lightning shall strike it, Most Worshipful!"

"Have a photograph made of this portrait: it will be needful to Moy Yen's admission to this land as a 'Native Daughter.' "

"And if she should be as beautiful as her picture shows her to be, wilt thou remit the greater debt?"

"Perhaps," said Quong Lung, eyeing him for a moment with disdain. "Now go!"

III

How Rhetoric May Serve Love

"Here is thy picture, Ho Chung," said Chin Lee when they met at the appointed hour.

"I could not sleep last night for thinking of it," responded Ho Chung, returning his money to the letter-writer, and concealing the precious miniature in his blouse.

"Sweetly shalt thou sleep tonight, young man, lulled by the consciousness that never fair woman received letter like this that thou shalt send to Moy Yen. But it is not fitting that such rhetoric as mine should be wasted in a roaring street. Come with me to the square below where, at least, there is grass with pleasant shadows thereon."

When they had reached Union Square, Chin Lee unrolled the papers in his hand, and read the following letter which he had indited:

"Moy Yen—Cherry Blossom!—to think that these my silly words shall take thine eyes!"

"Excellent!" interrupted Ho Chung; "I perceive thou hast suffered as I do."

Chin Lee acknowledged the compliment with a smile, and went on with his reading:

"—But to begin rightly: It hath been my good hap to meet with a Master of Rhetoric, one Chin Lee, who is not too old to have forgotten the thrill of the tender passion, and who hath suffered grievously in the cultivation of the affections. He hath much skill in the lofty art of the scrivener, for he hath labored all his life, and at all hours of the day and night, in the stony fields of poesy and expression. His skill is only less than my devotion, which he has herein transmuted into tender phrase and loving passage befitting thy surpassing excellence. What manner of man he is is hereunder told: His learning is only equalled by his benevolence, which is the talk of all people in this great and wondrous city of San Francisco, so that when any one hath good luck all men say, 'Herein is the hand of Chin Lee!' "

"But this is naught to Moy Yen, who would fain hear of me," broke in Ho Chung.

"The young are ever impatient," said Chin Lee, looking reprovingly over the top of his spectacles. "Patience is always rewarded." He then proceeded with his letter:

"What I would, first and last, impress upon thee, Dew of the Morning, is the superexcel-

lence of my Honorable Friend, Chin Lee, who hath toiled in the tea gardens of learning, where only the 'Orange Pekoe' of speech, so to speak, is cultivated."

"'Tis a fair sentence," said Chin Lee, looking up at Ho Chung; "'the Orange Pekoe of speech' is a fair phrase, and smacks rightly."

"Proceed," replied Ho Chung, kicking aside a pebble on the path.

Chin Lee, adjusting his spectacles, went on:

"But, whatsoever happens, always remember that Chin Lee is an Honorable Man—and my best friend."

"But this doth not touch me," said Ho Chung, with some irritation.

"Shall I, an uncredited man, act as a go-between for my honorable patrons and their correspondents who live where our speech is not spoken?" asked Chin Lee, with some heat.

"Perhaps thou art right—but I would dictate the rest of the letter. See, I will propitiate thee with favorable mention of thee to Moy Yen."

"Now nay, Ho Chung; bethink thee: shall one who is acquainted with the 'Four Books' and the 'Five Classics' yield to a mere goldsmith in matters pertaining to rhetoric? Shall I permit my perfect knowledge of the Confucian Analects to be trampled under foot even by a lover? Thy lack of learning should stand suppliantly in the presence of an understanding that comprehends the encyclopædia '*Wan heen tung kaou*,' compiled by the learned Ma Twan-lin." He finished with a lofty emphasis.

"Nevertheless, Chin Lee," replied Ho Chung, with a look of impatience on his face, "if I may not speak from my heart to Moy Yen's, I shall be compelled to employ the pen of Ah Moy who, they say, writeth as he is bidden."

"Ah Moy is a pig, and his father is a stray dog! He knoweth naught of the 'Ta-heo' (the Book of Great Learning), and he inditeth letters for coolies only to their filthy trulls—but thou art a *sing-song* (a gentleman), and hast done wisely to come to the only *sing-song* in my profession in San Francisco."

"Thy time is precious, Chin Lee; and I, too, must be about my day's work," said Ho Chung, turning his back on the letter-writer.

"Tchch, tchch!" clucked the latter, impatiently. "Pronounce, then, the words I must write, without regard to the lofty art of rhetoric, from thy untutored heart to Moy Yen's. I am but thy pen. Proceed. But fail not to speak favorably of me, as thou didst promise."

"The words thou hast written so far shall stand, Chin Lee," said the other, to conciliate the Master of Rhetoric, with whom rested the ultimate writing of the letter to Moy Yen—a letter not to be misconstrued for obvious reasons.

IV

Concerning a Vulgar Passion

When the scrivener was ready, Ho Chung dictated his message to the distant Moy Yen in the following terms:

"Beloved!—Soul of my Soul!—Bearing two hearts within thee! thou art blessed and decorated beyond the power of mere speech! But, ere I reach forth into the realms of words to dress thee with the praises that belong to thee, I am fain, first, to extol the good qualities of my Honorable Friend, Chin Lee——"

"Of 7793 Clay Street," interrupted the scrivener; "and I would add: 'He can speak thy language, and is famed for his modesty and benevolence.'"

"So be it set forth, but interrupt not again," said Ho Chung, with evident irritation, as he once more resumed his dictation. "Write now only what I shall say," and Chin Lee, reading Ho Chung's face aright, was henceforth silent, and wrote as follows:

"Our child?—hath it come, Cherry Blossom? Oh, the weary days until I see it, and hold it in my arms! But the thought that it is part thine and part mine, and that it rests on thy tender bosom, lies on my heart like the dew-pearls on the petals of a new-blown rose. Is it well—oh, it must be well with thee, and Ours! Tell me all that my heart is hungry for, Dawn of Love.

"As for me, I am still in the service of Quen Loy, and my work is in much demand, and holdeth me from early morn till early night;—Quen Loy will not suffer me to work longer lest harm befall mine eyes. My wage is more than passing fair—and even the lottery hath befriended me, so that I am able to send thee, herewith, twenty taels. *Two months hence, if my fortune change not, I shall send thee sufficient money to bring thee, and little Thine-and-Mine, to this fair country, where the sun shines more days in the year than elsewhere.*

"As for the people of this country, they are not the White Devils as set forth by the ignorant of our kind. The worst that can be said of them is that they obtrude themselves into the houses of our people, and have no reverence for our Gods or our shrines. I am told, too, that their women bare their bosoms and shoulders for the lewd to gaze upon, and that they dance in unseemly fashion in the embrace of men other than their husbands. This I have not seen, for mine eyes are for thy beauty alone, thou Spray of Jessamine!

"But, ah! the thought of thee, and of thy beauty, and of the Blossom—the babe, Thine-and-Mine!—are ever with me. It sustains me in my hours of work,—and then I have thy picture to look at! But it is at night, when the stimulus of work is over, that I feel most keenly that I am a stranger in a far country. Beloved, I awoke trembling last night: methought I was in Pekin with thee, and that I could hear thy gentle breathing; and then I stretched forth my hand; but, alas! thy place beside me was vacant, and I wept amain till the dawn came. Oh, cruel, cruel is the distance between us! and so is the vast wandering sea that separates us, and knows naught of our love, and careth less, and is indifferent to us. But if money can bring thee to me, I will faithfully work for it.

"Farewell, Orange Blossom. I breathe my benediction into the space in which this world spins, knowing that thou art somewhere in it, and that it will find thee.

"These from thy Husband,

"Ho Chung."

V

The Voice of Travail

To Ho Chung, two months after the despatch of the above letter, came the following reply from Moy Yen, which was thus translated to Ho Chung the next day, after the crafty Chin Lee had conferred with his Manchu agent:

"Best Beloved: Thy babe hath come!—and it is a Man-Child!

"Oh! my Lord, I have walked on a path that is hedged with death on both sides. Pain held my right hand, and Fear my left. The night was dark and clouded, and full of whisperings of mischance. And oft I should have failed and died, but the thought of Ours, and of my husband in a far and strange land toiling for me, sustained me. And then the babe Ho Sung was born, and the light returned.

"But the ever-fresh wonder of thy Man-Child! How may I tell it! Oh! Ho Chung, his hands are like the petals of a rose, and a cunning woman from Hindostan hath taught me how to stain his nails with henna.

"But the greater wonder of his feet, my Might! He kicked himself naked with them last night—and I can hold them both in one palm!

"He is so beautiful that I do not even fear

to put him to the breast that is stabbed with a thousand knives when he suckles.

"He hath speech, also, and it is in terms of two simple cries that convey impressions of pleasure and pain: his laughter is like a tiny, happy waterfall; and his wailings are melodious, too, save that they pierce my heart. And he groweth amain—I can scarce sustain him, though my breasts are never empty.

"Beloved, the twenty taels *thou didst send me have arrived. It is a thousand years till I get the rest of the moneys that shall take me to thee, and enable me to put Thine-and-Mine, as thou callest him, in thy arms.*

"From thine own,

"Moy Yen."

VI

The Withering of a Bud

"Ho Chung was overcome to the point of death when I read this to him," said Chin Lee, extending a letter to Quong Lung. "You see, he had knowledge through a previous letter that a notable babe had been born to him; and then came this letter, which, in his grief, he left with me."

Quong Lung took the paper, and read as follows:

"Best Beloved! Sharer of my joys and sorrows!—A great sorrow hath befallen us.

"But the babe—our babe, Thine-and-Mine!—was ever such a babe!

"How may I tell it!

"Yesterday some miscreant stole it from us. At first my heart filled with hope, because of the milk that flowed into my breasts, for, methought, that was a sign that our little one was still alive, and that I should, surely, suckle it again. But now my heart is full of pain, and my breasts are empty of milk!

"Strength of my Strength! call thy utmost strength to thy aid: thy man-child Ho Sung was stolen from my side as I slept, and today his body was found in the canal, and my milk, oh! my Lord, lay on his frozen lips."

"Thy honorable and aged parent in the Flowery Land is an 'artist,'" said Quong Lung, extending a cigar to Chin Lee.

"But *we* are ever more favored than our sires, for we reap the harvests sown by them. In fact, Chin Sen, my father, but followed out my directions," answered Chin Lee, eagerly.

Quong Lung proceeded to read as follows:

"Oh, my Lord, my babe being dead, and thou in a far land, my life droops. Oh, let me come to thee soon, soon, soon!

"From thy grief-stricken wife,

"Moy Yen."

"See to it that she comes soon," said Quong Lung, putting five double eagles on the table. "Her beauty will fade if she sorrow too long. Ah! I have it," he exclaimed. "My agent at Shanghai, Fan Wong, will despatch his next consignment of slave girls to me two months hence under charge of my wife, Suey See, who doth such errands for me. Moy Yen shall return as thy Californian daughter, Chin Lee, in fulfilment of the requirements of the Chinese Exclusion Act. Thy daughter shall have honorable escort."

"Thou art in merry mood this morning, Compeller. But greater honor would accrue to Moy Yen if she were to come as *thy* daughter—and no questions would be asked by the authorities on this side."

"No questions shall be asked in any case," said Quong Lung.

"Even the White Devils fear thee, Far Reacher! But the man Ho Chung is young and strong—and he might get knowledge of this matter—and my life is still precious to me. 'Twould place me on a dangerous path bordered by death, Most Merciful."

"Therefore do I order it," said Quong Lung, slowly, regarding Chin Lee with half-closed eyes. "But thou hast done well so far, Chin Lee; passing well. How much dost thou owe me?"

"One hundred and thirty-eight dollars, Fair Dealer;—and the rack of a scrap of paper that fell into thy hands. Consider: I have caused thy shadow to fall on a flower that hindered—and the flower hath withered. Thou wilt let that weigh with thee, Most Merciful."

"'Twas well done; very well done! 'Twas worth not less than the fifty dollars I herewith remit of thy debt to me in money," and Quong Lung wrote, and gave Chin Lee a receipt for that amount.

"But thou art not appraising the removal of the babe at fair value, Quong Lung."

"Fair enough, fair enough, when one considers that which was found ten years ago in Ross Alley in the hand of a dead man."

"Quong Lung, 'twere easier to confess all, than to live under the stress of thy shadow. Yes; to confess all—all!—some of thy misdeeds, too."

There was a battery connected with the chair on which Chin Lee sat, and, as he clasped its arms in the act of rising, Quong Lung switched on the current by an unperceived movement of his foot.

"The raising of thy voice, Chin Lee, would summon instant death. No man may threaten me, and live."

He held up a menacing finger, as his victim writhed in the toils of the Demon that Bestows Cramps.

"Call off thy Devil, Quong Lung; call him off! I am forever thy slave," whined Chin Lee.

"No man may threaten me, and live," repeated Quong Lung, impressively. "Yet see, I will be magnanimous to thee, for only the hem of my shadow hath fallen on thee this time—and I am mindful, too, of the bud that withered."

He shut off the current, whilst Chin Lee, almost dead with fear, sank into his chair and wiped the great drops from his forehead.

"Great is Quong Lung, and great are his spells!" he gasped. "I am his slave henceforth."

"Well spoken, Chin Lee. Now drink, for thou hast received the lesser discipline that I mete out to ingrates, and art in need of the assistance of *sam shu*," and Quong Lung set cups and a teapot filled with Chinese gin on the table that was between them.

"Nay, fear not, Chin Lee; the liquor is not poisoned. See," and Quong Lung filled a cup for himself, and drank its contents. Then, as his guest drank with a shaking hand, Quong Lung went on:

"Thou wert nearer a heavier discipline than that, Chin Lee. Stand a pace to the right of thy chair, and thou shalt see."

Chin Lee had scarcely complied with his command, when an arrow whizzed past him, and transfixed the chair from which he had just risen.

"Other means have I for subduing the recalcitrant. Never forget that thou art in my hands. And now some more *sam shu*; and resume thy seat," said Quong Lung, withdrawing the arrow from the chair.

"Thou wilt write to Moy Yen, in the name of Ho Chung, and direct her to the keeping of my wife Suey See who, also, will seek her with credentials purporting to come from Ho Chung."

"Thy wishes shall be obeyed, Subduer," returned the other, meekly. Then, with an air of sycophancy, he went on: "And when Moy Yen sends word of her coming, I will alter the date of her arrival here in the translation of the letter to Ho Chung, so that we may not be interrupted in any way in the taking of our pretty partridge to her cage. Ho, ho!"

"Thou art a worthy son of that worthy artist, thy honorable and aged father; and thy rhetoric shall yet advance thee. Drink once more."

VII

A Burial by Fire

"The brightness of the day is reflected in thy looks, my young friend," said Chin Lee with his best professional smile as he unfolded the letter Ho Chung had given him the day before—the third he was to translate and embellish with the flowers of his rhetoric for the young goldsmith.

"Ah, ha!" he went on, as he smoothed out the letter on his table; "I am, indeed, thy Luck. See what it is to have employed a man versed in languages, and who can summon happy words at his will. It is well known that I can pack more meaning into a sentence than Ah Moy, the hungry, can convey in a column. Not for nothing have I culled the flowers that abound in the *She king* of Confucius," and he shook his head with a nod of self-approval.

"Great, indeed, O Chin Lee, is the wonder of thy learning——"

"It is spoken of even among the barbarians who live on the borders of Thibet," interrupted the scrivener. "Even the Mandarins who sway the destinies of our great empire are fain to ease their so great and important functions with recitation of the odes I used to throw off in my idle moments. And when it was told to the Emperor that one Chin Lee, scrivener, prosodian, and rhetorician——"

"But this is barren talk," interrupted Ho Chung, looking hungrily at the letter in Chin Lee's hand.

"How headlong is youth!" exclaimed Chin Lee, in a tone of deprecation. "What a glowing sentence didst thou cool with the breath of thy impatience! The beauty of the young day, the expectant love beaming in thy youthful countenance, the news herein contained——"

"Oh, man of many words, is it good news?" once more interrupted Ho Chung, eagerly.

But the other held up his hand in remonstrance, and went on: "And the thought of the great task that the mightiest of Emperors had it in mind once to impose upon me, the task of compiling an encyclopædia that should rival that of Ma Twan-lin—all these had roused me to a height of poetic fervor that would have ended in a climax of rhetoric that should have thundered down the ages! Hast no love for literature? and do not the claims of posterity appeal to thee?"

"I have a passing strong love for Moy Yen, Chin Lee, and my heart knocketh for news of her. Give me the letter and I will go to Ah Moy, and leave thee to nourish thy 'poetic fervor,'" and Ho Chung extended an impatient hand.

"The heedlessness of youth passeth the comprehension of the wise! Well, if thou must obstruct the flow of rhythmic prose of which I feel capable even now, in spite of thy interruptions, I will translate the letter of thy Moy Yen. Sit down beside me, my headlong friend, while I improve the crude sentences wherewith the letter-writer of Moukden hath expressed the love of the beautiful Moy Yen for thee."

He wiped his spectacles deliberately, and proceeded to read as follows, interpolating and altering as suited the exigencies of the plot in which he was concerned:

"Ho Chung, Deliverer! oh, my hope is fulfilled! Yesterday came twenty other taels *from thee! And a kinsman, but lately found—who is an opium merchant, and hath been bereft of children, too—gave me other twenty for the journey, and yet another twenty to put into thy hand. See: before the moon is full again, they tell me I shall look once more upon my Beautiful Lord. The great vessel of iron moved by fire and steam, in which I shall cross the seas that separate us, will leave a month hence (Chin Lee substituted a 'month' for 'two weeks'), and I shall be with my sweet Lord ere the cherry blossoms show. I herewith send thee a paper that tells the name and date of departure of the vessel that shall bring me to thee.*

"But, oh, my Lord! how may I leave Thine-and-Mine behind me! Oh, the tender lips that I made, and the miracles of hands and feet; and the soft mouth that clung to me! Oh, Ho Chung, Ho Chung, how may I leave Thine-and-Mine behind me! Thou canst not understand it, my Lord, but the love of a woman for her babe—dead or alive—is beyond the comprehension of men. . . . And, too, a thousand deaths beset me in giving him birth—and then to lose him!

"Hasten, days and nights! Be propitious,

seas and stars!—so shall I soon clasp my beloved Lord once more.

"Oh, Ho Chung, I love thee, I love thee!

"From thy wife,

"Moy Yen."

As Ho Chung sat in rapt meditation over his impending happiness, Chin Lee spoke. "Never speaks heart to heart so sweetly," he began, "as in a first tender passion; and no one is so fit to interpret its soft utterances as a man of feeling and experience—and that am I. The bald sentences herein contained had bereft the day of sunlight for thee, but they glowed when they had been passed through the crucible of my fancy, my young goldsmith. Hadst thou followed thy foolish impulse to take the letter to Ah Moy—but why should I defile my mouth by further mention of him: he is a mere peddler of common speech; a coolie in literature! And see, my fond lover, it were better that the memory of my glowing translation should abide with thee than that somebody should expose to thee, in all its naked hideousness, the crude work of the scrivener who wrote this letter for Moy Yen. Let it have burial by fire"; and, before Ho Chung could guess his intention, Chin Lee had thrust the letter, that had to be destroyed, into the brazier at his feet.

"What hast thou done?" said Ho Chung, angrily. "Chin Lee, thou hast exceeded thy functions, and for small excuse I would chastise thee. Moy Yen's letters are my only comfort in a strange land."

"Stay thy hand, and repress thy wrath," said a stout Chinese merchant, regarding Ho Chung over the top of his spectacles. He had arrived in time to witness the burning of the letter by Chin Lee, and to hear Ho Chung's outbreak. It was Quong Lung, who maintained his evil supremacy by venturing abroad even when the Wars of the *Tongs* were at their height, although there was a reward on his head. But the See Yups are numerous, and he was practically surrounded by a body-guard of desperate hatchetmen sworn to his service. In the crowd of softly-shod Orientals who surrounded him, and who appeared to be but a part of the shifting crowd that ebbed and flowed along the street, were men ready to slay any one who made a movement that menaced Quong Lung. The house whence came a bullet that passed through his sleeve the preceding week was burnt the same night; and Chinatown laughed at the temerity of the *tong* whose hired assassin had fired the shot.

"Chin Lee," he went on, "thy rhetoric must be at fault to have roused the wrath of this worthy *sing-song.*"

"Dominator," replied Chin Lee, "I had it in mind to favor my young friend, Ho Chung, with the memories of a perfervid translation of a certain letter that lacked rhetorical merit. But Ho Chung hath no love for literature and rounded periods, and resented the destruction of the crude message translated by me."

"Young man," said Quong Lung, as he made a vivid mental note of Ho Chung, "it will comfort thee to know that Chin Lee, master of many words, doeth *me* much favor in the translation of certain letters that come from districts where they use speech unlike ours."

"And who art thou?" asked Ho Chung, with some heat.

"I am *that* Quong Lung known of all men in Chinatown."

"I have heard of thee—heard much ill of thee; and I like thee not," returned Ho Chung with warmth.

"Did they tell, too, that Chin Lee is my friend?" asked Quong Lung, apparently ignoring Ho Chung's exhibition of temper. "Nay? Well, hear it then from my lips; and, further, let me tell thee that those who honor him honor me. Of course, thou hast excuse for thy temper—and I will not notice it." Then, turning to the scrivener, he went on: "But, Chin Lee, see to it that whilst the letter thou hast destroyed is fresh in thy mind thou dost set it forth in thy loftiest terms in writing that shall serve as an ointment to this worthy *sing-song*'s hurt." And Quong Lung proceeded slowly along the street, apparently unaware of the fact that all men looked at him.

"Thou art, indeed, in luck this day, my rash

young friend," said Chin Lee, getting his writing implements ready. "It is not given to many men to express dislike of Quong Lung to his face, and be excused thereafter for so doing. But beware lest his Shadow fall upon thee: it is the Mantle of Death."

VIII

Le Roi Est Mort, Vive le Roi

Suey See had so schooled Moy Yen during the long voyage concerning the difficulty of landing in San Francisco except as Chin Lee's daughter, born in California, that the young woman made no demur when she was told that Ho Chung's absence from the wharf was absolutely necessary.

"Thy love for the beautiful goldsmith, thy husband, will betray thee in the presence of the officers of the law, and then they will send thee back across the cruel sea."

"Heaven be praised for having sent me such kind friends in my need; for consider, Suey See, I have been bereft of my babe, and I could not lose my lord, too."

Then, too, Quong Lung's influence with those who are concerned with the administration of the Chinese Exclusion Act had made Moy Yen's landing an easy matter.

In the hack in which she was taken to one of Quong Lung's "establishments" she was plied with *sam shu* so cunningly sophisticated that she was scarcely conscious as they thrust her into the padded room in which Suey See had said Ho Chung awaited her.

That same evening Chin Lee, partaking of "black smoke" on the mat in Quong Lung's inner chamber, addressed the latter thus: "Quong Lung, the destruction of an important writing witnessed by thee merits some reward, Fair Dealer. Its capture would have made trouble."

"Trouble for thee, doubtless, thou mere son of a great artist."

"Nay, Quong Lung, the aged and infirm Chin Sen, my honorable parent, had failed in his part had I not instructed him so carefully that he could not make a mistake. And, surely, he had nothing to do with the burning of Moy Yen's letter."

"'Twas a worthy burning, Chin Lee," said Quong Lung, somewhat thickly. He had been partaking unusually freely of whiskey since he had assisted at the formalities connected with the landing of his "covey of partridges," as he styled them; and the beauty of Moy Yen (who was now his property by process of the law that winks at such transactions) appealed strongly to him. "'Twas a worthy burning. What dost thou owe me now in money?"

"Eighty-eight dollars, O Soul of Generosity," answered Chin Lee.

"Write me a receipt for the amount, my Plotter, and I will sign it."

When Chin Lee had bestowed the receipt in his pocket-book, he said with all the nonchalance he could summon to his aid: "And Moy Yen, my daughter—she is comely?"

"She is most beautiful, Chin Lee. It is beyond the power of even thy rhetoric to compass her praises," returned Quong Lung with swelling nostrils, as he licked his lips.

"Doubtless, she is worth the scrap of paper that was found untowardly in Ross Alley ten years ago," said Chin Lee, tentatively, trying to repress any evidence of the anxiety that racked him.

Quong Lung laid down his pipe, and sat up on the mat. After looking among the papers in his pocket-book, he drew forth and handed one that was yellow with age to Chin Lee.

"Moy Yen is so beautiful, Chin Lee, and thou hast managed so well and faithfully in this matter, that I herewith release thee from all further service for placing her in my cage," and he lay down on the mat once more, and prepared some more opium for smoking.

As Chin Lee set fire to the fateful writing at the oil lamp on the tray beside him, and as he watched it burning till it was completely consumed, it seemed to him that the shadow of Quong Lung had fallen from his soul, and that he had at last laid the grim ghost that had haunted him for ten years at the bidding of the tyrant beside him. He should at last walk with greater confidence among his fellows, and the day should be brighter for him, he thought. If, under the stress of the paper that he had just destroyed, he had striven in the service of rhetoric, his fancy—now released from Bondage—should soar on freer pinions and in loftier flight. He should at last accomplish something that all men should talk about, and that should become a classic even in the few years that remained to him.

He had reached thus far in the pleasant reverie that was reflected in his face, when Quong Lung, noticing his rapt air and intuitively getting at the thought in his mind, spoke once more after he had finished his pipe:

"But always thou wilt remember, Chin Lee," he began, in deeper and more deliberate tones than he had yet used; "always thou wilt remember—whatever may happen—that thou art the father of Moy Yen, and will not fail in such paternal services as she may require from thee."

And the Shadow of Quong Lung, that had been lifted from the soul of Chin Lee for a moment, fell once more upon him with its gloomy oppression.

IX

The Sharpening of a Hatchet

Chin Lee slept but little that night. The waning fear of detection that was connected with the crime of ten years ago had been replaced by a greater dread of the very possible finding of Moy Yen by Ho Chung. And Ho Chung was young and strong. He was brave, too; for he had looked, without flinching, into the eyes of the mighty Quong Lung, and even spoken scornfully to him. And he was very much in love.

Better death than the tyranny of the fateful Quong Lung, who only lifted a lesser fear to impose a greater.

Was Quong Lung then invincible? Was he, indeed, Supreme Master in the art of plotting? Had not Chin Lee himself shown Quong Lung that he could plan and carry out a deep-laid scheme to the Master's satisfaction? Had not Quong Lung complimented him with the title of "plotter"?

When the dim morning light straggled into Chin Lee's room through the chinks between the shutters and barricades, it showed him gray and haggard, but with an unmistakable look of fixed resolve on his face; for he had thrown the die, although his life might be the forfeit of the game he was about to play.

One thing was in his favor: he would have the advantage of striking the first blow, and at a time of his own choosing. And, further, he would strike with a hatchet of his own sharpening!

When the day dawned that should bring the ship which carried Moy Yen to San Francisco, as Ho Chung fondly imagined, the young goldsmith sought Chin Lee. "Come with me," he began with a beaming countenance; "come with me, Chin Lee, and help me to welcome my wife, Moy Yen. I shall need the aid of thy rhetoric."

"That would necessitate the closing of my scrivener's stall for the day, thou worthy goldsmith;—and the scrivener's art is falling into decay by reason of the upspringing of coolie letter-writers who know naught of the encyclopædias which even the White Devils read and admire."

"And what is the price for the closing of thy stall for a day, Chin Lee?"

"The price, my affluent young friend, is hard to be appraised in terms of mere money: *posterity* will have to suffer if I accompany thee, for I am laboring and urgent this morning to bring forth sentences of exceeding merit, and one may not weigh pearls that perish against winged words possessing immortal youth and that shall enrich generations to come."

"Will five dollars suffice thee?" asked Ho Chung.

"Five dollars would scarcely recompense my conscience for withdrawing my accomplishments from the realm of letters for an entire day—the Gods expect service for the gifts they bestow. But in thy case—and seeing that thou hast discriminated between an artist and a coolie—I will waive the dues that are properly mine, and go with thee to meet thy Moy Yen."

After he had pocketed his fee, and placed his writing-table in the store of a friend, Chin Lee accompanied Ho Chung to the wharf, which they reached whilst the day was at noon.

There was hardly any one on the wharf, for the signallers at Point Lobos had seen no signs of the approach of the City of Peking.

To and fro walked Ho Chung and the scrivener, the latter trying to enliven the dragging hours with flowing sentences that fell on unheeding ears, for Ho Chung was more occupied in watching the point round which the steamer would come than in attending to Chin Lee.

"My stomach knocketh shrewdly," said Chin Lee in the middle of the afternoon. "'Twere well, my patron, to assist nature to bear up against the strain of this our waiting. Besides, thou, too, art worn; and it were no compliment to Moy Yen to greet her with a face of famine. How should I produce pearls of rhetoric when Hunger lays his hand on my mouth?" So Ho Chung unwillingly accompanied the famished and weary scrivener to a place of refreshment on Market Street, where even a Chinaman's money will procure food and drink.

Seeing that Ho Chung scarcely touched the food placed in front of him, Chin Lee pressed him: "Eat, my young friend. Thou mayst need all thy strength before the day is out."

"What dost thou mean?" asked Ho Chung, eyeing the other askance for a moment.

"We who have studied philosophy have gained mental strength and quietude which even disappointment may not disturb. But thou art young, and headlong, and impatient, and must brace thyself with food and drink lest disappointment come to thee and thy strength fail."

"Disappointment? What disappointment?" asked Ho Chung.

"Nay; how should I know? I spoke of disappointment in general terms. Thou wast disappointed this morning, for instance, because the ship did not arrive at the time set for it, and thy disappointment hath worn thee. Eat, therefore."

After they had finished their meal they returned to the wharf, and in deference to Chin Lee's weary feet they sat on an empty box at the end of the wharf and waited.

Presently the scene on the wharf became livelier, and, as the steamer hove into sight, the officials, who look after the landing of Chinese, came to the wharf, and Ho Chung joined them as he had been instructed to, Chin Lee accompanying him.

And now the happy moment had come when Ho Chung should once more have sight of his wife, Moy Yen. He was taken into the cabin set apart for Chinese women. "Moy Yen, Beloved," he called softly, with outstretched hands, as he entered the cabin. But no one responded. He eagerly scanned the dull, impassive faces of the women before him.

"She is, doubtless, in some other apartment," he said, addressing the interpreter. "Send for her."

"Moy Yen's name does not appear on the list of passengers. You must have made some mistake. Am I not right, sir?" asked the interpreter of the ship's officer who accompanied them.

"We did not carry any one of that name," was the answer.

A great fear came upon Ho Chung, and he trembled so that he was forced to clutch Chin Lee's arm as they left the vessel.

"Courage, my dear young friend! Call philosophy to thy aid," urged Chin Lee. But the only response he got was, "Oh! Moy Yen, Moy Yen! Where art thou, Beloved?"

Chin Lee led him to the seat they had occupied that morning at the end of the wharf. Here all was quiet and dark, save for the twinkling of the stars overhead.

X

That Laughter Is Not Always Pleasant

"Courage, my poor young Friend! Thou shalt yet find Moy Yen," began Chin Lee.

Orion's glittering belt, and glorious Sirius shining in the wonderful blue-black of the sky of a Californian night swept by a north wind, made no impression on Ho Chung, who moaned at intervals: "Oh, Moy Yen, Moy Yen! Where art thou?"

"Listen, Ho Chung; I will tell thee."

"What! thou canst tell me where Moy Yen is, and thou didst not tell me before!" said Ho Chung, clutching the other's arm. "Explain thyself, scrivener—and in few words; otherwise thou art treading the path that leads to death."

"I will tell thee a plain tale," replied Chin Lee, who had prepared himself for the occasion. "And if I appear to lie to thee, let this be the instrument of my destruction," and he drew a formidable knife from his mysterious blouse and handed it to Ho Chung.

"Ten years ago," he resumed, "I, too, had a mistress——"

"But Moy Yen is my *wife*!" interrupted Ho Chung.

"But a mistress is ever dearer than a wife, my inexperienced friend! Yes, Yu Moy was fairer even than my words can tell; and Shan Toy stole her from me. And, thereafter, he was found dead in Ross Alley, with a writing in his hand that would have given me to the rope of the white hangman; and the writing fell into the hands of Quong Lung—who hath done thee much wrong. For ten years Quong Lung hath——"

"But this relateth not to Moy Yen," said Ho Chung, impatiently.

"It lies closer to her than her garments," said Chin Lee. "Listen: With proof in his hand that would hang me, Quong Lung (than whom a more cruel and cunning fiend does not exist in hell!) has made me the slave of his iniquities. He hath stricken me dumb with the terror of his ever present shadow." He ceased for a moment while Ho Chung, never relaxing his grasp on Chin Lee's arm, took a deep breath with distended nostrils.

"Proceed."

"Oh, my Brother in Affliction!" resumed Chin Lee; "he hath wrought thee much wrong. But why waste words: thou didst flout him openly the first time thou sawest him, and it was told in Chinatown; and, so, the shadow of Quong Lung hath fallen upon thee, too."

"But Moy Yen—tell me of Moy Yen!"

"Quong Lung hath stricken thee through her."

"Is she dead?" demanded Ho Chung fiercely, increasing the pressure on the other's arm.

"No; there are things worse than death, and Moy Yen, by the laws of the White Devils, is now slave to Quong Lung, and penned up in his house of ill-fame on Waverley Place—nay, friend, the clutch of thy hand is too shrewd—and I am an old man—and my flesh is tender."

"And thou hadst knowledge of all this, and didst not tell me!" said Ho Chung, without heeding Chin Lee's last remark.

"It would not have availed thee, Ho Chung: Quong Lung hath many tools; and, besides, to have told thee would have involved thy taking off."

"That would have been merciful, at any rate. Proceed."

"See, Ho Chung, I am old enough to be thy father, and, therefore, wiser and more experienced. If thou wilt let me guide thee in this matter we will rid the world of a monster, and thou shalt have thy Moy Yen again."

"Have Moy Yen again!—Moy Yen dishonored! Ha, ha, ha!" and Ho Chung, who was ordinarily undemonstrative, after the manner of his race, went off into a shriek of hysterical laughter. "I loved Moy Yen—ho, ho, ho, ho!—and she was abducted from me—with thy knowledge—ha, ha, ha!—and I am to rid the world of Quong Lung to serve thy ends, and, as reward, receive Moy Yen, whose honor hath been soiled—oh, ye Gods! this is just cause for exceeding mirth—ha, ha, ha, ha——!"

At the first peal of wild laughter Chin Lee's heart beat fast, and a chill fear struck him. "Madness hath seized upon him," he thought. As Ho Chung proceeded, the scrivener's terror increased. With a sudden effort he wrenched himself free, and made a dash to escape.

"The shadow of Quong Lung hath covered thee tonight," shouted Ho Chung, as he overtook Chin Lee, and buried the knife to the hilt between his shoulders.

He tossed the dying man into the bay, and, after cleansing his hands and his weapon at a faucet on the wharf from which he had drunk that afternoon, he turned his steps towards Waverley Place—and Moy Yen.

XI

As Overheard in a Crowd

The house in which Moy Yen was at present confined consisted of a long passage, into which rooms but little larger than cells opened. Each room had a window with heavy iron bars, through which those who were in the passage could see the girls within.

Round each window, as Ho Chung entered, was a polyglot crowd, whose size was in proportion to the beauty of the occupant of the room. So thick was the press round one window that Ho Chung—though insistent and impatient, besides being heavier and taller than those present—could not force his way to the front, but had to wait his turn.

One glance over the heads of those in front of him showed him Moy Yen sitting on the side of a bed. She was dressed in black velvet, and her head gear was loaded with jewellery. In the lobes of her ears were heavy rings that hung almost to her shoulders; and on her wrists were massive jade bracelets. Ready to her hand, on the bed, lay a wicked-looking knife which her father had given her when he bade her good-by at Hong Kong. ("Let it guard thy honor, Little One, if need be," he had said.)

She had an expression of intense sadness on her face; and she appeared to look through and beyond the crowd gazing upon her.

"They say that she hath been but two weeks in San Francisco," said a young Chinese "blood" in the crowd to his pampered friend. "If these coolies would but remove themselves, we might at least look upon her beauty, which is much spoken of."

Ho Chung, who stood immediately behind the speaker, had it in mind to slay him there and then, but that would have interfered with far more important matters.

"She hath a sorrow that adds to her beauty, methinks," remarked the well-fed friend, who was in a better position to see Moy Yen. He put his head to one side critically, and smacked his lips as he regarded her.

"I overheard one say at the restaurant, last night, that Quong Lung gave Chin Lee the scrivener, whose daughter she is alleged to be, three thousand dollars for her," remarked the young Chinese man-about-town. (Ho Chung smiled grimly at this, and the thought of what had but just happened on the wharf shot one ray of comfort into the sorrow at his heart.)

"Quong Lung never made a better investment, Lee Yung, and he is no mean appraiser of flesh," returned the man who fulfilled the Psalmist's description of the ungodly, "whose eyes swell with fatness, and they do even what they lust."

"I am told, too, that she will admit no one into her room; not even a woman. Quey Lem, the old hag who looks after the girls here, told me last night that Quong had her put into this cell three days ago as a punishment, because she discouraged his advances with a knife——"

"It is on the bed beside her," interrupted the stout man, catching sight of the knife.

"It is a great telling, Nu Fong," went on the

man of fashion, and the crowd, whom he elegantly ignored, listened to his "telling." "I am in favor with Quey Lem for very good reasons," began Lee Yung: "I give her a trifle occasionally for taking thought of me"; and he looked round arrogantly at Ho Chung, who had trodden on his heel as he advanced an inch in the forward movement to the window.

"She was like a wild-cat newly caged, Quey Lem told me," resumed Lee Yung; "and she would have died of inanition—for she refused to eat or drink."

"What made her give so much trouble, Lee Yung?"

"Oh, she hath a lover, or a husband—some such obstacle—whom she expected to meet in San Francisco; and Quong Lung diverted her from him."

"Ho, ho, ho!" laughed Nu Fong. "Diverted is good! But why did she not die of starvation?"

"Thy academic career, Nu Fong, hath been sadly neglected. If you were a 'Native Son,' as I am, you would know that these White Devils can steal one's senses by poisoning the air one breathes; and that when one is in that condition they can feed him through tubes let into the stomach through the mouth."

"That is a joyless way of taking one's sustenance, Lee Yung; and an insult to the palate that hath its inalienable rights."

By this time they had advanced close enough to the window to give Lee Yung a full view of Moy Yen, who now sat listlessly with downcast eyes.

"By the Grave of my Father!" exclaimed Lee Yung; "rumor hath not lied for once. From the crown of her head to her little feet she is formed for the uses and offices of love." More he was not permitted to say, for Ho Chung, taking firm hold of the young men's queues, knocked their heads together.

"Have ye no respect for beauty in distress, ye pampered dogs?" he asked, angrily. "Nay; make no motion, lest ye die suddenly."

He thrust them to one side, and stepped to the window. The sound of his angry voice had attracted the other crowds in the passage, and, as they surged towards him, he warned them back with an imperious gesture.

"The young woman within is Moy Yen, my wife, who hath been stolen from me. I would have speech with her, and I would not be overheard. Let this argument persuade ye to keep back," and he drew a knife from his sleeve.

XII

That Iron Bars Are Ineffectual Sometimes

When Moy Yen heard Ho Chung's voice she raised her head and ran to the window; and when the crowd had fallen back at Ho Chung's bidding, he turned to Moy Yen, and clasped the hands she had extended through the bars.

"Oh! Moy Yen, Moy Yen, the Gods that were sworn to protect thee are false—and there are no Gods, but only devils of greater or lesser degree. Oh! Little One, how camest thou here?"

"My Beautiful Lord," she replied; "Suey See, the wife of one Quong Lung, showed me and my father letters in Hong Kong written for thee by Chin Lee, thy so great friend, and they said I was to put myself in charge of Suey See, who would give me honorable escort to San Francisco. And so I came."

"But *this* was to be the day of thy arrival."

"Thy letters, My Lord, said I was to start two weeks earlier than the time agreed upon, and I but obeyed thee. But now you will take me hence, my Lord and Master."

"Yes; thou shalt certainly escape hence, my Best Beloved; but the time for thy escape is short, and I have much to ask thee. Where wast thou taken on the day of thy arrival?"

"To the house of Quong Lung. But why dost thou ask, Ho Chung?" and she raised pleading eyes to his face.

"Tell me all, my Heart; and make haste, oh, make haste!—the time is short."

"Of anything that happened I am entirely innocent, my Husband; for they led me to a chamber where they said I should find thee—

but thou wast not there; and soon after, and whilst I wept, the drugged food and drink they had given me after I left the ship bereft me of my senses, and I fell into a deep sleep."

She stopped to weep awhile, until Ho Chung bade her proceed.

"When I woke, dear Master, a light burned in the room; and one, whom I now know to be Quong Lung, stood beside me with hungry eyes. And he spoke to me—such things as only lovers say to one another. But, when he laid a desecrating hand on my shoulder, I leapt from the bed and made at him with the knife that was concealed in my sleeve, and which I have so far managed to hide from my foes. So Quong Lung fled, and the door closed behind him with a snap; and I could not beat it down, nor wrench away the bars from the window. I was as a bird in a cage, and, therefore, I could but cry for help—but none came. Every night a strange heaviness comes upon me, and the air of my room becomes impregnated with a sweet heavy odor; and thereafter, in a half-swoon, I either see or dream that strange men and an old woman are about me; and when I wake I neither care to eat nor drink. And, because I persisted in repelling Quong Lung, I was brought here by means unknown to me; and here men, with hideous passions and evil looks, come and stare at me in my helpless captivity, and say abominable things to me. And I am to stay here till I yield myself to Quong Lung—but I would sooner die, Ho Chung, my Husband, as thou must know in thy heart. And now take me hence."

"Thou Brave, and Beautiful, and Faithful!—but, oh, Moy Yen, thou art, indeed, like a bird in a cage, and I am powerless to free thee—except in one way. Yes, indeed, thou must escape hence, for this is the abode of Dishonor, and better death than dishonor! Courage! the road to freedom is not so hard to travel. See, Little One, come nearer, for fear any one in the crowd should hear our speech and report to Quong Lung. So; press thy bosom to the bars, so that I may feel the beating of thy faithful heart. Now close thine eyes, for beautiful as they are thy face hath another beauty when thine eyes are closed—as I have often seen when thou hast slept."

Therefore Moy Yen closed her eyes, and pressed her bosom against the bars of the window.

"My husband," she murmured, "now thou art come, I am happy once more."

Ho Chung placed his hand where he could feel the beating of her heart.

"'Twas here Thine-and-Mine used to repose, Cherry Blossom!" As he spoke, he steadied the point of the knife with the hand he had laid on her breast, and, before any one in the crowd could guess his intention, he drove it through her heart with a swift blow from the other hand.

XIII

An Accident in Chinatown

The crowd broke and fled in wild disorder, as Ho Chung turned from the window. With Moy Yen's dying scream ringing in his ears, he strode rapidly towards Quong Lung's abode, whither he had been preceded—during his interview with Moy Yen—by Wau Shun, who acted as "bully" at the establishment on Waverley Place. He was one of the most dangerous highbinders in Chinatown, for he was backed by the full weight of Quong Lung's power; moreover, no man knew what he intended, or where he was looking, because of his atrocious squint. At present he was undergoing a severe castigation of words from Quong Lung, and writhing under the lash of his master's scorn.

"So; thou art not ashamed to take the wages of a man, and to run like a woman, Wau Shun! Doubtless, thy constant association with the women thou hast in keeping has turned thy blood to milk. Ho Chung is but a boy beside thee in years."

"Nay, Compeller, I am here in thy best interests, for Ho Chung will arrive presently, and I am come to protect thee."

"Protect me! Does the jackal protect the lion?"

"Nay, Most Powerful; but there is a killing forward, and thy honorable hands must not be soiled with blood."

"Oh! And why didst thou not do thy office at thy post, my considerate jackal? Thou hadst thy fangs with thee."

"I could not use powder and lead, Great Master, for fear of killing Moy Yen."

"Were thy knife and hatchet blunt, then?"

"Ho Chung's wrath was terrible to behold, Quong Lung; even the crowd fell back before it—for he is tall and strong, and he appeared to be demented."

"It is plainly to be seen that thy courage is no better than that of the women in thy charge. And to talk to me of blood!—and killing! As though a Master of Accidents hath any need to imbrue his hands in vulgar things! But stay in the room, and keep thy arguments of powder and lead in readiness lest they should be needed."

He walked down the passage, and bolted the barricade across it; it was a flimsy affair of latticed slats, and would readily yield to the pressure of a man's shoulder—but there was a thread stretched across the passage a foot in front of the barricade, which Quong Lung facetiously named "The Thread of Destiny."

Returning to the room, which was brilliantly illuminated, he threw the door open, so that he should be plainly seen by any one entering the passage; and leaning carelessly against the door-post, he smoked awhile in silence. Presently, he opened the door leading into the street by pressing on a spring, and calmly awaited events.

He had scarcely completed these details, when Ho Chung flung himself into the passage, brandishing a knife in his hands.

"Thou villain, Quong Lung!" he shouted, "thank the Gods, I have found thee!"

As Ho Chung put his weight against the barricade, he broke the thread in front of it, and a hundred-weight of iron descended on his head from a trap in the ceiling of the passage, and killed him instantly.

THE EDWARDIANS

Rogue: Cecil Thorold

The Fire of London

ARNOLD BENNETT

THE PROLIFIC ENOCH ARNOLD BENNETT (1867–1931) produced about a half-million words a year for more than twenty years and, consciously frugal, kept an exact count of the number and precisely how much he received as payment for his novels, stories, and plays. His reputation largely rested on his many works about the lower-middle-class people of the region in which he was born, Staffordshire, whose inhabitants were making pottery when the Romans invaded England and continue to do so to the present day. Such realistic novels as *The Old Wives' Tale* (1908), *Clayhanger* (1910), and *Riceyman Steps* (1923) were once regarded as among the first rank of English novels, though they have largely fallen out of favor in the twenty-first century.

Bennett frequently wrote mystery and crime fiction, notably *The Grand Babylon Hotel* (1902), a novel of pure detection; *The Statue* (1908), written in collaboration with the mystery novelist Eden Phillpotts, which lives up to its subtitle, *A Story of International Intrigue and Mystery*; and *The Night Visitor and Other Stories* (1931), which contains stories about people in a great hotel, including the adventure of the poet Lomax Harder, who kills a man for a very good reason in the classic story "Murder!" Perhaps Bennett's finest achievement in the crime genre is *The Loot of Cities* (1904), a collection of six stories about the combination Robin Hood/promoter/criminologist Cecil Thorold, "a millionaire in search of joy," whose unorthodox methods include kidnapping to further a romance and stealing to recover stolen goods.

"The Fire of London" was originally published in the June–November 1904 issue of *The Windsor Magazine*; it was first collected in *The Loot of Cities* (London, Alston Rivers, 1904).

THE FIRE OF LONDON

Arnold Bennett

I.

"YOU'RE WANTED on the telephone, sir."

Mr. Bruce Bowring, managing director of the Consolidated Mining and Investment Corporation, Limited (capital two millions, in one-pound shares, which stood at twenty-seven-and-six), turned and gazed querulously across the electric-lit spaces of his superb private office at the confidential clerk who addressed him. Mr. Bowring, in shirt-sleeves before a Florentine mirror, was brushing his hair with the solicitude of a mother who has failed to rear most of a large family.

"Who is it?" he asked, as if that demand for him were the last straw but one. "Nearly seven on Friday evening!" he added, martyrised.

"I think a friend, sir."

The middle-aged financier dropped his gold-mounted brush and, wading through the deep pile of the Oriental carpet, passed into the telephone-cabinet and shut the door.

"Hallo!" he accosted the transmitter, resolved not to be angry with it. "Hal*lo!* Are you there? Yes, I'm Bowring. Who are you?"

"*Nrrrr*," the faint, unhuman voice of the receiver whispered in his ear. "*Nrrrr. Cluck.* I'm a friend."

"What name?"

"No name. I thought you might like to know that a determined robbery is going to be attempted tonight at your house in Lowndes Square, a robbery of cash—and before nine o'clock. *Nrrrr.* I thought you might like to know."

"Ah!" said Mr. Bowring to the transmitter.

The feeble exclamation was all he could achieve at first. In the confined, hot silence of the telephone-cabinet this message, coming to him mysteriously out of the vast unknown of London, struck him with a sudden sick fear that perhaps his wondrously organised scheme might yet miscarry, even at the final moment. Why that night of all nights? And why before nine o'clock? Could it be that the secret was out, then?

"Any further interesting details?" he inquired, bracing himself to an assumption of imperturbable and gay coolness.

But there was no answer. And when after some difficulty he got the exchange-girl to disclose the number which had rung him up, he found that his interlocutor had been using a public call-office in Oxford Street. He returned to his room, donned his frock-coat, took a large envelope from a locked drawer and put it in his pocket, and sat down to think a little.

At that time Mr. Bruce Bowring was one of the most famous conjurers in the City. He had begun, ten years earlier, with nothing but a silk hat; and out of that empty hat had been produced, first the Hoop-La Limited, a South African gold-mine of numerous stamps and frequent dividends, then the Hoop-La No. 2 Limited, a mine with as many reincarnations as Buddha, and then a dazzling succession of mines and combination of mines. The more the hat emptied itself, the more it was full; and the emerging objects (which now included the house in Lowndes Square and a perfect dream of a place in Hampshire) grew constantly larger, and the conjurer more impressive and persuasive, and the audience more enthusiastic in its applause. At last, with a unique flourish, and a new turning-up of sleeves to prove that there was no deception, had come out of the hat the C.M.I.C., a sort of incredibly enormous Union Jack, which enwrapped all the other objects in its splendid folds. The shares of the C.M.I.C. were affectionately known in the Kaffir circus as "Solids"; they yielded handsome though irregular dividends, earned chiefly by flotation and speculation; the circus believed in them. And in view of the annual meeting of shareholders to be held on the following Tuesday afternoon (the conjurer in the chair and his hat on the table), the market price, after a period of depression, had stiffened.

Mr. Bowring's meditations were soon interrupted by a telegram. He opened it and read: "*Cook drunk again. Will dine with you Devonshire, seven-thirty. Impossible here. Have arranged about luggage.—Marie.*" Marie was Mr. Bowring's wife. He told himself that he felt greatly relieved by that telegram; he clutched at it; and his spirits seemed to rise. At any rate, since he would not now go near Lowndes Square, he could certainly laugh at the threatened robbery. He thought what a wonderful thing Providence was, after all.

"Just look at that," he said to his clerk, showing the telegram with a humorous affectation of dismay.

"Tut, tut," said the clerk, discreetly sympathetic towards his employer thus victimised by debauched cooks. "I suppose you're going down to Hampshire tonight as usual, sir?"

Mr. Bowring replied that he was, and that everything appeared to be in order for the meeting, and that he should be back on Monday afternoon or at the latest very early on Tuesday.

Then, with a few parting instructions, and with that eagle glance round his own room and into circumjacent rooms which a truly efficient head of affairs never omits on leaving business for the week-end, Mr. Bowring sedately, yet magnificently, departed from the noble registered offices of the C.M.I.C.

"Why didn't Marie telephone instead of wiring?" he mused, as his pair of greys whirled him and his coachman and his footman off to the Devonshire.

II.

The Devonshire Mansion, a bright edifice of eleven storeys in the Foster and Dicksee style, constructional ironwork by Homan, lifts by Waygood, decorations by Waring, and terracotta by the rood, is situated on the edge of Hyde Park. It is a composite building. Its foundations are firmly fixed in the Tube railway; above that comes the wine cellarage, then the vast laundry, and then (a row of windows scarcely level with the street) a sporting club, a billiard-room, a grill-room, and a cigarette-merchant whose name ends in "opoulos." On the first floor is the renowned Devonshire Mansion Restaurant. Always, in London, there is just one restaurant where, if you are an entirely correct person, "you can get a decent meal." The place changes from season to season, but there is never more than one of it at a time. That season it happened to be the Devonshire. (The *chef* of the Devonshire had invented tripe suppers, *tripes à la mode de Caen*, and these suppers—seven-and-six—had been the rage.) Consequently all entirely correct people fed as a matter of course at the Devonshire, since there was no other place fit to go to. The vogue of the restaurant favourably affected the vogue of the nine floors of furnished suites above the restaurant; they were always full; and the heavenward attics, where the servants took off their smart liveries and became human, held much wealth. The vogue of the restaurant also exercised a beneficial influence over the status of the Kitcat Club, which was a cock-and-hen club of the latest pattern and had its "house" on the third floor.

It was a little after half-past seven when Mr. Bruce Bowring haughtily ascended the grand staircase of this resort of opulence, and paused for an instant near the immense fireplace at the summit (September was inclement, and a fire burned nicely) to inquire from the head-waiter whether Mrs. Bowring had secured a table. But Marie had not arrived—Marie, who was never late! Uneasy and chagrined, he proceeded, under the escort of the head-waiter, to the glittering Salle Louis Quatorze and selected, because of his morning attire, a table half-hidden behind an onyx pillar. The great room was moderately full of fair women and possessive men, despite the month. Immediately afterwards a youngish couple (the man handsomer and better dressed than the woman) took the table on the other side of the pillar. Mr. Bowring waited five minutes, then he ordered Sole Mornay and a bottle of Romanée-Conti, and then he waited another five minutes. He went somewhat in fear of his wife, and did not care to begin without her.

"Can't you read?" It was the youngish man at the next table speaking in a raised voice to a squinting lackey with a telegraph form in his hand. "'Solids! Solids,' my friend. 'Sell—Solids—to—any—amount—tomorrow—and—Monday.' Got it? Well, send it off at once."

"Quite clear, my lord," said the lackey, and fled. The youngish man gazed fixedly but absently at Mr. Bowring and seemed to see through him to the tapestry behind. Mr. Bowring, to his own keen annoyance, reddened. Partly to conceal the blush, and partly because it was a quarter to eight and there was the train to catch, he lowered his face, and began upon the sole. A few minutes later the lackey returned, gave some change to the youngish man, and surprised Mr. Bowring by advancing towards him and handing him an envelope—an envelope which bore on its flap the legend "Kitcat Club." The note within was scribbled in pencil in his wife's handwriting, and ran: "*Just arrived. Delayed by luggage. I'm too nervous to face the restaurant, and am eating a chop here alone. The place is fortunately empty. Come and fetch me as soon as you're ready.*"

Mr. Bowring sighed angrily. He hated his wife's club, and this succession of messages telephonic, telegraphic, and calligraphic was exasperating him.

"No answer!" he ejaculated, and then he beckoned the lackey closer. "Who's that gentleman at the next table with the lady?" he murmured.

"I'm not rightly sure, sir," was the whispered reply. "Some authorities say he's the strong man at the Hippodrome, while others affirm he's a sort of American millionaire."

"But you addressed him as 'my lord.'"

"Just then I thought he was the strong man, sir," said the lackey, retiring.

"My bill!" Mr. Bowring demanded fiercely of the waiter, and at the same time the youngish gentleman and his companion rose and departed.

At the lift Mr. Bowring found the squinting lackey in charge.

"You're the liftman, too?"

"Tonight, sir, I am many things. The fact is, the regular liftman has got a couple of hours off—being the recent father of twins."

"Well—Kitcat Club."

The lift seemed to shoot far upwards, and Mr. Bowring thought the lackey had mistaken the floor, but on gaining the corridor he saw across the portals in front of him the remembered gold sign, "Kitcat Club. Members only." He pushed the door open and went in.

III.

Instead of the familiar vestibule of his wife's club, Mr. Bowring discovered a small antechamber, and beyond, through a doorway half-screened by a *portière*, he had glimpses of a rich, rose-lit drawing-room. In the doorway, with one hand raised to the *portière*, stood the youngish man who had forced him to blush in the restaurant.

"I beg your pardon," said Mr. Bowring, stiffly—"is this the Kitcat Club?"

The other man advanced to the outer door, his brilliant eyes fixed on Mr. Bowring's; his arm crept round the cheek of the door and came back bearing the gold sign; then he shut the door and locked it. "No, this isn't the Kitcat Club at all," he replied. "It is my flat. Come and sit down. I was expecting you."

"I shall do nothing of the kind," said Mr. Bowring disdainfully.

"But when I tell you that I know you are going to decamp tonight, Mr. Bowring——"

The youngish man smiled affably.

"Decamp?" The spine of the financier suddenly grew flaccid.

"I used the word."

"Who the devil are you?" snapped the financier, forcing his spine to rigidity.

"I am the 'friend' on the telephone. I specially wanted you at the Devonshire tonight, and I thought that the fear of a robbery at Lowndes Square might make your arrival here more certain. I am he who devised the story of the inebriated cook and favoured you with a telegram signed 'Marie.' I am the humorist who pretended in a loud voice to send off telegraphic instructions to sell 'Solids,' in order to watch your demeanour under the test. I am the expert who forged your wife's handwriting in a note from the Kitcat. I am the patron of the cross-eyed menial who gave you the note and who afterwards raised you too high in the lift. I am the artificer of this gold sign, an exact duplicate of the genuine one two floors below, which induced you to visit me. The sign alone cost me nine-and-six; the servant's livery came to two pounds fifteen. But I never consider expense when, by dint of a generous outlay, I can avoid violence. I hate violence." He gently waved the sign to and fro.

"Then my wife——" Mr. Bowring stammered in a panic rage.

"Is probably at Lowndes Square, wondering what on earth has happened to you."

Mr. Bowring took breath, remembered that he was a great man, and steadied himself.

"You must be mad," he remarked quietly. "Open this door at once."

"Perhaps," the stranger judicially admitted. "Perhaps a sort of madness. But do come and sit down. We have no time to lose."

Mr. Bowring gazed at that handsome face, with the fine nostrils, large mouth, and square clean chin, and the dark eyes, the black hair, and long, black moustache; and he noticed the long, thin hands. "Decadent!" he decided. Nevertheless, and though it was with the air of indulging the caprice of a lunatic, he did in fact obey the stranger's request.

It was a beautiful Chippendale drawing-room that he entered. Near the hearth, to which a morsel of fire gave cheerfulness, were two easy-chairs, and between them a small table. Behind was extended a fourfold draught-screen.

"I can give you just five minutes," said Mr. Bowring, magisterially sitting down.

"They will suffice," the stranger responded, sitting down also. "You have in your pocket, Mr. Bowring—probably your breast-pocket—fifty Bank of England notes for a thousand pounds each, and a number of smaller notes amounting to another ten thousand."

"Well?"

"I must demand from you the first-named fifty."

Mr. Bowring, in the silence of the rose-lit drawing-room, thought of all the Devonshire Mansion, with its endless corridors and innumerable rooms, its acres of carpets, its forests of furniture, its gold and silver, and its jewels and its wines, its pretty women and possessive men—the whole humming microcosm founded on a unanimous pretence that the sacredness of property was a natural law. And he thought how disconcerting it was that he should be trapped there, helpless, in the very middle of the vast pretence, and forced to admit that the sacredness of property was a purely artificial convention.

"By what right do you make this demand?" he inquired, bravely sarcastic.

"By the right of my unique knowledge," said the stranger, with a bright smile. "Listen to what you and I alone know. You are at the end of the tether. The Consolidated is at the same spot. You have a past consisting chiefly of nineteen fraudulent flotations. You have paid dividends out of capital till there is no capital left. You have speculated and lost. You have cooked balance-sheets to a turn and ruined the eyesight of auditors with dust. You have lived like ten lords. Your houses are mortgaged. You own an unrivalled collection of unreceipted bills. You are worse than a common thief. (Excuse these personalities.)"

"My dear, good sir——" Mr. Bowring interrupted, grandly.

"Permit me. What is more serious, your self-confidence has been gradually deserting you. At last, perceiving that some blundering person was bound soon to put his foot through the brittle shell of your ostentation and tread on nothing, and foreseeing for yourself an immediate future consisting chiefly of Holloway, you have by a supreme effort of your genius, borrowed £60,000 from a bank on C.M.I.C. scrip, for a week (eh?), and you have arranged, you and your wife, to—melt into thin air. You will affect to set out as usual for your country place in Hampshire, but it is Southampton that will see you tonight, and Havre will see you tomorrow. You may run over to Paris to change some notes, but by Monday you will be on your way to—frankly, I don't know where; perhaps Monte Video. Of course you take the risk of extradition, but the risk is preferable to the certainty that awaits you in England. I think you will elude extradition. If I thought otherwise, I should not have had you here tonight, because, once extradited, you might begin to amuse yourself by talking about me."

"So it's blackmail," said Mr. Bowring, grim.

The dark eyes opposite to him sparkled gaily.

"It desolates me," the youngish man observed, "to have to commit you to the deep with only ten thousand. But, really, not less than fifty thousand will requite me for the brain-tissue which I have expended in the study of your interesting situation."

Mr. Bowring consulted his watch.

"Come, now," he said, huskily; "I'll give you ten thousand. I flatter myself I can look facts in the face, and so I'll give you ten thousand."

"My friend," answered the spider, "you are a judge of character. Do you honestly think I don't mean precisely what I say—to sixpence? It is eight-thirty. You are, if I may be allowed the remark, running it rather fine."

"And suppose I refuse to part?" said Mr. Bowring, after reflection. "What then?"

"I have confessed to you that I hate violence. You would therefore leave this room unmolested, but you wouldn't step off the island."

Mr. Bowring scanned the agreeable features of the stranger. Then, while the lifts were ascending and descending, and the wine was sparkling, and the jewels flashing, and the gold chinking, and the pretty women being pretty, in all the four quarters of the Devonshire, Mr. Bruce Bowring in the silent parlour counted out fifty notes on to the table. After all, it was a fortune, that little pile of white on the crimson polished wood.

"*Bon voyage!*" said the stranger. "Don't

imagine that I am not full of sympathy for you. I am. You have only been unfortunate. *Bon voyage!*"

"No! By Heaven!" Mr. Bowring almost shouted, rushing back from the door, and drawing a revolver from his hip pocket. "It's too much! I didn't mean to—but confound it! what's a revolver for?"

The youngish man jumped up quickly and put his hands on the notes.

"Violence is always foolish, Mr. Bowring," he murmured.

"Will you give them up, or won't you?"

"I won't."

The stranger's fine eyes seemed to glint with joy in the drama.

"Then——"

The revolver was raised, but in the same instant a tiny hand snatched it from the hand of Mr. Bowring, who turned and beheld by his side a woman. The huge screen sank slowly and noiselessly to the floor in the surprising manner peculiar to screens that have been overset.

Mr. Bowring cursed. "An accomplice! I might have guessed!" he grumbled in final disgust.

He ran to the door, unlocked it, and was no more seen.

IV.

The lady was aged twenty-seven or so; of medium height, and slim, with a plain, very intelligent and expressive face, lighted by courageous, grey eyes and crowned with loose, abundant, fluffy hair. Perhaps it was the fluffy hair, perhaps it was the mouth that twitched as she dropped the revolver—who can say?—but the whole atmosphere of the rose-lit chamber was suddenly changed. The incalculable had invaded it.

"You seem surprised, Miss Fincastle," said the possessor of the bank-notes, laughing gaily.

"Surprised!" echoed the lady, controlling that mouth. "My dear Mr. Thorold, when, strictly as a journalist, I accepted your invitation, I did not anticipate this sequel; frankly I did not."

She tried to speak coldly and evenly, on the assumption that a journalist has no sex during business hours. But just then she happened to be neither less nor more a woman than a woman always is.

"If I have had the misfortune to annoy you——!" Thorold threw up his arms in gallant despair.

"Annoy is not the word," said Miss Fincastle, nervously smiling. "May I sit down? Thanks. Let us recount. You arrive in England, from somewhere, as the son and heir of the late Ahasuerus Thorold, the New York operator, who died worth six million dollars. It becomes known that while in Algiers in the spring you stayed at the Hôtel St. James, famous as the scene of what is called the 'Algiers Mystery,' familiar to English newspaper-readers since last April. The editor of my journal therefore instructs me to obtain an interview with you. I do so. The first thing I discover is that, though an American, you have no American accent. You explain this by saying that since infancy you have always lived in Europe with your mother."

"But surely you do not doubt that I am Cecil Thorold!" said the man. Their faces were approximate over the table.

"Of course not. I merely recount. To continue. I interview you as to the Algerian mystery, and get some new items concerning it. Then you regale me with tea and your opinions, and my questions grow more personal. So it comes about that, strictly on behalf of my paper, I inquire what your recreations are. And suddenly you answer: 'Ah! My recreations! Come to dinner tonight, quite informally, and I will show you how I amuse myself!' I come. I dine. I am stuck behind that screen and told to listen. And—and—the millionaire proves to be nothing but a blackmailer."

"You must understand, my dear lady——"

"I understand everything, Mr. Thorold,

except your object in admitting me to the scene."

"A whim!" cried Thorold vivaciously, "a freak of mine! Possibly due to the eternal and universal desire of man to show off before woman!"

The journalist tried to smile, but something in her face caused Thorold to run to a chiffonier.

"Drink this," he said, returning with a glass.

"I need nothing." The voice was a whisper.

"Oblige me."

Miss Fincastle drank and coughed.

"Why did you do it?" she asked sadly, looking at the notes.

"You don't mean to say," Thorold burst out, "that you are feeling sorry for Mr. Bruce Bowring? He has merely parted with what he stole. And the people from whom he stole, stole. All the activities which centre about the Stock Exchange are simply various manifestations of one primeval instinct. Suppose I had not—had not interfered. No one would have been a penny the better off except Mr. Bruce Bowring. Whereas——"

"You intend to restore this money to the Consolidated?" said Miss Fincastle eagerly.

"Not quite! The Consolidated doesn't deserve it. You must not regard its shareholders as a set of innocent shorn lambs. They knew the game. They went in for what they could get. Besides, how could I restore the money without giving myself away? I want the money myself."

"But you are a millionaire."

"It is precisely because I am a millionaire that I want more. All millionaires are like that."

"I am sorry to find you a thief, Mr. Thorold."

"A thief! No. I am only direct, I only avoid the middleman. At dinner, Miss Fincastle, you displayed somewhat advanced views about property, marriage, and the aristocracy of brains. You said that labels were for the stupid majority, and that the wise minority examined the ideas behind the labels. You label me a thief, but examine the idea, and you will perceive that you might as well call yourself a thief. Your newspaper every day suppresses the truth about the City, and it does so in order to live. In other words, it touches the pitch, it participates in the game. To-day it has a fifty-line advertisement of a false balance-sheet of the Consolidated, at two shillings a line. That five pounds, part of the loot of a great city, will help to pay for your account of our interview this afternoon."

"Our interview tonight," Miss Fincastle corrected him stiffly, "and all that I have seen and heard."

At these words she stood up, and as Cecil Thorold gazed at her his face changed.

"I shall begin to wish," he said slowly, "that I had deprived myself of the pleasure of your company this evening."

"You might have been a dead man had you done so," Miss Fincastle retorted, and observing his blank countenance she touched the revolver. "Have you forgotten already?" she asked tartly.

"Of course it wasn't loaded," he remarked. "Of course I had seen to that earlier in the day. I am not such a bungler——"

"Then I didn't save your life?"

"You force me to say that you did not, and to remind you that you gave me your word not to emerge from behind the screen. However, seeing the motive, I can only thank you for that lapse. The pity is that it hopelessly compromises you."

"Me?" exclaimed Miss Fincastle.

"You. Can't you see that you are in it, in this robbery, to give the thing a label. You were alone with the robber. You succoured the robber at a critical moment . . . 'Accomplice,' Mr. Bowring himself said. My dear journalist, the episode of the revolver, empty though the revolver was, seals your lips."

Miss Fincastle laughed rather hysterically, leaning over the table with her hands on it.

"My dear millionaire," she said rapidly, "you don't know the new journalism to which I have the honour to belong. You would know it better had you lived more in New York. All I have to announce is that, compromised or not, a full account of this affair will appear in my paper tomorrow morning. No, I shall not inform the police. I am a journalist simply, but a journalist I *am*."

"And your promise, which you gave me before going behind the screen, your solemn promise that you would reveal nothing? I was loth to mention it."

"Some promises, Mr. Thorold, it is a duty to break, and it is my duty to break this one. I should never have given it had I had the slightest idea of the nature of your recreations."

Thorold still smiled, though faintly.

"Really, you know," he murmured, "this is getting just a little serious."

"It is very serious," she stammered.

And then Thorold noticed that the new journalist was softly weeping.

V.

The door opened.

"Miss Kitty Sartorius," said the erstwhile liftman, who was now in plain clothes and had mysteriously ceased to squint.

A beautiful girl, a girl who had remarkable loveliness and was aware of it (one of the prettiest women of the Devonshire), ran impulsively into the room and caught Miss Fincastle by the hand.

"My dearest Eve, you're crying. What's the matter?"

"Lecky," said Thorold aside to the servant. "I told you to admit no one."

The beautiful blonde turned sharply to Thorold.

"I told him I wished to enter," she said imperiously, half closing her eyes.

"Yes, sir," said Lecky. "That was it. The lady wished to enter."

Thorold bowed.

"It was sufficient," he said. "That will do, Lecky."

"Yes, sir."

"But I say, Lecky, when next you address me publicly, try to remember that I am not in the peerage."

The servant squinted.

"Certainly, sir." And he retired.

"Now we are alone," said Miss Sartorius. "Introduce us, Eve, and explain."

Miss Fincastle, having regained self-control, introduced her dear friend the radiant star of the Regency Theatre, and her acquaintance the millionaire.

"Eve didn't feel *quite* sure of you," the actress stated; "and so we arranged that if she wasn't up at my flat by nine o'clock, I was to come down and reconnoitre. What have you been doing to make Eve cry?"

"Unintentional, I assure you——" Thorold began.

"There's something between you two," said Kitty Sartorius sagaciously, in significant accents. "What is it?"

She sat down, touched her picture hat, smoothed her white gown, and tapped her foot. "What is it, now? Mr. Thorold, I think *you* had better tell me."

Thorold raised his eyebrows and obediently commenced the narration, standing with his back to the fire.

"How perfectly splendid!" Kitty exclaimed. "I'm so glad you cornered Mr. Bowring. I met him one night and I thought he was horrid. And these are the notes? Well, of all the——!"

Thorold proceeded with his story.

"Oh, but you can't do *that*, Eve!" said Kitty, suddenly serious. "You can't go and split! It would mean all sorts of bother; your wretched newspaper would be sure to keep you hanging about in London, and we shouldn't be able to start on our holiday tomorrow. Eve and I are starting on quite a long tour tomorrow, Mr. Thorold; we begin with Ostend."

"Indeed!" said Thorold. "I, too, am going in that direction soon. Perhaps we may meet."

"I hope so," Kitty smiled, and then she looked at Eve Fincastle. "You really mustn't do *that*, Eve," she said.

"I must, I must!" Miss Fincastle insisted, clenching her hands.

"And she will," said Kitty tragically, after considering her friend's face. "She will, and our holiday's ruined. I see it—I see it plainly. She's in one of her stupid conscientious moods. She's fearfully advanced and careless and unconventional in theory, Eve is; but when it comes to practice——! Mr. Thorold, you have just got everything into a dreadful knot. Why did you want those notes so very particularly?"

"I don't want them so very particularly."

"Well, anyhow, it's a most peculiar predicament. Mr. Bowring doesn't count, and this Consolidated thingummy isn't any the worse off. Nobody suffers who oughtn't to suffer. It's your unlawful gain that's wrong. Why not pitch the wretched notes in the fire?" Kitty laughed at her own playful humour.

"Certainly," said Thorold. And with a quick movement he put the fifty trifles in the grate, where they made a bluish yellow flame.

Both the women screamed and sprang up.

"*Mr.* Thorold!"

"Mr. *Thorold*!" ("He's adorable!" Kitty breathed.)

"The incident, I venture to hope, is now closed," said Thorold calmly, but with his dark eyes sparkling. "I must thank you both for a very enjoyable evening. Some day, perhaps, I may have an opportunity of further explaining my philosophy to you."

Villain: Madame Sara

Madame Sara

L. T. MEADE & ROBERT EUSTACE

THE EARLY YEARS of the mystery short story featured quite a few female criminals, most of whom shared the traits of youth, beauty, charm, and a devoted male friend or gang. They tended also to be clever rogues who enjoyed the excitement and great good fun of stealing jewels, money, or a precious antique or painting.

Madame Sara, the creation of the prolific Elizabeth Thomasina Meade Smith (1844–1914), using the pseudonym L. T. Meade, and Dr. Robert Eustace Barton (1863–1948), using the pseudonym Robert Eustace, is a remarkably different sort of woman, carrying about her an air of mystery. Although she appears to be a beautiful young woman of no more than twenty-five years, the story notes that she attended a wedding thirty years earlier and looked exactly the same.

Madame Sara is also a ruthless murderer, counting both male and female victims among her triumphs. The six stories about her were collected in *The Sorceress of the Strand* (1903), one of more than sixty volumes of mystery, crime, and detection written by Meade; in all, she produced more than three hundred novels and short story collections in various genres.

Born in Ireland, Meade later moved to London, where she married, wrote prolifically, and became an active feminist and member of the Pioneer Club, a progressive women's club founded in 1892; members were identified by number, rather than name, to emphasize the unimportance of social position. In her spare time, she worked as the editor of *Atalanta*, a popular girls' magazine.

Robert Eustace collaborated with several authors, including Edgar Jepson, Gertrude Warden, and Dorothy L. Sayers, but most commonly with Meade. Although he worked with her on such significant books as *Stories from the Diary of a Doctor* (1894; second series, 1896), *A Master of Mysteries* (1898), *The Brotherhood of the Seven Kings* (1899), *The Gold Star Line* (1899), and *The Sanctuary Club* (1900), his name seldom appeared on the covers of the books, only on the title pages, so one wonders if it was due to the author's diffidence or the publisher's lack of respect.

"Madame Sara" was originally published in the October 1902 issue of *The Strand Magazine*; it was first collected in *The Sorceress of the Strand* (London, Ward, Lock, 1903).

MADAME SARA

L. T. Meade & Robert Eustace

EVERYONE IN TRADE and a good many who are not have heard of Werner's Agency, the Solvency Inquiry Agency for all British trade. Its business is to know the financial condition of all wholesale and retail firms, from Rothschild's to the smallest sweetstuff shop in Whitechapel. I do not say that every firm figures on its books, but by methods of secret inquiry it can discover the status of any firm or individual. It is the great safeguard to British trade and prevents much fraudulent dealing.

Of this agency I, Dixon Druce, was appointed manager in 1890. Since then I have met queer people and seen strange sights, for men do curious things for money in this world.

It so happened that in June, 1899, my business took me to Madeira on an inquiry of some importance. I left the island on the 14th of the month by the *Norham Castle* for Southampton. I embarked after dinner. It was a lovely night, and the strains of the band in the public gardens of Funchal came floating across the star-powdered bay through the warm, balmy air. Then the engine bells rang to "Full speed ahead," and, flinging a farewell to the fairest island on earth, I turned to the smoking-room in order to light my cheroot.

"Do you want a match, sir?"

The voice came from a slender, young-looking man who stood near the taffrail. Before I could reply he had struck one and held it out to me.

"Excuse me," he said, as he tossed it overboard, "but surely I am addressing Mr. Dixon Druce?"

"You are, sir," I said, glancing keenly back at him, "but you have the advantage of me."

"Don't you know me?" he responded, "Jack Selby, Hayward's House, Harrow, 1879."

"By Jove! so it is," I cried.

Our hands met in a warm clasp, and a moment later I found myself sitting close to my old friend, who had fagged for me in the bygone days, and whom I had not seen from the moment when I said goodbye to the "Hill" in the grey mist of a December morning twenty years ago. He was a boy of fourteen then, but nevertheless I recognised him. His face was bronzed and good-looking, his features refined. As a boy Selby had been noted for his grace, his well-shaped head, his clean-cut features; these characteristics still were his, and although he was now slightly past his first youth he was decidedly handsome. He gave me a quick sketch of his history.

"My father left me plenty of money," he said, "and The Meadows, our old family place, is now mine. I have a taste for natural history; that taste took me two years ago to South America. I have had my share of strange adventures, and have collected valuable specimens and trophies. I am now on my way home from Para, on the Amazon, having come by a Booth boat to Madeira and changed there to the Castle Line. But why all this talk about myself?" he added, bringing his deck chair a little nearer to mine. "What about your history, old chap? Are you settled down with a wife and kiddies of your own, or is that dream of your school days fulfilled, and are you the owner of the best private laboratory in London?"

"As to the laboratory," I said, with a smile, "you must come and see it. For the rest I am unmarried. Are you?"

"I was married the day before I left Para, and my wife is on board with me."

"Capital," I answered. "Let me hear all about it."

"You shall. Her maiden name was Dallas; Beatrice Dallas. She is just twenty now. Her father was an Englishman and her mother a Spaniard; neither parent is living. She has an elder sister, Edith, nearly thirty years of age, unmarried, who is on board with us. There is also a step-brother, considerably older than either Edith or Beatrice. I met my wife last year in Para, and at once fell in love. I am the happiest man on earth. It goes without saying that I think her beautiful, and she is also very well off. The story of her wealth is a curious one. Her uncle on the mother's side was an extremely wealthy Spaniard, who made an enormous fortune in Brazil out of diamonds and minerals; he owned several mines. But it is supposed that his wealth turned his brain. At any rate, it seems to have done so as far as the disposal of his money went. He divided the yearly profits and interest between his nephew and his two nieces, but declared that the property itself should never be split up. He has left the whole of it to that one of the three who should survive the others. A perfectly insane arrangement, but not, I believe, unprecedented in Brazil."

"Very insane," I echoed. "What was he worth?"

"Over two million sterling."

"By Jove!" I cried, "what a sum! But what about the step-brother?"

"He must be over forty years of age, and is evidently a bad lot. I have never seen him. His sisters won't speak to him or have anything to do with him. I understand that he is a great gambler; I am further told that he is at present in England, and, as there are certain technicalities to be gone through before the girls can fully enjoy their incomes, one of the first things I must do when I get home is to find him out. He has to sign certain papers, for we shan't be able to put things straight until we get his whereabouts. Some time ago my wife and Edith heard that he was ill, but dead or alive we must know all about him, and as quickly as possible."

I made no answer, and he continued:

"I'll introduce you to my wife and sister-in-law tomorrow. Beatrice is quite a child compared to Edith, who acts towards her almost like a mother. Bee is a little beauty, so fresh and round and young-looking. But Edith is handsome, too, although I sometimes think she is as vain as a peacock. By the way, Druce, this brings me to another part of my story. The sisters have an acquaintance on board, one of the most remarkable women I have ever met. She goes by the name of Madame Sara, and knows London well. In fact, she confesses to having a shop in the Strand. What she has been doing in Brazil I do not know, for she keeps all her affairs strictly private. But you will be amazed when I tell you what her calling is."

"What?" I asked.

"A professional beautifier. She claims the privilege of restoring youth to those who consult her. She also declares that she can make quite ugly people handsome. There is no doubt that she is very clever. She knows a little bit of everything, and has wonderful recipes with regard to medicines, surgery, and dentistry. She is a most lovely woman herself, very fair, with blue eyes, an innocent, childlike manner, and quantities of rippling gold hair. She openly confesses that she is very much older than she appears. She looks about five-and-twenty. She seems to have travelled all over the world, and says that by birth she is a mixture of Indian and Italian, her father having been Italian and her mother Indian. Accompanying her is an Arab, a handsome, picturesque sort of fellow, who gives her the most absolute devotion, and she is also bringing back to England two Brazilians from Para. This woman deals in all sorts of curious secrets, but principally in cosmetics. Her shop in the Strand could, I fancy, tell many a strange history. Her clients go to her there, and she does what is necessary for them. It is a fact that she occasionally performs small surgical operations, and there is not a dentist in London who can vie with her. She confesses quite naively that she holds some secrets for making false teeth cling to the palate that no one knows of. Edith Dallas is devoted to her—in fact, her adoration amounts to idolatry."

"You give a very brilliant account of this woman," I said. "You must introduce me tomorrow."

"I will," answered Jack, with a smile. "I should like your opinion of her. I am right glad I have met you, Druce, it is like old times. When we get to London I mean to put up at my town house in Eaton Square for the remainder of the season. The Meadows shall be re-furnished, and Bee and I will take up our quarters some time in August; then you must come and see us. But I am afraid before I give myself up to mere pleasure I must find that precious brother-in-law, Henry Joachim Silva."

"If you have any difficulty apply to me," I said. "I can put at your disposal, in an unofficial way, of course, agents who would find almost any man in England, dead or alive." I then proceeded to give Selby a short account of my own business.

"Thanks," he said presently, "that is capital. You are the very man we want."

The next morning after breakfast Jack introduced me to his wife and sister-in-law. They were both foreign-looking, but very handsome, and the wife in particular had a graceful and uncommon appearance. We had been chatting about five minutes when I saw coming down the deck a slight, rather small woman, wearing a big sun hat.

"Ah, Madame," cried Selby, "here you are. I had the luck to meet an old friend on board—Mr. Dixon Druce—and I have been telling him all about you. I should like you to know each other. Druce, this lady is Madame Sara, of whom I have spoken to you. Mr. Dixon Druce—Madame Sara."

She bowed gracefully and then looked at me earnestly. I had seldom seen a more lovely woman. By her side both Mrs. Selby and her sister seemed to fade into insignificance. Her complexion was almost dazzlingly fair, her face refined in expression, her eyes penetrating, clever, and yet with the innocent, frank gaze of a child. Her dress was very simple; she looked altogether like a young, fresh, and natural girl.

As we sat chatting lightly and about commonplace topics, I instinctively felt that she took an interest in me even greater than might be expected upon an ordinary introduction. By slow degrees she so turned the conversation as to leave Selby and his wife and sister out, and then as they moved away she came a little nearer, and said in a low voice:

"I am very glad we have met, and yet how odd this meeting is! Was it really accidental?"

"I do not understand you," I answered.

"I know who you are," she said, lightly. "You are the manager of Werner's Agency; its business is to know the private affairs of those people who would rather keep their own secrets. Now, Mr. Druce, I am going to be absolutely frank with you. I own a small shop in the Strand—a perfumery shop—and behind those innocent-looking doors I conduct the business which brings me in gold of the realm. Have you, Mr. Druce, any objection to my continuing to make a livelihood in perfectly innocent ways?"

"None whatever," I answered. "You puzzle me by alluding to the subject."

"I want you to pay my shop a visit when you come to London. I have been away for three or four months. I do wonders for my clients, and they pay me largely for my services. I hold some perfectly innocent secrets which I cannot confide to anybody. I have obtained them partly from the Indians and partly from the natives of Brazil. I have lately been in Para to inquire into certain methods by which my trade can be improved."

"And your trade is—?" I said, looking at her with amusement and some surprise.

"I am a beautifier," she said, lightly. She looked at me with a smile. "You don't want me yet, Mr. Druce, but the time may come when even you will wish to keep back the infirmities of years. In the meantime can you guess my age?"

"I will not hazard a guess," I answered.

"And I will not tell you. Let it remain a secret. Meanwhile, understand that my calling is quite an open one, and I do hold secrets. I should advise you, Mr. Druce, even in your professional capacity, not to interfere with them."

The childlike expression faded from her face as she uttered the last words. There seemed to ring a sort of challenge in her tone. She turned away after a few moments and I rejoined my friends.

"You have been making acquaintance with Madame Sara, Mr. Druce," said Mrs. Selby. "Don't you think she is lovely?"

"She is one of the most beautiful women I have ever seen," I answered, "but there seems to be a mystery about her."

"Oh, indeed there is," said Edith Dallas, gravely.

"She asked me if I could guess her age," I continued. "I did not try, but surely she cannot be more than five-and-twenty."

"No one knows her age," said Mrs. Selby, "but I will tell you a curious fact, which, perhaps, you will not believe. She was bridesmaid at my mother's wedding thirty years ago. She declares that she never changes, and has no fear of old age."

"You mean that seriously?" I cried. "But surely it is impossible?"

"Her name is on the register, and my mother knew her well. She was mysterious then, and I think my mother got into her power, but of that I am not certain. Anyhow, Edith and I adore her, don't we, Edie?"

She laid her hand affectionately on her sister's arm. Edith Dallas did not speak, but her face was careworn. After a time she said slowly: "Madame Sara is uncanny and terrible."

There is, perhaps, no business imaginable—not even a lawyer's—that engenders suspicions more than mine. I hate all mysteries—both in persons and things. Mysteries are my natural enemies; I felt now that this woman was a distinct mystery. That she was interested in me I did not doubt, perhaps because she was afraid of me.

The rest of the voyage passed pleasantly enough. The more I saw of Mrs. Selby and her sister the more I liked them. They were quiet, simple, and straightforward. I felt sure that they were both as good as gold.

We parted at Waterloo, Jack and his wife and her sister going to Jack's house in Eaton Square, and I returning to my quarters in St. John's Wood. I had a house there, with a long garden, at the bottom of which was my laboratory, the laboratory that was the pride of my life, it being, I fondly considered, the best private laboratory in London. There I spent all my spare time making experiments and trying this chemical combination and the other, living in hopes of doing great things some day, for Werner's Agency was not to be the end of my career. Nevertheless, it interested me thoroughly, and I was not sorry to get back to my commercial conundrums.

The next day, just before I started to go to my place of business, Jack Selby was announced.

"I want you to help me," he said. "I have been already trying in a sort of general way to get information about my brother-in-law, but all in vain. There is no such person in any of the directories. Can you put me on the road to discovery?"

I said I could and would if he would leave the matter in my hands.

"With pleasure," he replied. "You see how we are fixed up. Neither Edith nor Bee can get money with any regularity until the man is found. I cannot imagine why he hides himself."

"I will insert advertisements in the personal columns of the newspapers," I said, "and request anyone who can give information to communicate with me at my office. I will also give instructions to all the branches of my firm, as well as to my head assistants in London, to keep their eyes open for any news. You may be quite certain that in a week or two we shall know all about him."

Selby appeared cheered at this proposal, and, having begged of me to call upon his wife and her sister as soon as possible, took his leave.

On that very day advertisements were drawn up and sent to several newspapers and inquiry agents; but week after week passed without the slightest result. Selby got very fidgety at the delay. He was never happy except in my presence, and insisted on my coming, whenever I had time, to his house. I was glad to do so, for I took an interest both in him and his belongings, and as to Madame Sara I could not get her out of my head. One day Mrs. Selby said to me:

"Have you ever been to see Madame? I know she would like to show you her shop and general surroundings."

"I did promise to call upon her," I answered, "but have not had time to do so yet."

"Will you come with me tomorrow morning?" asked Edith Dallas, suddenly.

She turned red as she spoke, and the worried, uneasy expression became more marked on her face. I had noticed for some time that she had been looking both nervous and depressed. I had first observed this peculiarity about her on board the *Norham Castle*, but, as time went on, instead of lessening it grew worse. Her face for so young a woman was haggard; she started at each sound, and Madame Sara's name was never spoken in her presence without her evincing almost undue emotion.

"Will you come with me?" she said, with great eagerness.

I immediately promised, and the next day, about eleven o'clock, Edith Dallas and I found ourselves in a hansom driving to Madame Sara's shop. We reached it in a few minutes, and found an unpretentious little place wedged in between a hosier's on one side and a cheap print-seller's on the other. In the windows of the shop were pyramids of perfume bottles, with scintillating facet stoppers tied with coloured ribbons. We stepped out of the hansom and went indoors. Inside the shop were a couple of steps, which led to a door of solid mahogany.

"This is the entrance to her private house," said Edith, and she pointed to a small brass plate, on which was engraved the name—"Madame Sara, Parfumeuse." Edith touched an electric bell and the door was immediately opened by a smartly-dressed page-boy. He looked at Miss Dallas as if he knew her very well, and said:

"Madame is within, and is expecting you, miss."

He ushered us both into a quiet-looking room, soberly but handsomely furnished. He left us, closing the door. Edith turned to me.

"Do you know where we are?" she asked.

"We are standing at present in a small room just behind Madame Sara's shop," I answered. "Why are you so excited, Miss Dallas? What is the matter with you?"

"We are on the threshold of a magician's cave," she replied. "We shall soon be face to face with the most marvellous woman in the whole of London. There is no one like her."

"And you—fear her?" I said, dropping my voice to a whisper.

She started, stepped back, and with great difficulty recovered her composure. At that moment the page-boy returned to conduct us through a series of small waiting-rooms, and we soon found ourselves in the presence of Madame herself.

"Ah!" she said, with a smile. "This is delightful. You have kept your word, Edith, and I am greatly obliged to you. I will now show Mr. Druce some of the mysteries of my trade. But understand, sir," she added, "that I shall not tell you any of my real secrets, only as you would like to know something about me you shall."

"How can you tell I should like to know about you?" I asked.

She gave me an earnest glance which somewhat astonished me, and then she said: "Knowledge is power; don't refuse what I am willing to give. Edith, you will not object to waiting here while I show Mr. Druce through the rooms. First observe this room, Mr. Druce. It is lighted only from the roof. When the door shuts it automatically locks itself, so that any in-trusion from without is impossible. This is my sanctum sanctorum—a faint odour of perfume pervades the room. This is a hot day, but the room itself is cool. What do you think of it all?"

I made no answer. She walked to the other end and motioned to me to accompany her. There stood a polished oak square table, on which lay an array of extraordinary-looking articles and implements—stoppered bottles full of strange medicaments, mirrors, plane and concave, brushes, sprays, sponges, delicate needle-pointed instruments of bright steel, tiny lancets, and forceps. Facing this table was a chair, like those used by dentists. Above the chair hung electric lights in powerful reflectors, and lenses like bull's-eye lanterns. Another chair, supported on a glass pedestal, was kept there, Madame Sara informed me, for administering static electricity. There were dry-cell batteries for the continuous currents and induction coils for Faradic currents. There were also platinum needles for burning out the roots of hairs.

Madame took me from this room into another, where a still more formidable array of instruments was to be found. Here were a wooden operating table and chloroform and ether apparatus. When I had looked at everything, she turned to me.

"Now you know," she said. "I am a doctor—perhaps a quack. These are my secrets. By means of these I live and flourish."

She turned her back on me and walked into the other room with the light, springy step of youth. Edith Dallas, white as a ghost, was waiting for us.

"You have done your duty, my child," said Madame. "Mr. Druce has seen just what I want him to see. I am very much obliged to you both. We shall meet tonight at Lady Farringdon's 'At Home.' Until then, farewell."

When we got into the street and were driving back again to Eaton Square, I turned to Edith.

"Many things puzzle me about your friend," I said, "but perhaps none more than this. By what possible means can a woman who owns to being the possessor of a shop obtain the entrée to some of the best houses in London? Why does Society open her doors to this woman, Miss Dallas?"

"I cannot quite tell you," was her reply. "I only know the fact that wherever she goes she is welcomed and treated with consideration, and wherever she fails to appear there is a universally expressed feeling of regret."

I had also been invited to Lady Farringdon's reception that evening, and I went there in a state of great curiosity. There was no doubt that Madame interested me. I was not sure of her. Beyond doubt there was a mystery attached to her, and also, for some unaccountable reason, she wished both to propitiate and defy me. Why was this?

I arrived early, and was standing in the crush near the head of the staircase when Madame was announced. She wore the richest white satin and quantities of diamonds. I saw her hostess bend towards her and talk eagerly. I noticed Madame's reply and the pleased expression that crossed Lady Farringdon's face. A few minutes later a man with a foreign-looking face and long beard sat down before the grand piano. He played a light prelude and Madame Sara began to sing. Her voice was sweet and low, with an extraordinary pathos in it. It was the sort of voice that penetrates to the heart. There was an instant pause in the gay chatter. She sang amidst perfect silence, and when the song had come to an end there followed a furore of applause. I was just turning to say something to my nearest neighbour when I observed Edith Dallas, who was standing close by. Her eyes met mine; she laid her hand on my sleeve.

"The room is hot," she said, half panting as she spoke. "Take me out on the balcony."

I did so. The atmosphere of the reception-rooms was almost intolerable, but it was comparatively cool in the open air.

"I must not lose sight of her," she said, suddenly.

"Of whom?" I asked, somewhat astonished at her words.

"Of Sara."

"She is there," I said. "You can see her from where you stand."

We happened to be alone. I came a little closer.

"Why are you afraid of her?" I asked.

"Are you sure that we shall not be heard?" was her answer.

"She terrifies me," were her next words.

"I will not betray your confidence, Miss Dallas. Will you not trust me? You ought to give me a reason for your fears."

"I cannot—I dare not; I have said far too much already. Don't keep me, Mr. Druce. She must not find us together." As she spoke she pushed her way through the crowd, and before I could stop her was standing by Madame Sara's side.

The reception in Portland Place was, I remember, on the 26th of July. Two days later the Selbys were to give their final "At Home" before leaving for the country. I was, of course, invited to be present, and Madame was also there. She had never been dressed more splendidly, nor had she ever before looked younger or more beautiful. Wherever she went all eyes followed her. As a rule her dress was simple, almost like what a girl would wear, but tonight she chose rich Oriental stuffs made of many colours, and absolutely glittering with gems. Her golden hair was studded with diamonds. Round her neck she wore turquoise and diamonds mixed. There were many younger women in the room, but not the youngest nor the fairest had a chance beside Madame. It was not mere beauty of appearance, it was charm—charm which carries all before it.

I saw Miss Dallas, looking slim and tall and pale, standing at a little distance. I made my way to her side. Before I had time to speak she bent towards me.

"Is she not divine?" she whispered. "She bewilders and delights everyone. She is taking London by storm."

"Then you are not afraid of her tonight?" I said.

"I fear her more than ever. She has cast a spell over me. But listen, she is going to sing again."

I had not forgotten the song that Madame had given us at the Farringdons', and stood still to listen. There was a complete hush in the room. Her voice floated over the heads of the assembled guests in a dreamy Spanish song. Edith told me that it was a slumber song, and that Madame boasted of her power of putting almost anyone to sleep who listened to her rendering of it.

"She has many patients who suffer from insomnia," whispered the girl, "and she generally cures them with that song, and that alone. Ah! we must not talk; she will hear us."

Before I could reply Selby came hurrying up. He had not noticed Edith. He caught me by the arm.

"Come just for a minute into this window, Dixon," he said. "I must speak to you. I suppose you have no news with regard to my brother-in-law?"

"Not a word," I answered.

"To tell you the truth, I am getting terribly put out over the matter. We cannot settle any of our money affairs just because this man chooses to lose himself. My wife's lawyers wired to Brazil yesterday, but even his bankers do not know anything about him."

"The whole thing is a question of time," was my answer. "When are you off to Hampshire?"

"On Saturday."

As Selby said the last words he looked around him, then he dropped his voice.

"I want to say something else. The more I see"—he nodded towards Madame Sara—"the less I like her. Edith is getting into a very strange state. Have you not noticed it? And the worst of it is my wife is also infected. I suppose it is that dodge of the woman's for patching people up and making them beautiful. Doubtless the temptation is overpowering in the case of a plain woman, but Beatrice is beautiful herself and young. What can she have to do with cosmetics and complexion pills?"

"You don't mean to tell me that your wife has consulted Madame Sara as a doctor?"

"Not exactly, but she has gone to her about her teeth. She complained of toothache lately, and Madame's dentistry is renowned. Edith is constantly going to her for one thing or another, but then Edith is infatuated."

As Jack said the last words he went over to speak to someone else, and before I could leave the seclusion of the window I perceived Edith Dallas and Madame Sara in earnest conversation together. I could not help overhearing the following words:

"Don't come to me tomorrow. Get into the country as soon as you can. It is far and away the best thing to do."

As Madame spoke she turned swiftly and caught my eye. She bowed, and the peculiar look, the sort of challenge, she had given me before flashed over her face. It made me uncomfortable, and during the night that followed I could not get it out of my head. I remembered what Selby had said with regard to his wife and her money affairs. Beyond doubt he had married into a mystery—a mystery that Madame knew all about. There was a very big money interest, and strange things happen when millions are concerned.

The next morning I had just risen and was sitting at breakfast when a note was handed to me. It came by special messenger, and was marked "Urgent." I tore it open. These were its contents:

"My dear Druce, A terrible blow has fallen on us. My sister-in-law, Edith, was taken suddenly ill this morning at breakfast. The nearest doctor was sent for, but he could do nothing, as she died half an hour ago. Do come and see me, and if you know any very clever specialist bring him with you. My wife is utterly stunned by the shock. Yours, Jack Selby."

I read the note twice before I could realize what it meant. Then I rushed out and, hailing the first hansom I met, said to the man: "Drive to No. 192, Victoria Street, as quickly as you can."

Here lived a certain Mr. Eric Vandeleur, an old friend of mine and the police surgeon for the Westminster district, which included Eaton Square. No shrewder or sharper fellow existed than Vandeleur, and the present case was essentially in his province, both legally and professionally. He was not at his flat when I arrived, having already gone down to the court. Here I accordingly hurried, and was informed that he was in the mortuary.

For a man who, as it seemed to me, lived in a perpetual atmosphere of crime and violence, of death and coroners' courts, his habitual cheerfulness and brightness of manner were remarkable. Perhaps it was only the reaction from his work, for he had the reputation of being one of the most astute experts of the day in medical jurisprudence, and the most skilled analyst in toxicological cases on the Metropolitan Police staff. Before I could send him word that I wanted to see him I heard a door bang, and Vandeleur came hurrying down the passage, putting on his coat as he rushed along.

"Halloa!" he cried. "I haven't seen you for ages. Do you want me?"

"Yes, very urgently," I answered. "Are you busy?"

"Head over ears, my dear chap. I cannot give you a moment now, but perhaps later on."

"What is it? You look excited."

"I have got to go to Eaton Square like the

wind, but come along, if you like, and tell me on the way."

"Capital," I cried. "The thing has been reported then? You are going to Mr. Selby's, No. 34a; then I am going with you."

He looked at me in amazement.

"But the case has only just been reported. What can you possibly know about it?"

"Everything. Let us take this hansom, and I will tell you as we go along."

As we drove to Eaton Square I quickly explained the situation, glancing now and then at Vandeleur's bright, clean-shaven face. He was no longer Eric Vandeleur, the man with the latest club story and the merry twinkle in his blue eyes; he was Vandeleur the medical jurist, with a face like a mask, his lower jaw slightly protruding and features very fixed.

"The thing promises to be serious," he replied, as I finished, "but I can do nothing until after the autopsy. Here we are, and there is my man waiting for me; he has been smart."

On the steps stood an official-looking man in uniform, who saluted.

"Coroner's officer," explained Vandeleur.

We entered the silent, darkened house. Selby was standing in the hall. He came to meet us. I introduced him to Vandeleur, and he at once led us into the dining-room, where we found Dr. Osborne, whom Selby had called in when the alarm of Edith's illness had been first given. Dr. Osborne was a pale, under-sized, very young man. His face expressed considerable alarm. Vandeleur, however, managed to put him completely at his ease.

"I will have a chat with you in a few minutes, Dr. Osborne," he said; "but first I must get Mr. Selby's report. Will you please tell me, sir, exactly what occurred?"

"Certainly," he answered. "We had a reception here last night, and my sister-in-law did not go to bed until early morning; she was in bad spirits, but otherwise in her usual health. My wife went into her room after she was in bed, and told me later on that she had found Edith in hysterics, and could not get her to explain anything. We both talked about taking her to the country without delay. Indeed, our intention was to get off this afternoon."

"Well?" said Vandeleur.

"We had breakfast about half-past nine, and Miss Dallas came down, looking quite in her usual health, and in apparently good spirits. She ate with appetite, and, as it happened, she and my wife were both helped from the same dish. The meal had nearly come to an end when she jumped up from the table, uttered a sharp cry, turned very pale, pressed her hand to her side, and ran out of the room. My wife immediately followed her. She came back again in a minute or two, and said that Edith was in violent pain, and begged of me to send for a doctor. Dr. Osborne lives just round the corner. He came at once, but she died almost immediately after his arrival."

"You were in the room?" asked Vandeleur, turning to Osborne.

"Yes," he replied. "She was conscious to the last moment, and died suddenly."

"Did she tell you anything?"

"No, except to assure me that she had not eaten any food that day until she had come down to breakfast. After the death occurred I sent immediately to report the case, locked the door of the room where the poor girl's body is, and saw also that nobody touched anything on this table."

Vandeleur rang the bell and a servant appeared. He gave quick orders. The entire remains of the meal were collected and taken charge of, and then he and the coroner's officer went upstairs.

When we were alone Selby sank into a chair. His face was quite drawn and haggard.

"It is the horrible suddenness of the thing which is so appalling," he cried. "As to Beatrice, I don't believe she will ever be the same again. She was deeply attached to Edith. Edith was nearly ten years her senior, and always acted the part of mother to her. This is a sad beginning to our life. I can scarcely think collectedly."

I remained with him a little longer, and then,

as Vandeleur did not return, went back to my own house. There I could settle to nothing, and when Vandeleur rang me up on the telephone about six o'clock I hurried off to his rooms. As soon as I arrived I saw that Selby was with him, and the expression on both their faces told me the truth.

"This is a bad business," said Vandeleur. "Miss Dallas has died from swallowing poison. An exhaustive analysis and examination have been made, and a powerful poison, unknown to European toxicologists, has been found. This is strange enough, but how it has been administered is a puzzle. I confess, at the present moment, we are all nonplussed. It certainly was not in the remains of the breakfast, and we have her dying evidence that she took nothing else. Now, a poison with such appalling potency would take effect quickly. It is evident that she was quite well when she came to breakfast, and that the poison began to work towards the close of the meal. But how did she get it? This question, however, I shall deal with later on. The more immediate point is this. The situation is a serious one in view of the monetary issues and the value of the lady's life. From the aspects of the case, her undoubted sanity and her affection for her sister, we may almost exclude the idea of suicide. We must, therefore, call it murder. This harmless, innocent lady is struck down by the hand of an assassin, and with such devilish cunning that no trace or clue is left behind. For such an act there must have been some very powerful motive, and the person who designed and executed it must be a criminal of the highest order of scientific ability. Mr. Selby has been telling me the exact financial position of the poor lady, and also of his own young wife. The absolute disappearance of the step-brother, in view of his previous character, is in the highest degree strange. Knowing, as we do, that between him and two million sterling there stood two lives—*one is taken!*"

A deadly sensation of cold seized me as Vandeleur uttered these last words. I glanced at Selby. His face was colourless and the pupils of his eyes were contracted, as though he saw something which terrified him.

"What happened once may happen again," continued Vandeleur. "We are in the presence of a great mystery, and I counsel you, Mr. Selby, to guard your wife with the utmost care."

These words, falling from a man of Vandeleur's position and authority on such matters, were sufficiently shocking for me to hear, but for Selby to be given such a solemn warning about his young and beautiful and newly-married wife, who was all the world to him, was terrible indeed. He leant his head on his hands.

"Mercy on us!" he muttered. "Is this a civilized country when death can walk abroad like this, invisible, not to be avoided? Tell me, Mr. Vandeleur, what I must do."

"You must be guided by me," said Vandeleur, "and, believe me, there is no witchcraft in the world. I shall place a detective in your household immediately. Don't be alarmed; he will come to you in plain clothes and will simply act as a servant. Nevertheless, nothing can be done to your wife without his knowledge. As to you, Druce," he continued, turning to me, "the police are doing all they can to find this man Silva, and I ask you to help them with your big agency, and to begin at once. Leave your friend to me. Wire instantly if you hear news."

"You may rely on me," I said, and a moment later I had left the room. As I walked rapidly down the street the thought of Madame Sara, her shop and its mysterious background, its surgical instruments, its operating-table, its induction coils, came back to me. And yet what could Madame Sara have to do with the present strange, inexplicable mystery?

The thought had scarcely crossed my mind before I heard a clatter alongside the kerb, and turning round I saw a smart open carriage, drawn by a pair of horses, standing there. I also heard my own name. I turned. Bending out of the carriage was Madame Sara.

"I saw you going by, Mr. Druce. I have only just heard the news about poor Edith Dallas. I am terribly shocked and upset. I have been to the house, but they would not admit me. Have you heard what was the cause of her death?"

Madame's blue eyes filled with tears as she spoke.

"I am not at liberty to disclose what I have heard, Madame," I answered, "since I am officially connected with the affair."

Her eyes narrowed. The brimming tears dried as though by magic. Her glance became scornful.

"Thank you," she answered, "your reply tells me that she did not die naturally. How very appalling! But I must not keep you. Can I drive you anywhere?"

"No, thank you."

"Goodbye, then."

She made a sign to the coachman, and as the carriage rolled away turned to look at me. Her face wore the defiant expression I had seen there more than once. Could she be connected with the affair? The thought came upon me with a violence that seemed almost conviction. Yet I had no reason for it—none.

To find Henry Joachim Silva was now my principal thought. My staff had instructions to make every possible inquiry, with large money rewards as incitements. The collateral branches of other agencies throughout Brazil were communicated with by cable, and all the Scotland Yard channels were used. Still there was no result. The newspapers took up the case; there were paragraphs in most of them with regard to the missing step-brother and the mysterious death of Edith Dallas. Then someone got hold of the story of the will, and this was retailed with many additions for the benefit of the public. At the inquest the jury returned the following verdict:

"We find that Miss Edith Dallas died from taking poison of unknown name, but by whom or how administered there is no evidence to say."

This unsatisfactory state of things was destined to change quite suddenly. On the 6th of August, as I was seated in my office, a note was brought me by a private messenger. It was as follows:

"Norfolk Hotel, Strand.

"Dear Sir—I have just arrived in London from Brazil, and have seen your advertisements. I was about to insert one myself in order to find the whereabouts of my sisters. I am a great invalid and unable to leave my room. Can you come to see me at the earliest possible moment? Yours, Henry Joachim Silva."

In uncontrollable excitement I hastily dispatched two telegrams, one to Selby and the other to Vandeleur, begging of them to be with me, without fail, as soon as possible. So the man had never been in England at all. The situation was more bewildering than ever. One thing, at least, was probable—Edith Dallas's death was not due to her step-brother. Soon after half-past six Selby arrived, and Vandeleur walked in ten minutes later. I told them what had occurred and showed them the letter. In half an hour's time we reached the hotel, and on stating who I was we were shown into a room on the first floor by Silva's private servant. Resting in an armchair, as we entered, sat a man; his face was terribly thin. The eyes and cheeks were so sunken that the face had almost the appearance of a skull. He made no effort to rise when we entered, and glanced from one of us to the other with the utmost astonishment. I at once introduced myself and explained who we were. He then waved his hand for his man to retire.

"You have heard the news, of course, Mr. Silva?" I said.

"News! What?" He glanced up to me and seemed to read something in my face. He started back in his chair.

"Good heavens," he replied. "Do you allude to my sisters? Tell me, quickly, are they alive?"

"Your elder sister died on the twenty-ninth of July, and there is every reason to believe that her death was caused by foul play."

As I uttered these words the change that passed over his face was fearful to witness. He did not speak, but remained motionless. His claw-like hands clutched the arms of the chair, his eyes were fixed and staring, as though they would start from their hollow sockets, the colour of his skin was like clay. I heard Selby breathe quickly behind me, and Vandeleur stepped towards the man and laid his hand on his shoulder.

"Tell us what you know of this matter," he said sharply.

Recovering himself with an effort, the invalid began in a tremulous voice: "Listen closely, for you must act quickly. I am indirectly responsible for this fearful thing. My life has been a wild and wasted one, and now I am dying. The doctors tell me I cannot live a month, for I have a large aneurism of the heart. Eighteen months ago I was in Rio. I was living fast and gambled heavily. Among my fellow gamblers was a man much older than myself. His name was José Aranjo. He was, if anything, a greater gambler than I. One night we played alone. The stakes ran high until they reached a big figure. By daylight I had lost to him nearly £200,000. Though I am a rich man in point of income under my uncle's will, I could not pay a twentieth part of that sum. This man knew my financial position, and, in addition to a sum of £5,000 paid down, I gave him a document. I must have been mad to do so. The document was this—it was duly witnessed and attested by a lawyer—that, in the event of my surviving my two sisters and thus inheriting the whole of my uncle's vast wealth, half a million should go to José Aranjo. I felt I was breaking up at the time, and the chances of my inheriting the money were small. Immediately after the completion of the document this man left Rio, and I then heard a great deal about him that I had not previously known. He was a man of the queerest antecedents, partly Indian, partly Italian. He had spent many years of his life amongst the Indians. I heard also that he was as cruel as he was clever, and possessed some wonderful secrets of poisoning unknown to the West. I thought a great deal about this, for I knew that by signing that document I had placed the lives of my two sisters between him and a fortune. I came to Para six weeks ago, only to learn that one of my sisters was married and that both had gone to England. Ill as I was, I determined to follow them in order to warn them. I also wanted to arrange matters with you, Mr. Selby."

"One moment, sir," I broke in, suddenly. "Do you happen to be aware if this man, José Aranjo, knew a woman calling herself Madame Sara?"

"Knew her?" cried Silva. "Very well indeed, and so, for that matter, did I. Aranjo and Madame Sara were the best friends, and constantly met. She called herself a professional beautifier—was very handsome, and had secrets for the pursuing of her trade unknown even to Aranjo."

"Good heavens!" I cried, "and the woman is now in London. She returned here with Mrs. Selby and Miss Dallas. Edith was very much influenced by her, and was constantly with her. There is no doubt in my mind that she is guilty. I have suspected her for some time, but I could not find a motive. Now the motive appears. You surely can have her arrested?"

Vandeleur made no reply. He gave me a strange look, then he turned to Selby.

"Has your wife also consulted Madame Sara?" he asked, sharply.

"Yes, she went to her once about her teeth, but has not been to the shop since Edith's death. I begged of her not to see the woman, and she promised me faithfully she would not do so."

"Has she any medicines or lotions given to her by Madame Sara—does she follow any line of treatment advised by her?"

"No, I am certain on that point."

"Very well. I will see your wife tonight in order to ask her some questions. You must both leave town at once. Go to your country house and settle there. I am quite serious when I say that Mrs. Selby is in the utmost possible danger until after the death of her brother. We must leave you now, Mr. Silva. All business affairs must wait for the present. It is absolutely necessary that Mrs. Selby should leave London at once. Good night, sir. I shall give myself the pleasure of calling on you tomorrow morning."

We took leave of the sick man. As soon as we got into the street Vandeleur stopped.

"I must leave it to you, Selby," he said, "to judge how much of this matter you tell to your wife. Were I you I would explain everything. The time for immediate action has arrived, and she is a brave and sensible woman. From this moment you must watch all the foods and liquids that she takes. She must never be out of your sight or out of the sight of some other trustworthy companion."

"I shall, of course, watch my wife myself," said Selby. "But the thing is enough to drive one mad."

"I will go with you to the country, Selby," I said, suddenly.

"Ah!" cried Vandeleur, "that is the best thing possible, and what I wanted to propose. Go, all of you, by an early train tomorrow."

"Then I will be off home at once, to make arrangements," I said. "I will meet you, Selby, at Waterloo for the first train to Cronsmoor tomorrow."

As I was turning away Vandeleur caught my arm.

"I am glad you are going with them," he said. "I shall write to you tonight re instructions. Never be without a loaded revolver. Good night." By 6:15 the next morning Selby, his wife, and I were in a reserved, locked, first-class compartment, speeding rapidly west. The servants and Mrs. Selby's own special maid were in a separate carriage. Selby's face showed signs of a sleepless night, and presented a striking contrast to the fair, fresh face of the girl round whom this strange battle raged. Her husband had told her everything, and, though still suffering terribly from the shock and grief of her sister's death, her face was calm and full of repose. A carriage was waiting for us at Cronsmoor, and by half-past nine we arrived at the old home of the Selbys, nestling amid its oaks and elms. Everything was done to make the home-coming of the bride as cheerful as circumstances would permit, but a gloom, impossible to lift, overshadowed Selby himself. He could scarcely rouse himself to take the slightest interest in anything.

The following morning I received a letter from Vandeleur. It was very short, and once more impressed on me the necessity of caution. He said that two eminent physicians had examined Silva, and the verdict was that he could not live a month. Until his death precautions must be strictly observed.

The day was cloudless, and after breakfast I was just starting out for a stroll when the butler brought me a telegram. I tore it open; it was from Vandeleur:

"Prohibit all food until I arrive. Am coming down," were the words. I hurried into the study and gave it to Selby. He read it and looked up at me.

"Find out the first train and go and meet him, old chap," he said. "Let us hope that this means an end of the hideous affair."

I went into the hall and looked up the trains. The next arrived at Cronsmoor at 10:45. I then strolled round to the stables and ordered a carriage, after which I walked up and down on the drive. There was no doubt that something strange had happened. Vandeleur coming down so suddenly must mean a final clearing up of the mystery. I had just turned round at the lodge gates to wait for the carriage when the sound of wheels and of horses galloping struck on my ears. The gates were swung open, and Vandeleur in an open fly dashed through them. Before I could recover from my surprise he was out of the vehicle and at my side. He carried a small black bag in his hand.

"I came down by special train," he said, speaking quickly. "There is not a moment to lose. Come at once. Is Mrs. Selby all right?"

"What do you mean?" I replied. "Of course she is. Do you suppose that she is in danger?"

"Deadly," was his answer. "Come."

We dashed up to the house together. Selby, who had heard our steps, came to meet us.

"Mr. Vandeleur," he cried. "What is it? How did you come?"

"By special train, Mr. Selby. And I want to

see your wife at once. It will be necessary to perform a very trifling operation."

"Operation!" he exclaimed. "Yes; at once."

We made our way through the hall and into the morning-room, where Mrs. Selby was busily engaged reading and answering letters. She started up when she saw Vandeleur and uttered an exclamation of surprise.

"What has happened?" she asked. Vandeleur went up to her and took her hand.

"Do not be alarmed," he said, "for I have come to put all your fears to rest. Now, please, listen to me. When you visited Madame Sara with your sister, did you go for medical advice?"

The colour rushed into her face.

"One of my teeth ached," she answered. "I went to her about that. She is, as I suppose you know, a most wonderful dentist. She examined the tooth, found that it required stopping, and got an assistant, a Brazilian, I think, to do it."

"And your tooth has been comfortable ever since?"

"Yes, quite. She had one of Edith's stopped at the same time."

"Will you kindly sit down and show me which was the tooth into which the stopping was put?"

She did so.

"This was the one," she said, pointing with her finger to one in the lower jaw. "What do you mean? Is there anything wrong?"

Vandeleur examined the tooth long and carefully. There was a sudden rapid movement of his hand, and a sharp cry from Mrs. Selby. With the deftness of long practice, and a powerful wrist, he had extracted the tooth with one wrench. The suddenness of the whole thing, startling as it was, was not so strange as his next movement.

"Send Mrs. Selby's maid to her," he said, turning to her husband; "then come, both of you, into the next room."

The maid was summoned. Poor Mrs. Selby had sunk back in her chair, terrified and half fainting. A moment later Selby joined us in the dining-room.

"That's right," said Vandeleur; "close the door, will you?"

He opened his black bag and brought out several instruments. With one he removed the stopping from the tooth. It was quite soft and came away easily. Then from the bag he produced a small guinea-pig, which he requested me to hold. He pressed the sharp instrument into the tooth, and opening the mouth of the little animal placed the point on the tongue. The effect was instantaneous. The little head fell on to one of my hands—the guinea-pig was dead. Vandeleur was white as a sheet. He hurried up to Selby and wrung his hand.

"Thank heaven!" he said, "I've been in time, but only just. Your wife is safe. This stopping would hardly have held another hour. I have been thinking all night over the mystery of your sister-in-law's death, and over every minute detail of evidence as to how the poison could have been administered. Suddenly the coincidence of both sisters having had their teeth stopped struck me as remarkable. Like a flash the solution came to me. The more I considered it the more I felt that I was right; but by what fiendish cunning such a scheme could have been conceived and executed is still beyond my power to explain. The poison is very like hyoscine, one of the worst toxic-alkaloids known, so violent in its deadly proportions that the amount that would go into a tooth would cause almost instant death. It has been kept in by a gutta-percha stopping, certain to come out within a month, probably earlier, and most probably during mastication of food. The person would die either immediately or after a very few minutes, and no one would connect a visit to the dentist with a death a month afterwards."

What followed can be told in a very few words. Madame Sara was arrested on suspicion. She appeared before the magistrate, looking innocent and beautiful, and managed during her evidence completely to baffle that acute individual. She denied nothing, but declared that the poison must have been put into the tooth by one of the two Brazilians whom she had lately engaged to help her with her dentistry. She had her suspicions with regard to these men soon afterwards, and had dismissed them. She believed that they were in the pay of José Aranjo, but she could not tell anything for certain. Thus Madame escaped conviction. I was certain that she was guilty, but there was not a shadow of real proof. A month later Silva died, and Selby is now a double millionaire.

Rogue: Hamilton Cleek

The Affair of the Man Who Called Himself Hamilton Cleek

THOMAS W. HANSHEW

SUPERHEROES APPEAR TO BE LITERARY or comic book figures of recent vintage, but many criminals who appeared a century ago also had amazing abilities and powers. Hamilton Cleek, the creation of Thomas W. Hanshew (1857–1914), had the extraordinary ability to contort his face almost instantly, creating a dozen different visages in as many seconds, setting a living mask over his features without the aid of makeup.

He was variously known as "the Man of the Forty Faces" and as "the Vanishing Cracksman," a sobriquet he disliked, telling newspapers that describing him as merely a cracksman was akin to calling Paganini a fiddler. He insisted that he be referred to as "the Man Who Calls Himself Hamilton Cleek," promising journalists that for the courtesy he would henceforth provide them with the time and place of his next robbery. Furthermore, he informed Scotland Yard that he would send it a small portion of his haul on the following morning—as a souvenir.

Although he has several aliases, Cleek is actually Prince of Mauravania, a throne he abandons to marry Ailsa, the woman who is his partner in crime until she eventually convinces him to repent, after which he becomes a detective.

There are thirteen books featuring Hamilton Cleek, mostly published after Hanshew's death. The latter volumes were written by his wife, Mary E. Hanshew, at first produced from her husband's notes and ideas, then continued on her own. Most books were jointly bylined as by Thomas W. Hanshew and Mary E. Hanshew.

"The Affair of the Man Who Called Himself Hamilton Cleek," the first story in the series, was originally published in *The Man of the Forty Faces* (London, Cassell, 1910; the first American edition was titled, peculiarly, as the character worked only as a criminal, *Cleek, the Master Detective*; New York, Doubleday, 1918).

THE AFFAIR OF THE MAN WHO CALLED HIMSELF HAMILTON CLEEK

Thomas W. Hanshew

I

THE THING WOULDN'T have happened if any other constable than Collins had been put on point duty at Blackfriars Bridge that morning. For Collins was young, good-looking, and—knew it. Nature had gifted him with a susceptible heart and a fond eye for the beauties of femininity. So when he looked round and saw the woman threading her way through the maze of vehicles at "Dead Man's Corner," with her skirt held up just enough to show two twinkling little feet in French shoes, and over them a graceful, willowy figure, and over that an enchanting, if rather too highly tinted face, with almond eyes and a fluff of shining hair under the screen of a big Parisian hat—that did for him on the spot.

He saw at a glance that she was French—exceedingly French—and he preferred English beauty, as a rule. But, French or English, beauty is beauty, and here undeniably was a perfect type, so he unhesitatingly sprang to her assistance and piloted her safely to the kerb, revelling in her voluble thanks, and tingling as she clung timidly but rather firmly to him.

"Sair, I have to give you much gratitude," she said in a pretty, wistful sort of way, as they stepped on to the pavement. Then she dropped her hand from his sleeve, looked up at him, and shyly drooped her head, as if overcome with confusion and surprise at the youth and good looks of him. "Ah, it is nowhere in the world but Londres one finds these delicate attentions, these splendid sergeants de ville," she added, with a sort of sigh. "You are wonnerful—you are mos' wonnerful, you Anglais poliss. Sair, I am a stranger; I know not ze ways of this city of amazement, and if monsieur would so kindly direct me where to find the Abbey of the Ves'minster—"

Before P.C. Collins could tell her that if that were her destination, she was a good deal out of her latitude; indeed, even before she concluded what she was saying, over the rumble of the traffic there rose a thin, shrill piping sound, which to ears trained to the call of it possessed a startling significance.

It was the shrilling of a police whistle, far off down the Embankment.

"Hullo! That's a call to the man on point!" exclaimed Collins, all alert at once. "Excuse me, mum. See you presently. Something's up. One of my mates is a-signalling me."

"Mates, monsieur? Mates? Signalling? I shall

not understand the vords. But yes, vat shall that mean—eh?"

"Good Lord, don't bother me now! I—I mean, wait a bit. That's the call to 'head off' someone, and—By George! There he is now, coming head on, the hound, and running like the wind!"

For of a sudden, through a break in the traffic, a scudding figure had sprung into sight—the figure of a man in a grey frock-coat and a shining "topper," a well-groomed, well-set-up man, with a small, turned-up moustache and hair of that peculiar purplish-red one sees only on the shell of a roasted chestnut. As he swung into sight, the distant whistle shrilled again; far off in the distance voices sent up cries of "Head him off!" "Stop that man!" *et cetera;* then those on the pavement near to the fugitive took up the cry, joined in pursuit, and in a twinkling, what with cabmen, tram-men, draymen, and pedestrians shouting, there was hubbub enough for Hades.

"A swell pickpocket, I'll lay my life," commented Collins, as he squared himself for an encounter and made ready to leap on the man when he came within gripping distance. "Here! get out of the way, madmazelly. Business before pleasure. And, besides, you're like to get bowled over in the rush. Here, chauffeur!"—this to the driver of a big, black motor-car which swept round the angle of the bridge at that moment, and made as though to scud down the Embankment into the thick of the chase—"pull that thing up sharp! Stop where you are! Dead still. At once, at once, do you hear? We don't want you getting in the way. Now, then"—nodding his head in the direction of the running man—"come on, you bounder; I'm ready for you!"

And, as if he really heard that invitation, and really was eager to accept it, the red-headed man did "come on" with a vengeance. And all the time, "madmazelly," unheeding Collins's advice, stood calmly and silently waiting.

Onward came the runner, with the whole roaring pack in his wake, dodging in and out among the vehicles, "flooring" people who got in his way, scudding, dodging, leaping, like a fox hard pressed by the hounds—until, all of a moment he spied a break in the traffic, leapt through it, and—then there was mischief. For Collins sprang at him like a cat, gripped two big, strong-as-iron hands on his shoulders, and had him tight and fast.

"Got you, you ass!" snapped he, with a short, crisp, self-satisfied laugh. "None of your blessed squirming now. Keep still. You'll get out of your coffin, you bounder, as soon as out of my grip. Got you—got you! Do you understand?"

The response to this fairly took the wind out of him.

"Of course I do," said the captive, gaily; "it's part of the programme that you should get me. Only, for Heaven's sake, don't spoil the film by remaining inactive, you goat! Struggle with me—handle me roughly—throw me about. Make it look real; make it look as though I actually did get away from you, not as though you let me. You chaps behind there, don't get in the way of the camera—it's in one of those cabs. Now, then, Bobby, don't be wooden! Struggle—struggle, you goat, and save the film!"

"Save the what?" gasped Collins. "Here! Good Lord! Do you mean to say—?"

"Struggle—struggle—struggle!" cut in the man impatiently. "Can't you grasp the situation? It's a put-up thing: the taking of a kinematograph film—a living picture—for the Alhambra tonight! Heavens above, Marguerite, didn't you tell him?"

"Non, non! There was not ze time. You come so quick, I could not. And he—ah, le bon Dieu!—he gif me no chance. Officair, I beg, I entreat of you, make it real! Struggle, fight, keep on ze constant move. Zere!"—something tinkled on the pavement with the unmistakable sound of gold—"zere, monsieur, zere is the half-sovereign to pay you for ze trouble, only, for ze lot of goodness, do not pick it up while the instrument—ze camera—he is going. It is ze kinematograph, and you would spoil everything!"

The chop-fallen cry that Collins gave was lost in a roar of laughter from the pursuing crowd.

"Struggle—struggle! Don't you hear, you

idiot?" broke in the red-headed man irritably. "You are being devilishly well paid for it, so for goodness's sake make it look real. That's it! Bully boy! Now, once more to the right, then loosen your grip so that I can push you away and make a feint of punching you off. All ready there, Marguerite? Keep a clear space about her, gentlemen. Ready with the motor, chauffeur? All right. Now, then, Bobby, fall back, and mind your eye when I hit out, old chap. One, two, three—here goes!"

With that he pushed the chop-fallen Collins from him, made a feint of punching his head as he reeled back, then sprang toward the spot where the Frenchwoman stood, and gave a finish to the adventure that was highly dramatic and decidedly theatrical. For "mademoiselle," seeing him approach her, struck a pose, threw out her arms, gathered him into them—to the exceeding enjoyment of the laughing throng—then both looked back and behaved as people do on the stage when "pursued," gesticulated extravagantly, and, rushing to the waiting motor, jumped into it.

"Many thanks, Bobby; many thanks, everybody!" sang out the red-headed man. "Let her go, chauffeur. The camera men will pick us up again at Whitehall, in a few minutes' time."

"Right you are, sir," responded the chauffeur gaily. Then "toot-toot" went the motor-horn as the gentleman in grey closed the door upon himself and his companion, and the vehicle, darting forward, sped down the Embankment in the exact direction whence the man himself had originally come, and, passing directly through that belated portion of the hurrying crowd to whom the end of the adventure was not yet known, flew on and—vanished.

And Collins, stooping to pick up the half-sovereign that had been thrown him, felt that after all it was a poor price to receive for all the jeers and gibes of the assembled onlookers.

"Smart capture, Bobby, wasn't it?" sang out a deriding voice that set the crowd jeering anew. "You'll git promoted, you will! See it in all the evenin' papers—oh, yus! 'Orrible hand-to-hand struggle with a desperado. Brave constable has 'arf a quid's worth out of an infuriated ruffin!' My hat! won't your missis be proud when you take her to see that bloomin' film?"

"Move on, now, move on!" said Collins, recovering his dignity, and asserting it with a vim. "Look here, cabby, I don't take it kind of you to laugh like that; they had you just as bad as they had me. Blow that Frenchy! She might have tipped me off before I made such an ass of myself. I don't say that I'd have done it so natural if I had known, but—Hullo! What's that? Blowed if it ain't that blessed whistle again, and another crowd a-pelting this way; and—no!—yes, by Jupiter!—a couple of Scotland Yard chaps with 'em. My hat! what do you suppose that means?"

He knew in the next moment. Panting and puffing, a crowd at their heels, and people from all sides stringing out from the pavement and trooping after them, the two "plain-clothes" men came racing through the grinning gathering and bore down on P.C. Collins.

"Hullo, Smathers, you in this, too?" began he, his feelings softened by the knowledge that other arms of the law would figure on that film with him at the Alhambra tonight. "Now, what are you after, you goat? That French lady, or the red-headed party in the grey suit?"

"Yes, yes, of course I am. You heard me signal you to head him off, didn't you?" replied Smathers, looking round and growing suddenly excited when he realized that Collins was empty-handed, and that the red-headed man was not there. "Heavens! you never let him get away, did you? You grabbed him, didn't you—eh?"

"Of course I grabbed him. Come out of it. What are you giving me, you josser?" said Collins with a wink and a grin. "Ain't you found out even yet, you silly? Why, it was only a faked-up thing—the taking of a kinematograph picture for the Alhambra. You and Petrie ought to have been here sooner and got your wages, you goats. I got half a quid for my share when I let him go."

Smathers and Petrie lifted up their voices in one despairing howl.

"When you what?" fairly yelled Smathers. "You fool! You don't mean to tell me that you let them take you in like that—those two? You don't mean to tell me that you had him—had him in your hands—and then let him go? You did? Oh! you seventy-seven kinds of a double-barrelled ass! Had him—think of it!—had him, and let him go! Did yourself out of a share in a reward of two hundred quid when you'd only to shut your hands and hold on to it!"

"Two hundred quid? Two hun—W-what are you talking about? Wasn't it true? Wasn't it a kinematograph picture, after all?"

"No, you fool, no!" howled Smathers, fairly dancing with despair. "Oh, you blithering idiot! You ninety-seven varieties of a fool! Do you know who you had in your hands? Do you know who you let go? It was that devil 'Forty Faces'—'The Vanishing Cracksman'—the man who calls himself 'Hamilton Cleek'; and the woman was his pal, his confederate, his blessed stool-pigeon—'Margot, the Queen of the Apache'; and she came over from Paris to help him in that clean scoop of Lady Dresmer's jewels last week!"

"Heavens!" gulped Collins, too far gone to say anything else, too deeply dejected to think of anything but that he had had the man for whom Scotland Yard had been groping for a year—the man over whom all England, all France, all Germany wondered—close shut in the grip of his hands and then had let him go. The biggest and boldest criminal the police had ever had to cope with, the almost supernatural genius of crime, who defied all systems, laughed at all laws, mocked at all the Vidocqs, and Dupins, and Sherlock Holmeses, whether amateur or professional, French or English, German or American, that ever had been or ever could be pitted against him, and who, for sheer devilry, for diabolical ingenuity and for colossal impudence, as well as for a nature-bestowed power that was simply amazing, had not his match in all the universe.

Who or what he really was, whence he came, whether he was English, Irish, French, German, Yankee, Canadian, Italian, or Dutchman, no man knew and no man might ever hope to know unless he himself chose to reveal it. In his many encounters with the police he had assumed the speech, the characteristics, and, indeed, the facial attributes of each in turn, and assumed them with an ease and a perfection that were simply marvellous, and had gained for him the sobriquet of "Forty Faces" among the police, and of "The Vanishing Cracksman" among the scribes and reporters of newspaperdom. That he came, in time, to possess another name than these was due to his own whim and caprice, his own bald, unblushing impudence; for, of a sudden, whilst London was in a fever of excitement and all the newspapers up in arms over one of the most daring and successful coups, he chose to write boldly to both editors and police complaining that the title given him by each was both vulgar and cheap.

"You would not think of calling Paganini a 'fiddler,'" he wrote; "why, then, should you degrade me with the coarse term of 'cracksman'? I claim to be as much an artist in my profession as Paganini was in his, and I claim also a like courtesy from you. So, then, if in the future it becomes necessary to allude to me—and I fear it often will—I shall be obliged if you do so as 'The Man Who Calls Himself Hamilton Cleek.' In return for that courtesy, gentlemen, I promise to alter my mode of procedure, to turn over a new leaf, as it were, to give you at all times hereafter distinct information, in advance, of such places as I elect for the field of my operations, and of the time when I shall pay my respects to them, and, on the morning after each such visit, to bestow some small portion of the loot upon Scotland Yard as a souvenir of the event."

And to that remarkable programme he rigidly adhered from that time forth—always giving the police twelve hours' notice, always evading their traps and snares, always carrying out his plans in spite of them, and always, on the morning after, sending some trinket or trifle to Superintendent Narkom at Scotland Yard, in a little pink cardboard box, tied up with rose-coloured ribbon, and marked "With the compliments of The Man Who Calls Himself Hamilton Cleek."

The detectives of the United Kingdom, the detectives of the Continent, the detectives of America—each and all had measured swords with him, tried wits with him, spread snares and laid traps for him, and each and all had retired from the field vanquished.

And this was the man that he—Police Constable Samuel James Collins—had actually had in his hands; nay, in his very arms, and then had given up for half a sovereign and let go!

"Oh, so help me! You make my head swim, Smathers, that you do!" he managed to say at last. "I had him—I had the Vanishing Cracksman—in my blessed paws—and then went and let that French hussy—But look here; I say, now, how do you know it was him? Nobody can go by his looks; so how do you know?"

"Know, you footler!" growled Smathers, disgustedly. "Why shouldn't I know when I've been after him ever since he left Scotland Yard half an hour ago?"

"Left what? My hat! You ain't a-going to tell me that he's been there? When? Why? What for?"

"To leave one of his blessed notices, the daredevil. What a detective he'd a made, wouldn't he, if he'd only a-turned his attention that way, and been on the side of the law instead of against it? He walked in bold as brass, sat down, and talked with the superintendent over some cock-and-bull yarn about a 'Black Hand' letter that he said had been sent to him, and asked if he couldn't have police protection whilst he was in town. It wasn't until after he'd left that the super he sees a note on the chair where the blighter had been sitting, and when he opened it, there it was in black and white, something like this:

"'The list of presents that have been sent for the wedding tomorrow of Sir Horace Wyvern's eldest daughter make interesting reading, particularly that part which describes the jewels sent—no doubt as a tribute to her father's position as the greatest brain specialist in the world—from the Austrian Court and the Continental principalities. The care of such gems is too great a responsibility for the bride. I propose, therefore, to relieve her of it tonight, and to send you the customary souvenir of the event tomorrow morning. Yours faithfully,

"'The Man Who Calls Himself Hamilton Cleek.'

"That's how I know, dash you! Superintendent sent me out after him, hot foot; and after a bit I picked him up in the Strand, toddling along with that French hussy as cool as you please. But, blow him! he must have eyes all round his head, for he saw me just as soon as I saw him, and he and Frenchy separated like a shot. She hopped into a taxi and flew off in one direction; he dived into a crowd and bolted in another, and before you could say Jack Robinson he was doubling and twisting, jumping into cabs and jumping out again—all to gain time, of course, for the woman to do what he'd put her up to doing—and leading me the devil's own chase through the devil's own tangle till he was ready to bunk for the Embankment. And you let him go, you blooming footler! Had him and let him go, and chucked away a third of £200 for the price of half a quid!"

And long after Smathers and Petrie had left him, and the wondering crowd had dispersed, and point duty at "Dead Man's Corner" was just point duty again and nothing more, P.C. Collins stood there, chewing the cud of bitter reflection over those words, and trying to reckon up just how many pounds and how much glory had been lost to him.

II

"But, damme, sir, the thing's an outrage! I don't mince my words, Mr. Narkom—I say plump and plain the thing's an outrage, a disgrace to the police, an indignity upon the community at large; and for Scotland Yard to permit itself to be defied, bamboozled, mocked at in this appalling fashion by a paltry burglar—"

"Uncle, dear, pray don't excite yourself in

this manner. I am quite sure that if Mr. Narkom could prevent the things—"

"Hold your tongue, Ailsa—I will not be interfered with! It's time that somebody spoke out plainly and let this establishment know what the public has a right to expect of it. What do I pay my rates and taxes for—and devilish high ones they are, too, b'gad—if it's not to maintain law and order and the proper protection of property? And to have the whole blessed country terrorised, the police defied, and people's houses invaded with impunity by a gutter-bred brute of a cracksman is nothing short of a scandal and a shame! Call this sort of tomfoolery being protected by the police? God bless my soul! one might as well be in charge of a parcel of doddering old women and be done with it!"

It was an hour and a half after that exciting affair at "Dead Man's Corner." The scene was Superintendent Narkom's private room at headquarters, the dramatis personae, Mr. Maverick Narkom himself, Sir Horace Wyvern, and Miss Ailsa Lorne, his niece, a slight, fair-haired, extremely attractive girl of twenty, the only and orphaned daughter of a much-loved sister, who, up till a year ago, had known nothing more exciting in the way of "life" than that which is to be found in a small village in Suffolk, and falls to the lot of an underpaid vicar's only child. A railway accident had suddenly deprived her of both parents, throwing her wholly upon her own resources, without a penny in the world. Sir Horace had gracefully come to the rescue and given her a home and a refuge, being doubly repaid for it by the affection and care she gave him and the manner in which she assumed control of a household which hitherto had been left wholly to the attention of servants, Lady Wyvern having long been dead, and her two daughters of that type which devotes itself entirely to the pleasures of society and the demands of the world. A regular pepper-box of a man—testy, short-tempered, exacting—Sir Horace had flown headlong to Superintendent Narkom's office as soon as that gentleman's note, telling him of the Vanishing Cracksman's latest threat, had been delivered, and, on Miss Lorne's advice, had withheld all news of it from the members of his household and brought her with him.

"I tell you that Scotland Yard must do something—must! must! must!" stormed he as Narkom, resenting that stigma upon the institution, puckered up his lips and looked savage. "That fellow has always kept his word—always, in spite of your precious band of muffs—and if you let him keep it this time, when there's upwards of £40,000 worth of jewels in the house, it will be nothing less than a national disgrace, and you and your wretched collection of bunglers will be covered with deserved ridicule."

Narkom swung round, smarting under these continued taunts, these "flings" at the efficiency of his prided department, his nostrils dilated, his temper strained to the breaking-point.

"Well, he won't keep it this time—I promise you that!" he rapped out sharply. "Sooner or later every criminal, no matter how clever, meets his Waterloo—and this shall be his! I'll take this affair in hand myself, Sir Horace. I'll not only send the pick of my men to guard the jewels, but I'll go with them; and if that fellow crosses the threshold of Wyvern House tonight, by the Lord, I'll have him. He will have to be the devil himself to get away from me! Miss Lorne"—recollecting himself and bowing apologetically—"I ask your pardon for this strong language—my temper got the better of my manners."

"It does not matter, Mr. Narkom, so that you preserve my cousin's wedding-gifts from that appalling man," she answered with a gentle inclination of the head and with a smile that made the superintendent think she must certainly be the most beautiful creature in all the world, it so irradiated her face and added to the magic of her glorious eyes. "It does not matter what you say, what you do, so long as you accomplish that."

"And I will accomplish it—as I'm a living man, I will! You may go home feeling assured of that. Look for my men some time before dusk, Sir Horace—I will arrive later. They will come in one at a time. See that they are admitted by the area door, and that, once in, not one of them leaves the house again before I put in an appearance. I'll look them over when I arrive to be sure that there's no wolf in sheep's clothing amongst them. With a fellow like that—a diabolical rascal with a diabolical gift for impersonation—one can't be too careful. Meantime, it is just as well not to have confided this news to your daughters, who, naturally, would be nervous and upset; but I assume that you have taken some one of the servants into your confidence in order that nobody may pass them and enter the house under any pretext whatsoever?"

"No, I have not. Miss Lorne advised against it, and, as I am always guided by her, I said nothing of the matter to anybody."

"Was that wrong, do you think, Mr. Narkom?" queried Ailsa anxiously. "I feared that if they knew they might lose their heads, and that my cousins, who are intensely nervous and highly emotional, might hear of it, and add to our difficulties by becoming hysterical and demanding our attention at a time when we ought to be giving every moment to watching for the possible arrival of that man. And as he has always lived up to the strict letter of his dreadful promises heretofore, I knew that he was not to be expected before nightfall. Besides, the jewels are locked up in the safe in Sir Horace's consulting-room, and his assistant, Mr. Merfroy, has promised not to leave it for one instant before we return."

"Oh, well, that's all right, then. I dare say there is very little likelihood of our man getting in whilst you and Sir Horace are here, and taking such a risk as stopping in the house until nightfall to begin his operations. Still, it was hardly wise, and I should advise hurrying back as fast as possible and taking at least one servant—the one you feel least likely to lose his head—into your confidence, Sir Horace, and putting him on the watch for my men. Otherwise, keep the matter as quiet as you have done, and look for me about nine o'clock. And rely upon this as a certainty: the Vanishing Cracksman will never get away with even one of those jewels if he enters that house tonight, and never get out of it unshackled!"

With that, he suavely bowed his visitors out and rang up the pick of his men without an instant's delay.

Promptly at nine o'clock he arrived, as he had promised, at Wyvern House, and was shown into Sir Horace's consulting-room, where Sir Horace himself and Miss Lorne were awaiting him, and keeping close watch before the locked door of a communicating apartment in which sat the six men who had preceded him. He went in and put them all and severally through a rigid examination—pulling their hair and beards, rubbing their faces with a clean handkerchief in quest of any trace of "make-up" or disguise of any sort, examining their badges and the marks on the handcuffs they carried with them to make sure that they bore the sign which he himself had scratched upon them in the privacy of his own room a couple of hours ago.

"No mistake about this lot," he announced, with a smile. "Has anybody else entered or attempted to enter the house?"

"Not a soul," replied Miss Lorne. "I didn't trust anybody to do the watching, Mr. Narkom—I watched myself."

"Good. Where are the jewels? In that safe?"

"No," replied Sir Horace. "They are to be exhibited in the picture-gallery for the benefit of the guests at the wedding breakfast tomorrow, and as Miss Wyvern wished to superintend the arrangement of them herself, and there would be no time for that in the morning, she and her sister are in there laying them out at this moment. As I could not prevent that without telling them what we have to dread, I did not protest against it; but if you think it will be safer to return them to the safe after my daughters have gone to bed, Mr. Narkom—"

"Not at all necessary. If our man gets in, their lying there in full view like that will prove a tempting bait, and—well, he'll find there's a hook behind it. I shall be there waiting for him. Now go and join the ladies, you and Miss Lorne, and act as though nothing out of the common was in the wind. My men and I will stop here, and you had better put out the light and lock us in, so that there may be no danger of anybody finding out that we are here. No doubt Miss Wyvern and her sister will go to bed earlier than usual on this particular occasion. Let them do so. Send the servants to bed, too. You and Miss Lorne go to your beds at the same time as the others—or, at least, let them think that you have done so; then come down and let us out."

To this Sir Horace assented, and, taking Miss Lorne with him, went at once to the picture-gallery and joined his daughters, with whom they remained until eleven o'clock. Promptly at that hour, however, the house was locked up, the bride-elect and her sister went to bed—the servants having already gone to theirs—and stillness settled down over the darkened house. At the end of a dozen minutes, however, it was faintly disturbed by the sound of slippered feet coming along the passage outside the consulting-room, then a key slipped into the lock, the door was opened, the light switched on, and Sir Horace and Miss Lorne appeared before the eager watchers.

"Now, then, lively, my men—look sharp!" whispered Narkom. "A man to each window and each staircase, so that nobody may go up or down or in or out without dropping into the arms of one of you. Confine your attention to this particular floor, and if you hear anybody coming, lay low until he's within reach, and you can drop on him before he bolts. Is this the door of the picture-gallery, Sir Horace?"

"Yes," answered Sir Horace, as he fitted a key to the lock. "But surely you will need more men than you have brought, Mr. Narkom, if it is your intention to guard every window individually, for there are four to this room—see!"

With that he swung open the door, switched on the electric light, and Narkom fairly blinked at the dazzling sight that confronted him. Three long tables, laden with crystal and silver, cut glass and jewels, and running the full length of the room, flashed and scintillated under the glare of the electric bulbs which encircled the cornice of the gallery, and clustered in luminous splendour in the crystal and frosted silver of a huge central chandelier, and spread out on the middle one of these—a dazzle of splintered rainbows, a very plain of living light—lay caskets and cases, boxes and trays, containing those royal gifts of which the newspapers had made so much and the Vanishing Cracksman had sworn to make so few.

Mr. Narkom went over and stood beside the glittering mass, resting his hand against the table and feasting his eyes upon all that opulent splendour.

"God bless my soul! it's superb, it's amazing," he commented. "No wonder the fellow is willing to take risks for a prize like this. You are a splendid temptation; a gorgeous bait, you beauties; but the fish that snaps at you will find that there's a nasty hook underneath in the shape of Maverick Narkom. Never mind the many windows, Sir Horace. Let him come in by them, if that's his plan. I'll never leave these things for one instant between now and the morning. Good night, Miss Lorne. Go to bed and to sleep—you do the same, Sir Horace. My lay is here!"

With that he stooped and, lifting the long drapery which covered the table and swept down in heavy folds to the floor, crept out of sight under it, and let it drop back into place again.

"Switch off the light and go," he called to them in a low-sunk voice. "Don't worry yourselves, either of you. Go to bed, and to sleep if you can."

"As if we could," answered Miss Lorne agitatedly. "I shan't be able to close an eyelid. I'll try, of course, but I know I shall not succeed. Come, uncle, come! Oh, do be careful, Mr. Narkom; and if that horrible man does come—"

"I'll have him, so help me God!" he vowed. "Switch off the light, and shut the door as you go out. This is 'Forty Faces'' Waterloo at last."

And in another moment the light snicked out, the door closed, and he was alone in the silent room.

For ten or a dozen minutes not even the bare suggestion of a noise disturbed the absolute stillness; then of a sudden, his trained ear caught a faint sound that made him suck in his breath and rise on his elbow, the better to listen—a sound which came, not without the house, but from within, from the dark hall where he had stationed his men, to be exact. As he listened he was conscious that some living creature had approached the door, touched the handle, and by the swift, low rustle and the sound of hard breathing, that it had been pounced upon and seized. He scrambled out from beneath the table, snicked on the light, whirled open the door, and was in time to hear the irritable voice of Sir Horace say, testily: "Don't make an ass of yourself by your over-zealousness. I've only come down to have a word with Mr. Narkom," and to see him standing on the threshold, grotesque in a baggy suit of striped pyjamas, with one wrist enclosed as in a steel band by the gripped fingers of Petrie.

"Why didn't you say it was you, sir?" exclaimed that crestfallen individual, as the flashing light made manifest his mistake. "When I heard you first, and see you come up out of that back passage, I made sure it was him; and if you'd a struggled, I'd have bashed your head as sure as eggs."

"Thank you for nothing," he responded testily. "You might have remembered, however, that the man's first got to get into the place before he can come downstairs. Mr. Narkom," turning to the superintendent, "I was just getting into bed when I thought of something I'd neglected to tell you; and as my niece is sitting in her room with the door open, and I wasn't anxious to parade myself before her in my night clothes, I came down by the back staircase. I don't know how in the world I came to overlook it, but I think you ought to know that there's a way of getting into the picture gallery without using either the windows or the stairs, and that way ought to be both searched and guarded."

"Where is it? What is it? Why in the world didn't you tell me in the first place?" exclaimed Narkom irritably, as he glanced round the place searchingly. "Is it a panel? a secret door? or what? This is an old house, and old houses are sometimes a very nest of such things."

"Happily, this one isn't. It's a modern innovation, not an ancient relic, that offers the means of entrance in this case. A Yankee occupied this house before I bought it from him—one of those blessed shivery individuals his country breeds, who can't stand a breath of cold air indoors after the passing of the autumn. The wretched man put one of those wretched American inflictions, a hot-air furnace, in the cellar, with huge pipes running to every room in the house—great tin monstrosities bigger round than a man's body, ending in openings in the wall, with what they call 'registers,' to let the heat in, or shut it out as they please. I didn't have the wretched contrivance removed or those blessed 'registers' plastered up. I simply had them papered over when the rooms were done up (there's one over there near that settee), and if a man got into this house, he could get into that furnace thing and hide in one of those flues until he got ready to crawl up it as easily as not. It struck me that perhaps it would be as well for you to examine that furnace and those flues before matters go any further."

"Of course it would. Great Scott! Sir Horace, why didn't you think to tell me of this thing before?" said Narkom, excitedly. "The fellow may be in it at this minute. Come, show me the wretched thing."

"It's below—in the cellar. We shall have to go down the kitchen stairs, and I haven't a light."

"Here's one," said Petrie, unhitching a bull's-eye from his belt and putting it into Narkom's hand. "Better go with Sir Horace at once, sir. Leave the door of the gallery open and the light on. Fish and me will stand guard over the stuff till you come back, so in case the man is in one of them flues and tries to bolt out at this end, we can nab him before he can get to the windows."

"A good idea," commented Narkom. "Come on, Sir Horace. Is this the way?"

"Yes, but you'll have to tread carefully, and mind you don't fall over anything. A good deal of my paraphernalia—bottles, retorts, and the like—is stored in the little recess at the foot of the staircase, and my assistant is careless and leaves things lying about."

Evidently the caution was necessary, for a minute or so after they had passed on and disappeared behind the door leading to the kitchen stairway, Petrie and his colleagues heard a sound as of something being overturned and smashed, and laughed softly to themselves. Evidently, too, the danger of the furnace had been grossly exaggerated by Sir Horace, for when, a few minutes later, the door opened and closed, and Narkom's men, glancing toward it, saw the figure of their chief reappear, it was plain that he was in no good temper, since his features were knotted up into a scowl, and he swore audibly as he snapped the shutter over the bull's-eye and handed it back to Petrie.

"Nothing worth looking into, superintendent?"

"No—not a thing!" he replied. "The silly old josser! pulling me down there amongst the coals and rubbish for an insane idea like that! Why, the flues wouldn't admit the passage of a child; and even then, there's a bend—an abrupt 'elbow'—that nothing but a cat could crawl up. And that's a man who's an authority on the human brain! I sent the old silly back to bed by the way he came, and if—"

There he stopped, stopped short, and sucked in his breath with a sharp, wheezing sound. For, of a sudden, a swift pattering footfall and a glimmer of moving light had sprung into being and drawn his eyes upward; and there, overhead, was Miss Lorne coming down the stairs from the upper floor in a state of nervous excitement, and with a bedroom candle in her shaking hand, a loose gown flung on over her nightdress, and her hair streaming over her shoulders in glorious disarray.

He stood and looked at her, with ever-quickening breath, with ever-widening eyes, as though the beauty of her had wakened some dormant sense whose existence he had never suspected; as though, until now, he had never known how fair it was possible for a woman to be, how fair, how lovable, how much to be desired; and whilst he was so looking she reached the foot of the staircase and came pantingly toward him.

"Oh, Mr. Narkom, what was it—that noise I heard?" she said in a tone of deepest agitation. "It sounded like a struggle—like the noise of something breaking—and I dressed as hastily as I could and came down. Did he come? Has he been here? Have you caught him? Oh! why don't you answer me, instead of staring at me like this? Can't you see how nervous, how frightened, I am? Dear Heaven! will no one tell me what has happened?"

"Nothing has happened, miss," answered Petrie, catching her eye as she flashed round on him. "You'd better go back to bed. Nobody's been here but Sir Horace. The noise you heard was me a-grabbing of him, and he and Mr. Narkom a-tumbling over something as they went down to look at the furnace."

"Furnace? What furnace? What are you talking about?" she cried agitatedly. "What do you mean by saying that Sir Horace came down?"

"Only what the superintendent himself will tell you, miss, if you ask him. Sir Horace came downstairs in his pyjamas a few minutes ago to say as he'd recollected about the flues of the furnace in the cellar being big enough to hold a man, and then him and Mr. Narkom went below to have a look at it."

She gave a sharp and sudden cry, and her face went as pale as a dead face.

"Sir Horace came down?" she repeated, moving back a step and leaning heavily against the bannister. "Sir Horace came down to look at the furnace? We have no furnace!"

"What!"

"We have no furnace, I tell you, and Sir Horace did not come down. He is up there still. I know—I know, I tell you—because I feared for his safety, and when he went to his room I locked him in!"

"Superintendent!" The word was voiced by every man present, and six pairs of eyes turned toward Narkom with a look of despairing comprehension.

"Get to the cellar. Head the man off! It's

he—the Cracksman!" he shouted out. "Find him! Get him! Nab him, if you have to turn the house upside down!"

They needed no second bidding, for each man grasped the situation instantly, and in a twinkling there was a veritable pandemonium. Shouting and scrambling like a band of madmen, they lurched to the door, whirled it open, and went flying down the staircase to the kitchen and so to a discovery which none might have foreseen. For, almost as they entered they saw lying on the floor a suit of striped pyjamas, and close to it, gagged, bound, helpless, trussed up like a goose that was ready for the oven, gyves on his wrists, gyves on his ankles, their chief, their superintendent, Mr. Maverick Narkom, in a state of collapse, and with all his outer clothing gone!

"After him! After that devil, and a thousand pounds to the man that gets him!" he managed to gasp as they rushed to him and ripped loose the gag. "He was here when we came! He has been in the house for hours. Get him! get him! get him!"

They surged from the room and up the stairs like a pack of stampeded animals; they raced through the hall and bore down on the picture-gallery in a body, and, whirling open the now closed door, went tumbling headlong in.

The light was still burning. At the far end of the room a window was wide open, and the curtains of it fluttered in the wind. A collection of empty cases and caskets lay on the middle table, but man and jewels were alike gone! Once again the Vanishing Cracksman had lived up to his promise, up to his reputation, up to the very letter of his name, and for all Mr. Maverick Narkom's care and shrewdness, "Forty Faces" had "turned the trick" and Scotland Yard was "done"!

III

Through all the night its best men sought him, its dragnets fished for him, its tentacles groped into every hole and corner of London in quest of him, but sought and fished and groped in vain. They might as well have hoped to find last summer's partridges or last winter's snow as any trace of him. He had vanished as mysteriously as he had appeared, and no royal jewels graced the display of Miss Wyvern's wedding gifts on the morrow.

But it was fruitful of other "gifts," fruitful of an even greater surprise, that "morrow." For the first time since the day he had given his promise, no "souvenir" from "The Man Who Called Himself Hamilton Cleek," no part of last night's loot came to Scotland Yard; and it was while the evening papers were making screaming "copy" and glaring headlines out of this that the surprise in question came to pass.

Miss Wyvern's wedding was over, the day and the bride had gone, and it was half-past ten at night, when Sir Horace, answering a hurry call from headquarters, drove post haste to Superintendent Narkom's private room, and passing in under a red and green lamp which burned over the doorway, entered and met that "surprise."

Maverick Narkom was there alone, standing beside his desk, with the curtains of his window drawn and pinned together, and at his elbow an unlighted lamp of violet-coloured glass, standing and looking thoughtfully down at something which lay before him. He turned as his visitor entered and made an open-handed gesture toward it.

"Look here," he said laconically, "what do you think of this?"

Sir Horace moved forward and looked; then stopped and gave a sort of wondering cry. The electric bulbs overhead struck a glare of light down on the surface of the desk, and there, spread out on the shining oak, lay a part of the royal jewels that had been stolen from Wyvern House last night.

"Narkom! You got him, then—got him after all?"

"No, I did not get him. I doubt if any man could, if he chose not to be found," said Narkom bitterly. "I did not recover these jewels by any act of my own. He sent them to me; gave them up voluntarily."

"Gave them up? After he had risked so much to get them? God bless my soul, what a man! Why, there must be quite half here of what he took."

"There is half—an even half. He sent them tonight, and with them this letter. Look at it, and you will understand why I sent for you and asked you to come alone."

"'There's some good in even the devil, I suppose, if one but knows how to reach it and stir it up,'" Sir Horace read. "'I have lived a life of crime from my very boyhood because I couldn't help it, because it appealed to me, because I glory in risks and revel in dangers. I never knew where it would lead me—I never thought, never cared—but I looked into the gateway of heaven last night, and I can't go down the path to hell any longer. Here is an even half of Miss Wyvern's jewels. If you and her father would have me hand over the other half to you, and would have "The Vanishing Cracksman" disappear forever, and a useless life converted into a useful one, you have only to say so to make it an accomplished thing. All I ask in return is your word of honour (to be given to me by signal) that you will send for Sir Horace Wyvern to be at your office at eleven o'clock tonight, and that you and he will grant me a private interview unknown to any other living being. A red and green lantern hung over the doorway leading to your office will be the signal that you agree, and a violet light in your window will be the pledge of Sir Horace Wyvern. When these two signals, these two pledges, are given, I shall come in and hand over the remainder of the jewels, and you will have looked for the first time in your life upon the real face of "The Man Who Calls Himself Hamilton Cleek."'"

"God bless my soul! What an amazing creature—what an astounding request!" exclaimed Sir Horace, as he laid the letter down. "Willing to give up £20,000 worth of jewels for the mere sake of a private interview! What on earth can be his object? And why should he include me?"

"I don't know," said Narkom in reply. "It's worth something, at all events, to be rid of 'The Vanishing Cracksman' for good and all; and he says that it rests with us to do that. It's close to eleven now. Shall we give him the pledge he asks, Sir Horace? My signal is already hung out; shall we agree to the conditions and give him yours?"

"Yes, yes, by all means," Sir Horace made answer. And lighting the violet lamp, Narkom flicked open the pinned curtains and set it in the window.

For ten minutes nothing came of it, and the two men, talking in whispers while they waited, began to grow nervous. Then somewhere in the distance a clock started striking eleven, and without so much as a warning sound, the door flashed open, flashed shut again, a voice that was undeniably the voice of breeding and refinement said quietly: "Gentlemen, my compliments. Here are the diamonds and here am I!" and the figure of a man, faultlessly dressed, faultlessly mannered, with the slim-loined form, the slim-walled nose, and the clear-cut features of the born aristocrat, stood in the room.

His age might lie anywhere between twenty-five and thirty-five, his eyes were straight-looking and clear, his fresh, clean-shaven face was undeniably handsome, and, whatever his origin, whatever his history, there was something about him, in look, in speech, in bearing, that mutely stood sponsor for the thing called "birth."

"God bless my soul!" exclaimed Sir Horace, amazed and appalled to find the reality so widely different from the image he had drawn. "What monstrous juggle is this? Why, man alive, you're a gentleman! Who are you? What's driven you to a dog's life like this?"

"A natural bent, perhaps; a supernatural gift, certainly, Sir Horace," he made reply. "Look here! Could any man resist the temptation to use it when he was endowed by Nature with the power to do this?" His features seemed to writhe and knot and assume in as many moments a dozen different aspects. "I've had the knack of doing that since the hour I could breathe. Could any man 'go straight' with a fateful gift like that if the laws of Nature said that he should not?"

"And do they say that?"

"That's what I want you to tell me—that's why I have requested this interview. I want you to examine me, Sir Horace, to put me through those tests you use to determine the state of mind of the mentally fit and mentally unfit; I want to know if it is my fault that I am what I am, and if it is myself I have to fight in future, or the devil that lives within me. I'm tired of wallowing in the mire. A woman's eyes have lit the way to heaven for me. I want to climb up to her, to win her, to be worthy of her, and to stand beside her in the light."

"Her? What 'her'?"

"That's my business, Mr. Narkom, and I'll take no man into my confidence regarding that."

"Yes, my friend, but 'Margot'—how about her?"

"I'm done with her! We broke last night, when I returned and she learned——never mind what she learned! I'm done with her—done with the lot of them. My life is changed forever."

"In the name of Heaven, man, who and what are you?"

"Cleek—just Cleek; let it go at that," he made reply. "Whether it's my name or not is no man's business; who I am, what I am, whence I came, is no man's business either. Cleek will do—Cleek of the Forty Faces. Never mind the past; my fight is with the future, and so——examine me, Sir Horace, and let me know if I or Fate's to blame for what I am."

Sir Horace did.

"Absolutely Fate," he said, when, after a long examination, the man put the question to him again. "It is the criminal brain fully developed, horribly pronounced. God help you, my poor fellow; but a man simply could not be other than a thief and a criminal with an organ like that. There's no hope for you to escape your natural bent except by death. You can't be honest. You can't rise—you never will rise; it's useless to fight against it!"

"I will fight against it! I will rise! I will! I will! I will!" he cried out vehemently. "There is a way to put such craft and cunning to account; a way to fight the devil with his own weapons and crush him under the weight of his own gifts, and that way I'll take!

"Mr. Narkom"—he whirled and walked toward the superintendent, his hand outstretched, his eager face aglow—"Mr. Narkom, help me! Take me under your wing. Give me a start—give me a chance—give me a lift on the way up!"

"Good heaven, man, you—you don't mean——?"

"I do—I do. So help me heaven, I do. All my life I've fought against the law—now let me switch over and fight with it. I'm tired of being Cleek, the thief; Cleek, the burglar. Make me Cleek, the detective, and let us work together, hand in hand, for a common cause and for the public good. Will you, Mr. Narkom? Will you?"

"Will I? Won't I!" said Narkom, springing forward and gripping his hand. "Jove! what a detective you will make. Bully boy! Bully boy!"

"It's a compact, then?"

"It's a compact—Cleek."

"Thank you," he said in a choked voice. "You've given me my chance; now watch me live up to it. The Vanishing Cracksman has vanished forever, Mr. Narkom, and it's Cleek, the detective—Cleek of the Forty Faces from this time on. Now, give me your riddles—I'll solve them one by one."

Rogue: Arsène Lupin

The Mysterious Railway Passenger

MAURICE LEBLANC

NO CHARACTER IN THE WORLD of French mystery fiction is as beloved as the fun-loving criminal Arsène Lupin, created by Maurice Marie Émile Leblanc (1864–1941) for a new magazine in 1905; the stories were collected in book form two years later. They immediately became wildly popular, as successful in France as Sherlock Holmes stories were in England, and Leblanc achieved wealth and worldwide fame and was made a member of the French Legion of Honor. Although the tales are fast-paced, the amount and degree of action borders on the burlesque, with situations and coincidences often too far-fetched to be taken seriously.

Lupin, known as the Prince of Thieves, is a street urchin type who thumbs his nose—literally—at the police. He steals for the thrill of it more than for personal gain or noble motives. He is such a master of disguise that he was able to take the identity of the chief of the Sûreté and direct official investigations into his own activities. After several years as a successful criminal, Lupin decides to turn to the side of the law for personal reasons and assists the police, usually without their knowledge. He is not, however, a first-rate crime-fighter because he cannot resist jokes, women, and the derring-do of his freelance life as a crook.

"The Mysterious Railway Passenger" was first published in *Arsène Lupin, Gentleman-Cambrioleur* in Paris in 1907. The first English-language edition was *The Exploits of Arsène Lupin* (New York, Harper, 1907); it was reissued as *The Seven of Hearts* (New York, Cassell, 1908) and as *The Extraordinary Adventures of Arsène Lupin, Gentleman Burglar* (Chicago, Donohue, 1910). The book served as the basis for two silent films, *Lupin the Gentleman Burglar* (1914) and *The Gentleman Burglar* (1915).

THE MYSTERIOUS RAILWAY PASSENGER

Maurice Leblanc

I HAD SENT my motor-car to Rouen by road on the previous day I was to meet it by train, and go on to some friends, who have a house on the Seine.

A few minutes before we left Paris my compartment was invaded by seven gentlemen, five of whom were smoking. Short though the journey by the fast train be, I did not relish the prospect of taking it in such company, the more so as the old-fashioned carriage had no corridor. I therefore collected my overcoat, my newspapers, and my railway guide, and sought refuge in one of the neighboring compartments.

It was occupied by a lady. At the sight of me, she made a movement of vexation which did not escape my notice, and leaned towards a gentleman standing on the foot-board—her husband, no doubt, who had come to see her off. The gentleman took stock of me, and the examination seemed to conclude to my advantage; for he whispered to his wife and smiled, giving her the look with which we reassure a frightened child. She smiled in her turn, and cast a friendly glance in my direction, as though she suddenly realized that I was one of those well-bred men with whom a woman can remain locked up for an hour or two in a little box six feet square without having anything to fear.

Her husband said to her:

"You must not mind, darling; but I have an important appointment, and I must not wait."

He kissed her affectionately, and went away. His wife blew him some discreet little kisses through the window, and waved her handkerchief.

Then the guard's whistle sounded, and the train started.

At that moment, and in spite of the warning shouts of the railway officials, the door opened, and a man burst into our carriage. My travelling companion, who was standing up and arranging her things in the rack, uttered a cry of terror, and dropped down upon the seat.

I am no coward—far from it; but I confess that these sudden incursions at the last minute are always annoying. They seem so ambiguous, so unnatural. There must be something behind them, else . . .

The appearance of the new-comer, however, and his bearing were such as to correct the bad impression produced by the manner of his entrance. He was neatly, almost smartly, dressed; his tie was in good taste, his gloves clean; he had a powerful face. . . . But, speaking of his face, where on earth had I seen it before? For I had seen it: of that there was no possible doubt; or at least, to be accurate, I found within myself that sort of recollection which is left by the sight of an oft-seen portrait of which one has never beheld the original. And at the same time I felt the uselessness of any effort of memory that I might exert, so inconsistent and vague was that recollection.

But when my eyes reverted to the lady I sat astounded at the pallor and disorder of her features. She was staring at her neighbor—he was seated on the same side of the carriage—with an expression of genuine affright, and I saw one of her hands steal trembling towards a little travelling-bag that lay on the cushion a few inches from her lap. She ended by taking hold of it, and nervously drew it to her.

Our eyes met, and I read in hers so great an amount of uneasiness and anxiety that I could not help saying:

"I hope you are not unwell, madame. . . . Would you like me to open the window?"

She made no reply, but, with a timid gesture, called my attention to the individual beside her. I smiled as her husband had done, shrugged my shoulders, and explained to her by signs that she had nothing to fear, that I was there, and that, besides, the gentleman in question seemed quite harmless.

Just then he turned towards us, contemplated us, one after the other, from head to foot, and then huddled himself into his corner, and made no further movement.

A silence ensued; but the lady, as though she had summoned up all her energies to perform an act of despair, said to me, in a hardly audible voice:

"You know he is in our train."

"Who?"

"Why, he . . . he himself . . . I assure you."

"Whom do you mean?"

"Arsène Lupin!"

She had not removed her eyes from the passenger, and it was at him rather than at me that she flung the syllables of that alarming name.

He pulled his hat down upon his nose. Was this to conceal his agitation, or was he merely preparing to go to sleep?

I objected.

"Arsène Lupin was sentenced yesterday, in his absence, to twenty years' penal servitude. It is not likely that he would commit the imprudence of showing himself in public to-day. Besides, the newspapers have discovered that he has been spending the winter in Turkey ever since his famous escape from the Sante."

"He is in this train," repeated the lady, with the ever more marked intention of being overheard by our companion. "My husband is a deputy prison-governor, and the station-inspector himself told us that they were looking for Arsène Lupin."

"That is no reason why . . ."

"He was seen at the booking-office. He took a ticket for Rouen."

"It would have been easy to lay hands upon him."

"He disappeared. The ticket-collector at the door of the waiting-room did not see him; but they thought that he must have gone round by the suburban platforms and stepped into the express that leaves ten minutes after us."

"In that case, they will have caught him there."

"And supposing that, at the last moment, he jumped out of that express and entered this, our own train . . . as he probably . . . as he most certainly did?"

"In that case they will catch him here; for the porters and the police cannot have failed to see him going from one train to the other, and, when we reach Rouen, they will net him finely."

"Him? Never! He will find some means of escaping again."

"In that case I wish him a good journey."

"But think of all that he may do in the mean time!"

"What?"

"How can I tell? One must be prepared for anything."

She was greatly agitated; and, in point of fact, the situation, to a certain degree, warranted her nervous state of excitement. Almost in spite of myself, I said:

"There are such things as curious coincidences, it is true. . . . But calm yourself. Admitting that Arsène Lupin is in one of these carriages, he is sure to keep quiet, and, rather than bring fresh trouble upon himself, he will have no other idea than that of avoiding the danger that threatens him."

My words failed to reassure her. However she said no more, fearing, no doubt, lest I should think her troublesome.

As for myself, I opened my newspapers and read the reports of Arsène Lupin's trial. They contained nothing that was not already known, and they interested me but slightly. Moreover, I was tired, I had had a poor night, I felt my eye-lids growing heavy, and my head began to nod.

"But surely, sir, you are not going to sleep?"

The lady snatched my paper from my hands, and looked at me with indignation.

"Certainly not," I replied. "I have no wish to."

"It would be most imprudent," she said.

"Most," I repeated.

And I struggled hard, fixing my eyes on the landscape, on the clouds that streaked the sky. And soon all this became confused in space, the image of the excited lady and the drowsy man was obliterated in my mind, and I was filled with the great, deep silence of sleep.

It was soon made agreeable by light and incoherent dreams, in which a being who played the part and bore the name of Arsène Lupin occupied a certain place. He turned and shifted on the horizon, his back laden with valuables, clambering over walls and stripping country-houses of their contents.

But the outline of this being, who had ceased to be Arsène Lupin, grew more distinct. He came towards me, grew bigger and bigger, leaped into the carriage with incredible agility, and fell full upon my chest.

A sharp pain . . . a piercing scream . . . I awoke. The man, my fellow-traveller, with one knee on my chest, was clutching my throat.

I saw this very dimly, for my eyes were shot with blood. I also saw the lady in a corner writhing in a violent fit of hysterics. I did not even attempt to resist. I should not have had the strength for it had I wished to: my temples were throbbing, I choked . . . my throat rattled. . . . Another minute . . . and I should have been suffocated.

The man must have felt this. He loosened his grip. Without leaving hold of me, with his right hand he stretched a rope, in which he had prepared a slipknot, and, with a quick turn, tied my wrists together. In a moment I was bound, gagged—rendered motionless and helpless.

And he performed this task in the most natural manner in the world, with an ease that revealed the knowledge of a master, of an expert in theft and crime. Not a word, not a fevered movement. Sheer coolness and audacity. And there lay I on the seat, roped up like a mummy—I, Arsène Lupin!

It was really ridiculous. And notwithstanding the seriousness of the circumstances I could not but appreciate and almost enjoy the irony of the situation. Arsène Lupin "done" like a novice, stripped like the first-comer! For of course the scoundrel relieved me of my pocket-book and purse! Arsène Lupin victimized in his turn—duped and beaten! What an adventure!

There remained the lady. He took no notice of her at all. He contented himself with picking up the wrist-bag that lay on the floor, and extracting the jewels, the purse, the gold and silver knicknacks which it contained. The lady opened her eyes, shuddered with fright, took off her rings and handed them to the man as though she wished to spare him any superfluous exertion. He took the rings, and looked at her: she fainted away.

Then, calm and silent as before, without troubling about us further, he resumed his seat, lit a cigarette, and abandoned himself to a careful scrutiny of the treasures which he had captured, the inspection of which seemed to satisfy him completely.

I was much less satisfied. I am not speaking of the twelve thousand francs of which I had been unduly plundered: this was a loss which I accepted only for the time; I had no doubt that those twelve thousand francs would return to my possession after a short interval, together with the exceedingly important papers which my pocket-book contained: plans, estimates, specifications, addresses, lists of correspondents, letters of a coin-promising character. But, for the moment, a more immediate and serious care was worrying me: what was to happen next?

As may be readily imagined, the excitement caused by my passing through the Gare Saint-Lazare had not escaped me. As I was going to stay with friends who knew me by the name of Guillaume Berlat, and to whom my resemblance to Arsène Lupin was the occasion of many a friendly jest, I had not been able to disguise myself after my wont, and my presence had been discovered. Moreover, a man, doubtless Arsène Lupin, had been seen to rush from the express into the fast train. Hence it was inevitable and fated that the commissary of police at Rouen, warned by telegram, would await the arrival of the train, assisted by a respectable number of constables, question any suspicious passengers, and proceed to make a minute inspection of the carriages.

All this I had foreseen, and had not felt greatly excited about it; for I was certain that the Rouen police would display no greater perspicacity than the Paris police, and that I should have been able to pass unperceived: was it not sufficient for me, at the wicket, carelessly to show my deputy's card, collector at Saint-Lazare with every confidence? But how things had changed since then! I was no longer free. It was impossible to attempt one of my usual moves. In one of the carriages the commissary would discover the Sieur Arsène Lupin, whom a propitious fate was sending to him bound hand and foot, gentle as a lamb, packed up complete. He had only to accept delivery, just as you receive a parcel addressed to you at a railway station, a hamper of game, or a basket of vegetables and fruit.

And to avoid this annoying catastrophe, what could I do, entangled as I was in my bonds?

And the train was speeding towards Rouen, the next and the only stopping-place; it rushed through Vernon, through Saint-Pierre. . . .

I was puzzled also by another problem in which I was not so directly interested, but the solution of which aroused my professional curiosity: What were my fellow-traveller's intentions?

If I had been alone he would have had ample time to alight quite calmly at Rouen. But the lady? As soon as the carriage door was opened the lady, meek and quiet as she sat at present, would scream, and throw herself about, and cry for help!

Hence my astonishment. Why did he not reduce her to the same state of powerlessness as myself, which would have given him time to disappear before his twofold misdeed was discovered?

He was still smoking, his eyes fixed on the view outside, which a hesitating rain was beginning to streak with long, slanting lines. Once, however, he turned round, took up my railway guide, and consulted it.

As for the lady, she made every effort to continue fainting, so as to quiet her enemy. But a fit of coughing, produced by the smoke, gave the lie to her pretended swoon.

Myself, I was very uncomfortable, and had pains all over my body. And I thought . . . I planned.

Pont-de-l'Arche . . . Oissel . . . The train was hurrying on, glad, drunk with speed. . . . Saint-Etienne . . .

At that moment the man rose and took two steps towards us, to which the lady hastened to reply with a new scream and a genuine fainting fit.

But what could his object be? He lowered the window on our side. The rain was now falling in torrents, and he made a movement of annoyance at having neither umbrella nor overcoat. He looked up at the rack: the lady's *en-tout-cas* was there; he took it. He also took my overcoat and put it on.

We were crossing the Seine. He turned up his trousers, and then, leaning out of the window, raised the outer latch.

Did he mean to fling himself on the permanent way? At the rate at which we were going it would have been certain death. We plunged into the tunnel pierced under the Cote Sainte-Catherine. The man opened the door, and, with one foot, felt for the step. What madness! The darkness, the smoke, the din—all combined to give a fantastic appearance to any such attempt. But suddenly the train slowed up, the Westinghouse brakes counteracted the movement of the wheels. In a minute the pace from fast became normal, and decreased still more. Without a doubt there was a gang at work repairing this part of the tunnel; this would necessitate a slower passage of the trains for some days perhaps, and the man knew it.

He had only, therefore, to put his other foot on the step, climb down to the foot-board, and walk away quietly, not without first closing the door, and throwing back the latch.

He had scarcely disappeared when the smoke showed whiter in the daylight. We emerged into a valley. One more tunnel, and we should be at Rouen.

The lady at once recovered her wits, and her first care was to bewail the loss of her jewels. I gave her a beseeching glance. She understood, and relieved me of the gag which was stifling me. She wanted also to unfasten my bonds, but I stopped her.

"No, no; the police must see everything as it was. I want them to be fully informed as regards that blackguard's actions."

"Shall I pull the alarm-signal?"

"Too late. You should have thought of that while he was attacking me."

"But he would have killed me! Ah, sir, didn't I tell you that he was travelling by this train? I knew him at once, by his portrait. And now he's taken my jewels!"

"They'll catch him, have no fear."

"Catch Arsène Lupin! Never."

"It all depends on you, madam. Listen. When we arrive be at the window, call out, make a noise. The police and porters will come up. Tell them what you have seen in a few words: the assault of which I was the victim, and the flight of Arsène Lupin. Give his description: a soft hat, an umbrella—yours—a gray frock-overcoat . . ."

"Yours," she said.

"Mine? No, his own. I didn't have one."

"I thought that he had none either when he got in."

"He must have had . . . unless it was a coat which some one left behind in the rack. In any case, he had it when he got out, and that is the essential thing. . . . A gray frock-overcoat, remember. . . . Oh, I was forgetting . . . tell them your name to start with. Your husband's functions will stimulate the zeal of all those men."

We were arriving. She was already leaning out of the window. I resumed, in a louder, almost imperious voice, so that my words should sink into her brain:

"Give my name also, Guillaume Berlat. If necessary, say you know me . . . That will save time . . . we must hurry on the preliminary inquiries . . . the important thing is to catch Arsène Lupin . . . with your jewels. . . . You quite understand, don't you? Guillaume Berlat, a friend of your husband's."

"Quite . . . Guillaume Berlat."

She was already calling out and gesticulating. Before the train had come to a standstill a gentleman climbed in, followed by a number of other men. The critical hour was at hand.

Breathlessly the lady exclaimed:

"Arsène Lupin . . . he attacked us . . . he has stolen my jewels. . . . I am Madame Renaud . . . my husband is a deputy prison-governor. . . . Ah, here's my brother, Georges Andelle, manager of the Credit Rouennais. . . . What I want to say is . . ."

She kissed a young man who had just come up, and who exchanged greetings with the commissary. She continued, weeping:

"Yes, Arsène Lupin. . . . He flew at this gentleman's throat in his sleep. . . . Monsieur Berlat, a friend of my husband's."

"But where is Arsène Lupin?"

"He jumped out of the train in the tunnel, after we had crossed the Seine."

"Are you sure it was he?"

"Certain. I recognized him at once. Besides, he was seen at the Gare Saint-Lazare. He was wearing a soft hat . . ."

"No; a hard felt hat, like this," said the commissary, pointing to my hat.

"A soft hat, I assure you," repeated Madame Renaud, "and a gray frock-overcoat."

"Yes," muttered the commissary; "the telegram mentions a gray frock-overcoat with a black velvet collar."

"A black velvet collar, that's it!" exclaimed Madame Renaud, triumphantly.

I breathed again. What a good, excellent friend I had found in her!

Meanwhile the policemen had released me from my bonds. I bit my lips violently till the blood flowed. Bent in two, with my handkerchief to my mouth, as seems proper to a man who has long been sitting in a constrained position, and who bears on his face the blood-stained marks of the gag, I said to the commissary, in a feeble voice:

"Sir, it was Arsène Lupin, there is no doubt of it. . . . You can catch him if you hurry. . . . I think I may be of some use to you. . . ."

The coach, which was needed for the inspection by the police, was slipped. The remainder of the train went on towards Le Havre. We were taken to the station-master's office through a crowd of on-lookers who filled the platform.

Just then I felt a hesitation. I must make some excuse to absent myself, find my motor-car, and be off. It was dangerous to wait. If anything happened, if a telegram came from Paris, I was lost.

Yes; but what about my robber? Left to my own resources, in a district with which I was not very well acquainted, I could never hope to come up with him.

"Bah!" I said to myself. "Let us risk it, and stay. It's a difficult hand to win, but a very amusing one to play. And the stakes are worth the trouble."

And as we were being asked provisionally to repeat our depositions, I exclaimed:

"Mr. Commissary, Arsène Lupin is getting a start of us. My motor is waiting for me in the yard. If you will do me the pleasure to accept a seat in it, we will try . . ."

The commissary gave a knowing smile.

"It's not a bad idea . . . such a good idea, in fact, that it's already being carried out."

"Oh!"

"Yes; two of my officers started on bicycles . . . some time ago."

"But where to?"

"To the entrance to the tunnel. There they will pick up the clews and the evidence, and follow the track of Arsène Lupin."

I could not help shrugging my shoulders.

"Your two officers will pick up no clews and no evidence."

"Really!"

"Arsène Lupin will have arranged that no one should see him leave the tunnel. He will have taken the nearest road, and from there . . ."

"From there made for Rouen, where we shall catch him."

"He will not go to Rouen."

"In that case, he will remain in the neighborhood, where we shall be even more certain . . ."

"He will not remain in the neighborhood."

"Oh! Then where will he hide himself?"

I took out my watch.

"At this moment Arsène Lupin is hanging about the station at Darnetal. At ten-fifty—that is to say, in twenty-two minutes from now—he will take the train which leaves Rouen from the Gare du Nord for Amiens."

"Do you think so? And how do you know?"

"Oh, it's very simple. In the carriage Arsène Lupin consulted my railway guide. What for? To see if there was another line near the place where he disappeared, a station on that line, and a train which stopped at that station. I have just looked at the guide myself, and learned what I wanted to know."

"Upon my word, sir," said the commissary, "you possess marvellous powers of deduction. What an expert you must be!"

Dragged on by my certainty, I had blundered by displaying too much cleverness. He looked at me in astonishment, and I saw that a suspicion flickered through his mind. Only just, it is true; for the photographs despatched in every direction were so unlike, represented an Arsène Lupin so different from the one that stood before him, that he could not possibly recognize the original in me. Nevertheless, he was troubled, restless, perplexed.

There was a moment of silence. A certain ambiguity and doubt seemed to interrupt our words. A shudder of anxiety passed through me.

Was luck about to turn against me? Mastering myself, I began to laugh.

"Ah well, there's nothing to sharpen one's wits like the loss of a pocket-book and the desire to find it again. And it seems to me that, if you will give me two of your men, the three of us might, perhaps . . ."

"Oh, please, Mr. Commissary," exclaimed Madame Renaud, "do what Monsieur Berlat suggests."

My kind friend's intervention turned the scale. Uttered by her, the wife of an influential person, the name of Berlat became mine in reality, and conferred upon me an identity which no suspicion could touch. The commissary rose.

"Believe me, Monsieur Berlat, I shall be only too pleased to see you succeed. I am as anxious as yourself to have Arsène Lupin arrested."

He accompanied me to my car. He introduced two of his men to me: Honore Massol and Gaston Delivet. They took their seats. I placed myself at the wheel. My chauffeur started the engine. A few seconds later we had left the station. I was saved.

I confess that as we dashed in my powerful 35-h.p. Moreau-Lepton along the boulevards that skirt the old Norman city I was not without a certain sense of pride. The engine hummed harmoniously. The trees sped behind us to right and left. And now, free and out of danger, I had nothing to do but to settle my own little private affairs with the co-operation of two worthy representatives of the law. Arsène Lupin was going in search of Arsène Lupin!

Ye humble mainstays of the social order of things, Gaston Delivet and Honore Massol, how precious was your assistance to me! Where should I have been without you? But for you, at how many cross-roads should I have taken the wrong turning! But for you, Arsène Lupin would have gone astray and the other escaped!

But all was not over yet. Far from it. I had first to capture the fellow and next to take possession, myself, of the papers of which he had robbed me. At no cost must my two satellites be allowed to catch a sight of those documents, much less lay hands upon them. To make us of them and yet act independently of them was what I wanted to do; and it was no easy matter.

We reached Darnetal three minutes after the train had left. I had the consolation of learning that a man in a gray frock-overcoat with a black velvet collar had got into a second-class carriage with a ticket for Amiens. There was no doubt about it: my first appearance as a detective was a promising one.

Delivet said:

"The train is an express, and does not stop before Monterolier-Buchy, in nineteen minutes from now. If we are not there before Arsène Lupin he can go on towards Amiens, branch off to Cleres, and, from there, make for Dieppe or Paris."

"How far is Monterolier?"

"Fourteen miles and a half."

"Fourteen miles and a half in nineteen minutes . . . We shall be there before he is."

It was a stirring race. Never had my trusty Moreau-Lepton responded to my impatience with greater ardor and regularity. It seemed to me as though I communicated my wishes to her directly, without the intermediary of levers or handles. She shared my desires. She approved of my determination. She understood my animosity against that blackguard Arsène Lupin. The scoundrel! The sneak! Should I get the best of him? Or would he once more baffle authority, that authority of which I was the incarnation?

"Right!" cried Delivet. . . . "Left! . . . Straight ahead! . . ."

We skimmed the ground. The mile-stones looked like little timid animals that fled at our approach.

And suddenly at the turn of a road a cloud of smoke—the north express!

For half a mile it was a struggle side by side—an unequal struggle, of which the issue was certain—we beat the train by twenty lengths.

In three seconds we were on the platform in front of the second class. The doors were flung open. A few people stepped out. My thief was not among them. We examined the carriages. No Arsène Lupin.

"By Jove!" I exclaimed, "he must have recognized me in the motor while we were going alongside of him, and jumped!"

The guard of the train confirmed my supposition. He had seen a man scrambling down the embankment at two hundred yards from the station.

"There he is! . . . Look! . . . At the level crossing!"

I darted in pursuit, followed by my two satellites, or, rather, by one of them; for the other, Massol, turned out to be an uncommonly fast sprinter, gifted with both speed and staying power. In a few seconds the distance between him and the fugitive was greatly diminished. The man saw him, jumped a hedge, and scampered off towards a slope, which he climbed. We saw him, farther still, entering a little wood.

When we reached the wood we found Massol waiting for us. He had thought it no use to go on, lest he should lose us.

"You were quite right, my dear fellow," I said. "After a run like this our friend must be exhausted. We've got him."

I examined the skirts of the wood while thinking how I could best proceed alone to arrest the fugitive, in order myself to effect certain recoveries which the law, no doubt, would only have allowed after a number of disagreeable inquiries. Then I returned to my companions.

"Look here, it's very easy. You, Massol, take up your position on the left. You, Delivet, on the right. From there you can watch the whole rear of the wood, and he can't leave it unseen by you except by this hollow, where I shall stand. If he does not come out, I'll go in and force him back towards one or the other of you. You have nothing to do, therefore, but wait. Oh, I was forgetting: in case of alarm, I'll fire a shot."

Massol and Delivet moved off, each to his own side. As soon as they were out of sight I made my way into the wood with infinite precautions, so as to be neither seen nor heard. It consisted of close thickets, contrived for the shooting, and intersected by very narrow paths, in which it was only possible to walk by stooping, as though in a leafy tunnel.

One of these ended in a glade, where the damp grass showed the marks of footsteps. I followed them, taking care to steal through the underwood. They led me to the bottom of a little mound, crowned by a tumble-down lath-and-plaster hovel.

"He must be there," I thought. "He has selected a good post of observation."

I crawled close up to the building. A slight sound warned me of his presence, and, in fact, I caught sight of him through an opening; with his back turned towards me.

Two bounds brought me upon him. He tried to point the revolver which he held in his hand. I did not give him time, but pulled him to the ground in such a way that his two arms were twisted and caught under him, while I held him pinned down with my knee upon his chest.

"Listen to me, old chap," I whispered in his ear. "I am Arsène Lupin. You've got to give me back, this minute and without any fuss, my pocket-book and the lady's wrist-bag . . . in return for which I'll save you from the clutches of the police and enroll you among my friends. Which is it to be: yes or no?"

"Yes," he muttered.

"That's right. Your plan of this morning was cleverly thought out. We shall be good friends."

I got up. He fumbled in his pocket, fetched out a great knife, and tried to strike me with it.

"You ass!" I cried.

With one hand I parried the attack. With the other I caught him a violent blow on the carotid artery, the blow which is known as "the carotid hook." He fell back stunned.

In my pocket-book I found my papers and bank-notes. I took his own out of curiosity. On an envelope addressed to him I read his name: Pierre Onfrey.

I gave a start. Pierre Onfrey, the perpetrator of the murder in the Rue Lafontaine at Auteuil! Pierre Onfrey, the man who had cut the throats of Madame Delbois and her two daughters. I bent over him. Yes, that was the face which, in the railway-carriage, had aroused in me the memory of features which I had seen before.

But time was passing. I placed two hundred-franc notes in an envelope, with a visiting-card bearing these words:

"Arsène Lupin to his worthy assistants, Honore Massol and Gaston Delivet, with his best thanks."

I laid this where it could be seen, in the middle of the room. Beside it I placed Madame Renaud's wrist-bag. Why should it not be restored to the kind friend who had rescued me? I confess, however, that I took from it everything that seemed in any way interesting, leaving only a tortoise-shell comb, a stick of lip-salve, and an empty purse. Business is business, when all is said and done! And, besides, her husband followed such a disreputable occupation! . . .

There remained the man. He was beginning to move. What was I to do? I was not qualified either to save or to condemn him.

I took away his weapons, and fired my revolver in the air.

"That will bring the two others," I thought. "He must find a way out of his own difficulties. Let fate take its course."

And I went down the hollow road at a run.

Twenty minutes later a cross-road which I had noticed during our pursuit brought me back to my car.

At four o'clock I telegraphed to my friends from Rouen that an unexpected incident compelled me to put off my visit. Between ourselves, I greatly fear that, in view of what they must now have learned, I shall be obliged to postpone it indefinitely. It will be a cruel disappointment for them!

At six o'clock I returned to Paris by L'Isle-Adam, Enghien, and the Porte Bineau.

I gathered from the evening papers that the police had at last succeeded in capturing Pierre Onfrey.

The next morning—why should we despise the advantages of intelligent advertisement?—the *Echo de France* contained the following sensational paragraph:

> "Yesterday, near Buchy, after a number of incidents, Arsène Lupin effected the arrest of Pierre Onfrey. The Auteuil murderer had robbed a lady of the name of Renaud, the wife of the deputy prison-governor, in the train between Paris and Le Havre. Arsène Lupin has restored to Madame Renaud the wrist-bag which contained her jewels, and has generously rewarded the two detectives who assisted him in the matter of this dramatic arrest."

Rogue: Six-Eye

An Unposted Letter

NEWTON MACTAVISH

THIS ODD LITTLE STORY derives from an unlikely author: Newton McFaul MacTavish (1875–1941), a much-honored Canadian art critic and early art historian. Born in Staffa, Ontario, he began his career as a journalist at the age of twenty-one when he took a job as a reporter at *The Toronto Globe* and was assistant financial editor there until 1900. At that time he began to study English literature at McGill University while working as a correspondent and business representative of *The Globe* in Montreal. In 1906, MacTavish became the editor of *The Canadian Magazine* in Toronto, a position he held for twenty years. He acted as a trustee of the National Gallery of Canada in Ottawa from 1922 to 1933. He received honorary degrees in 1924 (M.A.) and 1928 (D.Litt.) from Acadia University, Nova Scotia. He was a member of the Civil Service Commission of Canada from 1926 to 1932. A founder of the Arts and Letters Club (Toronto), he served on the editorial advisory board of the *Encyclopedia of Canada* (1932–1935), to which he also was a contributor. In addition to his articles, essays, and short stories, MacTavish authored *Thrown In* (1923), a collection of essays about rural life in nineteenth-century Ontario; *The Fine Arts in Canada* (1925), the first full-length history of Canadian art; and *Ars Longa* (1938), stories about Canadian art and artists, with anecdotal reminiscences by the author. A fourth work, *Newton MacTavish's Canada: Selected Essays* (1963), was published posthumously.

"An Unposted Letter" was originally published in the February 1901 issue of *The Canadian Magazine*.

AN UNPOSTED LETTER

Newton MacTavish

OUTSIDE, A HAMMER POUNDED mockingly; the gallows were under construction. Through the iron bars of the prison window shone a few straggling shafts of sunlight. My client rested on his elbows, his chin in his hands. The light glistened on his matted hair. He heard the hammering outside.

"I guess I may's well write a line to Bill," he said, not raising his head. "Kin you get a pencil and paper?"

I got them, and then waited until he had written:

"Dear Bill,—By the sound of things, I reckon I've got to swing this trip. I've had a hope all along that they might git scent on the right track; but I see that Six-Eye'll be 'bliged to kick the bucket, with head up—the galleys is goin' up mighty fast.

"I say, Bill, there ain't no good in burglarin'. I swore once I'd quit it, and wish I had. But a feller can't allus do just as he fancies; I guess he can't allus do it, kin he, Bill? You never knew how I got into this scrape, did you?

"One day I was standin' around, just standin' around, nothin' doin', when I saw a pair of runaway horses a-comin' down the street like mad. I jumped out and caught the nigh one by the bridle. I hauled 'em up mighty sudden, but somethin' swung me round, and I struck my head agin the neck-yoke, kersmash.

"When I come to, I was sittin' back in the carriage with the sweetest faced girl bendin' over me, and wipin' my face with cool water. She asked where she would drive me home; and, do you know, Bill, for the first time, I was ashamed to say where. But I told her, and, so help me, she came clear down in there with me, and made Emily put me to bed. She left money, and every day till I got well she come out and sat and read the Bible and all them things. Do you know, Bill, it wasn't long afore things seemed different. I couldn't look at her pure, sweet face and plan a job. The last day she came I made up my mind I'd try somethin' else—quit burglarin'.

"I started out to get work. One man asked me what I'd served my time at. I said I'd served most of it in jail, and then he wouldn't have anythin' to do with me. A chap gave me a couple of days breakin' stones in a cellar. He said I did it so good he guessed I must have been in jail. After that I couldn't get nothin' to do, because no one wouldn't have nothin' to do with a jail-bird, and I had made up my mind to tell the truth.

"At last Emily began to kick and little Bob

to cry for grub. I got sick of huntin' for work, and it seemed as if everybody was pushin' me back to my old job. I got disgusted. I had to do somethin', so I sat down and planned to do a big house in the suburbs. I'd sized it up before.

"The moon was high that night, so I waited till it went down, long after midnight. I found the back door already open, so it was a snap to git in.

"I went upstairs and picked on a side room near the front. I eased the door and looked in. A candle flickered low, and flames danced from a few coals in the fireplace.

"I entered noiselessly.

"A high-backed chair was in front of the hearth. I sneaked up and looked over the top. A young girl, all dressed in white, with low neck and bare arms, laid there asleep. Her hair hung over her shoulders; she looked like as if she'd come home from a dance, and just threw herself there tired out.

"Just as I was goin' to turn away, the flames in the fireplace flickered, and I caught the glow of rubies at the girl's throat. How they shone and gleamed and shot fire from their blood-red depths! The candle burned low and sputtered; but the coals on the hearth flickered, the rubies glowed, and the girl breathed soft in her sleep.

"'It's an easy trick,' I said to myself, and I leaned over the back of the chair, my breath fanning the light hair that fell over marble shoulders. I took out my knife and reached over. Just then the fire burned up a bit. As I leaned over I saw her sweet, girlish face, and, so h'lp me, Bill, it was her, her whose face I couldn't look into and plan a job.

"Hardly knowing it, I bared my head, and stood there knife in hand, the blood rushin' to my face, and my feelin's someway seemin' to go agin me.

"I looked at her, and gradually closed my knife and straightened up from that sneakin' shape a feller gets into. I remembered a verse that she used to read to me, 'Ye shall not go forth empty-handed,' so I said to myself I'd try again. But just as I was turning to go, I heard a shot in the next room; then a heavy thud. I stood stock-still for a jiffy, and then ran out in time to see someone dart down the stairs. At the bottom I heard a stumble. I hurried along the hall and ran straight into the arms of the butler.

"I guess someone else was doin' that job that night. But they had me slicker'n a whistle. 'Twas no use; everythin' went agin me. I had on my big revolver, the mate to the one you got. As it happened, one chamber was empty, and the ball they took from the old man's head was the same size. I had a bad record; it was all up with me. The only thing they brought up in court to the contrary was the top of an ear they found in the hall, where someone must have hit agin somethin' sharp. But they wouldn't listen to my lawyer.

"Give up burglarin', Bill; see what I've come to. But I hope you'll do a turn for Emily if ever she's in need, and don't learn little Bob filchin'. Do this for an old pal's sake, Bill."

The doomed man stopped writing, as the last shaft of sunlight passed beyond the iron bars of the prison window. Outside the hammering had ceased; the scaffold was finished.

"You'll find Emily, my wife, in the back room of the basement at 126, River Street," said my client, handing me the letter. "She'll tell you where to find Bill."

I took the letter, but did not then know its contents. I started, but he called me back.

"You have a flower in your button-hole," he said. "I'd like to wrap it up and send it to Emily."

Next day, after the sentence of the law had been executed, I went to find Emily. I descended the musty old staircase at 126, River Street, where all was filth and squalor. At the back room I stopped and rapped. A towzy head was thrust out of the next door.

"They're gone," it said.

"Where?"

"Don't know. The woman went with some man."

"Did you know him?"

"I saw him here before sometimes, but the

top of his ear wasn't cut off then. They called him Bill—sort of pal."

"And where's the little boy?"

"He's gone to the Shelter."

I went out into the pure air, and, standing on the kerbstone, read the letter:

". . . The only thing they brought up in court to the contrary was the top of an ear. . . ."

When I had finished, I remembered the flower in my hand. I didn't throw it away; I took it to my office and have it there still, wrapped in the paper as he gave it to me.

Rogue: Smiler Bunn

The Adventure of "The Brain"

BERTRAM ATKEY

MOST REMEMBERED, if remembered at all, for the creation of Smiler Bunn, a not-quite-gentleman-crook, Bertram Atkey (1880–1952) also invented a wide range of eccentric and original characters for his many works of fiction, notably Winnie O'Wynn, a charming gold-digger; Prosper Fair, an amateur detective who is really Duke of Devizes; Hercules, a sportsman; Nelson Chiddenham, a crippled boy detective who has an immense knowledge of dogs and the countryside; Captain Cormorant, a widely traveled mercenary adventurer; and Sebastian Hope, a henpecked husband with a peculiar gift for disarming his wife by feeding her alibis of great verisimilitude.

It is the scores of stories about Smiler Bunn that continue to have charm in the present day. Also known as Mr. Wilton Flood, Bunn is an ingenious crook, blessed with great courage, resourcefulness, and humor, who "makes his living off society in a manner always devious and sometimes dark, but never mean." Bunn and his friend Lord Fortworth have lived in bachelor partnership for years, specializing in taking portable property (such as cash and jewels) from those who have no right to it, thereby avoiding encounters with the police.

Born in Wiltshire, Atkey moved to London as a teenager to write stories. He published his first book, *Folk of the Wild*, a collection of nature stories, in 1905. Two years later he created Smiler Bunn, later collecting the stories in *The Amazing Mr. Bunn* (1912), the first of nine books about the genial crook.

"The Adventure of 'The Brain'" was first published in the January 1910 issue of *The Grand Magazine*, and first collected in *The Amazing Mr. Bunn* (London, Newnes, 1912).

THE ADVENTURE OF "THE BRAIN"

Bertram Atkey

"I SHALL NOW PROCEED to give my celebrated imitation of a gentleman pinching a blood-orange," mused Mr. "Smiler" Bunn, the gifted pickpocket of Garraty Street, King's Cross, to himself, as he stood thoughtfully before a fruiterer's shop in a small street off Oxford Street. "A real gent hooking of the biggest blood-orange in the bunch!"

With this laudable intention he turned his gaze upon a fine pineapple that reposed aristocratically upon pink paper behind the plate-glass window, as the shopman came out and stood for a moment near the door, leaning against the shopfront extension, which was piled with fruit—chiefly oranges, "blood" and otherwise. This part of the shop was in front of the window, and was unprotected save by the watchful care of the shopman.

"Nice little pineapple, that," said Mr. Bunn casually.

"Pretty fair for the time of year," replied the shopman. "Will you take it?"

"Well, 'ow much is it?"

"Half a guinea," said the shopman.

Mr. Bunn shook his head. His resources at the moment totalled sevenpence only.

"Too dear," he decided, both hands plunged deep into his coat-pockets. "What's the little black-looking thing that keeps on running round the pineapple? Not a mouse, is it?"

The shopman plunged inside suddenly, with a frightful threat against all mice, and—Mr. Bunn's right hand flickered. Only flickered. Few people watching him would have cared to wager that his hand had left his pocket at all. Then he moved tranquilly away, and the biggest blood-orange on the shop-front went with him. The celebrated imitation was over, and the performer had strolled calmly round an adjacent corner before the shopman had given up his search for the mouse.

"Very well done, old man," muttered Mr. Bunn. "I ain't sure but what you ain't improving. Your 'and has not lost its cunning, nor your heye its quickness."

He turned into Oxford Street, feeling distinctly encouraged by this small success, and mingled unobtrusively with the crowd of women who were looking at the shop windows and wondering why their husbands did not earn as much as other women's husbands.

Mr. Bunn had skilfully worked his way through the thickest of the crowd for over a hundred yards before he marked a lady who seemed sufficiently careless in the handling of her bag to call for his closer attention. He moved quickly to her. She was a handsome woman of middle age, with a determined face, and rather too strong a chin. She was exceedingly well-dressed, and carried her bag in the bend of two fingers. At first she did not appear to be interested in the shops, but a hat dashingly displayed in a corner window suddenly caught her attention, and she stopped to look at it. Mr. Bunn paused for the fraction of a second immediately behind her. Then he went quietly on—round the corner (corners were a speciality of Smiler Bunn's). He did not look behind—he knew better. He simply lounged very slowly on, hoping the bag did not make too pronounced a bulge in his pocket. He looked quite the most unconcerned man in London, until he heard a sudden rustle of skirts behind him and felt a quick, firm grip on his arm.

"You are very unintelligent," said a sharp voice, and he turned to see the well-dressed woman who had been carrying her bag carelessly.

"Give me what you have in your right-hand coat-pocket at once," she requested him coldly.

"I dunno what you mean. I don't know *you*. What d'you mean?" asked Smiler, rather nervously.

"Do not let us have any nonsense, please," was her chilly comment. "Give it to me at once."

Smiler put his hand in his pocket with desperate calmness and drew out—a remarkably fine blood-orange.

"It's the only one I got, but you can have it——" he began; but she interrupted.

"Do you want me to call the police?" she said. "Give me the bag instantly."

Smiler gave a sickly smile, put his hand into the other pocket, and, with a badly-feigned start of surprise, produced the bag.

"Why, what's this? However did this get there? This ain't mine—it don't belong to me!" he began, making the best of a very bad job.

But she cut him short. She took the bag, her quick grey eyes playing over him in a singularly comprehensive glance. She saw a clean-shaven, rather stout, butlerish-looking man of about thirty-eight, with a good-humoured mouth and a solid chin. He was extremely shabby, but neat, and obviously was in a state of considerable embarrassment. She was about to speak, when Mr. Bunn pushed back his hat and passed his hand across his brow—a gesture evidently unconscious, and born of the mental stress of the moment. But her eyes brightened suddenly as they lighted upon his forehead, and her lips relaxed a little. For it was unquestionably a fine frontal development—a Brow among Brows. Assisted somewhat by a slight premature baldness, the forehead of Mr. Bunn was a feature of which its owner was acutely conscious. There was too much of it, in his opinion. It had never been of much use to him, and he was in the habit of considering its vast expanse a deformity rather than a sign of intellect. He was quite aware that it saved his features from being commonplace—he fancied it made them ridiculous instead. But evidently the lady of the bag did not think so. She was actually smiling to him.

"I should like to ask you a few questions," she said, "if you have no objection."

Mr. Bunn did not answer.

"*Have* you any objection?" she inquired sweetly, glancing across the road, where a dozen policemen were solemnly walking in Indian file towards their beats. Smiler regarded them for a moment—a most unpleasant sight, he considered.

Then, "No, no objection—not at all—not by no means," he said.

"Be good enough to accompany me, then," continued the woman, in a singularly business-like way. She moved slowly on, and Mr. Bunn walked by her side.

"Why are you a pickpocket?" she said curtly.

Mr. Bunn muttered to the effect that he was not—strike him lucky if he was. But the woman ignored his denial.

"It is so foolish," she said. "So obviously unsuitable a profession for a man with your intellect. Why, with your forehead you should be carving out a great future, a career, a reputation."

Smiler stared suspiciously at her.

"You leave my forrid alone," he requested her. "I can't help having a thing more like a balloon than a 'eadpiece on my shoulders, can I?"

"But, my good person, don't you see what a great thing it is to have such a brain, and what a terrible thing it is for such an intellect to lie dormant? If all men had such intellect as your forehead tells me plainly you possess, you do not think we women would ever have asked for votes? Certainly not. It is because not one man in a hundred thousand possesses such a brain as yours that we have decided to fight for our rights. And when I think of the possibilities of yours, when I think of the latent power in your glorious head, that only needs training and shaping to the Idea. When I think, here I have in its practically fallow state a Brain of Brains which belongs to me, and is my own to mould as I like—unless its owner wishes to be sent to prison for six months in the third division with hard labour—can you wonder that my whole spirit takes fire, and I cry aloud, yet again—'VOTES FOR WOMEN!' "

It was a truly lusty yell, and it gave Mr. Bunn an unpleasant shock. Everyone within hearing turned to stare at the woman, but she seemed blandly unconscious of their scrutiny. She gripped the unnerved Smiler's arm and became business-like again.

"Understand me," she said. "I consider you a Find, and I propose to keep you—unless, of course, you prefer to be handed over to the police. I can see that you are a man with immense possibilities, and those possibilities I intend to develop with the ultimate aim of devoting them to the Cause. Do you understand me? I propose to educate you. You shall become a lecturer, a champion of women's rights, a pursuer of the Vote. You shall be paid while you are being taught—and paid well—and when, in the course of time, I have stirred that great Brain out of its present inaction, it shall be devoted to our service and rewarded in proportion. No—not a word. Come with me. I am Lilian Carroway."

Mr. Bunn felt dazed. Lilian Carroway! He knew now with whom he had to deal. The Suffragette who knew more about jiu-jitsu than any European and most Japanese. The woman who a few months previously had wrestled her way into the House of Commons over the bodies of many half-stunned and wholly astonished policemen, and had threatened to put a strangulation lock on the Prime Minister himself if he did not promise to answer a plain question. Taken by surprise, he had promised, and Lilian, rather flurried, had put the following question to him:

"VOTES FOR WOMEN?"

"I must have notice of that question," had been the suave, non-committal reply of the Prime Minister, and before the Suffragette had quite thought it out, the police had taken her by storm and removed her.

Smiler Bunn remembered the incident well and congratulated himself on not having annoyed her.

She called a taxicab, and commanded him to get in. She gave the driver the address of the headquarters of the particular branch of the movement to which she belonged, and sat down beside the dazed pickpocket.

"Your fortune is made," she said briefly.

Mr. Bunn muttered "Certainly," in a very uncertain voice, and relapsed into a gloomy silence.

"I have no doubt that you consider yourself to be in a singularly unfortunate position, Mr.—er—what is your name?"

"Connaught," said Smiler, absently reading the first name he saw over a shop window, "Louisy Connaught."

"Louise Connaught! What an extraordinary name! How do you spell it? Louise is a woman's name."

"Well, some spell it one way and some another. I don't mind much."

"But it is a woman's name."

"Well, I was one of a twin," lied Mr. Bunn uncomfortably, wishing he had taken a name from some other shop window. "We was mixed a little at the christenin', and me sister's name is Thomas."

"I see. How unfortunate!" said the Suffragette. Then she spoke the name over to herself several times: "Louise Connaught—*Louis* Connaught. Why, it's a splendid name—Louis Connaught. It has a royal sort of ring. Mr. Louis Connaught, I really congratulate you upon your name."

"Louis" smiled uneasily and avoided meeting her eye.

Then the "taxi" turned suddenly into a courtyard at the side of a big block of flats near Whitehall, and pulled up.

"Here we are, Mr. Connaught," said the Suffragette, and paying the driver she gently impelled her captive into the building. He was not quite so anxious to bolt as he had been. That mention of payment had interested him, and, in any case, there seemed to be an uncomfortably large number of police in the neighbourhood. Mr. Bunn had recognised two plain-clothes men at the entrance to the side court.

He passively followed Mrs. Carroway into the lift, and from the lift into a large room on the second floor. This apartment was furnished like the board-room of a big company, but its business appearance was made slightly less severe by one or two little feminine touches here and there—a few flowers, a mirror or so, and some rather tasteful pictures. There were a dozen women of different ages scattered about the room.

Mrs. Carroway greeted them impulsively.

"My dears, I have discovered a Brain!" she cried.

The Brain blushed as he removed his hat, for he knew what was coming.

"Look at his forehead," said the enthusiastic Lilian. "Isn't it beautiful?"

"Wall, it's all right as regards quantity—there's a good square foot of it—if the quality is there," answered a rather obvious spinster of uncertain age, with a Scotch face and a New England accent. "What's the Brain's name?"

"Louis Connaught," announced Mrs. Carroway importantly, and several of the younger and less angular of the Suffragettes looked interested. It was certainly a high-sounding name.

"Wall, Louis, I'm glad you're here," said the American lady, "and the vurry fact of your being here shows that there's *something* behind that frontal freeboard of yours. Most men avoid this place as though it was a place of worship. You mustn't mind my candour; this strenuous pursuit of the Vote makes a girl candid."

The Brain bowed awkwardly. It was one of his few assets that he was not afraid of women. He was not even nervous with them, except when they were in a position, and looked likely to hand him over to the police. Some instinct deeply buried behind what the "girl" was pleased to term his "frontal freeboard" told him that Mrs. Carroway would not explain to the others the circumstances in which she had made his unwilling acquaintance.

A young and pretty girl came forward, smiling, offering her hand. It was hard to believe that such a lovely slip of feminine daintiness had done, to use a popular expression, "her two months in the second division," with the best of them. She was Lady Mary de Vott.

"We are very glad to have you fighting in our Cause, Mr. Connaught," she said charmingly.

Smiler shook hands as though he meant never to leave off.

"Glad—proud!" he said heavily. "Glad to oblige. Any little thing like that—any time."

Mrs. Carroway broke in.

"There is a rather curious little story to tell about Mr. Connaught," she said, "and in case anyone should notice and misconstrue any little mannerisms he may possess, I should like to tell his story, which explains them. Mr. Connaught probably will prefer not to be present. If so"—she turned to Smiler—"will you go to the waiting-room?"

She touched a bell, and a trim typist appeared.

"Show this gentleman into the waiting-room," ordered Lilian, and Smiler went out, feeling that, on the whole, he was travelling in the direction of a rich streak of luck. He dropped into a big, luxurious lounge, and gracefully lying at full length, proceeded, with many sounds of enjoyment, to demolish the large blood-orange he had so deftly acquired an hour before. He then took a little nap, and woke, thoroughly refreshed, to find Mrs. Carroway by the side of the lounge, staring with a rapt and wondering expression at his towering forehead.

"Ah, this is splendid!" she said. "I see that in common with many other great brains you have the knack of snatching an hour's rest at odd moments. Napoleon possessed it also, I believe."

"Napoleon who?" inquired Mr. Bunn, who could have beaten any brain in the world at the gentle art of resting.

"Bonaparte, my dear man!" said Mrs. Carroway good-humouredly. "Haven't you ever heard of Napoleon Bonaparte?"

Mr. Bunn thought.

"Heard the name somewhere or other. Hasn't he got a shop down by the Holborn end of Shaftesbury Avenue—fried fish and chips? Little dark man?"

Mrs. Carroway stared.

"I do not think so," she answered.

"Ah, some relation of his, I expect!" said Smiler airily, and dismissed the matter. He stood up. After his reception in the big committee-room he had lost much of his trepidation as to the result of his unfortunate little *contretemps* with the Suffragette leader's hand-bag.

"Well, how about this little lot?" He tapped his forehead significantly. "Was any offer made?"

"Ah, that is quite settled. We have agreed unanimously that—after a cursory examination by a skilled phrenologist—you shall be entered at once as a Special Organiser. Why, are you disappointed, Mr. Connaught?"

She had noticed his face fall.

"No; only I don't know a note of music. I can't tell one tune from another. I admit it don't want much thinking about, just turning a handle; but even a organ-grinder——"

Mrs. Carroway laughed.

"Oh, I see!" she smiled. "I said 'Organiser.'"

"Oh!" said Smiler, with an air of intense relief, wondering what an organiser was.

"Of course," the Suffragette continued, "I shall not expect big things from you at first. I think you had better begin by reading up the question of Women's Suffrage. Every morning you shall report to me at, say, ten, and we will talk over the chapters you have read. You will be able to tell me what conclusions you have come to, and what opinions you have formed on the subject, and I shall be able to correct any false impressions made upon you, and, no doubt, your intellect, as it becomes familiar with the question, will soon be discovering new and valuable interpretations of the old ideas, and giving new ideas and plans for the advancement of the Cause. After a few weeks of careful reading you will have to begin practising public speaking, and we all expect that by that time your own great natural gifts will assert themselves, and from being a—novice, let us say—you will become a leader both in thought and in action. During the first few weeks your remuneration will be three pounds a week—the League has plenty of funds—if that is agreeable to you."

She seemed to expect an answer, and Smiler managed to get his breath back in time to say that he thought three pounds a week would do "for a start."

"Well, that being settled, let us go into the committee-room. We've sent for a phrenologist, and he is waiting there for you; and, by the way, I've explained to our comrades that you were of almost noble birth, but, owing to a series of misfortunes, your education—both socially and—er—scholastically, has been slightly neglected. And now, Mr. Connaught, before we join the others, let me say that I believe in you, and I think you will prove a tremendous acquisition to the Cause. I do not see how one with so noble a forehead as yours can prove otherwise."

Mr. Bunn was almost touched.

"Lady," he said, with a singular emphasis, "you do me proud, strike me pink all over, if you don't. You're a *lady*, that's what you are, and I know when I'm dealing with a lady and I treat her *as* a lady. You'll see. Don't you worry about me. I shall be all right, once I get started. When I'm just joggin' along in my own quiet way, kids can play with me; but once I get started, I'm a rum 'un, and don't you forget it, lady. I only want to get started." He extended his hand. "Put it *there*, Mrs. Carroway!"

The Suffragette leader put her hand in his, and they shook in silence.

There were about thirty Suffragettes in the committee-room when the two re-entered, and a lean man in a frock coat and a flannel shirt, who was delivering a sort of lecture on phrenology. Smiler, with the instinct of one "crook" for another, glanced at his sharp, famished eyes and summed him up instantly as a charlatan—only "charlatan" was not the exact word which occurred to the new Organiser.

Mrs. Carroway introduced the two men, and the phrenologist indicated a chair, which Smiler took. In five minutes' talk with the ladies the phrenologist had gleaned precisely what they wanted for their money, and he proceeded to give it to them unstintingly.

He took Smiler's head in his hungry-looking hands and pressed it. He said:

"This is indeed a brain—a most unusual, indeed, an amazing brain. I have not often 'andled a brain of this description. This head which I hold in my 'and is an astonishing head!" He slid a clammy palm across the gratified Mr. Bunn's forehead. "I should term this head a phenomenal head. It is perplexing—it is what we call an Unexpected Head. It has every indication of being wholly undeveloped, while its natural force is stupendous. I consider it puzzling; it is a very difficult cranium!" He frowned, looked thoughtful, and finally dropped his hands suddenly. "Ladies," he said glibly, "I really couldn't afford to read this head for a guinea. This is as good a three-guinea head as ever I see under my 'and. This head should be charted properly; usually I charge a guinea extra for a No. 1 chart, but if you'll take a three-guinea readin' of this head, I'll throw in the chart, marked out in two colours, and framed in black oak, with pale green mount, with signed certificate and seal at the back, complete, with half-hour's verbal readin', any questions answered, for three pounds ten, cash, usual charge five guineas. Crowned heads twenty guineas and expenses. And that's a bargain."

Naturally, it being a bargain, every lady in the room agreed on the "three-pounds-ten readin'," and considered it cheap.

And then, to his intense astonishment and profound gratification, Mr. Bunn learnt among other things that he would, with a little practice, develop into an orator of a brilliance surpassing that of the late Mr. W. E. Gladstone, and rivalling that of Mark Antony, a statesman whose statecraft would be as iron-handed as that of Bismarck, as subtle as that of Abdul the Damned, as fearless as that of Nero, and as dazzling as that of the German Emperor; a lawgiver as unbiased and careful as Moses, a diplomat as finished as Talleyrand, a thinker as profound as Isaac Walton (the phrenologist probably meant Isaac Newton), a champion of rights as persuasive as Oliver Cromwell, and, finally, a politician "as honest as"—here the phrenologist faltered for a moment—"as honest a politician as—as—the best of them." A great deal of useful and equally valuable information having been imparted, the phrenologist announced that the sitting was at an end, drew his cheque, promised to send on the chart and certificate, volunteered to read the palms of any ladies present for five shillings per palm, offered to throw himself into a trance and communicate with the spirit of any dead relative of anyone present for two guineas per spirit, dealt round a pack of his business cards with the air of a pretty good poker-player, and finally took his departure.

The curious thing was that every woman—and there were many intelligent women there—seemed to believe in this shabby, flannel-shirted liar, and to respect him. Their congratulations as they surrounded the Brain were unmistakably genuine. Then, suddenly, the telephone-bell rang shrilly, and a message was received to the effect that the Prime Minister had been seen motoring in the direction of Walton Heath with a bag of golf clubs in the car. Mrs. Carroway gave a few swift instructions, and the room emptied like magic. In ten minutes Mr. Bunn was alone with the Suffragette leader. Smiler was a little dazed.

"Where've they all gone?" he asked.

"To Walton Heath, in taxicabs."

"Why?"

"To ask the Prime Minister when he's going to give Votes for Women, of course."

"Well, but that American woman took a darn great axe," said Smiler. "Surely she ain't going to ask with that!"

"One never knows," replied Mrs. Carroway darkly.

Mr. Bunn looked grieved.

"Pore bloke!" he said, with extraordinary earnestness. "Pore, *pore* bloke! It ain't all beer and skittles being Prime Minister, is it?"

"We do our best to see that it isn't!" said Mrs. Carroway modestly. "And now about your books. I've looked out a few to begin with. Here they are."

She indicated a pile of massive volumes on the floor at the foot of a big bookcase. Smiler's jaw fell.

"Well," he said, without enthusiasm, "brain or no brain, that little lot'll give me a thundering headache before I'm through 'em. They'd better be sent by Carter Paterson or Pickford, hadn't they?"

Mrs. Carroway thought a cab would be better, and sent for one. Then she produced her purse, and Smiler became more interested.

"You must not mind my mentioning it, Mr. Connaught, but it has just occurred to me that possibly you may be short of ready money. Are you?"

"Yes," replied Smiler, with manly simplicity. "I am, somethink astonishin'."

"In that case, then"—Mrs. Carroway opened the purse—"you may like to take two pounds of your first week's salary in advance. Would you?"

"I would," answered Smiler straightforwardly, and without false pride.

"Very well then"—she handed him two sovereigns. "Will you write your address on this envelope, and I will enter your name in the book of the League?"

Smiler did so.

"Garraty Street. What a quaint old name!" commented the lady as she read the address.

"Yes, ain't it?" said Smiler. "And it's a quaint, old-fashioned sort of street, too," he went on, "where everybody lives on fried fish, and the landlord's got to chain down the window sills to stop 'em from using 'em for firewood. I shall be leaving there pretty soon, directly I've developed me brain a little bit. And now I'll sling me hook. What time will you be expecting me tomorrow?"

"I think at two o'clock. You had better begin on this book." She handed him a somewhat massive volume entitled, *The Vote: What It Means and Why We Want It*, by Lilian Carroway. "You must make notes as you read, and we can discuss your notes tomorrow."

Smiler took the book and weighed it in his hand.

"Ye—es," he said, rather feebly, and turned to help the cabman carry the remaining books to the cab.

So Mr. Smiler Bunn, *alias* Louis Connaught, *alias* The Brain, became a Suffragette, and only the phrenologist seemed to know that he could never be more than a suffrajest at most.

He shook hands with Mrs. Carroway and went down to the cab. Waiting on the kerb near the entrance to the mansion was a man whose appearance seemed familiar to Mr. Bunn. This man stepped forward as Smiler entered the cab. It was the phrenologist.

"Excuse me, Brain," he said jauntily. "I'll give you a lift," and followed Smiler into the cab, closing the door behind him.

Smiler stared, then recollected the illuminated address the man had given him half an hour before, and grinned.

"All right," he said.

The phrenologist surveyed him with alert, black eyes that played over him like searchlights. He was a young man, painfully thin, hawk-nosed, and his movements were curiously deft and swift. He drew two long, thin, black, leathery-looking cigars from his breast-pocket, and handed one to Mr. Bunn.

"Hide behind that," he said, "if you like flavour and bite to a cigar."

Smiler did so, and waited for his companion to speak. The phrenologist lost no time.

"This has got to be worked properly, Mr. Connaught," he said. "There's lots of lovely money back there"—he jerked his thumb over his shoulder, indicating the Suffragettes' headquarters—"and you and me's got to magnetise it before any of the other grafters in this town gets on to it. Now, I'm going to play fair with you, Mr. Connaught. You got a pull with that bunch somehow; thanks to me, they reckon you'll be able to put King Solomon and all his wisdom in your ticket pocket after a week or two's study. On account of the shape of your head, I make it. Well, you and me's men of the world, and we can be frank where others fall out, and as a man of the world, I can tell you right away, Mr. Connaught, that the Brain idea is a dream. Why, say, the minute I feels your head under my 'and I found myself saying, 'Well, this is a High Brow all right, but it's hollow behind. There's nothin' to it—nix—vacant.' I mean nothing special. Of course there's brain there—about the average. Very near up to the average, say. But you ain't no Homer, any more than me or them daffy-down-dillies back to the mansions. The old girl seems to fancy herself at physiognomy, but she's trod on a banana-skin all right if she's risking real money on your dial. Well, now, I want to be friendly with you, Mr. Connaught. This town owes us both a living, and the only rule in the game is that we got to collect it. Well, now, let's put our cards on the table. I'm a palm-reader and phrenologist just now, but I'm going solid for bigger business bimeby. Now, what's your lay?"

"Well, the old girl *thought* I been picking her pocket," said Smiler, grinning, and the other scoundrel's eyes glittered with satisfaction.

"Why, that's great. Oh, you're sure enough gun; you got a gun's hand, all right. Say, shake. I knew you was a crook first glimp, and when I see your hands I wondered whether it was forgin' or picking pockets. Well now, that's settled. Now, I got a little place just off the Strand, here. You send this cab on with your books, and come to this office of mine, and we'll have a talk."

Smiler was willing; he was fascinated with his new acquaintance, and within five minutes the pair were closeted in the phrenologist's den in a back street off the Strand.

It took the "palm-reader" precisely ten minutes to outline the idea of a *coup* which he and Smiler could work together as partners.

"Now, brother," he began, "what you got to understand is that you ain't going to last with that bunch of vote-sharps longer than about a fortnight—if that. They got a lot of brains among 'em, and the old girl, she's got the brightest. But she's just happened to get hung up on your forrid, and her own idea of her physiognomy skill. But by the time you've read one or two of them books she'll have lost her interest. You'll give yourself away, sure, and then it'll be the street for yours, and the salary'll fold its tent and silently steal away—see? You see that, don't you?"

Smiler nodded. He had known that all along.

"Well, so what you get, you got to get quick. And now, listen to me——"

The palm-reader's voice dropped to a dry and rapid whisper.

"Now, my name's Mesmer La Touche, and my title's Perfessor, and I'm a man you can trust," he began, and straightway unfolded his scheme.

Precisely a week later the Suffragette cohort, under command of Mrs. Carroway, gave a greatly-boomed demonstration at King James's Hall. This demonstration had been enormously advertised. Entrance was free to all people of reasonably respectable appearance, and promised to be successful, if only because of the fact that the proceedings were not to consist of speeches but chiefly of a series of limelight illuminated tableaux. The idea of the tableaux was to re-enact on the platform various scenes which had marked the progress of the Women's Suffrage Movement, and with which scenes the Suffragettes were associated in the mind's eyes of the public.

For instance, Tableau No. 1 on the programme was to consist of about thirty Suffragettes clothed in prison raiment with feeding-bottles being held to their mouths by savage-looking men, their arms being held by brutal wardresses. The curtain would go up, revealing the "atrocity" in full swing against a back curtain painted to resemble masonry and prison bars. Tableau No. 2 again depicted the devoted thirty, chained and padlocked to a row of iron railings, staring defiantly at a back curtain painted like a Cabinet Minister's house, while, rapidly approaching, the heavy sound of the feet of a large body of reckless police could be heard—thanks to the energy of a shirt-sleeved scene-shifter in the wings, who was to manipulate various wood and drum contrivances built for the purpose of imitating the march of many men. And so on, through a series of about twenty similar tableaux. The first item on the programme was to be the singing of the famous Suffragette song:

"Women of England, arise in your might,
For the tyrant has nigh burnt his boats;
Man has done wrong too long, let him now
do aright
And give women votes"

by the thirty Suffragettes, who would, in this scene, wear their choicest evening toilets and all their jewels, in order to let the public see that, despite their desperate deeds, they were women of consequence, wealth, and position.

It was a well-conceived plan of entertainment, and advertisement, and the deadheads of London—and London is practically populated by deadheads—flocked to this free evening with a unanimity beyond either praise or blame. The doors opened at seven o'clock, and at 7:15 there was not even standing-room left. The curtain was due to go up at 7:30.

Behind the scenes there was a rushing sound of many silk skirts, wafts of expensive perfumes, the odour of flowers, excited whisperings of feminine tongues, the flash and flicker of diamonds, giggles and squirks and bubblings of mirth. The place was alive with women. Here and there a scene-shifter slouched in and out of dark angles and nooks, concerned with ropes and canvas frames. In a big dressing-room at the back was an uncomfortable-looking man in evening dress—Mr. Smiler Bunn. He seemed to be the only man in the place.

It may be explained that The Brain had not been fruitful of results during the previous week of study, and the development of his intellect appeared to be less than the improvement in his manners and speech. His ideas about Women's Suffrage were about where they were before he became the Brain; if anything, they were rather more confused on the subject than otherwise. He had disappointed Mrs. Carroway a little, but, thanks to a few points praising her book, which had been taught him by the phrenologist, she continued to expect big things from him.

But Smiler knew perfectly well that it was only a question of a week or two before his association with the Suffragettes would cease. He was a good pickpocket, but he was no political organiser, and he knew it. "Professor" La Touche had explained that to him too frequently for him to forget it. But Smiler did not care; he and the phrenologist had made their arrangements, and long before the tableaux were ended that night they would be carried out.

Mr. Bunn's duty that evening was to act as a sort of stage attendant to the thirty Suffragettes. He was to chain them to the railings, for instance, to help arrange the prison feeding scene, and so on. Mrs. Carroway had drilled him well, and she had no doubt he would do the thing thoroughly.

Now, there are about four back entrances to King James's Hall, three of which are in different streets, and as half-past seven drew near there rolled unobtrusively up to one of these entrances a neat one-horse brougham. Nobody got out of the brougham, nor did the coachman descend. He just pulled up and waited. A policeman strolled up and remarked that it was a "perishin' cold night." The coachman, in a voice curiously resembling that of Mesmer La Touche, palm reader and phrenologist, agreed with him, and volunteered the information that presently he had to take away a big dress-basket of costumes belonging to a titled Suffragette who was inside the hall. The intelligent constable gathered that if anybody happened to be about to lend a hand when the basket came down there would probably be a "dollar" floating about (Mesmer believed in boldness). The policeman decided to remain and lend a hand. This was one of the reasons why neither that efficient officer nor Mesmer La Touche saw a laundry-van—driven by a small and curiously unimportant-looking man—pull up at one of the back entrances farther round the building, and wait there in very much the same way as the brougham was waiting.

Inside the hall the opening song had been sung, and the Suffragettes were now posing in the prison scene, much to the appreciation of a sympathetic audience. Smiler Bunn, with an armful of short chains, was waiting in the wings with a group of scene-shifters bearing sections of strong iron railings. The curtain went down on the first tableau, and the women came pouring off the stage, hurrying to their dressing-rooms to change for the great "Chains" scene. In three minutes the railings were fixed, and Smiler Bunn was chaining the Suffragettes to the bars. And it was noticeable that while all the evening he had been wearing a distinctly worried look, now, as one by one the padlocks clicked, that worried look was replaced by a gradually widening smile. Mrs. Carroway noticed it, and wondered why The Brain was smiling.

The last Suffragette chained up, Mr. Bunn made a bolt for the back. He had about three minutes to work in, and a lot to do in that three minutes. He ran in and out of the dressing-rooms, exactly like a weasel working a rabbit warren. Each time he came out of a room he brought an armful of furs. In a minute and a half he had run through all the dressing-rooms, and was literally staggering under his bundle of furs. He dropped them all into a big dress-basket at the end of the corridor, jammed down the lid, and whistled softly. Instantly a man—the driver of the laundry-van—appeared, running silently to him, took one end of the basket, and Smiler taking the other end, the pair of them vanished. In twenty seconds the basket was in the laundry-van.

"Hurry up, for pity's sake!" sobbed Mr. Bunn, as he scrambled up beside his confederate. "Nearly half of 'em had left their diamonds on their dressing-tables"—his voice cracked with excitement—"and *by Gawd! I've got 'em all!*"

The van rolled down the back street and round a corner—corners, it has been explained, were a specialty of Mr. Smiler Bunn. He peered back as the van swung round, and caught a fleeting glimpse of a one-horse brougham waiting patiently outside another back door. And he grinned.

"Poor old Mesmer!" he chuckled. "He's a clever man, is Mesmer, but if he don't get off out of it, 'im and his brougham, he'll stand a darn good chance of getting copped. He's a good man at ideas, Mesmer is, but he's no good at carryin' of 'em out. Ah, well—round the corner, mate. The sooner we get this lot to Israelstein's the better I shall be pleased. I wonder what Lilian will say? It'll take 'em a good twenty minutes to file them chains!"

There was a sudden sound of galloping hoofs. Smiler turned, looking back just in time to see the brougham tear down the street they had just left, and a few yards behind it half a dozen policemen running like hares.

"There goes Mesmer—poor chap! The town certainly owes him a living, same as he said, but I don't reckon he'll be collecting any of it tonight—*not* tonight, I don't reckon," muttered The Brain.

And the laundry-van rumbled comfortably on towards the business-place of that genial receiver of stolen goods, Mr. Israelstein.

Rogue: Romney Pringle

The Kailyard Novel

CLIFFORD ASHDOWN

ONE OF THE MOST HIGHLY regarded practitioners of the pure detective story is Richard Austin Freeman (1862–1943), a giant of the Golden Age, though his early works preceded the era between the two World Wars, which loosely bracket that age; his first mystery was *The Red Thumb Mark* (1907), in which he introduced one of the most popular detective characters of all time, Dr. John Thorndyke. Freeman also invented the inverted detective story with the publication of *The Singing Bone* (1912), a short story collection in which the reader knows who the murderers are at an early stage of the tale. The suspense derives not from the chase, as in the traditional mystery, but from discovering how the detective will unravel the clues and capture the criminal.

Before his illustrious detective came on the scene, however, Freeman wrote under the pseudonym Clifford Ashdown, in collaboration with John James Pitcairn (1860–1936), an obscure prison medical officer, a series of connected stories about a gentleman crook named Romney Pringle.

Pringle is ostensibly a literary agent with an office in London, but that job is merely a front for his criminal activities. As a student of human nature and blessed with finely tuned observational powers, Pringle lives by his wits, never resorting to force or violence. When he notices curious behavior, he will pursue the individual to determine whether he will have the opportunity for self-enrichment. "The Kailyard Novel" presents Pringle with his greatest challenge: what to do when an actual manuscript shows up at his office.

"The Kailyard Novel" was originally published in the November 1902 issue of *Cassell's*; it was first collected in *The Adventures of Romney Pringle* (London, Ward, Lock, 1902).

THE KAILYARD NOVEL

Clifford Ashdown

THE POSTMAN with resounding knock insinuated half-a-dozen packages into the slit in the outer door. He breathed hard, for it was a climb to the second floor, and then with heavy foot clattered down the stone stairs into Furnival's Inn. As the cataract descended between the two doors Mr. Pringle dropped his newspaper and stretched to his full length with a yawn; then, rolling out of his chair, he opened the inner door and gathered up the harvest of the mail. It was mostly composed of circulars; these he carelessly flung upon the table, and turned to the single letter among them. It was addressed with clerkly precision, *Romney Pringle, Esq., Literary Agent, 33 Furnival's Inn, London, E.C.*

Such a mode of address was quite a novelty in Pringle's experience. Was his inexistent literary agency about to be vivified? and wondering, he opened the envelope.

"Chapel Street, Wurzleford,
"August 25th.

"Dear Sir,
"Having recent occasion to visit a solicitor in the same block in connection with the affairs of a deceased friend, I made a note of your address, and shortly propose to avail myself of your kind offices in publishing a novel on the temperance question. I intend to call it Drouthy Neebors, *as I have adopted the Scotch dialect which appears to be so very popular and, I apprehend, remunerative. Having no practical acquaintance with the same, I think of making a study of it on the spot during my approaching month's holiday—most likely in the Island of Skye, where I presume the language may be a fair guide to that so much in favour. I shall start as soon as I can find a substitute and, if not unduly troubling you, should be greatly obliged by your inserting the enclosed advertisement for me in the* Undenominational Banner. *Your kindly doing so may lead to an earlier insertion than I could obtain for it through the local agent and so save me a week's delay. Thanking you in anticipation, believe me to be your very grateful and obliged*

"Adolphus Honeyby (Pastor)."

Although "Literary Agent" stared conspicuously from his door, Pringle's title had never hitherto induced an author, of however aspiring a type, to disturb the privacy of his chambers, and it was with an amused sense of the perfection of his disguise that he lighted a cigarette and sat down to think over Mr. Honeyby's proposal.

Wurzleford—Wurzleford? There seemed to be a familiar sound about the name. Surely he had read of it somewhere. He turned to the Society journal that he had been reading when the postman knocked.

> *Since leaving Sandringham the Maharajah of Satpura has been paying a round of farewell visits prior to his return to India in October. His Highness is well known as the owner of the famous Harabadi diamond, which is said to flash red and violet with every movement of its wearer, and his jewels were the sensation of the various state functions which he attended in native costume last season.*
>
> *I understand that the Maharajah is expected about the end of next week at Eastlingbury, the magnificent Sussex seat of Lord Wurzleford, and, as a man of wide and liberal culture, his Highness will doubtless be much interested in this ancestral home of one of our oldest noble families.*

Mr. Honeyby ought to have no difficulty in getting a *locum tenens*, thought Pringle, as he laid down the paper. He wondered how it would be to——? It was risky, but worth trying! Why let a good thing go a-begging? He had a good mind to take the berth himself! Wurzleford seemed an attractive little place. Well, its attractiveness would certainly not be lessened for him when the Maharajah arrived! At the very least it might prove an agreeable holiday, and in any case would lead to a new and probably amusing experience of human nature. Smiling at the ludicrous audacity of the idea, Pringle strolled up to the mantelpiece and interrogated himself in the Venetian mirror. Minus the delible portwine mark, a pair of pince-nez, blackened hair, and a small strip of easily applied whisker would be sufficient disguise. He thoughtfully lighted another cigarette.

But the necessity of testimonials occurred to him. Why not say he had sent the originals with an application he was making for a permanent appointment, and merely show Honeyby the type-written copies? He seemed an innocent old ass, and Pringle would trust to audacity to carry him through. He could write to Wurzleford from any Bloomsbury address, and follow the letter before Honeyby had time to reply. He had little doubt that he could clinch matters when it came to a personal interview; especially as Honeyby seemed very anxious to be off. There remained the knotty point of doctrine. Well, the Farringdon Street barrows, the grave of theological literature, could furnish any number of volumes of sermons, and it would be strange if they could not supply in addition a very efficient battery of controversial shot and shell. In the meantime he could get up the foundation of his "Undenominational" opinions from the Encyclopædia. And taking a volume of the *Britannica*, he was soon absorbed in its perusal.

Mr. Honeyby's advertisement duly appeared in the *Banner*, and was answered by a telegram announcing the application of the "Rev. Charles Courtley," who followed close on the heels of his message. Although surprised at the wonderfully rapid effect of the advertisement, the pastor was disinclined to quarrel with his good luck, and was too eager to be released to waste much time over preliminary inquiries. Indeed, he could think of little but the collection of material for his novel, and fretted to commence it. "Mr. Courtley's" manner and appearance, to say nothing of his very flattering testimonials, were all that could be desired; his acquaintance with controversial doctrine was profound, and the pastor, innocently wondering how such brilliance had failed to attain a more eminent place in the denomination, had eagerly ratified his engagement.

"Well, I must say, Mr. Courtley, you seem to know so well what will be expected of you, that I really don't think I need wait over tonight," remarked Mr. Honeyby towards the end of the interview.

"I presume there will be no objection to my riding the bicycle I have brought with me?" asked Pringle, in his new character.

"Not at all—by no means! I've often thought of taking to one myself. Some of the church-members live at such a distance, you see. Besides, there is nothing derogatory in it. Lord Wurzleford, for instance, is always riding about, and so are some of the party he has down for the shooting. There is some Indian prince or other with them, I believe."

"The Maharajah of Satpura?" Pringle suggested.

"Yes, I think that is the name; do you know him?" asked Mr. Honeyby, impressed by the other's air of refinement.

"No—I only saw it mentioned in the *Park Lane Review*," said Pringle simply.

So Mr. Honeyby departed for London, *en route* for the north, by an even earlier train than he had hoped for.

About an hour afterwards Pringle was resting by the wayside, rather winded by cycling up one of the early undulations of the Downs which may be seen rising nearly everywhere on the Wurzleford horizon. He had followed the public road, here unfenced for some miles, through Eastlingbury Park, and now lay idle on the springy turf. The harebells stirred with a dry rustle in the imperceptible breeze, and all around him rose the music of the clumsy little iron-bells, clanking rhythmically to every movement of the wethers as they crisply mowed the herbage closer than any power of scythe. As Pringle drank in the beauty of the prospect, a cyclist made his appearance in the act of coasting down the hill beyond. Suddenly he swerved from side to side; his course grew more erratic, the zigzags wider: it was clear that he had lost control of the machine. As he shot with increasing momentum down the slope, a white figure mounted the crest behind, and pursued him with wild-waving arms, and shouts which were faintly carried onward by the wind.

In the valley beyond the two hills flowed the Wurzle, and the road, taking a sharp turn, crossed it by a little bridge with brick parapets; without careful steering, a cyclist with any way on, would surely strike one or other side of the bridge, with the prospect of a ducking, if not of a worse catastrophe. Quickly grasping the situation, Pringle mounted his machine, sprinted down to the bridge and over it, flinging himself off in time to seize the runaway by his handlebar. He was a portly, dark-complexioned gentleman in a Norfolk suit, and he clung desperately to Pringle as together they rolled into a ditch. By this time the white figure, a native servant, had overtaken his master, whom he helped to rise with a profusion of salaams, and then gathered up the shattered fragments of the bicycle.

"I must apologize for dragging you off your machine," said Pringle, when he too had picked himself up. "But I think you were in for a bad accident."

"No apology is necessary for saving my life, sir," protested the stout gentleman in excellent English. "My tire was punctured on the hill, so the brake refused to act. But may I ask your name?"

As Pringle handed him a card inscribed, "Rev. Charles Courtley," the other continued, "I am the Maharajah of Satpura, and I hope to have the pleasure of thanking you more fully on a less exciting occasion." He bowed politely, with a smile disclosing a lustrous set of white teeth, and leaning on the servant's arm, moved towards a group of cyclists who were cautiously descending the scene of his disaster.

In the jog-trot routine of the sleepy little place, where one day was very much like another, and in the study of the queer people among whom Pringle found himself a sort of deity, the days rapidly passed. To some of the church-members his bicycle had appeared rather a startling innovation, but his tact had smoothed over all difficulties, while the feminine Undenominationalists would have forgiven much to such an engaging personality, for Pringle well knew how to ingratiate himself with the more influential half of humanity. It was believed that his eloquence had, in itself, been the means of recalling several seceders to the fold, and it was even whispered that on several occasions gold coins graced the collection-plates—an event unprecedented in the history of the connection!

September had been an exceptionally hot month, but one day was particularly oppressive. Sunset had brought the slightest relief, and at Eastlingbury that evening the heat was emphatically tropical. The wide-open windows availed nothing to cool the room. The very candles drooped crescent-wise, and singed their shades. Although the clouds were scudding high aloft, and cast transient shadows upon the lawn, no leaf stirred within the park. The hour was late, and the ladies had long withdrawn, but the men still sat listening. It was a story of the jungle—of a fight between a leopard and a sambur-deer, and every one's pulse had quickened, and every one had wished the story longer.

"You are evidently an intrepid explorer, Mr. Courtley," commented the Earl, as his guest finished.

"And a keen observer," added the Maharajah. "I never heard a more realistic description of a fight. I have not had Mr. Courtley's good fortune to see such a thing in the jungle, although I frequently have wild-beast fights—*satmaris*, we call them—for the amusement of my good people of Satpura."

The Maharajah had found a little difficulty in inducing Lord Wurzleford to extend his hospitality to "Mr. Courtley." To begin with, the latter was an Undenominationalist, and only a substitute one at that! Then, too, the Maharajah had made his acquaintance in such a very unconventional manner. All the same, to please his Highness——

Pringle had thus a good deal of lee-way to make up in the course of the evening, and it says much for his success, that the ladies were unanimous in regretting the necessity for leaving the dinner-table. Indeed, from the very first moment of his arrival, he had steadily advanced in favour. He had not only talked brilliantly himself, but had been the cause of brilliancy in others—or, at least, of what passes for brilliancy in smart circles. His stories appeared to be drawn from an inexhaustible fund. He had literally been everywhere and seen everything. As to the Maharajah, who had of late grown unutterably bored by the smart inanities of the house-party, the poor man hailed him with unutterable relief. Towards the end of dinner, a youth had remarked confidentially to the lady beside him, that "that dissentin' fellow seemed a real good sort." He voiced the general opinion.

While Pringle, with the aid of a finger-bowl and some dessert-knives, was demonstrating the problem of the Nile *Barrage* to an interested audience, an earnest consultation was proceeding at the head of the table. The Maharajah, Lord Wurzleford, and the butler were in solemn conclave, and presently the first was seen to rise abruptly and retire in unconcealed agitation. So obviously did the host share this emotion, that the conversation flagged and died out; and amid an awkward pause, numerous inquiring glances, which good breeding could not entirely repress, were directed towards the head of the table, where the butler, with a pallid face, still exchanged an occasional word with his master.

With a view to breaking the oppressive silence, Pringle was about to resume his demonstration, when Lord Wurzleford anticipated him.

"Before we leave the table," said the peer in a constrained voice, "I want to tell you that a most unpleasant thing has happened under this roof. The apartments of the Maharajah of Satpura have been entered, and a quantity of jewellery is missing. I understand that some one was heard moving about the room only half-an-hour ago, and a strange man was met crossing the park towards Bleakdown not long after. I am sending into Eastlingbury for the police, and in the meantime the servants are scouring the park. Pray let the matter be kept secret from the ladies as long as possible."

Consternation was visible on every face, and amid a loud buzz of comment, the table was promptly deserted.

"Will you excuse me?" said Pringle as he approached Lord Wurzleford, whose self-possession appeared to have temporarily deserted him. "I know the Bleakdown road well, and have cycled over it several times. I rode out here on my machine, and perhaps I might be able to overtake the burglar. Every moment is of importance, and the police may be some time before they arrive."

"I am greatly obliged to you for the suggestion!" exclaimed the peer, adding with a dismal attempt at jocularity, "Perhaps you may succeed in doing his Highness a further service with your cycle."

Between four and five miles from Eastlingbury the high road leaves the park, and crosses the Great Southern Canal. The bridge is of comparatively low span, and a sloping way leads down from the road to the towing-path. As the gradient rose towards the bridge, Pringle slowed up, and steering on to the path, dismounted on the grass, and leant the machine against the hedge. He had caught sight of a man's figure, some eighty yards ahead, standing motionless on the hither side of the bridge; he appeared to be listening for sounds of pursuit. In the silence a distant clock was striking eleven, and the figure presently turned aside and disappeared. When Pringle reached the bridge, the grinding of feet upon the loose gravel echoed from beneath the arch, and stealing down the slope to the towing-path, he peered round the corner of the abutment.

The clouds had all disappeared by now, and the moon flashing from the water made twilight under the bridge. On his knees by the water's edge a man was busily securing a bundle with a cord. To and fro he wound it in criss-cross fashion, and then threaded through the network what looked like an ebony ruler, which he drew from his pocket. A piece of cord dangled from the bundle, and holding it in one hand, he felt with the other along the board which edged the towing-path at this point. Presently he found something to which he tied the cord, and then lowered bundle and all into the canal.

For some time past a sound of footsteps approaching on the road above had been plainly audible to Pringle, although it was lost on the other, absorbed as he was in his task; now, as he rose from his cramped position, and was in the act of stretching himself, he paused and listened. At this moment Pringle slightly changed his position, and loosened a stone which plunged into the water. The man looked up, and catching sight of him, retreated with a muttered curse to the far side of the arch. For a second he scowled at the intruder, and then turned and began to run down the towing-path in the shadow of the bank.

"There he goes—See! On the towing-path!" shouted Pringle, as he scrambled up to the road and confronted two members of the county constabulary who were discussing the portent of the deserted bicycle. Seeing further concealment was useless, the fugitive now took to his heels in earnest, and ran hot-foot beside the canal with the two policemen and Pringle in pursuit.

But Pringle soon dropped behind; and when their footsteps were lost in the distance, he made his way back to the road, and hoisting the machine on his shoulder, carried it down the slope and rested it under the bridge. Groping along the wooden edging, his hand soon encountered the cord, and hauling on it with both hands, for the weight was not inconsiderable, he landed the bundle on the bank. What had appeared to be a ruler now proved to be a very neat jemmy folding in two. Admiring it with the interest of an expert, he dropped it into the water, and then ripped up the towel which formed the covering of the bundle. Although he anticipated the contents, he was scarcely prepared for the gorgeous spectacle which saluted him, and as he ran his hands through the confused heap of gold and jewels, they glittered like a milky way of stars even in the subdued pallor of the moonlight.

The striking of the half-hour warned him that time pressed, and taking a spanner from his cycle-wallet, he unshipped the handle-bar, and deftly packed it and the head-tube with the treasure. Some of the bulkier, and perhaps also less valuable articles had to be left; so rolling them up again in the towel, he sent them to join the folding-jemmy. Screwing the nuts home, he carried the cycle up to the road again, and pedalled briskly along the downgrade to Eastlingbury.

"Hi! Stop there!"

He had forgotten to light his lamp, and as a bull's-eye glared upon him, and a burly policeman seized his handle-bar, Pringle mentally began to assess the possible cost of this outrage upon the county by-laws. But a semi-excited footman ran up, and turning another lamp upon him, at once saluted him respectfully.

"It's all right, Mr. Parker," said the footman. "This gentleman's a friend of his lordship's."

The policeman released the machine, and saluted Pringle in his turn.

"Sorry you were stopped, sir," apologized the footman, "but our orders is to watch all the roads for the burglar."

"Haven't they caught him yet?"

"No, sir! 'E doubled back into the park, and they lost 'im. One of the grooms, who was sent out on 'orseback, met the policemen who said they'd seen you, but didn't know where you'd got to after they lost the burglar. They were afraid 'e'd get back on to the road and make off on your bicycle, as you'd left it there, and they told the groom to ride back and tell us all to look out for a man on a bicycle."

"So you thought I was the burglar! But how did he get into the house?"

"Why, sir, the Indian king's 'ead man went up about ten to get the king's room ready. When 'e tried the door, 'e found 'e couldn't open it. Then 'e called some of the other Indians up, and when they couldn't open it either, and they found the door wasn't locked at all, they said it was bewitched."

Here the policeman guffawed, and then stared fixedly at the moon, as if wondering whether that was the source of the hilarity. The footman glanced reprovingly at him, and continued—

"They came down into the servants' 'all, and the one who speaks English best told us about it. So I said, 'Let's get in through the window.' So we went round to the tennis-lawn, underneath the king's rooms. The windows were all open, just as they'd been left before dinner, because of the 'eat. There's an old ivy-tree grows there, sir, with big branches all along the wall, thick enough for a man to stand on. So Mr. Strong, the butler, climbed up, and us after 'im. We couldn't see much amiss at first, but the king's 'ead man fell on 'is knees, and turned 'is eyes up, and thumped 'imself on the chest, and said 'e was a dead man! And when we said why? 'e said all the king's jewels were gone. And sure enough, some cases that 'eld diamond and ruby brooches, and necklaces, and things, were all burst open and cleaned out, and a lot of others for rings and small things were lying about empty. And we found the burglar 'd screwed wedges against the doors, and that was why they couldn't be opened. So we took them up and opened the doors, and Mr. Strong went down and reported it to 'is lordship, and 'e broke it to the king. But the 'ead man says the king took on about it terribly, and 'e's afraid the king'll take 'im and 'ave a wild elephant trample on 'is 'ead to execute 'im, when 'e gets back to India!"

Here the footman paused for breath, and the constable seized the opportunity to assert himself.

"So you'll know the man again, if you should see him, sir," he chimed in.

"That I shall," Pringle asseverated.

"A pleasant-spoken gentleman as ever was!" observed the footman as Pringle rode away, and the policeman grunted emphatic assent.

Walking down North Street, the principal thoroughfare in the village, next morning, Pringle was accosted by a stranger. He was small but wiry in figure, dressed very neatly, and had the cut of a gentleman's servant out of livery.

"Are you Mr. Courtley, sir?" respectfully touching his hat.

"Yes. Can I be of any service to you?"

"I should like to have a quiet talk with you, sir, if I may call upon you."

"Shall we say six this evening, then?"

"If you please, sir."

Opining that here was a possible recruit for the connection gained by his eloquence, Pringle went on his way. He had just received a letter from Mr. Honeyby announcing his return, and was not dissatisfied at the prospect of the evening seeing the end of his masquerade. Not that it had grown irksome, but having exhausted the predatory resources of Wurzleford, he began to sigh for the London pavement. The pastor wrote that having completed his philological studies in the Island of Skye, he had decided to return South at once. But the chief reason for thus curtailing his stay was the extreme monotony of the climate, in which, according to local opinion, snow is the only variant to the eternal rain. Besides, he feared that the prevalent atmosphere of herring-curing had seriously impaired his digestion! On the whole, therefore, he thought it best to return, and might be expected home about twelve hours after his letter. He trusted, however, that Mr. Pringle would remain his guest; at all events until the end of the month.

Mr. Honeyby's study was an apartment on the ground-floor with an outlook, over a water-butt, to the garden. It partook somewhat of the nature of a stronghold, the door being a specially stout one, and the windows having the protection—so unusual in a country town—of iron bars. These precautions were due to Mr. Honeyby's nervous apprehensions of burglary after "collection-days," when specie had to repose there for the night. It was none the less a cheerful room, and Pringle spent most of his indoor-time there. He was occupied in sorting some papers in readiness for the pastor's return, when, punctually as the clock struck six, the housekeeper knocked at his door.

"There's a young man come, sir, who says you're expecting him," she announced.

"Oh, ah! Show him in," said Pringle.

His chance acquaintance of the morning entered, and depositing his hat beneath a chair, touched his forehead and sat down. But no sooner had the door closed upon the woman than his manner underwent a complete change.

"I see you don't remember me," he said, leaning forward, and regarding Pringle steadily.

"No, I must confess you have rather the advantage of me," said Pringle distantly.

"And yet we *have* met before. Not so long ago either!"

"I have not the slightest recollection of ever having seen you before this morning," Pringle asserted tartly. He was nettled at the man's persistence, and felt inclined to resent the rather familiar manner in which he spoke.

"I must assist your memory then. The first time I had the pleasure of seeing you was last night."

"I should be glad to know where."

"Certainly!" Then very slowly and distinctly, "It was under a bridge on the Grand Southern Canal."

Pringle, in spite of his habitual composure, was unable to repress a slight start.

"I see you have not forgotten the circumstance. The time, I think, was about eleven P.M., wasn't it? Well, never mind that; the moon enabled me to get a better look at you than you got of me."

Pringle took refuge in a diplomatic silence, and the other walked across the room, and selecting the most comfortable chair, coolly produced a cigarette-case. Pringle observed, almost subconsciously, that it was a very neat gold one, with a monogram in one corner worked in diamonds.

"Will you smoke?" asked the man. "No? Well, you'll excuse me." And he leisurely kindled a cigarette, taking very detailed stock of Pringle while doing so.

"Now it's just as well we understood one another," he continued, as he settled himself in the chair. "My name is of no consequence, though I'm known to my associates as 'The Toff'; poor souls, they have such a profound respect for education! Now those who know me will tell you I'm not a man whom it pays to trifle with. Who you are, I don't know exactly, and I don't know that I very much care—it's rather an amusing thing, by the way, that no one else seems to be any the wiser! But what I do know"—here he sat straight up, and extended a menacing fist in Pringle's direction—"and what it'll be a healthy thing for you to understand, is, that I'm not going to leave here tonight without that stuff!"

"My good man, what on earth are you talking about?" indulgently asked Pringle, who by this time had recovered his imperturbability.

"Now don't waste time; you don't look altogether a fool!" "The Toff" drew a revolver from his pocket, and carelessly counted the chambers which were all loaded. "One, two, three, four, five, six! I've got six reasons for what I've said. Let's see now—First, you saw me hiding the stuff; second, no one else did; third, it's not there now; fourth, the Maharajah hasn't got it; fifth, there's no news of its having been found by any one else; sixth, and last, therefore you've got it!" He checked the several heads of his reasoning, one by one, on the chambers of the revolver as one might tell them on the fingers.

"Very logically reasoned!" remarked Pringle calmly. "But may I inquire how it is you are so positive in all these statements?"

"I'm not the man to let the grass grow under my feet," said "The Toff" vain-gloriously. "I've been making inquiries all the morning, and right up to now! I hear the poor old Maharajah has gone to Scotland Yard for help. But it strikes me the affair will remain a mystery 'forever and always,' as the people say hereabouts. And, as I said just now, you seem to be rather a mystery to most people. I spotted you right enough last night, but I wanted to find out all I could about you from your amiable flock before I tackled you in person. Well, I think I have very good grounds for believing you to be an impostor. That's no concern of mine, of course, but I presume you have your own reasons for coming down here. Now, a word to your principal, and a hint or two judiciously dropped in a few quarters round the place, will soon make it too hot for you, and so your little game, whatever it may be, will be spoiled."

"But supposing I am unable to help you?"

"I can't suppose any such thing! I am going to stick to you like tar, my reverend sir, and if you think of doing a bolt"—he glanced at the revolver, and then put it in his pocket—"take my advice and only *think* of it!"

"Is that all you have to say?" asked Pringle.

"Not quite. Look here now! I've been planning this job for the last four months and more, and I'm not going to take all the risk, and let you or any one else collar all the profit. By George, you've mistaken your man if you think that! I am willing to even go the length of recognizing you as a partner, and giving you ten per cent. for your trouble in taking charge of the stuff, and bringing it to a place of safety and so on, but now you've got to shell out!"

"Very well," said Pringle, rising. "Let me first get the housekeeper out of the way."

"No larks now!" growled "The Toff"; adding peremptorily, "I give you a couple of minutes only—and leave the door open!"

Without replying, Pringle walked to the door, and slipping through, closed and double-locked it behind him before "The Toff" had time to even rise from his chair.

"You white-livered cur! You—you infernal sneak!" vociferated the latter as Pringle crossed the hall.

Being summer-time, the fire-irons were absent from the study. There was no other lethal weapon wherewith to operate. Escape by the window was negatived by the bars. For the time then "The Toff" was a negligible quantity. Pringle ran down the kitchen-stairs. At the bottom was a gas-bracket, and stretching out his hand he turned on the gas as he passed. Out in the little kitchen there was much clattering of pots and dishes. The housekeeper was engaged in urgent culinary operations against Mr. Honeyby's return.

"Mrs. Johnson!" he bawled, as a furious knocking sounded from the study.

"Whatever's the matter, sir?" cried the startled woman.

"Escape of gas! We've been looking for it upstairs! Don't you smell it out here? You must turn it off at the main!" He rattled off the alarming intelligence in well-simulated excitement.

"Gas it is!" she exclaimed nervously, as the familiar odour greeted her nostrils.

Now the meter, as is customary, resided in the coal-cellar, and as the faithful creature opened the door and stumbled forwards, she suddenly found herself stretched upon the floor, while all became darkness. It almost seemed as if she had received a push from behind, and her head whirling with the unexpected shock, she painfully arose from her rocky bed, and slowly groped towards the door. But for all her pulling and tugging it held fast and never gave an inch. Desisting, as the truth dawned upon her that in some mysterious way she had become a prisoner, she bleated plaintively for help, and began to hammer at the door with a lump of coal.

Up the stairs again. Pringle glanced at the hall-door, then shot the bolts top and bottom, and put the chain up. "The Toff" seemed to be using some of the furniture as a battering-ram. Thunderous blows and the sharp splintering of wood showed that, despite his lack of tools, he was (however clumsily) engaged in the active work of his profession, and the door shivered and rattled ominously beneath the onslaught.

Pringle raced up-stairs, and in breathless haste tore off his clerical garb. Bang, bang, crash! He wished the door were iron. How "The Toff" roused the echoes as he savagely laboured for freedom! And whenever he paused, a feeble diapason ascended from the basement. The study-door would soon give at this rate. Luckily the house stood at the end of the town, or the whole neighbourhood would have been roused by this time. He hunted for his cycling suit. Where could that wretched old woman have stowed it? Curse her officiousness! He almost thought of rushing down and releasing her that she might disclose its whereabouts. Every second was priceless. At last! Where had that button-hook hidden itself now? How stiff the box-cloth seemed—he had never noticed it before. Now the coat. Collar and tie? Yes, indeed, he had nearly forgotten he still wore the clerical tie. No matter, a muffler would hide it all. Cap—that was all! Gloves he could do without for once.

Bang, crash, crack!

With a last look round he turned to leave the room, and faced the window. A little way down the road a figure was approaching. Something about it looked familiar, he thought; seemed to be coming from the direction of the railway-station, too. He stared harder. So it was! There was no doubt about it! Swathed in a Scotch maud, his hand grasping a portmanteau, the Rev. Adolphus Honeyby advanced blithely in the autumn twilight.

Down the stairs Pringle bounded, three at a time. "The Toff" could hear, but not see him as yet. The study-door was already tottering; one hinge had gone. Even as he landed with a thud at the foot of the stairs, "The Toff's" hand and arm appeared at the back of the door.

"I'd have blown the lock off if it wasn't for giving the show away," "The Toff" snarled through his clenched teeth, as loudly as his panting respiration would permit. "I'll soon be through now, and then we'll square accounts!" What he said was a trifle more full-flavoured, but this will suffice.

Crash! bang!! crack!!! from the study-door.

Rat-a-tat-a-tat! was the sudden response from the hall-door. It was Mr. Honeyby knocking! And, startled at the noise, "The Toff" took a momentary respite from his task.

Down to the basement once more. Mrs. Johnson's pummelling sounded louder away from the more virile efforts of the others. Fiercely "The Toff" resumed his labours. What an uproar! Mr. Honeyby's curiosity could not stand much more of that. He would be round at the back presently. The bicycle stood by the garden-door. Pringle shook it slightly, and something rattled; the precious contents of the head and handle-bar were safe enough. He opened the door, and wheeled the machine down the back-garden, and out into the little lane behind.

Loud and louder banged the knocker. But as a triumphant crash and clatter of wood-work resounded from the house, Pringle rode into the fast-gathering darkness.

Villain: Don Q.

The Parole of Gevil-Hay

K. & HESKETH PRICHARD

THE REMARKABLE HESKETH VERNON PRICHARD (later Hesketh-Prichard) (1876–1922) was an adventurer, big-game hunter (said, at one point, to be the best shot in the world), and author. He was rejected for service in World War I as too old (he was thirty-seven) but received a commission and trained snipers, earning a Distinguished Service Order.

At the age of twenty, he decided to eschew his law degree to become a writer, producing his first story, which his mother (Katherine O'Brien Prichard, 1851–1935) edited. They embarked on a writing career together under the noms de plume of H. Heron and E. Heron, finding success with a series of ghost stories about the character Flaxman Low, the first psychic detective of mystery fiction. Curiously, *Pearson's Magazine* promoted these tales as true stories. They were collected in 1899 under the title *Ghosts: Being the Experiences of Flaxman Low*, which is now a famously rare book in first edition.

K. and Hesketh Prichard created Don Q., a grim Spaniard who is not the lovable Robin Hood figure of fable but a charismatic bandit who is vicious toward the rich and evil but (relatively) kind to the poor and good. The stories were collected in *The Chronicles of Don Q.* (1904) and *New Chronicles of Don Q.* (1906; published in the United States as *Don Q. in the Sierra*). The authors also wrote a novel, *Don Q.'s Love Story* (1909), which served as the basis for the silent film *Don Q., Son of Zorro* (1925), starring Douglas Fairbanks. On his own, Hesketh Prichard wrote *November Joe: The Detective of the Woods* (1913), for which he used his background of hunting and outdoor experiences.

"The Parole of Gevil-Hay," the first Don Q. story, was originally published in the January 1898 issue of *Badminton Magazine*; it was first collected in *The Chronicles of Don Q.* (London, Chapman & Hall, 1904).

THE PAROLE OF GEVIL-HAY

K. & Hesketh Prichard

Chapter I

IF YOU TAKE A MAP of Spain and follow the Mediterranean coast, where, across the narrow seas, the mountains of Europe and the mountains of Africa stand up forever one against the other, you will find on the Spanish side the broad line of the Andalusian highlands stretching from Jerez to Almeria and beyond. Here is a wild, houseless country of silent forest and evergreen thicket climbing up towards barren, sun-tortured heights. It is patched with surfaces of smooth rock, and ravines strewn with tumbled boulders; lined by almost untrodden mule tracks, and sparsely dotted with the bottle-shaped *chozas* of the charcoal-burners and the herdsmen.

The lord of this magnificent desolation was locally, though not officially, acknowledged to be a certain brigand chief, known far and wide as Don Q., an abbreviation of the nickname Quebranta-Huesos, which is, being interpreted, the bone-smasher, a name by which the *neophron* or bone-breaking vulture goes in those parts. In answer to any question as to where the bandit came from or when he began to harry the countryside, one was told that he had been there always, which, though manifestly untrue, was, nevertheless, as near an approach to historical accuracy as may be found on many a printed page.

For Don Q., though perhaps not endowed with the sempiternal quality, had many other attributes of mysterious greatness. Few had seen him, but all knew him and feared him, and most had felt his power; he had cognizance of what was said or done, or, indeed, even thought of, throughout the length and the breadth of the wild region over which he held sway. He dealt out reward and punishment with the same unsparing hand. If a goatherd pleased him, the fellow was made rich for life; but no man lived to bring him false information twice.

From his hidden abiding-place in the black rock, a hundred feet above the general camp of his followers, he was to the surrounding country as a poised hawk to a covey of partridges.

The stories of his savageries were brought down to the plains by leather-clad mountaineers, and occasional expeditions were sent up against him by those in authority in the towns. But every attempt failed, and the parties of *guardias civiles* came back fewer in numbers, having built cairns over their dead, leaving them near lonely shrines, amongst the ravens and the big ragged birds of the sierra.

From all this it will be seen that the brigand chief was not a common brand of cut-throat; in fact, he belonged to that highest class known as *sequestradores*, or robbers who hold to ransom; and, though his methods were considered unpleasant, he carried through most of his affairs with satisfaction to himself, for he was an exceptionally good man of business.

No doubt, if any individual were to set up in the same line of life within twenty miles of a good-sized English or American town, the chances are that his career would end with something of suddenness. But in Spain it is always tomorrow, and the convenience of the system lies in the fact that there is always another tomorrow waiting to take up the deferred responsibilities. If Providence had seen fit to remove that fatal *mañana* from the Spanish vocabulary and the Spanish mind, the map might be differently coloured to-day.

A party of *civiles* had just returned from a particularly unlucky excursion into the mountains, and there was, therefore, the less excuse for the foolhardiness of Gevil-Hay, who declined to pay any heed to the warnings of H.B.M.'s consul on the seaboard or the deep hints of his host at the little inn under the mountains, but continued to pursue his journey across the sierra. He could not be brought to see why the will of a hill-thief should stand between him and his desire to wander where he liked.

Gevil-Hay's obstinacy sprang from a variety of causes. He was in bad health and worse spirits, and he had for the whole period of his manhood governed a small kingdom of wild and treacherous hill-men in the interests of the British Government, backed only by a handful of native police, and, what is more, had governed it with conspicuous success.

Besides, beneath a quiet exterior, Gevil-Hay was as hard to move as the nether millstone. After putting these facts together, it will not be difficult to see that when he started for his long solitary ride across the *Boca de Jabili* he only did what a man in his condition and with his temperament and experience would be likely to do.

He carried a revolver, it is true, but he found no use for it on a dim evening when something gripped his neck from behind. Indeed it was only after an interval that he understood vaguely how he came to be the centre of a hustling crowd of silent men who smelt offensively of garlic and leather. They tied him upon his horse and the party set their faces north-east towards the towering bulk of the higher sierra.

But for once in a way the spiders of Don Q. had taken a captive in their net of whom they could make nothing. In the dawn when they got him out of the cane-built hut in which they had passed the latter part of the night, they saw that he was tall and thin and rather stooped, with a statuesque face of extreme pallor. So far he was not so altogether uncommon. But the brigands were accustomed to see character come out strongly in similar circumstances, yet Gevil-Hay asked no questions, he evinced no trace of curiosity as to where they were taking him. He showed nothing but a cold indifference. A man in his position who asked no questions was a man of mark. He puzzled them.

The truth was that Gevil-Hay despised his warnings and took his ill-fortune in the same spirit of fatalism. He had been an Indian Civil servant of good prospects and bad health. In the end the bad health proved the stronger, and his country retired him on a narrow income. He was unemotionally heartbroken. There was a woman somewhere in the past, a woman to whom the man's lonely heart had clung steadfastly through the years while health slowly and surely deserted him. "Love me little, love me long" has its corresponding lines set deep throughout the character, and if Gevil-Hay was incapable of a passion of love or sorrow, he was not ignorant of the pang of a long renunciation and an enduring regret.

Don Q.'s men were no respecters of persons. The prisoner's reserve they finally put down to his being poor, probably deadly poor, for poverty is the commonest of all evils in Spain, and they treated him accordingly.

Rough handling and the keen winds of the upper sierra are not wholesome for a fever-shaken frame, but Gevil-Hay occupied himself with himself until he was brought into the presence of Don Q.

Late in the afternoon a halt was called, the prisoner was blindfolded and led through the scrub; then the wind blew more sharply in his face and Gevil-Hay knew that he trod on wiry grass, which in turn changed to a surface of bare echoing rock. Passing out of this tunnel he was secured by having his hands tied, and, when his eyes were uncovered, he found himself in a small enclosed valley with sheer precipitous sides. The ground was furred with coarse grass, but there were thickets of flowering shrubs on the higher ledges and a backing of wind-blown pines.

A couple of men hurried him up a winding pathway cut out of the cliff-face to the mouth of a cave, fronting which was a little natural terrace.

There they found Don Q., sitting in the sunshine, with a wide hat of felt drawn over his brows. Gevil-Hay saw nothing vulture-like but one lean hand like a delicate yellow claw that held the cloak about his neck.

"To whom have I the pleasure to address myself?" asked the brigand, with extreme and unexpected politeness.

Gevil-Hay's hands being loosed, he fixed his single eye-glass and glanced round the glen before he replied.

"Perhaps you will be good enough to give me some idea of your career, and we can go into the question of the ransom at the end of it," resumed Don Q. in his courteous manner, as the other finished speaking.

Gevil-Hay answered briefly in good Spanish, for an Indian civilian is supposed to start in life equipped with a knowledge of every language under the sun.

"Ah, then you have retired—well, been forced to retire—but with a pension? Yes!"

"Yes."

Don Q., like all other foreigners, entertained extravagant ideas as to the lavishness of the English Government. Perhaps by comparison it *is* lavish.

"How much?" he asked.

"£300 a year."

"Ah," the brigand hesitated while he made a mental calculation. "Your ransom, señor——" He stopped; he understood how to make a judicious use of suspense.

In the pause a shot re-echoed through the ravine, followed by a sound of loud, sudden brawling immediately below.

The Spaniard snatched off his hat and peered out over the end of the terrace. His cloak lay about him like a vulture's tumbled plumage, as he turned his face over his shoulder to listen with outstretched neck.

Then for the first time Gevil-Hay saw his face clearly, the livid, wrinkled eyelids, the white wedge-shaped bald head narrowing down to the hooked nose, the lean neck, the cruel aspect, all the distinctive features of the *quebranta-huesos* transmuted into human likeness.

A few sharp sibilant words hissed down the cliff, and the two swarthy quarrellers below fell apart with a simultaneous upward look of apprehension.

"Your punishment waits, my children," said the chief gently. "Go!"

The ruffians slunk away. They were curiously cowed and by a word. It was an object lesson to Gevil-Hay, and perhaps the brigand watched him covertly to see how he would take it. But the prisoner's calm face gave no sign.

"Señor," said Don Q., "you are a poor man you say, and you are lucky in that I believe you. I will name but a moderate sum, and after this conversation there will be no more about it. We will omit the subject while you remain my guest." The soft speech grew softer.

"There is no need to give my position a false name," answered Gevil-Hay; "I am your prisoner. Misfortune introduced us."

Above all things created, a man who defied him was abhorrent to the brigand, but now he saw one who looked him in the eyes without either fear or curiosity. Gevil-Hay interested him, but rather as a frog interests a vivisector.

"On one thing I pride myself, señor," he said presently. "When I speak, the thing which I say is unalterable. I am about to tell you the amount of your ransom. I will contrive to send down your message."

"You will have to give me time if you wish to get the money," said the other. "I have only my pension, and I must see if they will commute that."

"Your Government will pay," asserted Don Q. suavely. "They will not lose so valuable a servant."

"Do you care for a worn-out coat?" asked Gevil-Hay with a mirthless laugh. "Besides, I came here in spite of warnings that the roads were unsafe. I must bear the consequences."

Don Q.'s wrinkled eyelids quivered.

"Shall we say twenty thousand dollars?" he asked, as if deferring to his prisoner's opinion.

"You have said it, and that's the end," returned Gevil-Hay; "though," he added, "I don't think you are ever likely to see it. They will commute my pension on the scale of the probable duration of my life, and that will give no satisfactory average, I am afraid. I hope you may get fifteen thousand dollars. I doubt if you will get more."

"I trust for your sake I may get twenty thousand," replied the Spaniard, "otherwise a disappointment might lead to consequences—regrettable consequences."

He shook his head and blinked as he withdrew into the cave.

Meanwhile Gevil-Hay wrote out his appeal and a request to Ingham, the consul at the seaport under the mountains, that he would urge the matter forward. Then he sat and drearily watched the evening wind in the pines above the gorge, and wished vainly that he could do anything—anything but watch and wait.

It is a bad moment when a man believes his days of action are past, while his brain works strong and resolute as ever! He longed to beat the brigand at his own game, for he fancied he was a man worth beating.

In the gloom, when the fire was lit outside the cave, Don Q. returned. He took the sealed letter that Gevil-Hay held ready for dispatch.

"And now, señor, I regard you as my guest," said he; "and in all things but one you may command me. I assure you I will do my best to play the host well and to make your stay among us pleasant to you. I have your parole, señor?"

Gevil-Hay hesitated. The fever had laid its hand upon him, he shivered as he stood in the breeze, and the joints of his knees were unloosed with a creeping weakness. Not so many years ago the world seemed at his feet; he had striven hard for his position and won it—won more than that. He had tasted much of life's sweetness and the joy of power and growing success, yet to-day——

"Yes," he answered.

As the days went on Gevil-Hay found he had a good deal in common with the chief, who proved himself an attentive host. There was something kindred between the two men, and yet Gevil-Hay was alternately attracted and repelled.

Yielding to the charm of Don Q.'s fine courtesy he was led on to talk of many things, and he talked well, while the chilly thin-framed hearer, crouching in his cloak over the fire, listened with interest to a later view of the great world than lay within his own remembrance. Also the Englishman had been a wanderer in far countries; he was a man who spoke with authority, who understood the craft of administration and high affairs, so that he could converse on the level of actual knowledge and experience with one who held himself to be also a ruler and a lawgiver to no contemptible portion of mankind.

To Gevil-Hay Don Q. was a study. He watched him as a snake might be watched by an imaginative rabbit. He was always following the livid-lidded eyes, always speculating on the thoughts which worked in that ill-balanced brain. For Don Q. was a Spaniard of the Spaniards, having the qualities of his race in excess. He was quite fearless, proud to distraction, unsurpassed in the kindly courtesy of a nation of aristocrats, and cruel beyond belief. As this character developed itself, Gevil-Hay, like many another man who has thought himself tired of life, clung to his chances of escape as they hourly grew less before his eyes. For one thing was apparent—Don Q.'s peculiarities did not lean to the side of mercy.

A couple of days after his arrival in the glen he asked the brigand chief what had been done with the two young brawlers who had drawn knives upon each other under the terrace.

Don Q. removed his cigarette to answer.

"They will annoy you no more, señor," he said, with the anxiety of hospitality, "no more."

"What? Have you sent them away to some of your out-lying detachments?" asked Gevil-Hay, for he had learned by this time that the robbers were posted at many points in the mountains.

Don Q. laughed, a venomous sibilant laugh.

"They are gone—yes, with other carrion—the vultures alone know where!"

The chief was in one of his black moods of intense and brooding melancholy. They were common with him, but this was the first which Gevil-Hay had seen.

It suddenly struck him that some leaven of insanity might lurk behind the fierce, bird-like aspect. No wonder his followers obeyed him at the run. His generosity and his vengeance were out of all proportion to the deserving.

"Some day," said Gevil-Hay abruptly, "they will resent—this kind of thing. There are many ways; they might betray you, and then——"

Don Q. gave him a poisonous glance.

"I have made provision for that also; but no, señor, when I die, it shall be in my own manner and of my own will," and he relapsed again into musing.

It was then that Gevil-Hay found himself wishing his ransom might arrive in full, and wishing it with fervour. In a few minutes Don Q. spoke again.

"If you own a dog, he may love you; but a pack of wolves are kept in order with the lash. These," he waved his hand towards the gleaming camp fires in the hollow, "*are* wolves. Also many men desire to join us—many more than I care to take. So you perceive, señor, I can afford to lose a few who offend me."

He rose as he spoke, and, going back into the cave, brought forth his guitar.

"After all, what is life, that we should prize it so?" he asked, as his thin fingers touched the strings. "I live up here, feared and obeyed to satiety. Sometimes I have the honour of a gentleman's companionship, as I now have the honour of yours, señor. At other times I grow weary of life, and my restlessness drives me down the mountains; but—at all times I love the music of Spain."

Gevil-Hay looked askance at the guitar. Music was not one of the things for which he could declare any special fancy.

Don Q. placed his open palm across the twanging notes.

"If it displeases you," he said apologetically.

Gevil-Hay hastened to assure him to the contrary. And, indeed, if the listener had had the power of appreciation, he must have been touched and charmed, for Don Q.'s was a master hand. He lingered over mournful Andalusian melodies, and even sang in his strange sibilant voice long sad songs of old Spain and forgotten deeds and men.

Chapter II

So the days wore on, but one evening there was a new development.

Gevil-Hay, secured only by his parole, was allowed to wander at large about the glen, and on this occasion, after an ugly climb, he arrived at the head of a deep and narrow cleft in the higher rocks along the bottom of which a faint track was visible. As he stood and surveyed it with an involuntary thought of escape, he heard his name spoken. Of course it was some hidden sentinel, but he was surprised when the man repeated his call, in the same low voice, for Don Q.'s men were usually sullen. In their eyes a prisoner had but two uses. First he was saleable; second, if unsaleable, it was amusing to see him die.

"What do you want?" asked Gevil-Hay after a little hesitation.

"The thing I say must be forever between us two alone. You can help us, we can help you. That is the reason of my speaking. No, señor, stay where you are. If you promise, I will show you my face."

"I promise nothing."

"Ah, that is because you have not yet heard! Is it not true that my lord of the sierra is taking from you all your riches?"

"Yes."

"And you, like the rest of us, would do something to save them? Is not that also so?"

"It may be."

"Then do it. It is but a little thing, and in the doing should taste sweet. You will not betray me?"

"As I have not seen you I cannot."

"But you will not?"

"No."

"Then take it, señor. Here, look up towards the lentisco."

In the warm gloom of the lentisco shrub something cold and ominous passed from hand to hand, and Gevil-Hay's fingers closed on the butt of a revolver.

"You mean me to kill him?" he said slowly.

A laugh was the answer, and words followed the laugh.

"Yes, for you have opportunity. Then you shall go free, for we hate him."

"And you?"

There was another laugh.

"A pardon and the blood-money between us. Now go."

And it cannot be denied that in the soft southern dusk Charles Gerald Gevil-Hay was horribly tempted. He stood there in the silence and wrestled with the temptation. Arguments came to him freely. By firing that shot he would be serving his kind as well as himself. Tormented with thoughts he slid back into the glen and walked across the short, hard grass towards the terrace. He passed by the fires round which the men were gambling. Lean columns of smoke rose slowly into the higher air, strange cries filled the glen, for the *sequestradores* played high, and each voice rose and fell with its possessor's luck.

He mounted the sloping path to the terrace. Don Q., unsuspecting, was within the cave reading letters beside a cheap lamp. How easy—— Gevil-Hay stood outside in the herb-scented darkness and watched him. On the one side, the prisoner could look forward to a life of comfort at the least; and who could tell what else the future held? On the other hand, a hideous beggary in smoky, fish-scented lodgings, an existence worse than death! And in the night the man's honour wrestled with the man's temptations of expediency.

Presently he went in. Don Q. scowled at him and threw him an English newspaper. It was fourteen days old, and not one which Gevil-Hay was wont to buy when at home; but in the whirl of his thoughts he fled to it as to a refuge. He was about to open it, holding it at arm's length for the purpose, when his glance lit upon a notice in the obituary column.

"Hertford.—On March 10th, suddenly, at Frane Hall, Franebridge, George Chigwell Aberstone Hertford, eldest son of the late——"

He folded the paper with mathematical precision and read two columns of advertisements without seeing a word of what he read.

So George Hertford was dead at last! And Helen—free.

Don Q. looked furtively at him under the shadow of his wide hat, and saw that *El Palido*, as the men called him, was sitting there more white and more statuesque than ever. His eyes were blank and set. By his tense attitude Don Q. knew that some struggle was going on within the Englishman's mind, and his own face filled with an ominous light as he glanced at one of his letters.

"Señor," he said aloud, in a changed voice, "news of your ransom has come. Eighteen thousand dollars. I said twenty thousand."

Gevil-Hay started slightly, controlled himself, and said unconcernedly—

"And so?"

"And so, señor, I am prepared to stand by my side of the bargain," replied the chief with a poisonous politeness. "At the rising of the moon nine-tenths of you shall go free from the head of our glen!"

There was a silence, broken only by the noises in the camp.

Free? Gevil-Hay's thoughts were racing through his brain. Yes, free, and—Helen was free! Her husband dead. Then he took in the force of Don Q.'s words, and, rising, stood up and leaned against the rocky wall.

"Am I to be grateful?" he asked frigidly.

Don Q. smiled with a suave acquiescence.

"And because your conversation has interested me, señor, you shall have the privilege of choosing which tenth of yourself you will leave behind."

"In fact, not content with making me a beggar you will take from me all chance of regaining my losses?"

Don Q. bowed again and spoke with exceeding gentleness.

"It comes to that. I am very much afraid it comes to that," he said. "It is terribly unfortunate, I admit, but I do not see how it can be avoided. But you are a comparatively heavy man, señor; I think I should advise you to leave a limb behind you. One can yet live without a limb."

The brigand's callousness startled Gevil-Hay, well as he fancied he knew him. And in the breast of the slow-moving, phlegmatic man the temptation arose again with accumulated strength. A loaded revolver was under his hand, practical impunity waited upon the deed, and beyond that life—and Helen! What stood between him and all this? Why, a scruple, a scruple that should not hold good for a moment against such counteracting motives. It occurred to him with much force that the thin, bald-browed, malignant despot opposite would be much more wholesome of contemplation were his lips closed forever.

But he had passed his word, given his parole, and a man occasionally finds his honour an inconvenient possession.

Had it been a question of another man's life or person, Gevil-Hay would have had no hesitation in sending Don Q. to his appointed place. Moreover, he would have been delighted of the excuse for sending him there. As it was he held his hand.

In another hour he would be given over to the band for mutilation, and his talk in the dark with the sentinel, joined to his failure in making use of the opportunity offered him, would assuredly not lighten the manner of paying the penalty.

Through it all the bandit sat and watched him with blinking eyelids in the lamplight. Don Q.'s sight seemed not very good, but it served to show him what he wanted to see. He had broken down the indifference of Gevil-Hay.

But Gevil-Hay had not held himself well in hand during so many years of his life for nothing. He conquered now in the grimmest fight he had ever fought. But his soul rose at the man before him.

"I should certainly advise you to leave a limb," repeated Don Q. at last.

"You villain! You unutterable villain!"

Don Q.'s hand fell to his knife as he sprang to his feet and faced his captive.

"The one fact for which I am really sorry at this moment," went on Gevil-Hay, "is that I should have allowed such a thing as you to associate with me on equal terms! If I had guessed to what genus you belonged I would never have talked with you or remained near you except I had been held there by force! Now you know what I think of you, and I assure you, although I can guess the price I shall have to pay for the pleasure of saying so, it is cheap!"

Don Q.'s angled face was yellow. His figure shook. It must be remembered that Gevil-Hay had an exhaustive vocabulary of Spanish terms and knew the exact value of every word he distilled from the indignation within him. Also he had delivered his attack well and each word told.

The chief's livid eyelids were quivering.

"Señor, you have spoken as no man has ever spoken to me before," said Don Q., at last. "There are many ways of conducting those little scenes which lie between this moment and your departure. By the time the moon has risen it will be hard to recognize *El Palido*!"

There was a fierce significance in the last few words that at any other time might well have made Gevil-Hay's heart turn cold. But now with his blood up and the hopelessness of his position apparent, he merely turned his back with a stinging gesture of repulsion.

"You evil beast!" he repeated, "as long as I am not annoyed by the sight of you I can bear anything!"

So Gevil-Hay turned his back and stared out into the night. The noises below were hushed. The encampment was waiting for him—waiting—and for a third time temptation leaped upon him. And that was the worst spasm of all. When it left him, it left him exhausted. His mouth felt dry, his brow clammy.

He was still standing facing the opening of the cave, and after a pause a voice broke the silence.

"As you have a loaded revolver in your pocket, why do you not use it? Why do you not shoot me down, señor?"

"You know I could not," replied Gevil-Hay comprehensively.

"And are you not afraid of what is coming?"

Gevil-Hay turned and held out the revolver. Don Q.'s face was a study. He took no notice of the other's action, but asked—

"Because of your parole?"

He was answered by another question.

"How did you know about the revolver?"

"I instructed the man who gave it to you. I wished to see whether I had read you aright. Yet your inability to shoot me hurt you. Is not that so?"

"I wish I could do it now! At least there is no necessity for more talk between us. Maim me and let me go, or kill me! Only take away this revolver from me before I——"

Don Q. took the pistol and laid it with deliberation upon the table beside him, then he spoke.

"Señor," said he, "when I find one like you, I do not spoil the good God's work in him. You are not the type of man who comes to harm at my hands. A man who can keep his honour as you have done is worthy of life. Had you shot me, or rather had you attempted to do so—for I bear the charmed life of him who cares not whether he lives or dies—then the story of your death would have been related in the *posadas* of Andalusia for generations. But now, take your life, yes, take it from my hands.

"After tonight we shall see each other no more; but when you look back over your life, señor, you will always remember one man, who, like yourself, was afraid of nothing; a man worthy to stand beside you, Don Q., once of the noblest blood in Spain. A man——" The brigand checked himself in his flood of florid rhapsody and Spanish feeling. "Adios, señor."

Two hours later Gevil-Hay was alone upon the sierras. When he reached Gibraltar, which he did in due course, he was surprised to find himself almost sorry to hear that the Spanish Government, goaded on by ponderous British representations, had determined to cleanse the land of the presence of Don Q.

Since then Gevil-Hay's life has not been a failure. And sometimes in the midst of his work a thought comes back to him of the proud, unscrupulous, gallant brigand, whose respect he had once been lucky enough to win.

Rogue: Teddy Watkins

The Hammerpond Park Burglary

H. G. WELLS

ALTHOUGH HERBERT GEORGE WELLS (1866–1946) was one of the first and greatest of all writers of science fiction, for which he remains known today, he disliked being thought of as one, claiming that those works were merely a conduit for his social ideas. He had begun his adult life as a scientist and might, with a bit more encouragement, have made a successful career as a biologist, but instead was offered work as a journalist and quickly began to write fiction. His prolific writing career was loosely divided into three eras, but it is only the novels and short stories of the first, when he wrote fantastic and speculative fiction, that are much remembered today. Such early titles as *The Time Machine* (1895), *The Island of Doctor Moreau* (1896), *The Invisible Man* (1897), and *The War of the Worlds* (1898) are all milestones of the genre, though all feature Wells's dim view of mankind and society, which led him to the socialistic Fabian Society. He turned to more realistic fiction after the turn of the century with such highly regarded (at the time) novels as *Kipps* (1905), *Ann Veronica* (1909), *Tono-Bungay* (1909), and *Marriage* (1912). The majority of his works over the last three decades of his life were both fiction and nonfiction books reflecting his political and social views, and are as dated, unreadable, and insignificant as they are misanthropic.

More than a hundred films have been based on Wells's novels, with countless others using them as uncredited sources. Among the most famous are the classic *The Invisible Man* (1933), *Things to Come* (1936), *The First Men in the Moon* (1919 and 1964), *The Island of Dr. Moreau* (1996 and 1977, more capably filmed as *The Island of Lost Souls*, released in 1932), *The War of the Worlds* (1953 and 2005), and *The Time Machine* (1960 and 2002), among many others.

"The Hammerpond Park Burglary" was originally published in the July 5, 1894, issue of *Pall Mall Budget*; it was first collected in *The Short Stories of H. G. Wells* (London, Benn, 1927).

THE HAMMERPOND PARK BURGLARY

H. G. Wells

IT IS A MOOT POINT whether burglary is to be considered as a sport, a trade, or an art. For a trade, the technique is scarcely rigid enough, and its claims to be considered an art are vitiated by the mercenary element that qualifies its triumphs. On the whole it seems to be most justly ranked as sport, a sport for which no rules are at present formulated, and of which the prizes are distributed in an extremely informal manner. It was this informality of burglary that led to the regrettable extinction of two promising beginners at Hammerpond Park.

The stakes offered in this affair consisted chiefly of diamonds and other personal bric-a-brac belonging to the newly married Lady Aveling. Lady Aveling, as the reader will remember, was the only daughter of Mrs. Montague Pangs, the well-known hostess. Her marriage to Lord Aveling was extensively advertised in the papers, the quantity and quality of her wedding presents, and the fact that the honeymoon was to be spent at Hammerpond. The announcement of these valuable prizes created a considerable sensation in the small circle in which Mr. Teddy Watkins was the undisputed leader, and it was decided that, accompanied by a duly qualified assistant, he should visit the village of Hammerpond in his professional capacity.

Being a man of naturally retiring and modest disposition, Mr. Watkins determined to make this visit incognito, and after due consideration of the conditions of his enterprise, he selected the role of a landscape artist and the unassuming surname of Smith. He preceded his assistant, who, it was decided, should join him only on the last afternoon of his stay at Hammerpond. Now the village of Hammerpond is perhaps one of the prettiest little corners in Sussex; many thatched houses still survive, the flint-built church with its tall spire nestling under the down is one of the finest and least restored in the county, and the beech-woods and bracken jungles through which the road runs to the great house are singularly rich in what the vulgar artist and photographer call "bits." So that Mr. Watkins, on his arrival with two virgin canvases, a brand-new easel, a paint-box, portmanteau, an ingenious little ladder made in sections (after the pattern of the late lamented master Charles Peace), crowbar, and wire coils, found himself welcomed with effusion and some curiosity by half-a-dozen other brethren of the brush. It rendered the disguise he had chosen unexpectedly plausible, but it inflicted upon him a considerable amount of aesthetic conversation for which he was very imperfectly prepared.

"Have you exhibited very much?" said Young Person in the bar-parlour of the "Coach and Horses," where Mr. Watkins was skilfully accumulating local information, on the night of his arrival.

"Very little," said Mr. Watkins, "just a snack here and there."

"Academy?"

"In course. And the Crystal Palace."

"Did they hang you well?" said Porson.

"Don't rot," said Mr. Watkins; "I don't like it."

"I mean did they put you in a good place?"

"Whadyer mean?" said Mr. Watkins suspiciously. "One 'ud think you were trying to make out I'd been put away."

Porson had been brought up by aunts, and was a gentlemanly young man even for an artist; he did not know what being "put away" meant, but he thought it best to explain that he intended nothing of the sort. As the question of hanging seemed a sore point with Mr. Watkins, he tried to divert the conversation a little.

"Do you do figure-work at all?"

"No, never had a head for figures," said Mr. Watkins, "my miss—Mrs. Smith, I mean, does all that."

"She paints too!" said Porson. "That's rather jolly."

"Very," said Mr. Watkins, though he really did not think so, and feeling the conversation was drifting a little beyond his grasp added, "I came down here to paint Hammerpond House by moonlight."

"Really!" said Porson. "That's rather a novel idea."

"Yes," said Mr. Watkins, "I thought it rather a good notion when it occurred to me. I expect to begin tomorrow night."

"What! You don't mean to paint in the open, by night?"

"I do, though."

"But how will you see your canvas?"

"Have a bloomin' cop's—" began Mr. Watkins, rising too quickly to the question, and then realising this, bawled to Miss Durgan for another glass of cheer. "I'm goin' to have a thing called a dark lantern," he said to Porson.

"But it's about new moon now," objected Porson. "There won't be any moon."

"There'll be the house," said Watkins, "at any rate. I'm goin', you see, to paint the house first and the moon afterwards."

"Oh!" said Porson, too staggered to continue the conversation.

"They doo say," said old Durgan, the landlord, who had maintained a respectful silence during the technical conversation, "as there's no less than three p'licemen from 'Azelworth on dewty every night in the house—'count of this Lady Aveling 'n her jewellery. One'm won fower-and-six last night, off second footman–tossin'."

Towards sunset next day Mr. Watkins, virgin canvas, easel, and a very considerable case of other appliances in hand, strolled up the pleasant pathway through the beech-woods to Hammerpond Park, and pitched his apparatus in a strategic position commanding the house. Here he was observed by Mr. Raphael Sant, who was returning across the park from a study of the chalk-pits. His curiosity having been fired by Porson's account of the new arrival, he turned aside with the idea of discussing nocturnal art.

Mr. Watkins was apparently unaware of his approach. A friendly conversation with Lady Hammerpond's butler had just terminated, and that individual, surrounded by the three pet dogs, which it was his duty to take for an airing after dinner had been served, was receding in the distance. Mr. Watkins was mixing colour with an air of great industry. Sant, approaching more nearly, was surprised to see the colour in question was as harsh and brilliant an emerald green as it is possible to imagine. Having cultivated an extreme sensibility to colour from his earliest years, he drew the air in sharply between his teeth at the very first glimpse of this brew. Mr. Watkins turned round. He looked annoyed.

"What on earth are you going to do with that beastly green?" said Sant.

Mr. Watkins realised that his zeal to appear busy in the eyes of the butler had evidently betrayed him into some technical error. He looked at Sant and hesitated.

"Pardon my rudeness," said Sant; "but really, that green is altogether too amazing. It came as a shock. What do you mean to do with it?"

Mr. Watkins was collecting his resources. Nothing could save the situation but decision. "If you come here interrupting my work," he said, "I'm a-goin' to paint your face with it."

Sant retired, for he was a humorist and a peaceful man. Going down the hill he met Porson and Wainwright. "Either that man is a genius or he is a dangerous lunatic," said he. "Just go up and look at his green." And he continued his way, his countenance brightened by a pleasant anticipation of a cheerful affray round an easel in the gloaming, and the shedding of much green paint.

But to Porson and Wainwright Mr. Watkins was less aggressive, and explained that the green was intended to be the first coating of his picture. It was, he admitted in response to a remark, an absolutely new method, invented by himself. But subsequently he became more reticent; he explained he was not going to tell every passer-by the secret of his own particular style, and added some scathing remarks upon the meanness of people "hanging about" to pick up such tricks of the masters as they could, which immediately relieved him of their company.

Twilight deepened, first one then another star appeared. The rooks amid the tall trees to the left of the house had long since lapsed into slumbrous silence, the house itself lost all the details of its architecture and became a dark grey outline, and then the windows of the salon shone out brilliantly, the conservatory was lighted up, and here and there a bedroom window burnt yellow. Had anyone approached the easel in the park it would have been found deserted. One brief uncivil word in brilliant green sullied the purity of its canvas. Mr. Watkins was busy in the shrubbery with his assistant, who had discreetly joined him from the carriage-drive.

Mr. Watkins was inclined to be self-congratulatory upon the ingenious device by which he had carried all his apparatus boldly, and in the sight of all men, right up to the scene of operations. "That's the dressing-room," he said to his assistant, "and, as soon as the maid takes the candle away and goes down to supper, we'll call in. My! How nice the house do look, to be sure, against the starlight, and with all its windows and lights! Swopme, Jim, I almost wish I was a painter-chap. Have you fixed that there wire across the path from the laundry?"

He cautiously approached the house until he stood below the dressing-room window, and began to put together his folding ladder. He was much too experienced a practitioner to feel any unusual excitement. Jim was reconnoitring the smoking-room. Suddenly, close beside Mr. Watkins in the bushes, there was a violent crash and a stifled curse. Someone had tumbled over the wire which his assistant had just arranged. He heard feet running on the gravel pathway beyond. Mr. Watkins, like all true artists, was a singularly shy man, and he incontinently dropped his folding ladder and began running circumspectly through the shrubbery. He was indistinctly aware of two people hot upon his heels, and he fancied that he distinguished the outline of his assistant in front of him. In another moment he had vaulted the low stone wall bounding the shrubbery, and was in the open park. Two thuds on the turf followed his own leap.

It was a close chase in the darkness through the trees. Mr. Watkins was a loosely-built man and in good training, and he gained hand-over-hand upon the hoarsely panting figure in front. Neither spoke, but as Mr. Watkins pulled up alongside, a qualm of awful doubt came over him. The other man turned his head at the same moment and gave an exclamation of surprise. "It's not Jim," thought Mr. Watkins, and simultaneously the stranger flung himself, as it were, at Watkins's knees, and they were forthwith grappling on the ground together. "Lend a hand, Bill," cried the stranger as the third man came up. And Bill did—two hands in fact, and some accentuated feet. The fourth man, presumably Jim, had apparently turned aside and made off in a different direction. At any rate, he did not join the trio.

Mr. Watkins's memory of the incidents of the next two minutes is extremely vague. He has a dim recollection of having his thumb in the corner of the mouth of the first man, and feeling anxious about its safety, and for some seconds at least he held the head of the gentleman answering to the name of Bill to the ground by the hair. He was also kicked in a great number of different places, apparently by a vast multitude of people. Then the gentleman who was not Bill got his knee below Mr. Watkins's diaphragm, and tried to curl him up upon it.

When his sensations became less entangled he was sitting upon the turf, and eight or ten men—the night was dark, and he was rather too confused to count—standing round him, apparently waiting for him to recover. He mournfully assumed that he was captured, and would probably have made some philosophical reflections on the fickleness of fortune, had not his internal sensations disinclined him for speech.

He noticed very quickly that his wrists were not handcuffed, and then a flask of brandy was put in his hands. This touched him a little—it was such unexpected kindness.

"He's a-comin' round," said a voice which he fancied he recognised as belonging to the Hammerpond second footman.

"We've got 'em, sir, both of 'em," said the Hammerpond butler, the man who had handed him the flask. "Thanks to you."

No one answered this remark. Yet he failed to see how it applied to him.

"He's fair dazed," said a strange voice; "the villains half-murdered him."

Mr. Teddy Watkins decided to remain fair dazed until he had a better grasp of the situation. He perceived that two of the black figures round him stood side-by-side with a dejected air, and there was something in the carriage of their shoulders that suggested to his experienced eye hands that were bound together. Two! In a flash he rose to his position. He emptied the little flask and staggered—obsequious hands assisting him—to his feet. There was a sympathetic murmur.

"Shake hands, sir, shake hands," said one of the figures near him. "Permit me to introduce myself. I am very greatly indebted to you. It was the jewels of my wife, Lady Aveling, which attracted these scoundrels to the house."

"Very glad to make your lordship's acquaintance," said Teddy Watkins.

"I presume you saw the rascals making for the shrubbery, and dropped down on them?"

"That's exactly how it happened," said Mr. Watkins.

"You should have waited till they got in at the window," said Lord Aveling; "they would get it hotter if they had actually committed the burglary. And it was lucky for you two of the policemen were out by the gates, and followed up the three of you. I doubt if you could have secured the two of them—though it was confoundedly plucky of you, all the same."

"Yes, I ought to have thought of all that," said Mr. Watkins; "but one can't think of everything."

"Certainly not," said Lord Aveling. "I am afraid they have mauled you a little," he added. The party was now moving towards the house. "You walk rather lame. May I offer you my arm?"

And instead of entering Hammerpond House by the dressing-room window, Mr. Watkins entered it—slightly intoxicated, and inclined now to cheerfulness again—on the arm of a real live peer, and by the front door. "This," thought Mr. Watkins, "is burgling in style!" The "scoundrels," seen by the gaslight, proved to be mere local amateurs unknown to Mr. Watkins, and they were taken down into the pantry and there watched over by the three policemen, two gamekeepers with loaded guns, the butler, an ostler, and a carman, until the dawn allowed of their removal to Hazelhurst police-station.

Mr. Watkins was made much of in the salon. They devoted a sofa to him, and would not hear of a return to the village that night. Lady Aveling was sure he was brilliantly original, and said her idea of Turner was just such another rough, half-inebriated, deep-eyed, brave, and clever man. Some one brought up a remarkable little folding-ladder that had been picked up in the shrubbery, and showed him how it was put together. They also described how wires had been found in the shrubbery, evidently placed there to trip-up unwary pursuers. It was lucky he had escaped these snares. And they showed him the jewels.

Mr. Watkins had the sense not to talk too much, and in any conversational difficulty fell back on his internal pains. At last he was seized with stiffness in the back, and yawning. Everyone suddenly awoke to the fact that it was a shame to keep him talking after his affray, so he retired early to his room, the little red room next to Lord Aveling's suite.

The dawn found a deserted easel bearing a canvas with a green inscription, in the Hammerpond Park, and it found Hammerpond House in commotion. But if the dawn found Mr. Teddy Watkins and the Aveling diamonds, it did not communicate the information to the police.

Villain: Dr. Fu Manchu

The Zayat Kiss

SAX ROHMER

AS HAS BEEN DESCRIBED by Arthur Henry Sarsfield Ward (1883–1959), better known under his pseudonym of Sax Rohmer, a newspaper assignment sent him to Limehouse, London's Chinatown, an area so forbidding at the time that few white people ventured into it, even in daylight. For months, he sought a mysterious "Mr. King," who was said to rule all the criminal elements of the district, inspiring Rohmer to create the insidious Dr. Fu Manchu. He mentioned King by name in *Yellow Shadows* (1925), which, along with *Dope* (1919), helped clean up Limehouse and bring about government action on the drug trade. The Boxer Rebellion at the turn of the century had aroused fears of a "Yellow Peril" and convinced Rohmer that an "Oriental" arch-villain would be successful, so he began writing stories about sinister Chinese, notably the Devil Doctor. The first of the fourteen novels about the sinister Fu Manchu was *The Mystery of Dr. Fu-Manchu* (1913; published in the United States as *The Insidious Dr. Fu-Manchu*). Rohmer deliberately gave his character an impossible name, both "Fu" and "Manchu" being Chinese surnames; it was hyphenated only in the first three books.

Rohmer wrote more than fifty books but is best known for his creation of Fu Manchu, one of the greatest villains in literature. His early interest in the occult and Egyptology influenced his writing and caused him to join such societies as the Hermetic Order of the Golden Dawn along with other literary figures, including Arthur Machen, Aleister Crowley, and W. B. Yeats. Many of his books and stories are set in the mysterious East, including *Brood of the Witch Queen* (1918), *Tales of Secret Egypt* (1918), *The Golden Scorpion* (1919), and *Tales of East and West* (1932).

In their magazine appearances, the first adventures were simply titled *Fu-Manchu*, followed by the story title. For their book publication, they were disguised as a novel, lacking chapter titles.

"The Zayat Kiss," the first Fu Manchu story, was originally published in the October 1912 issue of *The Story-Teller*; it was first collected in *The Mystery of Dr. Fu-Manchu* (London, Methuen, 1913); the first American edition was titled *The Insidious Dr. Fu-Manchu* (New York, McBride, Nast & Co., 1913).

THE ZAYAT KISS

Sax Rohmer

I SANK INTO AN ARM-CHAIR in my rooms and gulped down a strong peg of brandy.

"We have been followed here," I said. "Why did you make no attempt to throw the pursuers off the track, to have them intercepted?"

Smith laughed.

"Useless, in the first place. Wherever we went, *he* would find us. And of what use to arrest his creatures? We could prove nothing against them. Further, it is evident that an attempt is to be made upon my life tonight—and by the same means that proved so successful in the case of poor Sir Crichton."

His square jaw grew truculently prominent, and he leapt stormily to his feet, shaking his clenched fists towards the window.

"The villain!" he cried. "The fiendishly clever villain! I suspected that Sir Crichton was next, and I was right. But I came too late, Petrie! That hits me hard, old man. To think that I knew and yet failed to save him."

He resumed his seat, smoking vigorously.

"Fu-Manchu has made the blunder common to all men of unusual genius," he said. "He has underrated his adversary. He has not given me credit for perceiving the meaning of the scented messages. He has thrown away one powerful weapon—to get such a message into my hands—and he thinks that, once safe within doors, I shall sleep, unsuspecting, and die as Sir Crichton died. But, without the indiscretion of your charming friend, I should have known what to expect when I received her 'information'—which, by the way, consists of a blank sheet of paper."

"Smith," I broke in, "who is she?"

"She is either Fu-Manchu's daughter, his wife, or his slave. I am inclined to believe the latter, for she has no will but his will, except"—with a quizzical glance—"in a certain instance."

"How can you jest with some awful thing—heaven knows what—hanging over your head? What is the meaning of these perfumed envelopes? How did Sir Crichton die?"

"He died of the Zayat Kiss. Ask me what that is, and I reply, 'I do not know.' The zayats are the Burmese caravanserais, or rest-houses. Along a certain route—upon which I set eyes, for the first and only time, upon Dr. Fu-Manchu—travellers who use them sometimes die as Sir Crichton died, with nothing to show the cause of death but a little mark upon the neck, face, or limb, which has earned, in those parts, the title of the 'Zayat Kiss.' The rest-houses along that route are shunned now. I have my theory, and I hope to prove it tonight, if I live. It will be one more broken weapon in his fiendish armoury, and it is thus, and thus only, that I can hope to crush him. This was my principal reason for not enlightening Dr. Cleeve. Even walls have ears where Fu-Manchu is concerned, so I feigned ignorance of the meaning of the mark, knowing that he would be almost certain to employ the same methods upon some other victim. I wanted an opportunity to study the Zayat Kiss in operation, and I shall have one."

"But the scented envelopes?"

"In the swampy forest of the district I have referred to, a rare species of orchid, almost green, and with a peculiar scent, is sometimes met with. I recognized the heavy perfume at once. I take it that the thing which kills the travellers is attracted by this orchid. You will notice that the perfume clings to whatever it touches. I doubt if it can be washed off in the ordinary way. After at least one unsuccessful attempt to kill Sir Crichton—you recall that he thought there was something concealed in his study on a previous occasion?—Fu-Manchu hit upon the perfumed envelopes. He may have a supply of these green orchids in his possession—possibly to feed the creature."

"What creature? How could any creature have got into Sir Crichton's room tonight?"

"You have no doubt observed that I examined the grate of the study. I found a fair quantity of fallen soot. I at once assumed, since it appeared to be the only means of entrance, that something had been dropped down; and I took it for granted that the thing, whatever it was, must still be concealed either in the study or in the library. But when I had obtained the evidence of the groom, Wills, I perceived that the cry from the lane or from the park was a signal. I noted that the movements of anyone seated at the study-table were visible, in shadow, on the blind, and that the study occupied the corner of a two-storeyed wing, and therefore had a short chimney. What did the signal mean? That Sir Crichton had leapt up from his chair, and either had received the Zayat Kiss or had seen the thing which someone on the roof had lowered down the straight chimney. It was the signal to withdraw that deadly thing. By means of the iron stairway at the rear of Major-General Platt-Houston's, I quite easily gained access to the roof above Sir Crichton's study—and I found this."

Out from his pocket Nayland Smith drew a tangled piece of silk, mixed up with which were a brass ring and a number of unusually large-sized split-shot, nipped on in the manner usual on a fishing-line.

"My theory proven," he resumed. "Not anticipating a search on the roof, they had been careless. This was to weigh the line and to prevent the creature clinging to the walls of the chimney. Directly it had dropped in the grate, however, by means of this ring, I assume that the weighted line was withdrawn and the thing was only held by one slender thread, which sufficed, though, to draw it back again when it had done its work. It might have got tangled, of course, but they reckoned on its making straight up the carved leg of the writing-table for the prepared envelope. From there to the hand of Sir Crichton—which, from having touched the envelope, would also be scented with the perfume—was a certain move."

"My God! How horrible!" I exclaimed, and glanced apprehensively into the dusky shadows of the room. "What is your theory respecting this creature—what shape, what colour——?"

"It is something that moves rapidly and silently. I will venture no more at present, but I think it works in the dark. The study was dark, remember, save for the bright patch beneath the reading-lamp. I have observed that the rear of this house is ivy-covered right up to, and above, your bedroom. Let us make ostentatious preparations to retire, and I think we may rely upon Fu-Manchu's servants to attempt my removal, at any rate—if not yours."

"But, my dear fellow, it is a climb of thirty-five feet at the very least."

"You remember the cry in the back lane? It suggested something to me, and I tested my idea—successfully. It was the cry of a dacoit. Oh, dacoity, though quiescent, is by no means extinct. Fu-Manchu has dacoits in his train, and probably it is one who operates the Zayat Kiss, since it was a dacoit who watched the window of the study this evening. To such a man an ivy-covered wall is a grand staircase."

The horrible events that followed are punctuated, in my mind, by the striking of a distant clock. It is singular how trivialities thus assert themselves in moments of high tension. I will proceed, then, by these punctuations, to the coming of the horror that it was written we should encounter.

The clock across the common struck two.

Having removed all traces of the scent of the orchid from our hands with a solution of ammonia, Smith and I had followed the programme laid down. It was an easy matter to reach the rear of the house, by simply climbing a fence, and we did not doubt that, seeing the light go out in the front, our unseen watcher would proceed to the back.

The room was a large one, and we had made up my camp-bed at one end, stuffing odds and ends under the clothes to lend the appearance of a sleeper, which device we also had adopted in the case of the larger bed. The perfumed envelope lay upon a little coffee-table in the centre of the floor, and Smith, with an electric pocket-lamp, a revolver and a brassy beside him, sat on cushions in the shadow of the wardrobe. I occupied a post between the windows.

No unusual sound, so far, had disturbed the stillness of the night. Save for the muffled throb of the rare all-night cars passing the front of the house, our vigil had been a silent one. The full moon had painted about the floor weird shadows of the clustering ivy, spreading the design gradually from the door, across the room, past the little table where the envelope lay, and finally to the foot of the bed.

The distant clock struck a quarter-past two.

A slight breeze stirred the ivy, and a new shadow added itself to the extreme edge of the moon's design.

Something rose, inch by inch, above the sill of the westerly window. I could see only its shadow, but a sharp, sibilant breath from Smith told me that he, from his post, could see the cause of the shadow.

Every nerve in my body seemed to be strung tensely. I was icily cold, expectant, and prepared for whatever horror was upon us.

The shadow became stationary. The dacoit was studying the interior of the room.

Then it suddenly lengthened, and, craning my head to the left, I saw a lithe, black-clad form, surmounted by a yellow face, sketchy in the moonlight, pressed against the window-panes!

One thin, brown hand appeared over the edge of the lowered sash, which it grasped—and then another. The man made absolutely no sound whatever. The second hand disappeared—and reappeared. It held a small square box.

There was a very faint *click*.

The dacoit swung himself below the window with the agility of an ape, as, with a dull, sickening thud, *something* dropped upon the carpet!

"Stand still, for your life!" came Smith's voice, high-pitched.

A beam of white light leapt out across the room and played fully upon the coffee-table in the centre.

Prepared as I was for something horrible, I know that I paled at sight of the thing that was running around the edge of the envelope.

It was an insect, full six inches long, and of a vivid, venomous red colour! It had something of the appearance of a great ant, with its long, quivering antennæ and its febrile, horrible vitality; but it was proportionately longer of body and smaller of head, and had numberless rapidly moving legs. In short, it was a giant centipede, apparently of the *scolopendra* group, but of a form quite new to me.

These things I realized in one breathless instant; in the next—Smith had dashed the thing's poisonous life out with one straight, true blow of the golf club!

I leapt to the window and threw it widely open, feeling a silk thread brush my hand as I did so. A black shape was dropping, with incredible agility, from branch to branch of the ivy, and, without once offering a mark for a revolver-shot, it merged into the shadows beneath the trees of the garden.

As I turned and switched on the light Nayland Smith dropped limply into a chair, leaning his head upon his hands. Even that grim courage had been tried sorely.

"Never mind the dacoit, Petrie," he said. "Nemesis will know where to find him. We know now what causes the mark of the Zayat Kiss. Therefore science is richer for our first brush with the enemy, and the enemy is poorer—unless he has any more unclassified centipedes. I understand now something that has been puzzling me since I heard of it—Sir Crichton's stifled cry. When we remember that he was almost past speech, it is reasonable to suppose that his cry was not 'The red hand!' but 'The red *ant*!' Petrie, to think that I failed, by less than an hour, to save him from such an end!"

EARLY TWENTIETH-CENTURY AMERICANS

Rogue: The Infallible Godahl

The Infallible Godahl

FREDERICK IRVING ANDERSON

JUST AS THE PERFECT MURDERER is someone who commits the crime without being suspected, perhaps even having the death seem accidental or natural, the Infallible Godahl has never even been *suspected* of a crime, much less been caught or convicted. He may well be the greatest criminal in the history of mystery fiction. Unlike such better-known thieves as A. J. Raffles, Arsène Lupin, and Simon Templar (the Saint), who rely on their wit, charm, intuition, and good luck to pull off a caper, Godahl has a purely scientific approach to jobs. His computer-like mind assesses every possibility in terms of logic and probabilities; his successes are triumphs of pure reason—the inevitable victory of superior intellect. His uninterrupted series of successes has made him wealthy enough to join the Pegasus Club, which has a membership restricted to fifty millionaires.

The New York Police Department is endlessly frustrated by the perfect crimes committed by Godahl, whose activities are known only to Oliver Armiston, a writer who has recorded some of his exploits. Godahl's only fear is of those afflicted with blindness or deafness, as he believes that the loss of any sense heightens the sensitivity of those that remain.

The exploits of Godahl are the product of one of America's most underrated mystery writers, Frederick Irving Anderson (1877–1947), who also created the only slightly better-known jewel thief Sophie Lang. Born in Aurora, Illinois, Anderson moved east and became a star reporter for the *New York World* from 1898 to 1908 and then became a successful and highly paid fiction writer for the top American and English magazines, notably *The Saturday Evening Post*, in which most of his mystery stories, and all six of his Godahl stories, were first published.

Anderson's stories are written in a slow, circuitous style that may discourage the impatient reader but have a subtle richness that rewards the careful one who will appreciate the events that transpire between the lines.

"The Infallible Godahl" was first published in the February 15, 1913, issue of *The Saturday Evening Post*; it was first collected in *The Adventures of the Infallible Godahl* (New York, Thomas Y. Crowell, 1914).

THE INFALLIBLE GODAHL

Frederick Irving Anderson

OLIVER ARMISTON never was much of a sportsman with a rod or gun—though he could do fancy work with a pistol in a shooting gallery. He had, however, one game from which he derived the utmost satisfaction. Whenever he went traveling, which was often, he invariably caught his trains by the tip of the tail, so to speak, and hung on till he could climb aboard. In other words, he believed in close connections. He had a theory that more valuable dollars-and-cents time and good animal heat are wasted warming seats in stations waiting for trains than by missing them. The sum of joy to his methodical mind was to halt the slamming gates at the last fraction of the last second with majestic upraised hand, and to stroll aboard his parlor-car with studied deliberation, while the train crew were gnashing their teeth in rage and swearing to get even with the gateman for letting him through.

Yet Mr. Armiston never missed a train. A good many of them tried to miss him, but none ever succeeded. He reckoned time and distance so nicely that it really seemed as if his trains had nothing else half so important as waiting until Mr. Oliver Armiston got aboard.

On this particular June day he was due in New Haven at two. If he failed to get there at two o'clock he could very easily arrive at three. But an hour is sixty minutes, and a minute is sixty seconds; and, further, Mr. Armiston, having passed his word that he would be there at two o'clock, surely would be.

On this particular day, by the time Armiston finally got to the Grand Central the train looked like an odds-on favorite. In the first place, he was still in his bed at an hour when another and less experienced traveler would have been watching the clock in the station waiting-room. In the second place, after kissing his wife in that absent-minded manner characteristic of true love, he became tangled in a Broadway traffic rush at the first corner. Scarcely was he extricated from this when he ran into a Socialist mass-meeting at Union Square. It was due only to the wits of his chauffeur that the taxicab was extricated with very little damage to the surrounding human scenery. But our man of method did not fret. Instead, he buried himself in his book, a treatise on Cause and Effect, which at that moment was lulling him with this soothing sentiment:

"There is no such thing as accident. The so-called accidents of every-day life are due to the preordained action of correlated causes, which is inevitable and over which man has no control."

This was comforting, but not much to the point, when Oliver Armiston looked up and discovered he had reached Twenty-third Street and had come to a halt. A sixty-foot truck, with an underslung burden consisting of a sixty-ton steel girder, had at this point suddenly developed weakness in its off hindwheel and settled down on the pavement across the right of way like a tired elephant. This, of course, was not an accident. It was due to a weakness in the construction of that wheel—a weakness that had from the beginning been destined to block street-cars and taxicabs at this particular spot at this particular hour.

Mr. Armiston dismounted and walked a block. Here he hailed a second taxicab and soon was spinning north again at a fair speed, albeit the extensive building operations in Fourth Avenue had made the street well-nigh impassable.

The roughness of the pavement merely shook up his digestive apparatus and gave it zest for the fine luncheon he was promising himself the minute he stepped aboard his train. His new chauffeur got lost three times in the maze of traffic about the Grand Central Station. This, however, was only human, seeing that the railroad company changed the map of Forty-second Street every twenty-four hours during the course of the building of its new terminal.

Mr. Armiston at length stepped from his taxicab, gave his grip to a porter and paid the driver from a huge roll of bills. This same roll was no sooner transferred back to his pocket than a nimble-fingered pickpocket removed it. This, again, was not an accident. That pickpocket had been waiting there for the last hour for that roll of bills. It was preordained, inevitable. And Oliver Armiston had just thirty seconds to catch his train by the tail and climb aboard. He smiled contentedly to himself.

It was not until he called for his ticket that he discovered his loss. For a full precious second he gazed at the hand that came away empty from his money pocket, and then:

"I find I left my purse at home," he said, with a grand air he knew how to assume on occasion. "My name is Mister Oliver Armiston."

Now Oliver Armiston was a name to conjure with.

"I don't doubt it," said the ticket agent dryly. "Mister Andrew Carnegie was here yesterday begging carfare to One Hundred and Twenty-fifth Street, and Mister John D. Rockefeller quite frequently drops in and leaves his dollar watch in hock. Next!"

And the ticket-agent glared at the man blocking the impatient line and told him to move on.

Armiston flushed crimson. He glanced at the clock. For once in his life he was about to experience that awful feeling of missing his train. For once in his life he was about to be robbed of that delicious sensation of hypnotizing the gatekeeper and walking majestically down that train platform that extends northward under the train-shed a considerable part of the distance toward Yonkers. Twenty seconds! Armiston turned round, still holding his ground, and glared concentrated malice at the man next in line. That man was in a hurry. In his hand he held a bundle of bills. For a second the thief-instinct that is latent in us all suggested itself to Armiston. There within reach of his hand was the money, the precious paltry dollar bills that stood between him and his train. It scared him to discover that he, an upright and honored citizen, was almost in the act of grabbing them like a common pickpocket.

Then a truly remarkable thing happened. The man thrust his handful of bills at Armiston.

"The only way I can raise this blockade is to bribe you," he said, returning Armiston's glare. "Here—take what you want—and give the rest of us a chance."

With the alacrity of a blind beggar miraculously cured by the sight of much money Armiston grabbed the handful, extracted what he needed for his ticket, and thrust the rest back into the waiting hand of his unknown benefactor. He caught the gate by a hair. So did his unknown friend. Together they walked down the platform, each matching the other's leisurely pace with his own. They might have been two potentates, so deliberately did they catch this train. Armiston would have liked very much to thank this person, but the other presented so forbidding an exterior that it was hard to find a point of attack. By force of habit Armiston boarded the parlor car, quite forgetting he did not have money for a seat. So did the other. The unknown thrust a bill at the porter. "Get me two chairs," he said. "One is for this gentleman."

Once inside and settled, Armiston renewed his efforts to thank this strange person. That person took a card from his pocket and handed it to Armiston.

"Don't run away with the foolish idea," he said tartly, "that I have done you a service willingly. You were making me miss my train, and I took this means of bribing you to get you out of my way. That is all, sir. At your leisure you may send me your check for the trifle."

"A most extraordinary person!" said Armiston to himself. "Let me give you my card," he said to the other. "As to the service rendered, you are welcome to your own ideas on that. For my part I am very grateful."

The unknown took the proffered card and thrust it in his waistcoat pocket without glancing at it. He swung his chair round and opened a magazine, displaying a pair of broad unneighborly shoulders. This was rather disconcerting to Armiston, who was accustomed to have his card act as an open sesame.

"Damn his impudence!" he said to himself. "He takes me for a mendicant. I'll make copy of him!"

This was the popular author's way of getting even with those who offended his tender sensibilities.

Two things worried Armiston: One was his luncheon—or rather the absence of it; and the other was his neighbor. This neighbor, now that Armiston had a chance to study him, was a young man, well set up. He had a fine bronzed face that was not half so surly as his manner. He was now buried up to his ears in a magazine, oblivious of everything about him, even the dining-car porter, who strode down the aisle and announced the first call to lunch in the dining-car.

"I wonder what the fellow is reading," said Armiston to himself. He peeped over the man's shoulder and was interested at once, for the stranger was reading a copy of a magazine called by the vulgar *The Whited Sepulcher.* It was the pride of this magazine that no man on earth could read it without the aid of a dictionary. Yet this person seemed to be enthralled. And what was more to the point, and vastly pleasing to Armiston, the man was at that moment engrossed in one of Armiston's own effusions. It was one of his crime stories that had won him praise and lucre. It concerned the Infallible Godahl.

These stories were pure reason incarnate in the person of a scientific thief. The plot was invariably so logical that it seemed more like the output of some machine than of a human mind. Of course the plots were impossible, because the fiction thief had to be an incredible genius to carry out the details. But nevertheless they were highly entertaining, fascinating, and dramatic at one and the same time.

And this individual read the story through without winking an eyelash—as though the mental effort cost him nothing—and then, to Armiston's delight, turned back to the beginning and read it again. The author threw out his chest and shot his cuffs. It was not often that such unconscious tribute fell to his lot. He took the card of his unknown benefactor. It read:

MR. J. BORDEN BENSON

THE TOWERS   NEW YORK CITY

"Humph!" snorted Armiston. "An aristocrat—and a snob too!"

At this moment the aristocrat turned in his

chair and handed the magazine to his companion. All his bad humor was gone.

"Are you familiar," he asked, "with this man Armiston's work? I mean these scientific thief stories that are running now."

"Ye—yes. Oh, yes," sputtered Armiston, hastily putting the other's card away. "I—in fact, you know—I take them every morning before breakfast."

In a way this was the truth, for Armiston always began his day's writing before breakfasting.

Mr. Benson smiled—a very fine smile at once boyish and sophisticated.

"Rather a heavy diet early in the morning, I should say," he replied. "Have you read this last one then?"

"Oh, yes," said the delighted author.

"What do you think of it?" asked Benson.

The author puckered his lips.

"It is on a par with the others," he said.

"Yes," said Benson thoughtfully. "I should say the same thing. And when we have said that there is nothing left to say. They are truly a remarkable product. Quite unique, you know. And yet," he said, frowning at Armiston, "I believe that this man Armiston is to be ranked as the most dangerous man in the world to-day."

"Oh, I say——" began Armiston. But he checked himself, chuckling. He was very glad Mr. Benson had not looked at his card.

"I mean it," said the other decidedly. "And you think so yourself, I fully believe. No thinking man could do otherwise."

"In just what way? I must confess I have never thought of his work as anything but pure invention."

It was truly delicious. Armiston would certainly make copy of this person.

"I will grant," said Benson, "that there is not a thief in the world to-day clever enough—brainy enough—to take advantage of the suggestions put forth in these stories. But some day there will arise a man to whom they will be as simple as an ordinary blueprint, and he will profit accordingly. This magazine, by printing these stories, is merely furnishing him with his tools, showing him how to work. And the worst of it is——"

"Just a minute," said the author. "Agreeing for the moment that these stories will be the tools of Armiston's hero in real life some day, how about the popular magazines? They print ten such stories to one of these by Armiston."

"Ah, my friend," said Benson, "you forget one thing: The popular magazines deal with real life—the possible, the usual. And in that very thing they protect the public against sharpers, by exposing the methods of those same sharpers. But with Armiston—no. Much as I enjoy him as an intellectual treat, I am afraid——"

He didn't finish his sentence. Instead he fell to shaking his head, as though in amazement at the devilish ingenuity of the author under discussion.

"I am certainly delighted," thought that author, "that my disagreeable benefactor did not have the good grace to look at my card. This is really most entertaining." And then aloud, and treading on thin ice: "I should be very glad to tell Oliver what you say and see what he has to say about it."

Benson's face broke into a wreath of wrinkles:

"Do you know him? Well, I declare! That is a privilege. I heartily wish you would tell him."

"Would you like to meet him? I am under obligations to you. I can arrange a little dinner for a few of us."

"No," said Benson, shaking his head; "I would rather go on reading him without knowing him. Authors are so disappointing in real life. He may be some puny, anemic little half-portion, with dirty fingernails and all the rest that goes with genius. No offense to your friend! Besides, I am afraid I might quarrel with him."

"Last call for lunch in the dinin' cy—yah—aa," sang the porter. Armiston was looking at his fingernails as the porter passed. They were manicured once a day.

"Come lunch with me," said Benson heartily.

"I should be pleased to have you as my guest. I apologize for being rude to you at the ticket window, but I did want to catch this train mighty bad."

Armiston laughed. "Well, you have paid my carfare," he said, "and I won't deny I am hungry enough to eat a hundred-and-ten-pound rail. I will let you buy me a meal, being penniless."

Benson arose, and as he drew out his handkerchief the card Armiston had given him fluttered into that worthy's lap. Armiston closed his hand over it, chuckling again. Fate had given him the chance of preserving his incognito with this person as long as he wished. It would be a rare treat to get him ranting again about the author Armiston.

But Armiston's host did not rant against his favorite author. In fact he was so enthusiastic over that man's genius that the same qualities which he decried as a danger to society in his opinion only added luster to the work. Benson asked his guest innumerable questions as to the personal qualities of his ideal, and Armiston shamelessly constructed a truly remarkable person. The other listened entranced.

"No, I don't want to know him," he said. "In the first place I haven't the time, and in the second I'd be sure to start a row. And then there is another thing: If he is half the man I take him to be from what you say, he wouldn't stand for people fawning on him and telling him what a wonder he is. That's about what I should be doing, I am afraid."

"Oh," said Armiston, "he isn't so bad as that. He is a—well, a sensible chap, with clean fingernails and all that, you know, and he gets a haircut once every three weeks, the same as the rest of us."

"I am glad to hear you say so, Mister—er——"

Benson fell to chuckling.

"By gad," he said, "here we have been talking with each other for an hour, and I haven't so much as taken a squint at your card to see who you are!"

He searched for the card Armiston had given him.

"Call it Brown," said Armiston, lying gorgeously and with a feeling of utmost righteousness. "Martin Brown, single, read-and-write, color white, laced shoes and derby hat, as the police say."

"All right, Mr. Brown; glad to know you. We will have some cigars. You have no idea how much you interest me, Mr. Brown. How much does Armiston get for his stories?"

"Every word he writes brings him the price of a good cigar. I should say he makes forty thousand a year."

"Humph! That is better than Godahl, his star creation, could bag as a thief, I imagine, let alone the danger of getting snipped with a pistol ball on a venture."

Armiston puffed up his chest and shot his cuffs again.

"How does he get his plots?"

Armiston knitted his ponderous brows. "There's the rub," he said. "You can talk about so-and-so much a word until you are deaf, dumb, and blind. But, after all, it isn't the number of words or how they are strung together that makes a story. It is the ideas. And ideas are scarce."

"I have an idea that I have always wanted to have Armiston get hold of, just to see what he could do with it. If you will pardon me, to my way of thinking the really important thing isn't the ideas, but how to work out the details."

"What's your idea?" asked Armiston hastily. He was not averse to appropriating anything he encountered in real life and dressing it up to suit his taste. "I'll pass it on to Armiston, if you say so."

"Will you? That's capital. To begin with," Mr. Benson said as he twirled his brandy glass with long, lean, silky fingers—a hand Armiston thought he would not like to have handle him in a rage—"To begin with, Godahl, this thief, is not an ordinary thief, he is a highbrow. He has made some big hauls. He must be a very rich man now—eh? You see that he is quite real to me. By this time, I should say, Godahl has acquired such a fortune that thieving for mere money is no longer an object. What does he do? Sit down and live on his income? Not much. He is a person of refined tastes with an eye for the esthetic. He desires art objects, rare porcelains, a gem of rare cut or color set by Benvenuto Cellini, a Leonardo da Vinci—did Godahl steal the *Mona Lisa,* by the way? He is the most likely person I can think of—or perhaps a Gutenberg Bible. Treasures, things of exquisite beauty to look at, to enjoy in secret, not to show to other people. That is the natural development of this man Godahl, eh?"

"Splendid!" exclaimed Armiston, his enthusiasm getting the better of him.

"Have you ever heard of Mrs. Billy Wentworth?" asked Benson.

"Indeed, I know her well," said Armiston, his guard down.

"Then you must surely have seen her white ruby?"

"White ruby! I never heard of such a thing. A white ruby?"

"Exactly. That's just the point. Neither have I. But if Godahl heard of a white ruby the chances are he would possess it—especially if it were the only one of its kind in the world."

"Gad! I do believe he would, from what I know of him."

"And especially," went on Benson, "under the circumstances. You know the Wentworths have been round a good deal. They haven't been overscrupulous in getting things they wanted. Now Mrs. Wentworth—but before I go on with this weird tale I want you to understand me. It is pure fiction—an idea for Armiston and his wonderful Godahl. I am merely suggesting the Wentworths as fictitious characters."

"I understand," said Armiston.

"Mrs. Wentworth might very well possess this white ruby. Let us say she stole it from some potentate's household in the Straits Settlements. She gained admittance by means of the official position of her husband. They can't accuse her of theft. All they can do is to steal the gem back from her. It is a sacred stone of course. They always are in fiction stories. And the usual tribe of jugglers, rug-peddlers, and so on—all disguised, you understand—have followed her to America, seeking a chance, not on her life, not to commit violence of any kind, but to steal that stone.

"She can't wear it," went on Benson. "All she can do is to hide it away in some safe place. What is a safe place? Not a bank. Godahl could crack a bank with his little finger. So might those East Indian fellows laboring under the call of religion. Not in a safe. That would be folly."

"How then?" put in Armiston eagerly.

"Ah, there you are! That's for Godahl to find out. He knows, let us say, that these foreigners in one way or another have turned Mrs. Wentworth's apartments upside down. They haven't found anything. He knows that she keeps that white ruby in that house. Where is it? Ask Godahl. Do you see the point? Has Godahl ever cracked a nut like that? No. Here he must be the cleverest detective in the world and the cleverest thief at the same time. Before he can begin thieving he must make his blueprints.

"When I read Armiston," continued Benson, "that is the kind of problem that springs up in my mind. I am always trying to think of some knot this wonderful thief would have to employ his best powers to unravel. I think of some weird situation like this one. I say to myself: 'Good! I will write that. I will be as famous as Armiston. I will create another Godahl.' But," he said with a wave of his hands, "what is the result? I tie the knot, but I can't untie it. The trouble is, I am not a Godahl. And this man Armiston, as I read him, is Godahl. He must be, or else Godahl could not be made to do the wonderful things he does. Hello! New Haven already? Mighty sorry to have you go, old chap. Great pleasure. When you get to town let me know. Maybe I will consent to meet Armiston."

Armiston's first care on returning to New York was to remember the providential loan by which he had been able to keep clean his record of never missing a train. He counted out the sum in bills, wrote a polite note, signed it "Martin Brown," and dispatched it by messenger boy to J. Borden Benson, The Towers. The Towers, the address Mr. Benson's card bore, is an ultra-fashionable apartment hotel in lower Fifth Avenue. It maintains all the pomp and solemnity of an English ducal castle. Armiston remembered having on a remote occasion taken dinner there with a friend, and the recollection always gave him a chill. It was like dining among ghosts of kings, so grand and funereal was the air that pervaded everything.

Armiston, who could not forbear curiosity as to his queer benefactor, took occasion to look him up in the Blue Book and the Club Directory, and found that J. Borden Benson was quite some personage, several lines being devoted to him. This was extremely pleasing. Armiston had been thinking of that white-ruby yarn. It appealed to his sense of the dramatic. He would work it up in his best style, and on publication have a fine laugh on Benson by sending him an autographed copy and thus waking that gentleman up to the fact that it really had been the great Armiston in person he had befriended and entertained. What a joke it would be on Benson, thought the author; not without an intermixture of personal vanity, for even a genius such as he was not blind to flattery properly applied, and Benson unknowingly had laid it on thick.

"And, by gad!" thought the author, "I will use the Wentworths as the main characters, as the victims of Godahl. They are just the people to fit into such a romance. Benson put money in my pocket, though he didn't suspect it. Lucky he didn't know what shifts we popular authors are put to for plots."

Suiting the action to the words, Armiston and his wife accepted the next invitation they received from the Wentworths.

Mrs. Wentworth, be it understood, was a lion hunter. She was forever trying to gather about her such celebrities as Armiston the author, Brackens the painter, Johanssen the explorer, and others. Armiston had always withstood her wiles. He always had some excuse to keep him away from her gorgeous table, where she exhibited her lions to her simpering friends.

There were many undesirables sitting at the table, idle-rich youths, girls of the fast hunting set, and so on, and they all gravely shook the great author by the hand and told him what a wonderful man he was. As for Mrs. Wentworth, she was too highly elated at her success in roping him for sane speech, and she fluttered about him like a hysterical bridesmaid. But, Armiston noted with relief, one of his pals was there—Johanssen. Over cigars and cognac he managed to buttonhole the explorer.

"Johanssen," he said, "you have been everywhere."

"You are mistaken there," said Johanssen. "I have never before tonight been north of Fifty-ninth Street in New York."

"Yes, but you have been in Java and Ceylon and the Settlements. Tell me, have you ever heard of such a thing as a white ruby?"

The explorer narrowed his eyes to a slit and looked queerly at his questioner. "That's a queer question," he said in a low voice, "to ask in this house."

Armiston felt his pulse quicken. "Why?" he asked, assuming an air of surprised innocence.

"If you don't know," said the explorer shortly, "I certainly will not enlighten you."

"All right; as you please. But you haven't answered my question yet. Have you ever heard of a white ruby?"

"I don't mind telling you that I have heard of such a thing—that is, I have heard there is a ruby in existence that is called the white ruby. It isn't really white, you know; it has a purplish tinge. But the old heathen who rightly owns it likes to call it white, just as he likes to call his blue and gray elephants white."

"Who owns it?" asked Armiston, trying his best to make his voice sound natural. To find in this manner that there was some parallel for the mystical white ruby of which Benson had told him appealed strongly to his super-developed dramatic sense. He was now as keen on the scent as a hound.

Johanssen took to drumming on the tablecloth. He smiled to himself and his eyes glowed. Then he turned and looked sharply at his questioner.

"I suppose," he said, "that all things are grist to a man of your trade. If you are thinking of building a story round a white ruby I can think of nothing more fascinating. But, Armiston," he said, suddenly altering his tone and almost whispering, "if you are on the track of *the* white ruby let me advise you now to call off your dogs and keep your throat whole. I think I am a brave man. I have shot tigers at ten paces—held my fire purposely to see how charmed a life I really did bear. I have been charged by mad rhinos and by wounded buffaloes. I have walked across a clearing where the air was being punctured with bullets as thick as holes in a mosquito screen. But," he said, laying his hand on Armiston's arm, "I have never had the nerve to hunt the white ruby."

"Capital!" exclaimed the author.

"Capital, yes, for a man who earns his bread and gets his excitement by sitting at a typewriter and dreaming about these things. But take my word for it, it isn't capital for a man who gets his excitement by doing this thing. Hands off, my friend!"

"It really does exist then?"

Johanssen puckered his lips. "So they say," he said.

"What's it worth?"

"Worth? What do you mean by worth? Dollars and cents? What is your child worth to you? A million, a billion—how much? Tell me. No, you can't. Well, that's just what this miserable stone is worth to the man who rightfully owns it. Now let's quit talking nonsense. There's Billy Wentworth shooing the men into the drawing-room. I suppose we shall be entertained this evening by some of the hundred-dollar-a-minute songbirds, as usual. It's amazing what these people will spend for mere vulgar display when there are hundreds of families starving within a mile of this spot!"

Two famous singers sang that night. Armiston did not have much opportunity to look over the house. He was now fully determined to lay the scene of his story in this very house. At leave-taking the sugar-sweet Mrs. Billy Wentworth drew Armiston aside and said:

"It's rather hard on you to ask you to sit through an evening with these people. I will make amends by asking you to come to me some night when we can be by ourselves. Are you interested in rare curios? Yes, we all are. I have some really wonderful things I want you to see. Let us make it next Tuesday, with a little informal dinner, just for ourselves."

Armiston then and there made the lion hunter radiantly happy by accepting her invitation to sit at her board as a family friend instead of as a lion.

As he put his wife into their automobile he turned and looked at the house. It stood opposite Central Park. It was a copy of some French château in gray sandstone, with a barbican, and overhanging towers, and all the rest of it. The windows of the street floor peeped out through deep embrasures and were heavily guarded with iron latticework.

"Godahl will have the very devil of a time breaking in there," he chuckled to himself. Late that night his wife awakened him to find out why he was tossing about so.

"That white ruby has got on my nerves," he said cryptically, and she, thinking he was dreaming, persuaded him to try to sleep again.

Great authors must really live in the flesh, at times at least, the lives of their great characters. Otherwise these great characters would not be so real as they are. Here was Armiston, who had created a superman in the person of Godahl the thief. For ten years he had written nothing else. He had laid the life of Godahl out in squares, thought for him, dreamed about him, set him to new tasks, gone through all sorts of queer adventures with him. And this same Godahl had amply repaid him. He had raised the author from the ranks of struggling amateurs to a position among the most highly paid fiction writers in the United States. He had brought him ease and luxury. Armiston did not need the money any more. The serial rights telling of the exploits of this Godahl had paid him handsomely. The books of Godahl's adventures had paid him even better, and had furnished him yearly with a never-failing income, like government bonds, but at a much higher rate of interest. Even though the crimes this Godahl had committed were all on paper and almost impossible, nevertheless Godahl was a living being to his creator. More—he was Armiston, and Armiston was Godahl.

It was not surprising, then, that when Tuesday came Armiston awaited the hour with feverish impatience. Here, as his strange friend had so thoughtlessly and casually told him was an opportunity for the great Godahl to outdo even himself. Here was an opportunity for Godahl to be the greatest detective in the world, in the first place, before he could carry out one of his sensational thefts.

So it was Godahl, not Armiston, who helped his wife out of their automobile that evening and mounted the splendid steps of the Wentworth mansion. He cast his eye aloft, took in every inch of the façade.

"No," he said, "Godahl cannot break in from the street. I must have a look at the back of the house."

He cast his eyes on the ironwork that guarded the deep windows giving on the street.

It was not iron after all, but chilled steel sunk into armored concrete. The outposts of this house were as safely guarded as the vault of the United States mint.

"It's got to be from the inside," he said, making mental note of this fact.

The butler was stone-deaf. This was rather singular. Why should a family of the standing of the Wentworths employ a man as head of their city establishment who was stone-deaf? Armiston looked at the man with curiosity. He was still in middle age. Surely, then, he was not retained because of years of service. No, there was something more than charity behind this. He addressed a casual word to the man as he handed him his hat and cane. His back was turned and the man did not reply. Armiston turned and repeated the sentence in the same tone. The man watched his lips in the bright light of the hall.

"A lip-reader, and a dandy," thought Armiston, for the butler seemed to catch every word he said.

"Fact number two!" said the creator of Godahl the thief.

He felt no compunction at thus noting the most intimate details of the Wentworth establishment. An accident had put him on the track of a rare good story, and it was all copy. Besides, he told himself, when he came to write the story he would disguise it in such a way that no one reading it would know it was about the Wentworths. If their establishment happened to possess the requisite setting for a great story, surely there was no reason why he should not take advantage of that fact.

The great thief—he made no bones of the fact to himself that he had come here to help Godahl—accepted the flattering greeting of his hostess with the grand air that so well fitted him. Armiston was tall and thin, with slender fingers and a touch of gray in his wavy hair, for all his youthful years, and he knew how to wear his clothes. Mrs. Wentworth was proud of him as a social ornament, even aside from his glittering fame as an author. And Mrs. Armiston was well born, so there was no jar in their being received in the best house of the town.

The dinner was truly delightful. Here Armiston saw, or thought he saw, one of the reasons for the deaf butler. The hostess had him so trained that she was able to catch her servant's eye and instruct him in this or that trifle by merely moving her lips. It was almost uncanny, thought the author, this silent conversation the deaf man and his mistress were able to carry on unnoticed by the others.

"By gad, it's wonderful! Godahl, my friend, underscore that note of yours referring to the deaf butler. Don't miss it. It will take a trick."

Armiston gave his undivided attention to his

hostess as soon as he found Wentworth entertaining Mrs. Armiston and thus properly dividing the party. He persuaded her to talk by a cleverly pointed question here and there; and as she talked, he studied her.

"We are going to rob you of your precious white ruby, my friend," he thought humorously to himself; "and while we are laying our wires there is nothing about you too small to be worthy of our attention."

Did she really possess the white ruby? Did this man Benson know anything about the white ruby? And what was the meaning of the strange actions of his friend Johanssen when approached on the subject in this house? His hostess came to have a wonderful fascination for him. He pictured this beautiful creature so avid in her lust for rare gems that she actually did penetrate the establishment of some heathen potentate in the Straits simply for the purpose of stealing the mystic stone. "Have you ever, by any chance, been in the Straits?" he asked indifferently.

"Wait," Mrs. Wentworth said with a laugh as she touched his hand lightly; "I have some curios from the Straits, and I will venture to say you have never seen their like."

Half an hour later they were all seated over coffee and cigarettes in Mrs. Wentworth's boudoir. It was indeed a strange place. There was scarcely a single corner of the world that had not contributed something to its furnishing. Carvings of teak and ivory; hangings of sweet-scented vegetable fibers; lamps of jade; queer little gods, all sitting like Buddha with their legs drawn up under them, carved out of jade or sardonyx; scarfs of baroque pearls; Darjeeling turquoises—Armiston had never before seen such a collection. And each item had its story. He began to look on this frail little woman with different eyes. She had been and seen and done, and the tale of her life, what she had actually lived, outshone even that of the glittering rascal Godahl, who was standing beside him now and directing his ceaseless questions. "Have you any rubies?" he asked.

Mrs. Wentworth bent before a safe in the wall. With swift fingers she whirled the combination. The keen eyes of Armiston followed the bright knob like a cat.

"Fact number three!" said the Godahl in him as he mentally made note of the numbers. "Five—eight—seven—four—six. That's the combination."

Mrs. Wentworth showed him six pigeon-blood rubies. "This one is pale," he said carelessly, holding a particularly large stone up to the light. "Is it true that occasionally they are found white?"

His hostess looked at him before answering. He was intent on a deep-red stone he held in the palm of his hand. It seemed a thousand miles deep.

"What a fantastic idea!" she said. She glanced at her husband, who had reached out and taken her hand in a naturally affectionate manner.

"Fact number four!" mentally noted Armiston. "Are not you in mortal fear of robbery with all of this wealth?"

Mrs. Wentworth laughed lightly.

"That is why we live in a fortress," she said.

"Have you never, then, been visited by thieves?" asked the author boldly.

"Never!" she said.

"A lie," thought Armiston. "Fact number five! We are getting on swimmingly."

"I do not believe that even your Godahl the Infallible could get in here," Mrs. Wentworth said. "Not even the servants enter this room. That door is not locked with a key; yet it locks. I am not much of a housekeeper," she said lazily, "but such housekeeping as is done in this room is all done by these poor little hands of mine."

"No! Most amazing! May I look at the door?"

"Yes, Mr. Godahl," said this woman, who had lived more lives than Godahl himself.

Armiston examined the door, this strange device that locked without a key, apparently indeed without a lock, and came away disappointed.

"Well, Mr. Godahl?" his hostess said tauntingly. He shook his head in perplexity.

"Most ingenious," he said; and then suddenly: "Yet I will venture that if I turned Godahl loose on this problem he would solve it."

"What fun!" she cried clapping her hands.

"You challenge him?" asked Armiston.

"What nonsense is this!" cried Wentworth, coming forward.

"No nonsense at all," said Mrs. Wentworth. "Mr. Armiston has just said that his Godahl could rob me. Let him try. If he can—if mortal man can gain the secret of ingress and egress of this room—I want to know it. I don't believe mortal man can enter this room."

Armiston noted a strange glitter in her eyes.

"Gad! She was born to the part! What a woman!" he thought. And then aloud:

"I will set him to work. I will lay the scene of his exploit in—say—Hungary, where this room might very well exist in some feudal castle. How many people have entered this room since it was made the storehouse of all this wealth?"

"Not six besides yourself," replied Mrs. Wentworth.

"Then no one can recognize it if I describe it in a story—in fact, I will change the material details. We will say that it is not jewels Godahl is seeking. We will say that it is a——"

Mrs. Wentworth's hand touched his own. The tips of her fingers were cold. "A white ruby," she said.

"Gad! What a thoroughbred!" he exclaimed to himself—or to Godahl. And then aloud: "Capital! I will send you a copy of the story autographed."

The next day he called at The Towers and sent up his card to Mr. Benson's apartments. Surely a man of Benson's standing could be trusted with such a secret. In fact it was evidently not a secret to Benson, who in all probability was one of the six Mrs. Wentworth said had entered that room. Armiston wanted to talk the matter over with Benson. He had given up his idea of having fun with him by sending him a marked copy of the magazine containing his tale. His story had taken complete possession of him, as always had been the case when he was at work dispatching Godahl on his adventures.

"If that ruby really exists," Armiston said, "I don't know whether I shall write the story or steal the ruby for myself. Benson is right. Godahl should not steal any more for mere money. He is after rare, unique things now. And I am Godahl. I feel the same way myself."

A valet appeared, attired in a gorgeous livery. Armiston wondered why any self-respecting American would consent to don such raiment, even though it was the livery of the great Benson family.

"Mr. Armiston, sir," said the valet, looking at the author's card he held in his hand. "Mr. Benson sailed for Europe yesterday morning. He is spending the summer in Norway. I am to follow on the next steamer. Is there any message I can take to him, sir? I have heard him speak of you, sir."

Armiston took the card and wrote on it in pencil:

"I called to apologize. I am Martin Brown. The chance was too good to miss. You will pardon me, won't you?"

For the next two weeks Armiston gave himself over to his dissipation, which was accompanying Godahl on this adventure. It was a formidable task. The secret room he placed in a Hungarian castle, as he had promised. A beautiful countess was his heroine. She had seen the world, mostly in man's attire, and her escapades had furnished vivacious reading for two continents. No one could possibly connect her with Mrs. Billy Wentworth. So far it was easy. But how was Godahl to get into this wonderful room where the countess had hidden this wonderful rare white ruby? The room was lined with chilled steel. Even the door—this he had noted when he was examining that peculiar portal—was lined with layers of steel. It could withstand any known tool.

However, Armiston was Armiston, and Godahl was Godahl. He got into that room. He got the white ruby!

The manuscript went to the printers, and the publishers said that Armiston had never done anything like it since he started Godahl on his astonishing career.

He banked the check for his tale, and as he did so he said: "Gad! I would a hundred times rather possess that white ruby. Confound the thing! I feel as if I had not heard the last of it."

Armiston and his wife went to Maine for the summer without leaving their address. Along in the early fall he received by registered mail, forwarded by his trusted servant at the town house, a package containing the envelope he had addressed to J. Borden Benson, The Towers. Furthermore it contained the dollar bills he had dispatched to that individual, together with his note which he had signed "Martin Brown." And across the note, in the most insulting manner, was written in coarse, greasy blue-pencil lines:

"Damnable impertinence. I'll cane you the first time I see you."

And no more. That was enough of course—quite sufficient.

In the same mail came a note from Armiston's publishers, saying that his story, "The White Ruby," was scheduled for publication in the October number, out September twenty-fifth. This cheered him up. He was anxious to see it in print. Late in September they started back to town.

"Aha!" he said as he sat reading his paper in the parlor car—he had caught this train by the veriest tip of its tail and upset the running schedule in the act—"Ah! I see my genial friend, J. Borden Benson, is in town, contrary to custom at this time of year. Life must be a great bore to that snob."

A few days after arriving in town he received a package of advance copies of the magazine containing his story, and he read the tale of "The White Ruby" as if he had never seen it before. On the cover of one copy, which he was to dispatch to his grumpy benefactor, J. Borden Benson, he wrote:

> Charmed to be caned. Call any time. See contents.
>
> Oliver Armiston.

On another he wrote:

> *Dear Mrs. Wentworth:* See how simple it is to pierce your fancied security!

He dispatched these two magazines with a feeling of glee. No sooner had he done so, however, than he learned that the Wentworths had not yet returned from Newport. The magazine would be forwarded to them no doubt. The Wentworths' absence made the tale all the better, in fact, for in his story Armiston had insisted on Godahl's breaking into the castle and solving the mystery of the keyless door during the season when the château was closed and strung with a perfect network of burglar alarms connecting with the *gendarmerie* in the near-by village.

That was the twenty-fifth day of September. The magazine was put on sale that morning.

On the twenty-sixth day of September Armiston bought a late edition of an afternoon paper from a leather-lunged boy who was hawking "Extra!" in the street. Across the first page the headlines met his eye:

> ROBBERY AND MURDER
> IN THE WENTWORTH MANSION!
>
> Private watchmen, summoned by burglar alarm at ten o'clock this morning, find servant with skull crushed on floor of mysterious steel-doored room. Murdered man's pockets filled with rare jewels. Police believe he was murdered by confederate who escaped.
>
> The Wentworth Butler, Stone Deaf, Had Just Returned From Newport to Open House at Time of Murder.

It was ten o'clock that night when an automobile drew up at Armiston's door and a tall man with a square jaw, square shoes, and a square mustache alighted. This was Deputy Police Commissioner Byrnes, a professional detective whom the new administration had drafted into the city's service from the government secret service.

Byrnes was admitted, and as he advanced to the middle of the drawing-room, without so much as a nod to the ghostlike Armiston who stood shivering before him, he drew a package of papers from his pocket.

"I presume you have seen all the evening papers," he said, spitting his words through his half-closed teeth with so much show of personal malice that Armiston—never a brave man in spite of his Godahl—cowered before him.

Armiston shook his head dumbly at first, but at length he managed to say: "Not all; no."

The deputy commissioner with much deliberation drew out the latest extra and handed it to Armiston without a word.

It was the *Evening News.* The first page was divided down its entire length by a black line. On one side and occupying four columns, was a word-for-word reprint of Armiston's story, "The White Ruby."

On the other, the facts in deadly parallel, was a graphic account of the robbery and murder at the home of Billy Wentworth. The parallel was glaring in the intensity of its dumb accusation. On the one side was the theoretical Godahl, working his masterly way of crime, step by step; and on the other was the plagiarism of Armiston's story, following the intricacies of the master mind with copybook accuracy.

The editor, who must have been a genius in his way, did not accuse. He simply placed the fiction and the fact side by side and let the reader judge for himself. It was masterly. If, as the law says, the mind that conceives, the intelligence that directs, a crime is more guilty than the very hand that acts, then Armiston here was both thief and murderer. Thief, because the white ruby had actually been stolen. Mrs. Billy Wentworth, rushed to the city by special train, attended by doctors and nurses, now confirmed the story of the theft of the ruby. Murderer, because in the story Godahl had for once in his career stooped to murder as the means, and had triumphed over the dead body of his confederate, scorning, in his joy at possessing the white ruby, the paltry diamonds, pearls, and red rubies with which his confederate had crammed his pockets.

Armiston seized the police official by his lapels.

"The butler!" he screamed. "The butler! Yes, the butler. Quick, or he will have flown."

Byrnes gently disengaged the hands that had grasped him.

"Too late," he said. "He has already flown. Sit down and quiet your nerves. We need your help. You are the only man in the world who can help us now."

When Armiston was himself again he told the whole tale, beginning with his strange meeting with J. Borden Benson on the train, and ending with his accepting Mrs. Wentworth's challenge to have Godahl break into the room and steal the white ruby. Byrnes nodded over the last part. He had already heard that from Mrs. Wentworth, and there was the autographed copy of the magazine to show for it.

"You say that J. Borden Benson told you of this white ruby in the first place."

Armiston again told, in great detail, the circumstances, all the humor now turned into grim tragedy.

"That is strange," said the ex-secret-service chief. "Did you leave your purse at home or was your pocket picked?"

"I thought at first that I had absent-mindedly left it at home. Then I remembered having paid the chauffeur out of the roll of bills, so my pocket must have been picked."

"What kind of a looking man was this Benson?"

"You must know him," said Armiston.

"Yes, I know him; but I want to know what he looked like to you. I want to find out how he happened to be so handy when you were in need of money."

Armiston described the man minutely.

The deputy sprang to his feet. "Come with me," he said; and they hurried into the automobile and soon drew up in front of The Towers.

Five minutes later they were ushered into the magnificent apartment of J. Borden Benson.

That worthy was in his bath preparing to retire for the night.

"I don't catch the name," Armiston and the deputy heard him cry through the bathroom door to his valet.

"Mr. Oliver Armiston, sir."

"Ah, he has come for his caning, I expect. I'll be there directly."

He did not wait to complete his toilet, so eager was he to see the author. He strode out in a brilliant bathrobe and in one hand he carried an alpenstock. His eyes glowed in anger. But the sight of Byrnes surprised as well as halted him.

"Do you mean to say this is J. Borden Benson?" cried Armiston to Byrnes, rising to his feet and pointing at the man.

"The same," said the deputy; "I swear to it. I know him well! I take it he is not the gentleman who paid your carfare to New Haven."

"Not by a hundred pounds!" exclaimed Armiston as he surveyed the huge bulk of the elephantine clubman.

The forced realization that the stranger he had hitherto regarded as a benefactor was not J. Borden Benson at all, but some one who had merely assumed that worthy's name while he was playing the conceited author as an easy dupe, did more to quiet Armiston's nerves than all the sedatives his doctor had given him. It was a badly dashed popular author who sat down with the deputy commissioner in his library an hour later. He would gladly have consigned Godahl to the bottom of the sea; but it was too late. Godahl had taken the trick.

"How do you figure it?" Armiston asked, turning to the deputy.

"The beginning is simple enough. It is the end that bothers me," said the official. "Your bogus J. Borden Benson is, of course, the brains of the whole combination. Your infernal Godahl has told us just exactly how this crime was committed. Now your infernal Godahl must bring the guilty parties to justice."

It was plain to be seen that the police official hated Godahl worse than poison, and feared him too.

"Why not look in the Rogues' Gallery for this man who befriended me on the train?"

The chief laughed.

"For the love of Heaven, Armiston, do you, who pretend to know all about scientific thievery, think for a moment that the man who took your measure so easily is of the class of crooks who get their pictures in the Rogues' Gallery? Talk sense!"

"I can't believe you when you say he picked my pocket."

"I don't care whether you believe me or not; he did, or one of his pals did. It all amounts to the same thing, don't you see? First, he wanted to get acquainted with you. Now the best way to get into your good graces was to put you unsuspectingly under obligation to him. So he robs you of your money. From what I have seen of you in the last few hours it must have been like taking candy from a child. Then he gets next to you in line. He pretends that you are merely some troublesome toad in his path. He gives you money for your ticket, to get you out of his way so he won't miss his train. His train! Of course his train is your train. He puts you in a position where you have to make advances to him. And then, grinning to himself all the time at your conceit and gullibility, he plays you through your pride, your Godahl. Think of the creator of the great Godahl falling for a trick like that!"

Byrnes's last words were the acme of biting sarcasm.

"You admit yourself that he is too clever for you to put your hands on."

"And then," went on Byrnes, not heeding the interruption, "he invites you to lunch and tells you what he wants you to do for him. And you follow his lead like a sheep at the tail of the bellwether! Great Scott, Armiston! I would give a year's salary for one hour's conversation with that man."

Armiston was beginning to see the part this queer character had played; but he was in a semi-hysterical state, and, like a woman in such a position, he wanted a calm mind to tell him the whole thing in words of one syllable, to verify his own dread.

"What do you mean?" he asked. "I don't quite follow. You say he tells me what he wants me to do."

Byrnes shrugged his shoulders in disgust; then, as if resigned to the task before him, he began his explanation:

"Here, man, I will draw a diagram for you. This gentleman friend of yours—we will call him John Smith for convenience—wants to get possession of this white ruby. He knows that it is in the keeping of Mrs. Billy Wentworth. He knows you know Mrs. Wentworth and have access to her house. He knows that she stole this bauble and is frightened to death all the time. Now John Smith is a pretty clever chap. He handled the great Armiston like hot putty. He had exhausted his resources. He is baffled and needs help. What does he do? He reads the stories about the great Godahl. Confidentially, Mr. Armiston, I will tell you that I think your great Godahl is mush. But that is neither here nor there. If you can sell him as a gold brick, all right. But Mr. John Smith is struck by the wonderful ingenuity of this Godahl. He says: 'Ha! I will get Godahl to tell me how to get this gem!'

"So he gets hold of yourself, sir, and persuades you that you are playing a joke on him by getting him to rant and rave about the great Godahl. Then—and here the villain enters—he says: 'Here is a thing the great Godahl cannot do. I dare him to do it.' He tells you about the gem, whose very existence is quite fantastic enough to excite the imagination of the wonderful Armiston. And by clever suggestion he persuades you to lay the plot at the home of Mrs. Wentworth. And all the time you are chuckling to yourself, thinking what a rare joke you are going to have on J. Borden Benson when you send him an autographed copy and show him that he was talking to the distinguished genius all the time and didn't know it. That's the whole story, sir. Now wake up!"

Byrnes sat back in his chair and regarded Armiston with the smile a pedagogue bestows on a refractory boy whom he has just flogged soundly.

"I will explain further," he continued. "You haven't visited the house yet. You can't. Mrs. Wentworth, for all she is in bed with four dozen hot-water bottles, would tear you limb from limb if you went there. And don't you think for a minute she isn't able to. That woman is a vixen."

Armiston nodded gloomily. The very thought of her now sent him into a cold sweat.

"Mr. Godahl, the obliging," continued the deputy, "notes one thing to begin with: The house cannot be entered from the outside. So it must be an inside job. How can this be accomplished? Well, there is the deaf butler. Why is he deaf? Godahl ponders. Ha! He has it! The Wentworths are so dependent on servants that they must have them round at all times. This butler is the one who is constantly about them. They are worried to death by their possession of this white ruby. Their house has been raided from the inside a dozen times. Nothing is taken, mind you. They suspect their servants. This thing haunts them, but the woman will not give up this foolish bauble. So she has as her major domo a man who cannot understand a word in any language unless he is looking at the speaker and is in a bright light. He can only understand the lips. Handy, isn't it? In a dull light or with their backs turned they can talk about anything they want to. This is a jewel of a butler.

"But," added Byrnes, "one day a man calls. He is a lawyer. He tells the butler he is heir to a fortune—fifty thousand dollars. He must go to Ireland to claim it. Your friend on the train—he is the man of course—sends your butler to Ireland. So this precious butler is lost. They must have another. Only a deaf one will do. And they find just the man they want—quite accidentally, you understand. Of course it is Godahl, with forged letters saying he has been in service in great houses. Presto! The great Godahl himself is now the butler. It is simple enough to play deaf. You say this is fiction. Let me tell you this: Six weeks ago the Wentworths actually changed butlers. That hasn't come out in the papers yet."

Armiston, who had listened to the deputy's review of his story listlessly, now sat up with a start. He suddenly exclaimed gleefully:

"But my story didn't come out till two days ago!"

"Ah, yes; but you forget that it has been in the hands of your publishers for three months. A man who was clever enough to dupe the great Armiston wouldn't shirk the task of getting hold of a proof of that story."

Armiston sank deeper into his chair.

"Once Godahl got inside the house the rest was simple. He corrupted one of the servants. He opened the steel-lined door with the flame of an oxyacetylene blast. As you say in your story that flame cuts steel like wax; he didn't have to bother about the lock. He simply cut the door down. Then he put his confederate in good humor by telling him to fill his pockets with the diamonds and other junk in the safe, which he obligingly opens. One thing bothers me, Armiston. How did you find out about that infernal contraption that killed the confederate?"

Armiston buried his face in his hands. Byrnes rudely shook him.

"Come," he said; "you murdered that man, though you are innocent. Tell me how."

"Is this the third degree?" said Armiston.

"It looks like it," said the deputy grimly as he gnawed at his stubby mustache. Armiston drew a long breath, like one who realizes how hopeless is his situation. He began to speak in a low tone. All the while the deputy glared at Godahl's inventor with his accusing eye.

"When I was sitting in the treasure room with the Wentworths and my wife, playing auction bridge, I dismissed the puzzle of the door as easily solved by means of the brazing flame. The problem was not to get into the house or into this room, but to find the ruby. It was not in the safe."

"No, of course not. I suppose your friend on the train was kind enough to tell you that. He had probably looked there himself."

"Gad! He did tell me that, come to think of it. Well, I studied that room. I was sure the white ruby, if it really existed, was within ten feet of me. I examined the floor, the ceiling, the walls. No result. But," he said, shivering as if in a draft of cold air, "there was a chest in that room made of Lombardy oak." The harassed author buried his face in his hands. "Oh, this is terrible!" he moaned.

"Go on," said the deputy in his colorless voice.

"I can't. I tell it all in the story, Heaven help me!"

"I know you tell it all in the story," came the rasping voice of Byrnes; "but I want you to tell it to me. I want to hear it from your own lips—as Armiston, you understand, whose deviltry has just killed a man; not as your damnable Godahl."

"The chest was not solid oak," went on Armiston. "It was solid steel covered with oak to disguise it."

"How did you know that?"

"I had seen it before."

"Where?"

"In Italy fifteen years ago, in a decayed castle, back through the Soldini pass from Lugano. It was the possession of an old nobleman, a friend of a friend of mine."

"Humph!" grunted the deputy. And then: "Well, how did you know it was the same one?"

"By the inscription carved on the front. It was—but I have told all this in print already. Why need I go over it all again?"

"I want to hear it again from your own lips. Maybe there are some points you did not tell in print. Go on!"

"The inscription was '*Sanctus Dominus.*'"

The deputy smiled grimly.

"Very fitting, I should say. Praise the Lord with the most diabolical engine of destruction I have ever seen."

"And then," said Armiston, "there was the owner's name—'Arno Petronii.' Queer name that."

"Yes," said the deputy dryly. "How did you hit on this as the receptacle for the white ruby?"

"If it were the same one I saw in Lugano—and I felt sure it was—it was certain death to attempt to open it—that is, for one who did not know how. Such machines were common enough in the Middle Ages. There was an obvious way to open it. It was meant to be obvious. To open it that way was inevitable death. It released tremendous springs that crushed anything within a radius of five feet. You saw that?"

"I did," said the deputy, and he shuddered as he spoke. Then, bringing his fierce face within an inch of the cowering Armiston, he said:

"You knew the secret spring by which that safe could be opened as simply as a shoebox, eh?"

Armiston nodded his head.

"But Godahl did not," he said. "Having recognized this terrible chest," went on the author, "I guessed it must be the hiding-place of the jewel—for two reasons: In the first place Mrs. Wentworth had avoided showing it to us. She passed it by as a mere bit of curious furniture. Second, it was too big to go through the door or any one of the windows. They must have gone to the trouble of taking down the wall to get that thing in there. Something of a task, too, considering it weighs about two tons."

"You didn't bring out that point in your story."

"Didn't I? I fully intended to."

"Maybe," said the deputy, watching his man sharply, "it so impressed your friend who paid your carfare to New Haven that he clipped it out of the manuscript when he borrowed it."

"There is no humor in this affair, sir, if you will pardon me," said Armiston.

"That is quite true. Go ahead."

"The rest you know. Godahl, in my story—the thief in real life—had to sacrifice a life to open that chest. So he corrupted a small kitchen servant, filling his pockets with these other jewels, and told him to touch the spring."

"You murdered that man in cold blood," said the deputy, rising and pacing the floor. "The poor deluded devil, from the looks of what's left of him, never let out a whimper, never knew what hit him. Here, take some more of this brandy. Your nerves are in a bad way."

"What I can't make out is this," said Armiston after a time. "There was a million dollars' worth of stuff in that room that could have been put into a quart measure. Why did not this thief, who was willing to go to all the trouble to get the white ruby, take some of the jewels? Nothing is missing besides the white ruby, as I understand it. Is there?"

"No," said the deputy. "Not a thing. Here comes a messenger boy."

"For Mr. Armiston? Yes," he said to the entering maid. The boy handed him a package for which the deputy signed.

"This is for you," he said, turning to Armiston as he closed the door. "Open it."

When the package was opened the first object to greet their eyes was a roll of bills.

"This grows interesting," said Byrnes. He counted the money. "Thirty-nine dollars. Your friend evidently is returning the money he stole from you at the station. What does he have to say for himself? I see there is a note."

He reached over and took the paper out of Armiston's hands. It was ordinary bond stationery, with no identifying marks of any consequence. The note was written in bronze ink, in a careful copperplate hand, very small and precise. It read:

"*Most Excellency Sir:* Herewith, most honored dollars I am dispatching complete. Regretful extremely of sad blood being not to be prevented. Accept trifle from true friend."

That was all.

"There's a jeweler's box," said Byrnes. "Open it."

Inside the box was a lozenge-shaped diamond about the size of a little fingernail. It hung from a tiny bar of silver, highly polished and devoid of ornament. On the back under the clasp-pin were several microscopic characters.

There were several obvious clues to be followed—the messenger boy, the lawyers who induced the deaf butler to go to Ireland on what later proved to be a wild-goose chase, the employment agency through which the new butler had been secured, and so on. But all of these avenues proved too respectable to yield results. Deputy Byrnes had early arrived at his own conclusions, by virtue of the knowledge he had gained as government agent, yet to appease the popular indignation he kept up a desultory search for the criminal.

It was natural that Armiston should think of his friend Johanssen at this juncture. Johanssen possessed that wonderful oriental capacity of aloofness which we Westerners are so ready to term indifference or lack of curiosity.

"No, I thank you," said Johanssen. "I'd rather not mix in."

The pleadings of the author were in vain. His words fell on deaf ears.

"If you will not lift a hand because of your friendship for me," said Armiston bitterly, "then think of the law. Surely there is something due justice, when both robbery and bloody murder have been committed!"

"Justice!" cried Johanssen in scorn. "Justice, you say! My friend, if you steal from me, and I reclaim by force that which is mine, is that injustice? If you cannot see the idea behind that, surely, then, I cannot explain it to you."

"Answer one question," said Armiston. "Have you any idea who the man was I met on the train?"

"For your own peace of mind—yes. As a clue leading to what you so glibly term justice—pshaw! Tonight's sundown would be easier for you to catch than this man if I know him. Mind you, Armiston, I do not know. But I believe. Here is what I believe:

"In a dozen courts of kings and petty princelings that I know of in the East there are Westerners retained as advisers—fiscal agents they usually call them. Usually they are American or English, or occasionally German.

"Now I ask you a question. Say that you were in the hire of a heathen prince, and a grievous wrong were done that prince, say, by a thoughtless woman who had not the least conception of the beauty of an idea she had outraged. Merely for the possession of a bauble, valueless to her except to appease vanity, she ruthlessly rode down a superstition that was as holy to this prince as your own belief in Christ is to you. What would you do?"

Without waiting for Armiston to answer, Johanssen went on:

"I know a man——You say this man you met on the train had wonderful hands, did he not? Yes, I thought so. Armiston, I know a man who would not sit idly by and smile to himself over the ridiculous fuss occasioned by the loss of an imperfect stone—off color, badly cut, and everything else. Neither would he laugh at the superstition behind it. He would say to himself: 'This superstition is older by several thousand years than I or my people.' And this man, whom I know, is brave enough to right that wrong himself if his underlings failed."

"I follow," said Armiston dully.

"But," said Johanssen, leaning forward and tapping the author on the knee—"but the task proves too big for him. What did he do? He asked the cleverest man in the world to help him. And Godahl helped him. That," said Johanssen, interrupting Armiston with a raised finger, "is the story of the white ruby. 'The Story of the White Ruby' you see, is something infinitely finer than mere vulgar robbery and murder, as the author of the Infallible Godahl conceived it."

Johanssen said a great deal more. In the end he took the lozenge-shaped diamond pendant and put the glass on the silver bar, that his friend might see the inscription on the back. He told him what the inscription signified—"Brother of a King," and, furthermore, how few men alive possessed the capacity for brotherhood.

"I think," said Armiston as he was about to take his leave, "that I will travel in the Straits this winter."

"If you do," said Johanssen, "I earnestly advise you to leave your Godahl and his decoration at home."

Villain: The Cisco Kid

The Caballero's Way

O. HENRY

IN "THE CABALLERO'S WAY," O. Henry, the pseudonym of William Sydney Porter (1862–1910), created a character who went on to become a beloved figure in motion pictures, radio, television, comic books, and comic strips, undergoing a major change from his original incarnation. The Cisco Kid is not a heroic figure in this short story, but the exact opposite, a killer and multiple murderer who is transformed in the first film, *In Old Arizona* (1929), into a sartorial, dressed-all-in-black, turn-of-the-century Mexican hero who captures outlaws and rescues damsels in distress. Warner Baxter won the Best Actor Oscar, the second ever given, for his portrayal of the Cisco Kid. There were multiple films about him, plus 156 half-hour television programs (among the first to be shot in color) between 1950 and 1956. He was played by Duncan Renaldo; his sidekick, Pancho (a character not in the original story), was played for comic effect by Leo Carrillo.

As O. Henry, Porter wrote approximately six hundred short stories that once were as critically acclaimed as they were popular. Often undervalued today because of their sentimentality, many nonetheless remain iconic and familiar, notably such classics as "The Gift of the Magi," "The Furnished Room," "A Retrieved Reformation" (better known for its several stage and film versions as *Alias Jimmy Valentine*), and "The Ransom of Red Chief." *The O. Henry Prize Stories*, a prestigious annual anthology of the year's best short stories named in his honor, has been published since 1919.

"The Caballero's Way" was originally published in the July 1907 issue of *Everybody's*; it was first published in book form in O. Henry's *Heart of the West* (New York, McClure, 1907).

THE CABALLERO'S WAY

O. Henry

THE CISCO KID had killed six men in more or less fair scrimmages, had murdered twice as many (mostly Mexicans), and had winged a larger number whom he modestly forbore to count. Therefore a woman loved him.

The Kid was twenty-five, looked twenty; and a careful insurance company would have estimated the probable time of his demise at, say, twenty-six. His habitat was anywhere between the Frio and the Rio Grande. He killed for the love of it—because he was quick-tempered—to avoid arrest—for his own amusement—any reason that came to his mind would suffice. He had escaped capture because he could shoot five-sixths of a second sooner than any sheriff or ranger in the service, and because he rode a speckled roan horse that knew every cow-path in the mesquite and pear thickets from San Antonio to Matamoras.

Tonia Perez, the girl who loved the Cisco Kid, was half Carmen, half Madonna, and the rest—oh, yes, a woman who is half Carmen and half Madonna can always be something more—the rest, let us say, was humming-bird. She lived in a grass-roofed *jacal* near a little Mexican settlement at the Lone Wolf Crossing of the Frio. With her lived a father or grandfather, a lineal Aztec, somewhat less than a thousand years old, who herded a hundred goats and lived in a continuous drunken dream from drinking *mescal.* Back of the *jacal* a tremendous forest of bristling pear, twenty feet high at its worst, crowded almost to its door. It was along the bewildering maze of this spinous thicket that the speckled roan would bring the Kid to see his girl. And once, clinging like a lizard to the ridge-pole, high up under the peaked grass roof, he had heard Tonia, with her Madonna face and Carmen beauty and humming-bird soul, parley with the sheriff's posse, denying knowledge of her man in her soft *melange* of Spanish and English.

One day the adjutant-general of the State, who is, *ex officio*, commander of the ranger forces, wrote some sarcastic lines to Captain Duval of Company X, stationed at Laredo, relative to the serene and undisturbed existence led by murderers and desperadoes in the said captain's territory.

The captain turned the colour of brick dust under his tan, and forwarded the letter, after adding a few comments, per ranger Private Bill Adamson, to ranger Lieutenant Sandridge, camped at a water hole on the Nueces with a squad of five men in preservation of law and order.

Lieutenant Sandridge turned a beautiful *couleur de rose* through his ordinary strawberry complexion, tucked the letter in his hip pocket, and chewed off the ends of his gamboge moustache.

The next morning he saddled his horse and rode alone to the Mexican settlement at the Lone Wolf Crossing of the Frio, twenty miles away.

Six feet two, blond as a Viking, quiet as a deacon, dangerous as a machine gun, Sandridge moved among the *jacales*, patiently seeking news of the Cisco Kid.

Far more than the law, the Mexicans dreaded the cold and certain vengeance of the lone rider that the ranger sought. It had been one of the Kid's pastimes to shoot Mexicans "to see them kick": if he demanded from them moribund Terpsichorean feats, simply that he might be entertained, what terrible and extreme penalties would be certain to follow should they anger him! One and all they lounged with upturned palms and shrugging shoulders, filling the air with *"quien sabes"* and denials of the Kid's acquaintance.

But there was a man named Fink who kept a store at the Crossing—a man of many nationalities, tongues, interests, and ways of thinking.

"No use to ask them Mexicans," he said to Sandridge. "They're afraid to tell. This *hombre* they call the Kid—Goodall is his name, ain't it?—he's been in my store once or twice. I have an idea you might run across him at—but I guess I don't keer to say, myself. I'm two seconds later in pulling a gun than I used to be, and the difference is worth thinking about. But this Kid's got a half-Mexican girl at the Crossing that he comes to see. She lives in that *jacal* a hundred yards down the arroyo at the edge of the pear. Maybe she—no, I don't suppose she would, but that *jacal* would be a good place to watch, anyway."

Sandridge rode down to the *jacal* of Perez. The sun was low, and the broad shade of the great pear thicket already covered the grass-thatched hut. The goats were enclosed for the night in a brush corral near by. A few kids walked the top of it, nibbling the chaparral leaves. The old Mexican lay upon a blanket on the grass, already in a stupor from his mescal, and dreaming, perhaps, of the nights when he and Pizarro touched glasses to their New World fortunes—so old his wrinkled face seemed to proclaim him to be. And in the door of the *jacal* stood Tonia. And Lieutenant Sandridge sat in his saddle staring at her like a gannet agape at a sailorman.

The Cisco Kid was a vain person, as all eminent and successful assassins are, and his bosom would have been ruffled had he known that at a simple exchange of glances two persons, in whose minds he had been looming large, suddenly abandoned (at least for the time) all thought of him.

Never before had Tonia seen such a man as this. He seemed to be made of sunshine and blood-red tissue and clear weather. He seemed to illuminate the shadow of the pear when he smiled, as though the sun were rising again. The men she had known had been small and dark. Even the Kid, in spite of his achievements, was a stripling no larger than herself, with black, straight hair and a cold, marble face that chilled the noonday.

As for Tonia, though she sends description to the poorhouse, let her make a millionaire of your fancy. Her blue-black hair, smoothly divided in the middle and bound close to her head, and her large eyes full of the Latin melancholy, gave her the Madonna touch. Her motions and air spoke of the concealed fire and the desire to charm that she had inherited from the *gitanas* of the Basque province. As for the humming-bird part of her, that dwelt in her heart; you could not perceive it unless her bright red skirt and dark blue blouse gave you a symbolic hint of the vagarious bird.

The newly lighted sun-god asked for a drink

of water. Tonia brought it from the red jar hanging under the brush shelter. Sandridge considered it necessary to dismount so as to lessen the trouble of her ministrations.

I play no spy; nor do I assume to master the thoughts of any human heart; but I assert, by the chronicler's right, that before a quarter of an hour had sped, Sandridge was teaching her how to plait a six-strand rawhide stake-rope, and Tonia had explained to him that were it not for her little English book that the peripatetic *padre* had given her and the little crippled *chivo*, that she fed from a bottle, she would be very, very lonely indeed.

Which leads to a suspicion that the Kid's fences needed repairing, and that the adjutant-general's sarcasm had fallen upon unproductive soil.

In his camp by the water hole Lieutenant Sandridge announced and reiterated his intention of either causing the Cisco Kid to nibble the black loam of the Frio country prairies or of haling him before a judge and jury. That sounded business-like. Twice a week he rode over to the Lone Wolf Crossing of the Frio, and directed Tonia's slim, slightly lemon-tinted fingers among the intricacies of the slowly growing lariata. A six-strand plait is hard to learn and easy to teach.

The ranger knew that he might find the Kid there at any visit. He kept his armament ready, and had a frequent eye for the pear thicket at the rear of the *jacal.* Thus he might bring down the kite and the humming-bird with one stone.

While the sunny-haired ornithologist was pursuing his studies the Cisco Kid was also attending to his professional duties. He moodily shot up a saloon in a small cow village on Quintana Creek, killed the town marshal (plugging him neatly in the centre of his tin badge), and then rode away, morose and unsatisfied. No true artist is uplifted by shooting an aged man carrying an old-style .38 bulldog.

On his way the Kid suddenly experienced the yearning that all men feel when wrong-doing loses its keen edge of delight. He yearned for the woman he loved to reassure him that she was his in spite of it. He wanted her to call his bloodthirstiness bravery and his cruelty devotion. He wanted Tonia to bring him water from the red jar under the brush shelter, and tell him how the *chivo* was thriving on the bottle.

The Kid turned the speckled roan's head up the ten-mile pear flat that stretches along the Arroyo Hondo until it ends at the Lone Wolf Crossing of the Frio. The roan whickered; for he had a sense of locality and direction equal to that of a belt-line street-car horse; and he knew he would soon be nibbling the rich mesquite grass at the end of a forty-foot stake-rope while Ulysses rested his head in Circe's straw-roofed hut.

More weird and lonesome than the journey of an Amazonian explorer is the ride of one through a Texas pear flat. With dismal monotony and startling variety the uncanny and multiform shapes of the cacti lift their twisted trunks, and fat, bristly hands to encumber the way. The demon plant, appearing to live without soil or rain, seems to taunt the parched traveller with its lush grey greenness. It warps itself a thousand times about what look to be open and inviting paths, only to lure the rider into blind and impassable spine-defended "bottoms of the bag," leaving him to retreat, if he can, with the points of the compass whirling in his head.

To be lost in the pear is to die almost the death of the thief on the cross, pierced by nails and with grotesque shapes of all the fiends hovering about.

But it was so with the Kid and his mount. Winding, twisting, circling, tracing the most fantastic and bewildering trail ever picked out, the good roan lessened the distance to the Lone Wolf Crossing with every coil and turn that he made.

While they fared the Kid sang. He knew but one tune and sang it, as he knew but one code and lived it, and but one girl and loved her. He was a single-minded man of conventional ideas. He had a voice like a coyote with bronchitis, but whenever he chose to sing his song he sang it. It was a conventional song of the camps and trail, running at its beginning as near as may be to these words:

Don't you monkey with my Lulu girl
Or I'll tell you what I'll do—

and so on. The roan was inured to it, and did not mind.

But even the poorest singer will, after a certain time, gain his own consent to refrain from contributing to the world's noises. So the Kid, by the time he was within a mile or two of Tonia's *jacal*, had reluctantly allowed his song to die away—not because his vocal performance had become less charming to his own ears, but because his laryngeal muscles were aweary.

As though he were in a circus ring the speckled roan wheeled and danced through the labyrinth of pear until at length his rider knew by certain landmarks that the Lone Wolf Crossing was close at hand. Then, where the pear was thinner, he caught sight of the grass roof of the *jacal* and the hackberry tree on the edge of the arroyo. A few yards farther the Kid stopped the roan and gazed intently through the prickly openings. Then he dismounted, dropped the roan's reins, and proceeded on foot, stooping and silent, like an Indian. The roan, knowing his part, stood still, making no sound.

The Kid crept noiselessly to the very edge of the pear thicket and reconnoitred between the leaves of a clump of cactus.

Ten yards from his hiding-place, in the shade of the *jacal*, sat his Tonia calmly plaiting a rawhide lariat. So far she might surely escape condemnation; women have been known, from time to time, to engage in more mischievous occupations. But if all must be told, there is to be added that her head reposed against the broad and comfortable chest of a tall red-and-yellow man, and that his arm was about her, guiding her nimble fingers that required so many lessons at the intricate six-strand plait.

Sandridge glanced quickly at the dark mass of pear when he heard a slight squeaking sound that was not altogether unfamiliar. A gun-scabbard will make that sound when one grasps the handle of a six-shooter suddenly. But the sound was not repeated; and Tonia's fingers needed close attention.

And then, in the shadow of death, they began to talk of their love; and in the still July afternoon every word they uttered reached the ears of the Kid.

"Remember, then," said Tonia, "you must not come again until I send for you. Soon he will be here. A *vaquero* at the *tienda* said to-day he saw him on the Guadalupe three days ago. When he is that near he always comes. If he comes and finds you here he will kill you. So, for my sake, you must come no more until I send you the word."

"All right," said the stranger. "And then what?"

"And then," said the girl, "you must bring your men here and kill him. If not, he will kill you."

"He ain't a man to surrender, that's sure," said Sandridge. "It's kill or be killed for the officer that goes up against Mr. Cisco Kid."

"He must die," said the girl. "Otherwise there will not be any peace in the world for thee and me. He has killed many. Let him so die. Bring your men, and give him no chance to escape."

"You used to think right much of him," said Sandridge.

Tonia dropped the lariat, twisted herself around, and curved a lemon-tinted arm over the ranger's shoulder.

"But then," she murmured in liquid Spanish, "I had not beheld thee, thou great, red mountain of a man! And thou art kind and good, as well as strong. Could one choose him, knowing thee? Let him die; for then I will not be filled with fear by day and night lest he hurt thee or me."

"How can I know when he comes?" asked Sandridge.

"When he comes," said Tonia, "he remains two days, sometimes three. Gregorio, the small son of old Luisa, the *lavendera*, has a swift pony. I will write a letter to thee and send it by him, saying how it will be best to come upon him. By

Gregorio will the letter come. And bring many men with thee, and have much care, oh, dear red one, for the rattlesnake is not quicker to strike than is '*El Chivato*,' as they call him, to send a ball from his *pistola*."

"The Kid's handy with his gun, sure enough," admitted Sandridge, "but when I come for him I shall come alone. I'll get him by myself or not at all. The Cap wrote one or two things to me that make me want to do the trick without any help. You let me know when Mr. Kid arrives, and I'll do the rest."

"I will send you the message by the boy Gregorio," said the girl. "I knew you were braver than that small slayer of men who never smiles. How could I ever have thought I cared for him?"

It was time for the ranger to ride back to his camp on the water hole. Before he mounted his horse he raised the slight form of Tonia with one arm high from the earth for a parting salute. The drowsy stillness of the torpid summer air still lay thick upon the dreaming afternoon. The smoke from the fire in the *jacal*, where the *frijoles* blubbered in the iron pot, rose straight as a plumb-line above the clay-daubed chimney. No sound or movement disturbed the serenity of the dense pear thicket ten yards away.

When the form of Sandridge had disappeared, loping his big dun down the steep banks of the Frio crossing, the Kid crept back to his own horse, mounted him, and rode back along the tortuous trail he had come.

But not far. He stopped and waited in the silent depths of the pear until half an hour had passed. And then Tonia heard the high, untrue notes of his unmusical singing coming nearer and nearer; and she ran to the edge of the pear to meet him.

The Kid seldom smiled; but he smiled and waved his hat when he saw her. He dismounted, and his girl sprang into his arms. The Kid looked at her fondly. His thick, black hair clung to his head like a wrinkled mat. The meeting brought a slight ripple of some undercurrent of feeling to his smooth, dark face that was usually as motionless as a clay mask.

"How's my girl?" he asked, holding her close.

"Sick of waiting so long for you, dear one," she answered. "My eyes are dim with always gazing into that devil's pincushion through which you come. And I can see into it such a little way, too. But you are here, beloved one, and I will not scold. *Que mal muchacho!* not to come to see your *alma* more often. Go in and rest, and let me water your horse and stake him with the long rope. There is cool water in the jar for you."

The Kid kissed her affectionately.

"Not if the court knows itself do I let a lady stake my horse for me," said he. "But if you'll run in, *chica*, and throw a pot of coffee together while I attend to the *caballo*, I'll be a good deal obliged."

Besides his marksmanship the Kid had another attribute for which he admired himself greatly. He was *muy caballero*, as the Mexicans express it, where the ladies were concerned. For them he had always gentle words and consideration. He could not have spoken a harsh word to a woman. He might ruthlessly slay their husbands and brothers, but he could not have laid the weight of a finger in anger upon a woman. Wherefore many of that interesting division of humanity who had come under the spell of his politeness declared their disbelief in the stories circulated about Mr. Kid. One shouldn't believe everything one heard, they said. When confronted by their indignant men folk with proof of the *caballero*'s deeds of infamy, they said maybe he had been driven to it, and that he knew how to treat a lady, anyhow.

Considering this extremely courteous idiosyncrasy of the Kid and the pride he took in it, one can perceive that the solution of the problem that was presented to him by what he saw and heard from his hiding-place in the pear that afternoon (at least as to one of the actors) must have been obscured by difficulties. And yet one could not think of the Kid overlooking little matters of that kind.

At the end of the short twilight they gathered around a supper of *frijoles*, goat steaks, canned peaches, and coffee, by the light of a lantern in the *jacal*. Afterward, the ancestor, his flock corralled, smoked a cigarette and became a mummy in a grey blanket. Tonia washed the few dishes while the Kid dried them with the flour-sacking towel. Her eyes shone; she chatted volubly of the inconsequent happenings of her small world since the Kid's last visit; it was as all his other home-comings had been.

Then outside Tonia swung in a grass hammock with her guitar and sang sad *canciones de amor*.

"Do you love me just the same, old girl?" asked the Kid, hunting for his cigarette papers.

"Always the same, little one," said Tonia, her dark eyes lingering upon him.

"I must go over to Fink's," said the Kid, rising, "for some tobacco. I thought I had another sack in my coat. I'll be back in a quarter of an hour."

"Hasten," said Tonia, "and tell me—how long shall I call you my own this time? Will you be gone again tomorrow, leaving me to grieve, or will you be longer with your Tonia?"

"Oh, I might stay two or three days this trip," said the Kid, yawning. "I've been on the dodge for a month, and I'd like to rest up."

He was gone half an hour for his tobacco. When he returned Tonia was still lying in the hammock.

"It's funny," said the Kid, "how I feel. I feel like there was somebody lying behind every bush and tree waiting to shoot me. I never had mullygrubs like them before. Maybe it's one of them presumptions. I've got half a notion to light out in the morning before day. The Guadalupe country is burning up about that old Dutchman I plugged down there."

"You are not afraid—no one could make my brave little one fear."

"Well, I haven't been usually regarded as a jack-rabbit when it comes to scrapping; but I don't want a posse smoking me out when I'm in your *jacal*. Somebody might get hurt that oughtn't to."

"Remain with your Tonia; no one will find you here."

The Kid looked keenly into the shadows up and down the arroyo and toward the dim lights of the Mexican village.

"I'll see how it looks later on," was his decision.

At midnight a horseman rode into the rangers' camp, blazing his way by noisy "halloes" to indicate a pacific mission. Sandridge and one or two others turned out to investigate the row. The rider announced himself to be Domingo Sales, from the Lone Wolf Crossing. he bore a letter for Senor Sandridge. Old Luisa, the *lavendera*, had persuaded him to bring it, he said, her son Gregorio being too ill of a fever to ride.

Sandridge lighted the camp lantern and read the letter. These were its words:

> *Dear One:* He has come. Hardly had you ridden away when he came out of the pear. When he first talked he said he would stay three days or more. Then as it grew later he was like a wolf or a fox, and walked about without rest, looking and listening. Soon he said he must leave before daylight when it is dark and stillest. And then he seemed to suspect that I be not true to him. He looked at me so strange that I am frightened. I swear to him that I love him, his own Tonia. Last of all he said I must prove to him I am true. He thinks that even now men are waiting to kill him as he rides from my house. To escape he says he will dress in my clothes, my red skirt and the blue waist I wear and the brown mantilla over the head, and thus ride away. But before that he says that I must put on his clothes, his *pantalones* and *camisa* and hat, and ride away on his horse from the *jacal* as far as the big road beyond the crossing and back again. This before he goes, so he can tell if I am true and if men are hidden to shoot him. It is a terrible thing. An hour before daybreak this is to be. Come, my dear one, and kill this man

and take me for your Tonia. Do not try to take hold of him alive, but kill him quickly. Knowing all, you should do that. You must come long before the time and hide yourself in the little shed near the *jacal* where the wagon and saddles are kept. It is dark in there. He will wear my red skirt and blue waist and brown mantilla. I send you a hundred kisses. Come surely and shoot quickly and straight.

Thine Own Tonia.

Sandridge quickly explained to his men the official part of the missive. The rangers protested against his going alone.

"I'll get him easy enough," said the lieutenant. "The girl's got him trapped. And don't even think he'll get the drop on me."

Sandridge saddled his horse and rode to the Lone Wolf Crossing. He tied his big dun in a clump of brush on the arroyo, took his Winchester from its scabbard, and carefully approached the Perez *jacal*. There was only the half of a high moon drifted over by ragged, milk-white gulf clouds.

The wagon-shed was an excellent place for ambush; and the ranger got inside it safely. In the black shadow of the brush shelter in front of the *jacal* he could see a horse tied and hear him impatiently pawing the hard-trodden earth.

He waited almost an hour before two figures came out of the *jacal*. One, in man's clothes, quickly mounted the horse and galloped past the wagon-shed toward the crossing and village. And then the other figure, in skirt, waist, and mantilla over its head, stepped out into the faint moonlight, gazing after the rider. Sandridge thought he would take his chance then before Tonia rode back. He fancied she might not care to see it.

"Throw up your hands," he ordered loudly, stepping out of the wagon-shed with his Winchester at his shoulder.

There was a quick turn of the figure, but no movement to obey, so the ranger pumped in the bullets—one—two—three—and then twice more; for you never could be too sure of bringing down the Cisco Kid. There was no danger of missing at ten paces, even in that half moonlight.

The old ancestor, asleep on his blanket, was awakened by the shots. Listening further, he heard a great cry from some man in mortal distress or anguish, and rose up grumbling at the disturbing ways of moderns.

The tall, red ghost of a man burst into the *jacal*, reaching one hand, shaking like a *tule* reed, for the lantern hanging on its nail. The other spread a letter on the table.

"Look at this letter, Perez," cried the man. "Who wrote it?"

"*Ah, Dios!* it is Senor Sandridge," mumbled the old man, approaching. "*Pues, senor,* that letter was written by '*El Chivato*,' as he is called—by the man of Tonia. They say he is a bad man; I do not know. While Tonia slept he wrote the letter and sent it by this old hand of mine to Domingo Sales to be brought to you. Is there anything wrong in the letter? I am very old; and I did not know. *Valgame Dios!* It is a very foolish world; and there is nothing in the house to drink—nothing to drink."

Just then all that Sandridge could think of to do was to go outside and throw himself face downward in the dust by the side of his humming-bird, of whom not a feather fluttered. He was not a *caballero* by instinct, and he could not understand the niceties of revenge.

A mile away the rider who had ridden past the wagon-shed struck up a harsh, untuneful song, the words of which began:

Don't you monkey with my Lulu girl
Or I'll tell you what I'll do—

Conscience in Art

O. HENRY

WILLIAM SYDNEY PORTER (1862–1910), under the pseudonym O. Henry, wrote approximately six hundred short stories and, with the possible exception of Edgar Allan Poe, is the most beloved short story writer America has produced.

Arrested for embezzlement from a bank in Austin, Texas, he served three years in an Ohio State Penitentiary, where he was befriended by a guard named Orrin Henry, who in all likelihood inspired the famous pseudonym.

His stories have been criticized for being overly sentimental, but they remain staples of the American literary canon. The master of the surprise ending, O. Henry has written such classics as "The Gift of the Magi," "The Last Leaf," "The Ransom of Red Chief," and "A Retrieved Reformation," which became better known when it was staged and later filmed as *Alias Jimmy Valentine*.

His most significant contribution to the mystery and crime genre is *The Gentle Grafter* (1908), selected by Ellery Queen for *Queen's Quorum* as one of the one hundred six greatest mystery story collections of all time. All the Grafter stories feature Jeff Peters and Andy Tucker, a couple of con artists who enjoy various levels of success. They are usually broke and struggle with the concept of being fair to their marks. They don't generally steal, and if their hapless target is too simpleminded, they endeavor to give him a little something in return for the money they bilk from him. The Grafter tales are more humorous than most of O. Henry's other stories, so many of which are poignant or dark.

"Conscience in Art" was originally published by the McClure Syndicate, appearing in numerous newspapers all around the United States at various dates; it was first collected in O. Henry's *The Gentle Grafter* (New York, McClure, 1908).

CONSCIENCE IN ART

O. Henry

"I NEVER COULD HOLD my partner, Andy Tucker, down to legitimate ethics of pure swindling," said Jeff Peters to me one day.

"Andy had too much imagination to be honest. He used to devise schemes of money-getting so fraudulent and high-financial that they wouldn't have been allowed in the bylaws of a railroad rebate system.

"Myself, I never believed in taking any man's dollars unless I gave him something for it—something in the way of rolled gold jewelry, garden seeds, lumbago lotion, stock certificates, stove polish, or a crack on the head to show for his money. I guess I must have had New England ancestors away back and inherited some of their stanch and rugged fear of the police.

"But Andy's family tree was in different kind. I don't think he could have traced his descent any further back than a corporation.

"One summer while we was in the middle West, working down the Ohio valley with a line of family albums, headache powders, and roach destroyer, Andy takes one of his notions of high and actionable financiering.

"'Jeff,' says he, 'I've been thinking that we ought to drop these rutabaga fanciers and give our attention to something more nourishing and prolific. If we keep on snapshooting these hinds for their egg money we'll be classed as nature fakers. How about plunging into the fastnesses of the skyscraper country and biting some big bull caribous in the chest?'

"'Well,' says I, 'you know my idiosyncrasies. I prefer a square, non-illegal style of business such as we are carrying on now. When I take money I want to leave some tangible object in the other fellow's hands for him to gaze at and to distract his attention from my spoor, even if it's only a Komical Kuss Trick Finger Ring for Squirting Perfume in a Friend's Eye. But if you've got a fresh idea, Andy,' says I, 'let's have a look at it. I'm not so wedded to petty graft that I would refuse something better in the way of a subsidy.'

"'I was thinking,' says Andy, 'of a little hunt without horn, hound, or camera among the great herd of the Midas Americanus, commonly known as the Pittsburg millionaires.'

"'In New York?' I asks.

"'No, sir,' says Andy, 'in Pittsburg. That's their habitat. They don't like New York. They go there now and then just because it's expected of 'em.'

"'A Pittsburg millionaire in New York is like

a fly in a cup of hot coffee—he attracts attention and comment, but he don't enjoy it. New York ridicules him for "blowing" so much money in that town of sneaks and snobs, and sneers. The truth is, he don't spend anything while he is there. I saw a memorandum of expenses for a ten days trip to Bunkum Town made by a Pittsburg man worth $15,000,000 once. Here's the way he set it down:

R. R. fare to and from	**$21 00**
Cab fare to and from hotel	**2 00**
Hotel bill @ $5 per day	**50 00**
Tips	**5,750 00**
Total	**$5,823 00**

"'That's the voice of New York,' goes on Andy. 'The town's nothing but a head waiter. If you tip it too much it'll go and stand by the door and make fun of you to the hat check boy. When a Pittsburger wants to spend money and have a good time he stays at home. That's where we'll go to catch him.'

"Well, to make a dense story more condensed, me and Andy cached our Paris Green and antipyrine powders and albums in a friend's cellar, and took the trail to Pittsburg. Andy didn't have any especial prospectus of chicanery and violence drawn up, but he always had plenty of confidence that his immoral nature would rise to any occasion that presented itself.

"As a concession to my ideas of self-preservation and rectitude he promised that if I should take an active and incriminating part in any little business venture that we might work up there should be something actual and cognizant to the senses of touch, sight, taste, or smell to transfer to the victim for the money so my conscience might rest easy. After that I felt better and entered more cheerfully into the foul play.

"'Andy,' says I, as we strayed through the smoke along the cinderpath they call Smithfield street, 'had you figured out how we are going to get acquainted with these coke kings and pig iron squeezers? Not that I would decry my own worth or system of drawing room deportment, and work with the olive fork and pie knife,' says I, 'but isn't the entree nous into the salons of the stogie smokers going to be harder than you imagined?'

"'If there's any handicap at all,' says Andy, 'it's our own refinement and inherent culture. Pittsburg millionaires are a fine body of plain, wholehearted, unassuming, democratic men.

"'They are rough but uncivil in their manners, and though their ways are boisterous and unpolished, under it all they have a great deal of impoliteness and discourtesy. Nearly every one of 'em rose from obscurity,' says Andy, 'and they'll live in it till the town gets to using smoke consumers. If we act simple and unaffected and don't go too far from the saloons and keep making a noise like an import duty on steel rails we won't have any trouble in meeting some of 'em socially.'

"Well Andy and me drifted about town three or four days getting our bearings. We got to knowing several millionaires by sight.

"One used to stop his automobile in front of our hotel and have a quart of champagne brought out to him. When the waiter opened it he'd turn it up to his mouth and drink it out of the bottle. That showed he used to be a glass-blower before he made his money.

"One evening Andy failed to come to the hotel for dinner. About 11 o'clock he came into my room.

"'Landed one, Jeff,' says he. 'Twelve millions. Oil, rolling mills, real estate, and natural gas. He's a fine man; no airs about him. Made all his money in the last five years. He's got professors posting him up now in education—art and literature and haberdashery and such things.

"'When I saw him he'd just won a bet of $10,000 with a Steel Corporation man that there'd be four suicides in the Allegheny rolling mills to-day. So everybody in sight had to walk up and have drinks on him. He took a fancy to me and asked me to dinner with him. We went to a restaurant in Diamond alley and sat on stools and had a sparkling Moselle and clam chowder and apple fritters.

"'Then he wanted to show me his bachelor apartment on Liberty street. He's got ten rooms over a fish market with privilege of the bath on the next floor above. He told me it cost him $18,000 to furnish his apartment, and I believe it.

"'He's got $40,000 worth of pictures in one room, and $20,000 worth of curios and antiques in another. His name's Scudder, and he's 45, and taking lessons on the piano and 15,000 barrels of oil a day out of his wells.'

"'All right,' says I. 'Preliminary canter satisfactory. But, kay vooly, voo? What good is the art junk to us? And the oil?'

"'Now, that man,' says Andy, sitting thoughtfully on the bed, 'ain't what you would call an ordinary scutt. When he was showing me his cabinet of art curios his face lighted up like the door of a coke oven. He says that if some of his big deals go through he'll make J. P. Morgan's collection of sweatshop tapestry and Augusta, Me., beadwork look like the contents of an ostrich's craw thrown on a screen by a magic lantern.

"'And then he showed me a little carving,' went on Andy, 'that anybody could see was a wonderful thing. It was something like 2,000 years old, he said. It was a lotus flower with a woman's face in it carved out of a solid piece of ivory.

"'Scudder looks it up in a catalogue and describes it. An Egyptian carver named Khafra made two of 'em for King Rameses II about the year B.C. The other one can't be found. The junkshops and antique bugs have rubbered all Europe for it, but it seems to be out of stock. Scudder paid $2,000 for the one he has.'

"'Oh, well,' says I, 'this sounds like the purling of a rill to me. I thought we came here to teach the millionaires business, instead of learning art from 'em?'

"'Be patient,' says Andy, kindly. 'Maybe we will see a rift in the smoke ere long.'

"All the next morning Andy was out. I didn't see him until about noon. He came to the hotel and called me into his room across the hall. He pulled a roundish bundle about as big as a goose egg out of his pocket and unwrapped it. It was an ivory carving just as he had described the millionaire's to me.

"'I went in an old second hand store and pawnshop a while ago,' says Andy, 'and I see this half hidden under a lot of old daggers and truck. The pawnbroker said he'd had it several years and thinks it was soaked by some Arabs or Turks or some foreign dubs that used to live down by the river.

"'I offered him $2 for it, and I must have looked like I wanted it, for he said it would be taking the pumpernickel out of his children's mouths to hold any conversation that did not lead up to a price of $35. I finally got it for $25.

"'Jeff,' goes on Andy, 'this is the exact counterpart of Scudder's carving. It's absolutely a dead ringer for it. He'll pay $2,000 for it as quick as he'd tuck a napkin under his chin. And why shouldn't it be the genuine other one, anyhow, that the old gypsy whittled out?'

"'Why not, indeed?' says I. 'And how shall we go about compelling him to make a voluntary purchase of it?'

"Andy had his plan all ready, and I'll tell you how we carried it out.

"I got a pair of blue spectacles, put on my black frock coat, rumpled my hair up and became Prof. Pickleman. I went to another hotel, registered, and sent a telegram to Scudder to come to see me at once on important art business. The elevator dumped him on me in less than an hour. He was a foggy man with a clarion voice, smelling of Connecticut wrappers and naphtha.

"'Hello, Profess!' he shouts. 'How's your conduct?'

"I rumpled my hair some more and gave him a blue glass stare.

"'Sir,' says I, 'are you Cornelius T. Scudder? Of Pittsburg, Pennsylvania?'

"'I am,' says he. 'Come out and have a drink.'

"'I've neither the time nor the desire,' says I, 'for such harmful and deleterious amusements. I have come from New York,' says I, 'on a matter of busi—on a matter of art.

"'I learned there that you are the owner of an Egyptian ivory carving of the time of Rameses II, representing the head of Queen Isis in a lotus flower. There were only two of such carvings made. One has been lost for many years. I recently discovered and purchased the other in a pawn—in an obscure museum in Vienna. I wish to purchase yours. Name your price.'

"'Well, the great ice jams, Profess!' says Scudder. 'Have you found the other one? Me sell? No. I don't guess Cornelius Scudder needs to sell anything that he wants to keep. Have you got the carving with you, Profess?'

"I shows it to Scudder. He examines it careful all over.

"'It's the article,' says he. 'It's a duplicate of mine, every line and curve of it. Tell you what I'll do,' he says. 'I won't sell, but I'll buy. Give you $2,500 for yours.'

"'Since you won't sell, I will,' says I. 'Large bills, please. I'm a man of few words. I must return to New York tonight. I lecture tomorrow at the aquarium.'

"Scudder sends a check down and the hotel cashes it. He goes off with his piece of antiquity and I hurry back to Andy's hotel, according to arrangement.

"Andy is walking up and down the room looking at his watch.

"'Well?' he says.

"'Twenty-five hundred,' says I. 'Cash.'

"'We've got just eleven minutes,' says Andy, 'to catch the B. & O. westbound. Grab your baggage.'

"'What's the hurry,' says I. 'It was a square deal. And even if it was only an imitation of the original carving it'll take him some time to find it out. He seemed to be sure it was the genuine article.'

"'It was,' says Andy. 'It was his own. When I was looking at his curios yesterday he stepped out of the room for a moment and I pocketed it. Now, will you pick up your suit case and hurry?'

"'Then,' says I, 'why was that story about finding another one in the pawn—'

"'Oh,' says Andy, 'out of respect for that conscience of yours. Come on.'"

Rogue: Robert Hooker

The Unpublishable Memoirs

A. S. W. ROSENBACH

PERHAPS THE GREATEST rare-book dealer in the history of the United States was Abraham Simon Wolf Rosenbach (1876–1952), who also was a collector of rare books and manuscripts. As a bookseller he was noted for his exceptional scholarship and business acumen.

He received his undergraduate and Ph.D. degrees from the University of Pennsylvania, where he was a teaching fellow for six years before joining with his brother to found the Rosenbach Company; he specialized in books and his brother in antiques. The firm soon became the most lucrative bookselling business in the world, boasting such clients as J. Pierpont Morgan and Henry Huntington. The Rosenbach Company acquired and sold an unimaginable eight Gutenberg Bibles and thirty Shakespeare first folios. During the course of his career, Rosenbach is said to have spent about seventy-five million dollars at auctions.

Among much else, he was particularly noted for his magnificent collection of children's books, ultimately donated to the Philadelphia Free Library. His book on the subject, *Early American Children's Books* (1933), is still regarded as a standard reference book. He was a frequent writer on bibliographical and literary subjects, producing numerous articles and books, including *Books and Bidders* (1927) and *A Book Hunter's Holiday* (1936). His one effort in fiction, *The Unpublishable Memoirs* (1917), features a bibliophile who finds methods of adding books to his collection that he might otherwise not have found attainable.

"The Unpublishable Memoirs" was originally published in *The Unpublishable Memoirs* (New York, Mitchell Kennerley, 1917).

THE UNPUBLISHABLE MEMOIRS

A. S. W. Rosenbach

IT WAS VERY CRUEL.

He was dickering for one of the things he had desired for a lifetime.

It was in New York at one of the famous book-stores of the metropolis. The proprietor had offered to him for one hundred and sixty dollars—exactly the amount he had in bank—the first and only edition of the "Unpublishable Memoirs" of Beau Brummel, a little volume issued in London in 1790, and one of two copies known, the other being in the famous "hidden library" of the British Museum.

It was a scandalous chronicle of fashionable life in the eighteenth century, and many brilliant names were implicated therein; distinguished and reputable families, that had long been honoured in the history of England, were ruthlessly depicted with a black and venomous pen. He had coveted this book for years, and here it was within his grasp! He had just told the proprietor that he would take it.

Robert Hooker was a book-collector. With not a great deal of money, he had acquired a few of the world's most sought after treasures. He had laboriously saved his pennies, and had, with the magic of the bibliophile, turned them into rare volumes! He was about to put the evil little book into his pocket when he was interrupted.

A large, portly man, known to book-lovers the world over, had entered the shop and asked Mr. Rodd if he might examine the Beau Brummel Memoirs. He had looked at it before, he said, but on that occasion had merely remarked that he would call again. He saw the volume on the table in front of Hooker, picked it up without ceremony, and told the owner of the shop that he would purchase it.

"Excuse me," exclaimed Hooker, "but I have just bought it."

"What!" said the opulent John Fenn, "I came especially to get it."

"I'm sorry, Mr. Fenn," returned the proprietor, "Mr. Hooker, here, has just said that he would take it."

"Now, look here, Rodd, I've always been a good customer of yours. I've spent thousands in this very shop during the last few years. I'll give you two hundred dollars for it."

"No," said Rodd.

"Three hundred!" said Fenn.

"No."

"Four hundred!"

"No."

"I'll give you five hundred dollars for it, and if you do not take it, I shall never enter this place again!"

Without another word Rodd nodded, and Fenn quickly grasped the little book, and placed it in the inside pocket of his coat. Hooker became angry and threatened to take it by bodily force. A scuffle ensued. Two clerks came to the rescue, and Fenn departed triumphantly with the secrets of the noble families of Great Britain securely in his possession.

Rodd, in an ingratiating manner, declared to Hooker that no money had passed between them, and consequently there had been no sale. Hooker, disappointed, angry, and beaten, could do nothing but retire.

At home, among his books, his anger increased. It was the old, old case of the rich collector gobbling up the small one. It was outrageous! He would get even—if it cost him everything. He dwelt long and bitterly upon his experience. A thought struck him. Why not prey upon the fancies of the wealthy! He would enter the lists with them; he would match his skill against their money, his knowledge against their purse.

Hooker was brought up in the mystic lore of books, for he was the son of a collector's son. He had always been a student, and half his time had been spent in the bookseller's shops, dreaming of the wonderful editions of Chaucer, of Shakespeare, of rare Ben Jonson, that some day he might call his own. He would now secure the priceless things dearest to the hearts of men, at no cost to himself!

He would not limit his choice to books, which were his first love, but he would help himself to the fair things that have always delighted the soul—pictures, like those of Raphael and da Vinci; jewels, like Cellini's; little bronzes, like Donatello's; etchings of Rembrandt; the porcelains (True Ming!) of old China; the rugs of Persia the magnificent!

The idea struck him at first as ludicrous and impossible. The more he thought of it, the more feasible it became. He had always been a good mimic, a fair amateur actor, a linguist, and a man of parts. He possessed scholarly attainments of a high order. He would use all of his resources in the game he was about to play. For nothing deceives like education!

And it had another side—a brighter, more fantastic side. Think of the fun he would get out of it! This appealed to him. Not only could he add to his collections the most beautiful treasures of the world, but he would now taste the keenest of joys—he would laugh and grow fat at the other man's expense. It was always intensely humorous to observe the discomfiture of others.

With particular pleasure Hooker read that evening in the *Post* this insignificant paragraph:

"John Fenn, President of the Tenth National Bank of Chicago, departs for home tonight."

He laid the paper down immediately, telephoned to the railroad office for a reservation in the sleeping-car leaving at midnight, and prepared for his first "banquet." Hooker shaved off his moustache, changed his clothes and his accent, and took the train for Chicago.

As luck would have it, John Fenn was seated next to him in the smoking-car, reading the evening papers. Hooker took from his pocket a book catalogue, issued by one of the great English auction houses. He knew that was the best bait! No book-lover that ever lived could resist dipping into a sale catalogue.

Hooker waited an hour—it seemed like five. Fenn read every word in the papers, even the advertisements. He dwelt long and lovingly over the financial pages, running his eyes up and down the columns of "to-day's transactions." He at last finished the perusal, and glanced at Hooker. He said nothing for awhile, and appeared restless, like a man with money weighing on his mind. This, of course, is a very distracting and unpleasant feeling. Several times he seemed on the verge of addressing his fellow-traveller, but desisted from the attempt. Finally he said:

"I see, friend, that you're reading one of Sotheby's catalogues."

"Yes," answered Hooker, shortly.

"You must be interested in books," pursued Fenn.

"Yes," was the brief response.

"Do you collect them?"

"Yes."

Fenn said nothing for five minutes. The stranger did not appear to be very communicative.

"Pardon me, Mr. ——, I am also a book-collector. I have quite a fine library of my own."

"Really?"

"Yes, I always visit the shops when I go to New York. Here is a rarity I picked up to-day."

The stranger expressed little interest until Fenn took from his pocket the "Unpublishable Memoirs." It was wrapped neatly in paper, and Fenn carefully removed the little volume from the wrappings. He handed it to the man who perused so assiduously the auction catalogue.

"How extraordinary!" he cried, "the lost book of old Brummel. My people were acquainted with the Beau. I suppose they are grilled right merrily in it! Of all places, how did you come to purchase it in the States?"

"That's quite a story. A queer thing how I bought it. I saw it the other day at Rodd's on Fifth Avenue. I did not buy it at first—the price was too high. Thought I would be able to buy it later for less. This morning, I went to see Rodd to make an offer on it, when I found that Rodd had just sold it to some young student. The confounded simpleton said it belonged to him! What did that trifler know about rare books? Now *I* know how to appreciate them."

"Naturally!" said the stranger.

"I've the finest collection in the West. I had to pay a stiff advance before the proprietor would let me have it. It was a narrow squeak—by about a minute. The young jackass tried to make a scene, but I taught him a thing or two. He'll not be so perky next time. How my friends will enjoy this story of the killing. I can't wait until I get home."

The stranger with the freshly-shaven face, the English clothes, and the austere eyes did not seem particularly pleased.

"How extraordinary!" he said, coldly, and returned to his reading.

Fenn placed the book in his pocket, a pleased expression on his face, as if he were still gloating over his conquest. He was well satisfied with his day, so intellectually spent among the banks and book-shops of New York!

"By the way, I am acquainted with this Rodd," said the Englishman, after a pause. "He told me a rather interesting story the other day, but it was in a way a boomerang. I don't like that man's methods. I'll never buy a book from him."

"Why not?" asked the inquisitive Mr. Fenn.

"Well, you'd better hear the tale. It appears he has a wealthy client in Chicago and he occasionally goes out to sell him some of his plunder. He did not tell me the name of his customer, but, according to Rodd, he is an ignoramus and knows nothing at all about books. Thinks it improves his social position. You know the type. Last winter Rodd picked up for fifty dollars a beautifully illuminated copy of Magna Charta issued about a hundred years ago. It's a fine volume, printed on vellum, the kind that Dibdin raved about, but always considered a 'plug' in England. Worth about forty guineas at the most. You know the book?"

Fenn nodded.

"Well, it worried Mr. Rodd how much he could ask his Western patron for it. He left for Chicago via Philadelphia and while he was waiting in the train there he thought he could ask two hundred dollars for it. The matter was on his mind until he arrived at Harrisburg, where he determined that three hundred would be about right. At Pittsburgh he raised the price to five hundred, and at Canton, Ohio, it was seven hundred and fifty! The more Rodd thought of the exquisite beauty of the volume, of its glowing colors and its lovely old binding, the more the price soared. At Fort Wayne, Indiana, it was a thousand dollars. When he arrived at Chicago the next morning, his imagination having had full swing, he resolved he would not under any circumstances part with it for less than two thousand dollars!"

"The old thief!" exclaimed Fenn, with feeling.

"It was a lucky thing," continued the stranger, "that his client did not live in San Francisco!"

At this Fenn broke forth into profanity.

"I always said that Rodd was an unprincipled, unholy, unmitigated—"

"Wait until you hear the end, sir," said the Englishman.

"That afternoon he called on the Western collector. He had an appointment with him at two o'clock. He left Rodd waiting in an outside office for hours. Rodd told me he was simply boiling. Went all the way to Chicago by special request and the brute made him cool his heels until four o'clock before he condescended to see him. He would pay dearly for it. When Rodd showed him the blooming book he asked three thousand five hundred for it—would not take a penny less—and he told me, sir, that he actually sold it for that price!"

"Don't you believe it," said Fenn, hotly. "Old Rodd is an unqualified liar. He sold it for five thousand dollars. That's what he did, the damn pirate!"

"How do you know, sir?"

"How do I know, *know, know!*" he repeated, excitedly. "I *ought* to know! I'm the fool that bought it!"

Without another word Fenn retired to his stateroom.

The next morning when Fenn arrived at his office in the Fenn Building, he called to one of his business associates, who, like his partner, was interested in the acquisition of rare and unusual books.

"I say, Ogden, I have something great to show you. Picked it up yesterday. In this package is the wickedest little book ever written!"

"Let me see it!" said Mr. Ogden, eagerly.

Fenn gingerly removed the paper in which it was wrapped, as he did not wish to injure the precious contents. He turned suddenly pale. Ogden glanced quickly at the title-page for fear he would be seen with the naughty little thing in his hands.

It was a very ordinary volume, entitled, "A Sermon on Covetousness, a Critical Exposition of the Tenth Commandment by the Rev. Charles Wesley."

"The devil!" exclaimed John Fenn.

"How the old dodge works," said Robert Hooker to himself on his way back to New York. "The duplicate package, known since the days of Adam! And how easy it was to substitute it under his very eyes! I shall call Beau Brummel's 'Unpublishable Memoirs' number *one* in my new library."

Rogue: J. Rufus Wallingford

The Universal Covered Carpet Tack Company

GEORGE RANDOLPH CHESTER

GEORGE RANDOLPH CHESTER (1869–1924) worked as a journalist, motion picture writer and director, and dramatist. Many of his short stories appeared in *The Saturday Evening Post* and other top-quality magazines, but his most popular and enduring work features Get-Rich-Quick Wallingford, a genial confidence man, and Blackie Daw, his partner in crime.

Wallingford, a "business buccaneer," uses *nearly* legal methods to earn fortunes in various enterprises, promptly spending the money on costly food, drink, and clothes. Suave and sophisticated, with a look of affluence, he inspires confidence in potential investors in his schemes who are eager to be connected to his "surefire" endeavors; he is equally eager to accept their contributions. His lovely young wife, Fanny, has a vague suspicion that he is not quite honest and feels guilty for not trusting her husband. His exploits are recounted in *Get-Rich-Quick Wallingford* (1908), *Young Wallingford* (1910), *Wallingford in His Prime* (1913), *Wallingford and Blackie Daw* (1913), all short story collections, and *The Son of Wallingford* (1921), a novel written by Chester and his wife, Lillian.

A very successful Broadway play was fashioned from the Wallingford stories by George M. Cohan in 1910, which in turn inspired a silent film series in 1916. Paramount distributed *Get-Rich-Quick Wallingford* in 1921; it is based on the present story.

"The Universal Covered Carpet Tack Company" was originally published in *Get-Rich-Quick Wallingford* (Philadelphia, Henry Altemus, 1908).

THE UNIVERSAL COVERED CARPET TACK COMPANY

George Randolph Chester

Chapter I

In Which J. Rufus Wallingford Conceives a Brilliant Invention

THE MUD WAS BLACK AND OILY where it spread thinly at the edges of the asphalt, and wherever it touched it left a stain; it was upon the leather of every pedestrian, even the most fastidious, and it bordered with almost laughable conspicuousness the higher marking of yellow clay upon the heavy shoes of David Jasper, where he stood at the curb in front of the big hotel with his young friend, Edward Lamb. Absorbed in "lodge" talk, neither of the oddly assorted cronies cared much for drizzle overhead or mire underfoot; but a splash of black mud in the face must necessarily command some attention. This surprise came suddenly to both from the circumstance of a cab having dashed up just beside them. Their resentment, bubbling hot for a moment, was quickly chilled, however, as the cab door opened and out of it stepped one of those impressive beings for whom the best things of this world have been especially made and provided. He was a large gentleman, a suave gentleman, a gentleman whose clothes not merely fit him but distinguished him, a gentleman of rare good living, even though one of the sort whose faces turn red when they eat; and the dignity of his worldly prosperousness surrounded him like a blessed aura. Without a glance at the two plain citizens who stood mopping the mud from their faces, he strode majestically into the hotel, leaving Mr. David Jasper and Mr. Edward Lamb out in the rain.

The clerk kowtowed to the signature, though he had never seen nor heard of it before—"J. Rufus Wallingford, Boston." His eyes, however, had noted a few things: traveling suit, scarf pin, watch guard, ring, hatbox, suit case, bag, all expensive and of the finest grade.

"Sitting room and bedroom; outside!" directed Mr. Wallingford. "And the bathroom must have a large tub."

The clerk ventured a comprehending smile as he noted the bulk before him.

"Certainly, Mr. Wallingford. Boy, key for 44-A. Anything else, Mr. Wallingford?"

"Send up a waiter and a valet."

Once more the clerk permitted himself a slight smile, but this time it was as his large guest turned away. He had not the slightest doubt that Mr. Wallingford's bill would be princely, he was positive that it would be paid; but a vague wonder had crossed his mind as to who would regrettingly pay it. His penetration was excellent, for at this very moment the new arrival's entire capitalized worth was represented by the less than one hundred dollars he carried in his pocket, nor had Mr. Wallingford the slightest idea of where he was to get more. This latter circumstance did not distress him, however; he knew that there was still plenty of money in the world and that none of it was soldered on, and a reflection of this comfortable philosophy was in his whole bearing. As he strode in pomp across the lobby, a score of bellboys, with a carefully trained scent for tips, envied the cheerfully grinning servitor who followed him to the elevator with his luggage.

Just as the bellboy was inserting the key in the lock of 44-A, a tall, slightly built man in a glove-fitting black frock suit, a quite ministerial-looking man, indeed, had it not been for the startling effect of his extravagantly curled black mustache and his piercing black eyes, came down the hallway, so abstracted that he had almost passed Mr. Wallingford. The latter, however, had eyes for everything.

"What's the hurry, Blackie?" he inquired affably.

The other wheeled instantly, with the snappy alertness of a man who has grown of habit to hold himself in readiness against sudden surprises from any quarter.

"Hello, J. Rufus!" he exclaimed, and shook hands. "Boston squeezed dry?"

Mr. Wallingford chuckled with a cumbrous heaving of his shoulders.

"Just threw the rind away," he confessed. "Come in."

Mr. Daw, known as "Blackie" to a small but select circle of gentlemen who make it their business to rescue and put carefully hoarded money back into rapid circulation, dropped moodily into a chair and sat considering his well-manicured finger-nails in glum silence, while his masterful host disposed of the bellboy and the valet.

"Had your dinner?" inquired Mr. Wallingford as he donned the last few garments of a fresh suit.

"Not yet," growled the other. "I've got such a grouch against myself I won't even feed right, for fear I'd enjoy it. On the cheaps for the last day, too."

Mr. Wallingford laughed and shook his head.

"I'm clean myself," he hastened to inform his friend. "If I have a hundred I'm a millionaire, but I'm coming and you're going, and we don't look at that settle-up ceremony the same way. What's the matter?"

"I'm the goat!" responded Blackie moodily. "The original goat! Came clear out here to trim a sucker that looked good by mail, and have swallowed so much of that citric fruit that if I scrape myself my skin spurts lemon juice. Say, do I look like a come-on?"

"If you only had the shaving-brush goatee, Blackie, I'd try to make you bet on the location of the little pea," gravely responded his friend.

"That's right; rub it in!" exclaimed the disgruntled one. "Massage me with it! Jimmy, if I could take off my legs, I'd kick myself with them from here to Boston and never lose a stroke. And me wise!"

"But where's the fire?" asked J. Rufus, bringing the end of his collar to place with a dexterous jerk.

"This lamb I came out to shear—rot him and burn him and scatter his ashes! Before I went dippy over two letter-heads and a nice round signature, I ordered an extra safety-deposit vault back home and came on to take his bank roll and house and lot, and make him a present of his clothes if he behaved. But not so! *Not*—so! Jimmy, this whole town blew right over from out of the middle of Missouri in the last cyclone. You've got to show everybody, and then turn it over and let 'em see the other side, and I haven't met the man yet that you could separate from a dollar without chloroform and an ax. Let me tell you what to do with that hundred, J. Rufe. Just get on the train and give it to the conductor, and tell him to take you as far ay-way from here as the money will reach!"

Mr. Wallingford settled his cravat tastefully and smiled at himself in the glass.

"I like the place," he observed. "They have tall buildings here, and I smell soft money. This town will listen to a legitimate business proposition. What?"

"Like the milk-stopper industry?" inquired Mr. Daw, grinning appreciatively. "How is your Boston corporation coming on, anyhow?"

"It has even quit holding the bag," responded the other, "because there isn't anything left of the bag. The last I saw of them, the thin and feeble stockholders were chasing themselves around in circles, so I faded away."

"You're a wonder," complimented the black-haired man with genuine admiration. "You never take a chance, yet get away with everything in sight, and you never leave 'em an opening to put the funny clothes on you."

"I deal in nothing but straight commercial propositions that are strictly within the pale of the law," said J. Rufus without a wink; "and even at that they can't say I took anything away from Boston."

"Don't blame Boston. You never cleaned up a cent less than five thousand a month while you were there, and if you spent it, that was your lookout."

"I had to live."

"So do the suckers," sagely observed Mr. Daw, "but they manage it on four cents' worth of prunes a day, and save up their money for good people. How is Mrs. Wallingford?"

"All others are base imitations," boasted the large man, pausing to critically consider the flavor of his champagne. "Just now, Fanny's in New York, eating up her diamonds. She was swallowing the last of the brooch when I left her, and this morning she was to begin on the necklace. That ought to last her quite some days, and by that time J. Rufus expects to be on earth again."

A waiter came to the door with a menu card, and Mr. Wallingford ordered, to be ready to serve in three quarters of an hour, at a choice table near the music, a dinner for two that would gladden the heart of any tip-hunter.

"How soon are you going back to Boston, Blackie?"

"Tonight!" snapped the other. "I was going to take a train that makes it in nineteen hours, but I found there is one that makes it in eighteen and a half, so I'm going to take that; and when I get back where the police are satisfied with half, I'm not going out after the emerald paper any more. I'm going to make them bring it to me. It's always the best way. I never went after money yet that they didn't ask me why I wanted it."

The large man laughed with his eyes closed.

"Honestly, Blackie, you ought to go into legitimate business enterprises. That's the only game. You can get anybody to buy stock when you make them print it themselves, if you'll only bait up with some little staple article that people use and throw away every day, like ice-cream pails, or corks, or cigar bands, or—or—or carpet tacks." Having sought about the room for this last illustration, Mr. Wallingford became suddenly inspired, and, arising, went over to the edge of the carpet, where he gazed down meditatively for a moment. "Now, look at this, for instance!" he said with final enthusiasm. "See this swell red carpet fastened down with rusty tacks? There's the chance. Suppose those tacks were covered with red cloth to match the carpet. Blackie, that's my next invention."

"Maybe there are covered carpet tacks," observed his friend, with but languid interest.

"What do I care?" rejoined Mr. Wallingford. "A man can always get a patent, and that's all I need, even if it's one you can throw a cat through. The company can fight the patent after I'm out of it. You wouldn't expect me to fasten myself down to the grease-covered details of an actual manufacturing business, would you?"

"Not any!" rejoined the dark one emphatically. "You're all right, J. Rufus. I'd go into your business myself if I wasn't honest. But, on the level, what do you expect to do here?"

"Organize the Universal Covered Carpet Tack Company. I'll begin tomorrow morning. Give me the list you couldn't use."

"Don't get in bad from the start," warned Mr.

Daw. "Tackle fresh ones. The particular piece of Roquefort, though, that fooled me into a Pullman compartment and kept me grinning like a drunken hyena all the way here, was a pinhead by the name of Edward Lamb. When Eddy fell for an inquiry about Billion Strike gold stock, he wrote on the firm's stationery, all printed in seventeen colors and embossed so it made holes in the envelopes when the cancellation stamp came down. From the tone of Eddy's letter I thought he was about ready to mortgage father's business to buy Billion Strike, and I came on to help him do it. Honest, J. Rufus, wouldn't it strike you that Lamb was a good name? Couldn't you hear it bleat?"

Mr. Wallingford shook silently, the more so that there was no answering gleam of mirth in Mr. Daw's savage visage.

"Say, do you know what I found when I got here?" went on Blackie still more ferociously. "I found he was a piker bookkeeper, but with five thousand dollars that he'd wrenched out of his own pay envelope, a pinch at a clip; and every time he takes a dollar out of his pocket his fingers creak. His whole push is like him, too, but I never got any further than Eddy. He's not merely Johnny Wise—he's the whole Wise family, and it's only due to my Christian bringing up that I didn't swat him with a brick during our last little chatter when I saw it all fade away. Do you know what he wanted me to do? He wanted me to prove to him that there actually was a Billion Strike mine, and that gold had been found in it!"

Mr. Wallingford had ceased to laugh. He was soberly contemplating.

"Your Lamb is my mutton," he finally concluded, pressing his finger tips together. "He'll listen to a legitimate business proposition."

"Don't make me fuss with you, J. Rufus," admonished Mr. Daw. "Remember, I'm going away tonight," and he arose.

Mr. Wallingford arose with him. "By the way, of course I'll want to refer to you; how many addresses have you besides the Billion Strike? A mention of that would probably get me arrested."

"Four: the Mexican and Rio Grande Rubber Company, Tremont Building; the St. John's Blood Orange Plantation Company, 643 Third Street; the Los Pocos Lead Development Company, 868 Schuttle Avenue; and the Sierra Cinnabar Grant, Schuttle Square, all of which addresses will reach me at my little old desk-room corner in 1126 Tremont Building, Third and Schuttle Avenues; and I'll answer letters of inquiry on four different letter-heads. If you need more I'll post Billy Riggs over in the Cloud Block and fix it for another four or five."

"I'll write Billy a letter myself," observed J. Rufus. "I'll need all the references I can get when I come to organize the Universal Covered Carpet Tack Company."

"Quit kidding," retorted Mr. Daw.

"It's on the level," insisted J. Rufus seriously. "Let's go down to dinner."

Chapter II

Wherein Edward Lamb Beholds the Amazing Profits of the Carpet-Tack Industry

There were twenty-four applicants for the position before Edward Lamb appeared, the second day after the initial insertion of the advertisement which had been designed to meet his eye alone. David Jasper, who read his paper advertisements and all, in order to get the full worth of his money out of it, telephoned to his friend Edward about the glittering chance.

Yes, Mr. Wallingford was in his suite. Would the gentleman give his name? Mr. Lamb produced a card, printed in careful imitation of engraving, and it gained him admission to the august presence, where he created some surprise by a sudden burst of laughter.

"Ex-cuse me!" he exclaimed. "But you're the man that splashed mud on me the other night!"

When the circumstance was related, Mr. Wallingford laughed with great gusto and shook hands for the second time with his visitor. The incident helped them to get upon a most cordial footing at once. It did not occur to either of them, at the time, how appropriate it was that Mr. Wallingford should splash mud upon Mr. Lamb at their very first meeting.

"What can I do for you, Mr. Lamb?" inquired the large man.

"You advertised——" began the caller.

"Oh, you came about that position," deprecated Mr. Wallingford, with a nicely shaded tone of courteous disappointment in his voice. "I am afraid that I am already fairly well suited, although I have made no final choice as yet. What are your qualifications?"

"There will be no trouble about that," returned Mr. Lamb, straightening visibly. "I can satisfy anybody." And Mr. Wallingford had the keynote for which he was seeking.

He knew at once that Mr. Lamb prided himself upon his independence, upon his local standing, upon his efficiency, upon his business astuteness. The observer had also the experience of Mr. Daw to guide him, and, moreover, better than all, here was Mr. Lamb himself. He was a broad-shouldered young man, who stood well upon his two feet; he dressed with a proper and decent pride in his prosperity, and wore looped upon his vest a watch chain that by its very weight bespoke the wearer's solid worth. The young man was an open book, whereof the pages were embossed in large type.

"Now you're talking like the right man," said the prospective employer. "Sit down. You'll understand, Mr. Lamb, that my question was only a natural one, for I am quite particular about this position, which is the most important one I have to fill. Our business is to be a large one. We are to conduct an immense plant in this city, and I want the office work organized with a thorough system from the beginning. The duties, consequently, would begin at once. The man who would become secretary of the Universal Covered Carpet Tack Company, would need to know all about the concern from its very inception, and until I have secured that exact man I shall take no steps toward organization."

Word by word, Mr. Wallingford watched the face of Edward Lamb and could see that he was succumbing to the mental chloroform. However, a man who at thirty has accumulated five thousand is not apt to be numbed without struggling.

"Before we go any further," interposed the patient, with deep, deep shrewdness, "it must be understood that I have no money to invest."

"Exactly," agreed Mr. Wallingford. "I stated that in my advertisement. To become secretary it will be necessary to hold one share of stock, but that share I shall give to the right applicant. I do not care for him to have any investment in the company. What I want is the services of the best man in the city, and to that end I advertised for one who had been an expert bookkeeper and who knew all the office routine of conducting a large business, agreeing to start such a man with a salary of two hundred dollars a month. That advertisement stated in full all that I expect from the one who secures this position—his expert services. I may say that you are only the second candidate who has had the outward appearance of being able to fulfill the requirements. Actual efficiency would naturally have to be shown."

Mr. Wallingford was now quite coldly insistent. The proper sleep had been induced.

"For fifteen years," Mr. Lamb now hastened to advise him, "I have been employed by the A. J. Dorman Manufacturing Company, and can refer you to them for everything you wish to know. I can give you other references as to reliability if you like."

Mr. Wallingford was instant warmth.

"The A. J. Dorman Company, indeed!" he exclaimed, though he had never heard of that concern. "The name itself is guarantee enough, at least to defer such matters for a bit while I show you the industry that is to be built in your city." From his dresser Mr. Wallingford produced a handful of tacks, the head of each one covered with a bit of different-colored bright cloth. "You have only to look at these," he continued, holding them forth, and with the thumb and forefinger of the other hand turning one red-topped tack about in front of Mr. Lamb's eyes, "to appreciate to the full what a wonderful business certainty I am preparing to launch. Just hold these tacks a moment," and he turned the handful into Mr. Lamb's outstretched palm. "Now come over to the edge of this carpet. I have selected here a tack which matches this floor covering. You see those rusty heads? Imagine the difference if they were replaced by this!"

Mr. Lamb looked and saw, but it was necessary to display his business acumen.

"Looks like a good thing," he commented; "but the cost?"

"The cost is comparatively nothing over the old steel tack, although we can easily get ten cents a paper as against five for the common ones, leaving us a much wider margin of profit than the manufacturers of the straight tack obtain. There is no family so poor that will use the old, rusty tinned or bronze tack when these are made known to the trade, and you can easily compute for yourself how many millions of packages are used every year. Why, the Eureka Tack Company, which practically has a monopoly of the carpet-tack business, operates a manufacturing plant covering twenty solid acres, and a loaded freight car leaves its warehouse doors on an average of every seven minutes! You cannot buy a share of stock in the Eureka Carpet Tack Company at any price. It yields sixteen per cent. a year dividends, with over eighteen million dollars of undivided surplus—and that business was built on carpet tacks alone! Why, sir, if we wished to do so, within two months after we had started our factory wheels rolling we could sell out to the Eureka Company for two million dollars; or a profit of more than one thousand per cent. on the investment that we are to make."

For once Mr. Lamb was overwhelmed. Only three days before he had been beset by Mr. Daw, but that gentleman had grown hoarsely eloquent over vast possessions that were beyond thousands of miles of circumambient space, across vast barren reaches where desert sands sent up constant streams of superheated atmosphere, with the "hot air" distinctly to be traced throughout the conversation; but here was something to be seen and felt. The points of the very tacks that he held pricked his palm, and his eyes were still glued upon the red-topped one which Mr. Wallingford held hypnotically before him.

"Who composes your company?" he managed to ask.

"So far, I do," replied Mr. Wallingford with quiet pride. "I have not organized the company. That is a minor detail. When I go searching for capital I shall know where to secure it. I have chosen this city on account of its manufacturing facilities, and for its splendid geographical position as a distributing center."

"The stock is not yet placed, then," mused aloud Mr. Lamb, upon whose vision there already glowed a pleasing picture of immense profits.

Why, the thing was startling in the magnificence of its opportunity! Simple little trick, millions and millions used, better than anything of its kind ever put upon the market, cheaply manufactured, it was marked for success from the first!

"Stock placed? Not at all," stated Mr. Wallingford. "My plans only contemplate incorporating for a quarter of a million, and I mean to avoid small stockholders. I shall try to divide the stock into, say, about ten holdings of twenty-five thousand each."

Mr. Lamb was visibly disappointed.

"It looks like a fine thing," he declared with a note of regret.

"Fine? My boy, I'm not much older than you are, but I have been connected with several large enterprises in Boston and elsewhere—if any one were to care to inquire about me they might drop a line to the Mexican and Rio Grande Rubber Company, the St. John's Blood Orange Plantation Company, the Los Pocos Lead Development Company, the Sierra Cinnabar Grant, and a number of others, the addresses of which I could supply—and I never have seen anything so good as this. I am staking my entire business judgment upon it, and, of course, I shall retain the majority of stock myself, inasmuch as the article is my invention."

This being the psychological moment, Mr. Wallingford put forth his hand and had Mr. Lamb dump the tacks back into the large palm that had at first held them. He left them open to view, however, and presently Mr. Lamb picked out one of them for examination. This particular tack was of an exquisite apple-green color, the covering for which had been clipped from one of Mr. Wallingford's own expensive ties, glued to its place and carefully trimmed by Mr. Wallingford's own hands. Mr. Lamb took it to the window for closer admiration, and the promoter, left to himself for a moment, stood before the glass to mop his face and head and neck. He had been working until he had perspired; but, looking into the glass at Mr. Lamb's rigid back, he perceived that the work was well done. Mr. Lamb was profoundly convinced that the Universal Covered Carpet Tack Company was an entity to be respected; nay, to be revered! Mr. Lamb could already see the smoke belching from the tall chimneys of its factory, the bright lights gleaming out from its myriad windows where it was working overtime, the thousands of workmen streaming in at its broad gates, the loaded freight cars leaving every seven minutes!

"You're not going home to dinner, are you, Mr. Lamb?" asked Mr. Wallingford suddenly. "I owe you one for the splash, you know."

"Why—I'm expected home."

"Telephone them you're not coming."

"We—we haven't a telephone in the house."

"Telephone to the nearest drug store and send a messenger over."

Mr. Lamb looked down at himself. He was always neatly dressed, but he did not feel equal to the glitter of the big dining room downstairs.

"I am not—cleaned up," he objected.

"Nonsense! However, as far as that goes, we'll have 'em bring a table right here." And, taking the matter into his own hands, Mr. Wallingford telephoned for a waiter.

From that moment Mr. Lamb strove not to show his wonder at the heights to which human comfort and luxury can attain, but it was a vain attempt; for from the time the two uniformed attendants brought in the table with its snowy cloth and began to place upon it the shining silver and cut-glass service, with the centerpiece of red carnations, he began to grasp at a new world—and it was about this time that he wished he had on his best black suit. In the bathroom Mr. Wallingford came upon him as he held his collar ruefully in his hand, and needed no explanation.

"I say, old man, we can't keep 'em clean, can we? We'll fix that."

The bellboys were anxious to answer summons from 44-A by this time. Mr. Wallingford never used money in a hotel except for tips. It was scarcely a minute until a boy had that collar, with instructions to get another just like it.

"How are the cuffs? Attached, old man? All right. What size shirt do you wear?"

Mr. Lamb gave up. He was now past the point of protest. He told Mr. Wallingford the number of his shirt. In five minutes more he was completely outfitted with clean linen, and when, washed and refreshed and spotless as to high lights, he stepped forth into what was now a perfectly appointed private dining room, he felt himself gradually rising to Mr. Wallingford's own height and able to be supercilious to the waiters, under whose gaze, while his collar was soiled, he had quailed.

It was said by those who made a business of dining that Mr. Wallingford could order a dinner worth while, except for the one trifling fault of over-plenty; but then, Mr. Wallingford himself was a large man, and it took much food and drink to sustain that largeness. Whatever other critics might have said, Mr. Lamb could have but one opinion as they sipped their champagne, toward the end of the meal, and this opinion was that Mr. Wallingford was a genius, a prince of entertainers, a master of finance, a gentleman to be imitated in every particular, and that a man should especially blush to question his financial standing or integrity.

They went to the theater after dinner—box seats—and after the theater they had a little cold snack, amounting to about eleven dollars, including wine and cigars. Moreover, Mr. Lamb had gratefully accepted the secretaryship of the Universal Covered Carpet Tack Company.

Chapter III

Mr. Wallingford's Lamb Is Carefully Inspired with a Flash of Creative Genius

The next morning, in spite of protests and warnings from his employer, Mr. Lamb resigned his position with the A. J. Dorman Company, and, jumping on a car, rode out to the far North Side, where he called at David Jasper's tumble-down frame house. On either side of this were three neat houses that David had built, one at a time, on land he had bought for a song in his younger days; but these were for renting purposes. David lived in the old one for exactly the same reason that he wore the frayed overcoat and slouch hat that had done him duty for many years—they made him as comfortable as new ones, and appearances fed no one nor kept anybody warm.

Wholesome Ella Jasper met the caller at the door with an inward cordiality entirely out of proportion to even a close friend of the family, but her greeting was commonplaceness itself.

"Father's just over to Kriegler's, getting his glass of beer and his lunch," she observed as he shook hands warmly with her. Sometimes she wished that he were not quite so meaninglessly cordial; that he could be either a bit more shy or a bit more bold in his greeting of her.

"I might have known that," he laughed, looking at his watch. "Half-past ten. I'll hurry right over there," and he was gone.

Ella stood in the doorway and looked after him until he had turned the corner of the house; then she sighed and went back to her baking. A moment later she was singing cheerfully.

It was a sort of morning lunch club of elderly men, all of the one lodge, the one building association, the one manner of life, which met over at Kriegler's, and "Eddy" was compelled to sit with them for nearly an hour of slow beer, while politics, municipal, state, and national, was thoroughly thrashed out, before he could get his friend David to himself.

"Well, what brings you out so early, Eddy?" asked the old harness maker on the walk home. "Got a new gold-mining scheme again to put us all in the poorhouse?"

Eddy laughed.

"You don't remember of the kid-glove miner taking anybody's money away, do you?" he demanded. "I guess your old chum Eddy saw through the grindstone that time, eh?"

Mr. Jasper laughed and pounded him a sledge-hammer blow upon the shoulder. It was intended as a mere pat of approval.

"You're all right, Eddy. The only trouble with you is that you don't get married. You'll be an old bachelor before you know it."

"So you've said before," laughed Eddy, "but I can't find the girl that will have me."

"I'll speak to Ella for you."

The younger man laughed lightly again.

"She's my sister," he said gayly. "I wouldn't lose my sister for anything."

David frowned a little and shook his head to himself, but he said nothing more, though the wish was close to his heart. He thought he was tactful.

"No, I've got that new job," went on young Lamb. "Another man from Boston, too. I'm in charge of the complete office organization of a brand-new manufacturing business that's to start up here. Two hundred dollars a month to begin. How's that?"

"Fine," said David. "Enough to marry on. But it sounds too good. Is he a sharper, too?"

"He don't need to be. He seems to have plenty of money, and the article he's going to start manufacturing is so good that it will pay him better to be honest than to be crooked. I don't see where the man could go wrong. Why, look here!" and from his vest pocket he pulled an orange-headed tack. "Carpet tack—covered with any color you want—same color as your carpet so the tacks don't show—only cost a little bit more than the cheap ones. Don't you think it's a good thing?"

David stopped in the middle of the sidewalk and put on his spectacles to examine the trifle critically.

"Is that all he's going to make—just tacks?"

"Just tacks!" exclaimed the younger man. "Why, Dave, the Eureka Tack Company, that has a practical monopoly now of the tack business in this country, occupies a plant covering twenty acres. It employs thousands of men. It makes sixteen per cent. a year dividends, and has millions of dollars surplus in its treasury—undivided profits! Long freight trains leave its warehouses every day, loaded down with nothing but tacks; and that's all they make—just tacks! Why, think, Dave, of how many millions of tacks are pulled out of carpets and thrown away every spring!"

Mr. Jasper was still examining the tack from head to point with deep interest. Now he drew a long breath and handed it back.

"It's a big thing, even if it is little," he admitted. "Watch out for the man, though. Does he want any money?"

"Not a cent. Why, any money I've got he'd laugh at. I couldn't give him any. He's a rich man, and able to start his own factory. He's going to organize a quarter of a million stock company and keep the majority of the stock himself."

"It might be pretty good stock to buy, if you could get some of it," decided Dave after some slow pondering.

"I wish I could, but there is no chance. What stock he issues is only to be put out in twenty-five-thousand-dollar lots."

Again David Jasper sighed. Sixteen per cent. a year! He was thinking now of what a small margin of profit his houses left him after repairs and taxes were paid.

"It looks to me like you'd struck it rich, my boy. Well, you deserve it. You have worked hard and saved your money. You know, when I got married I had nothing but a set of harness tools and the girl, and we got along."

"Look here, Dave," laughed his younger friend, whose thirty years were unbelievable in that he still looked so much like a boy, "some of these days I will hunt up a girl and get married, just to make you keep still about it, and if I have any trouble I'll throw it up to you as long as you live. But what do you think of this chance of mine? That's what I came out for—to get your opinion on it."

"Well," drawled Dave, cautious now that the final judgment was to be pronounced, "you want to remember that you're giving up a good job that has got better and better every year and that will most likely get still better every year; but, if you can start at two hundred a month, and are sure you're going to get it, and the man don't want any money, and he isn't a sharper, why, it looks like it was too good to miss."

"That's what I think," rejoined Mr. Lamb enthusiastically. "Well, I must go now. I want to see Mr. Lewis and John Nolting and one or two of the others, and get their advice," and he swung jubilantly on a car.

It was a pleasant figment this, Eddy Lamb's plan of consulting his older friends. He always went to them most scrupulously to get their advice, and afterward did as he pleased. He was too near the soil, however—only one generation away—to make many mistakes in the matter of caution, and so far he had swung his little financial ventures with such great success that he had begun to be conceited.

He found Mr. Wallingford at the hotel, but not waiting for him by any means. Mr. Wallingford was very busy with correspondence which, since part of it was to his wife and to "Blackie" Daw, was entirely too personal to be trusted to a public stenographer, and he frowningly placed his caller near the window with some new samples of tacks he had made that morning; then, for fifteen minutes, he silently wrote straight on, a course which allowed Mr. Lamb the opportunity to reflect that he was, after all, not entitled to have worn that air of affable familiarity with which he had come into the room. In closing his letter to Mr. Daw the writer added a postscript: "The Lamb is here, and I am now sharpening the shears."

His letters finished and a swift boy called to despatch them, Mr. Wallingford drew a chair soberly to the opposite side of the little table at which he had seated Mr. Lamb. Like every great captain of finance, he turned his back to the window so that his features were in shadow, while the wide-set, open eyes of Mr. Lamb, under their good, broad brow, blinked into the full light of day, which revealed for minute study every wrinkle of expression in his features.

"I forgot to warn you of one thing last night, and I hope you have not talked too much," Mr. Wallingford began with great seriousness. "I reposed such confidence in you that I did not think of caution, a confidence that was justified, for from such inquiries as I have made this morning I am perfectly satisfied with your record—and, by the way, Mr. Lamb, while we are upon this subject, here is a list of references to some of whom I must insist that you write, for my own satisfaction if not for yours. But now to the main point. The thing I omitted to warn you about is this," and here he sank his voice to a quite confidential tone: "I have not yet applied for letters patent upon this device."

"You have not?" exclaimed Mr. Lamb in surprise. The revelation rather altered his estimate of Mr. Wallingford's great business ability.

"No," confessed the latter. "You can see how much I trust you, to tell you this, because, if you did not know, you would naturally suppose that the patent was at least under way, and I would be in no danger whatever; but I am not yet satisfied on one point, and I want the device perfect before I make application. It has worried me quite a bit. You see, the heads of these tacks are too smooth to retain the cloth. It is very difficult to glue cloth to a smooth metal surface, and if we send out our tacks in such condition that a hammer will pound the cloth tops off, it will ruin our business the first season. I have experimented with every sort of glue I can get, and have pounded thousands of tacks into boards, but the cloth covering still comes off in such large percentage that I am afraid to go ahead. Of course, the thing can be solved—it is merely a question of time—but there is no time now to be lost."

From out of the drawer of the table he drew a board into which had been driven some dozens of tacks. From at least twenty-five per cent. of them the cloth covering had been knocked off.

"I see," observed the Lamb, and he examined the board thoughtfully; then he looked out of the window at the passing traffic in the street.

Mr. Wallingford tilted back his chair and lit a fat, black cigar, the barest twinkle of a smile playing about his eyes. He laid a mate to the cigar in front of the bookkeeper, but the latter paid no attention whatever to it. He was perfectly absorbed, and the twinkles around the large man's eyes deepened.

"I say!" suddenly exclaimed Mr. Lamb, turning from the window to the capitalist and throwing open his coat impatiently, as if to get away from anything that encumbered his free expression, "why wouldn't it do to roughen the heads of the tacks?"

His eyes fairly gleamed with the enthusiasm of creation. He had found the answer to one of those difficult problems like: "What bright genius can supply the missing letters to make up the name of this great American martyr, who was also a President and freed the slaves? L-NC-LN. $100.00 in GOLD to be divided among the four million successful solvers! *Send no money* until afterwards!"

Mr. Wallingford brought down the legs of his chair with a thump.

"By George!" he ejaculated. "I'm glad I found you. You're a man of remarkable resource, and I must be a dumbhead. Here I have been puzzling and puzzling with this problem, and it never occurred to me to roughen those tacks!"

It was now Mr. Lamb's turn to find the fat, black cigar, to light it, to lean back comfortably and to contemplate Mr. Wallingford with triumphantly smiling eyes. The latter gentleman, however, was in no contemplative mood. He was a man all of energy. He had two bellboys at the door in another minute. One he sent for a quart of wine and the other to the hardware store with a list of necessities, which were breathlessly bought and delivered: a small table-vise, a heavy hammer, two or three patterns of flat files, and several papers of tacks. Already in one corner of Mr. Wallingford's room stood a rough serving table which he had been using as a work bench, and Mr. Lamb could not but reflect how everything needed came quickly to this man's bidding, as if he had possessed the magic lamp of Aladdin. He was forced to admire, too, the dexterity with which this genius screwed the small vise to the table, placed in its jaws a row of tacks, and, pressing upon them the flat side of one of the files, pounded this vigorously until, upon lifting it up, the fine, indented pattern was found repeated in the hard heads of the tacks. The master magician went through this operation until he had a whole paper of them with roughened heads; then, glowing with fervid enthusiasm which was quickly communicated to his helper, he set Mr. Lamb to gluing bits of cloth upon these heads, to be trimmed later with delicate scissors, an extra pair of which Mr. Wallingford sent out to get. When the tacks were all set aside to dry the coworkers addressed themselves to the contents of the ice pail; but, as the host was pulling the cork from the bottle, and while both of them were perspiring and glowing with anticipated triumph in the experiment, Mr. Wallingford's face grew suddenly troubled.

"By George, Eddy"—and Mr. Lamb beamed over this early adoption of his familiar first name—"if this experiment succeeds it makes you part inventor with me!"

Eddy sat down to gasp.

Chapter IV

J. Rufus Accepts a Temporary Accommodation and Buys an Automobile

The experiment was a success. Immediately after lunch they secured a fresh pine board and pounded all the tacks into it. Not one top came off. The fact, however, that Mr. Lamb was part inventor, made a vast difference in the proposition.

"Now, we'll talk cold business on this," said Mr. Wallingford. "Of course, the main idea is mine, but the patent must be applied for by both as joint inventors. Under the circumstances, I should say that about one fourth of the value of the patent, which we shall sell to the company for at least sixty thousand dollars, would be pretty good for your few minutes of thought, eh?"

Mr. Lamb, his head swimming, agreed with him thoroughly.

"Very well, then, we'll go right out to a lawyer and have a contract drawn up; then we'll go to a patent attorney and get the thing under way at once. Do you know of a good lawyer?"

Mr. Lamb did. There was a young one, thoroughly good, who belonged to Mr. Lamb's lodge, and they went over to see him. There is no expressing the angle at which Mr. Lamb held his head as he passed out through the lobby of the best hotel in his city. If his well-to-do townsmen having business there wished to take notice of him, well and good; if they did not, well and good also. He needed nothing of them.

It was with the same shoulder-squared self-gratification that he ushered his affluent friend into Carwin's office. Carwin was in. Unfortunately, he was always in. Practice had not yet begun for him, but Lamb was bringing fortune in his hand and was correspondingly elated. He intended to make Carwin the lawyer for the corporation. Mr. Carwin drew up for them articles of agreement, in which it was set forth, with many a whereas and wherein, that the said party of the first part and the said party of the second part were joint inventors of a herein described new and improved carpet tack, the full and total benefits of which were to accrue to the said parties of the first part and the second part, and to their heirs and assigns forever and ever, in the proportion of one fourth to the said party of the first part and three fourths to the said party of the second part.

Mr. Carwin, as he saw them walk out with the precious agreement, duly signed, attested and sealed, was too timid to hint about his fee, and Mr. Lamb could scarcely be so indelicate as to call attention to the trifle, even though he knew that Mr. Carwin was gasping for it at that present moment. The latter had hidden his shoes carefully under his desk throughout the consultation, and had kept tucking his cuffs back out of sight during the entire time. There were reasons, however, why Mr. Wallingford did not pay the fee. In spite of the fact that everything was charged at his hotel, it did take some cash for the bare necessities of existence, and, in the past three days, he had spent over fifty dollars in mere incidentals, aside from his living expenses.

Mr. Lamb did not know a patent lawyer, but he had seen the sign of one, and he knew where to go right to him. The patent lawyer demanded a preliminary fee of twenty-five dollars. Mr. Lamb was sorry that Mr. Christopher had made such an unfortunate "break," for he felt that the man would get no more of Mr. Wallingford's business. The latter drew out a roll of bills, however, paid the man on the spot and took his receipt.

"Will a ten-dollar bill help hurry matters any?" he asked.

"It might," admitted the patent lawyer with a cheerful smile.

His office was in a ramshackle old building that had no elevator, and they had been compelled to climb two flights of stairs to reach it. Mr. Wallingford handed him the ten dollars.

"Have the drawings and the application ready by tomorrow. If the thing can be expedited we shall want you to go on to Washington with the papers."

Mr. Christopher glowed within him. Wherever this man Wallingford went he left behind him a trail of high hopes, a glimpse of a better day to dawn. He was a public benefactor, a boon to humanity. His very presence radiated good cheer and golden prospects.

As they entered the hotel, said Mr. Wallingford:

"Just get the key and go right on up to the room, Eddy. You know where it is. Make yourself at home. Take your knife and try the covering on those last tacks we put in. I'll be up in five or ten minutes."

When Mr. Wallingford came in Mr. Lamb was testing the tack covers with great gratification. They were all solid, and they could scarcely be dug off with a knife. He looked up to communicate this fact with glee, and saw a frowning countenance upon his senior partner. Mr. J. Rufus Wallingford was distinctly vexed.

"Nice thing!" he growled. "Just got a notice that there is an overdraft in my bank. Now, I'll have to order some bonds sold at a loss, with the market down all around; but that will take a couple of days and here I am without cash—without cash! Look at that! Less than five dollars!"

He threw off his coat and hat in disgust and loosened his vest. He mopped his face and brow and neck. Mr. Wallingford was extremely vexed. He ordered a quart of champagne in a tone which must have made the telephone clerk feel that the princely guest was dissatisfied with the house. "Frappé, too!" he demanded. "The last I had was as warm as tea!"

Mr. Lamb, within the past day, had himself begun the rise to dizzy heights; he had breathed the atmosphere of small birds and cold bottles into his nostrils until that vapor seemed the normal air of heaven; the ordinary dollar had gradually shrunk from its normal dimensions of a peck measure to the size of a mere dot, and, moreover, he considered how necessary pocket money was to a man of J. Rufus Wallingford's rich relationship with the world.

"I have a little ready cash I could help you out with, if you will let me offer it," he ventured, embarrassed to find slight alternate waves of heat flushing his face. The borrowing and the lending of money were not unknown by any means in Mr. Lamb's set. They asked each other for fifty dollars with perfect nonchalance, got it and paid it back with equal unconcern, and no man among them had been known to forget. Mr. Wallingford accepted quite gracefully.

"Really, if you don't mind," said he, "five hundred or so would be quite an accommodation for a couple of days."

Mr. Lamb gulped, but it was only a sort of growing pain that he had. It was difficult for him to keep up with his own financial expansion.

"Certainly," he stammered. "I'll go right down and get it for you. The bank closes at three. I have only a half hour to make it."

"I'll go right with you," said Mr. Wallingford, asking no questions, but rightly divining that his Lamb kept no open account. "Wait a minute. I'll make you out a note—just so there'll be something to show for it, you know."

He hurriedly drew a blank from his pocket, filled it in and arose from the table.

"I made it out for thirty days, merely as a matter of business form," stated Mr. Wallingford as they walked to the elevator, "but, as soon as I put those bonds on the market, I'll take up the note, of course. I left the interest in at six per cent."

"Oh, that was not necessary at all," protested Mr. Lamb.

The sum had been at first rather a staggering one, but it only took him a moment or two to get his new bearings, and, if possible, he held his head a trifle higher than ever as he walked out through the lobby. On the way to the bank the capitalist passed the note over to his friend.

"I believe that's the right date; the twenty-fifth, isn't it?"

"The twenty-fifth is right," Mr. Lamb replied, and perfunctorily opened the note. Then he stopped walking. "Hello!" he said. "You've made a mistake. This is for a thousand."

"Is that so? I declare! I so seldom draw less than that. Well, suppose we let it go at a thousand."

Time for gulping was passed.

"All right," said the younger man, but he could not make the assent as sprightly as he could have wished. In spite of himself the words drawled.

Nevertheless, at his bank he handed in his savings-book and the check, and, thoroughly permeated by the atmosphere in which he was now moving, he had made out the order for eleven hundred dollars.

"I needed a little loose change myself," he explained, as he put a hundred into his own pocket and passed the thousand over to Mr. Wallingford.

Events moved rapidly now. Mr. Wallingford that night sent off one hundred and fifty dollars to his wife.

"Cheer up, little girl," he wrote her. "Blackie came here and reported that this was a grouch town. I've been here three days and dug up a thousand, and there's more in sight. I've been inquiring around this morning. There is a swell little ten-thousand-dollar house out in the rich end of the burg that I'm going to buy to put up a front, and you know how I'll buy it. Also I'm going over tomorrow and pick out an automobile. I need it in my business. You ought to see what long, silky wool the sheep grow here."

The next morning was devoted entirely to pleasure. They visited three automobile firms and took spins in four machines, and at last Mr. Wallingford picked out a five-thousand-dollar car that about suited him.

"I shall try this for two weeks," he told the proprietor of the establishment. "Keep it here in your garage at my call, and, by that time, if I decide to buy it, I shall have my own garage under way. I have my eye on a very nice little place out in Gildendale, and if they don't want too much for it I'll bring on Mrs. Wallingford from Boston."

"With pleasure, Mr. Wallingford," said the proprietor.

Mr. Lamb walked away with a new valuation of things. Not a penny of deposit had been asked, for the mere appearance of Mr. Wallingford and his air of owning the entire garage were sufficient. In the room at the hotel that afternoon they made some further experiments on tacks, and Mr. Wallingford gave his young partner some further statistics concerning the Eureka Company: its output, the number of men it employed, the number of machines it had in operation, the small start it had, the immense profits it made.

"We've got them all beat," Mr. Lamb enthusiastically summed up for him. "We're starting much better than they did, and with, I believe, the best manufacturing proposition that was ever put before the public."

It was not necessary to supply him with any further enthusiasm. He had been inoculated with the yeast of it, and from that point onward would be self-raising.

"The only thing I am afraid of," worried Mr. Wallingford, "is that the Eureka Company will want to buy us out before we get fairly started, and, if they offer us a good price, the stockholders will want to stampede. Now, you and I must vote down any proposition the Eureka Company make us, no matter what the other stockholders want, because, if they buy us out before we have actually begun to encroach upon their business, they will not give us one fifth of the price we could get after giving them a good scare. Between us, Eddy, we'll hold six tenths of the stock and we must stand firm."

Eddy stuck his thumbs in his vest pocket and with great complacency tapped himself alternately upon his recent luncheon with the finger tips of his two hands.

"Certainly we will," he admitted. "But say; I have some friends that I'd like to bring into this thing. They're not able to buy blocks of stock as large as you suggested, but, maybe, we could split up one lot so as to let them in."

"I don't like the idea of small stockholders," Mr. Wallingford objected, frowning. "They are too hard to handle. Your larger investors are business men who understand all the details and are not raising eternal questions about the little things that turn up; but since we have this tack so perfect I've changed my plan of incorporation, and consequently there is a way in which your friends can get in. We don't want to attract any attention to ourselves from the Eureka people just now, so we will only incorporate at first for one thousand dollars, in ten shares of one hundred dollars each—sort of a dummy corporation in which my name will not appear at all. If you can find four friends who will buy one share of stock each of you will then subscribe for the other six shares, for which I will pay you, giving you one share, as I promised. These four friends of yours then, if they wish, may take up one block of twenty-five thousand when we make the final corporation, which we will do by increasing our capital stock as soon as we get our corporation papers. These friends of yours would, necessarily, be on our first board of directors, too, which will hold for one year, and it will be an exceptional opportunity for them."

"I don't quite understand," said Mr. Lamb.

"We incorporate for one thousand only," explained Mr. Wallingford, slowly and patiently, "ten shares of one hundred dollars each, all fully paid in. The Eureka Company will pay no attention to a one-thousand-dollar company. As soon as we get our corporation papers, we original incorporators will, of course, form the officers and board of directors, and we will immediately vote to increase our capitalization to one hundred thousand dollars, in one thousand shares of one hundred dollars each. We will vote to pay you and I as inventors sixty thousand dollars or six hundred shares of stock for our patents—applied for and to be applied for during a period of five years to come—in carpet-tack improvements and machinery for making the same. We will offer the balance of the forty thousand dollars stock for sale, to carry us through the experimental stage—that is, until we get our machinery all in working order. Then we will need one hundred thousand dollars to start our factory. To get that, we will reincorporate for a three-hundred-thousand capital, taking up all the outstanding stock and giving to each stockholder two shares at par for each share he then holds. That will take up two hundred thousand dollars of the stock and leave one hundred thousand for sale at par. You, in place of fifteen thousand dollars' worth of stock as your share for the patent rights, will have thirty thousand dollars' worth, or three hundred shares, and if, after we have started operating, the Eureka Company should buy us out at only a million, you would have a hundred thousand dollars net profit."

A long, long sigh was the answer. Mr. Lamb saw. Here was real financiering.

"Let's get outside," he said, needing fresh air in his lungs after this. "Let's go up and see my friend, Mr. Jasper."

In ten minutes the automobile had reported. Each man, before he left the room, slipped a handful of covered carpet tacks into his coat pocket.

Chapter V

The Universal Covered Carpet Tack Company Forms Amid Great Enthusiasm

The intense democracy of J. Rufus Wallingford could not but charm David Jasper, even though he disapproved of diamond stick-pins and red-leather-padded automobiles as a matter of principle. The manner in which the gentleman from Boston acknowledged the introduction, the fine mixture of deference due Mr. Jasper's age and of cordiality due his easily discernible qualities of good fellowship, would have charmed the heart out of a cabbage.

"Get in, Dave; we want to take you for a ride," demanded Mr. Lamb.

David shook his head at the big machine, and laughed.

"I don't carry enough insurance," he objected.

Mr. Wallingford had caught sight of a little bronze button in the lapel of Mr. Jasper's faded and threadbare coat.

"A man who went through the battle of Bull Run ought to face anything," he laughed back.

The shot went home. Mr. Jasper *had* acquitted himself with honor in the battle of Bull Run, and without further ado he got into the invitingly open door of the tonneau, to sink back among the padded cushions with his friend Lamb. As the door slammed shut, Ella Jasper waved them adieu, and it was fully three minutes after the machine drove away before she began humming about her work. Somehow or other, she did not like to see her father's friend so intimately associated with rich people.

They had gone but a couple of blocks, and Mr. Lamb was in the early stages of the enthusiasm attendant upon describing the wonderful events of the past two days—especially his own share in the invention, and the hundred thousand dollars that it was to make him within the year—when Mr. Wallingford suddenly halted the machine.

"You're not going to get home to dinner, you know, Mr. Jasper," he declared.

"Oh, we have to! This is lodge night, and I am a patriarch. I haven't missed a night for twenty years, and Eddy, here, has an office, too—his first one. We've got ten candidates tonight."

"I see," said Mr. Wallingford gravely. "It is more or less in the line of a sacred duty. Nevertheless, we will not go home to dinner. I'll get you at the lodge door at half past eight. Will that be early enough?"

Mr. Jasper put his hands upon his knees and turned to his friend.

"I guess we can work our way in, can't we, Eddy?" he chuckled, and Eddy, with equally simple pleasure, replied that they could.

"Very well. Back to the house, chauffeur." And, in a moment more, they were sailing back to the decrepit little cottage, where Lamb jumped out to carry the news to Ella. She was just coming out of the kitchen door in her sunbonnet to run over to the grocery store as Edward came up the steps. He grabbed her by both shoulders and dragged her out.

"Come on; we're going to take you along!" he threatened, and she did not know why, but, at the touch of his hands, she paled slightly. Her eyes never faltered, however, as she laughed and jerked herself away.

"Not much, you don't! I'm worried enough as it is with father in there—and you, of course."

He told her that they would not be home to supper, and, for a second time, she wistfully saw them driving away in the big red machine.

Mr. Wallingford talked with the chauffeur for a few moments, and then the machine leaped forward with definiteness. Once or twice Mr. Wallingford looked back. The two in the tonneau were examining the cloth-topped tacks, and both were talking volubly. Mile after mile they were still at it, and the rich man felt relieved of all responsibility. The less he said in the matter the better; he had learned the invaluable lesson of when not to talk. So far as he was concerned, the Universal Covered Carpet Tack Company was launched, and he was able to turn his attention to the science of running the car, a matter which, by the time they had reached their stopping point, he had picked up to the great admiration of the expert driver. For the last five miles the big man ran the machine himself, with the help of a guiding word or two, and when they finally stopped in front of the one pretentious hotel in the small town they had reached, he was so completely absorbed in the new toy that he was actually as nonchalant about the new company as he would have wished to appear. His passengers were surprised when they found that they had come twenty miles, and Mr. Wallingford showed them what a man who knows how to dine can do in a minor hotel. He had everybody busy, from the proprietor down. The snap of his fingers was as potent here as the clarion call of the trumpet in battle, and David Jasper, though he strove to disapprove, after sixty years of somnolence woke up and actually enjoyed pretentious luxury.

There were but five minutes of real business conversation following the meal, but five minutes were enough. David Jasper had called his friend Eddy aside for one brief moment.

"Did he give you any references?" he asked, the habit of caution asserting itself.

"Sure; more than half a dozen of them."

"Have you written to them?"

"I wrote this morning."

"I guess he wouldn't give them to you if he wasn't all right."

"We don't need the references," urged Lamb. "The man himself is reference enough. You see that automobile? He bought it this morning and didn't pay a cent on it. They didn't ask him to."

It was a greater recommendation than if the man had paid cash down for the machine; for credit is mightier than cash, everywhere.

"I think we'll go in," said Dave.

Think he would go in! It was only his conservative way of expressing himself, for he was already in with his whole heart and soul. In the five minutes of conversation between the three that ensued, David Jasper agreed to be one of the original incorporators, to go on the first board of directors, and to provide three other solid men to serve in a like capacity, the preliminary meeting being arranged for the next morning. Mr. Wallingford passed around his black cigars and lit one in huge content as he climbed into the front seat with the chauffeur, to begin his task of urging driver and machine back through the night in the time that he had promised.

That was a wonderful ride to the novices. Nothing but darkness ahead, with a single stream of white light spreading out upon the roadway, which, like a fast descending curtain, lowered always before them; a rut here, a rock there, angle and curve and dip and rise all springing out of the night with startling swiftness, to disappear behind them before they had given even a gasp of comprehension for the possible danger they had confronted but that was now past. Unconsciously they found themselves gripping tightly the sides of the car, and yet, even to the old man, there was a strange sense of exhilaration, aided perhaps by wine, that made them, after the first breathless five miles, begin to jest in voices loud enough to carry against the wind, to laugh boisterously, and even to sing, by-and-by, a nonsensical song started by Lamb and caught up by Wallingford and joined by the still firm voice of David Jasper. The chauffeur, the while bent grimly over his wheel, peered with iron-nerved intensity out into that mysterious way where the fatal snag might rise up at any second and smite them into lifeless clay, for they were going at a terrific pace. The hoarse horn kept constantly hooting, and every now and then they flashed by trembling horses drawn up at the side of the road and attached to "rigs," the occupants of which appeared only as one or two or three fish-white faces in the one instant that the glow of the headlight gleamed upon them. Once there was a quick swerve out of the road and back into it again, where the rear wheel hovered for a fraction of a second over a steep gully, and not until they had passed on did the realization come to them that there had been one horse that had refused, either through stubbornness or fright, to get out of the road fast enough. But what is a danger past when a myriad lie before, and what are dangers ahead when a myriad have been passed safely by? The exhilaration became almost an intoxication, for, in spite of those few moments when mirth and gayety were checked by that sudden throb of what might have been, the songs burst forth again as soon as a level track stretched ahead once more.

"Five minutes before the time I promised you!" exclaimed Mr. Wallingford in jovial triumph, jumping from his seat and opening the door of the tonneau for his passengers just in front of the stairway that led to their lodge-rooms.

They climbed out, stiff and breathless and still tingling with the inexplicable thrill of it all.

"Eleven o'clock in the morning, remember, at Carwin's," he reminded them as they left him, and afterward they wondered why such a simple exertion as the climbing of one flight of stairs should make their hearts beat so high and their breath come so deep and harsh. It would have been curious, later that night, to see Edward Lamb buying a quart of champagne for his friends, and protesting that it was not cold enough!

Mr. Wallingford stepped back to the chauffeur.

"What's your first name?" he inquired.

"Frank, sir."

"Well, Frank, when you go back to the shop you tell them that you're to drive my machine hereafter when I call for it, and when I get settled down here I want you to work for me. Drive to the hotel now and wait."

Before climbing into the luxury of the tonneau he handed the chauffeur a five-dollar bill.

"All right, sir," said Frank.

At the hotel, the man of means walked up to the clerk and opened his pocketbook.

"I have a little more cash than I care to carry around. Just put this to my credit, will you?" and he counted out six one-hundred-dollar bills.

As he turned away the clerk permitted himself that faint trace of a smile once more. His confidence was justified. He had known that somebody would pay Mr. Wallingford's acrobatic bill. His interesting guest strode out to the big red automobile. The chauffeur was out in a second and had the tonneau open before the stately but earnestly willing doorman of the hotel could perform the duty.

"Now, show us the town," said Wallingford as the door closed upon him, and when he came in late that night his eyes were red and his speech was thick; but there were plenty of eager hands to see safely to bed the prince who had landed in their midst with less than a hundred dollars in his possession.

He was up bright and vigorous the next morning, however. A cold bath, a hearty breakfast in his room, a half hour with the barber, and a spin in the automobile made him elastic and bounding again, so that at eleven o'clock he was easily the freshest man among the six who gathered in Mr. Carwin's office. The incorporators noted with admiration, which with wiser men might have turned to suspicion, that Mr. Wallingford was better posted on corporation law than Mr. Carwin himself, and that he engineered the preliminary proceedings through in a jiffy. With the exception of Lamb, they were all men past forty, and not one of them had known experience of this nature. They had been engaged in minor occupations or in minor business throughout their lives, and had gathered their few thousands together dollar by dollar. To them this new realm that was opened up was a fairyland, and the simple trick of watering stock that had been carefully explained to them, one by one, pleased them as no toy ever pleased a child. They had heard of such things as being vague and mysterious operations in the realms of finance and had condemned them, taking their tone from the columns of editorials they had read upon such practices; but, now that they were themselves to reap the fruits of it, they looked through different spectacles. It was a just proceeding which this genius of commerce proposed; for they who stood the first brunt of launching the ship were entitled to greater rewards than they who came in upon an assured certainty of profits, having waited only for the golden cargo to be in the harbor.

As a sort of sealing of their compact and to show that this was to be a corporation upon a friendly basis, rather than a cold, grasping business proposition, Mr. Wallingford took them all over to a simple lunch in a private dining room at his hotel. He was careful not to make it too elaborate, but careful, too, that the luncheon should be notable, and they all went away talking about him: what a wonderful man he was, what a wonderful business proposition he had permitted them to enter upon, what wonderful resources he must have at his command, what wonderful genius was his in manipulation, in invention, in every way.

There was a week now in which to act, and Mr. Wallingford wasted no time. He picked out his house in the exclusive part of Gildendale, and when it came to paying the thousand dollars down, Mr. Wallingford quietly made out a sixty-day note for the amount.

"I beg your pardon," hesitated the agent, "the first payment is supposed to be in cash."

"Oh, I know that it is supposed to be," laughed Mr. Wallingford, "but we understand how these things are. I guess the house itself will secure the note for that length of time. I am going to be under pretty heavy expense in fitting up the place, and a man with any regard for the earning power of money does not keep much cash lying loose. Do you want this note or not?" and his final tone was peremptory.

"Oh, why, certainly; that's all right," said the agent, and took it.

Upon the court records appeared the sale, but even before it was so entered a firm of decorators and furnishers had been given *carte blanche*, following, however, certain artistic requirements of Mr. Wallingford himself. The result that they produced within the three days that he gave them was marvelous; somewhat too garish, perhaps, for people of good taste, but impressive in every detail; and for all this he paid not one penny in cash. He was accredited with being the owner of a house in the exclusive suburb, Gildendale. On that accrediting the furnishing was done, on that accrediting he stocked his pantry shelves, his refrigerator, his wine cellar, his coal bins, his humidors, and had started a tailor to work upon half a dozen suits, among them an automobile costume. He had a modest establishment of two servants and a chauffeur by the time his wife arrived, and on the day the final organization of the one-thousand-dollar company was effected, he gave a housewarming for his associates of the Universal Covered Carpet Tack Company. Where Mr. Wallingford had charmed, Mrs. Wallingford fascinated, and the five men went home that night richer than they had ever dreamed of being; than they would ever be again.

Chapter VI

In Which an Astounding Revelation Is Made Concerning J. Rufus

The first stockholders' meeting of the Tack Company was a cheerful affair, held around a table that was within an hour or so to have a cloth; for whenever J. Rufus Wallingford did business, he must, perforce, eat and drink, and all who did business with him must do the same. The stockholders, being all present, elected their officers and their board of directors: Mr. Wallingford, president; Mr. Lamb, secretary; Mr. Jasper, treasurer; and Mr. Lewis, David Jasper's nearest friend, vice president, these four and Mr. Nolting also constituting the board of directors. Immediately after, they adopted a stock, printed form of constitution, voted an increase of capitalization to one hundred thousand dollars, and then adjourned.

The president, during the luncheon, made them a little speech in which he held before them constantly a tack with a crimson top glued upon a roughened surface, and alluded to the invaluable services their young friend, Edward Lamb, had rendered to the completion of the company's now perfect and flawless article of manufacture. He explained to them in detail the bigness of the Eureka Tack Manufacturing Company, its enormous undivided profits, its tremendous yearly dividends, the fabulous price at which its stock was quoted, with none for sale; and all this gigantic business built upon a simple tack!—Gentlemen, not nearly, not *nearly* so attractive and so profitable an article of commerce as this perfect little convenience held before them. The gentlemen were to be congratulated upon a bigger and brighter and better fortune than had ever come to them; they were all to be congratulated upon having met each other, and since they had been kind enough, since they had been trusting enough, to give him their confidence with but little question, Mr. Wallingford felt it his duty to reassure them, even though they needed no reassurance, that he was what he was; and he called upon his friend and their secretary, Mr. Lamb, to read to them the few letters that he understood had been received from the Mexican and Rio Grande Rubber Company, the St. John's Blood Orange Plantation Company, the Los Pocos Lead Development Company, the Sierra Cinnabar Grant, and others.

Mr. Lamb—Secretary Lamb, if you please—arose in self-conscious dignity, which he strove to taper off into graceful ease.

"It is hardly worth while reading more than one, for they're all alike," he stated jovially, "and if anybody questions our president, send him to his friend Eddy!" Whereupon he read the letters.

According to them, Mr. Wallingford was a gentleman of the highest integrity; he was a man of unimpeachable character, morally and financially; he was a genius of commerce; he had been sought, for his advice and for the tower of strength that his name had become, by all the money kings of Boston; he was, in a word, the greatest boon that had ever descended upon any city, and all of the gentlemen who were lucky enough to be associated with him in any business enterprise that he might back or vouch for, could count themselves indeed most fortunate. The letters were passed around. Some of them had embossed heads; most of them were, at least, engraved; some of them were printed in two or three rich colors; some had beautifully tinted pictures of vast Mexican estates, and Florida plantations, and Nevada mining ranges. They were impressive, those letter-heads, and when, after passing the round of the table, they were returned to Mr. Lamb, four pairs of eyes followed them as greedily as if those eyes had been resting upon actual money.

In the ensuing week the committee on factories, consisting of Mr. Wallingford, Mr. Lamb, and Mr. Jasper, honked and inspected and lunched until they found a small place which would "do for the first year's business," and within two days the factory was cleaned and the office most sumptuously furnished; then Mr. Wallingford, having provided work for the secretary, began to attend to his purely personal affairs, one of which was the private consulting of the patent attorney. Upon his first visit Mr. Christopher met him with a dejected air.

"I find four interferences against your application," he dolefully stated, "and they cover the ground very completely."

"Get me a patent," directed Mr. Wallingford shortly.

Mr. Christopher hesitated. Not only was his working jacket out at the elbows, but his street coat was shiny at the seams.

"I am bound to tell you," he confessed, after quite a struggle, "that, while I *might* get you some sort of a patent, it would not hold water."

"I don't care if it wouldn't hold pebbles or even brickbats," retorted Mr. Wallingford. "I'm not particular about the mesh of it. Just you get me a patent—any sort of a patent, so it has a seal and a ribbon on it. I believe it is part of your professional ethics, Mr. Christopher, to do no particular amount of talking except to your clients."

"Well, yes, sir," admitted Mr. Christopher.

"Very well, then; I am the only client you know in this case, and I say—get a patent! After all, a patent isn't worth as much as a dollar at the

Waldorf, except to form the basis of a lawsuit," whereat Mr. Christopher saw a great white light and his conscience ceased to bother him.

Meanwhile the majestic wheels of state revolved, and at the second meeting of the board of directors the secretary was able to lay before them the august permission of the Commonwealth to issue one hundred thousand dollars of stock in the new corporation. In fact, the secretary was able to show them a book of especially printed stock certificates, and a corporate seal had been made. Their own seal! Each man tried it with awe and pride. This also was a cheerful board meeting, wherein the directors, as one man, knowing beforehand what they were to do, voted to Mr. Wallingford and Mr. Lamb sixty thousand dollars in stock, for all patents relating to covered carpet tacks or devices for making the same that should be obtained by them for a period of five years to come. The three remaining members of the board of directors and the one stockholder who was allowed to be present by courtesy then took up five thousand dollars' worth of stock each and guaranteed to bring in, by the end of the week, four more like subscriptions, two of which they secured; and, thirty thousand dollars of cash having been put into the treasury, a special stockholders' meeting was immediately called. When this met it was agreed that they should incorporate another company under the name of the Universal Covered Tack Company, dropping the word "Carpet," with an authorized capital of three hundred thousand dollars, two hundred thousand of which was already subscribed.

It took but a little over a month to organize this new company, which bought out the old company for the consideration of two hundred thousand dollars, payable in stock of the new company. With great glee the new stockholders bought from themselves, as old stockholders, the old company at this valuation, each man receiving two shares of one hundred dollars face value for each one hundred dollars' worth of stock that he had held before. It was their very first transaction in water, and the delight that it gave them one and all knew no bounds; they had doubled their money in one day! But their elation was not half the elation of J. Rufus Wallingford, for in his possession he had ninety thousand dollars' worth, par value, of stock, the legitimacy of which no one could question, and the market price of which could be to himself whatever his glib tongue had the opportunity to make it. In addition to the nine hundred shares of stock, he had a ten-thousand-dollar house, a five-thousand-dollar automobile, and unlimited credit; and this was the man who had landed in the city but two brief months before, with no credit in any known spot upon the globe, and with less than one hundred dollars in his pocket!

It is a singular commentary upon the honesty of American business methods that so much is done on pure faith. The standing of J. Rufus Wallingford was established beyond question. Aside from the perfunctory inquiries that Edward Lamb had made, no one ever took the trouble to question into the promoter's past record. So far as local merchants were concerned, these did not care; for did not J. Rufus own a finely appointed new house in Gildendale, and did he not appear before them daily in a fine new automobile? This, added to the fact that he established credit with one merchant and referred the next one to him, referred the third to the second, and the fourth to the third, was ample. If merchant number four took the trouble to inquire of merchant number three, he was told: "Yes, we have Mr. Wallingford on our books, and consider him good." Consequently, Mrs. Wallingford was able to go to any establishment, in her own little runabout that J. Rufus got her presently, and order what she would; and she took ample advantage of the opportunity. She, like J. Rufus, was one of those rare beings of earth for whom earth's most prized treasures are delved, and wrought, and woven, and sewed; for transcendent beauty demands ever more beauty for its adornment. In all the city there was nothing too good for either of them, and they got it without money and without price. The provider of all this made no move toward paying even a retainer upon his automobile, for instance; but, when the subtle intuition within him warned that the dealer would presently make a demand, he calmly went in and selected the neat little runabout for his wife, and had it added to his bill. After he had seen the runabout glide away, the dealer was a little aghast at himself. He had firmly intended, the next time he saw Mr. Wallingford, to insist upon a payment. In place of that, he had only jeopardized two thousand dollars more, and all that he had to show for it were half a dozen covered tacks which J. Rufus had left him to ponder upon. In the meantime, Lamb's loan of one thousand had been increased, upon plausible pretext, to two thousand.

There began, now, busy days at the factory. In the third floor of their building a machine shop was installed. Three thousand dollars went there. Outside, in a large experimental shop, work was being rapidly pushed on machinery which would make tacks with cross-corrugated heads. Genius Wallingford had secretly secured drawings of tack machinery, and devised slight changes which would evade the patents, adding dies that would make the roughened tops. A final day came when, set up in their shop, the first faulty machine pounded out tacks ready for later covering, and every stockholder who had been called in to witness the working of the miracle went away profoundly convinced that fortune was just within his reach. They had their first patent granted now, and the sight of it, on stiff parchment with its bit of bright ribbon, was like a glimpse at dividends. It was right at this time, however, that one cat was let out of the bag. The information came first to Edward Lamb, through the inquiries of a commercial rating company, that their Boston capitalist was a whited sepulcher, so far as capital went. He had not a cent. The secretary, in the privacy of their office, put the matter to him squarely, and he admitted it cheerfully. He was glad that the *exposé* had come—it suited his present course, and he would have brought it about himself before long.

"Who said I had money?" he demanded. "I never said so."

"Well, but the way you live," objected Lamb.

"I have always lived that way, and I always shall. Not only is it a fact that I have no money, but I must have some right away."

"I haven't any more to lend."

"No, Eddy; I'm not saying that you have. I am merely stating that I have to have some. I am being bothered by people who want it, and I cannot work on the covering machine until I get it," and Mr. Wallingford coolly telephoned for his big automobile to be brought around.

They sat silently in the office for the next five minutes, while Lamb slowly appreciated the position they were in. If J. Rufus should "lay down on them" before the covering machine was perfected, they were in a bad case. They had already spent over twenty thousand dollars in equipping their office, their machine shop, and perfecting their stamping machine, and time was flying.

"You might sell a little of your stock," suggested Lamb.

"We have an agreement between us to hold control."

"But you can still sell a little of yours, and stay within that amount. I'm not selling any of mine."

Mr. Wallingford drew from his pocket a hundred-share stock certificate.

"I have already sold some. Make out fifty shares of this to L. W. Ramsay, twenty-five to E. H. Wyman, and the other twenty-five to C. D. Wyman."

Ramsay and the Wyman Brothers! Ramsay was the automobile dealer; Wyman Brothers were Wallingford's tailors.

"So much? Why didn't you sell them at least part from our extra treasury stock? There is twenty thousand there, replacing the ten thousand of the old company."

"Why didn't I? I needed the money. I got twenty-five hundred cash from Ramsay, and let him put twenty-five on account. I agreed to take one thousand in trade from Wyman Brothers, and got four thousand cash there."

The younger man looked at him angrily.

"Look here, Wallingford; you're hitting it up rather strong, ain't you? This makes six thousand five hundred, besides two thousand you borrowed from me, that you have spent in three months. You have squandered money since you came here at the rate of three thousand a month, besides all the bills I know you owe, and still you are broke. How is it possible?"

"That's my business," retorted Wallingford, and his face reddened with assumed anger. "We are not going to discuss it. The point is that I need money and must have it."

The automobile drew up at the door, and J. Rufus, who was in his automobile suit, put on his cap and riding coat.

"Where are you going?"

"Over to Rayling."

Lamb frowned. Rayling was sixty miles away.

"And you will not be back until midnight, I suppose."

"Hardly."

"Why, confound it, man, you can't go!" exclaimed Lamb. "They're waiting for you now over at the machine shop, for further instructions on the covering device."

"They'll have to wait!" announced J. Rufus, and stalked out of the door.

The thing had been deliberately followed up. Mr. Wallingford had come to the point where he wished his flock to know that he had no financial resources whatever, and that they would have to support him. It was the first time that he had departed from his suavity, and he left Lamb in a panic. He had been gone scarcely more than an hour when David Jasper came in.

"Where is Wallingford?" he asked.

"Gone out for an automobile trip."

"When will he be back?"

"Not to-day."

Jasper's face was white, but the flush of slow anger was creeping upon his cheeks.

"Well, he ought to be; his note is due."

"What note?" inquired Lamb, startled.

"His note for a thousand dollars that I went security on."

"You might just as well renew it, or pay it. I had to renew mine," said Lamb. "Dave, the man is a four-flusher, without a cent to fall back on. I just found it out this morning. Why didn't you tell me that he was borrowing money of you?"

"Why didn't you tell me he was borrowing money of you?" retorted his friend.

They looked at each other hotly for a moment, and then both laughed. The big man was too much for them to comprehend.

"We are both cutting our eye teeth," Lamb decided. "I wonder how many more he's borrowed money from."

"Lewis, for one. He got fifteen hundred from him. Lewis told me this morning, up at Kriegler's."

Lamb began figuring. To the eight thousand five hundred of which he already knew, here was twenty-five hundred more to be added—eleven thousand dollars that the man had spent in three months! Some bills, of course, he had paid, but the rest of it had gone as the wind blew. It seemed impossible that a man could spend money at the rate of one hundred and twenty-five dollars a day, but this one had done it, and that at first was the point which held them aghast, to the forgetting of their own share in it. They could not begin to understand it until Lamb recalled one incident that had impressed him. Wallingford had taken his wife and two friends to the opera one night. They had engaged a private dining room at the hotel, indulging in a dinner that, with flowers and wines, had cost over a hundred dollars. Their seats had cost fifty. There had been a supper afterward where the wine flowed until long past midnight. Altogether, that evening alone had cost not less than three hundred dollars—and the man lived at that gait all the time! In his home, even when himself and wife were alone, seven-course dinners were served. Huge fowls were carved for but the choicest slices, were sent away from the table and never came back again in any form. Expensive wines were opened and left uncorked after two glasses, because some whim had led the man to prefer some other brand.

Lamb looked up from his figuring with an

expression so troubled that his older friend, groping as men will do for cheering words, hit upon the idea that restored them both to their equilibrium.

"After all," suggested Jasper, "it's none of our business. The company is all right."

"That's so," agreed Lamb, recovering his enthusiasm in a bound. "The tack itself can't be beat, and we are making progress toward getting on the market. Suppose the man were to sell all his stock. It wouldn't make any difference, so long as he finishes that one machine for covering the tack."

"He's a liar!" suddenly burst out David Jasper. "I wish he had his machinery done and was away from us. I can't sleep well when I do business with a liar."

"We don't want to get rid of him yet," Lamb reminded him, "and, in the meantime, I suppose he will have to have money in order to keep him at work. You'd better get him to give you stock to cover your note and tell Lewis to do the same. We'll all go after him on that point, and get protected."

David looked troubled in his turn.

"I can't afford it. When I took up that five thousand dollars' worth of stock I only had fifteen hundred in the building loan, and I put a mortgage on one of my houses to make up the amount. If I have to stand this thousand I'll have to give another mortgage, and I swore I'd never put a plaster on my property."

"The tack's good for it," urged Lamb, with conviction.

"Yes, the tack's good," admitted Jasper.

That was the thing which held them all in line—the tack! Wallingford himself might be a spendthrift and a ne'er-do-well, but their faith in the tack that was to make them all rich was supreme. Lamb picked up one from his desk and handed it to his friend. The very sight of it, with its silken covered top, imagination carrying it to its place in a carpet where it would not show, was most reassuring, and behind it, looming up like the immense open cornucopia of Fortune herself, was the Eureka Company, the concern that would buy them out at any time for a million dollars if they were foolish enough to sell. After all, they had nothing to worry them.

David Jasper went up to the bank and had them hold the note until the next day, which they did without comment. David was "good" for anything he wanted. The next day he got hold of Wallingford to get him to renew the note and to give him stock as security for it. When J. Rufus came out of that transaction, in which David had intended to be severe with him, he had four thousand dollars in his pocket, for he had transferred to his endorser five thousand dollars of his stock and Jasper had placed another mortgage on his property. The single tack in his vest pocket had assumed proportions far larger than his six cottages and his home. It was the same with Lewis and one of the others, and, for a week, the inventor struggled with the covering machine.

No one seemed to appreciate the fact that here their genius was confronting a problem that was most difficult of solution. To them it meant a mere bit of mechanical juggling, as certain to be accomplished as the simple process of multiplication; but to glue a piece of cloth to so minute and irregular a thing as the head of a tack, to put it on firmly and leave it trimmed properly at the edges, to do this trick by machinery and at a rate rapid enough to insure profitable operation, was a Herculean task, and the stockholders would have been aghast had they known that J. Rufus was in no hurry to solve this last perplexity. He knew better than to begin actual manufacture. The interference report on the first patent led him to make secret inquiries, the result of which convinced him that the day they went on the market would be the day that they would be disrupted by vigorous suits, backed by millions of capital. He had been right in stating that a patent is of no value except as a basis for lawsuits.

There was only one thing which offset his shrewdness in realizing these conditions, and that was his own folly. Had he been content to devote himself earnestly to the accomplishment even of his own ends, the many difficulties into which he had floundered would never have existed. Always there was the pressing need for money. He was a colossal example of the fact that easily gotten pelf is of no value. His wife was shrewder than he. She had no social aspirations whatever at this time. They were both of them too bohemian of taste and habit to conform to the strict rules which society imposes in certain directions, even had they been able to enter the charmed circle. She cared only to dress as well as the best and to go to such places of public entertainment as the best frequented, to show herself in jewels that would attract attention and in gowns that would excite envy; but she did tire of continuous suspense—and she was not without keenness of perception.

"Jim," she asked, one night, "how is your business going?"

"You see me have money every day, don't you? There's nothing you want, is there?" was the evasive reply.

"Not a thing, except this: I want a vacation. I don't want to be wondering all my life when the crash is to come. So far as I have seen, this looks like a clean business arrangement that you are in now; but, even if it is, it can't stand the bleeding that you are giving it. If you are going to get out of this thing, as you have left everything else you were ever in, get out right away. Realize every dollar you can at once, and let us take a trip abroad."

"I can't let go just yet," he replied.

She looked up, startled.

"Nothing wrong in this, is there, Jim?"

"Wrong!" he exclaimed. "Fanny, I never did anything in my life that the law could get me for. The law is a friend of mine. It was framed up especially for the protection of J. Rufus Wallingford. I can shove ordinary policemen off the sidewalk and make the chief stand up and salute when I go past. The only way I could break into a jail would be to buy one."

She shook her head.

"You're too smart a man to stay out of jail, Jim. The penitentiary is full of men who were too clever to go there. You're a queer case, anyhow. If you had buckled down to straight business, with your ability you'd be worth ten million dollars to-day."

He chuckled.

"Look at the fun I'd have missed, though."

But for once she would not joke about their position.

"No," she insisted, "you're looking at it wrong, Jim. You had to leave Boston; you had to leave Baltimore; you had to leave Philadelphia and Washington; you will have to leave this town."

"Never mind, Fanny," he admonished her. "There are fifty towns in the United States as good as this, and they've got coin in every one of them. They're waiting for me to come and get it, and when I have been clear through the list I'll start all over again. There's always a fresh crop of bait-nibblers, and money is being turned out at the mint every day."

"Have it your own way," responded Mrs. Wallingford; "but you will be wise if you take my advice to accumulate some money while you can this time, so that we do not have to take a night train out in the suburbs, as we did when we left Boston."

Mr. Wallingford returned no answer. He opened the cellar door and touched the button that flooded his wine cellar with light, going down himself to hunt among his bottles for the one that would tempt him most. Nevertheless, he did some serious thinking, and, at the next board-of-directors' meeting, he announced that the covering machine was well under way, showing them drawings of a patent application he was about to send off.

It was a hopeful sign—one that restored confidence. He must now organize a selling department and must have a Chicago branch. They listened with respect, even with elation. After all, while this man had deceived them as to his financial standing when he first came among them, he was well posted, for their benefit, upon matters about which they knew nothing. Moreover, there was the great tack! He went to Chicago and appointed a Western sales agent. When he came back he had sold fifteen thousand dollars' worth of his stock through the introductions gained him by this man.

J. Rufus Wallingford was "cleaning up."

Chapter VII

Wherein the Great Tack Inventor Suddenly Decides to Change His Location

"In two weeks we will be ready for the market," Wallingford told inquiring members of the company every two weeks, and, in the meantime, the model for the covering device, in which change after change was made, went on very slowly, while the money went very rapidly. A half dozen of the expensive stamping machines had already been installed, and the treasury was exhausted. The directors began to look worried.

One morning, while Ella Jasper was at her sweeping in the front room, the big red automobile chugged up to the gate and J. Rufus Wallingford got out. He seemed gigantic as he loomed up on the little front porch and filled the doorway.

"Where is your father?" he asked her.

"He is over at Kriegler's," she told him, and directed him how to find the little German saloon where the morning "lunch club" gathered.

Instead of turning, he stood still for a moment and looked at her slowly from head to foot. There was that in his look which made her tremble, which made her flush with shame, and when at last he turned away she sat down in a chair and wept.

At Kriegler's, Wallingford found Jasper and two other stockholders, and he drew them aside to a corner table. For a quarter of an hour he was jovial with them, and once more they felt the magnetic charm of his personality, though each one secretly feared that he had come again for money. He had, but not for himself.

"The treasury is empty," he calmly informed them, during a convenient pause, "and the Corley Machine Company insist on having their bill paid. We owe them two thousand dollars, and it will take five thousand more to complete the covering machine."

"You've been wasting money in the company as you do at home," charged David, flaring up at once with long-suppressed grievances. "You had thirty thousand cash to begin with. I was down to the Corley Machine Company myself, day before yesterday, and I saw a pile of things you had them make and throw away that they told me cost nearly five thousand dollars."

"They didn't show you all of it," returned Wallingford coolly. "There's more. You don't expect to perfect a machine without experimenting, do you? Now you let me alone in this. I know my business, and no man can say that I am not going after the best results in the best way. You fellows figure on expense as if we were conducting a harness shop or a grocery store," he continued, whereat Jasper and Lewis reddened with resentment of the sort for which they could not find voice. "Rent, light, power, and wages eat up money every day," he reminded them, "and every day's delay means that much more waste. We *must* have money to complete this covering machine, and we must have it at once. There is twenty thousand dollars' worth of treasury stock for sale, aside from the hundred thousand held in reserve until we are ready to manufacture. That extra stock must be sold right away! I leave it to you," he concluded, rising. "I'm not a stock salesman," and with that brazen statement he left them.

The statement was particularly brazen because that very morning, after he left these men, he disposed of a five-thousand-dollar block of his own stock and turned the money over to his wife before he returned to the office in the afternoon. Lamb received him in a torrent of impatience.

"I feel like a cheat," he declared. "The Corley people were over here again, and say that they do not know us. They only know our money, and they want some at once or they will not proceed with the machinery."

"I have been doing what I could," replied Wallingford. "I put the matter up to Jasper and Lewis and Nolting this morning. I told them they would have to sell the extra treasury stock."

"You did!" exclaimed Lamb. "Why did you go to them? Why didn't you go out and sell the stock yourself?"

"I am not a stock salesman, my boy."

"You have been active enough in selling your private stock," charged Lamb.

"That's my business," retorted Mr. Wallingford. "I am strictly within my legal rights in disposing of my own stock. It is my property, to do with as I please."

"It is obtaining money under false pretenses, for until you have completed this machinery and made a market for our goods, the stock you have sold is not worth the paper it is printed on. It represents no value whatever."

"It represents as much value as treasury stock or any other stock," retorted Mr. Wallingford. "By the way, make a transfer of this fifty-share certificate to Thomas D. Caldwell."

"Caldwell!" exclaimed Lamb. "Why, he is one of the very men we have been trying to interest in some of this treasury stock. He is of our lodge. Last week we had him almost in the notion, but he backed out."

"When the right man came along he bought," said Wallingford, and laughed.

"This money should have gone into our depleted treasury," Lamb declared hotly. "I refuse to make the transfer."

"I don't care; it's nothing to me. I have the money and I shall turn over this certificate to Mr. Caldwell. When he demands the transfer you will have to make it."

"There ought to be some legal way to compel this sale to be made of treasury stock."

"Possibly," admitted Mr. Wallingford; "but there isn't. You will find, my boy, that everything I do is strictly within the pale of the law. I can go into any court and prove that I am an honest man."

Lamb sprang angrily from his chair.

"You're a thief," he charged, his eyes flashing.

"I'm not drawing any salary for it," replied Wallingford, and Lamb halted his anger with a sickened feeling. The two hundred dollars a month that he had been drawing lay heavily upon his conscience.

"I'm going to ask for a reduction in my pay at the next meeting," he declared. "I cannot take the money with a clear conscience."

"That's up to you," replied Wallingford; "but I want to remind you that unless money is put into this treasury within a day or so the works are stopped," and he went out to climb into his auto, leaving the secretary to some very sober thought.

Well, Lamb reflected, what was there to do? But one thing: raise the money by the sale of treasury stock to replenish their coffers and carry on the work. He wished he could see his friend Jasper. The wish was like sorcery, for no more was it uttered than David and Mr. Lewis came in. They were deeply worried over the condition into which affairs had been allowed to drift, but Lamb had cooled down by this time. He allowed them to hold an indignation meeting for a time, but presently he reminded them that, after all, no matter what else was right or wrong, it would be necessary to raise money—that the machine must be finished. They went over to the shop to look at it. The workmen were testing it by hand when they arrived, and it was working with at least a fair degree of accuracy. The inspection committee did not know that the device was entirely impractical. All that they saw was that it produced the result of a finished tack with a cover of colored cloth glued tightly to its head, and to them its operation was a silent tribute to the genius of the man they had been execrating. They came away encouraged. It was Mr. Lewis who expressed the opinion which was gaining ground with all of them.

"After all," he declared, "we're bound to admit that he's a big man."

The result was precisely what Wallingford had foreseen. These men, to save their company, to save the money they had already invested, raised ten thousand dollars among them. David

Jasper put another five-thousand-dollar mortgage on his property; Mr. Lewis raised two thousand, and Edward Lamb three thousand, and with this money they bought of the extra treasury stock to that amount. J. Rufus Wallingford returned in the morning. The stock lay open for him to sign; there was ten thousand dollars in the treasury, and a check to the Corley Machine Company, already signed by the treasurer, was also awaiting his signature.

The eight thousand dollars that was left went at a surprisingly rapid rate, for, with a love for polished detail, Wallingford had ordered large quantities of shipping cases, stamps to burn the company's device upon them, japanned steel signs in half a dozen colors to go with each shipment, and many other expensive incidentals, besides the experimental work. There were patent applications and a host of other accumulating bills that gave Lamb more worry and perplexity than he had known in all his fifteen years of service with the Dorman Company. The next replenishment was harder. To get the remaining ten thousand dollars in the treasury, the already committed stockholders scraped around among their friends to the remotest acquaintance, and placed scrip no longer in blocks of five thousand, but of ten shares, of five shares, even in driblets of one and two hundred dollars, until they had absorbed all the extra treasury stock; and in that time Wallingford, by appointing a St. Louis agent, had managed to dispose of twenty thousand dollars' worth of his own holdings. He was still "cleaning up," and he brought in his transfer certificates with as much nonchalance as if he were turning in orders for tacks.

Rapid as he now was, however, he did not work quite fast enough. He had still some fifteen thousand dollars' worth of personal stock when, early one morning, a businesslike gentleman stepped into the office where Lamb sat alone at work, and presented his card. It told nothing beyond the mere fact that he was an attorney.

"Well, Mr. Rook, what can I do for you?" asked Lamb pleasantly, though not without apprehension. He wondered what J. Rufus had been doing.

"Are you an officer of the Universal Covered Tack Company?" inquired Mr. Rook.

"The secretary, Edward Lamb."

"Quite so. Mr. Lamb, I represent the Invisible Carpet Tack Company, and I bring you their formal notification to cease using their device," whereupon he delivered to Edward a document. "The company assumes that you are not thoroughly posted as to its article of manufacture, nor as to its patents covering it," he resumed. "They have been on the market three years with this product."

From his pocket he took a fancifully embellished package, and, opening it, he poured two or three tacks into Edward's hand. With dismay the secretary examined one of them. It was an ordinary carpet tack, such as they were about to make, but with a crimson-covered top. Dazed, scarcely knowing what he was doing, he mechanically took his knife from his pocket and cut the cloth from it. The head was roughened for gluing precisely as had been planned for their own!

"Assuming, as I say, that you are not aware of the encroachment," the attorney went on, "the Invisible Company does not desire to let you invite prosecution, but wishes merely to warn you against attempting to put an infringement of their goods on the market. They have plenty of surplus capital, and are prepared to defend their rights with all of it, if necessary. Should you wish to communicate with me or have your counsel do so, my address is on that card," and, leaving the paper of tacks behind him, Mr. Rook left the office.

Without taking the trouble to investigate, Lamb knew instinctively that the lawyer was right, an opinion which later inquiry all too thoroughly corroborated. For three years the Invisible Carpet Tack Company had been supplying precisely the article the Universal Company was then striving to perfect. What there was of that trade they had and would keep, and a sickening realization came to the secretary that it meant a total loss to himself and his friends of practically everything they possessed. The machinery in which their money was invested was special machinery that could be used for no other purpose, and was worth but little more than the price of scrap iron. Every cent that they had invested was gone!

His first thought was for David Jasper. As for himself, he was young yet. He could stand the loss of five thousand. He could go back to Dorman's, take his old position and be the more valuable for his ripened experience, and there was always a chance that a minor partnership might await him there after a few more years; but as for Jasper, his day was run, his sun had set. It was a hard task that confronted the secretary, but he must do it. He called up Kriegler's and asked for David Jasper, and when David came to the telephone he told him what had happened. Over and over, carefully and point by point, he had to explain it, for his friend could not believe, since he could not even comprehend, the blow that had fallen upon him. Suddenly, Lamb found there was no answer to a question that he asked. He called anxiously again and again. He could hear only a confused murmur in the 'phone. There were tramping feet and excited voices, and he gathered that the receiver was left dangling, that no one held it, that no one listened to what he said. Hastily putting on his coat and hat, he locked the office and took a car for the North Side.

J. Rufus Wallingford himself was busy that morning, and in the North Side, too. His huge car whirled past the little frame houses that were covered with mortgages which would never be lifted, and stopped before the home of David Jasper. His jaw was hanging loosely, his big, red face was bloated and splotched, and his small eyes were bloodshot, though they glowed with a somber fire. He had been out all night, and this was one of the few times he had been indiscreet enough to carry his excesses over into the morning; usually he was alcohol proof. At first, blinking and blearing in the sunlight, he had been numb; but an hour's swift ride in the fresh air of the country had revived him, while the ascending sun had started into life again the fumes of the wine that he had drunk, so that all of the evil within him had come uppermost without the restraining caution that belonged to his sober hours. In his abnormal condition the thought had struck him that now was the time for the final coup—that he would dispose of his remaining shares of stock at a reduced valuation and get away, at last, from the irksome tasks that confronted him, from the dilemma that was slowly but surely encompassing him. In pursuance of this idea it had occurred to him, as it never would have done in his sober moments, that David Jasper could still raise money and that he could still be made to do so. Lumbering back to the kitchen door, he knocked upon it, and Ella Jasper opened it. Ella had finished her morning's work hurriedly, for she intended to go downtown shopping, and was already preparing to dress. Her white, rounded arms were bared to the elbow, and her collar was turned in with a "V" at the throat.

The somber glow in Wallingford's eyes leaped into flame, and, without stopping to question her, he pushed his way into the kitchen, closing the door behind him. He lurched suddenly toward her, and, screaming, she flew through the rooms toward the front door. She would have gained the door easily enough, and, in fact, had just reached it, when it opened from the outside, and her father, accompanied by his friend Lewis, came suddenly in. For half an hour, up at Kriegler's, they had been restoring David from the numb half-trance in which he had dropped the receiver of the telephone, and even now he swayed as he walked, so that his condition could scarcely have been told from that of Wallingford when the latter had come through the gate. But there was this difference between them: the strength of Wallingford had been dissipated; that of Jasper had been merely suspended. It was a mental wrench that had rendered him for the moment physically incapable. Now, however, when he saw the author of all his miseries, a hoarse cry of rage burst from him, and before his eyes there suddenly seemed to surge a red mist.

Hale and sturdy still, a young man in physique, despite his sixty years, he sprang like a tiger at the adventurer who had wrecked his prosperity and who now had held his home in contempt.

There was no impact of strained bodies, as when two warriors meet in mortal combat; as when attacker and defender prepare to measure prowess. Instead, the big man, twice the size and possibly twice the lifting and striking strength of David Jasper, having on his side, too, the advantage of being in what should have been the summit of life, shrank back, pale to the lips, suddenly whimpering and crying for mercy. It was only a limp, resistless man of blubber that David Jasper had hurled himself upon, and about whose throat his lean, strong fingers had clutched, the craven gurgling still his appeals for grace. Ordinarily this would have disarmed a man like David Jasper, for disgust alone would have stayed his hand, have turned his wrath to loathing, his righteous vengefulness to nausea; but now he was blind, blood-mad, and he bore the huge spineless lump of moral putty to the floor by the force of his resistless onrush.

"Man!" Lewis shouted in his ear. "Man, there's a law against that sort of thing!"

"Law!" screamed David Jasper. "Law! Did it save me my savings? Let me alone!"

The only result of the interference was to alter the direction of his fury, and now, with his left hand still gripping the throat of his despoiler, his stalwart fist rained down blow after blow upon the hated, fat-jowled face that lay beneath him. It was a brutal thing, and, even as she strove to coax and pull her father away, Ella was compelled to avert her face. The smacking impact of those blows made her turn faint; but, even so, she had wit enough to close the front door, so that morbid curiosity should not look in upon them nor divine her father's madness. Just as she returned to him, however, and even while his fist was upraised for another stroke at that sobbing coward, a spasmodic twitch crossed his face as he gasped deeply for air, and he toppled to the floor, inert by the side of his enemy. Age had told at last. In spite of an abstemious life, the unwonted exertion and the unwonted passion had wreaked their punishment upon him.

It was David's friend Lewis who, with white, set face, helped Wallingford to his feet, and, without a word, scornfully shoved him toward the door, throwing his crumpled hat after him as he passed out. With blood upon his face and two rivulets of tears streaming down across it, J. Rufus Wallingford, the suave, the gentleman for whom all good things of earth were made and provided, ran sobbing, with downstretched quivering lips, to his automobile. The chauffeur jumped out for a moment to get the hat and to dip his kerchief in the stream that he turned on for a moment from the garden hydrant; coming back to the machine, he handed the wet kerchief to his master, then, without instructions, he started home. When his back was thoroughly turned, the chauffeur, despite that he had been well paid and extravagantly tipped during all the months of his fat employment, smiled, and smiled, and kept on smiling, and had all he could do to prevent his shoulders from heaving. He was gratified—was Frank—pleased in his two active senses of justice and of humor.

Just as the automobile turned the corner, Edward Lamb came running down the street from Kriegler's, where he had gone first to find out what had happened, and he met Mr. Lewis going for a doctor. Without stopping to explain, Lewis jerked his thumb in the direction of the house, and Edward, not knocking, dashed in at the door. They had laid David on his bed in the front room, and his daughter bent over him, bathing his brow with camphor. David was speechless, but his eyes were open now, and the gleam of intelligence was in them. As their friend came to the bedside, Ella looked around at him. She tried to gaze up at him unmoved as he stood there so young, so strong, so dependable; she strove to look into his eyes bravely and frankly, but it had been a racking time, in which her strength had been sorely tested, and she swayed slightly toward him. Edward Lamb caught his sister in his arms, but when her head was pillowed for an instant upon his shoulder and the tears burst forth, lo! the miracle happened. The foolish scales fell so that he could see into his own heart, and detect what had lain there unnamed for many a long year—and Ella Jasper was his sister no longer!

"There, there, dear," he soothed her, and smoothed her tresses with his broad, gentle palm.

The touch and the words electrified her. Smiling through her tears, she ventured to look up at him, and he bent and kissed her solemnly and gently upon the lips; then David Jasper, lying there upon his bed, with all his little fortune gone and all his sturdy vigor vanished, saw, and over his wan lips there flickered the trace of a satisfied smile.

Hidden that night in a stateroom on a fast train, J. Rufus Wallingford and his wife, with but such possessions as they could carry in their suit cases and one trunk, whirled eastward.

Rogue: Boston Blackie

Boston Blackie's Code

JACK BOYLE

JACK BOYLE (1881–1928) wrote only one book about Boston Blackie, but the character resonated enough to inspire around ten silent films about him, followed by fourteen "B" movies made by Columbia from 1941 to 1949, all starring Chester Morris, who played him as much a detective as a criminal employing his unique skills, just outside the law, to bring about justice. The success of the films led to two radio series, one starring Morris and the second Richard Kollmar (1944–1950), and a television series (1951–1953) starring Kent Taylor.

In his introduction to *Boston Blackie* (1919), the author wrote about the ex-convict and cracksman, "To the police and the world he is a professional crook, a skilled and daring safe cracker, an incorrigible criminal made doubly dangerous by intellect. . . . But to me, . . . 'Blackie' is something more—a man with more than a spark of the Divine Spirit that lies hidden in the heart of even the worst of men. University graduate, scholar and gentleman, the 'Blackie' I know is a man of many inconsistencies and a strangely twisted code of morals."

Blackie does not consider himself a criminal; he is a combatant who has declared war on society. He is married to a pretty girl named Mary, his "best loved pal and sole confidante," who knows what he does and joins in his exploits.

Curiously, Blackie lives and works in San Francisco; Boston has nothing to do with the book and is never mentioned, just as it never served as a background in any of the films.

"Boston Blackie's Code" was first published in *Boston Blackie* (New York, H. K. Fly, 1919).

BOSTON BLACKIE'S CODE

Jack Boyle

HER THROAT TIGHTENED in an aching pain as her eye fell on the thin gold band that encircled a slender finger. Martin Wilmerding had stooped to kiss that hand and ring on the day it first was placed there.

"Dear little wife," he had said, "that ring is the symbol of a bond that never will be broken by me. Throughout all the years before us, whenever I see it, this hour will return, bringing back all the love and devotion that is in my heart now."

Recollection of the long-forgotten words swept her with a sudden revulsion of feeling, and she sprang to her feet. In that instant she realized for the first time why she had come to love Don Lavalle. It was because in his fresh, ardent, impulsive devotion he was so like the Martin Wilmerding who had kissed her hand and ring with a vow of lifetime fealty that had left her clinging to him in tearful ecstasy.

"Don," she said, "if you really love me, go—now, now."

Lavalle's arms, eagerly outstretched toward her, dropped to his side. It was not the answer he had awaited so confidently. A vague resentment against her tinged his disappointment with new bitterness.

"That is final, is it, Marian?" he asked.

"Yes, yes. Don't make it harder for me. Please go," she cried almost hysterically.

He slipped into his overcoat.

"Perhaps you will tell me why," he suggested with increasing asperity.

"Because of the boy and this," the woman said brokenly, laying a finger on her wedding-ring.

"Nonsense," he cried angrily. "What tie does that ring represent that Martin Wilmerding has not violated a hundred times? You have been faithful to it, we know, even though you admit you care for me. But has he? I have not the pleasure of your husband's acquaintance, but no man ever neglected a wife like you without a reason."

"Go, please, quickly," she pleaded, shivering.

"I will," he said, instinctively avoiding the blunder of combating her decision with argument.

He caught her in his arms, and stooping quickly, kissed her on the lips. She reeled away from him, sobbing.

"Our first and last kiss. Good-by, Marian," he said gently, and left the room.

She followed, clutching at the walls for support as she watched him from the doorway. He adjusted his muffler and caught up his hat without a backward glance, and she pressed her two hands to her lips to choke back a cry. Then as he opened the outer door, the crushing misery of her loneliness swept over her, overpowering self-restraint and resolution.

"Don, oh, Don!" she pleaded, stumbling toward him with outstretched arms.

In a second he was at her side, and she was crying against his breast.

"I can't let you go," she sobbed. "I tried, but I can't. Take me, Don. I will do as you wish."

From his hiding-place Blackie saw them re-enter the room. The woman stopped by the fireplace, drew off her wedding-ring and after holding it a second between shaking fingers, dropped it into the ashes.

"Dead and gone!" she said. "Dead as the love of the man who put it on my finger."

"My ring will replace it," said Lavalle tenderly, but with triumph in his eyes. "Wilmerding will want a divorce. He shall have it, and then you'll wear the wedding-ring of the man who loves you and whom you love—the only ring in the world that shouldn't be broken."

"Don, promise me that you will never leave me alone," she pleaded falteringly. "I don't ever want a chance to think, to reflect, to regret. I only want to be with you—and forget everything else in the world. Promise me."

"Love like mine knows no such word as separation," he answered. "From this hour we will never be apart. Don't fear regrets, Marian. There will be none."

"My boy," she suggested, "he will go with us. Poor little Martin! I wouldn't leave him behind fatherless and motherless."

"Of course not," he agreed. "And now you must get a few necessaries together quickly—just the things you will require on the steamer. You can get all you need when we reach Honolulu, but there is no time for anything now, for under the circumstances it is best that we go aboard the steamer before morning. Can you be ready in an hour?"

"In an hour!" she cried in surprise. "Yes, I can, but—but—how can we go aboard the steamer tonight? We can't, Don. Your passage is booked, but not mine."

"My passage is booked for Don Lavalle and wife," he informed her smilingly.

She turned away her head to hide the flush that colored her face.

"You were so sure as that!" she murmured, with a strangely new sense of disappointment.

"Yes," Lavalle answered, "for I knew love like mine could not fail to win yours. Will you pack a single trunk while I run back to my hotel and get my own things together? I can be back in an hour or less. Will you be ready?"

"Yes, I will be ready," she promised wearily. "I will only take a few things. I want nothing that my—husband ever gave me. I shall only take a few of my own things and the jewels in the safe that were in Mother's collection. They are my own, and they're very valuable, Don. It will not be safe to risk packing them in my baggage. I'll get them now and give them to you to keep until we can leave them in the purser's safe tomorrow. Be very careful of them, Don. They couldn't be replaced for a fortune."

Boston Blackie saw her hurry to the wall—saw the sliding door roll back; with a quickly indrawn breath, he watched the woman fumble nervously with the combination-dial. The safe-door swung open, and she rapidly sorted out a half-dozen jewel-cases and re-closed the safe.

"Here they are, Don," she said, handing the gems to Lavalle. "I have taken only those that came from my own people. And now you must leave me. I must pack, and I can't call the servants under these circumstances. I must get the boy up and ready; and also,"—she hesitated a second and then added—"I must write a note to Mr. Wilmerding telling him what I have done and why."

"Don't mail it until we are at the dock," warned the man. "Where is he—at his club or out of town?"

"He's at the Del Monte Hotel near Monterey—or was," she answered. "The letter won't reach him till tomorrow night."

"And tomorrow night we will be far out of sight of land," Lavalle cried. "That is as it should be. I am glad I never met him, for now I need never do so."

He stuffed the jewel-cases into his overcoat.

"I'll be back in my car in an hour," he warned. "Hurry, Marian, my love. Each minute until I am with you again will be a day."

He caught up his hat and ran down the steps to the street, where his car stood at the curbstone.

As the door closed behind him, Marian Wilmerding sank into a chair and clutched her throat to stifle choking sobs. Intuitive womanly fear of what she was to do paralyzed her. For many minutes she lay shaking convulsively as she tried to overcome the dread that chilled her heart. Then the dismal atmosphere of the masterless home began to oppress her with a sense of wretched loneliness.

She rose and with hard, reckless eyes shining hotly from behind wet lashes, ran upstairs to pack.

As Donald Lavalle threw open the door of his empty car, a man who had slipped behind him around the corner of the Wilmerding residence stepped to his side.

"I'm sorry to have to trouble you for my wife's jewels, Lavalle," he said.

The triumphant smile on Lavalle's face faded, and he shrank back in speechless consternation.

"Your wife's jewels!" he ejaculated, trying to recover from the shock of the utterly unexpected interruption. "You are—"

"Yes, I am Martin Wilmerding; and the happy chance that brought me home tonight also gave me the pleasure of listening from the window-seat of the living-room to your interesting tete-a-tete with my wife."

A gun flashed into Boston Blackie's hand and was jabbed sharply into Lavalle's ribs.

"Give me Marian's jewels," the pseudo-husband cried. "Hand them over before I blow your heart out. That's what I ought to do—and I may, anyway."

Lavalle handed over the cases that contained the Wilmerding collection of gems.

"Now," continued his captor, "I want a word with you."

A gun was thrust so savagely into Lavalle's face that it left a long red bruise.

"I have heard all you said tonight. I know all your plans for stealing away my wife," the inexorable voice continued, "and I've just a word of warning for you. You are dealing with a man, not a woman, from now on; and if you phone, write, telegraph, or ever again communicate in any way with Marian, I'll blow your worthless brains out if I have to follow you round the world to do it. Do you get that, Mr. Don Lavalle?"

"I understand you," said Lavalle helplessly.

Again the gun-muzzle bruised the flesh of his cheek.

"And as a last and kindly warning, Lavalle," Blackie continued, "I suggest that you take extreme precautions to see that you do not miss the *Manchuria* when she sails in the morning; because if you are not on board, you won't live to see another sunset if I have to kill you in your own club. Will you sail or die?"

"I'll sail," said Lavalle.

"Very well. That's about all that requires words between us, I believe. Go, and remember your life is in your own hands. One word of any kind to Marian, and you forfeit it. I don't know why I don't kill you now. I would if it were not for the scandal all this would cause when it came out before the jury that would acquit me. Now go."

Lavalle pressed the button that started the motor as Boston Blackie stepped back from his side.

"I've just one word I want to say to you, Wilmerding," Lavalle began, his foot on the clutch. "It's this: You have only yourself to blame. Don't accuse Marian. You forced her into the situation you discovered this evening, by your neglect of the finest little woman I ever met. I was forced into it by a love I admit frankly. Don't blame Marian for what you yourself have caused. I won't ever see or communicate with her again."

"That's the most decent speech I've heard from your lips tonight," said the man beside the car, dropping his gun back into an outside pocket. "I don't blame her. I've learned many important facts tonight—one of which is that the right place for a man is in his own home with his own wife. I'm going to remember that; and the wedding-ring that was dropped into the ashes tonight is going back on the finger it fits. Good night."

Lavalle without a word threw in the clutch, and his car sped away and was enveloped and hidden by the fog.

Halfway down the block, Boston Blackie came to another car standing at the curb with a well-muffled chauffeur sitting behind the wheel. As he climbed in, the driver, Mary, uttered a low, thankful cry.

"No trouble. I have the jewels here—feel the packages; and a whole lot happened," said Blackie with deep satisfaction. "I've a new story to tell you when we get home, Mary. It's the story of a big burglar named Blackie and a little boy named Martin Wilmerding and a still littler woolly dog named Rex, and a woman who guessed wrong. I think it will interest you. Let's go. I have several things to do before we go home."

When they reached the downtown district, Blackie had Mary drive him to the Palace Hotel. There he sought out the night stenographer.

"Will you take a telegram for me, please," he said. Then he dictated:

"'To Martin Wilmerding, Del Monte Hotel, Monterey:

"'The boy needs you. I do too. Please come.

"'Marian.'"

Though there was a telegraph-office in the hotel, he summoned a messenger-boy from a saloon and sent the message.

Then he went to another hotel and found a second stenographer, to whom he dictated a second message.

"'Mrs. Marian Wilmerding, 3420 Broadway, San Francisco:

"'The packages you gave me were what I really wanted. Thank you and good-by.

"'D. L.'"

Summoning another boy, he sent the second message from a different telegraph office.

"Those telegrams, and how they came to be sent, will be a mystery in the Wilmerding home to the end of time," he thought, deeply contented.

"Let's go home, Mary," he said then, returning to his car and climbing in. "I think I've finished my night's work, and I don't believe I've done such a bad job either."

He was silent for a moment.

"I've given a wife to a husband," he said half to himself. "I've given a father to a child; I've given a mother the right to look her son in the face without shame; and I've played square with the gamest little pal I ever want to know, Martin Wilmerding, Jr., and his dog, Rex. And for my pay I've taken the Wilmerding jewel-collection. I wonder who's the debtor."

Rogue: The Gray Seal

The Gray Seal

FRANK L. PACKARD

A POPULAR WRITER OF ADVENTURE fiction who was born in Canada of American parents, Frank Lucius Packard (1877–1942) made numerous trips to the Far East and elsewhere in search of adventure material, resulting in such popular works as *Two Stolen Idols* (1927), *Shanghai Jim* (1928), and *The Dragon's Jaws* (1937). His greatest success, however, came with the Jimmie Dale series, which sold more than two million copies.

Dale, like his namesake, O. Henry's Jimmy Valentine, is a safecracker who learned the skill from his father's safe-manufacturing business. A wealthy member of one of New York's most exclusive clubs, Dale leads a quadruple life. He is the Gray Seal, the mysterious thief who leaves his mark, a gray seal, at the scene of his crimes; Larry the Bat, a member of the city's underworld; Smarlinghue, a fallen artist; and Jimmie Dale, part of New York's social elite. In the Raffles tradition of so many other cracksmen in literature, Dale's burglaries are illegal, of course, but they are benevolently committed in order to right wrongs and they involve no violence. There are five books in the series, beginning with *The Adventures of Jimmie Dale* (1917) and concluding with *Jimmie Dale and the Missing Hour* (1935). Seven films were made from Packard's novels and short stories, most notably *The Miracle Man* (1932) starring Sylvia Sidney and Chester Morris; the story of another character, a con man, was released as a silent picture in 1919. Several two-reel silent films, starring E. K. Lincoln as Jimmie Dale, were based on short stories published in *The Adventures of Jimmie Dale* (1917).

"The Gray Seal" was originally published in *People's Ideal Fiction Magazine* in 1914; it was first collected in *The Adventures of Jimmie Dale* (New York, George H. Doran, 1917).

THE GRAY SEAL

Frank L. Packard

AMONG NEW YORK'S fashionable and ultra-exclusive clubs, the St. James stood an acknowledged leader—more men, perhaps, cast an envious eye at its portals, of modest and unassuming taste, as they passed by on Fifth Avenue, than they did at any other club upon the long list that the city boasts. True, there were more expensive clubs upon whose membership roll scintillated more stars of New York's social set, but the St. James was distinctive. It guaranteed a man, so to speak—that is, it guaranteed a man to be innately a gentleman. It required money, it is true, to keep up one's membership, but there were many members who were not wealthy, as wealth is measured nowadays—there were many, even, who were pressed sometimes to meet their dues and their house accounts, but the accounts were invariably promptly paid. No man, once in, could ever afford, or ever had the desire, to resign from the St. James Club. Its membership was cosmopolitan; men of every walk in life passed in and out of its doors, professional men and business men, physicians, artists, merchants, authors, engineers, each stamped with the "hall mark" of the St. James, an innate gentleman. To receive a two weeks' out-of-town visitor's card to the St. James was something to speak about, and men from Chicago, St. Louis, or San Francisco spoke of it with a sort of holier-than-thou air to fellow members of their own exclusive clubs, at home again.

Is there any doubt that Jimmie Dale was a gentleman—an *innate* gentleman? Jimmie Dale's father had been a member of the St. James Club, and one of the largest safe manufacturers of the United States, a prosperous, wealthy man, and at Jimmie Dale's birth he had proposed his son's name for membership. It took some time to get into the St. James; there was a long waiting list that neither money, influence, nor pull could alter by so much as one iota. Men proposed their sons' names for membership when they were born as religiously as they entered them upon the city's birth register. At twenty-one Jimmie Dale was elected to membership; and, incidentally, that same year, graduated from Harvard. It was Mr. Dale's desire that his son should enter the business and learn it from the ground up, and Jimmie Dale, for four years thereafter, had followed his father's wishes. Then his father died. Jimmie Dale had leanings toward more artistic pursuits than business. He was credited with sketching a little, writing a little; and he was credited with having received a very snug amount from the combine to which he sold out his safe-manufacturing interests. He lived a bachelor life—his mother had been dead many years—in the house that his father had left him on Riverside Drive, kept a car or two and enough servants to run his menage smoothly, and serve a dinner exquisitely when he felt hospitably inclined.

Could there be any doubt that Jimmie Dale was innately a gentleman?

It was evening, and Jimmie Dale sat at a small table in the corner of the St. James Club dining room. Opposite him sat Herman Carruthers, a young man of his own age, about twenty-six, a leading figure in the newspaper world, whose rise from reporter to managing editor of the morning *News-Argus* within the short space of a few years had been almost meteoric.

They were at coffee and cigars, and Jimmie Dale was leaning back in his chair, his dark eyes fixed interestedly on his guest.

Carruthers, intently engaged in trimming his cigar ash on the edge of the Limoges china saucer of his coffee set, looked up with an abrupt laugh.

"No; I wouldn't care to go on record as being an advocate of crime," he said whimsically; "that would never do. But I don't mind admitting quite privately that it's been a positive regret to me that he has gone."

"Made too good 'copy' to lose, I suppose?" suggested Jimmie Dale quizzically. "Too bad, too, after working up a theatrical name like that for him—the Gray Seal—rather unique! Who stuck that on him—you?"

Carruthers laughed—then, grown serious, leaned toward Jimmie Dale.

"You don't mean to say, Jimmie, that you don't know about that, do you?" he asked incredulously. "Why, up to a year ago the papers were full of him."

"I never read your beastly agony columns," said Jimmie Dale, with a cheery grin.

"Well," said Carruthers, "you must have skipped everything but the stock reports then."

"Granted," said Jimmie Dale. "So go on, Carruthers, and tell me about him—I dare say I may have heard of him, since you are so distressed about it, but my memory isn't good enough to contradict anything you may have to say about the estimable gentleman, so you're safe."

Carruthers reverted to the Limoges saucer and the tip of his cigar.

"He was the most puzzling, bewildering, delightful crook in the annals of crime," said Carruthers reminiscently, after a moment's silence. "Jimmie, he was the king-pin of them all. Clever isn't the word for him, or dare-devil isn't either. I used to think sometimes his motive was more than half for the pure deviltry of it, to laugh at the police and pull the noses of the rest of us that were after him. I used to dream nights about those confounded gray seals of his—that's where he got his name; he left every job he ever did with a little gray paper affair, fashioned diamond-shaped, stuck somewhere where it would be the first thing your eyes would light upon when you reached the scene, and—"

"Don't go so fast," smiled Jimmie Dale. "I don't quite get the connection. What did you have to do with this—er—Gray Seal fellow? Where do you come in?"

"I? I had a good deal to do with him," said Carruthers grimly. "I was a reporter when he first broke loose, and the ambition of my life, after I began really to appreciate what he was, was to get him—and I nearly did, half a dozen times, only—"

"Only you never quite did, eh?" cut in Jimmie Dale slyly. "How near did you get, old man? Come on, now, no bluffing; did the Gray Seal ever even recognise you as a factor in the hare-and-hound game?"

"You're flicking on the raw, Jimmie," Carruthers answered, with a wry grimace. "He knew me, all right, confound him! He favoured me with several sarcastic notes—I'll show 'em to you some day—explaining how I'd fallen down and how I could have got him if I'd done something else." Carruthers's fist came suddenly down on the table. "And I would have got him, too, if he had lived."

"Lived!" ejaculated Jimmie Dale. "He's dead, then?"

"Yes," averted Carruthers; "he's dead."

"H'm!" said Jimmie Dale facetiously. "I hope the size of the wreath you sent was an adequate tribute of your appreciation."

"I never sent any wreath," returned Carruthers, "for the very simple reason that I didn't know where to send it, or when he died. I said he was dead because for over a year now he hasn't lifted a finger."

"Rotten poor evidence, even for a newspaper," commented Jimmie Dale. "Why not give him credit for having, say—reformed?"

Carruthers shook his head. "You don't get it at all, Jimmie," he said earnestly. "The Gray Seal wasn't an ordinary crook—he was a classic. He was an artist, and the art of the thing was in his blood. A man like that could no more stop than he could stop breathing—and live. He's dead; there's nothing to it but that—he's dead. I'd bet a year's salary on it."

"Another good man gone wrong, then," said Jimmie Dale capriciously. "I suppose, though, that at least you discovered the 'woman in the case'?"

Carruthers looked up quickly, a little startled; then laughed shortly.

"What's the matter?" inquired Jimmie Dale.

"Nothing," said Carruthers. "You kind of got me for a moment, that's all. That's the way those infernal notes from the Gray Seal used to end up: 'Find the lady, old chap; and you'll get me.' He had a damned patronising familiarity that would make you squirm."

"Poor old Carruthers!" grinned Jimmie Dale. "You did take it to heart, didn't you?"

"I'd have sold my soul to get him—and so would you, if you had been in my boots," said Carruthers, biting nervously at the end of his cigar.

"And been sorry for it afterward," supplied Jimmie Dale.

"Yes, by Jove, you're right!" admitted Carruthers. "I suppose I should. I actually got to love the fellow—it was the *game*, really, that I wanted to beat."

"Well, and how about this woman? Keep on the straight and narrow path, old man," prodded Jimmie Dale.

"The woman?" Carruthers smiled. "Nothing doing! I don't believe there was one—he wouldn't have been likely to egg the police and reporters on to finding her if there had been, would he? It was a blind, of course. He worked alone, absolutely alone. That's the secret of his success, according to my way of thinking. There was never so much as an indication that he had had an accomplice in anything he ever did."

Jimmie Dale's eyes travelled around the club's homelike, perfectly appointed room. He nodded to a fellow member here and there, then his eyes rested musingly on his guest again.

Carruthers was staring thoughtfully at his coffee cup.

"He was the prince of crooks and the father of originality," announced Carruthers abruptly, following the pause that had ensued. "Half the time there wasn't any more getting at the motive for the curious things he did, than there was getting at the Gray Seal himself."

"Carruthers," said Jimmie Dale, with a quick little nod of approval, "you're positively interesting tonight. But, so far, you've been kind of scouting around the outside edges without getting into the thick of it. Let's have some of your experiences with the Gray Seal in detail; they ought to make ripping fine yarns."

"Not tonight, Jimmie," said Carruthers; "it would take too long." He pulled out his watch mechanically as he spoke, glanced at it—and pushed back his chair. "Great Scott!" he exclaimed. "It's nearly half-past nine. I'd no idea we had lingered so long over dinner. I'll have to hurry; we're a morning paper, you know, Jimmie."

"What! Really! Is it as late as that." Jimmie Dale rose from his chair as Carruthers stood up. "Well, if you must—"

"I must," said Carruthers, with a laugh.

"All right, O slave." Jimmie Dale laughed back—and slipped his hand, a trick of their old college days together, through Carruthers's arm as they left the room.

He accompanied Carruthers downstairs to the door of the club, and saw his guest into a taxi; then he returned inside, sauntered through the billiard room, and from there into one of the cardrooms, where, pressed into a game, he played several rubbers of bridge before going home.

It was, therefore, well on toward midnight when Jimmie Dale arrived at his house on Riverside Drive, and was admitted by an elderly manservant.

"Hello, Jason," said Jimmie Dale pleasantly. "You still up!"

"Yes, sir," replied Jason, who had been valet to Jimmie Dale's father before him. "I was going to bed, sir, at about ten o'clock, when a messenger came with a letter. Begging your pardon, sir, a young lady, and—"

"Jason"—Jimmie Dale flung out the interruption, sudden, quick, imperative—"what did she look like?"

"Why—why, I don't exactly know as I could describe her, sir," stammered Jason, taken aback. "Very ladylike, sir, in her dress and appearance, and what I would call, sir, a beautiful face."

"Hair and eyes—what color?" demanded Jimmie Dale crisply. "Nose, lips, chin—what shape?"

"Why, sir," gasped Jason, staring at his master, "I—I don't rightly know. I wouldn't call her fair or dark, something between. I didn't take particular notice, and it wasn't overlight outside the door."

"It's too bad you weren't a younger man, Jason," commented Jimmie Dale, with a curious tinge of bitterness in his voice. "I'd have given a year's income for your opportunity tonight, Jason."

"Yes, sir," said Jason helplessly.

"Well, go on," prompted Jimmie Dale. "You told her I wasn't home, and she said she knew it, didn't she? And she left the letter that I was on no account to miss receiving when I got back, though there was no need of telephoning me to the club—when I returned would do, but it was imperative that I should have it then—eh?"

"Good Lord, sir!" ejaculated Jason, his jaw dropped, "that's exactly what she did say."

"Jason," said Jimmie Dale grimly, "listen to me. If ever she comes here again, inveigle her in. If you can't inveigle her, use force; capture her, pull her in, do anything—do anything, do you hear? Only don't let her get away from you until I've come."

Jason gazed at his master as though the other had lost his reason.

"Use force, sir?" he repeated weakly—and shook his head. "You—you can't mean that, sir."

"Can't I?" inquired Jimmie Dale, with a mirthless smile. "I mean every word of it, Jason—and if I thought there was the slightest chance of her giving you the opportunity, I'd be more imperative still. As it is—where's the letter?"

"On the table in your studio, sir," said Jason, mechanically.

Jimmie Dale started toward the stairs—then turned and came back to where Jason, still shaking his head heavily, had been gazing anxiously after his master. Jimmie Dale laid his hand on the old man's shoulder.

"Jason," he said kindly, with a swift change of mood, "you've been a long time in the family—first with father, and now with me. You'd do a good deal for me, wouldn't you?"

"I'd do anything in the world for you, Master Jim," said the old man earnestly.

"Well, then, remember this," said Jimmie Dale slowly, looking into the other's eyes, "remember this—keep your mouth shut and your eyes open. It's my fault. I should have warned you long ago, but I never dreamed that she would ever come here herself. There have been times when it was practically a matter of life and death to me to know who that woman is that you saw tonight. That's all, Jason. Now go to bed."

"Master Jim," said the old man simply, "thank you, sir, thank you for trusting me. I've dandled you on my knee when you were a baby, Master Jim. I don't know what it's about, and it isn't for me to ask. I thought, sir, that maybe you were having a little fun with me. But I know now, and you can trust me, Master Jim, if she ever comes again."

"Thank you, Jason," said Jimmie Dale, his hand closing with an appreciative pressure on the other's shoulder "Good-night, Jason."

Upstairs on the first landing, Jimmie Dale opened a door, closed and locked it behind him—and the electric switch clicked under his fingers. A glow fell softly from a cluster of shaded ceiling lights. It was a large room, a very large room, running the entire depth of the house, and the effect of apparent disorder in the arrangement of its appointments seemed to breathe a sense of charm. There were great cozy, deep, leather-covered lounging chairs, a huge, leather-covered davenport, and an easel or two with half-finished sketches upon them; the walls were panelled, the panels of exquisite grain and matching; in the centre of the room stood a flat-topped rosewood desk; upon the floor was a dark, heavy velvet rug; and, perhaps most inviting of all, there was a great, old-fashioned fireplace at one side of the room.

For an instant Jimmie Dale remained quietly by the door, as though listening. Six feet he stood, muscular in every line of his body, like a well-trained athlete with no single ounce of superfluous fat about him—the grace and ease of power in his poise. His strong, clean-shaven face, as the light fell upon it now, was serious—a mood that became him well—the firm lips closed, the dark, reliant eyes a little narrowed, a frown on the broad forehead, the square jaw clamped.

Then abruptly he walked across the room to the desk, picked up an envelope that lay upon it, and, turning again, dropped into the nearest lounging chair.

There had been no doubt in his mind, none to dispel. It was precisely what he had expected from almost the first word Jason had spoken. It was the same handwriting, the same texture of paper, and there was the same old haunting, rare, indefinable fragrance about it. Jimmie Dale's hands turned the envelope now this way, now that, as he looked at it. Wonderful hands were Jimmie Dale's, with long, slim, tapering fingers whose sensitive tips seemed now as though they were striving to decipher the message within.

He laughed suddenly, a little harshly, and tore open the envelope. Five closely written sheets fell into his hand. He read them slowly, critically, read them over again; and then, his eyes on the rug at his feet, he began to tear the paper into minute pieces between his fingers, depositing the pieces, as he tore them, upon the arm of his chair. The five sheets demolished, his fingers dipped into the heap of shreds on the arm of the chair and tore them over and over again, tore them until they were scarcely larger than bits of confetti, tore at them absently and mechanically, his eyes never shifting from the rug at his feet.

Then with a shrug of his shoulders, as though rousing himself to present reality, a curious smile flickering on his lips, he brushed the pieces of paper into one hand, carried them to the empty fireplace, laid them down in a little pile, and set them afire. Lighting a cigarette, he watched them burn until the last glow had gone from the last charred scrap; then he crunched and scattered them with the brass-handled fender brush, and, retracing his steps across the room, flung back a portiere from where it hung before a little alcove, and dropped on his knees in front of a round, squat, barrel-shaped safe—one of his own design and planning in the years when he had been with his father.

His slim, sensitive fingers played for an instant among the knobs and dials that studded the door, guided, it seemed by the sense of touch alone—and the door swung open. Within was another door, with locks and bolts as intricate and massive as the outer one. This, too, he opened; and then from the interior took out a short, thick, rolled-up leather bundle tied together with thongs. He rose from his knees, closed the safe, and drew the portiere across the alcove again. With the bundle under his arm, he glanced sharply around the room, listened intently, then, unlocking the door that gave on the hall, he switched off the lights and went to his dressing room, that was on the same floor. Here, divesting himself quickly of his dinner clothes, he selected a dark tweed suit with loose-fitting sack coat from his wardrobe, and began to put it on.

Dressed, all but his coat and vest, he turned to the leather bundle that he had placed on a table, untied the thongs, and carefully opened it out to its full length—and again that curious, cryptic smile tinged his lips. Rolled the opposite away from that in which it had been tied up, the leather strip made a wide belt that went on somewhat after the fashion of a life preserver, the thongs being used for shoulder straps—a belt that, once on, the vest would hide completely, and, fitting close, left no telltale bulge in the outer garments. It was not an ordinary belt; it was full of stout-sewn, up-right little pockets all the way around, and in the pockets grimly lay an array of fine, blued-steel, highly tempered instruments—a compact, powerful burglar's kit.

The slim, sensitive fingers passed with almost a caressing touch over the vicious little implements, and from one of the pockets extracted a thin, flat metal case. This Jimmie Dale opened, and glanced inside—between sheets of oil paper lay little rows of *gray, adhesive, diamond-shaped seals.*

Jimmie Dale snapped the case shut, returned it to its recess, and from another took out a black silk mask. He held it up to the light for examination.

"Pretty good shape after a year," muttered Jimmie Dale, replacing it.

He put on the belt, then his vest and coat. From the drawer of his dresser he took an automatic revolver and an electric flashlight, slipped them into his pocket, and went softly downstairs. From the hat stand he chose a black slouch hat, pulled it well over his eyes—and left the house.

Jimmie Dale walked down a block, then hailed a bus and mounted to the top. It was late, and he found himself the only passenger. He inserted his dime in the conductor's little resonant-belled cash receiver, and then settled back on the uncomfortable, bumping, cushionless seat.

On rattled the bus; it turned across town, passed the Circle, and headed for Fifth Avenue—but Jimmie Dale, to all appearances, was quite oblivious of its movements.

It was a year since she had written him. *She!* Jimmie Dale did not smile, his lips were pressed hard together. Not a very intimate or personal appellation, that—but he knew her by no other. It *was* a woman, surely—the hand-writing was feminine, the diction eminently so—and had *she* not come herself that night to Jason! He remembered the last letter, apart from the one tonight, that he had received from her. It was a year ago now—and the letter had been hardly more than a note. The police had worked themselves into a frenzy over the Gray Seal, the papers had grown absolutely maudlin—and she had written, in her characteristic way:

Things are a little too warm, aren't they, Jimmie? Let's let them cool for a year.

Since then until tonight he had heard nothing from her. It was a strange compact that he had entered into—so strange that it could never have known, could never know a parallel—unique, dangerous, bizarre, it was all that and more. It had begun really through his connection with his father's business—the business of manufacturing safes that should defy the cleverest criminals—when his brains, turned into that channel, had been pitted against the underworld, against the methods of a thousand different crooks from Maine to California, the report of whose every operation had reached him in the natural course of business, and every one of which he had studied in minutest detail. It had begun through that—but at the bottom of it was his own restless, adventurous spirit.

He had meant to set the police by the ears, using his gray-seal device both as an added barb and that no innocent bystander of the underworld, innocent for once, might be involved—he had meant to laugh at them and puzzle them to the verge of madness, for in the last analysis they would find only an abortive attempt at crime—and he had succeeded. And then he had gone too far—and he had been caught—by *her*. That string of pearls, which, to study whose effect facetiously, he had so idiotically wrapped around his wrist, and which, so ironically, he had been unable to loosen in time and had been forced to carry with him in his sudden, desperate dash to escape from Marx's the big jeweler's, in Maiden Lane, whose strong room he had toyed with one night, had been the lever which, *at first*, she had held over him.

The bus was on Fifth Avenue now, and speeding rapidly down the deserted thoroughfare. Jimmie Dale looked up at the lighted windows of the St. James Club as they went by, smiled whimsically, and shifted in his seat, seeking a more comfortable position.

She had caught him—how he did not know—he had never seen her—did not know who she was, though time and again he had devoted all his energies for months at a stretch to a solution of the mystery. The morning following the Maiden Lane affair, indeed, before he had breakfasted, Jason had brought him the first letter from her. It had started by detailing his every move of the night before—and it had ended with an ultimatum: "The cleverness, the originality of the Gray Seal as a crook lacked but one thing," she had naively written, "and that one thing was that his crookedness required a leading string to guide it into channels that were worthy of his genius." In a word, *she* would plan the coups, and he would act at her dictation and execute them—or else how did twenty years in Sing Sing for that little Maiden Lane affair appeal to him? He was to answer by the next morning, a simple "yes" or "no" in the personal column of the morning *News-Argus*.

A threat to a man like Jimmie Dale was like flaunting a red rag at a bull, and a rage ungovernable had surged upon him. Then cold reason had come. He was caught—there was no question about that—she had taken pains to show him that he need make no mistake there. Innocent enough in his own conscience, as far as actual theft went, for the pearls would in due course be restored in some way to the possession of their owner, he would have been unable to make even his own father, who was alive then, believe in his innocence, let alone a jury of his peers. Dishonour, shame, ignominy, a long prison sentence, stared him in the face, and there was but one alternative—to link hands with this unseen, mysterious accomplice. Well, he could at least temporise, he could always "queer" a game in some specious manner, if he were pushed too far. And so, in the next morning's *News-Argus*, Jimmie Dale had answered "yes." And then had followed those years in which there had been *no* temporising, in which every plan was carried out to the last detail, those years of curious, unaccountable, bewildering affairs that Carruthers had spoken of, one on top of another, that had shaken the old headquarters on Mulberry Street to its foundations, until the Gray Seal had become a name to conjure with. And, yes, it was quite true, he had entered into it all, gone the limit, with an eagerness that was insatiable.

The bus had reached the lower end of Fifth Avenue, passed through Washington Square, and stopped at the end of its run. Jimmie Dale clambered down from the top, threw a pleasant "good-night" to the conductor, and headed briskly down the street before him. A little later he crossed into West Broadway, and his pace slowed to a leisurely stroll.

Here, at the upper end of the street, was a conglomerate business section of rather inferior class, catering doubtless to the poor, foreign element that congregated west of Broadway proper, and to the south of Washington Square. The street was, at first glance, deserted; it was dark and dreary, with stores and lofts on either side. An elevated train roared by overhead, with a thunderous, deafening clamour. Jimmie Dale, on the right-hand side of the street, glanced interestedly at the dark store windows as he went by. And then, a block ahead, on the other side, his eyes rested on an approaching form. As the other reached the corner and paused, and the light from the street lamp glinted on brass buttons, Jimmie Dale's eyes narrowed a little under his slouch hat. The policeman, although nonchalantly swinging a nightstick, appeared to be watching him.

Jimmie Dale went on half a block farther, stooped to the sidewalk to tie his shoe, glanced back over his shoulder—the policeman was not in sight—and slipped like a shadow into the alleyway beside which he had stopped.

It was another Jimmie Dale now—the professional Jimmie Dale. Quick as a cat, active, lithe, he was over a six foot fence in the rear of a building in a flash, and crouched a black shape, against the back door of an unpretentious, unkempt, dirty, secondhand shop that fronted on West Broadway—the last place certainly in all New York that the managing editor of the *News-Argus*, or anyone else, for that matter, would have picked out as the setting for the second debut of the Gray Seal.

From the belt around his waist, Jimmie Dale took the black silk mask, and slipped it on; and from the belt, too, came a little instrument that his deft fingers manipulated in the lock. A curious snipping sound followed. Jimmie Dale put his weight gradually against the door. The door held fast.

"Bolted," said Jimmie Dale to himself.

The sensitive fingers travelled slowly up and down the side of the door, seeming to press and feel for the position of the bolt through an inch of plank—then from the belt came a tiny saw, thin and pointed at the end, that fitted into the little handle drawn from another receptacle in the leather girdle beneath the unbuttoned vest.

Hardly a sound it made as it bit into the door. Half a minute passed—there was the faint fall of a small piece of wood—into the aperture crept the delicate, tapering fingers—came a slight rasping of metal—then the door swung back, the dark shadow that had been Jimmie Dale vanished, and the door closed again.

A round, white beam of light glowed for an instant—and disappeared. A miscellaneous, lumbering collection of junk and odds and ends blocked the entry, leaving no more space than was sufficient for a bare passageway. Jimmie Dale moved cautiously—and once more the flashlight in his hand showed the way for an instant—then darkness again.

The cluttered accumulation of secondhand stuff in the rear gave place to a little more orderly arrangement as he advanced toward the front of the store. Like a huge firefly, the flashlight twinkled, went out, twinkled again, and went out. He passed a sort of crude, partitioned-off apartment that did duty for the establishment's office, a sort of little boxed-in place it was, about in the middle of the floor. Jimmie Dale's light played on it for a moment, but he kept on toward the front door without any pause.

Every movement was quick, sure, accurate, with not a wasted second. It had been barely a minute since he had vaulted the back fence. It was hardly a quarter of a minute more before the cumbersome lock of the front door was unfastened, and the door itself pulled imperceptibly ajar.

He went swiftly back to the office now—and found it even more of a shaky, cheap affair than it had at first appeared; more like a box stall with windows around the top than anything else, the windows doubtless to permit the occupant to overlook the store from the vantage point of the high stool that stood before a long, battered, wobbly desk. There was a door to the place, too, but the door was open and the key was in the lock. The ray of Jimmie Dale's flashlight swept once around the interior—and rested on an antique, ponderous safe.

Under the mask Jimmie Dale's lips parted in a smile that seemed almost apologetic, as he viewed the helpless iron monstrosity that was little more than an insult to a trained cracksman. Then from the belt came the thin metal case and a pair of tweezers. He opened the case, and with the tweezers lifted out one of the gray-coloured, diamond-shaped seals. Holding the seal with the tweezers, he moistened the gummed side with his lips, then laid it on a handkerchief which he took from his pocket, and clapped the handkerchief against the front of the safe, sticking the seal conspicuously into place. Jimmie Dale's insignia bore no finger prints. The microscopes and magnifying glasses at headquarters had many a time regretfully assured the police of that fact.

And now his hands and fingers seemed to work like lightning. Into the soft iron bit a drill—bit in and through—bit in and through again. It was dark, pitch black—and silent. Not a sound, save the quick, dull rasp of the ratchet—like the distant gnawing of a mouse! Jimmie Dale worked fast—another hole went through the face of the old-fashioned safe—and then suddenly he straightened up to listen, every faculty tense, alert, and strained, his body thrown a little forward. *What was that!*

From the alleyway leading from the street without, through which he himself had come, sounded the stealthy crunch of feet. Motionless in the utter darkness, Jimmie Dale listened—there was a scraping noise in the rear—someone was climbing the fence that he had climbed!

In an instant the tools in Jimmie Dale's hands disappeared into their respective pockets beneath his vest—and the sensitive fingers shot to the dial on the safe.

"Too bad," muttered Jimmie Dale plaintively to himself. "I could have made such an artistic job of it—I swear I could have cut Carruthers' profile in the hole in less than no time—to open it like this is really taking the poor old thing at a disadvantage."

He was on his knees now, one ear close to the dial, listening as the tumblers fell, while the delicate fingers spun the knob unerringly—the other ear strained toward the rear of the premises.

Came a footstep—a ray of light—a stumble—nearer—the newcomer was inside the place now, and must have found out that the back door had been tampered with. Nearer came the steps—still nearer—and then the safe door swung open under Jimmie Dale's hand, and Jimmie Dale, that he might not be caught like a rat in a trap, darted from the office—but he had delayed a little too long.

From around the cluttered piles of junk and miscellany swept the light—full on Jimmie Dale. Hesitation for the smallest fraction of a second would have been fatal, but hesitation was something that in all his life Jimmie Dale had never known. Quick as a panther in its spring, he leaped full at the light and the man behind it. The rough voice, in surprised exclamation at the sudden discovery of the quarry, died in a gasp.

There was a crash as the two men met—and the other reeled back before the impact. Onto him Jimmie Dale sprang, and his hands flew for the other's throat. It was an officer in uniform! Jimmie Dale had felt the brass buttons as they locked. In the darkness there was a queer smile on Jimmie Dale's tight lips. It was no doubt *the* officer whom he had passed on the other side of the street.

The other was a smaller man than Jimmie Dale, but powerful for his build—and he fought now with all his strength. This way and that the two men reeled, staggered, swayed, panting and gasping; and then—they had lurched back close to the office door—with a sudden swing, every muscle brought into play for a supreme effort, Jimmie Dale hurled the other from him, sending the man sprawling back to the floor of the office, and in the winking of an eye had slammed shut the door and turned the key.

There was a bull-like roar, the shrill *cheep-cheep-cheep* of the patrolman's whistle, and a shattering crash as the officer flung his body against the partition—then the bark of a revolver shot, the tinkle of breaking glass, as the man fired through the office window—and past Jimmie Dale, speeding now for the front door, a bullet hummed viciously.

Out on the street dashed Jimmie Dale, whipping the mask from his face—and glanced like a hawk around him. For all the racket, the neighbourhood had not yet been aroused—no one was in sight. From just overhead came the rattle of a downtown elevated train. In a hundred-yard sprint, Jimmie Dale raced it a half block to the station, tore up the steps—and a moment later dropped nonchalantly into a seat and pulled an evening newspaper from his pocket.

Jimmie Dale got off at the second station down, crossed the street, mounted the steps of the elevated again, and took the next train uptown. His movements appeared to be somewhat erratic—he alighted at the station next above the one by which he had made his escape. Looking down the street it was too dark to see much of anything, but a confused noise as of a gathering crowd reached him from what was about the location of the secondhand store. He listened appreciatively for a moment.

"Isn't it a perfectly lovely night?" said Jimmie Dale amiably to himself. "And to think of that cop running away with the idea that I didn't see him when he hid in a doorway after I passed the corner! Well, well, strange—isn't it?"

With another glance down the street, a whimsical lift of his shoulders, he headed west into the dilapidated tenement quarter that huddled for a handful of blocks near by, just south of Washington Square. It was a little after one o'clock in the morning now and the pedestrians were casual. Jimmie Dale read the street signs on the corners as he went along, turned abruptly into an intersecting street, counted the tenements from the corner as he passed, and—for the eye of any one who might be watching—opened the street door of one of them quite as though he were accustomed and had a perfect right to do so, and went inside.

It was murky and dark within; hot, unhealthy, with lingering smells of garlic and stale cooking. He groped for the stairs and started up. He climbed one flight, then another—and one more to the top. Here, treading softly, he made an examination of the landing with a view, evidently, to obtaining an idea of the location and the number of doors that opened off from it.

His selection fell on the third door from the head of the stairs—there were four all told, two apartments of two rooms each. He paused for an instant to adjust the black silk mask, tried the door quietly, found it unlocked, opened it with a sudden, quick, brisk movement—and, stepping in side, leaned with his back against it.

"Good-morning," said Jimmie Dale pleasantly.

It was a squalid place, a miserable hole, in which a single flickering, yellow gas jet gave light. It was almost bare of furniture; there was nothing but a couple of cheap chairs, a rickety table—unpawnable. A boy, he was hardly more than that, perhaps twenty-two, from a posture in which he was huddled across the table with head buried in out-flung arms, sprang with a startled cry to his feet.

"Good-morning," said Jimmie Dale again. "Your name's Hagan, Bert Hagan—isn't it? And you work for Isaac Brolsky in the secondhand shop over on West Broadway—don't you?"

The boy's lips quivered, and the gaunt, hollow, half-starved face, white, ashen-white now, was pitiful.

"I—I guess you got me," he faltered "I—I suppose you're a plain-clothes man, though I never knew dicks wore masks."

"They don't generally," said Jimmie Dale coolly. "It's a fad of mine—Bert Hagan."

The lad, hanging to the table, turned his head away for a moment—and there was silence.

Presently Hagan spoke again. "I'll go," he said numbly. "I won't make any trouble. Would—would you mind not speaking loud? I—I wouldn't like her to know."

"Her?" said Jimmie Dale softly.

The boy tiptoed across the room, opened a connecting door a little, peered inside, opened it a little wider—and looked over his shoulder at Jimmie Dale.

Jimmie Dale crossed to the boy, looked inside the other room—and his lip twitched queerly, as the sight sent a quick, hurt throb through his heart. A young woman, younger than the boy, lay on a tumble-down bed, a rag of clothing over her—her face with a deathlike pallor upon it, as she lay in what appeared to be a stupor. She was ill, critically ill; it needed no trained eye to discern a fact all too apparent to the most casual observer. The squalor, the glaring poverty here, was even more pitifully in evidence than in the other room—only here upon a chair beside the bed was a cluster of medicine bottles and a little heap of fruit.

Jimmie Dale drew back silently as the boy closed the door.

Hagan walked to the table and picked up his hat.

"I'm—I'm ready," he said brokenly. "Let's go."

"Just a minute," said Jimmie Dale. "Tell us about it."

"'Twon't take long," said Hagan, trying to smile. "She's my wife. The sickness took all we had. I—I kinder got behind in the rent and things. They were going to fire us out of here—tomorrow. And there wasn't any money for the medicine, and—and the things she had to have. Maybe you wouldn't have done it—but I did. I couldn't see her dying there for the want of something a little money'd buy—and—and I couldn't"—he caught his voice in a little sob—"I couldn't see her thrown out on the street like that."

"And so," said Jimmie Dale, "instead of putting old Isaac's cash in the safe this evening when you locked up, you put it in your pocket instead—eh? Didn't you know you'd get caught?"

"What did it matter?" said the boy. He was twirling his misshappen hat between his fingers. "I knew they'd know it was me in the morning when old Isaac found it gone, because there wasn't anybody else to do it. But I paid the rent for four months ahead tonight, and I fixed it so's she'd have medicine and things to eat. I was going to beat it before daylight myself—I"—he brushed his hand hurriedly across his cheek—"I didn't want to go—to leave her till I had to."

"Well, say"—there was wonderment in Jimmie Dale's tones, and his English lapsed into ungrammatical, reassuring vernacular—"ain't that queer! Say, I'm no detective. Gee, kid, did you think I was? Say, listen to this! I cracked old Isaac's safe half an hour ago—and I guess there won't be any idea going around that you got the money and I pulled a lemon. Say, I ain't superstitious, but it looks like luck meant you to have another chance, don't it?"

The hat dropped from Hagan's hands to the floor, and he swayed a little.

"You—you ain't a dick!" he stammered. "Then how'd you know about me and my name when you found the safe empty? Who told you?"

A wry grimace spread suddenly over Jimmie Dale's face beneath the mask, and he swallowed hard. Jimmie Dale would have given a good deal to have been able to answer that question himself.

"Oh, that!" said Jimmie Dale. "That's easy—I knew you worked there. Say, it's the limit, ain't it? Talk about your luck being in, why all you've got to do is to sit tight and keep your mouth shut, and you're safe as a church. Only say, what are you going to do about the money, now you've got a four months' start and are kind of landed on your feet?"

"Do?" said the boy. "I'll pay it back, little by little. I meant to. I ain't no—" He stopped abruptly.

"Crook," supplied Jimmie Dale pleasantly. "Spit it right out, kid; you won't hurt my feelings none. Well, I'll tell you—you're talking the way I like to hear you—you pay that back, slide it in without his knowing it, a bit at a time, whenever you can, and you'll never hear a yip out of me; but if you don't, why it kind of looks as though I have a right to come down your street and get my share or know the reason why—eh?"

"Then you never get any share," said Hagan, with a catch in his voice. "I pay it back as fast as I can."

"Sure," said Jimmie Dale. "That's right—

that's what I said. Well, so long—Hagan." And Jimmie Dale had opened the door and slipped outside.

An hour later, in his dressing room in his house on Riverside Drive, Jimmie Dale was removing his coat as the telephone, a hand instrument on the table, rang. Jimmie Dale glanced at it—and leisurely proceeded to remove his vest. Again the telephone rang. Jimmie Dale took off his curious, pocketed leather belt—as the telephone repeated its summons. He picked out the little drill he had used a short while before, and inspected it critically—feeling its point with his thumb, as one might feel a razor's blade. Again the telephone rang insistently. He reached languidly for the receiver, took it off its hook, and held it to his ear.

"Hello!" said Jimmie Dale, with a sleepy yawn. "Hello! Hello! Why the deuce don't you yank a man out of bed at two o'clock in the morning and have done with it, and—eh? Oh, that you, Carruthers?"

"Yes," came Carruthers's voice excitedly. "Jimmie, listen—listen! The Gray Seal's come to life! He's just pulled a break on West Broadway!"

"Good Lord!" gasped Jimmie Dale. "You don't say!"

Villain: Lingo Dan

The Dignity of Honest Labor

PERCIVAL POLLARD

LINGO DAN (1903), one of the rarest books in the mystery genre with no copy catalogued or auctioned in a half-century, is a collection of stories about an extremely unusual fictional character. Receiving his sobriquet because of the flowery language he uses, he is a hobo, thief, con man, and a shockingly cold-blooded murderer—extremely unusual for nineteenth-century crooks. Although Lingo Dan also proves himself to be a patriotic American with a deep streak of sentimentality, he remains an unpleasant fellow who nonetheless has a significant position in the history of the mystery story: the year of the first story and the subsequent book makes him the first serial criminal in American literature.

Joseph Percival Pollard (1869–1911) was an important literary critic in his day, befriended both by Ambrose Bierce and H. L. Mencken. He wrote twelve books before his early death at the age of forty-two, but *Lingo Dan* was his only mystery. He was best known for his works of literary criticism, most successfully with *Their Day in Court* (1909).

In his scholarly work *The Detective Short Story: A Bibliography* (1942), Ellery Queen (a collector and scholar of mystery fiction as well as a bestselling novelist) quotes from an inscribed copy of the book in which Pollard wrote: "I expect for [Lingo Dan] neither the success of Sherlock Holmes, Raffles, etc., nor yet the immunity from comparison with those gentlemen. Yet it is at least one thing the others are not: American." Today, no one compares his character to those he cites, as Lingo Dan is an utterly forgotten figure in the literature of roguery.

"The Dignity of Honest Labor" was first published in book form in *Lingo Dan* (Washington, D.C., Neale Publishing Co., 1903).

THE DIGNITY OF HONEST LABOR

Percival Pollard

TO THE SOUND of the rattling husks being pulled from the yellow maize came the voice of Lingo Dan.

"It is passing wonderful," he said, "what a fascination your industry has for me, Billy! There is something so rare, so unusual, so bizarre, about it! Indeed, this past month or so—how quaint our lives have been. We have been engaged in honest toil——"

"You, eh?" Billy grunted, and stuffed some husks into a sack so viciously that the sharp edges of the dry leaves cut his hand like a knife. "Yes, you have—like Hell!" He wiped the scarred hand across his hair.

"My good Billy, you forget the ethic basis of the division of labor. It is true that yours has been of the hands—here is a handkerchief, Billy, to bind over that somewhat unsightly cut; a kerchief washed by Miss Mollie's own fair hands, I dare say—while mine has been of the head. I have been planning our deliverance, Billy. Do you think these elaborations come to me of their own accord? You judge me too highly." He stretched his legs out at full length, and, his hands clasped behind his head, stared out through a chink of the log-built crib. He sighed. From without came the monotonous buzzing of the cotton gin. "Why is it, Billy," he went on, "that we can not find contentment in these peaceful ways of life? Think, Billy—to watch the white fluffs of cotton blossoming on one's own land; to hear the wind whispering in the aisles of one's own cornfield; to feel that just so much of fair fresh air and sunshine was one's own—were it not pleasant?—I beg your pardon? Oh—really, Billy, your language is scarce academic. But you are right—we hardly seem the proper figures for that setting. We lack some atom of the elemental human; we are the victims of our versatilities." For a time there was no sound save that of the savage ripping with which Billy denuded the ears of corn. Then the other spoke again, in a voice from which the abstract and the dreamy was suddenly absent. "You are sure we were not noticed that Sunday?"

"Sure!" said Billy.

"And that you have your part of the business well in mind?"

"Dead easy."

"Then it becomes merely a question as to how soon that coquette, Opportunity, chooses to beckon to us. Hush a moment, Billy! Yes, our friend, the Deacon, approaches."

Billy handed over a sack that was half full of

the corn shucks. When the farmer whose hired men these two were opened the door of the crib and called them to dinner, Lingo Dan was husking the one ear of corn that had engaged his attention that day.

When his daughter Mollie was setting the table for supper that evening, Sam Travis, familiar to the fellow members of his church as Deacon Travis, came in from the kitchen chuckling to himself. "Been a'figuring things out," he said, "and dinged if the two of 'em's done a speck more'n one man's work o' shucking that there corn! One man's work—and we feeds the two of 'em. But the fact is I sort er reckin listening to the tall cuss is as good as reading a magazine. Ever know sech a gift o' gab, Mollie?"

"No. But he never learnt it on a farm!"

"That's right, too, Moll; but I ain't a'going to make no man's past lead me to the sin of curiosity, Moll—leastwise not in Texas. Ah—h! Wish your mother was alive to smell that cornbread o' yours, Moll!"

Molly smiled with pleasure. But as the others came in, and while she moved about serving the dishes, her face took on lines of pain. Presently her father noticed that she was making the merest pretence of eating. "Ain't you well, Moll?" he asked.

"One o' my headaches, dad," was the girl's answer.

"Too bad! An' tomorrow Sunday! The first Sunday 'the month; an' me not there to pass the plate!" Deacon Travis passed his cup for more tea, and sighed sadly.

"I'm sorry, dad. Can't you go without me?"

"No—sir! Not much! Got to see to your having camphor on your forehead right along."

There was a coughing noise from Lingo Dan. "If you really find yourself unable to go, would it be asking too much, might the buggy be allowed to take my companion and myself to holy worship? It is—not often," he paused and smiled wistfully at the Deacon, "that we have a chance."

Deacon Travis looked pleased. "Sure thing, you can have the team. Never thought you was given to churchgoing; might 'er asked you before. Sure you know the way?"

"Perfectly; it is very kind of you."

When they were alone with each other once more, Deacon Travis remarked to his daughter that it was perhaps a sort of special Providence that had given her a headache, so that two thirsty souls might have an opportunity to drink of the spiritual waters of the Word. Which philosophic point of view, however, was not completely cheering to Miss Mollie herself.

The little frame church, where the farmers of that region are wont to congregate every Sunday, stands on a slight lift of the prairie, where a narrow cross road leaves the North Road for the mountains. Nowhere else in the world would these hills be termed mountains; but here, contrasting vividly enough with the monotonous level of the prairie, they seem somehow to merit the title easily enough. Cedar-clad, these mountains make the horizon, at one point of the compass at least, green and fresh and picturesque. In the hot days, that are the rule in Texas, the shade of these cedars becomes a veritable oasis for travelers whose road takes them in that direction.

And it may be possible that many of the good farm folk being driven churchward that bright, torrid Sunday morning, would have preferred, in their heart of hearts, the cool of the cedar mountains to the hot church benches. Still, if such thoughts came to them while the white dust skurried with and behind their wheels, they put them away again as speedily as possible. They felt that they had every right to be proud of having a church at all. There were communities, in the same county, and not such a vast distance away, either, that were as godless as they were unprosperous. To feel that their own congregation was one made up of well-to-do folk, and to drive through the fields that showed such bountiful harvests was to be glad, also, that they had had the grace, years ago, to call to them a clergyman from the East, to build a church, to support it in every fitting, and, frequently, many a magnificent way. Good fortune, or good judgment, had ordained that the Rev. Martin Dawson prove himself exactly the best pastor in the world for that community. He was an oldish man, not too much the doctrinarian, a pleasant companion personally, and popular not only with the members of his congregation, but with the Eastern folk he had left when coming to Texas. His popularity, and the pleasant manner of his life reacted happily upon his congregation in another direction. After his old college chum, the Rev. James Langan, had paid him a visit some years ago, such glowing reports had been taken back East that thereafter this little Texas farm community had constantly the advantage of hearing many really admirable preachers in their little church. When their good pastor arose as the services opened, and introduced to them his "brother in the Lord" from say Hartford, and there followed a sermon as eloquent as occurs in the towns only where the pew rents are based on such incomes as millionaires have, these good people were no longer surprised. They listened, with interest and gratitude, and thanked fortune once more for giving them such a pastor. As for the visiting clergymen, such visits to their old friend Dawson were by way of holiday. That none of these visitors were the kind that might attempt any discourse tinctured with indoor rather than outdoor theology, was a point rigorously watched by Mr. Dawson.

The Rev. Martin Dawson was a bachelor. Alone with an old servant, who now acted as sexton, verger, and church warden rolled into one, he lived in a small house some two miles from the church, on the road that eventually passed Sam Travis's farm. Every Sunday morning these two old people betook themselves with surplice and sermon into the little road wagon, and allowed a lazy, easy-going grey mare to convey them leisurely to church. Then followed the duties of the day; the minister prayed and preached, his servant took up the collection. There were some moments in which the minister, his surplice laid aside, chatted cheerily with the members of his congregation, refusing, perhaps, many an invitation to dinner, and then home again, behind the grey mare to convey them leisurely to church. Frequently, to be sure, there was the clerical visitor also; and once or twice it had happened that the visitor had come alone with the old servant, the Rev. Dawson being heir to a gout that, at times, took him quite off his feet.

As the many vehicles of various shapes and capacities came bowling along the dusty roads that approached the church from the different points of the compass, one young farmer with sharper eyes than most people have, identified a buggy that was coming at right angles to his own.

"There's the Travis rig," he remarked to his wife.

"Mollie's been promising me a recipe for putting up Alexandrias; I hope to goodness she ain't forgot it today."

"I reckon," he went on, "you'll have to wait for that recipe. It's the Travis rig, but it ain't the folks. Looks more like some of parson's friends."

"Shaw—I'm sorry! One of Moll's headaches, I guess." And they drove on, joggedly.

In the Travis buggy, Lingo Dan was discoursing on the curious inconsistencies in human nature.

"A dear old soul, that parson! Eh, Billy—a dear old soul! But only human, after all. No strength of spiritual warp can break the bonds imposed by such coarse creature things as—as ourselves. I hardly think it likely he can break that rope unaided. And as for the partner of the righteous household, I believe you corded him up pretty securely, didn't you, Billy? Yes, I think we may be sure they are safely fettered for a while. Quite allegorical, this act of ours, Billy; do you not note the allegory? The fetters of the flesh—fetters of the flesh; if your education, Billy, had not been shamefully neglected, you would find many a Sunday school memory in that dear old phrase: The fetters of the flesh. In a measure I regret that force was necessary. A crude thing, after all, is force. If one had been able to obtain their promises, their holy oaths—how much finer, how much more of the age of Honor! But that—that was impossible. A dear old soul! But short in his breath—very short!

And then the inconsistency of him—did you note that? While he thought we merely came for common robbery, he seemed to feel little, save, perhaps regret for our misguided ways; but the instant I laid hands on his sermon and his surplice—Olympus, that was a mighty rage, eh, Billy! I was glad I had him bound by that time; had he been free just then, his rage—there is no telling what the dear old soul might not have done. A wonderfully inconsistent thing, human nature! Faceted like the brilliant; as full of surprises as—the weather!"

During all this monologue, jerked out with sudden silences, and laughings, at intervals, Billy sat stolidly binding a handkerchief about one hand.

"Bit me," he growled, "old beast!"

"Hush, Billy! A sexton—your late antagonist—a sexton, a man whose solemn office it is to aid materially the Last, the Great Divorce—the soul's decree of separation from the body—to call such a man a—a beast—oh, Billy!"

As they neared the church their eyes caught gladly the sight of the numerous vehicles standing about the fence, and approaching on the different highways.

"It is a case of 'Auspice Deo,'" Lingo Dan went on. "Eh, Billy? Nil desperandum, auspice Deo! Observe what a pleasant congregation we are to have. Glorious, glorious! You have the key to the vestry?"

"Right here," Billy tapped his pocket.

"And for my part—how delightful are the ways and means of modern civilization sometimes—the dear old soul's sermon is typewritten! Although," and here the speaker lowered his voice, as if unwilling to parade whatever had the least glimmer of vanity about it, "I dare say I should not be so utterly bad at an impromptu. I have known the time—in days that are now dead—"

"And buried!" This came from Billy like a fierce reproach. It was evident that gropings into the past had no more charms for him.

Lingo Dan looked slightly hurt. "True—most true. How close to the mark you do shoot, Billy—never a divergence, never a stroll into the abstract—ah, sometimes I believe I envy you, Billy."

But Billy only grunted. It was the grunt of unbelief.

In a few moments they had reached the vestry door. Billy hitched a rope from the bridle to the fence. Then he opened the vestry door, and the two of them stepped in. Billy noted with dull astonishment that his partner slipped into the surplice with apparent knowledge of its technique. Then the organ began the services of the day.

When the music ceased, a tall, pale figure arose beside the desk that faced the altar railings.

"Dearly beloved brethren," said the strange clergyman, "my portion in these services was merely to have been the sermon, but sudden indisposition coming to your good pastor, Mr. Dawson, I am here to make what shift I can as substitute."

There was a pause. The speaker's eyes swept about the church. Every seat was taken. But in every face he saw nothing save kind encouragement. Far in the last row, deep in shadows, loomed the face of him that was called Billy. All this the clergyman saw in a flash. Then he began, in the conventional voice of the preacher:

"Dearly beloved brethren, the Scripture moveth us in sundry places—" and thereafter the services continued drowsily and perfunctorily. There was nothing to show that the official of the occasion was not versed and practiced in these devotional functions. At times the congregation caught a note of fervor, of loving emphasis placed on some phrase that was more than usually freighted with the poetry that informs the Prayer book; in the mere elocution of the man they scented a sermon that would make them forget even the stifling heat.

From outside came the occasional whinnying of a horse, and the pawing of impatient feet. Beyond that, only the heat, quivering against the fences in visible form.

On the back bench Billy was exerting the last vestiges of his self-control to keep from snoring.

When the general "Amen" had closed the rehearsal of the Creed, the preacher moved to the pulpit. With bowed head he stood silent for some seconds. Then he folded his sermon to his liking. As he read the text he flushed for a space, but his voice never faltered. It was from the gospel of St. Matthew, and it read:

"Beware of false prophets, which come to you in sheep's clothing."

It was a pity that the Rev. Dawson could not have heard the eloquent delivery his sermon was given by his locum tenens. Use blunts the faculties somewhat, and it is certain that had its actual author preached this sermon it had not seemed half so powerful. As it was, each word, each phrase had behind it all the nervous vigor of a musical voice, a mind at high tension.

As he turned to the final page of the sermon an agonizing suspicion crossed the ear and the mind of the preacher. Was that a snore from the back bench?

If even the faintest chance of such a thing existed, it was necessary to grasp measures of force. Into the mere reading of another man's words it was possible to infuse but a limited amount of enthusiasm, after all.

Ostentatiously he closed the pamphlet from which he had been delivering his sermon. With eyes roving soulfully about the faces before him, he brought his voice to its most musical, gripping pitch.

"And so, my brethren," he exhorted, "sixthly and lastly, we approach the lesson to be learned. What is so rampant in the world today, as this hypocrisy, this wearing of the mask, the borrowed plume that Matthew warned against in the words of the text. The face is given man ofttimes but to hide the soul. New doctrines come and go; men prate of new religion and new science; the traders on the world's trend-to-believe make bargains in the market place. And who, of us here, dare say that some time in his life he has not played the hypocrite? Have all of us worn naught save these same garments, material and spiritual, that we stand in now? It is the one besetting sin; the cancer that is eating wholesome candor from the world. Here, in the open air, under the clear sky, you think the wearing of the mask can be but rarely. You err; the mask is worn, in city or in country. Look to your hearts and find the answer there. Look—" His voice roared up against the rafters, so that there was a quick shuffling heard from the rear bench, and the preacher's straining eyes caught the shine of Billy's amazement, and to himself he actually thanked God! "Look—deep in to your hearts!"

With something like a sob in his breath, the preacher turned his face to the East. "And now to the Father" muttered his voice. With the suspense over, the ring of eloquence was no longer necessary.

Then he turned to the table, looking apparently heavenwards, actually at Billy. As the latter lumbered up the aisle, the preacher droned in his monotone, standing with his hands folded in front of him.

"Let your light so shine before men, that they may see your good works."

With these well-known texts, he proceeded the while Billy passed the wooden plate nervously up and down the pews. The envelopes containing the contributions fell with a shuffling sound of paper upon paper. There were no casuals in this congregation; the actual sight of coin was hardly ever obtruded.

At last the collection was over. The plate, heaped up with white riches, stood beside the railing of the chancel. The preacher raced to the benediction.

After that, with a change in his voice, he came forward a step, and said:

"If the congregation will wait a few moments, I shall be glad to meet the individual members of it personally."

Those who watched him closely always declared that he had the most winning smile they had ever seen.

Then, with a quick snatch of the collection plate he hurried into the vestry. Into a corner went the surplice.

"Thank the Lord," he whispered to himself, "that this stuff's all folded in paper. Makes less noise." He slipped the money into a handkerchief and opened the outer door cautiously.

Another second or two and the Travis buggy was whirling over the highway to the mountains, a cloud of dust concealing it.

In the church the congregation awaited their meeting with one of the most eloquent preachers they had heard in many a day.

Several hours later, after a forced march through cedar brush that hid all tracks impenetrably, Lingo Dan and Billy stopped beside a mountain spring.

Spreading the contribution envelopes out on the cool rocks in the shadow of the hill that held the spring, Lingo Dan proceeded to open them, to count the gains from their adventure.

Billy got up with an oath.

Lingo Dan lay back on his back and roared with laughter. When he had breath enough, he said: "But Billy, do you count the sensation as nothing?"

Every contribution was a check.

Rogue: Napoleon Prince

The Eyes of the Countess Gerda

MAY EDGINTON

A NAME THAT RARELY RESONATES for readers of mystery fiction is May Edginton, the nom de plume of May Helen Marion Edginton Bailey (1883–1957), though she was a prolific writer of romances and has a connection to the American musical theater of perhaps greater import.

As H. M. Edginton, she wrote a novel, *Oh! James!* (1914), which inspired the 1919 stage play *My Lady Friends*, which lives in infamy in Boston because the owner of the Boston Red Sox sold Babe Ruth to the New York Yankees to finance it. The play in turn was the basis for the musical *No, No, Nanette* (1924), which, continuing to recycle the story, was adapted for film in 1930 and 1940 before again becoming a hit when it was revived on Broadway in 1971.

Among the many films based on her stories, novels, and plays were *The Prude's Fall* (1924), a silent film written by Alfred Hitchcock, who also was the assistant director; *Secrets* (1933), starring Mary Pickford, based on Edginton's play of the same title; and *Adventure in Manhattan* (1936), starring Jean Arthur, based on her story "Purple and Fine Linen."

The central character in *The Adventures of Napoleon Prince* (1912) has help, in the best tradition of Raffles, with his sidekick, Bunny, and, on the other side of the legal fence, Sherlock Holmes with his Watson. Aiding Prince in his nefarious schemes are his beautiful and devoted Gerda, described as his sister, and Dapper, his discreet and faithful servant.

"The Eyes of the Countess Gerda" was originally published in *The Adventures of Napoleon Prince* (New York, Cassell, 1912).

THE EYES OF THE COUNTESS GERDA

May Edginton

AMONG THE NEW TENANTS in the new block of very desirable flats not far from Victoria were a lady, young, charming and alone; a semi-paralytic man of any age from thirty to forty, accompanied by a pretty sister; and a tall, bronzed young man, who had apparently nothing more serious to do than to organise beautifully his bachelor housekeeping. The first named lady had been installed in Flat 24 for a month when the invalid and his sister moved into No. 20 of the flats below; the bronzed young man entered into possession of No. 23 a few days after the occupation of No. 20.

The young man, whose name, as testified by the indicator in the vestibule, was Mr. John Luck, had not been there many days before he made the acquaintance of the invalid and his sister. It was begun in quite an accidental fashion, as the hall porters saw—the trio most obviously never having met before—and it progressed casually and as politeness demanded, beneath the eyes of the same porters and a lift attendant of inquiring mind—just a "Good-morning, again!" or "Fine weather!" or "Beastly day!" and the like. A few days of these vestibule meetings resulted in the discussion of a camera which the invalid man was taking into the Green Park for the purpose of snapshotting winter scenes. It appeared Mr. John Luck knew a good deal of that make of camera; the invalid—Mr. Napoleon Prince, as testified by the indicator—had not used it before.

"You were just going out?" said the little paralytic pleasantly. "Only for a walk? Walk our way, won't you, for a few minutes, and go on telling me about this machine?"

So that Mr. John Luck walked out by the chair of Mr. Napoleon Prince, which he wheeled himself, and by the side of the very pretty girl, his sister. All of which was seen and observed by the porters and the lift-man.

"If people of our profession only realised, Johnnie," the little man in the chair observed as they passed out of the quadrangle, "what a deal depends on these seeming trivialities, there would be more genius rewarded, and fewer police triumphs."

"We have nothing definite in view, Nap?" the young man hazarded.

"No, no!" Napoleon replied. "Why should we? We are gourmets, not gourmands. We have enough for the present, *n'est-ce pas, mes enfants?*"

"Let's be good for a while, Nap," said the girl.

"You hear that, Luck," said Napoleon, smiling. "Mary tells us to be good. We will settle down for a few months, and be beneficent citizens, then. We'll do the theatres, and you shall take Mary to the races, and we will make the acquaintance of our neighbours, and entertain them innocently."

"Hurrah!" cried Mary. She wore a high-waisted coat of clinging lines, furs, and a wide hat, and she looked exquisite.

Johnnie Luck walked with freer step.

"Good!" he agreed. "Very good!"

"I believe," said Napoleon, glancing at them, one on either side of him, as he wheeled along past Buckingham Palace, "that you are both wretchedly respectable at bottom." They turned into the Green Park. "Leave me to run about and take my photographs, and philosophise on the profits of respectability, while you two take the brisk exercise that is good for you, and philosophise on—anything you like."

There was the faintest trace of a smile—a little grim or wistful—on his large pale face as he steered away from them. They walked about the Park for an hour, seeing nobody but each other, hearing nothing but their own low-toned talk, and forgetting entirely the size of the world—theirs being populated by two—until running wheels beside them brought them back to realisation of Napoleon.

"I am sorry," said he, "but I have used all my plates, and want my lunch. Johnnie, our acquaintance has ripened sufficiently, I imagine, for me to ask you to share the lunch."

The trio went home, and lunched together in the Princes' dining-room. After the meal:

"Mary is going to shop," said Napoleon. "She is going to the Stores, because it is so respectable. But you, Johnnie—"

Johnnie Luck looked hopefully at Mary, who, in the sweetest of frocks *à la Joséphine*, was standing to warm one small slippered foot at the fire.

"Don't take him with you, Mary," said Napoleon whimsically. "I want someone to talk to." Adding: "And you don't know him well enough, either."

She laughed, told Luck to stay, and left them.

"Get cigars, Johnnie," said the little man, "draw up that chair, put your feet on the mantelpiece—because it must be such a fine thing to be able to do—and make yourself generally comfortable."

They smoked at ease, each looking into the fire silently. Presently:

"Like your place, Johnnie? I've never asked."

"All right, thanks."

"I mentioned you should take number twenty-three or twenty-four. Better not to be on the same floor, you see."

"I see. Oh! yes, these little cautions are worth observing, of course. Number twenty-four was taken before we came, you know."

"So I suppose," said Napoleon, looking into the fire. A quarter of an hour ticked by before he roused himself to say anything further. Then it was, gently:

"Johnnie, you're seeing something in the fire, ain't you, old man? Don't be ashamed to be sentimental; be proud of it. I was seeing much the same sort of thing, I guess."

John Luck had seen the Joséphine girl's little face, of course, gleaming up at him, but—

"*You!*" he said, confounded, to Napoleon. "*You*, Nap!"

"Yes, I," said Napoleon, with a snap, looking up. "I've got a man's heart, I suppose, if I've only got half his body. And at *that* time, you see, I was whole. It was seven years ago, nearly."

Luck nodded, and looked at him in a man's silence of sympathy.

"It was the only time I've ever been done, Johnnie," said the little man. "Done, and not got my own back. You see, it was a woman. Like to hear? I'd like to tell you. I was travelling in Italy for the Cosmopolitans' gang I've told you about, and we'd got a great scoop on. I was their smartest man, and they gave the chief part to me. Well, I was in the Opera House in Florence one night, when I saw one woman among all the others. It was a crowded house—Royalty there—but after I'd looked at her I didn't see much else—you know. She was young and dark, with marvellous eyes; dressed in white with a scarlet cloak. She was with a man, and they sat close to the orchestra. I managed to follow them out, and to see her close. My word, Johnnie, magnificent! But, I thought, not happy. She had no gloves on, and there was no wedding ring—so she was, that far, free. I went home and dressed. Next morning—Ever been in Italy, Johnnie?"

Luck shook his head.

"Such mornings as you get!" said Napoleon. "It was spring, I remember, about March—Ever read poetry, Johnnie?

'. . . . white and wide,
Washed by the morning's water-gold,
Florence lay out on the mountain side.' "

The little man's voice caressed the words melodiously. He went on:

"I met her in the square, riding down to the river. I kept her in sight all the morning, and followed her when she rode at a foot pace back to an hotel. So I learned her address. I forgot all about the Cosmopolitans, and all that sort of truck. There seemed only one thing that mattered. . . . She was evidently staying at the hotel. I learned her name: the Countess Gerda di Veletto. I wrote to her, signing myself: 'A very mad Englishman,' and giving an address. Johnnie, boy, that same evening a page from the hotel brought me an answer. I have it here in my letter case. I've always carried it. Like to see it? Because I'd like to show it to you."

The folded sheet that he pulled out was worn almost to tatters at the creases. Johnnie Luck, feeling rather foolish and rather intrusive, read:

My Dear Stranger,

Your tribute pleased me. Did you suppose it would not? Don't you know that a woman can never receive too many kind words? Where did you sit in the Opera House? And I wonder if I saw you as you saw me? I do not think it, because, if so—— But I do not think I had better write what I was going to write. It would not be wise. I only want to thank you for the pleasure of your assurances, which come to me in a time of deep trouble and anxiety. And although I have never met—and never shall meet—my very mad Englishman, I am pleased to sign myself,

His friend,
Gerda di Veletto.

Luck passed this back in silence, and Napoleon returned it to the letter case, and thence to his inside breast pocket. He went on evenly.

"Johnnie, by that time I was loving her as I never loved a woman before, and never shall again. Her 'deep trouble and anxiety' gave me thought. I wrote her, crazed. Could I do something? Might her mad Englishman meet her at any hour and any place? Any way, would she command him? She wrote back that she could not see me that evening, as a friend would be dining with her. A friend? Who was this 'friend'? I got half mad with jealousy, and watched the hotel, as if I could pick out her visitor from the crowds. But when I saw the man who had been with her at the Opera go in, I knew that I had picked him out.

"I went home and wrote to her again. I begged her to make an appointment with me, let me do something for her if I could. She answered at once, as before, saying that I could call the next day, but she could see nobody till then. She was at her wits' end to escape from some trouble. I read a good deal between the lines of that letter, as she meant me to do. She knew how to leave room between the lines—which is an art, my dear Johnnie, of the highest order. I saw despair and fear in it. She said recklessly at the end that it was only monetary, her trouble. Five hundred pounds, after all, would clear her, and she was going to ask her friend for it that night. I remember phrases such as: 'I'm not that kind of woman, either, you very mad Englishman. . . . It goes cruelly hard . . . but there! he will be only too eager to give, as it will be only too bitter for me to take.' And then, with a sort of sudden return to formality, she added that she would be pleased to give me a few minutes' interview the next day.

"Johnnie, Gerda knew her book, boy. She realised, as very few people of our profession realise, what an important study is your book of psychology. Women, as a rule, are better at that game than men. Criminologists trace crime to heredity, to suggestion, to physical phenomena, to environment. But women go one better than that. They use the emotions; they know the weight of an eyelash, the value of the turn of a head, of a word, and more, of an unsaid word. It was what she did not say in that letter that made me see red and shake with absolute bestial rage. I thought of the chap at the Opera—recalled his face—his tricks of gesture, his age, all about him. He was a nice-looking, young dark fellow, but I got a vision of Mephistopheles. I imagined him driving a bargain with her for the five hundred. I had plenty of money—the Cosmopolitans' money—on me. I got notes for five hundred and put them into a letter, begging her to take them from the very mad Englishman, who would not even ask to see her in return, rather than from her 'friend.' But how I hoped for that meeting she'd promised! She sent an answer filled in between the lines—you know. I was to call and be thanked in person for 'the loan.' The next evening, at seven, I was to dine with her."

"And?" Luck asked, after a longish pause had fallen.

Napoleon replied tersely.

"I went, blindfold as I had acted, and shaking with excitement, to her hotel at seven o'clock. I came out at seven ten, sane. She had left early in the morning with, presumably, several articles of jewellery missed by other visitors, and my—or rather the Cosmopolitans'—five hundred pounds. Police inquiry—from the other victims, not me, Johnnie—elicited the fact that she had left Florence with her 'friend,' but they could not be traced. I cursed solid for some while—imagining her laughter."

Luck nodded.

"It must have been the softest thing she'd ever been on," said Napoleon, "and yet she was dealing with the cleverest man she had, in all probability, ever met with."

He made the assertion ruminatively, and with no conscious arrogance.

"Since then," he resumed, "I have relied less on science in my profession, less on logical sequence, and have recognised that chance, emotion, and adventure are very potent contingencies to be reckoned with. Her eyes had melted me. My science, my logic, my ingrained suspicion of the world, went by the board. It was, as I say, a very soft thing. She could not have expected to draw the money before she had granted me an interview, at least. And how she must have laughed when she did it! She and her friend! It must be the joke of their lives. And when you come to think of it, Johnnie, it is excruciatingly humorous that I—*I*—*I*—should have tumbled into *that*!"

There was nothing in the little man's pale face to betray that he had ever felt the excruciating humour of the situation, so John Luck did not laugh either.

"Logic is a fool to love," said Napoleon.

"It is an interesting story," Luck remarked.

"What reminded me of it," said Napoleon, turning his head, and fixing his auditor with his brief bright glance, "was seeing her eyes in the fire just now, as you were seeing someone else's, eh, Johnnie? I've never, these seven years, forgotten Gerda."

"Nor forgiven her?"

He evaded that. "And what called up those eyes, Johnnie, was seeing another pair very like them as I came out of the building this morning. She was a pretty woman named Muswell, the lift-man told me."

"My neighbour, I expect, in number twenty-four."

"That so? Do you know her? She looked wistful, worried, down on her luck, though Mary tells me her frock must have cost exactly ten pounds nineteen and eleven pence halfpenny."

"No, I don't know her. Often met her going up or down, of course. I've noticed the worried air. Perhaps she's just lonely. Seems a sin for a pretty woman like that to be living all by herself."

"She has eyes just like Gerda's," said Napoleon softly. He looked into the fire again, his chin sunk a little, his face merely a pale mask. Then he asked:

"Have you ever credited me with weakness, Johnnie?"

Luck smiled so broadly at this question that a spoken negative was unnecessary.

"Yet all men are weak," said Napoleon, answering the smile, "and my weakness, my soft spot, my tenderness, is for eyes like Gerda's. I loved her—and she hurt me. She had never set eyes on me—I just worshipped from my distance. Never mind. I loved her, and love is love, and, as I say, above all the logic in the world. I had a charwoman in Paris once with eyes a little like hers, and I did what I could to help that charwoman because of Gerda. Gerda wouldn't have done it, but never mind. Now I meet Mrs. Muswell here in these flats, and she has eyes that are the very duplicate of Gerda's. She looks lonely, unhappy, unlucky. Convention forbids Mary to call on her, and offer her some palliation of her loneliness, because it seems that she arrived here first. Apparently she will not call on us. And I want to do some good turn for a girl with Gerda's eyes. Arrange the matter for us, Johnnie."

"How?"

"Make her acquaintance, as she's next door. Make her talk. Make her tell you she's lonely. Then beg her to call on those nice people, the Princes, whose acquaintance you have made since coming here. And so on."

"How do I make her acquaintance, Nap?"

"Oh! run along, Johnnie!" said Napoleon, vastly tickled at this helplessness. "You are a very pretty young man—don't blush! You have the ordinary social gifts, and a pair of eyes to appreciate the blessings the gods grant you in the way of alluring neighbours. You have a charming flat next her own, and you are both solitary young people. The conditions are so favourable as to allow of positively no interesting obstacles to surmount at all."

Mary here returned from the Stores, and voted her shopping dull.

"Polly," said her brother, "Luck, here, is going to bring his neighbour, Mrs. Muswell, to call on you tomorrow afternoon. It is an old love-story——"

Mary looked frostily from one to the other.

"Of mine, child, not Johnnie's," Napoleon continued, preparing to wheel from the room; "an old love-story of which her eyes remind me. So we are going to be exceedingly kind to Mrs. Muswell, child, please."

A quite beautiful woman opened the door of her flat to Mr. John Luck the next morning. She was tall, dark, slight almost to leanness, and vivid; she looked any age from twenty-five to thirty, but it was most probably thirty. She wore an artful gown. Her eyes were very lovely—big, straight, innocent, appealing.

"I am sorry to trouble you," said Mr. John Luck, with his engaging smile, "but I have lost my kitten, and I think she must have come in to you, with the milk, or something. May I look, please?"

The lovely apparition looked Mr. Luck over.

"Come in," said she simply, and, closing the door behind him, led the way to a little drawing-room as artful as her frock. A very queer Eastern little drawing-room. She motioned him with frank kindness—her absence of all conventional mannerism was refreshing—to a seat, and inquired the name and description of the kitten.

"She answers to anything, but is generally called 'Puss,'" replied Mr. Luck admiringly, "and she is about the most spiritual cat I have ever met."

"What colour is your dear little kitten?"

"She is white," said Luck. "All spirits are, you know. I am sure you would love her. Are you fond of cats?"

"Very," she answered, smiling softly and doubtfully.

She stared at him much as a puzzled child might do. Then they rose and looked for the kitten all over the flat, but it could not be found. No answer came to any appeal of "Puss!" or any other name. The search proving futile, they returned to the drawing-room, and sat down again.

"I am your next-door neighbour, you know," he said, when one or two topics had been exhausted, and she gave him no unkind hint to go.

"Oh!—yes?" she said doubtfully.

"They are jolly flats, aren't they?"

"Yes."

"But even a flat is very lonely for one person, isn't it?"

"Yes." She added with great simplicity: "I am very lonely."

"What a sin, Mrs.—Mrs.——"

"Muswell," said she, hesitating over the name. He registered the hesitation. "I have no friends at all in London now." And she sighed.

"Why not call on some of the people here? The newer comers, you know."

"Oh, do you think they——"

"Would love it?" said Mr. Luck. "I do. There's a charming pair, brother and sister, just below you, whose acquaintance I've made since coming here. They'd be delighted, I know they would. Their name is Prince."

"Oh! Do you mean the poor little invalid gentleman, Mr.——?"

"My name is Luck. And I do mean the invalid and his sister. I say, are you very, very conventional?"

She shook her head, still smiling her doubtful, half timorous smile.

"No, I'm afraid I've lost touch with English conventions. I—I've been out of England so long."

A faint sigh again, and the words seemed to call up to the dark wells of her eyes some best-forgotten thing from fathoms deep.

"Then," he said, "do let me take you down to call this afternoon, Mrs. Muswell. Will you?"

After the necessary preliminary hesitations, she consented.

"Although," she said, "I am afraid of making friends. I——"

"Why should you deprive people?"

"My story," she said after a pause, "is rather an extraordinary one. I—I could hardly tell such a stranger, but——"

"Certainly not," replied Mr. Luck, promptly rising to take his leave. They skook hands by a sort of mutual impulse, she looking at him very straightly, he looking back very reassuringly. So he returned to his own demesne, anticipating with pleasure the hearing of this pretty woman's extraordinary story at a very near date, for he was but human. "In here after dinner," said he, looking thoughtfully round his drawing-room, "over coffee, with a dim light. Almost any cushions would suit her as a background."

He took her down that afternoon to call on the Princes, as prearranged.

The visit was a success. Afterwards Mary said, but kindly, that she looked like a woman with a story.

Luck assented grudgingly to the possibility.

Napoleon, with his mysterious smile, agreed with Mary. The young widow certainly had a story. He looked remotely into the fire. Probably he was seeing Gerda's eyes.

The young widow's extraordinary story was not long withheld from Johnnie Luck.

That same evening, having dined in his flat, he was seated at his piano, playing softly, and singing softly in a voice worth better things, some doggerel nigger melodies, when a lady was ushered in on him by the very discreet servitor whom Luck had engaged.

It was Mrs. Muswell.

She was in a simple black chiffon gown, and she looked appealing.

"You will think this very strange, I suppose," she began, as he jumped up with every manifestation of pleasure to meet her. "At least, I suppose you will think it strange—I forget just exactly what one may or may not do in England. Can I sit down?"

"I am sure you may do that," said he, smiling, and hastily dragging forward a chair which held cushions of the right colour for her complexion.

She dropped a soft black roll which she carried—it looked like a small hearthrug—and sank into the chair.

"*You* were so very kind to me this morning and this afternoon," she said hesitatingly, "that I would like to—to tell you about myself, unconventional as I suppose it seems. But then, as I told you, I have forgotten how to be properly conventional like your nice English girls."

She bit her lip, and her eyes looked as if they held tears.

"My dear Mrs. Muswell," he said interestedly, sitting down near her, "conventions are always wrong, because they indicate a state of things that calls for unnatural restraint. Whereas things are not in the least in that most deplorable state. Why can't we all be natural, and say what we like to each other? Why make acquaintance by the almanac?"

"Why, indeed?" she echoed innocently. "Can I, then, tell you everything, and ask your advice upon the situation, because I have no older friend than yourself here? Would a nice English girl do it?"

"She would love it," replied Luck earnestly.

She was very charmingly full of doubts and indecisions, half smiling. "I was brought up in England," she said; "my mother was English, but my father was Italian. You can see the Italian in me, can you not?"

The discreet servitor here brought in the coffee tray, to which he had discreetly added a second cup and saucer, and withdrew. Luck ministered to his guest; she tasted the coffee and gave a little exclamation.

"How good! I have not had it so good since I escaped from——"

She stopped. "We used to eat sweets with it there," she said rather faintly. "Rich, delicious sugary things like chocolate, marrons glacés, almond paste, crystallised violets, and Turkish delight all rolled together."

A box of chocolates, bought for Mary, was pushed away behind the furnishings of an occasional table. Luck found this, and, untying the ribbon, offered the sweets.

"It is the nearest thing I can do," said he apologetically.

She helped herself. She had very white teeth, over which her red lips crinkled back prettily. "Not that I want to remember anything about it," she sighed. "It is all too painful—too degrading—too——"

"I assure you that I will give you the best advice in my power."

"I know it, and I am going to tell you my story."

He sat before her, holding the open chocolate box; she began to talk, stopping now and again to help herself and nibble at the bonbons as a child may nibble sweets and tell a fairy tale.

"My mother, as I told you, was English, my father Italian. I was brought up during my childhood in England, but when I was eighteen I went with my parents to Paris. There my mother died, and I was left entirely to my father's care. It was not good care. Heaven forgive me for speaking ill of him, but it was very bad care. So bad for a girl of only eighteen, straight out of a convent school in England."

"A convent school?"

"Yes. I spent my holidays there as well as the terms. It was very peaceful and sweet; I loved it. One lived asleep. When I came out of that dear place the awakening was very sudden, crude, bewildering. But then I realised the world outside, and that I was alive in it. I simply threw myself into all the excitement my parents provided. When my mother died, my father went on providing excitements. I played, like a child still, with everything and everybody, till at last, seeing that I could not or would not understand that I was grown up, and what were his aims for me, my father spoke. 'Julie,' he said—in Paris it was, after a ball—'when are you going to marry?'

"The question was a horrid shock. I had not thought of marrying. I was happy. My world was Arcadia—not a dull one, of course, in Paris—but mentally Arcadia. 'I shall always stay with you, papa,' I said to him lightly. 'I have other plans for you, *ma chérie*,' said he to me heavily. And the next day he introduced me to Prince Mustapha. The prince had just come from Constantinople on a diplomatic mission, I understood. He was quite young, charming, and polished like our own men. I went about with him a great deal, my father dropping chaperonage when possible. I let the prince, as it were, into my Arcadia among all my other friends. I had very few women friends; but that, of course, was my father's fault. You believe me that it *was* Arcadia?"

She looked like a child afraid of the construction which may be put by an irreverent elder upon the truth which it is telling.

"I see you believe me," she resumed. "You are good, kind. Then came a horrible day; my father storming and telling me that I was talked about in every club and café in Paris; and Mustapha proposing marriage. I was so afraid of my father, so anxious to escape from such a blustering parent, that I accepted the prince. We were married in Paris—I, like an ignorant girl, not questioning the validity of the rite between one of his religion and one of mine, and we—my husband and I—travelled back together to Constantinople."

A long pause.

"I do not really think that I can go on," she said very faintly. But when she had dried her eyes and eaten a few more chocolates she insisted bravely on doing so.

"The prince had a harem——"

"Good heavens!" cried Luck.

"A harem. And I was one of his—called by courtesy—wives. I had been in his house twenty-four hours before I knew. I reproached him passionately. I said: 'If my father knew of this——' He replied: 'Your father knew well. I paid him twenty-five thousand francs to help him with his debts.' So I understood that it was a question of buying and selling. I, a free girl with English blood in my veins, had been sold! I saw what a broken reed I had to lean on in my father—my only reed, too! What could I do? I had been with Mustapha for a week. I—I stayed. I became one of the harem. One of the sleepy, fattening, decorated pets and slaves. I was that for eight years, and suddenly I revolted strongly enough to devise, with all the odds against me, my escape. I planned it for seven months, watching every sign and listening to every sound of life I could catch from outside to help me build a scheme. One thing I was resolved on: I would not go penniless.

"Just at that time there was a craze among us in the harem for making mats of black silk and wool an inch and a half thick. I had been for eight years Mustapha's favourite, and he had lavished jewels on me. As soon as I began to plan my escape, I commenced to hide these chains and necklaces in the weaving of my mat. One by one, very cunningly, I put my ornaments away, always keeping up to the last something to wear when Mustapha sent for me. I quarrelled with the other women, who had hated me from the beginning, and for seven months we hardly spoke, so I could sit away from them, and they never came to look at and handle my work, and chatter about it, as they did with one another's. By the time the mat was nearly finished my plans were ripe, and occasion came. We always walked at will on the roof garden. I went up alone with my mat one evening, and dropped myself right down from the roof into the top of a big fruit tree underneath. It seemed a sickening distance. I lay there and looked over the wall into the street. It was a comparatively quiet spot, away from the market place and principal squares. At last I dared to climb down and over the wall by the aid of the fruit trees that were trained along it. So I walked out free into a street for the first time in eight years. As free as I could be, that is. Of course, I went veiled. I got my passage money and an escort privately from the British Consul, and so I came back at last to England and to London."

She stopped to eat chocolates, and for some time there was a silence.

"Poor, poor girl!" said Johnnie Luck at last.

"You are good, kind," she said softly. "Advise me."

"What to do with your life? I couldn't."

"No, no!" said she. "What to do with my jewels. They represent my capital, you see. I have no money. I must sell them, yet very privately, because I could not bear anyone to hear this story—except you, of course, my good friend. The English are so prejudiced. I want to start a new life among them fairly. Besides, there is another reason why I must keep my secret." She looked reserved.

"Your story is, of course, perfectly safe with me."

"I know it. To return to the jewels, there must be at least ten thousand pounds' worth in the mat."

Luck looked respectfully at the soft black roll lying at their feet.

"Would you confide in the Princes?" he asked. "Napoleon Prince knows a great deal about—er—the—the curio markets of the world, and he might be able to assist you."

Reluctantly she consented to confide in Mr. Napoleon Prince at the earliest opportunity—on the morrow, if possible.

After she had gone, leaving a faint aroma of some Eastern perfume clinging to his cushions, Luck descended to No. 20. He found Napoleon up, smoking before a gorgeous fire, but Mary had retired early to bed.

"News, Johnnie?" said the little man, smiling slightly.

Luck related Mrs. Muswell's story. "Preposterous, eh?" he asked.

Napoleon had listened through it, merely nodding and commenting, with very little amazement. "Preposterous enough to be true," he replied oracularly. "You will learn not to discredit melodrama, Johnnie, presently. All the melodramas ever written are nothing to the melodramas that are lived every day."

"She's going to ask your advice on my recommendation, Nap."

"She couldn't come to a better quarter," replied Napoleon, looking into the fire.

"You will help her, then, in some way, like a good chap?"

"I shall help—Gerda's eyes!" said Napoleon, smiling.

"Good-night, Nap."

"Night-night, Johnnie."

And he was left looking at the eyes in the fire.

The tenant of No. 24 came, according to arrangement, the next afternoon to the Princes' flat. She carried with her a rolled-up black bundle—the mat woven, according to her story, in the harem of Prince Mustapha. Luck was there. Mary was charmingly kind. Napoleon pressed her hand in his left one, and said that he hoped she would not be vexed to know that Mr. Luck had already told them the story. Mr. Luck thought she might be glad to be saved the very painful recital.

No, she was not vexed. Yes, she was glad—thank you, kind people. She unrolled the black mat.

"Feel!" she said to Napoleon.

He felt, among the softness of the silk and wool, chains and layers here and there of hard, lumpy substances.

"Necklaces?" he queried.

She answered eagerly, frankly: "Two necklaces, nearly a dozen brooches, a girdle, a chain, many pairs of earrings, ruby, emerald and topaz. The necklaces are diamonds and pearls. How can I sell these things so as not to excite suspicion and call attention to myself? Mustapha may be looking for me, and I dare not attract his notice."

"He could not touch you in England, dear child," said the little man, with a fatherly air.

"But the story!" she said passionately. "The story! That would come out! And it must never be known—because I—I have so much at stake—I——"

Suddenly she put her handkerchief to her face and sobbed, her shoulders rocking. Napoleon watched her thoughtfully. Luck was really distressed. Mary administered what comfort she could give to a stranger and rang for tea.

During the dispensing of it the visitor recovered somewhat, and looked up with a quivering smile through tears that made her black eyes shine like jewels.

"What must you all think of me?" she gasped.

"I am sorry. I am very sorry. But, as I said, I have so much at stake. I—I am going to be married."

She sipped her tea, while Mary and Luck looked at her with exclamations of mutual sympathy and interest.

"You see," she said in a low voice, "I am not really Mustapha's wife. The marriage in Paris was not valid. In spite of my—my degradation, I am free. Let me tell you." She caught Mary's hand, looking with great understanding from her to Johnnie Luck. "You, dear girl, you will feel with me. On my way home to England I met, in Austria, a young officer of the Austrian army, on leave. We—we"—her eyes drooped—"we loved each other from the first moment," she said in a strangled voice, "and I promised to marry him. I tried to forget my story. Then I saw everything in what seemed its hideous impossibility, and I went on, without a word of good-bye to him. I dared not trust myself to say good-bye. But he followed me here."

"Delicious!" cried Mary warmly to Luck. He looked back at her as if to say: "Exactly as *I* should do!"

Their visitor went on: "And he found me yesterday. I renewed my promises to him, and we shall be married as soon as I have sold these and provided myself with a little money, and bought a trousseau, and so on. You see, ostensibly I am a young widow in comfortable circumstances. I am so afraid of the least hitch—of any inquiry leading to knowledge of what constitutes my capital"—she indicated the mat—"and then as to how I came by these Eastern-looking jewels—even if Mustapha does not trace me as I dispose of them. You understand—it's not a wicked deception? It is the happiness of two lives—mine and Friedrich's—that——"

"We understand perfectly," said the *Joséphine* girl sweetly. Napoleon was looking at the black roll.

"May we see some of the things?" he asked.

The visitor assented, and cutting the strands of the mat, they brought some of the ornaments to light. They were much as she had described them—rather roughly cut gems, some in heavy Eastern settings. Napoleon examined them one by one with the air of a connoisseur. He took little implements out of his waistcoat pocket, and tapped the stones, looking at them closely, their owner meanwhile looking closely at him. She grew a little pale during the examination, and spoke of the devotion of Mustapha, who would lavish ornaments to any value upon her.

"I think," Napoleon said at last, "that I might get you three thousand pounds for these in various markets that I know of. I am a bit of a traveller, as you may know, and through buying art curios I have been in touch with many dealers in Europe and Asia."

Her face fell. "You think they are not worth more?"

"They may be," he replied, "but that could be ascertained when they have been examined by experts. Sleep on the matter, my dear lady, and then let me know if you will put it into my hands."

"You are good," she said gratefully. "Good and kind, all of you. We may be able to talk further of it tomorrow. Friedrich is coming to dine with me tonight. Would you——" She looked from one to the other.

"Would you," Mary responded, "bring him down to us for coffee? We should be charmed."

The invitation being accepted with thanks and beaming smiles, Mrs. Muswell withdrew, Johnnie Luck accompanying her to carry the black roll to the flat above. She extolled the kindness of his friends and himself.

"Is he rich?" she asked plaintively, "your Mr. Prince?"

Receiving a cautious reply, she said childishly: "If he is, perhaps he would like to buy my jewels himself, and dispose of them at his leisure, at a big profit. It will be so hard for me to wait. So very, very hard. And I will not go to Friedrich without what they call a *dot*."

Accepting with a smile the compliments obviously to be turned on this, she vanished into her flat, and they saw her no more until nine thirty, when, charming and excited, she brought down Friedrich for a few minutes to be introduced to them. He was a dark, spruce, military-looking man, extremely smart. After coffee she took him back to her own flat again.

"Darling things!" said Mary. "Be kind to them, Nap."

"Yes," said Luck, "be kind to them, Nap."

"Children," said the little man, drinking a third cup of coffee in unwonted absence of mind, "I am already devising extensive plans of benevolence and philanthropy. All the world loves a lover. Here is to our pretty friend and her gallant Friedrich!" He drank the toast in coffee. "I anticipate that we may see her quite early in the morning."

It was comparatively early in the morning when Mrs. Muswell called at No. 20. Mary had gone out betimes to buy some articles of which her brother professed himself in instant need, for which she had to go half across London, and so would not be back before lunch. Johnnie Luck had, in response to a message from the paralytic, descended to No. 20. When he came, Napoleon had little to say, however, beyond desultory chat. He seemed to be listening. When a ring was heard, his face cleared and he smiled.

"I would lay you a hundred to one, Johnnie, that is the heroine of the Harem Melodrama."

"Do you mean to imply that you do not believe——"

"My dear Johnnie, I discredit nothing and credit nothing. I tell you she has Gerda's eyes, which is ample reason for my doing what I am about to do."

She was ushered in.

"Ah, my dear lady! We were speaking of angels. A very good morning to you!"

But she looked as though the morning were far from very good. She was *distraite*, worried. Under her arm she carried the black mat in a roll. When, seemingly too abstracted to give any formal greeting to either man, she had sat down, she said impulsively:

"Mr. Prince, I come to ask your immediate help in my trouble. Friedrich"—her eyes looked wet—"is ordered to rejoin his regiment. He is leaving England tonight."

They were all attention, making little murmurs of sympathy. She went on:

"He implored me yesterday evening—it was after we left you—to marry him before he left, to return to Austria with him. But first I want to get rid of these. I will not go to Friedrich's family—his cold, proud family—without a penny. Mr. Prince, what shall I do? Who will buy at a moment's notice?"

"Very few people, I am afraid, dear lady," said Napoleon.

She bit her lip and trembled. Her eyes were magnificent.

"I told you yesterday," he said, taking her unresisting hand, "that you could probably get three thousand for the lot without much haggling. *Probably*—not certainly. I do not trust my judgment to say certainly. You might get more, as I also told you, if you were content to wait and submit them to the really best experts——"

"No, no!" she exclaimed hurriedly. "I could not wait—now. Who would give me three thousand for them?"

"That," he replied, "I could not say at such short notice. I should have to find out. But I will give you two five for them down now, here, if you are willing to take it."

"Two thousand five hundred?"

"Yes. I do not offer you the full three thousand I suggested as their value, because, dear lady, I am a hard business man underneath my soft side, and you must give discount for cash, and for the trouble in store for me in disposing of the jewels. Also I may get barely more than my own money back, or even not as much. There *might* be a great deal more, I own, but the chances are as much for one as t'other. You see all this?"

"I see—I see." She began breathing lovely gratitude, but he stopped her.

"Don't thank me. I mentioned just now that soft side of mine, and my softness is for your eyes."

She looked at him, beautifully. He looked back full at her, appreciatively.

"You have the eyes," he said softly, "of someone I once loved. Luck, an errand, please."

Luck came forward.

"My bedroom is next door, and there's a little dispatch case on the table by my bed. If you don't mind—my wretched helplessness," he explained to her, as Johnnie Luck left the room. When the door closed, he added: "I want to claim a tremendous boon of you, dear lady, because you have the eyes of the girl I once loved."

"Ask it," said she, all softness.

"A kiss," said the little man.

In a moment Johnnie Luck would be back. She gave herself time for a little murmur of hesitation, surprise; then she rose from her chair, came close, and bent and kissed him. Her lips were very soft, and she kissed Napoleon on the lips. She sat down again. A flush swept up all over his pale face, passed, and was gone. The face was serene again when Luck came in with the dispatch case.

Napoleon unlocked it with his left hand, and found three crackling notes.

"I don't often keep this amount of money out of my bank," he explained. "It is pure coincidence, accident, what you will, that I have it to hand this morning. Later in the day it would have been paid to my account. They are three thousand-pound notes. Could you oblige me, somehow, with the change, dear lady?"

"Five hundred pounds," she considered.

"If you will hand over that, I will hand over this," he said with such charming apology that there could be no insult in the caution. "I am, as I said, a business man, and I do things in a business-like way."

"I can give you the notes, I believe," she answered. "I have about that amount, and I will go to get it. It is absolutely my all, of course, and it would not have been a *dot* fit for an Austrian officer's wife."

Luck sprang to open the door. She passed out smiling—not to her own flat, though, but hastily down to the street. Near the Army and Navy Stores her Friedrich waited.

Napoleon sat waiting her return, the fingers of his left hand drumming on the notes on the table, his eyes fixed rather absently on space. The black mat lay on the floor.

"Nap," said Luck, "ain't it risky, old man?"

"Her eyes, Johnnie!" said Napoleon. "Her eyes!"

He would say no more. In perhaps ten minutes the beautiful visitor hurried back. She was flushed and a little breathless, which condition she explained by the fact of the search she had had for the notes. She had put them securely away, under lock and key, forgotten where, and been terrified—so terrified—in consequence. But here they were, all safe and sound. Would Mr. Prince count them?

Mr. Prince counted them, thrust them into his breast pocket, and handed over three thousand-pound notes, enclosing them first in an envelope out of the dispatch box. He stretched out his left hand, and she put hers into it. He looked up at her, standing tall, vibrant, glowing, victorious.

"My congratulations to Friedrich," said he. "My felicitations to yourself. A very pleasant journey. Good-bye."

"Good-bye, kind, good friends." She shook hands with both. "I am going out now. Guess for what?"

"To be married?" Luck hazarded.

She nodded. "To be married. We leave for Austria to-day."

"Happy Friedrich!" said Luck.

"Happy Friedrich!" cried Napoleon.

The graceful creature went out, making an emotional leave-taking. The two men were left together, and the black mat lay on the floor. Napoleon's face had grown deathly.

"Mary will be amazed," began Luck.

"Oh! Ah!" He looked down at the mat. "Cart that truck away, there's a good fellow."

"Truck? I suppose you'll see your money back again all right?"

Napoleon looked—laughed noiselessly.

"Stuff's simply 'fake' all through, Johnnie, my dear good fool."

"What, Nap? And you knew it? Well, Nap, who's the fool?"

"Not I, Luck. 'Friedrich,' perhaps, and she. My notes were 'fake,' too."

Johnnie sat down.

"Ah! I can do notes. One of the things I've learned. Those were three of the kind the Cosmopolitans use, though, and were ready to hand."

"Her five hundred?"

"Real. Screaming humour? Rattling farce, eh?"

"So, after all—you cheated Gerda's eyes?"

"I cheated Gerda's wits."

Light began to show through for Luck. He gazed at the little man, now beginning to tremble in his invalid chair.

"We've been dealing with Gerda, you see, John Luck. And with her 'friend.' Who do you think, Johnnie, was the man she brought in to drink my coffee and liqueurs? The chap of the Florence Opera House! And what do you think is written inside the flap of that envelope I put her notes in?"

Luck shook his head.

"'To Gerda, from her very sane Englishman.' Funny, eh? Any questions, Johnnie?"

"Yes, Nap. Did you take these flats because you knew she was here?"

Napoleon nodded.

"Did you mean all through to get back at her, as soon as you had the chance?"

Napoleon nodded.

"Did you know what kind of story she'd come out with this time?"

Napoleon shook his head. "Know? Who does know, John Luck, what a woman plots and plans? Women lick men—they lick the rest of creation—at tricking. They don't work by logical sequence, but by accident. You can't insure against that kind of accident, either. There's no policy obtainable. Women—they haven't human science, but they're given monkey minds. Their mischief is more nimble than ours. They lay a plot like a three-volume novel about princes, and harems, and troubles and anxieties and love, and start creation playing their absurd melodramas and believing they're real. They feel your pulse, and they know all about you. And nature aids a woman—saturates her in the part she's taking. She can laugh and cry and quiver—her brain plays on her body like a bow on fiddle strings—and she's given lips that are so cursed soft, Johnnie—and eyes! And I've got my own back, Johnnie. There's no laugh any more, except for me. But do what I will, I'll never get the feel of her lips off mine—nor her eyes out of my heart—never exorcise her away."

Johnnie Luck got up very suddenly and quietly, and left the little man swayed against the table with his head on his arm.

The Willow Walk

SINCLAIR LEWIS

THE FIRST AMERICAN to win the Nobel Prize for Literature, Sinclair Lewis (1885–1951) wrote several novels that have given their names to the English language.

With *Babbitt* (1922), Lewis skewered the American businessman, personified by George F. Babbitt, an intellectually empty, immature man of weak morals. *Arrowsmith* (1925) is the name of a young doctor who battles to maintain his dignity in a dishonest world in which the medical profession is not spared. It was offered the Pulitzer Prize but Lewis refused the honor because the terms of the award required that it be given not just for a work of value but for a work that presents "the wholesome atmosphere of American Life," which it most assuredly did not. *Elmer Gantry* (1927) is an assault on religious hypocrisy, exemplified by the titular character's morals; the novel was the basis for the Oscar-winning 1960 film starring Burt Lancaster, Jean Simmons, and Shirley Jones.

An important American writer whose first great success was *Main Street* (1920), Lewis's reputation was soon superseded by such contemporary authors as Ernest Hemingway and F. Scott Fitzgerald. Lewis's later works were not very successful and he even found it difficult to find a publisher after World War II.

"The Willow Walk," the story of a "successful" embezzler, was originally published in the August 10, 1918, issue of *The Saturday Evening Post*; it was first collected in *Selected Short Stories of Sinclair Lewis* (New York, Doubleday, Doran, 1935).

THE WILLOW WALK

Sinclair Lewis

I

FROM THE DRAWER of his table Jasper Holt took a pane of window glass. He laid a sheet of paper on the glass and wrote, "Now is the time for all good men to come to the aid of their party." He studied his round business-college script, and rewrote the sentence in a small finicky hand, that of a studious old man. Ten times he copied the words in that false pinched writing. He tore up the paper, burned the fragments in his large ash tray, and washed the delicate ashes down his stationary washbowl. He replaced the pane of glass in the drawer, tapping it with satisfaction. A glass underlay does not retain an impression.

Jasper Holt was as nearly respectable as his room, which, with its frilled chairs and pansy-painted pincushion, was the best in the aristocratic boarding house of Mrs. Lyons. He was a wiry, slightly bald, black-haired man of thirty-eight, wearing an easy gray flannel suit and a white carnation. His hands were peculiarly compact and nimble. He gave the appearance of being a youngish lawyer or bond salesman. Actually he was senior paying teller in the Lumber National Bank in the city of Vernon.

He looked at a thin expensive gold watch. It was six-thirty, on Wednesday—toward dusk of a tranquil spring day. He picked up his hooked walking stick and his gray silk gloves and trudged downstairs. He met his landlady in the lower hall and inclined his head. She effusively commented on the weather.

"I shall not be there for dinner," he said amiably.

"Very well, Mr. Holt. My, but aren't you always going out with your swell friends though! I read in the *Herald* that you were going to be a star in another of those society plays in the Community Theater. I guess you'd be an actor if you wasn't a banker, Mr. Holt."

"No, I'm afraid I haven't much temperament." His voice was cordial, but his smile was a mere mechanical sidewise twist of the lip muscles. "You're the one that's got the stage presence. Bet you'd be a regular Ethel Barrymore if you didn't have to take care of us."

"My, but you're such a flatterer!"

He bowed his way out and walked sedately down the street to a public garage. Nodding to the night attendant, but saying nothing, he started his roadster and drove out of the garage, away from the center of Vernon, toward the suburb of Rosebank. He did not go directly to Rosebank. He went seven blocks out of his way, and halted on Fandall Avenue—one of those petty main thoroughfares which, with their motion-picture palaces, their groceries, laundries, undertakers' establishments, and lunch rooms, serve as local centers for districts of mean residences. He got out of the car and pretended to look at the tires, kicking them to see how much air they had. While he did so he covertly looked up and down the street. He saw no one whom he knew. He went into the Parthenon Confectionery Store.

The Parthenon Store makes a specialty of those ingenious candy boxes that resemble bound books. The back of the box is of imitation leather, with a stamping simulating the title of a novel. The edges are apparently the edges of a number of pages. But these pages are hollowed out, and the inside is to be filled with candy.

Jasper gazed at the collection of book boxes and chose the two whose titles had the nearest approach to dignity—*Sweets to the Sweet* and *The Ladies' Delight*. He asked the Greek clerk to fill these with the less expensive grade of mixed chocolates, and to wrap them.

From the candy shop he went to the drugstore that carried an assortment of reprinted novels, and from these picked out two of the same sentimental type as the titles on the book-like boxes. These also he had wrapped. He strolled out of the drugstore, slipped into a lunchroom, got a lettuce sandwich, doughnuts, and a cup of coffee at the greasy marble counter, took them to a chair with a table arm in the dim rear of the lunchroom and hastily devoured them. As he came out and returned to his car he again glanced along the street.

He fancied that he knew a man who was approaching. He could not be sure. From the breast up the man seemed familiar, as did the customers of the bank whom he viewed through the wicket of the teller's window. When he saw them in the street he could never be sure of them. It seemed extraordinary to find that these persons, who to him were nothing but faces with attached arms that held out checks and received money, could walk about, had legs and a gait and a manner of their own.

He walked to the curb and stared up at the cornice of one of the stores, puckering his lips, giving an impersonation of a man inspecting a building. With the corner of an eye he followed the approaching man. The man ducked his head as he neared, and greeted him, "Hello, Brother Teller." Jasper seemed startled; gave the "Oh! Oh, how are you!" of sudden recognition; and mumbled, "Looking after a little bank property."

The man passed on.

Jasper got into his car and drove back to the street that would take him out to the suburb of Rosebank. As he left Fandall Avenue he peered at his watch. It was five minutes to seven.

At a quarter past seven he passed through the main street of Rosebank and turned into a lane that was but little changed since the time when it had been a country road. A few jerry-built villas of freckled paint did shoulder upon it, but for the most part it ran through swamps spotted with willow groves, the spongy ground covered with scatterings of dry leaves and bark. Opening on this lane was a dim-rutted grassy private road which disappeared into one of the willow groves.

Jasper sharply swung his car between the crumbly gate posts and along on the bumpy private road. He made an abrupt turn, came in sight of an unpainted shed and shot the car into it without cutting down his speed, so that he almost hit the back of the shed with his front fenders. He shut off the engine, climbed out quickly and ran back toward the gate. From the shield of the bank of alder bushes he peered out. Two clattering women were going down the public road. They stared in through the gate and half halted.

"That's where that hermit lives," said one of them.

"Oh, you mean the one that's writing a religious book, and never comes out till evening? Some kind of a preacher?"

"Yes, that's the one. John Holt, I think his

name is. I guess he's kind of crazy. He lives in the old Beaudette house. But you can't see it from here—it's clear through the block, on the next street."

"I heard he was crazy. But I just saw an automobile go in here."

"Oh, that's his cousin or brother or something—lives in the city. They say he's rich, and such a nice fellow."

The two women ambled on, their clatter blurring with distance. Standing behind the alders Jasper rubbed the palm of one hand with the fingers of the other. The palm was dry with nervousness. But he grinned.

He returned to the shed and entered a brick-paved walk almost a block long, walled and sheltered by overhanging willows. Once it had been a pleasant path; carved wooden benches were placed along it, and it widened to a court with a rock garden, a fountain, and a stone bench. The rock garden had degenerated into a riot of creepers sprawling over the sharp stones; the paint had peeled from the fountain, leaving its iron cupids and naiads eaten with rust. The bricks of the wall were smeared with lichens and moss and were untidy with windrows of dry leaves and caked earth.

Many of the bricks were broken; the walk was hilly in its unevenness. From willows and bricks and scuffled earth rose a damp chill. But Jasper did not seem to note the dampness. He hastened along the walk to the house—a structure of heavy stone which, for this newish Midwestern land, was very ancient. It had been built by a French fur trader in 1839. The Chippewas had scalped a man in its dooryard. The heavy back door was guarded by an unexpectedly expensive modern lock. Jasper opened it with a flat key and closed it behind him. It locked on a spring. He was in a crude kitchen, the shades of which were drawn. He passed through the kitchen and dining room into the living room. Dodging chairs and tables in the darkness as though he was used to them he went to each of the three windows of the living room and made sure that all the shades were down before he lighted the student lamp on the game-legged table. As the glow crept over the drab walls Jasper bobbed his head with satisfaction.

Nothing had been touched since his last visit.

The room was musty with the smell of old green rep upholstery and leather books. It had not been dusted for months. Dust sheeted the stiff red velvet chairs, the uncomfortable settee, the chill white marble fireplace, the immense glass-fronted bookcase that filled one side of the room.

The atmosphere was unnatural to this capable business man, this Jasper Holt. But Jasper did not seem oppressed. He briskly removed the wrappers from the genuine books and from the candy-box imitations of books. One of the two wrappers he laid on the table and smoothed out. Upon this he poured the candy from the two boxes. The other wrapper and the strings he stuffed into the fireplace and immediately burned. Crossing to the bookcase he unlocked one section on the bottom shelf. There was a row of rather cheap-looking novels on this shelf, and of these at least six were actually such candy boxes as he had purchased that evening.

Only one shelf of the bookcase was given over to anything so frivolous as novels. The others were filled with black-covered, speckle-leaved, dismal books of history, theology, biography—the shabby-genteel sort of books you find on the fifteen-cent table at a secondhand bookshop. Over these Jasper pored for a moment as though he was memorizing their titles.

He took down *The Life of the Rev. Jeremiah Bodfish* and read aloud: "In those intimate discourses with his family that followed evening prayers I once heard Brother Bodfish observe that Philo Judaeus—whose scholarly career always calls to my mind the adumbrations of Melanchthon upon the essence of rationalism—was a mere sophist—"

Jasper slammed the book shut, remarking contentedly, "That'll do. Philo Judaeus—good name to spring."

He relocked the bookcase and went upstairs. In a small bedroom at the right of the upper hall an electric light was burning. Presumably the house had been deserted till Jasper's entrance, but a prowler in the yard might have judged from this ever-burning light that someone was in the residence. The bedroom was Spartan—an iron bed, one straight chair, a washstand, a heavy oak bureau. Jasper scrambled to unlock the bottom drawer of the bureau, yank it open, take out a wrinkled shiny suit of black, a pair of black shoes, a small black bow tie, a Gladstone collar, a white shirt with starched bosom, a speckly brown felt hat and a wig—an expensive and excellent wig with artfully unkempt hair of a faded brown.

He stripped off his attractive flannel suit, wing collar, blue tie, custom-made silk shirt, and cordovan shoes, and speedily put on the wig and those gloomy garments. As he donned them the corners of his mouth began to droop. Leaving the light on and his own clothes flung on the bed he descended the stairs. He was obviously not the same Jasper, but less healthy, less practical, less agreeable, and decidedly more aware of the sorrow and long thoughts of the dreamer. Indeed it must be understood that now he was not Jasper Holt, but Jasper's twin brother, John Holt, hermit and religious fanatic.

II

John Holt, twin brother of Jasper Holt, the bank teller, rubbed his eyes as though he had for hours been absorbed in study, and crawled through the living room, through the tiny hall, to the front door. He opened it, picked up a couple of circulars that the postman had dropped through the letter slot in the door, went out and locked the door behind him. He was facing a narrow front yard, neater than the willow walk at the back, on a suburban street more populous than the straggly back lane.

A street arc illuminated the yard and showed that a card was tacked on the door. John touched the card, snapped it with a nail of his finger to make sure it was securely tacked. In that light he could not read it, but he knew that it was inscribed in a small finicky hand: "Agents kindly do not disturb, bell will not be answered, occupant of the house engaged in literary work."

John stood on the doorstep until he made out his neighbor on the right—a large stolid commuter, who was walking before his house smoking an after-dinner cigar. John poked to the fence and sniffed at a spray of lilac blossoms till the neighbor called over, "Nice evening."

"Yes, it seems to be pleasant."

John's voice was like Jasper's but it was more guttural, and his speech had less assurance.

"How's the story going?"

"It is—it is very difficult. So hard to comprehend all the inner meanings of the prophecies. Well, I must be hastening to Soul Hope Hall. I trust we shall see you there some Wednesday or Sunday evening. I bid you good-night, sir."

John wavered down the street to the drugstore. He purchased a bottle of ink. In a grocery that kept open evenings he got two pounds of cornmeal, two pounds of flour, a pound of bacon, a half pound of butter, six eggs, and a can of condensed milk.

"Shall we deliver them?" asked the clerk.

John looked at him sharply. He realized that this was a new man, who did not know his customs. He said rebukingly: "No, I always carry my parcels. I am writing a book. I am never to be disturbed."

He paid for the provisions out of a postal money order for thirty-five dollars, and received the change. The cashier of the store was accustomed to cashing these money orders, which were always sent to John from South Vernon, by one R. J. Smith. John took the bundle of food and walked out of the store.

"That fellow's kind of a nut, isn't he?" asked the new clerk.

The cashier explained: "Yep. Doesn't even take fresh milk—uses condensed for everything! What do you think of that! And they say he burns up all his garbage—never has anything in the ashcan except ashes. If you knock at his door, he never answers it, fellow told me. All the time writing this book of his. Religious crank, I guess. Has a little income though—guess his folks were pretty well fixed. Comes out once in a while in the evening and pokes round town. We used to laugh about him, but we've kind of got used to him. Been here about a year, I guess it is."

John was serenely passing down the main street of Rosebank. At the dingier end of it he turned in at a hallway marked by a lighted sign announcing in crude house-painter's letters: "Soul Hope Fraternity Hall. Experience Meeting. All Welcome."

It was eight o'clock. The members of the Soul Hope cult had gathered in their hall above a bakery. Theirs was a tiny, tight-minded sect. They asserted that they alone obeyed the scriptural tenets; that they alone were certain to be saved, that all other denominations were damned by unapostolic luxury, that it was wicked to have organs or ministers or any meeting places save plain halls. The members themselves conducted the meetings, one after another rising to give an interpretation of the scriptures or to rejoice in gathering with the faithful, while the others commented with "Hallelujah!" and "Amen, brother, amen!" They were plainly dressed, not overfed, somewhat elderly, and a rather happy congregation. The most honored of them all was John Holt.

John had come to Rosebank only eleven months before. He had bought the Beaudette house with the library of the recent occupant, a retired clergyman, and had paid for them in new one-hundred-dollar bills. Already he had great credit in the Soul Hope cult. It appeared that he spent almost all his time at home, praying and reading and writing a book. The Soul Hope Fraternity were excited about the book. They had begged him to read it to them. So far he had only read a few pages, consisting mostly of quotations from ancient treatises on the Prophecies. Nearly every Sunday and Wednesday evening he appeared at the meeting and in a halting and scholarly way lectured on the world and the flesh.

Tonight he spoke polysyllabically of the fact that one Philo Judaeus had been a mere sophist. The cult were none too clear as to what either a Philo Judaeus or a sophist might be, but with heads all nodding in a row, they murmured: "You're right, brother! Hallelujah!"

John glided into a sad earnest discourse on his worldly brother Jasper, and informed them of his struggles with Jasper's itch for money. By his request the fraternity prayed for Jasper.

The meeting was over at nine. John shook hands all round with the elders of the congregation, sighing: "Fine meeting tonight, wasn't it? Such a free outpouring of the Spirit!" He welcomed a new member, a servant girl just come from Seattle. Carrying his groceries and the bottle of ink he poked down the stairs from the hall at seven minutes after nine.

At sixteen minutes after nine John was stripping off his brown wig and the funereal clothes in his bedroom. At twenty-eight after, John Holt had become Jasper Holt, the capable teller of the Lumber National Bank.

Jasper Holt left the light burning in his brother's bedroom. He rushed downstairs, tried the fastening of the front door, bolted it, made sure that all the windows were fastened, picked up the bundle of groceries and the pile of candies that he had removed from the booklike candy boxes, blew out the light in the living room and ran down the willow walk to his car. He threw the groceries and candy into it, backed the car out as though he was accustomed to backing in this bough-scattered yard, and drove along the lonely road at the rear.

When he was passing a swamp he reached down, picked up the bundle of candies, and steering with one hand removed the wrapping paper with the other hand and hurled out the candies. They showered among the weeds beside the road. The paper which had contained the candies, and upon which was printed the name of the Parthenon Confectionery Store, Jasper tucked into his pocket. He took the groceries item by item from the labeled bag containing them, thrust that bag also into his pocket, and laid the groceries on the seat beside him.

On the way from Rosebank to the center of the city of Vernon, he again turned off the main avenue and halted at a goat-infested shack occupied by a crippled Norwegian. He sounded the horn. The Norwegian's grandson ran out.

"Here's a little more grub for you," bawled Jasper.

"God bless you, sir. I don't know what we'd do if it wasn't for you!" cried the old Norwegian from the door.

But Jasper did not wait for gratitude. He merely shouted "Bring you some more in a couple of days," as he started away.

At a quarter past ten he drove up to the hall that housed the latest interest in Vernon society—The Community Theater. The Boulevard Set, the "best people in town," belonged to the Community Theater Association, and the leader of it was the daughter of the general manager of the railroad. As a well-bred bachelor Jasper Holt was welcome among them, despite the fact that no one knew much about him except that he was a good bank teller and had been born in England. But as an actor he was not merely welcome: he was the best amateur actor in Vernon. His placid face could narrow with tragic emotion or puff out with comedy, his placid manner concealed a dynamo of emotion. Unlike most amateur actors he did not try to act—he became the thing itself. He forgot Jasper Holt, and turned into a vagrant or a judge, a Bernard Shaw thought, a Lord Dunsany symbol, a Noel Coward man-about-town.

The other one-act plays of the next program of the Community Theater had already been rehearsed. The cast of the play in which Jasper was to star were all waiting for him. So were the ladies responsible for the staging. They wanted his advice about the blue curtain for the stage window, about the baby-spot that was out of order, about the higher interpretation of the rôle of the page in the piece—a rôle consisting of only two lines, but to be played by one of the most popular girls in the younger set. After the discussions, and a most violent quarrel between two members of the play-reading committee, the rehearsal was called. Jasper Holt still wore his flannel suit and a wilting carnation; but he was not Jasper; he was the Duc de San Saba, a cynical, gracious, gorgeous old man, easy of gesture, tranquil of voice, shudderingly evil of desire.

"If I could get a few more actors like you!" cried the professional coach.

The rehearsal was over at half-past eleven. Jasper drove his car to the public garage in which he kept it, and walked home. There, he tore up and burned the wrapping paper bearing the name of the Parthenon Confectionery Store and the labeled bag that had contained the groceries.

The Community Theater plays were given on the following Wednesday. Jasper Holt was highly applauded, and at the party at the Lakeside Country Club, after the play, he danced with the prettiest girls in town. He hadn't much to say to them, but he danced fervently, and about him was a halo of artistic success.

That night his brother John did not appear at the meeting of the Soul Hope Fraternity out in Rosebank.

On Monday, five days later, while he was in conference with the president and the cashier of the Lumber National Bank, Jasper complained of a headache. The next day he telephoned to the president that he would not come down to work—he would stay home and rest his eyes, sleep, and get rid of the persistent headache. That was unfortunate, for that very day his twin brother John made one of his frequent trips into Vernon and called at the bank.

The president had seen John only once before, and by a coincidence it had happened on this occasion also Jasper had been absent—had been out of town. The president invited John into his private office.

"Your brother is at home; poor fellow has a bad headache. Hope he gets over it. We think a great deal of him here. You ought to be proud of him. Will you have a smoke?"

As he spoke the president looked John over. Once or twice when Jasper and the president had been out at lunch Jasper had spoken of the remarkable resemblance between himself and his twin brother. But the president told himself that he didn't really see much resemblance. The features of the two were alike, but John's expression of chronic spiritual indigestion, his unfriendly manner, and his hair—unkempt and lifeless brown, where Jasper's was sleekly black about a shiny bald spot—made the president dislike John as much as he liked Jasper.

And now John was replying: "No, I do not smoke. I can't understand how a man can soil the temple with drugs. I suppose I ought to be glad to hear you praise poor Jasper, but I am more concerned with his lack of respect for the things of the spirit. He sometimes comes to see me, at Rosebank, and I argue with him, but somehow I can't make him see his errors. And his flippant ways—!"

"We don't think he's flippant. We think he's a pretty steady worker."

"But he's play-acting! And reading love stories! Well, I try to keep in mind the injunction, 'Judge not, that ye be not judged.' But I am pained to find my own brother giving up immortal promises for mortal amusements. Well, I'll go and call on him. I trust that some day we shall see you at Soul Hope Hall, in Rosebank. Good day, sir."

Turning back to his work, the president grumbled: "I am going to tell Jasper that the best compliment I can hand him is that he is not like his brother."

And on the following day, another Wednesday, when Jasper reappeared at the bank, the president did make this jesting comparison, and Jasper sighed, "Oh, John is really a good fellow, but he's always gone in for metaphysics and Oriental mysticism and Lord knows what all, till he's kind of lost in the fog. But he's a lot better than I am. When I murder my landlady—or say, when I rob the bank, Chief—you go get John, and I bet you the best lunch in town that he'll do his best to bring me to justice. That's how square he is!"

"Square, yes—corners just sticking out! Well, when you do rob us, Jasper, I'll look up John. But do try to keep from robbing us as long as you can. I'd hate to have to associate with a religious detective in a boiled shirt!"

Both men laughed, and Jasper went back to his cage. His head continued to hurt, he admitted. The president advised him to lay off for a week. He didn't want to, he said. With the new munition industries due to the war in Europe there was much increase in factory pay rolls, and Jasper took charge of them.

"Better take a week off than get ill," argued the president late that afternoon.

Jasper did let himself be persuaded to go away for at least a week-end. He would run up north, to Wakamin Lake, the coming Friday, he said; he would get some black-bass fishing, and be back on Monday or Tuesday. Before he went he would make up the pay rolls for the Saturday payments and turn them over to the other teller. The president thanked him for his faithfulness, and as was his not infrequent custom, invited Jasper to his house for the evening of the next day—Thursday.

That Wednesday evening Jasper's brother John appeared at the Soul Hope meeting in Rosebank. When he had gone home and magically turned back into Jasper this Jasper did not return the wig and garments of John to the bureau but packed them in a suitcase, took the suitcase to his room in Vernon, and locked it in his wardrobe.

Jasper was amiable at dinner at the president's house on Thursday, but he was rather silent, and as his head still throbbed he left the house early—at nine-thirty. Sedately carrying his gray silk gloves in one hand and pompously swinging his stick with the other, he walked from the president's house on the fashionable boulevard back to the center of Vernon. He entered the public garage in which he stored his car. He commented to the night attendant, "Head aches. Guess I'll take the 'bus out and get some fresh air."

He drove away at not more than fifteen miles an hour. He headed south. When he had reached the outskirts of the city he speeded up to a consistent twenty-five miles an hour. He settled down in his seat with the unmoving steadiness of the long-distance driver; his body quiet except for the tiny subtle movements of his foot on the accelerator, of his hand on the steering wheel—his right hand across the wheel, holding it at the top, his left elbow resting easily on the cushioned edge of his seat and his left hand merely touching the wheel.

He drove down in that southern direction for fifteen miles—almost to the town of Wanagoochie. Then by a rather poor side road he turned sharply to the north and west, and making a huge circle about the city drove toward the town of St. Clair. The suburb of Rosebank, in which his brother John lived, is also north of Vernon. These directions were of some importance to him; Wanagoochie eighteen miles south of the mother city of Vernon; Rosebank, on the other hand, eight miles north of Vernon, and St. Clair twenty miles north—about as far north of Vernon as Wanagoochie is south.

On his way to St. Clair, at a point that was only two miles from Rosebank, Jasper ran the car off the main road into a grove of oaks and maples and stopped it on a long-unused woodland road. He stiffly got out and walked through the woods up a rise of ground to a cliff overlooking a swampy lake. The gravelly farther bank of the cliff rose perpendicularly from the edge of the water. In that wan light distilled by stars and the earth he made out the reedy expanse of the lake. It was so muddy, so tangled with sedge grass that it was never used for swimming, and as its inhabitants were only slimy bullheads few people ever tried to fish there. Jasper stood reflective. He was remembering the story of the farmer's team which had run away, dashed over this cliff, and sunk out of sight in the mud bottom of the lake.

Swishing his stick he outlined an imaginary road from the top of the cliff back to the sheltered place where his car was standing. Once he hacked away with a large pocketknife a mass of knotted hazel bushes which blocked that projected road. When he had traced the road to his car he smiled. He walked to the edge of the woods and looked up and down the main highway. A car was approaching. He waited till it had passed, ran back to his own car, backed it out on the highway, and went on his northward course toward St. Clair, driving about thirty miles an hour.

On the edge of St. Clair he halted, took out his kit of tools, unscrewed a spark plug, and sharply tapping the plug on the engine block, deliberately cracked the porcelain jacket. He screwed the plug in again and started the car. It bucked and spit, missing on one cylinder, with the short-circuited plug.

"I guess there must be something wrong with the ignition," he said cheerfully.

He managed to run the car into a garage in St. Clair. There was no one in the garage save an old negro, the night washer, who was busy over a limousine with sponge and hose.

"Got a night repair man here?" asked Jasper.

"No, sir; guess you'll have to leave it till morning."

"Hang it! Something gone wrong with the carburetor or the ignition. Well, I'll have to leave it then. Tell him—Say will you be here in the morning when the repair man comes on?"

"Yes, sir."

"Well, tell him I must have the car by tomorrow noon. No, say by tomorrow at nine. Now, don't forget. This will help your memory."

He gave a quarter to the negro, who grinned and shouted: "Yes, sir; that'll help my memory a lot!" As he tied a storage tag on the car the negro inquired: "Name?"

"Uh—my name? Oh, Hanson. Remember now, ready about nine tomorrow."

Jasper walked to the railroad station. It was ten minutes of one. Jasper did not ask the night operator about the next train into Vernon. Apparently he knew that there was a train stopping here at St. Clair at one-thirty-seven. He did not sit in the waiting room but in the darkness outside, on a truck behind the baggage room. When the train came in he slipped into the last seat of the last car, and with his soft hat over his eyes either slept or appeared to sleep. When he reached Vernon he got off and came to the garage in which he regularly kept his car. He stepped inside. The night attendant was drowsing in a large wooden chair tilted back against the wall in the narrow runway which formed the entrance to the garage.

Jasper jovially shouted to the attendant: "Certainly ran into some hard luck. Ignition went wrong—I guess it was the ignition. Had to leave the car down at Wanagoochie."

"Yuh, hard luck, all right," assented the attendant.

"Yump. So I left it at Wanagoochie," Jasper emphasized as he passed on.

He had been inexact in this statement. It was not at Wanagoochie, which is south, but at St. Clair, which is north, that he had left his car.

He had returned to his boarding house, slept beautifully, hummed in his morning shower bath. Yet at breakfast he complained of his continuous headache, and announced that he was going up north, to Wakamin, to get some bass fishing and rest his eyes. His landlady urged him to go.

"Anything I can do to help you get away?" she queried.

"No, thanks. I'm just taking a couple of suitcases, with some old clothes and some fishing tackle. Fact, I have 'em all packed already. I'll probably take the noon train north if I can get away from the bank. Pretty busy now, with these pay rolls for the factories that have war contracts for the Allies. What's it say in the paper this morning?"

Jasper arrived at the bank, carrying the two suitcases and a neat, polite, rolled silk umbrella, the silver top of which was engraved with his name. The doorman, who was also the bank guard, helped him to carry the suitcases inside.

"Careful of that bag. Got my fishing tackle in it," said Jasper, to the doorman, apropos of one of the suitcases which was heavy but apparently not packed full. "Well, I think I'll run up to Wakamin today and catch a few bass."

"Wish I could go along, sir. How is the head this morning? Does it still ache?" asked the doorman.

"Rather better, but my eyes still feel pretty rocky. Guess I've been using them too much. Say, Connors, I'll try to catch the train north at eleven-seven. Better have a taxicab here for me at eleven. Or no; I'll let you know a little before eleven. Try to catch the eleven-seven north, for Wakamin."

"Very well, sir."

The president, the cashier, the chief clerk—all asked Jasper how he felt; and to all of them he repeated the statement that he had been using his eyes too much, and that he would catch a few bass at Wakamin.

The other paying teller, from his cage next to that of Jasper, called heartily through the steel netting: "Pretty soft for some people! You wait! I'm going to have the hay fever this summer, and I'll go fishing for a month!"

Jasper placed the two suitcases and the umbrella in his cage, and leaving the other teller to pay out current money he himself made up the pay rolls for the next day—Saturday. He casually went into the vault—a narrow, unimpressive, unaired cell with a hard linoleum floor, one unshaded electric bulb, and a back wall composed entirely of steel doors of safes, all painted a sickly blue, very unimpressive, but guarding several millions of dollars in cash and securities. The upper doors, hung on large steel arms and each provided with two dials, could be opened only by two officers of the bank, each knowing one of the two combinations. Below these were smaller doors, one of which Jasper could open, as teller. It was the door of an insignificant steel box, which contained one hundred and seventeen thousand dollars in bills and four thousand dollars in gold and silver.

Jasper passed back and forth, carrying bundles of currency. In his cage he was working less than three feet from the other teller, who was divided from him only by the bands of the steel netting.

While he worked he exchanged a few words with this other teller.

Once, as he counted out nineteen thousand dollars, he commented: "Big pay roll for the

Henschel Wagon Works this week. They're making gun carriages and truck bodies for the Allies, I understand."

"Uh-huh!" said the other teller, not much interested.

Mechanically, unobtrusively going about his ordinary routine of business, Jasper counted out bills to amounts agreeing with the items on a typed schedule of the pay rolls. Apparently his eyes never lifted from his counting and from the typed schedule which lay before him. The bundles of bills he made into packages, fastening each with a paper band. Each bundle he seemed to drop into a small black leather bag which he held beside him. But he did not actually drop the money into these pay-roll bags.

Both the suitcases at his feet were closed and presumably fastened, but one was not fastened. And though it was heavy it contained nothing but a lump of pig iron. From time to time Jasper's hand, holding a bundle of bills, dropped to his side. With a slight movement of his foot he opened that suitcase and the bills slipped from his hand down into it.

The bottom part of the cage was a solid sheet of stamped steel, and from the front of the bank no one could see this suspicious gesture. The other teller could have seen it, but Jasper dropped the bills only when the other teller was busy talking to a customer or when his back was turned. In order to delay for such a favorable moment Jasper frequently counted packages of bills twice, rubbing his eyes as though they hurt him.

After each of these secret disposals of packages of bills Jasper made much of dropping into the pay-roll bags the rolls of coin for which the schedule called. It was while he was tossing these blue-wrapped cylinders of coin into the bags that he would chat with the other teller. Then he would lock up the bags and gravely place them at one side.

Jasper was so slow in making up the pay rolls that it was five minutes of eleven before he finished. He called the doorman to the cage and suggested, "Better call my taxi now."

He still had one bag to fill. He could plainly be seen dropping packages of money into it, while he instructed the assistant teller: "I'll stick all the bags in my safe and you can transfer them to yours. Be sure to lock my safe. Lord, I better hurry or I'll miss my train! Be back Tuesday morning, at latest. So long; take care yourself."

He hastened to pile the pay-roll bags into his safe in the vault. The safe was almost filled with them. And except for the last one not one of the bags contained anything except a few rolls of coin. Though he had told the other teller to lock his safe, he himself twirled the combination—which was thoughtless of him, as the assistant teller would now have to wait and get the president to unlock it.

He picked up his umbrella and two suitcases, bending over one of the cases for not more than ten seconds. Waving good-by to the cashier at his desk down front and hurrying so fast that the doorman did not have a chance to help him carry the suitcases, he rushed through the bank, through the door, into the waiting taxicab, and loudly enough for the doorman to hear he cried to the driver, "M. & D. Station."

At the M. & D. R.R. Station, refusing offers of redcaps to carry his bags, he bought a ticket for Wakamin, which is a lake-resort town one hundred and forty miles northwest of Vernon, hence one hundred and twenty beyond St. Clair. He had just time to get aboard the eleven-seven train. He did not take a chair car, but sat in a day coach near the rear door. He unscrewed the silver top of his umbrella, on which was engraved his name, and dropped it into his pocket.

When the train reached St. Clair, Jasper strolled out to the vestibule, carrying the suitcases but leaving the topless umbrella behind. His face was blank, uninterested. As the train started he dropped down on the station platform and gravely walked away. For a second the light of adventure crossed his face, and vanished.

At the garage at which he had left his car on the evening before he asked the foreman: "Did you get my car fixed—Mercury roadster, ignition on the bum?"

"Nope! Couple of jobs ahead of it. Haven't had time to touch it yet. Ought to get at it early this afternoon."

Jasper curled his tongue round his lips in startled vexation. He dropped his suitcases on the floor of the garage and stood thinking, his bent forefinger against his lower lip.

Then: "Well, I guess I can get her to go—sorry—can't wait—got to make the next town," he grumbled.

"Lot of you traveling salesmen making your territory by motor now, Mr. Hanson," said the foreman civilly, glancing at the storage check on Jasper's car.

"Yep. I can make a good many more than I could by train."

He paid for overnight storage without complaining, though since his car had not been repaired this charge was unjust. In fact, he was altogether prosaic and inconspicuous. He thrust the suitcases into the car and drove away, the motor spitting. At another garage he bought another spark plug and screwed it in. When he went on, the motor had ceased spitting.

He drove out of St. Clair, back in the direction of Vernon—and of Rosebank where his brother lived. He ran the car into that thick grove of oaks and maples only two miles from Rosebank, where he had paced off an imaginary road to the cliff overhanging the reedy lake. He parked his car in a grassy space beside the abandoned woodland road. He laid a light robe over the suitcases. From beneath the seat he took a can of deviled chicken, a box of biscuits, a canister of tea, a folding cooking kit, and a spirit lamp. These he spread on the grass—a picnic lunch.

He sat beside that lunch from seven minutes past one in the afternoon till dark. Once in a while he made a pretense of eating. He fetched water from the brook, made tea, opened the box of biscuits and the can of chicken. But mostly he sat still and smoked cigarette after cigarette.

Once, a Swede, taking this road as a short cut to his truck farm, passed by and mumbled, "Picnic, eh?"

"Yuh, takin' the day off," said Jasper dully.

The man went on without looking back.

At dusk Jasper finished a cigarette down to the tip, crushed out the light and made the cryptic remark:

"That's probably Jasper Holt's last smoke. I don't suppose you can smoke, John—damn you!"

He hid the two suitcases in the bushes, piled the remains of the lunch into the car, took down the top of the car, and crept down to the main road. No one was in sight. He returned. He snatched a hammer and a chisel from his tool kit, and with a few savage cracks he so defaced the number of the car stamped on the engine block that it could not be made out. He removed the license numbers from fore and aft, and placed them beside the suitcases. Then, when there was just enough light to see the bushes as cloudy masses, he started the car, drove through the woods and up the incline to the top of the cliff, and halted, leaving the engine running.

Between the car and the edge of the cliff which overhung the lake there was a space of about one hundred and thirty feet, fairly level and covered with straggly red clover. Jasper paced off this distance, returned to the car, took his seat in a nervous, tentative way and put her into gear, starting on second speed and slamming her into third. The car bolted toward the edge of the cliff. He instantly swung out on the running board. Standing there, headed directly toward the sharp drop over the cliff, steering with his left hand on the wheel, he shoved the hand throttle up—up—up with his right. He safely leaped down from the running board.

Of itself, the car rushed forward, roaring. It shot over the edge of the cliff. It soared twenty feet out into the air, as though it were a thick-bodied aeroplane. It turned over and over, with a sickening drop toward the lake. The water splashed up in a tremendous noisy circle. Then silence. In the twilight the surface of the lake shone like milk. There was no sign of the car on the surface. The concentric rings died away. The lake was secret and sinister and still. "Lord!" ejaculated Jasper, standing on the cliff; then:

"Well, they won't find that for a couple of years anyway."

He turned to the suitcases. Squatting beside them he took from one the wig and black garments of John Holt. He stripped, put on the clothes of John, and packed those of Jasper in the bag. With the cases and the motor-license plates he walked toward Rosebank, keeping in various groves of maples and willows till he was within half a mile of the town. He reached the stone house at the end of the willow walk and sneaked in the back way. He burned Jasper Holt's clothes in the grate, melted down the license plates in the stove, and between two rocks he smashed Jasper's expensive watch and fountain pen into an unpleasant mass of junk, which he dropped into the cistern for rain water. The silver head of the umbrella he scratched with a chisel till the engraved name was indistinguishable.

He unlocked a section of the bookcase and taking a number of packages of bills in denominations of one, five, ten, and twenty dollars from one of the suitcases he packed them into those empty candy boxes which, on the shelves, looked so much like books. As he stored them he counted the bills. They came to ninety-seven thousand five hundred and thirty-five dollars.

The two suitcases were new. There were no distinguishing marks on them. But taking them out to the kitchen he kicked them, rubbed them with lumps of blacking, raveled their edges, and cut their sides, till they gave the appearance of having been long and badly used in traveling. He took them upstairs and tossed them up into the low attic.

In his bedroom he undressed calmly. Once he laughed: "I despise those pretentious fools—bank officers and cops. I'm beyond their fool law. No one can catch me—it would take me myself to do that!"

He got into bed. With a vexed "Hang it!" he mused, "I suppose John would pray, no matter how chilly the floor was."

He got out of bed and from the inscrutable Lord of the Universe he sought forgiveness—not for Jasper Holt, but for the denominations who lacked the true faith of Soul Hope Fraternity.

He returned to bed and slept till the middle of the morning, lying with his arms behind his head, a smile on his face.

Thus did Jasper Holt, without the mysterious pangs of death, yet cease to exist, and thus did John Holt come into being not merely as an apparition glimpsed on Sunday and Wednesday evenings but as a being living twenty-four hours a day, seven days a week.

III

The inhabitants of Rosebank were familiar with the occasional appearances of John Holt, the eccentric recluse, and they merely snickered about him when on the Saturday evening following the Friday that has been chronicled he was seen to come out of his gate and trudge down to a news and stationery shop on Main Street.

He purchased an evening paper and said to the clerk: "You can have the *Morning Herald* delivered at my house every morning—27 Humbert Avenue."

"Yuh, I know where it is. Thought you had kind of a grouch on newspapers," said the clerk pertly.

"Ah, did you indeed? The *Herald,* every morning, please. I will pay a month in advance," was all John Holt said, but he looked directly at the clerk, and the man cringed.

John attended the meeting of the Soul Hope Fraternity the next evening—Sunday—but he was not seen on the streets again for two and a half days.

There was no news of the disappearance of Jasper Holt till the following Wednesday, when the whole thing came out in a violent, small-city, front-page story, headed:

PAYING TELLER SOCIAL FAVORITE—
MAKES GET-AWAY

The paper stated that Jasper Holt had been missing for four days, and that the officers of the bank, after first denying that there was anything wrong with his accounts, had admitted that he was short one hundred thousand dollars—two hundred thousand, said one report. He had purchased a ticket for Wakamin, this state, on Friday and a trainman, a customer of the bank, had noticed him on the train, but he had apparently never arrived at Wakamin.

A woman asserted that on Friday afternoon she had seen Holt driving an automobile between Vernon and St. Clair. This appearance near St. Clair was supposed to be merely a blind, however. In fact, our able chief of police had proof that Holt was not headed north, in the direction of St. Clair, but south, beyond Wanagoochie—probably for Des Moines or St. Louis. It was definitely known that on the previous day Holt had left his car at Wanagoochie, and with their customary thoroughness and promptness the police were making search at Wanagoochie. The chief had already communicated with the police in cities to the south, and the capture of the man could confidently be expected at any moment. As long as the chief appointed by our popular mayor was in power, it went ill with those who gave even the appearance of wrongdoing.

When asked his opinion of the theory that the alleged fugitive had gone north the chief declared that of course Holt had started in that direction, with the vain hope of throwing pursuers off the scent, but that he had immediately turned south and picked up his car. Though he would not say so definitely the chief let it be known that he was ready to put his hands on the fellow who had hidden Holt's car at Wanagoochie.

When asked if he thought Holt was crazy the chief laughed and said: "Yes, he's crazy two hundred thousand dollars' worth. I'm not making any slams, but there's a lot of fellows among our political opponents who would go a whole lot crazier for a whole lot less!"

The president of the bank, however, was greatly distressed, and strongly declared his belief that Holt, who was a favorite in the most sumptuous residences on the Boulevard, besides being well known in local dramatic circles, and who bore the best of reputations in the bank, was temporarily out of his mind, as he had been distressed by pains in the head for some time past. Meantime the bonding company, which had fully covered the employees of the bank by a joint bond of two hundred thousand dollars, had its detectives working with the police on the case.

As soon as he had read the paper John took a trolley into Vernon and called on the president of the bank. John's face drooped with the sorrow of the disgrace. The president received him. John staggered into the room, groaning: "I have just learned in the newspaper of the terrible news about my brother. I have come—"

"We hope it's just a case of aphasia. We're sure he'll turn up all right," insisted the president.

"I wish I could believe it. But as I have told you, Jasper is not a good man. He drinks and smokes and play-acts and makes a god of stylish clothes—"

"Good Lord, that's no reason for jumping to the conclusion that he's an embezzler!"

"I pray you may be right. But meanwhile I wish to give you any assistance I can. I shall make it my sole duty to see that my brother is brought to justice if it proves that he is guilty."

"Good o' you," mumbled the president. Despite this example of John's rigid honor he could not get himself to like the man. John was standing beside him, thrusting his stupid face into his.

The president pushed his chair a foot farther away and said disagreeably: "As a matter of fact, we were thinking of searching your house. If I remember, you live in Rosebank?"

"Yes. And of course I shall be glad to have you search every inch of it. Or anything else I can do. I feel that I share fully with my twin brother in this unspeakable sin. I'll turn over the key of my house to you at once. There is also a shed at the back where Jasper used to keep his automobile when he came to see me." He produced a large, rusty, old-fashioned door key and held it out, adding: "The address is 27 Humbert Avenue, Rosebank."

"Oh, it won't be necessary, I guess," said the president, somewhat shamed, irritably waving off the key.

"But I just want to help somehow! What can I do? Who is—in the language of the newspapers—who is the detective on the case? I'll give him any help—"

"Tell you what you do: Go see Mr. Scandling, of the Mercantile Trust and Bonding Company, and tell him all you know."

"I shall. I take my brother's crime on my shoulders—otherwise I'd be committing the sin of Cain. You are giving me a chance to try to expiate our joint sin, and, as Brother Jeremiah Bodfish was wont to say, it is a blessing to have an opportunity to expiate a sin, no matter how painful the punishment may seem to be to the mere physical being. As I may have told you I am an accepted member of the Soul Hope Fraternity, and though we are free from cant and dogma it is our firm belief—"

Then for ten dreary minutes John Holt sermonized; quoted forgotten books and quaint, ungenerous elders; twisted bitter pride and clumsy mysticism into fanatical spider web. The president was a churchgoer, an ardent supporter of missionary funds, for forty years a pewholder at St. Simeon's Church, but he was alternately bored to a chill shiver and roused to wrath against this self-righteous zealot.

When he had rather rudely got rid of John Holt he complained to himself: "Curse it, I oughtn't to, but I must say I prefer Jasper the sinner to John the saint. Uff! What a smell of damp cellars the fellow has! He must spend all his time picking potatoes. Say! By thunder, I remember that Jasper had the infernal nerve to tell me once that if he ever robbed the bank I was to call John in. I know why, now! John is the kind of egotistical fool that would muddle up any kind of a systematic search. Well, Jasper, sorry, but I'm not going to have anything more to do with John than I can help!"

John had gone to the Mercantile Trust and Bonding Company, had called on Mr. Scandling, and was now wearying him by a detailed and useless account of Jasper's early years and recent vices. He was turned over to the detective employed by the bonding company to find Jasper. The detective was a hard, noisy man, who found John even more tedious. John insisted on his coming out to examine the house in Rosebank, and the detective did so—but sketchily, trying to escape. John spent at least five minutes in showing him the shed where Jasper had sometimes kept his car.

He also attempted to interest the detective in his precious but spotty books. He unlocked one section of the case, dragged down a four-volume set of sermons and started to read them aloud.

The detective interrupted: "Yuh, that's great stuff, but I guess we aren't going to find your brother hiding behind those books!"

The detective got away as soon as possible, after insistently explaining to John that if they could use his assistance they would let him know.

"If I can only expiate—"

"Yuh, sure, that's all right!" wailed the detective, fairly running toward the gate.

John made one more visit to Vernon that day. He called on the chief of city police. He informed the chief that he had taken the bonding company's detective through his house, but wouldn't the police consent to search it also?

He wanted to expiate—The chief patted John on the back, advised him not to feel responsible for his brother's guilt and begged: "Skip along now—very busy."

As John walked to the Soul Hope meeting that evening, dozens of people murmured that it was his brother who had robbed the Lumber National Bank. His head was bowed with the shame. At the meeting he took Jasper's sin upon himself, and prayed that Jasper would be caught and receive the blessed healing of punishment. The others begged John not to feel that he was guilty—was he not one of the Soul Hope brethren who alone in this wicked and perverse generation were assured of salvation?

On Thursday, on Saturday morning, on

Tuesday and on Friday, John went into the city to call on the president of the bank and the detective. Twice the president saw him, and was infinitely bored by his sermons. The third time he sent word that he was out. The fourth time he saw John, but curtly explained that if John wanted to help them the best thing he could do was to stay away.

The detective was out all four times.

John smiled meekly and ceased to try to help them. Dust began to gather on certain candy boxes on the lower shelf of his bookcase, save for one of them, which he took out now and then. Always after he had taken it out a man with faded brown hair and a wrinkled black suit, a man signing himself R. J. Smith, would send a fair-sized money order from the post office at South Vernon to John Holt, at Rosebank—as he had been doing for more than six months. These money orders could not have amounted to more than twenty-five dollars a week, but that was even more than an ascetic like John Holt needed. By day John sometimes cashed these at the Rosebank post office, but usually, as had been his custom, he cashed them at his favorite grocery when he went out in the evening.

In conversation with the commuter neighbor, who every evening walked about and smoked an after-dinner cigar in the yard at the right, John was frank about the whole lamentable business of his brother's defalcation. He wondered, he said, if he had not shut himself up with his studies too much, and neglected his brother. The neighbor ponderously advised John to get out more. John let himself be persuaded, at least to the extent of taking a short walk every afternoon and of letting his literary solitude be disturbed by the delivery of milk, meat, and groceries. He also went to the public library, and in the reference room glanced at books on Central and South America—as though he was planning to go south some day.

But he continued his religious studies. It may be doubted if previous to the embezzlement John had worked very consistently on his book about Revelation. All that the world had ever seen of it was a jumble of quotations from theological authorities. Presumably the crime of his brother shocked him into more concentrated study, more patient writing. For during the year after his brother's disappearance—a year in which the bonding company gradually gave up the search and came to believe that Jasper was dead—John became fanatically absorbed in somewhat nebulous work. The days and nights drifted together in meditation in which he lost sight of realities, and seemed through the clouds of the flesh to see flashes from the towered cities of the spirit.

It has been asserted that when Jasper Holt acted a rôle he veritably lived it. No one can ever determine how great an actor was lost in the smug bank teller. To him were imperial triumphs denied, yet he was not without material reward. For playing his most subtle part he received ninety-seven thousand dollars. It may be that he earned it. Certainly for the risk entailed it was but a fair payment. Jasper had meddled with the mystery of personality, and was in peril of losing all consistent purpose, of becoming a Wandering Jew of the spirit, a strangled body walking.

IV

The sharp-pointed willow leaves had twisted and fallen, after the dreary rains of October. Bark had peeled from the willow trunks, leaving gashes of bare wood that was a wet and sickly yellow. Through the denuded trees bulked the solid stone of John Holt's house. The patches of earth were greasy between the tawny knots of grass stems. The bricks of the walk were always damp now. The world was hunched up in this pervading chill.

As melancholy as the sick earth seemed the man who in a slaty twilight paced the willow walk. His step was slack, his lips moved with the intensity of his meditation. Over his wrinkled black suit and bleak shirt bosom was a worn overcoat, the velvet collar turned green. He was considering.

"There's something to all this. I begin to see—I don't know what it is I do see! But there's lights—supernatural world that makes food and bed seem ridiculous. I am—I really am beyond the law! I make my own law! Why shouldn't I go beyond the law of vision and see the secrets of life? But I sinned, and I must repent—some day. I need not return the money. I see now that it was given me so that I could lead this life of contemplation. But the ingratitude to the president, to the people who trusted me! Am I but the most miserable of sinners, and as the blind? Voices—I hear conflicting voices—some praising me for my courage, some rebuking—"

He knelt on the slimy black surface of a wooden bench beneath the willows, and as dusk clothed him round about he prayed. It seemed to him that he prayed not in words but in vast confusing dreams—the words of a language larger than human tongues. When he had exhausted himself he slowly entered the house. He locked the door. There was nothing definite of which he was afraid, but he was never comfortable with the door unlocked.

By candle light he prepared his austere supper—dry toast, an egg, cheap green tea with thin milk. As always—as it had happened after every meal, now, for eighteen months—he wanted a cigarette when he had eaten, but did not take one. He paced into the living room and through the long still hours of the evening he read an ancient book, all footnotes and cross references, about The Numerology of the Prophetic Books, and the Number of the Beast. He tried to make notes for his own book on Revelation—that scant pile of sheets covered with writing in a small finicky hand. Thousands of other sheets he had covered; through whole nights he had written; but always he seemed with tardy pen to be racing after thoughts that he could never quite catch, and most of what he had written he had savagely burned.

But some day he would make a masterpiece! He was feeling toward the greatest discovery that mortal man had encountered. Everything, he had determined, was a symbol—not just this holy sign and that, but all physical manifestations. With frightened exultation he tried his new power of divination. The hanging lamp swung tinily. He ventured: "If the arc of that moving radiance touches the edge of the bookcase, then it will be a sign that I am to go to South America, under an entirely new disguise, and spend my money."

He shuddered. He watched the lamp's unbearably slow swing. The moving light almost touched the bookcase. He gasped. Then it receded.

It was a warning; he quaked. Would he never leave this place of brooding and of fear, which he had thought so clever a refuge? He suddenly saw it all.

"I ran away and hid in a prison! Man isn't caught by justice—he catches himself!"

Again he tried. He speculated as to whether the number of pencils on the table was greater or less than five. If greater, then he had sinned; if less, then he was veritably beyond the law. He began to lift books and papers, looking for pencils. He was coldly sweating with the suspense of the test.

Suddenly he cried, "Am I going crazy?"

He fled to his prosaic bedroom. He could not sleep. His brain was smoldering with confused inklings of mystic numbers and hidden warnings.

He woke from a half sleep more vision-haunted than any waking thought, and cried: "I must go back and confess! But I can't! I can't, when I was too clever for them! I can't go back and let them win. I won't let those fools just sit tight and still catch me!"

It was a year and a half since Jasper had disappeared. Sometimes it seemed a month and a half; sometimes gray centuries. John's will power had been shrouded with curious puttering studies; long, heavy-breathing sittings with the ouija board on his lap, midnight hours when he had fancied that tables had tapped and crackling coals had spoken. Now that the second autumn of his seclusion was creeping into winter he was conscious that he had not enough initiative to carry out his plans for going to South America. The summer before he had boasted to himself that he would come out of hiding and go South, leaving such a twisty trail as only he could make. But—oh, it was too much trouble. He hadn't the joy in play-acting which had carried his brother Jasper through his preparations for flight.

He had killed Jasper Holt, and for a miserable little pile of paper money he had become a moldy recluse!

He hated his loneliness, but still more did he hate his only companions, the members of the Soul Hope Fraternity—that pious shrill seamstress, that surly carpenter, that tight-lipped housekeeper, that old shouting man with the unseemly frieze of whiskers. They were so unimaginative. Their meetings were all the same; the same persons rose in the same order and made the same intimate announcements to the Deity that they alone were his elect.

At first it had been an amusing triumph to be accepted as the most eloquent among them, but that had become commonplace, and he resented their daring to be familiar with him, who was, he felt, the only man of all men living who beyond the illusions of the world saw the strange beatitude of higher souls.

It was at the end of November, during a Wednesday meeting at which a red-faced man had for a half hour maintained that he couldn't possibly sin, that the cumulative ennui burst in John Holt's brain. He sprang up.

He snarled: "You make me sick, all of you! You think you're so certain of sanctification that you can't do wrong. So did I, once! Now I know that we are all miserable sinners—really are! You all say you are, but you don't believe it. I tell you that you there that have just been yammering, and you, Brother Judkins, with the long twitching nose, and I—I—I, most unhappy of men, we must repent, confess, expiate our sins! And I will confess right now. I st-stole—"

Terrified he darted out of the hall, and hatless, coatless, tumbled through the main street of Rosebank, nor ceased till he had locked himself in his house. He was frightened because he had almost betrayed his secret, yet agonized because he had not gone on, really confessed, and gained the only peace he could ever know now—the peace of punishment.

He never returned to Soul Hope Hall. Indeed for a week he did not leave his house save for midnight prowling in the willow walk. Quite suddenly he became desperate with the silence. He flung out of the house, not stopping to lock or even close the front door. He raced uptown, no topcoat over his rotting garments, only an old gardener's cap on his thick brown hair. People stared at him. He bore it with resigned fury.

He entered a lunch room, hoping to sit inconspicuously and hear men talking normally about him. The attendant at the counter gaped. John heard a mutter from the cashier's desk: "There's that crazy hermit!"

All of the half-dozen young men loafing in the place were looking at him. He was so uncomfortable that he could not eat even the milk and sandwich he had ordered. He pushed them away and fled, a failure in the first attempt to dine out that he had made in eighteen months; a lamentable failure to revive that Jasper Holt whom he had coldly killed.

He entered a cigar store and bought a box of cigarettes. He took joy out of throwing away his asceticism. But when, on the street, he lighted a cigarette it made him so dizzy that he was afraid he was going to fall. He had to sit down on the curb. People gathered. He staggered to his feet and up an alley.

For hours he walked, making and discarding the most contradictory plans—to go to the bank and confess, to spend the money riotously and never confess.

It was midnight when he returned to his house.

Before it he gasped. The front door was open. He chuckled with relief as he remembered that he had not closed it. He sauntered in. He was passing the door of the living room, going directly up to his bedroom, when his foot struck an object the size of a book, but hollow sounding. He picked it up. It was one of the booklike candy boxes. And it was quite empty. Frightened, he listened. There was no sound. He crept into the living room and lighted the lamp.

The doors of the bookcase had been wrenched open. Every book had been pulled out on the floor. All of the candy boxes, which that evening had contained almost ninety-six thousand dollars, were in a pile, and all of them were empty. He searched for ten minutes, but the only money he found was one five-dollar bill, which had fluttered under the table. In his pocket he had one dollar and sixteen cents. John Holt had six dollars and sixteen cents, no job, no friends—and no identity.

V

When the president of the Lumber National Bank was informed that John Holt was waiting to see him he scowled.

"Lord, I'd forgotten that minor plague! Must be a year since he's been here. Oh, let him—No, hanged if I will! Tell him I'm too busy to see him. That is, unless he's got some news about Jasper. Pump him, and find out."

The president's secretary sweetly confided to John:

"I'm so sorry, but the president is in conference just now. What was it you wanted to see him about? Is there any news about—uh—about your brother?"

"There is not, miss. I am here to see the president on the business of the Lord."

"Oh! If that's all I'm afraid I can't disturb him."

"I will wait."

Wait he did, through all the morning, through the lunch hour—when the president hastened out past him—then into the afternoon, till the president was unable to work with the thought of that scarecrow out there, and sent for him.

"Well, well! What is it this time, John? I'm pretty busy. No news about Jasper, eh?"

"No news, sir, but—Jasper himself! I am Jasper Holt! His sin is my sin."

"Yes, yes, I know all that stuff—twin brothers, twin souls, share responsibility—"

"You don't understand. There isn't any twin brother. There isn't any John Holt. I am Jasper. I invented an imaginary brother, and disguised myself—Why, don't you recognize my voice?"

While John leaned over the desk, his two hands upon it, and smiled wistfully, the president shook his head and soothed: "No, I'm afraid I don't. Sounds like good old religious John to me! Jasper was a cheerful, efficient sort of crook. Why, his laugh—"

"But I can laugh!" The dreadful croak which John uttered was the cry of an evil bird of the swamps. The president shuddered. Under the edge of the desk his fingers crept toward the buzzer by which he summoned his secretary.

They stopped as John urged: "Look—this wig—it's a wig. See, I am Jasper!"

He had snatched off the brown thatch. He stood expectant, a little afraid.

The president was startled, but he shook his head and sighed.

"You poor devil! Wig, all right. But I wouldn't say that hair was much like Jasper's!"

He motioned toward the mirror in the corner of the room.

John wavered to it. And indeed he saw that his hair had turned from Jasper's thin sleek blackness to a straggle of damp gray locks writhing over a yellow skull.

He begged pitifully: "Oh, can't you see I am Jasper? I stole ninety-seven thousand dollars from the bank. I want to be punished! I want to do anything to prove—Why, I've been at your house. Your wife's name is Evelyn. My salary here was—"

"My dear boy, don't you suppose that Jasper might have told you all these interesting facts? I'm afraid the worry of this has—pardon me if I'm frank, but I'm afraid it's turned your head a little, John."

"There isn't any John! There isn't! There isn't!"

"I'd believe that a little more easily if I hadn't met you before Jasper disappeared."

"Give me a piece of paper. You know my writing—"

With clutching claws John seized a sheet of bank stationery and tried to write in the round script of Jasper. During the past year and a half he had filled thousands of pages with the small finicky hand of John. Now, though he tried to prevent it, after he had traced two or three words in large but shaky letters the writing became smaller, more pinched, less legible.

Even while John wrote the president looked at the sheet and said easily: "Afraid it's no use. That isn't Jasper's fist. See here, I want you to get away from Rosebank—go to some farm—work outdoors—cut out this fuming and fussing—get some fresh air in your lungs." The president rose and purred: "Now, I'm afraid I have some work to do."

He paused, waiting for John to go.

John fiercely crumpled the sheet and hurled it away. Tears were in his weary eyes.

He wailed: "Is there nothing I can do to prove I am Jasper?"

"Why, certainly! You can produce what's left of the ninety-seven thousand!"

John took from his ragged waistcoat pocket a five-dollar bill and some change. "Here's all there is. Ninety-six thousand of it was stolen from my house last night."

Sorry though he was for the madman, the president could not help laughing. Then he tried to look sympathetic, and he comforted: "Well, that's hard luck, old man. Uh, let's see. You might produce some parents or relatives or somebody to prove that Jasper never did have a twin brother."

"My parents are dead, and I've lost track of their kin—I was born in England—Father came over when I was six. There might be some cousins or some old neighbors, but I don't know. Probably impossible to find out, in these war-times, without going over there."

"Well, I guess we'll have to let it go, old man." The president was pressing the buzzer for his secretary and gently bidding her: "Show Mr. Holt out, please."

From the door John desperately tried to add: "You will find my car sunk—"

The door had closed behind him. The president had not listened.

The president gave orders that never, for any reason, was John Holt to be admitted to his office again. He telephoned to the bonding company that John Holt had now gone crazy; that they would save trouble by refusing to admit him.

John did not try to see them. He went to the county jail. He entered the keeper's office and said quietly: "I have stolen a lot of money, but I can't prove it. Will you put me in jail?"

The keeper shouted: "Get out of here! You hoboes always spring that when you want a good warm lodging for the winter! Why the devil don't you go to work with a shovel in the sand pits? They're paying two-seventy-five a day."

"Yes, sir," said John timorously. "Where are they?"

A Retrieved Reformation

O. HENRY

SCORES OF PLAYS, motion pictures, and radio and television programs have been based on stories written by O. Henry, the pseudonym of William Sydney Porter (1862–1910), but no tale has proved to be as fecund as "A Retrieved Reformation" for inspiring dramatic works.

Seven years after the story's first publication in 1903, it began a successful Broadway run with the title that remains familiar more than a century later, *Alias Jimmy Valentine*. It was adapted by Paul Armstrong and starred H. B. Warner as the world's greatest safecracker, now retired because of his love for a woman. The play, and the films that followed, all closely adhere to the story line that places Jimmy in a hopeless dilemma. A 1921 stage revival, also successful, featured Otto Kruger in the title role.

The first film version starred Robert Warwick in a 1915 silent. A bigger-budget 1920 silent version featured Bert Lytell. A close remake of the silents with William Haines as Jimmy and Lionel Barrymore as the detective on his trail was released on November 15, 1928—Metro-Goldwyn-Mayer's first partially talking film. It was completed as a silent film; Irving Thalberg later sent Barrymore and Haines to repeat their performances for the last two reels, this time recording with sound. The first dramatic version with a title different from *Alias Jimmy Valentine* was *The Return of Jimmy Valentine* (1936) with Roger Pryor, in which a reporter writes a series of articles speculating about whether the legendary safecracker is still alive. He thinks he has tracked down the old criminal who now is a respected bank manager in a small town. The last film (though there were numerous later radio and television adaptations) was *Affairs of Jimmy Valentine* (1942), starring Dennis O'Keefe, in which the advertising agency for a radio program offers $10,000 to anyone who can find the real Valentine, now a middle-aged newspaper editor played by Roman Bohnen.

"A Retrieved Reformation" originally appeared in the April 1903 issue of *Cosmopolitan* under the title "A Retrieved Reform"; it was first collected in O. Henry's *Roads of Destiny* (New York, Doubleday, Page, 1909).

A RETRIEVED REFORMATION

O. Henry

IN THE PRISON SHOE-SHOP, Jimmy Valentine was busily at work making shoes. A prison officer came into the shop, and led Jimmy to the prison office. There Jimmy was given an important paper. It said that he was free.

Jimmy took the paper without showing much pleasure or interest. He had been sent to prison to stay for four years. He had been there for ten months. But he had expected to stay only three months. Jimmy Valentine had many friends outside the prison. A man with so many friends does not expect to stay in prison long.

"Valentine," said the chief prison officer, "you'll go out tomorrow morning. This is your chance. Make a man of yourself. You're not a bad fellow at heart. Stop breaking safes open, and live a better life."

"Me?" said Jimmy in surprise. "I never broke open a safe in my life."

"Oh, no," the chief prison officer laughed. "Never. Let's see. How did you happen to get sent to prison for opening that safe in Springfield? Was it because you didn't want to tell where you really were? Perhaps because you were with some lady, and you didn't want to tell her name? Or was it because the judge didn't like you? You men always have a reason like that. You never go to prison because you broke open a safe."

"Me?" Jimmy said. His face still showed surprise. "I was never in Springfield in my life."

"Take him away," said the chief prison officer. "Get him the clothes he needs for going outside. Bring him here again at seven in the morning. And think about what I said, Valentine."

At a quarter past seven on the next morning, Jimmy stood again in the office. He had on some new clothes that did not fit him, and a pair of new shoes that hurt his feet. These are the usual clothes given to a prisoner when he leaves the prison.

Next they gave him money to pay for his trip on a train to the city near the prison. They gave him five dollars more. The five dollars were supposed to help him become a better man.

Then the chief prison officer put out his hand for a handshake. That was the end of Valentine, Prisoner 9762. Mr. James Valentine walked out into the sunshine.

He did not listen to the song of the birds or look at the green trees or smell the flowers. He went straight to a restaurant. There he tasted the first sweet joys of being free. He had a good dinner. After that he went to the train station.

He gave some money to a blind man who sat there, asking for money, and then he got on the train.

Three hours later he got off the train in a small town. Here he went to the restaurant of Mike Dolan.

Mike Dolan was alone there. After shaking hands he said, "I'm sorry we couldn't do it sooner, Jimmy my boy. But there was that safe in Springfield, too. It wasn't easy. Feeling all right?"

"Fine," said Jimmy. "Is my room waiting for me?"

He went up and opened the door of a room at the back of the house. Everything was as he had left it. It was here they had found Jimmy, when they took him to prison. There on the floor was a small piece of cloth. It had been torn from the coat of the cop, as Jimmy was fighting to escape.

There was a bed against the wall. Jimmy pulled the bed toward the middle of the room. The wall behind it looked like any wall, but now Jimmy found and opened a small door in it. From this opening he pulled out a dust-covered bag.

He opened this and looked lovingly at the tools for breaking open a safe. No finer tools could be found any place. They were complete; everything needed was here. They had been made of a special material, in the necessary sizes and shapes. Jimmy had planned them himself, and he was very proud of them.

It had cost him over nine hundred dollars to have these tools made at a place where they make such things for men who work at the job of safe-breaking.

In half an hour Jimmy went downstairs and through the restaurant. He was now dressed in good clothes that fitted him well. He carried his dusted and cleaned bag.

"Do you have anything planned?" asked Mike Dolan.

"Me?" asked Jimmy as if surprised. "I don't understand. I work for the New York Famous Bread and Cake Makers Company. And I sell the best bread and cake in the country."

Mike enjoyed these words so much that Jimmy had to take a drink with him. Jimmy had some milk. He never drank anything stronger.

A week after Valentine, 9762, left the prison, a safe was broken open in Richmond, Indiana. No one knew who did it. Eight hundred dollars were taken.

Two weeks after that, a safe in Logansport was opened. It was a new kind of safe; it had been made, they said, so strong that no one could break it open. But someone did, and took fifteen hundred dollars.

Then a safe in Jefferson City was opened. Five thousand dollars were taken. This loss was a big one. Ben Price was a cop who worked on such important matters, and now he began to work on this.

He went to Richmond, Indiana, and to Logansport, to see how the safe-breaking had been done in those places. He was heard to say: "I can see that Jim Valentine has been here. He is in business again. Look at the way he opened this one. Everything easy, everything clean. He is the only man who has the tools to do it. And he is the only man who knows how to use tools like this. Yes, I want Mr. Valentine. Next time he goes to prison, he's going to stay there until his time is finished."

Ben Price knew how Jimmy worked. Jimmy would go from one city to another far away. He always worked alone. He always left quickly when he was finished. He enjoyed being with nice people. For all these reasons, it was not easy to catch Mr. Valentine.

People with safes full of money were glad to hear that Ben Price was at work trying to catch Mr. Valentine.

One afternoon Jimmy Valentine and his bag arrived in a small town named Elmore. Jimmy, looking as young as a college boy, walked down the street toward the hotel.

A young lady walked across the street, passed him at the corner, and entered a door. Over the door was the sign, "The Elmore Bank." Jimmy Valentine looked into her eyes, forgetting at once what he was. He became another man. She looked away, and brighter color came into her face. Young men like Jimmy did not appear often in Elmore.

Jimmy saw a boy near the bank door, and began to ask questions about the town. After a time the young lady came out and went on her way. She seemed not to see Jimmy as she passed him.

"Isn't that young lady Polly Simpson?" asked Jimmy.

"No," said the boy. "She's Annabel Adams. Her father owns this bank."

Jimmy went to the hotel, where he said his name was Ralph D. Spencer. He got a room there. He told the hotel man he had come to Elmore to go into business. How was the shoe business? Was there already a good shoe-shop?

The man thought that Jimmy's clothes and manners were fine. He was happy to talk to him.

Yes, Elmore needed a good shoe-shop. There was no shop that sold just shoes. Shoes were sold in the big shops that sold everything. All business in Elmore was good. He hoped Mr. Spencer would decide to stay in Elmore. It was a pleasant town to live in and the people were friendly.

Mr. Spencer said he would stay in the town a few days and learn something about it. No, he said, he himself would carry his bag up to his room. He didn't want a boy to take it. It was very heavy.

Mr. Ralph Spencer remained in Elmore. He started a shoe-shop. Business was good.

Also he made many friends. And he was successful with the wish of his heart. He met Annabel Adams. He liked her better every day.

At the end of a year everyone in Elmore liked Mr. Ralph Spencer. His shoe-shop was doing very good business. And he and Annabel were going to be married in two weeks. Mr. Adams, the small-town banker, liked Spencer. Annabel was very proud of him. He seemed already to belong to the Adams family.

One day Jimmy sat down in his room to write this letter, which he sent to one of his old friends:

Dear Old Friend:

I want you to meet me at Sullivan's place next week, on the evening of the 10th. I want to give you my tools. I know you'll be glad to have them. You couldn't buy them for a thousand dollars. I finished with the old business—a year ago. I have a nice shop. I'm living a better life, and I'm going to marry the best girl on earth two weeks from now. It's the only life—I wouldn't ever again touch another man's money. After I marry, I'm going to go further west, where I'll never see anyone who knew me in my old life. I tell you, she's a wonderful girl. She trusts me.

Your old friend, Jimmy.

On the Monday night after Jimmy sent this letter, Ben Price arrived quietly in Elmore. He moved slowly about the town in his quiet way, and he learned all that he wanted to know. Standing inside a shop, he watched Ralph D. Spencer walk by.

"You're going to marry the banker's daughter, are you, Jimmy?" said Ben to himself. "I don't feel sure about that!"

The next morning Jimmy was at the Adams home. He was going to a nearby city that day to buy new clothes for the wedding. He was also going to buy a gift for Annabel. It would be his first trip out of Elmore. It was more than a year now since he had done any safe-breaking.

Most of the Adams family went to the bank together that morning. There were Mr. Adams, Annabel, Jimmy, and Annabel's married sister with her two little girls, aged five and nine. They passed Jimmy's hotel, and Jimmy ran up to his room and brought along his bag. Then they went to the bank.

All went inside—Jimmy, too, for he was one of the family. Everyone in the bank was glad to see the good-looking, nice young man who was going to marry Annabel. Jimmy put down his bag.

Annabel, laughing, put Jimmy's hat on her head and picked up the bag. "How do I look?"

she asked. "Ralph, how heavy this bag is! It feels full of gold."

"It's full of some things I don't need in my shop," Jimmy said. "I'm taking them to the city, to the place where they came from. That saves me the cost of sending them. I'm going to be a married man. I must learn to save money."

The Elmore bank had a new safe. Mr. Adams was very proud of it, and he wanted everyone to see it. It was as large as a small room, and it had a very special door. The door was controlled by a clock. Using the clock, the banker planned the time when the door should open. At other times no one, not even the banker himself, could open it. He explained about it to Mr. Spencer. Mr. Spencer seemed interested but he did not seem to understand very easily. The two children, May and Agatha, enjoyed seeing the shining heavy door, with all its special parts.

While they were busy like this, Ben Price entered the bank and looked around. He told a young man who worked there that he had not come on business; he was waiting for a man.

Suddenly there was a cry from the women. They had not been watching the children. May, the nine-year-old girl, had playfully but firmly closed the door of the safe. And Agatha was inside.

The old banker tried to open the door. He pulled at it for a moment. "The door can't be opened," he cried. "And the clock—I hadn't started it yet."

Agatha's mother cried out again.

"Quiet!" said Mr. Adams, raising a shaking hand. "All be quiet for a moment. Agatha!" he called as loudly as he could. "Listen to me." They could hear, but not clearly, the sound of the child's voice. In the darkness inside the safe, she was wild with fear.

"My baby!" her mother cried. "She will die of fear! Open the door! Break it open! Can't you men do something?"

"There isn't a man nearer than the city who can open that door," said Mr. Adams, in a shaking voice. "My God! Spencer, what shall we do? That child—she can't live long in there. There isn't enough air. And the fear will kill her."

Agatha's mother, wild too now, beat on the door with her hands. Annabel turned to Jimmy, her large eyes full of pain, but with some hope, too. A woman thinks that the man she loves can somehow do anything.

"Can't you do something, Ralph? Try, won't you?"

He looked at her with a strange soft smile on his lips and in his eyes.

"Annabel," he said, "give me that flower you are wearing, will you?"

She could not believe that she had really heard him. But she put the flower in his hand. Jimmy took it and put it where he could not lose it. Then he pulled off his coat. With that act, Ralph D. Spencer passed away and Jimmy Valentine took his place.

"Stand away from the door, all of you," he commanded.

He put his bag on the table, and opened it flat. From that time on, he seemed not to know that anyone else was near. Quickly he laid the shining strange tools on the table. The others watched as if they had lost the power to move.

In a minute Jimmy was at work on the door. In ten minutes—faster than he had ever done it before—he had the door open.

Agatha was taken into her mother's arms.

Jimmy Valentine put on his coat, picked up the flower and walked toward the front door. As he went he thought he heard a voice call, "Ralph!" He did not stop.

At the door a big man stood in his way.

"Hello, Ben!" said Jimmy, still with his strange smile. "You're here at last, are you? Let's go. I don't care, now."

And then Ben Price acted rather strangely.

"I guess you're wrong about this, Mr. Spencer," he said. "I don't believe I know you, do I?"

And Ben Price turned and walked slowly down the street.

BETWEEN THE WORLD WARS

Villain: A Burglar

The Burglar

JOHN RUSSELL

THE POPULAR SHORT STORY WRITER, journalist, and screenwriter John Russell (1885–1956) is frequently confused with John Russell Fearn, a British writer of American pulp fiction often credited with some of Russell's stories.

Russell, an American born in Davenport, Iowa, was a reporter for the New York City News Association and the *New-York Tribune*. He began writing crime and adventure short stories for top magazines and newspapers, then moved to California to work for the motion picture industry. He wrote numerous silent films, his best-known being *Beau Geste* (1926), which starred Ronald Colman as the titular adventurer; he also worked, uncredited, on the iconic *Frankenstein* (1931), starring Boris Karloff.

"The Lost God," a short story originally published in *Collier's Weekly*, served as the basis for *The Sea God* (1930), a Paramount film written and directed by George Abbott. A South Seas adventure, the type of fiction for which Russell was best known, it tells the not-unfamiliar story of an explorer, Phillip "Pink" Barker (Richard Arlen), who becomes a god while battling with Square Deal McCarthy (Eugene Pallette) for the affections of Daisy (Fay Wray). The now lost silent film, *Where the Pavement Ends* (1923), was based on "The Passion Vine," a story from Russell's South Seas story collection, *Where the Pavement Ends* (1921); it was written and directed by Rex Ingram and starred Alice Terry and Ramon Novarro. *The Pagan* (1929), a part-silent, part-talking film that also starred Novarro, was based on a similar Russell story.

Russell's best stories were collected in *The Red Mark and Other Stories* (1919), *Where the Pavement Ends* (1921), *In Dark Places* (1923), and *Cops 'n Robbers* (1930).

"The Burglar," originally published in magazine form in the October 1913 issue of *New Story Magazine,* was first collected in *Cops 'n Robbers* (New York, W. W. Norton, 1930).

THE BURGLAR

John Russell

THREE STEPS SHORT of the third floor, and he stopped and grinned to himself inside the blinding mask of the dark, feeling with careful finger tips.

He found the wire at one side, plucked it out in a loop, and severed it neatly, finishing off each end with a scrape of the knife from mechanical habit of thoroughness. . . .

Then he lifted himself over, without even touching that step, as a wolf might break a snare and still shun it in sheer excess of wild caution. He crawled on to the landing. The house was dead as the tomb behind him as he slid along the passage to the rear room.

He was noiseless. He was sure. He was quick. His pulse kept a temperate beat in his throat. His muscles responded smoothly, slipping with silken, steely precision to do his will. His eyes were clear and steady as a cat's. His eardrums were tuned to finest perception. Every sense of his spare, wiry body was alert, thin drawn.

His was the keen, gaunt perfection of training that the starving thing of prey attains.

In some twenty hours he had not eaten. In some three weeks he had not known a full meal. In some twenty-six years, all he could boast, he had never enjoyed the chance to blunt his fine animal appetites or to dull his fine animal equipment with satiety.

It was in him to live, to endure, to keep his strength where the weaker went to the wall. His nature was the tough, tenacious, elastic, close-compacted metal that does not snap. . . .

Resistless poverty had ground him upon its whetting edge. Remorseless labor had shaped and hardened him. Relentless hunger had driven him forth at last, a cutting tool, finished and ready for crime.

And now he had found his work. . . .

Thin bands of moonlight cut in at an angle through the windows of the rear room. They were big windows, reaching from floor to ceiling, and barred to waist height with graceful iron grilles. They were wide open upon the garden below.

He curled in the heavy shadow along the wall near the door and watched, listened. . . .

Vagrant breaths of the summer night stirred the curtains. Vague rumors of the sleeping city stole mysteriously from the void. Nothing more.

Between winkings, almost without sensible movement, he was across the room to the far side, feeling out the shape and details of the wall cabinet, adjusting his sight to the ghostly reflection of moon glow.

The outer section of the cabinet was a writing desk. A blind, according to his tip. He slipped the bent end of the burnished implement he carried—his sole outfit—against the edge of the lock.

The smooth, lifting pressure gave him his first heave of effort, his first thrill of power. He had a ton at command in that leverage. And the lid came away like the top of a wet cardboard box.

He could make out the interior of the desk dimly. A model desk; there were pigeonholes, paper trays, two rows of shallow wooden drawers. At least, the veneer was of wood, and each inlaid panel was furnished with a neat little glass knob.

His tip saved him the trouble that would have been necessary to establish the incidental fact that behind the trays and the pigeonholes, behind the false fronts and the glass knobs, stood a solid foot of chrome steel plates. . . .

Swiftly, still relying on that valuable tip, he began to unscrew the little glass knobs from the imitation-drawer panels. As he drew each knob off he pressed the tiny screw shaft that was left standing in the wood, and each time he paused, expectant. Even the wonderful tip could not tell him which was the vital knob.

It proved to be the fourth on the left-hand row.

When he pressed, the fourth screw gave like a tiny plunger. The operating current closed. Springs released with an oily snicking. And the whole interior of the cabinet moved outward from the wall in a solid, silent swing like the shift of a scenic illusion.

It was a dainty job. The steps of it fitted like the parts of a jigsaw picture. No hitch, no hurry, no gap, no confusion. He foresaw, he judged, he made the adequate gesture. He applied the exact necessary force. And the act was complete—

It took him three minutes to open the small inner compartment. Three minutes that passed without a jar, without an audible breath, without a hasty movement. Three minutes, until he caught the shock of the snapping steel with deft balance of body, with perfect release of joint and sinew. . . .

He did not grab.

He searched the inner compartment lightly with one hand. When he drew it out, it brought a tiny, flat leather-bound casket. Kneeling there beside the open door of the safe at the edge of the moonlight band, he turned back the cover of the casket.

The moment of success is the test of the criminal. Achievement shows the nerve of the social wolf. Method, judgment, readiness retain their steadfast, savage purpose—or weaken and fumble in the flurry of desire.

He was under full control. His brain was level, cool. His heart had not jumped a stroke. He kept everything he had used about him. Nothing was mislaid. He knew his precise position. He was ready to flit on the instant, leaving no mark, no clue behind. He was fit. He proved it now.

Gently he picked out the Thing that nestled in the casket on its velvet bed.

He lifted the Thing between finger and thumb, as one might lift a sparrow's egg, and held it before him so that the moonlight fell upon it and was knotted there in a tangle of pale glory and was wafted through in delicate strands of spectral splendor. . . .

He gazed, quietly fascinated, not by the beauty of what he saw, but by what it meant to him.

A sound beat upon his ear—from close at hand—in the same room. He turned his head with birdlike quickness. For the rest he did not move, did not start.

"Keep it right there," said a voice dryly, calmly.

He kept it there.

"Just as you are," advised the voice.

He obeyed the suggestion.

"Pretty effect!"

A figure detached itself from the shadows about the doorway. As it advanced into the moonlight it was revealed as that of a man, tall, powerfully built, massively shouldered.

He was draped in an ample dressing gown, hanging loose and untied. He carried a big revolver in his fist carelessly, with the ease of habit. He had the air of one just aroused from a nap, and not at all excited by the incident.

He must have been a magnificent specimen of physical development at one time, this man. Even now he was little more than just beyond the ripeness of his powers. A fleshy droop under the eyes scarce marred his hard-cut features. A certain grossness about the body seemed no clog upon his strength. A heeling tread was as formidable without the spring and litheness it must once have owned.

He was still young, in spite of the marks of indulgence; easy, masterful, and sure in every gesture.

He stood regarding the glistening marvel in the moonshine for an appreciative moment. Then he reached out casually with his free hand.

"I'll take it. . . . Thanks!"

He turned his bold, confident face down upon the burglar with a grimly humorous smile. The burglar knelt staring up at him, immobile. Idly, almost indifferently, the big man's hand closed over the extended fingers, took the prize, weighed it an instant, and passed it to a waistcoat pocket.

His eyes were still fixed upon the burglar in lazy mockery. It was all so easy a triumph.

"Get up!"

The voice was deeper and shorter now that the dramatic effectiveness of the incident was complete.

The burglar stood up. . . .

The big man inspected him. His lip lifted as he took in the other's commonplace exterior. His glance sharpened as he noted each detail of lean wretchedness, of furtive shabbiness.

He dominated his captive in pride and arrogance, scowling down at him.

"And you're the lad who thought he could lift the Rangely diamond!" he exclaimed incredulously. "*You!*"

He continued his survey.

"Here's ambition!"

But his curious glance traveled beyond to the rifled safe, standing wide, and suddenly sarcasm was not adequate to him.

"Now tell me how in hell you did it?"

It rumbled from him in quick anger. The anger of privileged grievance and righteous disappointment.

"How the hell did you get that box open?"

The burglar said nothing.

The big head sank forward. The voice slid down another note.

"Look here," his restraint of word was ominous, "I think you'd better answer up promptly like a wise little man. I've a mind anyway to smash you like a bug! It'd please me a whole lot, and there's nothing to keep me, you know! . . .

"I want to hear how a poor sap like you managed to waltz right into that safe! . . . I'm waiting!"

There was something rawer and closer than menace in the tone.

"I got a tip," answered the burglar sullenly, at last.

"Where?"

"Off—a guy."

"What guy?"

"Usta work for a safe company."

There was silence between them for a time. A silence because the big man was pulling at the band of his collar.

"Never had to force it at all?"

"No."

"Never even figured to force it?"

"No."

"Well, you're some master hand, ain't you! Then what?"

"I watched."

"The house?"

"Yes."

"Go on!"

"And the newspapers."

"Well?"

"I saw where the old lady—where Mrs. Rangely was jumped to the hospital yest'd'y—and her husban' hired a room to stay near her."

"And—the son?"

"I saw where it said the son was livin' at some club or 'nother."

"Servants?"

"I saw the last of 'm go out two hours ago."

"Some student! Some clever crook, eh? . . . So then you thought you had your chance?"

"Yes."

"Having doped it all down to a fine point like they do in the books, you thought you'd just happen along and scoop up the Rangely diamond! You thought that?"

"Yes."

"And I bet you fell into the wires a dozen times on your way up. Do you know that stairway is wired?"

"Yeah."

"Do, eh? . . . Where?"

The burglar told him.

"And you dodged the connections?"

"I cut 'm."

Sudden wrath flared in the questioner.

"Why, damn your grubby little soul, anyway! Where did you get the brazen cheek to think of a job like this? Say—who the hell are you, anyhow?"

He gathered the slack of the dressing gown under an arm and took one heavy stride. The huge revolver jammed against the captive's ribs. The hard-jawed face sneered into his with brutal contempt. . . .

"Did you ever turn a big trick?"

"No."

"Did you ever blow a box?"

"No."

"Did you ever pull off anything above petty larceny in your life?"

He emphasized each question with the gun muzzle.

"No," muttered the burglar.

"Then what are you doing here? By Jove! I hoped it was somebody of some account. I hoped, anyway, it might *be* somebody! . . . Have you got any record of any kind?"

"Nah."

"And still you had the gall to go after the Rangely diamond! Didn't you know the best men in the business would have their work cut out to cop such a prize? Didn't you know the smartest operators in the world would be none too smart for this job? Men like Max Shimburn, or Perry, or even Meadow himself? And you sticking your dirty little paws into the game! . . ."

He gave a final thrust that sent the other spinning back upon the door of the safe.

The act of violence seemed to make him aware for the first time of the curious height to which his surge of personal resentment had risen.

He laughed at himself.

"Why look at me getting all fussed up!" he observed.

He considered a moment. When he spoke again his voice had regained something of its former dry calm. His manner, too, had reverted somewhat to the self-appreciatory dramatic. . . .

"We'll teach you a lesson," he decided. "We'll teach you to stick to frisking and till-banking and second-story work—where you belong!"

The burglar stared at him.

"You need to be shown, you guttersnipe! You need to be put in your proper place. Jobs like this are not for such as you. . . . I'll prove it!"

No whimsically cruel punishment would have seemed beyond the possible fancy of that contemptuous colossus.

"*Beat it!*" he growled.

The burglar still stared.

"That's what. You're not important enough! I'm giving you just what you're worth. I'm ignoring you. Understand? . . . On your way out of this house and don't linger!"

He stood there in the moonlight, a powerful, commanding figure, smiling to himself once more at his conceit, restored to casual amusement by his own fanciful disposal of the situation and the effective little play he had made of it. The picture of confidence, strength, and assurance.

For an instant longer the burglar stared, expressionless. Perhaps he was too crushed to understand. The big man banished him with a gesture.

He obeyed. . . .

He slid away from the safe. He glided along the side of the room. He did not even look back from the doorway. He passed through to the hall, to the head of the stairs. He began his descent, an audible descent.

He obeyed. . . .

But at the third stair from the top he introduced a trifling variation into the maneuver of retreat.

He stayed for an instant—just the fleeting fraction of a minute, while his weight bore upon the step; while he stooped; while his nimble fingers found the two free ends of the severed wire and touched, merely touched, the exposed tips of copper, one upon the other.

When he continued his flight it was as if he had not paused at all.

He obeyed.

But at the second floor he deviated again from the letter of his instructions.

He left the balustrade and crept down the hall toward the rear room, just as he had done at his first entrance. The rear room was similar to the one above. Like that, it was empty. Like that, its windows opened wide on the garden side. . . .

The burglar made straight to the farther window. He lifted himself over the ornamental grille. The frame gave him a handhold.

At the back of the house next to the Rangely residence was a one-story conservatory extension. It was vine-grown, flat-roofed.

He knew the exact measurement of the gap from the window ledge to the coping of that room. He bridged it in a step. For a space he was in the full eye of the moon. For such a space as a cat needs to dart across a fence. After that he disappeared from view at the extreme rear end of the conservatory roof in the black shadow of the chimney that raised its square bulk like a tower.

He had obeyed, now he waited. . . .

———

For all his alertness he was never quite certain whence came the first definite sign of results. Nor exactly when it came.

But presently there was some living presence in the garden below him. Presently, too, he knew that feet were softly astir in the basement of the Rangely house. At about the same time he was made aware of furtive movement in the side street, beyond the wall that hedged the garden two houses above. And glancing up at the sky line of the block he had a glimpse of a police cap spotted against the star dust for a wink. . . .

It was a circling attack, collected and delivered with a promptness, an energy, a cautious eagerness that offered startling proof of the standing of the Rangely family, the importance of the Rangely residence, and the value of the Rangely possessions in the anxious view of the authorities.

It came out of the void of the sleeping city, starting at the flicker of a needle on a dial, centering like a sweep of hornets, closing with a full cordon.

To an observer of ordinary police methods it might have seemed amazing, almost supernatural. To the initiated it might have furnished a cynic commentary on the efficiency that is reserved for the need of the wealthy and the great.

No slighting an emergency call from that locality. The response was swift and adequate. . . .

Meanwhile the man who crouched unseen in the shadow of the chimney on the observatory wing fixed his gaze upon the third-floor windows of the Rangely house.

Those windows were large. They were open from floor to ceiling. From his vantage some fifty feet away he was placed so as to command a low-angled sweep of vision over the sills.

He waited as a man in the pit waits for the rise of the curtain.

And when it did lift it went up on a smash of tense action. . . .

A muffled shout came from the depths of the house—the first challenge; the stamp of feet; then two bursting shots.

"*Stand!*" bellowed a bull voice. "Who's there? . . . Stand, or I'll fire again!"

The rush had checked on the stairs. Evidently a competent revolver was commanding that well.

"Inspector Lavery and ten men!" came the answer.

A pause, dropping in like the suck of a wave before its breaking. A pause that was tense with possibilities and indecision.

Then—

"Police?" rumbled the big voice. "What's all the excitement?"

The third-floor rear leaped with sudden radiance as the bulbs were switched on.

"All right, police!"

Upon the brilliantly lighted stage beyond the open windows appeared a knot of blue uniforms. Crowding in the doorway the policemen found themselves confronted by a young giant in a dressing robe who faced them coolly, a fisted weapon hanging by his side.

"Inspector Lavery?" he inquired. "Charmed, I'm sure! How did you get in?"

The inspector came forward.

"Walked in," he returned crisply. "The front door was open for all and sundry. And you, Mr.—"

"Rangely is my name."

The inspector looked him over.

"You live here?" he inquired, with considerably less rasp to his tone.

"At present, in the absence of my parents. But—I don't understand. The door open? The outer door?"

"And an alarm was touched from here about seven minutes ago."

"Alarm? Strange! . . . I rang no alarm."

"It was automatic. You have heard nothing? No disturbance in the house?"

"Not until I was wakened by tramping on the stairs and fired at random just now."

"You're quick with a gun!" commented the inspector grimly. "The servants?"

"Gone for the night."

The inspector turned his head.

"Well?"

"Nothing, sir," came a respectful answer from the hall. "Everything seems to be all right. We've covered the house."

"Is Devlin satisfied?"

"I'll ask him to report, sir."

The inspector looked again at the big, confident, easily interested young man who occupied the middle of the floor. Nothing could have been more reassuring, more solid and untroubled than that same young man.

"Perhaps I forgot to close the door when I came in," he was saying. "Perhaps I even touched the alarm. I'm not very familiar with the arrangements. Anyway—" He waved a casual hand while he dropped the revolver carelessly in his dressing-gown pocket. "Anyway—here is the house, and here am I. Quite at your service, but in no danger that I know of."

The inspector hesitated. . . .

In the pause, through the attendant group in the doorway, came thrusting an awkward, undersized man in common clothes who dropped a suit case at the inspector's feet with a bang and grinned with a most evil squint.

"Well, Devlin?"

"Front room—found 'em under th' bed in the front room," announced the newcomer, in a quaint, chuckling cackle. "Jes' give 'em the once over!"

He kicked open the suitcase as it lay.

Every man within eyeshot stood transfixed. . . .

"As classy a set of can openers as y'll ever see!" observed Mr. Devlin, rubbing his hands with extraordinary gusto. "Money can't buy no better. They ain't made no better. Poems! A package of poems in steel, sir. That's what they are—poems!"

The inspector looked up sharply.

"That all?"

"Except that the boy who owned 'em has been makin' hisself damn comfortable in that front room this evening! Reg'ler lordin' it. Must 'a' took a nap in there. Nerve! How about it for nerve?"

"You hear this, Mr.—Rangely?"

The host shrugged in frank surprise.

"Extraordinary! Apparently some one *has* been here—after all."

The meager individual who had brought the suitcase turned toward the speaker, dropping his head with a curious twist. A misshapen finger plucked the inspector's arm. . . .

"Who does he say he is?"

"Young Rangely."

"Huh! Well, he ain't," cackled Devlin, squinting. "Herbert Rangely's about the size an' shape of a stewed prune. This boy'd make six—*Look out!*"

A flash of steel from the dressing-gown pocket was swift, but no swifter than the thin spurt of yellow flame that jumped to meet it. . . .

The report was drowned in a shock of sound like the thunder of a torrent, prisoned and plunging for freedom, a roar that pulsed with the wild fury of untamed forces, cornered and struggling.

Through the haze of the electrics on that third-floor stage a gigantic figure flailed amid a writhing mass of blue, and drove with mighty limbs toward the nearest window.

Steadily it made its way, like some slow-moving polyp of the depths, impeded but unmastered by clinging incrustations.

It seemed that nothing could stop it.

It reached the window, it caught the grille, it hurled itself bodily at space in one magnificent heave. . . .

But there it stayed. . . .

The captors would not loosen. They were many, and others came to help. The whole invading force joined the tussle. And the many were too many—

After a moment of swaying doubt the center of the fight collapsed. The group bore back and drew its vortex with it. The roaring ceased. Silence, rushing in, was like an ache in the ears.

A rippling police whistle called the last of the inspector's reserves—

But there was no more resistance in the giant.

Standing once more in the middle of the room under the lights, half naked, great breast heaving, legs wide apart, he submitted while they snapped his wrists together behind his back, defiant, cursing them with his blazing beast's eyes, but beaten.

"By God!" broke from him in a gust. "You'd never 'a' got me if you hadn't put that bullet through my arm!"

"Don't y' fool y'rself!"

It was the detective, Devlin, who answered. He was peering up at the captive with button-bright eyes and rubbing his hands briskly.

"Don't y' fool y'rself. We got y' because y'r time had come! How about that for a little suggestion? Two years ago y'd 'a' popped through that window, bullet and all, cops and all, and hell itself couldn't 'a' stopped y'. Y' could 'a' done it then. But not now. Not now. It ain't in y' no more! . . . How d'y' like the notion?"

The prisoner snarled down at him, crimson-faced.

Devlin cackled.

"Don't like it, eh? It's true. Two years more of success—two years more of easy money—two years more of night clubs and speakeasies—two years more of loafin' and fifty-cent smokes, of gamblin' and women—that's what's done it for you, ol' boy!"

He plucked a roll of fat along the big man's ribs. He prodded his grossness. He pointed out the sag of the cheeks and the thinning at the temples, while the captive raged.

All with the veriest nonchalance, the impersonal interest of the clinical demonstrator. . . .

Only his glittering little eyes betrayed a more concrete meaning behind.

"That's what's the matter, ol' boy. Pret' tough! But you must 'a' seen it comin'. A man like you, with such opportunities! Hell, you must 'a' seen the time comin'. The time when y'd be done, like all the rest."

The big man had gone from poppy red to wax white.

"Damn you!" he choked. "Shut up, you little fiend. You don't know anything about me!"

"Oh, don't I?" cackled Devlin, springing back and pointing a crooked finger. "I wonder! I wonder if I don't—Mr. Meadow. Mr. Silver-gilt, Silk-stocking Meadow, Mr. Sportin'-life, Top-notcher Meadow, Mr. Jim Meadow, of Nowhere, wanted Everywhere, last seen Somewhere, and headed Anywhere! . . . I wonder if I don't!"

A babble of excited tongues burst at the name.

"Are you sure, Devlin?" cried the inspector. "*Meadow!* He's never been caught!"

"Look at his face," triumphed the detective. "It's writ there. He's never been caught, no! That's why I got his goat so easy. Look at him!"

In fact the prisoner could not control himself to put on a denial. Chagrin and rage held him helpless.

"James B. Meadow," chuckled Devlin. "Million-dollar thief, kid-glove crook, gentleman burglar—the master that never yet did a day in stir! I got one flash at him once, and that's as near as anybody has ever come to him before. . . .

"There he is! And we got him, because his time was come. *Ripe.* He was ripe and we picked him, that's all!"

It was a bit of theatricalism to have suited the taste of the prisoner himself, had the lines, and the supers, and the properties been somewhat altered.

He held the center. The police gathered about him with avid, exultant eyes, like a pack of hounds that have brought the biggest boar of the chase to bay.

"I only wish we'd got him at work," observed the inspector, dwelling on him fondly. "It's too tame a way to grab a guy with his record!"

But in the interval Devlin had discovered the wall cabinet. He swung it wide with a cackle.

"Oh, I guess it ain't so tame as you think! That's the Rangely safe, chief. You may have heard of it!"

"Cracked?"

"You bet!" Devlin's eyes were like points of fire. "And chief—this—this is where the Rangely diamond lives!"

But the inspector was the first to find the inner compartment—empty!

"Then it's moved," he commented dryly.

Devlin forgot to cackle.

"Don't tell me—" he began, and stopped.

He scratched his head.

"By golly, let's see them tools."

He swung around to the suitcase and pounced on the steel gems it contained.

"Meadow," he snapped, jumping up. "You never cracked that safe!"

"Didn't I?" sneered the prisoner.

Devlin was at the cabinet again, examining the mechanism.

"No, you didn't! The outer door's been worked with its proper combination. Not cracked at all. Them glass drawer knobs have something to do with it—and I shouldn't wonder—

"And if it was *you* who used the combination, why'd you bring all them tools, and a pint of soup? No! You came expectin' to blow her. Don't tell me!"

The prisoner smiled superior.

"The inner box has been forced all right," continued Devlin. "But the guy never had your beauty outfit. He wouldn't need it. He used a plain jimmy. And he didn't work like you!"

"No?"

"I know your signature, ol' boy. . . . See here, what's it mean?"

The prisoner shrugged.

Devlin shook an ugly finger under his nose.

"That diamond's been took, Meadow! If you got a pal—"

Meadow laughed at him.

"No, not that," acknowledged Devlin, totally at a loss. "You never took one. But there's been a hell of a funny evenin' around here, first and last. Come across, ol' boy. What was it?"

The prisoner smiled. . . .

Devlin watched him with bright, squinting eyes, head dropped askew, boring at him.

"By gol!" he breathed.

"By gol, I might have guessed! Of course. Somebody beat y' to it! Waterloo! It's y'r Waterloo, this night. Fat, and flabby, and off y'r game, and y' fall asleep in the next room while somebody beats you to it! The time had to come. It came tonight—all at once—all in a swoop. First y' lose one of the best cribs y' ever tackled, and then y' get pinched on the spot. Dished! Pinched beside another feller's leavin's! . . . Dished! . . . Done!"

He cackled into the captive's face.

Meadow had gone white again under the jeering lash of the detective so skillfully wielded. But he held himself with an effort.

"Think so?"

"I know so. And—tell y', Meadow. Let me tell y' one thing. . . . Listen—"

He laid finger into palm, and emphasized each word slowly.

"The crook that got that diamond—whoever he was—is a better crook than you. He may be a slob. He may be a green hand—likely he was, with that jimmy. But to come and crack the crib you was after, under your nose, and *such* a crib! And to get away with the plum!

"Meadow, I'm glad to get you. But if I had a chance to bargain I'd exchange you in a minute—yes—ten like you, like what you are now—for just *one good look* at that feller! . . .

"He's goin' to make trouble, big trouble. It may take years to find him. It may be years before he loses his punch and goes off his game like you. I tell you, you're done! You're no account! And him—he's just comin'!"

The quivering captive could endure no more. His pride, his self-love, his egotism—the monstrous bloated egotism of the criminal—had been slashed to the quick.

He cried out under it, as Devlin had meant he should.

"Is that so?" he yelled hoarsely. "Well, that's all the good you are, you shrimpy sleuth! Done? I may be a little out of training. I may have run into a rotten string of luck. But I'll show you whether I'm done or not.

"Yes, there was another guy on this job! Yes, he tried to butt in on my crib! And how far did he get with it, do you suppose? How far do you think I let him travel with my swag?

"He was a sniveling little wharf rat. Somehow, by dumb luck, he had picked up the combo of that safe. By more dumb luck he got the diamond. And then—I blew him back where he belonged. . . .

"I'm done, am I? Feel here—in what you've left of my vest. The right-hand pocket!"

Devlin sprang to him, smiling.

"I hand it to you, Jim," he cackled. "You're a wonder! Gents—"

He fumbled in the pocket while the bluecoats pressed eagerly around.

"Gents, we have here that well-known wonder of the world, famed in song and story—the Rangely diamond!"

There was a moment's strained silence in the rear room of the third floor, on that lighted stage offered to the windows of the night. . . .

Then Devlin's curiously hushed addition cut across it.

"Rangely h-ell! It's *glass*! . . . It's one of them blasted glass knobs *off—that—blasted—safe—front*!"

Such was the crisis of that impromptu midnight drama. It is likely that it might have afforded further interest.

But the audience did not wait to see. The audience had had enough. The audience was quite content to leave the action at that point, and to slip gently down the vine-laddered rear wall of the conservatory.

Safely started, he began a circumspect flight over the fences and through the yards to the far end of the block, unsuspected and unpursued. . . .

He was noiseless. He was sure. He was quick. He gave his undivided attention to the immediate problem of getting back to his lair. He was the keen hunting prowler of the night. He had made his kill. He had done more, he had stricken down and removed from the meat trail a competitor who had interfered with his quest, a rival whose cunning had failed to match his own, a fellow wolf whose day was done.

Now he was hurrying away with his unsatisfied hunger and his lusting appetite, hurrying toward the appeasement of that hunger and that lust. But even in his triumph, even in his hour of success, he did not slacken a nerve from his savage tension, his readiness, his craft, his precision. For he was perfectly fitted for the work of prey. And he had never yet known satiety. . . .

Only once he relaxed, when it was quite safe.

Under the edge of a garden wall, where the moonshine filtered among the lilac bushes, he took from his pocket and held in the cup of his hands for a moment a Thing, a glorious, delicate drop of shimmery light. . . . The Rangely diamond.

Villain: ?

Portrait of a Murderer

Q. PATRICK

OKAY, TRY TO FOLLOW THIS, if you can. The Q. Patrick pseudonym is one of three pen names (the others being Patrick Quentin and Jonathan Stagge) used in a complicated collaboration that began with Richard Wilson Webb (1902–1970) and Martha (Patsy) Mott Kelly (1906–2005) producing *Cottage Sinister* (1931) and *Murder at the Women's City Club* (1932). Webb then wrote *Murder at Cambridge* (1933) alone before collaborating with Mary Louise (White) Aswell (1902–1984) on *S.S. Murder* (1933) and *The Grindle Nightmare* (1935). He found a new collaborator, Hugh Callingham Wheeler (1912–1987), for *Death Goes to School* (1936) and six additional Q. Patrick titles, the last of which was *Danger Next Door* (1951); all were largely traditional British detective stories. Wheeler and Webb moved to the United States in 1934 and eventually became U.S. citizens.

Wheeler and Webb created the Patrick Quentin byline with *A Puzzle for Fools* (1936), which introduced Peter Duluth, a theatrical producer who stumbles into detective work by accident. The highly successful Duluth series of nine novels inspired two motion pictures, *Homicide for Three* (1948), starring Warren Douglas as Peter and Audrey Long as his wife, Iris, and *Black Widow* (1954), with Van Heflin (Peter), Gene Tierney (Iris), Ginger Rogers, George Raft, and Peggy Ann Garner. Webb dropped out of the collaboration in the early 1950s, and Wheeler continued using the Quentin name but abandoned the Duluth series to produce stand-alone novels until 1965.

Wheeler and Webb also collaborated on nine Jonathan Stagge novels, beginning with *Murder Gone to Earth* (1936; published in the United States the following year as *The Dogs Do Bark*). The series featured Dr. Hugh Westlake, a general practitioner in a small Eastern town, and his precocious teenage daughter, Dawn.

Wheeler went on to have a successful career as a playwright, winning the

Tony Award and the Drama Desk Award for Outstanding Book of a Musical in 1973, 1974, and 1979 for *A Little Night Music*, *Candide*, and *Sweeney Todd*.

"Portrait of a Murderer," written by Wheeler and Webb under the Q. Patrick byline, was originally published in the April 1942 issue of *Harper's Magazine*; it was first collected in *The Ordeal of Mrs. Snow* under the Patrick Quentin byline (London, Gollancz, 1961).

PORTRAIT OF A MURDERER

Q. Patrick

THIS IS THE STORY of a murder. It was a murder committed so subtly, so smoothly that I, who was an unwitting accessory both before and after the fact, had no idea at the time that any crime had been committed.

Only gradually, with the years, did that series of incidents, so innocuous-seeming at the time, fall into a pattern in my mind and give me a clear picture of exactly what happened during my stay at Olinscourt with Martin Slater.

Martin and I were at an English school together during the latter half of the First World War. In his fourteenth year Martin was a nondescript boy with light, untidy hair, quick brown eyes, and that generic schoolboy odor of rubber and chalk. There was little to distinguish him from the rest of us except his father, Sir Olin Slater.

Sir Olin, however, was more than enough to make Martin painfully notorious. Whereas self-respecting parents embarrassed their children by appearing at the school only on state occasions such as Sports Day or Prize-Giving, Sir Olin haunted his son like a passion. Almost every week this evangelical baronet could be seen, a pink, plump hippopotamus, walking about the school grounds, his arm entwined indecently round Martin. In his free hand he would carry a large bag of chocolates which he offered to all the boys he met with pious adjurations to lead nobler, sweeter lives.

Martin squirmed under these paraded embraces. It was all the worse for him in that his father suffered from a terrible disease of the throat which made every syllable he uttered a pathetic mockery of the English language. This disease (which was probably throat cancer) had no reality for Sir Olin. He did not believe that other people were even conscious of his mispronunciations. At least once every term, to our irreverent delight and to Martin's excruciating discomfort, he was invited to deliver before the whole school an informal address of a religious nature—or a pi-jaw as we called it. When I sat next to Martin in Big School, suppressing a disloyal desire to giggle, I used to watch my friend's knuckles go white as his father, from the dais, urged us "laddies" to keep ourselves strong and pure and trust in the Mercy of God, or, as he pronounced it, the "Murky of Klock."

Sir Olin's pious solicitude for his own beloved "laddie" expressed itself also in the written word. Every morning, more regular than the rising of the English sun, there lay on Martin's breakfast plate the blue envelope with the Slater coat-of-arms. Martin was a silent boy. He never spoke a word to hint that Sir Olin's effusiveness was a torment to him, even when the derisive titter parodied down the table: "Another lecker for the lickle lackie." But I noticed that he left these letters unopened unless his sensitive fingers, palpating the envelopes, could detect bank notes in them.

Most of the other boys tended to despise Martin for the solecism of such a parent. My own intimacy with him might well have been tainted with condescension had it not been for the hampers of "tuck" which Lady Slater sent from Olinscourt. Such tuck it was, too—coming at a period when German submarines were tightening all English belts. Being a scrawny and perpetually hungry boy, I was never more prepared to be chummy with Martin Slater than when my roommate and I sneaked off alone together to tackle those succulent tongues, those jellied chickens, those firm, luscious peaches, and those chocolate cakes stiffened with mouth-melting icing.

Martin shared my enthusiasm for these secret feasts, but he had another all-absorbing enthusiasm which I did not share. He was an inventor. He invented elaborate mechanical devices, usually from alarm clocks of which there were always five or six in his possession in different stages of disembowelment. He specialized at that period in burglar alarms. I can see now those seven or eight urchins that he used to lure into our room at night with sausage rolls and plum cake; I can almost hear my own heart beating as we waited in the darkness to witness in action Martin's latest contrivance for foiling house-breakers.

These thrilling episodes ended summarily, however, when an unfeeling master caught us at it, confiscated all Martin's clocks, and gave him a hundred lines for disturbing the peace.

Without these forbidden delights, the long, blacked-out nights of wartime seemed even darker and colder. It was Martin who evolved a system whereby we could dispel the dreary chill which settled every evening on the institution like a miasma, and warm up our cold beds and our undernourished bodies. He invented wrestling—or rather, he adapted and simplified the canons of the art to suit the existing contingency. His rules were simple almost to the point of being nonexistent. One took every possible advantage; one inflicted as much pain as one reasonably dared; one was utterly unscrupulous toward the single end of making one's opponent admit defeat with the phrase: "I give in, man. You win."

It didn't seem to do us much harm thus to work out on one another the sadism that is inherent in all children. It warmed and toughened us; perhaps in some subtle way it established in us an intimacy, a mutual respect.

Though Martin had the advantage of me in age and weight, I was, luckily, more wiry and possibly craftier. As I gradually got on to Martin's technic I began to develop successful counter measures. So successful were they, in fact, that I started to win almost nightly, ending up on top with monotonous regularity.

And that was the first, the greatest mistake I ever made in my dealings with Martin Slater. I should have known that it is unwise to win too often at any game. It is especially unwise when one is playing it with a potential murderer, who, I suspect, had already conceived for any subjugation, moral or physical, a hatred that was almost psychopathological and growing in violence.

I experienced its violence one night when, less scrupulous than Hamlet toward Claudius, he attacked me as I knelt shivering at my bedside going through the ritual of "saying my prayers." The assault was decidedly unfair. It occurred before the specified safety hour and while the matron was still prowling. Also, though props and weapons were strictly inadmissible, he elected on this occasion to initiate his attack by throwing a wet towel over my head, twisting it round my neck as he pulled me backward. It was a very wet towel too, so wet that breathing through it was quite out of the question.

With his initial, almost strangling jerk backward, my legs had shot forward, underneath the bed, where they could only kick feebly at the mattress springs, useless as leverage to shake off Martin, who had seated his full weight on my face, having pinioned my arms beneath his knees. I was a helpless prisoner with a wet towel and some hundred pounds of boy between me and any chance of respiration.

Frantically I gurgled my complete submission. I beat my hands on the floor in token of surrender. But Martin sat relentlessly on. For a moment I knew the panic of near suffocation. I clawed, I scratched, I bit; but I might have been buried a hundred feet under the earth. Then everything began to go black, including, as I afterward learned, my own face.

I was saved mercifully by the approach of the peripatetic matron who bustled in a few moments later and blew out the candle without being aware that one of her charges had almost become Martin Slater's first victim in homicide.

Martin apologized to me next morning but there was a strange expression on his face as he added: "You were getting too cocky, man, licking me every night."

His more practical appeasement took the form of inviting me to Olinscourt for the holidays. I weighed the disadvantages of four weeks under Sir Olin's pious tutelage against the prospect of tapping the source of those ambrosial hampers. Inevitably, my schoolboy stomach decided for me. I went.

To our delight, when we first arrived at Olinscourt we found Sir Olin away on an uplift tour of the reformatories and prisons of Western England. He might not have existed for us at all had it not been for the daily blue envelope on Martin's breakfast plate.

Lady Slater made an admirably unobtrusive hostess—a meek figure who trailed vaguely round in low-heeled shoes and snuff-colored garments which associate themselves in my mind with the word "gabardine." Apart from ordering substantial meals for us "growing boys" and dampening them slightly by an aroma of piety, she kept herself discreetly out of our way in some meditative boudoir of her own.

Left to our devices, Martin spent long days of feverish activity in his beautifully equipped workshop, releasing all the inventive impulses which had been frustrated at school and which, as he hinted apologetically, would be thwarted again on the return of Sir Olin. Being London-bred, there was nothing I enjoyed more than wandering alone round the extensive grounds and farm lands of Olinscourt, ploddingly followed by a dour Scotch terrier called Roddy.

The old rambling house was equally exciting, particularly since on the second day of my visit I discovered a chamber of mystery, a large locked room on the ground floor which turned out to be Sir Olin's study. Martin was as intrigued as I by the closure of this room which was normally much used. Inquiries from the servants elicited only the fact that there had been alterations of an unknown nature and that the room had been ordered shut until Sir Olin's return.

This romantic mystery, which only Sir Olin could solve, made us almost look forward to the Baronet's return. He arrived unexpectedly some nights later and appeared in our room, oozing plump affection, while we were having our supper—Martin's favorite meal and one he loved to spin out as long as possible. That evening, however, we were never to finish our luscious salmon mayonnaise. Ardent to resume his spiritual wrestling match with his beloved laddie, Sir Olin summarily dismissed our dishes and settled us down to a session known as "The Quiet Quarter," which was to prove one of the most mortifying of our daily ordeals at Olinscourt.

It started with a reading by Sir Olin from a book written and privately published by himself, entitled: *Five Minute Chats with a Growing Lad.* When this one-sided "chat" was over Sir Olin sat back, hands folded over his ample stomach, and invited us with an intimate smile to tell him of our problems, our recent sins and temptations. We wriggled and squirmed a while trying to think up some suitable sin or temptation;

then the Baronet relieved the situation by a long impromptu prayer, interrupted at last, thank heavens, by the downstairs booming of the dinner gong. Then, having laid benedictory hands on our heads, Sir Olin kissed us both—me on the forehead and Martin full on the mouth—and dismissed us to our beds.

There, for the first time since my arrival at Olinscourt, Martin leaped on me with a sudden savagery far surpassing anything he had shown at school. With his fingers pressed against my windpipe, I was helpless almost immediately and more than ready to surrender.

"Swear you won't tell the chaps at school about him kissing us good night," he demanded thickly.

"I swear, man," I stuttered.

"Nor about those pi-jaws he's going to give us every evening."

It was not until I had given my solemn oath that he released me.

Next morning it became immediately apparent that with Sir Olin's return the golden days were over. With his return too Lady Slater had departed on some missionary journeyings of her own, a fact which suggested that she enjoyed her husband's presence no more than we did. In the place of her short but fervent grace, Sir Olin treated us and the entire staff of servants to ten minutes of family prayers—all within sight and scent of the lemon glory of scrambled eggs, the glistening mahogany of sausage and kippers, which sizzled temptingly on the side table.

But at least the Baronet solved the mystery of the locked study, solved it quite dramatically too. Immediately after breakfast on his first day at home, he summoned us into the long, booklined room and announced with a chuckle: "Lickle surprise for you, Martin, laddie. Just you both watch that center bookcase."

We watched breathless as Sir Olin touched an invisible switch and smoothly, soundlessly, the bookcase swung out into the room, revealing behind it the dull metal of a heavy door. And in the center of this heavy door was a gleaming brass combination-dial.

"Oh, Father, it's a secret safe!" Martin's face lighted up with enthusiasm.

Sir Olin chuckled again and took out a heavy gold hunter watch. Opening the back of it as if to consult some combination number, he started to turn the brass knob to and fro. At length, as on oiled wheels, the heavy door rolled back, disclosing not a mere safe, but a square, vault-like chamber with a small desk and innumerable drawers of different sizes, suggesting the more modern bank-deposit strong rooms. He invited us to enter and we obeyed, trembling with excitement. Sir Olin showed us some of the wonders, explaining as he did so that his object in withdrawing his more liquid assets from his London bank had been to protect his beloved laddie's financial future from the destructive menace of German zeppelins. He twisted a knob and drew out a drawer glittering with golden sovereigns. He showed us other mysterious drawers containing all that was negotiable of the Slaters' earthly treasure, labeled with such titles as MORTGAGES, INSURANCE, STOCKS AND SHARES, TREASURE NOTES, etc., etc.

Confronted by this elaborate manifestation of parental solicitude, Martin asked the question I had expected: "Has it got a burglar alarm, Father?"

"No. No." Sir Olin's plump fingers caressed his son's hair indulgently. "Why don't you try your hand at making one, laddie, in your spare time?"

I was soon to learn, however, that spare time was a very rare commodity with Sir Olin about. The Baronet, a passionate English country gentleman himself, was determined to instill a similar enthusiasm in his only son and heir. Every morning after breakfast Martin, yearning for his workshop, was obliged to make the rounds of the estate with his father, following through barn and stable, over pasture and plowland, listening to an interminable monologue on how Sir Olin, the Eleventh Baronet, with the aid of God, was disposing everything perfectly for the Twelfth Baronet, the future Sir Martin Slater. I usually tagged along behind them with Sir Olin's only admirer, the dour Roddy, staring entrancedly at the sleek flanks of cows whose cream would enrich next term's tuck hampers; at pigs whose very shape suggested sausage rolls of the future; at poultry whose plumpness I translated dreamily into terms of drumsticks, second joints, and slices of firm white breast.

Every day Sir Olin brought us back from our cross-country tramps at exactly five minutes to one, which left us barely time to wash our hands for lunch. And after lunch until tea, the Baronet, eager to share Martin's playful as well as his weighty moments, took us riding or bowled googly lobs to us at the cricket nets, in a vain attempt to improve our batting style in a game that we both detested.

Tea at four-thirty was followed by our only real period of respite. For at five o'clock, punctual as Sir Olin's gold hunter, his estate agent arrived from Bridgewater, and the two of them were closeted together in the library until seven o'clock when the dressing gong sounded and Sir Olin put documents and ledgers into his strong room and the agent took his leave.

Needless to say, Martin and I daily blessed the estate agent's name, though it was, infelicitously enough, Ramsbotham. And, needless to say, his arrival was the signal for us to scoot off, me to my wanderings, Martin to his workshop, until suppertime.

Suppertime itself, once the most blissful moment of the day, lost its glory; for Sir Olin, unlike his wife, was quite indifferent to food. Eager for his "Quiet Quarter," he allowed us a scant twelve minutes to feed the inner boy. His appearance, dressed in a claret-colored dinner jacket, meant the instant removal of our plates, and many a succulent morsel did I see snatched from me. Martin loved good food as much as I did, but being a truer epicure than I, was incapable of gobbling. He frequently had to endure "The Quiet Quarter" and his father's goodnight kiss on an almost empty stomach.

A few days later Sir Olin introduced yet another torture for Martin. The Baronet decided that his son was now old enough to learn something about the business side of an estate that would one day be his. Three times a week, therefore, Martin was required to be present from five to seven o'clock in the library with his father and Ramsbotham. This left him only two hours on Tuesdays, Thursdays, and Saturdays for tinkering in his beloved workshop. It meant also that, at least three times a week, his supper period was even further curtailed.

I think it was about this time I began to notice a change in Martin. He became even more silent and his face was pale and set with dark lines under his eyes. These, I suspect, were caused partly by the fact that he made up for the lost time in his workshop by sneaking out to it in the middle of the night. I say I suspect this, for he never took me into his confidence; but on two occasions when I happened to wake after midnight his bed was empty and through the open window I could see a flickering light in the workshop.

My guess is that the final stage really started on Saturday night at the end of my third week at Olinscourt. The dressing gong had just sounded and, as I happened to pass the library, I heard the tinkle of a bell. I was surprised, since the telephone there rang very seldom and usually only for something important. Martin, who had joined me on the stairs, voiced my unspoken hope.

"Say, man, d'you think perhaps that's someone calling Father away or something jolly like that?"

And later, as I was hurrying through my bath, there was the sound of a car starting, and from the window Martin announced excitedly:

"There's old Ramsbum's car, and I do believe I see Father in it with him. He hasn't come up to dress yet. Wait while I go down to the library to see."

He returned in a few minutes with the good news that his father, not being there, had presumably left with Mr. Ramsbotham, which meant we could linger pleasantly over supper. It was a delicious supper too—fresh trout followed by raspberries and cream—and was brought up by no less a person than Pringle, the head butler. "Excuse me, Master Martin," he said with an apologetic cough, "but do you happen to know if Sir Olin will be down to dinner?"

"I think he went to Bridgewater with Mr. Ramsbotham." Martin's mouth was full of green peas. "I know he was asked to give a talk at the boys' reformatory there some Saturday. And someone rang him up on the telephone."

"I see, sir, but he didn't mention it to me, sir." Pringle withdrew in starchy disapproval and left us the pleasant realization that there would be no "Quiet Quarter" and no good-night kiss.

And there were no family prayers next morning, since Sir Olin had not returned. It was to be presumed that he had been exhausted by reforming reformatory boys and had consequently spent the night in Bridgewater with Mr. Ramsbotham. And, as it was a Sunday, no question was raised as to his absence.

Martin, bright-eyed, rushed off to his workshop immediately after breakfast and I decided on a stroll. It was then that happened one of those tiny incidents that seemed trivial at the time, but seen in later perspective, appear most significant.

I had whistled for Roddy, usually so anxious to share my walks abroad, but no scampering feet answered my summons. I whistled again. Then I started to look for him, calling:

"Hey, Roddy . . . rats . . . !"

The sound of whining from the study at last solved the problem. Roddy had apparently found a rat of his own, for he was scratching at the central bookcase with a strange crooning sound.

I induced him to follow me, but later when I turned to look back, he had vanished. And that, in itself, was quite unprecedented.

Another seemingly unimportant incident occurred later that morning when I arrived home from my walk. The day was hot and I had taken off my school blazer before going out, hanging it on a peg in the hall, near the front door. When I got back a blazer was there, but it was hanging upside down. As I unhooked it a number of letters dropped from the pockets. They were from Sir Olin to his son and I realized at once that Martin had gone in to lunch ahead of me, taking my blazer by mistake. I picked up the letters—all of them as I thought—shoved them back into the pockets and promptly forgot the whole thing. I doubt even if we bothered to effect an exchange of coats.

Next morning Martin did a rare thing. He got up before me and was at his place at the breakfast table when I came down. In front of him was an unopened letter and I immediately recognized the writing on the envelope as his father's.

As Pringle brought the coffee he said with his usual apologetic cough: "When I picked up the letters from the front hall, Master Martin, I took the liberty of observing there was one for you from Sir Olin. I was wondering if he mentions the date of his return."

"Just give me a sec, Pringle." Martin heaped his plate with kedgeree. "I'll read it and tell you."

After the dignified withdrawal of Pringle, Martin tore open the envelope and pulled out two pages of the familiar crabbed scrawl. He scanned the first page quickly, muttering: "Just the usual pi stuff."

"Does he say when he's coming back?" I asked.

"Wait, here's something at the end." As Pringle's footsteps sounded in the passage outside he handed me the first page and the envelope, saying urgently: "Here, shove those into the fire, man. I'd die rather than have Pringle see all that slosh."

As I speedily thrust the first page of slosh, together with the envelope, into the fire, I heard Martin's voice, studiedly casual for Pringle's benefit: "Here, Pat, read this. You're better at making out Father's writing."

He passed me the second sheet and I read:

And so, beloved lad, I shall be back with you in three or four days. In the meantime I pray that His Guidance . . . etc. . . . etc. . . .

The letter contained no hint as to his actual whereabouts.

We imparted the gist of this to Pringle and he seemed satisfied enough, though somewhat resentful that he had not been informed personally of his master's absence. Still more resentful and far less satisfied was Mr. Ramsbotham when he arrived at the usual hour that afternoon. No, he had not driven Sir Olin to Bridgewater or anywhere else. The talk at the reformatory had been definitely arranged for next Saturday. He had of course to accept the evidence of the letter which Martin duly presented but it was all very vexing . . . all very odd. It was more vexing and more odd when it came out that no one had driven Sir Olin to the station.

I don't know exactly when anyone became really alarmed at Sir Olin's continued absence, but at some stage Mr. Ramsbotham must have telephoned Lady Slater to come home. Even before her return, however, I had put the missing Baronet temporarily out of my mind and given myself up to thorough enjoyment of life without him.

To the adult it may seem odd that, in view of the circumstances narrated, I myself felt no uneasiness as to Sir Olin's safety. I can only say that a child's mind is not a logical one; that the events preceding the Baronet's disappearance had no sinister shape for me then; and it is only as I look back now and place each occurrence in its proper context that I can see the terrifying inevitability of the pattern that was forming.

The next piece of news I heard was exciting. The need to pay the staff and the monthly bills had made it essential that the vault, containing among its other riches all the Slater ready cash, be opened. Since Sir Olin alone knew its combination, arrangements were finally made to bring from London the workmen who had built it and who were to blast through the complicated lock.

We were warned to keep away during the period of the actual dynamite blast, but nothing could have kept me from the scene of operations. I lured a curiously reluctant Martin to join me, and we had hidden behind a couch in the dust-sheeted study by the time the men came in to set the fuse.

Even now I am able to recapture those tense moments of waiting behind the couch. I can smell the musty smell of the heavy brocade; I can hear Martin's breath coming faster and faster as we waited; I can see his face pale and set; I can hear the whispered words of the men as they set about their dangerous job.

And then, sooner than I had expected, came the blast. It was terrific, rocking the study and, so it seemed, rocking the very foundations of Olinscourt. Martin and I bumped heads painfully as we jumped up, but I did not notice the pain. I was watching the stream of black smoke which poured from the door of the vault. Through it we heard: "That ought to have done the trick. Here, lend a hand."

Martin and I watched as the men started to swing back the heavy door of the vault. Pringle was hovering fussily behind them. I could see him through the clearing smoke. I was conscious again of Martin's heavy breathing, of the inscrutable brown eyes staring fixedly at the door of the vault as it gradually opened.

Then I heard a smothered exclamation from one of the men, followed by the barking of Roddy who had somehow got into the room. Above it came Pringle's voice: "Good God in Heaven, it's Sir Olin!"

I saw it then—saw the body of a stout man slumped over the tiny desk inside the vault. I saw the dull gleam of a revolver in his hand, the purplish bloodstain above the right temple. I saw the men moving hesitatingly toward it to lift it up—and then Pringle's voice again, warningly: "Leave him for the police. He's dead. Shot 'isself."

For a moment I stared at that slumped body

with the fascination of a child who is seeing death for the first time. A vague odor invaded my nostrils. It was probably the odor of gunpowder, but to my childish mind it became the smell of death. I knew sudden, blinding terror. I pushed past Martin, running upstairs to the lavatory on the fourth floor. I was very sick.

I don't know how long I stayed there locked in the lavatory. I don't remember what my thoughts were except that I had a wild desire to get home—to walk if necessary back to zeppelin-raided London—away from the horror of the thing that I had seen in the vault.

I must have been there for hours.

Someone was calling my name. I emerged from the lavatory rather sheepishly to see Pringle on the landing below. He said: "Master Pat, you are wanted in Lady Slater's dressing room. You and Master Martin."

I found Martin hovering outside his mother's door. He looked as if he had been sick too. Lady Slater was sitting by the window in her boudoir. The snuff-colored gabardines had given place to funereal black, but there was no sign of grief or tears on her face. Even at that cruel moment it seemed beyond her scope to become human. Through a haze of pious phraseology she told us what I already knew—that Sir Olin had taken his own life.

"The terrible disease in his throat . . . we do not know how much he suffered . . . he explained it all in a letter to me . . . we must not judge him . . ."

And then she was holding out a thick envelope to Martin. "He left a letter for you too, my son."

Martin took the envelope, and I could not help noticing that his fingers instinctively palpated it to discover the lurking presence of bank notes, just as he had always done at school.

"And he left a parcel for you also." Lady Slater handed Martin a square carefully wrapped package. Then she continued: "The inscription on it is the same as on the letter. They are for you alone, Martin, to open and do with as you think fit."

After this Lady Slater took us downstairs to the great living room. The village constable was standing by the door. A gentleman of military deportment was talking with Pringle, the butler, and Mr. Ramsbotham. A dim, drooping figure hovered at their side—the local doctor.

From behind a bristling mustache, the military gentleman questioned Martin and myself about the day of Sir Olin's disappearance. Martin, surprisingly steady now, told our simple story. We had both thought we heard the telephone ringing in the library. Martin believed he had caught a glimpse of Sir Olin driving off with Mr. Ramsbotham. He assumed that his father had gone to give his lecture at the reformatory. Monday morning there had been a letter from Sir Olin on Martin's plate telling him that he would not return for several days.

The problem of that letter which had lulled everyone into a false sense of security was next considered. The mustache pointed out that it must have been one which Sir Olin had written to his son at some earlier date and which, by accident, had become confused with the morning post on the front-door mat. It was at this moment that I remembered how, in my hurry for lunch on the day after Sir Olin's disappearance, I had snatched at the blazer which had been hanging in the hall. I remembered how the unopened letters from Sir Olin to Martin had fallen from the pocket. With the conviction of sin known only to children, I saw the whole tragedy as my own fault. And, with more confusion than courage, I was stammering out my guilty secret.

Martin, watching me steadily, was able to corroborate my story, admitting with an awkward flush that he had not always opened his father's letters the moment they arrived. The military eyebrows were raised a trifle and there the matter of the letter stood. "Martin's little friend" had spilled some old unopened letters from Sir Olin out of Martin's blazer; he had failed to pick one of them up; next morning the butler had found it on the doormat and supposed it to be part of the regular morning post. . . . A most unfortunate accident.

The military gentleman then turned to Lady Slater: "There is one thing, Lady Slater. Sir Olin went into the vault on Saturday evening and he was never seen again. It is to be presumed that he did not come out. Indeed, he could not have opened that heavy door from the inside even if he had wished to."

Martin was watching the brisk mustache now, his eyes very bright.

"And yet, Lady Slater, Dr. Webb here tells me that your husband has actually been dead for less than twenty-four hours. Today is Thursday. This means that Sir Olin shot himself through the temple sometime yesterday. In other words he must have spent the three previous days alive in the vault."

He cleared his throat. "From this letter to you there is no question but that your husband took his own life, but I am wondering if you could—er—offer an explanation as to why he should have delayed so long—why he should have spent that uncomfortably long period in the vault. Why he should have waited until the oxygen must have been almost exhausted, why he should . . ."

"He had letters to write. Last bequests to make." Lady Slater's eyes blinked. She seemed determined to reduce the unpleasantness of her husband's death to its lowest possible terms.

"He wanted to make the final arrangements just right." Her voice sank to a whisper. "Such things take time."

"Time. Yes." The military gentleman gave almost an invisible shrug. "But not the better part of three days, Lady Slater."

"I think," replied Lady Slater, and with these words she seemed to lift the whole proceedings to a higher plane, "I think that Sir Olin probably spent the greater part of his last three days in—in prayer."

And indeed there was no answer to that.

We were dismissed almost immediately. In his mother's dressing room Martin carefully picked up the letter and the package which had been left for him by Sir Olin. He moved ahead of me toward the door.

Now that the ordeal was over I felt the need of human companionship, but Martin seemed eager to get away from everyone. Keeping a discreet distance, I followed him out into the sunlit afternoon. He made straight for his workshop, shutting the door behind him and leaving me with my face pressed dolefully against the window.

I don't think he was conscious of me, but I had no intention of spying on him. The loneliness of death was still with me and contact, however remote, with Martin was a comfort. As I watched, he put the letter down on his work bench. Then, casually, he started to unpack the parcel.

I was surprised to see that it was nothing more than an alarm clock, an ordinary alarm clock similar to the dozen or so that already stood on the workshop shelf, except for the fact that it seemed to have attached to it some sort of wire contrivance. I have a dim memory of thinking it odd that his father's last tangible bequest should be anything so meager, so commonplace as an alarm clock.

Martin hardly looked at the clock. He merely put it on the shelf with the others. Then he lighted one of the Bunsen burners with which his well-stocked workshop was provided. He picked up the letter his father had written him, the last of those many letters which he had received and which he had neglected to read. He did not even glance at the envelope. He thrust it quickly into the jet from the Bunsen burner and held it there until the flames must almost have scorched his fingers.

Then, very carefully, Sir Martin Slater, Twelfth Baronet, collected the ashes and threw them into the wastepaper basket.

I remained at Olinscourt for the funeral. Of the service itself I have only the shadowiest and most childish memories. Not so dim, however, are my recollections of the funeral baked meats. I am ashamed to say that I gorged myself. I have no doubt that Martin did so too.

The next day it was decided by my family that I should leave the Slaters alone to their grief. My reluctant departure was sweetened by a walnut cake left over from the funeral which I packed tenderly and stickily at the bottom of my portmanteau.

I never saw Martin Slater again. For some reason it was decided that he should leave the school where we had shivered and wrestled together and go straight to Harrow. For a while I missed the hampers from Olinscourt, but soon the war was over and my family moved to America. I forgot all about my old chum.

Not long ago a mood of nostalgia brought me to thinking of my childhood and Martin Slater again. Slowly, uncovering a fragment here, a fragment there, I found that I was able to restore this long obliterated picture of my visit at Olinscourt.

The facts of course had been in my mind all the time. All they had lacked was interpretation. Now, thanks to a more adult and detached eye, I can see as a whole something which, to my childish view, was nothing more than a disconnected sequence of happenings.

Perhaps I am doing an old school friend an atrocious wrong; perhaps I am cynically forcing a pattern onto what was, in fact, nothing more than a complex of unfortunate accidents and fantastic coincidences. But I am inclined to think otherwise. For I can grasp Martin Slater's character so much more clearly now than when we were children together. I see a boy teetering on the unstable brink of puberty, who revolted passionately from any physical or spiritual intrusion into his privacy; a boy of intense pride and fastidiousness who was mature enough to know he must fight to maintain his personal independence, yet not mature enough to have learned that in the wrestling match of life certain holds are barred—the death-lock, for example.

I see that boy stifled by the sincere but nauseating affection of a father who bombarded him with assiduous pieties that made him the laughingstock of his schoolfellows; of a father who, with his "Quiet Quarters," his sermonizings, his full-mouthed good-night kisses, turned Martin's home life into an incessant siege upon the sacred citadel of his privacy. I am sure that Martin's hatred of his father was something deeply ingrained in him which grew as he grew toward adolescence. That hatred was kept in check perhaps so long as the undeclared war of love was waged unknown to the outside world. It was different when I came to Olinscourt. For I represented the outside world, and in front of me Sir Olin stripped his son naked of all the decent reserves. Those kisses on the mouth were, I believe, to Martin the kisses of Judas. Sir Olin had betrayed him forever.

And Martin Slater was too young to know any other punishment for betrayal than—death.

The details of that crime speak, I think, plainly enough for themselves. During one of his nightly absences from our bedroom Martin could easily have stolen into his sleeping father's room and studied the combination of the safe in the back of the gold hunter. He could easily have slipped into the vault on the night before the crime and installed there some ingenious product of his workshop, some device manufactured from an alarm clock and set for the hour at which Sir Olin invariably entered the vault, which would either automatically have shut the heavy steel door behind the Baronet or have distracted his attention long enough for Martin to close the door upon him himself. Martin's inventive powers were more than adequate to have created that last and most successful "burglar alarm," just as his conversation with his father about installing the alarm, as witnessed by myself, would have provided an innocent explanation for the contrivance if it had been discovered later in the vault with Sir Olin.

From then on, with me as an unconscious and carefully exploited accessory, the rest must have been simple too—an invented glimpse of Sir Olin driving off in Mr. Ramsbotham's car, the clever trick of the old letter, steamed open probably and checked for content, planted among the morning post to put Pringle's mind at rest about his master's absence and to make certain that Sir

Olin would not be searched for until it was too late.

There was genuine artistry in Martin's use of me to cover his tracks. For it was I who innocently burned the first page and the envelope of that fatal letter whose date and postmark would otherwise have proved it to have been of earlier origin. It was I too, with my clumsy grab at the blazer, who was held responsible for that letter's having dropped "inadvertently" into the morning mail.

Yes, Martin Slater, at fourteen, showed a shrewd and native talent for murder. And, as a murderer, he must be considered an unqualified success. For he never even came under suspicion.

There was one person, however, who must have been only too conscious of Martin Slater's dreadful deed. And in that, to me, lies the real horror of the story. I try to keep myself from thinking of Sir Olin bustling into his safe to put away his papers as usual; Sir Olin hearing a little ting-a-ling like the whirring bell of an alarm clock; Sir Olin spinning round to see the great door of the safe closing behind him, shutting him into that soundproof vault; and somewhere, probably above the door, a curious amateur device composed of a clock and some lengths of wire.

I try not to think of the nightmare days that must have followed for him—days spent staring at that alarm-clock contrivance which he must have recognized as the lethal invention of his own son; days spent hoping against hope that Martin would relent and release him from that chamber where the oxygen was growing suffocatingly scarcer; days spent contemplating the terrible culmination of his "perfect" relationship with his beloved laddie.

I wonder if, during those hours of horror, Sir Olin Slater's evangelical faith in the intrinsic goodness of human nature ever faltered. Somehow I doubt it. His heroic manner of death gives me the clue. For Sir Olin, however frightfully he had mismanaged his life, made a triumphant success of death. I can see him, weakened with hunger and thirst, scarcely able to breathe; I can see him neatly, almost meticulously, wrapping up the telltale alarm clock which, if left to be discovered, might have pointed to Martin's complicity. I can see him writing a pious "suicide" note to his wife, and that other probably forgiving note, which was never to be read, to his son. I can see him producing a revolver from one of those brass-handled drawers in the wall of the vault—and gallantly taking his own life in order to shield his son's immense crime from detection.

Indeed, it may well be said of Sir Olin that nothing in his life became him like the leaving it.

Karmesin and the Big Flea

GERALD KERSH

ALTHOUGH THE TIRELESS GERALD KERSH (1911–1968) wrote more than a thousand magazine pieces and more than a thousand short stories, he is best known in the crime field for the few very short tales about Karmesin, a rogue who narrates his own adventures and has been described as "either the greatest criminal or the greatest liar of all time." Typical of these stories is "Karmesin and the Crown Jewels," in which the thief *may* have stolen the jewels from the Tower of London. For all his savoir faire and apparent elegance, there remains an undercurrent of smarminess; he could have been played by Sydney Greenstreet.

It is impossible to slot Kersh into any category of fiction, as his strange and powerful stories and novels cover the gamut from crime to fantasy to literary fiction, with many of the works straddling more than one genre. A somewhat bizarre young life—he was pronounced dead at four, only to sit up in his coffin at the funeral—continued through the early years of adulthood, in which he worked as a baker, nightclub bouncer, salesman, and professional wrestler. Although a successful writer, he moved to the United States after World War II to escape what he regarded as confiscatory taxation and became a naturalized citizen.

His most famous novel, *Night and the City* (1938), is set in the London underworld of professional wrestling and was the basis for the classic 1950 film noir directed by Jules Dassin and starring Richard Widmark; it was remade in 1992 with Robert De Niro and Jessica Lange. Most critics regard the 1957 novel *Fowler's End* to be Kersh's masterpiece and one of the great novels of the twentieth century, but it remains relatively unknown.

"Karmesin and the Big Flea" was originally published in the winter 1938/39 issue of *Courier*; it was first collected in *Karmesin: The World's Greatest Criminal—or Most Outrageous Liar* (Norfolk, Virginia, Crippen & Landru, 2003).

KARMESIN AND THE BIG FLEA

Gerald Kersh

A STREET PHOTOGRAPHER clicked his camera at us, and handed Karmesin a ticket. Karmesin simply said:—"Pfui!" and passed it to me. It was a slip of green paper, printed as follows:—

> **SNAPPO CANDID PHOTOS**
>
> 3 Film Shots have been made of
> *YOU*
> —by our cameraman.
> Post this ticket with P.O. value 1 /-,
> to SNAPPO, JOHN ROAD, E.I.
> For Three Lifelike Pictures.
>
> Name ....
> Address ....

"There is an opportunity for you," said Karmesin. "Procure nine or ten dummy cameras. Give them to nine or ten men, with your printed tickets. Have an accommodation address. A reasonable number of your tickets will come back with shillings. It will be quite a time before anybody complains. If anybody does, explain:—'Pressure of business: millions of customers.' In three or four weeks, you have made some money. Then you can start a mail-order business. By the time you are forty you may retire. *Voila.* I have set you up in life. I have done more for you than many fathers do for their sons. Give me a cigarette. Well, what are you laughing at?"

"Why don't you try the scheme yourself?"

Karmesin ignored this question and went on, in an undertone:—"On second thoughts, have real cameras and real films. That relieves you of the necessity for accomplices. Always avoid accomplices. Don't develop your film: just keep it. Then, if the police come, you say indignantly: 'Look, here are the pictures. Give a man a chance to develop them!' In this manner you can last for two or three months. Never trust any man. Work alone. And speaking of photography; keep out of the range of cameras. They are dangerous."

"Why?"

"I once blackmailed a man by means of a camera."

I was silent. Karmesin's huge, plum-like eyeballs swiveled round as he looked at me. Under his moustache, his lips curved. He said:—"You disapprove. Good! Ha!" and he let out a laugh which sounded like the bursting of a boiler.

I said: "I hate blackmailers."

"The man I blackmailed was a very bad man," said Karmesin.

"How bad?"

"He was a blackmailer," said Karmesin.

"Oh," was all I could say.

"It was a good example of the manner in which little fleas bite big fleas. The man whom he proposed to blackmail was myself."

"Make it a little clearer," I said.

"Certainly. It is very simple. We were going to blackmail Captain Crapaud, of the French Police. He, in his turn, was blackmailing a certain Minister. The man with whom I was working was a certain villain named Cherubini, also of the French Police. He, not content with blackmailing Captain Crapaud, also wanted to blackmail me."

"On what grounds?"

"He was going to blackmail me, because I was blackmailing Captain Crapaud; and blackmail is a criminal offence, even in France. All he had to do was obtain evidence that I was blackmailing Crapaud."

"All this is very complicated."

"Not at all. It is childishly simple," said Karmesin; and, having borrowed a cigarette, he proceeded to explain:—

Captain Crapaud (said Karmesin) was a man with whom it was impossible to feel sympathy. He was, if you will pardon the expression, a filthy pig. It is not usual to discover such men in high executive positions, in the police force of any great country, such as France. But as you know, such things happen. He had acquired a sort of hold upon a very great politician of the period. And he was using this man for all he was worth, which was plenty. This Crapaud was playing the devil. Like that other police officer, whose name, I think, was Mariani, he was using his office for purposes of personal profit. He organised burglaries, arranged the return of the loot, took rake-offs from this side and that; was responsible for many murders. He was a dangerous man to play with—a French equivalent of your own Jonathan Wild.

There is the basis of the situation: Captain Crapaud was holding a certain power, to the detriment of law and order; and his power was built upon a certain incriminating letter which he held.

You understand that? Good.

Now Crapaud had an underling, a species of stooge, a wicked little Corsican named Cherubini. This Cherubini was a bad man. He combined nearly all the vices, and, as is usual in such cases, was always short of money, although his income was far in excess of the normal. You know the type: his dependents starve, that he may bathe a couple of demi-mondaines in vintage champagne. *Pfui* on such wretches, I say! And *pfui*—and *pfui!* Tfoo! One spits at the very thought. Cherubini was little and rat-like. He had prominent front teeth, and no eyes worth mentioning. He would stop unhappy girls, and say "Be nice, or else . . ." But he had a weakness for the more elegant type of woman; and that kind of weakness costs money. Always beware, my friend, of the underling with luxurious tastes, for the time will come when he will nail you to the cross.

I met Cherubini in Cannes. He was going around like a Hungarian millionaire; with gardenias, and a gold-headed stick, and a diamond in his cravat, and an emerald like a walnut on his finger, and real Amber perfume on his moustache; smoking a Corona-Corona nearly as long as your arm . . . English clothes, English boots, silk shirts, polished nails—nothing was too good for this swine of a Cherubini.

I, needless to say, was a man of superlative elegance. I believe I have mentioned that my moustache was practically unrivalled in Europe. Yes, indeed, I am not exaggerating when I tell you that, while dressing, I used to keep my moustache out of the way by hanging it behind my ears. Nearly twenty-two inches, my friend, from tip to tip! However; it did not take me long to worm all the secrets out of the wretched little soul of this species of a Cherubini. He was second in command to the unspeakable Crapaud. Yes. That, in itself, was bad enough. But he was a traitor even to his master.

I will cut it short. Crapaud had a hold upon the Minister . . . let us call him Monsieur Lamoureux. Follow this carefully. Crapaud also had a hold upon Cherubini. Do you get that? Good. The Minister Lamoureux wanted very much to break away from the clutches of Crapaud, and was prepared to pay heavy money for the letter which Crapaud held.

Was this letter procurable? No. But there was an alternative to procuring it, and that was, to incriminate Crapaud in such a manner that he would be glad to part with the letter incriminating the Minister.

But how could one incriminate Crapaud?

Cherubini had a plan.

There was one thing which, in France, could never be forgiven or forgotten; and that was Treason. Out of any other charge, it was possible for a man with influence to wriggle; but not Treason. There was a spy scare at the time. (It was a little before the infamous Dreyfus affair.) If one could prove that Crapaud was receiving money from German agents, in return for information, then one had him.

"But is he?" I asked.

"Yes," said Cherubini, "Crapaud is the outlet through which so many confidential matters concerning internal policy leak through to Germany. He receives, in his apartment, Von Eberhardt of the German Embassy; and receives, in exchange for certain information, a certain sum of money. If only one could prove this . . ."

I asked:—"Have you means of getting into Crapaud's flat?"

"Yes."

"Then the whole matter is simple," I said. "Find out the exact moment when the money is likely to change hands, and take a photograph. A good photograph of Crapaud, taking money from Von Eberhardt, would be enough to hang him ten times over."

"Yes," said Cherubini.

"There is only one drawback," I said, "A camera is too cumbersome." This, you must remember, was before the days of the Candid Camera, and the lightning snapshot.

"Not at all," said Cherubini. "The police in Paris are beginning to use the portable camera invented by Professor Hohler. This camera can be concealed under an ordinary overcoat, and has a lens good enough to take a clear picture by strong gaslight."

"Can you get one?" I asked.

"Yes."

"Then what are you waiting for?"

"I am afraid," said Cherubini.

I paused; then asked:—"How much would there be in this?"

"How much? Why, two or three hundred thousand francs," said this rat of a man.

"Then have no fear. *I* will take the photograph, if you get me into Crapaud's flat at the right time."

Bon. It was agreed.

We arranged to go to Paris together, and settle the affair.

"I have entrée to the flat," said Cherubini, "and I know it like the palm of my hand. It is simple." And he added:—"But you must do the photography, mind."

All right. I will skip the tiresome details concerning the house, and so forth. It was a huge place in the Avenue Victor Hugo, with rooms as large as three rooms such as are built nowadays. The salon was something like a football field—vast, I tell you, and most luxuriously carpeted. The furniture in that room alone must have been worth four or five thousand pounds. Rare stuff. This pig-dog of a Crapaud did himself well. Near the window, there was a deep alcove, with another little window, or air-vent, at the back of it.

It was from this place that I was supposed to work. Cherubini had keys, and everything necessary. He also supplied me with the camera; a nice little piece of work, not dissimilar to the Leica or Contax camera of the present-day. I believe, in fact, that the Hohler Camera was the father of the candid camera. I was smuggled into the alcove, and there I waited for four hours, not daring to move. It was not very comfortable, my friend. However, in due course Crapaud arrived, with his friend Von Eberhardt. They sat. I was admirably in line with them. They conversed. I photographed them. They drank. Again I photographed them. They patted each other on the shoulder. Click! Again. Crapaud took out an enormous gold cigar-case, and offered Von Eberhardt a cigar. Again, click! Then, at last, the German took from his pocket a large roll of banknotes, and held it between his thumb and forefinger. Crapaud grinned and produced a sheet of paper. Then, as the paper and the money changed hands—click! Perfect.

Another hour passed before Von Eberhardt left. Then, as Crapaud went to escort his visitor to the door, I was up and out of the window, and away. You would never believe, looking at me now, how very agile I used to be. I thought I saw another figure slinking away in the shadows, but the night was too dark. I got to the street, and walked quietly home, where I developed my plates.

They were beautiful. The glaring gaslight, amply reflected in a dozen mirrors, was perfect. The photographs were as clear as figures seen by strong sunlight.

The next day, Cherubini came to see me. There was something in the manner of the wretch which disturbed me a little. He looked me up and down with an insolent grin, and said:—

"Captain Crapaud's apartment was broken into, last night."

"So?" I said.

"Watches, rings, trinkets, and money, to the value of fifty thousand francs were stolen," said Cherubini.

"Yes?"

"You were in the apartment, Monsieur," said Cherubini.

"Oh?"

"Yes. You see, Monsieur, *I* was behind *you*, also with a camera."

"Indeed?" I said.

"Indeed. And I am afraid that it will be my duty to have you arrested for the crime."

"Oh."

"Unless, of course, you are prepared to . . ."

"Pay you off, I suppose?" I said.

"Fifty thousand francs," said Cherubini.

"And otherwise?"

"Listen my friend," said Cherubini, throwing himself into a chair, "We are men of the world. I will put the cards on the table. The plates in your camera were duds, useless. You have no pictures. I, on the contrary, have some excellent ones of yourself in Captain Crapaud's flat."

"Any decent counsel could kick that case full of holes," I said.

"Oh no. Not by the time Crapaud and I have finished with it," said Cherubini. "Oh, my friend, my friend, you have no idea what evidence our boys would find, if once they searched your rooms."

"So I was caught, was I?" I asked.

"Like a fish in a net."

"But Von Eberhardt . . ."

Cherubini laughed. "Do you imagine that we would let you into the place with a camera? I mean, with a workable camera? With a camera loaded with proper plates? Be reasonable, Monsieur, be reasonable. There is nothing but your word, concerning Von Eberhardt. Who would believe you? No, no. You had better pay, my friend; you really had."

"And if I thought of all that, and took the precaution of changing the plates?" I asked.

"It would still have made no difference," said Cherubini, "The shutter of your camera would not work."

I rose, and seized him by the throat, slapped him in the face, and threw him to the floor.

"Listen," I said, "I would not trust you as far as I could see you. I saw through your game from the first. I had the shutter adjusted, the lens arranged, and the plates replaced. The camera was in perfect order. I will show you some pictures," I said; and showed him.

He was silent. Then I said:—"And now the ace of trumps. You remember how Crapaud offered Von Eberhardt a cigar?"

"Well?"

"Look," I said, and threw down a print. It was an excellent photo. One could see Eberhardt, Crapaud, and the unmistakable luxury of the salon. "Take that magnifying glass, and look at the cigar-case," I said. Cherubini took the large lens which I handed him, and looked; shrieked once, and looked at me.

Clearly defined in the polished lid of the case was an image of Cherubini, lurking behind the curtains, perfectly recognisable.

"Who wins?" I asked.

And Cherubini said:—"You win."

"And now who goes to Devil's Island?" I asked.

Cherubini simply said:—"How much for the plate?"

And I replied:—"Tell Crapaud this:—If he does not give me that letter of the Minister Lamoureux, then the day will come when one of his superior officers will hand him a revolver containing one cartridge."

"You are mad," said Cherubini. Nevertheless, three days later Crapaud's nerve broke, and I got the letter, which I returned to the Minister.

I asked Karmesin:—"What, you returned it free of charge?"

"Certainly," said Karmesin. "I simply asked him to pay my expenses."

"How much?"

"Chicken-feed. Fifty thousand francs," said Karmesin, "But am I a blackmailer? Bah."

"And Crapaud?"

"He left the country very suddenly, and, I believe, came to an evil end in the Belgian Congo, in the time of the Congo Atrocities. Probably some cannibal ate him. Or a lion. Who knows? Perhaps an elephant trod on him. I hope so. He was a villain. He was also a fool. He overreached himself. I was not the first person whom he had tried to blackmail in that manner. Only he was a little too clever. It should be a lesson to you: never be too clever. Also, beware of cameras. And furthermore, remember the folly of Crapaud, and if ever you come into possession of an incriminating document, you will know what to do."

"What?"

"Photograph it immediately," said Karmesin.

Rogue: DeLancey, King of Thieves

The Very Raffles-Like Episode of Castor and Pollux, Diamonds De Luxe

HARRY STEPHEN KEELER

FAIR WARNING: In more than a half-century of reading mystery fiction, I can point to no author who has confused me as frequently and comprehensively as Harry Stephen Keeler (1890–1967), whose zany, complex intrigue-farces are almost a genre to themselves. The prolific author produced scores of short stories and more than fifty novels, several of which were more than one hundred thousand words in length. It was common for him to interweave previously published stories into what passed for plot.

His "plots" were achieved by fishing through a large file cabinet that he filled with newspaper clippings that interested him and pulling out a handful at random, interweaving them into a story, using such eccentric devices as wacky wills, hitherto unknown religious tenets, insane (and nonexistent) laws, and, most commonly, coincidences that defy credulity. For all their lack of rationality and cohesion, Keeler's books had a wide and devoted following in the 1920s and '30s, but, as the books became more and more bizarre, his readership eroded and then all but vanished entirely, his many later novels being published only in Spain and Portugal. Keeler's wife of more than forty years, Hazel Goodwin, collaborated with him on dozens of books, often sharing a byline.

Thieves' Nights, Keeler's only short story collection, features Bayard DeLancey, King of Thieves, "whom lesser thieves feel honored to have known."

"The Very Raffles-Like Episode of Castor and Pollux, Diamonds De Luxe" was originally published in Keeler's *Thieves' Nights* (New York, Dutton, 1929).

THE VERY RAFFLES-LIKE EPISODE OF CASTOR AND POLLUX, DIAMONDS DE LUXE

Harry Stephen Keeler

I FIRST MET DELANCEY in London. The circumstances of that acquaintance hardly matter, except that I had about the best references that a crook could have. When he went over to Paris, I went back to New York with an understanding between us that I was to serve as the New York end of any big deal, and he had my address, and a code system by which we could communicate.

That he was mixed up in the Simon and Company robbery which he had broached to me at one time on Piccadilly, and that he had been successful, furthermore, was clearly proven by the interesting account I clipped from a New York paper on the second day of July. It read:

Protégé of Lord Albert Avistane Arrested in Paris.

(By cable) Paris: July 1. Bayard DeLancey, a protégé of Lord Albert Avistane of England, educated at Oxford by the nobleman, was arrested here today in connection with last night's robbery of Simon et Cie, 14 Rue Royale, in which two of the most well-known diamonds in the world were stolen.

The stones, known as Castor and Pollux to the trade, are similarly cut and weigh eight carats apiece. The total value of the two, considered by English experts to be well over £12,000, is due to the fact that one is a green, and the other a red diamond. Although certain circumstances point to DeLancey's complicity in the crime, the jewels were found neither in his possession nor at his rooms, and since sufficient definite proof in other directions is lacking, the authorities expect to be compelled to release him within a few days.

A few of the people who are known to have been with him the morning after the robbery are under surveillance, and it is hoped that the stones may ultimately be recovered from one or another of them.

Clever old DeLancey! It looked indeed as though that well-worked-out scheme he had outlined on Piccadilly had come to a successful conclusion.

As for myself, I had, of course, promised to be of assistance to DeLancey merely in getting the two stones into the hands of old Ranseer at his farm near Morristown, New Jersey, after which the split would be forthcoming and would be divided up according to our respective risks in the proceeding. This was the method which we had outlined when DeLancey first heard that I was personally acquainted with old Ranseer, the wealthy recluse who bought stolen rare jewels at nearly their face value.

Had the clipping itself, however, been insufficient evidence that DeLancey had scored one on the French police, his letter, which reached me a week and a half later, made everything clear.

The communication, which was, of course, in cipher, when translated ran as follows:

Gay Paree, July 4.
L. J.
—— Str.
New York.

Dear old Baltimore Rat:
Was it in the New York papers? Must have been. Pulled it off as slick as the proverbial whistle. The blooming beggars kept me locked up three days, though. But they were shy on proof—and besides, they were too late.

Rat, there is to be another man in our proposed crew. Never mind where I picked him up. I firmly believe he is the only man in Europe who will be able to get those gems across the pond. His name is Von Berghem. He called at my rooms the morning after the coup. I passed the stones to him, each one wrapped in a little cotton package, and tied with silk thread.

Now, Rat, he's bound for New York, taking the trip across England in easy stages as befits a gentleman traveling for his health, and according to our plans should embark on an ancient tub named the Princess Dorothy, which leaves Liverpool on July 6th, and arrives at New York nine days later. Immediately upon landing, he will call at your rooms.

As we have already arranged in London, you will have two of your friend Ranseer's carrier pigeons (the nesting birds, by all means) in a dark covered basket. Secure one stone to each pigeon so that if anything should go wrong, you could liberate them instantly through the window. With their known ability to cover as much as 500 miles, at a speed of 30 miles an hour, they would be able to reach the vicinity of Morristown in less than two hours, even taking into consideration darkness. At least, so my own map of your United States indicates.

As soon as things blow over, yours truly, DeLancey, will slide on toward your famous old N'Yawk, after which—heigh-ho, boy—the much-talked of white lights of America and ease for a time.

A last word as to Von Berghem. He wears glasses, has gray hair, and carries a mole on his left cheek. He will be accompanied by his fifteen-year-old son, as sharp a little rascal as ever spotted a Scotland Yard man fifty yards away.

Yours jubilantly,
DeL.

So Von Berghem, I reflected curiously, seemed to be the only man in Europe who could get those two sparklers across the pond?

Surely, I thought troubledly, if he had to get them out of Europe before the eyes of the police, and get them into the States before the eyes of the customs authorities, he would have to be sharp indeed, especially in view of the fact that a hue and cry had already been raised.

Everything was in readiness, though. The pigeons were cheeping in their covered basket. On the mantel were two small leather leg bags ready for the loot. I looked at my watch and found that it was after nine o'clock.

Strange that Von Berghem had not arrived. I had called the steamship offices by telephone at six o'clock and had learned that the *Princess Dorothy* had docked an hour before.

Then I fell to wondering why he had encumbered himself with his son. Unquestionably, he must have realized that in dealings such as ours, every extra man, constituting a possible weak link, meant just so much more chance of failure.

The clock struck ten.

Where had DeLancey found this fellow—this Von Berghem? I found myself asking myself. Was he sure of him? Did he understand the game as we did?

Everything that DeLancey did was always more or less mystifying. He seemed to know the name of every crook between the equator and the poles, and to understand just what part of an undertaking should logically be assigned to anyone. Without doubt he must have known what he was doing this time.

So Von Berghem, I told myself, was the only man that DeLancey believed capable of——

The clock struck ten-thirty.

I heard the slam of a taxicab door down on the street below.

A second later the bell of my New York apartment tinkled sharply.

I hurried to the front door and opened it quietly. In the outer hall stood a tall man wearing glasses. He had gray hair—and a mole on his left cheek. At his side was a boy of about sixteen.

"This is Rat," I whispered.

"Von Berghem," he answered, and stepped inside with the boy, while I closed the door behind them.

I passed down the narrow inner hall and threw open the library door. "In here," I said, and snapped on the lights. "How did you make out?"

Von Berghem seemed to be ill. The whiteness of his face and his halting gait, as he leaned heavily on the shoulder of his son, signified either sickness or——

Failure! Ah—that must be it, I told myself. My heart seemed to stop beating. Von Berghem must have been unsuccessful in his mission.

He sank heavily into a chair that the boy brought forth for him. The latter dropped down on a small footstool, nearby, and remained silent.

In the interval, I studied Von Berghem and perceived for the first time the horrible expression on his face. His eyes had the same haunting look that I had once seen on the face of a maniac in the state insane asylum in Wyoming, where I originally came from.

"Met with considerable trouble," he stated laconically, after a pause.

"Tell me about it," I said, half sympathetically and half suspiciously. His gaze, which had been roving aimlessly around the room, he directed toward me again. Then he commenced to talk.

"I called on DeLancey the morning after the robbery. He gave the two gems into my keeping at once. The lad was with me. He's a coming thief, is the lad. We took a cab at once for the station. Three hours afterward, DeLancey was nabbed.

"The lad and I boarded a train that morning for Calais. We reached there at one o'clock in the afternoon and spent the rest of the day in a hostel. From the hostel we made the boat safely that evening and got into Dover at midnight. So far, everything ran without a hitch. We stayed at a hostel in Dover till morning.

"No use to bore you telling you of our crawling progress across England. Only three hundred miles, but we spent four days covering it. Of course, we were just a gentleman and his son traveling for pleasure.

"But things began to liven up for us. We had hoped by this time that we were not being looked for after all, but apparently we were wrong. As we got off the train in the station at Liverpool, on the evening of July 5th, the lad, little lynx that he is, spots a man in a brown suit, carelessly watching all the passengers. He nudges me quickly.

"Now comes luck itself. A crazy emigrant, farther down the platform, pulls out a gun and commences shooting through the roof. Hell and confusion break loose. During the big rush of people that takes place, the lad notices a little door leading out to a side street. 'Quick, Daddy,' he says, 'we'll slip out this way.'

"Outside, he flags a cabby in a jiffy and we drive to a little dirty hostel on a side street, where we spend the night wondering whether the man in the brown suit was looking for us or for someone else.

"However, we're on our guard now. We don't feel quite so easy. Next morning we make the pier and board the *Princess Dorothy*, which boat, I may add, is one of the few going out of Liverpool that do not touch at Queenstown or any other point but New York, once she casts off from the Liverpool landing stage. Yes, friend Rat, every detail was figured out long in advance by DeLancey himself.

"As soon as we get aboard, I lie down in the stateroom and let the lad remain on deck. I'm not a well man, friend Rat, and traveling under the conditions and handicaps that we traveled under is hard on me. The following is the boy's account.

"As he says: No sooner had the ship pulled out from the landing stage and was headed about for the open water, than a motor car comes rushing pell-mell up to the wharf. Out jump four men—and one of 'em is our friend in the brown suit. The lad whips out the binoculars and watches their lips. 'Damn—too late—radio—' is what our brown-suited near-acquaintance appears to say.

"Well, in spite of the fact that, like all boats, we're equipped with wireless, nothing happens to us on board. But at no time do I forget the existence of the Atlantic Cable. What I figure is that they're trying to lull us into a false sense of security. At any rate, all the way across I take my meals in the stateroom and the lad prowls around deck trying to pick up some information. But, as I said before, everything's as peaceful as the grave.

"It's a mighty long nine days for us, friend Rat, but late in the afternoon of the fifteenth, we find we're within one hour of the Battery—and we realize now that things are very doubtful for us.

"As we step from the gangplank together, each of us suddenly finds a hand on our shoulder. In front of us stand three men, two of 'em fly-bulls with stars—the third a customs inspector. 'You're Von Berghem,' says one of 'em. 'Want you both to step in this little house at the end of the pier for a couple of hours. When we get done there won't be any further bother to you of a customs inspection, for the inspector himself here is going to help us out.' He laughed unpleasantly. 'Yep—we got a warrant,' adds the other in answer to my unspoken question.

"Well, my friend, I, Von Berghem, know my limitations. I didn't take the trouble to deny anything. Smilingly, I admitted that I was Von Berghem and that this was my son. Then I asked them what they intended to do. 'Just want to look you and your boy and your two suit-cases over,' admits one of them.

"In that little inspection house they locked the door. They drew down the shades and turned on the lights. They commanded us both to strip. When we had done this, they made us stand stark naked up against the wall. They began by examining our mouths, taking good care to look under our tongues. Then they combed out our hair with a fine-tooth comb. After a full fifteen minutes, in which they satisfied themselves that the jewels were not concealed on our bodies, they turned out the lights, and wheeled over some kind of a vertical metal standard that held a huge, powerful X-ray tube that could be moved up and down, and swung to left and right. The boy here is a little radio bug and can describe it and explain it far better than I. At any rate, standing us naked in turn in front of the tube, they slid it slowly up and down, from a point in our bodies about level with the esophagus and downward, literally peering through our very bodies with what I heard them refer to among themselves as a fluoroscope, which they handed back and forth from hand to hand. Of course I know enough about the X-rays and elementary physics to understand that they hoped to find a deep black opaque shadow that is always made, as I understand, by the crystalline carbon we call a diamond; they hoped to find such a shadow in our stomachs, or alimentary tracts, and had they done so, they could have watched its movement downward and corroborated matters for themselves. But, to cut a long story short, friend Rat, our alimentary tracts gave no opacities at all, outside of our bones which were fixed shadows and which they checked up on by moving the tube or the fluoroscope. For, you see, we made no errors of trying to swallow any big diamonds such as Castor or Pollux, if for no other reason than that your friend DeLancey had read all about this new customs instrument in the *London Illustrated News*, and had mentioned to us laughingly that if he ever tried to carry stolen jewels across the ocean himself, swallowing them was the last thing on earth he'd do.

"So as I say, after satisfying themselves unequivocally that the jewels were not in our hair or our mouths, on our bodies or in our bodies, they turned on the lights once more and started on our luggage. 'This is an outrage,' I grumbled.

"They dumped out the clothing in our suit-cases and placed it in one pile, together with that which we had been forced to discard. Then they commenced with our underclothing, which they examined seam by seam, button by button, square inch by square inch. Following that, our garters, our socks, our suspenders, were subjected to the same rigid examination.

"As fast as they finished with an article of clothing, they tossed it over to us and allowed whichever one of us was the owner to don it. In that way, we dressed, garment by garment, always protesting stoutly at the outrage.

"In the same manner they went through our neckties, most of which they ripped open; our shirts, collars, and vests followed next.

"When they came to our outer suits, not content with an exacting scrutiny, they brought out hammers and hammered every inch. Our shoes—look for yourself, friend Rat—are without heels; they tore them off, layer by layer. Our felt hats underwent similar treatment, for they removed the linings, replacing them later, loose.

"Our suit-cases were examined at buckle and seam, rivet and strap. At every place of possible concealment—every place which involved, say, a thickness greater than the diameter of Castor or Pollux—they pounded vigorously with their hammers, using enough force to smash steel balls, let alone brittle diamonds. And for every place that was thin, they gave a few vicious poundings for good measure.

"Friend Rat, we were in there three and a half hours, and had we had trunks, we might have been there yet. They left nothing unturned. Everything, though, has to come to an end. In disgust, they finally threw away their hammers. 'That lead from Liverpool's a phony one,' said one of the three to the two others. 'You're free, Von Berghem and son,' his companion added. 'It's a cinch you've not got the proceeds of the Simon Company's burglary at Paris. You and your boy can go.'

"This was about two hours ago. We have had no supper, for we took a taxicab and, with the exception of a couple of breakdowns on the way, came straight here in order to tell you of the situation in which we found ourselves."

I was crestfallen, disappointed, at the story I had heard. And I told Von Berghem so frankly.

"It's a shame," I commented bitterly. "DeLancey stakes his liberty on a bit of dangerous and clever work—and then sends a bungler across with the proceeds. Of course, man, they've got 'em by this time. It doesn't matter where in the stateroom you hid 'em—the woodwork, the carpet, the mattress—they've found 'em now. Well—we'll have to put it down as a failure—that's all."

He heard me through before he uttered a word. Then, dropping his glasses in his coat pocket, he answered me sharply.

"Failure? Who has said anything of failure? You do me a great injustice, friend Rat. Are your pigeons all in readiness? All right. Von Berghem never fails. Look!"

He pressed his hands to his face. For a moment I thought he was going to weep, for he made strange clawing motions with his fingers. Then he lowered his hands.

I sprang to my feet, suppressing a cry with difficulty. Where his eyes had been were now black, sightless sockets. On each of his palms lay a fragile, painted, porcelain shell—and in the hollow of each shell was a tiny cotton packet, tied with silk thread.

Villain: General Zaroff

The Most Dangerous Game

RICHARD CONNELL

ALTHOUGH A SUCCESSFUL AND PROLIFIC short story writer who also enjoyed some success in Hollywood, Richard Edward Connell (1893–1949) is known today mainly for "The Most Dangerous Game," one of the most anthologized stories ever written and the basis for numerous film versions, including the 1932 RKO film of the same title (called *The Hounds of Zaroff* in England), with Joel McCrea, Fay Wray, and Leslie Banks; *A Game of Death* (RKO, 1945, with John Loder, Edgar Barrier, and Audrey Long); and *Run for the Sun* (United Artists, 1956, with Richard Widmark, Jane Greer, and Trevor Howard). It has often served as the basis for slightly looser adaptations in other media (especially radio and television), sometimes credited and sometimes not.

At the age of eighteen, Connell became the city editor of *The New York Times*, then went to Harvard, where he was the editor of *The Harvard Lampoon* and *The Harvard Crimson*. Upon graduation, he returned to journalism but was soon offered a lucrative job writing advertising copy. After serving in World War I, he sold several short stories and became a full-time freelancer, becoming one of America's most popular and prolific magazine writers; he also produced four novels. Many of his stories served as the basis for motion pictures, notably *Brother Orchid* (1940, starring Edward G. Robinson, Ann Sothern, and Humphrey Bogart, based on his 1938 short story of the same name). Connell wrote original stories for several films, including *F-Man* (1936, with Jack Haley) and *Meet John Doe* (1941, directed by Frank Capra, starring Gary Cooper and Barbara Stanwyck), for which he was nominated for an Academy Award for Best Writing, Original Story. He was nominated for another Academy Award for Best Original Screenplay for *Two Girls and a Sailor* (1944, with June Allyson, Gloria DeHaven, and Van Johnson). He also wrote the screenplay for *Presenting Lily*

Mars (1943, starring Judy Garland and Van Heflin), based on Booth Tarkington's novel.

"The Most Dangerous Game" was originally published in the January 19, 1924, issue of *Collier's* magazine, winning the O. Henry Memorial Prize; it was first collected in Connell's *Variety* (New York, Minton Balch, 1925).

THE MOST DANGEROUS GAME

Richard Connell

"OFF THERE to the right—somewhere—is a large island," said Whitney. "It's rather a mystery—"

"What island is it?" Rainsford asked.

"The old charts called it Ship-Trap Island," Whitney replied. "A suggestive name, isn't it? Sailors have a curious dread of the place. I don't know why. Some superstition—"

"Can't see it," remarked Rainsford, trying to peer through the dank tropical night that pressed its thick warm blackness in upon the yacht.

"You've good eyes," said Whitney with a laugh, "and I've seen you pick off a moose moving in the brown fall bush at four hundred yards, but even you can't see four miles or so through a moonless Caribbean night."

"Nor four yards," admitted Rainsford. "Ugh! It's like moist black velvet."

"It will be light enough in Rio," promised Whitney. "We should make it in a few days. I hope the jaguar guns have come from Purdey's. We should have some good hunting up the Amazon. Great sport, hunting."

"The best sport in the world," agreed Rainsford.

"For the hunter," amended Whitney. "Not for the jaguar."

"Don't talk rot, Whitney. You're a big-game hunter, not a philosopher. Who cares how a jaguar feels?"

"Perhaps the jaguar does."

"Bah! They've no understanding."

"Even so, I rather think they understand one thing—fear. The fear of pain and the fear of death."

"Nonsense," laughed Rainsford. "This hot weather is making you soft, Whitney. Be a realist. The world is made up of two classes—the hunters and the huntees. Luckily you and I are hunters. Do you think we have passed that island yet?"

"I can't tell in the dark. I hope so."

"Why?"

"The place has a reputation—a bad one."

"Cannibals?"

"Hardly. Even cannibals wouldn't live in such a God-forsaken place. But it's gotten into sailor lore, somehow. Didn't you notice that the crew's nerves seemed a bit jumpy today?"

"They were a bit strange, now you mention it. Even Captain Nielsen."

"Yes, even that tough-minded old Swede, who'd go up to the devil himself and ask him for a light. Those fishy blue eyes held a look I never saw there before. All I could get out of him was: 'This place has an evil name among seafaring men, sir.' Then he said, gravely: 'Don't you feel anything?' Now you mustn't laugh but I did feel a sort of chill, and there wasn't a breeze. What I felt was a—a mental chill, a sort of dread."

"Pure imagination," said Rainsford. "One superstitious sailor can taint a whole ship's company with his fear."

"Maybe. Sometimes I think sailors have an extra sense which tells them when they are in danger . . . anyhow I'm glad we are getting out of this zone. Well, I'll turn in now, Rainsford."

"I'm not sleepy. I'm going to smoke another pipe on the after deck."

There was no sound in the night as Rainsford sat there but the muffled throb of the yacht's engine and the swish and ripple of the propeller.

Rainsford, reclining in a steamer chair, puffed at his favourite briar. The sensuous drowsiness of the night was on him. "It's so dark," he thought, "that I could sleep without closing my eyes; the night would be my eyelids—"

An abrupt sound startled him. Off to the right he heard it, and his ears, expert in such matters, could not be mistaken. Again he heard the sound, and again. Somewhere, off in the blackness, someone had fired a gun three times.

Rainsford sprang up and moved quickly to the rail, mystified. He strained his eyes in the direction from which the reports had come, but it was like trying to see through a blanket. He leaped upon the rail and balanced himself there, to get greater elevation; his pipe, striking a rope, was knocked from his mouth. He lunged for it; a short, hoarse cry came from his lips as he realized he had reached too far and had lost his balance. The cry was pinched off short as the blood-warm waters of the Caribbean Sea closed over his head.

He struggled to the surface and cried out, but the wash from the speeding yacht slapped him in the face and the salt water in his open mouth made him gag and strangle. Desperately he struck out after the receding lights of the yacht, but he stopped before he had swum fifty feet. A certain cool-headedness had come to him, for this was not the first time he had been in a tight place. There was a chance that his cries could be heard by someone aboard the yacht, but that chance was slender and grew more slender as the yacht raced on. He wrestled himself out of his clothes and shouted with all his power. The lights of the boat became faint and vanishing fireflies; then they were blotted out by the night.

Rainsford remembered the shots. They had come from the right, and doggedly he swam in that direction, swimming slowly, conserving his strength. For a seemingly endless time he fought the sea. He began to count his strokes; he could do possibly a hundred more and then—

He heard a sound. It came out of the darkness, a high, screaming sound, the cry of an animal in an extremity of anguish and terror. He did not know what animal made the sound. With fresh vitality he swam towards it. He heard it again; then it was cut short by another noise, crisp, staccato.

"Pistol shot," muttered Rainsford, swimming on.

Ten minutes of determined effort brought to his ears the most welcome sound he had ever heard, the breaking of the sea on a rocky shore. He was almost on the rocks before he saw them; on a night less calm he would have been shattered against them. With his remaining strength he dragged himself from the swirling waters. Jagged crags appeared to jut into the opaqueness; he forced himself up hand over hand. Gasping, his hands raw, he reached a flat place at the top. Dense jungle came down to the edge of the cliffs, and careless of everything but his weariness Rainsford flung himself down and tumbled into the deepest sleep of his life.

When he opened his eyes he knew from the position of the sun that it was late in the afternoon. Sleep had given him vigour; a sharp hunger was picking at him.

"Where there are pistol shots there are men. Where there are men there is food," he thought; but he saw no sign of a trail through the closely knit web of weeds and trees; it was easier to go along the shore. Not far from where he had landed, he stopped.

Some wounded thing, by the evidence a large animal, had crashed about in the underwood. A small glittering object caught Rainsford's eye and he picked it up. It was an empty cartridge.

"A twenty-two," he remarked. "That's odd. It must have been a fairly large animal, too. The hunter had his nerve with him to tackle it with a light gun. It is clear the brute put up a fight. I suppose the first three shots I heard were when the hunter flushed his quarry and wounded it. The last shot was when he trailed it here and finished it."

He examined the ground closely and found what he had hoped to find—the print of hunting boots. They pointed along the cliff in the direction he had been going. Eagerly he hurried along, for night was beginning to settle down on the island.

Darkness was blacking out sea and jungle before Rainsford sighted the lights. He came upon them as he turned a crook in the coast line, and his first thought was that he had come upon a village, as there were so many lights. But as he forged along he saw that all the lights were in one building—a château on a high bluff.

"Mirage," thought Rainsford. But the stone steps were real enough. He lifted the knocker and it creaked up stiffly as if it had never before been used.

The door, opening, let out a river of glaring light. A tall man, solidly built and black-bearded to the waist, stood facing Rainsford with a revolver in his hand.

"Don't be alarmed," said Rainsford, with a smile that he hoped was disarming. "I'm no robber. I fell off a yacht. My name is Sanger Rainsford of New York City."

The man gave no sign that he understood the words or had even heard them. The menacing revolver pointed as rigidly as if the giant were a statue.

Another man was coming down the broad, marble steps, an erect slender man in evening clothes. He advanced and held out his hand.

In a cultivated voice marked by a slight accent which gave it added precision and deliberateness, he said: "It is a great pleasure and honour to welcome Mr. Sanger Rainsford, the celebrated hunter, to my home."

Automatically Rainsford shook the man's hand.

"I've read your book about hunting snow leopards in Tibet," explained the man. "I am General Zaroff."

Rainsford's first impression was that the man was singularly handsome; his second, that there was a bizarre quality about the face. The general was a tall man past middle age, for his hair was white; but his eyebrows and moustache were black. His eyes, too, were black and very bright. He had the face of a man used to giving orders. Turning to the man in uniform, he made a sign. The fellow put away his pistol, saluted, withdrew.

"Ivan is an incredibly strong fellow," remarked the general, "but he has the misfortune to be deaf and dumb. A simple fellow, but a bit of a savage."

"Is he Russian?"

"A Cossack," said the general, and his smile showed red lips and pointed teeth. "So am I.

"Come," he said, "we shouldn't be chatting here. You want clothes, food, rest. You shall have them. This is a most restful spot."

Ivan had reappeared and the general spoke to him with lips that moved but gave forth no sound.

"Follow Ivan if you please, Mr. Rainsford. I was about to have my dinner, but will wait. I think my clothes will fit you."

It was to a huge beam-ceilinged bedroom with a canopied bed large enough for six men that Rainsford followed the man. Ivan laid out an evening suit and Rainsford, as he put it on, noticed that it came from a London tailor.

"Perhaps you were surprised," said the general as they sat down to dinner in a room which suggested a baronial hall of feudal times, "that I recognized your name; but I read all books on hunting published in English, French, and Russian. I have but one passion in life, and that is the hunt."

"You have some wonderful heads here," said Rainsford, glancing at the walls. "That Cape buffalo is the largest I ever saw."

"Oh, that fellow? He charged me, hurled me against a tree, and fractured my skull. But I got the brute."

"I've always thought," said Rainsford, "that the Cape buffalo is the most dangerous of all big game."

For a moment the general did not reply, then he said slowly: "No, the Cape buffalo is not the most dangerous." He sipped his wine. "Here in my preserve on this island I hunt more dangerous game."

"Is there big game on this island?"

The general nodded. "The biggest."

"Really?"

"Oh, it isn't here naturally. I have to stock the island."

"What have you imported, General? Tigers?"

The general grinned. "No, hunting tigers ceased to interest me when I exhausted their possibilities. No thrill left in tigers, no real real danger. I live for danger, Mr. Rainsford."

The general took from his pocket a gold cigarette case and offered his guest a long black cigarette with a silver tip; it was perfumed and gave off a smell like incense.

"We will have some capital hunting, you and I," said the general.

"But what game—" began Rainsford.

"I'll tell you. You will be amused, I know. I think I may say, in all modesty, that I have done a rare thing. I have invented a new sensation. May I pour you another glass of port?"

"Thank you, General."

The general filled both glasses and said: "God makes some men poets. Some he makes kings, some beggars. Me he made a hunter. But after years of enjoyment I found that the hunt no longer fascinated me. You can perhaps guess why?"

"No—why?"

"Simply this: hunting had ceased to be what you call a 'sporting proposition.' I always got my quarry . . . always . . . and there is no greater bore than perfection."

The general lit a fresh cigarette.

"The animal has nothing but his legs and his instinct. Instinct is no match for reason. When I realized this, it was a tragic moment for me."

Rainsford leaned across the table, absorbed in what his host was saying.

"It came to me as an inspiration what I must do."

"And that was?"

"I had to invent a new animal to hunt."

"A new animal? You are joking."

"I never joke about hunting. I needed a new animal. I found one. So I bought this island, built this house, and here I do my hunting. The island is perfect for my purpose—there are jungles with a maze of trails in them, hills, swamps—"

"But the animal, General Zaroff?"

"Oh," said the general, "it supplies me with the most exciting hunting in the world. Every day I hunt, and I never grow bored now, for I have a quarry with which I can match my wits."

Rainsford's bewilderment showed in his face.

"I wanted the ideal animal to hunt, so I said, 'What are the attributes of an ideal quarry?' and the answer was, of course: 'It must have courage, cunning, and, above all, it must be able to reason.' "

"But no animal can reason," objected Rainsford.

"My dear fellow," said the general, "there is one that can."

"But you can't mean—"

"And why not?"

"I can't believe you are serious, General Zaroff. This is a grisly joke."

"Why should I not be serious? I am speaking of hunting."

"Hunting? Good God, General Zaroff, what you speak of is murder."

The general regarded Rainsford quizzically. "Surely your experiences in the war—"

"Did not make me condone cold-blooded murder," finished Rainsford stiffly.

Laughter shook the general. "I'll wager you'll forget your notions when you go hunting with me. You've a genuine new thrill in store for you, Mr. Rainsford."

"Thank you, I am a hunter, not a murderer."

"Dear me," said the general, quite unruffled, "again that unpleasant word; but I hunt the scum of the earth—sailors from tramp ships—lascars, blacks, Chinese, whites, mongrels."

"Where do you get them?"

The general's left eyelid fluttered down in a wink. "This island is called Ship-Trap. Come to the window with me."

Rainsford went to the window and looked out towards the sea.

"Watch! Out there!" exclaimed the general, as he pressed a button. Far out Rainsford saw a flash of lights. "They indicate a channel where there's none. Rocks with razor edges crouch there like a sea-monster. They can crush a ship like a nut. Oh, yes, that is electricity. We try to be civilized."

"Civilized? And you shoot down men?"

"But I treat my visitors with every consideration," said the general in his most pleasant manner. "They get plenty of good food and exercise. They get into splendid physical condition. You shall see for yourself tomorrow."

"What do you mean?"

"We'll visit my training school," smiled the general. "It is in the cellar. I have about a dozen there now. They're from the Spanish bark *Sanlucar*, which had the bad luck to go on the rocks out there. An inferior lot, I regret to say, and more accustomed to the deck than the jungle."

He raised his hand and Ivan brought thick Turkish coffee. "It is a game, you see," pursued the general blandly. "I suggest to one of them that we go hunting. I give him three hours' start. I am to follow, armed only with a pistol of smallest calibre and range. If my quarry eludes me for three whole days, he wins the game. If I find him"—the general smiled—"he loses."

"Suppose he refuses to be hunted?"

"I give him the option. If he does not wish to hunt I turn him over to Ivan. Ivan once served as official knouter to the Great White Tsar, and he has his own ideas of sport. Invariably they choose the hunt."

"And if they win?"

The smile on the general's face widened. "To date I have not lost."

Then he added, hastily: "I don't wish you to think me a braggart, Mr. Rainsford, and one did almost win. I eventually had to use the dogs."

"The dogs?"

"This way, please. I'll show you."

The general led the way to another window. The lights sent a flickering illumination that made grotesque patterns on the courtyard below, and Rainsford could see a dozen or so huge black shapes moving about. As they turned towards him he caught the green glitter of eyes.

"They are let out at seven every night. If anyone should try to get into my house—or out of it—something regrettable would happen to him. And now I want to show you my new collection of heads. Will you come to the library?"

"I hope," said Rainsford, "that you will excuse me tonight. I'm really not feeling at all well."

"Ah, indeed? You need a good restful night's sleep. Tomorrow you'll feel like a new man. Then we'll hunt, eh? I've one rather promising prospect—"

Rainsford was hurrying from the room.

"Sorry you can't go with me tonight," called the general. "I expect rather fair sport. A big, strong black. He looks resourceful—"

The bed was good and Rainsford was tired, but nevertheless he could not sleep, and had only achieved a doze when, as morning broke, he heard, far off in the jungle, the faint report of a pistol.

General Zaroff did not appear till luncheon.

He was solicitous about Rainsford's health. "As for me," he said, "I do not feel so well. The hunting was not good last night. He made a straight trail that offered no problems at all."

"General," said Rainsford firmly, "I want to leave the island at once."

He saw the dead black eyes of the general on him, studying him. The eyes suddenly brightened. "Tonight," said he, "we will hunt—you and I."

Rainsford shook his head. "No, General," he said, "I will not hunt."

The general shrugged his shoulders. "As you wish. The choice rests with you, but I would suggest that my idea of sport is more diverting than Ivan's."

"You don't mean—" cried Rainsford.

"My dear fellow," said the general, "have I not told you I always mean what I say about hunting? This is really an inspiration. I drink to a foeman worthy of my steel at last."

The general raised his glass, but Rainsford sat staring at him. "You'll find this game worth playing," the general said, enthusiastically. "Your brain against mine. Your woodcraft against mine. Your strength and stamina against mine. Outdoor chess! And the stake is not without value, eh?"

"And if I win—" began Rainsford huskily.

"If I do not find you by midnight of the third day, I'll cheerfully acknowledge myself defeated," said General Zaroff. "My sloop will place you on the mainland near a town."

The general read what Rainsford was thinking.

"Oh, you can trust me," said the Cossack. "I will give you my word as a gentleman and a sportsman. Of course, you, in turn, must agree to say nothing of your visit here."

"I'll agree to nothing of the kind."

"Oh, in that case—but why discuss that now? Three days hence we can discuss it over a bottle of Veuve Cliquot, unless—"

The general sipped his wine.

Then a business-like air animated him. "Ivan," he said, "will supply you with hunting clothes, food, a knife. I suggest you wear moccasins; they leave a poorer trail. I suggest, too, that you avoid the big swamp in the southeast corner of the island. We call it Death Swamp. There's quicksand there. One foolish fellow tried it. The deplorable part of it was that Lazarus followed him. You can't imagine my feelings, Mr. Rainsford. I loved Lazarus; he was the finest hound in my pack. Well, I must beg you to excuse me now. I always take a siesta after lunch. You'll hardly have time for a nap, I fear. You'll want to start, no doubt. I shall not follow until dusk. Hunting at night is so much more exciting than by day, don't you think? Au revoir, Mr. Rainsford, au revoir."

As General Zaroff, with a courtly bow, strolled from the room, Ivan entered by another door. Under one arm he carried hunting clothes, a haversack of food, a leathern sheath containing a long-bladed hunting knife; his right hand rested on a cocked revolver thrust in the crimson sash about his waist. . . .

Rainsford had fought his way through the bush for two hours, but at length he paused, saying to himself through tight teeth, "I must keep my nerve."

He had not been entirely clear-headed when the château gates closed behind him. His first idea was to put distance between himself and General Zaroff and, to this end, he had plunged along, spurred by the sharp rowels of something approaching panic. Now, having got a grip on himself, he had stopped to take stock of himself and the situation.

Straight flight was futile for it must inevitably bring him to the sea. Being in a picture with a frame of water, his operations, clearly, must take place within that frame.

"I'll give him a trail to follow," thought Rainsford, striking off from the path into trackless wilderness. Recalling the lore of the foxhunt and the dodges of the fox, he executed a series of intricate loops, doubling again and again on his trail. Night found him leg-weary, with hands and face lashed by the branches. He was on a thickly wooded ridge. As his need for rest was imperative, he thought: "I have played the fox, now I must play the cat of the fable."

A big tree with a thick trunk and outspread branches was near by, and, taking care to leave no marks, he climbed into the crotch and stretched out on one of the broad limbs. Rest brought him new confidence and almost a feeling of security.

An apprehensive night crawled slowly by like a wounded snake. Towards morning, when a dingy grey was varnishing the sky, the cry of a startled bird focussed Rainsford's attention in its direction. Something was coming through the bush, coming slowly, carefully, coming by the same winding way that Rainsford had come. He flattened himself against the bough and, through a screen of leaves almost as thick as tapestry, watched.

It was General Zaroff. He made his way along, with his eyes fixed in concentration on the ground. He paused, almost beneath the tree, dropped to his knees and studied the ground. Rainsford's impulse was to leap on him like a panther, but he saw that the general's right hand held a small automatic.

The hunter shook his head several times as if he were puzzled. Then, straightening himself, he took from his case one of his black cigarettes; its pungent incense-like smoke rose to Rainsford's nostrils.

Rainsford held his breath. The general's eyes had left the ground and were travelling inch by inch up the tree. Rainsford froze, every muscle tensed for a spring. But the sharp eyes of the hunter stopped before they reached the limb where Rainsford lay. A smile spread over his brown face. Very deliberately he blew a smoke ring into the air; then he turned his back on the tree and walked carelessly away along the trail he had come. The swish of the underbrush against his hunting boots grew fainter and fainter.

The pent-up air burst hotly from Rainsford's lungs. His first thought made him feel sick and numb. The general could follow a trail through the woods at night; he could follow an extremely difficult trail; he must have uncanny powers; only by the merest chance had he failed to see his quarry.

Rainsford's second thought was more terrible. It sent a shudder through him. Why had the general smiled? Why had he turned back?

Rainsford did not want to believe what his reason told him was true—the general was playing with him, saving him for another day's sport. The Cossack was the cat; he was the mouse. Then it was that Rainsford knew the meaning of terror.

"I will not lose my nerve," he told himself, "I will not."

Sliding down from the tree, he set off into the woods. Three hundred yards from his hiding-place he stopped where a huge dead tree leaned precariously on a smaller, living one. Throwing off his sack of food, he took his knife from its sheath and set to work.

When the job was finished, he threw himself down behind a fallen log a hundred feet away. He did not have to wait long. The cat was coming back to play with the mouse.

Following the trail with the sureness of a bloodhound came General Zaroff. Nothing escaped those searching black eyes, no crushed blade of grass, no bent twig, no mark, no matter how faint, in the moss. So intent was the Cossack on his stalking that he was upon the thing Rainsford had made before he saw it. His foot touched the protruding bough that was the trigger. Even as he touched it, the general sensed his danger, and leaped back with the agility of an ape. But he was not quite quick enough; the dead tree, delicately adjusted to rest on the cut living one, crashed down and struck the general a glancing blow on the shoulder as it fell; but for his alertness he must have been crushed beneath it. He staggered but he did not fall; nor did he drop his revolver. He stood there, rubbing his injured shoulder, and Rainsford, with fear again gripping his heart, heard the general's mocking laugh ring through the jungle.

"Rainsford," called the general, "if you are within sound of my voice let me congratulate you. Not many men know how to make a Malay man catcher. Luckily for me I, too, have hunted in Malacca. You are proving interesting, Mr. Rainsford. I am now going to have my wound dressed; it is only a slight one. But I shall be back. I shall be back."

When the general, nursing his wounded shoulder, had gone, Rainsford again took up his flight. It was flight now, and it carried him on for some hours. Dusk came, then darkness, and still he pressed on. The ground grew softer under his moccasins; the vegetation grew ranker, denser; insects bit him savagely. He stepped forward and his foot sank into ooze. He tried to wrench it back, but the mud sucked viciously at his foot as if it had been a giant leech. With a violent effort he tore his foot loose. He knew where he was now. Death Swamp and its quicksand.

The softness of the earth had given him an idea. Stepping back from the quicksand a dozen feet, he began, like some huge prehistoric beaver, to dig.

Rainsford had dug himself in, in France, when a second's delay would have meant death. Compared to his digging now, that had been a placid pastime. The pit grew deeper; when it was above his shoulders he climbed out and from some hard saplings cut stakes, sharpening them to a fine point. These stakes he planted at the bottom of the pit with the points up. With flying fingers he wove a rough carpet of weeds and branches and with it covered the mouth of the pit. Then, wet with sweat and aching with tiredness, he crouched behind the stump of a lightning-blasted tree.

By the padding sound of feet on the soft earth he knew his pursuer was coming. The night breeze brought him the perfume of the general's cigarette. It seemed to the hunted man that the general was coming with unusual swiftness; that he was not feeling his way along, foot by foot. Rainsford, from where he was crouching, could not see the general, neither could he see the pit. He lived a year in a minute. Then he heard the sharp crackle of breaking branches as the cover of the pit gave way; heard the sharp scream of pain as the pointed stakes found their mark. Then he cowered back. Three feet from the pit a man was standing with an electric torch in his hand.

"You've done well, Rainsford," cried the general. "Your Burmese tiger pit has claimed one of my best dogs. Again you score. I must now see what you can do against my whole pack. I'm going home for a rest now. Thank you for a most amusing evening."

At daybreak Rainsford, lying near the swamp, was awakened by a distant sound, faint and wavering, but he knew it for the baying of a pack of hounds.

Rainsford knew he could do one of two things. He could stay where he was. That was suicide. He could flee. That was postponing the inevitable. For a moment, he stood there thinking. An idea that held a wild chance came to him, and, tightening his belt, he headed away from the swamp.

The baying of the hounds drew nearer, nearer. Rainsford climbed a tree. Down a watercourse, not a quarter of a mile away, he could see the bush moving. Straining his eyes, he saw the lean figure of General Zaroff. Just ahead of him Rainsford made out another figure, with wide shoulders, which surged through the jungle reeds. It was the gigantic Ivan and he seemed to be pulled along. Rainsford realized that he must be holding the pack in leash.

They would be on him at any moment now. His mind worked frantically, and he thought of a native trick he had learned in Uganda. Sliding down the tree, he caught hold of a springy young sapling and to it fastened his hunting knife, with the blade pointing down the trail. With a bit of wild grape-vine he tied back the sapling . . . and ran for his life. As the hounds hit the fresh scent, they raised their voices and Rainsford knew how an animal at bay feels.

He had to stop to get his breath. The baying of the hounds stopped abruptly, and Rainsford's heart stopped, too. They must have reached the knife.

Shinning excitedly up a tree, he looked

back. His pursuers had stopped. But the hope in Rainsford's brain died, for he saw that General Zaroff was still on his feet. Ivan, however, was not. The knife, driven by the recoil of the springing tree, had not wholly failed.

Hardly had Rainsford got back to the ground when, once more, the pack took up the cry.

"Nerve, nerve, nerve!" he panted to himself as he dashed along. A blue gap showed through the trees dead ahead. The hounds drew nearer. Rainsford forced himself on towards that gap. He reached the sea, and across a cove could see the grey stone of the château. Twenty feet below him the sea rumbled and hissed. Rainsford hesitated. He heard the hounds. Then he leaped far out into the water.

When the general and his pack reached the opening, the Cossack stopped. For some moments he stood regarding the blue-green expanse of water. Then he sat down, took a drink of brandy from a silver flask, lit a perfumed cigarette, and hummed a bit from *Madame Butterfly.*

General Zaroff ate an exceedingly good dinner in his great panelled hall that evening. With it he had a bottle of Pol Roger and half a bottle of Chambertin. Two slight annoyances kept him from perfect enjoyment. One was that it would be difficult to replace Ivan; the other, that his quarry had escaped him. Of course—so thought the general, as he tasted his after-dinner liqueur—the American had not played the game.

To soothe himself, he read in his library from the works of Marcus Aurelius. At ten he went to his bedroom. He was comfortably tired, he said to himself, as he turned the key of his door. There was a little moonlight, so before turning on the light he went to the window and looked down on the courtyard. He could see the great hounds, and he called: "Better luck another time." Then he switched on the light.

A man who had been hiding in the curtains of the bed was standing before him.

"Rainsford!" screamed the general. "How in God's name did you get here?"

"Swam. I found it quicker than walking through the jungle."

The other sucked in his breath and smiled. "I congratulate you. You have won the game."

Rainsford did not smile. "I am still a beast at bay," he said, in a low, hoarse voice. "Get ready, General Zaroff."

The general made one of his deepest bows. "I see," he said. "Splendid. One of us is to furnish a repast for the hounds. The other will sleep in this very excellent bed. On guard, Rainsford. . . ."

He had never slept in a better bed, Rainsford decided.

Four Square Jane

EDGAR WALLACE

IN THE "EDITOR'S NOTE" for the first edition of *Four Square Jane* (1929), the only book devoted to the young rogue's exploits, the "heroine" is described as an "extremely ladylike crook, an uncannily clever criminal who exercises all her female cunning on her nefarious work, makes the mere male detectives and policemen who endeavor to be on her tracks look foolish."

Jane is pretty, young, slim, and chaste, and leaves her calling card at the scene of her robberies: a printed label with four squares and the letter "J" in the middle. She makes sure to do this so that none of the servants will be accused of the theft. She has a coterie of loyal associates on whom she calls as they are needed.

During the height of his popularity in the 1920s as the most successful thriller writer who ever lived, Richard Horatio Edgar Wallace (1875–1932) is reputed to have been the author of one of every four books sold in England. After dropping out of school at an early age, he joined the army and was sent to South Africa, where he wrote war poems and later worked as a journalist during the Boer War. Returning to England with a desire to write fiction, he self-published *The Four Just Men* (1905), a financial disaster, but went on to produce 173 books and 17 plays.

Wallace's staggering popularity assured a market for anything he wrote and the top magazines competed for his work, paying him princely sums, but the stories in *Four Square Jane* appear to have been written directly for the book, with no prior periodical appearance. None of the stories has a title.

"Four Square Jane" was originally published in *Four Square Jane* (London, Readers Library, 1929).

FOUR SQUARE JANE

Edgar Wallace

MR. JOE LEWINSTEIN slouched to one of the long windows which gave light to his magnificent drawing-room and stared gloomily across the lawn.

The beds of geraniums and lobelias were half-obscured by a driving mist of rain, and the well-kept lawns that were the pride of his many gardeners were sodden and, in places, under water.

"Of course it had to rain to-day," he said bitterly.

His large and comfortable wife looked up over her glasses.

"Why, Joe," she said, "what's the good of grousing? They haven't come down for an al fresco fête; they've come down for the dance and the shooting, and anything else they can get out of us."

"Oh, shut up, Miriam," said Mr. Lewinstein irritably; "what does it matter what they're coming for? It's what I want them for myself. You don't suppose I've risen from what I was to my present position without learning anything, do you?" Mr. Lewinstein was fond of referring to his almost meteoric rise in the world of high finance, if not in the corresponding world of society. And, to do him justice, it must be added that such companies as he had promoted, and they were many, had been run on the most straightforward lines, nor had he, to use his own words, risked the money of the "widows and orphans." At least, not unnecessarily.

"It's knowing the right kind of people," he continued, "and doing them the right kind of turns that counts. It's easier to make your second million than your first, and I'm going to make it, Miriam," he added, with grim determination. "I'm going to make it, and I'm not sticking at a few thousands in the way of expenses!"

A housewifely fear lest their entertainment that night was going to cost them thousands floated through Mrs. Lewinstein's mind, but she said nothing.

"I'll bet they've never seen a ball like ours is tonight," her husband continued with satisfaction, as he turned his back on the window and came slowly towards his partner, "and the company will be worth it, Miriam, you believe me. Everybody who's anybody in the city is coming. There'll be more jewels here tonight than even I could buy."

His wife put down her paper with an impatient gesture.

"That's what I'm thinking about," she said.

"I hope you know what you're doing. It's a big responsibility."

"What do you mean by responsibility?" asked Joe Lewinstein.

"All this loose money lying about," said his wife. "Don't you read the paper? Don't any of your friends tell you?"

Mr. Lewinstein burst into a peal of husky laughter.

"Oh, I know what's biting you," he said. "You're thinking of Four Square Jane."

"Four Square Jane!" said the acid Mrs. Lewinstein. "I'd give her Four Square Jane if I had her in this house!"

"She's no common burglar," said Mr. Lewinstein shaking his head, whether in admonition or admiration it was difficult to say. "My friend, Lord Belchester—my friend, Lord Belchester, told me it was an absolute mystery how his wife lost those emeralds of hers. He was very worried about it, was Belchester. He took about half the money he made out of Consolidated Grains to buy those emeralds, and they were lost about a month after he bought them. He thinks that the thief was one of his guests."

"Why do they call her Four Square Jane?" asked Mrs. Lewinstein curiously.

Her husband shrugged his shoulders.

"She always leaves a certain mark behind her, a sort of printed label with four squares, and the letter J in the middle," he said. "It was the police who called her Jane, and somehow the name has stuck."

His wife picked up the paper and put it down again, looking thoughtfully into the fire.

"And you're bringing all these people down here to stop the night, and you're talking about them being loaded up with jewellery! You've got a nerve, Joe."

Mr. Lewinstein chuckled.

"I've got a detective, too," he said. "I've asked Ross, who has the biggest private detective agency in London, to send me his best woman."

"Goodness gracious," said the dismayed Mrs. Lewinstein, "you're not having a woman here?"

"Yes, I am. She's a lady, apparently one of the best girls Ross has got. He told me that in cases like this it's much less noticeable to have a lady detective among the guests than a man. I told her to be here at seven."

Undoubtedly the Lewinstein's house-party was the most impressive affair that the county had seen. His guests were to arrive by a special train from London and were to be met at the station by a small fleet of motor cars, which he had pressed to his service from all available sources. His own car was waiting at the door ready to take him to the station to meet his "special" when a servant brought him a card.

"Miss Caroline Smith," he read. On the corner was the name of the Ross Detective Agency.

"Tell the young lady I'll see her in the library."

He found her waiting for him. A personable, pretty girl, with remarkably shrewd and clever eyes that beamed behind rimless glasses and a veil, she met him with an elusive smile that came and went like sunshine on a wintry day.

"So you're a lady detective, eh?" said Lewinstein with ponderous good humour; "you look young."

"Why, yes," said the girl, "even way home, where youth isn't any handicap, I'm looked upon as being a trifle under the limit."

"Oh, you're from America, are you?" said Mr. Lewinstein, interested.

The girl nodded.

"This is my first work in England, and naturally I am rather nervous."

She had a pleasant voice, a soft drawl, which suggested to Mr. Lewinstein, who had spent some years on the other side, that she came from one of the Southern States.

"Well, I suppose you pretty well know your duties in the game to suppress this Four Square woman."

She nodded.

"That may be a pretty tough proposition. You'll give me leave to go where I like, and do practically what I like, won't you? That is essential."

"Certainly," said Mr. Lewinstein; "you will dine with us as our guest?"

"No, that doesn't work," she replied. "The time I ought to be looking round and taking notice, my attention is wholly absorbed by the man who is taking me down to dinner and wants my views on prohibition.

"So, if you please, I'd like the whole run of your house. I can be your young cousin, Miranda, from the high mountains of New Jersey. What about your servants?"

"I can trust them with my life," said Mr. Lewinstein.

She looked at him with a half-twinkle in her eyes.

"Can you tell me anything about this she-Raffles?" she asked.

"Nothing," said her host, "except that she is one of these society swells who frequent such—well, such parties as I am giving tonight. There will be a lot of ladies here—some of the best in the land—that is what makes it so difficult. As likely as not she will be one of them."

"Would you trust them all with your life?" she asked mischievously, and then going on: "I think I know your Four Square woman. Mind," she raised her hand, "I'm not going to say that I shall discover her here."

"I hope to goodness you don't," said Joe heartily.

"Or if I do find her I'm going to denounce her. Perhaps you can tell me something else about her."

Mr. Lewinstein shook his head.

"The only thing I know is that when she's made a haul, she usually leaves behind a mark."

"That I know," said the girl nodding. "She does that in order that suspicion shall not fall upon the servants."

The girl thought a moment, tapping her teeth with a pencil, then she said:

"Whatever I do, Mr. Lewinstein, you must not regard as remarkable. I have set my mind on capturing Four Square Jane, and starting my career in England with a big flourish of silver trumpets." She smiled so charmingly that Mrs. Lewinstein in the doorway raised her eyebrows.

"It is time you were going, Joseph," she said severely. "What am I to do with this young woman?"

"Let somebody show her her room," said the temporarily flustered Mr. Lewinstein, and hurried out to the waiting car.

Mrs. Lewinstein rang the bell. She had no interest in detectives, especially pretty detectives of twenty-three.

Adchester Manor House was a large establishment, but it was packed to its utmost capacity to accommodate the guests who arrived that night.

All Mrs. Lewinstein had said—that these pretty women and amusing men had been lured into Buckinghamshire with a lively hope of favours to come—might be true. Joe Lewinstein was not only a power in the City, with the control of four great corporations, but the Lewinstein interests stretched from Colorado to Vladivostock.

It was a particularly brilliant party which sat down to dinner that night, and if Mr. Lewinstein swelled a little with pride, that pride was certainly justified. On his right sat Lady Ovingham, a thin woman with the prettiness that consists chiefly in huge appealing eyes and an almost alarming pallor of skin. Her appearance greatly belied her character, for she was an unusually able business woman, and had partnered Mr. Lewinstein in some of his safer speculations. An arm covered from wrist to elbow with diamond bracelets testified to the success of these ventures in finance, for Lady Ovingham had a way of investing her money in diamonds, for she knew that these stones would not suddenly depreciate in value.

The conversation was animated and, in many cases, hilarious, for Mr. Lewinstein had mixed his guests as carefully as his butler had mixed the cocktails, and both things helped materially towards the success of the evening.

It was towards the end of the dinner that the first disagreeable incident occurred. His butler leant over him, ostensibly to pour out a glass of wine, and whispered:

"That young lady that came this afternoon, sir, has been taken ill."

"Ill!" said Mr. Lewinstein in dismay. "What happened?"

"She complained of a bad headache, was seized with tremblings, and had to be taken up to her room," said the butler in a low voice.

"Send into the village for the doctor."

"I did, sir," said the man, "but the doctor had been called away to London on an important consultation."

Mr. Lewinstein frowned. Then a little gleam of relief came to him. The detective had asked him not to be alarmed at anything that might happen. Possibly this was a ruse for her own purpose. She ought to have told him though, he complained to himself.

"Very good, wait till dinner is over," he said.

When that function was finished, and the guests had reached the coffee and cigarette stage before entering the big ballroom or retiring to their cards, Mr. Lewinstein climbed to the third floor to the tiny bedroom which had been allocated by his lady wife as being adequate for a lady detective.

He knocked at the door.

"Come in," said a faint voice.

The girl was lying on the bed, covered with an eiderdown quilt, and she was shivering.

"Don't touch me," she said. "I don't know what's the matter with me even."

"Good Lord!" said Mr. Lewinstein in dismay, "you're not really ill, are you?"

"I'm afraid so; I'm awfully sorry. I don't know what has happened to me, and I have a feeling that my illness is not wholly accidental. I was feeling well until I had a cup of tea, which was brought to my room, when suddenly I was taken with these shivers. Can you get me a doctor?"

"I'll do my best," said Mr. Lewinstein, for he had a kindly heart.

He went downstairs a somewhat anxious man. If, as the girl seemed to suggest, she had been doped, that presupposed the presence in the house either of Four Square Jane or one of her working partners. He reached the hall to find the butler waiting.

"Excuse me, sir," said the butler, "but rather a fortunate thing has happened. A gentleman who has run short of petrol came up to the house to borrow a supply——"

"Well?" said Mr. Lewinstein.

"Well, sir, he happens to be a doctor," said the butler. "I asked him to see you, sir."

"Fine," said Mr. Lewinstein enthusiastically, "that's a good idea of yours. Bring him into the library."

The stranded motorist, a tall young man, came in full of apologies.

"I say, it's awfully good of you to let me have this juice," he said. "The fact is, my silly ass of a man packed me two empty tins."

"Delighted to help you, doctor," said Mr. Lewinstein genially; "and now perhaps you can help me."

The young man looked at the other suspiciously.

"You haven't anybody ill, have you?" he asked, "I promised my partner I wouldn't look at a patient for three months. You see," he explained, "I've had rather a heavy time lately, and I'm a bit run down."

"You'd be doing us a real kindness if you'd look at this young lady," said Mr. Lewinstein earnestly. "I don't know what to make of her, doctor."

"Setheridge is my name," said the doctor. "All right, I'll look at your patient. It was ungracious of me to pull a face I suppose. Where is she? Is she one of your guests by the way? I seem to have butted in on a party."

"Not exactly," Mr. Lewinstein hesitated, "she is—er—a visitor."

He led the way up to the room, and the young man walked in and looked at the shivering girl with the easy confident smile of the experienced practitioner.

"Hullo," he said, "what's the matter with you?"

He took her wrist in his hand and looked at his watch, and Mr. Lewinstein, standing in the open doorway, saw him frown. He bent down and examined the eyes, then pulled up the sleeve of his patient's dress and whistled.

"Is it serious?" she asked anxiously.

"Not very, if you are taken care of; though you may lose some of that hair," he said, with a smile at the brown mop on the pillow.

"What is it?" she asked.

"Scarlet fever, my young friend."

"Scarlet fever!" It was Mr. Lewinstein who gasped the words. "You don't mean that?"

The doctor walked out and joined him on the landing, closing the door behind him.

"It's scarlet fever, all right. Have you any idea where she was infected?"

"Scarlet fever," moaned Mr. Lewinstein; "and I've got the house full of aristocracy!"

"Well, the best thing you can do is to keep the aristocracy in ignorance of the fact. Get the girl out of the house."

"But how? How?" wailed Mr. Lewinstein.

The doctor scratched his head.

"Of course, I don't want to do it," he said slowly; "but I can't very well leave a girl in a mess like this. May I use your telephone?"

"Certainly, use anything you like; but, for goodness' sake, get the girl away!"

Mr. Lewinstein showed him the library, where the young man called up a number and gave some instructions. Apparently his telephone interview was satisfactory, for he came back to the hall, where Mr. Lewinstein was nervously drumming his fingers on the polished surface of a table, with a smile.

"I can get an ambulance out here, but not before three in the morning," he said; "anyway, that will suit us, because your guests will be abed and asleep by then, and most of the servants also, I suppose. And we can get her out without anybody being the wiser."

"I'm awfully obliged to you, doctor," said Mr. Lewinstein, "anything you like to charge me——"

The doctor waved fees out of consideration.

Then a thought occurred to Mr. Lewinstein.

"Doctor, could that disease be communicated to the girl by means of a drug, or anything?"

"Why do you ask?" said the other quickly.

"Well, because she was all right till she had a cup of tea. I must take you into my confidence," he said, lowering his voice. "She is a detective, brought down here to look after my guests. There have been a number of robberies committed lately by a woman who calls herself 'Four Square Jane,' and, to be on the safe side, I had this girl down to protect the property of my friends. When I saw her before dinner she was as well as you or I; then a cup of tea was given to her, and immediately she had these shiverings."

The doctor nodded thoughtfully.

"It is curious you should say that," he said; "for though she has the symptoms of scarlet fever, she has others which are not usually to be found in scarlet fever cases. Do you suggest that this woman, this Four Square person, is in the house?"

"Either she or her agent," said Mr. Lewinstein. "She has several people who work with her by all accounts."

"And you believe that she has given this girl a drug to put her out of the way?"

"That's my idea."

"By jove!" said the young man, "that's rather a scheme. Well, anyway, there will be plenty of people knocking about tonight, and your guests will be safe for tonight."

The girl had been housed in the servants' wing, but fortunately in a room isolated from all the others. Mr. Lewinstein made several trips upstairs during the course of the evening, saw through the open door the doctor sitting by the side of the bed, and was content. His guests retired towards one o'clock and this agitated Mrs. Lewinstein, to whom the news of the catastrophe had been imparted, having been successfully induced to go to bed, Mr. Lewinstein breathed more freely.

At half-past one he made his third visit to the door of the sick room, for he, himself, was not without dread of infection, and saw through the open door the doctor sitting reading a book near the head of the bed.

He stole quietly down, so quietly that he almost surprised a slim figure that was stealing along the darkened corridor whence opened the bedrooms of the principal guests.

She flattened herself into a recess, and he passed her so closely that she could have touched him. She waited until he had disappeared, and then crossed to one of the doors and felt gingerly at the key-hole. The occupant had made the mistake of locking the door and taking out the key, and in a second she had inserted one of her own, and softly turning it, had tip-toed into the room.

She stood listening; there was a steady breathing, and she made her way to the dressing-table, where her deft fingers began a rapid but silent search. Presently she found what she wanted, a smooth leather case, and shook it gently. She was not a minute in the room before she was out again, closing the door softly behind her.

She had half-opened the next door before she saw that there was a light in the room and she stood motionless in the shadow of the doorway. On the far side of the bed the little table-lamp was still burning, and it would, she reflected, have helped her a great deal, if only she could have been sure that the person who was lying among the frilled pillows of the bed was really asleep. She waited rigid, and with all her senses alert for five minutes, till the sound of regular breathing from the bed reassured her. Then she slipped forward to the dressing-table. Here, her task was easy. No less than a dozen little velvet and leather cases lay strewn on the silk cover. She opened them noiselessly one by one, and put their glittering contents into her pocket, leaving the cases as they had been.

As she was handling the last of the jewels a thought struck her, and she peered more closely at the sleeping figure. A thin pretty woman, it seemed in the half-light. So this was the businesslike Lady Ovingham. She left the room as noiselessly as she had entered it, and more quickly, and tried the next door in the passage.

This one had not been locked.

It was Mrs. Lewinstein's own room, but she was not sleeping quietly. The door had been left open for her lord, who had made a promise to see his wife to make arrangements for the morrow. This promise he had quite forgotten in his perturbation. There was a little safe let into the wall, and the keys were hanging in the lock; for Mr. Lewinstein, who, being a prudent, careful man, was in the habit of depositing his diamond studs every night.

The girl's fingers went into the interior of the safe, and presently she found what she wanted. Mrs. Lewinstein stopped breathing heavily, grunted, and turned, and the girl stood stock-still. Presently the snoring recommenced, and she stole out into the corridor.

As she closed each door she stopped only long enough to press a small label against the surface of the handle before she passed on to the next room.

Downstairs in the library, Mr. Lewinstein heard the soft purr of a motor car, and rose with a sigh of relief. Only his butler had been let into the secret, and that sleepy retainer, who was dozing in one of the hall chairs, heard the sound with as great relief as his employer. He opened the big front door.

Outside was a motor-ambulance from which two men had descended. They pulled out a stretcher and a bundle of blankets, and made their way into the hall.

"I will show you the way," said Mr. Lewinstein. "You will make as little noise as possible, please."

He led the procession up the carpeted stairs, and came at last to the girl's room.

"Oh, here you are," said the doctor, yawning. "Set the stretcher by the side of the bed. You had better stand away some distance, Mr. Lewinstein," he said, and that gentleman obeyed with alacrity.

Presently the door opened and the stretcher

came out, bearing the blanket-enveloped figure of the girl, her face just visible, and she favoured Mr. Lewinstein with a pathetic smile as she passed.

The stairs were negotiated without any difficulty by the attendants, and carefully the stretcher was pushed into the interior of the ambulance.

"That's all right," said the doctor; "if I were you I would have that bedroom locked up and fumigated tomorrow."

"I'm awfully obliged to you, doctor. If you will give me your address I would like to send you a cheque."

"Oh, rubbish," said the other cheerfully, "I am only too happy to serve you. I will go into the village to pick up my car and get back to town myself."

"Where will you take this young woman?" asked Mr. Lewinstein.

"To the County Fever Hospital," replied the other carelessly. "That's where you're taking her, isn't it?"

"Yes, sir," said one of the attendants.

Mr. Lewinstein waited on the steps until the red lights of the car had disappeared, then stepped inside with the sense of having managed a very difficult situation rather well.

"That will do for the night," he said to the butler. "Thank you for waiting up."

He found himself walking, with a little smile on his lips, along the corridor to his own room.

As he was passing his wife's door he stumbled over something. Stooping, he picked up a case. There was an electric switch close by, and he flooded the corridor with light.

"Jumping Moses!" he gasped, for the thing he held in his hand was his wife's jewel case.

He made a run for her door, and was just gripping the handle, when the label there caught his eye, and he stared in hopeless bewilderment at the sign of Four Square Jane.

An ambulance stopped at a cross-road, where a big car was waiting, and the patient, who had long since thrown off her blankets, came out. She pulled after her a heavy bag, which one of the two attendants lifted for her and placed in the car. The doctor was sitting at the wheel.

"I was afraid I was going to keep you waiting," he said. "I only just got here in time."

He turned to the attendant.

"I shall see you tomorrow, Jack."

"Yes, doctor," replied the other.

He touched his hat to Four Square Jane, and walked back to the ambulance, waiting only to change the number plates before he drove away in the opposite direction to London.

"Are you ready?" asked the doctor.

"Quite ready," said the girl, dropping in by his side. "You were late, Jim. I nearly pulled a real fit when I heard they'd sent for the local sawbones."

"You needn't have worried," said the man at the wheel, as he started the car forward. "I got a pal to wire calling him to London. Did you get the stuff?"

"Yards of it," said Four Square Jane laconically. "There will be some sad hearts in Lewinstein's house tomorrow."

He smiled.

"By the way," she said, "that lady detective Ross sent, how far did she get?"

"As far as the station," said the doctor, "which reminds me that I forgot to let her out of the garage where I locked her."

"Let her stay," said Four Square Jane. "I hate the idea of she-detectives, anyway—it's so unwomanly."

Rogue: Edward Farthindale

A Fortune in Tin

EDGAR WALLACE

THE ENORMOUS SUCCESS that Richard Horatio Edgar Wallace (1875–1932) enjoyed in the 1920s and '30s extended beyond the United Kingdom to the United States, but *Elegant Edward* (1928) was suffused with a kind of humor that evidently did not appeal to Americans, as the collection of short stories was never published on the other side of the Atlantic.

Unlike most of the many criminal characters created by Wallace, Edward Farthindale, known to one and all as Elegant Edward, was not a brilliant mastermind who arrogantly laughed at the police who tried to capture him. He is described thus by the editor:

> He is a droll character. His crimes are not conceived in a spirit of overwhelming and deadly seriousness. There is a light touch in all his performances. Nor is his skill always of such a high order that he outwits the police. His encounters with them are almost in the nature of a friendly game in which the better man, whoever he may happen at the time to be, wins, with no lasting ill-feeling on the part of his opponent.

As the most popular writer in the world in the 1920s and '30s, Wallace earned a fortune—reportedly more than a quarter of a million dollars a year during the last decade of his life, but his extravagant lifestyle left his estate deeply in debt when he died.

"A Fortune in Tin" was originally published in *Elegant Edward* (London, Readers Library, 1928).

A FORTUNE IN TIN

Edgar Wallace

ELEGANT EDWARD dealt in a stable line of goods, and, in the true sense of the word, he was no thief. He was admittedly a chiseller, a macer, a twister, and a get-a-bit. His stock-in-trade consisted either of shares in derelict companies purchased for a song, or options on remote properties, or genuine gold claims, indubitable mineral rights, and oil propositions. Because of his elegance and refinement, he was able to specialize in this high-class trade and make a living where another man would have starved.

Mr. Farthindale had emerged from a welter of trouble with almost all the capital which had been his a week before. He had tracked down certain disloyal partners who had sold property of his, and had forced them to disgorge their ill-gotten gains, and from the fence who had illegally purchased his property, he had obtained the rest.

The police were seeking a certain Scotty Ferguson, the partner in question, and because Edward had no desire to give evidence against his some-time confederate, he had changed his lodgings, and was considering the next move in his adventurous game.

It came as a result of a chance meeting with an itinerant vendor of novelties, who stood on the kerb of a London street selling 100,000 mark notes for twopence. Insensibly Edward's mind went to the business he understood best. In the city of London was a snide bucket-shop keeper with whom he was acquainted. This gentleman operated from a very small office in a very large building. A picture of the building was on his note-paper, and country clients were under the impression that the Anglo-Imperial Stock Trust occupied every floor and overflowed to the roof. To him, Edward repaired, and found him playing patience, for business was bad.

"How do, Mr. Farthindale. Come in and sit down."

"How's it going?" asked Edward conventionally.

The Anglo-Imperial Stock Trust made a painful face.

"Rotten," he said. "I sent out three thousand circulars last week, offering the finest oil ground in Texas at a hundred pounds an acre. I got one reply—from an old lady who wanted to know if I'd met her son who lives in Texas City. The suckers are dying, Mr. Farthindale."

Edward scratched his chin.

"Oil's no good to me," he said. "I've worked oil in Scotland. What about mines?"

"Gold or silver?" asked the Anglo-Imperial, rising with alacrity. "I've got a peach of a silver mine——"

"I've worked silver mines," said the patient Edward, "in Wales. Silver never goes as well as gold."

"What about tin?" asked The Trust anxiously. "The Trevenay Tin Mine Corporation? The mine's been working since the days of the Pernicions, or Phinocians . . . prehistoric dagoes . . . *you* know?"

Elegant Edward had a dim idea that the Phœnicians were pretty old, and was mildly impressed.

"I've got a hundred and twenty thousand shares out of a hundred and fifty thousand. It's a real mine, too—about forty years ago a thousand people used to work on it!" The Trust continued. "The other thirty thousand are owned by an old Scotsman—a professor or something—and he won't part. I offered him twenty pounds for 'em, too. Not that they're worth it, or rather at the time they weren't," added The Trust hastily, realizing that Edward stood in the light of a possible purchaser.

"But the land and machinery are worth money?" suggested Edward.

The Trust shook his head.

"The company only holds mining rights, and the royalty owner has got first claim on the buildings—such as they are. But the company looks good, and the new share certificates I had printed look better. You couldn't have a finer proposition, Mr. Farthindale."

There were hagglings and bargainings, scornful refusings and sardonic comments generally before Elegant Edward was able to take the trail again, the owner of a hundred and twenty thousand shares in a tin company, which was genuine in all respects, except that it contained no tin.

"If you're going to Scotland, see that professor," said The Trust at parting. "You ought to get the rest of the stock for a tenner."

It was to Scotland, as a needle to a magnet, that Elegant Edward was attracted. A desire to get "his own back," to recoup himself for his losses, in fact to "show 'em" brought him to a country he loathed.

He had come to sell to the simple people of Scotia, at ten shillings per share, stock which he had bought at a little less than a farthing. And, since cupidity and stupidity run side by side in the mental equipment of humanity, he succeeded.

It was in the quietude of an Edinburgh lodging that Edward ran to earth Professor Folloman.

The professor was usually very drunk and invariably very learned—a wisp of a man, with long, dirty-white hair and an expression of woe. Five minutes after the two boarders met in the dismal lodging-house "drawing-room," the professor, a man without reticence, was retailing his troubles.

"The world," said Professor Folloman, "neglects its geniuses. It allows men of my talent to starve, whilst it gives fortunes to the charlatan, the faker, and the crook. *O mores, o tempores!*"

"*Oui, oui,*" said Elegant Edward misguidedly.

The professor came naturally to his favourite subject, which was the hollowness and chicanery of patent medicines. It was his illusion that his life had been ruined, his career annihilated, and the future darkened by the popularity of certain patent drugs which are household words to the average Briton. That his misfortune might be traced to an early-acquired habit of making his breakfast on neat whisky—a practice which on one occasion had almost a tragical result—never occurred to him.

"Here am I, sir, one of the best physicians of the city of Edinburgh, a man holding degrees which I can only describe as unique, and moreover, the possessor of shares in one of the richest tin mines in Cornwall, obliged to borrow the price of a drink from a comparative stranger."

Elegant Edward, recognizing this description of himself, made an heroic attempt to nail down the conversation to the question of tin mines, but the professor was a skilful man.

"What has ruined me?" he demanded, fixing his bright eyes on Edward with a hypnotic glare. "I'll tell you, my man! Biggins' Pills have ruined me, and Walkers' Wee Wafers and Lambo's Lightning Lung-tonic! Because of this pernicious invasion of the healing realm, I, John Walker Folloman, am compelled to live on the charity of relations—let us have a drink."

Such a direct invitation, Elegant Edward could not refuse. They adjourned to a near-by bar, and here the professor took up the threads of the conversation.

"You, like myself, are a gentleman. The moment I saw you, my man, I said: 'Here is a professional.' None but a professional would have his trousers creased, and wear a tail-coat. None but a professional would pay the scrupulous attention to his attire and the glossiness of his hat—don't drown it, my lass! whisky deserves a better fate—you're a doctor, sir?"

Edward coughed. He had never before been mistaken for a doctor. It was not an unpleasing experience.

"Not exactly," he said.

"Ah! A lawyer!"

"I've had a lot to do with the law," said Elegant Edward truthfully, "but I'm not exactly a lawyer."

"Something that makes money, I have no doubt," said the old man gloomily. "I could have been a millionaire, had I descended to the manufacture of noxious quack medicines instead of following my profession. I should have been a millionaire had somebody with my unique knowledge of metallurgy been in control of the Trevenay Mines——"

"Tin mines?" asked Elegant Edward. "There's no money in tin. I always tell my friends—I'm in the stock-broking business—'If you've got tin shares, sell 'em.'"

"I'll no' sell mine," said the old man grimly. "No, sir! I'll hold my shares. A dear friend of mine, Professor Macginnis, is in Cornwall and has promised to give me a report—Macginnis is the greatest authority on tin in this world, Sir. I have his letter," he fumbled in his pocket unsuccessfully, "no, I have left it in my other jacket. But it doesn't matter. He is taking a holiday in the south, and has promised to thoroughly examine the ground."

"His—his report won't be published in the papers, will it?" asked Edward anxiously.

"It will not," said the professor, and pushed his glass across the counter. "Repeat the potion, Maggie, and let your hand be as generous as your heart, my lass!"

A few days later, and on a raw December morning, with leaden clouds overhead and the air thick with driving sleet, Elegant Edward came out of the station and gazed disconsolately upon so much of the town as was visible through the veil of the blizzard.

"So this is Dundee!" said Elegant Edward, unconsciously paraphrasing a better-known slogan. He had chosen Dundee for the scene of his operations, mainly because it was not Glasgow. Gathering up his rug and his bag, he beckoned the one cab in sight and gave his instructions.

At the little hotel where he was set down, he found a letter awaiting him. It was addressed to Angus Mackenzie (he had signed the register in that name) and its contents were satisfactory. The small furnished office which he had engaged by letter was waiting his pleasure, the key was enclosed, together with a receipt for the rent he had paid in advance.

To trace the progress of Mr. Farthindale through the months that followed his arrival on the Tay would be more or less profitless; to tell the story of his limited advertising campaign, his clever circularization and the pleasing volume of business which came his way, and divers other incidentals, would be to elongate the narrative to unpardonable length.

Margaret Elton came to him on the third day after his arrival. She was tall, good-looking and, moreover, she believed in miracles. But although she was, by the admission of one who loved her best, masterful, she could not master the cruel fate which had hitherto denied her sufficient money to support an ailing mother without having recourse to the limited income of a young man who found every day a new reason for marrying at once.

"It is no use, John," she said firmly. "I'm not going to let you marry the family. When I can make mother independent I'll marry."

"Margaret," he said, "that means waiting another fifty years—but I'll wait. What is your new boss like?"

"He's English and inoffensive," she said tersely.

Which in a sense was true, though Elegant Edward had his own doubts about his inoffensiveness.

Edward would have fired her the day she came, only he couldn't summon sufficient courage. Thereafter, he was lost. She took control of the office, the business, and Elegant Edward. It was she who had the idea for appointing the travellers to carry the joyous news about the Trevenay Tin Mine to the remotest parts of Scotland; she who discharged them when their expense accounts came in; she who saw the printers and corrected the proofs of the circular describing the history of the Trevenay Mine; she who bought the typewriter, and insisted upon Edward coming to the office at ten o'clock every morning. She liked Edward; she told him so. Usually such a declaration, coming from so charming a female, would have set Edward's head wagging. But she had so many qualifications to her admiration that he was almost terrified at her praise.

"I don't like that moustache. Why do you wax it, Mr. Mackenzie?" she demanded. "It looks so ridiculous! I wonder how you would look clean-shaven?"

Now Edward's moustache was the pride of his life, and he made one great effort to preserve it intact.

"My personal appearance——" he began with tremulous hauteur.

"Take it off; I'd like to see you without it," she said, "unless you've got a bad mouth. Most men wear moustaches because their mouths won't stand inspection."

The next morning Edward came clean-shaven, and she looked at him dubiously.

"I think you had better grow it again," she said. It was her only comment.

Money was coming in in handsome quantities—Mr. Farthindale's new profession was paying handsome dividends.

One day there floated into his office an acquaintance of other days, Lew Bennyfold—an adventurer at large. Happily the dominant Margaret was out at lunch.

"Thought it was you," said Lew, seating himself uninvited. "I spotted you coming into the building yesterday; it took me all the morning to locate you. What's the graft?"

Edward gazed upon the apparition in dismay. He had some slight acquaintance with this confidence man—he did not wish to improve upon it.

"This is no graft, Mr. Bennyfold," he said gently, "but honest toil and labour—I'm running a mine."

"Go on?" said the other incredulously. "You're not the What-is-it Tin Mine, are you?"

Edward nodded.

"That explains everything," said Mr. Lew Bennyfold gravely, and rose to his feet. "Well, I won't stay—I don't want to be in this."

"What do you mean?" asked Edward.

Mr. Bennyfold smiled pityingly.

"From what I've heard of you, you're a fly mug," he said; "in fact, you've got a name for being clever but easy. But how any grafter could sit here in an office, working with a 'nose' and not be wise to it, beats me."

"A nose!" said the startled Edward.

Mr. Bennyfold nodded again.

"I've been working Dundee, and 'work's' a good word. It has been perishing hard work. And I've been here long enough to see things. How do you think I came to be watching this office?"

Edward had wondered that too.

"I've been tailing up Sergeant Walker and his girl," said Lew. "I happen to lodge opposite the sergeant—he's the smartest 'busy' in Dundee. And I've noticed that he's always with a girl. Meets her after dark and they go long walks. So I got on the track of the girl. And she led me here."

"Here?" gasped Edward turning pale. "You don't mean to tell me——?"

"She's Miss Margaret Elton," said Bennyfold, "and if you've let her know anything about your business, you're as good as jugged."

Elegant Edward wiped his warm forehead.

His business was an honest one—only an insider who knew the office secrets could prove otherwise. Usually, Elegant Edward did not allow an insider to know much, but this bossy girl had taken the office workings into her own hands.

"He's sweet on her—there's no doubt about that," said Bennyfold. "My landlady told me they're going to be married. But that's worse for you, because she'll do anything for him and swear anything. Mr. Farthindale, I wouldn't be in your shoes for a million!"

He left with this, and his anxiety to avoid complications added to Edward's distress.

When the girl came back from lunch he regarded her with a new and a fearful interest. There was something very remorseless about her mouth; her eyes, he thought, were pitiless, her profile made him shudder.

"Our agent in Ayr isn't doing much business," she said brusquely. "I think we had better fire him and get another man."

He opened his mouth to speak, but no words came. Now he understood her bossiness. She had behind her the power and authority of the law.

Late in the afternoon she interrupted his gloomy meditations.

"Will you excuse me for a few minutes? A friend of mine wants to see me."

"Certainly, Miss Elton," he said, almost humbly.

When she had left the room, he went to the window and looked out.

A tall, stern-looking young man was pacing the sidewalk on the opposite side, from time to time looking up at the office window. With him was an older man—a typical chief constable in mufti.

Edward saw the girl join them, watched the earnest conversation between them, and once saw the girl look up to the window where he was standing. She saw him and said something and all three looked up.

Edward drew back quickly out of sight.

So Lew was right. He was trapped!

Now Edward was a quick thinker and a man to whom inspiration came very readily. He was inspired now. The scheme came to him in a flash—the greatest wangle that had ever entered his mind. He waited until the girl came back.

"I'm sorry I was so long. That young gentleman you saw me with—I noticed you were looking—is my fiancé, and the other gentleman is a house agent. Willie is buying a house, though I doubt if he'll ever put it to the use he intends."

"Indeed," said Edward politely. "I'll be going to my lawyers for a few minutes to get my will made. Will you witness it for me?"

She looked at him in surprise.

"Thinking of dying?" she asked suspiciously.

Edward had the feeling that to die without her permission would be regarded by her as an unfriendly act.

The little lawyer who had fixed up his tenancy was in.

"I want a short deed drawn up, transferring my business to a young lady," said Edward. "I want it done right away so that I can get it signed."

The lawyer was puzzled.

"A deed? I don't think it is necessary. A receipt would be sufficient. I'll draw it up for you. How much is being paid?"

"Half-a-crown," said Edward. He didn't think Margaret would part with more without explanation. "But it has got to have her signature."

"I see—a nominal transfer," said the lawyer, and drew up the document on the spot.

Edward carried the paper back to his office.

"You sign this here," he said, as he wrote his name across the stamp, "and to make this document legal you've got to put your name under mine and give me half-a-crown."

"Why? I've got no half-crowns to throw away!"

Eventually and on the promise that the money would be returned, she consented, signed the paper, paid, and was repaid the money.

Edward put the document into an envelope, sealed it, and placed it in his little safe.

"Now everything's all right," he said and smiled seraphically.

The next morning came fifty inquiries for Trevenay Shares. The afternoon post brought forty more. He went to his bank and drew six hundred pounds. He must be ready to move at a moment's notice.

Edward had often lived on the edges of volcanoes and thrived in the atmosphere of sulphur, but he was more than usually nervous that day and the next; and on the evening of the second day the blow fell.

He was leaving his office when he saw the tall stern young man come quickly towards him. Elegant Edward stood stock still.

"I want you, Mr. Mackenzie," said the officer.

"I don't know what you want me for," said Edward loudly, and at that moment Margaret Elton came out into the street.

"You may want this young lady, but you certainly don't want me."

The officer stared at him.

"I don't understand you," he said.

"You don't? Well, I'll tell you something—the business belongs to her. If you'll step inside I'll show you."

Edward led the way back to his sanctum, opened the safe, took out and opened the envelope.

"Here you are," he said, "read this."

Sergeant Walker read in silent amazement the document that transferred to Margaret Elton, "the business known as the Trevenay Share Syndicate, together with all shares held by that company, exclusive of monies standing to the credit of the syndicate, furniture, leaseholds, and all properties whatsoever."

"You mean . . . this is Miss Elton's business?" gasped Walker.

Edward nodded gravely.

"I gave it to her as—as a wedding present," he said, "there's the key of the safe—bless you, my children!"

He was out of the office before they could stop him.

"What does it mean?" asked the amazed girl.

Sergeant Walker shook his head.

"I don't know—it must be that miracle you're always talking about," he said. "I stopped him in the street to ask him if he could give you a fortnight's holiday and come to the wedding and he sprung this on me. How did he know we were getting married?"

The first person Edward saw on Edinburgh railway station was the professor, and he was sober. The recognition was mutual and the professor waved a cheery greeting.

"Going south, eh? So am I. Yes, sir, thanks to the activities of the quacks, I haven't seen London for thirty years."

The old man got into the carriage and deposited his bag on the hat rack, and as the train began to move slowly out of the station on its non-stop run to Newcastle, he explained the object of his journey.

"I'm going to meet my dear friend, Macginnis, who has made me a rich man. The Trevenay Mine, sir, is a gold mine! I am speaking figuratively, of course. A new tin deposit has been discovered, the shares which were not worth the paper they are written on, are now worth a pound—perhaps two pounds. You said you had some? I congratulate you. . . ."

Edward did not hear any more. He had swooned.

Rogue: Fidelity Dove

The Genuine Old Master

DAVID DURHAM

TWO VERY ORIGINAL CHARACTERS, each quite different from the other, highlight the accomplishments of William Edward Vickers (1889–1965), who wrote under the nom de plume of Roy Vickers. *The Exploits of Fidelity Dove* (1924) recounts the adventures of the angelic-looking girl whose ethereal beauty has made emotional slaves of many men. She is a fearless and inventive crook, whose "gang" consists of a lawyer, a businessman, a scientist, and other devoted servants. She always wears gray, partly because the color matches well with her violet eyes but also because it reflects her strict, puritanical life. She is committed to righting wrongs, to helping those who cannot help themselves, while also being certain that the endeavor is profitable to herself. Her frustrated adversary, Detective Inspector Rason, finds greater success when he joins the Department of Dead Ends, Vickers's other memorable series. *The Exploits of Fidelity Dove* was published under the pseudonym David Durham and is one of the rarest volumes of crime fiction of the twentieth century; it was reissued eleven years later by Roy Vickers.

The Department of Dead Ends is an obscure branch of Scotland Yard that has the unenviable task of trying to solve crimes that have been abandoned as hopeless. The stories in this series are "inverted" detective tales in which the reader witnesses the crime being committed, is aware when the incriminating clue is discovered, and follows the police methods that lead to the arrest. The department's unusual cases are recorded in several short story collections, beginning with *The Department of Dead Ends* (1947); the British edition of 1949 has mainly different stories.

Vickers's novel *The Girl in the News* (1937) was released on film in 1940 to mostly good reviews. It was directed by Carol Reed, with a screenplay by Sidney Gilliat, and starred Margaret Lockwood, Barry K. Barnes, and Emlyn Williams.

"The Genuine Old Master" was originally published in *The Exploits of Fidelity Dove* (London, Hodder & Stoughton, 1924).

THE GENUINE OLD MASTER

David Durham

THE UNFRIENDLY CRITICS of Fidelity Dove have urged that her ingenuity, her courage, and her resource have been grossly exaggerated. They point to the fact that she worked with a company of metallurgists, electricians, mechanics, and artists. They suggest that these men supplied the daring and the originality, and that Fidelity was little more than a competent actress.

In point of fact, as the episode of the Old Master amply proves, Fidelity was a great deal more than a competent actress. She was a shrewd little psychologist with a decided *flair* for calculating just how the human brain would act in a given set of circumstances—and as she was generally the one to "give" the circumstances, she was nearly always right. Ask Sir Rufus Blatch to tell you about his Old Master.

"Clery's 'Sister of Charity,'" murmured Fidelity, gazing up at the picture. "You have seen reproductions, of course, Sir Rufus?"

Sir Rufus Blatch, the button-stick baronet—his fortune and title had come to him through the contract to supply the entire Forces of the Crown with button-sticks during the Great War—removed his eyes hastily from Fidelity's angelic face and, looking up at the Clery, said that of course he had seen many reproductions. He stared at the oval face, enclosed so straitly by the stiff, winged coif of a nun, and the pale hands folded upon a breviary. "Very little life in it," was his private opinion.

"No reproduction can give those velvet shadows their value or suggest the true beauty of the flesh-tints," murmured Fidelity, still gazing up at the picture. It hung above the carved mantelpiece in the room she called "the study," a stately apartment that afforded a rich setting to her own ethereal beauty.

Sir Rufus admired the Clery volubly. He was ready to admire anything that Fidelity admired. He had that day had the privilege of entertaining Fidelity to lunch in his gilded Kensington residence, packed with *objets d'art.* He had driven her home after lunch in one of his smaller cars, and afterwards, at her request, entered her house to see the "Sister of Charity."

"I congratulate you on such a valuable possession, my dear," said Sir Rufus, and hastily added, as Fidelity's limpid eyes rested upon his—"Miss Dove."

Fidelity waved a slender hand up at the picture.

"If you really like it so much, Sir Rufus," she said, "you will only be doing me a kindness by taking it off my hands. I know it would be useless to offer it to you as a present for you would not take it. You may pay me what I gave for it." There was a tiny pause, and then: "Ten thousand pounds."

Sir Rufus coughed. It was a nasty shock, and he did not quite know how to deal with it. It was impossible to believe that with those eyes, that voice, that grave *naïveté*, she had deliberately led him to this point.

"Really, my dear young lady, you're most generous, but—your proposition is rather sudden, as it were. I would not for a moment dispute the worth of the picture, but ten thousand pounds is a great deal of money, even if I felt—"

"Not to you, Sir Rufus," said Fidelity. "They say you are one of the richest men in London."

Sir Rufus beamed. He had not at that moment the smallest intention of buying the picture, but it was pleasant to be regarded as one of the richest men in London. He looked down at Fidelity. If, by purchasing the picture, he could make sure of the fair owner—well, he could afford to do that sort of thing if he wanted to. But he would not be rushed into it. Fidelity must make her intentions clearer first.

"I'll think it over, Miss Dove," he said, eyeing her with mingled shrewdness and desire, "and I'll let you know tomorrow. Dear me! Half-past three! I must be going."

"Please take ample time for consideration," said Fidelity with silver sweetness. "You have perhaps friends whose opinion you value. It will be a pleasure to afford them a view of the picture."

"Ah, thanks. Yes." Sir Rufus had brightened. Apparently Fidelity's final suggestion had reminded him of someone. "I'll let you know later on. Good-bye."

As the bulky form of the button-stick baronet disappeared, another and much younger man sauntered into the study by way of the conservatory at the far end. He approached the picture, moistened his finger and touched it, then drew back. Fidelity watched him with enigmatic kindliness.

"The frame," he said slowly, "is not a bad piece of gilding. I value that at about four pounds. For the picture itself, as it is a quite passably good copy, I would allow twelve guineas. H'm! There's a bit of careful work about the eyes done by a man who is no amateur. Call it twenty pounds. Total twenty-four. What did you pay for it, Fidelity?"

"Forty guineas," said Fidelity.

"Then you've not been too badly swindled," said Garfield. (You will remember Garfield's picture in the Academy a few years ago—you see now the reason behind his sensational disappearance.) "The original 'Sister of Charity,' by the way, is in the possession of Lord Doucester—unless the poor old dear has been compelled to part with it. It's a long way from being a national treasure, but it's worth quite fifteen hundred."

Fidelity transferred her clear and shining gaze to the shadows of the big room. She appeared to drift into a state of spiritual exaltation. When Garfield spoke again, she came back to herself with a start.

"What is my part in the scheme, Fidelity? For I suppose it *is* a scheme?"

Fidelity bent her pale-gold head in assent.

"It is a scheme, or will be. The essence of it flashed into my mind when Sir Rufus was driving me back through the Park. A friend of his saluted us. It was Mr. Garstein."

Garfield stared. It seemed only the other day that they had relieved Mr. Garstein of a considerable sum of money in circumstances that had left him no legal remedy.

"What are my orders, Fidelity?" asked Garfield, repressing his curiosity.

"I have none to give," returned Fidelity with an upward glance that sent the blood pounding through Garfield's veins. "You have all done wonders in our recent ventures, my dear friend, and deserve a rest. I shall not ask your assistance on this occasion."

II

Sir Rufus Blatch returned to his house to find his friend Garstein awaiting him. Sir Rufus was none too pleased to see Garstein. The Jew had been associated with him more than once in various deals. And Sir Rufus did not wish to think of business just then. He wished to think of Fidelity.

"Hullo! Garstein," he said somewhat coldly. "What can I do for you?"

"It ithn't what you can do for me, it'th what I can do for you," said Mr. Garstein, who could really speak English quite well except in moments of excitement, when he would lisp intermittently. "I can stop you making the biggest mistake of your life." He lowered his voice and added: "I thaw who wath with you in the car."

Sir Rufus Blatch bristled.

"If you've got a word to say against Miss Dove, Garstein, I trust for the sake of our old friendship it will not be said in my presence," said Sir Rufus.

"Ah!" said Garstein triumphantly. "You want to marry her, I dare thay."

"Well—er—in a sense, I do, and—er—in a sense, I don't mind admitting it," said Sir Rufus.

"And if she won't marry you it'th jutht occurred to you in passing that she might conthent to become your adopted daughter," continued Garstein. Sir Rufus started. Garstein went on: "I know. I've been through it. She didn't marry me in a sense or any other way, and she didn't be adopted. But I paid twenty thousand pounds for thinking that she would."

"What!" exploded Sir Rufus. "You mean to tell me——"

"I mean to tell you that she's the thmarteth crook in London." There followed an anecdote in support of the charge.

At the end of the anecdote Sir Rufus gasped, but was still only half convinced. He could scarcely believe that Fidelity Dove was the girl in the Garstein case. Then he remembered the rather strange manner in which the Old Master had been sprung upon him. He related that to Garstein.

"Pah! You can bet that picture'th a fake," said Garstein. "She'll lead you on to buying it and look goo-goo at you until you don't mind whether it'th a fake or not, and she'll cash your cheque and you'll not thee her again."

Sir Rufus glared at Garstein as one glares at a man who tells what may prove to be an unpleasant truth.

"It's all speculation," said Sir Rufus irritably. "You're saying that it's a fake. She says it isn't. And, after all, Garstein, there is the bare possibility of mistaken identity. She may not be the same."

"I know a bit about pictureth," said Garstein. "I'm not an exthpert, but I've got a friend who ith. What'th thith picture called?"

Sir Rufus told him and Garstein picked up the receiver of the telephone and presently was talking to his "friend," a well-known art dealer.

"Know anything about a 'Thithter of Charity,' by Clery?" asked Garstein. . . . "You do? . . . Well, look it up and make sure, ma tear, I'll wait." A couple of minutes passed and then the Jew murmured his thanks and banged down the receiver.

"You've theen that picture in her houth this afternoon, ain't it?" asked Garstein. "Well, that picture what you've theen in her house this afternoon is in Lord Doucester's houth at the present moment. Come along and we'll thee it."

Throughout the short drive to Bloomsbury Garstein baited Sir Rufus.

The house in Bloomsbury was in need of a coat of paint and suggested that his lordship had seen better days, as indeed was the case.

"If I were you I'd buy the picture—then you've got the girl at your merthy," advised Garstein. "Thay my friend recommended you."

Lord Doucester, a kindly, faded man, readily consented to showing the picture. It was in a long, high room which held the relics of a great collection.

"That is the Clery," said Lord Doucester,

and Sir Rufus gazed with eyes that were more than a little bloodshot upon the original. To Sir Rufus it was indistinguishable from the copy, for in spite of the *objets d'art* at home he knew nothing whatsoever about pictures. It came to him that Fidelity must have been laughing immoderately at him as well as planning to rob him.

He wheeled round, his mind made up.

"Would you care to accept fifteen hundred pounds for this picture, Lord Doucester?" he asked.

"I'm afraid not," said Lord Doucester.

"Two thousand," said Sir Rufus.

"I regret that I am not in a position to offer it for sale at all," said Lord Doucester. "If you are making an art collection, however, I have here a vase which may possibly appeal to you. I——"

Sir Rufus and Garstein managed to get out.

"I've got her without the picture," snapped Sir Rufus. "I must say, Garstein, I'm obliged to you for opening my eyes. I——"

"You can liquidate the obligation by letting me help you land her," said Garstein with relish.

Back at the house the two men put their heads together. As a result of the consultation, Sir Rufus presently picked up a pen and wrote:

> *"Dear Miss Dove, I have been thinking over your proposition that I should buy your picture 'The Sister of Charity,' by Clery, for ten thousand pounds. As it is a considerable sum of money, even to me, I must ask you to give me your written assurance that the picture is genuine. If you will do this, and will bring it to my house tomorrow morning at eleven, I will have pleasure in handing you my cheque. I am, yours very sincerely, Rufus Blatch (Bart.)."*

"That's all right," said Garstein eagerly. "Now we'll get off to Scotland Yard. But give her notheth, not a cheque. Thafer. You'll get 'em back at the polithe thtathion. You mutht pay her or the crime is not complete. Thee?"

Sir Rufus saw, and the two friends set off to Scotland Yard.

III

At ten-thirty on the following morning—so as to be in good time—Detective-Inspector Rason and Talbot his junior, enclosed themselves in two huge curtains that hung over the bow window in Sir Rufus Blatch's spacious library. Behind a screen in a corner of the room stood Mr. Garstein in the rôle of entirely independent witness. Astride the hearth stood Sir Rufus Blatch himself, inwardly fuming, but outwardly presenting a very over-acted indifference.

Sir Rufus constantly rehearsed what he would say when Fidelity Dove came in. He had ample time for rehearsal between ten-thirty and eleven, the hour at which Fidelity was expected. At five minutes to eleven he was suffering badly from stage-fright. By five minutes past eleven the stage-fright was less pronounced. By a quarter past eleven it had given way to irritation.

By twenty past eleven Sir Rufus was seized with exasperation.

"The whole thing's a frost!" he cried out. "She's got wind of what's happening and has been frightened off." He spoke to the room at large. From behind the screen came a thin voice:

"Let'th give it till twelve o'clock. I don't mind waiting."

"Quiet, please!" ordered Detective-Inspector Rason from behind the curtains. "There's a car drawing up outside."

Sir Rufus Blatch strode to the window. Fidelity Dove's limousine had stopped in the road below and out of it stepped Fidelity herself. She was, as always, in grey—the grey of cathedral cloisters. While Sir Rufus watched, the chauffeur sprang from his seat and followed his mistress into the house, carrying the picture.

Sir Rufus reported events in a hoarse whisper and waited.

"Miss Dove," announced the butler.

Sir Rufus Blatch bustled forward, contorting his mouth to a sickly smile while his eyes remained furious.

"Good morning, Miss Dove. I see you've brought the picture!" he remarked with quite commendable brightness.

"Of course, Sir Rufus!" said Fidelity. "Did I not promise? And is not the given word the greatest of all pledges? Where shall my man put the Clery?"

"Oh, anywhere, anywhere," said Sir Rufus airily. "If he'll put it down against the wall there it will do for the present."

Sir Rufus offered Fidelity a chair and himself fussed until the chauffeur was out of the room.

"You have not forgotten the guarantee?" asked Sir Rufus, trying to make his voice sound merely conversational.

"Assuredly not," said Fidelity, and added: "I agree with you that in transactions between friends the very strictest etiquette should prevail. Friendship seems to me like one of those beautiful sunflowers—you may handle it with freedom but you must never lean upon the stem. I beg you to read this guarantee with the utmost particularity. If you can, Sir Rufus, pretend for the moment that I am an entirely unscrupulous person."

Sir Rufus managed a throaty laugh as with trembling fingers he took the guarantee.

" 'To Sir Rufus Blatch,' " he read aloud. " 'Sir, I guarantee that the picture "Sister of Charity," for which you have offered me the sum of ten thousand pounds, is by Josef Clery and is in every respect genuine. (Signed) Fidelity Dove.'

"That is quite satisfactory, Miss Dove," said Sir Rufus, a gleam of triumph in his eyes. He opened a drawer in his desk. "Here are notes to the value of ten thousand pounds. If you will be good enough to count them you will then perhaps sign this receipt."

Fidelity took the notes and placed them in her bag.

"You must allow me a woman's privilege of departing from my own principles," she said, her voice like the call of birds at evensong. "I am going to trust you where I would not let you trust me. May I have this pen?"

In a rounded, schoolgirlish hand, Fidelity Dove signed the receipt for ten thousand pounds, blotted it, and handed it to Sir Rufus. Then she rose.

"Something in the air, Sir Rufus, tells me that you are busy. It makes me just a little frightened, and I'm going to run away as fast as I can."

"No, you don't, ma tear, not this time!"

Fidelity gave a little cry of alarm as the screen was precipitated with a crash and Mr. Julius Garstein thrust himself forward between herself and the door. At the same moment the curtains parted, and Detective-Inspector Rason and his assistant Talbot stepped into the room.

"Sir Rufus!" cried Fidelity in alarm. "What does this mean?"

"It means, Miss Dove," replied Sir Rufus ponderously, "that in the presence of three witnesses you have sold to me for ten thousand pounds a picture which you know perfectly well to be an impudent fake."

Fidelity looked from Sir Rufus to Detective-Inspector Rason on the one hand and Garstein on the other. She swayed a little and caught the back of a chair to steady herself.

"I don't understand!" she said. She looked like a child who has been struck for the first time in its life.

"That's just it," snapped Sir Rufus. "You haven't understood anything from the first. You thought I'd be fool enough to pay ten thousand pounds for a picture without making any inquiries about it—just to see you smile. You thought I could go on swallowing drivel about friendship and sunflowers and what not—"

"There's no need for this, Sir Rufus," said Rason stepping forward. "Miss Dove will accompany me to the station, I hope of her own free will."

"Am I under arrest?" gasped Fidelity.

"Yes," said Rason. "And I'd take it quietly, if I were you, Miss Dove."

Fidelity looked at Garstein as if a light were breaking over her.

"Oh, I see it all," she said. "Mr. Garstein once accused me of robbing him. He has poisoned your mind, Sir Rufus. I beg you for your own sake rather than mine——"

"I always thought you'd take defeat gamely when it came, Miss Dove," said Rason, disappointment in his voice.

From the bag that contained ten thousand pounds in notes, Fidelity took a handkerchief. Sobbing bitterly, she allowed Detective-Inspector Rason to lead her downstairs and into a waiting taxi.

"All right, you follow on behind," said Rason to his junior.

As the taxi started, a change came over Fidelity Dove. The handkerchief was whisked back into the deep velvet bag. Detective-Inspector Rason noted with sudden alarm that her eyes were quite dry.

"This is our second little taxi-ride together, Mr. Rason. Last time, if I remember rightly, it was the prelude to a very thrilling little incident." The detective said nothing, and she added in a confidential whisper in his ear: "There's going to be just as exciting an incident at the end of this one."

Rason drew an automatic pistol from his hip pocket and held it on his knee.

"If any of your friends attempt to rescue you, Miss Dove, the law allows me to use this."

"The law allows you to deal death for the protection of Sir Rufus Blatch's ill-gotten gains!" murmured Fidelity. She took out the ten thousand pounds and gazed sorrowfully at the notes. "How many of these flimsy scraps of paper, Mr. Rason, must be cast into the scale to balance a human life?"

"I don't know, I'm sure," said Detective-Inspector Rason, and then as the taxi slowed: "Your pals have missed their chance. Here we are, Miss Dove."

Fidelity was again sobbing as Detective-Inspector Rason led her into the charge-room.

IV

Sir Rufus stated the charge without reluctance. A relish was added to the proceedings by an occasional broken protest, an intermittent choking sob from Fidelity Dove. Sir Rufus contrived to delay until Fidelity, still sobbing, was led away to the cells. The ten thousand pounds, he noted, was impounded by the sergeant in charge.

Garstein had contributed his quota, and the two friends returned to Sir Rufus's house for the purpose of taking lunch and each other's congratulations.

The lunch tended to elongate itself. Sir Rufus made a clean breast of his experiences with Fidelity Dove, and the anecdotes were many if, for the most part, imaginary. It was three o'clock before they had finished their coffee, and then their serenity was disturbed by the reappearance of Detective-Inspector Rason.

The confidence had vanished from the detective's manner. He looked positively haggard.

"I'd be obliged if you two gentlemen would accompany me to the station," he said. He kept on saying it, and would say no more, and in the end they went.

In the charge-room they came face to face with Lord Doucester, who bowed distantly. By his side was Mr. Edgar Bloomfield, one of the foremost art authorities in the country. It was the sergeant who explained. Rason retired to a far corner and turned his back upon the scene.

"About this charge you made against Miss Dove of selling you a fake picture, Sir Rufus," began the sergeant. "This gentleman here—his lordship—says he sold the original picture to Miss Dove this morning; she told him at the time that she wished to sell it to you. This other gentleman, I understand, is an expert. He has examined the picture that was brought here and says there's no doubt about it."

Sir Rufus removed his silk hat and mopped his brow. The sergeant had to explain the whole thing over again before he grasped it. Sir Rufus in bewilderment turned to Lord Doucester.

"When I saw you last night, Lord Doucester, you told me that your picture was not for sale."

"Pardon me," said Lord Doucester coldly, "I told you I was not at liberty to sell it to you. I was not. I had received the day before one hundred pounds from Miss Fidelity Dove for the option to purchase that picture within three months for two thousand pounds. She had also requested secrecy regarding the arrangement. Miss Dove called this morning and paid me the two thousand pounds, mentioning quite frankly that she intended to sell it to you at a profit."

Sir Rufus gasped.

"Five hundred per thent!" came the feeble wail from Garstein. "And that letter you wrote wath a contract to purchase. You can't get out of it."

A voluble discussion followed. Assurances by Lord Doucester and Mr. Bloomfield were repeated. The sergeant again cut in.

"I presume you drop the charge against Miss Dove, Sir Rufus?" asked the sergeant.

For a moment Sir Rufus hesitated.

"There's no charge to make," said Lord Doucester contemptuously. "If you have finished with me, sergeant, I will go."

"May I wait and speak to Miss Dove?" asked Sir Rufus. It was a mild breach of the regulations but in the tangled circumstances the sergeant consented. A couple of minutes later Fidelity was brought in.

"The charge against you has been dropped, Miss Dove," said the sergeant while he signed the necessary papers. "I have to return you your property."

The sergeant handed her the big grey bag. Fidelity counted the notes and gave the sergeant a receipt, glanced at Rason's immovable back, bade him a soft good-afternoon, and then appeared for the first time to catch sight of Sir Rufus.

Sir Rufus breathed deeply.

"I ask you, Miss Dove, in the presence of the police, whether you are going to return that ten thousand to me," he said.

"If you are discontented with your bargain you can communicate with my solicitors," said Fidelity with dignity. She gave him a little bow and cast down her eyes modestly.

"Cut your loss," muttered Garstein to Sir Rufus.

"That is very good advice, Mr. Garstein," said Fidelity without looking up. "Sir Rufus, in your hour of tribulation I perceive that you have a good friend to advise you. Would you like to cut your loss, Sir Rufus?"

"Are you offering me a compromise?" demanded Sir Rufus.

"Certainly," said Fidelity. "I feel that you are more sinned against than sinning, Sir Rufus. Your heart was poisoned and your head confused. I will be generous."

"Generous?" clamoured Sir Rufus. *"Generous?"*

"And my generosity," went on Fidelity, "shall be rewarded by the contemplation of yours. The other day you showed me your pocket chequebook. If you have it on you, as I am sure you have, I suggest that you write a cheque for a thousand pounds to the Police Orphanage. If you will do that, I will telephone my solicitors to stop the action against you for malicious arrest and imprisonment. The cheque should be handed to Detective-Inspector Rason."

Rason made a violent movement, which he as violently checked. Garstein looked affronted. Sir Rufus waved his arm foolishly.

The sergeant was seized with a coughing fit. Like every true policeman, he was more than ready to do his bit for the Orphanage.

"Miss Dove has been in touch with her solicitors, I can vouch for that, sir," he put in to aid Sir Rufus in forming a decision.

"You would have the barefathed impudenth—" began Garstein.

"Sir Rufus has digged a pit for me and fallen into it himself," said Fidelity, and her voice was exquisitely sad. "He must clamber out of it as best he can. To redeem my good name I would gladly endure the full glare of publicity upon every detail of the affair."

Sir Rufus leant heavily against the sergeant's desk. His hand went to his breast-pocket and then he dashed it away again.

"The police often risk their lives in the discharge of their duty," said Fidelity almost with reverence. "Mr. Rason will tell you that he was once in grave peril from a giant crane. For myself, I would gladly forego my rights if the Orphanage were to benefit. Charity, Sir Rufus, covers a multitude of sins."

Sir Rufus snatched the sergeant's pen. Rason, white with fury, accepted the cheque.

Fidelity after 'phoning her solicitors, breathed a benediction upon her foes and went forgivingly away.

Rogue: Colonel Humphrey Flack

The Colonel Gives a Party

EVERETT RHODES CASTLE

LARGELY FORGOTTEN TODAY, Everett Rhodes Castle (1894–1968) was a hugely popular short story writer for decades, appearing with regularity in the pages of the best-paying magazines in America, including *Redbook*, *Collier's*, and *The Saturday Evening Post*, to which he sold his first story in 1917.

Born in Cleveland, Ohio, his goal had been to be a cartoonist, but he instead became a journalist before becoming an advertising copywriter while creating gently humorous stories that mostly featured business, romance, and crime on the side.

Castle is best known for his long series about Colonel Humphrey Flack, a con man who swindles other swindlers with the aid of his partner, Uthas P. ("Patsy") Garvey. They serve a role akin to Robin Hood figures, turning over their ill-gotten gains to the deserving while retaining a percentage "for expenses." The magazine stories inspired a humorous, family-oriented television series for the Dumont network titled *Colonel Humphrey Flack* that ran from October 7, 1953, to July 2, 1954; it was revived for a thirty-nine-episode syndicated series that aired from October 5, 1958, to July 5, 1959, with the title *Colonel Flack*.

"The Colonel Gives a Party" was first published in the May 8, 1943, issue of *The Saturday Evening Post*.

THE COLONEL GIVES A PARTY

Everett Rhodes Castle

THE OLD GENTLEMAN with the crimson face and sweeping white mustaches picked up the telephone and asked, in an amiable bass, for the cashier. His watery blue eyes, pendent in bulging brassières of flesh, twinkled good-naturedly. His free hand, a massive paw speckled with brown spots, fondled a brandy and soda. A vintage cigar, also speckled with brown spots, rode jauntily above his huge, glistening, winged collar.

"This is Colonel Humphrey Flack in Suite Nine-o-two," he said, after a moment. "Mr. Garvey and I are checking out in the morning. Ha. . . . Exactly. . . . Eh? . . . No, no. Everything has been eminently satisfactory. Quite. I—we are merely going South. To my place in Palm Beach. Will you see that my chit is ready immediately after breakfast? Ha. . . . Good. Very good. Incidentally, there will be a few—hum—additions to the account this evening. I—ha—am giving a little farewell party."

The younger man with his hands thrust deep into the trouser pockets of his blue flannel suit turned away from the window. His dark eyes smoldered with resentment.

"It ought to be a pleasure to hear you speak the truth for once," he fumed. "But it isn't! The Colonel gives the party! What else have you been doing twice a week for the past weeks? Poker, he calls it! Ever thought of what that gang of highbinders you've been having in here probably call it?" His thin, bitter laugh curdled the twilight.

The old gentleman by the telephone gestured meekly with his sweating glass. "But it's been fun," he protested mildly. "And at seventy-one a man must seize the few—hum—pleasures which come his way."

Mr. Uthas Garvey's nervous fingers flecked the ash from his cigarette. "That's your trouble," he snapped. "You're living in the past. You're a hangover from the good old days when suckers bought the Brooklyn Bridge, gold bricks, went for the wire racket, the tear-up, and all the other bewhiskered gyps of the Gay Nineties."

The Colonel dipped his aristocratic puce beak into his glass, came up smiling. "I live by my wits," he admitted benignly. "Ha. I admit it, frankly. But so do you, my dear chap. The pot libels the kettle, eh?"

"I'm fed up with wits!" Mr. Garvey assured him sourly. "What's it got me in the two years we've been playing around together? Right now I've got three dollars and ten cents in cash and a case of stomach ulcers. And what have you laid by, fine-feathered friend? Two bucks and a bad case of dementia grandeur. Some balance sheet, eh?"

"It could be worse, my dear boy."

"How?" Mr. Garvey dropped his voice to a mocking imitation of his associate's rumble. "Get my bill ready, my good man! I'm leaving for the South, my good man." His voice edged up. "Where does the lettuce come from to pay the bill? The railroad tickets? Where will you get the dough you'll lose tonight trying to make a four-card flush stand up against three mop squeezers?"

"Maybe I'll hold the three queens tonight, my dear chap. Ha. Exactly."

"Against Billings?" Mr. Garvey's laughter was abrupt, derisive. "That goon used to be a dealer in Moxey Manning's gambling joint in Denver. Purdy? He just beat a rap for selling fake cemetery lots to the widow-and-orphan trade by an eyelash. And Spertz! A crooked stock rigger under indictment right now. And Dolan! A bottom-of-the-deck artist. A fine gang of playmates."

"Don't forget Captain Ferdinand Smythe-Calder," the Colonel implored him meekly. "Of course, he isn't a captain and Calder isn't his real name. But he has a very quick brain. Ha. Indubitably."

"As opposed to senile decay!" Mr. Garvey muttered wrathfully.

The Colonel rubbed his lower lip tenderly. "It's heartening, the interest people take in the aged and mentally infirm," he observed placidly. "At my last little poker party, Eddie, the bell captain, delivered some cigars. Yesterday he took the time and—hum—trouble to hint that my guests—particularly the Captain—were residents of Queer Street, as the English say. Ha. Exactly. I gathered the Captain had done the dirty, as they say, to some friend of the lad's. A nice boy. Ha. Eddie, I mean. Did you know this was his last day at the hotel? He's leaving in the morning. The Marines, I believe. A noble service. I must not forget to leave him a substantial remembrance."

"And they lock up poor jerks who only imagine that they're Nero or Napoleon or Lincoln," Mr. Garvey mourned.

The Colonel was humming one of his favorite tunes now. A little number entitled *A Violet Plucked from Mother's Grave.* It was more than flesh could take.

"For God's sake, quit that dirge!" Mr. Garvey screamed.

"Dirge?" The watery orbs were mildly reproving. "Hardly, my dear fellow. A most interesting little lyric. By a chap named J. P. Skelly. He was known as the Bible House Plumber in his day. He wrote over four hundred songs. All on brown wrapping paper. Ha. Exactly. Most interesting, eh?"

"I'm enthralled," Mr. Garvey snarled. "You've opened up an entirely new world to me." He dropped down abruptly on a putty-colored settee that cornered the far side of the parlor. "My ulcers!" he moaned.

With quick solicitude the Colonel dug up the telephone and called for room service. He ordered bicarbonate, and then, almost as a casual afterthought, added two quarts of Scotch, a bottle of brandy, one of bourbon, charged water, ginger ale, cigarettes, and a box of cigars.

"And—hah—a large platter of turkey, ham and cheese sandwiches later, eh? About ten-thirty."

Mr. Garvey's stomach writhed in agony, but his mind was busy with a bitter sum in mental arithmetic. "How typical of our partnership," he observed brightly. "Everything fifty-fifty! A dose of baking soda for Garvey and forty dollars' worth of high living for Colonel Humphrey."

The old gentleman ignored the crack. He gulped his drink and reached again for the telephone. "The desk," he commanded.

When the connection was made, he requested the immediate installation of a radio. He hung up with a flourish.

"Eat, drink and be merry, for tomorrow we die," Mr. Garvey quoted petulantly. Then his mind backtracked to the flourish. His eyes narrowed suspiciously. "Or could I be wrong?"

"About a hangover from the old days when suckers went for the wire racket and all the other bewhiskered gyps of the Gay Nineties? My dear boy!"

"Spare me those trained dewlaps quivering with reproach." The younger man stood up and started for the array of glasses and bottles on the side table near the older man. Then he sighed and twisted away. "You don't like radio," he pointed out accusingly over his shoulder. "You've said so a hundred times. The blatting—"

"But I do like the—hah—manly art of self-defense, my dear lad," the Colonel pointed out glibly. "And so do my guests." The massive gold chain attached to his stomach watch twitched with logic—or something. "Young Cooney is battling Stanley Peyskisk for the light-heavyweight championship tonight. Ha. Exactly. I—I was reading about it over luncheon today. Hum. On the sports page. Then I happened to notice that the bout would also be on a local station at eleven o'clock. What a marvelous age we are living in, my dear boy! It—it makes one think, doesn't it?"

"Cooney will cut him to pieces," Mr. Garvey predicted. "And don't tell me all the wise money is going on the Polack. I know it is. But wise dough has been wrong before."

The Colonel was making himself another drink. He held glass and bottle high, squinting tenderly at the golden liquid threading into the glass. "I wasn't thinking of the two contestants," he chirruped blithely. "My—my mind was traveling back. Years ago we had to—hum—depend on the telegraph for sporting results—"

"I'm not interested."

But the old goat was off, teetering on his toes, one hand tugging reminiscently at his port mustache.

Mr. Garvey sighed, shrugged his shoulders wearily, and wished the bicarbonate would arrive.

"I was thinking of the old wire racket you mentioned," the Colonel pattered on. "Remember how it worked? Contact was made with a—hum—gullible and—and avaricious gentleman with money. It was explained to this easy mark that the contactor was a close friend or relative of a telegraph operator. This operator had agreed to hold up the news of certain race results. Ha. Exactly. At the same time he would pass along the names of the winning horses to his friend. The friend would thus be able to place a bet on the winning horse with some bookie joint—hah—after the race was won. It—it was absolutely sure. The contactor explained that he was without the necessary funds to make a big killing, quick. Hence the opportunity for the easy mark. Of course, the whole thing was a plant. After letting the mark win a few small bets, they took him in—hah—a big way and—hum—fled."

Mr. Garvey draped his feet over the end of the settee and lit a cigarette. The tableau was one of complete disinterest.

"I was just thinking—" the Colonel went on with a sly, ruminative grin, as his younger partner sent smoke rings twisting toward the ceiling—"ha—how the magic of modern science and invention has made such small stratagems—hum—quite obsolete. You agree?"

Mr. Garvey yawned, loudly and ostentatiously.

A waiter arrived, pushing a white-clothed cart covered with bottles before him. Mr. Garvey sat up with a quick sigh of relief. The Colonel signed the check with the dash and confidence of the Federal Reserve System. He added a tip to the bottom of the card. The smile on the waiter's face made Mr. Garvey wince as he stirred his bicarbonate.

Then the old boar was at the telephone again. This time he wanted the bell captain. "Eddie? Ha. . . . Oh, I see. This is Colonel Flack. Will you tell him I'd like to see him for a minute as soon as he returns? Tell him it is—hah—very important."

Garvey eyed him thoughtfully over the cloudy glass. The Colonel grinned.

Something—either the bicarbonate or the grin—made the younger man feel better. "So I was wrong, eh?"

"What time have you, my dear fellow?"

Garvey stared at his wrist. "Five to eight."

"Your watch is three minutes slow. I checked with the telephone company just before you returned from dinner. Please set it."

"What difference does three minutes make when—"

The Colonel returned his huge gold hunter to his white linen vest. "Timing is one of the most important things in life, my dear Garvey. In business. In—hah—the drama. Even in paying one's hotel bill. Ha. Exactly. Quite."

Mr. Uthas P. Garvey dragged his coat sleeve away from his wrist for the fifth time in twenty minutes. It was exactly five minutes after ten. Nearly an hour to go! Mr. Garvey lit another cigarette and sat back to brood. Why couldn't the old goat come right out and say what the angle was? He had insisted that the younger man could carry out his part of the deal more naturally, and, consequently, with a better chance for success, if he did not know what was going on. But that was always his line.

Mr. Garvey inhaled savagely. At three minutes after eleven o'clock—not one moment sooner—he was to turn on the radio.

After pretending to fiddle with the tuning controls, he was to bring in the local station carrying the fight. What did that make him? A stooge for a cheap hotel radio, Mr. Garvey thought bitterly. The smoke from his cigarette was flat and unstimulating in his lungs. Nothing added up. The old crocodile had intimated, with one of his sly cat-and-canary smiles, that the Garvey bewilderment augured well for the success of his scheme. It proved, he said, the psychological soundness of the basic thought.

So what? So where? So how? Mr. Garvey ground out his cigarette with savage thoroughness. The old ram had intimated that his ulcers were nothing but attacks of nervous indigestion. Well, for once, Mr. Garvey hoped the old bull was right. Ulcers or no ulcers, he had to have a drink! A big drink! The six men around the green-covered table in the middle of the room paid no attention to him as he crossed to the bottle-littered table by the door.

"All pink," a flat voice announced as he reached for rye. "Sorry, Colonel. They don't seem to be running, do they?"

Mr. Garvey recognized the voice. He wondered if Dolan had dealt his flush from the bottom of the pack.

But apparently the Colonel entertained no such suspicion. He took a hearty pull from the glass beside him.

"That's the third time I've had three of a kind topped," he announced, with a chuckle. "Perhaps I'm allergic to the—hah—digit, eh? Ha. Quite. Well, we shall see. . . . Your deal, Billings."

The news caused Mr. Garvey to add still another jigger of liquor to his drink. He gulped thirstily and then sauntered over to stand behind the Colonel. His dark eyes took a swift inventory of the chips. He gulped again. They were playing five-card stud, five-dollar limit. As Mr. Garvey stood there, a little man in his shirt sleeves across the table bet a red chip on an exposed ace. He had eyebrows like Harpo Marx and a mouth like a barracuda. A tall man next to him saw the red chip with long, delicate-looking fingers and added a yellow one. His exposed card was a knave of diamonds. And Captain Ferdinand Smythe-Calder looked like a knave, Mr. Garvey thought. A very elegant knave.

A beefy man whose baldness and horn-rimmed glasses made him look like a gremlin's wicked uncle grunted and turned down his hand. The next man did the same with a shrug and a thin smile.

The Colonel hiccuped gently. His shirt sleeves ballooned out of his bulging vest. His white mustaches seemed to reach out and clutch at the drifting smoke which brooded over the table. His eyes seemed to be at full tide.

"Purdy," he said to the gremlin's wicked uncle, "you ought to have more faith in the—hah—future. Ha. Exactly. . . . Spertz, did I see you turn down a nine? Observe my little trey of hearts, gentlemen. Now take heed of my confidence in a beneficent providence." He hiccuped again and the ashes from his cigar cascaded gently down the front of his vest. "Here is Billings's original bet. Here is Calder's raise. Ha. And here is my answer to them both." He pushed another yellow chip forward.

Billings saw the raise and added a yellow chip on his own account. His eyebrows twitched greedily. Calder, the tall man with the long white fingers, lit a fresh cigarette and raised them both. The Colonel beamed delightedly.

Tight-lipped, Mr. Garvey watched the hand through. Eyebrows won it with aces back-to-back. His hairy arms, bare to the elbow, went out to garner the harvest. Mr. Garvey turned away from the slaughter with a groan he found difficult to stifle. The old mark was getting tighter by the minute.

His journey back to the grateful dimness of the putty-colored settee in the corner was broken by the shrill summons of the telephone. Mr. Garvey crossed to the instrument. A male voice asked for Colonel Flack.

"For you," Mr. Garvey said, gesturing with the receiver.

The Colonel levered himself upward with difficulty.

"Flack here. . . . Eh? What? . . . Oh, Parker! No, I haven't given the matter any—hah—further consideration. I—I'm leaving for the South in the morning. . . . Eh? . . . Yes, I know. But consider the low coupon rate, my dear man. Suppose I bought ten thousand dollars' worth? . . . I know they're high-grade bonds. Ha. Without question. But at one hundred and seven, the yield is less than three per cent. . . . Eh? . . . So am I. Some later offering, perhaps."

He pattered back to the table in the center of the room. The old chump's guests were impatiently awaiting his return. Jackals awaiting their prey, Mr. Garvey thought. He plucked nervously at his wrist. Nearly a half hour to go.

"Broker chap," the Colonel explained to the table. "Well, well. Perhaps the fellow changed my luck. Ha. Eh? . . . Another stack of chips, my dear Calder."

This washes me up, Mr. Garvey assured himself fervidly. When I get out of this jam I'm traveling on my own.

His ulcers began to yell. A waiter brought two great platters of sandwiches. Mr. Garvey closed his eyes. The next time he looked at his watch, it was one minute after eleven.

He arose and stretched with elaborate carelessness. The Colonel, busily engaged in an unsuccessful attempt to draw to an inside straight, seemed to miss the movement completely. Mr. Garvey moved aimlessly in the direction of the radio.

"Now they're out in the middle of the ring, ladies and gentlemen. One minute and fifteen seconds of this fifteen-round bout for the light-heavyweight championship is over. And the boys—"

The Colonel bounded out of his chair. "Bless my soul!" he sputtered. "The Cooney-Peyskisk go! I—I had forgotten all about it. . . . Leave it on, my dear Garvey! Leave it on!"

"Cooney will cut that guy to pieces," Mr. Garvey predicted for the second time that night.

The Colonel's eyes popped with interest. "You think so, my dear boy? Really? Of—of course, I don't know much about boxing myself. Next to—hah—nothing. But Eddie, the bell captain here, was talking about it to me this morning. He seems to think it will be all Peyskisk. Ha. Without a doubt. Apparently, he had made quite a substantial wager on the chap. Betting with the wise money was the way—hum—he put it."

Mr. Garvey stared at the mountain of chips before Billings, swiveled his eyes to the Captain's pile and went on to take in the substantial assets of the remaining guests.

"I'm afraid the poor chump doesn't know any more about wise money than you do, Colonel," he sneered.

Billings spoke around his cigar, "Meaning what, Claude High-pocket?"

Mr. Garvey felt the color flood his face at this insulting reference to his financial conservatism. But the Colonel halted the angry retort which rose to his younger associate's tightly pressed lips.

"Now, now, gentlemen!" he pleaded hastily. "No personalities, eh? A—a friendly little gathering. My—my young friend here is not well. He—hum—suffers from ulcers. . . . I—I'm sorry if his dislike for cards seemed to reflect on your—er-r—luck, Billings. Ha. . . . I'm sure nothing of the kind was intended, eh, my dear boy?"

Mr. Garvey eyed him stonily, obstinately.

"How about a little bet on the outcome of the event?" the Colonel proposed, obviously covering the awkward situation as best he could. "Garvey, here, likes Cooney. But he's not a—hah—betting man. The wise money seems to prefer Peyskisk. Ha. Exactly. Whom do you gentlemen prefer? Billings? Purdy?"

The radio bellowed: "Cooney lands two light rights to the face. Another right and a left. The Polished Pole took the last two going away. Now both men are back in the middle of the ring. Now it's Peyskisk who's handing it out. A looping right which caught Cooney on the side of the face, and then two hard lefts to the champion's midriff and one in the face. They go into a clinch. Peyskisk—And there's the bell, for Round One, ladies and gentlemen. Now George Maxwell for Bellows Shaving Lotion. Come in, George."

"Sounds like an even match." The drawling observation came from the elegant Captain lounging in the doorway leading into the bedroom. The bathroom lay beyond the bedroom. The self-styled military man had carelessly sauntered out of the parlor just as the Colonel's challenge had been pinched off by the increased volume of the radio.

The Colonel turned, pivoting on another hiccup. "How about you, Calder?"

The Captain lit a languid cigarette. "I always trail along with the wise money your friend Mr. Garvey seems to dislike," he said, with a smile which bared even white teeth beneath a small elegant mustache. "I like Peyskisk. Would you like a hundred or two on Cooney, just to put a little extracurricular interest into the broadcast?"

"I'll take five hundred!"

"You're a—a—Don't be a fool!" Mr. Garvey snarled. "The odds are seven to five on Peyskisk. I—I was only giving you my personal opinion."

"I have great confidence in your—hah—fistic judgment, my dear boy," the Colonel chided him with unheeding cheerfulness. "Ha. Hic! Indeed." His watery eyes swiveled challengingly around the room. "Any other supporters of—hah—the Pole?"

"I'll take a couple of hundred," the gremlin's uncle said eagerly. He spoke after one quick look at the Captain.

"A hundred," Dolan, the alleged bottom-of-the-deck artist, said quickly. He licked his gray lips.

"Calder usually knows what he's doing," Spertz said over a poised siphon. He made the observation sound like a question. "A hundred for me," he said suddenly.

Garvey heard them through an agony of apprehension. He faced the teetering old fool savagely.

"Don't be a patsy!" he cried with passionate earnestness. "You—you're tight as a fiddler's toupee! I—I only said I thought Cooney—"

"You mustn't—hah—deprecate your—er-r—talents, my dear Garvey," the old monkey reproved him. He tugged gently at his port mustache. "No. No. Besides, I have a hunch that Cooney may change my—hum—recent bad luck."

". . . The referee is now between the two men," the staccato voice of the announcer rattled on as the Colonel paused to lift his glass. "Cooney's right eye apparently was slightly hurt by Peyskisk in that volley during the closing seconds of the first round. He keeps brushing it with his right. Now the contender tries two lefts to the chin and another looping right to the head. Now they're trading rights and lefts to the body. The Pole tries a left hook and the men go into a clinch as the bell rings. . . . Now back to George Maxwell and a message from the makers of the shaving lotion with a lift."

Mr. Garvey suddenly resolved never to use

a bottle of the stuff as long as he lived. Words foamed up to his lips and were smothered in helpless rage. While the rest of the party munched sandwiches and lapped up liquor, the announcer spattered the room with four more rounds of give and take. Too much take on the part of Cooney to keep the fever from glistening in Garvey's eyes.

"Telephone down for another spot of soda, my dear chap," the Colonel begged him after the fifth round. In this round Cooney's right optic was realistically described by the announcer as bearing a startling resemblance to an oyster with high blood pressure.

"I'm having a double rye," Mr. Garvey informed him thickly. He started recklessly for the array of bottles and glasses. He was busy pouring when the seventh round began. In the middle of the operation he replaced both the bottle and the glass on the table and started unsteadily for the bedroom. Cooney was down. He was up at the count of five, however, but Mr. Garvey did not stop. He went through the darkened room and snapped on the lights in the bathroom. For several minutes he ran cold water on his wrists. Then he sprinkled some of the Colonel's imported toilet water on his forehead and eyelids.

Back in the bedroom he sat down on the edge of the far bed and lit a cigarette. He wondered how many years a first offender got under the Defrauding-an-Innkeeper Act.

Time has a hackneyed habit of standing still in moments of great mental stress. Mr. Garvey had no idea how long he sat there on the bed, before the door leading into the parlor was suddenly flung open to flood his harassed, weary eyes with a blaze of golden radiance.

"Garvey! My dear boy! Where are you? Ha. Come out! Come out immediately! Your judgment has been vindicated! Ha. Completely! Cooney retains his title!"

Garvey made him out finally. The Colonel stood on the threshold. The light from behind caught the triumphant ends of his mustaches and danced gleefully on his huge bald pate.

"What—" he managed to say before the Colonel was off again.

"In the eleventh round, my dear boy. Ha. A miracle! Exactly. Without a doubt. The—the Pole had battered him to a—hum—pulp. Ha. Quite. But our boy did not give up. No! No! The—the typical American spirit. He kept boring in. And then a lucky punch! A—a truly lethal affair. Come out, my dear fellow. Our—our guests wish to congratulate you on your—hum—acumen."

The world rolled gently off Mr. Garvey's chest. He stood up. He tugged his red-and-green foulard out from under his ear, whither it had slipped during his stay in the bathroom.

"I told you Cooney would cut him to pieces," he said for the third time since dinner.

But he still was not done with the observation. Two hours later, when the parlor of Suite 902 was a quiet shambles of empty bottles, sandwich fragments, ashes, and scattered poker chips, he perched himself on the arm of one of the room's easy chairs and repeated it again.

The Colonel was seated at the big table in the center of the room, busy with pencil and paper as he hummed another of his favorite tunes. It was *The Letter Edged in Black*.

For a moment Mr. Garvey digressed. "How much?" he inquired eagerly.

The Colonel sat back in his chair and removed the heavy horn-rimmed reading glasses which he had adjusted at the start of his bookkeeping.

"After—hah—adequate allowance for my poker losses of recent weeks and setting aside all moneys due and owing our hostel," he reported with a broad smile, "I find that we are in the black to the extent of three hundred and fifteen dollars and—hum—sixty-five cents. Ha. Three hundred and fifteen dollars. Not bad, eh? By the way, did you notice how the other guests seemed to—hah—regard the gallant Captain with marked disfavor after the fight?"

Mr. Garvey's nod started out to be gay

enough, but before it could flower fully it became slightly frostbitten.

"Suppose Cooney had lost?" he inquired with a shiver.

The Colonel had risen from his bookkeeping labors to mix himself a nightcap. His huge head twisted benignly at the question.

"Eh? Then I wouldn't have bet on him, my dear boy. I would have maneuvered the situation so that my money would have been on Peyskisk. Ha. Exactly. Perhaps by offering odds which would have appealed to my—hum—sporting guests. Or, if that failed, I had in mind suggesting that each of us put one hundred dollars into a pool. The money to go to the man picking the winning round. Or then I might have recouped our battered fortunes by betting them I could name the round in which the fight would end. Ha. I fancy this would have got me some—hum—juicy odds."

Mr. Garvey slid down into the easy chair.

"Am I gazing at a seventh son of a seventh son?" he demanded incredulously. "Am I looking at Swami Flack in the flesh? Were those hiccups of yours really phonies? Are you standing there telling me in all sobriety that you knew Cooney was going to win that fight in the eleventh round by a lucky punch?"

The old gentleman stirred his drink thoughtfully. He looked like a sporting peer after a hard day at Ascot. "Put it this way, my dear boy," he said blandly: "I did not know Cooney was going to win the fight—in advance. Ha. No. No. But I did know that he had won the fight in the eleventh round—before I made any wagers."

Mr. Garvey thought of something. "That telephone call! Parker!"

The Colonel took a long, appreciative pull at his nightcap.

"Eddie, the bell captain," he corrected the younger man softly. "He told me it was Cooney."

"But that couldn't be," said Mr. Garvey. "The—the fight didn't go on until eleven o'clock."

The Colonel brushed the golden drops from his mustaches. His watery eyes twinkled merrily. "Earlier in the evening," he rumbled benignly, "you called me a confidence man. Ha. Eh? Exactly. I—I protested that I lived by my wits. The two aren't necessarily synonymous. This evening—my little party—is a case in point. I arranged it after I noticed by the paper that this fight was being carried by the local radio station, starting at eleven o'clock. Ha. Exactly. It struck me that this was rather a late hour for a—hum—bout of this importance."

"A difference of time could account for that," Mr. Garvey pointed out.

"It could, but it didn't. I took the trouble to call up the radio station and inquire. I was informed that because of prior commercial commitments the station could not carry the fight at ten o'clock—when it actually occurred. So they were carrying an electrical transcription of the entire affair, exactly as it occurred, at eleven o'clock. Ha. Exactly. A rebroadcast."

A quick grin broke like a breaker over Mr. Garvey's tanned face. "That was why you were so particular about the time I turned the radio on. If we had caught the first minutes of the broadcast, we—your guests would have realized that it was a transcription and—and—" He paused. "I suppose you cut off the closing announcement too?"

"Exactly."

Mr. Garvey stood up. His ulcers had disappeared.

"Clever!" he said admiringly. "And—and my natural anxiety made it look like the McCoy, didn't it?" he added with thoughtful modesty.

"A great job, my dear boy," the Colonel agreed, and Mr. Garvey's suddenly suspicious eyes found only guileless enthusiasm in the crimson face behind the words. "Splendid. Ha. Quite. But perhaps it didn't work quite the way I've just described it at all."

The younger man sat down suddenly. "I—I don't get you."

"Ask yourself these two questions," the old gentleman suggested solicitously: "Wouldn't it have been rather—hum—dangerous for me to assume that a group of gamblers—to—hah—

name them gently—would not know the exact time of a big-time bout?"

"Lots of people don't stop to think about things they read in the paper," Mr. Garvey pointed out. "I didn't." Then he added hastily, "What's the second question?"

"Didn't it strike you that the boys were a bit—hah—avid to get their money down on Peyskisk?"

"That was Calder. He's a smart cooky. You said so yourself. They followed his lead."

"Exactly."

Mr. Garvey lit a cigarette. He blew smoke at his partner. "So what?"

The Colonel beamed over his fondly clasped nightcap. Then he sat down and crossed his plump knees tenderly. "Eh? Oh. So I took out some insurance, my dear boy. Ha. Just in case. Or I protected my exposed flank, as they say in—hah—military circles."

"I get my military news over the radio," Mr. Garvey pointed out sourly.

Colonel Humphrey Flack ignored both the acid and the observation. "Put yourself in the wily, quick-thinking Captain's shoes," he urged gently. "A slightly—hah—inebriated, innocent old gentleman of means with whom he has been playing cards—at a profit—is leaving town. At a farewell party given by this old gentleman a radio happens to be turned on about eleven o'clock, just in time to catch the opening minutes of the first round of a prize fight. The wily Captain, being a follower of such things, knows the fight really started at ten o'clock, hence this must be a rebroadcast. Luckily, this fact is not apparent, because the radio was not tuned in when the opening announcement was made. Ha. Quite. Now! Even as the wily Captain is figuring on how to turn this situation to his financial—hum—advantage, the old gentleman hands him the idea on a platter—with a convincing hiccup."

"The bet?"

"Right. So what happens? The Captain saunters unobtrusively in the direction of the bathroom. But his real destination is the telephone in the bedroom. The radio will cover his—er-r—quick, guarded inquiry. A moment later he emerges. He offers to bet on the man whom he has just been told has won the fight. Exactly. Peyskisk! He is betting on a sure thing. He can't lose. The fight is over. Ha. Hum. A wink is as good as a word to his friends. Ha. Indubitably. They hasten to—hah—get in their wagers."

"The guy he telephoned gave him the wrong boy." Mr. Garvey's dark head nodded understandingly. Then he frowned. "But it still doesn't add up," he protested plaintively. "How could you be sure Calder would get the wrong boy? How could you control his call? He might have called some pal or a newspaper office or a dozen different gambling joints?"

The Colonel finished his nightcap and arose. He pulled out his stomach watch and stared at it.

"Nearly two o'clock, my dear chap. And we must be up and away to the sun-drenched Southland in the morning. . . . Eh? Oh, the telephone call, of course. It was very simple. Elementary. I had stressed the fact that Eddie, the bell captain, had a substantial wager on the fight, that he was a rabid boxing enthusiast. Remember? To be sure. Calder had no time to waste. The sucker might cool off while he was waiting around for a number. Ha. Then there was always the danger that if he did too much talking he might be overheard. Against all this was the simple, quick, and direct path! Pick up the telephone. Ask for the bell captain. Inquire about the fight. A few seconds and the whole thing was over. It was just the bait for a wily captain."

The Colonel lowered his eyes modestly.

"And of course with Eddie having it in for the guy anyway and leaving to join the Marines in the morning—"

Mr. Garvey grinned. Then he thought of something else. "What gave you the idea, in the first place?"

The Colonel looked longingly at the bottle-covered table, sighed and turned resolutely toward the bedroom. "I—I was living in the past, my dear boy," he chuckled from the threshold. "Ha. Just so. Remember our talking about the old wire racket earlier in the evening? How the—er-r—confidence man ensnared his victim by pretending to get advance notice of racing results. Ha. I see you do. Well, I just got to wondering how one of the wonders of—hum—modern science—like radio, for instance—might be adapted to this be-whiskered gyp of the Gay Nineties—in reverse, so to speak."

Villain: Dr. B. Edward Loxley

Footsteps of Fear

VINCENT STARRETT

CHARLES VINCENT EMERSON STARRETT (1886–1974), one of the greatest bibliophiles in the history of the American book world, produced innumerable essays, biographical works, critical studies, and bibliographical pieces on a wide range of authors, all while managing the "Books Alive" column for the *Chicago Tribune* for many years. His autobiography, *Born in a Bookshop* (1965), should be required reading for bibliophiles of all ages.

He also wrote numerous mystery short stories and several detective novels, including *Murder on "B" Deck* (1929), *Dead Man Inside* (1931), and *The End of Mr. Garment* (1932). His 1934 short story, "Recipe for Murder," was expanded to the full-length novel *The Great Hotel Murder* (1935), which was the basis for the film of the same title and released the same year; it starred Edmund Lowe and Victor McLaglen.

Few would argue that Starrett's most outstanding achievements were his writings about Sherlock Holmes, most notably *The Private Life of Sherlock Holmes* (1933) and "The Unique 'Hamlet,'" described by Sherlockians for decades as the best pastiche ever written.

A charming story involves his young daughter, who offered the best tombstone inscription for anyone who is a Dofob—Eugene Field's useful word for a "damned old fool over books"—as Starrett admitted to being. When a friend called at his home, Starrett's daughter answered the door and told the visitor that her father was "upstairs, playing with his books."

"Footsteps of Fear" was originally published in the April 1920 issue of *Black Mask*—the magazine's first issue. It was first collected in Starrett's *The Quick and the Dead* (Sauk City, Wisconsin, Arkham House, 1965).

FOOTSTEPS OF FEAR

Vincent Starrett

DR. B. EDWARD LOXLEY (jocularly called "Bedward" by the gossip columnists), the wife-murderer for whom hundreds of police had been scouring the city for three weeks, sat quietly at his desk in the great Merchandise Exchange reading his morning mail. The frosted glass door beyond his outer office read simply *William Drayham, Rare Books. Hours by Appointment.* After three weeks of security he was beginning to feel complacent. For three weeks he had not left his hiding place and he had no intention of leaving it immediately, except feet first.

It had all been thought out beforehand. The office had been rented a month before the murder of Lora Loxley, and he had quietly taken possession and begun his new personality buildup as William Drayham. He had been accepted by his neighbors in the sixth floor corridor. The elevator starter was getting to know him. He breakfasted, lunched, and dined at the several restaurants in the building, was shaved by a favorite barber, and was—he had every reason to believe—an accepted fixture. His neighbors were inoffensive, unimaginative workers who did not question his identity, and the words *Rare Books* on the door were formidable enough to frighten away casual visitors.

Lora Loxley, murdered by suffocation, had long been buried and even the newspapers were beginning to minimize the sensational story. The feeling was growing that Loxley, himself, also might have been murdered and a desultory search for his body continued when the police had nothing better to occupy them. As his window overlooked the river where, in addition to the normal traffic, police boats occasionally plied, he was enabled to watch their activities with amused appreciation of their effort. He had now spent two lonely Sundays watching the holiday traffic with a pair of binoculars, waiting for any active renewal of police attention. He was on excellent terms with the watchmen in his part of the building, who were accustomed to seeing him around at unlikely hours.

The Merchandise Exchange was a city within a city. It contained everything he needed—restaurants, laundries, barbershops, tobacconists, dentists, news stands, banking facilities, a gymnasium, even a postal station. He was known by name in the restaurants and barbershops. He bought all the newspapers. Occasionally he dictated a letter to a public stenographer, ordering or rejecting books. As William Drayham he had a sufficient banking account downstairs for his immediate needs. The rest of his wealth, in cash, was in Paris with Gloria.

His principal bogies had been watchmen and cleaning women. He had little fear, however, of the cleaning women, a friendly trio who liked candy and who readily agreed to visit his office while he was having a late dinner. His domestic arrangements were simple. He slept on a couch in his inner office, which held also a vault to which he could retire in an emergency. To date there had been no emergency.

Dr. Loxley pushed the mail aside impatiently. Too early perhaps to expect a response to the little ad he was running in a Sunday book supplement. But not too early for the coffee that Miss Marivole Boggs served at all hours. What luck to have found so admirable a creature in the same corridor, and even in the same line. Rare books and antiques went very well together. She had been responsible for a number of his infrequent customers. He glanced at his expensive wristwatch and left William Drayham's rare books behind him without a pang.

M. Boggs, Antiques, as she described herself on the show window of her small shop at the end of the corridor, looked up at his entrance.

"Hello," she said. "I was hoping you would come in."

"I couldn't miss," he said. His brown eyes took in the familiar room, resting for a moment on the suit of antique armor that dominated one corner of the shop and the Spanish chest that was Miss Boggs's pride and joy. "Well, I see nobody has bought either of them yet." It was one of their standing jokes that some day, when the rare book business was better, he would write a check for them himself.

As she poured his coffee she said, "The newspaper stories about that doctor are getting shorter every day. I'm beginning to believe he really *was* murdered."

They often discussed the missing Dr. Loxley, as indeed the whole city was doing. At first it had been Miss Boggs's idea that the "society doctor" had murdered his wife over some glamorous patient who was now living in sin with him somewhere on the Riviera.

Dr. Loxley had thought not. "Too romantic, Boggs. I still think he's in the river or somewhere on his way to the Gulf of Mexico. That scarf they found on the river banks looks like it."

"Anyway, the police seem to have stopped looking," said M. Boggs.

"Anyway, this is good coffee, Boggs. I hope you'll leave me the recipe. Do you still plan to leave this month?"

"At once," she said. "I'm flying to New York tomorrow, if I can get away. I want to be in London for the Exhibition; then on to Paris, Rome, Switzerland, and what have you. I'm enormously relieved that you'll be here to keep an eye on things, Bill. Coffee at all hours, eh?"

"Morning, noon, and night," he agreed, rising to leave. Her change of plan had startled him for a moment; but he was quick enough to see an advantage in it for himself. "Never fear, I'll be here waiting for you when you return."

Strolling back to his own shop, humming a jaunty air, he became aware of a man leaving the doorway of the office directly opposite his own. Something about the man's carriage seemed familiar. He was turning toward the elevators and walking fast. In an instant they would meet.

And suddenly Dr. Loxley realized that the man was, indeed, familiar. He was his own brother-in-law, Laurence Bridewell.

His first instinct was to turn and flee, his second to turn back to *M. Boggs, Antiques.* His final decision, made in a split second, was to see the encounter through. His disguise had fooled better men than Larry Bridewell, although none who knew him better. With his neat little beard and moustache gone, and his blue eyes transformed by brown contact lenses, he was another man. After an appalling moment of indecision, he fumbled for a cigarette, realizing that after three weeks of complacent safety, he was about to face a supreme test.

He tried and failed to light the cigarette. . . . Then they were face to face, looking at each other as men do in passing, and the test was over.

Or was it? Bridewell continued on his way to the elevators, walking fast, and Loxley stumbled to his own door.

Dared he look back? Had Bridewell turned to look back at *him*? Moving casually, he stole a glance along the corridor. There was no doubt about it—Larry was looking back, too. Perhaps he had merely been troubled by a fancied resemblance. . . .

Dr. Loxley made some difficulty about opening his own door, and just before he closed it, it occurred to him to look at the name on the door of the office from which his brother-in-law had emerged. Actually he knew very well what he would find there: *Jackson & Fortworth, Attorneys at Law.* And below, the significant word *Investigations.*

He tried to take himself in hand and was annoyed to find himself shaking. Experimentally he ventured a little drink to see what it would do for him. It helped considerably. But the whole incident haunted him and gave him a bad night. In the morning, however, his fears had vanished. He was his confident self again until, a few hours later, a second incident shook his nerve. Returning from the cigar stand in the lobby he had to pass the De Luxe Dog Salon in one of the street level corridors and paused, as he had often done before, to look in at the windows at the fashionable dogs in process of being barbered, an amusing spectacle. But as he turned away an appalling thing happened.

A well-dressed woman was approaching the salon with a sprightly French poodle on a leash. She looked familiar. God's teeth! She *was* familiar, and so was the dog. She was Mrs. Montgomery Hyde, no less, an old patient. His heart seemed to stop beating. Would she recognize him?

It was the dog that recognized him. With a yelp of joy the poodle jerked the leash from the woman's hand and flung himself rapturously against the doctor's legs.

With an effort Loxley recovered his balance and somehow recovered his poise. It was his worst moment to date. Automatically he disengaged himself from the poodle's embrace and pulled the black ears.

"There, there fellow," he said to the excited animal in a voice that he hoped was not his own. "I beg your pardon, Madam. Your dog appears to have made a mistake."

To his intense relief, Mrs. Montgomery Hyde agreed.

"Do forgive Toto's impulsiveness," she begged, snatching up the leash. "He loves everybody."

Dr. Loxley left the scene in almost a hurry. She had not recognized him! It seemed to him a miracle, but again he was annoyed to find himself shaking. And yet, could it not be a good omen? If Mrs. Hyde and his own brother-in-law had failed to recognize him, what was there to fear? Immediately he began to feel better. But when he had returned to his office William Drayham again treated himself to a stiff drink.

In a moment of alert intelligence he realized that for three weeks he had been too complacent. His meeting with Mrs. Hyde had taught him something that was important to remember. He had almost spoken her name. In his first moment of panic he might well have betrayed himself. If it was important for him not to be recognized, it was equally important that *he* must not recognize someone by accident.

It was clear to him that this cat-and-mouse existence could not go on indefinitely. He must remain in hiding only until it was safe for him to emerge and get out of the country. Then William Drayham would ostentatiously pack his books and remove to New York. After that, the world was wide.

For several days the chastened doctor lived cautiously, visiting *M. Boggs, Antiques* at intervals for coffee and to admire the suit of armor and the Spanish chest, which continued to fascinate him. He had promised Boggs, now on her travels, not to cut the price on either.

Twice, returning from the antique shop, again he had caught a glimpse of his brother-in-law entering the law office of Jackson & Fortworth, and had hastened to lock himself in his own quarters before Larry could emerge. What the devil did the fellow want with a firm of investigators anyway?

The visit of Jackson, the lawyer, to the bookshop one morning took him by surprise or he might have locked the door.

"I've been intending to look in on you for some time, Mr. Drayham," said the lawyer cordially. "I'm Jackson, just across from you. Rare books have always interested me. Mind if I look around?"

Loxley rose from his chair abruptly, knocking a book from his desk to the floor. An icy fear had entered his heart. Was this *it*, at last, he wondered.

He shook hands effusively. "Glad to know you, Mr. Jackson. Sure, look around. Is there anything I can show you?"

But Jackson was already looking around. When he had finished he strolled to the window. "Nice view of the river you have," he said appreciatively. "My windows all look out on a court." He strolled to the door. "Just wanted to meet you. I'll come in again when I have more time."

"Any time," said Loxley with perfunctory courtesy.

Dr. Loxley sat down at his desk and reached for the lower drawer. Another little drink wouldn't hurt him. What had the fellow really wanted? What had he hoped to find? Or was he really one of the many idiots who collected books?

One thing at last was clear. Any day now he might have to leave the building and the city. If he was suspected, the blow would fall swiftly. At any minute the door might open again, and perhaps Jackson would not be alone. Why not get the hell out of this trap immediately? What was there to stop him? His stock—three hundred volumes of junk bought at a storage house—could be left behind if necessary.

What stopped him was Gloria's cable from Paris: "Trouble here. Phoning Friday night."

This was Thursday. Whatever else, he had to wait for Gloria's call. His hand moved toward the lower drawer, then was withdrawn. Coffee, not whiskey, was what he needed; and after luncheon he spent most of the afternoon with M. Boggs's weird collection of antiques. There, he had a fair view of Jackson's door, and was not himself conspicuous. If Larry Bridewell was among the lawyer's visitors, Loxley did not see him.

Exploring the antique shop he paused, as always to admire its two star exhibits, the almost frightening suit of armor and the massive Spanish chest. In a pinch, either would do as a hiding place—if there were time to hide.

That evening he was startled to find his picture in the paper again. The familiar face of Dr. B. Edward Loxley as he had looked with the neat little beard and moustache before he murdered his wife. It appeared that he had been arrested by an alert Seattle policeman, but had denied his identity.

Dr. Loxley drew a long breath of relief. After all, perhaps he was still safe. But what could Gloria have to say to him that required a call from Paris? Bad news of some kind. Bad for somebody.

In spite of his new fears he hated to leave the building that had been his refuge. It had been his hope to live there indefinitely, undetected; never again to venture into the streets until Dr. Loxley was as forgotten as Dr. Crippen.

Again he slept off his fears and spent an uninterrupted morning with his view and newspapers. He was beginning to feel almost at ease again, indeed, when the insufferable Jackson knocked on his locked door and called a hearty greeting. There was somebody with him. Through the frosted pane the shadowy outline of another man was visible.

"May we come in?" asked the lawyer. "I've got a couple of friends here who want to meet you."

Loxley rose uncertainly to his feet and moved to the door. So it *had* come at last! He had been right about his damned brother-in-law and this sneaking lawyer. This is *it*! And suddenly he knew what he had to do.

He unlocked and threw open the door. "Come in, gentlemen," he said without emotion. "What can I do for you?"

Jackson was beaming. "These are my friends,

Sergeants Coughlin and Ripkin, from Headquarters. They hope you will come quietly." He laughed heartily at his own witticism.

"Come in, gentlemen, and sit down." Loxley forced a smile. He seated himself at his desk, stamped and addressed an envelope, and stood up. "I was just going to the mail chute with an important letter. I'll be back in a couple of minutes."

"Sure," said the two cops genially. "Take your time."

Dr. Loxley closed the outer door behind him and almost ran for *M. Boggs, Antiques.* As he locked the antique shop door he was relieved to see the corridor was still empty. They would follow him, of course. Every office in the building would be searched, probably this one first.

It *had* to be the chest!

It stood open as always, and he squeezed down inside—an uncomfortable fit—then lowered the heavy lid until only a thin crack remained for air. Faintly now he could hear footsteps in the corridor. He drew a deep breath and closed the lid.

There was a sharp *click*, then only intense darkness and suffocating silence. . . .

———

Twenty minutes later Sergeant Ripkin said to his partner, "Wonder what's keeping that guy. We've still got sixty tickets to sell, Pete."

"Oh, leave them with me," said Jackson. "I'll see that you get your money. Drayham's a good fellow."

The two policemen, who had been hoping to dispose of a block of tickets for a benefit ball game, departed leisurely.

The disappearance of William Drayham, a "rare book dealer" in the Merchandise Exchange, attracted less attention than that of Dr. B. Edward Loxley; but for a few days it was a mild sensation.

Returning from Europe, a month later, M. Boggs wondered idly when Bill would drop in for a cup of coffee. He had told her he would be here when she returned.

She puttered happily among her treasures. Some fool, she noted, had automatically locked the chest by closing it. One of these days she'd have to unlock it and raise the lid. . . .

Rogue: Sophie Lang

The Signed Masterpiece

FREDERICK IRVING ANDERSON

FREDERICK IRVING ANDERSON (1877–1947), the creator of Sophie Lang, the charming and creative jewel thief, has been largely forgotten by modern readers, having produced two books about farming and only three books of mystery and crime; many additional stories were published only in magazines, mainly *The Saturday Evening Post*, and never collected in book form.

Perhaps his best-known character is the delightful young woman who appeared in the single volume *The Notorious Sophie Lang* (1925), a thief of such daring and unmatched success that she is often regarded as a legend who doesn't actually exist. Much of Sophie Lang's fame derives from a series of 1930s Paramount films recounting her adventures. She was portrayed by Gertrude Michael in all three.

In *The Notorious Sophie Lang* (1934), the police use a French thief to capture her, but she and the thief fall in love and escape. In *The Return of Sophie Lang* (1936), which also starred Ray Milland, the reformed adventuress is on an ocean liner traveling to the United States with her elderly benefactress when she recognizes a "distinguished" fellow passenger; he is actually a jewel thief planning to involve Sophie in the disappearance of a diamond on which he has set his sights. The final film in the series, *Sophie Lang Goes West* (1937), which also stars Lee Bowman and Buster Crabbe, recounts Lang's predicament when she evades the police by boarding a train to California. It is not long before she becomes involved with fellow travelers, including a brash but charming Hollywood press agent and a desperate sultan who hopes the valuable gem he is carrying will be stolen. Curiously, although the films had some success, the only volume of Sophie's adventures was never published in America.

Anderson's other two mystery collections were *Adventures of the Infallible Godahl* (1914) and *The Book of Murder* (1930), selected by Ellery Queen as one of the 106 greatest collections of mystery stories ever published. Deputy Parr, who is outwitted by Godahl in one book and Sophie Lang in another, again has his hands full with assorted crooks in the third and last of Anderson's fiction works.

"The Signed Masterpiece" was first published in the *McClure's* June/July 1921 issue; it was first collected in *The Notorious Sophie Lang* (London, Heinemann, 1925).

THE SIGNED MASTERPIECE

Frederick Irving Anderson

NUMBER 142, on the south side of the street, was an English basement dwelling of that commodious Van Bibber era of yesterday when Manhattan was still a native island and its inhabitants retained elbow room and a sense of substantial living. Most of the town had taken the hint and moved north, but Number 142 and a few other stalwarts with shiny plate-glass windows, scoured doorsteps and pull-bells still held their ground, with supercilious apartment houses and gilt hotels jostling them on all sides.

Number 142 was occupied by the widow of Amos P. Huntington. The departed, a drab, inoffensive little person, had only once achieved newspaper notoriety, when he blew himself into eternity while compounding synthetic rubber. The relict was a little Dresden china affair; as evidence of her quality she drove a smart plum-coloured brougham drawn by a smarter pair of roached hackneys of a water too luxurious for this day and age; on the box sat a coachman and footman in plum-colour, two stern middle-aged males, close-shaven and showing that curious prison pallor acquired by upper servants who spend most of their days in the semi-obscurity of old-fashioned basements.

This former fashionable section had begun its migration north some years before. One by one the brownstone residences on the north side that faced Number 142 and its few companions had been converted into red-brick stables with sharp roofs, cottage windows, and wide doorways. For a brief period the *ancien régime* had inhaled the fumes of ammonia and horse liniment and witnessed the capers of a superior class of equines that were led off to the Park afternoons by cockney grooms, to rack and amble for the benefit of the digestions of over-fed masters and mistresses.

Then the superior horses disappeared and in their stead came superior artists who raised north lights over the old hay-lofts, filled the air with the odours of turpentine and wet clay, and for the most part dined unromantically in a pastry-shop around the corner. Then the city, like a rank forest encroaching on a forsaken meadow, wiped the artists and their studios out of the picture, and set up in their place unsightly garages and machine shops for sick motors. The sunny side of the street became slippery with grease from leaky oil pans, the air thick with the odour of gas and rubber. At the curb at all hours of the day and far into the night diseased insides of broken-down automobiles strewed the sidewalks, while the begrimed mechanics tinkered and tested. Through all these vicissitudes the old guard hung on grimly, Number 142 and its companions, by protest, seeming to grow more immaculate. Mrs. Huntington, in addition to these aggressions on her domestic peace, had suffered the further indignity of being dragged from her sheltered grief into open court by the insurance guarantors of her departed husband, who maintained that anyone so temerarious as to tamper with synthetic rubber could have but one motive—suicide. Twice the little widow had won the sympathy of the jury, who in two suits had awarded her the full amount of her claim, a quarter of a million dollars.

Directly across the street, in Number 143, was a machine shop which in grime, odour, and noisy clamour differed in no respects from its neighbours. An observant person might have noted, with some stirring of curiosity, that all of its mechanics were young, stood six feet, and weighed 185 pounds. Unknown and unsuspected, Number 143 was of the police; it was one of that series of carefully masked deadfalls which that arch man-hunter, Deputy Parr of Headquarters, had planted in unexpected corners throughout the city. Crime is sporadic; nevertheless it is also regional and vocational. Here through his minions he eavesdropped on the night-birds indigenous to Automobile Alley. In Broad Street he maintained a bucket shop, manned with mammoth messenger boys and clerks; in Maiden Lane a platinum refinery, whose wrinkled old alchemist could tell him at a moment's notice the chemical signature of any batch of platinum in existence; in Fourth Avenue he had a two-by-four office among the brokers of raw silk, a commodity that attracts thieves as honey does flies; and in Central Park West he conducted, under an able lieutenant, a spook parlour for table-tilting and slate-writing, where occasionally a wire got through from the other shore. Many a poor wight languishing behind bars wondered, but would never know, how he had come so summarily to his doom. It was simple enough, merely getting acquainted and being neighbourly.

At ten of an early winter morning a car of some consequence came to a jerking, sputtering stop, sighed, and died at the curb in front of Number 142. The driver, a man of six feet, weighing 185 pounds, got down, opened the hood, and stood regarding his ailing motor with the forlorn look of a medico whose patient had gone beyond his skill. A red-headed mechanic, six feet of height, 185 pounds of weight, came out. He evinced sympathetic interest and put his head under the hood.

"The Chief," said the driver, bending down and speaking in the mechanic's ear, "wants a report on Number 142."

The mechanic re-connected a high-tension wire with a spark plug terminal, thus restoring the consequential motor to its full faculties, should an emergency arise. He tore a blue ticket in two along the line of perforation, handed one half to the driver with the remark, "No tickee—no washee!" and tied the other half by a stout cord to the windshield of the automobile. The chauffeur strolled away to a backroom haunt of chauffeurs and mechanics, and whiled away a few hours getting acquainted. The mechanic pretended to resume tinkering, meantime studying out of the tail of his eye that respectable domicile opposite, Number 142, vaguely speculating on what turn of the weathercock had brought the Dresden china widow under the surveillance of the police.

An hour later Mrs. Amos P. Huntington descended the steps and entered her brougham. She had small feet encased in trim high boots which she displayed by a modishly short skirt; her complexion was very white, her eyes hazel, and her hair of that peculiar shade of mahogany which can be retained only by unremitting attention; she was in full mourning, of a rich correctness that suggested one of those fashionable specialty shops in the next block just off the avenue which devote themselves exclusively to the millinery of grief. Her footman wrapped her in moleskin and mounted the box; her mincing pair moved off in perfect step as if in time to the tinkle of some antique gavotte. At this moment the red-headed mechanic, scratching his auburn thatch with a grim set of fingers, seemed to come to the decision that a trial run was necessary. He started his hypochondriac motor and rolled along in the wake of the plum-coloured brougham, bending a sympathetic ear to catch some symptomatic murmur from the engine.

At Columbus Circle, that eternal whirligig of traffic, the traffic signal fell against the plum-coloured brougham and the horses came to a stop, snorting motors on all sides instantly piling up with the fecundity of a log jam. A man in a brown derby on the sidewalk had his attention arrested by the flapping of the blue ticket of the motor behind the brougham. He halted at the curb, and casually catching the eye of the red-headed mechanic, he took off his brown derby, though it was freezing weather, and mopped his forehead. The red-headed mechanic answered by blowing his nose in a red bandana; and turning, he stared stupidly at the plum-coloured brougham. The traffic sluice was opened, the jam started to move; and the red-headed mechanic now lost interest in the plum-coloured brougham. He turned east and in ten minutes was back at his machine shop.

"Does anyone follow, William?" asked the Dresden china widow in her speaking-tube.

"No, ma'am," responded William the footman, speaking out of the corner of his mouth, without moving his lips, into the receiver at his shoulder. "There was one," he added encouragingly. "The mechanic opposite—but he turned off."

Mrs. Huntington did not permit herself to be lulled by a sense of security. For a long period the gracious lady of Number 142 had never driven out without inquiring sooner or later, "Does anyone follow, William?" It might have intimated a vanity or a fear. There had been occasions which seemed to the capable William to hold forth a promise. But these promises were never fulfilled. Always the particular person or vehicle that had attracted the suspicious scrutiny of William would be lost in the ceaseless traffic of the city streets, much as the red-headed mechanic, who had momentarily aroused William's interest, was now lost.

That afternoon two studious young men called at Number 142 to test the electric meter. This task, having to do with slide rules and logarithmic calculations and shiny instruments, was spread out on the basement stairway with the interested servants watching now and then, and obligingly handing the two scientists, by request, tools whose nickel-plated surfaces had been especially prepared for finger-prints. The next day telephone linemen asked for and received permission to pass through the house to the roof to untangle some wires. An inspector for the Water Department, a most entertaining fellow, looked over the taps for leaks. Some dispute having arisen in an obscure quarter as to the encroachment on the building line of this row of houses, a young man must enter and open every window from the inside, to measure the protruding sills with a rule. Once when he was leaning far out of the drawing-room window he asked politely over his shoulder would Mrs. Huntington please pass him his magnifying glass, which the little widow did graciously, picking it up quite unconsciously in the hand which held her lace handkerchief. In departing he offered her his fountain pen to sign his call slip, but not seeing his gesture, she used her own pen instead. There were other callers at the basement door, all civil, and, to the outward eye at least, simple. By the end of the week a complete dossier of Number 142 was in the hands of Mr. Parr. It had to do with the mistress and her *ménage*, down to microscopic details. If she had nursed a fancied sense of sanctified privacy, she must have been horror-stricken to know how easy it had been for Parr's camera-eyed sleuths to turn Number 142 inside out and upside down. In the preparation of the report, in only one point had they failed—they carried away nothing bearing the imprint of the pink finger-tips of the pathetic widow herself, although her household had been most obliging in this respect. The magnifying glass, when developed in Centre Street Headquarters, yielded only a hazy replica of her dainty kerchief.

II

"I know it is the fashion," said Deputy Parr, settling himself in his favourite elbow-chair by Oliver Armiston's desk, "to assign us cops the rôle of solid ivory in modern detective drama. A thick cop always makes a hit!" He shot a venomous gleam at Oliver, who, running his fingers through his single grey lock, looked up from his work but did not deign to reply. "Some bright young man," went on Mr. Parr ponderously, "might make a name for himself by endowing one of us with a glimmer of brains." He selected a cigar for himself from the paste-board box by Oliver's elbow. "I realize," he said, nipping off the tip with his finger-nails, "that there is a popular prejudice against it. But it could be done—it could be done." He struck a match with a single magic twist in the air, applied the light, and drew a few meditative puffs, eyeing Oliver through half-closed lids.

Armiston, the extinct author, was merely another phase of Deputy Parr's amazing versatility. For the most part Parr practised logic, not intuition. Through long experience of the habits and resorts of the creatures he hunted, he set his traps in what he knew to be good game country. Then he retired to wait for some prowling creature to spring them. But occasionally his traps yawned empty, not so much as the snap of a dry twig rewarded his longest vigil along well-proved runways. Then, like his prototype, the savage hunter, Parr would withdraw stealthily to consult his Medicine. Armiston occupied this position. Armiston had been a weaver of tall tales, thrillers. On one occasion he had been too realistic; a cunning thief had actually dramatized Oliver's fiction as fact, with murder as its outcome. The ensuing sensation had driven the hectic author into retirement. Here the argus-eyed Deputy found him. If fiction could be done into fact, then why not fact into fiction? So reasoned the deputy of police.

His method was direct but subtle. An insoluble mystery or a hesitating *dénouement* aroused the dormant faculties of the extinct author as the clang of a gong revives the pensioned fire horse. Parr would dress the stage for Oliver with characters and scenery, ring up the curtain on a frozen plot—and in his most ingratiating manner invite Armiston to "go to it." The results had occasionally been startling. They always, to the matter-of-fact policeman, bordered on the mystic. Oliver's imagination, once touched off, had an uncanny fecundity.

Now the deputy, with the sigh of too much girth, picked up his left foot encased in a Number 12 boot, and deposited it on his right knee; he tapped the sole significantly, it was a new sole, a very slab of a sole, spiked into place, designed for wear, not stealth.

"It cost me two seventy-five," he said lugubriously. "It used to cost fifty cents. Even the price of detecting crime has gone up. Sole leather!" he exclaimed with some vehemence, "that's what achieves results in my business. Whenever I take on a new man, I look at his feet, not his head."

He paused. Oliver by continued silence seemed to reserve judgment.

"As a matter of fact," said Parr confidentially, "we don't detect crime. Crime detects itself."

"It's too bad the perpetrators aren't so obliging," put in Oliver.

"But, my dear fellow, they are! That's just the point!" said Parr expansively.

"They detect themselves?"

"Oh, absolutely, inevitably. That is—eventually. The element of time enters, of course. We simply wait," explained the policeman blandly. "Sooner or later every crook revisits his usual haunts. I have a man sitting on the doorstep waiting for him." Parr smiled childishly.

"You must admit it, it requires some intelligence on your part to pick the right doorstep," said Armiston.

"Not at all!" retorted Parr. "That's the least of our worries. They give us the address!" He chuckled. Armiston returned to his ciphering. He had the hurt air of a too credulous child who has been imposed on.

"Every dog has its flea," said Parr, nodding solemnly at the fat Buddha in the corner of the study. "Every crook has his squealer. I have never known it fail, Oliver. If I ever caught up with the squeals that fall on my desk every morning I would close shop and call it a day." He added gruffly: "I haven't had a day off in twenty years. Failures? We have no failures. Unfinished business, yes. Sooner or later somebody blabs—blabs to me! That's what I am here for." He jabbed his chest fiercely. "Let me illustrate," he went on gravely. "Did you ever hear of Sophie Lang? I suspect not." He smiled oddly. "The public never hears of successful crooks. It is only when they fail, when we catch them, that they become notorious. Sophie has yet to stub her toe."

Armiston shook his head; the name meant nothing to him. But it had a tang, either in its accidental combination of letters, or in the way Parr pronounced it, that suggested inherent possibilities. The man-hunter became mellow in a reminiscent mood.

"We used to have a habit of assigning our bright young men to the Sophie Lang case. It was like sending a machinist's apprentice for a left-handed monkey wrench, or a quart of auger holes." He laughed. "So far as my bright young men are concerned, she was only a rumour."

"Oh, a legendary crook! I say, that's beautiful!" exclaimed Armiston.

"Legendary is right," assented the deputy, snapping his jaws shut. "None of us ever saw her. We knew her only by her works. When we came a cropper we'd say 'That's Sophie.' When something particularly slick was turned, Sophie again! We used to say that Sophie signed her serious work, like any other artist. Well, finally," said Parr, thrusting his hands into his pockets and stretching luxuriously, "we filed Sophie away as 'unfinished business.' "

He fixed his fierce little eyes on Armiston and waited. Oliver too waited.

"Sophie has turned up," said Parr softly.

"In bracelets?" ejaculated Armiston.

"Not yet. But soon!"

"A squeal?"

"Certainly! What else? Haven't I been telling you?"

"But who—who squealed?"

Parr assumed a hurt look.

" 'Who?' " he replied. "How the devil do I know? What the devil do I care? An anonymous letter," he grunted. "They drop on my desk like the gentle dew from heaven. If they stopped coming I'd be out of a job. As it is," he added, with a queer smile, "I am assigning myself, in my old age, to the Sophie Lang case. Do you get the humour of that, Oliver? But this time she is more than a rumour. Sophie is"—he paused for effect—"Sophie is Mrs. Huntington."

"The widow—the insurance widow?"

Parr nodded slowly, his eyes gleaming.

Armiston eased himself back in his chair and said disgustedly: "You don't believe that, Parr?"

"I am certain of it."

"I've been meeting her around for several years, among the very best people. She's—she's eminently respectable," protested Oliver.

"Sophie would be," said Parr, chuckling.

Armiston found Parr's complacency irritating.

"Is there anything definite to suggest Sophie?" he demanded.

"There is that quarter of a million dollars," chuckled Parr.

"Forget your feet, Parr," said Oliver sarcastically. Then suddenly, with sudden inspiration: "Has she signed it? You say, she does, or did."

"There isn't a flaw in her case," said Parr. "That's her usual signature. Limpid. She has beaten the insurance company twice, your sheltered little widow. They put the burden of proof on her. It wasn't any burden—for Sophie!" He guffawed. "She hasn't got the boodle yet—they are marking time for another appeal. They will only get themselves disliked, for picking on a poor helpless female. Helpless female is good!" and Parr fairly shook with mirth.

"Have you looked her up?" demanded Armiston.

"Naturally. Everybody has looked her up. Clean slate! Too clean! That's Sophie. Sophie doesn't react to the ordinary methods," the deputy said. "That's why I have come to you. I thought maybe you would like to undertake a little psychic research."

Lowering his voice instinctively with a cautious look around for eavesdroppers, the deputy explained how he had been prying into the sanctified privacy of the insurance widow during the past week—with no results. Except for the one negative fact that the pathetic widow had avoided leaving the imprints of her pink fingertips on his carefully prepared instruments, the record was blank. Parr volunteered the further information that he had just entered a new line of business—window cleaning. One of his best operatives was weekly polishing Number 142. Then there was the red-headed mechanic, and—unknown to the latter—two casual loafers haunting the block. Sophie's time was pretty well accounted for.

"What's her line, Parr?" asked Armiston when Parr finished.

"Anything. Sophie isn't squeamish," said Parr. He added with a vacant stare: "I've got a paper-weight in my museum collection with some human hair on it—and some finger-marks. I have always thought I would like to see Sophie's finger-prints."

He arose and began buttoning his coat, looking down on Armiston, smiling.

"There are a certain number of obvious things I might point out to you," he said. "But I won't. They might obstruct the psychic machinery." He had his little laugh.

There was a full silence. The fire crackled on the hearth, the grandfather clock at the head of the room was emphasizing the passage of time, with dull sedate thuds. Suddenly, as if to recall the two men, it began to intone the hour. Towards the end of its count of noon, a little gilt magpie of a clock on the mantel woke up and joined in briskly. The deputy looked at his watch; and from his watch to Armiston, whom he regarded with a pleased smile. Oliver was brushing his white lock with contemplative fingers. Helping himself to a fresh cigar, the deputy took his departure.

III

"Does anyone follow, William?"

The sheltered widow smiled almost wistfully as she whispered the inquiry through the speaking-tube.

"The mechanic from across the street, ma'am," replied William out of the corner of his mouth without moving his lips. The faithful sentry added that the red-headed mechanic was on foot this time. "Now he passes under the red cigar sign."

"Drive slowly," commanded the bereaved woman. "Don't hurry him."

But the red-headed mechanic, who of course had no suspicion that he was the object of so much thoughtfulness on the part of his widow, straightway began to lag; he discovered an interest in window shopping, particularly in those windows displaying tires of renovated rubber, of which there were many in this neighbourhood. Shortly he seemed to find what he sought, for he entered a shop—and that was the last of him for this time. But that same afternoon when she was about to turn into the avenue—at that misty hour of winter twilight when the street lamps awake with sickly blinks, and gorgeous limousines, whose interiors present charming Rodney groups of women and children, moved hub to hub in opposing tides—she picked him up again in her busybody mirror. Mrs. Huntington's pair had come to a prancing stop at the avenue corner ready for their cue to join the ceremonial procession, when the red-headed mechanic, exercising another sick car, pulled up behind, his bumper grazing milady's wheel felloes. In the mirror the cut of his jib fairly screamed his origin and purpose to the experienced eyes of the widow. Police? No doubt of it! Now, abruptly, the avenue stream broke in two at the traffic signal, opening the sluices for the cross current. William whirled his whip, his stylish pair danced on their tender toes and slowly wheeled into their place in the parade. The flutter of the motor sounded behind.

"Careful, William—pocket him!" cautioned the lady.

"He's gone, ma'am—gone 'cross town," said the disconsolate William.

Now suddenly Sophie Lang became all alert. Like a wily fox that has been idly scratching fleas waiting for the hunt to come within mouthing distance again, Sophie instinctively gathered her faculties, aware of a pleasing thrill. Figuratively she nosed the air to catch the tell-tale taint; figuratively she cocked an ear for the distant song of the pack. It had been a long wait, this last one, for the bay of the hounds, years of ennui and respectability, shared with a colourless husband. Husbands merely as such did not appeal to Sophie.

"Did you see him pass the 'office,' William?"

William had not detected anything.

Undoubtedly the "office"—she had unconsciously dropped into the argot of her craft—had been passed. It was not coincidence that her red-headed mechanic had found an errand to take him in her direction whenever she drove out these last few days; nor had it been coincidence that he lost interest in her before they had gone half a mile through the teeming streets. They were hunting her in relays! Sophie preened herself. This was genuine subtlety on the part of the police. It was her due; her dignity demanded it. She laughed softly, almost the first genuine revelation of amusement she had permitted herself since her widowhood. Instantly she closed her pretty lips over her pretty teeth again. Out of the corners of her long eyes she examined her neighbours in the procession. Among them she knew must be one tied to her heels like a noonday shadow. But the faces she looked into were blankly anonymous. She tried her bag of tricks one by one; like the wily fox, doubling, back-tracking, side-stepping, taking to earth, to water, to fallen timber. But with no results—except certainty! When finally that afternoon she returned to her domicile by devious ways, her red-headed mechanic was tinkering with still another sick motor at the curb in front of his shop; he did not even raise his eyes when her brougham drove up and drove away.

From that moment Mrs. Amos P. Huntington gradually faded out of the picture. The outer semblance of that quondam widow remained—her clothes, her speech, her aspect of grief; but beneath it all was Sophie. She watched with bead-like eyes. For several days she devoted her talents to catching her red-headed mechanic in the act of passing her bodily to the tender mercies of his relay. But never did she surprise the actual moment. This was finesse. Maybe it was the great Parr himself! She thrilled for an instant on this note. Then she decided on a stroke wholly characteristic.

When William had tucked her in among her moleskins he crossed to the red-headed man and, with that curious condescension upper servants bestow on mere artizans, informed him that his mistress would have speech with him.

"What is your name?" she asked, when the red-headed man stood respectfully, cap in hand, at her carriage door.

"Hanrahan, ma'am—John Hanrahan," he replied.

"I have had my eyes on you for some time, John, without your suspecting it," said she kindly. She had her eyes on him at that moment; and as he met them he had the startling impression that he and she understood each other perfectly. The impression was fugitive.

"You are to enter my service," she informed him, with a large air of conferring an inestimable favour; and without awaiting an answer she informed John that he was to go with William to bring home a new car which she named—

she was giving up her pair because the pavements were too hard on their feet. William was instructed to take John to the tailor and have him outfitted. All this with a gracious smile while she complimented John on the way he carried himself—John's particular uprightness was the regulation product of the police gymnasium. The widow spoke in a little thread of a voice, which broke here and there, when she would close her eyes with a sigh. If the red-headed man had been a thousand devils he could not have refused so pathetic a figure. But the element of humour in the transaction was the ultimate appeal.

A few days later Parr himself, held up by one of his own regal traffic cops at a busy corner, had the grim satisfaction of seeing Sophie taking his red-headed mechanic out for an airing. The new car itself was quite as perfect in its way as had been her prancing pair—a town car imported from France, where they do themselves well in such things.

The motor occupied a glistening bandbox up forward. Sophie was enclosed in a gorgeous candybox away aft. The red-headed mechanic was exposed to the world and the weather as the only living thing abroad, perched on a slender capstan of a seat rising out of the bare deck amidships. She was making a Roman holiday of her prize. Parr could not repress a chuckle. It was so like Sophie!

The Dresden china widow—or what remained of her for popular consumption—did not vary her surface routine by a jot. At home and abroad her shuttle-like eyes were always moving slowly back and forth under the screen of her long lashes. Before many days had passed she had isolated her red-headed mechanic's pack brothers. One was a man with a brown derby who always chewed a cold cigar. The other was a frayed taxi-driver with a moth-eaten beard who had a stand just off the avenue. She never hurried them, never lost them; she nursed them as tenderly as she did her man on the box. They were merely the hounds following blindly. It was the huntsman behind whom she must uncover. She examined bolts, bars, locks, window ledges, painted surfaces for tell-tale marks. In the act of crossing her boudoir she would pause, only her eyes moving, her senses alert and as receptive as if in the very cloister of her retreat she had already half-uncovered the thing that lurked and would strike when the time came. She knew the tricks and pace of her pursuers, and she timed her wits and pace to theirs.

Her telephone she handled with the utmost delicacy—they had tapped that, of course. Whenever she used it, she would set it down softly, then instantly pick it up again and listen, for minutes on end. It was filled with voices, disembodied, inarticulate, and far-off, that swirled and eddied through the ceaseless river of speech. Nothing there—it required exquisite patience. And then one day as she eavesdropped, under her very elbow someone yawned incautiously, groaned lazily, "Oh, dear! Oh, dear!" Sophie showed herself her little white teeth in the mirror that looked down on her eavesdropping. Her nimble mind drew a picture: it would be a big bare room with a lazy man in a blue uniform, with receivers strapped to his ears, seated at a desk. And this police ear grafted to her wire would always be open and attentive.

Once Sophie was rewarded by hearing a door open in that vague room. Again she caught the tread of feet; then the murmur of hushed voices. But it was the ticking of a clock—two of them, in fact—that pleased her most of all. How like a stupid cop, to lie in wait breathless at the mouthpiece of a telephone, with a blatant clock at his elbow. Sophie giggled. While she crouched up wind, watching those who watched her, she savoured the old intoxication of the game rising in her blood. This was *réclame*! She had had enough of stodgy respectability. After she had executed her last great coup Sophie had solemnly assured herself she would go out to grass for the remainder of her days. She had devoted years to this end. And yet, at the first fillip to the vanity of her legendary aloofness—Sophie, the uncaught!—she was off again.

Meantime our friend Mr. Parr, who had

assigned himself, in his mature age, to the Sophie Lang case, was gloomy and bad company. The end of the fourth week found him scowling. There was the daily harvest of squeals falling on his desk. Betrayed crooks, with bracelets on, came home to roost as inevitably as raindrops trickle back to the ocean. But, just as all the rivers flow into the sea and yet the sea is not full, so Parr was conscious of an aching void. He had the uncomfortable sensation of being laughed at.

"The damned thing is frozen—solid!" he muttered, settling himself heavily in his favourite elbow-chair by Armiston's desk.

Armiston said nothing. It wasn't frozen to him. It was merely that the element of time had entered in. This yarn had "written" itself, as he would say professionally. He had merely brushed the tips of his clairvoyant fingers across the oracular keys of his faithful typewriter, and the congealed action which Parr had laid at the feet of his Medicine had straightway come to life, started to move. It had developed the impetus of the inevitable. He had written Finis and locked his typewriter and packed for Lakewood. Then he waited for his friend Parr to call on him.

Leaning back in his chair Oliver idly tinkered with some electrical indicating instrument. The grandfather clock ticked, the fire crackled, and the deputy scowled misanthropically at the fat Buddha in the corner. Silence did not embarrass Oliver. In fact it was his observation that if silence were maintained long enough, the other fellow would say something interesting. Parr seemed tongue-tied. As if tired of waiting for animate things to take the initiative, the needle of the instrument Oliver held in his hand made a spontaneous gesture. It swung over to the middle of a calibrated arc—and stayed there, as if intent on something. Armiston with a yawn set the thing down and presently picked up the telephone. He rested on one elbow watching his friend Parr while he waited.

"Rotten service!" he mumbled after a long wait. Parr nodded gloomily.

"Parr," said Oliver abruptly, over the top of the telephone, "have you made any effort to find the husband? He is the one that squealed, of course. I suppose the poor devil got tired hiding out."

The effect of these words, or rather of this act, on the deputy of police was electric. He reached out with one gorilla-like hand and snatched the telephone from Oliver's grasp. The loose receiver cluttered to the floor, and Parr picked it up and replaced it. He glared at Armiston.

"Was she on there?" he demanded threateningly.

"Certainly," said Oliver easily.

He pointed to the electric needle that still trembled over the middle of the card. That telltale needle gave warning every time the receiver was lifted off its hook in Number 142. To the two watchers at that moment, that tremulous needle personified the woman herself, the eavesdropper, probably at that instant cocking her pretty head with the swift movement of a startled doe.

"So you tip her off—under my nose, eh? Eh?" snarled Parr.

The sudden brainstorm that evoked these words gave him a look ape-like in its ferocity. His huge hands clamped themselves on the extinct author's shoulder. Oliver could almost feel the bones crunch. He gritted his teeth, but continued to watch the spying needle on his desk. It was the needle itself at this juncture that came to the rescue. Abruptly, as if released by an unseen force, it flopped back to zero, nothing, on the calibrated scale. It was as significant as the snap of a dry twig. The lurker was withdrawing, on tiptoe.

For another instant Parr sat there glaring into Oliver's eyes. Then as if he too were in the grip of some unseen force, the deputy jammed his hat down on his ears, turned up his collar and rushed from the room as if the very devil were prodding him on.

While the Lakewood train was picking its way across the drawbridges that span the estuaries of Newark Bay, the Dresden china widow was rolling over hill and dale through the bleak fawn-colour of the winter landscape to Byam, a little lake among the hills where her stylish hackneys were acquiring a winter coat and new hoofs in drowsy ease. On the spur of the moment this morning she had thought of her beloved horses with a tinge of self-accusation. It was honest John Hanrahan, the red-headed mechanic, who as usual conducted her. Some distance behind, coming into sight now and again as her car topped a rise, followed the man in the brown derby, only for this occasion he had discarded his derby for a cap, thrown away his cold cigar, and acquired a moustache.

Life had become a bed of thorns for the red-headed mechanic. Perched out there in the open where the widow could watch him breathe wasn't his idea of being a detective; and so little had transpired in these four weeks that he was beginning to have grave doubts of the infallibility of his great Chief. But ahead of him this morning was a taste of paradise. Arriving at the farm, he went over his car, like a good mechanic, while he waited to take the widow back to town. This done, he entered the kitchen to get warm. Settling himself in a gloomy corner by the stove, he waited, sourly meditating on life. There entered a pert little French maid, a round pink person of Chippendale pattern, on high heels, which gave to her walk the tilt of a Gallic poodle. She caught the reflection of herself in a mirror—a pier-glass that had obviously been banished from above—and before the astonished eyes of John, she began to rehearse those very arts of coquetry which he in his ignorance had always supposed to be spontaneous, when exercised on helpless males.

In the act, she caught sight of him. She was not at all abashed. Indeed, quite the contrary. She tripped daintily over to him, sat down on the edge of his bench and indicated with a propelling shove that he was to move over—not too much. She folded her hands primly on her little lace apron, regarded him under her lashes; a dimple appeared on the apple-tinted cheek she presented to his gaze. Then, in the sudden effulgence of being well met, they both fixed their eyes on the wood-box and sighed happily.

An hour later, when his lady upstairs called for her motor, the red-headed mechanic—city bred—had changed his ideas about the attractions of the country.

It was the little maid who handed his lady into the car. The lady had found some fresh sweet grief here among the bucolic penates of her departed spouse, and she was crying and blowing her nose under her veil. As the pert maid handed her in, the maid boldly—behind the weeping lady's shoulder—pressed a tiny hand in John's ample paw. The motor rounded the drive, and as it passed the gate city-ward, the maid rising on tiptoe tossed a kiss to the moon-struck sleuth.

IV

In West Broadway, among the spaghetti factories, the junk-shops, and the holes in walls where artificial flowers grow, the windows are always dingy, their ledges covered with a thick fall of grime. The Elevated trains growl all day and night, peering in, as they pass, on the upper floors where life is frankly uncurtained. The air is full of the aroma of roasting coffee from the warehouses near-by, and the sour smell of glue from the piano factories.

A man in a seamy uniform and a brass-bound cap, with a number that proclaimed him an Elevated motorman, examined doorway after doorway, always with a glance at the upper windows, as he picked his way up the street. Finally he came to a halt at a broken-down stoop, and ascending three rickety steps he rang a bell. In response there appeared, after a wait, a capacious Sicilian woman with a baby squatting on one hip. She could understand nothing; with a twitch of a shoulder and an upturning movement of one hand, she conferred upon him the freedom of the house. Indeed there was nothing worth stealing. The motorman ascended a creaking flight of stairs, and on the first landing, after some hesitation, picked out a door towards the front of the house and rapped sharply. He listened in open-mouthed concern. Then he rapped again and again, louder, and louder. Doors above him opened and shut; tousled heads peered down on him over the banisters. But the door stared at him blankly.

He retraced his steps to the street, walked briskly north a block, then turned and walked as briskly in the other direction. At a corner he sighted a policeman sampling the wares of a fruit vendor. The motorman whispered to the policeman.

"What's that?" demanded the policeman, bending his head. He gave more careful heed to the motorman's rapid flow of words. Together they crossed the street swiftly. Their unusual pace attracted a crowd. Before they had gone a block their followers were looking at each other expectantly. Many halted and turned to watch. So slight an incident as a policeman moving faster than his wont will rivet the attention of the casuals of such a street.

"There!" said the motorman, bringing the policeman to a halt. He pointed through the lattices of the Elevated structure. "I think that man is dead. He has been sitting in that window for thirty-six hours. At first," he said, in the tone of one speaking of a long time ago, "he was reading a newspaper. But not lately."

He went on to explain that he had passed and repassed that face in the window on his day and night shift, at the controller of his train—until finally it got on his nerves so he had to come on foot to see what was up. He added that he hadn't been able to sleep last night for seeing that face, and—— The policeman, businesslike, pushed his way through the halted traffic and stamped up the stairs. The crowd banked against the door like a swarm of bees. He put his shoulder to the door above and it fell with a weak, splintering smash.

The man was dead—quite. The officer threw up a smeared window and blew his whistle, paying no more heed to the man in the chair. Shortly, other policemen appeared, running, and buffeted lanes through the rising throng below. A little while later a black wagon backed up to the door and carried away the man in the chair covered with a horse blanket. Another wagon bore off the fat Sicilian woman and her baby, and several other terrified denizens of the house. They said he had been a lodger for some months, a poor man. Oh, yes, very poor! It was his habit to sit in that window by the hour, by the day sometimes. Had he any friends come to see him? Who could say? The whole world might pass up and down that dingy staircase without question. The wagons moved off; in a moment the crowd was fluid again; in five minutes it was all forgotten.

In a pawnshop, any pawnshop, timorous clients are apt to be made more timid by the stare of a six-foot man, 185 pounds, who lounges at one end of the counter idly puffing a cigar, and watching, as they beg and haggle. Well they may be: it is one of Parr's invincibles.

In the little building on the river front at the foot of East 26th Street, where black wagons drive up at all hours of the day and night, to deposit burdens covered with horse blankets, just such a man stands, smoking the same cigar, quite as idly, and quite as languidly interested as his brothers in the pawnshops. Dead souls come here; they must be inspected, suspected, like any object offered in pawn. Distraught people come here, anxious mothers, brothers, next friends, seeking. An attendant pulls out drawer after drawer for their inspection. Sometimes a shriek, heard in the street, tells the hangers-on that a quest has ended. Outside undertakers, like flies, flock about them when they emerge.

A stocky man, evidently a mason who had come directly from his work, was whispering to the attendant, trembling. They all whisper and tremble when they come here. The attendant knew the world only as fearful people who whispered and trembled. The attendant listened and nodded. He knew—yes, it was here; he hauled out a drawer. The mason inclined his head, brushing his eyes with a plaster-stained hand. His brother, he said. The attendant made a grimace over a shoulder; and the man with the cigar approached, eyeing the mason with a bleary look. He took out a note-book and they talked in low tones, the policeman making entries as the other answered.

"You will have to be corroborated, of course," said the policeman, not unkindly. "Anyone could come here and pick what they wanted, otherwise."

"But why?" ejaculated the mason, horrified at the idea of anyone having use for a dead body and going to the city morgue to pick out one to his liking. The policeman said he couldn't say why—it had been done, and they must be careful. The mason produced his union card and other credentials to establish his identity.

Outside the tip had gone forth. The grisly hangers-on lay in wait for him, and he gruffly selected one, who led him triumphantly to his near-by store. The next day a little funeral party departed from that side street "parlour" with what pomp the poor can give to their dead. There were four carriages, three of them empty, the blinds drawn and, in the first the only mourner, the mason. Drivers in battered silk hats urged decrepit black nags to a sharp trot over the bridge and far away. The service of the obscure dead must move at a sharp trot—there are hundreds between sunsets.

On their return, the policeman with the cigar met the foremost carriage—there were some papers to sign for the records. When the mason stepped down he looked up and saw the porticoed door of a big building, with massive towers and turrets of red brick and terra-cotta. He drew back involuntarily; but the man with the cigar had a double twist on his coat-sleeve.

"Come along quietly, and don't start anything," he said amiably, and led the mourner up the stone steps, down the corridor, and into a big room in which sat a man at a desk. The door closed behind him. The man at the desk was Parr, deputy commissioner of police.

"Ha, ha! At last! Well, how did it go?" asked Parr, looking up.

The mason crouched like an animal, one hand stealing behind him to try the door. He straightened up, breathing hard.

"Sophie almost got away with it," said Parr. "Knocking the old duffer off like that, with arsenic in his dope! And turning the stiff over to us, to hand out to the first comer that identified it! You thought you weren't even taking a chance, didn't you, William?"

It was William, the footman—William redrawn, some lines erased, as plausible as a raised cheque, nevertheless, it was William. He swallowed hard.

"Come over here. I want a good look at you," commanded Parr.

The man obeyed sullenly. Parr pointed to a glass paper-weight on his desk. "Did you ever see that before? Answer me!" he bawled, with sudden ferocity. William looked from Parr to the paper-weight, and back again, but maintained silence.

"What did Amos P. Huntington call himself ten years ago, when he left his finger-prints on that paper-weight, in the Park Place murder?"

Parr referred to a crime that had gone down in the annals as a celebrated mystery. It was a mystery no more. The obscure man who was found dead in his chair in West Broadway had the same finger-prints. That was why the man with the cigar had been so polite to the mason when he called on his sad errand. William did not answer. His eyes roved round the room, avoiding the one thing he feared.

"What did you blow up in your rubber plant, William?" asked Parr. "Was it a basket of cats—or dogs—or did you borrow another of your brothers from East Twenty-sixth Street? Sophie put the remains through the crematory so fast we didn't have a look-in."

Parr laughed. So did William. By that laugh Parr knew that questions were useless. At that moment the door opened and Oliver Armiston came in, back from Lakewood, in picturesque polo cloak and cap, swinging a stick.

"Take him downstairs!" growled Parr to an attendant. "Charge him with—charge him with complicity in the murder of John Doe, alias Amos P. Huntington."

Armiston dropped his stick with a clatter and started back with such a genuine movement of amazement that the policeman who was ushering him in actually grabbed him, thinking him the murderer.

"No! No! Not that one! This one!" said Parr. Parr's eyes twinkled.

When William had been taken away, he said to Oliver with some relish: "As a matter of fact, Oliver, you ought to be downstairs on that charge!"

"But how—what—I got your wire. I came right in. Is there—did she——"

"Certainly," responded Parr, nodding. "You are a wonder, Oliver!" Parr rubbed his hands comfortably. "What put it into your head to start Sophie after her husband? Don't tell me you didn't," said the deputy, as Armiston tried to break in with a word. "I heard you! You knew she was listening in, on the telephone, the other day, in your study, when you told me in a loud voice to go out and find her husband—that he had squealed on her. Squealed on her!" cried Parr. "On the level, Oliver, I could have strangled you at that moment. I thought you were squealing on me. Then it all came over me—just like that!" and he snapped his fingers to indicate the suddenness of light. He pounded Oliver on one knee. "You've got the goods! You're all right, Oliver."

"Well, it was the obvious thing to do, of course," agreed Oliver, now preening himself. "I knew you couldn't find him. I knew the only way was to scare her into starting after him herself. Then you could trail along behind. It was—it made a very good ending of the story, I thought," said Oliver, rubbing his hands. "Your men trailed her, of course?"

"Well, as a matter of fact," said Parr weakly, "she got the jump on us. You know Sophie! So we just sat back and waited."

"Waited?" ejaculated Armiston, his jaw dropping.

"Oh, Sophie did her part—she produced him all right," said Parr. "Dead!" he added grimly. He related swiftly how the bogus Amos P. Huntington, who had been blown up by synthetic rubber and cremated, in the end came to his death and burial in so obscure a manner that the police would never have known who he was, except for one thing that Sophie overlooked.

"My window washer," said Parr, "he's a wonder, too. He managed to borrow a razor, among other personal effects of Amos P. Huntington. Sophie had packed it away in a box. We found finger-prints on it that corresponded to that," he said, pointing at the glass paper-weight, grisly souvenir of the famous Park Place mystery. "When his dead body turned up, with the same finger-prints, the rest was simple enough. We merely sat on the doorstep and waited." And Parr, who had complacently compassed the murder of a murderer, by neglecting to follow Sophie too closely, leaned back in his chair smiling in a grim way. "Oh, they all come to pot sooner or later," he said, in his philosophic mood again.

"But—Sophie——"

"Oh, she is on her way down-town now," said Parr. "Sit still. You will see her."

The Dresden china widow, an hour before, had set out on her afternoon drive to air her red-headed mechanic. At Forty-second Street a policeman said gruffly, "Drive up to the curb, young fellow," and the red-headed mechanic had obeyed with alacrity, not knowing at the moment if he was wanted for some infraction of the traffic rules, or by his Chief. "Let me have your keys," commanded the traffic policeman. He took the proffered keys and calmly locked the door of the candy-box tonneau. Sophie could not escape now, except by smashing glass. "Take her to Headquarters!" commanded the traffic man, who had his instructions.

While Parr and Oliver sat talking, Sophie was announced. A graceful little woman clothed in a cloud of black entered, weeping, and sniffling in her handkerchief under her veil.

"Lift up the curtain, Sophie," said Parr, with a full breath of elation. "This is where you stop for the night, Sophie."

She lifted the veil, disclosing a tear-stained face pathetically pretty. Parr, with an oath, lifted himself out of his chair. His hands strained at the arms till the veins stood out like whipcords. He stared like a wooden man.

"What's the joke, Hanrahan?" he bawled at the red-headed mechanic.

"Joke, sir? Joke!" protested Hanrahan.

"Look at her, you fool!" snarled the deputy, coming out from behind his desk. "Look what you have brought here—this rag doll done up in *crêpe.*"

The lady here burst into a torrent of words.

"I not understand!" she wailed, in French accents. "I am Madam 'Untington maid! She move—I come to town—three—four days—to make ready! She move. This afternoon I go out—to get littl' air! The policeman—he lock me in! Oh, he lock me in! I scream! I cry! I knock the window! I come here! This man he say 'don't start nothings—' "

But Hanrahan was holding his head. He was reviving that episode in the kitchen that made the country seem so attractive to him a few days gone by. If this was the maid, who then was that piece of pert prettiness with whom he had philandered?

"Where did you get those clothes?" demanded Parr roughly.

"Madam—she give them to me—she no want them any more—my 'usband, he is dead—*Il est mort!*"

"Take her away!" roared Parr.

"What is the charge?" asked the meek Hanrahan.

"Oh, anything—anything," snarled Parr, "to keep it out of the papers! You a detective! You on the Sophie Lang case! Oh dear, oh dear!"

When the door closed on the two figures it was Armiston who broke the painful silence.

"After all," he said dreamily, fingering his grey lock, "it was a signed masterpiece! Eh, Parr?"

That was the end of the Sophie Lang case. There were loose ends of course, such as William, and the maid, and the jettisoned quarter of a million dollars. The underlings proved to be very faithful ignorant tools of the lady, who took their medicine, slight doses, maintaining to the end their lack of knowledge of such a purely legendary person as Sophie Lang.

Villain: Mr. Ottermole

The Hands of Mr. Ottermole

THOMAS BURKE

THE BIRTH OF THE MYSTERY/DETECTIVE STORY is generally conceded to have occurred in 1841 with the publication of Edgar Allan Poe's "The Murders in the Rue Morgue." It is probably impossible to count the number of stories in the genre that were published in the ensuing century. A few years after that centenary, in 1949, a panel of twelve experts was called upon to name the greatest of them all, and the story given that extraordinary honor was "The Hands of Mr. Ottermole" by Sydney Thomas Burke (1886–1945), a tale inspired by the Jack the Ripper murders.

Burke was born in the London suburb of Clapham, but when he was only a few months old his father died, and he was sent to the East End to live with his uncle until the age of ten, when he was put into a home for respectable middle-class children without means. Burke sold his first story, "The Bellamy Diamonds," when he was fifteen. His first book, *Nights in Town: A London Autobiography*, was published in 1915, soon followed by the landmark volume *Limehouse Nights* (1916), a collection of stories that had originally been published in the magazines *The English Review*, *Colour*, and *The New Witness*. This volume of romantic but violent stories of the Chinese district of London was enormously popular and, though largely praised by critics, there were objections to the depictions of interracial relationships, opium use, and other "depravities."

"The Hands of Mr. Ottermole" was originally published in the author's collection *The Pleasantries of Old Quong* (London, Constable, 1931); it was published in the United States as *A Tea-Shop in Limehouse* (Boston, Little, Brown, 1931).

THE HANDS OF MR. OTTERMOLE

Thomas Burke

AT SIX O'CLOCK of a January evening Mr. Whybrow was walking home through the cobweb alleys of London's East End. He had left the golden clamour of the great High Street to which the tram had brought him from the river and his daily work, and was now in the chessboard of byways that is called Mallon End. None of the rush and gleam of the High Street trickled into these byways. A few paces south—a flood tide of life, foaming and beating. Here—only slow-shuffling figures and muffled pulses. He was in the sink of London, the last refuge of European vagrants.

As though in tune with the street's spirit, he too walked slowly, with head down. It seemed that he was pondering some pressing trouble, but he was not. He had no trouble. He was walking slowly because he had been on his feet all day, and he was bent in abstraction because he was wondering whether the Missis would have herrings for his tea, or haddock; and he was trying to decide which would be the more tasty on a night like this. A wretched night it was, of damp and mist, and the mist wandered into his throat and his eyes, and the damp had settled on pavement and roadway, and where the sparse lamplight fell it sent up a greasy sparkle that chilled one to look at. By contrast it made his speculations more agreeable, and made him ready for that tea—whether herring or haddock. His eye turned from the glum bricks that made his horizon, and went forward half a mile. He saw a gas-lit kitchen, a flamy fire, and a spread tea table. There was toast in the hearth and a singing kettle on the side and a piquant effusion of herrings, or maybe of haddock, or perhaps sausages. The vision gave his aching feet a throb of energy. He shook imperceptible damp from his shoulders, and hastened towards its reality.

But Mr. Whybrow wasn't going to get any tea that evening—or any other evening. Mr. Whybrow was going to die. Somewhere within a hundred yards of him another man was walking: a man much like Mr. Whybrow and much like any other man, but without the only quality that enables mankind to live peaceably together and not as madmen in a jungle. A man with a dead heart eating into itself and bringing forth the foul organisms that arise from death and corruption. And that thing in man's shape, on a whim or a settled idea—one cannot know—had said within himself that Mr. Whybrow should never taste another herring. Not that Mr. Whybrow had injured him. Not that he had any dislike of

Mr. Whybrow. Indeed, he knew nothing of him save as a familiar figure about the streets. But, moved by a force that had taken possession of his empty cells, he had picked on Mr. Whybrow with that blind choice that makes us pick one restaurant table that has nothing to mark it from four or five other tables, or one apple from a dish of half a dozen equal apples; or that drives Nature to send a cyclone upon one corner of this planet, and destroy five hundred lives in that corner, and leave another five hundred in the same corner unharmed. So this man had picked on Mr. Whybrow, as he might have picked on you or me, had we been within his daily observation; and even now he was creeping through the blue-toned streets, nursing his large white hands, moving ever closer to Mr. Whybrow's tea table, and so closer to Mr. Whybrow himself.

He wasn't, this man, a bad man. Indeed, he had many of the social and amiable qualities, and passed as a respectable man, as most successful criminals do. But the thought had come into his mouldering mind that he would like to murder somebody, and, as he held no fear of God or man, he was going to do it, and would then go home to *his* tea. I don't say that flippantly, but as a statement of fact. Strange as it may seem to the humane, murderers must and do sit down to meals after a murder. There is no reason why they shouldn't, and many reasons why they should. For one thing, they need to keep their physical and mental vitality at full beat for the business of covering their crime. For another, the strain of their effort makes them hungry, and satisfaction at the accomplishment of a desired thing brings a feeling of relaxation towards human pleasures. It is accepted among non-murderers that the murderer is always overcome by fear for his safety and horror at his act; but this type is rare. His own safety is, of course, his immediate concern, but vanity is a marked quality of most murderers, and that, together with the thrill of conquest, makes him confident that he can secure it, and when he has restored his strength with food he goes about securing it as a young hostess goes about the arranging of her first big dinner—a little anxious, but no more. Criminologists and detectives tell us that *every* murderer, however intelligent or cunning, always makes one slip in his tactics—one little slip that brings the affair home to him. But that is only half true. It is true only of the murderers who are caught. Scores of murderers are not caught: therefore scores of murderers do not make any mistake at all. This man didn't.

As for horror or remorse, prison chaplains, doctors, and lawyers have told us that of murderers they have interviewed under condemnation and the shadow of death, only one here and there has expressed any contrition for his act, or shown any sign of mental misery. Most of them display only exasperation at having been caught when so many have gone undiscovered, or indignation at being condemned for a perfectly reasonable act. However normal and humane they may have been before the murder, they are utterly without conscience after it. For what is conscience? Simply a polite nickname for superstition, which is a polite nickname for fear. Those who associate remorse with murder are, no doubt, basing their ideas on the world legend of the remorse of Cain, or are projecting their own frail minds into the mind of the murderer, and getting false reactions. Peaceable folk cannot hope to make contact with this mind, for they are not merely different in mental type from the murderer: they are different in their personal chemistry and construction. Some men can and do kill, not one man, but two or three, and go calmly about their daily affairs. Other men could not, under the most agonising provocation, bring themselves even to wound. It is men of this sort who imagine the murderer in torments of remorse and fear of the law, whereas he is actually sitting down to his tea.

The man with the large white hands was as ready for his tea as Mr. Whybrow was, but he had something to do before he went to it. When he had done that something, and made no mistake about it, he would be even more ready for it, and would go to it as comfortably as he went to it the day before, when his hands were stainless.

Walk on, then, Mr. Whybrow, walk on; and as you walk, look your last upon the familiar features of your nightly journey. Follow your jack-o'-lantern tea table. Look well upon its warmth and colour and kindness; feed your eyes with it, and tease your nose with its gentle domestic odours; for you will never sit down to it. Within ten minutes' pacing of you a pursuing phantom has spoken in his heart, and you are doomed. There you go—you and phantom—two nebulous dabs of mortality, moving through green air along pavements of powder blue, the one to kill, the other to be killed. Walk on. Don't annoy your burning feet by hurrying, for the more slowly you walk, the longer you will breathe the green air of this January dusk, and see the dreamy lamplight and the little shops, and hear the agreeable commerce of the London crowd and the haunting pathos of the street organ. These things are dear to you, Mr. Whybrow. You don't know it now, but in fifteen minutes you will have two seconds in which to realise how inexpressibly dear they are.

Walk on, then, across this crazy chessboard. You are in Lagos Street now, among the tents of the wanderers of Eastern Europe. A minute or so, and you are in Loyal Lane, among the lodging houses that shelter the useless and the beaten of London's camp followers. The lane holds the smell of them, and its soft darkness seems heavy with the wail of the futile. But you are not sensitive to impalpable things, and you plod through it, unseeing, as you do every evening, and come to Blean Street, and plod through that. From basement to sky rise the tenements of an alien colony. Their windows slot the ebony of their walls with lemon. Behind those windows strange life is moving, dressed with forms that are not of London or of England, yet, in essence, the same agreeable life that you have been living, and tonight will live no more. From high above you comes a voice crooning "The Song of Katta." Through a window you see a family keeping a religious rite. Through another you see a woman pouring out tea for her husband. You see a man mending a pair of boots; a mother bathing her baby. You have seen all these things before, and never noticed them. You do not notice them now, but if you knew that you were never going to see them again, you would notice them. You never *will* see them again, not because your life has run its natural course, but because a man whom you have often passed in the street has at his own solitary pleasure decided to usurp the awful authority of nature, and destroy you. So perhaps it's as well that you don't notice them, for your part in them is ended. No more for you these pretty moments of our earthly travail: only one moment of terror, and then a plunging darkness.

Closer to you this shadow of massacre moves, and now he is twenty yards behind you. You can hear his footfall, but you do not turn your head. You are familiar with footfalls. You are in London, in the easy security of your daily territory, and footfalls behind you, your instinct tells you, are no more than a message of human company.

But can't you hear something in those footfalls—something that goes with a widdershins beat? Something that says: *Look out, look out. Beware, beware.* Can't you hear the very syllables of *mur-der-er, mur-der-er*? No; there is nothing in footfalls. They are neutral. The foot of villainy falls with the same quiet note as the foot of honesty. But those footfalls, Mr. Whybrow, are bearing on to you a pair of hands, and there *is* something in hands. Behind you that pair of hands is even now stretching its muscles in preparation for your end. Every minute of your days you have been seeing human hands. Have you ever realised the sheer horror of hands—those appendages that are a symbol for our moments of trust and affection and salutation? Have you thought of the sickening potentialities that lie within the scope of that five-tentacled member? No, you never have; for all the human hands that you have seen have been stretched to you in kindness or fellowship. Yet, though the eyes can hate, and the lips can sting, it is only that dangling member that can gather the accumulated essence of evil, and electrify it into currents of destruction. Satan may enter into man by many doors, but in the hands alone can he find the servants of his will.

Another minute, Mr. Whybrow, and you will know all about the horror of human hands.

You are nearly home now. You have turned into your street—Caspar Street—and you are in the centre of the chessboard. You can see the front window of your little four-roomed house. The street is dark, and its three lamps give only a smut of light that is more confusing than darkness. It is dark—empty, too. Nobody about; no lights in the front parlours of the houses, for the families are at tea in their kitchens; and only a random glow in a few upper rooms occupied by lodgers. Nobody about but you and your following companion, and you don't notice him. You see him so often that he is never seen. Even if you turned your head and saw him, you would only say "Good-evening" to him, and walk on. A suggestion that he was a possible murderer would not even make you laugh. It would be too silly.

And now you are at your gate. And now you have found your door key. And now you are in, and hanging up your hat and coat. The Missis has just called a greeting from the kitchen, whose smell is an echo of that greeting (herrings!) and you have answered it, when the door shakes under a sharp knock.

Go away, Mr. Whybrow. Go away from that door. Don't touch it. Get right away from it. Get out of the house. Run with the Missis to the back garden, and over the fence. Or call the neighbours. But don't touch that door. Don't, Mr. Whybrow, don't open . . .

Mr. Whybrow opened the door.

That was the beginning of what became known as London's Strangling Horrors. Horrors they were called because they were something more than murders: they were motiveless, and there was an air of black magic about them. Each murder was committed at a time when the street where the bodies were found was empty of any perceptible or possible murderer. There would be an empty alley. There would be a policeman at its end. He would turn his back on the empty alley for less than a minute. Then he would look round and run into the night with news of another strangling. And in any direction he looked nobody to be seen and no report to be had of anybody being seen. Or he would be on duty in a long-quiet street, and suddenly be called to a house of dead people whom a few seconds earlier he had seen alive. And, again, whichever way he looked nobody to be seen; and although police whistles put an immediate cordon around the area, and searched all houses, no possible murderer to be found.

The first news of the murder of Mr. and Mrs. Whybrow was brought by the station sergeant. He had been walking through Caspar Street on his way to the station for duty, when he noticed the open door of No. 98. Glancing in, he saw by the gaslight of the passage a motionless body on the floor. After a second look he blew his whistle, and when the constables answered him he took one to join him in a search of the house, and sent others to watch all neighbouring streets, and make inquiries at adjoining houses. But neither in the house nor in the streets was anything found to indicate the murderer. Neighbours on either side, and opposite, were questioned, but they had seen nobody about, and had heard nothing. One had heard Mr. Whybrow come home—the scrape of his latchkey in the door was so regular an evening sound, he said, that you could set your watch by it for half past six—but he had heard nothing more than the sound of the opening door until the sergeant's whistle. Nobody had been seen to enter the house or leave it, by front or back, and the necks of the dead people carried no finger prints or other traces. A nephew was called in to go over the house, but he could find nothing missing; and anyway his uncle possessed nothing worth stealing. The little money in the house was untouched, and there were no signs of any disturbance of the property, or even of struggle. No signs of anything but brutal and wanton murder.

Mr. Whybrow was known to neighbours and

workmates as a quiet, likeable, home-loving man; such a man as could not have any enemies. But, then, murdered men seldom have. A relentless enemy who hates a man to the point of wanting to hurt him seldom wants to murder him, since to do that puts him beyond suffering. So the police were left with an impossible situation: no clue to the murderer and no motive for the murders; only the fact that they had been done.

The first news of the affair sent a tremor through London generally, and an electric thrill through all Mallon End. Here was a murder of two inoffensive people, not for gain and not for revenge; and the murderer, to whom, apparently, killing was a casual impulse, was at large. He had left no traces, and, provided he had no companions, there seemed no reason why he should not remain at large. Any clear-headed man who stands alone, and has no fear of God or man, can, if he chooses, hold a city, even a nation, in subjection; but your everyday criminal is seldom clear-headed, and dislikes being lonely. He needs, if not the support of confederates, at least somebody to talk to; his vanity needs the satisfaction of perceiving at first hand the effect of his work. For this he will frequent bars and coffee shops and other public places. Then, sooner or later, in a glow of comradeship, he will utter the one word too much; and the nark, who is everywhere, has an easy job.

But though the doss houses and saloons and other places were "combed" and set with watches, and it was made known by whispers that good money and protection were assured to those with information, nothing attaching to the Whybrow case could be found. The murderer clearly had no friends and kept no company. Known men of this type were called up and questioned, but each was able to give a good account of himself; and in a few days the police were at a dead end. Against the constant public gibe that the thing had been done almost under their noses, they became restive, and for four days each man of the force was working his daily beat under a strain. On the fifth day they became still more restive.

It was the season of annual teas and entertainments for the children of the Sunday Schools, and on an evening of fog, when London was a world of groping phantoms, a small girl, in the bravery of best Sunday frock and shoes, shining face, and new-washed hair, set out from Logan Passage for St. Michael's Parish Hall. She never got there. She was not actually dead until half past six, but she was as good as dead from the moment she left her mother's door. Somebody like a man, pacing the street from which the Passage led, saw her come out; and from that moment she was dead. Through the fog somebody's large white hands reached after her, and in fifteen minutes they were about her.

At half past six a whistle screamed trouble, and those answering it found the body of little Nellie Vrinoff in a warehouse entry in Minnow Street. The sergeant was first among them, and he posted his men to useful points, ordering them here and there in the tart tones of repressed rage, and berating the officer whose beat the street was. "I saw you, Magson, at the end of the lane. What were you up to there? You were there ten minutes before you turned." Magson began an explanation about keeping an eye on a suspicious-looking character at that end, but the sergeant cut him short: "Suspicious characters be damned. You don't want to look for suspicious characters. You want to look for *murderers.* Messing about . . . and then this happens right where you ought to be. Now think what they'll say."

With the speed of ill news came the crowd, pale and perturbed; and on the story that the unknown monster had appeared again, and this time to a child, their faces streaked the fog with spots of hate and horror. But then came the ambulance and more police, and swiftly they broke up the crowd; and as it broke the sergeant's thought was thickened into words, and from all sides came low murmurs of "Right under their noses." Later inquiries showed that four people of the district, above suspicion, had passed that entry at intervals of seconds before the murder, and seen nothing and heard nothing. None of them had passed the child alive or seen her dead. None of them had seen anybody in the street except themselves. Again the police were left with no motive and with no clue.

And now the district, as you will remember, was given over, not to panic, for the London public never yields to that, but to apprehension and dismay. If these things were happening in their familiar streets, then anything might happen. Wherever people met—in the streets, the markets, and the shops—they debated the one topic. Women took to bolting their windows and doors at the first fall of dusk. They kept their children closely under their eye. They did their shopping before dark, and watched anxiously, while pretending they weren't watching, for the return of their husbands from work. Under the Cockney's semi-humorous resignation to disaster, they hid an hourly foreboding. By the whim of one man with a pair of hands the structure and tenor of their daily life were shaken, as they always can be shaken by any man contemptuous of humanity and fearless of its laws. They began to realise that the pillars that supported the peaceable society in which they lived were mere straws that anybody could snap; that laws were powerful only so long as they were obeyed; that the police were potent only so long as they were feared. By the power of his hands this one man had made a whole community do something new: he had made it think, and left it gasping at the obvious.

And then, while it was yet gasping under his first two strokes, he made his third. Conscious of the horror that his hands had created, and hungry as an actor who has once tasted the thrill of the multitude, he made fresh advertisement of his presence; and on Wednesday morning, three days after the murder of the child, the papers carried to the breakfast tables of England the story of a still more shocking outrage.

At 9:32 on Tuesday night a constable was on duty in Jarnigan Road, and at that time spoke to a fellow officer named Petersen at the top of Clemming Street. He had seen this officer walk down that street. He could swear that the street was empty at that time, except for a lame bootblack whom he knew by sight, and who passed him and entered a tenement on the side opposite that on which his fellow officer was walking. He had the habit, as all constables had just then, of looking constantly behind him and around him, whichever way he was walking, and he was certain that the street was empty. He passed his sergeant at 9:33, saluted him, and answered his inquiry for anything seen. He reported that he had seen nothing, and passed on. His beat ended at a short distance from Clemming Street, and, having paced it, he turned and came again at 9:34 to the top of the street. He had scarcely reached it before he heard the hoarse voice of the sergeant: "Gregory! You there? Quick. Here's another. My God, it's Petersen! Garotted. Quick, call 'em up!"

That was the third of the Strangling Horrors, of which there were to be a fourth and a fifth; and the five horrors were to pass into the unknown and unknowable. That is, unknown as far as authority and the public were concerned. The identity of the murderer *was* known, but to two men only. One was the murderer himself; the other was a young journalist.

This young man, who was covering the affairs for his paper, the *Daily Torch*, was no smarter than the other zealous newspaper men who were hanging about these byways in the hope of a sudden story. But he was patient, and he hung a little closer to the case than the other fellows, and by continually staring at it he at last raised the figure of the murderer like a genie from the stones on which he had stood to do his murders.

After the first few days the men had given up any attempt at exclusive stories, for there was none to be had. They met regularly at the police station, and what little information there was they shared. The officials were agreeable to them, but no more. The sergeant discussed with them the details of each murder; suggested possible explanations of the man's methods; recalled from the past those cases that had some similarity; and on the matter of motive reminded them of the motiveless Neill Cream and the wanton John Williams, and hinted that work was being done which would soon bring the business to an end; but about that work he would not say a word. The Inspector, too, was gracefully garrulous on the thesis of Murder, but whenever one of the party edged the talk towards what was being done in this immediate matter, he glided past it. Whatever the officials knew, they were not giving it to newspaper men. The business had fallen heavily upon them, and only by a capture made by their own efforts could they rehabilitate themselves in official and public esteem. Scotland Yard, of course, was at work, and had all the station's material; but the station's hope was that they themselves would have the honour of settling the affair; and however useful the coöperation of the Press might be in other cases, they did not want to risk a defeat by a premature disclosure of their theories and plans.

So the sergeant talked at large, and propounded one interesting theory after another, all of which the newspaper men had thought of themselves.

The young man soon gave up these morning lectures on the Philosophy of Crime, and took to wandering about the streets and making bright stories out of the effect of the murders on the normal life of the people. A melancholy job made more melancholy by the district. The littered roadways, the crestfallen houses, the bleared windows—all held the acid misery that evokes no sympathy: the misery of the frustrated poet. The misery was the creation of the aliens, who were living in this makeshift fashion because they had no settled homes, and would neither take the trouble to make a home where they *could* settle, nor get on with their wandering.

There was little to be picked up. All he saw and heard were indignant faces, and wild conjectures of the murderer's identity and of the secret of his trick of appearing and disappearing unseen. Since a policeman himself had fallen a victim, denunciations of the force had ceased, and the unknown was now invested with a cloak of legend. Men eyed other men, as though thinking: It might be *him*. It might be *him*. They were no longer looking for a man who had the air of a Madame Tussaud murderer; they were looking for a man, or perhaps some harridan woman, who had done these particular murders. Their thoughts ran mainly on the foreign set. Such ruffianism could scarcely belong to England, nor could the bewildering cleverness of the thing. So they turned to Roumanian gipsies and Turkish carpet sellers. There, clearly, would be found the "warm" spot. These Eastern fellows—they knew all sorts of tricks, and they had no real religion—nothing to hold them within bounds. Sailors returning from those parts had told tales of conjurors who made themselves invisible; and there were tales of Egyptian and Arab potions that were used for abysmally queer purposes. Perhaps it *was* possible to them; you never knew. They were so slick and cunning, and they had such gliding movements; no Englishman could melt away as they could. Almost certainly the murderer would be found to be one of that sort—with some dark trick of his own—and just because they were sure that he *was* a magician, they felt that it was useless to look for him. He was a power, able to hold them in subjection and to hold himself untouchable. Superstition, which so easily cracks the frail shell of reason, had got into them. He could do anything he chose: he would never be discovered. These two points they settled, and they went about the streets in a mood of resentful fatalism.

They talked of their ideas to the journalist in half tones, looking right and left, as though *HE* might overhear them and visit them. And though all the district was thinking of him and ready to pounce upon him, yet, so strongly had he worked upon them, that if any man in the street—say, a small man of commonplace features and form—had cried "*I* am the Monster!" would their stifled fury have broken into flood and have borne him down and engulfed him? Or would they not suddenly have seen something unearthly in that everyday face and figure, something unearthly in his everyday boots, something unearthly about his hat, something that marked him as one whom none of their weapons could alarm or pierce? And would they not momentarily have fallen back from this devil, as the devil fell back from the Cross made by the sword of Faust, and so have given him time to escape? I do not know; but so fixed was their belief in his invincibility that it is at least likely that they would have made this hesitation, had such an occasion arisen. But it never did. To-day this commonplace fellow, his murder lust glutted, is still seen and observed among them as he was seen and observed all the time; but because nobody then dreamt, or now dreams, that he was what he was, they observed him then, and observe him now, as people observe a lamp-post.

Almost was their belief in his invincibility justified; for, five days after the murder of the policeman Petersen, when the experience and inspiration of the whole detective force of London were turned towards his identification and capture, he made his fourth and fifth strokes.

At nine o'clock that evening, the young newspaper man, who hung about every night until his paper was away, was strolling along Richards Lane. Richards Lane is a narrow street, partly a stall market, and partly residential. The young man was in the residential section, which carries on one side small working-class cottages, and on the other the wall of a railway goods yard. The great wall hung a blanket of shadow over the lane, and the shadow and the cadaverous outline of the now deserted market stalls gave it the appearance of a living lane that had been turned to frost in the moment between breath and death. The very lamps, that elsewhere were nimbuses of gold, had here the rigidity of gems. The journalist, feeling this message of frozen eternity, was telling himself that he was tired of the whole thing, when in one stroke the frost was broken. In the moment between one pace and another silence and darkness were racked by a high scream and through the scream a voice: "Help! help! *He's here!*"

Before he could think what movement to make, the lane came to life. As though its invisible populace had been waiting on that cry, the door of every cottage was flung open, and from them and from the alleys poured shadowy figures bent in question mark form. For a second or so they stood as rigid as the lamps; then a police whistle gave them direction, and the flock of shadows sloped up the street. The journalist followed them, and others followed him. From the main street and from surrounding streets they came, some risen from unfinished suppers, some disturbed in their ease of slippers and shirt sleeves, some stumbling on infirm limbs, and some upright, and armed with pokers or the tools of their trade. Here and there above the wavering cloud of heads moved the bold helmets of policemen. In one dim mass they surged upon a cottage whose doorway was marked by the sergeant and two constables; and voices of those behind urged them on with "Get in! Find him! Run round the back! Over the wall!" and those in front cried: "Keep back! Keep back!"

And now the fury of a mob held in thrall by unknown peril broke loose. He was here—on the spot. Surely this time he *could not* escape. All minds were bent upon the cottage; all energies thrust towards its doors and windows and roof; all thought was turned upon one unknown man and his extermination. So that no one man saw any other man. No man saw the narrow, packed lane and the mass of struggling shadows, and all forgot to look among themselves for the monster who never lingered upon his victims. All forgot, indeed, that they, by their mass crusade of vengeance, were affording him the perfect hiding place. They saw only the house, and they heard only the rending of woodwork and the smash of glass at back and front, and the police giving orders or crying with the chase; and they pressed on.

But they found no murderer. All they found was news of murder and a glimpse of the ambulance, and for their fury there was no other object than the police themselves, who fought against this hampering of their work.

The journalist managed to struggle through

to the cottage door, and to get the story from the constable stationed there. The cottage was the home of a pensioned sailor and his wife and daughter. They had been at supper, and at first it appeared that some noxious gas had smitten all three in mid-action. The daughter lay dead on the hearthrug, with a piece of bread and butter in her hand. The father had fallen sideways from his chair, leaving on his plate a filled spoon of rice pudding. The mother lay half under the table, her lap filled with the pieces of a broken cup and splashes of cocoa. But in three seconds the idea of gas was dismissed. One glance at their necks showed that this was the Strangler again; and the police stood and looked at the room and momentarily shared the fatalism of the public. They were helpless.

This was his fourth visit, making seven murders in all. He was to do, as you know, one more—and to do it that night; and then he was to pass into history as the unknown London horror, and return to the decent life that he had always led, remembering little of what he had done, and worried not at all by the memory. Why did he stop? Impossible to say. Why did he begin? Impossible again. It just happened like that; and if he thinks at all of those days and nights, I surmise that he thinks of them as we think of foolish or dirty little sins that we committed in childhood. We say that they were not really sins, because we were not then consciously ourselves: we had not come to realisation; and we look back at that foolish little creature that we once were, and forgive him because he didn't know. So, I think, with this man.

There are plenty like him. Eugene Aram, after the murder of Daniel Clarke, lived a quiet, contented life for fourteen years, unhaunted by his crime and unshaken in his self-esteem. Dr. Crippen murdered his wife, and then lived pleasantly with his mistress in the house under whose floor he had buried the wife. Constance Kent, found Not Guilty of the murder of her young brother, led a peaceful life for five years before she confessed. George Joseph Smith and William Palmer lived amiably among their fellows untroubled by fear or by remorse for their poisonings and drownings. Charles Peace, at the time he made his one unfortunate essay, had settled down into a respectable citizen with an interest in antiques. It happened that, after a lapse of time, these men were discovered, but more murderers than we guess are living decent lives to-day, and will die in decency, undiscovered and unsuspected. As this man will.

But he had a narrow escape, and it was perhaps this narrow escape that brought him to a stop. The escape was due to an error of judgment on the part of the journalist.

As soon as he had the full story of the affair, which took some time, he spent fifteen minutes on the telephone, sending the story through, and at the end of the fifteen minutes, when the stimulus of the business had left him, he felt physically tired and mentally dishevelled. He was not yet free to go home; the paper would not go away for another hour; so he turned into a bar for a drink and some sandwiches.

It was then, when he had dismissed the whole business from his mind, and was looking about the bar and admiring the landlord's taste in watch chains and his air of domination, and was thinking that the landlord of a well-conducted tavern had a more comfortable life than a newspaper man, that his mind received from nowhere a spark of light. He was not thinking about the Strangling Horrors; his mind was on his sandwich. As a public-house sandwich, it was a curiosity. The bread had been thinly cut, it was buttered, and the ham was not two months stale; it was ham as it should be. His mind turned to the inventor of this refreshment, the Earl of Sandwich, and then to George the Fourth, and then to the Georges, and to the legend of that George who was worried to know how the apple got into the apple dumpling. He wondered whether George would have been equally puzzled to know how the ham got into the ham sandwich, and how long it would have been before it occurred to him that the ham could not have got there unless somebody had put it there. He got up to order another sandwich, and in that moment a little active corner of his mind settled the affair. If there was ham in his sandwich, somebody must have put it there. If seven people had been murdered, somebody must have been there to murder them. There was no aeroplane or automobile that would go into a man's pocket; therefore that somebody must have escaped either by running away or standing still; and again therefore——

He was visualising the front-page story that his paper would carry if his theory were correct, and if—a matter of conjecture—his editor had the necessary nerve to make a bold stroke, when a cry of "Time, gentlemen, please! All out!" reminded him of the hour. He got up and went out into a world of mist, broken by the ragged discs of roadside puddles and the streaming lightning of motor buses. He was certain that he had *the* story, but, even if it were proved, he was doubtful whether the policy of his paper would permit him to print it. It had one great fault. It was truth, but it was impossible truth. It rocked the foundations of everything that newspaper readers believed and that newspaper editors helped them to believe. They might believe that Turkish carpet sellers had the gift of making themselves invisible. They would not believe this.

As it happened, they were not asked to, for the story was never written. As his paper had by now gone away, and as he was nourished by his refreshment and stimulated by his theory, he thought he might put in an extra half hour by testing that theory. So he began to look about for the man he had in mind—a man with white hair, and large white hands; otherwise an everyday figure whom nobody would look twice at. He wanted to spring his idea on this man without warning, and he was going to place himself within reach of a man armoured in legends of dreadfulness and grue. This might appear to be an act of supreme courage—that one man, with no hope of immediate outside support, should place himself at the mercy of one who was holding a whole parish in terror. But it wasn't. He didn't think about the risk. He didn't think about his duty to his employers or loyalty to his paper. He was moved simply by an instinct to follow a story to its end.

He walked slowly from the tavern and crossed into Fingal Street, making for Deever Market, where he had hope of finding his man. But his journey was shortened. At the corner of Lotus Street he saw him—or a man who looked like him. This street was poorly lit, and he could see little of the man: but he *could* see white hands. For some twenty paces he stalked him; then drew level with him; and at a point where the arch of a railway crossed the street, he saw that this was his man. He approached him with the current conversational phrase of the district: "Well, seen anything of the murderer?" The man stopped to look sharply at him; then, satisfied that the journalist was not the murderer, said:

"Eh? No, nor's anybody else, curse it. Doubt if they ever will."

"I don't know. I've been thinking about them, and I've got an idea."

"So?"

"Yes. Came to me all of a sudden. Quarter of an hour ago. And I'd felt that we'd all been blind. It's been staring us in the face."

The man turned again to look at him, and the look and the movement held suspicion of this man who seemed to know so much. "Oh? Has it? Well, if you're so sure, why not give us the benefit of it?"

"I'm going to." They walked level, and were nearly at the end of the little street where it meets Deever Market, when the journalist turned casually to the man. He put a finger on his arm. "Yes, it seems to me quite simple now. But there's still one point I don't understand. One little thing I'd like to clear up. I mean the motive. Now, as man to man, tell me, Sergeant Ottermole, just *why* did you kill all those inoffensive people?"

The sergeant stopped, and the journalist stopped. There was just enough light from the sky, which held the reflected light of the continent of London, to give him a sight of the sergeant's face, and the sergeant's face was turned to him with a wide smile of such urbanity and charm that the journalist's eyes were frozen as they met it. The smile stayed for some seconds. Then said the sergeant: "Well, to tell you the truth, Mr. Newspaper Man, I don't know. I really don't know. In fact, I've been worried about it myself. But I've got an idea—just like you. Everybody knows that we can't control the workings of our minds. Don't they? Ideas come into our minds without asking. But everybody's supposed to be able to control his body. Why? Eh? We get our minds from lord-knows-where—from people who were dead hundreds of years before we were born. Mayn't we get our bodies in the same way? Our faces—our legs—our heads—they aren't completely ours. We don't make 'em. They come to us. And couldn't ideas come into our bodies like ideas come into our minds? Eh? Can't ideas live in nerve and muscle as well as in brain? Couldn't it be that parts of our bodies aren't really us, and couldn't ideas come into those parts all of a sudden, like ideas come into—into"—he shot his arms out, showing the great white-gloved hands and hairy wrists; shot them out so swiftly to the journalist's throat that his eyes never saw them—"into *my hands*!"

Rogue: Richard Verrell (Blackshirt)

"His Lady" to the Rescue

BRUCE GRAEME

GRAHAM MONTAGUE JEFFRIES (1900–1982), pseudonym Bruce Graeme, was working as a young literary agent and submitted his own novel to a publisher. When it was rejected, he tried writing a short story, a ten-thousand-word Blackshirt adventure, which was immediately accepted by a magazine, with a commission to write seven more. The British publishing house T. Fisher Unwin used the eight Blackshirt stories to launch a series of cheap "novels" in 1925 and sold more than a million copies of *Blackshirt* over the next fifteen years. The sequel, *The Return of Blackshirt* (1927), sold just as well.

Richard Verrell is known as Blackshirt because of the costume he affects when on a safecracking job, dressing entirely in black, including his mask. By day Verrell is a wealthy member of high society; at night he is an audacious burglar. A bestselling author, he continues his life of crime in the name of adventure.

Secure in his anonymity, his tranquility is shattered when his identity is discovered by a beautiful young woman who anonymously calls him on the telephone. Threatening to expose him, she forces him to change from a mere thief to a kind of Robin Hood. He soon thinks of her as his "Lady on the Phone." By the second volume in the series, they are married with a son, who has similar adventures.

"'His Lady' to the Rescue" was originally published in *New Magazine* in 1925; it was first collected in *Blackshirt* (London, T. Fisher Unwin, 1925).

"HIS LADY" TO THE RESCUE

Bruce Graeme

RICHARD VERRELL, the author, suddenly realised that although at least two hours had elapsed since he had lain his head upon the pillow, he had not yet fallen asleep. He referred to his watch, and found that his imaginary two hours was in reality only a matter of forty to forty-five minutes. Nevertheless, this was unusual, because as a general rule he automatically dropped asleep as soon as he switched off the light of his reading-lamp. Up to the present time the fact that he, a well-known novelist, was at the same time Blackshirt, now of a sudden as equally notorious, had given him no undue qualms of conscience; but tonight he felt strangely stirred, moved by some new emotion which he found impossible to define.

Restless, sleepless, he lit a cigarette and gave his chaotic thoughts full play; analysed his individuality, dissected his personality. In this turmoil there comes to him flashes of his boyhood, memories of dismal surroundings, of cruel and hated foster-parents. He lives again the night when he became lost in a maze of streets, parted from parents of whom now he had no memory. He dares not ask the people who pass, who, to his terrified imagination, assume the stature of giants, whilst he runs helter-skelter from the one man who would have been his salvation—the man in blue, the policeman at the corner. This man to the childish imagination, instilled into it by a stupid seventeen-year-old nursemaid, is an ogre from whom all good boys who say their prayers properly every night should shrink, for is he not the punisher of sins?

He glimpses himself shrinking into the shadows, sick with fear; a hairy hand gripping his shoulder till he shrieks with pain, and a beery voice mumbling incoherently; then a whirlwind of motion, clattering horses, jostling people, yells and shouts, and countless ogres, from whom, too, the man of the hairy hand also shrinks.

Next, a broken-down hovel, a slatternly woman, high words, and, if he could have only understood it then, a dawning look of comprehension and admiration on the woman's face as she whispers: "You aren't 'alf a slick 'un, Alf, after all."

Then a pseudo word of comfort to the trembling boy.

Follows then a faint, misty remembrance of brutal blows, of lessons in the art of picking pockets. With frequent practice his arms become quick and his fingers nimble. A turned back, a hasty dig from his tormentor, and the next moment an apple, a cake, a cheap piece of jewellery—anything upon which he can lay his hands—is transferred into his small pocket.

Through a hazy recollection of lessons and more lessons, of scaling walls, of slipping window-catches, he pictures himself growing taller and stronger. He remembers the pride with which he discovered one day that his head was actually level with the mantelpiece.

Then follows the period when his soul awakens from the emancipation of a shivering, nervous boy to a youth with a growing intuition of virile manliness, conscious also that his recent hatred of his unlawful escapades has turned to a joyful eagerness to embark more and more upon these nocturnal adventures, which inclination becomes emphasised as he grows older.

Even then, however, it was not for what he secured that he carried on, but for the thrill, the excitement, the risk in the obtaining thereof. Then the day that he is free of his tyrants, no more to witness with disgust the drunken orgies, to listen to their fights, their vile language. His finer feelings are urging him to escape his environment, to leave behind the sordid slums. He does so, and his finely keyed intelligence becomes aware that he is ignorant, uneducated, and uncouth.

Then years of study, with interludes of more thrills and more excitements, for which his soul craves, during which he becomes possessed of the wherewithal to live and carry on.

So the years pass until the transition is complete, and the slum-bred grub emerges into the polished, educated gentleman of the West End, perhaps, for all he knew, the ultimate position to which he had been predestined by virtue of his birth.

He stirred uneasily in his bed. Had he, however, achieved that ultimate end? Was he the man his birth demanded? As Richard Verrell, well-known author, decidedly yes; but as Blackshirt—Blackshirt, the mysterious man upon whom the detectives of Scotland Yard had long wished to lay hands; the man who robbed how, when, and where he could, matching his perfect solo-play against the team-work of the myrmidons of the law, and winning by the superiority of his wits, his subtlety, and his counter-play—Verrell shook his head. If he had been the natural-born son of the man and woman who were so long his foster-parents, and who were not even married, then, indeed, even as Blackshirt he had raised himself in life; for, though a criminal, he was at least better than the drunken, cringing sycophants that were his foster-parents.

He smiled sarcastically, and wondered why these twinges of conscience were suddenly inflicting themselves upon him, but his smile softened as he remembered a telephone conversation of a night or two before.

"Why do you do it?" had asked his Lady of the 'Phone.

He had thought and turned the matter over in his mind, but in the end he shrugged his shoulders, to confess weakly that he knew not why, which had been no more than the truth.

Why was he what he was? How was it that he lived a double life—on the one hand a gentleman, a respected member of society; and on the other an outlaw, a thief of the night?

He did not attempt to mince his language. He could not, for, whatever his faults, his sins of commission and omission, he abhorred hypocrisy—he that lived a life of hypocrisy, his one life a living lie to the other. He himself knew not why, why he was this, a man of dual personality; but one who could have known him well would have instantly laid his finger on the root of the trouble. His hidden life was nothing more or less than his excessive craving for excitement, an outlet of his dynamic forces, an opportunity to play a living game of chess. As a thief he was superb; as a detective he would have been prominent; but Fate had cast him on the wrong side of the law, and if any one person other than himself was to be blamed for his misdeeds, it was the seventeen-year-old nursemaid who had one day neglected her charge for the more amusing, if less onerous, distraction of a passing Grenadier Guardsman.

The throbbing boom of an adjacent church clock echoed twice through the quiet, still air, and still Verrell had not yet succeeded in sleeping; in fact, he was more wide awake than ever.

He switched on the reading-lamp, lit another cigarette, and picked up the book which he had been reading earlier in the evening; but, after having read two or three pages, and discovering that he had not consciously assimilated a single word, he threw the book away from him in disgust.

His nerves were tingling with a throbbing sensation, which he was too well aware was usually a prelude to one of his night excursions. The pounding of his heart seemed almost to call continually to him: "Come, come, come!"

Resolutely he attempted to ignore the call, and picked up an evening paper which lay folded and so far unread on the table next his bed. He opened it out, and as he did so his gaze was arrested by startling headlines, in which stood out one word—"Blackshirt."

With a feeling of amusement, not unmixed with a tinge of anxiety, for the first time he commenced to read about himself in print; that is to say, his secret self:

"BLACKSHIRT"

"Mysterious Master Criminal at Large"
"Scotland Yard Admits Failure"

"Through sources which it can command, and which have been the means more than once in the past of the *Evening Star* achieving some of the world's greatest newspaper scoops, we have recently learned that there is at large, and has been for many years, a mysterious criminal, known to members of the C.I. Department at Scotland Yard as 'Blackshirt,' a sobriquet well chosen by reason of the fact that this criminal invariably wears a black shirt when engaged on his nefarious enterprises.

"Blackshirt has been engaged on a series of remarkable crimes, all of which have so far been of a burglarious nature, and, notwithstanding the vigilance of the Metropolitan Police, and the recognised efficiency of our detective force, has so far successfully evaded all attempts at his capture. It speaks well of our police force that up to the present moment no whisper of this fact has been allowed to reach the general public, who are prone, in their anxiety, to be of assistance to the police, to be the means of blocking their very worthy efforts, and thus helping the criminal to escape his well-earned deserts.

"On the first rumours of Blackshirt reaching the sensitive pulses of the *Evening Star* office our crime expert immediately got into touch with officials at Scotland Yard, who can, however, add little information to that contained above.

"Amongst the recent robberies of which no trace has been found of the perpetrator, and which are assumed to be the work of Blackshirt, are the theft of Lady Carrington's diamond pendant, Mrs. Sylvester-ffoulkes's 'Study of the Infant Christ,' by Michael Angelo, Sir George Hayes's valuable stamp collection, and Lord Walker's famous statue of Apollo, in malachite. It will be seen, therefore, that Blackshirt is extremely versatile in his choice of booty, but he is even more so in his method of attack. In one instance he was successful in his coup by impersonating a policeman, whilst in another case he made his appearance disguised as a Frenchman."

There was much more to this effect, and by the time he had finished reading he was shaking in silent merriment. The *Evening Star* was the yellowest of the yellow journals, and the writer had not hesitated to draw upon his imagination.

For instance, it was the first time that Blackshirt became aware he had ever impersonated a policeman, though it was the truth that he had once taken the part of a foreigner—an Italian.

He flung the paper away in disgust. The Yellow Press could always be depended upon to make out the worst of a man and ignore the best.

An insidious, insistent voice was calling, and with a gesture of impotence he flung the bedclothes from him. He knew it was useless to struggle further.

A few minutes later Richard Verrell disappeared, and in his place stood Blackshirt. Outwardly he was dressed as a man about town, with the regulation silk hat, dress overcoat, and scarf, but this last-named article did more than keep his collar clean, for it hid his black shirt underneath, just as his shirt covered a broad elastic belt containing a complete outfit for opening any kind of door, window, or safe.

The next question which he had to consider was where to go, and as he stood hesitatingly at the window of his apartment the church clock struck the half-hour.

He grinned suddenly. He was still boyish enough to appreciate a joke, and he determined that he would walk aimlessly about until his wrist-watch showed three o'clock. Whichever house he should be nearest at that time he would enter. He was about to leave when he caught sight of the crumpled newspaper. Once again he smiled. He would tear out the columns about Blackshirt and leave it in place of whatever goods he should purloin, as a mute and poignant reminder that Blackshirt was still at large.

A clock near by struck the hour of three, and Blackshirt halted. He had wandered aimlessly up this road and down the next, caring not whether he went north, south, east, or west.

Relegating the fact that when three o'clock struck he had other work to do to the background, he had spent a happy half-hour in dreaming of his Lady of the 'Phone.

To him she was just a voice which was beginning to mean all the world to him; even now he hung upon every word she spoke, memorising every syllable, every intonation of the sweet music of her conversation.

For a full half-hour he had dreamed dreams in which appeared but two people, himself and his Lady of the Voice, as he imagined her to be—an unknown, mystical figure.

As the last stroke of the clock echoed away in the distance his dreams were banished, and he became once more his alert self, keen in his work, happy in its dangers.

He found himself in a short road, evidently an avenue, judging by the fact that plane trees lined it. There were but few houses, each one detached, standing in its own grounds. Obviously a rich neighbourhood.

Blackshirt chuckled to himself. He would have more pleasure in helping himself to a rich man's goods.

He gave a quick, searching glance up and down the road, and noted with satisfaction that there was not a soul to be seen. With a quick athletic spring he vaulted the low brick wall, and emerged into the shadows of the other side.

He covered his face with a black silk mask, and encased his hands in a pair of black silk gloves, thus making himself more invisible than ever, so that he appeared merely a black blur which crept noiselessly across the small lawn.

At the edge of the lawn he paused a moment, memorising the geography of the front of the house, and then proceeded to the back, where he hoped he would be more secluded and less likely to be seen.

In this he was not disappointed, for the back of the house was hidden from the adjacent households by a ring of trees.

He noted several points of similarity between the back and the front of the house, and concluded from this that the lower rooms stretched the whole length of the house; one, which he surmised to be a reception-room, opened out on to a small balcony through long, handsome French windows.

He judged the balcony to be undoubtedly his best means of entry into the house, and before another twenty seconds had elapsed he was standing in front of one of the windows.

There was a slight click as the latch was forced back by an instrument which he pulled from his elastic waist-belt, but he was disappointed, for the window did not give way immediately. It was evident that it was bolted as well as latched.

Another tool came into play, and presently the windows opened noiselessly inwards, and the black shadow that was Blackshirt entered and closed them behind him.

For a time he stood there, his ears alert for the slightest sound, but the house seemed absolutely silent.

Next a tiny pin-prick of light from his pocket-torch travelled round the room, moving on from one object to another.

He was surprised to note that, notwithstanding the fact that the house was built apparently in the early Victorian era, it was scarcely typical of this country, and the furnishing seemed to Blackshirt to hint somewhat of the Continent; nothing tangible, nothing which he could positively say belonged to any other country than his own, yet, nevertheless, he was distinctly of the impression that he was in the residence of a foreigner.

His light came to rest eventually on a handsome, ornate secretaire, and the artist within him gazed with delight at its graceful lines, its exquisite inlaid pattern. Obviously an *objet d'art*, the possession of a connoisseur.

Blackshirt wished that he could have taken the desk away with him. He would cheerfully have left everything else could he have done this.

He tried to draw his attention away from the desk, but each time his eyes wandered glitteringly back to it, and at length he determined that he would at least glance within, not so much in search of anything that might be there—for he did not believe that it contained anything of any value—but more to taste of the splendid work which he knew would be carried out inside as well as externally.

He found it locked, but anticipated no difficulty in opening it, suspecting that it was kept closed by the usual type of lock.

To his surprise he discovered that the lock was of an unusually intricate pattern, and it was only after great difficulty that he was successful in forcing it, but he did not regret the waste of time. Undoubtedly the desk was one of the most beautiful he had seen.

Within were scattered papers and letters. With a smile he picked up one, as he thought to himself he might just as well know exactly where he was. The envelope was addressed to:

Count de Rogeri,
Versailles House,
Maddox Gardens.

Blackshirt raised his eyebrows. Maddox Gardens! Why, he had heard of this neighbourhood often, but, although he knew whereabouts it was, this was the first time he had actually set foot here.

He had indeed come to an affluent district.

What was wealth compared to the desk? If ever Blackshirt regretted having to leave anything behind he did so this time. His supple hands wandered lovingly over the carving, whilst his flashlight revealed its extravagant design.

His sensitive finger-tips came in contact with a slack panel, and he frowned. Evidently its owner was careless. He wondered how loose it was, and moved it slightly.

The next moment there was a click, and Blackshirt spun round, his light disappearing as he did so. He stood there, tense with nervous excitement, but could hear nothing; no voice was challenging him, no revolver threatening him, all was dark, still, and silent.

Uneasily he turned again towards the desk. He did not like mysterious sounds, but as he resumed his examination of the bureau the cause of the noise was revealed to him as, where before had been a plain piece of panelling, there was now an open drawer.

By the merest coincidence Blackshirt had discovered a secret recess.

With sparkling eyes, which were synonymic of the happy excitement he felt in this discovery, he noted that there were papers within.

Curiosity urged him to glance through them, but on opening the first one he was annoyed to find the contents in German. Of this language he knew a little, though not much, so he was about to thrust them back into the drawer when two or three stray words which he recognised caught his eye and arrested his attention.

For the next few minutes his puzzled brain was gradually translating the manuscript. When he had finished he remained motionless, unable to connect his thoughts together coherently, his discovery numbing his senses.

When Marshall retired from the C.I. Department of Scotland Yard he was fortunate in securing a small, self-contained flat over a greengrocer's shop in Shepherd's Bush, and here he settled down to finish the rest of his days. He was not entirely happy in his new occupation of a retired gentleman of leisure, for he was that type of man whose enjoyment was solely in his work, and this was particularly so where he was concerned, who considered his employment the spice of life.

He missed the routine, the discipline, and, above all, the interest. There was to him as much pleasure in capturing a criminal as there is in discovering a piece of Chippendale to an antique collector.

Every now and again he was fortunate in being engaged as a private detective, but cases in which he really took interest happened so few and far between that they were not nearly enough to keep him satisfied. Most of his undertakings seemed to be in connection with divorce, in which, apart from the simplicity of the work, he discovered that usually his sympathy was with the poor, misguided people he shadowed. Eventually he came to the conclusion that if all husbands and wives were all like the people who employed him, he would remain better off as he was—single.

He lived by himself, attended only by a housekeeper, who came every morning; but as he was usually out most of the day, and very often during the night as well, he did not suffer from loneliness.

This night, for once, he had found himself what he would have termed "at a loose end," and when ten-thirty struck he went to bed in disgust, and very soon dropped into a heavy slumber.

Presently he dreamed—a weird, monstrous nightmare, in which the main plot was that everybody he knew would pick him up and throw him about, till he tired of this, and awoke to find himself looking into the muzzle of a revolver.

"Good God!" he muttered, and then glanced at the man who sat on the side of his bed, shaking him by the shoulder with his free hand.

There was no mistaking the black mask, the black shirt.

"Blackshirt!" he gasped involuntarily.

"At your service, Marshall," mocked the other.

"What the hell are you doing here?" exploded the detective.

"My dear Marshall, that is precisely what I am about to explain; but in the meantime please do not make any movement, as I happen to be, as you will observe, covering you with a revolver, which, by the way, is your own, and which I took the liberty of borrowing from beneath your pillow. I hope you do not object?"

Marshall did not answer, but merely grunted with an amazed air.

"Thank you," continued Blackshirt; "then I may take it you do not object. To continue, I have a great admiration for you, Marshall, and when I say this I want you to believe that I mean it sincerely; I am not just mocking you. I have several things about which I wish to speak to you, and I am not particularly keen to tire my arm out holding this gun out in this threatening attitude. Give me your word, Marshall, that you will make no attempt at my capture until I have left this building, and I will talk to you as man to man on a matter beside which my capture and your fame are as nothing, for it concerns what is more important to both of us—our own country."

The detective thought rapidly. Should he or should he not give the required promise, and if he did, would he keep it? On this latter point he very soon made up his mind. He knew, come what might, he could not break his word to any man, not even to Blackshirt, for whose capture he would give his right hand. On the other hand, if he did not give the undertaking Blackshirt asked he might, by awaiting his opportunity, turn the tables.

Blackshirt read his mind. "It's no good your thinking that, Marshall, for unless you agree I shall clear out now. I think you know me better than to give you the chance which you think might be yours if you don't do as I wish."

The detective shrugged his shoulders. "Well, I suppose you're right. Yes, I give you my assurance."

Blackshirt seemed relieved, and cast the revolver down on the bed beside Marshall.

"Thanks, Marshall; though I took the trouble to extract your ammunition beforehand."

"Hang!" muttered the detective. "If I'd known that——"

"Yes, I dare say," interrupted Blackshirt, not giving him time to finish, and smiled in his winning way, which even the black mask could not entirely cover. "I felt sure that I would arouse your curiosity sufficiently."

Marshall gazed at him admiringly. "You're a cool card, whatever else you may be. However, what is it you want to tell me, and will you have a whisky-and-soda while you are saying it?"

Blackshirt laughed. "Not for me; thanks all the same, though. It's apt to spoil one's work to imbibe in the middle of it. But now to business.

"Tonight I went to bed—for a change, you are no doubt thinking; but, nevertheless, I do sometimes act as any other law-abiding citizen.

"For some reason or other I was restless, and was not successful, as novelists say, in the wooing of Morpheus, so I picked up an evening newspaper, and, greatly to my delight and amusement, had the pleasure of reading all about myself."

"Yes, I read all that, too. They made it a bit hot towards the end." Marshall grinned.

"Ah, well, that's the penalty of being famous, eh, Marshall? To continue. The article had an unfortunate effect upon me, I confess, for it roused me to action. So you can therefore imagine me, an hour or so back, getting inside this picturesque outfit of mine, which has its uses. It will be a boon to the cartoonist in tomorrow's paper.

"Having no fixed destination in mind, I determined to wander around until a clock struck three, and then to break into the nearest mansion, help myself to the valuables in the accredited way, and go back home to bed a richer and more sleepy man."

His voice suddenly dropped its bantering tone, and Marshall sensed that he was coming to the point to which he owed this unexpected visit.

"Marshall, by some stroke of Fate, when the clock struck three I was outside what I afterwards discovered to be the residence of Count de Rogeri, who lives at Versailles House, Maddox Gardens.

"A few minutes later I was inside and examining a wonderful desk, an example of Italian art in the sixteenth century. Whilst doing so, by pure accident I touched a hidden spring, and a secret drawer was exposed to my view. There were papers within, and my curiosity urged me to look through them, to find they were in German."

He paused, and unconsciously Marshall uttered an impatient "Go on, man!" so intent was he upon the narrative which was slowly being unfolded.

"I read those papers, though my knowledge of German is none too good, but it was sufficient for me to realise that what I held in my hand were the plans and specifications of the latest R.A.F. machine."

"Good heavens! A spy!"

"Precisely."

Again the silence, whilst the two men revolved in their minds the sudden revelation.

Presently Marshall spoke. "Why have you come to me?" he asked curiously.

"For several reasons, one of which I have already explained to you—that I trust you. Secondly, this spy must be unmasked. Obviously, were I, as Blackshirt, to write and inform Scotland Yard of this fact, the probability is that they would give no credence to my accusation. On the other hand, if I were to sign the name by which I am known to the world at large—such few people as I do know—my identity would be revealed, and Blackshirt would promptly see the inside of a prison, which is the last thing I desire.

"Again, there is no knowing when the Count is likely to go to that desk again. Perhaps by the time Scotland Yard had made up its mind, and arrived at his house for the proof, these papers might be on the way to Germany, and then there would be just my accusations against Count de Rogeri's word. I have, therefore, brought the papers with me."

Marshall shook his head. "You were wrong to do that. As it happens I was on the Special Section of the C.I. Department during the war, which, as perhaps you may know, devoted itself to spies, so that I learned quite a lot of the methods of this country in dealing with foreign agents.

"During the war it was just a question of capture, trial and execution; but in peace-time, no. We play a far more subtle game than that. Once a man is identified as a spy to our certain knowledge, from that time forward he is watched day and night. Every letter he writes, every parcel he sends, is intercepted, whilst every communication to him is copied before he receives it. In this way, not only does our own Secret Service become aware of every scrap of information which may be sent out of the country, but it also discovers the names and addresses of other spies who may get into touch with the one who was originally watched.

"Blackshirt—for this is the only name I can call you—by hook or by crook you must return those papers, and leave everything as you found it, so that your presence there will be positively unsuspected.

"Tomorrow I shall go to the Yard. In the meantime, for heaven's sake get them back again."

Blackshirt glanced at his watch. The time was twelve minutes past four. He pursed his lips.

"It can't be done, Marshall. It's too late. For all we know some of the maids may already be astir." But Marshall knew that, despite what he said, he had already determined in his mind to act as the detective suggested.

Like a shadow Blackshirt disappeared, and a few seconds later Marshall heard the whir of an electric starter. Evidently Blackshirt had a car. He felt tempted to rush to the window and note the number, but he resisted. He could not play the dirty on the other, as he so aptly put it to himself.

Meanwhile, Blackshirt was speeding back towards Maddox Gardens. The car was a borrowed one. At the end of Maddox Road was a garage, from which Blackshirt had helped himself.

It was still dark when he was back at Versailles House once more, having returned the automobile, but there was a suspicious greyness in the east, and he calculated that the first streaks of daylight would be showing within half an hour.

Once again he crept across the lawn and round to the back of the house, and once more climbed up on to the balcony and entered the room through the tall French windows.

He listened intently, but there was not a sound. The tiny pin-prick of light from his torch travelled slowly round the room, but nothing had been moved. He breathed a sigh of relief. Apparently his presence had not been discovered, so that it would be a simple matter to return the papers.

With a quick, silent step he crossed the room, and, opening the desk, which he had left unlocked, he returned the papers to their hiding-place.

This time he knew it would be necessary to re-lock the desk, and he knelt down before it. He brought his delicate little instruments to work, and presently a faint click informed him that he had been successful.

No sooner had this occurred when he experienced an extraordinary sensation. At the back of his brain he felt an intuition that something had gone wrong. This communicated itself to the rest of his body, and his sensitive nerves jumped in unison.

He could not define what it was, but he seemed to sense that someone was watching him, that there was somebody else present in the room besides himself.

He listened acutely; there was not a sound to be heard. The house was as silent as a graveyard; yet the feeling became more insistent, till at last he became positively assured that he was under observation.

He almost groaned, for, were this indeed the case, and the unseen watcher the Count himself, what Marshall feared most would probably happen. Undoubtedly the Count's suspicions would be aroused on seeing a man before the desk, when there was more valuable booty in another part of the room.

What must he do to allay this supposition? Before he could act the room was suddenly flooded with light.

He whirled round; the room was still empty. Incredulous and bewildered, he gazed in every direction, and confirmed that fact that only he himself was present. Instinctively, as he realised this fact, he stepped towards the window, but——

"Ah, so you are not armed!"

The heavy portière was flung aside, to reveal a man in evening dress.

"Good evening," he said, with a pleasant smile, which was contradicted by the glitter in his eyes, and the menacing revolver which he held in his hand, pointing with unpleasant directness at the pit of Blackshirt's stomach.

Despite the seriousness of his position, it flashed through Blackshirt's mind that it was not an entirely dissimilar situation to that in which he had been less than an hour ago, but then it was he who held the whip-hand.

He glanced at the newcomer, and gathered, as he had assumed, that he was Count de Rogeri himself. Dressed and groomed immaculately in the English style, there was to be recognised a faint soupçon of foreign blood, and Blackshirt wondered if he were not of mixed parentage, possibly French and German. A correct supposition, could he have known it, the Count's mother being an Alsatian Frenchwoman, and his father a Prussian.

"Why, may I ask, have I the honour of this visit?" There was a fixed intensity in the Count's voice, which confirmed the suspicion in his eyes.

Blackshirt turned over in his mind on what grounds he should meet the Count. Should he be an ignorant housebreaker, or should he remain just Blackshirt? He decided upon the latter course. With any luck the Count had read the papers.

Blackshirt shrugged his shoulders. "Why does one usually break into other people's houses?"

The Count raised his eyebrows. "An educated voice, I observe. Forgive me if I smoke?" he asked with irony, and with his left hand he took out a handsome gold cigarette-case from his coat pocket, snapped it open, and placed a cigarette in his mouth, which he afterwards lit, never for a moment allowing his revolver to waver a hair's breadth from the direction of Blackshirt's body.

"I regret I cannot offer you one also," he remarked presently, "but I prefer to see your hands remain where they are." He paused. "Really, you look remarkably picturesque for an ordinary burglar."

"But then, you see, my dear sir, I like to think that I am not an ordinary housebreaker."

"Ah, I see. An Arsène Lupin!"

"And you, Ganimand!"

"Your choice of books is evidently picked with care, for I judge you have read the book."

"In the original."

"Ah, my admiration for you increases every moment! You are indeed worthy to be captured. If I talk much longer to you I shall almost regret having to call your big, flat-footed policemen."

"There's many a slip, my dear Count, many a slip."

"Banal." The Count paused, and then with startling suddenness he asked: "How did you know my name?"

If he thought to catch Blackshirt off his guard he was mistaken, for by this time the prisoner had planned his campaign, though with a sinking heart he realised that even if he were successful in persuading the Count that he was there only for a commonplace burglary, the more he did so the more likely it would be that the Count would have him arrested.

For a brief moment he thought of buying his liberty with his knowledge of the Count's secret intrigues, but this he dismissed almost as soon as it occurred to him.

"An up-to-date and modern housebreaker plans his attack with as much care and foresight as a field-marshal directing his army. I have been watching this house for the last two or three weeks, so naturally I knew who you were directly you appeared so disconcertingly from behind the portière."

The Count blew a swirling, eddying smoke-ring into the air, and, watching it, he inquired casually: "And the desk, monsieur—did you expect to find many Bank of England notes there?"

Blackshirt laughed scornfully.

"Scarcely. There are sometimes papers which are more valuable than banknotes."

He was watching the Count intently, and saw him stiffen up with an infinitesimal start. For a moment his glance rested piercingly upon his unexpected visitor, only to look casually away again, and Blackshirt knew that the Count's suspicions were now thoroughly aroused, a point to which he had been working.

"Papers!" asked the Count. "What kind of papers?"

"Letters, Count de Rogeri, letters! You are a woman's man."

It was a shot in the dark, but it hit home.

"Perhaps, and so——"

"Sometimes letters pass between a man and his mistress. Such letters are valuable."

"Blackmail!" The Count laughed sneeringly, but Blackshirt detected the note of relief in his voice. His suspicions, roused to a point when they became almost certainties, were suddenly allayed. Even so he meant to take no chances.

"And may I ask whether you were successful?"

Blackshirt became suddenly despondent.

"I regret to say you arrived about five or ten minutes too soon. That pretty desk of yours has an unusually tough lock, and I had been unable to crack it when you made your appearance."

Still keeping Blackshirt covered, the Count warily crossed to the desk and tried it, and notwithstanding his expressionless face, Blackshirt caught the relief which he could not keep from his eyes.

With the knowledge that he was safe he became instantly more domineering, more the man with the whip-hand. Before he had been merely fencing, not sure of his ground.

"Now we will quit fooling. What is your name?"

"That, Count de Rogeri, is a thing that many would like to know, which many have tried to discover. They have been singularly unsuccessful."

"Perhaps they did not have you at the wrong end of a revolver, as have I."

"A forcible argument, I admit. Under the circumstances I suppose it is necessary for me to tell you that my name is Blackshirt."

"Ah, Blackshirt! I had the pleasure of reading about you in tonight's paper. Well, well! Supposing you take off that mask! I remember now that the paper stated that you had never been seen without a mask."

"I regret I must refuse, however much it might be my pleasure to do you the honour, Count de Rogeri, of being the first one of having that privilege."

The Count thrust his chin a little forward. "You will take that mask off, or——" He patted his revolver significantly. "It would be quite easy for me to look at your face *afterwards.*"

"That would be murder, and murder is a hanging matter in England."

The Count chuckled unpleasantly. "Not murder, my dear Blackshirt, but justifiable manslaughter. I have another revolver upstairs. It would be only necessary to put it in your hand to prove my point."

Blackshirt felt tiny beads of perspiration forcing themselves through his skin, and despair took hold of him. Unfortunately he knew that what the Count had said was only too true. There would be no witnesses to prove that he had been deliberately murdered. In his own mind he believed the Count thoroughly capable of doing what he had threatened. Discovery seemed inevitable. His glance wandered desperately away from the penetrating gaze of his captor.

What was it he had just said to himself? "Discovery seemed inevitable!" Perhaps; but not this evening, for he had just seen a tiny, shapely hand creeping slowly round the edge of the portière and shake a warning to him.

At all costs he must delay the evil moment for unmasking for just a few seconds. Perhaps rescue was at hand, for otherwise why the stealthy attitude of the person behind the curtain?

"Count de Rogeri, I admit defeat. You have got the better of me."

"Very kind of you to grant me that," answered the other sarcastically, "but the mask—I am waiting."

Whoever was behind the curtain was gradually advancing into view, and Blackshirt suddenly thrilled. It was a woman.

"Please give me half a minute," he asked desperately, "while I explain my circumstances to you. Count de Rogeri, I am rich and wealthy. I move in your own circle. I, too, am a gentleman, and I carry on my midnight adventures for the sake of excitement only."

The woman was heavily veiled. Out of the corner of his eye he noticed this fact, and saw, too, that she was still steadily moving forward. Another three yards—no, two and a half yards, and she would be behind the Count.

"You would not like to go to prison any more than I. It must be hateful! Think of it, seven years of torture; seven years of damnation, perhaps more, and it will be on your conscience that you have sent me there. Please, please," he cried, in an agonised voice, "let me go!"

The woman was almost behind the Count now; another step or two, and the scarf which she was holding in both hands would be around her quarry.

"Bah! A coward!" The scorn in his voice was galling, and, acting up to his part, Blackshirt straightened up suddenly as if the moral blow had gone home, glanced despairingly at the revolver, and slumped again into a dejected attitude.

The Count sneered again, and relaxed the tension of the hand which was holding the weapon.

At that moment the mysterious new-comer stretched out her arms and enveloped the Count's face with a scarf, and simultaneously Blackshirt sprang forward and wrested the revolver from the Count's grasp. The tables were turned.

"You can let him go," said Blackshirt to his unknown rescuer, and covered the Count with the pistol.

Trembling with rage and fury, the Count gazed evilly at him.

"Not quite such a coward, eh, Count de Rogeri?" mocked Blackshirt, and the Count realised that his late captive had been acting a part.

"I am sorry I can't ask you to unmask or

anything of that sort," continued Blackshirt, "but I am afraid it will be necessary for me to request that you sit on one of those chairs, and perhaps my lady friend, as she has evidently come here to rescue me, will kindly tie your arms and legs securely. No, not that scarf. It doesn't do to leave behind a possible clue. His own silk handkerchief will do quite well, whilst I can supply another one which is absolutely unmarked."

In another few seconds, Count de Rogeri was trussed hand and foot to one of his own chairs, and gagged by one of his own cushion-covers.

Blackshirt gazed at their joint work admiringly. "I trust that you are perfectly comfortable, Count de Rogeri, for I am afraid you will be under the painful necessity of remaining in the same attitude until your servants awake to release you, and as you are a ladies' man, and probably sleep late, it would not surprise me if they were not more or less later than the usual household.

"I am sorry that I was not able to unmask, but had I done so I should have felt more like Cinderella, who was changed from the belle of the ballroom, dressed in silks and jewellery, into a poor little scullery-maid. So should I have ceased to be unknown, and doubtless would have spent seven long years in prison through your instrumentality. *Au revoir*, Monsieur le Comte, or should I say 'Adieu'?" The next moment Blackshirt and his rescuer disappeared.

In the front, securely hidden from prying eyes by a large elm tree, they stopped.

"Say, I'll tell the world that that was the cutest piece of play I have ever seen!" said the woman suddenly.

Blackshirt started with delight. "My Lady of the 'Phone!" he muttered involuntarily.

"Say, is that what you call me? Well, now, isn't that sweet?"

Blackshirt felt his cheeks flushing, and was glad of the protecting darkness.

"You may remove your mask, Mr. Verrell," continued the other, "and we had best be on our way before any further unpleasant events transpire."

"And if I do," he whispered softly, "will you not lift your veil?"

"I should say not!" she answered decisively.

"Oh, won't you, please?" he pleaded, but she shook her head.

"Then you will 'phone me up?"

"I will."

"Very often?" he said, catching her hand within his own.

For a moment she left it there, and Blackshirt felt the warmth of her soft fingers stealing into his, even through his gloves; then she withdrew it.

"Perhaps," she whispered, so softly that it sounded more like the sighing of the wind.

He swayed towards her, and the magic of the moment gripped them both. Shaking in every limb, his arms crept slowly towards and around her, and for one brief moment she stood there, a trembling, palpitating woman. Just then a distant church clock struck the hour of five.

She pushed him away sharply.

"Quick! You go along to the wall and see if the coast is clear, and I will follow you, and you can help me over."

"Yes, yes, I will do that; but before we go tell me how did you know where I was, and that I was in such an awkward situation?"

"That is my secret," she answered gaily. "Now go."

"But you must tell me," he commanded.

"I will—one day." And she pushed him forward with her hands, and he knew her answer was final.

He crept towards the wall, and, observing that there was no one near, he leapt lightly over and turned round to assist his Lady of the 'Phone, but she had disappeared. He waited half a minute, but when there was still no sign of her he knew that she intended to remain the mystery that she was.

He tore off the mask from his face, and

slipped off his black silk gloves, turned up the collar of his light rainproof, and sprung out his opera hat, which fitted into a special pocket of the coat. This he set rakishly upon his head, and became once again a gentleman of the world as he started home.

"Curse that clock!" he muttered savagely.

In the garage at the end of Maddox Gardens a bewildered chauffeur scratched his head and gazed, bewitched, at the car in front of him. "Well, I never!" he muttered, "but I could have swore that I cleaned the car last night!"

Rogue: Anthony Newton

On Getting an Introduction

EDGAR WALLACE

"ANTHONY NEWTON was a soldier at sixteen; at twenty-six he was a beggar of favors." Thus Richard Horatio Edgar Wallace (1875–1932) introduces the young man who finds success as a con man and thief. After his military service, Newton makes every effort to gain honest employment but without luck. He does find that his quick wit and amusing tongue make him a successful scam artist, so he devotes his energies to that endeavor.

Newton is merely one of many rogues created by Wallace. As a populist writer, Wallace found that common people related to his rogues—criminals who were not violent or physically dangerous but whose talents and inclinations led them to the other side of the law. Others include Anthony Smith (*The Mixer*, 1927), "Elegant" Edward Farthindale (*Elegant Edward*, 1928), and Four Square Jane (*Four Square Jane*, 1929). Readers rooted for these and other of Wallace's numerous literary criminals, who always stole from the wealthy and powerful.

The prolific Wallace reputedly wrote one hundred seventy novels, eighteen stage plays, nine hundred fifty-seven short stories, and elements of numerous screenplays and scenarios, including the first British sound version of *The Hound of the Baskervilles*; one hundred sixty films, both silent and sound, have been based on his books and stories.

"On Getting an Introduction" was first published in *The Brigand* (London, Hodder & Stoughton, 1927).

ON GETTING AN INTRODUCTION

Edgar Wallace

POLITE BRIGANDAGE has its novel aspects and its moments of fascination. Vulgar men, crudely furnished in the matter of ideas, may find profit in violence, but the more subtle and the more delicate nuances of the art of gentle robbery had an especial attraction for one who, in fulfilment of the poet's ambition, could count the game before the prize.

So it came about that Mr. Newton found himself in an awkward situation. The two near wheels of his car were in a ditch; he with some difficulty had maintained himself at the steering wheel, though the branches of the overhanging hedge were so close to him that he had to twist his head on one side. Nevertheless, he maintained an attitude of supreme dignity as he climbed out of his car, and the eyes that met the girl's alarmed gaze were full of gentle reproach.

She sat bolt upright at the wheel of her beautiful Daimler, and for a while was speechless.

"You were on the wrong side of the road," said Tony gently.

"I'm awfully sorry," she gasped. "I sounded my horn, but these wretched Sussex lanes are so blind . . ."

"Say no more about it," said Anthony. He surveyed the ruins of his car gravely.

"I thought you would see me as you came down the hill," she said in excuse. "I saw you and I sounded my horn."

"I didn't hear it," said Anthony, "but that is beside the question. The fault is entirely mine, but I fear my poor car is completely ruined."

She got out and stood beside him, the figure of penitence, her eyes fixed upon the drunken wreck.

"If I had not turned immediately into the ditch," said Anthony, "there would have been a collision. And it is better that I should ruin my car than I should occasion you the slightest apprehension."

She drew a quick sigh.

"Thank goodness it is only an old car," she said. "Of course, Daddy will—"

Anthony could not allow the statement to pass unchallenged.

"It looks old now," he said gently; "it looks even decrepit. It has all the appearance of ruin which old age, alas, brings, but it is not an old car."

"It is an old model," she insisted. "Why, that's about twenty years old—I can tell from the shape of the wing."

"The wings of my car," said Anthony, "may

be old fashioned. I am an old fashioned man, and I like old fashioned wings. In fact, I insisted upon having those old fashioned wings put on this perfectly new car. You have only to look at the beautiful coach work—the lacquer—"

"You lacquered it yourself," she accused him. "Anybody can see that that has been newly done." She touched the paint with her finger, and it left a little black stain. "There," she said triumphantly, "It has been done with 'Binko,' you can see the advertisements in all the papers: 'Binko dries in two hours.'" She touched the paint again and looked at the second stain on her finger. "That means you painted it a fortnight ago," she said, "it always takes a month to dry."

Anthony said nothing. He felt that her discovery called for silence. Moreover, he could not, for the moment, think of any appropriate rejoinder.

"Of course," she went on more warmly, "it was very fine of you to take such a dreadful risk. My father, I know, will be very grateful."

She looked at the car again.

"You don't think you could get it up," she said.

Anthony was very sure he could not restore the equilibrium of his car. He had bought it a week before for thirty pounds. The owner had stuck out for thirty-five, and Anthony had tossed him thirty pounds or forty, and had won. Anthony always won those tosses. He kept a halfpenny in his pocket which had a tail on each side, and since ninety-nine people out of a hundred say "heads" when you flip a coin in the air, it was money for nothing.

"Shall I drive you into Pilbury?" she said.

"Is there anywhere I can find a telephone?" asked Anthony.

"I'll take you back to the house," said Jane Mansar suddenly. "It's quite near, you can telephone from there, and I'd like you to have a talk with father. Of course, we will not allow you to lose by your unselfish action, though I did sound my horn as I came round the corner."

"I didn't hear it," said Anthony gravely.

He climbed in, and she backed the car into a gateway, turned and sped at a reckless pace back the way she had come. She turned violently from the road, missed one of the lodge gates by a fraction of an inch and accelerated up a broad drive to a big white house that showed sketchily between the encircling elms. She braked suddenly and Anthony got out with relief.

Mr. Gerald Mansar was a stout, bald man, whose fiery countenance was relieved by a pure white moustache and bristling white eyebrows. He listened with thunderous calm whilst his pretty daughter told the story of her narrow escape.

"You sounded your horn?" he insisted.

"Yes, father, I am sure I sounded the horn."

"And you were going, of course, at a reasonable pace," said Mr. Mansar.

In his early days he had had some practice at the law in the County Courts. Anthony Newton recognised the style and felt it was an appropriate moment to step in.

"You quite understand, Mr. Mansar, that I completely exonerate Miss Mansar from any responsibility," he interjected. "I am perfectly sure she sounded the horn, though I did not hear it. I am completely satisfied and can vouch for the fact that she was proceeding at a very leisurely pace, and whatever fault there was, was mine."

Anthony Newton was a very keen student of men, particularly of rich men. He had studied them from many angles, and one of the first lessons he learnt in presenting a claim, was to exonerate these gentlemen from any legal responsibility. The rich hate and loathe the onus of legal responsibility. They will spend extravagant sums in law costs to demonstrate to the satisfaction of themselves and the world that they are not legally responsible for the payment of a boot-black's fee. The joy of wealth is generosity. There was never a millionaire born who would not prefer to give a thousand than to pay a disputed penny.

Mr. Mansar's puckered face relaxed.

"I shall certainly not allow you to be the loser, Mr.—"

"Newton is my name."

"Newton. You are not in the firm of Newton, Boyd, and Wilkins, are you, the rubber people?"

"No," said Anthony. "I never touch rubber."

"You are not the pottery Newton, are you?" asked Mr. Mansar hopefully.

"No," said Anthony gravely, "we have always kept clear of pots."

After Mr. Mansar had, by cross-examination, discovered that he wasn't one of the Warwickshire Newtons, or Monmouth Newtons, or a MacNewton of Ayr, or one of those Irish Newtons, or a Newton of Newton Abbot, but was just an ordinary London Newton, his interest momentarily relaxed.

"Well, my dear," he said, "what shall we do?"

The girl smiled.

"I think at least we ought to ask Mr. Newton to lunch," she said and the old man, who seemed at a loss as to how the proceedings might reasonably be terminated or developed, brightened up at the suggestion.

"I noticed that you mentioned me by name. Of course, my daughter told you—" he said.

Anthony smiled.

"No, sir," he replied, "but I know the city rather well and, of course, your residence in this part of the world is as well known as—"

"Naturally," said Mr. Gerald Mansar. He had no false ideas as to his fame. The man who had engineered the Nigerian oil boom, the Irish linen boom, who floated the Milwaukee paper syndicate for two millions, could have no illusions about his obscurity.

"You are in the city yourself, Mr. Newton?"

"Yes," admitted Anthony.

He was in the city to the extent of hiring an office on a first floor of a city building; and it was true he had his name painted on the door. It was an office not big enough to swing a cat, as one of his acquaintances had pointed out. Anthony however, did not keep cats. And if he had kept them, he would certainly have never been guilty of such cruelty.

The lunch was not an unpleasant function, for a quite unexpected factor had come into his great scheme. Nobody knew better than Anthony Newton that it was Mr. Mansar himself who every Saturday morning drove the Daimler into Pullington, and when Anthony had purchased his racketty car, spending many hours in the application of "Binko" to endow it with a more youthful complexion, he had not dreamt that the adventure would end so pleasantly. He knew that Mr. Millionaire Mansar had a daughter—he had a vague idea that somebody had told him she was pretty. He did not anticipate when he engineered his accident so carefully, that it would be at her expense.

For, whatever else he was, Anthony Newton was an honest adventurer. He had decided that there was money in honest adventure; he had reached this conclusion after he had made a careful study of the press. There were other adventurers whose names figured conspicuously in the police court reports. They were all ingenious and painstaking men, but their ingenuity and foresight were employed in ways which made no appeal to one who had strict, but not too strict, views on the sacredness of property.

Some of these adventurers had walked into isolated post offices, a mask over their faces and a revolver in their hands and had carried off the contents of the till, amidst the loud protests of postal officials who were on the spot. Others had walked into banks similarly disguised and had drawn out balances which were certainly not due to them.

And Anthony, thinking out the matter, decided that it was quite possible, by the exercise of his mental talent, to secure quite a lot of money without taking the slightest risks.

He wished to know Mr. Mansar. Mr. Mansar, in ordinary circumstances, was unapproachable. To step into his office and demand an interview was almost as futile as stepping up to the stamp counter in St. Martin's-le-Grand, and asking to see the Postmaster-General. Mr. Mansar was surrounded by guards, inner and outer, by secretaries, by heads of departments, by general managers and managing directors, to say nothing of commissionaires, doorkeepers, messengers, and plain clerks.

There are two ways of getting acquainted with the great. One is to discover their hobbies, which is the weakest side of their defence, and the other is to drop in upon them on their holidays. The man you cannot meet in the City of London is very accessible in the Hotel de la Paix.

But apparently Mr. Mansar never took a holiday, and his only hobby was keeping alive an illusion of his profound genius.

Lunch over, and Anthony's object achieved, there seemed no excuse for his lingering. He awaited, with some confidence, the grave intimation that a car was ready to take him to the station, and that Mr. Mansar would be glad if he would dine with him at his London house on Thursday. Maybe it would be Wednesday. Possibly, thought Anthony, the function might be deferred for a week or two. But the intimation did not come. He was treated as though he had arrived for a permanent stay.

Mr. Mansar showed him the library, and told him to make himself comfortable, pointing out certain books which had amused him (Mr. Mansar) in his moments of leisure.

Anthony Newton cooed and settled himself, not perhaps to read, but to think large and beautiful thoughts of great financial coups which he might engineer with this prince of financiers, of partnerships maybe, certainly of profits.

There was a big window looking out upon a marble terrace and as he read, or pretended to read, Mr. and Miss Mansar paced restlessly along the paved walk. They were talking in a low voice and Anthony, having surrendered all sense of decorum, crept nearer to the window and listened as they passed.

"He is much better looking than the last one," murmured Jane, and he saw Mr. Mansar nod.

Much better looking than the last one? Anthony scratched his head.

Presently they came back.

"He has a very clever face," said Jane, and Mr. Mansar grunted.

Anthony had not the slightest doubt as to whom they were talking about. When she said "clever face" he knew it was himself.

They did not return again, and Anthony waited on, a little impatient, a little curious; he had decided that he himself would make a move to go, when Mr. Mansar came into the library and carefully closed the door behind him.

"I want a little talk with you, Mr. Newton," he said solemnly. "It has occurred to me that you might be of the very greatest service to my firm."

Anthony cleared his throat. The same thought had occurred to him also.

"Do you know Brussels at all?"

"Intimately," said Anthony promptly. He had never been to Brussels, but he knew that he could get a working knowledge of the city from any guide book.

Mr. Mansar stroked his chin, pursed his lips, frowned, and then:

"It is providential, your arriving," he said. "I have a very confidential mission which I have been looking for somebody to undertake. In fact, I thought of going to town this afternoon to find a man for the purpose but, as I say, your arrival has been miraculously providential. I have been discussing it with my daughter, I hope you will forgive that little impertinence," he said, courteously.

Anthony Newton forgave him there and then.

"My daughter, who is a judge of character, is rather impressed by you."

It was clear to Anthony now that he had been the subject of the conversation he had overheard. He was tingling with curiosity to discover exactly the nature of the mission which was to be entrusted to him. Mr. Mansar did not keep him waiting long.

"I want you to go by tonight's train to Brussels. You will arrive on Sunday morning, and remain there until Wednesday morning. Have you sufficient money for your journey?"

"Oh, yes," said Anthony, airily.

"Good." Mr. Mansar nodded gravely, as though he had never had any doubt upon the matter. "You will carry with you a sealed envelope, which you will open on Wednesday morning in the presence of my Brussels agent, Monsieur Lament, of the firm of Lament and Lament, the great financiers, of whom you must have heard."

"Naturally," said Anthony.

"I want you to keep your mission a secret, tell nobody, you understand?"

Anthony understood perfectly.

"I leave the method of travel to you. There is a train to London in half an hour; here is the letter."

He took it from his inside pocket. It was addressed to Mr. Anthony Newton, and marked "To be opened in the presence of Monsieur Cecil Lament, 119, Rue Partriele, Brussels."

"I do not promise you that you will be paid very well or even be paid at all, for undertaking this mission," said the millionaire. "But I rather fancy this experience will be useful to you in more ways than one."

Anthony detected a certain significance in this cautious promise and smiled happily.

"I think I'll go along now, sir," he said briskly. "When I carry out these missions—and as you may guess, this is not the first time that I have been—entrusted with important errands—I prefer that I should lose no time."

"I think you're wise," said Mr. Mansar soberly.

Anthony hoped to see the girl before he went, but here he was disappointed. It was a very ordinary chauffeur who drove him to the station and, passing the wreckage of his car stranded in the ditch, Anthony did not regret one single penny of his expenditure. Anyway, the car would still sell for the price of old iron.

He reached Brussels in time for breakfast on Sunday morning, and on the Monday he made a call at Monsieur Lament's office. Monsieur Lament was a short, stout man, with a large and bushy beard, and seemed surprised at the advent of this spruce and mysterious young Englishman.

"From M'sieur Mansar," he said with respect, even veneration. "M'sieur Mansar did not tell me he was sending anybody. Is it in connection with the Rentes?"

"I am not at liberty to say," said Anthony discreetly. "In fact, sir, I am, so to speak, under sealed orders."

Monsieur Lament heard the explanation and nodded.

"I honour your discretion, M'sieur," he said. "Now is there anything I can do for you while you are in Brussels? Perhaps you would dine with me tonight at my club."

Anthony was very happy to dine with him at his club, because he had brought with him a grossly insufficient sum to pay his expenses.

Over the dinner that night, Monsieur Lament spoke reverently of the great English financier.

"What a wonderful man," he said, with an expressive gesture. "You are a friend of his, M'sieur Newton?"

"Not exactly a friend," said Anthony carefully, "how can one be a friend of a monument? One can only stand at a distance and admire."

"True, true," said the thoughtful Monsieur Lament. "He is indeed, a remarkable character. And his daughter—" he kissed the tips of his fingers, "what charm, what intelligence, what beauty!"

"Ah!" said Anthony, "what!"

So charming a companion was he, that Monsieur Lament asked him to lunch with him the next day, and this time the Belgian showed some curiosity as to the object of Anthony's visit.

"Is it in connection with the Turkish loan?" he asked.

Anthony smiled.

"You will, I am sure, agree with me that I must maintain the utmost secrecy," he said firmly.

"Naturally! Of course! Certainly!" said Monsieur Lament hastily. "I honour your discretion. But if it is in connection with the Turkish loan, or the Viennese Municipal loan—"

Anthony raised his hand with a gesture of gentle insistence.

Monsieur Lament dissolved into apologies.

Anthony was himself curious and he attended M. Lament's office on Wednesday morning with a joyous sense of anticipation.

In that rosewood-panelled room standing with his back to the white marble fireplace, he tore the flap of the envelope with fingers that shook, for he realised that he might be at the very crisis of his career; and that his good plan to drop into financial society had succeeded beyond his wildest hope.

To his amazement, the letter was from Jane Mansar, and he read it, open-mouthed.

Dear Mr. Newton:
Daddy wants to hand you over to the police or have you ducked in the pond. I chose this method of giving you a graceful exit from the scene, because I feel that such a man of genius and valour should not be subjected to so ignominious a fate. You are the thirty-fourth person who has secured an introduction to my father by novel, and in some cases, painful, methods. I have been rescued from terrifying tramps (who have been hired by my rescuer) some six times. I have been pushed into the river and rescued twice. Daddy has had three people accidentally wounded by him when he has been shooting rabbits, and at least five who have got into the way of his car when he has been driving between the house and the station.

We do recognize and appreciate the novelty of your method, and I confess that for a moment I was deceived by the artistic wreckage of your poor little car. To make absolutely sure that I was not doing you an injustice, I telephoned the local garage, and found, as I expected, that you had kept the car there for a fortnight before the "accident." Poor Mr. Newton, better luck next time.

Yours sincerely,
Jane Mansar.

Anthony read the letter three times, and then looked mechanically at the slip of paper which was enclosed. It ran:

To MONSIEUR LAMENT,
Pay Mr. Anthony Newton a sum sufficient to enable him to reach London, and to support him on the journey.

Gerald Mansar.

Monsieur Lament was watching the dazed young man.

"Is it important?" he asked eagerly. "Is it to be communicated to me?"

Anthony was never wholly overcome by the most tremendous circumstances. He folded the letter, put it in his pocket, looked at the slip again.

"I regret that I cannot tell you all that this contains," he said. "I am leaving immediately for Berlin. From Berlin I go to Vienna, from Vienna to Istanbul; from there I must make a hurried journey to Rome, and from Rome I have to get to Tangier. Then I shall reach Gibraltar in a month's time, and fly to England."

He handed the slip to Monsieur Lament.

"Pay Mr. Anthony Newton a sufficient sum to enable him to reach London and support him on the journey."

Monsieur Lament looked at Anthony. "How much will you require, M'sieur?" he asked respectfully.

"About nine hundred pounds, I think," said Anthony softly.

Monsieur Lament gave him the money then and there and when Mansar got the account he was justifiably annoyed.

He came into Jane, storming.

"That . . . that . . ." he spluttered, "rascal . . ."

"Which rascal, Daddy, you know so many," she was half smiling.

"Newton . . . as you know, I gave Lament an order to pay his expenses to London?"

She nodded.

"Well, he drew nine hundred pounds."

The girl opened her eyes with joyous amazement.

"He told Lament that he was coming home by way of Berlin, Vienna, Istanbul, and Rome," groaned Mr. Mansar. "Thank God the trans-Siberian railway isn't working!" he added. It was the one source of comfort he had.

Rogues (?): Doctors

The Fifteen Murderers

BEN HECHT

THE REMARKABLE BEN HECHT (1894–1964) was a child prodigy on the violin, giving a concert in Chicago at the age of ten. As a young teenager, he spent his summer vacations in Wisconsin touring as an acrobat with a small circus. He ran away to Chicago at sixteen, owning and managing an "art theater" before becoming a successful journalist, first as a crime reporter and then as a foreign correspondent.

He was an integral part of the Chicago literary renaissance in the 1920s, writing newspaper columns, short stories, novels, and dramas. Cowriting *The Front Page* with Charles MacArthur made him famous and wealthy; it has been produced on the stage frequently since it opened in New York in 1928 and has served as the basis for numerous motion pictures under its original title and others, including *His Girl Friday*.

It is fair to say that Hecht was the most successful screenwriter in Hollywood history, both critically and in terms of the popularity of his films. Among his nearly one hundred screen credits are *Underworld* (1927), winner of the first Academy Award for Original Screenplay, *The Front Page* (1931), *Scarface* (1932), *Gunga Din* (1939), *Wuthering Heights* (1939), *It's a Wonderful World* (1939), *Spellbound* (1945), *Notorious* (1946), and *Kiss of Death* (1947). Films on which he worked extensively but did not receive screen credit include *Stagecoach* (1939), *Gone With the Wind* (1939), *Foreign Correspondent* (1940), *The Thing from Another World* (1951), *The Hunchback of Notre Dame* (1956), and *Mutiny on the Bounty* (1962).

"The Fifteen Murderers" was first published in the January 16, 1943, issue of *Collier's Magazine*. It was first collected in *The Collected Stories of Ben Hecht* as "The Miracle of the Fifteen Murderers" (New York, Crown, 1945).

THE FIFTEEN MURDERERS

Ben Hecht

THERE IS ALWAYS an aura of mystery to the conclaves of medical men. One may wonder whether the secrecy with which the fraternity surrounds its gatherings is designed to keep the layman from discovering how much it knows or how much it doesn't know. Either knowledge would be unnerving to that immemorial guinea pig who submits himself to the abracadabras of chemicals, scalpels, and incantations under the delusion he is being cured rather than explored.

Among the most mysterious of medical get-togethers in this generation have been those held in New York City by a group of eminent doctors calling themselves the X Club. Every three months this little band of healers have hied them to the Walton Hotel overlooking the East River and, behind locked doors and beyond the eye of even medical journalism, engaged themselves in unknown emprise lasting till dawn.

What the devil had been going on in these conclaves for twenty years no one knew, not even the ubiquitous head of the American Medical Association, nor yet any of the colleagues, wives, friends, or dependents of the X Club's members. The talent for secrecy is highly developed among doctors who, even with nothing to conceal, are often as close-mouthed as old-fashioned bomb throwers on their way to a rendezvous.

How then do I know the story of these long-guarded sessions? The answer is—the war. The war has put an end to them, as it has to nearly all mysteries other than its own. The world, engaged in re-examining its manners and its soul, has closed the door on minor adventure. Nine of the fifteen medical sages who comprised the X Club are in uniform and preside over combat-zone hospitals. Deficiencies of age and health have kept the others at home—with increased labors. There is a part of science which retains a reluctant interest in the misfortunes of civilians and has not yet removed its eye entirely from the banal battlefields on which they ignominiously keep perishing.

"Considering that we have disbanded," Dr. Alex Hume said to me at dinner one evening, "and that it is unlikely we shall ever assemble again, I see no reason for preserving our secret. Yours is a childish and romantic mind, and may be revolted by the story I tell you. You will undoubtedly translate the whole thing into some sort of diabolical tale and miss the deep human and scientific import of the X Club. But I am not the one to reform the art of fiction, which must substitute sentimentality for truth, and Cinderella for Galileo."

And so on. I will skip the rest of my friend's all-knowing prelude. You may have read Dr. Hume's various books, dealing with the horseplay of the subconscious. If you have, you know this baldheaded mastermind well enough. If not, take my word for it that he is a genius. There is nobody I know more adept at prancing around in the solar-plexus swamps out of which most of the world's incompetence and confusion appear to rise. He has, too, if there is any doubt about his great talent, the sneer and chuckle which are the war whoop of the superpsychologist. His face is round and his mouth is pursed in a chronic grimace of disbelief and contradiction. You can't help such an expression once you have discovered what a scurvy and detestable morass is the soul of man. Like most subterranean workers, my friend is almost as blind as a bat behind his heavy glasses. And like many leading psychiatrists, he favors the short and balloonlike physique of Napoleon.

The last dramatic meeting of the X Club was held on a rainy March night. Despite the hostile weather, all fifteen of its members attended, for there was an added lure to this gathering. A new member was to be inducted into the society.

Dr. Hume was assigned to prepare the neophyte for his debut. And it was in the wake of the round-faced soul fixer that Dr. Samuel Warner entered the sanctum of the X Club.

Dr. Warner was unusually young for a medical genius—that is, a recognized one. And he had never received a fuller recognition of his wizardry with saw, ax, and punch hole than his election as a member of the X Club. For the fourteen older men who had invited him to be one of them were leaders in their various fields. They were the medical peerage. This does not mean necessarily that any layman had ever heard of them. Eminence in the medical profession is as showy at best as a sprig of edelweiss on a mountaintop. The war, which offers its magic billboards for the vanities of small souls and transmutes the hunger for publicity into sacrificial and patriotic ardors, has not yet disturbed the anonymity of the great medicos. They have moved their bushels to the front lines and are busy under them, spreading their learning among the wounded.

The new member was a tense and good-looking man with the fever of hard work glowing in his steady dark eyes. His wide mouth smiled quickly and abstractedly, as is often the case with surgeons who train their reactions not to interfere with their concentration.

Having exchanged greetings with the eminent club members, who included half of his living medical heroes, Dr. Warner seated himself in a corner and quietly refused a highball, a cocktail, and a slug of brandy. His face remained tense, his athletic body straight in its chair as if it were poised for a sprint rather than a meeting.

At nine o'clock Dr. William Tick ordered an end to all the guzzling and declared the fifty-third meeting of the X Club in session. The venerable diagnostician placed himself behind a table at the end of the ornate hotel room and glared at the group ranged in front of him.

Dr. Tick had divided his seventy-five years equally between practising the art of medicine and doing his best to stamp it out—such, at least, was the impression of the thousands of students who had been submitted to his irascible guidance. As Professor of Internal Medicine at a great Eastern medical school, Dr. Tick had favored the Education by Insult theory of pedagogy. There were eminent doctors who still winced when they recalled some of old bilious-eyed, arthritic, stooped Tick's appraisals of their budding talents, and who still shuddered at the memory of his medical philosophy.

"Medicine," Dr. Tick had confided to flock after flock of students, "is a noble dream and at the same time the most ancient expression of error and idiocy known to man. Solving the mysteries of heaven has not given birth to as many abortive findings as has the quest into the mysteries of the human body. When you think of yourselves as scientists, I want you always to remember everything you learn from me will probably be regarded tomorrow as the naïve confusions of a pack of medical aborigines. Despite all our toil and progress, the art of medicine still falls somewhere between trout casting and spook writing.

"There are two handicaps to the practice of medicine," Tick had repeated tenaciously through forty years of teaching. "The first is the eternal charlatanism of the patient who is full of fake diseases and phantom agonies. The second is the basic incompetence of the human mind, medical or otherwise, to observe without prejudice, acquire information without becoming too smug to use it intelligently, and most of all, to apply its wisdom without vanity."

From behind his table old Tick's eyes glared at the present group of "incompetents" until a full classroom silence had arrived, and then turned to the tense, good-looking face of Dr. Warner.

"We have a new medical genius with us tonight," he began, "one I well remember in his prewizard days. A hyperthyroid with kidney disfunction indicated. But not without a trace of talent. For your benefit, Sam, I will state the meaning and purpose of our organization."

"I have already done that," said Dr. Hume, "rather thoroughly."

"Dr. Hume's explanations to you," Tick continued coldly, "if they are of a kind with his printed works, have most certainly left you dazed if not dazzled."

"I understood him quite well," Warner said.

"Nonsense," old Tick said. "You always had a soft spot for psychiatry and I always warned you against it. Psychiatry is a plot against medicine. And who knows but it may someday overthrow us? In the meantime it behooves us not to consort too freely with the enemy."

You may be sure that Dr. Hume smiled archly at this.

"You will allow me," Tick went on, "to clarify whatever the learned Hume has been trying to tell you."

"Well, if you want to waste time." The new member smiled nervously and mopped his neck with a handkerchief.

Dr. Frank Rosson, the portly and distinguished gynecologist, chuckled. "Tick's going good tonight," he whispered to Hume.

"Senility inflamed by sadism," said Hume.

"Dr. Warner," the pedagogue continued, "the members of the X Club have a single and interesting purpose in their meeting. They come together every three months to confess to some murder any of them may have committed since our last assembly. I am referring, of course, to medical murder. Although it would be a relief to hear any one of us confess to a murder performed out of passion rather than stupidity. Indeed, Dr. Warner, if you have killed a wife or polished off an uncle recently, and would care to unbosom yourself, we will listen respectfully. It is understood that nothing you say will be brought to the attention of the police or the A.M.A."

Old Tick's eyes paused to study the growing tension in the new member's face.

"I am sure you have not slain any of your relatives," he sighed, "or that you will ever do so except in the line of duty.

"The learned Hume," he went on, "has undoubtedly explained these forums to you on the psychiatric basis that confession is good for the soul. This is nonsense. We are not here to ease our souls but to improve them. Our real purpose is scientific. Since we dare not admit our mistakes to the public and since we are too great and learned to be criticized by the untutored laity and since such inhuman perfection as that to which we pretend is not good for our weak and human natures, we have formed this society. It is the only medical organization in the world where the members boast only of their mistakes.

"And now," Tick beamed on the neophyte, "allow me to define what we consider a real, fine professional murder. It is the killing of a human being who has trustingly placed himself in a doctor's hands. Mind you, the death of a patient does not in itself spell murder. We are concerned only with those cases in which the doctor, by a wrong diagnosis or by demonstrably wrong medication or operative procedure, has killed off a patient who, without the aforesaid doctor's attention, would have continued to live and prosper."

"Hume explained all this to me," the new member muttered impatiently, and then raised his voice: "I appreciate that this is my first meeting and that I might learn more from my distinguished colleagues by listening than by talking. But I have something rather important to say."

"A murder?" Tick asked.

"Yes," said the new member.

The old Professor nodded. "Very good," he said. "And we shall be glad to listen to you. But we have several murderers on the docket ahead of you."

The new member was silent and remained sitting bolt upright in his chair. It was at this point that several, including Hume, noticed there was something more than stage fright in the young surgeon's tension. The certainty filled the room that Sam Warner had come to his first meeting of the X Club with something violent and mysterious boiling in him.

Dr. Philip Kurtiff, the eminent neurologist, put his hand on Warner's arm and said quietly, "There's no reason to feel bad about anything you're going to tell us. We're all pretty good medical men and we've all done worse—whatever it is."

"If you please," old Tick demanded, "we will have silence. This is not a sanatorium for doctors with guilt complexes. It is a clinic for error. And we will continue to conduct it in an orderly, scientific fashion. If you want to hold Sam Warner's hand, Kurtiff, that's your privilege. But do it in silence."

He beamed suddenly at the new member.

"I confess," he went on, "that I'm as curious as anybody to hear how so great a know-it-all as our young friend Dr. Warner could have killed off one of his customers. But our curiosity will have to wait. Since five of you were absent from our last gathering I think that the confession of Dr. James Sweeney should be repeated for your benefit."

Dr. Sweeney stood up and turned his lugubrious face and shining eyes to the five absentees. Of all present, Sweeney was considered next to old Tick the ablest diagnostician in the East.

"Well," he said in his preoccupied monotone, "I told it once, but I'll tell it again. I sent a patient to my X-ray room to have a fluoroscopy done. My assistant gave him a barium meal to drink and put him under the fluoroscope. I walked in a half hour later to observe progress and when I saw the patient under the fluoroscopic screen I observed to my assistant, Dr. Kroch, that it was amazing and that I had never seen anything like it. Kroch was too overcome to bear me out.

"What I saw was that the patient's entire stomach and lower esophagus were motionless and dilated, apparently made out of stone. And as I studied this phenomenon, I noticed it was becoming clearer and sharper. The most disturbing factor in the situation was that we both knew there was nothing to be done. Dr. Kroch, in fact, showed definite signs of hysteria. Shortly afterward the patient became moribund and fell to the floor."

"Well, I'll be damned!" several of those who had been absent cried in unison, Dr. Kurtiff adding, "What was it?"

"It was simple," said Sweeney. "The bottom of the glass out of which the patient had drunk his barium meal was caked solid. We had filled him up with plaster of Paris. I fancy the pressure caused a fatal coronary attack."

"Good Lord," the new member said. "How did it get into the glass?"

"Through some pharmaceutical error," said Sweeney mildly.

"What, if anything, was the matter with the patient before he adventured into your office?" Dr. Kurtiff inquired.

"The autopsy revealed chiefly a solidified stomach and esophagus," said Sweeney. "But I think from several indications that there may have been a little tendency to pyloric spasm, which caused the belching for which he was referred to me."

"A rather literary murder," said old Tick. "A sort of Pygmalion in reverse."

The old Professor paused and fastened his red-rimmed eyes on Warner. "By the way, before we proceed," he said, "I think it is time to tell you the full name of our club. Our full name is the X Marks the Spot Club. We prefer, of course, to use the abbreviated title as being a bit more social sounding."

"Of course," said the new member, whose face now appeared to be getting redder.

"And now," announced old Tick, consulting a scribbled piece of paper, "our first case on tonight's docket will be Dr. Wendell Davis."

There was silence as the elegant stomach specialist stood up. Davis was a doctor who took his manner as seriously as his medicine. Tall, solidly built, gray-haired and beautifully barbered, his face was without expression—a large, pink mask that no patient, however ill and agonized, had ever seen disturbed.

"I was called late last summer to the home of a workingman," he began. "Senator Bell had given a picnic for some of his poorer constituency. As a result of this event, the three children of a steamfitter named Horowitz were brought down with food poisoning. They had overeaten at the picnic. The Senator, as host, felt responsible, and I went to the Horowitz home at his earnest solicitation. I found two of the children very sick and vomiting considerably. They were nine and eleven. The mother gave me a list of the various foods all three of them had eaten. It was staggering. I gave them a good dose of castor oil.

"The third child, aged seven, was not as ill as the other two. He looked pale, had a slight fever, felt some nausea—but was not vomiting. It seemed obvious that he too was poisoned to a lesser degree. Accordingly I prescribed an equal dose of castor oil for the youngest child—just to be on the safe side.

"I was called by the father in the middle of the night. He was alarmed over the condition of the seven-year-old. He reported that the other two children were much improved. I told him not to worry, that the youngest had been a little late in developing food poisoning but would unquestionably be better in the morning, and that his cure was as certain as his sister's and brother's.

"When I hung up I felt quite pleased with myself for having anticipated the youngest one's condition and prescribed the castor oil prophylactically. I arrived at the Horowitz home at noon the next day and found the two older children practically recovered. The seven-year-old, however, appeared to be very sick indeed. They had been trying to reach me since breakfast. The child had 105 degrees' temperature. It was dehydrated, the eyes sunken and circled, the expression pinched, the nostrils dilated, the lips cyanotic and the skin cold and clammy."

Dr. Davis paused. Dr. Milton Morris, the renowned lung specialist, spoke. "It died within a few hours?" he asked.

Dr. Davis nodded.

"Well," Dr. Morris said quietly, "it seems pretty obvious. The child was suffering from acute appendicitis when you first saw it. The castor oil ruptured its appendix. By the time you got around to looking at it again, peritonitis had set in."

"Yes," said Dr. Davis slowly. "That's exactly what happened."

"Murder by castor oil," old Tick cackled, "plus an indifference to the poor."

"Not at all," Dr. Davis said. "All three children had been at the picnic, overeaten alike and revealed the same symptoms."

"Not quite the same," Dr. Hume said.

"Oh, you would have psychoanalyzed the third child?" Dr. Davis smiled.

"No," said Hume. "I would have examined its abdomen like any penny doctor, considering that it had some pain and nausea, and found it rigid with both direct and rebound tenderness."

"Yes, it would have been an easy diagnosis for a medical student," Dr. Kurtiff agreed. "But unfortunately, we have outgrown the humility of medical students."

"Dr. Davis's murder is morally instructive," old Tick announced, "but I find it extremely dull. I have a memo from Dr. Kenneth Wood. Dr. Wood has the floor."

The noted Scotch surgeon, famed in his college days as an Olympic Games athlete, stood up. He was still a man of prowess, large-handed, heavy-shouldered and with the purr of masculine strength in his soft voice.

"I don't know what kind of murder you can call this." Dr. Wood smiled at his colleagues.

"Murder by butchery is the usual title," Tick said.

"No, I doubt that," Dr. Morris protested. "Ken's too skillful to cut off anybody's leg by mistake."

"I guess you'll have to call it just plain murder by stupidity," Dr. Wood said softly.

Old Tick cackled. "If you'd paid a little more attention to diagnosis than to shot-putting you wouldn't be killing off such hordes of patients," he said.

"This is my first report in three years," Wood answered modestly. "And I've been operating at the rate of four or five daily, including holidays."

"My dear Kenneth," Dr. Hume said, "every surgeon is entitled to one murder in three years. A phenomenal record, in fact—when you consider the temptations."

"Proceed with the crime," Tick said.

"Well"—the strong-looking surgeon turned to his hospital colleague, the new member—"you know how it is with these acute gall bladders, Sam."

Warner nodded abstractedly.

Dr. Wood went on: "Brought in late at night. In extreme pain. I examined her. Found the pain in the right upper quadrant of the abdomen. It radiated to the back and right shoulder. Completely characteristic of gall bladder. I gave her opiates. They had no effect on her, which, as you know, backs up any gall-bladder diagnosis. Opiates never touch the gall bladder."

"We know that," said the new member nervously.

"Excuse me," Dr. Wood smiled. "I want to get all the points down carefully. Well, I gave her some nitroglycerin to lessen the pain then. Her temperature was 101. By morning the pain was so severe that it seemed certain the gall bladder had perforated. I operated. There was nothing wrong with her gall bladder. She died an hour later."

"What did the autopsy show?" Dr. Sweeney asked.

"Wait a minute," Wood answered. "You're supposed to figure it out, aren't you? Come on—you tell me what was the matter with her."

"Did you take her history?" Dr. Kurtiff asked after a pause.

"No," Wood answered.

"Aha!" Tick snorted. "There you have it! Blind man's buff again."

"It was an emergency." Wood looked flushed. "And it seemed an obvious case. I've had hundreds of them."

"The facts seem to be as follows," Tick spoke up. "Dr. Wood murdered a woman because he misunderstood the source of a pain. We have, then, a very simple problem. What besides the gall bladder can produce the sort of pain that that eminent surgeon has described?"

"Heart," Dr. Morris answered quickly.

"You're getting warm," said Wood.

"Before operating on anyone with so acute a pain, and in the absence of any medical history," Tick went on, "I would most certainly have looked at the heart."

"Well, you'd have done right," said Wood quietly. "The autopsy showed an infraction of the descending branch of the right coronary artery."

"Which a cardiogram would have told you," said old Tick. "But you didn't have to go near a cardiograph. All you had to do is ask one question. If you had even called up a neighbor of the patient she would have told you that previous attacks of pain came on exertion—which would have spelled heart, and not gall bladder.

"Murder by a sophomore," old Tick pronounced wrathfully.

"The first and last," said Wood quietly. "There won't be any more heart-case mistakes in my hospital."

"Good, good," old Tick said. "And now, gentlemen, the crimes reported thus far have been too infantile for discussion. We have learned nothing from them other than that science and stupidity go hand in hand, a fact already too well known to us. However, we have with us tonight a young but extremely talented wielder of the medical saws. He has been sitting here for the last hour, fidgeting like a true criminal, sweating with guilt and a desire to tell all. Gentlemen, I give you our new and youngest culprit, Dr. Samuel Warner."

Dr. Warner faced his fourteen eminent colleagues with a sudden excitement in his manner. His eyes glittered and the dusty look of hard work and near exhaustion already beginning to mark his youth lifted from his face.

The older men regarded him quietly and with various degrees of irritation. They knew, without further corroboration than his manner, that this medico was full of untenable theories and half-baked medical discoveries. They had been full of such things themselves once. And they settled back to enjoy themselves. There is nothing as pleasing to a graying medical man as the opportunity of slapping a dunce cap on the young of science. Old Tick, surveying his colleagues, grinned. They had all acquired the look of pedagogues holding a switch behind their backs.

Dr. Warner mopped his neck with his wet handkerchief and smiled knowingly at the medical peerage.

"I'll give you this case in some detail," he said, "because I think it contains as interesting a problem as you can find in practice."

Dr. Rosson, the gynecologist, grunted, but said nothing.

"The patient was a young man, or rather a boy," Warner went on eagerly. "He was seventeen, and amazingly talented. He wrote poetry. That's how I happened to meet him. I read one of his poems in a magazine, and it was so impressive I wrote him a letter."

"Rhymed poetry?" Dr. Wood asked, with a wink at old Tick.

"Yes," said Warner. "I read all his manuscripts. They were sort of revolutionary. His poetry was a cry against injustice. Every kind of injustice. Bitter and burning."

"Wait a minute," Dr. Rosson said. "The new member seems to have some misconception of our function. We are not a literary society, Warner."

"And before you get started," Dr. Hume grinned, "no bragging. You can do your bragging at the annual surgeons' convention."

"Gentlemen," Warner said, "I have no intention of bragging. I'll stick to murder, I assure you. And as bad a one as you've ever heard."

"Good," Dr. Kurtiff said. "Go on. And take it easy and don't break down."

"Yes." Dr. Wood grinned. "I remember when Morris here made his first confession. We had to pour a quart of whisky into him before he quit blubbering."

"I won't break down," Warner said. "Don't worry. Well, the patient was sick for two weeks before I was called."

"I thought you were his friend," Dr. Davis said.

"I was," Warner answered. "But he didn't believe in doctors."

"No faith in them, eh?" old Tick cackled. "Brilliant boy."

"He was," said Warner eagerly. "I felt upset when I came and saw how sick he was. I had him moved to a hospital at once."

"Oh, a rich poet," Dr. Sweeney said.

"No," said Warner. "I paid his expenses. And I spent all the time I could with him. The sickness had started with a severe pain on the left side of the abdomen. He was going to call me, but the pain subsided after three days, so the patient thought he was well. But it came back in two days and he began running a temperature. He developed diarrhea. There was pus and blood, but no amoeba or pathogenic bacteria when he finally sent for me.

"After the pathology reports I made a diagnosis of ulcerative colitis. The pain being on the left side ruled out the appendix. I put the patient on sulfaguanidin and unconcentrated liver extract, and gave him a high protein diet—chiefly milk. Despite this treatment and constant observation the patient got worse. He developed generalized abdominal tenderness, both direct and rebound, and rigidity of the entire left rectus muscle. After two weeks of careful treatment the patient died."

"And the autopsy showed you'd been wrong?" Dr. Wood asked.

"I didn't make an autopsy," said Warner. "The boy's parents had perfect faith in me. As did the boy. They both believed I was doing everything possible to save his life."

"Then how do you know you were wrong in your diagnosis?" Dr. Hume asked.

"By the simple fact," said Warner irritably, "that the patient died instead of being cured. When he died I knew I had killed him by a faulty diagnosis."

"A logical conclusion," said Dr. Sweeney. "Pointless medication is no alibi."

"Well, gentlemen," old Tick cackled from behind his table, "our talented new member has obviously polished off a great poet and close personal friend. Indictments of his diagnosis are now in order."

But no one spoke. Doctors have a sense for things unseen and complications unstated. And nearly all the fourteen looking at Warner felt there was something hidden. The surgeon's tension, his elation and its overtone of mockery, convinced them there was something untold in the story of the dead poet. They approached the problem cautiously.

"How long ago did the patient die?" Dr. Rosson asked.

"Last Wednesday," said Warner. "Why?"

"What hospital?" asked Davis.

"St. Michael's," said Warner.

"You say the parents had faith in you," said Kurtiff, "and still have. Yet you seem curiously worried about something. Has there been any inquiry by the police?"

"No," said Warner. "I committed the perfect crime. The police haven't even heard of it. And even my victim died full of gratitude." He beamed at the room. "Listen," he went on, "even you people may not be able to disprove my diagnosis."

This brash challenge irritated a number of the members.

"I don't think it will be very difficult to knock out your diagnosis," said Dr. Morris.

"There's a catch to it," said Wood slowly, his eyes boring at Warner.

"The only catch there is," said Warner quickly, "is the complexity of the case. You gentlemen evidently prefer the simpler malpractice type of crime, such as I've listened to tonight."

There was a pause, and then Dr. Davis inquired in a soothing voice, "You described an acute onset of pain before the diarrhea, didn't you?"

"That's right," said Warner.

"Well," Davis continued coolly, "the temporary relief of symptoms and their recurrence within a few days sounds superficially like ulcers—except for one point."

"I disagree," Dr. Sweeney said softly. "Dr. Warner's diagnosis is a piece of blundering stupidity. The symptoms he has presented have nothing to do with ulcerative colitis."

Warner flushed and his jaw muscles moved angrily. "Would you mind backing up your insults with a bit of science?" he said.

"Very easily done," Sweeney answered calmly. "The late onset of diarrhea and fever you describe rule out ulcerative colitis in ninety-nine cases out of a hundred. What do you think, Dr. Tick?"

"No ulcers," said Tick, his eyes studying Warner.

"You mentioned a general tenderness of the

abdomen as one of the last symptoms," said Dr. Davis smoothly.

"That's right," said Warner.

"Well, if you have described the case accurately," Davis continued, "there is one obvious fact revealed. The general tenderness points to a peritonitis. I'm certain an autopsy would show that this perforation had walled off and spilled over and that a piece of intestine was telescoped into another."

"I don't think so," Dr. William Zinner, the cancer-research man, said. He was short, bird-faced and barely audible. Silence fell on the room, and the others waited attentively for his soft voice.

"It couldn't be an intussusception such as Dr. Davis describes," he went on. "The patient was only seventeen. Intussusception is unusual at that age unless the patient has a tumor of the intestines. In which case he would not have stayed alive that long."

"Excellent," old Tick spoke.

"I thought of intussusception," said Warner, "and discarded it for that very reason."

"How about a twisted gut?" Dr. Wood asked. "That could produce the symptoms described."

"No," said Dr. Rosson. "A volvulus means gangrene and death in three days. Warner says he attended his patient for two weeks and that the boy was sick for two weeks before Warner was called. The length of the illness rules out intussusception, volvulus, and intestinal tumor."

"There's one other thing," Dr. Morris said. "A left-sided appendix."

"That's out, too," Dr. Wood said quickly. "The first symptom of a left-sided appendix would not be the acute pain described by Warner."

"The only thing we have determined," said Dr. Sweeney, "is a perforation other than ulcer. Why not go on with that?"

"Yes," said Dr. Morris. "Ulcerative colitis is out of the question considering the course taken by the disease. I'm sure we're dealing with another type of perforation."

"The next question," announced old Tick, "is what made the perforation?"

Dr. Warner mopped his face with his wet handkerchief and said softly, "I never thought of an object perforation."

"You should have," Dr. Kurtiff stated.

"Come, come," old Tick interrupted. "Let's not wander. What caused the perforation?"

"He was seventeen," Kurtiff answered, "and too old to be swallowing pins."

"Unless," said Dr. Hume, "he had a taste for pins. Did the patient want to live, Warner?"

"He wanted to live," said Warner grimly, "more than anybody I ever knew."

"I think we can ignore the suicide theory," said Dr. Kurtiff. "I am certain we are dealing with a perforation of the intestines and not of the subconscious."

"Well," Dr. Wood spoke, "it couldn't have been a chicken bone. A chicken bone would have stuck in the esophagus and never got through to the stomach."

"There you are, Warner," old Tick said. "We've narrowed it down. The spreading tenderness you described means a spreading infection. The course taken by the disease means a perforation other than ulcerous. And a perforation of that type means an object swallowed. We have ruled out pins and chicken bones. Which leaves us with only one other normal guess."

"A fishbone," said Dr. Sweeney.

"Exactly," said Tick.

Warner stood listening tensely to the voices affirming the diagnosis. Tick delivered the verdict.

"I think we are all agreed," he said, "that Sam Warner killed his patient by treating him for ulcerative colitis when an operation removing an abscessed fishbone would have saved his life."

Warner moved quickly across the room to the closet where he had hung his hat and coat.

"Where are you going?" Dr. Wood called after him. "We've just started the meeting."

Warner was putting on his coat and grinning.

"I haven't got much time," he said, "but I want to thank all of you for your diagnosis. You were right about there being a catch to the case. The catch is that my patient is still alive. I've been treating him for ulcerative colitis for two weeks and I realized this afternoon that I had wrongly diagnosed the case—and that he would be dead in twenty-four hours unless I could find out what really was the matter with him."

Warner was in the doorway, his eyes glittering.

"Thanks again, gentlemen, for the consultation and your diagnosis," he said. "It will enable me to save my patient's life."

A half hour later, the members of the X Club stood grouped in one of the operating rooms of St. Michael's Hospital. They looked different from the men who had been playing a medical Halloween in the Walton Hotel. There is a change that comes over doctors when they face disease. The oldest and the weariest of them draw vigor from a crisis. The shamble leaves them and it is the straight back of the champion that enters the operating room. Confronting the problem of life and death, the tired, red-rimmed eyes become full of greatness and even beauty.

On the operating table lay the unconscious body of a Negro boy. Dr. Warner in his surgical whites stood over him.

The fourteen other X Club members watched Warner operate. Wood nodded approvingly at his speed. Rosson cleared his throat to say something, but the swift-moving hands of the surgeon held him silent. No one spoke. The minutes passed. The nurses quietly handed instruments to the surgeon. Blood spattered their hands.

Fourteen great medical men stared hopefully at the pinched and unconscious face of a colored boy who had swallowed a fishbone. No king or pope ever lay ill with more medical genius holding its breath around him.

Suddenly the perspiring surgeon raised something aloft in his forceps.

"Wash this off," he muttered to the nurse, "and show it to these gentlemen."

He busied himself placing drains in the abscessed cavity and then powdered some sulfanilamide into the opened abdomen to kill the infection.

Old Tick stepped forward and took the object from the nurse's hand.

"A fishbone," he said.

The X Club gathered around it as if it were a treasure indescribable.

"The removal of this small object," old Tick cackled softly, "will enable the patient to continue writing poetry denouncing the greeds and horrors of our world."

That, in effect, was the story Hume told me, plus the epilogue of the Negro poet's recovery three weeks later. We had long finished dinner and it was late night when we stepped into the war-dimmed streets of New York. The headlines on the newsstands had changed in size only. They were larger in honor of the larger slaughters they heralded.

Looking at them you could see the death-strewn wastes of battles. But another picture came to my mind—a picture that had in it the hope of a better world. It was the hospital room in which fifteen famed and learned heroes stood battling for the life of a Negro boy who had swallowed a fishbone.

Rogue: Simon Templar (The Saint)

The Damsel in Distress

LESLIE CHARTERIS

SIMON TEMPLAR, the adventurer created by Leslie Charteris (1907–1993), although commonly known as the Saint, is anything but. He is a romantic hero who works outside the law and has grand fun doing it. Like so many crooks in literature, he is imbued with the spirit of Robin Hood, which suggests that it is perfectly all right to steal, so long as it is from someone with wealth. Most of the more than forty books about the Saint are collections of short stories or novellas, and in the majority of tales, he also functions as a detective. Unconstricted by being an official policeman, he steps outside the law to retrieve money or treasure that may not have been procured in an honorable fashion, either to restore it to its proper owner or to enrich himself. Not unlike James Bond, a remarkable number of his cases involve damsels in distress.

"Maybe I am a crook," Templar muses, "but in between times I'm something more. In my simple way I am a kind of justice."

In addition to the many books about the Saint, there were more than twenty films about him, the good ones starring George Sanders or Louis Hayward, as well as a comic strip, a radio series that ran for much of the 1940s, and a television series starring Roger Moore that was an international success with one hundred eighteen episodes.

Charteris was born in Singapore but spent most of his life in London, even after becoming an American citizen in 1946.

"The Damsel in Distress" was first published in the November 19, 1933, issue of *Empire News* under the title "The Kidnapping of the Fickle Financier." It was first collected under its more familiar title in *Boodle* (London, Hodder & Stoughton, 1934); the American title is *The Saint Intervenes* (New York, Doubleday, 1934).

THE DAMSEL IN DISTRESS

Leslie Charteris

"YOU NEED BRAINS in this life of crime," Simon Templar would say sometimes; "but I often think you need luck even more."

He might have added that the luck had to be consistent.

Mr. Giuseppe Rolfieri was lucky up to a point, for he happened to be in Switzerland when the astounding Liverpool Municipal Bond forgery was discovered. It was a simple matter for him to slip over the border into his own native country; and when his four partners in the swindle stumbled down the narrow stairway that leads from the dock of the Old Bailey to the terrible blind years of penal servitude, he was comfortably installed in his villa at San Remo with no vengeance to fear from the Law. For it is a principle of international law that no man can be extradited from his own country, and Mr. Rolfieri was lucky to have retained his Italian citizenship even though he had made himself a power in the City of London.

Simon Templar read about the case—he could hardly have helped it, for it was one of those sensational scandals which rock the financial world once in a lifetime—but it did not strike him as a matter for his intervention. Four out of the five conspirators, including the ringleader, had been convicted and sentenced; and although it is true that there was a certain amount of public indignation at the immunity of Mr. Rolfieri, it was inevitable that the Saint, in his career of shameless lawlessness, sometimes had to pass up one inviting prospect in favour of another nearer to hand. He couldn't be everywhere at once—it was one of the very few human limitations which he was ready to admit.

A certain Domenick Naccaro, however, had other ideas.

He called at the Saint's apartment on Piccadilly one morning—a stout bald-headed man in a dark blue suit and a light blue waistcoat, with an unfashionable stiff collar and a stringy black tie and a luxuriant scroll of black moustache ornamenting his face—and for the first moment of alarm Simon wondered if he had been mistaken for somebody else of the same name but less respectable morals, for Signor Naccaro was accompanied by a pale pretty girl who carried a small infant swathed in a shawl.

"Is this-a Mr. Templar I have-a da honour to spik to?" asked Naccara, doffing his bowler elaborately.

"This is one Mr. Templar," admitted the Saint cautiously.

"Ha!" said Mr. Naccaro. "It is-a da Saint himself?"

"So I'm told," Simon answered.

"Then you are da man we look-a for," stated Mr. Naccaro, with profound conviction.

As if taking it for granted that all the necessary formalities had therewith been observed, he bowed the girl in, bowed himself in after her, and stalked into the living-room. Simon closed the door and followed the deputation with a certain curious amusement.

"Well, brother," he murmured, taking a cigarette from the box on the table. "Who are you, and what can I do for you?"

The flourishing bowler hat bowed the girl into one chair, bowed its owner into another, and came to rest on its owner's knees.

"Ha!" said the Italian, rather like an acrobat announcing the conclusion of a trick. "I am Domenick Naccaro!"

"That must be rather nice for you," murmured the Saint amiably. He waved his cigarette towards the girl and her bundle. "And is this the rest of the clan?"

"That," said Mr. Naccaro, "is-a my daughter Maria. And in her arms she hold-as a leedle baby. A baby," said Mr. Naccaro, with his black eyes suddenly swimming, "wis-a no father."

"Careless of her," Simon remarked. "What does the baby think about it?"

"Da father," said Mr. Naccaro, contradicting himself dramatically, "is-a Giuseppe Rolfieri."

Simon's brows came down in a straight line, and some of the bantering amusement fell back below the surface of his blue eyes. He hitched one hip on to the edge of the table and swung his foot thoughtfully.

"How did this happen?" he asked.

"I keep-a da small-a restaurant in-a Soho," explained Mr. Naccaro. "Rolfieri, he come-a there often to eat-a da spaghetti. Maria, she sit at-a da desk and take-a da money. You, *signor*, you see-a how-a she is beautiful. Rolfieri, he notice her. When-a he pay his bill, he stop-a to talk-a wis her. One day he ask-a her to go out wis him."

Mr. Naccaro took out a large chequered handkerchief and dabbed his eyes. He went on, waving his hands in broken eloquence.

"I do not stop her. I think-a Rolfieri is-a da fine gentleman, and it is nice-a for my Maria to go out wis him. Often, they go out. I tink-a that Maria perhaps she make-a presently da good-a marriage, and I am glad for her. Then, one day, I see she is going to have-a da baby."

"It must have been a big moment," said the Saint gravely.

"I say to her, 'Maria, what have-a you done?' " recounted Mr. Naccaro, flinging out his arms. "She will-a not tell-a me." Mr. Naccaro shut his mouth firmly. "But presently she confess it is-a Rolfieri. I beat-a my breast." Mr. Naccaro beat his breast. "I say, 'I will keell-a heem; but first-a he shall marry you.' "

Mr. Naccaro jumped up with native theatrical effect.

"Rolfieri does-a not come any more to eat-a da spaghetti. I go to his office, and they tell me he is-a not there. I go to his house, and they tell me he is-a not there. I write-a letters, and he does-a not answer. Da time is going so quick. Presently I write-a da letter and say: 'If you do not-a see me soon, I go to da police.' He answer that one. He say he come soon. But he does-a not come. Then he is-a go abroad. He write again, and say he come-a to see me when he get back. But he does not-a come back. One day I read in da paper that he is-a da criminal, and da police are already look-a for him. So Maria she have-a da baby—and Rolfieri will-a never come back!"

Simon nodded.

"That's very sad," he said sympathetically. "But what can I do about it?"

Mr. Naccaro mopped his brow, put away his large chequered handkerchief, and sat down again.

"You are-a da man who help-a da poor people, no?" he said pleadingly. "You are-a da Saint, who always work-a to make justice?"

"Yes, but—"

"Then it is settled. You help-a me. Listen,

signor, everyting, everyting is-a arrange. I have-a da good friends in England and in-a San Remo, and we put-a da money together to make-a this right. We kidnap-a Rolfieri. We bring him here in da aeroplane. But we do not-a know anyone who can fly. You, *signor*, you can fly-a da aeroplane." Mr. Naccaro suddenly fell on his knees and flung out his arms. "See, *signor*—I humble myself. I kiss-a your feet. I beg-a you to help us and not let Maria have-a da baby wis-a no father!"

Simon allowed the operatic atmosphere to play itself out, and thereafter listened with a seriousness from which his natural superficial amusement did not detract at all. It was an appeal of the kind which he heard sometimes, for the name of the Saint was known to people who dreamed of his assistance as well as to those who lived in terror of his attentions, and he was never entirely deaf to the pleadings of those troubled souls who came to his home with a pathetic faith in miracles.

Mr. Naccaro's proposition was more practical than most.

He and his friends, apparently, had gone into the problem of avenging the wickedness of Giuseppe Rolfieri with the conspiratorial instinct of professional vendettists. One of them had become Mr. Rolfieri's butler in the villa at San Remo. Others, outside, had arranged the abduction down to a precise time-table. Mr. Naccaro himself had acquired an old farmhouse in Kent at which Rolfieri was to be held prisoner, with a large field adjoining it at which an aeroplane could land. The aeroplane itself had been bought, and was ready for use at Brooklands Aerodrome. The only unit lacking was a man qualified to fly it.

Once Rolfieri had been taken to the farmhouse, how would they force him through the necessary marriage?

"We make-a him," was all that Naccaro would say, but he said it with grim conviction.

When the Saint finally agreed to take the job, there was another scene of operatic gratitude which surpassed all previous demonstrations. Money was offered; but Simon had already decided that in this case the entertainment was its own reward. He felt pardonably exhausted when at last Domenick Naccaro, bowing and scraping and yammering incoherently, shepherded his daughter, his illegitimate grandchild, and his own curling whiskers out of the apartment.

The preparations for his share in the abduction occupied Simon Templar's time for most of the following week. He drove down to Brooklands and tested the aeroplane which the syndicate had purchased—it was an ancient Avro which must have secured its certificate of airworthiness by the skin of its ailerons, but he thought it would complete the double journey, given luck and good weather. Then there was a halfway refuelling base to be established somewhere in France—a practical necessity which had not occurred to the elemental Mr. Naccaro. Friday had arrived before he was able to report that he was ready to make the trip; and there was another scene of embarrassing gratitude.

"I send-a da telegram to take Rolfieri on Sunday night," was the essence of Mr. Naccaro's share in the conversation; but his blessings upon the Saint, the bones of his ancestors, and the heads of his unborn descendants for generations, took up much more time.

Simon had to admit, however, that the practical contribution of the Naccaro clan was performed with an efficiency which he himself could scarcely have improved upon. He stood beside the museum Avro on the aerodrome of San Remo at dusk on the Sunday evening, and watched the kidnapping cortège coming towards him across the field with genuine admiration. The principal character was an apparently mummified figure rolled in blankets, which occupied an invalid chair wheeled by the unfortunate Maria in the uniform of a nurse. Her pale lovely face was set in an expression of beatific solicitude at which Simon, having some idea of the fate which awaited Signor Rolfieri in England, could have hooted aloud. Beside the invalid chair stalked a sedate spectacled man whose rôle was obviously that of the devoted physician. The airport officials, who had already checked the papers of pilot and passengers, lounged boredly in the far background, without a single disturbing suspicion of the classic getaway that was being pulled off under their noses.

Between them, Simon and the "doctor" tenderly lifted the mummified figure into the machine.

"He will not wake before you arrive, *signor*," whispered the man confidently, stooping to arrange the blankets affectionately round the body of his patient.

The Saint grinned gently, and stepped back to help the "nurse" into her place. He had no idea how the first stage of the abduction had been carried out, and he was not moved to inquire. He had performed similar feats himself, no less slickly, without losing the power to stand back and impersonally admire the technique of others in the same field. With a sigh of satisfaction he swung himself up into his own cockpit, signalled to the mechanic who stood waiting by the propeller of the warmed-up engine, and sent the ship roaring into the wind through the deepening dusk.

The flight north was consistently uneventful. With a south wind following to help him on, he sighted the three red lights which marked his fuelling station at about half-past two, and landed by the three flares that were kindled for him when he blinked his navigating lights. The two men procured from somewhere by Mr. Naccaro replenished his tank while he smoked a cigarette and stretched his legs, and in twenty minutes he was off again. He passed over Folkestone in the early daylight, and hedge-hopped for some miles before he reached his destination so that no inquisitive yokel should see exactly where he landed.

"You have him?" asked Mr. Naccaro, dancing about deliriously as Simon climbed stiffly down.

"I have," said the Saint. "You'd better get him inside quickly—I'm afraid your pals didn't dope him up as well as they thought they had, and from the way he was behaving just now I shouldn't be surprised if he was going to have-a da baby, too."

He stripped off his helmet and goggles, and watched the unloading of his cargo with interest. Signor Giuseppe Rolfieri had recovered considerably from the effects of the drug under whose influence he had been embarked; but the hangover, combined with some bumpy weather on the last part of the journey, restrained him hardly less effectively from much resistance. Simon had never known before that the human skin could really turn green; but the epidermis of Signor Rolfieri had literally achieved that remarkable tint.

The Saint stayed behind to help the other half of the reception committee—introduced as Mr. Naccaro's brother—wheel the faithful Avro into the shelter of a barn; and then he strolled back to the farmhouse. As he reached it the door opened, and Naccaro appeared.

"Ha!" he cried, clasping the Saint's shoulders. "Meester Templar—you have already been-a so kind—I cannot ask it—but you have-a da car—will you go out again?"

Simon raised his eyebrows.

"Can't I watch the wedding?" he protested. "I might be able to help."

"Afterwards, yes," said Naccaro. "But we are not-a ready. *Ecco*, we are so hurry, so excited, when we come here we forget-a da mos' important tings. We forget-a da soap!"

Simon blinked.

"Soap?" he repeated. "Can't you marry him off without washing him?"

"No, no, no!" spluttered Naccaro. "You don't understand. Da soap, she is not-a to wash. She is to persuade. I show you myself, afterwards. It is my own idea. But-a da soap we mus' have. You will go, please, please, *signor*, in your car?"

The Saint frowned at him blankly for a moment; and then he shrugged.

"Okay, brother," he murmured. "I'd do more than that to find out how you persuade a bloke to get married with a cake of soap."

He stuffed his helmet and goggles into the pocket of his flying coat, and went round to the barn where he had parked his car before he took off for San Remo. He had heard of several strange instruments of persuasion in his time, but it was the first time he had ever met common or household soap in the guise of an implement of torture or moral coercion. He wondered whether the clan Naccaro had such a prejudiced opinion of Rolfieri's personal cleanliness that they thought the mere threat of washing him would terrify him into meeting his just obligations, or whether the victim was first smeared with ink and then bribed with the soap, or whether he was made to eat it; and he was so fascinated by these provocative speculations that he had driven nearly half a mile before he remembered that he was not provided with the wherewithal to buy it.

Simon Templar was not stingy. He would have stood any necessitous person a cake of soap, any day. In return for a solution of the mystery which was perplexing him at that moment, he would cheerfully have stood Mr. Naccaro a whole truckload of it. But the money was not in his pocket. In a moment of absent-mindedness he had set out on his trip with a very small allowance of ready cash; and all he had left of it then was two Italian lire, the change out of the last meal he had enjoyed in San Remo.

He stopped the car and scowled thoughtfully for a second. There was no place visible ahead where he could turn it, and he had no natural desire to back half a mile down that narrow lane; but the road had led him consistently to the left since he set out, and he stood up to survey the landscape in the hope that the farmhouse might only lie a short distance across the fields as the crow flies or he could walk. And it was by doing this that he saw a curious sight.

Another car, of whose existence nobody had said anything, stood in front of the farmhouse; and into it Mr. Naccaro and his brother were hastily loading the body of the unfortunate Signor Rolfieri, now trussed with several fathoms of rope like an escape artist before demonstrating his art. The girl Maria stood by; and as soon as Rolfieri was in the car she followed him in, covered him with a rug, and settled herself comfortably on the seat. Naccaro and his brother jumped into the front, and the car drove rapidly away in the opposite direction to that which the Saint had been told to take.

Simon Templar sank slowly back behind the wheel and took out his cigarette-case. He deliberately paused to tap out a cigarette, light it, and draw the first two puffs as if he had an hour to spare; and then he pushed the gear lever into reverse and sent the great cream and red Hirondel racing back up the lane at a speed which gave no indication that he had ever hesitated to perform the manœuvre.

He turned the car round in the farmhouse gates and went on with the cut-out closed and his keen eyes vigilantly scanning the panorama ahead. The other car was a saloon, and half the time he was able to keep the roof in sight over the low hedges which hid the open Hirondel from its quarry. But it is doubtful whether the possibility of pursuit ever entered the heads of the party in front, who must have been firm in their belief that the Saint was at that moment speeding innocently towards the village to which they had directed him. Once, at a fork, he lost them; and then he spotted a tiny curl of smoke rising from the grass bank a little way up one turning, and drove slowly up to it. It was the lighted stub of a cigar which could not have been thrown out at any place more convenient for a landmark, and the Saint smiled and went on.

In a few seconds he had picked up the saloon again; and very shortly afterwards he jammed on his brakes and brought the Hirondel to a sudden halt.

The car in front had stopped before a lonely cottage whose thatched roof was clearly visible. In a flash the Saint was out of his own seat and walking silently up the lane towards it. When the next turn would have brought him within sight of the car, he slipped through a gap in the hedge and sprinted for the back of the house. In broad daylight, there was no chance of further concealment; and it was neck or nothing at that point. But his luck held; and so far as he could tell he gained the lee of his objective unobserved. And once there, an invitingly open kitchen window was merely another link in the chain of chance which had stayed with him so benevolently throughout that adventure.

Rolfieri and the Naccaro team were already inside. He could hear the muffled mutter of their voices as he tiptoed down the dark passage towards the front of the house; and presently he stood outside the door of the room where they were. Through the keyhole he was able to take in the scene. Rolfieri, still safely trussed, was sitting in a chair, and the Naccaro brothers were standing over him. The girl Maria was curled up on the settee, smoking a cigarette and displaying a remarkable length of stocking for a betrayed virgin whose honour was at stake. The conversation was in Italian, which was only one language out of the Saint's comprehensive repertoire; and it was illuminating.

"You cannot make me pay," Rolfieri was saying; but his stubbornness could have been more convincing.

"That is true," Naccaro agreed. "I can only point out the disadvantages of not paying. You are in England, where the police would be very glad to see you. Your confederates have already been tried and sentenced, and it would be a mere formality for you to join them. The lightest sentence that any of them received was five years, and they could hardly give you less. If we left you here, and informed the police where to find you, it would not be long before you were in prison yourself. Surely twenty-five thousand pounds is a very small price to pay to avoid that."

Rolfieri stared sullenly at the floor for a while and then he said: "I will give you ten thousand."

"It will be twenty-five thousand or nothing," said Naccaro. "Come, now—I see you are prepared to be reasonable. Let us have what we ask, and you will be able to leave England again before dark. We will tell that fool Templar that you agreed to our terms without the persuasion of the soap, and that we hurried you to the church before you changed your mind. He will fly you back to San Remo at once, and you will have nothing more to fear."

"I have nothing to fear now," said Rolfieri, as if he was trying to hearten himself. "It would do you no good to hand me over to the police."

"It would punish you for wasting so much of our time and some of our money," put in the girl, in a tone which left no room for doubt that that revenge would be taken in the last resort.

Rolfieri licked his lips and squirmed in the tight ropes which bound him—he was a fat man, and they had a lot to bind. Perhaps the glimpse of his well-fed corporation which that movement gave him made him realise some of the inescapable discomforts of penal servitude to the amateur of good living, for his voice was even more half-hearted when he spoke again.

"I have not so much money in England," he said.

"You have a lot more than that in England," answered the other Naccaro harshly. "It is deposited in the City and Continental Bank under the name of Pierre Fontanne; and we have a cheque on that bank made out ready for you. All we require is your signature and a letter in your own hand instructing the bank to pay cash. Be quick and make up your mind, now—we are losing patience."

It was inevitable that there should be further argument on the subject, but the outcome was a foregone conclusion.

The cheque was signed and the letter was written; and Domenick Naccaro handed them over to his brother.

"Now you will let me go," said Rolfieri.

"We will let you go when Alessandro returns with the money," said Domenick Naccaro. "Until then, you stay here. Maria will look after you while I go back to the farm and detain Templar."

The Saint did not need to hear any more. He went back to the kitchen with soundless speed, and let himself out of the window by which he had entered. But before he left he picked up a trophy from a shelf over the sink.

Domenick Naccaro reached the farmhouse

shortly after him, and found the Saint reading a newspaper.

"Rolfieri has-a marry Maria," he announced triumphantly, and kissed the Saint on both cheeks. "So after all I keep-a da secret of my leedle trick wis-a da soap. But everyting we owe to you, my friend!"

"I guess you do," Simon admitted. "Where are the happy couple?"

"Ha! That is-a da romance. It seems that Signor Rolfieri was always fond of Maria, and when he hear that she have-a da baby, and he see her again—*presto!* he is in love wis her. So now they go to London to get-a da clothes, queeck, so she can go wis him for da honeymoon. So I tink we drink-a da wine till they come back."

They spent a convivial morning, which Simon Templar would have enjoyed more if caution had not compelled him to tip all his drinks down the back of his chair.

It was half-past one when a car drew up outside, and a somewhat haggard Rolfieri, a jubilant Alessandro Naccaro, and a quietly smiling Maria came in. Domenick jumped up.

"Everything is all right?" he asked.

"Pairfect," beamed Alessandro.

That was as much as the Saint was waiting to hear. He uncoiled himself from his chair and smiled at them all.

"In that case, boys and girls," he drawled, "would you all put up your hands and keep very quiet?"

There was an automatic in his hand; and six eyes stared at it mutely. And then Domenick Naccaro smiled a wavering and watery smile.

"I tink you make-a da joke, no?" he said.

"Sure," murmured the Saint amiably. "I make-a da joke. Just try and get obstreperous, and watch me laugh."

He brought the glowering Alessandro towards him and searched his pockets. There was no real question of anybody getting obstreperous, but the temptation to do so must have been very near when he brought out a sheaf of new banknotes and transferred them one-handed to his own wallet.

"This must seem rather hard-hearted of me," Simon remarked, "but I have to do it. You're a very talented family—if you really are a family—and you must console yourselves with the thought that you fooled me for a whole ten days. When I think how easily you might have fooled me for the rest of the way, it sends cold shivers up and down my spine. Really boys, it was a rather brilliant scheme, and I wish I'd thought of it myself."

"You wait till I see you da next time, you pig," said Domenick churlishly.

"I'll wait," Simon promised him.

He backed discreetly out of the room and out of the house to his car; and they clustered in the doorway to watch him. It was not until he pressed the starter that the fullest realisation dawned upon Signor Rolfieri.

"But what happens to me?" he screamed. "How do I go back to San Remo?"

"I really don't know, Comrade," answered the Saint callously. "Perhaps Domenick will help you again if you give him some more money. Twenty-five thousand quid instead of five years' penal servitude was rather a bargain price, anyway."

He let in the clutch gently, and the big car moved forward. But in a yard or two he stopped it again, and felt in one of his pockets. He brought out his souvenir of a certain fortunate kitchen, and lobbed it towards the empurpled Domenick.

"Sorry, brother," he called back over his shoulder. "I forget-a da soap!"

THE PULP ERA

Villain: ?

After-Dinner Story

WILLIAM IRISH

ARGUABLY THE GREATEST WRITER of suspense fiction of all time, Cornell George Hopley-Woolrich (1903–1968) was born in New York City, grew up in Mexico and New York, and was educated at Columbia University, to which he left his literary estate.

Writing as Cornell Woolrich, William Irish, and George Hopley, he was a sad and lonely man, pathetically dedicating books to his typewriter and to his hotel room. An alcoholic and almost certainly a closeted homosexual, Woolrich was so antisocial and reclusive that he refused to leave his hotel room when his leg became infected, ultimately resulting in its amputation.

Not surprisingly, the majority of his work has an overwhelming darkness, and few of his characters, whether good or evil, have much hope for happiness—or even justice. Although his novels and stories require a good deal of suspension of disbelief, relying on an inordinate amount of coincidence, no twentieth-century author equaled Woolrich's ability to create tension.

Hollywood producers recognized the cinematic quality of his narratives of the everyday gone wrong, and few writers have had as many films based on their work as Woolrich has, including *Convicted* (1938), starring Rita Hayworth, based on "Face Work"; *Street of Chance* (1942), with Burgess Meredith and Claire Trevor, based on *The Black Curtain* (1941); *The Leopard Man* (1943), with Dennis O'Keefe and Jean Brooks, based on *Black Alibi* (1942); *Phantom Lady* (1944), with Ella Raines and Alan Curtis, based on the novel of the same title (published in 1942); *Deadline at Dawn* (1946), with Susan Hayward, based on the novel of the same title (published in 1944); *Rear Window* (1954), with Grace Kelly and James Stewart, based on "It Had to Be Murder"; and sixteen others, including two directed by François Truffaut: *The Bride Wore Black* (1968), with Jeanne

Moreau, based on the novel of the same title (published 1940); and *Mississippi Mermaid* (1969), with Catherine Deneuve, based on *Waltz into Darkness* (1947).

"After-Dinner Story" was originally published in the January 1938 issue of *Black Mask Magazine*; it was first collected in *After-Dinner Story* (Philadelphia, J. B. Lippincott, 1944).

AFTER-DINNER STORY

William Irish

MACKENZIE GOT ON the elevator at the thirteenth floor. He was a water-filter salesman and had stopped in at his home office to make out his accounts before going home for the day. Later on that night he told his wife, half-laughingly, that that must have been why it happened to *him*, his getting on at the thirteenth floor. A lot of buildings omit them.

The red bulb bloomed and the car stopped for him. It was an express, omitting all floors, both coming and going, below the tenth. There were two other men in it when he got on, not counting the operator. It was late in the day, and most of the offices had already emptied themselves. One of the passengers was a scholarly-looking man with rimless glasses, tall and slightly stooped. The time came when MacKenzie learned all their names. This was Kenshaw. The other was stout and cherubic looking, one of two partners in a struggling concern that was trying to market fountain pens with tiny lightbulbs in their barrels—without much success. He was fiddling with one of his own samples on the way down, clicking it on and off with an air of proud ownership. He turned out to be named Lambert.

The car was very efficient looking, very smooth running, sleek with bronze and chromium. It appeared very safe. It stopped at the next floor down, the twelfth, and a surly-looking individual with bushy brows stepped in, Prendergast. Then the number 11 on the operator's call board lit up, and it stopped there too. A man about MacKenzie's own age and an older man with a trim white mustache were standing there side by side when the door opened. However, only the young man got on; the elder man gripped him by the arm in parting and turned away remarking loudly, "Tell Elinor I was asking for her." The younger answered, "'Bye, Dad," and stepped in. Hardecker was his name. Almost at the same time 10 was flashing.

The entry from 11 had turned to face the door, as all passengers are supposed to do in an elevator for their own safety. MacKenzie happened to glance at the sour-pussed man with the bushy brows at that moment; the latter was directly behind the newest arrival. He was glaring at the back of Hardecker's head with baleful intensity; in fact MacKenzie had never seen such a hundred-watt glower anywhere before except on a movie "heavy." The man's features, it must be admitted, lent themselves to just such an expression admirably; he had a swell head start even when his face was in repose.

MacKenzie imagined this little by-play was due to the newcomer's having inadvertently trodden on the other's toe in turning to face forward. As a matter of fact, he himself was hardly conscious of analyzing the whole thing thus thoroughly; these were all just disconnected thoughts.

Ten was still another single passenger, a bill collector judging by the sheaf of pink, green, and canary slips he kept riffling through. He hadn't, by the gloomy look he wore, been having much luck today; or maybe his feet hurt him. This one was Megaffin.

There were now seven people in the car, counting the operator, standing in a compact little group facing the door, and no more stops due until it reached street level. Not a very great crowd; certainly far from the maximum the mechanism was able to hold. The framed notice, tacked to the panel just before MacKenzie's eyes, showed that it had been last inspected barely ten days before.

It never stopped at the street floor.

MacKenzie, trying to reconstruct the sequence of events for his wife that night, said that the operator seemed to put on added speed as soon as they had left the tenth floor behind. It was an express, so he didn't think anything of it. He remembered noticing at this point that the operator had a boil on the back of his neck, just above his uniform collar, with a Maltese cross of adhesive over it. He got that peculiar sinking sensation at the pit of his stomach many people get from a too-precipitated drop. The man near him, the young fellow from the eleventh, turned and gave him a half-humorous, half-pained look, so he knew that he must be feeling it too. Someone farther back whistled slightly to show his discomfort.

The car was a closed one, all metal, so you couldn't see the shaft doors flashing up. They must have been ticking off at a furious rate, just the same. MacKenzie began to get a peculiar ringing in his ears, like when he took the subway under the East River, and his knee joints seemed to loosen up, trying to buckle under him.

But what really first told him—and all of them—that something had gone wrong and this was not a normal descent, was the sudden, futile, jerky way the operator was wangling the control lever to and fro. It traveled the short arc of its orbit readily enough, but the car refused to answer to it. He kept slamming it into the socket at one end of the groove, marked Stop for all eyes to read, and nothing happened. Fractions of seconds, not minutes, were going by.

They heard him say in a muffled voice, "Look out! We're going to hit!" And that was all there was time for.

The whole thing was a matter of instants. The click of a camera shutter. The velocity of the descent became sickening; MacKenzie felt as if he were going to throw up. Then there was a tremendous bang like a cannon, an explosion of blackness, and of bulb glass showering down as the light went out.

They all toppled together in a heap, like a bunch of ninepins. MacKenzie, who had gone over backward, was the luckiest of the lot; he could feel squirming bodies bedded under him, didn't touch the hard-rubber floor of the car at all. However, his hip and shoulder got a bad wrench, and the sole of his foot went numb, through shoe and all, from the stinging impact it got flying up and slapping the bronze wall of the car.

There was no opportunity to extricate one's self, to try to regain one's feet. They were going up again—on springs or something. It was a little sickening too, but not as bad as the coming down had been. It slackened, reversed into a drop, and they banged a second time. Not with the terrific impact of the first, but a sort of cushioned bang that scrambled them up even more than they were already. Somebody's shoe grazed MacKenzie's skull. He couldn't see it but quickly caught it and warded it aside before it kicked him and gave him a fracture.

A voice near him was yelling, "Stop it! Cut it out!" half-hysterically, as though the jockeying up and down could be controlled. Even MacKenzie, badly frightened and shaken up as he was, hadn't lost his head to that extent.

The car finally settled, after a second slight bounce that barely cleared the springs under it at all, and a third and almost unnoticeable jolt. The rest was pitch darkness, a sense of suffocation, a commingling of threshing bodies like an ant heap, groans from the badly hurt and an ominous sigh or two from those even beyond groaning.

Somebody directly under MacKenzie was not moving at all. He put his hand on him, felt an upright, stiff collar, and just above it a small swelling, crisscrossed by plaster. The operator was dead. There was an inertness that told MacKenzie, and the rubber matting beneath the operator's skull was sticky.

He felt then for the sleek metal wall of the enclosure that had buried them all alive, reached up it like a fly struggling up glass, with the heels of his hands and the points of his elbows. He squirmed the rest of his body up after these precarious grips. Upright again, he leaned against cold bronze.

The voice—there's always one in every catastrophe or panic—that had been pleading to "Cut it out!" was now begging with childish vehemence: "Get me outa here! For the love of Mike, I've got a wife and kids. Get me outa here!"

MacKenzie had the impression it was the surly-looking follow with the bushy eyebrows. The probabilities, he felt, were all for it. Such visible truculence and toughness are usually all hollow inside, a mask of weakness.

"Shut up," he said, "I've got a wife too. What's that got to do with it?"

The important thing, he recognized, was not the darkness, nor their trapped position at the bottom of a sealed-up shaft, nor even any possible injuries any of them had received. But the least noticeable of all the many corollaries of their predicament was the most dangerous. It was that vague sense of stuffiness, of suffocation. Something had to be done about that at once. The operator had opened the front panel of the car at each floor, simply by latch motion. There was no reason why that could not be repeated down here, even though there was no accompanying opening in the shaft wall facing it. Enough air would filter down the crack between the jammed-in car and the wall, narrow though it was, to keep them breathing until help came. They were going to need that air before this was over.

MacKenzie's arms executed interlocking circles against the satiny metal face of the car, groping for the indented grip used to unlatch it. "Match," he ordered. "Somebody light a match. I'm trying to get this thing open. We're practically airtight in here."

The immediate, and expected, reaction was a howl of dismay from the tough-looking bird, like a dog's craven yelp.

Another voice, more self-controlled, said, "Wait a minute." Then nothing happened.

"Here I am; here, hand 'em to me," said MacKenzie, shoveling his upturned hand in and out through the velvety darkness.

"They won't strike, got all wet. Glass must have cut me." And then an alarmed "My shirt's all covered with blood!"

"All right, it mayn't be yours," said MacKenzie steadyingly. "Feel yourself before you let loose. If it is, hold a handkerchief to it. That bulb glass isn't strong enough to pierce very deep." And then in exasperation he hollered out, "For the love of God! Six men! Haven't any of you got a match to give me?" Which was unfair, considering that he himself had run short just before he left his office, and had been meaning to get a folder at the cigar store when he got off the car. "Hey, you, the guy that was fiddling with that trick fountain pen coming down, how about that gadget of yours?"

A new voice, unfrightened but infinitely crestfallen, answered disappointedly: "It—it broke." And then with a sadness that betokened there were other, greater tragedies than what had happened to the car: "It shows you can't drop it without breakage. And that was the chief point of our whole advertising campaign." Then an indistinct mumble: "Fifteen hundred dollars capital! Wait'll Belman hears what a white elephant we've got on our hands." Which, under the circumstances, was far funnier than was intended.

At least he's not yellow, whoever he is, thought MacKenzie. "Never mind," he exclaimed suddenly. "I've got it." His fingertips had found the slot at the far end of the seamless cast-bronze panel. The thing didn't feel buckled in any way but if the concussion had done that to it, if it refused to open . . .

He pulled back the latch, leaning over the operator's lifeless body to do so, and tugged at the slide. It gave, fell back about a third of its usual orbit along the groove, then stalled unmanageably. That was sufficient for their present needs, though there was no question of egress through it. The rough-edged bricks of the shaft wall were a finger's width beyond the lips of the car's orifice; not even a venturesome cat could have gotten a paw between without jamming it. What mattered was that they wouldn't asphyxiate now, no matter how long it took to free the mechanism, raise it.

"It's all right, fellows," he called reassuringly to those behind him, "I've got some air into the thing now."

If there was light farther up the shaft, it didn't reach down this far. The shaft wall opposite the opening was as black as the inside of the car itself.

He said, "They've heard us. They know what's happened. No use yelling at the top of your voice like that, only makes it tougher for the rest of us. They'll get an emergency crew on the job. We'll just have to sit and wait, that's all."

The nerve-tingling bellows for help, probably the tough guy again, were silenced shamefacedly. A groaning still kept up intermittently from someone else. "My arm, oh, Gawd, it hurts!" The sighing, from an injury that had gone deeper still, had quieted suspiciously some time before. Either the man had fainted, or he, too, was dead.

MacKenzie, matter-of-factly but not callously, reached down for the operator's outflung form, shifted it into the angle between two of the walls, and propped it upright there. Then he sat himself down in the clear floor space provided, tucked up his legs, wrapped his arms around them. He wouldn't have called himself a brave man; he was just a realist.

There was a momentary silence from all of them at once, one of those pauses. Then, because there was also, or seemed to be, a complete stillness from overhead in the shaft, panic stabbed at the tough guy again. "They gonna leave us here all night?" he whimpered. "What you guys sit there like that for? Don't you wanna get out?"

"For Pete's sake, somebody clip that loudmouth on the chin!" urged MacKenzie truculently.

There was a soundless indrawn whistle. "My arm! Oh, my arm!"

"Must be busted," suggested MacKenzie sympathetically. "Try wrapping your shirt tight around it to kill the pain."

Time seemed to stand still, jog forward a few notches at a time every so often, like something on a belt. The rustle of a restless body, a groan, an exhalation of impatience, an occasional cry from the craven in their midst, whom MacKenzie sat on each time with increasing acidity as his own nerves slowly frayed.

The waiting, the sense of trapped helplessness, began to tell on them, far more than the accident had.

"They may think we're all dead and take their time," someone said.

"They never do in a case like this," MacKenzie answered shortly. "They're doing whatever they're doing as fast as they can. Give 'em time."

A new voice, that he hadn't heard until then, said to no one in particular, "I'm glad my father didn't get on here with me."

Somebody chimed in, "I wish I hadn't gone back after that damn phone call. It was a wrong number, and I coulda ridden down the trip before this."

MacKenzie sneered, "Ah, you talk like a bunch of ten-year-olds! It's happened; what's the good of wishing about it?"

He had a watch on his wrist with a luminous dial. He wished that he hadn't had, or that it had gone out of commission like the other man's trick fountain pen. It was too nerve-racking; every minute his eyes sought it, and when it seemed like half an hour had gone by, it was only five minutes. He wisely refrained from mentioning it to any of the others; they would have kept asking him, "How long is it now?" until he went screwy.

When they'd been down twenty-two and one-half minutes from the time he'd first looked at it, and were all in a state of nervous instability bordering on frenzy, including himself, there was a sudden unexpected, unannounced thump directly overhead, as though something heavy had landed on the roof of the car.

This time it was MacKenzie who leaped up, pressed his cheek flat against the brickwork outside the open panel, and funneled up the paper-thin gap: "Hello! Hello!"

"Yeah," a voice came down, "we're coming to you, take it easy!"

More thumping for a while, as though somebody were jigging over their heads. Then a sudden metallic din, like a boiler factory going full blast. The whole car seemed to vibrate with it, it became numbing to touch it for long at any one point. The confined space of the shaft magnified the noise into a torrent of sound, drowning out all their remarks. MacKenzie couldn't stand it, finally had to stick his palms up flat against his ears. A blue electric spark shot down the narrow crevice outside the door from above. Then another, then a third. They all went out too quickly to cast any light inside.

Acetylene torches! They were having to cut a hole through the car roof to get at them. If there was a basement opening in the shaft, and there must have been, the car must have plunged down even beyond that, to subbasement level, wound up in a dead end cul-de-sac at pit bottom. There was apparently no other way.

A spark materialized eerily through the ceiling. Then another, then a semicircular gush of them. A curtain of fire descended halfway into their midst, illuminating their faces wanly for a minute. Luckily it went out before it touched the car floor.

The noise broke off short and the silence in its wake was deafening. A voice shouted just above them: "Look out for sparks, you guys below, we're coming through. Keep your eyes closed, get back against the walls!"

The noise came on again, nearer at hand, louder than before. MacKenzie's teeth were on edge from the incessant vibration. Being rescued was worse than being stuck down here. He wondered how the others were standing it, especially that poor guy with the broken wing. He thought he heard a voice scream: "Elinor! Elinor!" twice, like that, but you couldn't be sure of anything in that infernal din.

The sparks kept coming down like a dripping waterfall; MacKenzie squinted his eyes cagily, kept one hand shielded up over them to protect his eyesight. He thought he saw one spark shoot across horizontally, instead of down vertically, like all the others; it was a different color too, more orange. He thought it must be an optical illusion produced by the alternating glare and darkness they were all being subjected to; either that, or a detached splinter of combusted metal from the roof, ricocheting off the wall. He closed his eyes all the way, just to play safe.

There wasn't much more to it after that. The noise and sparks stopped abruptly. They pried up the crescent-shaped flap they had cut in the roof with crowbars, to keep it from toppling inward and crushing those below. The cool, icy beams of torches flickered through. A cop jumped down into their midst and ropes were sent snaking down after him. He said in a brisk, matter-of-fact way: "All right, who's first now? Who's the worst hurt of yez all?"

His torch showed three forms motionless at the feet of the others in the confined space. The operator, huddled in the corner where MacKenzie had propped him; the scholarly-looking man with the rimless glasses (minus them now, and a deep gash under one eye to show what had become of them) lying senseless on his side; and the young fellow who had got on at the eleventh, tumbled partly across him, face down.

"The operator's dead," MacKenzie answered as spokesman for the rest, "and these two're out of their pain just now. There's a guy with a busted arm here, take him first."

The cop deftly looped the rope under the armpits of the ashen-faced bill collector, who was knotting the slack of one sleeve tightly in his other hand and sweating away like a fish in the torchlight.

"Haul away!" the cop shouted toward the opening. "And take your time, the guy's hurt."

The bill collector went up through the ceiling, groaning, legs drawn up under him like a trussed-up fowl.

The scholarly-looking man went next, head bobbing down in unconsciousness. When the noose came down empty, the cop bent over to fasten it around the young fellow still on the floor.

MacKenzie saw him change his mind, pry open one eyelid, pass the rope on to the tough-looking mug who had been such a crybaby, and who was shaking all over from the nervous reaction to the fright he'd had.

"What's the matter with him?" MacKenzie butted in, pointing to the floor.

"He's dead," the cop answered briefly. "He can wait, the living come first."

"Dead! Why, I heard him say he was glad his father didn't get on with him, long after we hit!"

"I don't care what you heard him say!" the cop answered. "He coulda said it, and still be dead now! Nuts. Are you telling me my business? You seem to be pretty chipper for a guy that's just come through an experience like this!"

"Skip it," said MacKenzie placatingly. He figured it was no business of his anyway, if the guy had seemed all right at first and now was dead. He might have had a weak heart.

He and the disheartened fountain pen entrepreneur seemed to be the only two out of the lot who were totally unharmed. The latter, however, was so brokenhearted over the failure of his appliance to stand up under an emergency, that he seemed hardly to care whether he went up or stayed down or what became of him. He kept examining the defective gadget even on his way up through the aperture in the car roof, with the expression of a man who has just bitten into a very sour lemon.

MacKenzie was the last one up the shaft, except the two fatalities. He was pulled in under the lip of the basement opening, from which the sliding doors had been taken down bodily. It was a bare four feet above the roof of the car; in other words the shaft continued on down past it for little more than the height of the car. He couldn't understand why it had been built that way, and not ended flush with the basement, in which case their long imprisonment could have been avoided. It was explained to him later, by the building superintendent, that it was necessary to give the car additional clearance underneath, else it would have run the risk of jamming each time it came down to the basement.

There were stretchers there in the basement passageway, and the bill collector and the scholarly-looking man were being given first aid by a pair of interns. The hard-looking egg was gulping down a large glass of spirits of ammonia between clicking teeth. MacKenzie let one of the interns look him over, at the latter's insistence; was told what he knew already, that he was okay. He gave his name and address to the lieutenant of police in charge, and walked up a flight of stairs to the street level, thinking: The old-fashioned way's the best after all.

He found the lobby of the building choked with a milling crowd, warded off a number of ambulance chasers who tried to tell him how badly hurt he was. "There's money in it, buddy, don't be a sucker!" MacKenzie phoned his wife from a nearby booth to shorten her anxiety, then he left the scene for home.

His last fleeting impression was of a forlorn figure standing there in the lobby, a man with a trim white mustache, the father of the young fellow lying dead below, buttonholing every cop within reach, asking over and over again, "Where's my son? Why haven't they brought my son up yet?" And not getting any answer from any of them—which was an answer in itself. MacKenzie pushed out into the street.

Friday, that was four days later, the doorbell rang right after supper and he had a visitor. "MacKenzie? You were in that elevator Monday night, weren't you, sir?"

"Yes," MacKenzie grinned, he sure was.

"I'm from Police Headquarters. Mind if I ask you a few questions? I've been going around to all of 'em checking up."

"Come in and sit down," said MacKenzie interestedly. His first guess was that they were trying to track down labor sabotage, or some violation of the building laws. "Matter, anything phony about it?"

"Not for our money," said the dick, evidently because this was the last leg of what was simply a routine questioning of all the survivors, and he refused to differ from his superiors. "The young fellow that was lying dead there in the bottom of the car—not the operator but young Wesley Hardecker—was found by the examiner to have a bullet embedded in his heart."

MacKenzie, jolted, gave a long-drawn whistle that brought his Scotty to the door questioningly. "Whew! You mean somebody shot him while we were all cooped up down there in that two-by-four?"

The dick showed, without being too pugnacious about it, that he was there to ask the questions, not answer them. "Did you know him at all?"

"Never saw him in my life before, until he got on the car that night. I know his name by now, because I read it in the papers next day; I didn't at the time."

The visitor nodded, as though this was the answer he'd gotten from all the others too. "Well, did you hear anything like a shot while you were down there?"

"No, not before they started the blowtorches. And after that, you couldn't have heard one anyway. Matter of fact, I had my hands over my ears at one time. I did see a flash, though," he went on eagerly. "Or at least I remember seeing one of the sparks shoot *across* instead of dropping down, and it was more orange in color."

Again the dick nodded. "Yeah, a couple of others saw that too. That was probably it, right there. Did it light up anyone's face behind it, anything like that?"

"No," MacKenzie admitted, "my eyes were all pinwheels, between the coal blackness and these flashing sparks coming down through the roof; we'd been warned, anyway, to keep them shut a minute before." He paused thoughtfully, went on: "It doesn't seem to hang together, does it? Why should anyone pick such a time and place to—"

"It hangs together beautifully," contradicted the dick. "It's his old man, the elder Hardecker, that's raising a stink, trying to read something phony into it. It's suicide while of unsound mind, and has been all along; and that's what the findings of the coroner's inquest are going to be too. We haven't turned up anything that throws a doubt on that. Old man Hardecker himself hasn't been able to identify a single one of you as having ever known or seen his son—or himself—before six o'clock last Monday evening. The gun was the fellow's own, and he had a license for it. He had it with him when he got in the car. It was under his body when it was picked up. The only fingerprints brought out on it were his. The examiner finds the wound a contact wound, powder burns all around it."

"The way we were crowded together down there, any kind of a shot at anyone would have been a contact," MacKenzie tried to object.

The dick waved this aside. "The nitrate test shows that his fingers fired the shot. It's true that we neglected to give it to anyone else at the time, but since there'd been only one shot fired out of the gun, and no other gun was found, that don't stack up to much. The bullet, of course, was from that gun and no other, ballistics has told us. The guy was a nervous, high-strung young fellow. He went hysterical down there, cracked up, and when he couldn't stand it any more, took himself out of it. And against this, his old man is beefing that he was happy, he had a lovely wife, they were expecting a kid, and he had everything to live for."

"Well, all right," objected MacKenzie mildly, "but why should he do it when they were already working on the roof over us, and it was just a matter of minutes before they got to us? Why not before? That don't sound logical. Matter of fact, his voice sounded calm and unfrightened enough while we were waiting."

The detective got up, as though the discussion were ended, but condescended to enlighten him on his way to the door: "People don't crack up at a minute's notice; it was after he'd been down there twenty minutes, half an hour, it got him. When you heard him say that, he was probably trying to hold himself together, kid himself he was brave or something. Any psychiatrist will tell you what noise'll do to someone already under a strain or tension. The noise of the blowtorches gave him the finishing touch; that's why he did it then, couldn't think straight any more. As far as having a wife and expecting a kid is concerned, that would only make him lose his head all the quicker. A man without ties or responsibilities is always more cold-blooded in an emergency."

"It's a new one on me, but maybe you're right. I only know water filters."

"It's my job to be right about things like that. Good night, Mr. MacKenzie."

The voice on the wire said, "Mr. MacKenzie? Is this the Mr. Stephen MacKenzie who was in an elevator accident a year ago last August? The newspapers gave—"

"Yes, I was."

"Well, I'd like you to come to dinner at my house next Saturday evening, at exactly seven o'clock."

MacKenzie cocked his brows at himself in the wall mirror. "Hadn't you better tell me who you are, first?"

"Sorry," said the voice, crisply. "I thought I had. I've been doing this for the past hour or so, and it's beginning to tell on me. This is Harold Hardecker, I'm head of the Hardecker Import and Export Company."

"Well, I still don't place you, Mr. Hardecker," MacKenzie said. "Are you one of the men who was on that elevator with me?"

"No, my son was. He lost his life."

"Oh," said MacKenzie. He remembered now. A man with a trim white mustache, standing in the milling crowd, buttonholing the cops as they hurried by . . .

"Can I expect you then at seven next Saturday, Mr. MacKenzie? I'm at—Park Avenue."

"Frankly," said MacKenzie, who was a plain soul not much given to social hypocrisy, "I don't see any point to it. I don't believe we've ever spoken to one another before. Why do you single me out?"

Hardecker explained patiently, even good-naturedly, "I'm not singling you out, Mr. MacKenzie. I've already contacted each of the others who were in the car that night with my son, and they've all agreed to be there. I don't wish to disclose what I have in mind beforehand; I'm giving this dinner for that purpose. However, I might mention that my son died intestate, and his poor wife passed away in childbirth in the early hours of the following morning. His estate reverted to me, and I am a lonely old man, without friends or relatives, and with more money already than I know what to do with. It occurred to me to bring together five perfect strangers, who shared a common hazard with my son, who were with him during the last few moments of his life." The voice paused, insinuatingly, to let this sink in. Then it resumed, "If you'll be at my house for dinner Saturday at seven, I'll have an announcement of considerable importance to make. It's to your interest to be present when I do."

MacKenzie scanned his water-filter-salesman's salary with his mind's eye, and found it altogether unsatisfactory, as he had done not once but many times before. "All right," he agreed, after a moment's consideration . . .

Saturday at six he was still saying, "You can't tell me. The guy isn't in his right mind, to do a thing like this. Five people that he don't know from Adam, and that don't know each other. I wonder if it's a practical joke?"

"Well, if you feel that way, why didn't you refuse him?" said his wife, brushing off his dark blue coat.

"I'm curious to find out what it's all about. I want to see what the gag is." Curiosity is one of the strongest of human traits. It's almost irresistible. The expectation of getting something for nothing is no slouch either. MacKenzie was a good guy, but he was a guy after all, not an image on a stained-glass window.

At the door she said with belated anxiety, "Steve, I know you can take care of yourself and all that, but if you don't like the looks of things, I mean if none of the others show up, don't stay there alone."

He laughed. He'd made up his mind by now, had even spent the windfall ahead of time, already. "You make me feel like one of those innocents in the old silent pictures, that were always being invited to a big blowout and when they got there they were alone with the villain and just supper for two. Don't worry, Toots, if there's no one else there, I turn around and come back."

The building had a Park Avenue address, but was actually on one of the exclusive side streets just off that thoroughfare. A small ultra-ultra cooperative, with only one apartment to a floor. "Mr. Harold Hardecker?" asked Mr. MacKenzie in the lobby. "Stephen MacKenzie."

He saw the hallman take out a small typed list of five names, four of which already had been penciled out, and cross out the last one. "Go right up, Mr. MacKenzie. Third floor."

A butler opened the single door in the elevator foyer for him, greeted him by name and took his hat. A single glance at the money this place spelled would have been enough to restore anyone's confidence. People that lived like this were perfectly capable of having five strangers in to dinner, subdividing a dead son's estate among them, and chalking it off as just that evening's little whimsy. The sense of proportion alters above a certain yearly income.

He remembered Hardecker readily enough as soon as he saw him coming toward him along the central gallery that seemed to bisect the place like a bowling alley. It took him about three and a half minutes to get up to him, at that. The man had aged appreciably from the visual snapshot that was all he'd had of him at the scene of the accident. He was slightly stooped, very thin at the waist, looked as though he'd suffered. But the white mustache was as trim and needle-pointed as ever, and he had on one of the new turned-over soft collars under his dinner jacket, which gave him a peculiarly boyish look in spite of the almost blinding white of his undiminished hair, cropped close as a Prussian's.

Hardecker held out his hand, said with just the right mixture of dignity and warmth, "How do you do, Mr. MacKenzie, I'm very glad to know you. Come in and meet the others and have a pickup."

There were no women present in the living room, just the four men sitting around at ease. There was no sense of strain, of stiffness; an advantage that stag gatherings are apt to have over mixed parties anyway, not through the fault of women, but through men's consciousness of them.

Kenshaw, the scholarly-looking man, had a white scar still visible under his left eye where his glasses had broken. The cherubic Lambert had deserted the illuminated fountain pen business, he hurriedly confided, unasked, to MacKenzie, for the ladies' foundation-girdle business. No more mechanical gadgets for him. Or as he put it, unarguably, "A brassière they gotta have, or else. But who needs a fountain pen?" The hard-bitten mug was introduced as Prendergast, occupation undisclosed. Megaffin, the bill collector, was no longer a bill collector. "I send out my own now," he explained, swiveling a synthetic diamond around on his pinky.

MacKenzie selected Scotch, and when he'd caught up with the rest the butler came to the door, almost as though he'd been timing him through a knothole. He just looked in, then went away again.

"Let's go and get down to business now, gentlemen, shall we?" Hardecker grinned. He had the happy faculty, MacKenzie said to himself, of making you feel perfectly at home, without overdoing it, getting in your hair. Which looks easier than it is.

No flowers, candles, or fripperies like that were on the table set for six; just good substantial man's board. Hardecker said, "Just sit down anywhere you choose, only keep the head for me." Lambert and Kenshaw took one side, Prendergast and Megaffin the other. MacKenzie sat down at the foot. It was obvious that whatever announcement their host intended making was being kept for the end of the meal, as was only fitting.

The butler had closed a pair of sliding doors beyond them after they were all in, and he stayed outside. The waiting was done by a man. It was a typical bachelor's repast, plain, marvelously cooked, without dainty or frivolous accessories to detract from it, salads, vegetables, things like that. Each course had its vintage corollary. And at the end no cloying sweets—Roquefort cheese and coffee with the blue flame of Courvoisier flickering above each glass. It was a masterpiece. And each one, as it ended, relaxed in his chair in a haze of golden daydreams. They anticipated coming into money, money they hadn't had to work for, maybe more money than they'd ever had before. It wasn't such a bad world after all.

One thing had struck MacKenzie, but since he'd never been waited on by servants in a private home before, only in restaurants, he couldn't determine whether it was unusual or customary. There was an expensive mahogany buffet running across one side of the dining room, but the waiter had done no serving or carving on it, had brought in each portion separately, always individually, even the roast. The coffee and the wines, too, had been poured behind the scenes, the glasses and the cups brought in already filled. It gave the man a lot more work and slowed the meal somewhat, but if that was the way it was done in Hardecker's house, that was the way it was done.

When they were already luxuriating with their cigars and cigarettes, and the cloth had been cleared of all but the emptied coffee cups, an additional dish was brought in. It was a silver chalice, a sort of stemmed bowl, holding a thick yellowish substance that looked like mayonnaise. The waiter placed it in the exact geometrical center of the table, even measuring with his eye its distance from both sides, and from the head and foot, and shifting its position to conform. Then he took the lid off and left it open. Threads of steam rose sluggishly from it. Every eye was on it interestedly.

"Is it well mixed?" they heard Hardecker ask.

"Yes, sir," said the waiter.

"That will be all, don't come in again."

The man left by the pantry door he had been using, and it clicked slightly after it had closed behind him.

Somebody—Megaffin—asked cozily: "What's *that* got in it?" evidently on the lookout for still more treats.

"Oh, quite a number of things," Hardecker answered carelessly, "whites of eggs, mustard, as well as certain other ingredients all beaten up together."

MacKenzie, trying to be funny, said, "Sounds like an antidote."

"It is an antidote," Hardecker answered, looking steadily down the table at him. He must have pushed a call button or something under the table, for the butler opened the sliding doors and stood between them, without coming in.

Hardecker didn't turn his head. "You have that gun I gave you? Stand there, please, on the other side of those doors and see that no one comes out of here. If they try it, you know what to do."

The doors slipped to again, effaced him, but not before MacKenzie, facing that way, had seen something glimmer in his hand.

Tension was slow in coming on, the change was too abrupt, they had been too steeped in the rosy afterglow of the meal and their own imminent good fortune. Then too, not all of them were equally alert mentally, particularly Megaffin, who had been on such a fourth dimensional plane of unaccustomedness all evening he couldn't tell menace from hospitality, even when a gun was mentioned.

Its first focal point was Hardecker's own face—that went slowly white, grim, remorseless. From there it darted out to MacKenzie and Lambert, caught at them, paled them too. The rest grew allergic to it one by one, until there was complete silence at the table.

Hardecker spoke. Not loudly, not angrily, but in a steely, pitiless voice. "Gentlemen, there's a murderer in our midst."

Five breaths were sharply indrawn together, making a fearful "Ffff!" sound around the table. Not so much aghast at the statement itself, as aghast at the implication of retribution that lurked just behind it. And behind that was the shadowy suspicion that it had already been exacted.

No one said anything.

The hard, remorseless cores of Hardecker's eyes shot from face-to-face. He was smoking a long slim cigar, cigarette-thin. He pointed it straight out before him, indicated them all with it without moving it much, like a dark finger of doom. "Gentlemen, one of you killed my son." Pause. "On August 30, 1936." Pause. "And hasn't paid for it yet."

The words were like a stone going down into a deep pool of transparent water, and the ripples spreading out from them spelled fear.

MacKenzie said slowly, "You're setting yourself above the properly constituted authorities? The findings of the coroner's inquest were suicide while of unsound mind. Why do you hold them incompe—"

Hardecker cut him short like a whip. "This isn't a discussion. It's—" a long pause, then very low, but very audible, "an execution."

There was another of those strangling silences. They took it in a variety of ways, each according to his temperament. MacKenzie just kept staring at him, startled, apprehensive. Apprehensive, but not inordinately frightened, any more than he had been that night on the elevator. The scholarly-looking Kenshaw had a rebuking look on his face, that of a teacher for an unruly pupil, and the scar on his cheek stood out whitely. Megaffin looked shifty, like some small weasel at bay, planning its next move. The pugnacious-looking guy was going to cave in again in a minute, judging by the wavering of his facial lines. Lambert pinched the bridge of his nose momentarily, dropped his hand, mumbled something that sounded like, "*Oy*, I give up my pinochle club to come here, yet!"

Hardecker resumed, as though he hadn't said anything unusual just now. "I know who the man is. I know which one among you the man is. It's taken me a year to find out, but now I know, beyond the shadow of a doubt." He was looking at his cigar now, watching the ash drop off of its own weight onto his coffee saucer. "The police wouldn't listen to me, they insisted it was suicide. The evidence was insufficient to convince them the first time, and for all I know it still may be." He raised his eyes. "But I demand justice for the taking of my son's life." He took an expensive, dime-thin, octagonal watch out of his pocket, placed it face up on the table before him. "Gentlemen, it's now nine o'clock. In half an hour, at the most, one of you will be dead. Did you notice that you were all served separately just now? One dish, and one alone out of all of them, was deadly. It's putting in its slow, sure work right as we sit here." He pointed to the silver tureen, equidistant from all of them. "There's the answer. There's the antidote. I have no wish to set myself up as executioner above the law. Let the murderer be the chooser. Let him reach out and save his life and stand convicted before all of you. Or let him keep silent and go down to his death without confessing, privately executed for what can't be publicly proved. In twenty-five minutes collapse will come without warning. Then it will be too late."

It was Lambert who voiced the question in all their minds. "But are you sure you did this to the right—"

"I haven't made any mistake, the waiter was carefully rehearsed, you are all perfectly unharmed but the killer."

Lambert didn't seem to derive much consolation from this. "Now he tells us! A fine way to digest a meal," he brooded aloud. "Why didn't you serve the murderer first, so then the rest of us could eat in peace at least?"

"Shut up," somebody said, terrifiedly.

"Twenty minutes to go," Hardecker said, tonelessly, as a chime signal over the radio.

MacKenzie said, without heat, "You can't be sane, you know, to do a thing like this."

"Did you ever have a son?" was the answer.

Something seemed to snap in Megaffin. His chair jolted back. "I'm gettin' out of here," he said hoarsely.

The doors parted about two inches, silently as water, and a black metal cylinder peered through. "That man there," directed Hardecker. "Shoot him where he stands if he doesn't sit down."

Megaffin shrank down in his seat again like a whipped cur, tried to shelter himself behind Prendergast's shoulder. The doors slipped together again into a hairline crack.

"I couldn't," sighed the cherubic-faced Lambert, "feel more at home if I was in the Brown House at Munich!"

"Eighteen minutes," was the comment from the head of the table.

Prendergast suddenly grimaced uncontrollably, flattened his forearms on the table, and ducked his head onto them. He sniveled aloud. "I can't stand it! Lemme out of here! *I* didn't do it!"

A wave of revulsion went around the table. It was not because he'd broken down, analyzed MacKenzie, it was just that he didn't have the face for it. It should have been Lambert with his kewpie physiognomy, if anyone. The latter, however, was having other troubles. He touched the side of his head, tapped himself on the chest. "Whoof!" he murmured. "What heartburn! He should live so long, I don't take this up with my lawyer!"

"This is no way," said MacKenzie surlily. "If you had any kind of a case—"

"This is my way," was Hardecker's crackling answer. "I've given the man his choice. He needn't have it this way; he has his alternative. Fourteen minutes. Let me remind you, the longer the antidote's delayed, the more doubtful its efficacy will be. If it's postponed too long, it may miss altogether."

Conscious of a sticking sensation in his stomach, as though a mass of concrete had lodged there, MacKenzie felt a burning sensation shoot out from it. There is such a thing as nervous indigestion, he knew, but . . . He eyed the silver goblet reflectively.

But they were all doing that almost incessantly. Prendergast had raised his head again, but it remained a woebegone mask of infantile fretfulness. Megaffin was green in the face and kept moistening his lips. Kenshaw was the most self-controlled of the lot; he had folded his arms and just sat there, as though waiting to see which one of the others would reach for the salvation in the silver container.

MacKenzie could feel a painful pulsing under his solar plexus now, he was in acute discomfort that verged on cramp. The thought of what this might be was bringing out sweat on his forehead.

Lambert reached out abruptly, and they all quit breathing for a minute. But his hand dodged the silver tureen, plunged into a box of perfectos to one side of it. He grabbed up two, stuck one in his breast pocket, the other between his teeth. "On you," he remarked resentfully to Hardecker.

Somebody gave a strained laugh at the false alarm they had all had. Kenshaw took off his glasses, wiped them ruefully, as though disappointed it hadn't been the payoff after all.

MacKenzie said, "You're alienating whatever sympathy's due you, by pulling a stunt like this."

"I'm not asking for sympathy," was Hardecker's coldly ferocious answer. "It's atonement I want. Three lives were taken from me: my only son, my daughter-in-law, their prematurely born child. I demand payment for that!"

Lambert said aloud, for his own benefit, "Jennie won't believe this when I tell her."

Prendergast clutched his throat all at once, whimpered: "I can't breathe! He's done it to *me*, so help me!"

MacKenzie, hostile now to Hardecker, tried to steady him just on general principle. "Gas around the heart, maybe. Don't fall for it if you're not sure."

"Don't fall for it," was the ungrateful yelp, "and if I drop dead are *you* gonna bring me back?"

"He ought to be arrested for this," said Kenshaw, displaying emotion for the first time. His glasses had clouded over, giving him a peculiarly sightless look.

"Arrested?" snapped Lambert. He wagged his head from side to side. "He's going to be sued like no one was ever sued before! When I get through with him he'll go on relief."

Hardecker threw him a contemptuous look. "About ten minutes," he said. "He seems to prefer the more certain way. Stubborn, eh? He'd rather die than admit it."

MacKenzie gripped the seat of his chair, his churning insides heaving. He thought, "If this is the McCoy that I'm feeling now, I'm going to bash his head in with a chair before I go. I'll give him something to poison innocent people about!"

Megaffin was starting to swear at their tormentor, in a whining, guttural singsong.

"*Mazzeltov*," seconded Lambert, with a formal nod of approval. "Your breath, but my ideas."

"Five minutes. It will almost certainly fail if it's not downed within the next thirty seconds." Hardecker pocketed his watch, as though there were no further need for consulting it.

MacKenzie gagged, hauled at the knot of his tie, undid his collar button. A needle of suffocating pain had just splintered into his heart.

Only the whites of Prendergast's eyes showed, he was going off into some fit or fainting spell. Even Lambert quit pulling at his cigar, as though it sickened him. Kenshaw took off his glasses for the third time in five minutes, to clear them.

A pair of arms suddenly shot out, grasped the silver bowl, swung it. It was uptilted over someone's face and there was a hollow, metallic groaning coming from behind it, infinitely gruesome to hear. It had happened so quickly, MacKenzie couldn't be sure who it was for a minute, long as he had been sitting at the macabre table with all of them. He had to do it by a quick process of elimination. Man sitting beside Lambert—Kenshaw, the scholarly-looking one, the man who had had least to say since the ordeal had begun! He was gulping with a convulsive rising and falling of his Adam's apple, visible in the shadow just below the lower rim of the bowl.

Then suddenly he flung it aside, his face was visible again, the drained receptacle clanged against the wall where he'd cast it, dropped heavily to the floor. He couldn't talk for a minute or two, and neither could anyone else, except possibly Hardecker, and he didn't, just sat staring at the self-confessed culprit with pitiless eyes.

Finally Kenshaw panted, checks twitching, "Will it—will it—save me?"

Hardecker folded his arms, said to the others, but without taking his eyes off Kenshaw: "So now you know. So now you see whether I was right or not."

Kenshaw was holding his hands pressed tightly to the sides of his head. A sudden flood of words was unloosed from him, as though he found it a relief to talk now, after the long unbearable tension he'd been through. "Sure you were right, and I'd do it over again! I'm glad he's gone. The rich man's son that had everything. But that wasn't enough for him, was it? He had to show off how good he was—Horatio Alger stuff, paddle your own canoe from riches to more riches! He couldn't take a job with your own firm, could he? No, people might say you were helping him. He had to come to the place *I* worked and ask for a job. Not just anonymously. No, he had to mention whose son he was, to swing the scales in his favor! They were afraid to offend you, they thought maybe they'd get a pull with you, through him. It didn't count that I'd been with them all the best years of my life, that I had someone home too, just like he had, that I couldn't go anywhere else and mention the name of an influential father! They fired me."

His voice rose shrilly. "D'you know what happened to me? D'you know or care how I tramped the streets in the rain, at my age, looking for work? D'you know my wife had to get down on her knees and scrub dirty office corridors? D'you know how I washed dishes, carried sandwich boards through the streets, slept on park benches, all on account of a smart aleck with Rover Boy ideas? Yes, it preyed on my mind, why wouldn't it? I suppose you found the threatening letters I wrote him, that's how you knew."

Hardecker just shook his head slightly in denial.

"Then he got on the elevator that day. He didn't see me, probably wouldn't have known me if he had, but I saw him. I knew him. Then we fell—and I hoped he was dead, I hoped he was dead! But he wasn't. The idea took hold of me slowly, waiting down there in the dark. The torches started making noise, and I grabbed him, I was going to choke him. But he wrenched himself free and took out his gun to defend himself against what I guess he thought was a fear-crazed man. I wasn't fear-crazed, I was revenge-crazed, I knew what I was doing!

"I grabbed his hand. Not the gun, but the hand that was holding it. I turned it around the other way, into his own heart. He said 'Elinor, Elinor!' but that didn't save him; that was the wrong name, that was *his* wife not mine. I squeezed the finger he had on the trigger with my own, and he fired his own weapon. So the police were right, it was suicide in a way.

"He leaned against me, there wasn't room enough in there to fall. I flung myself down first under him, so they'd find us that way, and eased him down on top of me. He bled on me a little while and then he quit. And when they came through I pretended I'd fainted."

Hardecker said, "Murderer. Murderer." Like drops of ice water. "He didn't *know* he'd done all that to you; oh, why didn't you give him a chance at least, why weren't you a man? Murderer! Murderer!"

Kenshaw started reaching downward to the floor, where he'd dropped his glasses when he had seized the antidote. His face was on a level with the tabletop. He scowled: "No matter what they've all heard me say just now, you'll never be able to prove I did it. Nobody saw me. Only the dark."

A whisper sounded: "And that's where you're going. Into the dark."

Kenshaw's head vanished suddenly below the table. The empty back of his chair whirled over sidewise, cracked against the floor.

They were all on their feet now, bending over him. All but Hardecker. MacKenzie got up from his knees. "He's dead!" he said. "The antidote didn't work in time!"

Hardecker said, "That wasn't the antidote, that was the poison itself. He hadn't been given any until he gulped that down. He convicted himself and carried out sentence upon himself with one and the same gesture. I hadn't known which one of you it was until then. I'd only known it hadn't been my son's own doing, because, you see, the noise of those torches wouldn't have affected him much, he was partly deaf from birth."

He pushed his chair back and stood up. "I didn't summon you here under false pretenses; his estate will be divided in equal parts among the four of you that are left. And now I'm ready to take my own medicine. Call the police, let them and their prosecutors and their courts of law decide whether I killed him or his own guilty conscience did!"

Villain: Dr. Yen Sin

The Mystery of the Golden Skull

DONALD E. KEYHOE

DONALD EDWARD KEYHOE (1897–1988) had two careers—wildly divergent except to cynics. He became an international sensation for his book *The Flying Saucers Are Real* (1950), which grew from a *True* magazine article and sold five hundred thousand copies. He averred that the U.S. government knew that UFOs existed but kept it silent to avoid a public panic. He wrote several additional books on the subject of extraterrestrials and made a controversial appearance on television to discuss his findings, only to have CBS cut off all audio on the live broadcast.

He was a successful writer for *The Nation*, *The Saturday Evening Post*, and *Reader's Digest*, before turning to pulp fiction in the 1920s and 1930s, creating fantastic stories for the prestigious *Weird Tales*, as well as thrilling aviation stories for *Flying Aces*, *Dare-Devil Aces*, *Battle Aces*, and *Sky Birds*. His major contribution to the pulps was Dr. Yen Sin, also known as the "Invisible Emperor," the "Yellow Doctor," and the "Cobra."

Dr. Yen Sin was the titular villain in a short-lived (three-issue) pulp magazine that superseded a similar magazine from the same publishers titled *The Mysterious Wu Fang*, which had ceased publication in March 1936. The title characters of both magazines were "Yellow Peril" villains in the mold of Dr. Fu Manchu.

In Washington, D.C., Yen Sin employs modern technology as well as such diabolical weapons as death rays, inventions from his scientific laboratories, blow guns, and dacoits. He is opposed by Michael Traile, who professes that he has not slept for twenty-seven years, having lost the power of sleep at age two because of a brain injury. The Hindu doctor performing the operation had to remove the portion of the brain that controlled sleep. Traile's parents engaged a fakir who taught him the yoga trick of complete relaxation and, to avoid boredom, he was educated constantly, his intelligence developing rapidly as a result. He is expert at everything.

"The Mystery of the Golden Skull" was originally published in the July/August 1936 issue of *Dr. Yen Sin*.

THE MYSTERY OF THE GOLDEN SKULL

Donald E. Keyhoe

Chapter 1

The Man Who Did Not Sleep

THE ROARING VOICE of the city had died away to a murmur. It was the hour when Manhattan slumbered. High up in a dark building near Fifth Avenue, a furtive figure sat at the window of an unlighted room, a pair of binoculars raised to his eyes. His pose had the instinctive stealth of the East, though the man on whom he was spying was almost two blocks away.

Suddenly a faint buzzing sounded in the phones which covered his ears. He bent his head, spoke into the mouthpiece strapped to his chest.

"Control, Group Two." His voice was strained, for he had been watching constantly for more than six nerve-racking hours.

"Observer Nine," came a muffled voice. "Neither Michael Traile nor Eric Gordon has left the building."

"I can see Traile," grated the man at the window, "but he has been alone for two hours."

"Gordon must be in some other room," muttered the second voice. "We've kept the place covered—"

"Resume position," curtly ordered the man in the darkened room. As he leaned over the sill, dim light from the street far below fell on the sallow features of a Eurasian.

He lifted the binoculars again, gazed out into the night. A deep blue had begun to tinge the blackness above the skyscraper canyons, but it was still two hours until dawn. Beyond an expanse of lower buildings, a tall structure loomed. The man trained his glasses on a yellow rectangle near the top and almost at his own level.

The powerful lenses bridged the intervening space, seemed to bring that lighted window to within a few yards of him. He was looking into a large room, apparently intended for a den. But the furnishing was not complete, for the library table was littered with curios, books, and various objects. A huge packing box stood on the Persian rug which covered the floor.

A man was moving back and forth, emptying the box. He was very tall, and his lean face was tanned to the color of bronze. It was a keen face, and strong. The pleasant set of his lips relieved a hint of grimness about the jaw.

The hidden watcher swore to himself. This man Traile showed no sign of weariness, yet the reports proved he had not slept in thirty-one hours. The spy kept the glasses focused as the other man went back and forth from the box to the table. Traile seemed to be hunting for something.

With growing bewilderment, the spy saw the objects which appeared. Already the packing box had yielded a pair of foils, a violin, a jeweler's lathe, and several pieces of chemical apparatus. In quick succession, Traile produced a set of boxing gloves, three cameras of varying sizes, and a dozen pistols ranging from a small French derringer to a Colt .45 automatic. Books and a score of cartons and bundles followed. One carton was torn, and as Traile lifted it some theatrical make-up materials spilled to the floor. He tossed the things onto the table, turned and drew a leather-covered case from the packing box.

This was evidently the object of his search. He laid the case on a pedestal beside a big easy chair. Seating himself, he started to unsnap the buckles. Then he paused, and the spy saw a tired expression cross his tanned face. He stretched his long arms, sank back. For a moment the hidden observer thought he was going to sleep. But instead, Traile idly lighted a cigarette and looked out into the night.

Though he was two blocks away, the spy jerked back, for Traile's dark eyes, as seen through the glasses, appeared to be boring straight into him. The impression persisted as he forced himself to keep watching. Even at that distance, he could feel the power of that motionless figure.

A peculiar, far-off expression came into Traile's dark eyes. He seemed to be thinking intently. He finished the cigarette, lighted another, then picked up a newspaper from the arm of his chair. His movements were oddly lazy.

The spy gave a sigh of relief as that penetrating gaze was cut off. He laid down the binoculars, wiped his damp brow.

Several minutes passed.

He was about to lift the glasses again when a queer signal buzzed in his phones. He hurriedly pressed a button at the base of the mouthpiece. There was a double click, then a calm, sibilant voice spoke in Chinese.

"Main Control. Summarize the latest reports on Michael Traile."

The words were in an obscure dialect. The Eurasian replied nervously in the same tongue.

"Personal observation transferred from Number Nine to Group Control at eight fifty-nine. At nine one, suspected apartment entered by Traile and unknown man. Obtained photograph of latter by telephoto camera with night lens."

"Very good," came the emotionless comment. "As I supposed, it is one of the new secret stations for the Q-Unit operating against the Invisible Empire. Proceed."

"Unknown man left at ten seventeen. At ten forty-five Eric Gordon entered apartment, bringing small black box, probably a portable radio."

"What report from the observer detailed to Gordon?" inquired the unseen Chinese.

"Gordon came directly from laboratories of World Radio and Cables," answered the spy. "Observer Eight reports rumor of Government arrangement with the company for Gordon's service."

"Continue the report on Michael Traile," came the toneless command.

"Examined the black box, moved out of my range to the left. Returned in two minutes, conversed with Gordon until one o'clock. Gordon then disappeared, but Observer Nine reports he did not leave building. Believe he is in another room, sleeping. But there is something strange about the man Traile. He has not slept since Group Two took over observation."

There was a sound as of harshly indrawn breath.

"Impossible! He had already gone without sleep for the forty-eight hours he was observed by Group One. You must be mistaken."

"No, Master," said the spy, nervously. "I am certain. And there is another odd point. From the material he has unpacked, he must have a hundred hobbies."

"I am aware of that," the unseen Chinese answered curtly. "But this other matter is vitally important. You are sure he is still awake?"

"Yes, I can see him clearly." The half-caste lifted the binoculars. "He has just put down the paper he was reading. He is smoking a cigarette . . . *Ai!* This is puzzling! A few minutes ago he seemed tired. Now he looks refreshed, as though he had slept for hours."

"There is only one explanation," said the other man rapidly. "The cigarette must contain some mysterious drug which enables him to do without sleep for long periods. Watch closely—what is he doing now?"

The spy carefully focused the glasses, gazed into the distant room.

"Master, you will think me mad—he has opened a case of child's toys! . . . He is standing up—he has gone out of my range—now he is coming back with the black box which Gordon brought. . . . He is connecting it with wires to a toy church. . . . He is looking at the clock in the church steeple."

"That is enough," interrupted the man he had called Master. "I think I understand now."

There was a long pause.

"An expert rifleman could easily kill him from this observation point," ventured the half-caste.

"The secret of that drug is more valuable to me than his death," came the emotionless answer. "Here are my orders." He spoke swiftly for a minute. "Report at once if he leaves at four o'clock."

The phones clicked twice. The spy looked down at the luminous hands of his wristwatch. It was ten minutes to four.

As the carton of make-up material spilled to the floor, Michael Traile glanced quickly toward the adjacent room. The sound had not awakened Eric. He could see the young Southerner where he lay sprawled, half-dressed, on the only bed the "Q-Station" boasted. Eric's hair was rumpled, and even in sleep his face had a boyishly genial look. He was breathing deeply.

For an instant, as Traile picked up the scattered materials, a bitter light came into his eyes. If only he, too, could know that precious gift of sleep—could shut out everything for even one short hour. But Death was the only sleep he would ever know.

He turned back to the packing box, his thoughts still somber.

It had been twenty-seven years since that childhood injury which had made him a man apart. It had happened in India, where his parents were traveling. He had been only two years old, but he knew the story by heart. A skull fracture . . . a hasty operation by a Hindu surgeon . . . then the discovery that the man had damaged the lobe of the brain controlling the function of sleep. Sleepless nights and days when they feared that he would die . . . the Yogi who had trained him to relax his body completely, even though his mind would ever be awake. His strange boyhood back in the States . . . a day and a night tutor, to keep his wakeful brain occupied with one subject after another . . . a physical instructor to balance that strenuous mental life with games, exercise, sports.

Traile found the leather case he bad been seeking. He sat down, started to open it, then paused, realizing a sudden weariness. He stretched, relaxing his tall form to the utmost, then sat back and idly lighted a cigarette. For a few minutes he stared out into the night, through the bulletproof window.

If he were right, somewhere in the vastness of Manhattan was hidden the most dangerous man in the world—Dr. Yen Sin, malignant wizard of crime, and head of that unholy organization, the Invisible Empire. Traile's jaw hardened. The Yellow Doctor had escaped him in Washington, and now he would be fully on guard. But there was one advantage. Dr. Yen Sin would be looking for five Q-men—instead of one man connected with five Federal departments.

He lighted another cigarette; the tobacco helped him to relax. With his mind still on the Yellow Doctor, he opened his newspaper. For a week he had watched for something that would give a clue to Dr. Yen Sin's activities, if he were really in New York.

His restless eyes flicked over the headlines. A gang killing . . . a senator's speech, warning of the danger of inflation . . . a hint of sabotage in the sinking of a new submarine, on its trial runs before being delivered to the Navy . . . a murder trial . . . a rehash story on the week-old disappearance of John J. Meredith, prominent Wall Street figure, and a missing-persons item hooked up with it.

Traile's eyes narrowed thoughtfully as he read the last story. Two of the cases were believed murder, but the bodies had not been found. The police knew of no motives. . . .

He put down the paper and turned quickly to the leather box. His bronzed face was now alert; all his tired expression had vanished during that brief "relax-period." He opened the case. At first glance, it appeared to be filled with toys, each one clipped separately to the canvas lining. There was a tiny church, with a clock in its steeple; a brass soldier, with a bayoneted rifle; a small model ship; a toy pistol hardly two inches long; and a score of other similar objects.

Traile stood up briskly, crossed the room and brought back a small black box. It was a special microwave radio, a new self-powered type, developed by World Radio and Cables. It was still switched on, but so far he had failed to hear the strange Chinese code which Eric and one of the company engineers had caught two nights ago.

He connected two wires with tiny binding posts at the back of the toy church. Like most of his collection of "miniaturia," the church was not what it seemed. It was a diminutive radio, with a sensitive directional indicator.

As he sat back, waiting, his eyes strayed over the things which cluttered the room. They were like monuments down the long vista of sleepless years, even to the language books on the table. He had been a linguist at ten. At fifteen, his mind had been that of a mature man. Since then his life had been a constant seeking for new hobbies, new problems to ward off the desolation of endless nights. It was this which had accidentally led him into the web of the Yellow Doctor's criminal empire.

A faint hum from the toy church told him that the miniature tubes were warm. He glanced at the black box. The standard broadcast and licensed shortwave bands were tuned out. Anything which came in now would be from an unlicensed station, transmitting in the micro-frequencies no ordinary receiver would catch. He set the dials again at the point where the mysterious code had been heard. But there was only silence. He waited a minute or two, then stood up and moved restlessly about the den. It was not quite four. There would be a long, lonely stretch before Eric would awaken. He picked up a hobby magazine, rummaged through it.

Suddenly, from the room where Eric slept, a low-pitched buzzer sounded. He hurried into the room, slid open a small panel which hid a special switchboard. There were several numbered sockets. A bulb was flashing over the symbol "Q-5," which was his designation when he was working with the Department of Justice. The line was a direct wire to the Bureau of Investigation, at Washington.

"Michael?" came a barked query as he plugged in the phone. He recognized the voice of Director John Glover.

"Right," he said. Back of him, Eric stirred.

"I've a lead on Doctor Yen Sin," Glover said hastily. "The son of Peter Courtland was stabbed to death half an hour ago at the entrance to my hotel. It was done by a Chinese who got away. Before he died, young Courtland gasped out something about his father and the Invisible Empire. He had just arrived from New York, and was evidently bringing me a message."

"You haven't notified your Manhattan office?"

"No, the State Department says you're in full charge of the Invisible Empire case."

"Give me fifteen minutes," said Traile swiftly.

"Then phone Lexington Street to send two squads of agents to surround the Courtland place on Riverside Drive. Tell them to close in quietly. I'll fire a shot if I need help."

"Got it," barked Glover. He hung up, and Traile turned to find Eric Gordon dressing.

"What's up?" Eric asked eagerly.

Traile told him while he slipped off his smoking jacket and fastened a shoulder harness in place.

"You'd better take a gun, too," he advised, as he put on his coat. "If Courtland is mixed up with Doctor Yen Sin, we may run into anything."

Eric was ready in less than a minute. He hurried after Traile as the taller man strode into the den. They were almost at the steel-backed door to the hall when a sharp *da-dit-da-dit* rasped from the micro-set. Traile snatched up a pencil and pad.

"Here—you can take code faster than I can! I'll check the direction."

Eric began a hasty scribble, but the code abruptly ended. There was a long buzz, then from the silence which followed came a sinister, toneless voice.

"Main Control. Interpreter, Group Six, stand by."

Traile went rigid. It was the voice of the Invisible Emperor!

"Holy smoke!" Eric said tensely. "It's Doctor Yen Sin!"

Traile motioned him to silence, for the Yellow Doctor was speaking again. This time the words were Chinese. After a few moments there was a pause.

"What did he say?" Eric exclaimed.

Traile wheeled to a wall map of Greater New York.

"He simply counted from one to ten in Shamo dialect. What was that first code?"

"X-three-D, repeated," said Eric.

"Probably the call number of this 'Group Six,'" muttered Traile. He took up a ruler, looked at the hour hand of the tiny church-steeple clock. "The bearing is just about a hundred and sixty degrees."

"—eleven, twelve, thirteen," came the calm words of the Invisible Emperor. "Alternate two-five interval, Interpreter."

"Look!" said Eric excitedly. "Your bearing line goes within a block of Chinatown, between Pell Street and the East River."

Traile seized a strap from a bundle and swiftly fastened the micro-set to the miniature church.

"Come on," he said, thrusting the set under his arm. "We can take a cross-bearing on the way to the Courtland place, and trace the station later."

"Why not follow it now?" demanded Eric as they went into the hall.

Traile set a special lock on the steel-backed door.

"The Courtland lead is more important. We might be hours locating the transmitter, and even then they may be operating it by remote control."

Chapter 2

The Corpse with the Twisted Head

The elevator came up, and they descended to the first floor. The lobby was deserted except for the desk clerk and two drowsy bellhops.

"You're up early again, Mr. Scott," yawned the clerk. "Don't you ever sleep?"

"In the daytime," Traile replied tersely. He led the way to the garage at the rear of the apartment hotel, and in a few moments his car was rolling out into the night. Free of building interference, the micro-set brought the voice of Dr. Yen Sin to an audible note.

"—at one-minute intervals, Group Six," came the silken accents both he and Eric had grown to hate. A monotonous buzzing followed.

"Watch the indicator," Traile said as he turned westward.

"All Group Controls, attention!" the voice of the Invisible Emperor came with a sharpened note. "On suspicion of treachery, Female Agent Twenty-two is being removed—"

"No, no!" a woman screamed. "You can't do this—I haven't betrayed you!"

The words faded out with a moan. Eric whirled frantically.

"That was Sonya Damitri's voice! For God's sake, Michael, follow that bearing!"

Instead, Traile jammed his foot down on the throttle, sent the car racing across Sixth Avenue.

"Doctor Yen Sin forced her to trick you before! Don't fall for it again."

"But that yellow fiend's going to kill her!" Eric cried wildly. "She saved our lives that night—we've got to help her!"

"The whole thing is a plant," rapped Traile. "I was a fool not to see—"

The shriek of a police siren drowned the rest. Eric spun around.

"It's a prowl car." He clutched the strapped set. "I'm going to take these and ask them to help me find her!"

"Stay where you are," muttered Traile. He slowed as the police car drew alongside, then with a swift movement turned his spotlight handle. The beam fell on a dark and vicious face under a low-drawn police cap. Traile saw a bloody rip in the man's half-buttoned blue coat just in time.

The pseudo-policeman snarled an oath, and then the driver jerked the police car into Traile's path. Traile stood on the brakes, snatched at his .38.

"*San hai!*" yelled the dark man.

Three crouching figures leaped up in the rear of the prowl car. They were outside with the swiftness of rats. Traile fired pointblank. The first man went down with a screech. Traile threw the gears into reverse. A yellow face flashed through the spotlight beam. Eric's gun blasted around the right side of the windshield. The Chinese pitched over.

The prowl car roared backward as Traile reversed. The third Chinese sprang to its running board. Before Traile could fire, he leaped across and landed on the hood of the sedan. Eric lunged around his side of the windshield, gun leveled.

A stream of dark vapor shot from a pear-shaped bulb in the hand of the yellow assassin. Eric's finger tightened convulsively on the trigger as he slumped back. His gun roared, spurted red flame. The Chinese gave a gurgling cry and toppled down against the windshield.

As Eric sagged back, a cold fury swept over Traile. He whipped the .38 toward the prowl car. Two shots crashed, and the man with the bloody coat fell limply over the door. The driver cut his wheels with a desperate speed. As the two machines scraped together, he twisted hastily in his seat. The ringed snout of a silenced gun poked across at Traile.

Traile's shot and the jump of the silenced weapon were simultaneous. A bullet ripped the seat cushion near Traile's shoulder. Then the prowl car raked past with a dead man at its wheel.

Above the scraping of fenders, as the cars pulled free, came the trill of a whistle. It was echoed by another not far off, then a siren wailed out in the night. Traile braked to turn, sent the car charging ahead. Those might be real police, or they might be more of the Yellow Doctor's agents. He took the next corner on two wheels, rolling the dead Chinese into the street. Without slowing, he switched off his lights, plunged into the first alley he saw.

As the whistle blasts faded away, he stopped, anxiously bent over Eric. With relief, he felt the other man move. He quickly propped him up at the window. Eric began to breathe more normally, and in a few moments he opened his eyes. He tried to sit up.

"Take it easy, old man," said Traile. "You'll be all right in a minute."

"What happened?" Eric asked dazedly.

"That killer sprayed you with some kind of anesthetic. They must have had orders to take us alive."

"I remember now," Eric mumbled. "It

smelled like incense, then everything turned black."

"I was afraid at first he'd killed you," Traile said grimly. "Thank Heaven the Yellow Doctor overplayed his hand and gave me warning. But we'd better get out of this area in case he has others looking for us."

He started the car, and they emerged cautiously from the alley. He switched on the lights, zigzagged through the Fifties, and swung into Broadway at Fifty-seventh Street. By this time Eric had almost recovered.

"How'd you know they were fake cops?" he asked huskily.

"I wasn't sure," said Traile. "But it was obvious he wanted us to follow that bearing into a trap of some kind. When the police car appeared so quickly, I had a hunch they were Yen Sin's killers."

"Then they must've bumped off the real cops to get their uniforms and the car," said Eric.

Traile's bronzed face was hard.

"Undoubtedly. I saw a bloody knife-slit in one man's coat. And the blood was fresh, so this thing must have been very recently planned."

"But I still don't see," said Eric, "how Yen Sin knew you'd be tuned in to catch those messages."

Traile gazed thoughtfully ahead as the sedan crossed Columbus Circle. "There's only one answer. He's spotted that Q-station. I was evidently being watched from somewhere—unless Doctor Yen Sin learned through someone at the company that we were going to listen in for that code."

"I never spilled a word," Eric said indignantly. "And I sneaked out the set without anybody seeing me."

"Then the first idea must be right. It's clear that the messages were designed to lead us into a trap. From the way those last signals faded, they were obviously using a narrow beam pointed straight at the building. If it hadn't been for Glover's call, I'd probably have followed that lead—at least until Yen Sin brought Sonya into it. That was plainly intended to bring you racing to help her. And he knew I wouldn't let you go alone."

"I still can't believe she did it on purpose," Eric said miserably.

Traile slowly shook his head.

"You'll save yourself many heartaches if you forget her, Eric. Even though she's an unwilling agent, remember she's still in his power. Yen Sin holds her father prisoner at his base in China, ready to torture him—or kill him if she should betray him."

A stricken look filled Eric's boyish face.

"Then you checked on her story?" he asked in a low tone.

Traile glanced at the dash clock, increased the car's speed.

"Yes, through a source in Shanghai. Her father is Grand Duke Sergius Damitri—one of the old Czarist regime. When the Revolution broke out, he fled with Sonya and her mother. They tried to reach Spain—Sonya's mother was Spanish—but they couldn't get out of the Orient. The Grand Duke became mixed up in espionage. His wife died, and Sonya was practically brought up to become an agent for the White Russians. Then a year ago Doctor Yen Sin drew her father into his web, held him as a hostage, and since then has forced her to act as a spy for the Invisible Empire."

Eric's blue eyes blazed.

"The damned fiend! To think of his having a white woman in his power!"

"She's only one of hundreds. Iris Vaughan is another example. He enslaved her through opium, so he'd have a spy in the British Embassy at Washington."

"Too bad the Embassy protected her after the raid on Yen Sin's hideout," said Eric. "She might have told plenty."

The sedan reached Seventy-second Street. Traile slowed, turned toward Riverside Drive, speeded up again.

"She was to be turned over to us next day, but she escaped that night," he said with a trace of glumness. "I thought we were clever when we managed to trace her to San Francisco. I know now that Yen Sin had her lead us there so we'd think he had fled to the Coast. And then she vanished right under my nose."

"Anyway, it did some good," Eric pointed out. "We linked our San Francisco communications with the other Q-stations."

"Thanks to your work," assented Traile. He turned northward into the drive which paralleled the Hudson. A faint grayness had come into the sky, against which the rows of towering apartments, broken by an occasional mansion, bulked in dark silhouette.

"We're almost there," Eric said quickly, as Traile leaned out around the windshield.

"Yes, I know." A sharp alertness had come into the taller man's face. "I was looking to see if by chance the D.J. cars had beat us to the place."

"You really think Courtland is working with Doctor Yen Sin?" exclaimed Eric.

"Not willingly. But the Yellow Doctor may have found some shady spot in old Courtland's life. In that event, he'll be a potential enemy."

A moment later, the car swung in toward the entrance of the Courtland place, which comprised one whole square block. Suddenly, Traile put on the brakes. The huge gates were open, but there in the center and barring the way was a shining crimson pole. In the headlights it was the color of blood.

"Good Lord!" Traile whispered. He leaped out.

"What is it?" Eric gasped as he caught up.

"It's a Chinese funeral pole!" Traile said tensely. "I'm afraid we're going to be too late."

He raced up the curving drive with Eric close at his heels. No lights shone from the mansion. He ran up the steps. The door was open, and from somewhere beyond there came an eerie will-o'-the-wisp glow. The silence all but shrieked.

Traile tiptoed to the doorway through which the flickering light showed. It led to a drawing room. He took one step inside, then halted, appalled, with Eric gazing white-faced past his shoulder.

Two yellow Chinese candles shone down from the head of an open coffin directly before them. An icy shudder went over Traile. He was looking down on the back of a corpse—but the dead man's face was staring upward!

With horror, Traile saw the bloodstains which had dyed the man's white collar. Peter Courtland had been decapitated, and his head sewn on again—backward!

Chapter 3

The Golden Skull

Eric turned away, sickened, as Traile stepped closer to stare in amazement. Just beyond the candles, on a stand beneath a mirror, a queer bright object was gleaming. Leering down at the pale dead face below was a small golden skull.

Eric gazed blankly at it, but Traile's dark eyes suddenly filled with consternation.

"My God! The *Chuen Gin Lou*!"

"What do you mean?" Eric asked thickly.

"The Circle of the Golden Skull—one of the oldest, most dreaded secret societies of China. It's supposed to have died out. Doctor Yen Sin must have revived it, made it part of the Invisible Empire."

Eric looked back at the dead man and shivered.

"It's horrible enough, murdering him, but to sew on his head that way—"

"It's part of their ritual, based on the Chinese penal code," said Traile, as Eric broke off. "When a Chinese criminal is beheaded, it is the custom to sew his head on backward before giving the body to his relatives. Courtland must have been about to betray Yen Sin. This thing has been staged as a warning to others in the Empire."

Eric gripped his gun, peered around into the shadows.

"It's like a tomb," he whispered. "I wonder if they killed all the servants, too."

"We'll search the place as soon as those agents arrive," Traile answered. His eyes had hardly left the golden skull. There was a curious fascination about it. It had been molded by a master hand, and with diabolical artistry. Its proportions were perfect, though it was less than half the size of a human skull. In the flickering candlelight, a mocking grin seemed to play across its hideous metal face. Eric looked at it, startled.

"Lord! For a second, I thought it was moving!"

"It's only the light," said Traile. He thrust out his hand as Eric came closer. "Don't touch it. There may be some solid basis for that old fantastic story."

Eric stared at him.

"What story?"

Traile hesitated before he answered.

"The *Chuen Gin Lou* is said to have been a mysterious murder cult ruled by a golden skull. The skull was supposed to have the power of death. Only the members ever knew the truth, but there are well-educated Chinese who still believe that 'He who looks upon the Golden Skull must either kill or die.'"

Eric's jaw dropped.

"Don't tell me you believe that!"

Traile's dark eyes were somber.

"Eric, I've seen strange things in the East. I am not easily affected, but there is something about that skull—"

He stopped, glanced quickly at his watch.

"Those D.J. agents should be here in a few minutes. You know Bill Allen, and he'll probably be in charge. I wish you'd meet him—tell him to hurry in here. I'll examine Courtland's body, meanwhile."

Eric grimaced.

"You're welcome to that part. I'll be glad to get out of here."

As he went out, Traile stooped over the dead man. The beheading had been done by a skilled hand, for the cut was straight. The bloodstained stitches also gave evidence of surgical knowledge. Traile's lips tightened. Unless he was badly mistaken, this was the work of the Yellow Doctor himself.

He holstered his automatic, started to search Courtland's pockets. He did it cautiously, knowing Yen Sin's predilection for setting deathtraps in unlikely places. The dead man's pockets were empty. Traile turned, was bending over the golden skull when he heard something from the left side of the house. It grew swiftly into the sound of a woman's footsteps, a woman who was running desperately, fearfully.

Traile stepped back quickly into the shadows, took a hasty glance about him. The nearest concealment was a large urn on a taboret. He crouched behind it. The next instant a girl darted in from a door at the side. With a start, Traile recognized the pretty face of the blonde English girl, Iris Vaughan.

Her head was bare, and her bright hair shone in the light of the candles. She halted for a moment, cast a fearful look about the room. From the half-opened bag on her arm she had taken a small, pearl-handled pistol.

She gasped as she saw the coffin and its terrible occupant. For a second, Traile thought she would faint. But the desperate light came back into her eyes, and she forced herself to go on. With her gaze averted, she passed the dead man's bier. She had reached the stand under the mirror when Traile silently moved from behind the urn. He kept to one side, so that she would not see his reflection. He was within a few feet of her, the thick rug muffling his step, when she suddenly turned. All the color went out of her face.

"Michael Traile!" she moaned. She stood as though paralyzed, then with a frantic motion tried to snatch up the gun she had laid down. Traile's long fingers closed on the weapon. He calmly dropped it into his pocket. The girl shrank back with a little cry. Traile's dark eyes searched her frightened face.

"So the Doctor didn't intend the Golden Skull to be left here."

She tried to speak, made a helpless gesture. Traile looked down at the gruesome figure of Peter Courtland.

"Once before, I told you there was no diplomatic immunity for murder."

"I had nothing to do with it," she said wildly. "I never even knew!"

"Then why are you here?" Traile interrupted.

"*He* sent me—" The words broke in a sob. "Please let me go—I swear I knew nothing of this awful murder!"

Traile eyed her sternly.

"Where is Doctor Yen Sin hidden?"

"I don't know!" she whispered. "All my orders come indirectly—"

"You're lying," said Traile, but part of the sternness went out of his face. She was dangerous, yet there was something pitiful about her.

He hesitated. "If you will give me the information I need, I'll see that you are protected against his vengeance."

"You're mad!" she cried. "Nothing could save me! In God's name, give me the skull—let me go—"

"What is its secret?" Trail demanded.

Iris Vaughan turned deathly pale. "I can't tell you—I don't know!"

"Perhaps you would rather tell the police," Traile said calmly.

With a trembling hand, she took something from the vanity bag on her arm. He reached out quickly, thinking it was another weapon. To his astonishment, she opened a jeweler's box and an enormous oval-shaped diamond blazed up at him. "Here!" she said tensely. "This is worth a thousand times the gold in that skull. Take it!"

Traile stared down at the shimmering jewel.

"The Vare Diamond!"

"It's not stolen, if that's what you're thinking," she said in a breathless whisper. "But it's yours—in exchange for the skull."

"I'm sorry." Traile lifted his head as the sound of hastily applied brakes came from outside. "But you have one last chance to talk, before the Department of Justice men get here."

She caught at him with frantic hands.

"Please don't let them take me!"

He could feel the warmth of her body as she clung to him. He looked down, steeling himself against the passionate appeal in her upturned face. For an instant, her very soul seemed to be in her eyes.

"Save me!" she whispered. "I promise I shall not forget!"

He reached up to disentangle her arms. Outside, another car stopped with tires squealing. Iris moved back despairingly as a thud of feet sounded from the reception hall. But suddenly a wild hope flashed into her eyes.

Traile shot a look at the mirror. A bulky figure had plunged into the room. In that split second, he saw a strange gray face. Then he dived headlong back of the coffin.

The silenced gun he had seen gave a muffled *clunk*. The slug tore through the coffin, and wood splintered three inches above his head. He rolled over, came up with his .38 blasting. The other man jumped back, gun arm dangling. He made a vain attempt to shift the weapon and reload.

"Drop it!" clipped Traile.

The man's queer gray face jerked spasmodically, and the silenced gun slipped from his fingers. His eyes, small and deep-sunken, never moved from Traile. Hoarse voices abruptly were audible, then a French window to the conservatory burst open. Traile half-wheeled, expecting to see Bill Allen's agents. But to his dismay, he was looking on three more gray-faced men.

As the three leaped into the drawing room, Iris struck at Traile's elbow. The .38 roared, drilled a hole in the wall. Its crashing report was followed by the ominous click of another silenced pistol. The mirror back of Traile shattered into a thousand fragments. He flung a swift-aimed shot at the first of the trio of Gray Men.

The man screamed hoarsely, stumbled and fell in a heap. Traile hurled himself toward the coffin as the other two leveled their guns. A sweep of his hand, and the candles went to the floor. In the darkness he heard a venomous hiss of lead from the raiders' pistols.

From the direction of Riverside Drive, an exhaust whistle throbbed four times. Instantly, a beam of light swept the lawn beyond the veranda. A fifth Gray Man dashed into the room.

"Come on!" he rasped. "They're surrounding the place."

"But the Golden Skull!" snarled another voice. "We haven't found it."

"I have it!" came the panicky voice of Iris Vaughan. "But we'll never escape now."

Traile leaped toward her as she started to run to the window. By the faint light from the shifting searchlight of the D.J. men, he saw the gleam of gold. He tore the skull from her hands, whirled toward the urn. In the shadows back of him, Iris gave a scream.

"It's gone! Someone—"

A crash of gunfire drowned her cry. The shots came from behind the mansion. Two of the Gray Men were silhouetted as they hastily picked up their dead comrade, carried him through the French window. Traile had barely placed the skull inside the urn and wheeled to the hall doorway when a flashlight probed through the dark. The man he had wounded snarled an alarm. Bullets plunked into the doorframe as Traile charged into the hall.

He dodged through the library, hurriedly opened a window, and dropped to the ground outside. A powerful spotlight in the hands of an agent covered him at once.

"Get 'em up!" the man ordered sharply.

"Hold it, Johnson," snapped another voice. The lanky form of Bill Allen appeared, with Eric close behind.

"They're getting away on the other side," Traile said hastily, as Allen recognized him. Even as he spoke, there was another burst of shots. He and the others sprinted around the front of the mansion. A big car was racing down the exit drive. It swerved suddenly, charged across the lawn and plunged through the hedge which bordered the yard. Behind it came a second machine, engine roaring. It whirled through the beam of an agent's searchlight, and for a moment Traile saw the terrified face of Iris Vaughan, where she cringed down by one of the Gray Men.

Bill Allen had raised a tommy gun for a burst at the car. At sight of the girl, he swore and pointed the weapon lower. A stuttering blast ripped at the wheels, but the bullets missed the tires. At furious speed, the car tore through the break in the hedge and was swallowed up in the gloom. Down near the main entrance to the estate, a D.J. car roared away in hot pursuit.

Traile swung quickly to Bill Allen, as several D.J. men ran toward the senior agent.

"The police will be here in a few minutes. I want them to think that Eric and I are agents of yours—that we arrived here at the same time you did. Here's your story: You had a tip from Washington, dashed out here, and ran into a fight with some gangsters who got away."

"That bird I saw with the girl didn't look like any gangster," Bill Allen muttered. "He looked like a corpse."

"You'll find a real one inside," Traile said grimly. "But pass that word to your men, and then have them search the place. I've something to show you."

Allen gave hasty instructions to his men, and they scattered to search the mansion. Traile had drawn Eric aside.

"You recognized her?" he said in an undertone.

Eric nodded, his blue eyes still wide with excitement.

"Sure, it was Iris Vaughan—but where on earth were she and those—"

"I'll explain in a minute. But don't tell anyone but Allen that we know who she was."

Bill Allen strode back and joined them.

"Now, would you mind telling me what the hell—"

"Come on," Traile cut in. "We've no time to waste."

He led the way to the drawing room, tersely

explaining what had happened. The lights were on, and one of the agents was just starting on to the conservatory, after an amazed stare at Courtland's body. Traile waited till he had gone, then retrieved the golden skull from the urn, while Allen gingerly examined the dead man.

"I don't want the police to know about this skull," Traile said rapidly. "It must have some tremendous importance. The Gray Men were sent here to recover it. Not only that, the Vaughan girl offered me the Vare Diamond in exchange."

Bill Allen gaped at him.

"The Vare Diamond! Why, that stone's worth a third of a million if it's worth a penny."

"I know that." Traile scanned the floor near the coffin. "I thought she dropped it, but she evidently found it again."

Eric pointed to a pool of blood nearer the opened window.

"You must've finished one of those Gray Men, all right."

Traile's tanned face was flinty.

"If he'd been a better shot, I'd be stretched out here with poor old Courtland."

Allen shook his head bewilderedly.

"I thought you were screwy tonight, when I got Glover's order and you told me about Doctor Yen Sin and the Invisible Empire. But after this—"

"This is only a hint of Yen Sin's diabolical methods," interrupted Traile. "We're likely to have more than a hint when he finds we have the skull."

All three gazed at the golden object for a second.

"I can't see what anybody'd want of that thing," grated Bill Allen. "Unless they were to melt it down—"

"And tonight's work proves it's not that," rapped Traile. He lit a cigarette, took a turn back and forth. "From all the rumors and stories about it, the Golden Skull must be a sacred symbol. If you knew Chinese superstition, you'd understand Doctor Yen Sin's desperate efforts to regain possession of it. Millions of Chinese blindly worship lesser things than this."

"Then why did they leave it here?" asked Eric, puzzled.

Traile frowned down at the skull. "It may have been used in the ritual. The red funeral pole bears that out; it means, literally, that 'a man lies in a coffin within this house.' But someone must have left the skull by mistake."

A whine of sirens announced the approach of the police.

"Eric, you and I had better slip outside," Traile said quickly. "We want to be as inconspicuous as possible while the police investigate this."

As they were hurrying out with Bill Allen, one of the D.J. agents came downstairs.

"No sign of anybody up there, sir," he told the senior agent. "And Johnson reports the servants' quarters deserted."

"The servants have probably been kidnapped," Traile said as they reached the main entrance. "If I know the Yellow Doctor, they won't be seen again."

"By Heaven, he can't get away with this!" said Allen angrily.

A police car had come to a halt before the funeral pole and a strongly Irish voice was heard in a profane outburst.

"At least they're real cops," Traile muttered. He hid the golden skull under his coat. "Explain things as fast as you can, Bill. Eric and I will stay back with your men until you've arranged it so we can leave."

"I'll do my best," said the lanky agent.

But it was almost an hour before he could finish explaining to the satisfaction of the homicide squad. By this time police and reporters were swarming over the place, and a crowd had gathered at the gates.

Several of the D.J. men grouped themselves about Traile as he went out to his car, and the bulge under his coat apparently passed unnoticed. Bill Allen climbed into the rear of Traile's car, with two agents armed with tommy guns.

Two machines filled with the rest of the D.J. men formed a close escort in the dash for Lexington Avenue.

Traile drove as fast as he dared through the early morning traffic. His bronzed face was stonily set, and his dark eyes flicked ceaselessly from right to left at each new intersection. By now, Yen Sin would undoubtedly know the truth. There probably had been spies in that crowd back at the mansion. But there seemed to be no one following, and it would be difficult for anyone to pick them up on the zigzag route he was taking.

On the front seat between him and Eric reposed the mysterious, gleaming skull. Eric kept looking down at it with a morbid fascination. Suddenly he stared across at Traile's hard-set face.

"Michael, you remember what you said: 'He who looks upon the—' "

"Yes, I remember," said Traile. "Why?"

"It's already come true," Eric exclaimed. "You looked at the skull, and in a few minutes you killed a man. If you hadn't, you would have died."

"Only a coincidence," muttered Traile. But he glanced down at the thing beside him. The Golden Skull seemed to leer back mockingly at him.

Chapter 4

The Invisible Emperor

In an otherwise dark room hidden beneath Manhattan, one eye of a small Buddha suddenly glowed with emerald light. A yellow hand reached out from the gloom, and a sharp-nailed finger touched the rim of what appeared to be a roulette wheel. As the numbered wheel turned, the second eye of the Buddha became green, until it glowed with the same intensity as the first.

"Report," came the emotionless voice of the man seated beside the Buddha.

"Control, Group Three," a whisper came from the lips of the Buddha. "The police and Federal agents still hold position H. Number Ninety-three, using reporter's credentials, penetrated grounds and mansion. No prisoners observed, and no sign of—the Skull." The last two words were in an oddly altered tone.

A pointed saffron face, like a mocking picture of Satan, appeared for a moment above the wheel. In the emerald glow from the Buddha's eyes it was a weird hue.

"Police statements in regard to Citizen Fourteen?" the Yellow Doctor inquired.

"Removal believed underworld vengeance for refusing tribute to racketeers," was the muffled response from the Buddha. "This evidently based on report from Department of Justice agent in charge."

The tawny eyes slowly narrowed.

"Maintain close observation on the Federal officers. For some reason, they are withholding information. Courtland's son mentioned the Invisible Empire before he died."

The eyes of the idol dimmed, then one went dark. Doctor Yen Sin leaned over the table on which the wheel and the Buddha stood. There was a row of pearl buttons in an onyx panel. He pressed the second button from the right. A faint, irregular buzzing sounded from the idol, and the numbered wheel began to rotate slowly.

The Crime Emperor sat back, a shadowy figure in the fan-backed Bilibid chair. A minute passed, and the wheel began its second revolution. Suddenly it stopped, swung back through an arc of forty degrees. Doctor Yen Sin reached out a yellow claw, and the buzzing signal ceased. Instantly the Buddha's eyes lit up.

"Group One," a sullen voice said.

The Yellow Doctor leaned forward.

"Your signal was transmitted at four fifty-three and five nineteen," he said coldly.

"I heard it, but couldn't answer," the other

man said with a trace of harshness. "A bullet damaged the set, and I've just repaired it."

Yen Sin gazed down at the numbered wheel. It was still moving, but almost imperceptibly.

"You have had time to reach Headquarters B. Why are you still in motion?"

"It's taken all this time to shake off the police," came the muttered retort. "We're lucky we weren't killed."

The Crime Emperor looked unseeingly at the green eyes of the Buddha.

"Present orders revoked," he said with a return to his usual emotionless voice. "You will bring the Skull at once to Headquarters A."

There was a pause, then the Buddha rasped out the answer.

"We didn't get it! There was a mix-up—Agent Eighty-five had it—someone got it away from her in the dark."

A look of fury swept over the malignant face of Doctor Yen Sin. But when he spoke, his voice was icily controlled.

"Full report," he ordered.

"When we reached there," the voice from the idol said hoarsely, "Number Three entered, with Two and Five following. I heard a shot and ran after the others. I found Number Three slightly wounded, and Agent Eighty-five captured by a man who was evidently a police officer. This man shot and killed Number Two, then knocked over the candles. Agent Eighty-five was fleeing with the Skull when it was snatched from her hands. The place was almost surrounded—we barely had time to carry out Number Two and escape."

In the green light from the Buddha's eyes, the Crime Emperor's face held a furious look.

"Transfer to Agent Eighty-five," he directed.

"She escaped in the other car," was the sullen reply from the idol. "We separated at once."

There was a long interval, during which faint sounds of traffic came through from the microphone in the distant car.

"Follow these orders," Doctor Yen Sin said abruptly. He spoke for two minutes, then depressed a button. The Buddha's eyes dimmed, glowed again as the indicator wheel swung to its former position.

"Control, Group Three."

"Main Control," Yen Sin now said swiftly. "The Golden Skull was not recovered. Concentrate for necessary action. Groups Four and Five will reinforce you. Report at once any movement on part of the Federal men."

As the light faded from the idol's eyes, he stood up, the silken folds of his mandarin costume falling about his figure. Though the room was now completely dark, he stretched out his hand to the exact spot where a light switch was located. A soft luminance spread over the room, revealing the details of the secret chamber. A richly colored Arabian rug, hung like a tapestry, covered most of one wall. Across from it was a large blackboard, on which were written words in both English and Chinese. In the center of the board was a sketch not unlike that of some intricate football maneuver.

On a rosewood table beside a divan was a tray bearing a teapot, a cup, and an empty dish, testimony to the sparse diet to which the Yellow Doctor adhered. Books and a number of photographs, the latter varying from miniatures to enlargements, cluttered one corner. A map case partly obscured a full-length mirror of peculiarly dark glass.

Doctor Yen Sin turned to an odd diagram which had been painted on one wall. It appeared to be a sketch showing the arrangement of streets in a small village. Colored lights showed at the ends of the streets and at some intersections. Beneath the diagram was a switchboard with a built-in Dictaphone.

The Crime Emperor inserted a plug in a socket, and one of the lights immediately flickered. He spoke in Chinese for a few moments, made another connection.

"Yes, Master?" came the hasty query, also in Chinese.

"What report from Group Six concerning the captives?" Doctor Yen Sin asked a trifle sharply.

"They have not appeared or reported, Master," the other man replied anxiously.

"Broaden the beam and search the area near Position D," ordered the Yellow Doctor. "There is a chance they have been forced into the other headquarters. Let me know the result."

"Yes, Master." The Dictaphone clicked. Doctor Yen Sin turned away. He crossed the room, moving with an almost feline step, and halted before the map case. He stood there a moment, his weird eyes flitting over the crayon lines which had been drawn on a chart of Long Island Sound. In the slant of his cheekbones, and by his height—for he was taller than most Chinese—an expert might have traced the Manchurian blood which coursed in the veins of the Yellow Doctor.

He glanced aside, stooped, and picked up one of the enlarged photographs. It was a gruesome scene—a tableau of murder. A crumpled body upon the floor . . . a dark stain on the man's shirtfront . . . the half-crouched form of the murderer, with a dripping knife in his hand, and his startled, ghastly face turned toward the camera. . . .

Doctor Yen Sin's thin lips curled. There was something comical about that look of horror and dismay. The poor fool had thought himself so clever. He had never dreamed that he had been led every step of the way into committing that murder. But since then there had been time for him to learn.

A sudden clicking, as of distant castanets, caused the Crime Emperor to wheel quickly. A bright red light was shining above the painted diagram. Another light was blinking where two lines intersected. Doctor Yen Sin hastily crossed to the switchboard. As he plugged a connection, a rough voice became audible through the Dictaphone.

"Don't be a little fool! What's one Chink more or less?"

"Are you crazy?" a feminine voice gasped. "The Emperor will kill you for this."

"If he's so tough," came the grated answer, "why's he scared to show himself? I've still got to see the Chink I can't handle."

The girl moaned something, but the man cut her short.

"Get smart, baby! I've been watching you, and you got class enough for Ricco. We can take it on the lam before anybody gets wise. I can get a hundred grand for that rock, out on the Coast. You play along with Ricco, and you'll—"

"Let go of me!" the girl cried out.

Sounds of a scuffle came through the Dictaphone. Doctor Yen Sin calmly pressed a button, reached toward a switch at one side.

"You she-devil!" came a snarl from the unseen man. "I was goin' to give ya a break, but now—"

The sepulchral note of a deep-toned gong broke into his angry threat. In the same moment, light shone through the dark glass at one side of the secret room. The Yellow Doctor glanced toward the glass as footsteps echoed through the amplifier. A short passage was visible, its walls decorated with scores of red-and-gold circles. Each had a black center.

In a second, two figures came into view. The first was Iris Vaughan. Her blonde hair was flying, and her pretty face was transfixed with a look of terror. Both greed and fear showed on the swarthy face of the man who pursued her. With a sudden leap, he caught the girl by one shoulder and spun her around. A brutal jerk, and he tore the jewel case from her fingers. A violent shove sent her back against the dark glass.

The deep-toned gong struck, and there followed a thudding sound from beyond the turn of the passage. The thief's swarthy face turned pasty. He whirled, the jewel case in one hand, a blood-smeared stiletto raised in the other. As he turned, the Yellow Doctor coolly threw a switch. The dark glass slid silently into a niche, and Iris Vaughan stumbled, almost fell into the room.

There was another thud, and a massive gate

settled into place where the passage turned. As the gangster saw his escape cut off he sprang around with an oath. Then he froze.

From each of those red-and-gold circles a dark-stained blade was swiftly moving outward!

"You yellow butcher!" Ricco screamed. He hurled himself at the Crime Emperor. The stiletto flashed up—and scraped to a stop in midair. Behind the clear glass panel which had replaced the dark one, Doctor Yen Sin slowly smiled.

"You expressed a desire to see me, Mr. Ricco?" came his sibilant voice from some spot above the passage.

A tortured shriek burst from the gangster's lips as the swords began to gash his sides. He twisted around madly, pounding upon the glass.

"For God's sake, don't kill me! I didn't mean it—I'll do anything!"

The last word rose to a cry of mortal anguish. Iris Vaughan cowered away, hiding her face in her hands. The Yellow Doctor reached out toward the switchboard, and the faint whir of a hidden motor rose to a whine. One last dreadful scream rang out. Then Ricco's pierced body sagged, quivering, on the blades which had taken his life.

Without emotion, Doctor Yen Sin opened the heavy glass panel. He picked up the jewel case, calmly glanced at its contents. Stepping back into the secret room, he turned to the Dictaphone.

"The post of Number Five, Group Eight, is vacant," he announced tonelessly. "Correct the rolls and make the following disposal of the body." He spoke briefly in Chinese, then turned his tawny eyes on Iris Vaughan. The girl's face was sick with fear.

"I couldn't help it," she whispered. "He was hiding there at the third entrance. He sprang and killed Lun Shan—"

"The book of Mr. Ricco has been closed," said the Yellow Doctor. "But there is another matter—of real importance."

At the sudden harshness in his voice, the girl spoke breathlessly.

"I was hurrying to tell you. I reached the mansion ahead of—"

"The details have been reported," interrupted the Crime Emperor. "All but one." His weird eyes bored into her. "Who has the Golden Skull?"

"Michael Traile," she answered, and there was renewed dread in her face.

The pupils of Yen Sin's eyes enlarged with incredible swiftness, until they were black pools of fury. He took a step toward the girl, one yellow claw clenched.

"I did all I could!" she cried piteously. "But he tricked even the Gray Men."

There was a sharp buzzing, and the eyes of the Buddha glowed with green light. Doctor Yen Sin opened a sliding door which had been concealed by a tapestry.

"Be in readiness at your station," he curtly ordered. As the blonde girl hurried out he closed the door and stooped over the idol. "Main Control. What report on Position H?"

"Federal men leaving in three cars," was the hasty reply. "Believe the Golden Skull in second car. Man observed carrying something under his coat. Did not observe personally but from description believe him to be Michael Traile. Senior Agent Allen and two men with machine guns in rear seat. Machine guns also in cars forming close escort. Success of direct action extremely doubtful."

Doctor Yen Sin looked down. The numbered wheel was moving very slowly.

"Maintain contact without arousing suspicion," he ordered. "Repeat this order to cooperating groups, then shift to Number Three waveband. Further instructions will follow."

As the wheel ceased to move, the Buddha's eyes changed to clear white light.

"Send Sonya to me at once," Yen Sin directed. "Then stand by for special code to Headquarters B."

Two minutes later a girl entered from the direction in which Iris Vaughan had disappeared. She was lovely, with a foreign, exotic beauty in which the warmth of sunny Spain and the cool aloofness of a Russian aristocrat were oddly blended. Her dark eyes, as she faced the Yellow Doctor, had a tragic, hopeless look. Yen Sin smiled mirthlessly at her.

"I have need of your talents, my dear Sonya." The tone was a deliberate mockery.

The girl's glance shifted to the gruesome figure suspended on the bloody swords in the passage. She stepped back in horror.

"No, it is neither of our expected—guests," said the Crime Emperor silkily. "They have been delayed, unfortunately." He had spoken in Chinese, but he abruptly changed to Russian. As he finished speaking, Sonya faced him with blazing eyes.

"No! I will not do it!" she cried defiantly. "This is some trick to make me help trap them again."

The oblique eyes of Doctor Yen Sin drew into slits.

"I have a photograph of your honorable father, taken as he received your last little—gift. Perhaps if I let you see it—"

All the fiery rebellion died out of her face.

"I'll go," she said in a broken voice. Her shoulders were drooping as she turned away. When she had gone, Doctor Yen Sin turned again to the Buddha. White light flashed, then swiftly he began his instructions.

Chapter 5

The Rainbow Death

Traile's eyes searched the street ahead. "We're too well-guarded for him to try a mass attack," he said grimly. "If he strikes, it will be something unexpected."

"It's only three more blocks," said Eric. "Looks as though we'll get through O.K."

"I still think you've got this Yellow Doctor overrated," Bill Allen grunted from the rear seat. "I'll admit he pulled a fast one out there at the Courtland place, but he can't buck the whole police system of New York City."

Trail swung the car into Lexington Avenue.

"You still don't understand the Invisible Empire. Yen Sin's spies keep him informed, and he gets around the police by trickery."

"Well, I'd like to see him get around these tommy guns," retorted the lanky D.J. man.

Traile looked down at the miniature radio set.

"Too bad we didn't get a good cross-bearing," he said to Eric. "We've lost our chance to locate that station."

Eric's face shadowed, and Traile knew he was thinking of Sonya Damitri.

The leading D.J. car slowed as they neared the building which housed the F.B.I. offices. The hour was not yet seven, and there were but few cars parked along the street. Traile pulled in close to the first machine, and the other D.J. car stopped behind him.

Early pedestrians stared as the agents jumped out with their guns poised. Traile thrust the golden skull under his coat and motioned for Eric to bring the radios. Allen and his men closed in as they went toward the building.

They were almost at the entrance when there came a crash of shots from back of them. Traile wheeled. A limousine was drawing up at the curb across the avenue. Fifty feet behind it, and darting in diagonally, was a taxicab. Guns were blazing from the rear of the cab, and Traile saw one of the limousine windows shatter.

Three or four D.J. men were racing toward the spot. Two more shots crashed from the taxi, then a pinched yellow face glared around toward the running agents. A look of terror crossed the features of the Chinese. He frantically swerved his pistol.

Two tommy guns roared simultaneously. The Chinese toppled back, riddled with lead. The bloody face of a second Oriental was visible as the taxi wildly leaped ahead. As he slumped from view, another machine gun burst drilled both tires on the left side. The taxi skidded crazily, plunged headlong against a lamppost and overturned. The driver fell out limply, lay still.

As the firing began, Traile shot a hurried look around the entrance and into the lobby. This might be an attempt by Yen Sin to draw attention so that other spies of the Invisible Empire could regain the skull. But there was no sign of an attack.

A crowd was beginning to gather in the street. A big man, of powerful build, had jumped from the rear of the limousine. As two of Allen's men approached, Traile saw the big man motion anxiously, then all three bent over the crumpled form of the limousine chauffeur.

"Jumping Jupiter!" Allen erupted. "That's Mark Bannister those Chink gunmen tried to rub out!"

"Another millionaire," Traile muttered, half to himself. "I wonder what Yen Sin is after."

In a moment Bannister hurried toward them with one of the agents. Traile would hardly have recognized the financier, though he had seen pictures of him. In addition to being a financial power, with his hotels, his steamship line, and his brokerage house, Mark Bannister was known as a Beau Brummel. But now his handsome face was haggard with fear and strain. His cheeks were unshaven, and there were dark circles under his eyes. Blood was dripping from a small cut on his jaw, where flying glass had struck.

"Which one?" he rasped to the man beside him, as he reached the group.

"This is Special Agent Allen," said the other, indicating the lanky D.J. man.

The millionaire jerked around to Allen.

"I'm Mark Bannister. I want to see you—alone!"

Allen hesitated, glanced at Traile. Traile spoke in an undertone.

"You question him first, while I examine the skull up in your lab."

Allen motioned to one of his men.

"Take charge, Weller. Find out all you can, and explain to the cops what happened."

Traile and Eric entered an elevator with the millionaire and Bill Allen. The operator looked, wide-eyed, from Allen's tommy gun to the cut on Bannister's jaw. The financier glared at him, stamped out at the fourteenth floor, almost falling over a wrinkled old charwoman who was mopping up the corridor.

As Bannister and Allen disappeared into an office, Traile nodded for Eric to follow him into the laboratory. The technician on duty was a pleasant-faced agent named Jim Stone. Traile knew him from a former visit, when Director Glover had introduced him as Roger Scott, a private criminologist who was to be given the run of the place.

"What happened down below?" Stone asked, after Traile introduced Eric. "I heard the shooting, but couldn't see much from the window."

Traile explained briefly.

"Hell's bells!" said Stone. "That and the Courtland murder will split the town wide open."

"How did you know about Courtland?" Traile asked sharply. "Police teletype?"

"No, there was a radio news flash almost an hour ago. All about his head being sewed on backward and—" Stone stared as Traile brought the gold skull from under his coat. "What the devil is the idea of that?"

"That's what we want to know," said Traile as he put the skull down on a table. "Let me have a magnifying glass, will you? I haven't had time for a careful examination."

"You mean you found this thing?" exclaimed Stone, amazed.

Traile hesitated only a moment.

"It was at the head of Courtland's coffin, but don't mention that to anyone. I'm explaining to you because there's some danger connected with it, and it will have to be closely guarded."

Professional interest quickly conquered Stone's first astonishment. He brought a magnifying glass, switched on a bright light. Traile took the glass, bent over the gleaming skull, and looked through the eye sockets. After a brief scrutiny he carefully turned it upside down and peered in through the throat opening. The skull was empty, and except for a few scratches the interior of the metal shell was unmarked.

"What did you expect to find?" asked Eric, as Traile straightened up with a look of disappointment.

"I thought some secret of the cult might be engraved inside," Traile answered a trifle shortly. The puzzle was beginning to annoy him.

"Maybe it's written so small that this glass won't show it up," suggested Stone. "I can put it under the big microscope."

"I don't think there's anything to see," said Traile. "But you might as well try it."

Stone started to pick up the skull, then grasped it in both hands. "Say, that thing's heavy! I wouldn't mind having what it's worth in cash."

"It's probably worth about ten thousand dollars," stated Traile. "But I've had proof that it's valued for some other reason."

"Ten thousand bucks would be plenty of reason for me," said Eric.

"Same here," grinned Stone. He carried the skull over to a large compound microscope and was placing it on the stage when Allen hastily entered the room. Behind the agent came Bannister. Allen closed the door, turned to Traile and addressed him by the name he had temporarily assumed.

"Scott, I've already told Mr. Bannister that you're working with us on this Courtland case. He has some information that should help us.

"It's help for myself I want," the millionaire said bluntly. His hard eyes probed at Traile. "You saw what happened down there—I escaped death by a miracle—my bodyguard was murdered—"

"Bodyguard?" said Traile.

"He was acting as chauffeur," snapped Bannister, "because the regular man disappeared—vanished like five more of my employees! I tell you it's maddening—knowing there's something closing in on you—knowing there are eyes watching you all the time."

He looked around fiercely at Eric and Stone, who were both staring at him, then pulled a crumpled paper from his coat pocket.

"Here's a sample of what I mean. Read that, and for 'Citizen Nine' substitute 'Mark Bannister'!"

The message was typewritten in green ink. Traile's dark eyes passed quickly over the words.

SECRET REPORT 31 ON CITIZEN NINE
DATE: JULY 17, 8 P.M. TO MIDNIGHT

At 8:03, Citizen 9 called from his penthouse apartment on top Hotel Lordmore, speaking by direct wire to the hotel manager. Gave instructions that Citizens 12 and 14 were to be brought up secretly from garage in basement—

"Think of it!" rasped Bannister. "One of my own hotels—my private wire! But go on—go on!"

Citizens 12 and 14 arrived by private penthouse elevator at 8:10. During dinner, Citizen 14 produced copy of latest secret report on his movements. Announced he was going to the police. Citizens 9 and 12 argued against this, but at 10:35 he left for that purpose. At 11:15, Citizen 12 departed after phoning down to his private detective escort to meet him on mezzanine floor. Citizen 9 stationed special guard at switchboard controlling the private elevator, with orders to keep current shut off. Retired at 11:50, after searching entire apartment.

Traile looked up slowly.

"Is this report accurate?"

"It's exact!" the millionaire said harshly. "The thing is uncanny. Our conference didn't start until dinner had been served and my servants had been sent downstairs.

Traile studied the lower edge of the paper.

"A piece had been cut off here. Did you do it?"

Bannister did not answer for a moment.

Then he rammed his hands into his coat pockets and spoke abruptly.

"All right, I'll tell you! I've received thirty of those damned reports, some even describing things I thought nobody could possibly know. Each one has contained mention of something private, personal." He made a savage gesture. "Every man in my position has made mistakes on the way up. But how these devils ever learned—"

"Then it's blackmail?" Traile asked calmly.

"It must be!" grated Bannister. "But they haven't asked a cent. After each report—except this one—I've had a mysterious phone call. I've been told to go to a certain place to meet someone—but a different spot has been named every time. I've gone three times, with private detectives hiding nearby—but no one appeared."

"If you'd come to us sooner—" began Allen, but the millionaire cut him off with a snort.

"Never mind about that! I'm here now and I want protection. I heard the news that Courtland's been murdered, and after what just occurred I know I must be next on the list."

Traile looked at him keenly.

"The man called 'Citizen Fourteen' in this message was Peter Courtland, wasn't he?"

Bannister started.

"What makes you think that?"

"It's evident that no rich man complained to the police about being threatened," said Traile, "or the detectives on the Courtland case would have seen a connection. It's fair to assume that he was seized on his way to Centre Street."

The haggard expression came back into the millionaire's face. "You're right, it was old Courtland. He and Merton Cloyd came last night to help me form a scheme to fight this mysterious group. They were getting reports like this, too."

Allen cleared his throat.

"You and the others hadn't any idea, then, who was back of the letters?"

Bannister started to shake his head, then paused.

"Cloyd and I didn't, but something last night made me think that Courtland knew more than he was telling. I asked him if he'd made contact with these devils. He denied it, but the way he acted—"

A woman's querulous voice was suddenly audible from out in the hall. Its shrill accents were cut off by a muttered snarl and the sound of a blow. As Allen ran to the side door there was a stifled cry, and a clatter of something against the panels.

"Be careful!" rapped Traile. "Stand to one side when you open it!"

Allen gripped the knob, jumped back. As the door opened, the handle of a mop slid down and struck the floor. Just beyond, the old charwoman was struggling to her feet, a bruise on her wrinkled face. Traile helped her up.

"Thanks, sir—but I'll be all right now," she said in a quavering voice.

"What happened?" Allen demanded.

The old woman whimpered, rubbing her bruised cheek.

"It was a man, sir—I come on him sudden-like, and there he was, with his ear to the door, listenin'—"

"What did he look like? Which way did he go?" Allen broke in impatiently.

"His face was queer—almost like a dead man's." The old woman looked fearfully toward the stairs to the lower floors. "You'd best be careful—he's a bad one."

"It must have been one of the Gray Men," Traile said to Allen in a lowered voice. "If you work fast, you may be able to catch him."

Allen dashed toward the front offices, and in a few moments his agents were spreading out in a hasty search. The old charwoman picked up her mop and bucket, shuffled down the hall. Traile turned back into the laboratory as he saw that Stone had come into the hall with Bannister and Eric.

"We shouldn't have left the skull unguarded," he said anxiously.

"Nobody could've come through from the front," replied the technician. "There are always three or four men up there."

Traile locked the door as Bannister and Eric followed him into the room. Stone switched on one of the special illuminators attached to the microscope.

The millionaire gave a puzzled look at the skull, then glanced back at Traile.

"You appear to have influence here. I want some of your agents to guard me."

"My connection is unofficial," said Traile. "But Allen can probably arrange it."

As he started out with Bannister, he turned to Eric.

"You'd better stay here with Stone. Keep your gun ready, in case you hear anyone else at that door."

When they reached Allen's office, the senior agent was just putting down the phone.

"No luck yet," be said irritably, "but I'm having all entrances watched."

The millionaire gruffly stated his request for D.J. agents to guard him. Allen hesitated.

"So far, Mr. Bannister, it's not a Federal case. The Courtland murder and the attack on you are police matters. Those secret reports don't actually constitute a crime."

"What about the abduction of my servants—my two secretaries?" rasped Bannister. "I came here because I don't want publicity. The police will spread it all over the papers. You people have a reputation for doing things quietly."

Allen gave Traile a sidewise glance. "What do you think?"

Traile's dark eyes rested on the millionaire's haggard face.

"Mr. Bannister, have you ever heard of the Invisible Empire?"

Bannister shook his head.

"No, what is it?"

"It's the organization back of those reports," replied Traile.

An angry color darkened Bannister's face. "If you already know about this business, why didn't you say so?"

"I didn't know about the letters," Traile said calmly. "But from the Courtland evidence—"

He stopped as Eric Gordon burst into the office.

"Come on!" Eric exclaimed. There was an excited light in his blue eyes. "Stone's found out something."

All three men jumped to their feet.

"What is it?" clipped Traile, as they hurried toward the laboratory.

"I don't know," Eric said tensely. "He said one of the light rays showed up some writing that seemed to be inside the metal. Then all of a sudden he got a scared look, and sent me back here to get you."

"It may be the key to the whole thing," Allen said in an eager voice.

Traile nodded, started through the room adjoining the laboratory. He was halfway to the connecting door when a muffled hissing became audible from the other room. Then a voice rose in a scream of agony.

"It's Stone!" shouted Allen.

Traile sprang for the door. He flung it open, then jumped back in amazement. A cloud of weirdly beautiful smoke was swirling within the laboratory. In its opaque, shimmering haze shone every hue of the rainbow.

Somewhere from the depths of that pastel-colored smoke came a terrible, frenzied cry. It died away, and there was only the muffled hissing which had been heard at first.

The opening of the door had brought some of the smoke billowing into the other room. It puffed into Traile's face, stinging his eyes. He stumbled against Bannister. Then, realizing that the smoke was not immediately poisonous, he drew a deep breath of fresh air and dashed into the laboratory.

Through the eddying smoke he glimpsed something jerking around madly near the center of the room. He could vaguely see flashes of colored light, like fireworks seen through a heavy fog. The hissing came from that spot.

Half-blinded, he managed to find a window and raise it. Not until the colored smoke had blown away from where he stood did he risk taking a breath. The rest of the room was still hidden from view. He could hear Allen coughing, and the others stumbling around in the smoke.

"Keep back until it's clear!" he called out.

A figure staggered toward him, almost collapsed at the open window. It was Bannister.

"What is it?" gasped the millionaire.

"I don't know," Traile answered tautly. He strained his eyes for a sign of Jim Stone. The hissing began to diminish, and in a few moments it had ended. The eerie smoke dissipated rapidly as fresh air blew into the room.

As Allen and Eric Gordon appeared in the colored haze, Traile stepped toward the center of the laboratory. The queer flashes of light had ceased with the hissing, but the last of that strange and beautiful smoke still hovered over the spot.

As it started to fade, a bony hand became visible. Then swiftly the smoke thinned, revealing the dreadful thing which lay beneath. Traile stared down in stark horror.

There on the floor was a rainbow-colored skeleton! It was all that remained of Jim Stone.

Chapter 6

The Woman in Rags

Allen swayed back, white and sick. "Oh, my God!" he whispered.

Eric and Bannister looked down with stunned faces at the shimmering, gruesome figure. Faint wisps of colored smoke still eddied around the rainbow-hued skeleton. The effect was one of horrible beauty, more dreadful than bleached white bones would have been.

"Oh, God!" Allen said again. He pulled his eyes away, looked dazedly at Traile. "What terrible thing—"

Traile shook his head, then knelt down, his lean face pale under its tan. A slight breeze was blowing in from the opened window. Suddenly the left arm of the skeleton quivered, then a tiny cloud of bright ashes fluttered into the air. The next moment the hand and forearm crumbled into rainbow-colored dust.

Traile stood up and quickly closed the window. But the crumbling process continued, until in a minute, only a vague-shaped, sinister pile of colored ash remained on the marble floor. He gazed at it a moment longer, then with a start turned to the big microscope. In the horror of his discovery, he had forgotten the golden skull. Allen followed his swift glance.

"It's gone!" he said hoarsely.

Traile bent over the mounting stage to which the skull had been fastened. One side was mottled with the same colors as those of the rainbow ashes. He heard an exclamation, looked up into Allen's tortured face.

"The stuff that killed him must have been a part of the skull!" rasped the D.J. man.

"No," Traile said grimly, "he was killed by something else, so that someone could get the skull out of here. Look at this clamp. It's twisted from a jerk, and there's a scraping of gold on the setscrew."

Eric Gordon ran across to the hall door.

"It's still locked," he exclaimed.

"A master key would take care of that," rapped Traile. He wheeled to the half-dazed Allen. "They'll be trying to get it out of the building. It's doubly important now—"

A savage look replaced the sickness in the senior agent's eyes.

"By God, if I catch the fiend who did this—" The rest was lost as he ran toward the front offices.

His whirlwind exit sent a flurry of rainbow ash into the air. Bannister stared at it and shivered. Traile turned to Eric.

"Did Stone give you any other hint of what he learned about the skull?"

"Not a word," mumbled Eric. "But whatever he saw, it gave him a bad scare. He jumped back and told me to get you as fast as I could. I may be wrong, but I think it was something beside the writing that scared him."

"I should have had a dozen men in here guarding him," Traile said self-accusingly. "I might have known something would happen."

"Why was that little gold skull so important?" Bannister interposed curiously.

Traile's bronzed face was stern. "Because Courtland's murderers left it at the head of his coffin."

The millionaire started.

"But why, in Heaven's name?" Traile was hurrying from window to window, examining the ledges.

"I believe it was a mistake," he answered. "Since then, agents of the Invisible Empire have tried desperately to recover it. And now they've succeeded, unless—" He stopped short.

"What's the matter?" Eric asked.

"The charwoman!" Traile whirled toward the door to the hall. "I was a fool not to guess it before."

He jerked open the door, then spun around to Bannister. "Warn Allen not to let that woman get out of the building! We'll be searching for her at once." Eric raced after him to the rear elevator shafts. When a car came up, Traile shot a sharp look at the attendant and then spoke. "Have you seen the charwoman who works on this floor?"

"Ya mean the new one?" said the operator. "She's up on Sixteen. I saw her a few minutes ago."

Traile sprang into the car.

"Take us up!" When they reached the floor, he flung a crisp order at the man. "Go back to Fourteen and find Mr. Allen—Bureau of Investigation. Tell him to rush a squad up here!"

"Yes, sir!" gulped the operator. The car started down. Traile drew a fresh cartridge clip from a leather pocket under his belt.

"Take the left corridor," he whispered to Eric, as he rammed the magazine into his gun. "She'll probably have other spies helping her, so be on your guard."

A determined look came into Eric's youthful face. He hurried away on tiptoe. Traile took the other hall, watching each door that he passed. It was only seven thirty, and all the offices still appeared to be deserted. He made a right-angle turn, was almost to the next one when he saw an open window at the end of a side corridor leading to a fire escape. As he started toward it, Eric appeared from the other direction.

"No sign of her—" the younger man began.

"Quiet," whispered Traile. He leaned out warily, then straightened. "There's a window open in the second office to the left. Cover the door while I sneak in from this direction."

He stole out onto the fire escape, noiselessly made his way to the office window. As he reached it he heard a gasp, then he saw the charwoman run for the door. She threw it open, then gave a moan as Eric confronted her in the shadowy entrance. Traile saw her cringe away from him, a wretched figure in tattered black, her streaked gray hair tumbling down over her eyes.

"Watch her, Eric!" he said sharply. "She's a cold-blooded murderess!"

Eric made no answer. Traile climbed through the window, after a quick glance to be sure that no one else was in the room. As he saw the torment in Eric's eyes, he grasped their captive's shoulder and pulled her around. A strange sight met his gaze.

Gone were the wrinkled features of the old charwoman. Only a smudge of make-up here and there remained to betray the secret. An oval face, lovely with a foreign, exotic charm, looked up at him in despair.

"Good God!" he said, half under his breath. He reached out toward the tangled hair. Two slim hands, no longer gnarled, flew up to her head, but it was too late. As he lifted away the wig, the lustrous black hair of a beautiful woman was revealed. The last faint hope vanished from Eric Gordon's blue eyes.

"Sonya!" he groaned. "To think you could do that awful thing!"

A haunted look crossed her face.

"I didn't kill him," she said in a shaken voice. "It was only intended to drive him from the room while—"

"While you stole the golden skull," Traile finished grimly. "But you killed him, nevertheless."

"No, no! I was not the—" She broke off, drew herself up with a quiet dignity. "Arrest me if you will. I am a criminal—yes. But I have never killed anyone."

Eric had come into the room, was watching her in misery. But at her last words some of the hope came back into his face.

"Michael, she's telling the truth! Look at her eyes—you can see—"

Traile smiled bitterly.

"I'm afraid your infatuation has blinded you, Eric."

"It's not infatuation!" Eric burst out hotly. "If she weren't any good, I'd never care—"

A slow flush came into Sonya Damitri's pale cheeks as he left the sentence unfinished.

Traile broke in coldly before she could speak.

"Even if you're telling the truth, you're still an accessory to murder."

"Didn't you hear?" Eric cried fiercely. "She wasn't the one who did it—she's innocent!"

The girl gave him a sad smile from under her long black lashes.

"I shall never forget—that you believed in me," she said softly.

There was a sudden movement in the doorway.

"Good work," came a muffled snarl. "Raise your hands—you two!"

Traile had wheeled as the man appeared. There in the doorway stood one of the gray-faced men. His oddly sunken eyes glared over a leveled gun. For a split second, Traile hesitated, but Eric was in his line of fire. Slowly, he raised his hands. The Gray Man stepped into the room. He closed the door, snatched Eric's gun and thrust it into his pocket.

"Get the other one," he harshly ordered Sonya. His bloodless lips seemed hardly to move when he spoke.

The girl hastily took Traile's gun, laid it on a desk. He saw her wince before the look in Eric's eyes.

"Where is the Golden Skull?" demanded the Gray Man. His queer eyes flicked toward the dirty water in the bucket which Sonya had carried.

"It's still in there," she said in a low voice. "They haven't dropped the line."

"It will be down in a few seconds," said the man. "Be ready to hook on the bucket while I take care of these two."

A frightened light came into her great black eyes.

"You can't kill them!" Her expression quickly altered, under his penetrating glare. "The last orders were that they were to be taken alive."

"There's no chance for that now," retorted the Gray Man. "I'd better finish them."

"You know the penalty for disobeying!" the girl exclaimed. "Tie them up, or lock them in that closet."

Something scraped, out on the fire escape. Sonya picked up the bucket and carried it to the window. As the Gray Man drove the two captives toward the closet, Traile saw a hook dangling just outside. The girl grasped it, and in a moment he saw the bucket disappear upward.

"Hurry up and finish changing," the Gray Man muttered nervously. "Those agents may be up here any minute."

Sonya took up a thick briefcase from the desk, and ran into the room adjoining the office. The man twitched his gun toward Eric.

"Reach back and open that door. And don't try any tricks."

Eric obeyed in angry silence. The Gray Man cast a hasty look into the closet, evidently searching for something to bind and gag the two men. Traile had not moved, after being forced back toward the wall, but his dark eyes never left their captor's face. Suddenly the Gray Man stiffened.

"Turn around!" he said in a muffled tone.

Eric started to obey, but Traile halted him with a swift warning.

"Watch out! He intends to slug you!"

The Gray Man lunged toward him, stopped

with a snarled oath, swerving his gun back and forth to cover them.

"Turn around, both of you!" he rasped. "Unless you want a dose of lead!"

Eric tensed, but Traile signaled with a jerk of his head.

"Hold it! He doesn't dare kill us."

There was a gasp, and Sonya reappeared. The ragged dress of the charwoman had been replaced by a smart knitted suit, and a small sport hat covered her dark hair. Instead of the shabby shoes, she wore a pair of modish pumps. "What are you doing?" she demanded. "I told you—*look out!*"

Her cry was directed at Eric. In the brief instant when the Gray Man's gaze jerked toward her, Eric had crouched for a spring. But the other man had whirled, lifting his gun for a furious blow. Traile hurtled between him and Eric. The butt of the pistol, descending with a force that would have crushed Eric's skull, struck Traile's shoulder.

That sudden leap had knocked Eric backward into the closet. The impact of the gun numbed Traile's left arm, swung him around. He lashed out with his right, and the Gray Man's pistol jetted flame toward the ceiling. But before Traile could wrest the gun from his hand, a vicious blow to the stomach sent him reeling. The door slammed as he fell against Eric, then the lock clicked, and the voices of Sonya and the Gray Man quickly died away.

It was half a minute before Traile could get his breath from that blow to his solar plexus. Eric frantically bent over him in the dark.

"Michael! Oh, good Lord, he's been shot!"

"No—only took my wind," Traile managed to groan. He pulled himself to his feet. "We've got to break out of here."

He turned his uninjured shoulder, and together they crashed against the door. At the second attempt, a panel splintered. As the door burst open, Allen and three of his men charged into the room.

"What the hell?" yelped the senior agent as he recognized them.

"No time to explain!" said Traile. "They hauled the skull up to the roof!"

"They must be crossing to the next building," snapped Allen. He and his agents raced for the elevators.

Traile's gun was still lying on the desk. He picked it up, went out into the hall. Another squad of agents appeared. Traile tersely described Sonya while Eric stood by unhappily. The operatives quickly separated to look for her and continue their search for the Gray Man. Traile and Eric silently went down to the fourteenth floor.

Ten minutes later a glum-faced group assembled in Allen's office.

"They're a slick outfit, all right," growled the senior agent. "They got away clean."

"What about the girl?" Eric asked, staring at the floor.

The agent named Weller spoke up.

"She went right out the front way, before we got the second warning." He grinned ruefully. "When you're looking for an old charwoman, you don't stop a classy dame like that."

Traile was the only one who saw the relief in Eric's eyes. There was a brief silence, then he turned to Bannister.

"Do you happen to know whether Harley Kent still owns the Vare Diamond?"

The millionaire looked surprised.

"So far as I know. Why?"

"I want to pay him a visit." Traile looked at Allen. "I think you'd better come, too."

"What about the protection I asked for?" said Bannister. In the last half-hour, his unshaven face had become more haggard than ever.

"You can go along with us," said Allen. "We'll talk over the details on the way."

As they went out, two men came along the hall which led to the laboratory. They were carefully carrying a porcelain tray with a pane of glass for a cover. As Traile glanced down, the hall lights sparkled in the rainbow dust which had once been a man.

Chapter 7

"You Have Till Midnight to Live"

For almost half an hour, the talking Buddha had been silent. Before the idol, the Yellow Doctor sat like some grim statue of Satan. His glittering, tawny eyes were fixed in space. Only the restless tapping of his talon-like fingers betrayed the tension within him.

Suddenly the eyes of the Buddha glowed bright green. The Crime Emperor swiftly leaned forward.

"Main Control!" The words all but crackled.

"The Golden Skull is recovered," a voice said rapidly. "A Federal technician examining it was destroyed. Operating group safely withdrawn, and Agent Twenty-two also clear. No clues left unless by the Gray Man cooperating."

Dr. Yen Sin slowly sat back in his chair.

"What report on Michael Traile?"

"Left the building ten minutes ago with man known as Citizen Nine, Gordon, and Agent Allen," was the reply from the idol. "Gordon carried small black box strapped to what appeared to be a toy church. Party was delayed at the door by arrival of Police Commissioner, presumably investigating Courtland case, also by detectives covering the action in Lexington Avenue. Traile and Allen conferred privately with the commissioner, then followed Gordon and Citizen Nine into a car. Personal observation transferred to Group Two."

The Crime Emperor touched one of the buttons before him. A buzzing was audible, and the numbered wheel began to rotate slowly. In a few seconds the Buddha's eyes, which had dimmed, shone brightly again.

"Group Two." A husky voice spoke against a muffled background of traffic sounds. "On Fifth Avenue, following car containing—"

"I am already informed," Dr. Yen Sin interrupted, "as to the occupants. Notify me at once when they arrive at Hotel Lordmore."

"They're not going to the Lordmore," came the hurried reply from the talking Buddha. "Observer in crowd overheard senior agent's orders to the escort, to follow them to residence of Harley Kent."

The Yellow Doctor's robed figure stiffened.

"This should have been reported at once!"

"We tried, but the signal wasn't answered," began the other nervously. "I thought—"

"Break contact!" said Dr. Yen Sin. "Proceed as rapidly as possible to the Kent residence. Assign one man to carry out these instructions." He spoke incisively for almost a minute. "Act at once on his signal. I shall delay the escorting agents, but count on no more than two minutes."

As the eyes of the idol darkened, the Crime Emperor quickly bent over the row of buttons before him.

With Eric Gordon at the wheel, the sedan swung away from the curb, moving slowly through the crowd which had gathered. Michael Traile, seated in the rear with Bannister, glanced back carelessly. The car with the escorting agents was following at a short distance.

"I hope you don't expect another attack," Bannister said uneasily.

Traile shook his head.

"It's not likely, now. Besides, this car is armored and the windows are bulletproof."

The millionaire drew a breath of relief.

"Thank Heaven for that! I've had enough to last me for a long time."

"It beats me," Allan grated from the front seat, "how they've got away with everything. The Courtland affair was bad enough—but that damned business right in a Federal building—"

"I told you we were fighting a master criminal," Traile said a trifle wearily. He lighted a cigarette, leaned back and relaxed his tightened muscles. "Every important move he makes is planned like a military maneuver, with detailed orders to every man—or woman—involved."

From his position at the right, he could see Eric flush. Bannister shook his head.

"It's incredible, a thing like that here in

Manhattan. If I hadn't had proof through those secret reports—"

"I was going to ask you about those," said Traile. His words had an oddly lazy note, the result of his complete relaxation. "Have you tried to trace the sender?"

"Yes, but it was useless," growled the millionaire. "Some came by ordinary mail, some by messengers who could give only vague descriptions of the person who paid for them. They've been sent to my Wall Street office, my hotels—even to my yacht."

Traile's dark eyes were on the rear-vision mirror up forward.

"The one this morning?" he asked absently.

Bannister scowled.

"It was at the desk when I hurried down. One of the clerks had heard the radio flash about poor old Courtland, and knowing our association he called me at once. When I reached the desk, he told me the letter had been brought in by a special messenger, about an hour before. It was marked *Urgent*."

Traile gazed through the smoke from his cigarette.

"If we only knew his exact motive," he mused. "Blackmail, yes—but if I know the Invisible Emperor that's only a means to an end."

A queer hunted expression came into Bannister's eyes.

"Until this morning," he began slowly, "I never considered anything but plain blackmail. But after Courtland's murder—and those Chinese gunmen—" He hesitated, made an impatient gesture. "It's ridiculous, I suppose, but I suddenly recalled an episode which occurred in China almost six years ago."

Both Allen and Eric started, and Traile's bronzed face lost its indolent look.

"I didn't know you'd been in China," he said quickly.

The millionaire nodded.

"It was in connection with my importing business—my freight steamship line. I was there about a year, and I'd put over some pretty shrewd deals, when strange things began to happen. One of my ships caught fire—two of my confidential men disappeared—I was threatened with death unless I paid tribute to some mysterious Chinese. I fought back, but things became so bad that I had to leave. The officials at Shanghai told me that they were helpless—that this devil called the *Shek* would revenge himself if I ever returned."

"You're lucky to be alive," Traile said in a grim voice. "The man they called the 'Cobra' was none other than Doctor Yen Sin, the man we are seeking."

Bannister looked at him in consternation. "What! You mean to say this Invisible Emperor is a Chinese?"

"Right—and in my opinion the most dangerous man alive! A super-scientist, an evil genius with the ruthless will of a dictator—and an Oriental hatred for the white race that amounts to a mania."

There was perspiration on the millionaire's forehead, and Traile saw the fear in his eyes.

"Then I was right," Bannister said hoarsely. "It's personal vengeance he's after."

Traile's eyes were again on the rear-vision mirror.

"Perhaps so," he muttered. "But in these other cases—" He whirled, stared through the window behind him.

"What's the matter?" exclaimed Allen.

"A suspicious-looking car has been following along with the traffic," Traile answered. "I noticed it at one side of the escort machine when we left Lexington Avenue. It just now turned and dashed into Forty-fifth Street."

"You mean that black delivery truck?" cut in Eric.

"That's the one," said Traile. "But I've a hunch that it was no ordinary truck. There was no name on it. The driver and the man with him looked foreign. Also, that black glass in the side looked like the old speakeasy-door kind, the type you can see through and not be seen. There may have been more men inside."

As he spoke, Traile leaned down and switched on the miniature radio set.

"What's the idea of that?" queried Bannister.

Traile lifted the set to his knee.

"Doctor Yen Sin is using a special microwave radio to transmit orders to his agents. We caught one message, but—" He bent over quickly as one hand in the church-steeple quivered. "We're in the beam! He must be sending a message to those men in the truck."

"Then why don't we hear it?" objected Allen.

"They've shifted to a waveband out of our range, but the indicator is wired higher and it registers." Traile stared down at the trembling needle. "Step on it, Eric! Get to Kent's place as fast as you can!"

The sedan shot forward, grazed a bus, wove swiftly through traffic. At Forty-seventh Street, a policeman whistled peremptorily for them to slow down. Allen had already jerked his gold F.B.I. shield from an inner pocket. He flashed it, shouted at the officer. The sedan sped on. Two minutes later, as Eric was swinging left in the upper Fifties, Allen gave a startled exclamation.

"Wait a minute! We've lost the other car."

"We can't stop now," said Traile. "That may be part of the scheme, to cut them off."

"What do you think they're up to?" Bannister asked in alarm.

"It must be connected with the Vare Diamond," Traile responded crisply.

It was only half a block from Fifth Avenue to the old brownstone house which served as bachelor quarters for Harley Kent, well-known collector of rare jewels. As the sedan slid to a halt in front of the building, Traile looked quickly down the street. Then, still holding the micro-set, he jumped out and motioned for the others to follow.

"There's a chance they may have—" He stopped, as the door opened and a frightened-looking manservant came running down the steps.

"What's wrong?" Allen demanded.

"Mr. Kent—he's been murdered!" cried the man.

"Good Lord," rasped the F.B.I. agent. He sprang up the steps. Traile and the others quickly followed with the servant. As they entered, Traile shoved the strapped set under his arm and drew his .38.

"When did it happen?" he asked the manservant in a low tone.

"I don't know, sir," the man wailed. "I just came in and found him there—" He pointed a trembling hand into the library.

Traile pushed him ahead, cast a keen glance around the hall before following Bannister and Eric into the room. Allen stood transfixed, a few feet from the doorway. Traile looked, then he, too, stopped in his tracks.

In a high-backed chair at the head of the library table sat Harley Kent. His hands were tied behind the chair, keeping his body from falling forward. A wide strip of purplish tape covered his lips, except at one spot where dark blood had oozed out and was slowly dropping. The dead man's eyes were open with an agonized stare.

But that tortured face, terrible as it was, held Traile's eyes only a moment. For Harley Kent had been stripped to the waist, and his bared chest stabbed three times with a red-hot iron. The three ugly wounds formed a triangle, with one hole over the heart, and directly in the center of the triangle was a tiny gilt seal. It was in the shape of a skull.

For a moment no one moved. Then Traile stepped close to the dead man.

"Another murder in the name of the *Chuen Gin Lou*," he said in a hard voice.

Eric looked down at the seal, and a grimace twitched his lips.

"Michael, that thing has the same hideous expression as the Golden Skull!"

Traile slowly nodded, stooped to look at the mutilating wounds in Harley Kent's breast. As he straightened, he saw the manservant shudder and turn away. Mark Bannister was gazing with a horrified fascination at the corpse.

"God!" he said thickly. "He must have gone through hell before he died."

Allen had not spoken since he entered. But as the servant stepped back, the lanky F.B.I. man suddenly bent over. He stood up with a large plush jewel case in his hands.

"This must be the answer," he said harshly. "The devils probably got away with some valuable stones."

Just as he started to open it, Traile caught a furtive movement near the door.

"Wait!" he rapped out. But it was too late. Even as he spoke, Allen pressed the catch. The lid of the jewel case flew open, and a dark, fragrant vapor instantly poured forth.

"The incense!" Eric cried thickly. He took a blind step forward, fell to his knees. Traile had sprung toward the doorway, where the servant was stealing out. But as the fragrant anesthetic engulfed him, an unwanted weakness sent him staggering. Allen and Bannister were both crumpling to the floor. A terrific pain shot through his head. He caught at the table, then as he saw the servant's tense face in the entry he let himself fall with a groan. The next second he heard the man racing up the hall toward the front of the house.

He pulled himself up, stumbled toward the door. While his sleepless brain refused to yield to the drug, a feeling of exhaustion threatened to overcome him. He forced himself on, gripped the knob and pulled the door open. The fresh air from the hall was like a dash of cold water in his face. He gulped in a deep breath, tightened his grasp on the pistol, which had almost slipped from his fingers.

From the entrance of the house came a peculiar whistle. Traile lunged toward the vestibule, sucking deep breaths into his lungs. As he reached the door, he saw the false servant signal hastily toward the street, then a motor roared, and the black truck swiftly drew up in front.

Abruptly, the other man turned and saw Traile. His pinched face contorted in amazement and terror. Then, like a cornered rat, he sprang. Traile's gun was already lifted. He slashed it fiercely along the side of the spy's head. With a howl, the man teetered backward, rolled down the steps.

Two men had leaped from the front seat of the truck. Dismay spread over their features as Traile appeared. One of them jumped back, shouting toward the rear of the machine. Instantly, a section of dark glass slid open in the side of the truck. The muzzled snout of a silenced machine gun poked up at Traile.

Traile flung himself down, firing as he dropped. The man behind the machine gun toppled to the floor of the truck. Another figure sprang to take his place, but the driver stopped him with a furious yell.

"You fool! We've got to get him alive!"

"It's too late!" The false servant had scrambled to his feet, blood streaming down his face. "Beat it! G-men!"

A taxi was thundering down the street from the direction of Fifth Avenue. In a hurried sideglance, Traile saw two of Allen's agents on the running boards. With frantic haste, the Invisible Emperor's spies jumped into the speed-truck and fled. Traile stood up, pumped two shots at the rear of the machine, but it raced on and was quickly swallowed up in traffic.

"Let it go!" Traile exclaimed, as one of the agents shot a hasty question at him. "I need your help inside."

He had left the library door open, and when he and the first of the squad entered they found the three victims beginning to stir. Traile and the others carried them out into the hall, and they soon revived. Bannister was the first one able to speak.

"What the devil happened?"

"We walked into a neat trap," Traile said with a slight note of curtness. "Kent had been dead hours before we got here—but Yen Sin twisted it to his advantage and nearly won."

Ten minutes later, the entire group returned to the library for a final examination of the scene while they waited for the police. Suddenly a clicking sounded from the micro-set which

Traile had laid on the table. Then, to his astonishment, the voice of the Yellow Doctor spoke.

"I congratulate you, Mr. Traile, but you have only delayed our meeting."

There was a hush as the assembled men stared at the miniature radio. Then the sibilant voice of Yen Sin continued.

"And to Citizen Nine, I give this final message: You have until midnight to live!"

Chapter 8

Murder Garden

Night had fallen over Manhattan. From the roof of the towering Hotel Lordmore, the vast expanse of lighted streets below was pleasantly remote, a picturesque background for Mark Bannister's sumptuous penthouse.

Along the stone guard-wall at one end of the roof, Michael Traile stood with a field glass raised to his eyes. The millionaire paced restlessly back and forth beside him.

"It's after ten," Bannister grated out. "If Allen's coming up with more men, why isn't he here?"

Traile did not seem to have heard him. He moved the glass slowly over the twinkling lights on the East River, on out toward the Sound, then back to the nearest skyscraper.

"An excellent view," he said as he put down the glass.

"To hell with the view!" exploded the millionaire. "Do you realize I'm likely to go like Kent and poor old Courtland?"

"I don't think you need worry," Traile said calmly. "This place is almost impregnable."

Bannister stared back through the gloom, to where Eric Gordon and two F.B.I. men stood near the brightly lighted penthouse.

"That's what I thought," he muttered. "But from all you've told me, this Doctor Yen Sin must be almost superhuman. And now that Cloyd has disappeared—"

He shook his head gloomily.

Traile turned a moment later, as Eric quickly approached them.

"Your elevator signal is buzzing," Eric said to Bannister.

Bannister strode toward the penthouse. Traile and Eric followed him through a Japanese gate, one of the curios the millionaire had brought back from the East. It opened into a walled Oriental garden, partly roofed and rather flamboyantly blending Chinese and Japanese motifs. A pale purple moon shone dimly on a tiny arched bridge, under which ran an artificial brook. Back in the shadows stood a pagoda-shaped shrine. Colored lanterns, farther on, illuminated an open display of Samurai swords, Chinese highbinder hatchets, and other Oriental weapons of a past day.

The millionaire scowled about him as he stalked through the garden.

"This place is going to be changed. After today, I don't want anything Chinese around me!"

"I don't blame you," said Eric. "Even the sight of a Chink laundryman gives me the jitters now."

In the large reception hall, Bannister stopped before his private switchboard. He spoke into a phone, listened, then turned a knob marked *Elevator*.

"It's Allen and his men," he grunted.

Traile's dark eyes were watching the indicator. The car came up swiftly, stopped automatically. Bannister peered through the observation panel, touched the release which opened the double doors. Allen and the operative named Johnson stepped out. Bannister frowned.

"Where are the rest of your men?"

The lanky senior agent shrugged.

"Helping the cops search Chinatown. After Weller phoned me about the layout up here, I didn't think we'd need any more."

The millionaire glowered at him. Allen rubbed his jaw, looked around curiously.

"Weller said the elevator is the only way to get up here. I guess this job's a cinch."

"I told him there was also an emergency exit," snapped Bannister. He pointed to a heavy door with massive double locks. "However, it can be opened only from this side, and there's a similar door—locked the same way—at the bottom of the steps. It opens into the hall of the floor below. Both doors are connected with these burglar-alarm bells on the switchboard."

Allen nodded, glanced at Traile.

"I guess we won't see the Yellow Doctor tonight. . . . By the way, here's your gun. You left it at the Kent place."

Bannister gave Traile a sour look. "A lot of help you'd have been, if anything had happened while we were driving to the hotel tonight. They might have kidnapped me—and I'd probably have died like Harley Kent."

Traile inspected the magazine of the .38, slid it back into the butt.

"In that case," he said, "you would have died very quickly."

"It's plain he was tortured," snapped the millionaire. "How do you know how he died?"

"I should know," Traile said coolly. "I was the one who killed him."

Bannister took a step backward.

"*You?*" he rasped. Then the angry glare returned to his eyes. "This is no time for jokes!"

"I'm not joking," said Traile. He looked at Eric and Johnson, who were staring at him in amazement. Then he turned back to the millionaire. "I killed him in self-defense. Harley Kent was the Gray Man I shot at the Courtland mansion."

Bannister looked from him to Allen. The senior agent nodded.

"That's right. The slug found in Kent's heart tallied exactly in rifling marks with a test bullet fired from that .38."

"But I don't understand," Bannister said dazedly.

"It's quite simple," Traile told him. "They were attempting to cover up the truth. From the medical examiner's report, Kent's body must have been brought to his home soon after the Gray Men escaped from the Courtland place. They bound it as you saw, then stabbed it with a red-hot poker, also plunging the iron into the bullet hole in his left side so it would look like the other wounds. Either they forgot the bullet in their haste, or they had no means of probing for it."

"But—Harley Kent, a criminal!" Bannister exclaimed. "Why, it's impossible!"

Traile's deep-tanned face was stern.

"He was evidently driven to it by desperation. If I'm right, the Gray Men are rich and influential victims of the Yellow Doctor. Perhaps one or two are willing members, actuated by greed in joining the Invisible Empire. But I think most of them have been trapped by blackmail or some other insidious scheme, and then forced to do Yen Sin's bidding."

The millionaire looked horrified.

"Then that's what he intended to do with me!"

"It looks that way," Traile said grimly.

"What about the gray faces of those men?" put in Agent Johnson. "You think they were made up, like that girl this morning?"

Eric Gordon winced. Traile shook his head.

"Nothing that complicated. I believe they wear some kind of thin rubber masks which conform partly with their real features, yet conceal their identity. That adhesive tape on Kent's mouth gave me a hint. I found sticky spots where something had adhered to his face. I thought of a mask, and that fitted in with what I noticed about that wound. They must wear the masks so they will be able to distinguish each other when they're carrying out some mission, and still be disguised from other members of the Invisible Empire—perhaps even from one another."

"The thing's fantastic," Bannister said incredulously. "What possible good could it do this Invisible Emperor?"

As Traile replied he led the way out to the unlighted sun deck.

"Getting them more deeply involved would be the initial reason. I suspect that he's building toward some tremendous goal, and he wants to get those men completely in his power so that they can't rebel at the last. But whatever it is, the stakes are sure to be enormous."

Allen savagely bit off the end of a cigar.

"After what happened to Jim Stone, I'd like just one minute with that yellow fiend!"

He scratched a match on the guard-wall. Bannister jumped nervously at the sound. Allen paused with the blazing match half-raised to his cigar.

"By the way, where're Murdock and Weller?"

"On the other side," volunteered Eric.

"Let's go around there," said Allen.

As they started along the dark walk by the guard-wall, the musical sound of chimes came from somewhere in the penthouse.

"Eleven o'clock!" Bannister said in a strained voice. "By God, I'm going in where it's light!"

He wheeled back along the sun deck, but he had not taken four steps when a voice rose in a shout from the other side of the roof.

"Help! Something's happened to Weller!"

Traile whirled to Eric Gordon and Allen.

"You two stay here with Bannister!"

Johnson snapped on a flashlight as he ran after Traile.

"Hold it out to the side," Traile flung over his shoulder.

The light swerved and, as they reached the Japanese gate, fell on the chunky figure of Agent Murdock. The man's round face had a stunned expression.

"This way!" he jerked out hoarsely.

They followed him through the garden. Beyond the little arched bridge Murdock halted, pointing dumbly to the floor. Kneeling there before the shrine, bent over with his forehead to a prayer mat, was Weller. His face, as seen from the side, was the color of old parchment.

Traile shot a swift look backward, then stooped over the silent figure. The man did not move as he touched him. He grasped the agent's shoulder, shook it. Weller toppled over sidewise, his body rigidly retaining its queer, kneeling pose.

"He's dead!" gasped Johnson.

Traile wheeled, took the flashlight, and swept it about the garden.

"Did you see it happen?" he demanded of Murdock.

Before Murdock could answer, Bannister and the others appeared from the direction of the sun deck. Eric Gordon and Allen were trying to keep the millionaire back. But he pulled away from them.

"I insist on knowing what—" He broke off as he saw the queerly rigid body. "My God, he's been killed!"

"Weller!" groaned Allen. He sprang forward, but Traile stopped him.

"Wait! Don't touch him yet." He probed the flashlight around again, then turned quickly to Bannister. "Those colored lanterns don't help much. Switch on some bright lights."

Bannister shook his head.

"The lanterns are the only ones connected in the garden."

Traile bent for a hasty scrutiny of Weller's body. Then, at his direction, Murdock and Johnson carried the dead agent into the reception hall. He closed the glass door to the garden, handed Allen the flashlight.

"Keep it pointed at that door. Eric, you and Johnson watch toward the sides of the roof. Fire at anything that moves."

"I thought you searched this place," Alien muttered.

"We did," Traile said grimly. He looked at Murdock. "Now, let's hear what you know."

The man tore his eyes away from the grotesquely stiffened form on the floor.

"I thought he was somewhere near me. He'd been wandering around in the garden. Then I heard something buzz, like a bee, right close to my ear. It gave me a start, and I began looking for Weller. When I found him he was bent down in front of that heathen shrine, just like he was praying. He was shaking as though he was scared to death, and he wouldn't say a word. That's when I yelled for help."

Allen took his gaze from the glass door for a brief stare at the dead man. "He must've had some kind of fit. But I never heard of rigor mortis setting in so fast."

Traile motioned to Bannister. "Help me turn him over."

The millionaire recoiled.

"I wouldn't even touch him! You can't tell what killed him."

"I can guess," Traile said shortly. He turned the dead agent onto his back. Weller's head was still bent, and his limbs rigidly fixed in their curious position. Traile looked at the wildly dilated eyes, then pointed to a small brown spot under Weller's jaw.

"There's the answer. A tiny dart or needle went in there. That smear is *lakta*, a Malay poison. There's enough left on the outside to stop a full-grown tiger."

As he stood up the others looked at him with horror.

"Then that buzz I heard—" Murdock said, ashen-faced.

"Was either that dart—or another one meant for you," Traile finished.

Bannister suddenly turned and closed the door to the sun deck.

"Leave it open," Traile said quickly.

"You're crazy!" rasped the millionaire. "The dart must have been shot from the top of that office building across the street. They may shoot another at any second."

"None of Yen Sin's killers are on top of that building," snapped Traile. "The danger is here on this roof."

"Then why are you standing here idle?" stormed Bannister. He made a furious gesture. "You've bungled it from start to finish—had me get rid of my bodyguards—refused to call in the police—"

Traile went after him as he spun around toward his private telephone.

"What are you going to do?"

"Get some real protection up here!" snarled Bannister. "You've let one man be murdered, and I'm likely to be the next!"

"You will be," Trails said sharply, "if you try to send that signal!"

Bannister froze, glaring down at Traile's leveled gun.

"Have you lost your senses?" he said hoarsely.

Traile's dark eyes drilled into the other man's face.

"The game's up, Bannister. You're a good actor—but not good enough."

The millionaire tamed a chalky white.

"You're stark mad!" he cried. "Grab his gun, one of you!"

Johnson jumped toward Traile, but Allen halted him with a brusque command. Traile searched the millionaire, handed a Mannlicher pistol to Eric.

"Keep him covered. Don't let him get near that switchboard. He'd signal Yen Sin's agents down in the hotel—and there may be two or three dozen of them planted in different rooms, waiting to come up here."

Eric's blue eyes were wide with astonishment.

"Then he's really a member of the Invisible Empire?"

"Probably its chief agent in New York," Traile answered. The attack in Lexington Avenue was a fake. Doctor Yen Sin deliberately sacrificed those Chinese gunmen for effect, so that Bannister wouldn't be suspected while he helped to recover the gold skull."

"I tell you you're crazy," fumed the millionaire. "I never heard of him until today—except as the 'Cobra.'"

A cold smile lighted Traile's lean face.

"The secret reports and those other half-truths were clever business, Bannister—but you gave yourself away when you played the role of the Gray Man. You see, while you were unconscious at Kent's home, I found one of the rubber gloves you wore as a Gray Man. Later Allen turned the glove inside out and took the fingerprints. They matched perfectly with those on the report you'd been handling."

Murderous fury leaped into the other man's eyes.

"I knew I should have killed you!"

Traile motioned with the .38.

"Turn around. Face the wall and keep your hands up against it."

Bannister obeyed with an oath. Traile stepped back close to Allen, took from his pocket what appeared to be a thick toy pistol.

"Use this on him if you have to," he whispered. He put the miniature gun on a stand by the F.B.I. man. "We don't want to shoot him. I'm almost positive he's Yen Sin's key man in New York, and if we can make him talk we'll wipe the Invisible Empire off the map."

Allen had his left hand partway out of his coat pocket. He dropped whatever he had been about to withdraw.

"Then you're not ready for—"

"Not yet," Traile said in an undertone. "It's clear that one of the Yellow Doctor's assassins has been smuggled onto the roof. I think I know where he's hiding."

"Then take Murdock and Johnson and go after him," Allen said hastily.

"No, you don't know those devils. If he found he was trapped, he'd be sure to get one or two of us before he died. I've a plan for nabbing him. Give me a minute or so to steal around on the sun-deck side, and get near the gate. Then turn the flashlight away from the garden."

"All right," Allen agreed reluctantly. "But for Heaven's sake be careful."

With a final glance about him, Traile stepped through the door at his right and was soon hidden in the shadows. He had left the flashlight pointed toward the garden so that no one could see beyond it and observe his departure. He tiptoed along in the darkness, with his gun poised for a quick shot. His movements had the stealth of a stalking tiger.

He paused until his eyes were accustomed to the gloom, then went on toward the gate. He was moving now with infinite caution, making sure of each deep shadow. The glow from the flashlight shone through from the other end of the garden. He stopped, crouched down by the gate, waiting for the light to be shifted.

It was turned away in a few seconds, and he could see through the glass door at the farther end. Bannister was still facing the paneled wall, with Eric covering him. Allen and his two men were looking nervously about them. Only the dim light of the colored lanterns shone in the garden.

It was then that Traile noticed that the artificial moon had been turned off. He edged past the gate, moved silently toward the shrine. Within a few feet of it he suddenly halted. Was it imagination, or had a faint sound come from the shadows near the display of Oriental weapons?

He crouched at one side of the shrine, staring toward the spot. A minute passed. He heard Bannister's angry voice, muffled by the glass door, and Allen's curt response. Then silence again, a silence which grew more tense with every passing second.

From somewhere in the penthouse the sweet, musical sound of the chimes was audible again. Bannister at once burst into another angry protest. And in that moment the shrine began to move!

Traile sprang back, flattened himself against the decorated wall of the garden. His suspicion was right. The chimes were a signal to Bannister, controlled from the hiding place of the assassin.

Pivoting at one corner, the shrine swung open on noiseless hinges. Traile held his breath, for it was the side next to him which had swung away from the wall. Motionless, he waited, almost as dark as the shadow where he stood. As the shrine ceased to move, his finger took up the slack of his trigger.

No one appeared. Traile strained his eyes to pierce the darkness back of the shrine. Finally a faint *pat-pat* came to his ears, accompanied by a low, swishing sound. A shadowy figure seemed to rise from out of the floor. Traile watched in brief amazement, then the truth burst on him.

The shrine had concealed a secret stairway to a room on the floor below.

The man ascending the stairs was almost at the top, when, to Traile's dismay, whispering voices sounded from below. The full peril of the situation struck him like a blow. A dozen of the Yellow Doctor's spies must be coming up those steps.

Before he could hurl himself against the shrine, a robed form came into view. Traile's pulses gave a leap.

It was Doctor Yen Sin!

Chapter 9

The Three Hatchets

Traile sprang and rammed his gun against the Yellow Doctor's side, forcing him to block the narrow opening.

"Don't move!" he said fiercely.

For just an instant, fear showed in the Satanic face before him. Then the cold mockery came back to Yen Sin's eyes.

"So you decided to hasten our meeting, Mr. Traile?"

A low, metallic clink sounded from the other side of the garden. Traile half-whirled, trying to watch both directions. There stood a glaring Chinese with a hatchet!

As the man's arm whipped forward, Traile desperately hurled himself sidewise. The hatchet buried itself in the shrine, just beyond his shoulder.

There was a rush of feet, and three men leaped from the stairway as Yen Sin stepped aside. Already off balance, Traile was thrown to the floor. A hand gripped his throat, cutting off his attempt at a shout. He jerked the gun toward the man's head, but it was wrenched away.

As he was held down, one of the men hastily taped his mouth. Two more twisted his arms, then brought him to his feet at the Crime Emperor's low-spoken command. He looked hopefully toward the penthouse door, but Bannister was still haranguing furiously and the muffled sounds of that silent battle had gone unheard.

Doctor Yen Sin calmly surveyed the scene beyond the glass door, from his vantage point in the gloom. Then he turned, spoke in a low tone to a sallow-skinned Eurasian. The half-caste went back toward the secret stairway, reappeared with a girl. As she tore herself free from the man's grasp, Traile recognized the beautiful face of Sonya Damitri. The Yellow Doctor fixed his weird eyes on her.

"You will go with Kang Fu, and do as I instructed."

She turned, hopelessly, with the Eurasian and two more spies closely following. They disappeared to the left of the arched bridge. Doctor Yen Sin nodded to the men holding Traile.

"To the right," he said in whispered Chinese. "And move exactly as I ordered."

Twisting his arms so that he was forced to walk on tiptoe, Traile's captors marched him toward the side of the penthouse. As they neared the door to the reception hall, he saw Allen looking anxiously around the room. Eric had Bannister covered, but the millionaire's head was twisted around and he was snarling something over his shoulder.

There was a sudden crash from the dim-lit garden. Allen jumped toward the glass door, and his two agents raced after him. Instantly, Traile's captors plunged into the hall with him, and at the same moment Sonya appeared from the sun-deck side, two armed men crouching back of her.

Eric had whirled as the two doors burst open. He jerked his gun toward the left, then stood paralyzed at sight of Sonya. Bannister was on him in a flash. He snatched at the Mannlicher, and in a moment both men were on the floor, struggling for the gun.

Allen and the two agents had spun around at the first sound of action. After an instant of amazement, Murdock sprang at the men holding Traile. Something buzzed by Traile's shoulder, and a dark spot appeared on Murdock's cheek. The agent jerked to a stop, his eyes bulging. His lips opened convulsively, then his knees buckled and he fell to the floor.

The glass door was swiftly flung open, and three Burmese dacoits leaped at Allen and Johnson. With an ape-like jump, one of the thugs hurled himself onto Johnson's back. The agent went down with the dacoit's fingers locked around his throat. His head struck the floor with a thump, and he ceased to move.

The two other thugs seized Allen before he could turn. His right arm was wrenched around behind him with bone-breaking force. He groaned, let his pistol fall. With despair, Traile saw that Bannister had gained possession of the Mannlicher. Eric was writhing on the floor from a vicious blow to the groin.

As the millionaire jumped up, there was momentary silence. Then from the shadows of the garden, Doctor Yen Sin slowly came forward. He glanced around the room without emotion, turned to Bannister.

"If you had followed instructions," he said icily, "this would not have been necessary."

Bannister had a frightened look.

"I didn't have a chance. Traile was onto me."

The Yellow Doctor smiled contemptuously.

"I am afraid you lack in courage, my friend."

"I'm in a spot," the millionaire said harshly. "He guessed the truth this morning. They've probably got agents here in the building, ready to grab me."

"They will not trouble you," replied Doctor Yen Sin. He looked sardonically at Allen. "You should have advised at least some of your men not to ask for rooms on the topmost floors."

Allen lunged at him.

"You yellow devil! What have you done with them?"

His captors hauled him back. The Crime Emperor regarded him without expression, then turned.

"And you, Mr. Traile—I gave you credit for more ingenuity."

Traile met his gaze coolly. Doctor Yen Sin looked at his taped lips, beckoned to Traile's guards.

"Bring him closer." When they had obeyed, he fixed his strange, tawny eyes on Traile's face. "I shall not insult your intelligence by any pretense about your eventual end. But I shall make it more swift in exchange for certain information."

He signaled to the Eurasian who had used Sonya as a shield.

"Kang Fu, assist Mr. Traile to speak."

The half-caste approached with an ugly grin. Traile set his jaw. Kang Fu reached out, brutally ripped away the tape. It was like a fiery lash across Traile's lips, but he made no sound. Doctor Yen Sin gave him a thin smile.

"An heroic display of bravery, Mr. Traile. And now, the first question. What is the drug which enables you to go without sleep for so long?"

Traile made no answer. The Yellow Doctor frowned, then nodded to the men holding him. They forced Traile against the wall, twisting his arms until it seemed they would be torn from their sockets. Drops of perspiration stood out on his forehead. He saw Sonya close her eyes, shuddering. A red-hot agony shot through his ever-wakeful brain. Then, abruptly, that torturing pull was relaxed.

"He would faint before he would speak," he heard Yen Sin mutter. "Hold him there. We will try another way."

Eric Gordon had almost recovered from Bannister's cruel blow. As he staggered to his feet, the Crime Emperor gestured curtly to the millionaire.

"Keep him back." He turned, whispered to the Chinese whom Traile had seen in the garden. The man disappeared, came back quickly. In spite of himself, Traile started as he saw the three hatchets the Chinese carried.

"I see you have heard of this ceremony," Doctor Yen Sin said with ironic amusement. "Perhaps you are ready to answer the first question?"

Traile's eyes shifted for an instant to Allen. The F.B.I. man was looking helplessly toward the door to the darkened sun deck. Yen Sin quickly followed Traile's glance, but Allen was now staring at the floor. The Yellow Doctor motioned to the waiting hatchet man. Eric burst out with a cry as the Chinese took his position.

"Tell him, Michael, for God's sake!"

"It would do no good," said Traile, grimly.

His captors drew away on each side, still holding his arms twisted so that he was forced against the wall. He felt them tense as the Chinese drew back the first hatchet.

"One," said Doctor Yen Sin.

The hatchet man's arm shot forward. With a savage swish, the weapon dashed toward Traile. For an instant it seemed aimed straight between his eyes. Then it whirled past and thudded into the wall an inch from his head. The quivering handle almost touched his ear.

The Crime Emperor looked at him with slitted eyes.

"Now, are you ready to speak?"

Before Traile had time to reply, Eric recklessly leaped past Bannister and struck at Traile's nearest guard.

"Get back!" Traile groaned. "They'll only kill you, too."

Kang Fu and a dacoit seized Eric, pulled him away. Doctor Yen Sin gazed shrewdly from Traile to Eric.

"I perceive a swifter means for my purpose," he said to the millionaire.

At his brief order, Traile was hustled to one side, and Eric pinioned against the wall in his place. Sonya Damitri ran toward Yen Sin, but he thrust her aside. She turned wildly to Traile.

"You brought him into this! Save him, while there is yet time."

The Crime Emperor's yellow face darkened.

"I will have no more of your maudlin sympathy for this young American!" He gave a command, and a ferocious-looking Burmese dragged the girl out of the way. Then he turned to Traile. "Her suggestion, however, is the one I intended to make. I will free him when it is safe—if you answer my two questions. The first one you know. The second: What are the names of the other Q-men?"

Traile faced him stonily.

"I'll tell you, if you include Allen and Johnson—and swear by the bones of your ancestors that you'll free them."

Yen Sin's brows drew together, then he looked around at Allen and the unconscious agent on the floor.

"I agree," he said, shortly. "But they will not be liberated in this country."

"Very well," Traile said. "Then here are your answers. There is no drug—I can't sleep because of an accident. And there are no other Q-men."

The Yellow Doctor stiffened, then the pupils of his queer eyes dilated with a violent passion.

"Do you expect me to believe such childish lies?" He whirled to the hatchet man, pointed at Eric. "Finish your work!"

"Wait!" Traile cried. "I've told you the truth!"

But the second hatchet was already whizzing through the air. Sonya screamed, and Traile turned cold with fear. Then, with a tremendous surge of relief, he saw that Eric fortunately had not tried to dodge. The hatchet had half-buried itself in the paneled wall, so that now the two handles kept his head from moving.

Yen Sin turned a look of icy hate on Traile.

"A last chance! Answer—or the third hatchet goes squarely between the others!"

Eric's boyish face was white, but his lips were trying to smile.

"All right!" Trails said desperately. "I'll tell you! Here in the back of my wristwatch . . . a supply of the capsules. . . ."

Yen Sin's tawny eyes lit with an eager flame. At his sharp command, the dacoit at Traile's right loosened his grasp to unstrap the watch. Traile jerked his arm free, swung with all his might at the man on his left. The thug's head snapped back from the blow, and Traile dived madly for the toylike gun on the stand. The first dacoit plunged after him with a snarl of fury. Traile snatched up the miniature weapon, but the Burmese was on him before he could touch the trigger. Three more of Yen Sin's agents were racing to the spot. Traile slammed his fist into the dacoit's throat. As the man's clawing hands fell away, he pressed the stubby trigger.

Zip! A cartridge of tear-gas concentrate burst against the wall. The steamy vapor almost instantly filled the room. Traile had frantically rolled to one side as he fired the tear-gas gun. He could dimly see two of Yen Sin's men pile over the one he had crippled.

He jumped up, trying to find Allen. Pandemonium had broken loose behind him. Suddenly, a hazy figure bumped against him. A wild blow scraped along his shoulder, and he heard the other man curse. "Allen!" he rapped out.

"Where's the doorway?" the agent said thickly.

Above the clamor, Yen Sin's choked voice rose with a note of rage. Traile pushed Allen in the other direction. He heard the door being opened, felt cool air on his face. The senior agent stumbled outside. He was about to follow when a vague figure lunged into view. There was a gun in the man's extended hand. He sprang, tore the weapon away. The man struck blindly at him, missed. Traile landed a left hook, sent him reeling backward.

Three shrill blasts of a whistle sounded from outside on the roof. They were echoed almost at once from somewhere near. Trail dashed through the doorway, leaped to one side. A fan of white light was spreading from the top of the building diagonally across the street. It flashed toward the hotel roof, then the whistle blasts were drowned by the piercing shriek of a siren.

Chapter 10

Death Trap

Three or four staggering figures were brilliantly outlined in the glare which swept the garden. One of the spies dashed his hand across his streaming eyes. When he caught sight of a man crouching down by the guard wall, he fiercely lifted his arm. Traile fired as he saw the man's raised hatchet.

The Chinese lurched back, and the weapon dropped from his hand. He doubled over and fell. At the same moment Allen's whistle shrilled another signal. From behind the floodlight, a tommy gun began to chatter. The spies in back of the hatchet man wilted to the floor.

As the tommy gun ceased to pound, the siren on the office building roof lessened its piercing shriek. From four directions, down in the streets of Manhattan, that shriek was quickly answered. Traile plunged back into the penthouse. The tear gas was being sucked out toward the garden, and he could now see the spot where Eric had stood. The two hatchets still protruded from the wall, but there was no sign of the young Southerner.

He stumbled over Murdock's body, felt his way toward the glass door. Panicky voices were audible from the direction of the elevator. He ran toward it, but the doors had clicked shut. Through the steamy whiteness of the tear gas, the observation panel was visible. He dimly saw the group which had crowded into the car. Eric was struggling in the hands of Kang Fu and Bannister. In front of Sonya and two Asian spies stood Doctor Yen Sin.

Traile leaped toward the switchboard, but the car was starting to move and the special switch had no effect. He had a last glimpse of the Crime Emperor's malignant face, then the car dropped from sight. He dashed out onto the roof. Allen was shouting through cupped hands at the squad of F.B.I. men over on the other building.

"Come on!" Traile broke in. "They've escaped and taken Eric!"

They ran past the bullet-torn gate. The dying hatchet man cursed them in Chinese as they hurried by. Traile turned to the shrine.

"Why not the emergency doors?" exclaimed Allen.

"Bannister has the keys," clipped Traile. He poised the automatic, went down the narrow stairway, with Allen close behind. They emerged in one room of a special suite. A faint odor of incense was perceptible. The windows were closed and shuttered.

There were signs of hasty flight as they rushed through the other rooms, but no one was to be found. Traile led the way into the hall, just as more Federal agents with drawn guns appeared from the main elevators.

"Three of you stay up here—hunt for Clark's squad!" yelled Allen. "The rest of you come along!"

They ran to the first elevator. As it shot downward, Traile fired a query at the frightened operator.

"How many doors to the penthouse shaft?"

"Three beside the roof, sir," gasped the man. "Top floor, main, and the garage in the basement."

"Drop us all the way," rapped Traile. He looked at the leader of the squad. "Are the police closing in all right?"

"Yes, but I heard some shooting," the agent replied quickly.

When they reached the basement, they found a scene of wild confusion. An F.B.I. man dashed up to Allen, a bloody arm dangling.

"That Chinese and the bunch with him got away! They had a dozen men in cop's uniforms hidden around, and we got mixed up."

Traile ran toward the first car he saw, a big Duesenberg. Allen and three others tumbled in after him, and he sent the machine speeding up the ramp. As they reached the street, the senior agent called something to a policeman in a squad car. The police machine roared ahead, with Traile keeping close behind.

"They're heading toward the East River," Allen yelled above the howl of the sirens.

Traile grimly nodded.

"They'll probably make for Bannister's yacht on Long Island Sound."

Three minutes later the cars halted by a small dock opposite Blackwell's Island. Nearby, a motorcycle man lay dead under his wrecked machine. Another officer, obviously wounded, ran toward them, cursing and groaning.

"They jumped on an express cruiser! They're going up the West Channel!"

A red-faced lieutenant ran for the nearest phone, but it was several minutes before a fast police boat swung in to the dock. Traile and the others jumped aboard, and the boat sped ahead in pursuit of the fleeing craft. As they approached Ward Island, the man at the searchlight gave an exclamation.

"There's a cruiser runnin' without lights!"

The darkened boat heeled to pass through the narrow channel. As it swung into the wider expanse of the East River, south of the Bronx, a green rocket flared up from the gloom beyond. It was answered by a red rocket from the commuting-cruiser. The searchlight man swerved the beam toward the spot from which the green signal had come. It fell on a trim white yacht some distance ahead.

"Hell!" he said, startled. "Why, that's the *Mahola*—Mark Bannister's yacht!"

"Keep your light on the cruiser," Traile said hurriedly. "They'll trick us if they get the chance."

After one attempt to dodge out of the beam, the commuter ploughed straight for the yacht. Traile frowned thoughtfully at the smaller craft.

"There's something odd about this," he muttered to Allen. "Even if we can't stop it, they must know that the yacht will be caught before it reaches open sea."

"Maybe we've been fooled," Allen said hastily. "They might not be aboard at all."

Traile looked at the searchlight man.

"Have you a pair of field glasses?"

"Right back of you," said the policeman.

Traile focused them on the cruiser. He could see several figures in the luxuriously-fitted cockpit at the stern. Doctor Yen Sin was looking back impassively. He saw Kang Fu, and he thought he glimpsed Eric lying helpless at the half-caste's feet. Bannister seemed to be arguing with the Crime Emperor. Yen Sin shook his head, turned, and vanished within the cabin.

"Don't let them out of your beam for a second," Traile said to the man at the searchlight. "The most dangerous criminal alive is in that boat."

"You don't mean Bannister?" the cop gasped.

"No, but he's mixed up in it," said Traile.

"The yacht's lights are going on," exclaimed Allen.

Traile stared toward the vessel. Only the riding lights had been showing. Now, lighted portholes made two strings of yellow dots along the yacht's side. Another light glowed, up on the bridge, then a powerful searchlight swept around toward the police boat. Traile shielded his eyes, tried to see ahead. In a moment the searchlight shifted, and he saw another police boat putting out from Flushing Bay. He raised the field glasses. Bannister and Doctor Yen Sin were now visible up in the deckhouse, as the cruiser slowed and turned in toward the *Mahola*. He saw Kang Fu and another man drag Eric to his feet.

The commuting-boat passed out of sight on the other side of the yacht. Traile put down the glasses, took out his pistol. Allen followed suit, and his agents made ready to board the yacht. It was almost two minutes before they reached the *Mahola*. The police boat quickly circled around to the starboard side, where the express cruiser rode at the gangway, empty.

Muffled voices could be heard aboard the yacht. Traile flung a warning to the agents and police as he jumped to the gangway.

"Be on guard every second! That devil's up to something. And watch out for the girl and a prisoner."

The deck was deserted. The boarding party spread out, covering port and starboard sides. Traile and Allen hastily searched the bridge, ran aft toward the main salon. The muffled voices seemed to come from below. There was a peculiar background of throbbing, metallic sounds which made the words and the source hard to determine.

Several of the others joined them as they stole down the main companionway. The dining saloon was as empty as the one above, but the voices were somewhat louder. Suddenly Traile heard Bannister's grating accents.

"But it cost me more than a million!"

"What are a few millions compared with all there is at stake?" came the calm retort of Doctor Yen Sin.

Traile ran silently into the passage aft of the dining saloon. As the others followed, Bannister's harsh voice was heard again in protest.

"I tell you this is madness! We'll be trapped like rats!"

"Traile and those others will be the ones to die," the Yellow Doctor's response sounded from behind a closed door. "After that, no one will guess the truth."

"You butcher!" Traile heard Eric Gordon cry out fiercely. "They'll get you some day for—"

The sound of a blow cut off his outburst. Traile motioned swiftly for the agents and police to group themselves at the sides of the door.

"Is the device ready?" Yen Sin's query came from inside.

"Not quite," said a nervous voice Traile did not recognize. "We want to be sure."

There was a sudden, high whine, like the whistle of a speaking tube. Then someone rasped a few indistinct words.

"What's the matter?" Traile heard Bannister demand.

"It's Fricht!" shrilled the man with the nervous voice. "The fool says he left his set on the—"

"Michael! Allen!" Eric's shout rang out behind the door. "For Heaven's sake get off—"

The words ended with a moan, then there was stark silence. Traile seized the doorknob, jumped aside and flung open the door. The agents and police sprang forward with guns leveled. Then they stared at each other in blank amazement.

There was not a soul in the stateroom.

The red-faced lieutenant jumped inside, yanked open the only visible door. Nothing but a small closet was revealed. He kicked at the back of it, looked around in bewilderment.

"Where th' hell did they go? They couldn't have got out that porthole."

Traile gazed hurriedly around the stateroom. A box of long, black cigarettes lay on the lower bunk, near a small leather satchel like a man's overnight kit. He bent over the partly open satchel. For a moment he stared, puzzled, at its contents. Then a dismayed look flashed across his face and he whirled around.

"Get off the yacht as fast as you can!"

There was a hasty exodus from the stateroom. Traile snatched up the leather satchel and dashed after Allen.

"What is it?" the senior agent said breathlessly.

"No time to explain!" snapped Traile.

As the police charged out on deck, the alarmed coxswain started his engine. The officers and F.B.I. men tumbled down the gangway. While the last ones were still scrambling aboard, the coxswain started the boat ahead. Allen made a flying leap and landed on the gunwale.

"Hold on!" he bellowed. "There's one more man."

The distance was already too great for Traile to hurdle. He turned and raced toward the bow. Gripping the satchel, he jumped. The impact tore one of the handles from his grasp. Before he could prevent it, the satchel opened and spilled its contents into the water. He let go of the bag, struck out toward the police boat. He was within twenty feet of it when a terrific explosion blasted the night.

The concussion, coming through the water, was like a sudden blow. The police boat rocked violently, and he saw several men thrown down. He dived to escape the heat of the blast, came up on the other side of the boat. As Allen helped him aboard he could partly make out the wrecked yacht through the glare of the flames.

The explosion had occurred amidships, and had practically blown the vessel apart. Even as he looked, he saw it break in two, and the blazing bow and stern sections begin to sink. He cast an anxious glance across the water.

"Where's the boat that came out from Flushing?"

A grizzled harbor policeman shook has head.

"They were lying close by the port side. I'm afraid they're done for."

"Poor devils," muttered Traile. He turned to the coxswain. "You'd better head for the darkest spot along shore. We may not be safe yet."

The boat swerved. Allen stared at Traile.

"But what could happen now? Yen Sin and his mob are at the bottom of the East River—what's left of them."

Traile gazed toward the sinking wreckage of the yacht. He slowly nodded.

"I still don't get all of it," Allen said. "I can see that Yen Sin and those others must have been behind some secret door in the stateroom. But what was he trying to do?"

Traile looked at the listening policemen. "He intended to finish us, but the scheme backfired," he replied briefly.

Allen shivered.

"That poor kid Gordon—and the girl! It's hard, their going like that. But at least we're rid of the Yellow Doctor."

The grizzled harbor man eyed Traile curiously.

"What gets me, how did you know it was goin' to happen?"

"I read the first lines of a message in that satchel," Traile answered. "That gave me the hint."

"Well, thank God for that!" said the policeman fervently.

But as he went forward, Traile drew Allen away from the other men.

"Can you stand a shock?" he said in an undertone.

"Huh?" said Allen. "What do you mean?"

"I want all the others to think that Doctor Yen Sin is dead."

Allen started.

"But, good Lord, he couldn't be alive! You yourself—"

"I admitted he was at the bottom of the East River. Unfortunately, he's very much alive. The *Mahola* was torpedoed."

"Torpedoed!" Allen whispered dazedly. Then he swore under his breath. "Jumping Jupiter! That lost-submarine business that's been in all the papers!"

"Exactly," Traile said in a grim voice. "I read about it myself, and never even suspected. But it's a perfect means of escape for Yen Sin, if he's too closely pressed."

"I see it now," Allen said savagely. "Bannister's a director of the Lodin Submarine Corporation. He worked it so that a bunch of crooks were in the crew on the test runs, and they took command by force."

"And they've simply been hiding somewhere, or lying submerged in the daytime," assented Traile, "getting signals from Yen Sin or Bannister. Tonight, they evidently came up on the other side of the yacht and took off everyone from the express cruiser. Then they submerged to the periscope, eased off a little way in the dark, and waited until we were on board the yacht before firing the torpedo."

"But how the devil did you get wise?" Allen queried.

"The man called Fricht was evidently on the yacht to maintain communication with the sub and with Dr. Yen Sin. That satchel contained a compact two-way radio. There was an extension cord for plugging in the transmitter, but the receiver was already switched on. Fricht must have left it that way in his hurry to escape."

"So that's how we heard them!" interjected Allen. Then he added excitedly: "We can still capture them. With your Navy connection, you can get some destroyers out in the Sound—they could drop nets or depth bombs, and bottle the sub up—"

Traile gravely shook his head.

"Eric is a prisoner, and I'm going to save him if it's humanly possible. Yen Sin will think he's safe now. He'll hide out for a day or two to make sure, and then shift to some base in New York. He won't give up this mysterious scheme of his, you can bank on that."

"I believe you're right," Allen said quickly. "He wouldn't have built up that group of Gray Men and all his spy system, unless he was after something big."

"Today's events, with that desperate business about the Golden Skull, prove that." Traile gazed soberly across the water toward the distant skyline of Manhattan. "Allen, I've a feeling that we haven't heard the last of the *Chuen Gin Lou*."

Chapter II

The Hong Kong Chest

Outside the Q-Station, purple dusk was settling over the city, but within Michael Traile's heavily curtained den the lights were blazing. Traile stood before the wall map of Greater New York, his eyes on the area known as Chinatown. There was weariness in the pose of his tall figure. The bronze of his face had paled somewhat from long hours spent indoors.

He turned restlessly, went into the adjoining room. His glance passed over Eric Gordon's bed, and the sad look in his eyes deepened. It had been four days since Eric had vanished as a prisoner of Doctor Yen Sin. He slid back the panel which covered the special telephone system that Eric had installed. One of the lines was a direct wire to his contact officer at the Brooklyn Navy Yard. He plugged the connection.

"Q-four," he said, when a voice answered. "Any further report from the patrol?"

"Not a thing, sir," the officer replied. "I'm afraid they got away."

"Hold to the same schedule," said Traile. He disconnected, was about to make another call when his door buzzer rasped. He went to the vestibule, glanced up at the mirror which was placed to show whoever was outside. It was Allen.

"I was about to call you," he said as he admitted the F.B.I. man. A hopeful look replaced his weariness as he saw the excited expression on the lanky agent's face. "What's happened?" he asked.

"It's not about Eric, I'm sorry to say," Allen responded. "But I'll bet my shirt it's connected with Yen Sin."

Traile closed the steel-backed door. Allen was hastily taking an X-ray film from a large manila envelope.

"It's got me going in circles," he exclaimed. "This was just one of several routine jobs done in the last three days. It was an exposure made of an ordinary document we suspected of being a forgery. But here's what we found!"

He lifted the shade from a table lamp and held the film close to the light. Traile leaned down, stared at the X-ray picture. The typewritten words of the document stood out clearly against a blurred but terrible background. A diabolical face looked out from behind the legal lettering, a face like some hideous thing seen in a nightmare. It had no ears, and its lips were stretched wide so that the teeth showed from jaw to jaw. The eyes were two slits of staring horror, and the lower part of the nose had been cut away.

"Good Heaven!" Traile whispered.

"I damn near fell out of my chair when I saw it," Allen said. "Then I realized it was a picture of some poor guy that had been tortured. Right away I thought of Doctor Yen Sin—"

He started, for Traile had snatched the film and was bending over it feverishly.

"I got men after the bird we think forged it," he began, but Traile cut him short.

"We'll have to go to your office! My microscope outfit is in Washington."

"But what's the idea?" said Allen, blankly.

Without answering, Traile held the film almost against the lamp. The face was still blurred, and the close-spaced lines of the document obscured much of the detail, but he could catch the general effect. The cheeks were shrunken, and the emptiness of the eyes was more horrible than it had seemed at first. The forehead, where the legal writing did not cover it, was marked with a mass of tiny blurred scratches or cuts, suggestive of slow, deliberate torture.

"Hellish!" Traile muttered as he straightened up. "Only one man in the world would ever have thought of it."

"What I don't see," said Allen, "is why or how it was ever printed on that paper. It must have been done with invisible ink, of course, but what idea could they—"

He stopped as Traile laid down the film and went rummaging through a pile of newspaper clippings on his desk. In a moment Traile returned with the photograph of a gaunt, elderly man. He penciled the eyes to a solid blackness, blocked out the ears and altered the mouth and nose. As he held it up beside the film, Allen jumped. Then he stared at the name under the photograph.

"Holy mackerel! It's John J. Meredith—the broker who disappeared two weeks ago."

Traile's dark eyes held a strange light.

"It's part of the answer, Allen! We should have seen it before."

He put the film and the clipping into the envelope.

"Look here," said Allen aggrievedly, "if you've figured out something, you might—"

They both turned at the sound of the buzzer. Traile stepped to the door, glanced up at the angled mirror. With a puzzled look, he beckoned to Allen. The F.B.I. man stared up into the glass. The reflection showed a tall Hong Kong chest, beautifully carved, standing on end just outside the door. There was no one in sight.

"How many people know about that X-ray?" Traile whispered.

"Only myself and Griel—the assistant lab man who took Stone's place," Allen replied. "But why?"

"It couldn't be that, then," Traile said, as though to himself. He pushed a wall-switch button, and a bright light outside shone down on the carved chest. Several Chinese characters, painted on the lid, were at once discernible. The mirror reversed them, and it took Traile a few seconds to read the short inscription. Suddenly he turned pale, sprang to unlock the door.

"Watch your step," Allen said tensely. "It may be a trick to bump you off."

But Traile heedlessly ran out, and with shaking hands unfastened the brass clamps of the long lid. It swung open like a door. A broken cry came to his lips as he looked inside. Within the chest was a stiffened form, held upright by three web belts. And the white, waxen face which showed in the light was the face of Eric Gordon!

"My God!" groaned Allen. "They've killed him."

Traile, after his first short cry, made no other sound. He reached out one hand, touched the pale cheek of that pitiful figure. It was as cold as marble. Like a man in a stupor, he turned to Allen.

"We must—take him—inside," he said dully.

They closed the lid, laid the chest flat, and then carried it into the second room. Without a word, Traile unfastened the belts. He shook his head as Allen bent to help him. Unaided, he lifted Eric's body and laid it upon the bed. For more than a minute he stood looking down at the cold white face.

"Eric!" he whispered. "Eric. . . ."

Allen's eyes blurred. But after a moment he touched Traile's arm.

"You can't let it get you like this. He wouldn't want you to—" He stopped, pointed down. "Look, there's something in his left hand."

Traile gently pried apart the stiff fingers. The object was a small glass bottle with a paper rolled up inside. He removed the paper, saw that it was a message in Chinese. Dull anger, then a sudden wild hope, came into his eyes as he read. He whirled toward the den. Allen followed, stared in amazement as Traile switched on his microwave set and fumbled with the dial.

"What's up?" he asked in a startled voice, but the taller man was now springing to the window. A few minutes after Traile threw back the heavy curtains, a low hum became audible from the miniature radio. Then a mocking voice spoke.

"I am sorry, Mr. Traile, to have caused you these moments of grief."

Traile's face was stony, but Allen flushed with rage.

"It's Yen Sin!" he rasped.

Traile motioned him to keep silent.

"You will tilt your desk lamp so that it shines directly on your face," the voice of the Yellow Doctor went on silkily. Then, as Traile obeyed, "That is better . . . stand back a little farther, if you please."

"For God's sake, Traile, are you crazy?" Allen burst out "He'll kill you!"

"The glass is bulletproof," Traile muttered over his shoulder.

"Keep your face toward the window," came the sharpened accents of Doctor Yen Sin. "And for Mr. Allen's benefit, it will do no good to take a bearing on this station. It will be moved within five minutes."

Allen let out an explosive gasp. There was a pause, then the suave voice continued.

"As you probably have guessed, Mr. Traile, you are being observed through binoculars. The observer is a lip-reader. You will enunciate clearly to avoid mistake."

"I understand," Traile said bitterly. "What are your conditions for reviving Eric Gordon?"

There was another pause.

"He is alive now," was the Crime Emperor's calm reply. "However, he is in a state of completely suspended animation, and I am the only one who can restore his normal functions. I warn you, if you attempt to use adrenalin or a similar preparation, it will kill him instantly."

"What are your conditions?" Traile repeated, this time harshly.

Again there was a pause, evidently while the lip-reader relayed his query.

"Your agreement to surrender yourself unarmed, alone, within an hour," answered

Doctor Yen Sin. "The proper drug will then be delivered to any surgeon you designate. It is simply a matter of an intravenous injection."

"I agree," Traile said grimly. He waved Allen back as the agent frantically tried to protest.

He could hear the hiss of the Yellow Doctor's indrawn breath.

"I accept your word," Yen Sin spoke rapidly. "It is now almost eight o'clock. You will leave the building exactly at eight. A private car will draw up at the Forty-eighth Street entrance, and the chauffeur will address you as 'Mr. Scott'—in keeping with your present role. You will enter. He will take you to another location, where one of my agents will give you further instructions. If there is any attempt to have yourself followed, or any variation from this order, your young companion will never awaken."

"I have your sworn word that you'll send the drug?" Traile demanded.

"You have," said the Yellow Doctor, "on condition that you are my—guest—by nine o'clock."

The miniature radio became silent. As Traile stepped out of the glare of light by the window, Allen made a helpless gesture.

"I think you've lost your senses. Eric couldn't be alive. Yen Sin's lying just to get you in his power."

Traile went past him, into the room where Eric Gordon lay. He knelt, felt for a heartbeat, then held a small mirror to Eric's nostrils.

"You see?" Allen said. "There's not a sign of life."

"That doesn't mean anything," Traile answered. "I've seen a Hindu miracle man go into a similar trance and let himself be buried alive for two weeks. But I never could learn what drug he took, or what they used to revive him."

"You can't go through with this," Allen persisted desperately, as Traile took off his shoulder harness. "It's suicide."

Traile looked down at Eric's pallid face while he put on his coat.

"If I don't, it will be murder." He turned abruptly and went into the other room. At the door he paused, looked sharply at the Federal man. "No rush call to your men, to try to have me followed. Until Eric is revived I'm holding you also to the promise I made Yen Sin."

Allen's face was a picture of misery.

"Damn it, I can't let you go, knowing what—"

"You'll help me by staying here with Eric," Traile broke in. "After eight o'clock, call the best doctor you know and have him waiting."

He put out his hand. Allen gripped it, swore helplessly. Traile went to the elevator. He rang, and the car came up. He went down to the lobby, was almost at the Forty-eighth Street side when he remembered about the X-ray film. He had intended to tell Allen. He hesitated, but already the clock was striking eight.

He turned and went on out. A long black car was sliding up to the curb. It was, he thought with grim humor, vaguely like a hearse.

Chapter 12

The Room of the Dolls

In the dimly-lighted chamber which contained the talking Buddha, a panel had silently opened. Doctor Yen Sin paused in the aperture, spoke in Mandarin dialect to someone in the passage behind him.

"I have finished with him. Prepare the scene as I directed earlier, so that it will make the proper impression upon our friends."

"*Tche*, Master," the other man answered hastily.

The Yellow Doctor stepped into the room, and the panel closed behind him. He paused, glanced impassively at the clock, then began to remove the long rubber gloves which covered his hands. There was blood on the tips, and in place of his usual embroidered robes he wore a jacket similar to a surgeon's operating gown, save that it was shorter and was decorated with silken braid.

He laid the gloves aside, was about to remove the surgical gown, when the eyes of the Buddha glowed with white light. Impatiently, he touched a long-nailed finger to a button on the table before him.

"I ordered that all routine reports were to be received by Kang Fu."

"This is an emergency, Master," the half-caste's anxious voice came from the idol. "I believe the man Traile is trying to betray you in spite of his promise."

The Crime Emperor gazed fixedly at the Buddha.

"Condensed report," he directed.

"Followed instructions at his hotel and while being transferred," Kang Fu said hurriedly. "Met Agent Eighty-five at Position E, entered car with her, apparently not followed. No police or Federal men seen on arrival of car outside the Black Dragon, but on descending to the lower floor he was immediately noted by three men, one now identified as Department of Justice operative. The three men have stationed themselves in position to relay signals. One is watching Traile, another is on the balcony, and the third at a window on the rear court."

"Where are Traile and Agent Eighty-five now?" the Yellow Doctor inquired.

"Near the roulette table in the Lotus Room," replied the Eurasian. "Agent Eighty-five was signaled to delay until further instructions."

Doctor Yen Sin turned and looked at the diagram painted on the opposite wall.

"It is a simple problem." He rapidly gave instructions, adding: "Allow ten minutes for Group Seven to get placed. Also, make arrangements to escort Citizens Five and Eight by one of the other entrances instead of through the Black Dragon."

"Citizen Five has already been admitted," came the reply from the Buddha. "He arrived early, and was taken to the usual room."

"Very well, proceed with your orders," directed Doctor Yen Sin.

The light faded from the eyes of the idol. The Crime Emperor gazed down with a thoughtful look on his saffron face. Then with sudden decision, he crossed to the Dictaphone under the painted diagram. He inserted a plug, and one of the lights on the diagram flickered.

"Advise Citizen Five that I will speak with him," Doctor Yen Sin said coldly.

"But, Master, he has not yet arrived," was the quick answer.

The Yellow Doctor stiffened.

"He was admitted some time ago, through Entrance Three?"

"Something must be wrong, Master," the unseen man replied in alarm. "The Frenchman, Lecoste, went to escort him here, twenty minutes ago, but they did not return. I wondered at his being so early—"

The word was broken as Yen Sin snatched the plug from its socket. With a look of rage, the Crime Emperor whirled to the Buddha. He jabbed a button, spoke fiercely in Chinese, then slid open the hidden panel and hurried into the passage. A few seconds later a similar panel opened in one side of a small octagonal room. The section which the Yellow Doctor had entered was almost in darkness. A partition had been built across the center of the room, almost touching the walls on both sides. Back of it was a heavy chair, placed so that the occupant could easily see through the special black glass in the middle of the partition, and yet be invisible from the other side. A microphone and several switches were mounted on a small shelf just under the rectangular black glass.

Yen Sin hurriedly passed through the narrow space between the left side of the partition and the wall. A light shone down on the other half of the octagonal room, revealing three glass panels which formed a bay at the front. The panel at the left had been partly slid back into a niche in the wall. Beyond the three panels a long room with a table and chairs was visible. A ceremonial pedestal stood just inside the center panel.

After one furious glance at the opened section. Doctor Yen Sin turned swiftly toward the front of the partition. Directly under the rectangle of black glass was a cabinet about three feet square. It was almost filled with hideous-faced masculine dolls. There were two rows of them, all dressed in men's attire, like ugly little puppets in some wholly male farce.

On the upper shelf, between the third and fifth doll, was an empty space. Where the fourth puppet had been, two insulated wires had been neatly clipped. As the Yellow Doctor saw the space and the severed wires, a murderous flame blazed up in his tawny eyes. He went to the side of the partition, stepped back of it to where the microphone stood. One talonlike hand raked at a switch.

"Kang Fu!" he rasped out.

"Yes, Master!" came the frightened half-caste's answer.

"Warn all searching parties!" the Yellow Doctor snarled. "Citizen Five and Lecoste have stolen one of the dolls!"

In the softly-lighted Lotus Room, under the ornate restaurant known as the Black Dragon, Michael Traile stood coolly waiting. From the moment he had entered with Iris Vaughan, he had been aware of furtive movements among the group of men and women who filled the room. The wooden-faced croupier at the roulette table, a German by his appearance, was watching him from the corner of his eye.

As another minute passed, Traile turned to the blonde girl beside him.

"Since we are to await the Doctor's pleasure," he said carelessly, "we may as well sit down."

He motioned toward a divan, but Iris Vaughan, who had been nervously watching the other end of the room, shook her head.

"No, we are to go on now," she whispered. Her pretty face was colorless under her rouge. Traile looked down at her, as he followed into the hall.

"One would think you were to be the victim," he said ironically.

Her luminous blue eyes, too bright from opium, took on a certain hardness.

"It is not my fault if you choose to be a fool. You came here of your own free will."

They had turned toward the right. Traile saw three or four men near a door a few yards away. A dark-haired girl in a red evening gown, with a light cloak thrown over her shoulders, was just entering. She glanced around quickly, gave a start as she glimpsed Traile.

It was Sonya Damitri.

For a fraction of a second, her black, mysterious eyes seemed to be trying to convey some message. Then she hurried on into the room. The men near the door closed about Traile as he followed with Iris. His eyes swept quickly about the room. It appeared to be the office for the gambling establishment. A fat Chinese sat behind a desk, a benevolent smile on his face.

He was looking toward Sonya, who had turned to a large wardrobe cabinet at one side, when a muffled cry sounded—apparently from the wall behind the cabinet. In the same instant, the phone on the desk rang shrilly.

Before the Chinese could pick up the instrument, the doors of the cabinet burst open. Sonya gasped and stepped back. A man leaped out, a pair of brass knuckles on each hand. A small, bloody spike protruded from the center knuckle on each hand.

"Lecoste!" Sonya cried out in astonishment. "What are you—"

"Get out of my way!" rasped the Frenchman. He whirled toward the hall. The men near Traile sprang after him. The Frenchman struck viciously with the spiked knuckles. One man fell back with a shriek. Lecoste drove his left fist into another man's face. Suddenly the Chinese gave a screech of terror as a second man appeared from the passage back of the cabinet.

The light showed the rubber mask of a Gray Man. But it was not this which had brought that squeal of terror to the Oriental's lips. His slanting eyes were fixed on a hideous little doll the man carefully gripped in both hands. As Iris Vaughan saw the doll she, too, gave a cry of fear, then turned and fled.

Sonya had leaped back into one corner. The

two remaining men struggling with Lecoste suddenly jumped for the hall. Holding the puppet vertically with both hands, the Gray Man stepped through the cabinet, made for the doorway. In his haste, he stumbled over the doorsill, fell headlong on the doll.

Instantly, there was a flash of rainbow fire. As the weirdly-colored blaze leaped up, Traile threw himself back. A terrific heat swept out after him, then the room began to fill with the rainbow smoke.

The Gray Man's voice rose in a frightful scream, the same frenzied cry which Jim Stone had given before he died. Gasping for breath, Traile felt his way along the wall. Cool air from somewhere led him on. He reached the cabinet, vaguely glimpsed Sonya as she ran into the passage.

He quickly followed. She went down a flight of steps, vanished around a turn. Above the hissing of the Rainbow Death, and the clamor from beyond the office, Traile heard her give a stifled exclamation. He reached the bottom of the steps, saw a heavy door standing ajar. A Chinese lay dead nearby, two ugly wounds in temple and throat showing where Lecoste's knuckle-spikes had stabbed him.

There was a telephone in a small recess just inside the entry. The wires had been cut. Traile stepped over the dead man, looked swiftly along the passage. There was but a single light, and its glow was feeble. He could barely see the girl as she paused before the seemingly solid brick wall at the end. She reached up, pushed at a spot about the height of her shoulder. A section of the brickwork lifted like a gate, and she stepped through. The section descended quickly.

Traile ran to the end of the passage, felt around for the hidden release. One brick moved inward under his hasty pressure, and the gate slid up. He found himself in another passage, wider than the first. It led off into blackness. He listened intently, caught the sound of Sonya's swift footsteps from the dark. Brushing one hand along the wall to guide him, he followed as silently as possible.

The footsteps ceased and he halted immediately. From somewhere back of him, but at a distance, he could hear a commotion. Two shots made muffled reports, and he thought someone screamed.

Then, suddenly, light showed through a vertical crack ahead, as a door was slowly opened. He waited, unmoving. The slit widened into a rectangle, and he saw the girl's slender figure silhouetted in the opening. She looked back into the darkness, then hurried inside. Traile ran on tiptoe, caught the edge of the door as it started to close. In a second he was in the room.

Sonya's back was turned, and she seemed to be looking down in horror at something on a black table. Her figure screened it from Traile's view. He hastily glanced around. One look, and he knew he was in the torture chamber of Doctor Yen Sin.

Back in the gloom stood a darkened suit of armor, with a row of gas jets which could be turned upon it, after some luckless victim was placed inside. From a beam overhead hung a stained pair of saw-toothed leg irons, mute testimony to the manner in which some ill-fated wretch had been suspended in agony. A rack, an iron boot by a forge, and a score of other torture devices gave evidence to the horrors which had taken place within this chamber.

They were all ranged along one side of the room. The other wall was bare, and of an odd, shiny blackness. But Traile had only a moment to inspect it. For Sonya, after that horrified glance down at the table, was turning away. He was at her side in a flash, one hand raised to stop the cry he expected. Her red lips parted in amazement, but only a moan came.

"Are you mad?" she whispered. "Why didn't you escape when you had the chance, up there?"

He started to reply, then he saw the thing on the table. For a second, he thought he was looking again on the mutilated body of Peter Courtland. There, on a decorated black velvet pall, lay a corpse in evening clothes. Like Courtland's, his head had been cut off and sewed on again, backward. Two tall candles shone down on the distorted face of the dead man. And there between them was the Golden Skull!

Traile stared in fascination at the gleaming metal face, while Sonya frantically tugged at his arm. Then he shook her off, took a quick step and bent over the corpse. It was only after a second glance that he recognized the agonized features of Merton Cloyd.

"You must get away," Sonya was saying wildly. "You should never have followed me."

Traile's lean face was cold.

"You know why I am here."

"You can never hope to capture him," she said hopelessly. "He is too well guarded."

Traile's dark eyes bored into her.

"I am not trying to capture Yen Sin. I came to save the man who unfortunately has fallen in love with you."

Astonishment filled her lovely eyes.

"But I don't—" She turned, with a suddenly frightened look. At the same moment Traile thought he heard a faint scuffing from the black gloom of the torture chamber. As he wheeled for an anxious glance, Sonya gasped and seized his arm. But before she could pull him aside, there was a swishing sound from above.

Then a noose flashed down over their heads.

Traile caught desperately at the rope, but it was already tightening about their necks. Sonya was swiftly drawn against him, her white hands futilely clutching at the noose. He had a brief glimpse of a snarling brown face, where a dacoit had crawled out on the beam above. Then a sibilant voice spoke hurriedly, and through the door he had left open came the Yellow Doctor.

A look of disappointment shot over the Burmese's face. He kept the noose taut, but ceased his pull on the rope. Dr. Yen Sin calmly approached, a scalpel gleaming in one claw-like hand.

"You are a few minutes late, Mr. Traile—but since you have already broken our agreement, it is no matter."

"I've kept my word," Traile said, his voice thick from the pressure of the noose against his throat. "I could have escaped when that fire bomb went off."

The Yellow Doctor gave him a sneering smile.

"You are lying. I have already had a report. You followed Sonya through the secret entrance, thinking your agents were close behind you."

Sonya was struggling to widen the noose. She flung an angry look up at the dacoit.

"Clumsy fool!" she said in Hindustani. "I drew him straight under you. You did not have to catch me, too."

"It will be only a brief inconvenience," Doctor Yen Sin said smoothly. "Kang Fu will be here with help in a moment."

He had stopped close to Traile, the scalpel half-raised with a mocking significance.

"I am sorry to tell you, Mr. Traile, that your men have been intercepted."

Traile's face hardened.

"I obeyed your instructions to the letter. If I was followed, I know nothing of it."

The Crime Emperor smiled contemptuously.

"Lies will not help you now. You chose to break faith, and for that, your friend will die."

"I've surrendered myself," Traile retorted fiercely. "I demand that you send the drug to revive him."

Sonya Damitri twisted around, her great black eyes fixed on him with a strange expression. The dacoit up on the beam growled something in his throat. Doctor Yen Sin looked up sharply. In the same moment, light showed through the shiny black wall, disclosing that it was glass. Several figures were moving in the adjoining room. Desperation came over Traile as he saw Kang Fu and three of Yen Sin's killers. In another second, they would be entering through some secret door, and his last chance would be gone.

He stole a look toward the beam. The rope

was pulled halfway around an upright to the ceiling, but the dacoit's eyes were on the Yellow Doctor, as he started to mutter something. Traile's hands shot up and gripped the rope. Doctor Yen Sin sprang forward with a snarl. But that sudden, violent jerk had done its work.

Pulled off-balance, the killer came plunging down headfirst. Yen Sin jumped back just in time. The hurtling form of the Burmese struck against his arm, and the scalpel fell from his hand. Then the dacoit thudded against the floor.

Traile's fingers were frantically widening the noose. As he cast it aside, the Yellow Doctor whirled to seize the knife. Traile crashed into him with a force that sent him back against the wall. Then he snatched up the scalpel and dashed for the door he had entered.

Sonya had sped out into the passage. Traile pulled at the door as he raced past, and it closed to a narrow slit. He was about to run in the direction from which he had come when the girl reappeared, caught at his arm.

"This way!" she whispered tensely.

He hastily followed her around a bend in the bricked tunnel. A connecting passage and two doors were dimly visible in the gloom.

"Take the second door," she said in a low tone. "Hide inside until I can come back."

Her voice rang out in a scream as he sprang into the darkness back of the opened door. He hauled the door almost shut, his pulses pounding as he heard the howls of Yen Sin's assassins in answer to Sonya's cry. In a few seconds there was a rush of feet, then a fierce jabbering of foreign voices.

"The left passage!" he heard Sonya tell them. The snarling voices and sounds of running feet died away. Traile waited, then to his dismay the voice of the Crime Emperor came from only a few feet away. It was harsh with anger.

"If you had signaled from Entrance Three, he would have been caught before this could have happened."

"But the wires had been cut," Sonya protested in a voice that trembled. "And the rainbow fire had so frightened me—"

"Return and find Agent Eighty-five," the Yellow Doctor interrupted coldly. "I wish to question her, after the council meeting."

"I am sure she was not to blame," Sonya began, but Doctor Yen Sin peremptorily cut her short. Traile heard her move away, and after a moment he caught the soft footsteps of the Crime Emperor as he also departed.

He waited a minute, then cautiously opened the door. Indistinct sounds came from both directions outside. He looked back into his hiding place. It was a small room, littered with boxes—some empty, some of them unopened. He saw several trunks, two of them heavily roped. There was another door. He closed the one where he stood, moved across in the dark and tried the other. It was locked.

He stood in the dark, thinking intently. Yen Sin's killers might return and search this area when they failed to find him. It was doubtful that Sonya could get back in time to help him, and he was still not sure of her. At any moment, her dread of the Yellow Doctor might cause her to change her mind.

There was a slim chance that he could escape through the Black Dragon restaurant and return with a huge raiding party. But it was the only way he could see to force Yen Sin to save Eric.

He started to open the door, holding the scalpel partly up his sleeve. Suddenly there was a click from behind him, and without further warning the other door swung open.

There stood one of the Gray Men!

Chapter 13

The Cult of the Golden Skull

As the light from the passage beyond fell on Traile, the Gray Man jumped back with an oath. His right hand plunged under his coat. Traile leaped, whirling the scalpel out of his sleeve. The Gray Man gave a cry of fear, threw himself aside. The blade scraped the edge of the door.

The Gray Man's hand reappeared with an automatic. Traile dropped the knife, seized the arm with the gun. A furious twist, and the weapon clattered to the floor. A muffled howl of pain came through the mouth-slit of the rubber mask. Then Traile's fist crashed on the other man's jaw. The Gray Man staggered, then came back with a snarl.

He swung wildly with his left. Traile shifted, landed an uppercut that sent the Gray Man reeling. Before he could recover, Traile snatched the mask away. The hate-filled eyes of Mark Bannister glared into his.

"I thought so!" Traile said grimly.

With a sudden lunge, Bannister dived at the gun. But Traile had seen the purpose which tensed the millionaire's face. As Bannister's head went down, Traile swung with all his might. There was a crack like a half-muffled shot, and the millionaire sagged to the floor.

Traile bent over him, made sure that the man was not shamming. A hasty glance showed him that Bannister had been alone. The passage through which he had come ended with a dark glass door, of the type which he had seen before. The wall was decorated with red-and-gold circles. He closed the door, took out his cigarette lighter and lit it. With this to guide him, he cut the rope from one of the trunks. After a quick scrutiny, he removed Bannister's coat and tie, then bound the unconscious man. He substituted the millionaire's tie and coat for his own, pressed the adhesive edges of the rubber mask onto his face, and dropped Bannister's gun into his pocket. There was a signet ring on the millionaire's right middle finger. He slipped it onto his own.

A minute later he stepped out into the other passage. He had left the millionaire concealed as much as possible behind the boxes and trunks, and had improvised a gag. If luck were with him, he would be out of the secret base and on his way to phone for help before Bannister recovered or was found.

They were about the same height, and though Bannister was slightly heavier, the difference would not be easily noticed. In the left lapel of the millionaire's coat was a peculiar little ribbon which Traile suspected was a mark of identification. That and the gray mask should carry him through.

He was nearing the door to the torture chamber when he saw a similar door about twenty feet farther on. It was open, and a stolid Chinese was following another of the Gray Men inside.

Traile paused, waiting for the door to be closed, but it remained open. He started on, intending to pass by hastily. But before he could reach it, the door to the torture chamber slid silently back, and the candlelight from the gruesome scene within fell squarely upon him.

The man who had opened the door was Kang Fu. He looked sharply at Traile, then glanced at the ribbon in his lapel. Then he turned and spoke toward the center of the gloomy room.

"Here he is now, Master."

The malignant face of the Yellow Doctor appeared in the candle glow. He beckoned imperiously to Traile.

"Come in, I have a final instruction for you."

Traile's heart sank. If he attempted to escape now, the alarm would be flashed before he could reach the entrance. He stepped inside, and Kang Fu closed the door. The Crime Emperor motioned the Eurasian out of earshot.

"I am anticipating trouble with Citizen Ten," he said in an ominous voice. "He is already in the Council Room. Go in and keep close watch on him until the others arrive. Do not forget your part. You, also, are supposed to be an unwilling member of the Empire."

"I know," Traile said in a harsh tone which closely resembled Bannister's voice.

The Yellow Doctor's weird eyes probed at his masked face.

"There is no occasion for fear about tonight's affair," he said impatiently, "if that is what troubles you. My men are searching, and Traile cannot escape. The deaths of Citizen Five and Lecoste have already been covered. Nothing can ruin our plans now."

Traile silently nodded. Doctor Yen Sin gestured to Kang Fu.

"When you have played the role of escort for Mr. Bannister, bring me one of the skull seals."

The half-caste looked at the gruesome display on the table, and Traile saw that the Golden Skull was gone.

"It has been returned to its proper place," the Crime Emperor said curtly. "I decided not to use it, as long as Traile knows the way into this room and is still at large."

At the mention of Traile's name, Kang Fu's sallow face took on an ugly expression. He looked significantly at the torture devices.

"When he is captured, Master, I hope you will let me take part in—"

"We will speak of that later," Doctor Yen Sin halted him. He waved a yellow claw, and the Eurasian opened the door. Traile followed him out into the passage. His hand closed around the butt of Bannister's gun as they started on, but his plan was abruptly thwarted. A searching party with flashlights was coming through the tunnel, and a burly Sikh was now standing guard at the secret gate in the brick wall.

The door through which the other Gray Man had gone was still open. Kang Fu stepped aside to let Traile precede him. Traile entered, a helpless feeling coming over him that some irresistible Fate had him in its hands. Then he thought of the cold, white face of Eric Gordon, and the grim set came back to his jaw.

The room he had entered was not unlike the reception room of a small club, except that there was an Oriental touch to the furnishings. A thickset Chinese with horn-rimmed glasses began to open a record book on a desk, but after a second glance at Traile he stood up and drew aside a tapestry. A narrow corridor lay beyond. It was only about twelve feet in length, and as Traile neared the other end a solid door noiselessly opened.

It closed behind him as he went in. He looked back and saw that Kang Fu had disappeared. Then he heard a sound and glanced around. The Gray Man he had already seen was turning hastily. Traile guessed that he had been trying to peer through one of the sections of dark glass which formed the wall.

The man stared at him through the eye-slits of his rubber mask, then abruptly seated himself near the end of a long table. Traile saw that numbers had been neatly painted on the table, running in sequence from 1 to 16. The Gray Man had seated himself before the number 10.

Traile moved his eyes swiftly about the room. The walls on his right and left were composed of the peculiar black glass. Steel uprights divided the glass into sections six feet wide, and these were further divided into squares, so that they appeared like huge, dark French windows. He could see nothing beyond them.

At the other end of the room was a clear glass bay, formed of three heavy panels connected by metal frames and extending upward at least nine feet. This bay closed off the space behind it. Directly back of the center glass panel was a tall ceremonial pedestal. There was a round hole in its top.

A light was shining at an angle from the high ceiling. Its rays slanted down on the front of a wide partition behind the glass bay. In the middle of this partition, and just under a black rectangle, was an open-faced cabinet. Traile barely hid a start as he saw it. The cabinet was almost filled with ugly little puppets like the one which had caused the Rainbow Death.

There was something gruesomely suggestive about the faces of those hideous dolls. He stepped forward, moving carelessly, aware that sharp eyes were probably observing him from behind the dark glass walls. The Gray Man at the table jerked around as he passed.

"Be careful, you fool!" he said in a harsh whisper.

The door at the rear of the council room opened before Traile could reply. Two more of the masked men appeared. Kang Fu and two Chinese were briefly visible before the door closed. The newcomers stared at the cabinet, then silently took places at the table.

Traile sat down in front of the space marked *9*. His chair was the first on the left, at the end near the glass bay. Citizen Ten was at his right, and the other men were seated across the table and farther down. The one at the space marked *6* looked again at the cabinet, and Traile saw him tremble.

The man's eyes seemed to be fixed on a puppet in the lower right-hand corner. It was a grotesque little figure, perhaps a foot high, with a bald, ugly head too large for its body. On the front of its tiny shirt was a red splotch, like a drop of blood, as though the puppet represented a man who had been stabbed.

The heads of the other dolls were also too large for their bodies, each being about the size of a man's clenched fist. Their lips and nostrils were sewn together with thread, and their eyes were tiny, vacant slits.

A wave of horror suddenly swept over Traile. He had been partly prepared; Allen's X-ray film had hinted at the fate of Meredith. But that frightful puppet show turned him sick and cold, as he realized the truth about those hideous dolls.

Each one bore the shrunken head of a murdered man!

Behind the rubber mask an icy perspiration bathed Traile's forehead. For a moment he thought that nausea would overcome him. But by a tremendous effort he controlled his sickened stomach.

A terrible fascination drew his eyes back to the puppets. He had seen shrunken heads before, in the Jivaro Indian country of South America. He had even witnessed the grim procedure which followed a head-hunting raid upon an enemy tribe. The slitting of the scalp from the hairline to the back of the neck . . . the removal of the skull . . . the sewing up of the scalp, the mouth, nostrils, and ears to retain the hot sand which kept the features intact while the empty head was boiled and toughened.

That had been bad enough, even in a savage atmosphere, with the victims as deadly as their killers. But this horrible display before him almost froze his blood.

The rear door opened again, and seven other Gray Men entered. He saw each one look toward the shrunken heads, and in more than one man's hasty stare he read despair and horror.

Without a word, the masked men took their seats. Only their strained breathing broke the hush of the room. Traile watched them from behind his mask, saw their tight-clenched hands, saw their bodies go taut with fear. The tension swiftly increased.

From somewhere behind the glass bay came the sharp clash of a gong. Every man at the table jumped. As Traile jerked around he saw a dim light shine up through the hole in the tall, carved pedestal. Then, slowly, a gleaming object moved up into view.

It was the Golden Skull.

The jangling clash of the gong faded away. Traile gazed at the leering face of the skull, concealing a shudder as he thought of its grim secret. He started in spite of himself as an almost toneless voice came from those golden jaws.

"It is unfortunate that two more members of the *Chuen Gin Lou* will be absent—permanently."

The words were somewhat muffled by the thick glass, but Traile recognized the voice of Yen Sin.

"Citizen Five bribed an agent of the Invisible Empire," continued the voice from the Skull. "He attempted to withdraw from the *Chuen Gin Lou*, but met with a misfortune. His end was—colorful."

The man next to Traile shivered. Traile looked at the cabinet. He was close enough to see two severed wires where the death's-head doll had been fastened. It was obvious that an alarm had been disconnected. He remembered that Sonya had mentioned "rainbow fire." Evidently Doctor Yen Sin had placed a chemical bomb inside each puppet, arranged so that a slight impact or even tilting would set it off.

"The absence of Citizen Thirteen will be explained later—if necessary," the Yellow Doctor went on sibilantly. "But you have been summoned here for more important matters."

Traile heard a click, then one section of the dark glass swung back. A light went on in a vault, at the front of which was a large stack of engraved certificates.

"Citizen Seven, you will examine a few of the exhibits," directed the Invisible Emperor.

The Gray Man addressed went quickly to the vault. He picked up three or four of the certificates.

"They're bonds!" he exclaimed. "Good Heaven, there must be—" He broke off, hastily turned. "They're stolen! These four were stolen in the Union Trust robbery a year ago!"

"Your memory is excellent," came the mocking reply from the Skull. "You need not examine the rest. They are in the same category."

Three or four of the Gray Men gasped. Traile looked in amazement at the pile of bonds. There were, he knew from his reading of financial journals, almost a billion dollars' worth of stolen bonds in the United States. Normally only a small portion would ever be recovered or sold as legitimate bonds through dishonest brokerage houses. But it was plain that the Yellow Doctor had, through his vast criminal empire, drawn the larger part of the stolen securities from their various hiding places. The possibilities staggered his already taut brain.

"Details are unnecessary," he heard the silky voice of the Invisible Emperor. "The bonds will be equally divided, for sale through your banks and brokerage offices. It will be forty-eight hours before the truth is generally known. By that time—"

"But, my God!" cried Citizen Seven. "The losses have already been paid by the insurance companies. The market will have to absorb them again—it'll mean a panic worse than Twenty-nine!"

"I am not interested in the stock market of America," the hidden Chinese said coldly. "Here are my orders: As rapidly as the bonds are sold, they will be converted into foreign securities or jewels, as I direct, and these will be delivered to me by—"

"You're mad!" the man next to Traile broke in furiously. "It'll wreck the country—ruin us all—"

"Silence!" rasped the Invisible Emperor.

But Citizen Ten whirled frantically to the others.

"You damned fools, are you going to let him finish us? We'll be ruined—they'll jail us for—"

The crash of the unseen gong cut him off. He turned, shaking, looked toward the Golden Skull. There was a dead silence as the reverberations of the gong ceased. Then the Crime Emperor spoke in an icy tone.

"Perhaps you would rather go to the electric chair for—murder!"

"You tricked me into killing him!" the Gray Man said hoarsely. "By Heaven, I'll take my chances with the police!"

Traile had slid his hand into his pocket, was watching tensely. If the rest should rebel, there might be a chance. . . .

"May I suggest," said the Invisible Emperor softly, "that you turn and look to your right?"

The Gray Man turned, went rigid. Diagonally across from the vault, another section of the dark glass had opened, revealing the torture room.

Though Traile had already seen the mutilated corpse, a chill ran down his spine. For beside the dead man's bier was a small guillotine. Its slanting blade was raised, and an ugly stain covered most of the surface. In the background stood several shadowy figures.

"Cloyd!" the Gray Man whispered as he saw the face of the corpse. He stumbled backward, dropped heavily into his chair. There was a sound like a faint mirthless laugh from the Golden Skull.

"I trust," said the Invisible Emperor, "there will be no further objections."

Citizen Ten buried his head in his hands. No one spoke. The pivoted black glass slowly began to close. It was almost shut when from the passage beyond the torture chamber came the unmistakable crack of a pistol shot.

Traile and several of the Gray Men leaped to their feet. A bright light flashed on in the torture chamber, as the waiting assassins whirled and ran for the passage. Then the Yellow Doctor's voice crackled from the amplifier back of the Skull.

"There is no cause for alarm. My men have obviously captured a certain spy who has been hiding in the base."

Traile was tightly gripping his gun. This might be a break. . . .

There was a sound of fierce struggling, as the passage door opened. A dozen of Yen Sin's killers appeared, dragging two men with them. Traile silently groaned as he recognized Bill Allen. His eyes shifted to the second man. Then he stood paralyzed.

It was Eric!

Chapter 14

The End of the Rainbow

In that first moment, Traile almost doubted his senses. But the Yellow Doctor's men viciously shoved their captive into the lighted room and he saw that it was really Eric Gordon. The deathly pallor of the young Southerner's face had given way to an angry flush. He struggled for a second more, then gave up as he saw its futility.

Traile had instinctively sprung forward to help the two men. But even as he moved, he knew it was useless, and he transformed his hasty action into a threatening gesture. Bill Allen cursed him, and Eric gave him a savage glare.

Behind the group of dacoits and Chinese killers, three more figures appeared. Traile's eyes narrowed back of his mask slits as he saw Sonya with Iris Vaughan and Kang Fu. Then he realized that she could not know him, that she had not been able to return to the room where he had left Bannister.

Above the confusion and jabber of voices, an imperious command came from the Golden Skull.

"Kang Fu! Explain this, at once!"

The Eurasian gave Eric a half-frightened look.

"How this man recovered, I do not know, Master. He was leading the other one and a small party of Federal agents when Agent Eighty-five gave the alarm."

There was a short pause, and Traile guessed that the Yellow Doctor was looking at Iris Vaughan through the rectangle of dark glass. The blonde girl came forward nervously.

"I know nothing about it, either—I had just come in through Entrance Four when I saw them." She motioned to Sonya. "I was with her. We were unable to use the other entrance."

"What of the raiding party?" the Invisible Emperor demanded.

It was Kang Fu who answered.

"One of the men was killed. The others were shut out when we closed the emergency door. Group Five has been sent to take care of them."

"And you still have not found the man Traile?" came a harsh query from the Skull.

"No, Master, but it is impossible for him to escape," the half-caste replied hastily.

"Are you blind?" the Invisible Emperor said in a fierce voice. "This entire affair is a conspiracy. Traile must have known about the drug, and he simply pretended to agree to my conditions so he could discover the base. He must have some scheme to wreck our plans."

For just an instant, Traile caught a strange look in Sonya Damitri's eyes. And he knew, then, how Eric had been revived. But Kang Fu's next words snatched his mind from that brief, revealing thought.

"These two must know what Traile intends, Master. It should not take long to make them talk."

Before Yen Sin could answer, Traile wheeled toward the glass bay, which he knew shielded the Yellow Doctor.

"Let me handle them!" he said harshly. "I've a score to settle with both of them."

He thought Sonya gave a start, in spite of his careful imitation of the millionaire's grating voice. But Yen Sin's answer showed he had no suspicion.

"Very well. Kang Fu will assist you."

The tight band about Traile's heart relaxed. He nodded to the Eurasian. Kang Fu ordered the others to take out the captives. They were starting through the opening to the torture room when, without the slightest warning, the black section next to the vault whirled open on its pivots.

Then Mark Bannister plunged into the room.

There was a stifled exclamation from the Golden Skull, and Yen Sin's voice rose sharply.

"Kang Fu! Seize the man behind you!"

Traile had leaped back the instant he saw the millionaire. Kang Fu spun around, halted with a look of stupefaction. As Traile snatched the gun from his pocket, the half-caste frantically raised his own pistol.

Traile fired. Kang Fu crumpled to the floor, and Bannister tripped over him in his furious charge. One of the Gray Men clawed out at Traile's gun hand. Traile jumped sidewise, stiff-armed the other man.

In the sudden confusion, Eric had wrenched away from his captors. He hurled himself down after the half-caste's pistol. A squealing Chinese dashed after him with a knife. Traile drilled the man through the head. Two of the Gray Men were almost on him. He slammed the gun across the nearer one's face. The rubber mask tore away, and he saw a bleeding gash. Before the second man could reach him, Traile hurdled a chair and jumped onto the table.

The second Gray Man dived at his legs. He lashed out, kicked the man squarely under the jaw. The Gray Man fell back with a strangled groan. Traile flung a look upward, crouched swiftly. Two dacoits were springing to drag him down. He leaped up with all his might, hooked one arm over the top of the center bay-panel.

Clutching hands caught at his feet. He kicked backward, felt the thud of his foot against flesh. His gun had slipped from his fingers as he grasped the top of the panel, pulled himself up with both hands.

Back of the partition, the Satanic face of the Yellow Doctor glared up at him. As he swung himself over the top, a gun blasted from the council room. The slug made a scar on the bulletproof panel, ricocheted up to the ceiling. Two more shots crashed against the glass as he dropped.

He struck beside the pedestal. Like a flash, the black rectangle was slid aside, and the snout of a peculiar weapon appeared. He threw himself flat. There was a twang, and a steel dart buried itself in the side of the pedestal.

As Yen Sin stepped back to recharge the gun, Traile sprang to his feet. The Crime Emperor stabbed a yellow talon at a button before him, and the right bay-panel swished back into a niche. Bannister and four of Yen Sin's killers darted toward the opening.

Traile whirled, snatched one of the death's-head dolls, and hurled it toward the onrushing men. A horrified look shot into Bannister's face as he saw the doll. He jumped back, threw his hand before his eyes.

There was a brilliant flash, an awful shriek, and the millionaire was lost in a blaze of rainbow fire. As Yen Sin ran toward the other side, Traile saw two more groups closing in. He turned desperately and jerked one after another of the deadly puppets from their wires. He saw it land near the pile of bonds, and another blaze up near the door to the torture room.

Alarm bells were clanging wildly above the hiss of the Rainbow Death and the screams of the dying men. Traile felt his way toward the right side of the bay, to the opening through which Yen Sin had fled.

The Yellow Doctor's voice was audible from across the council room. As Traile ran toward the spot, the rainbow-colored smoke billowed from a sudden draft. He saw three or four of the Gray Men dashing to the rear door. Eric was hastily drawing Sonya away from the flames. The girl swayed against him, almost overcome by the smoke.

From the direction of the torture chamber came a rattle of shots. Traile heard Allen bawl out something. He stumbled on toward the other side of the room. The pile of stolen bonds was blazing fiercely, and by the glare he caught sight of a yellow-robed figure only a few yards away. He leaped to bar the opening for which Doctor Yen Sin was making.

The Crime Emperor gave a baffled snarl, whirled to spring past the heap of blazing paper. The flames eddied out at him. He threw one hand before his eyes, staggered back into the vault. Then a wall of rainbow fire billowed across the entrance.

The heat forced Traile back. His feet struck Kang Fu's body, and as he tripped to his knees he saw part of a rainbow skeleton where Bannister had dropped. The draft sent the smoke whirling again, and he saw Allen and two of his men charge into the room, handkerchiefs held at their nostrils.

"Watch out!" Traile called huskily as they neared him. "Some of Yen Sin's killers may still be here."

The senior agent limped toward him, his mouth bleeding, and his clothes torn half from him.

"I think the damned rats are taking it on the lam," he said thickly through the handkerchief. "The other four squads finally got in through that restaurant."

Traile quickly pointed toward the blazing bonds.

"Keep your guns trained over there. Yen Sin was forced into that vault, and if the smoke hasn't stupefied him he'll try to make a break."

A few moments later Eric reappeared, but Sonya was not to be seen. Eric met his gaze firmly.

"I helped her escape, Michael."

Traile slowly nodded.

"I understand, old man. I hope she gets away."

Allen came over to them, stared through one of the open bay panels at the Golden Skull. Traile saw the grimace which came to his face.

"Then you guessed what that X-ray was?"

The F.B.I. man grimly wagged his head.

"Yes, when Eric told me that Yen Sin had threatened to cut off his head and shrink it for a present to you. I doped it out then that Meredith's shrunken head was inside the Golden Skull. Poor old Stone must have made an X-ray of the skull at the last minute. Nobody thought to look at the machine, and later that forged paper must have been X-rayed on the same film."

"It was a fiendish idea," Traile muttered. "The original Golden Skull was probably only a symbol, but Yen Sin used this one to keep a merciless hold on the Gray Men. I suspect that he tricked a number of them into helping kill Meredith, perhaps by threat of torture. Those tiny marks we saw on the forehead are undoubtedly the signatures of the members of the cult."

The two agents with Allen stared in astonishment at Traile's revelations. He peered toward the vault, went on hurriedly.

"After cutting off the ears, and mutilating the nose and lips, he simply plated the head with gold to hide what it really was and to preserve the signatures. That way, he had the corpus delicti and what amounted to a signed confession in form he could easily move from one place to another. Those other shrunken heads evidently served the same purpose for later members. If someone hadn't taken the real skull to

Courtland's home instead of one of the seals, we'd probably never have known."

"Well, we'll know plenty when we get another X-ray and read those names," muttered Allen.

Traile's dark eyes were grave.

"We'd better forget the Gray Men, Allen. To publish the truth about this might wreck Wall Street—and the country. Better by far to drop the skull in that fire and destroy the heads later. After all, most of those poor wretches were driven by torture and blackmail, and tricked into those killings."

Allen looked fiercely toward the vault.

"I hope I'm there to see it when they strap Yen Sin in the chair!"

Traile shook his head.

"I'm afraid it's too late for that. The yellow butcher is probably roasted by now."

To his amazement, the voice of Yen Sin replied sonorously through the Golden Skull.

"I am sorry to disappoint you, Mr. Traile. The 'Yellow Butcher' is quite alive—as you may soon regret."

Traile stared down, speechless.

"Holy Moses!" Eric breathed. "He's evidently got away to some other part of the base."

Traile looked grimly at the now silent skull.

"That vault looked solid. But I was a fool not to suspect there was another entrance."

"We might still catch him!" grated Allen.

A briefly bitter smile came to Traile's lips.

"No, he wouldn't have mocked us if he hadn't already been safe." Then his eyes fell on the colored flames consuming the stolen bonds. "But there's one thing certain. He'll find no pot of gold at the end of that rainbow."

Villains: Multiple

We Are All Dead

BRUNO FISCHER

THE MULTITALENTED BRUNO FISCHER (1908–1992; sometimes recorded as 1995) began his writing career as a contributor to literary journals, which were as nonlucrative in the 1930s as they are today. When he discovered pulp magazines, he knew he had found his home and produced more than three hundred stories between the late 1930s and the late 1950s.

Under his own name but even more frequently using the pseudonyms Russell Gray and Harrison Storm, Fischer gravitated toward stories of terror in the short-lived subgenre known as "weird menace" pulps. Deformed and depraved villains were abundant, as were beautiful women to stalk, torture, and terrorize—frequently saved by stalwart heroes, although not always, which maintained a level of suspense.

When censors pressed for a shutdown or tempering of that violent horror market, Fischer learned to write crime stories for such pulps as *Black Mask*, *Dime Detective*, and *Real Detective Tales*, among many others. As the pulps began to die in the late 1940s, he became one of the first authors to switch to the paperbacks that had pushed the magazines aside and published twenty-five novels, about half of which were published by various hardcover houses, though his most successful book was a Gold Medal paperback original, *House of Flesh* (1950), which sold nearly two million copies.

A lifelong Socialist, he was the editor of *The Socialist Call*, the official weekly of the Socialist Party, until his pulp writing was too great a drain on his time and energy. He retired in order to divide his time between New Mexico and a Socialist cooperative community in New York's Putnam County.

"We Are All Dead" was originally published in the May 1955 issue of *Manhunt*.

WE ARE ALL DEAD

Bruno Fischer

I

THE CAPER went off without a hitch except that Wally Garden got plugged.

There were five of us. My idea had been that three would be enough, figuring the less there were the bigger the cut for each. But Oscar Trotter made the decisions.

Looking at Oscar, you might take him for a college professor—one of those lean, rangy characters with amused, intelligent eyes behind horn-rimmed glasses. He sounded like one, too, when he didn't feel like sounding like somebody else. Maybe he'd been one once, among all the other things he'd ever been.

But there was no question of what he was now. He could give the toughest hood the jitters by smiling at him a certain way, and he could organize and carry out a caper better than any man I knew.

He spent a couple of weeks casing this job and then said five men would be needed, no more and no less. So there were four of us going in soon after the payroll arrived on a Friday afternoon. The fifth, Wally Garden, was cruising outside in a stolen heap.

Wally was far and away the youngest of us, around twenty-three, and he wasn't a regular. I didn't know where Oscar had picked him up; somebody had recommended him, he'd said. It must have been somebody Oscar had a lot of confidence in because Oscar was a mighty careful guy. Wally was supposed to be very good with a car, but I think what made Oscar pick him was that he was moon-faced and clear-eyed and looked like he was always helping old ladies across streets.

Protective coloration, Oscar called it. Have one appearance during the job and another while making the getaway.

So there was the kid, and Oscar Trotter who could pass for a professor, and Georgie Ross who had a wife and two children and made like a respectable citizen except for a few days a year, and Tiny who was an old-time Chicago gorilla but could have been your kindly gray-haired Uncle Tim.

As for me, I'd been around a long, long time in thirty-four years of living. I'd almost been a lawyer, once. I'd almost married a decent woman, once. I'd almost . . .

Never mind. I was thirty-four years old

and had all my features in the right places, and whenever Oscar Trotter had a job I was there at his side.

Wally Garden's part was to swipe a car early in the afternoon and pick us up on a country road and drop us off at the factory and drive slowly for five hundred feet and make a U-turn and drive slowly back. He picked out a nice car—a shiny big Buick.

The factory manufactured plastic pipe. It was in New Jersey, on the outskirts of Coast City where real estate was cheap. The office of the large, low, sprawling plant was in a wing off by itself. From that wing a side door opened directly out to a two-lane blacktop road that had little traffic. There was an armed guard who arrived with the payroll and stayed until it was distributed, but he was an old man who was given that job because he couldn't work at anything else.

Oscar decided it would be a cinch. And it was.

We were in and out in seventy seconds—five seconds under the schedule Oscar had worked out. We barged in wearing caps and T-shirts and denim work pants, and we had Halloween masks on our faces and guns in our hands. Tiny had the guard's gun before the sluggish old man knew what was up. Seven or eight others were in the office, men and women, but they were too scared to cause trouble. Which was just as well. We weren't after hurting anybody if we could help it. We were after dough, and there it was on a long table in an adjoining room, in several hundred little yellow envelopes.

Seventy seconds—and we were coming out through the side door with two satchels holding the payroll, pulling off our masks and sticking away our guns before we stepped into the open air, then striding to the Buick Wally Garden was rolling over to us.

Some hero in the office got hold of a gun and started to fire it.

The newspapers next day said it was a bookkeeper who had it in his desk. One thing was sure—he didn't know a lot about how to use it. He stood at a window and let fly wildly.

None of the slugs came near us. Anyway, not at the four of us out in the open he was firing at. But he got Wally who was still a good twenty feet away. Got him through the car window as if he'd been an innocent bystander.

The car jerked as his foot slipped off the throttle and it stalled and stopped after rolling a few more feet. Through the windshield we saw Wally slump over the wheel.

Oscar yelled something to me, but I knew what to do. Sometimes I could think for myself. I ran around to the left front door.

The shooting had stopped. No more bullets, I supposed.

Wally turned a pale, agonized face to me as I yanked open the car door. "I'm hit," he moaned.

"Shove over," I said.

He remained bowed over the wheel. I pushed him. Oscar got into the car through the opposite door and pulled him. Groaning, Wally slid along the seat. Georgie and Tiny were piling into the back seat with the satchels. There was plenty of screaming now in the office, but nobody was coming out, not even the hero. I took Wally's place and got the stalled engine started and away we went.

Sagging between Oscar and me on the front seat, Wally started to cough, shaking all over.

"Where's it hurt, son?" Oscar asked gently.

Wally pushed his face against Oscar's shoulder, the way a frightened child would against his mother's bosom.

He gasped, "I feel . . . it stabs . . . my insides . . . bleeding."

He was the only one of us wearing a jacket. Oscar unbuttoned it and pulled it back. I glanced sideways and saw blood soaking a jagged splotch on the right side of his shirt. It looked bad.

Nobody said anything.

2

Tiny sat twisted around on the back seat watching through the rear window. It wasn't what was behind us we had to worry about as much as what was ahead. Pretty soon there would be roadblocks.

We traveled three and two-tenths miles on that road, according to plan. Then I swung the Buick left, off blacktop and onto an oiled country road running through fields and woods.

It was a bright spring afternoon, the kind of day on which you took deep breaths and felt it was good to be alive. Beside me Wally Garden started to claw at his right side. Oscar had to hold his hand to keep him from making the wound worse than it was.

Again I made a left turn. This time there was no road to turn onto but only an open field. Wally screamed between clenched teeth as the rough ground jounced the car.

Beyond the field were woods—big stuff, mostly, oaks and maples, with a fringe of high shrubs. Two cars, a Ford and a Nash, were where we'd left them this morning behind the shrubs. I rolled the hot car, the Buick, quite a way in among the trees.

It was dim in there, and cool and quiet. Wally's eyes were closed; he'd stopped squirming in agony. He would have toppled over if Oscar hadn't been holding him.

"Passed out?" I asked.

"Uh-huh," Oscar said.

Getting out of the car, he eased Wally's head and shoulder down on the seat. Wally lay on his side twitching and moaning and unconscious.

The Buick was going to be left right here—after, of course, we'd wiped off all our prints. The way we planned it, we'd hang around for two-three hours before starting back to New York in the two other cars. Until then we had plenty of time on our hands. We used some of it to make a quick count of the loot in the two satchels.

When Oscar Trotter had cased the job, he'd estimated that the take would be between forty and fifty grand. Actually it was around twenty-two grand.

What the hell! After a while you get to be part realist and part cynic, if the two aren't the same thing in this rotten racket. Nothing is ever as good as you plan or hope or dream. You're doing all right if you get fifty percent, and don't lose your life or freedom while doing it.

Every now and then I'd leave the others to go over for a look at Wally. The third time I did his eyes were open.

"How d'you feel, kid?"

He had trouble speaking. He managed to let me know he was thirsty.

There wasn't any water, but Georgie had a pint of rye. Wally, lying cramped on that car seat, gulped and coughed and gulped and pushed the bottle away. I thought it probably did him more harm than good.

"I'm burning up," he moaned.

I felt his brow. He sure was.

I went over to where Oscar and Georgie and Tiny were changing their clothes beside the Nash. This would be an important part of our protective coloration—completely different and respectable clothes.

The alarm was out for five men in a Buick, at least four of whom had been seen wearing caps and T-shirts and denim pants. I felt kind of sorry for anybody within a hundred miles who would be in T-shirts and denim pants. But we wouldn't be. We'd be wearing conservative business suits and shirts and neckties, and we'd be driving two in a Ford Georgie owned legally and three in a Nash Oscar owned legally, and why would any cop at a roadblock or toll gate waste time on such honest-looking citizens?

Except that in one of the cars there would be a wounded man. This was one contingency Oscar hadn't foreseen.

I said to Tiny who was standing in his underwear, "Give me a hand with the kid. He'll be more comfortable on the ground."

Oscar stopped buttoning a freshly laundered white shirt. "Leave him where he is."

"For how long?" I said.

There was a silence. I'd put our plight into words. This was as good a time as any to face it.

Oscar tossed me a smile. About the worst thing he did was smile. It was twisted and almost never mirthful.

"Until," he said, "somebody blunders into these woods and finds him." He tucked his shirt-tail into his pants and added hopefully, "It might take days."

Wally was nobody to me. But I said, "We can't do that."

"Have you a better idea, Johnny?" Oscar said.

"You're the big brain," I said.

"Very well then." Oscar, standing among us tall and slightly stooped, took off his horn-rimmed glasses. "Gentlemen, let us consider the situation."

This was his professorial manner. He could put it on like a coat, and when he did you knew he was either going to show how bright he was or pull something dirty.

"The odds are highly favorable," he drawled, "that before midnight we four will be out of New Jersey and in New York and each safe and snug at home. But not if we're burdened by a wounded and probably dying man. We'll never make it. If by chance we do make it, what do we do with him? At the least he needs a doctor. A doctor finds the bullet wound and calls in the police. Perhaps Wally wouldn't talk. Perhaps he will. He may be delirious and not know he's talking." Oscar's smile broadened. "There's no question, gentlemen, that we'd deserve to have our heads chopped off if we stuck our necks out so far."

Tiny said uneasily, "Yeah, but we can't just leave him here to die."

"Certainly not." Oscar's eyeglasses swung gently from his fingers. "He might die too slowly or scream and attract a passing car. There is, I'm afraid, only one alternative."

All right, but why did he have to say it in that mocking, lecturing manner, and why did he have to keep smiling all the time?

Georgie was down on one knee lacing his shoes so he wouldn't have to look at anybody. Tiny was scratching his hairy chest unhappily. I was a little sick to my stomach. And Oscar Trotter smiled.

"Tiny, your knife, please," Oscar drawled. "A gun would be too noisy."

Tiny dug his switchblade knife out of a pair of pants draped over the hood of the Nash. Oscar took it from him and moved to the Buick as if taking a stroll through the woods.

I turned away. I couldn't stop him, and if I could I wouldn't have. I'd seen that kid only twice in my life before today, the first time less than a week ago. I didn't know a thing about him except his name. He was nobody at all to me. But I turned away and my hands shook as I set fire to a cigarette.

Then Oscar was coming back.

"Well, Johnny," he taunted me, "from the first you wanted less men to cut in on the loot, didn't you?"

I had an impulse to take a swing at him. But of course I didn't.

3

Much of the next three days I watched Stella jiggle about Oscar's apartment. She was a bit on the buxom side, but in a cozy-looking, cuddly-looking way. She went in for sheer, tight sweaters and little else, and she had what to jiggle with. She belonged to Oscar.

I didn't know what the dames saw in him. He was no longer young and you couldn't call him handsome by a long shot, but he always had a woman around who had both youth and looks. Like Stella, who was merely the current one. She was also a fine cook.

I was staying with them in Oscar's two-bedroom apartment on Riverside Drive. I'd come down from Boston for that New Jersey caper, and afterward there was nothing to take me back to Boston. Oscar was letting me use the spare room while I was making up my mind whether to stay in New York or push on to wherever the spirit moved me.

On that third day Oscar and I went up to the Polo Grounds to take in a ball game. When Stella heard us at the door, she came out to meet us in the foyer.

"There's a friend of yours in the living

room," she told Oscar. "A Mr. Brant. He's been waiting over an hour."

I stepped to the end of the foyer and looked into the living room. The meaty man sitting on the sofa and sucking a pipe was definitely no friend of Oscar's. Or of mine. He was Bill Brant, a city detective attached to the DA's office, which meant he was a kind of free-wheeling copper.

Oscar touched my arm. "I expected this. Merely the MO. I'll do the talking." He turned to Stella. "Go do your work in the kitchen."

"I haven't any. Dinner's cooking."

"Go find something to do in the kitchen," he snapped.

She flounced away, wiggling almost as much as she jiggled. But the thing is that she obeyed.

Oscar trained his women right. She was used to being sent out of the room or sometimes clear out of the apartment when business was being discussed. She was no innocent, of course, but in his book the less any woman knew, the better. It might be all right to trust Stella today, but who knew what the situation would be tomorrow? So she went into the kitchen and we went into the living room.

"Well, what d'you know!" Bill Brant beamed at me. "Johnny Worth too! Another piece fits into the picture. I guess you came to town for the Jersey stickup?"

"I did?" I said and went over to the portable bar for a drink. I didn't offer the cop any.

"What's this about New Jersey?" Oscar was asking.

"We're cooperating with the police over there. You're a local resident. So was Wallace Garden, who was found dead in the Buick."

"You misunderstood my question." Oscar was using his mocking drawl. "I'm not interested in the jurisdictional problems of the police. I'm simply curious as to the reason for your visit."

"Come off it," Brant said. "That payroll stickup has all your earmarks."

I helped myself to another drink. I hadn't been very much worried, but now I felt better. That, as Oscar had guessed, was all they seemed to have—the MO, the modus operandi, the well-planned, perfectly timed and executed armed robbery that cops identified with Oscar.

"Earmarks!" Oscar snorted. "Do they arrest citizens for that these days?"

"No, but it helps us look in the right direction." Brant sucked on his pipe. "That killing too. It's like you not to leave loose ends, even if it means sticking a knife into one of your own boys." He twisted his head around to me. "Or did he have you do the dirty work, Johnny?"

That was one thing about Oscar, I thought—he did his own dirty work. Maybe because he enjoyed it.

Aloud I said, "What the hell are you talking about?"

Brant sighed. What had he expected, that we'd up and confess all as soon as he told us he had a suspicion? We knew as well as he did that he didn't even have enough to take us to headquarters and sweat us, and likely never would have. But he was paid to try, and he hung around another ten minutes, trying. That got him nothing, not even a drink.

After he was gone, Stella came in from the kitchen and said dinner would be ready soon.

4

Another day passed and another. I was on edge, restless. I took walks along the Drive, I dropped in on friends, I went to the movies. Then I'd come back to Oscar's apartment and there would be Stella jiggling.

Understand me. I didn't particularly hanker for her—certainly not enough to risk fooling around with anything of Oscar Trotter's. Besides, I doubted that she would play. She seemed to like me, but strictly as her husband's friend. She was completely devoted to him.

No, it was just that any juicy dame within constant eyesight made my restlessness so much harder to take.

We were playing Scrabble on the cardtable, Oscar and Stella and I, when the doorbell rang.

It was evening, around eight-thirty. Oscar, of course, was way ahead; he was unbeatable at any game that required brains. Stella was way behind. I was in the middle, where I usually found myself in everything. As it was Stella's turn to play, I went to answer the doorbell.

A girl stood in the hall—a fairhaired, blue-eyed girl in a simple gray dress and a crazy little gray hat.

"Mr. Trotter?" she said.

"You're right, I'm not," I said. "He's inside."

Without being invited in, she stepped over the threshold and closed the door behind her. "Please tell him Mrs. Garden would like to see him."

"Sure." I started to turn and stopped. "Garden?" I said. "Any relative of—"

I caught myself. In my racket you became cautious about naming certain names under certain circumstances, especially when you weren't supposed to know them. There were all kinds of traps.

Gravely she said, "I was Wally's wife." She put her head back. "You must be Johnny. Wally told me about you."

I gawked at her. Standing primly and trimly in the foyer, she made me think of golden fields and cool streams and the dreams of youth.

I said, "Wait here," and went into the living room. Stella was scowling at the Scrabble board and Oscar was telling her irritably to do something or pass. I beckoned to him. He rose from the cardtable and came over to me.

"Wally's wife is in the foyer," I said.

Oscar took off his eyeglasses, a sign that he was disturbed. "He never mentioned a wife to me."

"To me either. He wasn't much of a talker."

"What does she want?"

"Seems to me," I said, "our worry is what does she know. If Wally—"

And then she was in the living room. Having waited maybe thirty seconds in the foyer, she wasn't waiting any longer. She headed straight for Oscar.

"You must be Mr. Trotter," she said. "I'm Abby Garden."

Abby, I thought—exactly the name for a lovely girl of twenty, if she was that old.

Oscar put his glasses back on to stare at her. He seemed as startled as I'd been that such a dish could have been the moon-faced kid's wife. But he didn't say anything to her. In fact, his nod was rather curt. Then he looked across the room at Stella.

Stella was twisted around on her chair, giving Abby Garden that feminine once-over which in a moment took in age, weight, figure, clothes, make-up. Stella didn't look enthusiastic. Which was natural enough, considering that whatever she had the other girl had better.

"Baby," Oscar said to Stella, "take a walk to Broadway and buy a pack of cigarettes."

There were cigarettes all over the apartment. At another time he might have given her the order in one word, "Blow!" but this evening he was being polite about it in front of a guest. It amounted to the same thing. Stella undulated up the length of the room, and on the way her eyes never left the girl. No doubt she didn't care for being chased out for her. But she left, all right.

Me, whenever I told a dame to do anything, she either kicked up a fuss or ignored me. What did Oscar have?

I fixed drinks for the three of us. Abby wanted a rye highball without too much gingerale. Her hand brushed mine as she took the glass from me. That was sheer accident, but all the same my fingers tingled.

"Now then, Mrs. Garden," Oscar said. His long legs stretched from the armchair in which he lounged. "What's your business with me?"

She rolled her glass between her palms. "Wally told me his share would come to thousands of dollars."

"And who," he said, "might Wally be?"

"Please, Mr. Trotter." Abby leaned forward. "We can be open and aboveboard. Wally had no secrets from me. I didn't like it when he told me he was going in on that—that robbery. He'd already done one stretch. Six months for stealing cars. Before I met him." She bit her lower lip. "I tried to stop him, but he wouldn't listen to me."

Oscar looked utterly disgusted. He had no use for a man who blabbered to anybody, including his wife. Wally may very well have endangered us all.

"So?" Oscar said.

"Oh, you needn't worry I told the police. They asked me, of course. They questioned me for hours after they found poor Wally. But I told them I knew nothing about any holdup or who was in it." She gave him a piece of a small smile. "You see, I didn't want to get into trouble. After all, if I'd known beforehand, I was a kind of accessory, wasn't I?"

"So?" Oscar said again.

"There was one detective especially—a fat man named Brant. He kept asking me if I knew you." She looked Oscar straight in the eye. "He said you killed Wally."

"Now why would I do any such thing?"

"Brant said Wally was wounded during the getaway and then you or one of the others killed him with a knife to get him out of the way."

"My dear," Oscar said, more in sorrow than in anger, "can it be possible you fell for that line?"

"Is it a line? That's what I want to know."

Oscar sighed. "I see you're not familiar with police tricks. This is a particularly shabby one. Don't you see they made up this story to induce you to talk?"

"Then he wasn't killed with a knife?"

"No, my dear. The bullet killed him. He died in my arms. Wasn't that so, Johnny?"

"Yes," I said.

5

That word was my first contribution to the conversation, and my last for another while. Nursing a Scotch-on-the-rocks, I sat on the hassock near Abby's legs. They were beautifully turned legs. I looked up at her face. She was drinking her highball, and over the rim of the glass her wide blue eyes were fixed with rapt attention on Oscar, who was, now, being a salesman.

He was as good at that as at anything else. His honeyed voice was hypnotic, telling her how he'd loved Wally like a son, how he would have given his right arm to have saved him after that dastardly bookkeeper had plugged him, how the conniving, heartless coppers were out to make her hate him and thus betray him with that fantastic yarn that he, Oscar Trotter, would either have harmed or permitted anybody else to have harmed a hair of one of his own men.

He was good, and on top of that she apparently wasn't too bright. He sold her and she bought.

"Wally always warned me not to trust a cop." She split a very warm smile between both of us. "You look like such nice men. So much nicer than that fat detective."

Oscar purred, "Then I take it we're friends, Abby?"

"Oh, yes." She put her highball glass down on the coffee table. "And in a way we're partners, aren't we? When will I get my share?"

Suddenly there was frost in the room. The cheekbones ridged Oscar's lean face.

"What share?" he said softly.

"Why, Wally's share. He earned it, didn't he?" She was completely relaxed; she was free and easy and charming. "I read in the papers that there were twenty-two thousand dollars. One-fifth of that—"

"Young lady," Oscar cut in, "are you trying to blackmail me?"

"Not at all. I simply ask for what I'm entitled to. If money is owed to a man who dies, it goes to his wife."

She said that wide-eyed and innocent-faced, her earnest manner holding no hint of threat—merely a young and probably destitute widow wanting to clean up financial matters after her husband's untimely demise.

Huh! A few minutes ago I'd thought she wasn't so bright. Now I changed my mind.

I spoke up. "She's got something there, Oscar."

"You keep out of this."

"Not this time," I said. "I suggest we each give her five hundred bucks."

Oscar pushed his fingers under his glasses to rub his eyes. Then he nodded. He had no choice. We'd be in a bad way if she were to chirp to the cops.

"How much will that come to?" Abby asked me.

"Two grand. Wally wouldn't have gotten a fifth anyway. He was only the driver. Believe me, we're being more than fair."

"I'm sure you are," she said, and gave me a smile.

This was why I'd jumped in to negotiate—to get some such smile out of her, a smile of sheer joyous gratitude. A man has already gone quite a distance with a dame who thinks she's beholden to him for money. And with this one I was after going on and on and maybe never stopping.

"Just a minute," Oscar said.

Abby and I shifted our attention from each other to him.

"Prove you're Wally's wife," he said.

"But I am."

Oscar looked stern. "I know every switch on every con game. We don't even know Wally had a wife. If he did, we don't know you were the one. Prove it."

"Why, of course," she said. "I have my marriage license and other things at home. If you want me to bring—"

"I've a better idea," I said. I wasn't one to pass up any chance when I was on the make. I got off the hassock so quickly I almost spilled what was left in my glass. "I'll go with you right now and look over whatever you have."

"That's so good of you," she said so sweetly that my heart did a complete flip.

Oscar nodded and closed his eyes. When we left, he appeared to have fallen asleep in the armchair.

6

According to the marriage license, they'd been married seven months ago by the county clerk here in New York.

I sat in the only decent chair in the place. Nearby a train rumbled on the Third Avenue El. She didn't quite live in a slum, but the difference wasn't great. There wasn't much to this room, and there was less to the bedroom and kitchen and bathroom. They were all undersized and falling apart.

Wally's cut of the loot would have meant a lot to him and her, if he'd lived through it.

I handed the marriage license back to Abby. She fed me other stuff out of the shoebox on her lap—snapshots of her and Wally, his discharge papers from the army, the deposit book of a joint savings account containing less than fifty dollars, a letter from her mother from somewhere in Iowa complaining because she'd gone and married a man named Wallace Garden whom none of the family had met.

"Good enough," I said.

"How soon will I get the money?"

"Soon as I collect it from the others. Maybe tomorrow."

"Two thousand dollars," she reminded me.

"That's right," I said.

Abby put the lid on the shoebox and carried it into the bedroom. She didn't jiggle and wiggle like Stella. Her tight, slender figure in that trim gray dress seemed to flow when in motion.

I wanted her as I hadn't wanted anybody or anything in a very long time.

Take it easy, I warned myself while waiting for her to return. I could mark myself lousy in her book by rushing. All right, she'd been married to that round-faced kid, who'd been what he'd been, meaning no better than I, and she hadn't acted particularly upset over his death.

But I didn't yet know what made her tick. I only knew that she looked like moonlight and roses and that it would be wise to handle her accordingly. She was already grateful to me. She'd be a lot more grateful when I brought her the two grand. Then would be time enough to take the next step—a big step or small step, depending on how she responded.

So I was a perfect little gentleman that evening. She put up a pot of coffee and we sat opposite each other at the table and she was as pleasant to talk to as to look at. She spoke of her folks' farm in Iowa and I spoke of my folks' farm in Indiana.

When I was leaving, she went to the door with me and put her hand in mine. And she said, "I'll see you soon, Johnny."

"Do you want to see me or the money?"

"Both," she said and squeezed my hand holding hers.

I walked on a cloud clear across town and then a couple of miles uptown to Oscar's apartment. I hadn't as much as kissed her good-night, or tried to, but what of that? My hand still tingled from the feel of hers.

I laughed at myself. Johnny Worth, the cynical hard guy, acting like a love-sick schoolboy! But I laughed at myself happily.

Oscar and Stella were in bed when I let myself in. Oscar heard me and came out of his bedroom in a bath-robe.

"She was Wally's wife, all right," I told him. "Tomorrow I'll go collect the dough from Georgie and Tiny."

"You seem anxious," he said with an amused twist to his mouth.

I shrugged. "We promised her."

"I can read you like a book, Johnny." He nudged my ribs with his elbow. "Make much headway with her?"

I shrugged again.

"I guess not if you're back so early," Oscar said, leering amiably. "I can't imagine what she saw in that punk Wally. She has class. Well, good hunting."

"Good-night," I said and went into my room.

7

Next afternoon I set forth to make the collection for Abby. Oscar had given me his five hundred in the morning, and of course I had my own, so that left Georgie and Tiny to go.

Georgie Ross lived out in Queens, in a neat frame house with a patch of lawn in front. His wife and two teen-aged daughters hadn't any notion of how he picked up extra money to support them. His regular job, as a traveling salesman in housewares, didn't keep him very busy or bring in much income. He had time on a weekday afternoon to be mowing his lawn.

He stopped mowing when he saw me come up the street. He stood middle-aged and potbellied.

"For God's sake," he complained when I reached him, "you know better than to come here."

"Relax. You can say I'm a bill collector."

"Just don't come around, that's all I ask. What d'you want?"

"To collect a bill. Five C's for Wally Garden's widow."

His eyes bugged out. "You're kidding," he said. Meaning, if I knew him, not about the widow but about the money.

I told him I wasn't kidding and I told him about Abby's visit last evening.

"Listen," Georgie said, taking out a handkerchief and wiping his suddenly sweaty face, "I'm not shelling out that kind of dough for anybody's wife. I have my own family to think of. My God, do you know what my two girls cost me? Just their clothes! And my oldest, Dinah, is starting college next year. Is that expensive! I got to hang onto every penny."

"Some of those pennies were supposed to have gone to Wally."

"It's his tough luck he wasn't around to collect." He leaned against the handle of the mower. "I tell you this: we give her two grand now, she thinks she has us over a barrel and keeps coming back for more. Oscar ought to handle her different."

"How?"

"Well, he handled her husband," Georgie said.

That was a quiet, genteel street, and he fitted into it, by looking at him, the way anybody else in sight did. He resumed mowing his lawn.

I tagged after him. "Use your head, Georgie."

"You don't get one damn penny out of me."

I knew I was licked. I'd ask Oscar to try. He could persuade him if anybody could. I left Georgie plodding stolidly behind the mower.

Tiny was harder to find. He was like me, without anywhere to stay put. He was paying rent on a mangy room he'd sublet downtown, but he only slept in it. I made the rounds of the neighboring ginmills. What with lingering in this place and that and shooting the breeze with guys I knew, I didn't come across Tiny until after nine o'clock.

He was sitting wide-shouldered and gray-haired at the bar, drinking beer. He was always drinking beer.

He said, "Gee, am I glad to see you." Picking up his glass, he slid off the stool and we went to an isolated table. "I've been trying to get Oscar on the phone," he said, "but he ain't in. Stella says she don't know where he went." He glanced around. "Johnny, there's been a city dick asking me questions this afternoon. A fat guy."

"Brant?"

"Yeah, that's the name. He's got it, Johnny. He knows who was in on it and what happened to Wally and all."

I thought of Abby.

"Go on," I said.

"Remember last Wednesday when the five of us went over the route in Oscar's car? It was hot and when we came back through the Holland Tunnel from Jersey we stopped for beer on Tenth Avenue. Remember?"

"I remember."

"Somebody that knew us saw the five of us sitting in that booth together."

I let out my breath. Not Abby.

"Who was it?" I asked.

"Search me. This Brant, he wasn't telling. Some goddamn stoolie. He knew four of us—me and you, Oscar and Georgie. The one break is he hadn't never seen Wally before. Brant is one cagy cookie, but I wasn't born yesterday. I figure they showed the stoolie Wally's picture, but he wasn't sure. If he'd been sure, they'd be piling on us."

"That's right," I said. "The cops can't make any move officially unless they can link us to Wally. I saw Georgie this afternoon and he didn't mention being questioned."

"He's been by now, I guess. The way I figure, this stoolie didn't spill till today." Tiny took a slug of beer and wiped his mouth with the back of his hand. "But I don't get it, Johnny. A stoolie sees four of us and a strange guy in a beer joint. What makes this Brant so all-fired smart he can tell from that Wally was the strange guy and we was the ones did the job way over in Jersey a couple days later?"

"Because Oscar is too good."

"Come again?"

"The caper bore the marks of genius," I said, "and Oscar is a genius. Then Brant drops into Oscar's apartment a few days ago and finds me staying there, so he's got two of us tagged. Then he learns we two plus you and Georgie were drinking beer with a fifth guy who could've been Wally Garden, and he's got us all."

"The hell he has! All he's got is thoughts running in his head. He needs evidence. How'll he get it if we sit tight?"

"He won't," I said.

This was a good time to tell him about Abby. I told him.

When I finished, Tiny complained, "What's the matter with Oscar these days? First he lets us all be seen together in a beer joint—"

"I don't remember any of us objected. In fact, I remember it was your idea we stop off."

"Sure, but Oscar should know better. He's supposed to have the brains. Then he don't know the kid had a wife and would blab every damn thing to her. Where'd he pick up Wally, anyway?"

"He never told me," I said. "But there's the widow and we promised her two grand. I want five C's from you."

Tiny thought about it, and he came up with what, I had to concede, was a good question. "You said you saw Georgie this afternoon. Did he shell out?"

"Not yet."

"Expect him to?"

"Sure."

"Bet he don't?"

"Look, Oscar will get it out of him. I'm asking you."

Tiny said cheerfully. "Tell you what I'll do, Johnny. When Georgie shells out, I'll shell out."

And he looked mighty pleased with himself. He had confidence in Georgie's passion for hanging onto a buck.

8

So after chasing around for hours I had only the thousand I'd started out with. Well, that wasn't hay and the evening was young. I could bring the thousand to Abby and tell her it was part payment. She would be grateful. She would thank me. One thing could lead to another—and perhaps tonight would be the night, the beginning.

I took a hack to her place.

Through her door I heard music going full blast. I knocked. No answer, which wasn't surprising considering all the row a hot dance band was making. I knocked louder. Same result. I turned the knob and found the door unlocked.

Abby wasn't in the living room. The bedroom and the bathroom doors were both closed. The band music, coming from a tiny table radio, stopped and a disc jockey's voice drooled. In the comparative quiet I heard a shower running in the bathroom. I sat down to wait for her to come out.

The music started up again. It was too raucous; my mood was for sweet stuff. I reached over the table to turn off the radio, and my hand brushed a pair of horn-rimmed eyeglasses. She hadn't worn them when I'd seen her, but women were vain about such things. Probably only reading glasses.

She'd stopped showering. Now with the radio off, there was no sound in the apartment. Suddenly it occurred to me that I ought to let her know she had a visitor. Thinking she was alone, she might come trotting out without anything on. I wouldn't mind, but she might, and I was still on the perfect little gentleman technique.

I went to the bathroom door and said, "Abby."

"I'll be right out."

I hadn't time to wonder why she hadn't sounded surprised to hear a man in her apartment and why at the least she hadn't asked who I was. The explanation came almost at once—from the bedroom.

"What did you say, baby?" a man called.

"I'll be right out," she repeated.

Then it was quiet again except for the thumping of my heart.

I knew that man's voice. If there was any doubt about it, there were those eyeglasses on the table. A minute ago I'd given them hardly a glance because I hadn't any reason then to take a good look to see if they were a woman's style and size. They seemed massive now, with a thick, dark frame.

The bathroom doorknob was turning. I moved away from there until the table stopped me, and Abby came out. She was wearing a skimpy towel held around her middle and not another thing.

Her body was very beautiful. But it was a bitter thing for me to see now.

She took two or three steps into the room, flowing with that wonderful grace of hers, before she realized that the man standing by the table wasn't the one who had just spoken to her from the bedroom—wasn't the one for whom she didn't at all mind coming out like this. It was only I—I who had been dreaming dreams. Her free hand yanked up and across her breasts in that age-old gesture of women, and rage blazed in her blue eyes.

"You have a nerve!" She said harshly.

Again he heard her in the bedroom and again he thought she was speaking to him. He called, "What?" and the bedroom door opened, and he said, "With this door closed I can't hear a—" and he saw me.

Oscar Trotter was without jacket and shirt, as well as without his glasses.

I had to say something. I muttered, "The radio was so loud you didn't hear me knock. I came in." I watched Abby sidling along the wall toward the bedroom, clinging to that towel and keeping her arm pressed in front of her, making a show of modesty before me, the intruder, the third man. "I didn't expect she was having this kind of company," I added.

He shrugged.

A door slammed viciously. She had ducked into the bedroom, where her clothes would be. He picked up his glasses from the table and put them on.

There was nothing to keep me here. I started to leave.

"Just a minute, Johnny. I trust you're not sore."

I turned. "What do you expect me to be?"

"After all, you had no prior claim on her." Oscar smiled smugly. "We both saw her at the same time."

He stood lean and slightly stooped and considerably older than I, and dully I wondered why everything came so easily to him—even this.

"Next time," I said, "remember to lock the door."

"I didn't especially plan this. I asked her out to dinner. My intention was chiefly business. Chiefly, I say, for I must confess she had—ah—impressed me last night."

This was his high-hat manner, the great man talking down to a lesser being. Some day, I thought wearily, I'd beat him up and then he'd kill me, unless I killed him first.

"You understand," he was drawling, "that I was far from convinced that our problem with her would be solved by giving her two thousand dollars. I had to learn more about her. After dinner we came up here for a drink." That smug smile again. "One thing led to another. You know how it is."

I knew how it was—how I'd hoped it would be with me. And I knew that he had never for one single moment made the mistake of acting the little gentleman with her.

I had forgotten about the money in my pocket. I took it out and dropped it on the table.

"Georgie and Tiny weren't keen about contributing," I told him. "There's just this thousand. You've earned the right to worry about the balance."

"I doubt that it will be necessary to give her anything now. You see, I'll be paying all her bills. She's moving in with me."

"How nice," I said between my teeth. "I'll be out of there as soon as I pack my bags."

His head was bent over the money. "Take your time," he said as he counted it into two piles. "I still have to tell Stella. Any time tomorrow will do." He pushed one pile across the table. "Here's yours."

So I had my five hundred bucks back, and that was all I had. Before I was quite out of the apartment, Oscar, in his eagerness, was already going into the bedroom where Abby was.

I went out quietly.

9

That night I slept in a hotel. I stayed in bed most of the morning, smoking cigarettes and looking up at the ceiling. Then I shaved and dressed and had lunch and went to Oscar's apartment for my clothes.

I found Stella all packed and about to leave. She was alone in the apartment. I could guess where Oscar was.

"Hello, Johnny," she said. "I'm leaving for good."

She wasn't as upset as I'd expected. She was sitting in the living room with her legs crossed and taking a final drink of Oscar's liquor.

"I know," I said. "When's she moving in?"

"Tonight, I guess." She looked into her glass. "You know, the minute she walked into this room the other night I had a feeling. Something in the way Oscar looked at her."

"I'm sorry," I said.

She shrugged. "I'm not sure I am. He was too damn bossy."

I went into the guest bedroom and packed my two bags. When I came out, Stella was still there.

"Johnny," she said, "have you any plans?"

"No."

"I called up a woman I know. She owns a rooming house off Columbus Avenue. She says she has a nice furnished apartment to let on the second floor, with kitchenette and bath. She says the room is large and airy and nicely furnished. A young married couple just moved out."

"Are you taking it?"

"I think I will." She uncrossed her knees and pulled her skirt over them. "Two people can be very comfortable."

I looked at her sitting there rather primly with eyes lowered—a placid, cozy, cuddly woman with a bosom made for a man to rest his weary head on. She wasn't Abby, but Abby was a ruined dream, and Stella was real.

"You and me?" I murmured.

"If you want to, Johnny."

I picked up my bags. "Well, why not?" I said.

10

Stella was very nice. We weren't in love with each other, but we liked each other and got along, which was more than could be said of a lot of couples living together.

We weren't settled a week in the rooming house near Columbus Avenue when Oscar phoned. Stella answered and spoke to him. I dipped the newspaper I was reading and listened to her say we'd be glad to come over for a drink that evening.

I said, "Wait a minute."

She waved me silent and told Oscar we'd be there by nine. When she hung up, she dropped on my lap, cuddling the way only she could.

"Honey, I want to go just to show I don't care for him any more and am not jealous of that Abby. You're sweeter than he ever was. Why shouldn't we all still be friends?"

"All right," I said.

Oscar answered the doorbell when we got there. Heartily he shook Stella's hand and then mine and said Abby was in the kitchen and would be out in a minute. Stella went into the kitchen to give Abby a hand and Oscar, with a hand on my shoulder, took me into the living room.

Georgie and Tiny were there. Georgie hadn't brought his wife, of course; he kept her strictly away from this kind of social circle. They were drinking cocktails, even Tiny who was mostly a beer man.

"Looks like a caper reunion," I commented dryly. "Except that there's one missing. Though I guess we could consider that his widow represents him."

There was an uncomfortable silence. Then Oscar said pleasantly, "Here, sour-puss, maybe this will cheer you up," and thrust a cocktail at me.

I took it and sipped.

Then Abby came in, bearing a plate of chopped liver in one hand and a plate of crackers in the other. She had a warm smile for me—the impersonal greeting of a gracious hostess. Stella came behind her with potato chips and pretzels, and all of a sudden Stella's jiggling irritated me no end.

Abby hadn't changed. There was no reason why I had expected she would. She still made me think of golden fields and cool streams, as she had the first time I'd laid eyes on her.

I refilled my glass from the cocktail shaker and walked to a window and looked out at the Hudson River sparkling under the sinking sun.

"Now that was the way to handle her," Georgie said. He had come up beside me; he was stuffing into his mouth a cracker smeared with liver. "Better than paying her off. Not only saves us dough. This way we're sure of her."

"That's not why he did it."

"Guess not. Who needs a reason to want a looker like that in his bed? But the result's the same. And you got yourself Stella, so everybody's happy."

Everybody was happy and everybody was gay and got gayer as the whiskey flowed. But I wasn't happy and the more I drank the less gay I acted. Long ago I'd learned that there was nowhere a man could be lonelier than at a party. I'd known it would be a mistake to come, and it was.

Suddenly Georgie's face turned green and he made a dash for the bathroom. Oscar sneered that he'd never been able to hold his liquor and Tiny grumbled that the only drink fit for humans was beer and I pulled Stella aside and told her I wanted to go home.

She was not only willing; she was anxious. "Fact is, I don't feel so good," she said. "I need air."

We said our good-byes except to Georgie whom we could hear having a bad time in the bathroom. An empty hack approached when we reached the sidewalk and I whistled. In the hack, she clung to me, shivering, and complained, "My throat's burning like I swallowed fire. My God, his whiskey wasn't that bad!"

"You must be coming down with a cold," I said.

She wobbled when we got out of the hack and she held her throat. I had to half-carry her up the steps of the brownstone house and into our room. As I turned from her to switch on the light, she moaned, "Johnny!" and she was doubled over, clutching at her stomach.

For the next hour I had my hands full with her. She seemed to be having quite an attack of indigestion. I undressed her and put her to bed and piled blankets on her because she couldn't stop shivering. I found baking soda in the kitchen and fed her a spoonful and made tea for her. The cramps tapered off and so did the burning in her throat.

"Something I ate," she said as she lay huddled under the blankets. "But what? We didn't have anything for dinner that could hurt us. How do you feel, honey?"

"Fine."

"I don't understand it. That Abby didn't serve anything to speak of. Nothing but some chopped liver and—" She paused. "Honey, did you have the liver?"

"No. I can't stand the stuff."

"Then it was the liver. Something wrong with it. Call up Oscar and see if the others are all right."

I dialed his number. Oscar answered after the bell had rung for some time. His voice sounded weak.

"How are you over there?" I asked.

"Terrible. All four of us sick as dogs. And you?"

"I'm all right, but Stella has indigestion. We figure it was the chopped liver because that was the one thing she ate that I didn't."

"Could be," Oscar said. "Georgie seems to be in the worst shape; he's sleeping it off in the spare room. Tiny left a short time ago. Abby's in bed, and that's where I'll be in another minute. What bothers me most is a burning in my throat."

"Stella complained of the same thing. First I ever heard of indigestion making your throat burn."

"All I know," Oscar said, "is that whatever it is I have plenty of company in my misery. Abby is calling me."

He hung up.

I told Stella what he'd said. "The liver," she murmured and turned on her side.

That was at around one o'clock. At three-thirty a bell jarred me awake. I slipped out of bed and staggered across the room to the phone.

"I need you at once," Oscar said over the wire.

"Do you feel worse?"

"About the same. But Georgie has become a problem."

"Is he that bad?"

"Uh-huh. He went and died on my hands. I need your help, Johnny."

II

Georgie lay face-down on the bed in the guest room. He was fully dressed except for his shoes.

"Tiny took him in here before he left," Oscar told me. "After that I didn't hear a sound out of Georgie. I assumed he was asleep. Probably he went into a coma and slipped off without waking. When I touched him half an hour ago, he was already cold."

Oscar's face was the color of old putty. He could hardly stand without clinging to the dresser. Abby hadn't come out of the other bedroom.

I said, "Died of a bellyache? And so quickly?"

"I agree it must have been the chopped liver, which would make it ptomaine poisoning. But only Georgie ate enough of the liver to kill him. Abby says she remembers he gorged himself on it." Oscar held his head. "One thing's sure—he mustn't be found here. Brant is enough trouble already."

"This is plainly an accidental death."

"Even so, the police will use it as an excuse to get as tough as they like with us. We can't afford that, Johnny, so soon after the Coast City job. Best to get the body out."

I looked him over. He didn't seem in much better condition than the man on the bed.

"I can't do it alone," I said.

He dug his teeth into his lower lip and then fought to draw in his breath. "I'll help you."

But most of it had to fall on me. I fished car keys out of Georgie's pocket and went looking for his Ford. I found it a block and a half up Riverside Drive and drove it around to the service entrance of the apartment building. At that late hour it was possible to park near where you wanted to.

Oscar was waiting for me on the living room sofa. He roused himself and together we got that inanimate weight that had been pot-bellied Georgie Ross down the three flights of fire stairs and, like a couple of men supporting a drunk, walked it between us out of the building and across the terribly open stretch of sidewalk and shoved it into the Ford. For all we could tell, nobody was around to see us.

That was about as far as Oscar could make it. He was practically out on his feet. I told him to go back upstairs and I got behind the wheel and drove off with Georgie slumped beside me like a man asleep.

On a street of dark warehouses over on the east side, I pulled the car over to the curb and got out and walked away.

Stella was up when I let myself in. She asked me if I'd gone to Oscar's.

"I was worried about them," I told her. "Tiny and Georgie left. Oscar and Abby are about in your shape. How're you?"

"Better, though my stomach is very queazy."

I lay in bed wondering what the odds were on chopped liver becoming contaminated and if a burning throat could possibly be a symptom of ptomaine poisoning. I watched daylight trickle into the room and listened to the sounds of traffic building up in the street, and I was scared the way one is in a nightmare, without quite knowing of what.

Eventually I slept. It was past noon when I woke and Stella was bustling about in the kitchen. She was pretty much recovered.

Toward evening I went out for a newspaper. When I returned, Brant was coming down the stoop. Being a cop, he wouldn't have had trouble finding out where I'd moved too.

"Nice arrangement," he commented. "You shack up with Oscar's woman and Oscar with Wally Garden's widow. This way nobody gets left out in the cold."

"You running a gossip column now?" I growled.

"If I were, I'd print an item like this: How come Johnny Worth's pals are getting themselves murdered one by one?"

I held onto myself. All I did was raise an eyebrow. "I don't get it."

"Haven't you heard? George Ross was found dead this morning in his car parked near the East River Drive."

He had already spoken to Stella, but I didn't have to worry that she'd told him about last night's party and who'd been there. She wouldn't tell a cop anything about anything.

I said, "That's too bad. Heart attack?"

"Arsenic."

I wasn't startled. Maybe, after all, it was no surprise to me. Arsenic, it seemed, was a poison that made your throat burn.

I lit a cigarette. Brant watched my hands. They were steady. I blew smoke at him. "Suicide, I suppose."

"Why suicide?"

"It goes with poison."

"Why would he want to die?"

"I hardly knew the guy," I said.

"You've been seeing him. You were in a beer joint with him a week ago Wednesday."

"Was I? Come to think of it, I dropped in for a beer and there were some guys I knew and I joined them."

Brant took his pipe out of his fat face. "Two days later you and he were both in on that Coast City stickup."

"Who says?"

A cop who was merely following a hunch didn't bother me. We sparred with words, and at the end he sauntered off by himself. He hadn't anything. He couldn't even be sure that Georgie hadn't been a suicide.

But I knew, didn't I? I knew who had murdered him and had tried to murder all of us.

12

Oscar didn't say hello to me. He opened the door of his apartment and just stood there holding onto the doorknob, and his eyes were sick and dull behind his glasses. Though it was after six o'clock, he was still in his pajamas. His robe was tied sloppily, hanging crooked and twisted on his long, lean body. He needed a shave. He looked, to put it mildly, like hell.

I stepped into the foyer and moved on past him into the living room. He shambled after me.

I said, "I suppose Brant came to see you before he did me."

"Yes."

"So you know what killed Georgie."

He nodded tiredly.

"Abby still in bed?" I asked.

"I made her dress and go to a doctor when I learned it was arsenic. Don't want him coming here, not with the cops snooping. Whatever he gives her for it, I'll take too."

"Better not," I said. "Likely she'll mix more arsenic with it."

Oscar took off his eyeglasses. "Explain that, Johnny."

"I don't have to. You know as well as I do why she put arsenic in the chopped liver."

He stood swinging his glasses and saying nothing. He was not the man I had known up until the time I had left the party last night, and it was not so much because he was ill. It was as if a fire had burned out in him.

"Boy, did she sucker you!" I said. "Me too, I admit. But it was mostly our own fault. We knew she didn't fall for your line that you hadn't killed Wally. We kidded ourselves she'd be willing to forgive and forget if we paid her off. We wanted to believe that because we wanted her. Both of us did. Well, you got her. Or the other way around—she got you. She got you to bring her to live here where she could get all of us together and feed us arsenic."

"No," he mumbled. He looked up. "She ate the liver too. She's been sick all night and all day. She's still in a bad way even though she managed to get out of bed and dressed."

"Huh! She had to put on an act."

"No, I can tell. And she wouldn't poison me. Look what she'd give up—this nice home, plenty of money. Why? For a stupid revenge? No. And she's fond of me. Loves me, I'm sure. Always affectionate. A wonderful girl. Never knew anybody like her. So beautiful and warm."

He was babbling. He was sick with something worse than poison, or with a different kind of poison. It was the sickness of sex or love or whatever you cared to call it, and it had clouded that brain that always before had known all the answers.

"Try to think," I said. "Somebody put arsenic in the chopped liver. Who but Abby would have reason?"

"Somebody else." That old twisted smile, which was not really a smile at all, appeared on his thin lips. "You, for instance," he said softly.

"Me?"

"You," he repeated. "You hate my guts for having gotten Abby. You hate her for being mine instead of yours."

I said, "Does it make sense that I'd want to kill Georgie and Tiny and Stella also?"

"There was a guy put a time bomb on an airplane and blew a lot of people to hell because he wanted to murder his wife who was on the plane. Last night was your first chance to get at Abby and me—and what did you care what happened to the others?"

"My God, you're so crazy over her you'd rather believe anything but the truth."

"The truth?" he said and kept smiling that mirthless smile. "The truth is you're the only one didn't eat the liver." He put on his glasses. "Now get out before I kill you."

"Are you sure she'll let you live that long?"

"Get out!"

I left. There was no use arguing with a mind in that state, and with Oscar it could be mighty dangerous besides.

The usual wind was sweeping up Riverside Drive. I stood on the sidewalk and thought of going home to eat and then I thought of Tiny. What had happened to him since he had left Oscar's apartment last night and had dragged himself to his lonely little room? At the least I ought to look in on him.

I walked over to Broadway and took the subway downtown. I climbed two flights of narrow, smelly stairs in a tenement and pushed in an unlocked door. There was just that one crummy room and the narrow bed against the wall and Tiny lying in it on his back with a knife sticking out of his throat.

13

I must have expected something like this, which was why I'd come. There had been four of us involved in the killing of Wally Garden. Now only two of us were left.

I touched him. He wasn't long dead; rigor mortis had not yet begun to set in. She had left her apartment on the excuse that she was going to a doctor and had come here instead.

There was no sign of a struggle. Tiny wouldn't have suspected anything. Lying here sick and alone, he'd been glad to see her—to see anybody who would minister to him, but especially the boss's lovely lady. She had bent over him to ask how he felt, and he must have been smiling up at that clean fresh young face when she had pushed the knife into his throat, and then she had quickly stepped back to avoid the spurting blood.

That was a switchblade knife, probably Tiny's own, the knife Oscar had borrowed from him to kill Wally Garden. Which would make it grim justice, if you cared for that kind of justice when you also were slated to be on the receiving end.

I got out of there.

When I was in the street, I saw Brant. He was making the rounds of Georgie's pals and he was up to Tiny. It was twilight and I managed to step into a doorway before he could spot me. He turned into the tenement I had just left.

I went into a ginmill for the drink I needed and had many drinks. But I didn't get drunk. When I left a couple of hours later, my head was clear and the fear was still jittering in the pit of my stomach.

I'd never been much afraid of anybody, not even of Oscar, but I was afraid of Abby.

It was her life or ours. I had to convince Oscar of that. Likely he would see the light now that Tiny had been murdered too, because who but Abby had motive? If he refused to strangle her, I would, and be glad to do it, squeezing that lilywhite throat until the clear blue eyes bulged and the sweet face contorted.

I got out of a hack on Riverside Drive. The wind was still there. I huddled against it a moment and then went up to the apartment.

Abby answered the door. She wore a sleazy housecoat hugging that slender body of hers. She looked limp and haggard and upset.

"Johnny," she said, touching my arm, "I'm glad you're here. The police took Oscar away."

"That so?" I stepped into the apartment.

She closed the door and tagged after me. "They wouldn't tell why they took him away. Was it because of Georgie?"

"No. I guess they're going to ask him how Tiny got a knife in his throat."

Abby clutched her bosom—the kind of gesture an actress would make, and she was acting. "It couldn't have been Oscar. He wasn't out of the house."

"But you were, weren't you?" I grinned at her. "You got only one of us with the arsenic, so you're using other methods, other weapons. Have you anything special planned for my death?"

She backed away from me. "You're drunk. You don't know what you're saying."

"You blame all four of us for Wally's death. You're out to make us pay for it."

"Listen, Johnny!" She put out a hand to ward me off. "I didn't care very much for Wally. When I married him, yes, but after a while he bored me. He was such a kid. He didn't tell me a thing about the holdup. Not a word. All I found out about it was from the police, when they questioned me later. I heard your name and Oscar's from that detective, Brant. So I tried to make some money on it. That's all I was after—a little money."

"You didn't take the money. Instead you worked it so Oscar would bring you to live with him where you could get at all of us."

"I like Oscar. Honest."

"Don't you mind sleeping with the man who killed your husband?"

She tossed her blonde hair. "I don't believe he did. He's so sweet. So kind."

I hit her. I pushed my fist into her lying face. She'd meant death for Georgie and Tiny, and she would mean death for me unless I stopped her.

She bounced off a chair and fell to the floor and blood trickled from her mouth. I hadn't come to hit her but to strangle her. But something besides fear possessed me. Maybe, heaven help me, I was still jealous of Oscar. I swooped down on her and grabbed her by her housecoat and yanked her up to her feet. The housecoat came open. I shook her and her breasts bobbed crazily and I slapped her face until blood poured from her nose as well as her mouth.

Suddenly I let go of her. She sank to the floor, holding her bloody face and moaning. At no time had she screamed. Even while I was beating her, she'd had enough self-possession not to want to bring neighbors in on us. She started to sob.

I'd come to do more to her, to stop her once and for all. But I didn't. I couldn't. I looked down at her sobbing at my feet, lying there slim and fair-haired, battered and bleeding, feminine and forlorn, and there was nothing but emptiness left in me.

After all, hadn't we killed her husband? Not only Oscar, but Georgie and Tiny and I as well were in a community of guilt.

I turned and walked out of the apartment. I kept walking to the brownstone house, and there in the room Stella and I shared a couple of plainclothes men were waiting for me.

14

They grabbed me, and Stella rose from a chair and flung herself at me.

"Honey, are you in trouble?"

I said dully, "Not much with the cops," and went with them.

For the rest of that night they sweated me in the station house. No doubt they had Oscar there too, but we didn't see each other. They kept us apart.

Sometimes Brant was there, sucking his pipe as he watched the regular cops give me the business. There was no more fooling around. They still had questions about Wally and about Georgie, but mostly they wanted to know about the murder of my pal Tiny.

Once, exhausted by their nagging, I sneered at them like a defiant low-grade mug, "You'll never get us."

Brant stepped forward and took his pipe out of his mouth. "Maybe we won't get you," he said gently, "but somebody else is doing it. Three of you already."

After that I stopped sneering. I stopped saying anything. And by morning they let me go.

Before I left, I asked a question. I was told Oscar had been released a couple of hours before.

I made my way home and Stella was waiting and I reached for her.

But there was no rest for my weariness against her cuddly body. She told me Oscar had been here looking for me with a gun.

"When was this?"

"Half an hour ago," she said. "He looked like a wild man. I'd never seen him like that. He was waving a gun. He said you'd beaten up Abby and he was going to kill you. Honey, did you really beat her up?"

I had taken my jacket off. I put it on.

Stella watched me wide-eyed. "If you're running away, take me with you."

"I'm not running," I said.

"But you can't stay. He said he'd be back."

"Did he?" I said hollowly.

I got my gun from where I'd stashed it and checked the magazine and stuck the gun into my jacket pocket.

She ran to me. "What are you going to do? What's going on? Why don't you tell me anything?"

I said, "I don't want to die," and pushed her away from me.

I went only as far as the top of the stoop and waited there, leaning against the side of the doorway. I could watch both directions of the cheerful sun-washed street, and it wasn't long before Oscar appeared.

He looked worse than he had yesterday afternoon. His unshaven face was like a skeleton head. There was a scarecrow limpness about his lean body. All that seemed to keep him going was his urge to kill me.

Maybe if I were living with Abby, had her to love and to hold, I wouldn't give a damn what suspicions I had about her and what facts there were to back them up. I'd deny anything but my need for her body, and I'd be gunning for whoever had marred that lovely face.

I knew there was no use talking to him. I had seen Oscar Trotter in action before, and I knew there was only one thing that would stop him.

I walked down the steps with my right hand in my pocket. Oscar had both hands in his pockets. He didn't check his stride. He said, "Johnny, I—"

I wasn't listening to him. I was watching his right hand. When it came out of his pocket, so did mine. I shot him.

15

And now we are all dead.

There were five of us on that caper. Four are in their graves. I still have the breath of life in me, but the difference between me and the other four is only a matter of two days, when I will be burned in the chair.

It was a short trial. A dozen witnesses had seen me stand in the morning sunlight and shoot down Oscar Trotter. I couldn't even plead self-defense because he'd had no gun on him. And telling the truth as I knew it wouldn't have changed anything. The day after the trial began the jury found me guilty.

I sent for Stella. I didn't expect her to come, but she did. Yesterday afternoon she was brought here to the death house to see me.

She didn't jiggle. Something had happened to her—to her figure, to her face. Something seemed to have eaten away at her.

"Congratulations," I said.

Stella's voice had changed too. It was terribly tired. "Then you've guessed," she said.

"I've had plenty of time to think about it. Oscar didn't have a gun on him. I know now what he was about to do when he took his hand out of his pocket. He was going to offer me his hand. He had started to say, 'Johnny, I made a mistake.' Something like that. Because he still had a brain. When he'd learned that Tiny had been knifed in bed, he'd realized I'd been right about Abby. But the irony is that I hadn't been right. I'd been dead wrong."

"Yes, Johnny, you were wrong," she said listlessly.

"At the end you got yourself two birds with one stone. You told me a lie about Oscar gunning for me, and it turned out the way you hoped. I killed him and the state will kill me. I've had plenty of time to think back—how that night at Oscar's, as soon as we arrived you hurried into the kitchen to give Abby a hand. Why so friendly so quickly with Abby who'd taken your man from you? I saw why. You'd gone into the kitchen to put arsenic in the chopped liver."

"You can't prove it, Johnny," she whispered.

"No. And it wouldn't save me. Well, I had my answer why you were so eager to take up with me the minute Oscar was through with you. You had to hang around his circle of friends, and you had to bide your time to work the killings so you wouldn't be suspected. You succeeded perfectly, Stella. One thing took me a long time to understand, and that was why."

"Wally," she said.

I nodded. "It had to be. If you'd hated Oscar for throwing you over for Abby, you mightn't have cared if you killed the others at that party as long as you got those two. But there was Tiny's death—cold, deliberate, personal murder. The motive was the same as I'd thought was Abby's. The same master plan—those who'd been in on Wally's death must die. And so it had to be you and Wally."

Stella moved closer to me. Her pretty face was taut with intensity.

"I loved him," she said. "That wife of his, that Abby—she was a no-good louse. First time I ever saw her was when she came up to the apartment to see Oscar, but I knew all about her. From Wally. That marriage was a joke. You wouldn't believe this—you were crazy over her yourself, like Oscar was—but she was after anything wore pants. That was all she gave a damn for, except maybe money."

"I believe you," I said. "You must have been the one who persuaded Oscar to take Wally in on the caper."

"We fell for each other, Wally and I. One of those screwy, romantic pickups on a bus. We saw each other a few times and then planned to go away together. But we hadn't a cent. I knew Oscar was planning a big job. He thought he kept me from knowing anything that was going on. But I knew. Always. And I was smarter. I got a guy who owed me a favor to bring Oscar and Wally together. Oscar took him in on it." Her mouth went bitter. "How I hated the rackets! I wanted to get out of them. I hated Oscar. We had it all figured. We'd take Wally's cut, the few thousand dollars, and go out west and live straight and clean. A little house somewhere and a decent job and children." Her head drooped. "And Oscar killed him."

"He might have died anyway from the bullet wound."

"But not to give him at least a chance!" Stella hung onto her handbag with both hands. "You know why I came when you sent for me? To gloat. To tell you the truth if you didn't know it already and laugh in your face."

But she didn't laugh. She didn't gloat. She looked as sick and tired of it all as I was. She looked as if, like me, she no longer gave a damn about anything.

"It doesn't give you much satisfaction, does

it?" I said. "It doesn't bring Wally back. It doesn't make it easy to live with yourself."

She swayed. "Oh, God! So much death and emptiness. And I can't sleep, Johnny. I've had my revenge, but I can't sleep."

"Why don't you try arsenic?" I said softly.

She looked at me. Her mouth started to work, but she didn't say anything. Then she was gone.

That was yesterday. Today Bill Brant visited me and told me that Stella had taken poison and was dead.

"Arsenic?" I said.

"Yeah. The same way Georgie Ross died. What can you tell me about it?"

"Nothing, copper," I said.

So that makes five of us dead, and very soon now I will join them, and we will all be dead. Except Abby, and she was never part of the picture.

Wasn't she?

Stella was kidding herself by thinking she'd killed Oscar and me. Georgie and Tiny and finally herself, yes, but not us.

I needn't have been so quick with my gun on the street outside the brownstone house. I could have waited another moment to make sure that it was actually his life or mine.

Now, writing this in my cell in the death house, I can face up to the truth. I had shot him down in the clear bright morning because he had Abby.

Villain: Doctor Satan

Horror Insured

PAUL ERNST

PAUL FREDERICK ERNST (1900–1983) was a frequent contributor to *Weird Tales*, notably with his series about Dr. Satan, "the world's weirdest criminal," whose nemesis is the occult detective Ascott Keane. The series ran in the mid-1930s. Ernst claimed that most of these stories, and his other supernatural tales, came to him in dreams so perfectly constructed, which he remembered in the morning, that he merely had to sit down and transcribe them.

Doctor Satan wears a red cloak, red gloves, a red mask, and a skull cap with horns on it. We never learn who (or what) he is. Doctor Satan is assisted by the ugly, monkey-like dwarf Girse and the legless giant Bostiff. Keane is accompanied by his secretary, with whom he is in love, the beautiful Beatrice Dale.

The Doctor Satan series lasted only eight episodes. Ernst created works in a wide variety of genres, including mystery, horror, and, most famously, his pseudonymous hero character, The Avenger, written as Kenneth Robeson. The Robeson byline was used by Lester Dent for a long run of *Doc Savage* magazines, one of the most successful pulps of its time. Because of the tremendous sales in recounting the adventures of "The Man of Bronze," the publisher convinced Ernst to write about "The Man of Steel," The Avenger, which the author claimed was the worst writing he ever did, though fans disagreed and his twenty-four novelettes were later reprinted as paperback books.

"Horror Insured" was originally published in the January 1936 issue of *Weird Tales*; it was first collected in *The Complete Tales of Doctor Satan* (Boston, Altus, 2013).

HORROR INSURED

Paul Ernst

IT WAS NOON. The enormous National State Building hummed like a beehive with the activity of its tenants. Every office spewed forth men and women on their way to lunch. The express elevators dropped like plummets from the seventy-ninth floor, while the locals handled the crowds from the fortieth floor down.

At the top floor an express elevator tarried beyond its usual schedule. The operator paid no attention to the red flash from the starter downstairs signaling the Up cages to start down as soon as possible. He acted as though he was beyond schedules, as indeed he was.

This elevator, though not entirely private, was at the disposal of Martial Varley, owner of the building, whose offices took up the top floor. Others could ride in it, but they did so with the understanding that at morning, noon, and evening the elevator waited to carry Varley, whose appearances at his office occurred with time-clock regularity. Hence, if the cage waited inactively those in it knew why and did not exhibit signs of impatience.

There were half a dozen people in the elevator that paused for Varley to ride down. There was an elderly woman, Varley's office manager, and two secretaries; and there were two big business men who had been conferring with Varley and were now waiting to go to lunch with him.

The six chatted in pairs to one another. The cage waited, with the operator humming a tune. Around them, in the big building, the prosaic business of prosaic people was being done. The glass-paneled doors to Varley's office opened. The operator snapped to attention and those in the cage stopped talking and stared respectfully at the man who came to the cage doors.

Varley was a man of sixty, gray-haired, with a coarse but kindly face dominated by a large nose which his enemies called bulbous. He wore the hat that had made him famous—a blue-gray fedora which he ordered in quantity lots and wore exclusive of all other colors, fabrics, or fashions.

"Sorry to keep you waiting, Ed," Varley boomed to one of the two business men in the cage. "Phone call. Held me up for a few minutes."

He stepped into the elevator, nodding to the others. "Let's go," he said to the operator.

The cage started down.

The express elevators were supposed to fall like a plummet. They made the long drop to the ground in a matter of seconds, normally. And this one started like a plummet.

"Damn funny, that phone call I got just before I came out of my office," Varley boomed to the two men he was lunching with. "Some joker calling himself Doctor Satan—" He stopped, and frowned. "What's wrong with the elevator?" he snapped to the operator.

"I don't know, sir," the boy said.

He was jerking at the lever. Ordinarily, so automatic was the cage, he did not touch the controls from the time the top floor doors mechanically closed themselves till the time the lobby was reached. Now he was twitching the control switch back and forth, from Off to On.

And the elevator was slowing down.

The swift start had slowed to a smooth crawl downward. And the crawl was becoming a creep. The floor numbers that had flashed on the little frosted glass panel inside the cage as fast as you could count were now forming themselves with exasperating slowness. Sixty-one, sixty, fifty-nine . . .

"Can't you make it go faster?" said Varley. "I never saw these cages go so slow. Is the power low?"

"I don't think so, sir," said the operator. He jammed the control against the fast-speed peg. And the cage slowed down still more.

"Something's wrong," whispered one of the girl secretaries to the other. "This slow speed . . . And it's getting warm in here!"

Evidently Varley thought so too. He unbuttoned his vest and took his fedora off and fanned himself.

"I don't know what the hell's the matter," he growled to the two men with him. "Certainly have to have the engineer look into this. There's supposed to be decent ventilation in these shafts. And if they call this express service . . . Gad, I'm hot!"

Perspiration was bursting out on his forehead now. He began to look ghastly pale.

Fifty-two, fifty-one, fifty . . . the little red numbers appeared on the frosted glass indicator ever more slowly. The elevator would take five minutes to descend, at this pace.

"Something's the matter with me," gasped Varley. "I've never felt like this before." One of the secretaries was standing near him. She looked at him suddenly, with wide eyes in which fear of something beyond normal comprehension was beginning to show. She shrank back from him.

"Get this cage down," Varley panted. "I'm—sick."

The rest looked at each other. All were beginning to feel what the girl, who had been nearest him, had felt. Heat was beginning to radiate from Varley's corpulent body as if he were a stove!

"Good heavens, man!" said one of the two business men. He laid his hand on Varley's arm, took it away quickly. "Why—you're burning up with fever. What's wrong?"

Varley tried to answer, but couldn't. He staggered back against the wall of the cage, leaned there with arms hanging down and lips hanging slack. There was no longer perspiration on his face. It was dry, feverishly dry; and the skin was cracking on his taut, puffed cheeks.

"Burning!" he gasped. "Burning up!"

The girl secretary screamed, then. And the man who had put his hand on Varley's arm jerked at the operator's shoulder.

"For heaven's sake get this cage down! Mr. Varley's ill!"

"I—I can't," gasped the boy. "Something's the matter—it never acted like this before—"

He jerked at the controls, and the elevator did not respond. Slowly, monotonously, it continued its deliberate descent.

And abruptly a scream tore from Varley's cracking lips. "*Burning!* Help me, somebody—"

The slowly dropping cage became a thing of horror, a six-foot square of hell from which there was no escape because there were no doors opening onto the shaft at the upper levels, and which could not be speeded up because it did not respond to the controls.

Screaming with every breath he drew, Varley sank to the floor. And those who might otherwise have tried to help him cowered away from him as far as they could get. For from his body now was radiating heat that made a tiny inferno of the elevator.

"God!" whispered one of the men. "Look at him—he really *is* burning up!"

The heat from Varley's body had become so intense that the others in the cage could hardly stand it. But far worse than their bodily torment was the mental agony of watching the thing that for a week had New York City in a chaos.

Varley had stopped screaming now. He lay staring up at the gilded roof of the elevator with frightful, glazing eyes. His chest heaved with efforts to draw breath. Heaved, then was still.

"*He's dead!*" shrieked one of the secretaries. "Dead—"

Her body fell to the floor of the cage near Varley's. The elderly woman quietly sagged to her knees, then in a huddled heap in the corner as her senses fled under the impact of a shock too great to be endured.

But the horror that had gripped Varley went on. "*Look! Look! Look!*" panted the office manager.

But he had no need to pant out the word. The rest were looking all right. They'd have turned their eyes away if they could, but there is a fascination to extremes of horror that makes the will powerless. In every detail they were forced to see the thing that happened.

Varley's dead body was beginning to disappear. The corpulent form of the man who a moment ago had been one of the biggest figures in the nation seemed to have been turned to wax, which was melting and vaporizing.

His face was a shapeless mass now; and the flesh of his body seemed to be melting and running together. As it did so, his limbs writhed and twitched as if still imbued with life. Writhed, and shriveled.

"*Burning up!*" whispered the office manager, his eyes bulging with horror behind their thick lenses. "*Melting away . . . burning up. . . .*"

It was so incredible, so unreal that it was dream-like.

The cage descended slowly, slowly, like the march of time itself which no man could hasten. The operator stood like a wooden image at the controls, staring with starting eyes at the heap on the floor which had been Varley. The two business men shrank together, hands to their mouths, gnawing the backs of their hands. The office manager was panting, "Look . . . look . . . look . . ." with every breath, like a sobbing groan. And Varley was a diminishing, shapeless mass on the floor.

"Oh, God, let me out of here!" screamed one of the business men.

But there was no way out. No doors opened onto the shaft here. All in the cage were doomed to stay and watch the spectacle that would haunt them till they died.

On the cage floor there was a blue-gray fedora hat, and a mound of blackened substance that was almost small enough to have been contained in it.

Twenty-nine, twenty-eight, twenty-seven . . . The cage descended with its horrible, unchangeable slowness.

Twenty-five, twenty-four . . .

On the floor was Varley's hat. That was all.

The operator was last to go. Eleven, ten, the red numerals on the frosted glass panel read. Then his inert body joined the senseless forms of the others on the floor.

The cage hit the lobby level. Smoothly, marvelous mechanisms devised by man's ingenuity, the doors opened by themselves; opened, and revealed seven fainting figures—around a gray-blue fedora hat.

Three o'clock. On the stage of the city's leading theater, the show, *Burn Me Down*, was in the middle of the first act of its matinee performance.

The show was a musical comedy, built around

a famous comedian. His songs and dances and patter carried it. To see him, and him alone, the crowds came. Worth millions, shrewd, and at the same time as common as the least who saw him from the galleries, he was the idol of the stage.

He sat on a stool in the wings now, chin on fist, moodily watching the revue dance of twenty bare-legged girls billed as the world's most beautiful. His heavy black eyebrows were down in a straight line over eyes like ink-spots behind comedy horn-rimmed glasses. His slight, lithe body was tense.

"Your cue in a minute, Mr. Croy," warned the manager.

"Hell, don't you suppose I know it?" snapped the comedian.

Then his scowl disappeared for a moment. "Sorry."

The manager stared. Croy's good humor and even temper were proverbial in the theater. No one had ever seen him act like this before.

"Anything wrong?" he asked.

"Yeah, I don't feel so hot," said Croy, scowling again. "Rather, I feel *too* hot! Like I was burning up with a fever or something."

He passed a handkerchief over his forehead. "And I feel like trouble's coming," he added. He took a rabbit's foot from his vest pocket and squeezed it. "Heavy trouble."

The manager bit his lip. Croy was the hit of the show—*was* the show. "Knock off for the afternoon if you feel bad," he advised. "We'll have Charley do your stuff. We can get away with it at a matinee—"

"And have the mob on your neck," interrupted Croy, without false modesty. "It's me they come to see. I'll go on with it, and have a rest afterward . . ."

The twenty girls swept forward in a last pirouette and danced toward the wings. Croy stood up.

"It must be a fever," he muttered, mopping at his face again. "Never felt like this before, though."

The stage door attendant burst into the wings and ran toward the manager. The manager started to reprimand him for leaving his post, then saw the afternoon newspaper he was waving.

He took it from the man's hand, glanced at the headlines.

"What!" he gasped. "A man burn up? They're crazy! How could a . . . Varley—biggest man in the city! . . ."

He started toward the comedian.

"My God, could it be the same thing happening here? . . . *Croy! Croy—wait—*"

But the famous comedian was already on the stage, catapulting to the center of it in the ludicrous stumble, barely escaping a fall, that was his specialty.

The manager, clutching the newspaper, stood in the wings with death-white face, and watched. Croy went into a dance to the rhythm of the theme song of the show. He was terribly pale, and the manager saw him stagger over a difficult step. Then his voice rose with the words of the song:

"Burn me down, baby. Don't say maybe. Put your lips against my lips—*and burn me down!*"

The audience half rose. Croy had fallen to his knees on a dance turn. The manager saw that the perspiration that had dewed his forehead no longer showed. His skin looked dry, cracked.

Croy got up. The audience settled back again, wondering if the fall had been part of his act. Croy resumed his steps and his singing. But his voice was barely audible beyond the fifth row:

"Burn me down, Sadie. Oh-h-h, lady! Look into my eyes and *burn me—*"

Croy stopped. His words ended in a wild high note. Then he screamed almost like a woman and his hands went to his throat. They tore at his collar and tie.

"Burning!" he screamed. "*Burning—*"

The manager leaned, shaking against a pillar. The newspaper, with the account in it of what had happened to Varley, rattled to the floor.

It was the same! The same awful thing was happening to Croy! "Curtain!" he croaked. "Bring down the curtain!"

Now the audience was standing up, some of them indeed climbing to their seats to see what was happening on the stage. Croy was prone on the boards, writhing, shrieking. The canvas backdrop billowed a little with the heat coming from his body.

"Curtain!" roared the manager. "For God's sake—are you deaf?"

The curtain dropped. Croy's convulsed body was hidden from the sight of the audience. With the curtain's fall, he stopped screaming. It was as though the thing had sliced through the sound like a great descending guillotine. But it was not the curtain that had killed the sound.

Croy was dead. His limbs still jerked and writhed. But it was not the movement of life. It was the movement of a twisted roll of paper that writhes and jerks as it is consumed in flame.

The manager drew a deep breath. Then, with his knees trembling, he walked out onto the stage.

"Ladies and gentlemen," he announced, trying to make his voice sound out over the pandemonium that ruled over the theater. "Mr. Croy has had a heart attack. The show will not go on. You may get your money at the box-office on the way out."

He fairly ran from the stage and back of the curtain, where terrified girls and men were clumped around Croy's body—or what was left of it. Heart attack! The manager's mouth distorted over that description.

Croy's body had shrunk—or, rather, *melted*—to half its normal size. His features were indistinguishable, like the features of a wax head with a fire under it. His clothes were smoldering. The heat was such that it was hard to stand within a yard of him. The big, horn-rimmed glasses slid from his face. His body diminished, diminished . . .

A stage hand came racing back. Behind him trotted a plump man in black with rimless spectacles over his eyes.

"I got a doctor," the stage hand gasped. "From the audience."

He stopped. And the doctor stared at the place where Croy had lain, and then gazed around at the faces of the others.

"Well?" he said. "Where is Croy? I was told he was dangerously ill."

No one answered. One after another stared back into his face with the eyes of maniacs. "Where is he, I say?" snapped the doctor. "I was told—"

He stopped, aware at last that something far worse than ordinary illness was afoot back here.

The manager's lips moved. Words finally came. "Croy is—*was*—there."

His pointing finger leveled tremulously at a spot on the stage. Then he fell, pitching forward on his face like a dead man.

And the point on the stage he had designated was empty. Only a blackened patch was there, with a little smoke drifting up from it. A blackened patch—with a pair of comedy horn-rimmed glasses beside it.

2

In the elevator control room of the Northern State Building, a man in the coveralls of an electrician bent over the great switchboard. He was examining the automatic control switch of the elevator in which Varley had ridden down from his top-floor office for the last time in life; had ridden down—but never reached the bottom!

Grease smeared the man's face and hands. But an especially keen observer would have noted several things about the seeming electrician that did not match his profession.

He would have noticed that the man's body was as lithe and muscular as that of a dancer; that his hands were only superficially smeared with grease, and were without calluses; that his fingers were the long, steely strong ones of a great surgeon or musician. Then, if he were one of the very few in New York capable of the identification, he might have gone further and glanced into the man's steely eyes under coal-black eyebrows, and stared at his patrician nose and strong chin and firm, large mouth—and have named him as Ascott Keane.

The building manager stood beside Keane. He had treated Keane as an ordinary electrician while the building engineer was near by. Now he gave him the deference due one of the greatest criminal investigators of all time. "Well, Mr. Keane?" he said.

"It's about as I thought," Keane said. "A device on the order of a big rheostat was placed on the switch circuit. In that way the descent of the elevator could be slowed as much as the person manipulating the switch desired."

"But why was the elevator Mr. Varley rode down in made to go slower? Did the slowness have anything to do with his death?"

"No, it had to do only with the spectacle of his death!" Keane's face was very grim. His jaw was a hard square. "The man who killed Varley wanted to be sure that his death, and dissolution, were witnessed lingeringly and unmistakably, so that the full terror of it could be brought out."

He straightened up, walked toward the door. "You've set an office aside for me?"

"Yes. It's next to my own on the sixtieth floor. But you aren't going to it yet, are you?"

"Yes. Why not?"

"Well, there might be fingerprints. Whoever tampered with the control board might not have been careful about clues."

A mirthless smile appeared on Keane's firm lips. "Fingerprints! My dear sir! You don't know Doctor Satan, I'm afraid."

"Doctor Sat—"

The building manager clenched his hands excitedly. "Then you already know about the phone call to Mr. Varley just before he died."

"No," said Keane, "I don't."

"But you named the man who called—"

"Only because I know who did this—have known since I first heard of it. Not from any proofs I've found or will ever find. Tell me about the phone call."

"There isn't much. I'd hardly thought of it till you spoke of a Doctor Satan . . . Varley was leaving his office for lunch when his telephone rang. I was in his office about a lease and I couldn't help hearing a little of it—his words, that is. I gathered that somebody calling himself Doctor Satan was talking to Varley about insurance."

"Insurance!"

"Yes. Though what a physician should be doing selling insurance, I couldn't say—"

"Doctor Satan is not exactly a physician," Keane interrupted dryly. "Go on."

"That's all there is to tell. The man at the other end of the wire calling himself Doctor Satan seemed to want to insist that Varley take out some sort of insurance, till finally Varley just hung up on him. He turned to me and said something about being called by cranks and nuts, and went out to the elevator."

Keane walked from the control room, with the building manager beside him. He went to the elevator shafts.

"Sixty," he said to the operator.

In the elevator, he became the humble workman again. The manager treated him as such. "When you're through with the faulty wiring in sixty, come to my office," he said.

Keane nodded respectfully, then got out at the sixtieth floor.

A suite of two large offices had been set aside for him. There was a door through a regular anteroom, and a smaller, private entrance leading directly into the rear of the two offices.

Keane went through the private entrance. A girl, seated beside a flat-topped desk, got up. She was tall, quietly lovely, with dark blue eyes and copper-brown hair. This was Beatrice Dale, Keane's more-than-secretary.

"Visitors?" said Keane, as she handed a calling-card to him.

She nodded. "Walter P. Kessler, one of the six you listed as most likely to receive Doctor Satan's first attentions in this new scheme of his."

Keane was running a towel over his face, taking off the grease—which was not grease but dark-colored soap. He took off the electrician's coveralls, emerging in a perfectly tailored blue serge suit complete save for his coat. The coat he took from a closet, shrugging into it as he approached the desk and sat down.

"What did you find out, Ascott?" said Beatrice.

Her face was pale, but her voice was calm, controlled. She had worked with Keane long enough to know how to face the horrors devised by Doctor Satan calmly, if not fearlessly.

"From the control room?" said Keane. "Nothing. The elevator was slowed simply to make the tragic end of Varley more spectacular. And there is Doctor Satan's autograph! The spectacular! All of his plans are marked by it."

"But you found out nothing of the nature of his plans?"

"I got a hint. It's an insurance project."

"Insurance!"

Keane smiled. There was no humor in the smile. There had been no humor in his smiles—or in his soul—since he had first met Doctor Satan, and there would be none till finally, somehow, he overcame the diabolical person who, already wealthy beyond the hopes of the average men, was amusing himself by gathering more wealth in a series of crimes as weird as they were inhuman.

"Yes, insurance. Send in Kessler, Beatrice."

The girl bit her lip. Keane had told her nothing. And the fact that she was burning to know what scraps of information he had picked up showed in her face. But she turned obediently and went to the door leading into the front office.

She came back in a moment with a man who was so anxious to get in that he almost trod on her heels. The man, Walter P. Kessler, was twisting a felt hat to ruins in his desperate fingers, and his brown eyes were like the eyes of a horrified animal as he strode toward Keane's desk.

"Keane!" He paused, looked at the girl, gazed around the office. "I still can't quite understand this. I've known you for years as a rich man's son who never worked in his life and knew nothing but polo and first editions. Now they tell me you are the only man in the world who can help me in my trouble."

"If your trouble has to do with Doctor Satan—and of course it has—I may be able to help," said Keane. "As for the polo and first editions—it is helpful in my hobby of criminology to be known as an idler. You will be asked to keep my real activities hidden."

"Of course," gasped Kessler. "And if ever I can do anything for you in return for your help now—"

Keane waved his hand. "Tell me about the insurance proposition," he said.

"Are you a mind-reader?" exclaimed Kessler.

"No. There's no time to explain. Go ahead."

Kessler dug into his inside coat pocket.

"It's about insurance, all right. And it's sponsored by a man who calls himself Doctor Satan. Though how you knew?"

He handed a long envelop to Keane. "This came in this morning's mail," he said. "Of course I paid no attention to it. Not *then*! In fact, I threw it in my waste basket. I only fished it out again after reading the early afternoon papers—and finding out what happened to poor old Varley—"

He choked, and stopped. Keane read the folded paper in the long business envelope:

Mr. Kessler: You are privileged, among a few others in New York City, to be among the first to be invited to participate in a new type of insurance plan recently organized by me. The insurance will be taken out against an emotion, instead of a tangible menace. That emotion is horror. In a word, I propose to insure you against feeling horror. The premium for this benevolent insurance is seven hundred and fifty thousand dollars. If the premium is not paid, you will be subjected to a rather unpleasant feeling of horror concerning something that may happen to you. That something is death, but death in a new form: If you do not choose to take out my horror insurance, you shall burn in slow fire till you are utterly consumed. It may be next month or next year. It may be tomorrow. It may be in the privacy of your room, or among crowds. Read in this afternoon's paper of what will shortly happen to two of the town's leading citizens. Then decide whether or not the premium payment asked is not a small price to pay for allaying the horror the reading of their fates will inspire in you.

Signed, DOCTOR SATAN.

Keane tapped the letter against his palm. "Horror insurance," he murmured. "I can see Doctor Satan's devilish smile as he coined that phrase. I can hear his chuckle as he 'invites' you to take out a 'policy.' Well, are you going to pay it?"

Kessler's shudder rattled the chair he sat in. "Certainly! Am I mad, that I should refuse to pay—after reading what happened to Varley and Croy? Burned alive! Reduced to a shapeless little residue of consumed flesh—and then to nothingness! Certainly I'll pay!"

"Then why did you come to me?"

"To see if we couldn't outwit this Doctor Satan in future moves. What's to keep him from demanding a sum like that every year as the price of my safety? Or every month, for that matter?"

"Nothing," said Keane.

Kessler's hand clenched the chair-arm. "That's it. I'll have to pay this one, because I daren't defy the man till some sort of scheme is set in motion against him. But I want you to track him down before another demand is presented. I'll give you a million dollars if you succeed. Two million . . ."

The look on Keane's face stopped him. "My friend," said Keane, "I'd double your two million, personally, if I could step out and destroy this man, now, before he does more horrible things."

He stood up. "How were you instructed to pay the 'premium'?"

For a moment Kessler looked less panic stricken. A flash of the grim will that had enabled him to build up his great fortune showed in his face.

"I was instructed to pay it in a way that may trip our Doctor Satan up," he said. "I am to write ten checks of seventy-five thousand dollars each, payable to the Lucifex Insurance Company. These checks I am to bring to this building tonight. From the north side of the building I will find a silver skull dangling from a wire leading down the building wall. I am to put the checks in the skull. It will be drawn up and the checks taken by someone in some room up in the building."

His jaw squared. "That ought to be our chance, Keane! We can have men scattered throughout the National State Building—"

Keane shook his head. "In the first place, you'd have to have an army here. There are seventy-nine floors, Kessler. Satan's man may be in any room on any of the seventy-nine floors on the north side of the building. Or he may be on the roof. In the second place, expecting to catch a criminal like Doctor Satan in so obvious a manner is like expecting to catch a fox in a butterfly net. He probably won't be within miles of this building tonight. And you can depend on it that his man, who is to draw up the skull with the checks in it, won't be in any position where he can be caught by the police or private detectives."

Kessler's panic returned in full force. He clawed at Keane's arm. "What can we do, then?" he babbled. "What can we do?"

"I don't know, yet," admitted Keane. "But we've got till tonight to figure out a plan. You come to the building as instructed, with the checks to put in the skull. By then I'll have weapons with which to fight"—his lips twisted—"the Lucifex Insurance Company."

3

The National State Building is situated on a slanting plot in New York City. The first floor on the lower side is like a cavern—dark, with practically no light coming in the windows from the canyon of a street.

Near the center of that side was an unobtrusive small shop with "Lucian Photographic

Supplies" lettered on it. The window was clean-looking, yet it was strangely opaque. Had a person looked at it observantly he would have noticed, with some bewilderment, that while nothing seemed to obstruct vision, he still could not see what was going on behind it. But there are few really observant eyes; and in any event there was nothing about the obscure place to attract attention.

At the back of the shop there was a large room completely sealed against light. On the door was the sign, "Developing Room."

Inside the light-proof room the only illumination came from two red light bulbs, like and yet strangely unlike the lights used in developing-rooms. But the activities in the room had nothing to do with developing pictures!

In one corner were two figures that seemed to have stepped out of a nightmare. One was a monkey-like little man with a hair-covered face from which glinted bright, cruel eyes. The other was a legless giant who swung his great torso, when he moved, on arms as thick as most men's thighs. Both were watching a third figure in the room, more bizarre than either of them.

The third figure bent over a bench. It was tall, spare, and draped from throat to ankles in a blood-red robe. Red rubber gloves were drawn over its hands. The face was covered by a red mask which concealed every feature save the eyes—which were like black, live coals peering through the eye-holes. A skullcap fitted tightly over the head; and from this, in sardonic imitation of the fiend he pretended to be, were two projections like horns.

Doctor Satan stared broodingly at the things on the bench which were engaging his attention. These, innocent enough in appearance, still had in them somehow a suggestion of something weird and grotesque.

They were little dolls, about eight inches high. The sheen of their astonishingly life-like faces suggested that they were made of wax. And they were so amazingly well sculptured that a glimpse revealed their likeness to living persons.

There were four of the little figures clad like men. And any reporter or other person acquainted with the city's outstanding personalities would have recognized them as four of the nation's business titans. One of them was Walter P. Kessler.

Doctor Satan's red-gloved hand pulled a drawer open in the top of the bench. The supple fingers reached into the drawer, took from it two objects, and placed them on the bench.

And now there were six dolls on the bench, the last two being a man and a woman.

The male doll was clad in a tiny blue serge suit. Its face was long-jawed, with gray chips for eyes, over which were heavy black brows. An image of Ascott Keane.

The female doll was a likeness of a beautiful girl with coppery brown hair and deep blue eyes. Beatrice Dale.

"Girse." Doctor Satan's voice was soft, almost gentle.

The monkey-like small man with the hairy face hopped forward.

"The plate," said Doctor Satan.

Girse brought him a thick iron plate, which Doctor Satan set upon the bench.

On the plate were two small, dark patches; discolorations obviously made by the heat of something being burned there. The two little discolorations were all that was left of two little dolls that had been molded in the image of Martial Varley, and the comedian, Croy.

Doctor Satan placed the two dolls on the plate that he had taken from the drawer: the likeness of Beatrice Dale and Ascott Keane.

"Kessler went to Keane," Doctor Satan said, the red mask over his face stirring angrily. "We shall tend to Kessler—after he has paid tonight. We shall not wait that long to care for Keane and the girl."

Two wires trailed over the bench from a wall socket. His red-gloved fingers twisted the wires to terminals set into the iron plate. The plate began to heat up.

"Keane has proved himself an unexpectedly competent adversary," Satan's voice continued. "with knowledge I thought no man on earth save myself possessed. We'll see if he can escape *this* fate—and avoid becoming, with his precious secretary, as Varley and Croy became."

Small waves of heat began to shimmer up from the iron plate. It stirred the garments clothing the two little dolls. Doctor Satan's glittering eyes burned down on the mannikins. Girse and the legless giant, Bostiff, watched as he did . . .

Fifty-nine stories above the pseudo-developing shop, Keane smiled soberly at Beatrice Dale. "I ought to fire you," he said.

"Why on earth—" she gasped.

"Because you're such a valuable right-hand man, and because you're such a fine person."

"Oh," Beatrice murmured. "I see. More fears for my safety?"

"More fears for your safety," nodded Keane. "Doctor Satan is out for your life as well as mine, my dear. And—"

"We've had this out many times before," Beatrice interrupted. "And the answer is still: No. I refuse to be fired, Ascott. Sorry."

There was a glint in Keane's steel-gray eyes that had nothing to do with business. But he didn't express his emotions. Beatrice watched his lips part with a breathless stirring in her heart. She had been waiting for some such expression for a long time.

But Keane only said: "So be it. You're a brave person. I oughtn't to allow you to risk your life in this private, deadly war that no one knows about but us. But I can't seem to make you desert, so—"

"So that's that," said Beatrice crisply. "Have you decided how you'll move against Doctor Satan tonight?"

Keane nodded. "I made my plans when I first located him."

"You know where he is?" said Beatrice in amazement.

"I do."

"How did you find it out?"

"I didn't. I thought it out. Doctor Satan seems to have ways of knowing where I am. He must know I've located here in the National State Building. The obvious thing for him to do would be to conceal himself on the other side of town. So, that being the expected thing, what would a person as clever as he is, do?"

Beatrice nodded. "I see. Of course! He'd be—"

"Right here in this building."

"But you told Kessler he was probably miles away!" said Beatrice.

"I did. Because I knew Kessler's character. If he knew the man who threatened him was in the building, he'd try to do something like organizing a raid. Fancy a police raid against Doctor Satan! So I lied and said he was probably a long distance off." Keane sighed. "I'm afraid the lie was valueless. I can foretell pretty precisely what Kessler will do. He will have an army of men scattered through the building tonight, in spite of what I said. He will attempt to trace Doctor Satan through collection of the checks—and he will die."

Beatrice shuddered. "By burning? What a horrible way to—"

She stopped.

"What is it?" said Keane urgently, at the strained expression that suddenly molded her face.

"Nothing, I guess," replied Beatrice slowly. "Power of suggestion, I suppose. When I said 'burning' I seemed to feel hot all over, myself."

Keane sprang from his chair. "My God—why didn't you tell me at once! I—"

He stopped too, and his eyes narrowed to steely slits in his rugged face. Perspiration was studding his own forehead now.

"It's come!" he said. "The attack on us by Satan. But it wasn't wholly unexpected. The suitcase in the corner—get it and open it! Quickly!"

Beatrice started toward the suitcase but stopped and pressed her hands to her cheeks. "Ascott—I'm . . . burning up . . . I—"

"Get that suitcase!"

Keane sprang to the desk and opened the wide lower drawer. He took a paper-wrapped parcel from it, ripped it open. An odd array was disclosed; two pairs of things like cloth slippers, two pairs of badly proportioned gloves, two small rounded sacks.

Beatrice was struggling with the snaps on the suitcase. Both were breathing heavily now, dragging their arms as if they weighed tons.

"Ascott—I can't stand it—I'm burning—" panted the girl.

"You've got to stand it! Is the case open? Put on the smaller of the two garments there. Toss me the other."

The garments in question were two suits of unguessable material that were designed to fit tightly over a human body—an unclothed human body.

Beatrice tossed the larger of the two to Keane, who was divesting himself of his outer garments with rapid fingers.

"Ascott—I can't change into *this*—here before—"

"Damn modesty!" grated Keane. "Get into those things! You hear! Quickly!"

Both were no longer perspiring. Their faces were dry, feverish. Heat was radiating from their bodies in a stifling stream.

Beatrice stood before Keane in the tight single garment that covered body and arms and legs.

"These gloves on your hands!" snapped Keane. "The sack over your head. The shoes on your feet!"

"Oh, God!" panted Beatrice.

Then she had done as Keane commanded. From soles to hair she was covered by the curious fabric Keane had devised. And the awful burning sensation was allayed.

There were eye-slits in the sacks each wore. They stared at each other with eyes that were wide with a close view of death. Then Beatrice sighed shudderingly.

"The same thing Varley and Croy went through?" she said.

"The same," said Keane. "Poor fellows! Doctor Satan thought he could deal us the same doom. And he almost did! If we'd been a little farther away from these fabric shields of ours—"

"How do they stop Doctor Satan's weapon?" said Beatrice. "And how can he strike—as he does—from a distance?"

"His weapon, and this fabric I made," said Keane, "go back a long way beyond history, to the priesthood serving the ancestors of the Cretans. They forged the weapon in wizardry, and at the same time devised the fabric to wear as protection against their enemies who must inevitably learn the secret of the weapon too. It is the father of the modern voodoo practise of making a crude image of an enemy and sticking pins into it."

He drew a long breath.

"A small image is made in the likeness of the person to be destroyed. The image is made of substance pervious to fire. In the cases of Croy and Varley, I should say after descriptions of how they perished, of wax. The image is then burned, and the person in whose likeness it is cast burns to nothingness as the image does—*if* the manipulator knows the secret incantations of the Cretans, as Doctor Satan does. But I'll give you more than an explanation; I'll give you a demonstration! For we are going to strike back at Doctor Satan in a manner I think he will be utterly unprepared for!"

He went to the opened suitcase, looking like a being from another planet in the ill-fitting garments he had thrown together after analyzing Varley's death. He took from the suitcase a thing that looked like a little doll. It was an image of a monkey-like man with a hairy face and long, simian arms.

"How hideous!" exclaimed Beatrice. "But isn't that Doctor Satan's assistant Girse?"

Ascott Keane nodded. "Yes. I wish it were the image of Satan himself, but that would be useless. Satan, using the ancient death, would too obviously be prepared for it just as I was."

Beatrice stared at the image for a moment,

perplexity in her eyes. "But—Ascott! Didn't you tell me that Girse was dead? Wasn't he—consumed instead of you when . . . ?"

Keane nodded. "Yes, he was—and I was foolish enough for a while to believe what I saw as final. But Doctor Satan knows as much about the ancient evil arts as I do—at least as much—and I know of a way to bring a dead person back, even if the body is destroyed, so long as I had the foresight to preserve some parts like hair or nail-clippings. I forgot that any close associate of Doctor Satan must be killed twice, so long as Satan is free to work his magic. That is why I made this image of Girse as soon as I realized what Doctor Satan is doing. There's just a chance that he hasn't prepared any protection for Girse, on the assumption that I already considered Girse out of the picture forever."

"It's made of wax?" said Beatrice, understanding and awe beginning to glint in her eyes.

"Made of wax," Keane nodded.

He looked around the office, saw no metal tray to put the little doll on, and flipped back a corner of the rug. The floor of the office was of smooth cement. He set the image on the cement. With her hand to her breast, Beatrice watched. The proceeding, seeming inconsequential in itself, had an air of deadliness about it that stopped the breath in her throat.

Keane looked around the office again, then strode to the clothes he and Beatrice had flung to the floor in their haste a moment ago.

"Sorry," he said, taking her garments with his own and piling them on the cement. "We'll have to send down to Fifth Avenue for more clothes to be brought here. I need these now."

On the pile of cloth he placed the image of Girse. Then he touched a match to the fabric . . .

In the developing room, Doctor Satan fairly spat his rage as he stared at the two wax dolls on the red-hot iron plate. The dolls were not burning! Defying all the laws of physics and, as far as Satan knew, of wizardry, the waxen images were standing unharmed on the metal that should have consumed them utterly.

"Damn him!" Doctor Satan whispered, gloved hands clenching. "Damn him! He has escaped again! Though how—"

He heard breathing begin to sound stertorously beside him. His eyes suddenly widened with incredulity behind the eye-holes in his mask. He whirled.

Girse was staring at him with frenzy and horror in his eyes. The breath was tearing from his corded throat, as though each would be his last.

"Master!" he gasped imploringly. "Doctor Satan! Stop—"

The skin on his face and hands, dry and feverish-looking, suddenly began to crack. "*Stop the burning!*" he pleaded in a shrill scream.

But Doctor Satan could only clench his hands and curse softly, whispering to himself, "I did not foresee it, Girse. I brought you back with the essential salts, one of the most guarded of all occult secrets, and I was sure that Ascott Keane would never suspect. But he did, damn him, and he was ready for me . . ."

Girse shrieked again, and fell to the floor. Then his screams stopped; he was dead, and this time there would be no return; the essential salts could be used to restore a man only once. Girse's body moved on, jerking and twisting as a tight-rolled bit of paper twists and jerks in a consuming fire.

"Keane!" whispered Doctor Satan, staring at the floor where a discolored spot was all that remained of his follower. His eyes were frightful. "By the devil, my master, he'll pay for that a thousand times over!"

4

At half-past twelve that night a solitary figure walked along the north side of the National State Building. The north side was the one the Lucian Photographic Supplies shop faced on, the side street. It was deserted save for the lone man.

The man slowed his pace as he saw a shining object hanging from the building wall about waist-high, a few yards ahead of him. He clenched his hands, then took out his handkerchief and wiped his forehead.

The man was Walter P. Kessler. And the flourish of the white handkerchief in the dimness of the street was a signal.

Across the street four floors up in a warehouse, a man with a private detective's badge in his pocket and a pair of binoculars to his eyes. He watched Kessler, saw the shining object he was approaching, and nodded.

Kessler drew from his pocket an unaddressed envelope. In it were ten checks made out to the Lucifex Insurance Company. He grasped the receptable for the checks in his left hand.

The receptacle was a cleverly molded skull, of silver, about two-thirds life size. There was a hole in the top of it. Kessler thrust the envelope securely into the hole.

The skull began to rise up the building wall, toward some unguessable spot in the tremendous cliff formed by seventy-nine stories of cut stone. Across the street the man with the binoculars managed at last to spot the thin wire from which the silver skull was suspended. He followed it up with his gaze.

It came from a window almost at the top of the building. The man grasped a phone at his elbow.

He did not dial operator. The phone had a direct line to the building across the way. He simply picked up the receiver and said softly: "Seventy-second floor, eighteenth window from the east wall. *Hop it!*"

In the National State Building a man at an improvised switchboard on the ground floor turned to another. "Seventy-second floor, eighteenth window from the east. Get everybody."

The second man ran toward the night elevator. He went from floor to floor. At each floor he opened the door and signaled. And on each floor two men, who had been watching the corridors along the north side, ran silently toward the other local elevators, which had shaft doors on every floor all the way up to the top. At the same time a third man, at the stairs, drew his gun as he prepared to guard more carefully yet the staircase, rarely used, threading up beside the shafts.

And on the ground floor within fifty yards of the man at the switchboard, a chuckle came from the masked lips of a red-robed figure who stood straight and tall in a red-lit room.

Across the street the man with the binoculars suddenly picked up the phone again.

"Damn it—they tricked us. Somebody took the money in on the sixty-third floor!"

Changed orders vibrated through the great building. And the red-robed figure in the room at the heart of the maze chuckled again—and moved toward the bench.

Doctor Satan picked up one of the dolls remaining there. It was the image of Kessler. He placed it on the iron plate, which was already heated by the wires trailing from the socket. He watched the little doll broodingly.

It writhed and twisted as the heat melted its wax feet. It fell to the plate. And from the street, far away, sounded a horrible scream.

Doctor Satan's head jerked back as if the shriek were music to his ears. Then, once more, his hissing chuckle sounded out.

"For disobeying commands, my friend," he muttered. "But I knew you'd be obstinate enough to try it—"

He stopped. For a second he stood as rigid as a statue swathed in red. Then, slowly, he turned; and in his coal-black, blazing eyes was fury—and fear.

There was an inner door to the developing-room, but the door was locked, and it still stood locked. It had not been touched. Neither had the outer door. Yet in that room with the red-robed figure was another figure now. That of Ascott Keane.

He stood as rigid as Doctor Satan himself, and stared at his adversary out of steel-gray, level eyes.

"It seems we are alone," Keane said slowly. "Bostiff, I suppose, is retrieving the money from Kessler. And Girse? Where is he?"

Doctor Satan's snarl was the only answer. He moved toward Keane, red-swathed hands clenching as he came. Keane stood his ground. Satan stopped.

"How—" he asked.

"Surely *you* do not need to ask that," said Keane. "You must have penetrated the secret of transferring substance, including your own, from one place to another by sheer power of thought."

"I have not!" rasped Doctor Satan. "Nor have you!"

Keane shrugged. "I am here."

"You discovered my hiding-place and hid here while I was out, a short time ago!"

Keane's smile was a deadly thing. "Perhaps I did. Perhaps not. You can provide your own answer. The only thing of importance is that I *am* here—"

"And shall stay here!" Doctor Satan's soft voice lifted. The fear was fading from his eyes and leaving only fury there. "You have interfered in my plans once too often, Keane!"

As he spoke he raised his right hand with the thumb and forefinger forming an odd, eery angle.

"'Out of the everywhere into the here,'" he quoted softly. "I have servants more powerful than Girse, whom you destroyed, Ascott Keane. One comes now—*to your own destruction!*"

As he spoke, a strange tensity seized the air of the dim room. Keane paled a little at the blaze in the coal-black eyes. Then he stared suddenly at a spot in thin air to Doctor Satan's right.

Something was happening there. The air was shimmering as though it danced over an open fire. It wavered, grew misty, swayed in a sinuous column.

"'Out of the everywhere into the here,'" Doctor Satan's voice was raised in final triumph. "The old legends had a basis, Keane. The tales of dragons . . . There was such a thing, *is* such a thing. Only the creations the ancients called dragons do not ordinarily roam Earth in visible form."

The sinuous misty column at the right of the red-robed form was materializing into a thing to stagger a man's reason.

Keane found himself gazing at a shimmering figure that looked like a great lizard, save that it was larger than any lizard, and had smaller legs. It was almost like a snake with legs, but it was a snake two feet through at its thickest part, and only about fourteen feet long, which is not typical serpentine proportion. There were vestigial stubs of wings spreading from its trunk about a yard back of its great, triangular head; and it had eyes such as no true lizard ever had—eight inches across and glittering like evil gems.

"A dragon, Keane," Doctor Satan purred. "You have seen old pictures of some such thing, painted by artists who had caught a glimpse of these things that can only visit earth when some necromancer conjures them to. A 'mythical' creature, Keane. But you shall feel how 'mythical' it is when it attacks you."

A hiss sounded in the dim room. The serpentine form was so solidly materialized now that it would scarcely be seen through. And in a few more seconds it was opaque. And weighty! The floor quivered a little as it moved—toward Keane.

Its great, gem-like eyes glinted like colored glass as it advanced, foot by foot, on the man who had pitted himself against Doctor Satan till the death of one of them should end the bitter war. But, Keane did not move. He stood with shoulders squared and arms at his sides, facing the red-robed form.

"'Out of the everywhere into the here,'" he murmured. His lips were pale but his voice was calm. "There is another saying, Doctor Satan. It is a little different . . . 'Out of the *hereafter* into the here!'"

The unbelievable thing Doctor Satan had called into being in the midst of a city that would have scoffed at the idea of its existence suddenly halted its slow, deadly approach toward Keane. Its hiss sounded again, and it raised a taloned foot and clawed the thin air in a direction to Keane's left.

It retreated a step, slinking low to the floor, its talons and scales rattling on the smooth cement. It seemed to see something beyond the reach of mortal eyes. But in a moment the things it saw were perceptible to the eyes of the two men, too. And as Doctor Satan saw them an imprecation came from his masked lips.

Three figures, distorted, horrible, yet familiar! Three things like statues of mist that became less misty and more solid-seeming by the second!

Three men who writhed as though in mortal torment, and whose lips jerked with soundless shrieks—which gradually became not entirely soundless but came to the ears of Satan and Keane like far-off cries dimly heard.

And the three were Varley and Croy and Kessler.

A gasp came from Doctor Satan's concealed lips. He shrank back, even as the monstrosity he had called into earthly being shrank back.

"'Out of the hereafter into the here,'" Keane said. "These three you killed, Doctor Satan. They will now kill you!"

Varley and Croy and Kessler advanced on the red-robed form. As they came they screamed with the pain of burning, and their blackened hands advanced, with fingers flexed, toward Satan. Such hatred was in their dead, glazed eyes, that waves of it seemed to surge about the room like a river in flood.

"They're shades," panted Doctor Satan. "They're not real, they can't actually do harm—"

"You will see how real they are when they attack you," Keane paraphrased Satan's words.

The three screaming figures converged on Doctor Satan. From death they had come, and before them was the man who had sent them to death. Their eyes were wells of fury and despair.

"My God!" whispered Doctor Satan, cowering. And the words, though far from lightly uttered, seemed doubly blasphemous coming from the lips under the diabolical red mask.

The hissing of the dragon-thing he had called into existence was inaudible. Its form was hardly to be seen. It was fleeing back into whatever realm it had come from. But the screaming three were advancing ever farther into our earthly plane as they crept toward the cowering body of Doctor Satan.

"*My God!*" Satan cried. "Not that! Not deliverance into the hands of those I—"

The three leaped. And Keane, with his face white as death at the horror he was witnessing, knew that the fight between him and the incarnate evil known as Doctor Satan was to end in this room.

The three leaped, and the red-robed figure went down . . .

There was a thunderous battering at the door, and the bellow of men outside: "Open up, in the name of the law!"

Keane cried out, as though knife-blades had been thrust under his nails. Doctor Satan screamed, and thrust away from the three furies, while the three themselves mouthed and swayed like birds of prey in indecision over a field in which hunters bristle suddenly.

"Open this door!" the voice thundered again. "We know there's somebody in here—"

The shock of the change from the occult and unreal back to prosaic living was like the shock of being rudely waked from sound sleep when one has walked to the brink of a cliff and opens dazed eyes to stare at destruction. The introduction of such a thing as police, detectives, into a scene where two men were evoking powers beyond the ability of the average mortal even to comprehend, was like the insertion of an iron club into the intricate and fragile mechanism of a radio transmitting-station.

Keane literally staggered. Then he shouted: "For God's sake—get away from that door—"

"Open up, or we'll break in," the bellowing voice overrode his own.

Keane cursed, and turned. The three revengeful forces he had evoked for the destruction of Doctor Satan were gone, shattered into non-existence again with the advance of the prosaic. And Doctor Satan—

Keane got one glimpse of a torn red robe, with dots of deeper crimson on its arm, as the man slid through the inner door of the room and out to—God knew where. Some retreat he had prepared in advance, no doubt.

And then the door crashed down and the men Kessler had stubbornly and ruinously retained in his fight with Doctor Satan burst in.

They charged toward Keane. "You're under arrest for extortion," the leader, a bull-necked man with a gun in his hand, roared out. "We traced the guy that took the dough from the skull here before we lost him."

Keane only looked at him. And at something in his stare, though the detective did not know him from Adam, he wilted a little. "Stick out your hands while I handcuff you," he tried to bluster.

Then the manager of the building ran in. "Did you get him?" he called to the detective. "Was he in here?" He saw the man the detective proposed to handcuff. "*Keane!* What has happened?"

"Doctor Satan has escaped," said Keane. "That's what has happened. I had him"—he held his hand out and slowly closed it—"like that! Then these well-intentioned blunderers broke in, and—"

His voice broke. His shoulders sagged. He stared at the door through which the red-robed figure had gone. Then his body straightened and his eyes grew calm again—though they were bleak with a weariness going far beyond physical fatigue.

"Gone," he said, more to himself than to anyone in the red-lit room. "But I'll find him again. And *next* time I'll fight him in some place where no outside interference can save him."

Rogue: Countess d'Yls

A Shock for the Countess

C. S. MONTANYE

THE STORIES OF CARLETON STEVENS MONTANYE (1892–1948) appeared in numerous pulp magazines, including *Argosy*, *Top-Notch*, *Pep Stories*, *Thrilling Detective*, *Complete Stories*, and he achieved the peak of any pulp writer's career by selling numerous stories to *Black Mask*, beginning with the May 1920 issue and continuing through the issue of October 1939.

His most famous character, Captain Valentine, made his *Black Mask* debut on September 1, 1923, with "The Suite on the Seventh Floor," and appeared nine more times in two years, concluding with "The Dice of Destiny" in the July 1925 issue. The gentleman rogue was also the protagonist of the novel *Moons in Gold*, published in 1936, in which the debonair Valentine, accompanied by his amazingly ingenious Chinese servant Tim, is in Paris, where he has his eye on the world's most magnificent collection of opals.

Among his other characters were Johnny Castle, a private eye; detective Dave McClain; the Countess d'Yls, a wealthy, beautiful, brilliant, and laconic old-fashioned international jewel thief; Monahan, a tough, not-too-bright yegg; and Rider Lott, inventor of the perfect crime. Montanye also was one of the writers of the Phantom Detective series under the house name Robert Wallace.

"A Shock for the Countess" first appeared in the March 15, 1923, issue of *Black Mask*.

A SHOCK FOR THE COUNTESS

C. S. Montanye

FROM THE TERRACES of the Chateau d'Yls, the valley of Var was spread out below Gattiere, threaded with the broad bed of the River Var, swirling over its stony reaches from its cradle in the Hautes-Alpes. The snow-crowned mountains frowned ominously down but in the valley summertime warmth prevailed—quietude disturbed only by the song of birds and the voice of the river.

On the shaded promenade of the Chateau, the pretty Countess d'Yls stared thoughtfully at the unwinding river of the dust-powdered highway, twisting off into the dim distance. Beside her, a tall, well-built young man in tweeds absently flicked the ash from his cigarette and tinkled the ice in the thin glass he held.

Once or twice he surreptitiously considered the woman who reclined so indolently in the padded depths of a black wicker chair. The Countess seemed rarely lovely on this warm, lazy afternoon.

Her ash-blond hair caught what sunshine came in under the sand-colored awning above. Her blue eyes were dreamy and introspective, her red lips meditatively pursed. Yet for all of her abstraction there was something regal and almost imperious in her bearing; a subtle charm and distinction that was entirely her own.

"I do believe," the Countess remarked at length, "we are about to entertain visitors."

She motioned casually with a white hand toward the dust-filled road. The man beside her leaned a little forward. A mile or less distant he observed an approaching motor car that crawled up the road between clouds of dust.

"Visitors?"

The Countess inclined her head.

"So it would appear. And visitors, *mon ami*, who have come a long way to see us. Observe that the machine is travel-stained, that it appears to be weighted down with luggage. Possibly it is our old friend Murgier," she added almost mischievously.

The face of the man in tweeds paled under its tan.

"Murgier!" he exclaimed under his breath.

The Countess smiled faintly.

"But it is probably only a motoring party up from Georges de Loup who have wandered off the main road, Armand."

The man in tweeds had torn the cigarette

between his fingers into rags. As if held in the spell of some strange fascination he watched the motor grow larger and larger.

"There are men in it!" he muttered, when the dusty car was abreast the lower wall of the Chateau. "Four men!"

The woman in the wicker chair seemed suddenly to grow animated.

"*Mon Dieu!*" she said in a low voice. "If it is *he*, that devil!"

The man she addressed made no reply, only the weaving of his fingers betraying his suppressed nervousness. The hum of the sturdy motor was heard from the drive, way among the terraces now.

There was an interlude—voices around a bend in the promenade—finally the appearance of a liveried automaton that was the butler.

"Monsieur Murgier, madame."

The man in tweeds stifled a groan. The Countess turned slowly in her chair.

"You may direct Monsieur Murgier here, Henri."

The butler bowed and turned away. The man in tweeds closed his hands until the nails of them bit into the palms.

"God!"

The Countess laid a tense hand on his arm.

"*Smile!*" she commanded.

The Monsieur Murgier who presently sauntered down the shaded promenade of the Chateau was a tall, loose-jointed individual with a melancholy mustache and a deeply wrinkled face. A shabby, dusty suit hung loosely and voluminously about his spare figure. A soft straw hat was in one hand; he was gray at the temples.

When he bowed over the slender fingers of the Countess there was a hidden glow in his somber eyes.

"To be favored by the presence of the great!" the woman murmured softly. "Monsieur, this is an honor! May I make you acquainted with the Marquis de Remec?"

She introduced the visitor to the man in tweeds, who bowed stiffly. Somewhere back around the corner of the promenade the drone of the voices of those who had been in the car sounded faintly.

"A liqueur, m'sieu?" the Countess asked. "A cigar?"

Her visitor shook his head, gazed on the peaceful panorama of the valley of the Var.

"Thank you, no. My time is limited. My journey has been a long one and I must make a start for Paris with all due haste. You," he explained courteously, "and the Marquis will put yourselves in readiness with as much rapidity as possible. You are both my guests for the return journey!"

The man in tweeds whitened to the lips. His startled glance darted to the Countess. The woman had settled herself back in the black wicker chair again and had joined her fingers, tip to tip.

"Accompany you to Paris?" she drawled. "Are you quite serious?"

The wrinkled face of Monsieur Murgier grew inflexible, brass-like!

"Quite serious," he replied. "You are both under arrest—for the theft of the de Valois pearls!"

For a week, intermittently, Paris had known rain—the cold, chilly drizzle of early springtime. Because of the weather cafés and theatres were crowded, fiacres and taxis in constant demand, omnibuses jammed and the drenched boulevards deserted by their usual loungers.

From Montmartre to Montparnasse, scudding, gray clouds veiled the reluctant face of the sun by day and hid a knife-edged moon by night.

The steady, monotonous drizzle pattered against the boudoir windows in the house of the Countess d'Yls, mid-way down the Street of the First Shell. Within, all was snug, warm, and comfortable. A coal file burned in a filigree basket-grate, the radiance of a deeply shaded floor lamp near the toilette table, where a small maid hovered like a mother pigeon about the Countess, diffused a subdued, mellow glow.

The evening growl of Paris came as if from faraway, a lesser sound in the symphony of the rain.

"Madame will wear her jewels?"

The Countess turned and lifted her blue eyes.

"My rings only, Marie, if you please."

The maid brought the jewel casket, laid it beside her mistress, and at the wardrobe selected a luxurious Kolinsky cape which she draped over an arm. The Countess slipped on her rings, one by one—flashing, blue-white diamonds in carved, platinum settings, an odd Egyptian temple ring, a single ruby that burned like a small ball of crimson fire.

When the last ring glinted on her white fingers she dropped the lid of the casket, stood and turned to a full length cheval mirror back of her.

The glass reflected the full perfection of her charms, the sheer wonder of her sequin-spangled evening gown, the creamy luster of her bare, powdered arms, shoulders and rounded, contralto throat. Standing there, the soft light on her hair, she was radiant, incomparable, a reincarnated Diana whose draperies came from the most expert needles of the Rue de la Paix.

"I think," the Countess said aloud, "those who go to fashionable affairs to witness and copy will have much to occupy their pencils on the morrow. My gown is clever, is it not, Marie?"

"It is beautiful!" the maid breathed.

With a little laugh the Countess took the Kolinsky cape.

"Now I must hasten below to the Marquis. Poor boy, it is an hour—or more—that I have kept him cooling his heels. Marie, suspense, they say, breeds appreciation but there is such a thing as wearing out the patience of a cavalier. The really intelligent woman knows when not to overdo it. You understand?"

"Perfectly, madame," the maid replied.

The Countess let herself out and sought the stairs. She moved lightly down steps that were made mute by the weight of their waterfall of gorgeous carpet. Murals looked down upon her progress to the lower floor, tapestries glittered with threads of flame, the very air seemed somnolent with the heaviness of sybaritic luxury.

Humming a snatch of a boulevard *chansonette*, the Countess turned into a lounge room that was to the right of the entry-hall below. The aroma of cigarette smoke drifted to her. When she crossed the threshold the Marquis de Remec stood, a well-made, immaculately groomed individual in his perfectly tailored evening clothes.

"Forgive me, Armand," the Countess pleaded. "Marie was so stupid tonight—all thumbs. I thought she would never finish with me."

The Marquis lifted her fingers to his lips.

"How lovely you are!" he cried softly. "Ah, dear one, will you never say the word that will make me the happiest man in all France? For two years we have worked together shoulder to shoulder, side by side—for two years you have been a star to me, earth-bound, beautiful beyond all words! Two years of—"

The Countess interrupted with a sigh.

"Of thrills and danger, Armand! Of plots and stratagems, plunder and wealth! I think, *mon ami*," she said seriously, "if we are successful tonight I will marry you before April ends. But wait, understand me. It will be a secret. I will still be the Countess d'Yls and you will remain the Marquis de Remec to all the world but me. Then, my friend, if either of us suffers disaster one will not drag the other down. You see?"

She seated herself beside the Marquis, considering him wistfully.

"But *tonight*?" he said in a stifled voice. "The de Valois affair is the hardest nut we have yet attempted to crack! Tonight we will need all of our cunning, all of our wits!"

The Countess lifted airy brows.

"Indeed?"

The Marquis leaned closer to her.

"There is not," he explained rapidly, "only Monsieur Murgier of the Surete to consider—the knowledge that he has been blundering after us for months—but the Wolf as well! An hour ago only, François picked up some gossip across the river, in some dive. The Wolf steals from his lair tonight *questing the de Valois pearls*! Do you understand? We must face double enemies—the net of Murgier, the fangs of the animal who sulks among the Apache brigands of the river front. And this is the task you give to set a crown upon my every hope!"

The Countess d'Yls touched his hand with her pretty fingers.

"Does the threat of Murgier and the presence of the Wolf pack dismay you?" she questioned lightly. "You, the undaunted! You who have been the hero of so many breathless adventures! Armand, you—you annoy me."

De Remec stood.

"But this is different!" he cried. "Here I have something at stake more precious than gold or jewels—your promise! I—I tremble—"

The Countess laughed at his melodrama.

"Silly boy! We shall not fail—we will snatch the famous pearls from under the very noses of those who would thwart and destroy us. *Voilà!* I snap my fingers at them all. Come now, it grows late. Had we not better start?"

The other glanced at his watch.

"Yes. François is waiting with the limousine—"

When they were side by side in the tonneau of the purring motor, the Countess glanced at the streaming windows and shivered.

"Soon it will be late spring," she said quietly. "Soon it will be our privilege to rest city-weary eyes on the valley of the Var. I intend to open the Chateau in six weeks, *mon ami.* It will seem like heaven after the miserable winter and the rain, the rain!"

The car shaped a course west, then south. Paris lifted a gaudy reflection to the canopy of the frowning clouds, flashing past in its nightly pursuit of pleasure. The Countess eyed the traffic tide idly. Her thoughts were like skeins of silk on a loom that was slowly being reversed. She thought of yesterday—of the little heap of jewels in the boudoir of the villa at Trouville that had been the scene of that week-end party, of herself stealing through the gloom to purloin them—of the Marquis bound on the same errand—of their meeting—surprise—their pact and the bold, triumphant exploits they had both planned and carried out.

The red lips of the Countess were haunted by a smile.

It had all been so easy, so exciting, so simple. True, the dreaded Murgier of the Law had pursued them relentlessly but they had always outwitted him, had always laughed secretly at his discomfiture, rejoicing together over their spoils.

Now, tonight, it was the de Valois pearls—that famous coil the woman had had strung in Amsterdam by experts. Tomorrow Madame de Valois would be bewailing its loss and the necklace—the necklace would be speeding to some foreign port, safe in the possession of the agent who handled all their financial transactions.

"The Wolf!" the Countess thought.

Surely there was nothing to fear from the hulk of the Apache outlaw—a man whose cleverness lay in the curve of a knife, the slippery rope of the garroter, the sandbag of the desperado. How could the Wolf achieve something that required brains, delicate finesse? It was only the chance that Murgier might upturn some carefully hidden clew that was perilous—

"You are silent," the Marquis observed.

"I am thinking," the Countess d'Yls replied dreamily.

A dozen more streets and the motor was in the Rue de la Saint Vigne, stopping before a striped canopy that stretched from the door to the curb that fronted the Paris home of Madame de Valois. The windows of the building were brightly painted with light. The whisper of music crept out. Set in the little, unlighted park that surrounded it, the house was like a painted piece of scenery on a stage.

A footman laid a gloved hand on the silver knob of the limousine door and opened it. The Marquis de Remec assisted the Countess to alight. Safe from the rain under the protection of the awning they went up the front steps and entered the house.

"You," the Countess instructed cautiously, "watch for Murgier and I will take care of the Wolf whelps! If the unexpected transpires we will meet tomorrow at noon in the basement of the Café of the Three Friends. François has been instructed?"

"He will keep the motor running—around the corner," the Marquis whispered.

Then, pressing her hand: "Courage, dear one, and a prayer for success!"

To the Countess d'Yls it seemed that all the wealth and beauty of the city had flocked to the ballroom which they entered together.

Under the flare of crystal chandeliers Fashion danced in the arms of Affluence. Everywhere jewels sparkled, eyes laughed back at lips that smiled. Perfumes were like the scents of Araby on a hot, desert breeze. Conversation blended with the swinging lilt of the orchestra on the balcony—the shuffle of feet and the whisper of silks and satins filled the room with a queer dissonance.

Separating from the Marquis, the Countess, greeting those who addressed her with a friendly word, a smile or bow, promptly lost herself in the crush. Murgier's assistants she left to the attention of de Remec. She decided, first, to mark the presence of Madame de Valois and the pearls—after that she would seek the Wolf or his agents in the throng.

After some manoeuvering the Countess discovered the location of Madame de Valois. The woman was dancing with a gray-bearded Senator—an ample, overdressed burden from whose fat neck the famous rope of pearls swayed with every step. The Countess watched the woman drift past and then turned to seek the footprints of the Wolf.

In and out among the crowd she circulated, disregarding those she knew, scanning anxiously the faces and appearance of those she had never before seen. An hour sped past before she believed she had at last discovered the man she sought. This was a beardless youth in shabby evening attire who lingered alone in a foyer that adjoined the south end of the ballroom.

Watching, the Countess touched the elbow of a woman she knew, discreetly indicated the youth and asked a question.

"That," her friend replied, "is a Monsieur Fernier. He is a young composer of music from the Latin Quarter. Madame de Valois invited him tonight so that he might hear the orchestra play one of his own dance compositions. He is so melancholy, do you not think?"

"From the Latin Quarter," the Countess told herself when she was alone again. "I will continue to watch you, Monsieur Fernier!"

A few minutes later the Marquis de Remec approached.

"Three agents of Murgier present!" he breathed, drifting past. "The doors are guarded. Be cautious, dear one!"

Another sixty minutes passed.

It was midnight precisely when the Countess saw the putative student from the Latin Quarter make his first move. The youth took a note from his pocket and handed it to a footman, with a word of instruction. The servant threaded a way among the crowd and delivered the message to Madame de Valois. The woman excused herself to those about her, opened the note, read it, and after several more minutes began to move slowly toward the ballroom doors. The Countess, tingling, tightened her lips. A glance over her shoulder showed her that Fernier had left the foyer.

What was the game?

A minute or two after Madame de Valois had disappeared through the doors of the ballroom the Countess had reached them. She looked out in time to behold the other woman crossing the entry-hall and disappearing through the portieres of the reception room beyond. There was no one in evidence. Certain she was on the right trail and filled with a growing anticipation, the Countess waited until the portieres opposite ceased to flutter before moving swiftly toward them.

The metallic jar of bolts being drawn, a scraping sound and then a damp, cool current of air told the Countess that without question the long, French windows in the reception room, opening out on a balcony that overlooked one side of the park, had been pushed wide. She parted the portieres cautiously and looked between them.

The chamber was in darkness—Madame de Valois was a bulky silhouette on the balcony outside—and voices mingled faintly.

On noiseless feet the Countess picked a stealthy way down the room. Close to the open windows she drew back into a nest of shadows, leaned a little forward and strained her ears.

There came to her the perplexed query of Madame de Valois:

"But why do you ask me to come out here? Who are you? What is the secret you mention in your note?"

A pause—the suave, silky tones of a man:

"A thousand pardons, Madame. This was the only way possible under the circumstances. My secret is a warning—unscrupulous people are within who would prey upon you!"

"You mean?" Madame de Valois stammered.

"I mean," the man replied, "your pearls!"

Another pause—plainly one of agitation for the woman on the balcony—then the man again:

"Madame, allow me to introduce myself. Possibly you have heard of me. Paris knows me as the Wolf! Madame will kindly make neither outcry nor move—my revolver covers you steadily and my finger is on the trigger! I will take care of your pearls and see that no one takes them. Madame will be so kind as to remove the necklace immediately!"

Madame de Valois's gasp of dismay followed hard on the heels of a throaty chuckle. Came unexplainable sounds, the words:

"Thank you. Adieu!"

—then the woman tottering in through the open windows, a quivering mountain of disconcerted flesh, making strange, whimpering sounds.

Madame de Valois had hardly reached the middle of the reception room before the Countess was out on the balcony and was over its rail. A single glance showed her the shadowy figure of the Wolf hastening toward the gates at the far end of the park that opened on the avenue beyond.

With all the speed at her command the Countess ran to the other door in the street wall that was to the right of the house. The door was unlocked. She flung it open and surged out onto the wet pavement, heading toward the avenue, running with all speed while her fingers found and gripped the tiny revolver she had hidden under the overskirt of her evening creation.

She reached the gates at the northern end of the park at the same minute footsteps sounded on the other side of them. They gave slowly, allowing a stout, bearded man to pass between them. The Countess drew back and waited until he turned to close the gates after him.

Then she took two steps forward and sank the muzzle of her weapon into the small of his back.

"Do not trouble yourself to move, Monsieur Wolf," she said sweetly. "Just keep facing the way you are and I will help myself to the pearls without bothering you."

She could feel the quiver of the man's back under the nose of the gun.

"You will die for this!" the Wolf vowed.

The Countess found the smooth, lustrous coil of Madame de Valois's necklace in his side pocket and stuffed it hastily into her bodice.

"Possibly," she agreed amiably. "But this is no time to discuss the question. Pay attention to what I say. If you move before two minutes elapse I will shoot you down in your tracks! Continue to keep your face glued to the—gates—and—"

Dropping her weaponed hand, the Countess surged around the turn of the wall where the avenue joined the side street and raced across the petrol-polished asphalt toward François and the waiting limousine. Hazily aware of the growing tumult in the house itself, the Countess was stunned by the sudden crack of a revolver, the whistle of a bullet flying past her, the hoarse bellow of the Wolf's voice:

"Police! . . . Police! . . . Thieves! There she goes! . . . In that car . . ."

Pausing only to fire twice at the howling Apache, the Countess, sensitive to the fact that a machine was rolling down the street toward her, climbed into the limousine.

"Quick!" she cried breathlessly. "Off with you, François!"

Like a nervous thoroughbred, the car sprang toward the junction of the avenue beyond. The Countess pressed her face to the rear window. The other motor was a thousand rods behind, a car with pale, yellow lamps—a police car—one of the machines of the Surete.

"Across the river!" the Countess directed through the open front glass of the limousine. "We will shake them off on the other side of the Seine!"

Across a bridge—over the night-painted river—past cafés and then into a district of gaunt, silent warehouses, the limousine panted. Twice more the Countess looked back. The pale, yellow lamps behind followed like an avenging nemesis.

"Round the next corner and slow down," the Countess commanded crisply. "The minute I swing off, speed up and head for the open country—"

On two wheels the limousine shot around into the black gully of a narrow, cobble-paved side street. Its brakes screamed as it slowed for a minute before lunging forward again. Shrinking back behind a pile of casks that fronted one of the warehouses, the Countess laughed as the second car whirled past.

"The long arm of Murgier!" she sneered. "What rubbish!"

Still laughing a little, she moved out from behind the casks—to stiffen suddenly and dart back behind them again. A motorcycle had wheeled into the silent street and a man was jumping off it.

The Countess, frantic fingers clutching the pearls of Madame de Valois, knew it was the Wolf even before his level tones came to her.

"Mademoiselle," the Apache said. "I know you are there. I saw the shimmer of your gown before you stepped back behind those casks. You cannot escape me. *Hand the necklace over!*"

"The theft of the de Valois pearls?" the Countess d'Yls cried softly. "Monsieur is joking!"

Murgier, on the shaded promenade of the Chateau, touched the tips of his disconsolate mustache.

"There is really," he said almost wearily, "no use in pretending surprise or indignation. Four days ago we bagged the Wolf—he made a full and complete confession . . ."

The sunlit quiet of the promenade was broken by the throaty cry of the Countess d'Yls. She jumped up, her blue eyes cold, blazing stars.

"Yes, you devil!" she said unsteadily. "Yes, Monsieur Ferret, we took the pearls—*I* took the pearls! The Wolf did not get them! No one else shall! I have hidden them well! Take me, take us both—jail us—you will never find the necklace—no one ever will!"

Murgier snapped his fingers twice. The men who had come up the dusty road in the travel-stained motor rounded the corner of the walk. The Countess laughed insolently at the man who faced her.

"In a measure," Murgier said quietly, "your statement is true. No one will ever reclaim the de Valois pearls. Let me tell you something. When the Wolf made his appearance that night at the warehouse, you saved the necklace from him by dropping it into the mouth of an open cask. Is that not correct? You marked this cask so you might distinguish it again. When you foiled the Wolf your agent began a search for the cask. It had been stored away in the warehouse—there were difficulties—so far your aid has not been able to locate it—but you have hopes. Madame Countess, it is my duty to disillusion both you and—" he nodded toward de Remec—"your husband. There was one thing you overlooked—the contents of the cask in question—"

The Countess drew a quick breath, leaning forward as if to read the meaning of the other's words.

"The contents?"

Murgier smiled.

"The cask," he explained, "we found to be half full of vinegar. The pearls are no more—eaten up like that! Pouf! Let us be going."

Rogue: Mr. Amos Clackworthy

A Shabby Millionaire

CHRISTOPHER B. BOOTH

AS WAS TRUE for so many writers for the pulp magazines of the 1920s and 1930s, Christopher Belvard Booth (1889–1950) was prolific, producing ten mysteries under his own name between 1925 and 1929 and another eight crime novels between 1924 and 1935 under the pseudonym John Jay Chichester. Approximately fifty short crime stories, published in Street & Smith's *Detective Story Magazine*, all appeared in the 1920s and 1930s as well. Booth also wrote a number of Western stories, five of which were filmed. After that avalanche of fiction, Booth appears to have vanished, as no works attributed to him appeared in the 1940s or after. Booth, born in Centralia, Missouri, also worked as a journalist for the *Chicago Daily News* and later owned his own newspaper.

Mr. Clackworthy appears in two short story collections, *Mr. Clackworthy* (1926) and *Mr. Clackworthy, Con Man* (1927); in both of them he preys on victims who deserve to be swindled: greedy bankers, crooked stock brokers, and their ilk. Readers rooted for the grifter even though, like so many of the crooks of the era, he did not play the part of Robin Hood; he kept the money. Clackworthy was described by his publisher as "a master confidence man, smooth-spoken, grandiloquent, full of clever schemes for the undoing of rascals more unscrupulous than himself." His partner, James Early, is a roughneck henchman who was so well known to the Chicago police that he was given the nickname "The Early Bird."

"A Shabby Millionaire" was originally published in *Detective Story Magazine*; it was first collected in *Mr. Clackworthy, Con Man* (New York, Chelsea House, 1927).

A SHABBY MILLIONAIRE

Christopher B. Booth

THAT GENIAL HARVESTER of "easy money," Mr. Amos Clackworthy, was again in funds. And none too soon; for eight unprofitable months he had seen his best-laid plans miscarry, his shrewdest schemes come to naught but approaching bankruptcy.

When it had seemed as if the ebb tide would sweep his last dollar from him, together with his sumptuous establishment in Sheridan Road, where he had lived for more than three years in ease and luxury, there had come a turn in his luck. Even without working capital—that confidence-inspiring display of wealth which had lured so many wealthy victims—he had been able to trim a certain Mr. MacDowell, and a canny Scot at that, to the merry tune of twenty thousand dollars.

Not a great sum for a man who had accustomed himself to the spending pace of a millionaire, but it had certainly saved Mr. Clackworthy from the humiliation of bankruptcy court, and the rich furnishings of his apartment from the auctioneer's hammer. The immediate future was safe.

Mr. Clackworthy sat in a high-backed chair beside his rosewood library table, the elbows of his dinner coat resting upon the arms, and the tips of his long, slender fingers touching lightly. Upon his face there was a pensive expression, as he looked at the far wall, where there hung a small painting.

Across the room was Mr. Clackworthy's friend and chief assistant, James Early, nicknamed in those crass days, when his movements were of extreme and often embarrassing interest to the police, "The Early Bird." The latter occupied his favorite seat by the window which looked down upon Sheridan Road and its endless procession of motor vehicles.

The master confidence man's thoughtful mood, his meditative abstraction, gave James an expectant thrill. Perhaps, he told himself hopefully, a new scheme was under way. In funds or out of funds, The Early Bird knew only complete happiness when they were engaged in one of those fascinating adventures to which he referred as "raking in the coin."

Some minutes had passed in silence; presently Mr. Clackworthy relighted his cigar which had gone out, exhaled a cloud of rich, blue smoke, and reached to the table for a magazine. The Early Bird's thin shoulders heaved a sigh, and a groan of disappointment escaped him.

"Something seems to trouble your peace of

mind, James," murmured the master confidence man, and there was the suspicion of a twinkle in his eye.

"My piece of mind, huh?" growled The Early Bird. "Mebbe I ain't got no eight-cylinder noodle on me; mebbe I'm only a light four and only hittin' on three cylinders at that, but I can tell *you* something."

"I never turn a deaf ear to words of wisdom, James," chuckled Mr. Clackworthy. "Pray, proceed, although, before you do, I must assure you that I intended no reflection upon your mentality."

"Yeah, I gotcha, boss," grunted The Early Bird, "but I'm gonna spill you an earful just the same. When I see you sittin' there, lookin' like a medium gone into a trance, I says to myself, 'The boss is cookin' up somethin'; the boss has got a hen on, and in a couple of minutes I'm gonna hear biddie doin' a proud cackle.' And now there you go, stickin' your nose inside one of them there magazines. Huh, readin' that truck ain't gonna help us to grab any new kale!"

Mr. Clackworthy laughed, as he fingered the point of his Vandyke beard.

"Evidently," he said, "you observed my thoughtful mood, as I sat here looking at my little painting on yonder wall. I was wondering what price it would have brought at a forced sale."

"Mebbe five bucks," ventured The Early Bird, who depreciated art as well as literature.

"Oh, come, James!" remonstrated the master confidence man. "You forget that picture is a Hulbert. Haven't I told you that I paid two thousand five hundred dollars for it?"

"Say, boss, don't waste no time talkin' about pitchers when we've busted our hoodoo and has got things breakin' our way again. What if we did get our mitts on twenty thousand smackers when we throwed the hooks into that Scottish goof? I ain't denyin' that there's been times when a century note looked like all the dough in the world, but, the way you're livin', it ain't gonna last forever. Huh, there was days, when you was hittin' it up good, that fifty thou' wasn't so much."

Mr. Clackworthy's mood became more sober, and he nodded his head in agreement with the remarks of his coplotter against the safety of carelessly chaperoned bank balances.

"James, you are right; there were those days when we had twenty or thirty thousand in cash that we could risk on a turn of the wheel and take a loss without embarrassment. More than once I have seen our personal fortune come very close to a quarter of a million.

"However, my friend, as I sat here speculating what that painting would have brought under the auctioneer's hammer, it forced me to a fresh realization of how narrow was our escape from disaster, and how important it is—"

"That we step out an' clip another woolly lamb," finished The Early Bird, with a grin of delight. He hitched forward in his chair in an attitude of engrossed attention. "Crank up the old talkin' machine, boss, an' lemme listen to that favorite record, 'We're gonna go fishin' for suckers.' Boss, lemme in on the who, when, and how of this new trimmin' expedition."

"The plan so far, James," responded Mr. Clackworthy, "is, I regret to say, in a somewhat nebulous state, but—"

"Whatcha mean neb-nebulous state?" interrupted the other. "Trim down them words to my size an' lemme have the facts in first-reader langwich. Y'know I ain't chummy with that Webster guy like you are."

"I mean that the scheme is not in definite shape—little more than a bare idea, the details of which are to be decided. The next victim on our list is as yet unknown. The how is a bit hazy, too, but as to the when I can answer you. Immediately, James, immediately. Also, my dear friend, I can answer you where. We shall very shortly depart for that popular resort where the ailments of the rich are taken and left behind upon their return. It's a good rule, when seeking wealth, to go to a place where wealth is to be found. And it is a foregone conclusion that we shall find such surplus wealth at Boiling Springs."

The Early Bird wrinkled his shallow forehead and stared at the master confidence man, with a dubious and questioning expression.

"Y'mean, boss," he demanded incredulously, "that you're gonna grab a rattler for this Boilin' Springs place without knowin' who you're gonna throw the hooks into, or how you're gonna do it?" Since Mr. Clackworthy usually had his schemes perfected to precise detail, this mode of procedure was somewhat surprising.

The master confidence man smiled blandly.

"When one goes fishing, James," he answered, "there is no way of knowing what particular fish will be caught, but when one fishes in a stream where the finny tribe is plentiful, uses good bait, and has a little patience, there's a rather good chance that the hook will be swallowed."

"But what's the bait?" The Early Bird urged pleadingly. "Ain'tcha just said that you didn't know how you was gonna—" The question jarred to a stop, as Mr. Clackworthy picked up the magazine from the table and began to turn the pages.

"I have noticed here, James, an article that has ensnared my interest; it is, in a way, a biography. The subject thereof is none other than Mr. Rufus Gilbanks."

Across the face of The Early Bird there flashed an expression of joy.

"Gee, boss! The millionaire oil man!" he exclaimed, leaping to his feet. "Whatcha mean is that Gilbanks is puttin' up at Boilin' Springs, and that we're gonna trot down there an' skim off a few thousand barrels of flowin' gold. Lead us to 'im, boss!"

"Not so fast, James. I have not said that Rufus Gilbanks was to contribute to the rehabilitation of our fortune. In fact, I have no such thought in mind. Calm yourself and allow me to read you a few extracts from this most interesting article.

"In the first place, Mr. Gilbanks is referred to as 'the silent mystery man of American oil.' He rose from obscurity and remains in as much obscurity as he can manage. He detests publicity and the spotlight; he has never sat for a photograph. Except for a very poor snapshot now and then, the curious public can merely speculate as to what Mr. Rufus Gilbanks, one of the country's richest men, looks like. He never talks for publication; he moves in a cloak of mystery. Let me read you a brief word picture of the man."

"Spiel," grunted The Early Bird. Mr. Clackworthy turned to the magazine and read:

> "A tall man with a beard, which would seem to serve the purpose of shielding his features from exposure to the gaze of a curious public, Rufus Gilbanks might be considered distinguished in appearance, except for a carelessness of attire that is almost shabby. His clothes, ready made and inexpensive, cling to him in a wrinkled mass. His collars never fit him and are usually a trifle soiled. No jewelry, except a heavy watch chain spread across his vest, and to this chain there is fastened a worn silver dollar said to bear the date of 1867, and generally supposed to be the first dollar which the multimillionaire oil man ever earned."

The master confidence man put down the magazine and smiled; the smile broadened into a grin, and a throaty chuckle reached The Early Bird's ears, as the latter struggled in vain to understand just what the other was driving at.

"Boss," he complained, "I don't getcha—I don't getcha a-tall."

Mr. Clackworthy's hand went to his pocket and reappeared with an ancient silver dollar. He tossed it into the air, with a flip of his fingers, and the coin described a brief arc across the room. The Early Bird caught it and saw that it bore the date of 1867.

"Is—is it Gilbanks's dollar?" he gasped. "Y'mean that you've had somebody lift it offn him?"

"Not Mr. Gilbanks's dollar, James, but one like Mr. Gilbanks's dollar. If you think it's easy to lay hands on a coin like that, try it. I got it from a dealer, and it cost me fifty."

"A good-luck piece?" inquired The Early Bird, being able to think of no other plausible explanation.

"I trust so, James, and I have a hunch that it's going to bring us quite a bit of good luck—the coin, along with a few other properties. A watch chain with heavy gold links, a supply of collars too large for me, and a couple of hand-me-down suits badly in need of pressing. I already have the beard."

The Early Bird's eyes widened, and across his face there came a look of extreme apprehension.

"Holy pet goldfish, boss!" he exclaimed in a hoarse whisper. "Whatcha mean is that you're gonna go down there to Boilin' Springs an' tell them rich guys that—that you're Rufus Gilbanks? Nix on that stuff, boss! It's five years in stir, if they catch us at that sort of game."

"I shall tell no one any such thing," Mr. Clackworthy retorted severely. "I shall deny it. Moreover, I shall deny it extensively and repeatedly." He paused for a moment and then laughed. "You know, James, the human mind is peculiar; if you deny a thing often enough you convince a considerable number of people that it must be true. It is upon that bit of psychology that I am building our plans of taking our next victim to a trimming. Ring for Nogo, and we shall drink a toast to the success of our new adventure."

Crimson Shackles

FREDERICK C. DAVIS

IN ADDITION to nearly sixty full-length novels, Frederick C. Davis (1902–1977) wrote more than a thousand short stories, producing more than a million words a year during the 1930s and 1940s. He created several series characters, including Professor Cyrus Hatch under his own name, Lieutenant Lee Barcello under the Stephen Ransome byline, and twenty pulp thrillers about Operator 5 as Curtis Steele. None of his creations, however, was more popular than the Moon Man—Stephen Thatcher, a policeman by day and a notorious robber by night.

The son of the police chief, Sergeant Thatcher was utterly dedicated to helping those unable to handle the trials of America's Great Depression, even if it meant breaking the law. In the tradition of Robin Hood, he stole from the wealthy to give to the poor.

To keep his true identity a secret, Thatcher donned the most peculiar disguise in all of pulp fiction—not a mask, but a dome made of highly fragile one-way glass, fitted with a breathing apparatus that filtered air. The glass, known as Argus glass, was manufactured in France and was, at the time, unknown in the United States. As the perpetrator of innumerable crimes, he was the most-hunted criminal in the city, saving lives in equally impressive numbers along the way.

There were thirty-nine adventures about the Moon Man, all published in *Ten Detective Aces* between May/June 1933 and January 1937.

"Crimson Shackles" was originally published in the March 1934 issue of *Ten Detective Aces*; it was first collected in Davis's *The Night Nemesis* (Bowling Green, Ohio, Purple Prose Press, 1984).

CRIMSON SHACKLES

Frederick C. Davis

Chapter I

Nemesis in Scarlet

A RED LIGHT FLICKERED on the switchboard in police headquarters. Phone Sergeant Doyle plugged in. Over the wire came a strident voice:

"They're robbing the place! They're robbing the museum! Send the police!"

Doyle jerked up straight. "Who's calling? What museum? Talk fast!"

"The Van Ormond collection. They're taking it! Men in red masks. They're—*he-elp!*"

The cry was prolonged, piercing. Doyle, pressing the earphones close, heard a clattering thump that told of the distant telephone being dropped to the floor. Then there was another scream, far away:

"They've got me!"

The line went dead even as Doyle plugged into the socket labeled "Broadcasting Studio." "Hell's hinges!" Doyle gasped. As the studio answered he blurted: "Mason! Squad call! The museum in the Van Ormond place is being robbed! Snap it out!"

"On the air!" Mason sang back.

Across the corridor, in a room half filled with filing cabinets, the announcer pushed the phone away. His lips worked fast as he leaned toward the microphone and threw a cam.

"Calling cars Five, Ten, Fifty-one, Seventy-four! Calling Five, Ten, Five-one, Seven-four! Top speed to the Van Ormond place, Glassford and Buckingham Streets. The private museum is being robbed. All other cars stand by for further reports!"

Through the night air the invisible power of the radio antenna lightninged.

Squad call!

The police sedan cruising along the side of City Park was not a squad car, though it was one of the police fleet. Its radio was tuned to the headquarters wave length, and its loud-speaker was rattling.

"Top speed to the Van Ormond place! The museum is being robbed by men wearing red masks."

Red masks!

The two men in the car jerked startled eyes toward each other. The grim-faced detective at the wheel muttered: "By damn!" One dismayed moment his jaw-muscles bunched hard beneath his leathery skin. Then his foot thrust against the accelerator and he swung the sedan through a sharp U-turn.

Detective Lieutenant Gilbert McEwen, ace sleuth of the plain-clothes division of police headquarters, born hunter of men, sent the police car whizzing up the avenue with all the power eight cylinders could furnish.

"Red masks!" the young man beside McEwen exclaimed. "Sounds like—"

"The Red Six!"

Detective Sergeant Stephen Thatcher, son of the chief of police, realized even more keenly than McEwen the startling import of the frenzied squad call. The Red Six, the most daring criminal combine that had ever operated, were at work again—preying even at that moment on the famed, priceless Van Ormond collection.

Tires whined as McEwen swerved around a corner. At the far end of the block the Van Ormond home stood, an imposing edifice of white stone. The museum wing extended along the street up which McEwen sped the car. As he trod on the brakes he saw other cars lined up at the curb, with men guarding them—masked men.

Black-masked faces turned toward McEwen's sedan as it creaked to a stop.

Swiftly he ducked out, grabbing at his service gun. Steve Thatcher eased to the sidewalk beside him. Except for the parked cars, the street was empty. None of the radio patrol machines had yet appeared. Seconds would bring them—but even as McEwen ran toward the entrance of the museum, its broad door opened and half a dozen masked men crowded out.

Gun metal flashed in the light of the street lamps. The nozzles of the masked men's revolvers became black spots pointed at McEwen's hurrying figure.

"Stay back and you won't be harmed!" a voice called in sharp warning.

McEwen fired.

The quiet of the street disappeared in the thunder of roaring revolvers. The masked men answered McEwen's bullet with a fusillade. Slugs clacked against the buildings beyond and caromed screamingly off the sidewalk. Hornets of lead flew as McEwen ducked for the shelter of a doorway and yelled to Steve Thatcher:

"Cover, Steve!"

The blasting bullets separated Thatcher from McEwen in one swift moment. He ducked into the shelter of a car standing by the curb. Another blasting chorus of reports rang out, and again lead whined, forcing McEwen deep into the doorway and Thatcher low behind the car.

The black-masked men were like an advancing army. Separating from the door, alert, ready to fire again should either McEwen or Thatcher dare show themselves, they left a clear space across the sidewalk. Instantly other men appeared, some carrying suitcases, some bearing paintings still in their frames, others carrying glass display racks.

As they scrambled inside the cars at the curb with their priceless booty, still more masked men appeared in the doorway of the museum. And the faces of these men, the last to appear, unlike the others were covered with red. On the foreheads of their masks were Roman numerals: II, III, IV, V, VI.

As the pillagers hurried into the waiting cars, the whine of a siren sounded far away—the shrill warning of one of the squad cars coming like a banshee down the next avenue.

McEwen risked another shot. Bullets swarmed at him and he ducked back, cursing. Steve Thatcher was crouching low in the shadow of the car. He saw masked men advancing toward him, closing him in. He crouched to spring away; but at that instant light flashed down the street, and tires rubbed the pavement as a squad car swung into view.

Instantly there was a shout, and the masked men whirled to attack the car. Bullets rained at it, crashing against the windshield. The men in the seat huddled back before the storm of gunfire. For one instant attention was distracted from Steve Thatcher—and one instant was enough for his quick, sure move.

He was crouched behind a heavy roadster. He twisted the rumble-seat handle and leaped up. Swiftly he slid into the hollow darkness of the rear compartment, and let the seat click back into place.

The blasting guns sounded muffled as Steve Thatcher crouched. He lay on his side, gun directed at the closed rumble lid. He heard heels beating on the pavement. Then the car swayed as some one stepped on the running board, and the starter ground.

Swiftly the car lurched away.

Gil McEwen stood backed in the doorway, grimly gripping his revolver. His coat was ripped in two places where bullets had cut through. His hat was punctured. Breathing hard, he reached out and risked a shot as the cars snarled past him.

Withering fire answered his attack. The hot breath of bullets forced McEwen to drop, gasping. One short moment, and the cars of the museum thieves were streaking away, a black, mechanical herd.

"After 'em!" McEwen yelled at the squad car stopped near the corner.

Motors were roaring. The wail of the siren was growing louder. A second squad car darted into sight as McEwen sprinted toward the first. A third swung from the opposite direction. A fourth was streaking down the avenue toward the intersection. McEwen scrambled through the door of the foremost car as it started up in chase.

The plunderers were already at the farther corner, turning both ways. All the black fleet twisted out of sight as McEwen's sedan reached the halfway point of the block. Behind him the other squad cars were racing. They picked up speed swiftly as the intersection neared. Then—

McEwen yelled hoarsely: "Look out!"

From a hidden spot beyond the corner, a huge van appeared. It looked as big as a box car as it swung to enter the street. A moving barricade, its length crossed the pavement—and there it stopped. Two men leaped from its seat and sprang away. Before the radio cars could stop, the two men had darted out of sight beyond the corner buildings—and the outlet of the street was blocked.

Brakes screeched as McEwen's car slowed. He thumped against the windshield, thrown forward. Shouts came from the cars behind as brakes smoked and bumpers clashed. McEwen stumbled out, gun in hand, and ran past the huge hulk of the van.

Far up and down the avenue flanking the park, black cars were racing.

McEwen sprang back. "Get after 'em! Corner 'em! Get around the block! By damn, you've got to move fast!"

Gears snarled. Bumpers clanked again. Engines raced as the squad cars backed. McEwen climbed into the van and spent a wrathful moment trying to start its engine, but the ignition had been locked. When he climbed down, the radio cars, jouncing over the curbs in their frantic haste to chase the escaping thieves, were rushing toward the far and unbarricaded corner.

"Yeah," McEwen said sourly as they swerved out of sight. "'Get after 'em and corner 'em.'" He started grimly for the open doorway of the Van Ormond museum. "A swell chance they've got. A swell chance!"

Complete darkness enveloped Steve Thatcher. The exhaust of the rushing roadster rumbled in the closed space around him. He was swayed back and forth by the turning of the car as it swung past corners. For long minutes he lay listening, gun in hand, as the roadster sped over smooth pavement.

Then it began to tremble over rougher streets. Steve Thatcher guessed bricks or cobbles. This continued for moments. Thatcher tried to reason where the car was, but it was hopeless. There were more turns, and a continued trembling of the car chassis; and then, abruptly, a swerve and a stop.

The men in the front of the car got out. There were quick, muffled voices, and heels tapping the pavement. The purring of other cars sounded close. Gradually the sounds lessened, then vanished completely. Thatcher waited, listening, through long moments of silence.

He edged forward, and pushed at the padded rumble-seat cover. It held firm. It was latched in place; and there was no handle on the inside. Thatcher had had no opportunity to slip something in the crack to keep the catch from clicking into its socket. He was locked securely in.

He fumbled out a folder of matches and struck a light. Turning on his back, he could see the latch-belt resting in its socket. He thrust at it, and it moved. Striking another light, he brought out a key, and used it to press the bolt back. It was almost free when—

A click sounded. The rumble seat swung up. Over the edge appeared a hand gripping an automatic. The barrel of the gun looked down at Steve Thatcher as he stared.

"Come out!" a voice commanded.

Thatcher dragged himself up quickly. Doing so, he saw another hand and another gun pointing at him from the opposite side. Now two heads appeared, two faces that were masked in black. The same voice commanded curtly:

"Drop your gun and climb out!"

The beam of a flash light sprang into the rumble space, blinding Thatcher. Wry-faced, helpless in the stare of the two guns, he obeyed orders; he dropped his own weapon. He climbed over the side, while the two masked men covered him.

"Enjoy your trip?" one asked tartly.

"You knew I was in there all the time, did you?" Thatcher asked disgustedly.

"Certainly. This way, if you please."

The firm direction of the guns belied the suave politeness of the suggestion. Thatcher's arms were taken by curling fingers. He was led across a black sidewalk. Glancing around quickly, he saw a dark, deserted alleyway, flanked by sooted brick walls. A lifetime of living in the city gave Thatcher no clue to his whereabouts. Abruptly he was stopped before a placarded door.

The door was opened, and he was pushed through it. He found himself in a vast, musty room. It was filled with old furniture piled high. A single bulb threw black shadows on the brick walls. With the gun prodding him, Thatcher was led along a lane through the furniture, toward another door.

There the hands left his arms. The guns prodded him again. The voice commanded:

"Go inside."

Steve Thatcher stepped past the sill. The door was closed behind him. Bright light dazzled him a moment. His returning vision revealed to him a small room contrasting utterly with the larger one he had just left.

This one was hung with tapestries. Old paintings hung on the walls. Statuettes stood on pedestals. Valuable, all of them; Thatcher realized that at a glance. But his gaze left them at once, and centered on a desk in the room, over which soft light was flooding.

Behind that desk a man was sitting. His face was masked with a red domino. On its forehead was the Roman numeral II.

"Good evening," he said, "Mr. Moon Man!"

Chapter II

Secundus Speaks

Steve Thatcher's muscles jerked tight. He peered appalled at the smiling face of the man at the desk. Words struggled behind his pressed lips, words of protest that would not form.

"You are, of course, Mr. Thatcher," the red-masked one went on, "the Moon Man. Allow me to introduce myself. I am Secundus. I am the chief of what was until recently the Red Six, and what is now the Red Five."

Stephen Thatcher could do no more than stare.

"I was really very gratified to see you lock yourself in the rumble seat of my roadster," Secundus continued smoothly. "I had been planning to get in touch with you. Now that we are alone, we can talk."

"Talk—about what?" Thatcher blurted.

"If you recall the late Primus, which you no doubt do," said the red-masked man, "you scarcely need ask. Sit down, Mr. Thatcher. Sit down."

Thatcher sank into a luxurious chair because his legs were threatening to give way. He stared dismayed at the man who called himself Secundus as that gentleman, still smiling, poured whisky from a decanter into two glasses and shot seltzer into them. He pushed one highball toward Thatcher and settled back comfortably.

"No doubt this is an unpleasant surprise to you, Mr. Thatcher," Secundus remarked. "You thought you were free of the Red Six, did you not? You believed that no one save Primus knew you to be the Moon Man. A mistake, Mr. Thatcher. I knew."

Secundus sipped. Thatcher did not even move to touch his drink. His eyes clung fascinatedly to the red mask.

"By the simple expedient of overhearing you talking with Primus when he called you to our headquarters a month ago, Mr. Thatcher. I learned then that your thumbprint matches perfectly that of the Moon Man which is on file at police headquarters. I learned, Mr. Thatcher, your secret."

Thatcher could not move.

"Interesting, indeed," Secundus went on. "Knowing that Detective Sergeant Thatcher, son of the chief of police, is leading a double life. That, on the one hand, he is a respected officer of the law, and on the other the most notorious criminal wanted by police headquarters.

"Interesting indeed. The chief of police bending every effort to capture the Moon Man, not knowing the Moon Man is his own son. Gilbert McEwen striving his utmost to bring the Moon Man to justice, not dreaming that the Moon Man is his closest friend, the young man engaged to marry his only daughter."

Thatcher asked hoarsely: "Why—why did you have me brought in here? What do you want? If—"

Secundus' smile returned. "Your crimes, I believe, as the Moon Man, include innumerable robberies—so many that you should be sent to jail for the rest of your life, Mr. Thatcher. I believe, also, there is the matter of several kidnapings and a murder. I suspect that you are innocent of the murder, but you could never prove that now. Could you, Mr. Thatcher?"

"I asked, what do you want?"

"I'm coming to that. The point I am making is that if you were caught, you'd doubtless die in the electric chair. But that, I fancy, is the least horrible consequence your exposure would bring about. Even more terrible would be the tragedy it would bring into the life of your father. And the girl you love, Gil McEwen's daughter—what would she do if she learned that her fiancé is the Moon Man?"

"God! Don't—"

"Naturally," Secundus continued, sipping, "you dread exposure worse than death. Well, then, let us not think of it. I intend to keep your secret, Mr. Thatcher—on the same terms made to you by the late Primus, who introduced you into the organization of the Red Six—now the Red Five."

"You can't force me to—"

"Co-operate with us? I think I can, Mr. Thatcher. You must realize that you are inescapably caught. You will again become one of us, you will again follow our orders. You will again act as our special informer on police activities. You will serve us loyally, Mr. Thatcher, as long as we wish you to—unless you desire that your father, and McEwen, and your sweetheart shall learn that you are, in fact, the notorious Moon Man."

Thatcher said grimly: "You know I didn't rob for the sake of the money. You know I played the Moon Man and robbed to help—"

"That doesn't matter, Mr. Thatcher. You are the Moon Man, and that is the whole point. Let's not argue."

Thatcher leaned forward tensely. "You're right," he said in a sibilant whisper. "To me exposure would be worse than death. I'll face anything rather than that. I'll—I'll even commit murder. Do you understand that? Murder."

"You're threatening me, Mr. Thatcher."

"I won't allow you to hold that weapon over my head. I won't allow you—"

"I?" Secundus rose quickly. "I alone, Mr. Thatcher? You are laboring under a delusion. I am not the only one of us who knows your secret. Look!"

Secundus stepped to the side of the room and pulled a cord. A tapestry drew back from the wall. Disclosed behind it was an open, glassless window. Beyond it lay another room like the one in which Thatcher stood. Seated in that room, facing Thatcher now through the opening, were four men.

All of them were masked. All the masks were numbered. On the scarlet foreheads were the consecutive Roman numerals III, IV, V, and VI.

"They, you see," said Secundus, "have listened to our little conversation. You see how futile protest is, Mr. Thatcher—unless you choose to attempt five murders here and now. That, I suggest, would scarcely be wise."

Thatcher stared at the red-masked faces beyond as the voice of Secundus lost its suavity and hissed.

"One move of treachery on your part, Thatcher, one suspicious action, and your secret will be disclosed instantly to your father, the chief of police. Remember—always remember—'*We give silence for silence!*'"

Steve Thatcher's mind whirled. Echoing in his memory were words once spoken, in grim determination, by Gil McEwen. By McEwen, who had sworn some day to bring the Moon Man to justice:

"Nothing'll stop me from putting that crook in the electric chair—not even if you were the Moon Man, Steve."

Slowly Steve Thatcher pushed open the door labeled "Chief of Police" on the second floor of headquarters. He found Gil McEwen pacing the floor wrathfully. He found his father, Chief Peter Thatcher, silver-haired and kindly-faced, seated in his cushioned chair behind the old rolltop desk. Chief Thatcher came erect and Gil McEwen stopped short when Steve Thatcher entered.

"Steve!" McEwen blurted. "Where've you been?"

Thatcher answered grimly: "I made a try at following that gang, Gil, but I didn't get very far."

"Well, by damn, you're safe, anyway," McEwen growled. "'Didn't get very far'! Neither've I. It's the damnedest thing I ever ran up against!"

"What did they get out of the museum, Gil?" Thatcher asked.

"Everything they could take! All they left were the pieces too big to carry out. Alarms, guards, nothing stopped 'em. They had plenty of nerve!"

Thatcher asked tightly: "No clues?"

"Clues!" McEwen snarled. "Clues, Steve, are sadly lacking. You think a shrewd gang like that would leave any clues about? Not one! Only it's plain as day that the job was pulled with inside help. It had to be done that way.

"The electric alarms were switched off. The two night watchmen were surprised and tied up. Somebody inside had to throw off the switches, and unbolt the outer door—that's the way they got in. But who?

"Blake and Eswell are at the place now, grilling hell out of the servants, but they won't get anywhere. The servants weren't in on it. Most of 'em were off duty. It was a maid that found out what was going on—she'd been out too, but she came back early, and saw the masked men and the cars outside. She ran in to a phone by another entrance. I'm telling you, none of the servants were working with the gang—it goes higher than that."

"Gil," Chief Thatcher said quietly, "you can't mean that one of the family actually helped the crooks rob their own museum?"

"That's exactly what I do mean, chief. If it wasn't the servants who opened the way to the gang, then it's got to be one of the Van Ormonds. What's worse, trying to find out which one of 'em did it is hopeless. The crime ring is so powerful and so feared that nobody connected with it dares talk. If there's any danger of their talking, you know what happens to 'em. The same thing that happened to Amos Colchester a month ago—and he died of lockjaw.

"Tetanus got him. Lord, it was horrible! He received a little brass head as a warning. It's fear of dying the same frightful way that keeps the members of the crime ring silent. If they don't keep their mouths shut, tetanus will make 'em!"

McEwen jerked open a drawer of the chief's desk and lifted an object wrapped in paper. It was the size of an apple, the modeled head of a man done in brass. The face was a grotesque mask, the lips drawn into a sardonic grin, the eyes protruding. McEwen peered at the ghastly image and shuddered.

"Colchester looked like that when he died. Well, he—one of the biggest men of the city—had been drawn into the crime ring, and he died because there was danger of his talking. That's the way they work, those crooks—they blackmail respectable people into helping them pull off their crimes. The people they hook have position and influence and are able to give them valuable tips. They follow orders because they dread exposure—and death by tetanus."

Steve Thatcher swallowed hard as he listened.

"How the hell're we going to break up an organization like that?" McEwen demanded, thrusting the brass image back into the drawer. "An organization that works in complete secret and has such a powerful hold on their tools? By damn, for all we know half the *élite* of this town are members of the gang. Politicians, bankers, big business men, society women, debs—anybody. Yes, and it's possible that the crime ring's got a man right here in this headquarters as a spy!"

Steve Thatcher winced.

Gil McEwen was pacing the floor. "There's only one thing I'm sure of, Chief. One thing. The master mind behind this gang is the Moon Man."

Steve Thatcher asked through a dry throat: "How can you be sure of that, Gil?"

"How? The Moon Man ran the show during the robbery of the Embassy Ball last month, didn't he? I saw him myself, didn't I, directing the whole thing? Certainly! The Moon Man's the ringleader."

"But—" Thatcher's words came with difficulty—"perhaps the Moon Man is only a tool of the real ringleaders, Gil. Perhaps he's been forced into helping execute crimes, as others have been. If the real ringleaders found out, somehow, who the Moon Man is, and used that information to force him to work with them under threat of exposure—"

McEwen humphed. "Maybe you're right, Steve, but I don't think so. I believe he's the master mind. Ten times I've had him cornered, and each time he's slipped away. His luck can't last forever. The day's coming when I'll crack down on him—crack down so hard—"

The knob rattled and the door opened. A girl stepped into the room eagerly. She was smartly dressed, young, pretty. She was Sue McEwen, Gil's only daughter and Steve Thatcher's fiancée. She stepped to him smiling, and he took her in his arms.

"Steve darling—" She kissed him warmly. "I hoped I'd find you here. I want you to drive me home, and then we're going to have a good, long talk."

She greeted her father and Chief Thatcher as Steve Thatcher frowned. He forced a smile and answered: "Sue, dear, there's nothing I'd like better—"

"Because it's not very long now until we'll be married," she said softly, turning back, "and there are so many things we've got to plan. It's so wonderful, Steve—dreaming it all out and—"

"But I can't, Sue. I can't go with you tonight."

"Steve!" Sue drew back, hurt. "But I won't let you do anything else tonight. What is there more important? You're *going* to drive me home and—"

"Please, Sue," Steve Thatcher pleaded. "I know I've been treating you shamefully, and I'd go with you if it were possible—but it isn't. Believe me. I—"

He stumbled into silence. The disappointment in Sue's eyes sent a twinge through him.

"Steve," she said quietly, coming toward him, "you're troubled about something. I can see it in your eyes. What is it? Won't you tell me? Let's go home together and talk it all over and—"

Tell her!

White-faced, cold, Steve Thatcher stepped past Sue quickly. "Nothing's wrong," he mumbled, and she called pleadingly, "Steve!" but he closed the door. He dared not even glance back as he ran down the steps, and hurried out of the entrance of police headquarters.

Agony shone in his eyes as he crossed the street. He hurried into the corner drug store, shouldered into a telephone booth, and hesitated with the receiver in his hands. Looking up, he could see the lighted windows of the chief's office.

In that room were the three people dearest to him. Sue—his father—Gil McEwen. Three people who must never learn Steve Thatcher's secret—never.

Thatcher called a number. It was a very private number known only to him and one other. In a moment a voice answered.

"Angel!" Thatcher said quickly.

"Boss!"

The voice was Ned Dargan's—Dargan, the ex-pug, secret lieutenant of the Moon Man. Side by side they had worked in defiance of the written law, bound by deepest friendship and loyalty. For long months not even Dargan had known that Steve Thatcher was the notorious criminal who robbed and robbed again, cloaked in a robe of black and masked with silver glass. The secret learned, they had become bound even closer by it. And now Steve Thatcher spoke swiftly to the one man in the world he could trust.

"Angel, they've trapped me again!"

"Boss! The Red Six? Gosh, I thought you'd broken clear of 'em! Gosh, Boss, you can't let 'em drive you—"

"Listen fast, Angel. The Red Six is now the Red Five. They're at work again. I found out tonight that Secundus, who's taken the place of Primus as chief of the crime ring, knows that I'm the Moon Man. He's got me cornered—"

"Boss, you can't let 'em—"

"They've got me, Angel. What they're going to do with me this time I don't know—but we've got to act fast, or they'll use me as the Moon Man again. McEwen's gunning for me, thinking that the Moon Man is the leader. Somehow we've got to get at the Red Five and stop 'em before—"

"Anything you say, Boss!"

"Bless you, Angel. Listen. You can get over to the Royale Apartments in a few minutes. The headquarters of the Red Five is on the top floor. I want you to watch that place. Trail anybody you see leaving the secret headquarters. If we can find out who the Red Five are, Angel, we'll hold trump cards. But it's dangerous—damn' dangerous."

"Never mind that, Boss!"

"Watch yourself, Angel."

"Depend on me, Boss. I'm leaving now."

Steve Thatcher hung up the receiver. For a moment he sat in the booth, white-faced, filled with anxiety. He remembered the brass image in Chief Thatcher's desk—the metal face twisted into the horrible *risor sardonicus* of lockjaw. He recalled the way Amos Colchester had died the month previous—in horrible agony. Ghastly death because he had dared defy the red-masked crooks.

"Angel," Steve Thatcher moaned, "watch yourself!"

Chapter III

The Brass Horror

The imposing building of the Royale Apartments stood in the shadow of the city's tallest skyscraper, the Apex Building. Tonight the street flanking it was deserted except for occasional passers-by. It was almost midnight when a young man went striding past the elaborate door of the apartment house, coat collar turned up and head lowered.

The brim of his hat shadowed his cauliflower ear. The tilt of his chin hid the fact that he had no neck.

Ned Dargan.

Dargan glanced into the lobby as he passed. It was quiet and empty. The grille of one of the elevators was standing open, and the operator was sitting inside it—a huge man with a brutal, apelike face. Trudging on, Dargan glanced up, toward the cornices. On the top floor curtained windows were glowing with soft light.

The headquarters of the Red Five was in use.

Dargan walked the length of the block, crossed the street, and turned. When he reached the lobby of the Apex Building he stepped inside it. He stood in the shadow of a pillar, peering across the street into the foyer of the Royale.

Long, empty minutes passed.

Then Dargan saw the brutelike elevator operator turn, step into the cage, and close the grille. Immediately Dargan darted out of the shadow and across the street. Quietly he stepped into the foyer and walked back to the elevator door.

Only one car was in use at this time of night. The indicator above the bronze panels was moving. Dargan watched it swing farther and farther as the car slid upward in the shaft. At last the needle paused, showing that the cage had stopped at the top floor of the building.

Dargan had learned what he had come to learn. Some one was coming down from the secret headquarters of the Red Five. He slipped out of the foyer quickly, recrossed the street, and ducked again into the shadow of the Apex entrance. Another long minute passed. Dargan could see the floor-indicator of the elevator moving again. Presently the grille opened, and a man stepped out.

He was a stocky man, dressed expensively. He walked out of the foyer and onto the sidewalk. Glancing right and left, he turned, striding briskly away. Dargan watched him alertly until he reached the next corner.

Then Dargan followed. Keeping to the opposite side of the street, eyes fast on the man who had left the headquarters of the Red Five, he quickly swung his short legs. He turned when his man turned, crossed, and eased closer.

So Dargan shadowed his quarry along two dark blocks. Then again the man turned past a corner. Dargan hurried. He reached the corner—and hesitated.

The sidewalk beyond was empty.

Dargan went on, eyes shifting right and left. He saw that there were no doorways along the first half of the block into which his man could have ducked. Two sedans were parked at the curb, but they seemed empty, and Dargan dared not move closer to peer into them. Anxiously he hurried on, to the next corner.

The intersecting street was also empty. Dargan's quarry had vanished.

Covering his consternation by keeping on the move, Dargan turned back on the opposite side of the street. His shifting eyes found no answer to the disappearance of the man he had been following. Again, at the far corner, he turned back.

So he spent long moments, stealthily searching—and finding no sign of his quarry.

Quickly he went on, seething with disgust. He walked again past the front of the Apex Building, glancing toward the top floor of the Royale. Now the highest windows were dark.

"Nobody else there," Dargan muttered.

Saying blasphemous things about himself as

a shadower, he walked away. The room which he had rented under a false name was not far. He hurried toward it. Head still bent, scowling at his failure, he was not aware that, a block behind him, a man was following.

He was the expensively dressed man whom Dargan had been trailing—and now he was trailing Dargan.

Dargan reached the house in which he lived, climbed the steps, and pushed in without glancing back.

Three minutes later the expensively dressed man entered a cigar store a block away and sidled into a telephone booth. He called a number from memory. A voice answered:

"Oriental Importing Company."

"Quintus calling."

"Secundus. You may speak."

"Leaving headquarters a few minutes ago, I was trailed by some one. I ducked into a parked car, and he lost me. I trailed him to his room. He lives there under the name of Sam Daniels."

"Who is he?"

"I don't know. He may be a detective. Possibly he's one of our number. It does not matter. He has been indiscreet, and he may be dangerous."

"I recommend action, Quintus."

"I'll take action—at once."

The man who called himself Quintus—V of the Red Five—pronged the receiver. Immediately he called another number from memory. He talked quickly, in low tones that could not possibly carry through the double glass panels of the phone booth. When, a short minute later, he stepped out, his eyes were glittering grimly and his mouth was a thin, cruel line.

Ned Dargan climbed a flight of stairs. He inserted a key in the lock of a front room. He stepped in, clicking the light switch. He was in the act of flinging off his hat when his muscles froze.

A young man was seated in a chair beside the table—Steve Thatcher.

"Boss!"

Thatcher sprang up. "Angel, have you been on the job? What did you learn?"

Dargan made a disgusted noise. "Boss, I'm lousy. I spotted a guy coming out of the Royale, and lost him—lost him, damn it! I didn't even get a good look at his face."

"He learned you were following him?"

"I guess so," Dargan moaned. "I had a swell chance to spot one of the Red Five, and I muffed it. But next time, Boss—next time I'll hang on!"

Steve Thatcher's eyes were narrowed and thoughtful. "I hope to God there'll be a next time, Angel, but—Listen! You've got to move out of here. You've got to beat it—tonight."

"What? Why, Boss?"

"Because it's too dangerous to stay. You may've been spotted by the man you tried to follow. If you have been—Lord, Angel, do you realize what that means?"

"If anybody makes a pass at me," Dargan threatened, doubling one huge fist, "I'll—"

Steve Thatcher gestured impatiently. "You know what happened to Amos Colchester last month. You know how he died. Tetanus! Once the germs get into you, Angel, you're lost. Any little scratch on the skin, even so small you wouldn't notice it—and you're done for. Nothing that doctors can do will stop the infection once it sets in. God, Angel, I don't want that to happen to you!"

"Yeah, but—what about you, Boss? You're in a damn' sight tighter place than I—"

"Never mind that, Angel. Get your grip packed. Get out of this room tonight—now."

"Boss, I'm not going to run out on you when—"

"You can take a room under another name in some other part of town, Angel. I tell you you've got to do it! If you've been spotted, it's the only way—"

Steve Thatcher broke off as a knock sounded on the door. Ned Dargan turned sharply. His hand slipped toward his hip pocket, where an automatic nestled, as they peered at the panels. Thatcher quickly stepped close.

"Who's there?"

"Western Union."

Thatcher hesitated, frowning, then stepped back and gestured Dargan to answer the summons. Dargan, squaring his shoulders, turned the knob. His hand was still on his gun; but when he saw the uniformed boy outside, his fingers unflexed.

"Sure that's for me?"

"Sam Daniels?"

Dargan peered at the small, square box in the boy's hand. Quickly he signed, and took the parcel. He closed the door, heard the messenger going down the stairs, and looked up to find Steve Thatcher staring at him widely.

"Careful, Angel!"

Thatcher jerked gloves from his pocket and pulled them on. He took the box from Dargan's blunt fingers and tore at the string. He ripped off the paper and lifted the cover. An inarticulate gasp broke through his lips as he peered at the thing inside.

It was the modeled brass head of a man, the eyes bulging, the lips drawn into a horrible grin—the grimace that denoted death by tetanus!

Dargan lifted horrified eyes to Steve Thatcher's face. Thatcher recoiled from the box, and blurted:

"It's their—warning!"

"Gosh, Boss! They have spotted me!"

Thatcher's face was deathly white. "Angel, put on gloves—quick!" As Dargan complied with alacrity, Thatcher strode to the window and looked out upon the empty street. Quickly he drew the shade. "Don't touch anything—not anything you can avoid touching. Don't even pack now, Angel."

"Gosh, Boss, I—"

"There might be a pin somewhere in your stuff. A pin dipped in *bacilli tetani* and placed so that it'll prick you. That would be enough, Angel. Come on—we're going."

Dargan muttered angrily. "Okay, Boss, I'll beat it. But you can't come with me. What if somebody saw us leaving together? They'd know then that you're working with me—and you'd get one of those ugly brass heads yourself!"

"I'm taking that chance. I'm going with you, Angel, because it's up to me to see that you get out of here safe. Grab that hat, and come on!"

Steve Thatcher stepped to the hallway door and inched it open. Dargan shouldered beside him as he stepped out. The corridor was silent and empty. They went down the steps together, alert, tense.

At the outer door Thatcher paused, listening. He turned his coat collar up, pulled his hat brim down. He twisted the knob, glanced out, and stepped across the sill.

"Grab the first taxi you see, Angel. Better stay at some hotel tonight. Tomorrow find another room. Get yourself all new clothes, and let me know—"

"Boss! Look out!"

They were halfway down the steps. Dargan cried out as a shadow moved in the darkness below. A man raised from a huddled position and sprang in front of Thatcher and Dargan. His movement was so swift that Thatcher did not have time to pause before he lunged.

The unknown man's right hand swung up, and the blade of a knife glittered in the street lights.

"Look out, Boss!"

Dargan snapped it, twisting forward. His right fist shot beyond Thatcher's shoulder. His hard knuckles cracked against the assailant's jaw. The man jerked back. The knife, slashing downward, hissed close to Thatcher's face.

"Look out for it—poisoned!" Thatcher gasped.

He leaped aside as the unknown man straightened, still clutching the knife. Dargan ducked low, arms thrown into the defense position of a professional boxer. His eyes glittered as he danced out, toward the man with the knife. Again the arm swung, the knife glittered.

Cloth ripped. Steve Thatcher groaned as he heard the sound. Dargan raised on tiptoes, slamming out his fists. The other man rushed in desperately. Dargan snatched at the knife and caught the man's wrist as their bodies strained in a clinch.

Suddenly they dropped, rolling over. Thatcher saw the knife glittering between the two of them. He was leaping toward Dargan when Dargan broke free and jumped up. The other man lay on the pavement, writhing. Dargan's fists grabbed into his clothes; he jerked the man up.

One terrific straight-armed clout, smashing full into the assailant's face, sent him sprawling in the gutter.

Dargan whirled.

"Skip, Boss!"

He raced along the sidewalk with Thatcher at his side. Past the next corner they darted. Headlights were shining in the street; a car was approaching. Colored lights proclaimed it a taxi. Thatcher signaled it to a stop and jerked the door open.

"Inside, Angel! Did he get you?"

"Sliced through my coat, Boss—never touched me! If any of them saw you with me—"

"Take it fast, Angel!"

"So-long, Boss!"

Thatcher slammed the door. The taxi spurted away, with Dargan peering out the window. Thatcher hesitated as it rolled past the intersection into the darkness of the street beyond. His impulse was to rush back to the man who had attacked them; but he checked it.

Turning, walking swiftly, he lost himself in the darkness of the streets.

"Thank God, Angel," he moaned, "they didn't get you!"

Chapter IV

The Scarlet Power

Black headlines streamed across the front page of the afternoon newspaper:

LLOYD VAN ORMOND DYING OF TETANUS!

Seated in his father's chair, in the chief's office in police headquarters, Steve Thatcher read the account for the twentieth time.

Lloyd Van Ormond, youngest son of the noted family, had collapsed at the breakfast table that morning. Rushed to the hospital, his case was diagnosed as tetanus. There was a small cut on his arm, evidently made by a sharp knife, through which the bacilli had entered his body.

Grimly Steve Thatcher read that. It was Van Ormond then, a tool in the hands of the Red Five, who had attacked Dargan and Thatcher on the steps of the rooming house. In the fight with Dargan the poisoned blade had cut him. Now he was gripped in the throes of lockjaw—dying.

"No hope is held out for his recovery," the newspaper article read.

Steve Thatcher glanced up as the door banged open. Gil McEwen marched in, red of face. He dropped into a chair, chewing angrily on a cigar. Steve Thatcher half rose and asked anxiously: "Did he talk any, Gil?"

"Talk?" McEwen blurted. "He couldn't talk. Jaw's locked. Got sent to the hospital too late. Haven't I been there all day, trying to get something out of him? I tried to make him write what he knew, but all he would write was that it was an accident."

McEwen sighed wearily. "Maybe. On the other hand, it's a certainty that Van Ormond had been drawn into the crime ring. They'd forced him to be one of them. He was forced to help them steal his father's collection. Poor guy—dying like that. You ought to know, Steve. You saw Colchester die."

"I know," Thatcher said quietly.

Only too well he knew. But for the swift power of an ex-pug's fists, the man dying in the hospital tonight might have been Ned Dargan—or Steve Thatcher.

"Van Ormond's death will only tighten the hold of the crime ring on the others. It'll make 'em still more afraid of dying the same way. By damn, it's driving me crazy! Trying to fight—"

The telephone clattered sharply. McEwen

broke off with a growl as Thatcher took up the instrument. A suave voice came over the wire.

"Good evening, Stephen Thatcher. I recognize your voice. This is Secundus talking."

Thatcher's hand went white around the phone as he sent a sharp glance toward McEwen. "What do you want?"

"You are to be at our headquarters within ten minutes, Mr. Thatcher. Ten minutes at the outside. Orders are waiting for you."

Thatcher breathed hard. "And if I don't come?" he demanded grimly.

"You know full well the absolutely certain result that would have. Your father and McEwen will be informed of your secret identity. You will not forget that—*we give silence for silence.*"

Thatcher swallowed hard. "All right. All right."

"Within ten minutes."

And the line went dead.

Steve Thatcher rose stiffly. McEwen was eyeing him. The leather-faced detective grimaced. "What do you think about this thing, Steve? Who do *you* think is behind it?"

Thatcher's throat tightened. "I—I'm stumped, Gil," he said strainedly. He put on his hat and strode to the door, as McEwen eyed him strangely. "Just got an important call—I've got to go."

McEwen's bright eyes haunted him as he ran down the stairs. In the police garage he climbed into his roadster. He started off, swinging into the street, hands clamped white to the steering wheel. "Within ten minutes," Secundus had commanded inexorably, and Steve Thatcher was obeying.

Rendezvous with the red power!

Steve Thatcher walked quickly from his car into the richly decorated lobby of the Royale Apartments. He stepped into the elevator and the huge, brutal-faced operator clacked the door upon him. The giant's eyes pierced Steve Thatcher during the ride up. When the cage stopped, Steve crossed an empty corridor.

He pressed a button at a door. An electric lock clicked. Stepping through, Thatcher found himself in a small, curtained room. Except for a table at one side, it was empty. Thatcher's gaze dropped to an object lying on the table—a black domino mask.

A voice came from behind the curtains: "Cover your face, if you please."

Feverishly, Steve Thatcher obeyed. In a moment the curtains parted, and two men came through. They were attired in tuxedoes, and their faces were also covered with black dominos. They stationed themselves beside Thatcher and suggested politely:

"This way."

Impotent rebellion tore at Steve Thatcher's mind as he was led along a dim corridor. A door was opened before him. He was led across a room to a chair which was facing a wall. He was gestured into it, and when he sat the two black-masked men withdrew.

Silence in the room. Steve Thatcher rose and crossed quickly to the door. He found it locked. Another door in the room was also firmly fastened. The window was thickly curtained. Puzzled, Steve Thatcher returned to the chair, and sat again facing the wall.

Startled, he saw an image appear on it. The image was being thrown across the room, through a small porthole in the opposite wall, through which a lens looked. The picture was that of another room, richly furnished, brightly lighted. In the center sat a desk, and behind the desk was seated a man wearing a red mask, on the forehead of which was the Roman numeral II.

The image moved as Thatcher watched it. The lips of Secundus parted and suddenly a voice spoke in the room where Steve Thatcher sat.

"What you see," came the voice of Secundus, "is an image produced by wired television, Mr. Thatcher. I am in an adjoining room, speaking to you. I cannot see or hear you—indeed, no one can while you remain locked in—but you will be able to witness everything that is said and done in this office during the next few minutes. The wired television apparatus will allow you to look in upon me exactly as though you were present, and a microphone and loud-speaker will reproduce every word.

"Watch!"

The flickering image of Secundus had been looking straight at Steve Thatcher. Now the red-masked man sat back, and pressed a button on his desk. A moment of silence followed, while Steve Thatcher watched, puzzled, fascinated. Then a door, on the far side of the room in which Secundus sat, opened swiftly.

A girl took three swift steps inward and stopped. At sight of her, Steve Thatcher jerked to his feet and cried out in anguish. The girl's face was clearly visible on the screen, and her name burst explosively from Thatcher's lips: "Sue!"

The sound of Thatcher's voice brought no response from the image of the girl on the screen. She could not hear him. She was standing, rooted with surprise, gazing at the red-masked man at the desk. As her lips moved, her reproduced voice echoed in the room with Thatcher: "Where is my father?"

Secundus said, gesturing: "Sit down, Miss McEwen."

"I came here because I received a telephone message that my father had been hurt," Sue McEwen said quickly. "Where is he? Who are you? Why are you masked?"

"Permit me," Secundus said, rising and gesturing again toward the chair. "The message concerning your father was only a trick, I must confess. So far as I know, he is in perfect health, and certainly is not here. It was only a means of bringing you here, Miss McEwen."

Steve Thatcher moaned again as he watched: "Sue!" The girl turned and strode to the door through which she had entered; but her pulls at the knob were futile; now it was locked. She was pale now, and frightened. She exclaimed: "You're one of the Red Six!"

"Chief of the Red Five," Secundus corrected politely. "Please sit down. I have very interesting information for you. You will not be harmed, of course. You won't sit down?"

Sue McEwen stood defiantly. "What do you mean? Is this a kidnaping? Don't you realize that I will be missed and that—"

"You will be released in a few minutes, Miss McEwen. I will explain quickly. This, you see, is our headquarters—where the organization of the Red Five is centered. Here we make our plans. You have become a part of them—an important part."

Sue McEwen blurted: "You must be mad! Once you let me go, I'll have this building surrounded by radio cars in five minutes! You and your headquarters will—"

"You won't do that, Miss McEwen. Because, you see, you are about to become one of our workers. You are a young woman with many important connections, some of them in police headquarters. We will make valuable use of you. Through your friends, on and off the detective force—"

"Absurd!" Sue exclaimed. "How do you think you can force me to do as you say? I demand that you let me go at once."

"In a moment, Miss McEwen. You will work with us quite willingly, I'm sure, and keep our secret as faithfully as our other workers keep it. For, you see, I am about to make a disclosure to you. Some one very close to you is a member of this organization—and you wouldn't want him arrested as a criminal, would you, Miss McEwen?"

Steve Thatcher, watching the image, stood stunned.

The girl's voice came: "I don't believe that!"

"It's quite true. I am speaking, Miss McEwen, of your fiancé, Stephen Thatcher."

Steve Thatcher moaned in anguish. Intently he watched the image of the girl. She took a quick step closer to Secundus.

"Steve! One of you? That's preposterous!"

"Not at all, Miss McEwen. He is not only a member of this organization. He is also the notorious criminal known as the Moon Man."

Cold weakness overcame Steve Thatcher. He sank appalled into the chair. His eyes clung haggardly to the image on the wall.

Sue McEwen laughed shortly. "You're talking like a madman. Steve Thatcher is the finest person alive. He could never—"

"A difficult thing to believe, I'm sure, Miss McEwen," came the voice of Secundus. "A difficult thing to convince you of. I shan't try—I shall leave that to you. There is one means of proving conclusively that Steve Thatcher is the Moon Man."

Again the girl declared indignantly: "I don't believe it!"

"Your father, Gil McEwen, has the thumbprint of the Moon Man on file at headquarters. No doubt you are thoroughly familiar with it. It will be a simple matter, you know, to compare Steve Thatcher's thumbprint with that of the Moon Man. I assure you, you will find them identical."

The girl was staring transfixed at Secundus. The red-masked man was smiling suavely. And still Steve Thatcher watched, paralyzed.

"I have only one further thing to say, Miss McEwen," Secundus continued. "Until you convince yourself that what I say is true, I advise you to remain silent concerning this visit you have paid me. If you decided, prematurely, to send the police crashing into this headquarters it would result, certainly, in the arrest of Steve Thatcher as the Moon Man.

"It has been a hard shock to you, to learn his secret. It would be a severe blow to Steve Thatcher's father—no doubt it would break the old man's heart and perhaps kill him. It would even crush Gilbert McEwen to discover that his daughter's fiancé is the Moon Man.

"I urge discretion upon you, Miss McEwen. You had best remain silent. And, when orders come to you from us, obey them without question. Now—good-night."

The girl was still standing, gazing dumfounded at Secundus. Now the door opened, and two masked men advanced. They led the girl toward the door, and she dazedly went with them through it. It closed—shutting her from view.

Suddenly the televised image vanished off the wall.

Steve Thatcher jerked to his feet in the dim light. He swiftly crossed the room and strained at the door knob; but the door would not give. Throat tight, chilled to the core, he stood motionless.

"Sue!" came in agony through his lips.

One of the three who must never know—had learned. The girl Steve Thatcher loved. The girl he was engaged to marry. Sue, who had once contemptuously called the Moon Man "nothing but a petty pilferer." In her was bred the creed of her father—hatred for the Moon Man's kind. And now she knew!

"Sue!"

The latch of the door clicked. Steve Thatcher snatched at the knob. He jerked over the sill and stopped short. Two black-masked men were in the corridor. In their hands automatics were gripped, leveled. Behind them stood Secundus, a smile on his lips.

"You dared do that!" Thatcher blurted.

"I fancy," Secundus answered calmly, "you now find additional reason for loyalty to us—since the young lady has become one of us."

"I'll kill you for that!"

The leveled guns stopped Steve Thatcher's furious step forward. Secundus's smile did not fade. His hand slipped inside his coat and he withdrew an envelope, proffering it to Thatcher.

"So we grow strong," he said. "Your orders, Number Thirteen. You will obey them, of course, to the letter."

Steve Thatcher found the envelope in his hands, and he fumbled it into his pocket. Secundus strode down the hallway and disappeared through a door. The guns prodded Steve Thatcher. He was forced along the corridor, into the curtained vestibule.

There he was suddenly left alone. He sensed

that the automatics were still trained on him behind the curtains, but he gave no heed to the threat. He ripped the black mask off his face. Swiftly he stepped through the doorway into the corridor.

It was empty. Frantically he punched the button of the elevator. The torture within him made the minutes seem ages until the car appeared. With the evil eyes of the brutelike operator studying him, he rode to the foyer. He ran out it, glancing swiftly up and down the street.

Sue McEwen was not in sight. One agonized moment Thatcher hesitated. Then, grimly, he ran to his parked roadster. The starter snarled, and he jerked away from the curb. Swiftly he drove in the direction of Sue McEwen's home.

Chapter V

Moon Man's Orders

Thatcher's roadster bucked to a stop in front of a modest house in an outlying residential district. He ran to the porch, and punched the bell button. He waited anxiously until a shadow crossed the pane of the door.

The latch clicked, and Sue McEwen looked out. Steve Thatcher could not speak. The girl gazed at him silently a long minute, deep into his eyes.

"Sue, I've got to come in."

"Of course, Steve. Do come in."

Her voice was not strained now. She stepped back, and he entered. He kissed her, pressing feverish lips to her cool mouth. Quickly he strode into the living room beyond. In the lighter light, he saw that Sue's cheeks were flushed, her eyes clouded with worry. She came toward Steve, forcing a smile.

"It's the first time we've been alone in a long while, Steve."

"Yes. I—I've got to talk with you."

"What—about?"

She turned her eyes from him and sat down. Her manner puzzled him. She was trying to seem her old self, but the pain in her eyes, the lingering doubt, betrayed her. She looked up at Thatcher and smiled again.

"You know," she said, "I've just heard a perfectly horrible story about a—a very dear friend of mine, and it's upset me. I'll be all right in a little while. I don't believe it at all—I simply don't."

Thatcher sat down stiffly, peering at her. "Would it matter a great deal if it were true, dear?" he asked softly.

She gazed at him, not answering, as the color left her face. The moment of silence was torture to Thatcher. At last the girl smiled again.

"But I don't believe it, so it can't matter. A cigarette, please, Steve?"

He drew his silver case from his vest, eyes fast upon hers. He was startled when she took from him, not a cigarette, but the case. She peered at it—peered closer. The cold shock that passed through Thatcher was like a physical blow.

She was studying a smudge on the smooth silver—a print left by Steve Thatcher's thumb.

"Darling—oh, God!" he blurted. "Please don't!"

Now her eyes were wide, her lips parted in hurt amazement as she searched his eyes. He took the case from her and tucked it away. He tried to speak, but words choked him. It was her soft whisper that broke the strained silence.

"Steve! You *are*—"

"Sue, darling! Listen!" Thatcher caught her cold hands in his. "It's true. I confess it's true. But let me explain. I've got to tell you the truth—"

Her hands in his were unresponsive. She was stunned, her face blank. Words now poured past his lips.

"I did it—only to help, Sue! To help people who had to be helped—or they would die. You—you've been in social work. You know how terrible conditions have been—whole families starving—ill—human bodies broken by privation. You know that the city charities act slowly, and can't take care of every one. It's what I tried to do, Sue—to help those that couldn't be helped otherwise—because it was more than I would bear to see them suffer."

Sue did not speak.

"Once you called the Moon Man a petty pilferer, Sue. Because he stole small sums as well as large. He did it—I did it—because that money was necessary to save lives, to feed starving people. It was breaking the written law—I know. It was a higher law I was obeying, Sue—the law of humanity. I couldn't stand by and see people starving and cold and sick. And so I stole—to help them.

"Yes, Sue. I'm the Moon Man. I'm the crook your father has sworn to send to the chair. I swear to you, Sue, that every penny I stole went to the needy. If I did anything more than steal it was because I was forced to do it to get money for them. There's a murder charged against the Moon Man—but I'm innocent of that, before God! I swear it, Sue—I swear I'm telling the truth!"

Still Sue was silent, gazing deep into Steve Thatcher's eyes.

"You have only my word for it, Sue, but you've got to believe me. Oh, Sue, believe what I'm telling you!"

Silence.

Steve Thatcher's voice came quietly. "Perhaps it's too much to ask, Sue. Perhaps it makes too much difference to you. Perhaps you can't love a man—who's done what I've done—'a petty pilferer.' Perhaps you could never bring yourself to marry a man like me. I hope to God—"

He broke off, gazing at her in anguish.

"I love you, Sue—love you more than any one else in the world. It'd kill me if you stopped loving me but—I wouldn't blame you. I wouldn't blame you, Sue."

She took her hands from his. She rose quietly and stood rigidly erect. He came to his feet beside her and searched for an answer in her eyes.

"Steve—please go."

"Sue! You must—"

"Please go, Steve!"

He drew back. His face was haggard, his lips dry, his throat throbbing and tight. He said slowly: "I'll go."

She stood without moving as he took up his hat and walked to the door. He glanced back once, to see her still standing there, not looking at him. A tear glistened on her cheek as he closed the door; a single sob broke through her lips. And then sight of her was shut from him.

Hunched at the wheel, staring blankly into the gleam of his headlights, Steve Thatcher drove his roadster. A country road unrolled as his foot pressed hard to the accelerator; his engine roared and miles flashed past.

For an hour he had been driving, scarcely aware of his own actions, scarcely aware of where he was. The pinching pain in his heart had grown sharper with the moments. Leaden fatigue loaded him. At last, catching his bearings, he turned his car and drove back toward the city.

In front of police headquarters he parked. While minutes passed he sat slumped at the wheel. He was dropping the ignition key into his pocket when he heard the rattle of paper, and drew out a legal envelope, sealed.

"Your orders," Secundus had said.

Grimly Thatcher tore the envelope open. He spread the closely typewritten page. To it a flat key was attached. He read by the light of the dash:

> *To:* Number 13.
> *Concerning:* Operations on the Municipal National Bank.
> *Subject:* Orders.
>
> Tomorrow night, the night following your receipt of these orders, the Municipal National Bank is regularly open from seven until nine o'clock P.M.
>
> At exactly eight-fifty P.M. you will enter the bank. You will carry with you a small case containing the back robe and the

glass mask which comprise the regalia of the Moon Man.

"Oh, God!" Steve Thatcher moaned.

You will ask to be allowed to look into safe-deposit box Number 109. This box, part of our preparations, is rented under the name of Milton Argyle. You will step into one of the booths provided for the purpose of handling the contents of such boxes and immediately garb yourself in the regalia of the Moon Man.

With sickened eyes Steve Thatcher read the remainder of the orders—orders which were part of a plan for looting one of the largest banks in the city—orders commanding him, as the Moon Man, to appear to control the movements of the criminal band which was to swoop down on the bank. The words swam in Thatcher's vision as he finished.

He remembered the anguish in Sue McEwen's eyes.

He read again the inexorable command: "Garb yourself in the regalia of the Moon Man!"

Chapter VI

Menace in Scarlet

Eight-fifteen, read the old clock in the office of Chief of Police Peter Thatcher. It ticked sonorously in the empty silence of the room.

Steve Thatcher thrust the door open. He closed it tightly behind him and strode to the desk. He sat with hand upon the receiver of the telephone, eyes narrowed, lips pressed together, waiting.

Almost twenty-four hours had passed since the orders of the Red Five had been placed in his hands. Almost twenty-four hours had passed since he had last seen Sue McEwen.

Anxiously Thatcher waited with the phone in his hands. The seconds ticked by. And suddenly the bell shrilled. Instantly Thatcher had the receiver to his ear.

"Steve?" asked Doyle, the phone sarge downstairs. "Call for you."

"Put it on!"

A new voice came over the wire. "Hello—Steve Thatcher?"

Thatcher said in a breath: "Angel!"

"Right, Boss!"

"Thank God you got my note, Angel! I sent it as soon as I heard from you—and a package."

"I got 'em both, Boss. I waited to call you right on the dot, like you asked. Say. I don't like it, calling you at headquarters when—"

"There was no other way, Angel. Is that package safe? You read that letter carefully?"

"I know it by heart, Boss!"

"It means a lot, Angel—everything. The plan's got to click through to the split second. You've got to be careful—damn' careful."

"Trust me, Boss! But what about you? You'll be taking an awful chance—"

"There's no other way. For God's sake, Angel, watch yourself. Remember—remember the brass head—the warning."

"I'm not forgetting it! Time's short now. I've got to go if—"

"Bless you, Angel—and good luck!"

Thatcher hung up the receiver. He glanced at the ticking clock as he rose. Quietly he left the office and trod down the stairs. He was passing the door which connected with the headquarters garage when he heard a voice booming—the voice of Gil McEwen.

Steve Thatcher paused, looking into the garage. McEwen was standing beyond the door, facing into the vast room. Against the walls a score of squad cars were lined. In the center space were forty-odd men, wearing police uniforms, members of the squad car crew. McEwen was snapping at them angrily.

"A swell bunch you are—fine!" he rasped. "You moved so damn' slow that every one of the crooks' cars got away from you the other night.

What the hell do you do while on duty, anyway? Go off somewhere and eat picnic lunches? Stop in every speak-easy in every block? Look for blondes to pick up! By damn, no matter what you've been doing, from now on you're going to be on the job!"

Steve Thatcher listened grimly.

"Every time after this a squad call goes out, you're going to be clocked. If it takes you more than sixty seconds by the watch to answer the call, you're sunk. Every damn' one of you'll go back to pounding the gas-house beats. You're not worth a damn unless you move fast. You'll move fast, all right, after this. You will—or else!"

Thatcher turned away, but McEwen's voice stopped him again.

"I've got a hunch that something's going to break tonight—something big—and my hunches are never wrong. I want double patrols in the downtown section. I'm going to be in one of the cars myself—just on that hunch. And if a squad call comes—you're going to move faster than you've ever moved before, I promise you!

"That's all—dismissed!"

Anxiously Thatcher turned away, glancing at his watch. Minutes had passed. It was nearly time for the orders of the Red Five to be executed. As Steve Thatcher hurried from the door of headquarters, McEwen's words rang in his ears.

Double patrol! Got a hunch something's going to break tonight—something big. I'm going to be in one of the cars myself.

Loaded with worry, Thatcher hurried to his roadster. He lifted the rumble cover and peered into the compartment, at a small black case lying there—the case containing the precious regalia of the Moon Man. With a sigh he climbed to the wheel and tramped on the starter.

Just as his car moved off, another drew to a stop on the far side of the entrance. A girl got out of it quickly. She was Sue McEwen, her face drawn, her eyes anxious. She saw Steve Thatcher at the wheel of the rolling roadster and took quick steps after him.

"Steve!" she called.

He did not hear. His roadster picked up speed as she called again. One moment she hesitated anxiously. Then, turning quickly, she returned to the wheel of her own car. Starting up, she began to follow the roadster that was carrying Steve Thatcher toward the Municipal National bank.

A red light stopped her, and Thatcher's roadster gained. She spurted ahead several blocks, and then was surprised to see the other car swerve to the curb and stop. Steve Thatcher got out of it almost directly in front of the lighted windows of the Municipal National.

High overhead the clock in the spire of the Apex Building was indicating the hour: eight-forty-nine.

Steve Thatcher swung the black case from the rumble compartment of the roadster. He did not see Sue McEwen's car stopping in the next clear space fifty yards behind. He walked through the swinging doors of the bank, into the lobby.

Bright light filled the bank. At the bronze grilles of the tellers' windows queues of people had formed, waiting in line. Behind the counters employees of the bank were busy. As Steve Thatcher, cold and grim, crossed toward the grilled partition, his gaze went to one man standing in the file of depositors.

His hair was flaxen, falsely so. One of his ears was cauliflowered. He had no neck.

Ned Dargan.

Dargan was carrying a fat brief case. His eyes found Steve Thatcher and moved away quickly without a glint of recognition coming into them. Steve Thatcher moved on, to the grille door, and when a girl stepped close he said:

"I want box one hundred and nine. The name is Argyle."

"Step this way, sir."

Thatcher strode through the opened door. The girl took the key from him and suggested he wait in Booth B. As she strode back toward the open vault, Steve Thatcher sidled into the small, partitioned space.

He glanced at his watch.

Eight-fifty and a half.

The zero hour of the Red Five was at hand.

Latching the door, Thatcher quickly opened the small case he had carried in. From it he unrolled a long, voluminous black robe. He drew it over his shoulders swiftly. On his hands he pulled black gloves. He lifted carefully from the suitcase a sphere of silver glass—the precious mask of the Moon Man—and placed it over his head.

Steve Thatcher vanished and the Moon Man appeared.

Again he glanced at his watch. The globular mask seemed as bright and opaque from the outside as a mirror, but through it the Moon Man could see as clearly as though it were finest crystal. Seconds were ticking by. Into his black-gloved hand the Moon Man took an automatic.

The orders of the Red Five were singing through his tortured mind as he waited.

Suddenly, outside, in the lobby of the bank—a shrill whistle.

Instantly the Moon Man thrust wide the door. His black robe flapped as he strode toward the open vault. Against the wall, desks were arranged. A bound put him on top of one of them. He whirled, turning his gun upon the startled tellers behind the grille. Through his shell of a mask his voice rang muffled:

"Hands up! Everybody hands up!"

Startled cries rang out. Some hands lifted. A second of tense, alarmed silence followed. During it, the Moon Man's eyes shifted quickly right and left behind his silver mask.

He jerked; a gasp of agony crossed his lips. His gaze paused on a girl standing in the lobby of the bank—a girl separated from the others—a girl peering at him in consternation.

Sue McEwen!

———

While the Moon Man's command still echoed, the doors of the bank swung open sharply. Cars had drawn up outside, and from them men were pouring—masked men. Faces hidden behind black dominos appeared as if by magic. Guns flashed in the light. Into the Municipal National came the masked swarm.

Commands rang: "All hands up! Form lines against the wall!"

From his high vantage point, the Moon Man still stared at the girl who was gazing in horror at him. He tore his eyes from her, and peered at the door. Hordes of black-masked men were appearing. Two lines of them had formed outside the door, guarding the entrance, holding passers-by back.

Others were crowding the depositors against the wall, commanding them to raise their hands. One who was forced to comply with Ned Dargan. He lifted his arms, still holding the fat brief case. He saw Sue McEwen standing motionless; his eyes shifted in terror to the black apparition which was the Moon Man; and a sob caught in his throat.

The Moon Man leaped down. The orders from the Red Five had revealed to him the location of the electric button controlling the grille door which gave into the space behind the tellers' desks. He pushed it, and the latch chattered. Instantly black-masked men came crowding through.

Then red-masked men appeared. They darted in from the sidewalk, guns leveled, eyes glittering. The Moon Man glimpsed Secundus, stationing himself in the center of the lobby. Tertius—III—sprang toward the grille door with Quintus—V—at his side. The others darted to positions of advantage. While women screamed, while men cried out hoarsely, the masked men moved swiftly.

Tertius stepped briskly behind one of the tellers' cages. He saw the young man there desperately pressing a button on the floor with his foot. An expression of amazement was on the teller's face. Tertius's voice came swiftly.

"No use! The batteries on that alarm are dead—we've seen to that. Every alarm in the place is out of commission. Keep your hands up!"

The teller in the next cage, listening through the mesh partition, heard the amazing announcement. Instantly he whirled, and snatched at the telephone in his booth. He grabbed up the receiver and called huskily.

"Police! Robbery—"

He got no farther. Quintus was crowding in upon him. The gun in the hand of the red-masked man belched fire. The rocking report shocked through the room. In the tense silence that followed, the teller twisted away from the telephone. It dropped from his hands as red gushed upon his shirt. With a strangled moan he fell.

Murder!

"That's a warning!" rang the voice of Quintus shrilly.

The Moon Man straightened, peering at the red mask numbered V. Behind the silver glass, his unseen face grew hard and grim. Cold fury turned his gun toward Quintus.

Then, a warning call froze him. He jerked, to see Secundus staring at him through the grille. Secundus's glittering gun was directed at the black-covered form of the Moon Man. And the voice of the red-masked one rang in a hushed whisper:

"Silence for silence!"

Tertius shouted to the black-masked band: "Follow orders!"

The black-faced crooks were already swarming into the tellers' cages, into the vault. Before their threatening guns the clerks and bookkeepers quailed. Canvas bags were whisked into view from the coats of the masked band. Money began tingling into the bags; fistfuls of currency were thrust into them. In the vault, three men were dragging from its place the huge safety drawer in which the cash reserve of the bank was stored.

The Moon Man's eyes darted to one of the figures lined against the wall—Dargan, holding his hands straight up, the brief case clenched in one hand.

"Now, Angel!" he whispered softly. "Now!"

Dargan's hands were moving. While guns faced him he dared click open the catch of the brief case. One hand slipped inside and came out gripping a shiny, elongated object. Swiftly Dargan tossed it, straight into the middle of the foyer.

A crash. A hollow report. White fumes sprang into the air.

Tear-gas!

There were other bombs in the case which Dargan held—bombs taken from the headquarters supply—sent to Dargan by Steve Thatcher during the day.

A shout of consternation broke from the masked men. They whirled as the blinding, choking fumes swelled to enormous volume. As they swung back, Dargan's hand hurled another bomb.

The crashing puff released a fresh cloud of vapor, and the room filled with the stinging mist.

A gun barked, and a bullet tore through Dargan's coat. He sprang toward the base of a stairway which led into the foyer and upward to a balcony overhead onto which doors opened. As he leaped up the steps bullets cracked at him; but the blinding gas was having its effect, and the aim of the gunners was untrue. Bounding, Dargan tossed another bomb, and another.

He bumped into some one on the stairs. He saw the face of Sue McEwen. She was peering at him, startled.

"Out of the way!" he gasped. "Up the stairs!"

Thicker fog blanketed him as he forced the girl higher. On the balcony, with Sue recoiling against the far wall, he paused and tossed more bombs. Now the room was full of muttered cursing, coughing, shouts of pain. Dargan, finding his case empty, grimly grabbed a gun from his pocket and retreated to Sue's side.

"I'll keep 'em away from you!"

The Moon Man, at the first crash, had begun

working his way behind the grille toward the electrically-operated door. As he edged through it, he saw several black-masked men writhing on the floor, disabled. Tears were streaming from the eyes of the others. The Moon Man was edging toward the main entrance, gun leveled against possible attack, when he was startled by a sudden burst of gunfire in the street.

He wheeled, peered out. Police cars were swarming over the pavement outside. Uniformed men were leaping from them, guns out, rushing toward the doors. Flame and lead clashed again as the Moon Man backed away.

The clerk's quick telephone call had brought results!

The black-masked men outside were retreating before the blasting fire of the squad car cops.

A bedlam of alarmed shouts rang inside the bank as the Moon Man whirled away. He groped through the choking fog, glimpsing red- and black-masked faces. And as he moved he heard a shout from outside:

"Fill that door!"

The voice of Gil McEwen!

Twisting back, the Moon Man saw McEwen leaping for the bank entrance. The black-masked gang had recoiled and the way was open. Those inside were crowding down upon McEwen as he pushed through. The detective drew up short, face-to-face with a red-masked man with leveled gun.

One instant, through the swirling fumes, they glared at each other—McEwen and Quintus.

The automatic in the hand of Quintus snapped out fire as McEwen bellowed and leaped. He dropped to one knee, his gun flashing in the dimmed light. Twice he fired, with deadly speed, with grim accuracy. And two bullets drilled into the chest of Quintus.

The red-masked man crumpled, clawing the air. He sprawled on the floor, gun dropping from his hands. McEwen leaped up again with a bellow of savage satisfaction.

Death to Quintus, murderer of the teller, sender of the brass warning to Ned Dargan.

The Moon Man was on the stairs now. As McEwen leaped farther into the bank, eyes streaming scalding tears, he retreated a few steps. McEwen paused, peering up.

He saw the glistening silver globe that was the Moon Man's head. He saw the black-robed figure in the fog. A triumphant cry rang from his lips as he leaped forward.

McEwen's gun crashed.

The Moon Man felt the bullet tug at his robe as he sagged back. He gasped in anguish. Swiftly he fired in return—sent a bullet which he prayed would miss McEwen. Then, leaping black lightning, he bounded to the balcony above, and raced along it.

He saw a door closing, glimpsed Dargan's strained face an instant. He sprang to it. He pushed through, and whirled.

He backed to the door of the directors' room, and behind his silver mask his streaming eyes widened upon Sue McEwen.

Dargan had forced her into the room, away from the gas and the bullets. She had retreated against the table. She stood immobile, peering at the black-robed figure with the globular head of silver. Her lips parted with a silent sob; and from the Moon Man's shell of a mask came a groan.

Footfalls sounded on the balcony outside. Twisting, he shot the latch of the door. Fists crashed against the panels. McEwen's voice came:

"Open up!"

Dargan gasped: "Gosh, Boss—it's him! He's got you cornered!"

The Moon Man tore his hidden eyes from the face of Sue McEwen. He crossed the room swiftly, to the windows on the opposite side. Swiftly he threw one up, and peered down. An alleyway lay below. It was deserted now; but in a few seconds, the Moon Man knew, the squad car men would be swarming into it.

Then the Moon Man saw a telephone pole

within reach, a pole that reached as high as the building.

"Climb up, Angel!" he gasped, whirling back. "You can make it! You'll be safe up there until you can get away without being seen!"

"Boss! I'm not leaving you now! Not when McEwen's got you cor—"

"Up, Angel! Quick!"

The Moon Man forced Dargan across the room to the window. With savage insistence he obliged Dargan to climb through. Poised on the sill, Dargan peered back.

"Boss! Oh, God, Boss!"

"You did your work well, Angel! The Red Five'll think it was the clerk's telephone call that broke up the plan. Quick, Angel—up!"

"Don't worry about me, Boss! I'll get away, all right! Good luck, Boss—so-long!"

Dargan reached out, and gripped the pole. Swiftly he climbed, wrapping arms and legs around it. As he rose higher, fists pounded again on the door behind the Moon Man, and McEwen's voice shouted:

"Break down that door! He's in there! We've got him cornered this time!"

Now Dargan was near the top of the pole. He reached out a leg, steadied himself against the edge of the roof, then pushed over. He disappeared from view quickly.

The Moon Man turned. One quick glance he gave the pale, strained face of Sue McEwen. She was still staring at him, transfixed.

"Sue!"

She gave no answer.

With a moan, the Moon Man reached out the window for the pole. His fingers had not yet touched it when there was a rush of feet across the pavement below. He glimpsed men running into the alleyway—uniformed men—members of the squad car crew.

Swiftly he ducked back.

From below came a hoarse shout: "Cover those windows!"

The Moon Man retreated. Shouts continued to come from below. The door was still shaking with the hammering of McEwen's fists. Now a shoulder crashed against the panels, and the wood cracked.

Sue McEwen took a quick step toward the Moon Man. She sobbed: "Steve, Steve!" He stood erect—a black-garbed figure with shining silver head—looking down at her.

"Sue!"

Quickly he lifted the mask of Argus glass from his head. His eyes were streaming with tears from the sting of the gas. He had been obliged to place his automatic on the table to remove the mask; and as he lowered it he saw, startled, Sue's small hand snatch up the gun.

She leveled it.

"Take off the robe!"

"Sue—for God's sake—"

"Take it off!"

Not understanding, he obeyed. When the robe and gloves were flung onto the table beside the mask, Sue stepped forward again. Her face was grim and drawn as she turned the gun in her hand. Swiftly she swung it—struck out with it—and the hard metal cracked to the side of Steve Thatcher's head.

He recoiled, stunned. The bruise beside his temple was livid red, but he did not even feel the pain of it. He was peering dazed into Sue's desperate eyes.

The girl quickly snatched up the robe and gloves and mask. She jerked open the drawer of a filing cabinet which sat in the corner. Quickly she stuffed the regalia into it, dropped the gun in. She slammed it shut; and then, without a glance at Steve Thatcher, she hurried across to the door.

She drew the latch.

Gil McEwen thrust in. He stopped short, gun leveled. His eyes snapped from the white face of his daughter to the haggard features of Steve Thatcher.

"Where is he—the Moon Man?" he demanded. "I saw him come in here!"

"He—he hit Steve with a gun—and climbed

out through the window. He went down into the alleyway, Dad!"

McEwen leaped for the window. His voice roared down at the men below:

"Look for the Moon Man! He got down there! Scatter and grab him!"

Whirling back, halfway across the room, Gil McEwen stopped short.

"By damn, if he's got away again! By damn, we've saved the bank from being robbed anyway! We've got one man, with a red mask, dead, and a full dozen of the others! We're cracking into this gang! But the Moon Man—by damn—"

"He got out minutes ago, Dad!" Sue said swiftly. "I couldn't open the door because Steve was—hurt so badly—"

McEwen strode to the door and stopped again. His eyes glittered back.

"What the hell are you two doing here, anyway?"

"We—we came here—seeing about the house we're going to live in when we're married, Dad. This bank holds a mortgage on it, and—we came to talk terms. We were going to surprise you—"

McEwen tore himself away. He went running down the stairs shouting orders to "get the Moon Man!" Sue McEwen turned slowly, and her eyes sought Steve Thatcher's. He was gazing at her in amazed confusion.

"Steve!"

Sue McEwen went into his arms. He crushed her body close to his. Her cheeks pressed his warmly and her lips, close to his ear, whispered.

"I'll never tell them, Darling—I'll never tell!"

"God bless you!" murmured Steve Thatcher. "God bless you, Sue!"

"I can't let it matter, Steve—not now. I understand. We can't let it matter."

From below Gil McEwen's voice rang gruffly: "Get the Moon Man—get the Moon Man!" And in the room on the balcony the Moon Man clasped close to him the girl he loved.

Rogue: Vivian Legrand

The Adventure of the Voodoo Moon

EUGENE THOMAS

ALTHOUGH THE GREAT PULP MAGAZINES of the 1920s and 1930s were noted for their fiction, *Detective Fiction Weekly*, one of the most successful of the mystery pulps, liked to run two or three true-crime stories in each issue. Easily one of the most popular series featured a female spy named Vivian Legrand, who was not identified as a heroine.

Beautiful, intelligent, and resourceful, she was also a liar, blackmailer, thief, and the murderer of her own father. Her exploits, which were reported by Eugene Thomas (1894–?), began to appear so regularly that doubt was cast upon their veracity—with good reason. Without apology, *DFW* continued to run stories about the woman dubbed "The Lady from Hell," now acknowledging that the tales were fictional. Were any of the stories true? Was there really a woman named Vivian Legrand? There is little evidence either way, but only the most gullible would accept the notion that all the stories published as true had any genesis in reality.

Thomas, the author of five novels, created another series character, Chu-Seng, typical of many other fictional "Yellow Peril" villains. A Chinese deaf-mute with paranormal abilities, he works with the Japanese in their espionage activities against the United States in *Death Rides the Dragon* (1932), *The Dancing Dead* (1933), and *Yellow Magic* (1934). He is thwarted by Bob Nicholson, an American agent, Lai Chung, a Mongol prince, and a team of lamas who counteract Chu-Seng's powers with their white magic.

"The Adventure of the Voodoo Moon" was originally published in the February 1, 1936, issue of *Detective Fiction Weekly*.

THE ADVENTURE OF THE VOODOO MOON

Eugene Thomas

Chapter I

Crooks on Holiday

THE LADY FROM HELL was standing on the upper deck of the little inter-island steamer as it neared the coast of Haiti. Her crown of flaming red hair was beaten back from her smooth forehead and her white dress modeled tightly to her body by the strong trade wind.

She and her companion in crime, Adrian Wylie, had just completed one of the most amazing coups in their whole career, and were now on a vacation. The Lady from Hell had been emphatic on that point before leaving Havana.

"Nothing is to tempt us into mingling business with pleasure," she had told Wylie. "Not even if we stumble across the vaults of a bank wide open and unguarded."

Now, the second day out from Havana, the sun was just rising over the blue bubbles dreaming on the horizon that were the mountains of Haiti, and still she could not account for the vague sense of disquiet, the little feeling of apprehension that had been growing in her ever since the steamer passed between Morro Castle and its smaller counterpart on the other side of Havana harbor.

No one on the little steamer dreamed that she was the notorious Lady from Hell, whose fame had already filtered even to the West Indies. And if they had, it would have seemed incredible that this graceful, beautiful woman could have started her career by poisoning her own father; could have escaped from a Turkish prison—the only time in her career that the net of the law had closed about her—could have held up and robbed the Orient Express, a deed that had filled the press of the world, although her part in it had never even been suspected.

The daring coup in Havana that had added a large sum to the bank account of Adrian Wylie, her chief of staff, and herself had not been brought to the attention of the Cuban police. And, although the police of half a dozen European countries knew her well and swore when her name was mentioned, there was not a single thing with which she could be charged, so cleverly had her tracks been covered, so adroitly her coups planned.

She turned away and began to stride up and down the deck. More than one passenger turned to stare at her as she passed with a rippling grace of motion, a little lithe stride that told of perfect muscles and the agility of a cat.

A sound made her turn as a passenger came up behind her and fell into step with her.

"Good evening, Mrs. Legrand," he said in English, with the faintest of accents. "You are up early."

"I was eager to catch a sight of Haiti," Vivian responded with a smile. "The mountains there are lovely."

"They are lovely," he responded, "even though Haiti is my home I never tire of seeing her mountains grow about the horizon line." Then he added, "We dock in a few hours. See that headland there," and he pointed to an amethyst bulk that thrust itself out into the sea. "That is Cap St. Feral. The port is just beyond it."

There was an impression of power, perfectly controlled, about Carlos Benedetti that was perfectly evident to Vivian Legrand as she surveyed him for a fleeting instant through narrowed eyes. His face was unhealthily pale, the nose slightly crooked, the black eyes very sharp and alert, beneath the close-cropped and sleek black hair. He had the air of one to whom the world had been kind, and from it he had learned assurance and a kind of affability.

But behind his assurance—this affability—the Lady from Hell sensed something that was foreign to the face he presented to the world, something that made her cautious.

"Do we dock?" she queried. "I thought that we landed in small boats."

"The word was incorrectly used," he admitted. "I should have said that we arrive. Cap St. Feral is not modern enough to possess a dock for a ship of this size, small as the vessel is." He hesitated a moment. "I assume that you are not familiar with Cap St. Feral."

"No," Vivian said. "This is my first visit to Haiti."

The man's oblique stare was annoying her. Not that she was unaccustomed to the bold stare that men give beautiful women. But this was different. Had the man been wiser he might have taken warning at the hard light that lay in the depths of her geenish eyes.

But he went on suavely:

"To those of us who know the island it offers little in the way of entertainment," he said, "but to a stranger it might be interesting. If you care to have me, I should be glad to offer my services as a guide while you are in port."

A casual enough courtesy offered to a stranger by a native of a place. Vivian thanked him and watched, with a calculating eye, as he bowed and walked on down the deck. The man was sleek, well groomed and obviously wealthy. His spotless Panama was of the type that cannot, ordinarily, even be bought in Equador, where they are woven. A hat so fine and silky that usually they are reserved as gifts to persons in high position. And the white suit that he wore had not come from an ordinary tailor.

It was made of heavy white silk—Habatui silk that in the East sells for its weight in gold, literally.

Adrian Wylie found Vivian on deck. In a few swift words she told him of the invitation and of the intuitive warning she had felt.

Wylie nodded slowly. "That explains something that had been puzzling me," he said. "For an hour last night the purser insisted on buying me drinks in the smoking room and casually asking questions about the two of us. And hardly five minutes after he left me I saw him talking earnestly to Benedetti at the door of the purser's office. Evidently the man hunted you up for the first thing this morning, after his talk with the purser."

Benedetti, they knew from the ship's gossip, was an exceedingly wealthy sugar planter, who owned the whole of an exceedingly fertile island called Ile de Feral, not far from the port of Cap St. Feral. The Haitian Sugar Centrals—actually the sugar trust, so ship gossip ran—had attempted to drive him out of business, and failed miserably. Despite a price war, he had managed to undersell the trust and still make a profit. Then he had been offered a staggering sum for the island, and had refused. The offer was still open, so she had been told, and any time he cared to sell the sugar trust would be only too eager to buy him out.

A little smile formed on Vivian's lips. Benedetti, she suspected, was accustomed to having his own way where women were concerned. And the Lady from Hell knew full well her own attractiveness as a woman.

But even the Lady from Hell, astute as she was, could not have fathomed the dark reason that lay behind Benedetti's advances.

Chapter II

Danger's Warning

The faint sound of drums somewhere in the distance; a regular, rhythmic beat, as though a gigantic heart, the heart of Black Haiti were beating in the stillness of the blazing moon, hung over the little city of Cap St. Feral as the Lady from Hell, Wylie, and Benedetti rode through the sun-washed streets.

The heat that hung about them like a tangible thing seemed to be intensified and crystalized by the monotonous beating of the lonely drums.

The Lady from Hell turned to Benedetti with a question, the brilliant sunlight through the trees overarching the road catching her hair and turning it into a halo of flame about her exquisitely lovely face.

"Voodoo drums," he said. "The night of the Voodoo Moon is approaching. The drums will keep on sounding until the climax of the Snake Dance. They're beating like this all over the island, even in Port-au-Prince. Worshipers in the cathedral can hear the sound of the drums from the hills outside the city drifting through the intoning of the mass. Then, almost as if they had been silenced by a gigantic hand, they will all stop at the same moment—the climax of the Snake Dance."

Vivian stole another glance at the people along the roadside as their car passed. Voodoo. It was something out of a book to her, something a little unsettling to come so closely in contact with. And it seemed difficult to believe that the happy, smiling faces were the faces of people who had run mad through the streets of Port-au-Prince, so history said, tearing President Guillaume Sam to bloody bits while he still lived.

Benedetti caught the thought in her mind.

"You have not lived here, Mrs. Legrand," he said quietly. "You cannot understand the place that Voodoo holds in these people's lives; the grip it has upon them. And you are not familiar with the effect of rhythms upon the nerve centers. It does strange things to blacks, and to whites things stranger still."

He leaned forward and flung a few words in Creole French at the driver—words that Vivian Legrand, fluent as her French was, could barely follow. The car stopped before a long, rambling structure, of gleaming white *coquina*, half hidden behind crimson hibiscus bushes.

"I brought you here for lunch," he said. "It would be unbearably hot on the ship and there is no hotel at which you would want to eat, even if you could, in the town itself. This is a little house that I maintain, so that I may have a comfortable place to stay when necessity or business compels me to be in town. I took the liberty of assuming that Dr. Wylie and yourself would have lunch with me here."

Vivian looked about her curiously as their host opened the little gate and ushered them into the flower garden that surrounded the house.

From the whitewashed, angular, stone walls of the old house, almost smothered in pink Flor de Amour, her eyes went to the table set beneath a flowering Y'lang-y'lang tree in the center of the close-cropped lawn. An old woman stood beside it, an ancient crone with more than a trace of white blood in her, one of those incredibly ancient people that only primitive races can produce. Her face was a myriad of tiny wrinkles and her parchment skin had the dull, leathery hue and look that is common in the aged of the Negro race.

The woman turned slowly as the trio approached and her eyes fastened on Vivian. In her cold, yellow eyes was a look almost of fear. Something that was like lurking terror coiled in the depths of those alert, flashing eyes and rendered them stony, glassy, shallow.

And then, as Benedetti and Wylie went on past her she made a gesture, an unmistakable gesture for Vivian to halt, and her voice, lowered until it was barely a sibilant whisper, came to Vivian's ears in French.

"Do not stay here," she said. "You must not stay."

There was definite horror in her eyes, and fear also, as her glance flitted from Vivian toward Benedetti. Despite the whisper to which her voice had been lowered there was fear to be distinguished in her tones also.

Her face was impassive as she turned away. Only her eyes seemed alive. They were cold, deadly bits of emerald. The Lady from Hell abhorred the unknown. All through her criminal career the unsolved riddle, the unsolved personality, the unexplained situation, inflamed her imagination. She would worry over it as a dog worries a bone.

And how her mind hovered over this problem with relentless tenacity, her brain working swiftly, with smooth precision. Her intuition had been right, after all. The feeling of danger, of disquiet, of apprehension that had haunted her ever since the coast line of Haiti came in sight over the horizon had not been wrong. She knew now, beyond a shadow of doubt, that danger hovered over her like a vulture.

The fear that she had glimpsed in the old woman's eyes, Vivian reasoned, was fear for herself should she be caught warning the white woman. But what was the danger against which she was warned, and why should this old woman, who had never seen her before, take what was obviously a risk to warn her against it?

Luncheon was just over when a long hoot sounded from the steamer.

"The warning whistle," Benedetti told her. "A signal to the passengers that the steamer will sail in an hour."

He turned to Vivian.

"My roses," he said, "are so lovely that I took the liberty of requesting Lucilla to cut an armful of them for you to take back to the ship as a remembrance."

There was a distinct warning in the old woman's veiled eyes as Vivian stretched out her hands for the big bunch of pale yellow roses that Lucilla brought; not only warning, but that same terror and fear that had stood starkly in them a short time before. Instinctively Vivian stiffened and looked about her, her nerves tense. Was the danger, whatever it was, ready to spring? But the scene seemed peaceful enough.

"How lovely they are!" she exclaimed, and wondered if it could be her imagination that made the old woman seem reluctant to part with the flowers. Then she gave a little exclamation of pain as she took them from Lucilla. "Like many other lovely things, there are thorns," she said ruefully, gazing at the long, thorny stems, still slightly damp from standing in water.

"That is true," Benedetti said, and there seemed to be an expression of relief in his eyes. "Our Haitian roses are lovely, but they have longer and sharper thorns than any other roses I know."

"Don't you think we had better be leaving?" Vivian queried, glancing at her watch. The shimmering heat haze that covered everything seemed to have blurred her vision, and she had to peer closely at the little jewelled trinket to make out the time. "It's a long drive back to the ship."

"There is still plenty of time," Benedetti assured her. "The warning whistle is supposed to sound an hour before sailing time, but it always is nearer two hours." Then he gave a little exclamation of concern. "But you are ill," he said as Vivian swayed a little.

"Just the heat," she said. "I am not yet accustomed to it."

The flowers she had been holding tumbled to the table and thence to the ground. The long-stemmed yellow blossoms gave no hint of the fact that from the moment Benedetti's message had been delivered to the old woman until the moment before they had been placed in Vivian's hands their stems and thorns had been soaking in a scum-covered fluid brewed by Lucilla herself.

"You must go inside for a few moments. You must rest," Benedetti said sharply. "I should have realized that you were not accustomed to heat. It might be fatal for you to drive back to the ship in this sun without a rest."

Wylie, a look of concern on his face, took Vivian's arm and helped her to her feet. Even then, with her vision blurred and an overpowering drowsiness creeping over her, the Lady from Hell did not realize that she had been drugged. It was not until she reached the threshold of the room to which she had been guided that the truth burst upon her dulled senses with the force of a thunderbolt.

Stacked neatly against the whitewashed walls of the room was the baggage she had left in her cabin on the steamer!

Dizzily, clutching at the door for support, she turned . . . just in time to see a short heavy club descend with stunning force on Wylie's head. And then, even as her companion crumpled to the stone flooring, blackness flooded her brain.

Chapter III

Vivian Legrand Trapped

Dusk had fallen with tropic swiftness before Vivian awoke. She had not been conscious of her journey, wrapped in coco fiber matting from the house where she had been drugged, to Benedetti's launch, nor of the subsequent trip to the man's home on the Ille de Feral.

Now, anger smoldering in her greenish eyes, she faced him across the dining room table. In the dim room the table floated in a sea of amber candlelight. Barefooted black girls passed in and out, their voices keyed to the soft stillness, a thing of pauses and low voices. The whole thing, to Vivian, seemed to take on a character of unreality—a dream in which anything might happen.

She waited for Benedetti to speak after the slender black girl drew out her chair for her. But the man did not, so finally she broke the silence herself.

"What do you hope to gain by this?" she queried.

"Won't you try your soup?" he said bitterly. "I am sure that you will find it very good."

He halted as one of the girls stopped beside his chair and said something in Creole in a low voice. He rose to his feet.

"Will you pardon me?" he said. "There is someone outside, with a message. I shall be gone only a moment."

He disappeared through the door beside the staircase, the door that Vivian imagined led to the rear of the house.

Swiftly she beckoned the black maid to her, slipped the glittering diamond from her finger, and folded the girl's hand about it.

"Come to my room tonight," she whispered tensely, "when it is safe. No one will ever know. And in Port-au-Prince or Cap St. Feral you can sell that ring for sufficient to live like a *blanc* millionaire for the rest of your days."

The girl's face paled to a dusky brown, she glanced furtively from the glittering jewel in her hand to the pale face of the woman who had given it to her. Vivian caught the hesitation.

"I have others in my room," she urged desperately. "You shall choose from them what you want—two—three—when you sell them there will never have been another girl in Haiti as rich as you will be."

"I will come," the girl said in a whisper and stepped back against the wall. A moment later Benedetti returned.

"I regret to have been so poor a host as to leave you alone for even so short a time," he said.

"Please," Vivian said shortly, and there was in her manner no indication of the triumph that filled her breast. "Why dissemble. You've brought me here for a purpose. Why not tell me what it is?"

Already a scheme was forming in that agile mind of hers. When the girl came to her room that night she would persuade her to find weapons—guide Wylie and herself to a boat so that they might escape. But was Wylie still alive?

Benedetti's answer interrupted her thoughts.

"It is not so much what I hope to gain, as what I hope to keep," he said smoothly. He paused, and through the silence there came to her ears that queer rise and fall of notes from drums that had followed her ever since she arrived in Haiti—the drums of the Voodoo Moon, Benedetti had called it. He leaned forward.

"You might as well know now," he said abruptly. "You have until tomorrow midnight to live."

"Unless?" Vivian queried meaningly. She was very sure that she knew what the man meant.

Benedetti calmly placed the spoon in his plate and pushed it aside.

"There is no proviso. I know nothing of your personal life—of your finances. They are no concern of mine. You may be extremely rich, or completely poor—that does not enter into the matter at all. You have nothing that I care to buy. All I know is that you are young and extremely beautiful." He studied her with a cold dispassionate interest, then sighed, a bit regretfully, it seemed. "That is the reason you must die tomorrow night."

The thing was utterly fantastic. Vivian listened in amazed fascination. She could hardly bring herself to believe that she had heard correctly. So sure had she been that the man's interest in her rose from the fact that he was attracted to her that the thought there might be another, more sinister motive behind the drugging and kidnaping had not occurred to her.

Her green eyes narrowed a trifle—only that, but there was the impression of a steel spring tightening. Then she said quietly:

"Why must I die?"

"Because," he answered, "tomorrow night is the night of the Voodoo Moon—the night when the Papaloi and the Mamaloi present Ogoun Badagri, the Bloody One, with the Goat Without Horns."

"The Goat Without Horns?" Vivian repeated, uncomprehendingly. "What is that?"

"You," the man said tersely. "Tomorrow at midnight, when the Voodoo Moon is fullest, you will be offered as a sacrifice to Ogoun Badagri, the snake god."

For a moment the Lady from Hell stared at him, a chill feeling clutching at her breast. Then an alert look came into her eyes, a look that she quickly veiled. She was listening intently.

"You're not actually in earnest?" she asked quietly. Every nerve was strained to catch that sound again—the drone of an airplane engine that had come faintly to her ears. It was louder now. "You are trying to frighten me, to trap me into something. You will find that I am not easily frightened or trapped."

The sound of the plane was louder now. She shot a furtive glance at Benedetti. Could aid be on the way? Could Benedetti's plans have gone wrong, and a search be underway for them?

"I am very much in earnest," the man opposite her said. "You see, that is the secret of my successful defiance of the sugar trust, the secret of why my laborers never leave me, the secret of why I can manufacture sugar at a cost that the sugar trust cannot possibly equal and still make a profit. Once a year I present the Papaloi and the Mamaloi, the high priest and priestess of Voodoo, with a human sacrifice—a white man or woman—and in turn these two guardians of the great snake see to it that my laborers do not leave, and are kept content with the lowest pay scale in the island of Haiti."

He broke off and smiled.

"You may relax, Mrs. Legrand," he said. "That plane that you hear will not land here. It is the marine mail plane that passes over the island every night between eleven thirty and twelve o'clock."

Vivian looked at him blankly. "Plane?" she said vaguely. "Oh, yes, that is a plane, isn't it? Quite honestly, I had not noticed the sound before you spoke."

It was so well done that it fooled him. She picked up the slender silver fruit knife that lay on the table in front of her, twisting it so that it shone in her fingers, a pale, metallic splinter of light. She regarded him with eyes that had turned mysteriously dark, and leaned forward a little. Her voice, when she spoke, was very soft, and it held a quality of poignancy.

"You seem to live alone here," she said, and her eyes regarded him warmly. "Don't you ever become—lonely?"

There was a world of promise and invitation in the soft tone, in the alluring lips.

He looked at her and tightened his lips.

"That is useless," he said. "You are beautiful, one of the most beautiful women that I have ever seen, but a dozen such women as you could not make up to me for the loss of my plantation. No, my dear, your charm is useless."

"But you wouldn't dare," she said. "A woman cannot simply disappear from a steamer without inquiries being made. This is not the Haiti of twenty years ago. The Americans are in control—they are the police . . ."

Benedetti shook his head. "Do not raise false hopes. You sent the purser of the steamer a note saying that you had unexpectedly found friends in Cap St. Feral and were breaking your voyage here. The same man who brought the note took yours and your companion's baggage off the ship. By now he has probably forgotten your existence.

"There is nothing to connect you with me, and if inquiries should be made it will simply be assumed that you either left the island or were murdered by a wandering Caco. And as for an Haitian, who might know something of your disappearance, aside from the fact that the secrets of Voodoo are something that are never discussed, there is an island saying: '*Z affaires negres, pas z'z affaires blancs.*' And you will find that the affairs of the Negroes are not the affairs of the whites. And then," his voice was bland as he made the significant statement, "there is rarely any proof—left—when the great green snake god has completed his sacrifice."

"And my companion—Dr. Wylie—what have you done with him?" Vivian queried steadily. A bright spark glowed in her narrowed green eyes for a moment. It died slowly.

"He is safe, quite safe," Benedetti assured her, "for the time being. He also will be a sacrifice to Ogoun Badagri."

He said it with simple, sincere ruthlessness; undisguised, but neither vindictive nor cruel.

"You are quite sure of yourself," Vivian said softly, and had Wylie been there he would have recognized the meaning of that tone; the threat of that greenish glow at the back of her eyes. He had seen that cold light in her eyes before. But Benedetti, even had he glimpsed it, would not have known that it was like the warning rattle of a snake before it strikes.

Now, with a swift movement she flung the silver fruit knife she held at the gleaming shirt front of the man opposite her. Her aim was deadly, for few people could throw a knife with the skill and precision of the Lady from Hell.

But Benedetti had caught the glitter of the candlelight on the metal a split second before she launched the knife. His agile mind perceived her intention and he flung himself to one side just in time. The knife thudded into the high back of the chair in which he had been sitting and rested there, quivering.

"You are a fool," the man commented curtly. Striding to the French windows he flung them wide, letting moonlight stream into the room. The sound of the drums came in louder, a barbaric rhythm beating in strange tempo with the pulse in her wrist.

"Look at that," he said, flinging out an arm.

At the edge of the veranda, which ran along the front of the house, lounged a white cotton-clad Haitian, a three-foot cane knife clasped in his fist. Further along, at the edge of the beach, another man leaned against the bole of a coconut tree, and the glitter of the moonlight on steel betrayed the fact that he also was armed with a cane knife.

"Even if you had killed me," he said quietly, "you would have been no better off. You could not escape from the island. There are no boats here. Even the launch on which you arrived has been sent away and will not return until after the ceremony. And if you had attempted to swim, the sea swarms with sharks."

It was after midnight when Vivian went upstairs to her room again. Benedetti escorted her to the door.

"I am locking you in," he told her. "It is really quite useless to do so. You could not escape. There is absolutely no possibility of success. But it is a precaution I always take with my annual—visitors."

Then he drew from his pocket the diamond ring that Vivian had, earlier in the evening, given to the little black maid.

"You will find," he said with a smile, "that it is useless to attempt to bribe my servants. The fear of the Voodoo in them is greater than the greed for money."

With a slight bow he closed the door, leaving her staring at the blank panels with a sinking feeling in her heart. She was a prisoner in a prison without walls, and yet the sea that girdled the land was a barrier as effective as stone ramparts and iron bars. Instead of one jailer she had dozens—perhaps hundreds—for she realized that every laborer on the island was a potential guard, alert to halt any attempt to escape. She did not attempt to deceive herself by thinking that every native of the place did not know of her presence and the fate for which she was destined.

She wondered what prompted the old woman—Benedetti's servant—to take her life in hand and warn her, back there in Cap St. Feral? The woman had, of course, realized Benedetti's purpose in bringing her here, since it had been she who had prepared the drugged rose stems. It was not for a long time, and then only by accident, that Vivian was to discover that in a Haitian the desire for revenge can transcend even the fear of Voodoo, and that it was to avenge what she considered a wrong that the old woman had warned her.

Vivian turned her thoughts back to her position. She believed she knew where Wylie was being held. On her way down to the dining room a little earlier she had encountered one of the black maids with a tray; had noted the door through which the girl had passed. That, she reasoned, must be the room in which Wylie was held prisoner, unless there were other prisoners in the house of whom she knew nothing.

She smiled a trifle grimly at the thought of being locked in her room. If Benedetti only knew of how little importance a lock—particularly an old-fashioned one such as this—was to her. Opening her suitcase she took out a hand mirror with a long handle. Unscrewing the handle, she removed from the hollow interior a long slender rod of thin steel. This she forced slowly into the thin opening between door and jamb. The rod scraped on metal. She worked it up and down, slowly pressing inward. Bit by bit the sloping tongue of the lock was forced back into its sheath, until the blade slipped through. A twist of the door handle and Vivian was peering out into the corridor.

Darkness hung before her eyes. It was as if a curtain of some impenetrable texture hung before her. She knew nothing of the floor plan of the big, rambling house, but she knew that the room she had seen the girl entering was the last on her side of the corridor, and accordingly she made her way cautiously in that direction, feeling her way, finger-tips trailing the wall, listening intently every step or so for some sound that might warn her of the presence of another person.

Her hand trailing along the wall touched a door—the fifth one she had passed. This was the door she sought. Gently she tried the knob. It was locked. A few minutes' work with the thin steel rod and the door swung inward with only the faintest of sounds. But even that was sufficient to betray her presence to Wylie's alert ears.

"Who is it?" he queried.

"Shhh," she whispered warningly, and, closing the door, crossed swiftly toward the chair where he sat beside the window.

In low, tense whispers she told him of her conversation with Benedetti and of the fate that was in store for both of them.

"We've got to get away tonight," she finished. "It's our only chance. There must be some way—perhaps we can make a raft. At least we can try."

Chapter IV

The First Victim

With Wylie by her side she made her way to the door; peered cautiously outside. By diligent practice the Lady from Hell had long ago acquired the chatoyant eye—the cat's—good for prowling about and seeing things in the dark, but here in the corridor the blackness was intense, with a tangible quality that was numbing to the senses. The utter opacity was tactile, half fluid, like fog. She crept down the hallway with feline assurance, passing her fingers delicately over objects that came into her path with a touch light enough to stroke a butterfly's wing. The house was a sea of silence, and on its waves the slightest noise made long and screeching journeys.

To Vivian's hearing, sandpapered by suspense, the slight give of the polished boards of the staircase beneath their slow steps produced a terrific noise. By making each step a thing of infinite slowness, they crept forward safely. Each downward step was a desperate and long-drawn-out achievement, involving an exactly calculated expenditure of muscular energy, an unceasing, muscular alertness.

Once, as they reached the bottom of the stairs, there came from the dining room in which they stood the rattle of a clock preparing to ring out a quarter hour. It struck Vivian's tense nerves as a thing of abominable violence—like countless, swift hammer strokes on the innumerable frayed ends of her nerves. She had the sensation of being driven into the woodwork of the floor upon which she stood, of being crushed under an immense and lightning-like pressure.

After what seemed an eternity they reached the further side of the dining room. Under her careful manipulation the latch of the door slipped slowly back. The door moved silently, slowly. A brilliant line of moonlight appeared. Vivian caught her breath sharply.

Standing there in the open ground in front of the veranda stood a Haitian, alert, watchful, armed with a machete.

There was no escape that way. Weaponless, they were helpless before the menace of that shining three-foot length of steel, even if they could cross the moonlit space that lay between the veranda and the man without being detected.

"The back of the house," Vivian whispered to Wylie, her voice barely perceptible.

She knew that the door to the kitchen was beside the staircase they had descended. That much she had observed during her interview with Benedetti earlier in the evening. By locating the staircase first in the blackness, she found the door she sought and opened it. A passageway opened before them, dimly illuminated by a shaft of silver that poured through a half opened door at its further end.

Silently they made their way down the passage and cautiously peered through the partly opened door. Another disappointment.

It was a small room, one wall covered with shelves, boxes and bags stacked high on the other side with a single window, half way up the wall, through which moonlight poured. A storeroom of some sort.

Vivian reached out and caught Wylie's arm,

drew him silently into the little room and closed the door.

"There may be weapons here," she said. But she was mistaken. The nearest approach was a broken kitchen knife used, probably, to slash open the burlap bags which stood against the wall.

It was a poor substitute for a weapon, but Vivian took it thankfully. And then she gave a gasp. Her hand, exploring a shelf, had come in contact with something clammy and sticky that clung and would not be shaken off. Her first thought was that it was some monstrous tropical insect. It seemed alive, it clung so persistently, despite her efforts to shake it loose.

Then, as Wylie snapped his cigarette lighter into flame, the tiny glow illuminated an oblong of sticky fly paper fastened to her hand. There was a pile of the sheets upon the shelf. Despite the tenseness of the situation she almost laughed at the uncanny feeling the thing had given her there in the darkness.

In the dim flame of Wylie's lighter they searched again for anything that might prove of assistance to them in their predicament. Bags of flour. Bags of potatoes. Kegs of pig tails and pig snouts in brine—evidently food for the laborers. A half-emptied case of bacale—dried codfish, a staple article of diet in the West Indies—and a can of phosphorescent paint. Also row after row of canned food. But nothing that might be of assistance to them.

Climbing upon a box Vivian peered through the window, then turned back to Wylie, excitement in her voice.

"We can get out this way," she whispered. "There is the limb of a tree almost against the window and shrubbery around the tree."

"Anybody in sight?" Wylie queried.

"No one," Vivian said, and pried the latch of the window with her broken knife blade. It came open with a tearing shriek that sounded like thunder in the silence. Disregarding the noise Vivian slipped through the window and swung on to the limb of the tree. Wylie followed her, and in a moment they stood on the ground in the midst of dense shrubbery.

"We will have to keep in the shadow," she said as they crept silently through the bushes, only an occasional rustling leaf marking their passage. "The moment we step in the moonlight we'll be seen, if anyone is watching."

Even there in the bushes the brilliant moonlight illuminated the ground about them. A faint drumming ebbed to them through the brilliance, faintly touching the dark membrane of the night as they emerged on what seemed to be a well-defined path leading toward the beach.

A sudden opening in the trail, a burst of moonlight, and they stood on a strip of white sand with breakers creaming softly in front of them.

"There," Vivian said, still keeping her voice low. "See that pile of driftwood. We'll make a raft of that. Drag it to the water's edge while I cut vines to lash it together."

Feverishly they worked, Wylie dragging the heavy logs into position, lashing them firmly together with the vines that Vivian cut from the jungle's edge, until at last a crazy-looking affair bobbed up and down in the ripple at the edge of the beach. Makeshift, clumsy, but it would float and it was an avenue of escape, the only avenue that had presented itself.

Vivian returned from a final trip to the jungle, dragging behind her three bamboo poles.

"We can use two of these to shove the thing with, until we get into deep water," she said. "The other we can lash upright as a mast and use my dress as a sail."

At that instant, from the path behind them, came the sound of voices. Vivian flashed a frantic glance at the jungle rearing up behind them, and then leaped on board the raft. Wylie followed. It dipped and swayed, but held their weight. The voices came nearer. Desperately Vivian braced her pole against the sandy bottom and shoved. Wylie followed suit. Sluggishly the clumsy craft moved away from the shore—five feet—ten feet—and than half a dozen men poured through the opening in the jungle and raced across the sand, splashed through the shallow water and surrounded the little craft, gleaming machetes raised threateningly.

Vivian did not see Benedetti when they returned to the house with their captors that night, nor was he visible when she awoke the next morning after a night spent in futile speculation and planning, and descended to the dining room.

A black girl served them breakfast. Golden sunlight poured through the wide French windows, beyond which they could see the beach and the green cove. Nowhere was there evidence of the fate that hung over them. But both knew, and the fact of that knowledge was evident in their eyes, in their short jerky words, that Death's wings were already casting their shadows across them.

The sun was well up when they went on to the veranda. There should have been the click of machetes in the cane fields and the low, lazy laughter of the workers. But everything was still, and that stillness held an ominous meaning.

Wylie was frankly without hope—more so as the day wore on, and Vivian, although she had never admitted defeat, admitted to herself that she saw no way out of the impasse. Benedetti, she saw now, had made no mistake when he told her that escape was impossible.

The day wore on, and still Benedetti did not put in an appearance. Once Vivian asked one of the maids where he could be found and received in answer a queer jumble of Creole French that held no meaning. Later, they essayed a walk to the Sugar Central, whose smokestacks rose on the other side of the cane fields, but one of the ever-present natives stepped slowly in their path, his machete openly in evidence. From the corner of her eyes Vivian could see others, alert, ready, at the edge of the jungle. Their captors were taking no chances.

On the far side of the cleared space Vivian could see a break in the jungle where a path ended. From this path men kept coming and going, and this, she surmised, must lead to the place where they were scheduled to die that night.

It was after dinner when Benedetti made his appearance, and with him stalked tragedy.

Vivian and Wylie were on the broad veranda, walking up and down. Something—some sixth sense—warned Vivian of danger, even before she heard the quick, catlike tread behind her. She made an attempt to swing around an instant too late. Someone leapt on her. A strong arm was locked about her throat. A hand was clamped over her mouth. A knee dug into the small of her back. She wrenched, tore at the gripping hands, even as she saw other hands seizing Wylie; she was aware of Benedetti's face, his features hard as stone. In the same second something dropped over her head and blotted the world into darkness.

How long she was held there motionless on the veranda she did not know. Then came a quick gabble of Creole in Benedetti's voice and the smothering hand was removed.

She flashed a glance around. The place was deserted save for herself, Benedetti and one tall native who stood beside the veranda steps, the ever-present machete in evidence. Obviously a guard.

The man interpreted her look.

"Your companion is gone. You will never see him again," he said, and his voice was indifferent. He might have been speaking of some trivial object that had disappeared. He turned back toward the dining room, where candlelight made a soft glow. Vivian followed. The house seemed curiously still, as if all life had departed from it save these two.

"Gone—you mean—" she could not finish the sentence.

Benedetti nodded and selected a cigarette from a box on a little side table; lit it at one of the candles.

"He will be the first sacrifice to Ogoun Badagri. When the great green snake god has finished with him they will come for you. You will be the climax of the ceremony," he told her brutally.

"You mean that you—a white man—will actually permit these men to make a sacrifice of us?" she queried. She knew, before she said it, that any appeal to him would be useless, but her mind was going around frantically, seeking a method of warding off the death that was imminent.

"What is your life and that of your companion to me?" he asked. "Nothing—not so much as the ash from the cigarette—compared with the fact that your death means that I keep my plantation a year longer. I refused close to half a million dollars from the sugar trust for the island. Do you think, then, that I would permit a little thing like your life to rob me of it?"

Chapter V

Voodoo Death

Vivian did not answer. Her eyes roamed around the room, although already every article in it had been photographed indelibly on her retina. A fly had alighted on the border of the sticky fly paper that lay in the center of the mahogany table. It tugged and buzzed, but the sticky mess held it too firmly.

"You may comfort yourself with the thought," Benedetti went on, "if the fact is any comfort, that you are not the first. There have been others. The little dancing girl from the Port-au-Prince cabaret, a Spanish girl from Santo Domingo . . ."

He was not boastful, purely meditative as he sat there and smoked and talked, telling Vivian of the victims whose lives had paid for his hold on his sugar plantation. Vivian's eyes were fastened on the feebly fluttering fly on the sticky paper. They, too, were caught like flies in a trap, and unless she could do something immediately—she faced the fact calmly; it would be the end.

Abruptly she leaned forward. There was a stillness in her pose, a stillness in her opaque eyes. Her hands coiled like springs. She found it difficult to keep her detached poise as the scheme began to unfold and take shape in her brain.

She smiled thinly. The air was suddenly electrical, filled with the portent of danger. Benedetti caught the feel of it, and peered at her suspiciously for a moment. The Lady from Hell knew that it was a thousand to one that she would lose. But, if her scheme worked, she could save Wylie's live and her own, and Benedetti might be made to pay for the thing he had attempted—pay as he had never dreamed that he would have to pay.

Reaching out one hand she moved the candle in front of her, so that its glow fell more on Benedetti's face than her own. Her voice, as she spoke, was quiet, almost meditative. But her eyes told a different story.

"How much time have I to live?" she said.

The man glanced at his watch.

"Roughly, two hours," he said. He might have been estimating the departure time of a steamer, his voice was so calm. "It might be a trifle more or less—the time of my workers is not accurate. When the drums stop they will come for you. And when they start again—well, you will be there then."

She rose to her feet, leaning lightly on the table.

"If I am to die," she said hysterically, "I will die beautiful." Then she added as an explanation, "My makeup is in my room."

But he was on his feet too, alert, wary. "You must not leave my presence," he said. "I cannot permit it. The sacrifice must go to the arms of Ogoun Badagri alive, not a corpse."

His dark eyes held no recognition of the fact that she was a very beautiful woman. Vivian sensed, and rightly, that to him she was merely a woman who might thwart his plans. But she caught the implication in his last sentence.

"I shall not take poison," she said. "You may come with me—watch me, if you wish."

She took a step or two and groped blindly at the table for support. Instinctively he stretched out a hand to steady her.

That was the moment for which she had planned, the instant for which she had been waiting. Benedetti made the fatal mistake that many men had made with the Lady from Hell as an opponent—of underestimating her as an adversary.

Like a striking snake her hand darted to the table, seized one of the heavy candlesticks. Before Benedetti could interfere, had even divined her purpose, the heavy metal fell across his forehead with stunning force. He crumpled to the floor without a murmur.

Leaving him where he had fallen, Vivian ran to the door and peered out. The gigantic black on guard at the veranda steps had heard nothing. He was still standing there, unaware of the drama being enacted within the dining room.

Swiftly she turned back and her slender fingers searched the drawers of the carved mahogany sideboard against the wall until she found what she sought—a heavy, sharp carving knife. She balanced it speculatively in her hand. It would do, she decided.

The man was still standing there when she peered out the door again. He never saw the slender blade as it flew through the air, sped by a hand that had learned its cunning from the most expert knife thrower in Shanghai. The blade went through, sinking into the flesh at the base of his throat as though it had been butter. He died without an outcry.

Now she must work fast, if she were to escape and save Wylie too. Benedetti she bound and gagged and rolled against the sideboard where he was out of the way. But first she had taken his revolver from his side pocket.

Trip after trip she made, first to the flat tin roof of the house, and then to the front of the house. Finally she was satisfied with what she had done, and, snatching up a flashlight from the sideboard fled toward the path in the jungle that she knew led to the place of sacrifice.

A tropical squall was rising out of the sea beyond the little cove. A cloud, black in the light of the moon, was rising above the horizon. She glanced at it anxiously. Then she plunged into the jungle.

The valences of the palms were motionless against the moonlit sky. The atmosphere, as she pushed her way along, seemed saturated with mystery, dew dripping, bars of green moonlight between the trunks of the trees; the cry of night birds, the patter of something in the dark mystery of the tree roof overhead, the thudding of the drums that had never ceased. Out of that familiar hollow rhythm of drums that had begun to emerge a thread of actual melody—an untraditional rise and fall of notes—a tentative attack, as it were, on the chromatic scale of the beat. A tentative abandonment of Africa. It was a night of abandonment, anyhow, a night of betrayal and the peeling off of blanketing layers down to the raw.

Once she stopped short with a sudden emptiness in her chest at sight of what she thought was a man in the path ahead. But it was only a paint-daubed, grinning skull on a bamboo stake planted in the ground—a voodoo *ouanga*. Then she went ahead again. Evidently there were no guards posted. With every inhabitant of the island concerned in the ceremony in one way or another there would be no need for guards to be posted now.

The rapid sequence of events had edged Vivian's nerves, and the boom of the drums—heavy, maddening, relentless, did nothing to soothe them. That passage through the jungle was galling, fraying the nerve ends like an approaching execution.

A red glow came to her through the trees, and seemed to spread and spread until it included the whole world about her in its malignancy. The drums, with that queer rise and fall of notes that it seemed impossible to achieve with taut skins stretched over drum heads, beat upon her senses, pounded until the air was filled with sounds that seemed to come from the earth, the sky, the forest; dominated the flow of blood with strange excitations.

She had formulated no plan for rescuing Wylie. She could not, until she reached the spot and saw what she had to contend with. She had the gun she had taken from Benedetti, but six cartridges against a horde of drum-maddened blacks—that was only a last resort.

And then she stood on the edge of a clearing that seemed sunk to the bottom of a translucent sea of opalescent flame.

Something that was age-old was happening in that crimson-bathed clearing, something old and dark, buried so deeply under the subtleties of civilization that most men go through life without ever knowing it is there, was blossoming and flowering under the stark madness of those thudding drums.

Coconut fibre torches, soaked in palm oil, flaring red in the blackness of the night lit up the space in front of her like a stage, the torchlight weaving strange scarlet and mauve shadows. Tall trees, lining the clearing opposite her, seemed to shelter masses of people, darker shadows against the red glow of the burning torches.

Two enormous drums, taut skins booming under the frenzied pounding of the palms of two drummers, stood on one side. A dozen, two dozen dancing black figures, male and female, spun and danced in the center of the clearing, movements graceful and obscene—animal gestures that were identical with similar dances of their ancestors hundreds of years before in Moko or the Congo.

And then she saw Wylie. He was tied to a post in the center of the clearing, and the dancers were milling about him. Beside him stood a woman whom Vivian instinctively knew must be the Mamaloi, the priestess of whom Benedetti had spoken.

Now and then the priestess gave vent to a sound that seemed to stir the dancers to greater activity—to spur the slowly humming throng of watchers to a point of frenzy; a sound such as Vivian had never heard before and never hoped to hear again. When she stopped, it would hang, incredibly high-pitched, small, like a black thrill in the shadow. It was shocking and upsetting out of that ancient thin figure.

Her eyes shifted from the aged figure to the sky line above the trees. The black cloud that, a short time before had been no larger than the palm of her hand on the horizon, was visible through the branches of the trees now. Even as she looked a faint flicker of heat lightning laced through it.

And then, as if at a conductor's signal, more torches flowered on the edge of the clearing, and in their light the Lady from Hell saw half a dozen men staggering forward with an enormous thing of bamboo—a cage—and in that cage was a great snake; a boa constrictor, perhaps, or a python, although neither of them, she seemed to remember, was native to Haiti.

Chapter VI

White Man's Voodoo

They placed the cage in the center of the clearing, and Vivian saw that it had been placed so that a small door in the cage was directly opposite Wylie's bound figure. The significance of that fact went through her like a breath of cold wind. If she failed, she also would be bound to that stake. Mentally she could see the little door in the cage opening, the great triangular head of the snake gliding slowly . . .

Swiftly she bent over and caught up a handful of the black leaf mold underfoot, smeared it over her face, her arms, her neck, her shoulders. A section of the dress she was wearing was ripped off and made into a turban that hid the flaming crown of her hair. More earth was rubbed onto the white of her dress.

Then, with swift leaps, she was on the outer fringe of the dancers, and the chaos of moving arms and legs caught her up and swallowed her as a breaking wave on the beach swallows a grain of sand.

It was a mad thing to do, a desperate thing.

She knew that, normally, her crude disguise would not have fooled the natives. The Haitian black seems to have the ability to almost smell the presence of a *blanc*, much as an animal can smell the presence of another. But, in that flickering torchlight, the crudeness of disguise would not be so apparent, and in that unceasing madness of drums that went on like a black echo of something reborn, she hoped that her alien presence would pass unnoticed long enough for her to accomplish her object.

Slowly she worked her way through the writhing, dancing mass of figures toward the center. She knew that her time was short—that the lesser ceremony was approaching its height. Even as she reached the inner ring of dancers she saw the ancient Mamaloi joining in the dance, while the others kept a respectful distance from her. Monotonously, maddeningly, the priestess twisted and turned and shivered, holding aloft a protesting fowl. Faster and faster she went, and while all eyes were fastened on that whirling figure Vivian managed to reach Wylie's bound figure.

A swift slash with the knife she had hidden beneath her dress and his hands were free.

"Keep still . . . don't let them see that you're not bound," she whispered. Another motion and the bonds that fastened his ankles to the post were free.

Vivian moved about Wylie with graceful motions, imitating the movements of the blacks about her, and her voice came to him in broken, desperate whispers:

"Signal . . . you'll recognize it . . . don't move until then . . . dead tree by the edge of the clearing . . . that's the path . . . I'll be waiting there . . . it's only chance . . ."

Then she was gone, breasting her way through the black figures that danced like dead souls come back from Hell in the evil glow of the sputtering torches. And then came a great shout as the Mamaloi caught the chicken she held by the head and whirled it around and around.

Throom . . . throom . . . throom. The drums were like coalescing madness. A moan went up from the onlookers and a chill went through Vivian.

She knew from what Benedetti had told her that the chicken was the prelude of what would happen to Wylie. Next, the old woman would slash Wylie's throat . . . let his life blood spurt into a bowl with which the dancers would be sprinkled. Then would come the lesser ceremony, while the guard at the house would start with her for the ceremony that would end with the door in the great snake's cage being opened . . .

Vivian snatched a torch from the hands of one of the dancers. The man did not even seem to be aware of the fact that it had been taken away. From beneath her dress she took a stick of dynamite with fuse attached—part of her loot from the storeroom—and touched the fuse to the flame of the torch.

It sputtered and she hurled it with all her strength at her command toward the overhanging tree beneath which the drummers sat, then fled for the bare naked branches of the dead tree that stood where the path entered the clearing—the spot where she had told Wylie she would meet him.

She had barely reached the spot when there came a tremendous concussion that shook the earth, and a gush of flame. The thing was as startling, as hideously unexpected to the drum maddened Haitians as a striking snake. Scream after scream—long, jagged screams that ripped red gashes through the dark, were followed by a swift clacking of tongues, a terrified roar as dancers and onlookers milled about, black bodies writhing in the light of the remaining torches. A black tide, rising, filled the clearing with terrified clamor. A moment later there was the sound of running feet and Wylie was at her side.

"This way," she whispered, and guided him into the path.

Both of them knew that it would be only a moment before the startled natives recovered their wits and discovered that their victim was gone. Then they would take up their trail again immediately.

"Where are we going?" Wylie asked her as he ran behind her along the winding jungle trail.

"The house," she answered tersely.

"The house?" He almost halted in his amazement. "But Vivian—that's the first place they'll make for. Even if you've found weapons we can't hold them off forever."

"Wait," she said. "No time to explain now . . . But if things work out, we'll be off this island before morning, safe and sound."

From behind them a quavering yell rose on the air and the two fugitives knew that Wylie's escape had been discovered. It was a matter of yards and of minutes now. Then they burst from the shadow of the jungle into the moonlight clearing.

"Follow me," she said quickly. "Don't take the path," and he followed her footsteps as she twisted and twined about the space toward the steps.

At the steps he halted a moment in wonder at what he saw there, and then, in spite of the gravity of the situation, a chuckle broke from his panting lips.

"So that's it," he said, and Vivian nodded.

"That's it. Be careful. It's a slim enough chance, but there is just a chance it'll work—the only chance we've got."

"But even that," he said, a thought striking him, as he threaded his way carefully up the steps to the veranda, "will only be temporary. Even if it holds them at bay until dawn—when daylight comes . . ."

"I know," she said a trifle impatiently, "but long before then . . ." She broke off suddenly as their pursuers appeared, breaking out from under the palms, just as a flash of lightning came.

"They're here," he whispered. "If the scheme won't work, then it's all up with us."

"It will work," Vivian said confidently.

But, although her tone was cool, confident, there was anxiety in her eyes as she watched the black figures pouring out of the jungle. Vivian knew that her own and Wylie's lives were hanging by the slenderest margin in their criminal career.

The Papaloi, the giant negro with the white lines and scar ridges criss-crossing his muscular torso, was the first to see them as another flash of lightning illuminated the veranda where they stood. He uttered a single bellow, a stentorian cry, which seemed to shake the house, and bounded toward the stairs. Behind him came part of his followers, while others rushed for the other pair of stairs.

The Papaloi leaped for the steps, his men close behind him. His feet landed in something that slid quickly under him, that clung to his soles. He lost his balance, fell asprawl, his followers in a momentary confusion that quickly increased to panic—the panic of the primitive mind confronted with something unseen that it cannot understand.

The hands of the gigantic black Papaloi were glued now to squares of sticky fly paper that he could not shake off—the fly paper that The Lady from Hell had taken from the storeroom and spent so much precious time placing upon the steps and around the veranda without encountering it, save along the narrow, tortuous trail along which Vivian had led Wylie.

There was a square of fly paper on the Papaloi's face now, clinging there, flapping a little as if alive, persistent as a vampire bat. There were more on the side of his body where he had slipped. He struck at them and accumulated more.

The Mamaloi, that ancient crone, was in trouble also. She had slipped and in falling, had a sheet of fly paper plastered squarely across her eyes. She was uttering shrill cries of distress as she pawed at her face with hands that were covered with sticky fly paper and glue. All about the two, men and women were struggling, shouting in alarm. The silent attack had materialized out of nothing with such appalling swiftness, and continued with such devastating persistence that it robbed them of every thought save alarm.

Robbed of their spiritual leaders, terror was striking at the hearts of the voodoo worshipers. At the edge of the veranda, black men writhed in horror, snatching at one another for support, tearing at the horrible things that clung as if with a million tiny sucking mouths. Their machetes, covered with glue and flapping fly paper, had been dropped, forgotten in the confusion. Torches had dropped underfoot, forgotten, so that the struggle was in darkness, illuminated only by the light of the moon through the clouds and the flashes of lightning. Flypaper in their hair, across their eyes, clinging, hampering, maddening them with the knowledge that some frightful voodoo, stronger than their Papaloi or Mamaloi, had laid hands upon them.

A flare of lightning slashed from the very center of the storm cloud that was now hanging overhead. Its brilliance illuminated, for a moment, the figure of The Lady from Hell, standing at the edge of the veranda, her arms uplifted as if calling down the wrath of the heavens upon them. A shattering blast of thunder followed and a gust of wind swept across the clearing.

That gust of wind was the crowning touch, the straw that was needed to break the camel's back of resistance in that struggling, milling black throng. It set all the loose ends of the flypaper fluttering, where it was not fastened to bodies. And, more than that, it caught up the sticky squares that were still unattached and sent them dancing through the air.

There rose a howl of fear. The demons of these *blancs*, not content with lying in wait and springing out upon them, were now flying through the air; attacking them from the heavens, sucking from their bodies all their strength.

What use to resist when even the magic of the Papaloi and the Mamaloi was not sufficient to fight off the demons.

They bolted headlong, flypaper sticking to every part of their anatomy. They fell, scaled with the awful things, and promptly acquired more. Women fell and shrieked as they were trampled upon, not from the pain of the trampling feet, but from the fear that they might be left behind at the mercy of the demons. Men, blinded by the sticky things, ran in circles and clutched at whatever they came in contact with.

Then came the low drone of an airplane engine in the distance, flying low because of the storm. Turning, Vivian ran back into the dining room, where Benedetti still lay, bound upon the floor, his eyes glaring hatred at her. Calmly she sat down and wrote upon one of his letterheads which she found in the desk there. Then she snatched off the gag that muffled his mouth.

"The danger is all over," she told the man, "for us. But for you trouble is just beginning."

"You can't escape," he raved at her viciously. "I don't know what you've done, but you won't be able to leave the island. In an hour, two hours—by daylight at least—they will return, and what they will do to you won't be pleasant."

Vivian smiled. The invisible plane seemed to be circling the house now. She waved the paper she had written to dry the ink.

"What the American authorities in Port-au-Prince do to you will not be pleasant, either," she told Benedetti. "Voodoo is forbidden by law. You have not only aided and abetted voodoo ceremonies, but you have also procured human sacrifices for the ceremonial. There was the little French girl from the Port-au-Prince cabaret, and the girl from Santo Domingo—you should not have boasted. For you murdered them as surely as if you had driven a knife in their hearts, and the law will agree with me."

"You'll never live to tell the Americans, even if they believed the tale," he scoffed.

"Oh, yes I will," she mocked. Her voice was as dry and keen as a new ground sword. "Within an hour I shall be on my way to Cape Hatien. Hear that," and she raised an admonitory hand. In the silence the plane could be heard. She threw open the French windows. From where he lay Benedetti could see a Marine plane slanting down toward the comparatively sheltered waters of the little cove.

"In less than ten minutes," she said, "the plane will have taxied up to the beach and the Marine pilot and his observer will be in this room, asking if we need aid. You see," and her smile was completely mocking and scornful now, "you yourself brought about your own downfall—planted the idea in my brain when you told me that the plane passed overhead every night at about this time. There was a can of luminous paint in your storeroom. I saw it, and there he is coming to see what it's all about—and to take you to Cape Hatien—unless . . ."

"Unless what?" he queried eagerly.

"Unless you sign this memorandum. It deposes that I have purchased this plantation from you—that you have received the purchase price—and that proper legal transfer to it will be made later."

There was a calculating gleam in the man's eyes as he made assent. His gaze flickered out through the open door to where the plane had already landed on the surface of the cove.

Vivian had caught that gleam. "Of course," she went on smoothly, "we will have the Marine officers sign it as witnesses in your presence. Then you can accompany us back to Cape Hatien in the plane, and the lawyers of the Haitian Sugar Central will be glad to see that memorandum is put in proper legal form before I, in turn, resell the plantation to them. I shall not refuse the price they are willing to pay—and it will not matter to the sugar trust whether you or I are the owner." She gazed at him for a moment. "Well, do you agree?—or do you go to Cape Hatien a prisoner?"

Benedetti shot a glance at the trim, uniformed figure coming cautiously up from the beach. Feverishly he scribbled his name at the bottom of the memorandum.

The Copper Bowl

GEORGE FIELDING ELIOT

BEST KNOWN FOR HIS MILITARY WRITINGS, George Fielding Eliot (1894–1971) was born in Brooklyn, New York, but his family moved to Australia when he was eight. He fought in the Australian army at the Dardanelles in 1915, then at the battles of the Somme, Passchendaele, Arras, and Amiens. He moved back to the United States after the war and joined the U.S. Army Reserves as a lieutenant. He studied military history and, after reading a 1926 pulp magazine, *War Stories*, decided he could earn extra money by writing and sold *War Stories* a narrative of a war experience, thereby beginning his life as a full-time writer, albeit only intermittently writing for the pulps. He took a job writing for *The Infantry Journal* in 1928, and produced the full-length novels *The Eagles of Death* (1930) and *Federal Bullets* (1936), a G-Man adventure. The first of his many books about the military, *If War Comes* (1937), written with Major Richard Ernest Dupuy, was a well-received survey of war zones; his *The Ramparts We Watch* (1938) was a prescient warning to America that its military needed to be prepared to defend Canada and South America against the combined attacks of Germany, Italy, and Japan. He was a military writer for the *New York Herald Tribune* from 1939 and worked as a correspondent for CBS during World War II, after which he was a columnist for the *New York Post* before syndicating his own column in 1950.

The straightforward analysis of Eliot's highly regarded military books fail to prepare the reader for the extremity, both of language and subject, in his pulp fiction, and this "Yellow Peril" story is infamous among pulp fiction experts as one of the most brutal ever published.

"The Copper Bowl" was originally published in the December 1928 issue of *Weird Tales*.

THE COPPER BOWL

George Fielding Eliot

YUAN LI, the mandarin, leaned back in his rosewood chair.

"It is written," he said softly, "that a good servant is a gift of the gods, whilst a bad one—"

The tall, powerfully built man standing humbly before the robed figure in the chair bowed thrice, hastily, submissively.

Fear glinted in his eye, though he was armed, and moreover was accounted a brave soldier. He could have broken the little smooth-faced mandarin across his knee, and yet . . .

"Ten thousand pardons, beneficent one," he said. "I have done all—having regard to your honourable order to slay the man not nor do him permanent injury—I have done all that I can. But—"

"But he speaks not!" murmured the mandarin. "And you come to me with a tale of failure? I do not like failures, Captain Wang!"

The mandarin toyed with a little paper knife on the low table beside him. Wang shuddered.

"Well, no matter for this time," the mandarin said after a moment. Wang breathed a sigh of most heartfelt relief, and the mandarin smiled softly, fleetingly. "Still," he went on, "our task is yet to be accomplished. We have the man—he has the information we require; surely some way may be found. The servant has failed; now the master must try his hand. Bring the man to me."

Wang bowed low and departed with considerable haste.

The mandarin sat silent for a moment, looking across the wide, sunlit room at a pair of singing birds in a wicker cage hanging in the farther window. Presently he nodded—one short, satisfied nod—and struck a little silver bell which stood on his beautifully inlaid table.

Instantly a white-robed, silent-footed servant entered, and stood with bowed head awaiting his master's pleasure. To him Yuan Li gave certain swift, incisive orders.

The white-robed one had scarcely departed when Wang, captain of the mandarin's guard, reentered the spacious apartment.

"The prisoner, Benevolent!" he announced.

The mandarin made a slight motion with his slender hand; Wang barked an order, and there entered, between two heavily muscled, half-naked guardsmen, a short, sturdily built man, barefooted, clad only in a tattered shirt and khaki trousers, but with fearless blue eyes looking straight at Yuan Li under the tousled masses of his blonde hair.

A white man!

"Ah!" said Yuan Li, in his calm way, speaking faultless French. "The excellent Lieutenant Fournet! Still obstinate?"

Fournet cursed him earnestly, in French and three different Chinese dialects.

"You'll pay for this, Yuan Li!" he wound up. "Don't think your filthy brutes can try the knuckle torture and their other devil's tricks on a French officer and get away with it!"

Yuan Li toyed with his paper knife, smiling.

"You threaten me, Lieutenant Fournet," he answered, "yet your threats are but as rose petals wafted away on the morning breeze—unless you return to your post to make your report."

"Why, damn you!" answered the prisoner. "You needn't try that sort of thing—you know better than to kill me! My commandant is perfectly aware of my movements—he'll be knocking on your door with a company of the Legion at his back if I don't show up by tomorrow at reveille!"

Yuan Li smiled again.

"Doubtless—and yet we still have the better part of the day before us," he said. "Much may be accomplished in an afternoon and evening."

Fournet swore again.

"You can torture me and be damned," he answered. "I know and you know that you don't dare to kill me or to injure me so that I can't get back to Fort Deschamps. For the rest, do your worst, you yellow-skinned brute!"

"A challenge!" the mandarin exclaimed. "And I, Lieutenant Fournet, pick up your glove! Look you—what I require from you is the strength and location of your outpost on the Mephong River. So—"

"So that your cursed bandits, whose murders and lootings keep you here in luxury, can rush the outpost some dark night and open the river route for their boats," Fournet cut in. "I know you, Yuan Li, and I know your trade—mandarin of thieves! The military governor of Tonkin sent a battalion of the Foreign Legion here to deal with such as you, and to restore peace and order on the frontier, not to yield to childish threats! That is not the Legion's way, and you should know it. The best thing you can do is to send in your submission, or I can assure you that within a fortnight your head will be rotting over the North Gate of Hanoi, as a warning to others who might follow your bad example."

The mandarin's smile never altered, though well he knew that this was no idle threat. With Tonkinese tirailleurs, even with Colonial infantry, he could make some sort of headway, but these thrice-accursed Legionnaires were devils from the very pit itself. He—Yuan Li, who had ruled as king in the valley of the Mephong, to whom half a Chinese province and many a square mile of French Tonkin had paid tribute humbly—felt his throne of power tottering beneath him. But one hope remained: down the river, beyond the French outposts, were boats filled with men and with the loot of a dozen villages—the most successful raiding party he had ever sent out. Let these boats come through, let him have back his men (and they were his best), get his hands on the loot, and perhaps something might be done. Gold, jewels, jade—and though the soldiers of France were terrible, there were in Hanoi certain civilian officials not wholly indifferent to these things. But on the banks of the Mephong, as though they knew his hopes, the Foreign Legion had established an outpost—he must know exactly where, he must know exactly how strong; for till this river post was gone, the boats could never reach him.

And now Lieutenant Fournet, staff officer to the commandant, had fallen into his hands. All night his torturers had reasoned with the stubborn young Norman, and all morning they had never left him for a minute. They had marked him in no way, nor broken bones, nor so much as cut or bruised the skin—yet there are ways! Fournet shuddered all over at the thought of what he had gone through, that age-long night and morning.

To Fournet, his duty came first; to Yuan Li, it was life or death that Fournet should speak. And he had taken measures which now marched to their fulfilment.

He dared not go to extremes with Fournet;

nor yet could French justice connect the mandarin Yuan Li with the bandits of the Mephong.

They might suspect, but they could not prove; and an outrage such as the killing or maiming of a French officer in his own palace was more than Yuan Li dared essay. He walked on thin ice indeed those summer days, and walked warily.

Yet—he had taken measures.

"My head is still securely on my shoulders," he replied to Fournet. "I do not think it will decorate your gate spikes. So you will not speak?"

"Certainly not!"

Lieutenant Fournet's words were as firm as his jaw.

"Ah, but you will. Wang!"

"Magnanimous!"

"Four more guards. Make the prisoner secure."

Wang clapped his hands.

Instantly four additional half-naked men sprang into the room: two, falling on their knees, seized Fournet round the legs; another threw his corded arms round the lieutenant's waist; another stood by, club in hand, as a reserve in case of—what?

The two original guards still retained their grip on Fournet's arms.

Now, in the grip of those sinewy hands, he was held immobile, utterly helpless, a living statue.

Yuan Li, the mandarin, smiled again. One who did not know him would have thought his smile held an infinite tenderness, a divine compassion.

He touched the bell at his side.

Instantly, in the farther doorway, appeared two servants, conducting a veiled figure—a woman, shrouded in a dark drapery.

A word from Yuan Li—rough hands tore the veil aside, and there stood drooping between the impassive servants a vision of loveliness, a girl scarce out of her teens, dark-haired, slender, with the great appealing brown eyes of a fawn: eyes which widened suddenly as they rested on Lieutenant Fournet.

"Lily!" exclaimed Fournet, and his five guards had their hands full to hold him as he struggled to be free.

"You fiend!" he spat at Yuan Li. "If a hair of this girl's head is touched, by the Holy Virgin of Yvetot I will roast you alive in the flames of your own palace! My God, Lily, how—"

"Quite simply, my dear Lieutenant," the mandarin's silky voice interrupted. "We knew, of course—every house-servant in North Tonkin is a spy of mine—that you had conceived an affection for this woman; and when I heard you were proving obdurate under the little attentions of my men, I thought it well to send for her. Her father's bungalow is far from the post—indeed, it is in Chinese and not French territory, as you know—and the task was not a difficult one. And now—"

"André! André!" the girl was crying, struggling in her turn with the servants. "Save me, André—these beasts—"

"Have no fear, Lily," André Fournet replied. "They dare not harm you, any more than they dare to kill me. They are bluffing—"

"But have you considered well, Lieutenant?" asked the mandarin gently. "You, of course, are a French officer. The arm of France—and it is a long and unforgiving arm—will be stretched out to seize your murderers. The gods forbid I should set that arm reaching for me and mine. But this girl—ah, that is different!"

"Different? How is it different? The girl is a French citizen—"

"I think not, my good Lieutenant Fournet. She is three-quarters French in blood, true; but her father is half Chinese, and is a Chinese subject; she is a resident of China—I think you will find that French justice will not be prepared to avenge her death quite so readily as your own. At any rate, it is a chance I am prepared to take."

Fournet's blood seemed to turn to ice in his veins. The smiling devil was right! Lily—his lovely white Lily, whose only mark of Oriental blood was the rather piquant slant of her great eyes—was not entitled to the protection of the tricolour.

God! What a position! Either betray his flag, his regiment, betray his comrades to their deaths—or see his Lily butchered before his eyes!

"So now, Lieutenant Fournet, we understand each other," Yuan Li continued after a brief pause to let the full horror of the situation grip the other's soul. "I think you will be able to remember the location and strength of that outpost for me—now?"

Fournet stared at the man in bitter silence, but the words had given the quick-minded Lily a key to the situation, which she had hardly understood at first.

"No, no, André!" she cried. "Do not tell him. Better that I should die than that you should be a traitor! See—I am ready."

Fournet threw back his head, his wavering resolution reincarnate.

"The girl shames me!" he said. "Slay her if you must, Yuan Li—and if France will not avenge her, I will! But traitor I will not be!"

"I do not think that is your last word, Lieutenant," the mandarin purred. "Were I to strangle the girl, yes—perhaps. But first she must cry to you for help, and when you hear her screaming in agony, the woman you love, perhaps then you will forget these noble heroics!"

Again he clapped his hands; and again silent servants glided into the room. One bore a small brazier of glowing charcoal; a second had a little cage of thick wire mesh, inside of which something moved horribly; a third bore a copper bowl with handles on each side, to which was attached a steel band that glittered in the sunlight.

The hair rose on the back of Fournet's neck. What horror impended now? Deep within him some instinct warned that what was now to follow would be fiendish beyond the mind of mortal man to conceive. The mandarin's eyes seemed suddenly to glow with infernal fires. Was he in truth man—or demon?

A sharp word in some Yunnan dialect unknown to Fournet—and the servants had flung the girl upon her back on the floor, spreadeagled in pitiful helplessness, upon a magnificent peacock rug.

Another word from the mandarin's thin lips—and roughly they tore the clothing from the upper half of the girl's body. White and silent she lay upon that splendid rug, her eyes still on Fournet's: silent, lest words of hers should impair the resolution of the man she loved.

Fournet struggled furiously with his guards, but they were five strong men, and they held him fast.

"Remember, Yuan Li!" he panted. "You'll pay! Damn your yellow soul—"

The mandarin ignored the threat.

"Proceed," he said to the servants. "Note carefully, Monsieur le Lieutenant Fournet, what we are doing. First, you will note, the girl's wrists and ankles are lashed to posts and to heavy articles of furniture, suitably placed so that she cannot move. You wonder at the strength of the rope, the number of turns we take to hold so frail a girl? I assure you, they will be required. Under the copper bowl, I have seen a feeble old man tear his wrist free from an iron chain."

The mandarin paused; the girl was now bound so tightly that she could scarce move a muscle of her body.

Yuan Li regarded the arrangements.

"Well done," he approved. "Yet if she tears any limb free, the man who bound that limb shall have an hour under the bamboo rods. Now—the bowl! Let me see it."

He held out a slender hand. Respectfully a servant handed him the bowl, with its dangling band of flexible steel. Fournet, watching with eyes full of dread, saw that the band was fitted with a lock, adjustable to various positions. It was like a belt, a girdle.

"Very well." The mandarin nodded, turning the thing over and over in fingers that almost seemed to caress it. "But I anticipate—perhaps the lieutenant and the young lady are not familiar with this little device. Let me explain, or rather, demonstrate. Put the bowl in place, Kan-su. No, no—just the bowl, this time."

Another servant, who had started forward,

stepped back into his corner. The man addressed as Kan-su took the bowl, knelt at the side of the girl, passed the steel band under her body and placed the bowl, bottom up, on her naked abdomen, tugging at the girdle till the rim of the bowl bit into the soft flesh. Then he snapped the lock fast, holding the bowl thus firmly in place by the locked steel belt attached to its two handles and passing round the girl's waist. He rose, stood silent with folded arms.

Fournet felt his flesh crawling with horror—and all this time Lily had said not one word, though the tight girdle, the pressure of the circular rim of the bowl, must have been hurting her cruelly.

But now she spoke, bravely.

"Do not give way, André," she said. "I can bear it—it does—it does not hurt!"

"God!" yelled André Fournet, still fighting vainly against those clutching yellow hands.

"It does not hurt!" the mandarin echoed the girl's last words. "Well, perhaps not. But we will take it off, notwithstanding. We must be merciful."

At his order the servant removed the bowl and girdle. An angry red circle showed on the white skin of the girl's abdomen where the rim had rested.

"And still I do not think you understand, Mademoiselle and Monsieur," he went on. "For presently we must apply the bowl again—and when we do, under it we will put—this!"

With a swift movement of his arm he snatched from the servant in the corner the wire cage and held it up to the sunlight.

The eyes of Fournet and Lily fixed themselves upon it in horror. For within, plainly seen now, moved a great grey rat—a whiskered, beady-eyed, restless, scabrous rat, its white chisel-teeth shining through the mesh.

"*Dieu de Dieu!*" breathed Fournet. His mind refused utterly to grasp the full import of the dreadful fate that was to be Lily's; he could only stare at the unquiet rat—stare—stare . . .

"You understand now, I am sure," purred the mandarin. "The rat under the bowl—observe the bottom of the bowl, note the little flange. Here we put the hot charcoal—the copper becomes heated—the heat is overpowering—the rat cannot support it—he has but one means of escape: he gnaws his way out through the lady's body! And now about that outpost, Lieutenant Fournet?"

"No—no—no!" cried Lily. "They will not do it—they are trying to frighten us—they are human; men cannot do a thing like that. Be silent, André, be silent, whatever happens; don't let them beat you! Don't let them make a traitor of you! Ah—"

At a wave from the mandarin, the servant with the bowl again approached the half-naked girl. But this time the man with the cage stepped forward also. Deftly he thrust in a hand, avoided the rat's teeth, jerked the struggling vermin out by the scruff of the neck.

The bowl was placed in position. Fournet fought desperately for freedom—if only he could get one arm clear, snatch a weapon of some sort!

Lily gave a sudden little choking cry.

The rat had been thrust under the bowl.

Click! The steel girdle was made fast—and now they were piling the red-hot charcoal on the upturned bottom of the bowl, while Lily writhed in her bonds as she felt the wriggling, pattering horror of the rat on her bare skin, under that bowl of fiends.

One of the servants handed a tiny object to the impassive mandarin.

Yuan Li held it up in one hand.

It was a little key.

"This key, Lieutenant Fournet," he said, "unlocks the steel girdle which holds the bowl in place. It is yours—as a reward for the information I require. Will you not be reasonable? Soon it will be too late!"

Fournet looked at Lily. The girl was quiet now, had ceased to struggle; her eyes were open, or he would have thought she had fainted.

The charcoal glowed red on the bottom of the copper bowl. And beneath its carved surface, Fournet could imagine the great grey rat stirring restlessly, turning around, seeking escape from the growing heat, at last sinking his teeth in that soft white skin, gnawing, burrowing desperately . . .

God!

His duty—his flag—his regiment—France! Young Sous-lieutenant Pierre Desjardins—gay young Pierre—and twenty men, to be surprised and massacred horribly, some saved for the torture, by an overwhelming rush of bandit-devils, through his treachery? He knew in his heart that he could not do it.

He must be strong—he must be firm.

If only he might suffer for Lily—gentle, loving little Lily, brave little Lily who had never harmed a soul.

Loud and clear through the room rang a terrible scream.

André, turning in fascinated horror, saw that Lily's body, straining upward in an arc from the rug, was all but tearing asunder the bonds which held it. He saw, what he had not before noticed, that a little nick had been broken from one edge of the bowl—and through this nick and across the white surface of the girl's heaving body was running a tiny trickle of blood!

The rat was at work.

Then something snapped in André's brain. He went mad.

With the strength that is given to madmen, he tore loose his right arm from the grip that held it—tore loose, and dashed his fist into the face of the guard. The man with the club sprang forward unwarily; the next moment André had the weapon, and was laying about him with berserk fury. Three guards were down before Wang drew his sword and leaped into the fray.

Wang was a capable and well-trained soldier. It was cut, thrust, and parry for a moment, steel against wood—then Wang, borne back before that terrible rush, had the reward of his strategy.

The two remaining guards, to whom he had signalled, and a couple of the servants flung themselves together on Fournet's back and bore him roaring to the floor.

The girl screamed again, shattering the coarser sounds of battle.

Fournet heard her—even in his madness he heard her. And as he heard, a knife hilt in a servant's girdle met his hand. He caught at it, thrust upward savagely: a man howled; the weight on Fournet's back grew less; blood gushed over his neck and shoulders. He thrust again, rolled clear of the press, and saw one man sobbing out his life from a ripped-open throat, while another, with both hands clasped over his groin, writhed in silent agony upon the floor.

André Fournet, gathering a knee under him, sprang like a panther straight at the throat of Wang the captain.

Down the two men went, rolling over and over on the floor. Wang's weapons clashed and clattered—a knife rose, dripping blood, and plunged home.

With a shout of triumph André Fournet sprang to his feet, his terrible knife in one hand, Wang's sword in the other.

Screaming, the remaining servants fled before that awful figure.

Alone, Yuan Li the mandarin faced incarnate vengeance.

"The key!"

Hoarsely Fournet spat out his demand; his reeling brain had room for but one thought:

"The key, you yellow demon!"

Yuan Li took a step backward into the embrasured window, through which the jasmine-scented afternoon breeze still floated sweetly.

The palace was built on the edge of a cliff; below that window ledge, the precipice fell a sheer fifty feet down to the rocks and shallows of the upper Mephong.

Yuan Li smiled once more, his calm unruffled.

"You have beaten me, Fournet," he said, "yet I have beaten you, too. I wish you joy of your victory. Here is the key." He held it up in his hand; and as André sprang forward with a shout, Yuan Li turned, took one step to the window ledge, and without another word was gone into space, taking the key with him.

Far below he crashed in red horror on the rocks, and the waters of the turbulent Mephong closed forever over the key to the copper bowl.

Back sprang André—back to Lily's side. The blood ran no more from under the edge of the bowl; Lily lay very still, very cold . . .

God! She was dead!

Her heart was silent in her tortured breast.

André tore vainly at the bowl, the steel girdle—tore with bleeding fingers, with broken teeth, madly—in vain.

He could not move them.

And Lily was dead.

Or was she? What was that?

In her side a pulse beat—beat strongly and more strongly . . .

Was there still hope?

The mad Fournet began chafing her body and arms.

Could he revive her? Surely she was not dead—could not be dead!

The pulse still beat—strange it beat only in one place, on her soft white side, down under her last rib.

He kissed her cold and unresponsive lips.

When he raised his head the pulse had ceased to beat. Where it had been, blood was flowing sluggishly—dark venous blood, flowing in purple horror.

And from the midst of it, out of the girl's side, the grey, pointed head of the rat was thrusting, its muzzle dripping gore, its black eyes glittering beadily at the madman who gibbered and frothed above it.

So, an hour later, his comrades found André Fournet and Lily his beloved—the tortured maniac keening over the tortured dead.

But the grey rat they never found.

POST-WORLD WAR II

The Cat-Woman

ERLE STANLEY GARDNER

THE AMAZINGLY PROLIFIC Erle Stanley Gardner (1889–1970) created countless series characters for the pulp magazines before he wrote his first Perry Mason novel, *The Case of the Velvet Claws* (1933). He had studied law on his own and never got a degree, but passed the bar exam in 1911, practicing for about a decade. He made little money, so he started to write fiction, selling his first mystery to a pulp magazine in 1923. For the next decade, he published approximately 1.2 million words a year, the equivalent of a full-length novel every three weeks.

Mason, the incorruptible lawyer, went on to become the bestselling mystery character in American literature, with three hundred million copies sold of more than eighty novels (though Mickey Spillane's Mike Hammer outsold him on a per-book basis). The books inspired the *Perry Mason* television series that starred Raymond Burr for nine hugely successful years (1957–1966), which had followed on the heels of the equally popular radio series that ran from 1943 to 1955.

Gardner found popular success with virtually everything he wrote, including the stories about Ed Jenkins, known as the Phantom Crook, whose adventures appeared in the prestigious *Black Mask* magazine. A master of disguise and con artist, Jenkins was a self-confessed "outlaw, desperado, and famous lone wolf." He worked both as a detective and as a crook, frequently informing on his fellow criminals—always for the sole purpose of enriching himself.

"The Cat-Woman" was originally published in the February 1927 issue of *Black Mask*; it was first collected in *Dead Men's Letters* (New York, Carroll & Graf, 1990).

THE CAT-WOMAN

Erle Stanley Gardner

BIG BILL RYAN slid his huge bulk into the vacant chair opposite my own and began toying with the heavy watch chain which stretched across the broad expanse of his vest.

"Well," I asked, showing only mild annoyance, for Big Ryan had the reputation of never wasting time, his own or anyone else's.

"Ed, I hear you've gone broke. I've got a job for you."

He spoke in his habitual, thin, reedy voice. In spite of his bulk his mouth was narrow and his tone shrill. However, I fancied I could detect a quiver of excitement underlying his words, and I became cold. News travels fast in the underworld. He knew of my financial setback as soon as I did, almost. My brokers had learned my identity—that I was a crook, and they had merely appropriated my funds. They were reputable business men. I was a crook. If I made complaint the courts would laugh at me. I've had similar experiences before. No matter how honest a man may appear he'll always steal from a crook—not from any ethical reasons, but because he feels he can get away with it.

"What's on your mind?" I asked Ryan, not affirming or denying the rumor concerning my financial affairs.

His pudgy fingers seemed to be fairly alive as he twisted and untwisted the massive gold chain.

"It's just a message," he said, at length, and handed me a folded slip of paper.

I looked it over. It was a high class of stationery, delicately perfumed, bearing a few words in feminine handwriting which was as perfect and characterless as copper plate.

> *"Two hours after you get this message meet me at Apartment 624, Reedar Arms Apartments. The door will be open.*
>
> *H. M. H."*

I scowled over at Ryan and shook my head. "I've walked into all the traps I intend to, Ryan."

His little, pig eyes blinked rapidly and his fingers jammed his watch chain into a hard knot.

"The message is on the square, Ed. I can vouch for that. What the job will be that opens up I can't tell. You'll have to take the responsibility of that; but there won't be any police trap in that apartment."

I looked at the note again. The ink was dark. Evidently the words had been written some little time ago. The message did not purport to be to anyone in particular. Big Ryan was a notorious fence, a go-between of crooks. Apparently he had been given the note with the understanding that he was to pick out the one to whom it was to be delivered. The note would clear his skirts, yet he must be in on the game. He'd have to get in touch with the writer after he made a delivery of the note so that the time of the appointment would be known.

I reached a decision on impulse, and determined to put Ryan to the test. "All right, I'll be there."

I could see a look of intense relief come over his fat face. He couldn't keep back the words. "Bully for you, Ed Jenkins!" he shrilled. "After I heard you were broke I thought I might get you. You're the one man who could do it. Remember, two hours from now," and, with the words, he pulled out his turnip watch and carefully checked the time. Then he heaved up from the chair and waddled toward the back of the restaurant.

I smiled to myself. He was going to telephone "H. M. H." and I filed that fact away for future reference.

Two hours later I stepped from the elevator on the sixth floor of the Reedar Arms Apartments, took my bearings and walked directly to the door of 624. I didn't pause to knock but threw the door open. However, I didn't walk right in, but stepped back into the hallway.

"Come in, Mr. Jenkins," said a woman's voice.

The odor of incense swirled out into the hall, and I could see the apartment was in half-light, a pink light which came through a rose-colored shade. Ordinarily I trust the word of no man, but I was in desperate need of cash, and Big Bill Ryan had a reputation of being one who could be trusted. I took a deep breath and walked into the apartment, closing the door after me.

She was sitting back in an armchair beneath a rose-shaded reading lamp, her bare arm stretched out with the elbow resting on a dark table, the delicate, tapering fingers holding a long, ivory cigarette holder in which burned a half-consumed cigarette. Her slippered feet were placed on a stool and the light glinted from a well-proportioned stretch of silk stocking. It was an artistic job, and the effect was pleasing. I have an eye for such things, and I stood there for a moment taking in the scene, appreciating it. And then I caught the gaze of her eyes.

Cat eyes she had; eyes that seemed to dilate and contract, green eyes that were almost luminous there in the half-light.

I glanced around the apartment, those luminous, green eyes studying me as I studied the surroundings. There was nothing at all in the apartment to suggest the personality of such a woman. Everything about the place was suggestive merely of an average furnished apartment. At the end of the room, near the door of a closet, I saw a suitcase. It merely confirmed my previous suspicion. The woman had only been in that apartment for a few minutes. She rented the place merely as a meeting ground for the crook she had selected to do her bidding. When Big Bill Ryan had picked a man for her, he had telephoned her and she had packed her negligee in the suitcase and rushed to the apartment.

She gave a little start and followed my gaze, then her skin crinkled as her lips smiled. That smile told me much. The skin seemed hard as parchment. She was no spring chicken, as I had suspected from the first.

The cat-woman shrugged her shoulders, reached in a little handbag and took out a blue-steel automatic which she placed on the table. Then she hesitated, took another great drag at the cigarette and narrowed her eyes at me.

"It is no matter, Mr. Jenkins. I assure you that my desire to conceal my identity, to make it appear that this was my real address, was to protect myself only in case I did not come to terms with the man Ryan sent. We had hardly expected to be able to interest a man of your ability in the affair, and, now that you are here, I shan't let you go, so there won't be any further need of the deception. I will even tell you who I am and where I really live—in a moment."

I said nothing, but watched the automatic. Was it possible she knew so little about me that she fancied I could be forced to do something at the point of a pistol?

As though she again read my mind, she reached into the handbag and began taking out crisp bank notes. They were of five-hundred-dollar denomination, and there were twenty of them. These she placed on the table beside the gun.

"The gun is merely to safeguard the money," she explained with another crinkling smile. "I wouldn't want you to take the cash without accepting my proposition."

I nodded. As far as possible I would let her do the talking.

"Mr. Jenkins, or Ed, as I shall call you now that we're acquainted, you have the reputation of being the smoothest worker in the criminal game. You are known to the police as The Phantom Crook, and they hate, respect, and fear you. Ordinarily you are a lone wolf, but because you are pressed for ready cash, I think I can interest you in something I have in mind."

She paused and sized me up with her cat-green eyes. If she could read anything on my face she could have read the thoughts of a wooden Indian.

"There are ten thousand dollars," she said, and there was a subtle, purring something about her voice. "That money will be yours when you leave this room if you agree to do something for me. Because I can trust you, I will pay you in advance."

Again she stopped, and again I sat in immobile silence.

"I want you to break into a house—my own house—and steal a very valuable necklace. Will you do it?"

She waited for a reply.

"That is all you wish?" I asked, killing time, waiting.

She wrinkled her cheeks again.

"Oh yes, now that you speak of it, there is one other thing. I want you to kidnap my niece. I would prefer that you handle the entire matter in your own way, but I will give you certain suggestions, some few instructions."

She paused waiting for a reply, and I let my eyes wander to the cash piled on the table. Very evidently she had intended that the actual cash should be a strong point in her argument and it would disappoint her if I didn't look hungrily at it.

"How long shall I hold your niece captive?"

She watched me narrowly, here eyes suddenly grown hard.

"Ed Jenkins, once you have my niece you can do anything with her or about her that you want. You must keep her for two days. After that you may let her go or you may keep her."

"That is all?" I asked.

"That is all," she said, and I knew she lied, as she spoke.

I arose. "I am not interested, but it has been a pleasure to have met you. I appreciate artistry."

Her face darkened, and the corners of her upper lip drew back, the feline snarl of a cat about to spring. I fancied her hand drifted toward the automatic.

"Wait," she spat, "you don't know all."

I turned at that, and, by an effort, she controlled herself. Once more the purring note came into her voice.

"The necklace you will steal is my own. I am the legal guardian of my niece and I will give you my permission to kidnap her. What is more, I will allow you to see her first, to get her own permission. You will not be guilty of any crime whatever."

I came back and sat down in the chair.

"I have the necklace and it is insured for fifty thousand dollars," she said in a burst of candor. "I must have the money, simply must. To sell the necklace would be to cause comment of a nature I cannot explain. If I secrete the necklace I will be detected by the insurance company. If the notorious Ed Jenkins breaks into my house, steals my necklace, kidnaps my niece, the insurance company will never question but what the theft was genuine. You will, of course, not actually take the necklace. You will take a paste copy. The insurance company will pay me fifty thousand dollars, and, when occasion warrants, I can again produce the necklace."

I nodded. "You intend then that I shall be identified as the thief, that the police shall set up a hue and cry for me?"

She smiled brightly. "Certainly. That's why I want you to kidnap my niece. However, that should mean nothing to you. You have a reputation of being able to slip through the fingers of the police any time you wish."

I sighed. I had enjoyed immunity from arrest in California because of a legal technicality; but I was broke and in need of cash. All honest channels of employment were closed to me, and, after all, the woman was right. I had been able to laugh at the police.

I reached forward and took the money, folded the crisp bills and put them in my pocket.

"All right. I will accept. Remember one thing, however, if you attempt to double-cross me, to play me false in any way, I will keep the money and also get revenge. Whatever your game is you must keep all the cards on the table as far as my own connection with it is concerned. Otherwise . . . ?"

I paused significantly.

"Otherwise?" she echoed, and there was a taunt in her voice.

I shrugged my shoulders. "Otherwise you will be sorry. Others have thought they could use Ed Jenkins for a cat's-paw, could double-cross him. They never got away with it."

She smiled brightly. "I would hardly give you ten thousand dollars in cash unless I trusted you, Ed. Now that we've got the preliminaries over with we may as well get to work and remove the stage setting."

With that she arose, stretched with one of those toe stretching extensions of muscles which reminded me of a cat arising from a warm sofa, slipped out of the negligee and approached the suitcase. From the suitcase she took a tailored suit and slipped into it in the twinkling of an eye. She threw the negligee into the suitcase, took a hat from the closet, reached up and switched out the light.

"All right, Ed. We're ready to go."

She had her own machine in a nearby garage, a long, low roadster of the type which is purchased by those who demand performance and care nothing for expense of operation. I slipped into the seat and watched her dart through the traffic. She had skill, this cat-woman, but there was a ruthlessness about her driving. Twice, pedestrians barely managed to elude the nickeled bumpers. On neither occasion did she so much as glance backward to make sure she had not given them a glancing blow in passing.

At length we slowed up before an impressive house in the exclusive residential district west of Lakeside. With a quick wriggle she slipped out from behind the steering wheel, vaulted lightly to the pavement and extended her long, tapering fingers to me. "Come on, Ed. Here's where we get out."

I grinned as she held the door open. Whatever her age she was in perfect condition, splendidly formed, quick as a flash of light, and she almost gave the impression of assisting me from the car.

I was shown into a drawing-room and told to wait.

While the cat-woman was gone I looked about me, got the lay of the land, and noticed the unique furnishings of the room. Everywhere were evidences of the striking personality of the woman. A tiger rug was on the floor, a leopard skin on the davenport. A huge painted picture hung over the fireplace, a picture of a cat's head, the eyes seeming to have just a touch of luminous paint in them. In the semi-darkness of the nook the cat's eyes blazed forth and dominated the entire room. It was impossible to keep the eyes away from that weird picture; those steady, staring eyes drew my gaze time after time.

At length there was the rustle of skirts and I rose.

The cat-woman stood in the doorway. On her arm was a blonde girl attired in flapper style, painted and powdered, and, seemingly, a trifle dazed.

"My niece, Jean Ellery, Ed. Jean, may I present Mr. Ed Jenkins. You folks are destined to see a good deal of each other so you'd better get acquainted."

I bowed and advanced. The girl extended her hand, a limp, moist morsel of flesh. I took it and darted a glance at the cat-woman. She was standing tense, poised, her lips slightly parted, her eyes fixed upon the girl, watching her every move.

"Hullo, Ed, Mr. Jenkins. I understand you're goin' to kidnap me. Are you a cave-man or do you kidnap 'em gently?"

There was a singsong expression about her voice, the tone a child uses in reciting a piece of poetry the import of which has never penetrated to the brain.

"So you want to be kidnapped, do you, Jean?"

"Uh, huh."

"Aren't you afraid you may never get back?"

"I don't care if I never come back. Life here is the bunk. I want to get out where there's somethin' doin', some place where I can see life. Action, that's what I'm lookin' for."

With the words she turned her head and let her vacant, blue eyes wander to the cat-woman. Having spoken her little piece, she wanted to see what mark the teacher gave her. The cat-woman flashed a glance of approval, and the doll-faced blonde smiled up at me.

"All right, Jean," she said. "You run along. Mr. Jenkins and I have some things to discuss."

The blonde turned and walked from the room, flashing me what was meant to be a roguish glance from over her shoulder. The cat-woman curled up in a chair, rested her head on her cupped hands, and looked at me. There in the half-light her eyes seemed as luminous as those of the cat in the painting over the fireplace.

"Tomorrow at ten will be about right, Ed. Now, here are some of the things you must know. This house really belongs to Arthur C. Holton, the big oil man, you know. I have been with him for several years as private secretary and general house manager. Tomorrow night our engagement is to be announced and he is going to present me with the famous tear-drop necklace as an engagement present. I will manage everything so that the presentation takes place at about nine-thirty. Just before ten I will place the necklace on my niece to let her wear the diamonds for a few minutes, and she will leave the room for a moment, still wearing the diamonds.

"Really, I'll slip the genuine necklace in my dress and put an imitation around my niece's neck. She will leave the room and an assistant will bind and gag her and place her in a speedy roadster which I have purchased for you and is to be waiting outside. Then you must show your face. It won't look like a kidnapping and a theft unless I have some well-known crook show himself for a moment at the door.

"You can pretend that you have been double-crossed in some business deal by Mr. Holton. You suddenly jump in the doorway and level a gun at the guests. Then you can tell them that this is merely the first move in your revenge, that you will make Mr. Holton regret the time he double-crossed you. Make a short speech and then run for the machine. I have a little cottage rented down on the seashore, and I have had Jean spend several days there already, under another name, of course, and you can go there as Jean's husband, one who has just returned from a trip East. You will be perfectly safe from detection because all the neighbors know Jean as Mrs. Compton. You will pose as Mr. Compton and adopt any disguise you wish. But, remember; you must not stop and open the luggage compartment until you reach the cottage.

She spilled all that and then suddenly contracted her eyes until the pupils seemed mere slits.

"That may sound unimportant to you, Ed, but you've got to play your part letter perfect. There is a lot that depends on your following instructions to the letter. In the meantime I will give you plenty of assurance that I will shoot square with you."

I sat there, looking at this cat-woman curled up in the chair before the crackling fire, and had all I could do to keep from bursting out laughing right in her face. I've seen some wild, farfetched plots, but this had anything cheated I had ever heard of.

"Think how it will add to your reputation,"

she went on, the singing, purring note in her soothing tone.

I yawned. "And you can double-cross me and have me arrested ten minutes later, or tip the police off to this little cottage you have reserved for me, and I'll spend many, many years in jail while you laugh up your sleeve."

She shook her head. "What earthly reason would I have for wanting to have you arrested? No, Ed, I've anticipated that. Tomorrow we go to a notary public and I'll execute a written confession of my part in the affair. This confession will be placed in safekeeping where it will be delivered to the police in the event you are caught. *That* will show you how my interests are the same as your own, how I cannot afford to have you captured. This paper will contain my signed statement that I have authorized you to steal the jewels, and my niece will also execute a document stating the kidnapping is with her consent. Think it over, Ed. You will be protected, but I must have that insurance money, and have it in such a way that no one will suspect me."

I sat with bowed head, thinking over the plan. I had already digested everything she had told me. What I was worrying about was what she hadn't told me.

I arose and bowed.

"I'll see you tomorrow then?"

She nodded, her green eyes never leaving my face.

"Meet me at the office of Harry Atmore, the lawyer, at eleven and ask for Hattie M. Hare. He will see that you are protected in every way. I guarantee that you won't have any cause for alarm about my double-crossing you."

Apparently there was nothing more to be gained by talking with this woman and I left her.

I had ten thousand dollars in my pocket, a cold suspicion in my mind and a determination to find out just what the real game was. I didn't know just how deep Big Ryan was mixed in this affair—not yet I didn't, but I proposed to find out. In the meantime I wasn't taking any chances, and I slipped into my apartment without any brass band to announce my presence.

At first I thought everything was in proper order, and then I noticed something was missing. It was a jade handled, Chinese dagger, one that I had purchased at a curio store not more than a month ago. What was more, the Chinaman who sold it to me had known who I was. That dagger could be identified by the police as readily as my signature or my fingerprints.

I sat down by the window in my easy chair and thought over the events of the evening. I couldn't see the solution, not entirely, but I was willing to bet the cat-woman wouldn't have slept easily if she had known how much I was able to put together. Right then I could have dropped the whole thing and been ten thousand dollars ahead; but there was big money in this game that was being played. I couldn't forget how Big Bill Ryan had twisted and fumbled at his watch chain when he had delivered that note to me. He was a smooth fence, was Big Ryan, and he wouldn't have let his fat fingers get so excited over a mere thirty or forty thousand dollar job. There was a million in this thing or I missed my guess.

At last I figured I'd checked things out as far as I could with the information I had, and rolled in.

At eleven on the dot I presented myself at the office of Harry Atmore. Atmore was a shyster criminal lawyer who charged big fees, knew when and where to bribe, and got results for his clients. I gave the stenographer my name, told her that I had an appointment, and was shown into the private office of Henry Atmore, attorney-at-law.

Atmore sat at a desk, and his face was a study. He was trying to control his expression, but his face simply would twitch in spite of himself. He held forth a flabby hand, and I noticed that his palm was moist and that his hand trembled. To one side of the table sat the cat-woman and the blonde. Both of them smiled sweetly as I bowed.

Atmore got down to business at once. He passed over two documents for my inspection. One was a simple statement from Hattie M. Hare to the effect that I had been employed by her to steal the Holton, "tear-drop" necklace, and that we were jointly guilty of an attempt to defraud the insurance company. The other was a statement signed by Jean Ellery to the effect that I had arranged with her to kidnap her, but that she gave her consent to the kidnapping, and that it was being done at her request.

I noticed that the Hare statement said nothing about the kidnapping, and the other said nothing about the necklace. I filed those facts away for future reference.

"Now here's what we'll do, Jenkins," Atmore said, his moist hand playing with the corners of some papers which lay on his desk, "we'll have both of these statements placed in an envelope and deposited with a trust company to be held indefinitely, not to be opened, and not to be withdrawn. That will prevent any of the parties from withdrawing them, but if you should ever be arrested the district attorney, or the grand jury could, of course, subpoena the manager of the trust company and see what is in the envelope. The idea of these statements is not to give you immunity from prosecution, but to show you that Miss Hare is as deep in the mud as you are in the mire. She can't afford to have you arrested or to even let you get caught. Of course, if you *should* get arrested on some other matter we're relying on you to play the game. You've never been a squealer, and I feel my clients can trust you."

I nodded casually. It was plain he was merely speaking a part. His plan had already been worked out.

"I have one suggestion," I said.

He inclined his head. "Name it."

"That you call in a notary public and have them acknowledge the confessions."

The lawyer looked at his client. He was a beady-eyed, sallow-faced rat of a man. His great nose seemed to have drawn his entire face to a point, and his mouth and eyes were pinched accordingly. Also his lip had a tendency to draw back and show discolored, long teeth, protruding in front. He was like a rat, a hungry, cunning rat.

The cat-woman placed her ivory cigarette holder to her vivid lips, inhaled a great drag and then expelled two streams of white smoke from her dilated nostrils. She nodded at the lawyer, and, as she nodded, there was a hard gleam about her eyes.

"Very well," was all she said, but the purring note had gone from her voice.

Atmore wiped the back of his hand across his perspiring forehead, called in a notary, and, on the strength of his introduction, had the two documents acknowledged. Then he slipped them in one of his envelopes, wrote "Perpetual Escrow" on the back, signed it, daubed sealing wax all over the flap, and motioned to me.

"You can come with me, Jenkins, and see that I put this in the Trust Company downstairs."

I arose, accompanied the lawyer to the elevator and was whisked down to the office of the Trust Company. We said not a word on the trip. The lawyer walked to the desk of the vice-president, handed him the envelope, and told him what he wanted.

"Keep this envelope as a perpetual escrow. It can be opened by no living party except with an order of court. After ten years you may destroy it. Give this gentleman and myself a duplicate receipt."

The vice-president looked dubiously at the envelope, weighed it in his hand, sighed, and placed his signature on the envelope, gave it a number with a numbering machine, dictated a duplicate receipt, which he also signed, and took the envelope to the vaults.

"That should satisfy you," said Atmore, his beady eyes darting over me, the perspiration breaking out on his forehead. "That is all fair and above board."

I nodded and started toward the door. I could see the relief peeping in the rat-like eyes of the lawyer.

At the door I stopped, turned, and clutched the lawyer by the arm. "Atmore, do you know what happens to people who try to double-cross me?"

He was seized with a fit of trembling, and he impatiently tried to break away.

"You have a reputation for being a square

shooter, Jenkins, and for always getting the man who tries to double-cross you."

I nodded.

There in the marble lobby of that trust company, with people all around us, with a special officer walking slowly back and forth, I handed it to this little shyster.

"All right. You've just tried to double-cross me. If you value your life hand me that envelope."

He shivered again.

"W-w-w-what envelope?"

I gave him no answer, just kept my eyes boring into his, kept his trembling arm in my iron clutch, and kept my face thrust close to his.

He weakened fast. I could see his sallow skin whiten.

"Jenkins, I'm sorry. I told her we couldn't get away with it. It was her idea, not mine."

I still said nothing, but kept my eyes on his.

He reached in his pocket and took out the other envelope. My guess had been right. I knew his type. The rat-like cunning of the idea had unquestionably been his, but he didn't have the necessary nerve to bluff it through. He had prepared two envelopes. One of them had been signed and sealed before my eyes, but in signing and sealing it he had followed the mental pattern of another envelope which had already been signed and sealed and left in his pocket, an envelope which contained nothing but blank sheets of paper. When he put the envelope with the signed confession into his coat pocket he had placed it back of the dummy envelope. The dummy envelope he had withdrawn and deposited in his "perpetual escrow."

I took the envelope from him, broke the seals, and examined the documents. They were intact, the signed, acknowledged confessions.

I turned back to the shyster.

"Listen, Atmore. There is a big fee in this for you, a fee from the woman, perhaps from someone else. Go back and tell them that you have blundered, that I have obtained possession of the papers and they will expose you, fire you for a blunderer, make you the laughing stock of every criminal rendezvous in the city. If you keep quiet about this no one will ever know the difference. Speak and you ruin your reputation."

I could see a look of relief flood his face, and I knew he would lie to the cat-woman about those papers.

"Tell Miss Hare I'll be at the house at nine forty-five on the dot," I said. "There's no need of my seeing her again until then."

With that I climbed into my roadster, drove to the beach and looked over the house the cat-woman had selected for me. She had given me the address as well as the key at our evening interview, just before I said good night. Of course, she expected me to look the place over.

It was a small bungalow, the garage opening on to the sidewalk beneath the first floor. I didn't go in. Inquiry at a gasoline station showed that the neighbors believed Compton was a traveling salesman, away on a trip, but due to return. The blonde had established herself in the community. So much I found out, and so much the cat-woman had expected me to find out.

Then I started on a line she hadn't anticipated.

First I rented a furnished apartment, taking the precaution first to slip on a disguise which had always worked well with me, a disguise which made me appear twenty years older.

Second, I went to the county clerk's office, looked over the register of actions, and found a dozen in which the oil magnate had been a party. There were damage suits, quiet title actions, actions on oil leases, and on options. In all of these actions he had been represented by Morton, Huntley, & Morton. I got the address of the lawyers from the records, put up a good stall with their telephone girl, and found myself closeted with old H. F. Morton, senior member of the firm.

He was a shaggy, grizzled, gray-eyed old campaigner and he had a habit of drumming his fingers on the desk in front of him.

"What was it you wanted, Mr. Jenkins?"

I'd removed my disguise and given him my right name. He may or may not have known my original record. He didn't mention it.

I shot it to him right between the eyes.

"If I were the lawyer representing Arthur C. Holton I wouldn't let him marry Miss Hattie Hare."

He never batted an eyelash. His face was as calm as a baby's. His eyes didn't even narrow, but there came a change in the tempo of his drumming on the desk.

"Why?" he asked.

His tone was mild, casual, but his fingers were going rummy-tum-tum; rummy-tum-tum; rummy-tum-tummy-tum-tummy-tum-tum.

I shook my head. "I can't tell you all of it, but she's in touch with a shyster lawyer planning to cause trouble of some kind."

"Ah, yes, Mr.-er-Jenkins. You are a friend of Mr. Holton?"

I nodded. "He doesn't know it though."

"Ah, yes," rummy-tum-tum; rummy-tum-tum; "what is it I can do for you in the matter?"

"Help me prevent the marriage."

Rummy-tum-tum; rummy-tum-tum.

"How?"

"Give me a little information as a starter. Mr. Holton has a great deal of property?"

At this his eyes did narrow. The drumming stopped.

"This is a law office. Not an information bureau."

I shrugged my shoulders. "Miss Hare will have her own personal attorney. If the marriage should go through and anything should happen to Mr. Holton another attorney would be in charge of the estate."

He squirmed at that, and then recommenced his drumming.

"Nevertheless, I cannot divulge the confidential affairs of my client. This much is common knowledge. It is street talk, information available to anyone who will take the trouble to look for it. Mr. Holton is a man of great wealth. He owns much property, controls oil producing fields, business property, stocks, bonds. He was married and lost his wife when his child was born. The child was a boy and lived but a few minutes. Mr. Holton created a trust for that child, a trust which terminated with the premature death of the infant. Miss Hare has been connected with him as his secretary and general household executive for several years. Mr. Holton is a man of many enemies, strong character, and few friends. He is hated by the working class, and is hated unjustly, yet he cares nothing for public opinion. He is noted as a collector of jewels and paintings. Of late he has been influenced in many respects by Miss Hare, and has grown very fond of her.

"How do you propose to prevent his marriage, and what do you know of Miss Hare?"

I shook my head.

"I won't tell you a thing unless you promise to give me all the information I want, and keep me posted."

His face darkened. "Such a proposition is unthinkable. It is an insult to a reputable attorney."

I knew it, but I made the stall to keep him from finding out that I had all the information I wanted. I only wanted a general slant on Holton's affairs, and, most of all, I wanted a chance to size up his attorney, to get acquainted with him so he would know me later.

"Stick an ad in the personal columns of the morning papers if you want to see me about anything," I said as I made for the door.

He watched me meditatively. Until I had left the long, book-lined corridor, and emerged from the expensive suite of offices, I could still hear his fingers on the desk.

Rummy-tum-tum; rummy-tum-tum; rummy-tum-tummy-tum-tummy-tum-tum.

I went to a hotel, got a room and went to sleep. I was finished with my regular apartment. That was for the police.

At nine-forty-five I sneaked into the back door of Holton's house, found one of the extra servants waiting for me, and was shown into a closet near the room where the banquet was taking place. The servant was a crook, but one I couldn't place. I filed his map away for future reference, and he filed mine.

Ten minutes passed. I heard something that

might or might not have been a muffled scream, shuffling footsteps going down the hall. Silence, the ringing of a bell.

I stepped to the door of the banquet room, and flung it wide. Standing there on the threshold I took in the scene of hectic gaiety. Holton and the cat-woman sat at the head of the table. Couples in various stages of intoxication were sprinkled about. Servants stood here and there, obsequious, attentive. A man sat slightly apart, a man who had his eyes riveted on the door of an ante-room. He was the detective from the insurance company.

For a minute I stood there, undiscovered.

The room was a clatter of conversation. The detective half arose, his eyes on the door of the ante-room. Holton saw me, stopped in the middle of a sentence, and looked me over.

"Who are you, and what do you want?"

I handed it out in bunches. "I'm Ed Jenkins, the phantom crook. I've got a part of what I want. I'll come back later for the rest."

The detective reached for his hip, and I slammed the door and raced down the corridor. Taking the front steps in a flying leap I jumped into the seat of the powerful speedster, noticed the roomy luggage compartment, the running engine, the low, speedy lines, slammed in the gear, slipped in the clutch, and skidded out of the drive as the detective started firing from the window.

I didn't go direct to the beach house.

On a dark side-road I stopped the car, went back and opened up the luggage compartment and pulled out the bound and gagged girl. She was one I had never seen before, and she was mad. And she was the real Jean Ellery or else I was dumb.

I packed her around, parked her on the running board, took a seat beside her, left on the gag and the cords, and began to talk. Patiently, step by step, I went over the history of the whole case, telling her everything. When I had finished I cut the cords and removed the gag.

"Now either beat it, go ahead and scream, or ask questions, whichever you want," I told her.

She gave a deep breath, licked her lips, wiped her face with a corner of her party gown, woefully inspected a runner in the expensive stockings, looked at the marks on her wrists where the ropes had bitten, smoothed out her garments and turned to me.

"I think you're a liar," she remarked casually.

I grinned.

That's the way I like 'em. Here this jane had been grabbed, kidnapped, manhandled, jolted, forced to sit on the running board of a car and listen to her kidnapper talk a lot of stuff she naturally wouldn't believe, and then was given her freedom. Most girls would have fainted. Nearly all of 'em would have screamed and ran when they got loose. Here was a jane who was as cool as a cucumber, who looked over the damage to her clothes, and then called me a liar.

She was a thin slip of a thing, twenty or so, big, hazel eyes, chestnut hair, slender figure, rosebud mouth, bobbed hair and as unattainable as a girl on a magazine cover.

"Read this," I said, and slipped her the confession of the cat-woman.

She read it in the light of the dash lamp, puckered her forehead a bit, and then handed it back.

"So you are Ed Jenkins—Why should auntie have wanted me kidnapped?"

I shrugged my shoulders. "That's what I want to know. It's the one point in the case that isn't clear. Want to stick around while I find out?"

She thought things over for a minute.

"Am I free to go?"

I nodded.

"Guess I'll stick around then," she said as she climbed back into the car, snuggling down next to the driver's seat. "Let's go."

I got in, started the engine, and we went.

A block from the beach house I slowed up.

"The house is ahead. Slip out as we go by this palm tree, hide in the shadows and watch what happens. I have an idea you'll see some action."

I slowed down and turned my face toward her, prepared to argue the thing out, but there was no need for argument. She was gathering her skirts about her. As I slowed down she jumped. I drove on to the house, swung the car so it faced the door of the garage and got out.

I had to walk in front of the headlights to fit the key to the door of the garage, and I was a bit nervous. There was an angle of this thing I couldn't get, and it worried me. I thought something was due to happen. If there hadn't been so much money involved I'd have skipped out. As it was, I was playing my cards trying to find out what was in the hand of the cat-woman.

I found out.

As though the swinging of the garage door had been a signal, two men jumped out from behind a rosebush and began firing at the luggage compartment of the car.

They had shotguns, repeaters, and they were shooting chilled buckshot at deadly range through the back of that car. Five times they shot, and then they vanished, running like mad.

Windows began to gleam with lights, a woman screamed, a man stuck his head out into the night. Around the corner there came the whine of a starting motor, the purr of an automobile engine, the staccato barks of an exhaust and an automobile whined off into the night.

I backed the speedster, turned it and went back down the street. At the palm tree where I'd left the flapper I slowed down, doubtfully, hardly expecting to see her again.

There was a flutter of white, a flash of slim legs, and there she was sitting on the seat beside me, her eyes wide, lips parted. "Did you get hurt?"

I shook my head and jerked my thumb back in the direction of the luggage compartment.

"Remember, I wasn't to stop or open that compartment until I got to the beach house," I said.

She looked back. The metal was riddled with holes, parts of the body had even been ripped into great, jagged tears.

"Your beloved auntie didn't want you kidnapped. She wanted you murdered. Right now she figures that you're dead, that I am gazing in shocked surprise at the dead body of a girl I've kidnapped, the police on my trail, the neighborhood aroused. Naturally she thinks I'll have my hands full for a while, and that she won't be bothered with me any more, either with me or with you."

The girl nodded.

"I didn't say so before, but I've been afraid of Aunt Hattie for a long time. It's an awful thing to say about one's own aunt, but she's absolutely selfish, selfish and unscrupulous."

I drove along in silence for a while.

"What are you going to do?" asked the kid.

"Ditch this car, get off the street, hide out for a few days, and find out what it's all about. Your aunt tried to double-cross me on a deal where there's something or other at stake. I intend to find out what. She and I will have our accounting later."

She nodded, her chin on her fist, thinking.

"What are *you* going to do?"

She shrugged her shoulders. "Heaven knows. If I go back I'll probably be killed. Having gone this far, Aunt Hattie can't afford to fail. She'll have me killed if I show up. I guess I'll have to hide out, too."

"Hotel?" I asked.

I could feel her eyes on my face, sizing me up, watching me like a hawk.

"I can't get a room in a hotel at this hour of the night in a party dress."

I nodded.

"Ed Jenkins, are you a gentleman?"

I shook my head. "Hell's fire, no. I'm a crook."

She looked at me and grinned. I could feel my mouth soften a bit.

"Ed, this is no time to stand on formalities. You know as well as I do that I'm in danger. My aunt believes me dead. If I can keep under cover, leaving her under that impression, I'll stand a chance. I can't hide out by myself. Either my aunt or the police would locate me in no time. You're an experienced crook, you know all the dodges, and I think I can trust you. I'm coming with you."

I turned the wheel of the car.

"All right," I said. "It's your best move, but I wanted you to suggest it. Take off those paste diamonds and leave 'em in the car. I've got to get rid of this car first, and then we'll go to my hideout."

An hour later I showed her into the apartment. I had run the car off the end of a pier. The watchman was asleep and the car had gurgled down into deep water as neatly as a duck. The watchman had heard the splash, but that's all the good it did him.

The girl looked around the place.

"Neat and cozy," she said. "I'm trusting you, Ed Jenkins. Good night."

I grinned.

"Good night," I said.

I slept late the next morning. I was tired. It was the girl who called me.

"Breakfast's ready," she said.

I sat up in bed and rubbed my eyes.

"Breakfast?"

She grinned.

"Yep. I slipped down to the store, bought some fruit and things, and brought you the morning papers."

I laughed outright. Here I had kidnapped a girl and now she was cooking me breakfast. She laughed, too.

"You see, I'm about broke, and I can't go around in a party dress. I've got to touch you for enough money to buy some clothes, and it's always easier to get money out of a man when he's well-fed. Aunt Hattie told me that."

"You've got to be careful about showing yourself, too," I warned her. "Some one is likely to recognize you."

She nodded and handed me the morning paper.

All over the front page were smeared our pictures, hers and mine. Holton had offered a reward of twenty thousand dollars for my arrest. The insurance company had added another five.

Without that, I knew the police would be hot on the trail. Their reputation was at stake. They'd leave no stone unturned. Having the girl with me was my best bet. They'd be looking for me alone, or with a girl who was being held a prisoner. They'd hardly expect to find me in a downtown apartment with the girl cooking me breakfast.

I handed Jean a five-hundred-dollar bill.

"Go get yourself some clothes. Get quiet ones, but ones that are in style. I'm disguising myself as your father. You look young and chic, wear 'em short, and paint up a bit. Don't wait, but get started as soon as we eat."

She dropped a curtsey.

"You're so good to me, Ed," she said, but there was a wistful note in her voice, and she blinked her eyes rapidly. "Don't think I don't appreciate it, either," she added. "You don't have to put up with me, and you're being a real gentleman. . . ."

That was that.

I was a little nervous until the girl got back from her shopping. I was afraid some one would spot her. She bought a suit and changed into that right at the jump, then got the rest of her things. She put in the day with needle and thread, and I did some thinking, also I coached the girl as to her part. By late afternoon we were able to buy an automobile without having anything suggest that I was other than an elderly, fond parent and the girl a helter-skelter flapper.

"Tonight you get educated as a crook," I told her.

"Jake with me, Ed," she replied, flashing me a smile. Whatever her thoughts may have been she seemed to have determined to be a good sport, a regular pal, and never let me see her as other than cheerful.

We slid our new car around where we could watch Big Bill Ryan's place. He ran a little café where crooks frequently hung out, and he couldn't take a chance on my having a spotter in the place. One thing was certain. If he was really behind the play he intended to have me caught and executed for murder. He knew me too well to think he could play button, button, who's got the button with me and get away with it.

We waited until eleven, parked in the car I'd purchased, watching the door of the café and

Big Ryan's car. It was crude but effective. Ryan and the cat-woman both thought I had been left with the murdered body of Jean Ellery in my car, a car which had to be got rid of, a body which had to be concealed, and with all the police in the state on my track. They hardly expected I'd put in the evening watching Big Ryan with the kid leaning on my shoulder.

At eleven Ryan started out, and his face was all smiles. He tried to avoid being followed, but the car I'd purchased had all sorts of speed, and I had no trouble in the traffic. After that I turned out the lights and tailed him into West Forty-ninth Street. I got the number of the house as he stopped, flashed past once to size it up and then kept moving.

"Here's where you get a real thrill," I told the girl as I headed the car back toward town. "I've a hunch Harry Atmore's mixed up in this thing as a sort of cat's-paw all around, and I want to see what's in his office."

We stopped a block away from Atmore's office building. I was a fatherly-looking old bird with mutton chop whiskers and a cane.

"Ever done any burglarizing?" I asked as I clumped my way along the sidewalk.

She shook her head.

"Here's where you begin," I said, piloted her into the office building, avoided the elevator, and began the long, tedious climb.

Atmore's lock was simple, any door lock is, for that matter. I had expected I'd have to go take a look through the files. It wasn't necessary. From the odor of cigar smoke in the office there'd been a late conference there. I almost fancied I could smell the incense-like perfume of the cat-woman and the aroma of her cigarettes. Tobacco smoke is peculiar. I can tell just about how fresh it is when I smell a room that's strong with it. This was a fresh odor. On the desk was a proof of loss of the necklace, and a memo to call a certain number. I looked up the number in the telephone book. It was the number of the insurance company. That's how I found it, simply looked up the insurance companies in the classified list and ran down the numbers.

The insurance money would be paid in the morning.

That house on West Forty-ninth Street was mixed up in the thing somehow. It was a new lead, and I drove the kid back to the apartment and turned in. The situation wasn't ripe as yet.

Next morning I heard her stirring around, getting breakfast. Of course it simplified matters to eat in the apartment; but if the girl was going to work on the case with me she shouldn't do all the housework. I started to tell her so, rolled over, and grabbed another sleep. It was delicious lying there, stretching out in the warm bed, and hearing the cheery rattle of plates, knives and forks, cups and spoons. I had been a lone wolf so long, an outcast of society, that I thrilled with a delicious sense of intimacy at the idea of having Jean Ellery puttering around in my kitchen. Almost I felt like the father I posed as.

I got up, bathed, shaved, put on my disguise and walked out into the kitchen. The girl was gone. My breakfast was on the table, fruit, cream, toast in the toaster, coffee in the percolator, all ready to press a button and eat. The morning paper was even propped up by my plate.

I switched on the electricity, and wondered about the girl. Anxiously I listened for her step in the apartment. She was company, and I liked her. The kid didn't say much, but she had a sense of humor, a ready dimple, a twinkle in her eyes, and was mighty easy to look at.

She came in as I was finishing my coffee.

"Hello, Ed. I'm the early bird this morning, and I've caught the worm. That house out on Forty-ninth Street is occupied by old Doctor Drake. He's an old fellow who used to be in San Francisco, had a breakdown, retired, came here, lost his money, was poor as could be until three months ago, and then he suddenly blossomed out with ready money. He's retiring, crabbed, irascible, keeps to himself, has no practice and few visitors."

I looked her over, a little five-foot-three flapper, slim, active, graceful, but looking as though she had nothing under her chic hat except a hair bob.

"How did you know I wanted to find out about that bird; and how did you get the information?"

She ignored the first question, just passed it off with a wave of the hand.

"The information was easy. I grabbed some packages of face powder, went out in the neighborhood and posed as a demonstrator representing the factory, giving away free samples, and lecturing on the care of the complexion. I even know the neighborhood gossip, all the scandals, and the love affairs of everyone in the block. Give me some of that coffee, Ed. It smells good."

I grinned proudly at her. The kid was there. It would have been a hard job for me to get that information. She used her noodle. A doctor, eh? Big Ryan had gone to see him when he knew he would have the insurance money. The aunt wanted the girl killed. The engagement had been announced. Then there was the matter of my jade-handled dagger. Those things all began to mill around in my mind. They didn't fit together exactly, but they all pointed in one direction, and that direction made my eyes open a bit wider and my forehead pucker. The game was drawing to the point where I would get into action and see what could be done along the line of checkmating the cat-woman.

A thought flashed through my mind. "Say, Jean, it's going to be a bit tough on you when it comes time to go back. What'll you tell people, that you were kidnapped and held in a cave or some place? And they'll have the police checking up on your story, you know?"

She laughed a bit and then her mouth tightened. "If you had been one of the soft-boiled kind that figured you should have married me or some such nonsense I wouldn't have stayed. It was only because you took me in on terms of equality that I remained. You take care of your problems and I'll take care of mine; and we'll both have plenty."

"That being the case, Jean," I told her, "I'm going to stage a robbery and a burglary tonight. Are you coming?"

She grinned at me.

"Miss Jean Ellery announces that it gives her pleasure to accept the invitation of Ed Jenkins to a holdup and burglary. When do we start?"

I shrugged my shoulders. "Some time after eight or nine. It depends. In the meantime we get some sleep. It's going to be a big night."

With that I devoted my attention to the paper. After all, the kid was right. I could mind my own business and she could mind hers. She knew what she was doing. Hang it, though, it felt nice to have a little home to settle back in, one where I could read the papers while the girl cleaned off the table, humming a little song all the while. All the company I'd ever had before had been a dog, and he was in the hospital recovering from the effects of our last adventure. I was getting old, getting to the point where I wanted company, someone to talk to, to be with.

I shrugged my shoulders and got interested in what I was reading. The police were being panned right. My reputation of being a phantom crook was being rubbed in. Apparently I could disappear, taking an attractive girl and a valuable necklace with me, and the police were absolutely powerless.

Along about dark I parked my car out near Forty-ninth Street. I hadn't much that was definite to go on, but I was playing a pretty good hunch. I knew Big Ryan's car, and I knew the route he took in going to the house of Dr. Drake. I figured he'd got the insurance money some time during the day. Also I doped it out that the trips to the house of Dr. Drake were made after dark. It was pretty slim evidence to work out a plan of campaign on, but, on the other hand, I had nothing to lose.

We waited there two hours before we got action, and then it came, right according to schedule. Big Bill Ryan's car came under the street light, slowed for the bad break that was in the gutter at that point, and then Big Ryan bent forward to shift gears as he pulled out of the hole. It was a bad spot in the road and Bill knew it was there. He'd driven over it just the same way the night I'd followed him.

When he straightened up from the gearshift he was looking down the business end of a wicked pistol. I don't ordinarily carry 'em, preferring to use my wits instead, but this job I wanted to look like the job of somebody else anyway, and the pistol came in handy.

Of course, I was wearing a mask.

There wasn't any need for argument. The gun was there. Big Bill Ryan's fat face was there, and there wasn't three inches between 'em. Big Bill kicked out the clutch and jammed on the brake.

There was a puzzled look on his face as he peered at me. The big fence knew every crook in the game, and he probably wondered who had the nerve to pull the job. It just occurred to me that he looked too much interested and not enough scared, when I saw what I'd walked into. Big Bill had the car stopped dead before he sprung his trap. That was so I couldn't drop off into the darkness. He wanted me.

The back of the car, which had been in shadow, seemed to move, to become alive. From beneath a robe which had been thrown over the seat and floor there appeared a couple of arms, the glint of the street light on metal arrested my eye; and it was too late to do anything, even if I could have gotten away with it.

There were two gunmen concealed in the back of that car. Big Bill Ryan ostensibly was driving alone. As a matter of fact he had a choice bodyguard. Those two guns were the best shots in crookdom, and they obeyed orders.

Big Bill spoke pleasantly.

"I hadn't exactly expected this, Jenkins, but I was prepared for it. You see I credit you with a lot of brains. How you found out about the case, and how you learned enough to intercept me on this little trip is more than I know. However, I've always figured you were the most dangerous man in the world, and I didn't take any chances.

"You're a smart man, Jenkins; but you're running up against a stone wall. I'm glad this happened when there was a reward out for you in California. It'll be very pleasant to surrender you to the police, thereby cementing my pleasant relations and also getting a cut out of the reward money. Come, come, get in and sit down. Grab his arms, boys."

Revolvers were thrust under my nose. Grinning faces leered at me. Grimy hands stretched forth and grabbed my shoulders. The car lurched forward and sped away into the night, headed toward the police station. In such manner had Ed Jenkins been captured by a small-time crook and a couple of guns. I could feel myself blush with shame. What was more, there didn't seem to be any way out of it. The guns were awaiting orders, holding fast to me, pulling me over the door. Ryan was speeding up. If I could break away I'd be shot before I could get off of the car, dead before my feet hit ground. If I stayed where I was I'd be in the police station in ten minutes, in a cell in eleven, and five minutes later the reporters would be interviewing me, and the papers would be grinding out extras.

It's the simple things that are hard to beat. This thing was so blamed simple, so childish almost, and yet, there I was.

We flashed past an intersection, swung to avoid the lights of another car that skidded around the corner with screeching tires, and then we seemed to be rocking back and forth, whizzing through the air. It was as pretty a piece of driving as I have ever seen. Jean Ellery had come around the paved corner at full speed, skidding, slipping, right on the tail of the other machine, had swung in sideways, hit the rear bumper and forced Ryan's car around and over, into the curb, and then she had sped on her way, uninjured. Ryan's car had crumpled a front wheel against the curb, and we were all sailing through the air.

Personally, I lit on my feet and kept going. I don't think anyone was hurt much, although Ryan seemed to make a nosedive through the windshield, and the two guns slammed forward against the back of the front seat and then pitched out. Being on the running board, I had just taken a little loop-the-loop through the atmosphere, gone into a tail spin, and pancaked to the earth.

The kid was there a million. If she had come up behind on a straight stretch there would have been lots of action. Ryan would have spotted her, and the guns would have gone into action. She'd either have been captured with me, or we'd both have been shot. By slamming into us from around a corner, however, she'd played her cards perfectly. It had been damned clever driving. What was more it had been clever headwork. She'd seen what had happened when I stuck the gun into Ryan's face, had started my car, doubled around the block, figured our speed to a nicety, and slammed down the cross street in the nick of time.

These things I thought over as I sprinted around a house, through a backyard, into an alley, and into another backyard. The kid had gone sailing off down the street, and I had a pretty strong hunch she had headed for the apartment. She'd done her stuff, and the rest was up to me.

Hang it! My disguise was in my car, and here I was, out in the night, my face covered by a mask, a gun in my pocket, and a reward out for me, with every cop in town scanning every face that passed him on the street. Oh well, it was all in a lifetime and I had work to do. I'd liked to have handled Bill Ryan; seeing I couldn't get him, I had to play the next best bet, Dr. Drake.

His house wasn't far, and I made it in quick time. I was working against time.

I took off my mask, walked boldly up the front steps and rang the doorbell.

There was the sound of shuffling feet, and then a seamed, sallow face peered out at me. The door opened a bit, and two glittering, beady eyes bored into mine.

"What d'yuh want?"

I figured him for Doctor Drake. He was pretty well along in years, and his eyes and forehead showed some indications of education. There was a glittering cupidity about the face, a cunning selfishness that seemed to be the keynote of his character.

"I'm bringing the money."

His head thrust a trifle farther forward and his eyes bored into mine.

"What money?"

"From Bill Ryan."

"But Mr. Ryan said he would be here himself."

I shrugged my shoulders.

I had made my play and the more I kept silent the better it would be. I knew virtually nothing about this end of the game. He knew everything. It would be better for me to let him convince himself than to rush in and ruin it trying to talk too much of detail.

At length the door came cautiously open.

"Come in."

He led the way into a sort of office. The furniture was apparently left over from some office or other, and it was good stuff, massive mahogany, dark with years; old-fashioned bookcases; chairs that were almost antiques; obsolete text books, all of the what-nots that were the odds and ends of an old physician's office.

Over all lay a coating of gritty dust.

"Be seated," said the old man, shuffling across to the swivel chair before the desk. I could see that he was breaking fast, this old man. His forehead and eyes retained much of strength, indicated some vitality. His mouth was sagging, weak. Below his neck he seemed to have decayed, the loose, flabby muscles seemed incapable of functioning. His feet could hardly be lifted from the floor. His shoulders lurched forward, and his spine curved into a great hump. Dandruff sprinkled over his coat, an affair that had once been blue serge and which was now spotted with egg, grease, syrup, and stains.

"Where is the money?"

I smiled wisely, reached into an inner pocket, half pulled out a wallet, then leered at him after the fashion of a cheap crook, one of the smart-aleck, cunning kind.

"Let's see the stuff first."

He hesitated, then heaved out of his chair and approached a bookcase. Before the door he suddenly stiffened with suspicion. He turned, his feverish eyes glittering wildly in the feeble light of the small incandescent with which the room was redly illuminated.

"Spread out the money on the table."

I laughed.

"Say, bo, the coin's here, all right; but if you want to see the long green you gotta produce."

He hesitated a bit, and then the telephone rang, a jangling, imperative clamor. He shuffled back to the desk, picked up the receiver in a gnarled, knotty hand, swept back the unkempt hair which hung over his ear, and listened.

As he listened I could see the back straighten, the shoulders straighten. A hand came stealing up the inside of the coat.

Because I knew what to expect I wasn't surprised. He bent forward, muttered something, hung up the receiver, spun about and thrust forward an ugly pistol, straight at the chair in which I had been sitting. If ever there was desperation and murder stamped on a criminal face it was on his.

The only thing that was wrong with his plans was that I had silently shifted my position. When he swung that gun around he pointed it where I had been, but wasn't. The next minute I had his neck in a stranglehold, had the gun, and had him all laid out for trussing. Linen bandage was available, and it always makes a nice rope for tying people up with. I gagged him on general principles and then I began to go through that bookcase.

In a book on interior medicine that was written when appendicitis was classified as fatal inflammation of the intestines, I found a document, yellow with age. It was dated in 1904 but it had evidently been in the sunlight some, and had seen much had usage. The ink was slightly faded, and there were marks of old folds, dog-eared corners, little tears. Apparently the paper had batted around in a drawer for a while, had perhaps been rescued at one time or another from a wastebasket, and, on the whole, it was genuine as far as date was concerned. It couldn't have had all that hard usage in less than twenty-two years.

There was no time then to stop and look at it. I took out my wallet, dropped it in there, and then went back to the bookcase, turning the books upside down, shaking them, fluttering the leaves, wondering if there was something else.

I was working against time and knew it. Big Bill Ryan wouldn't dare notify the police. He wouldn't want to have me arrested at the home of Doctor Drake; but he would lose no time in getting the house surrounded by a bunch of gunmen of his own choosing, of capturing me as I sought to escape the house, and then taking me to police headquarters.

It was a matter of seconds. I could read that paper any time; but I could only go through that bookcase when I was there, and it looked as though I wouldn't be in that house again, not for some time. At that I didn't have time to complete the search. I hadn't covered more than half of the books when I heard running steps on the walk, and feet came pounding up the steps.

As a crook my cue was to make for the back door, to plunge out into the night, intent on escape. That would run me into the guns of a picked reception committee that was waiting in the rear. I knew Big Ryan, knew that the hurrying impatience of those steps on the front porch was merely a trap. I was in a house that was surrounded. The automobile with engine running out in front was all a part of the stall. Ryan had probably stopped his machine half a block away, let out his men, given them a chance to surround the house, and then he had driven up, stopped the car with the engine running and dashed up the steps. If Dr. Drake had me covered all right; if I had managed to overpower the old man, I would break and run for the rear.

All of these things flashed through my mind in an instant. I was in my element again. Standing there before the rifled bookcase, in imminent danger, I was as cool as a cake of ice, and I didn't waste a second.

The door of the bookcase I slammed shut. The books were in order on the shelves. As for myself, I did the unexpected. It is the only safe rule.

Instead of sneaking out the back door, I reached the front door in one jump, threw it open and plunged my fist into the bruised, bleeding countenance of Big Bill Ryan. That automobile windshield hadn't used him too kindly, and he was badly shaken. My maneuver took him by surprise. For a split fraction of a second I saw him standing like a statue. The next instant my fist had crashed home.

From the side of the house a revolver spat. There was a shout, a running of dark figures, and I was off. Leaping into the driver's seat of the empty automobile, I had slammed in the gears, shot the clutch, stepped on the throttle and was away.

I chuckled as I heard the chorus of excited shouts behind, the futile rattle of pistol shots. There would be some explaining for Big Bill Ryan to do. In the meantime I was headed for the apartment. I was going to decorate Jean Ellery with a medal, a medal for being the best assistant a crook ever had.

I left the car a couple of blocks from the apartment and walked rapidly down the street. I didn't want the police to locate the stolen car too near my apartment, and yet I didn't dare to go too far without my disguise. The walk of two blocks to my apartment was risky.

My own machine, the one in which Jean had made the rescue, was parked outside. I looked it over with a grin. She was some driver. The front bumper and license plate had been torn off, and the paint on the radiator was scratched a bit, but that was all.

I worried a bit about that license number. I'd bought that car as the old man with the flapper daughter, and I had it registered in the name I had taken, the address as the apartment where Jean and I lived. Losing that license number was something to worry about.

I made record time getting to the door of the apartment, fitting the latchkey and stepping inside. The place was dark, and I pressed the light switch, then jumped back, ready for anything. The room was empty. On the floor was a torn article of clothing. A shoe was laying on its side over near the other door. A rug was rumpled, a chair overturned. In the other room there was confusion. A waist had been ripped to ribbons and was lying by another shoe. The waist was one that Jean had been wearing. The shoes were hers.

I took a quick glance around, making sure the apartment was empty, and then I got into action. Foot by foot I covered that floor looking for something that would be a clue, some little thing that would tell me of the persons who had done the job. Big Bill had acted mighty quick if he had been the one. If it had been the police, why the struggle? If it was a trap, why didn't they spring it?

There was no clue. Whoever it was had been careful to leave nothing behind. I had only a limited amount of time, and I knew it. Once more I was working against time, beset by adverse circumstances, fighting overwhelming odds.

I made a run for the elevator, got to the ground floor, rushed across the street, into the little car Jean had driven, and, as I stepped on the starter and switched on the lights, there came the wail of a siren, the bark of an exhaust, and a police car came skidding around the corner and slid to a stop before the apartment house.

As for me, I was on my way.

Mentally I ran over the characters in the drama that had been played about me, and I picked on Harry Atmore. The little, weak, clever attorney with his cunning dodges, his rat-like mind, his cowering spirit was my meat. He was the weak point in the defense, the weak link in the chain.

I stopped at a telephone booth in a drug store. A plastered-haired sheik was at the telephone fixing up a couple of heavy dates for a wild night. I had to wait while he handed out what was meant to be a wicked line. Finally he hung up the receiver and sauntered toward his car, smirking his self-satisfaction. I grabbed the instrument and placed the warm receiver to my ear.

Atmore wasn't at the house. His wife said I'd find him at the office. I didn't call the office. It would suit me better to walk in unannounced if I could get him by himself. I climbed into my machine and was on my way.

I tried the door of Atmore's office and found

it was open. There was a light in the reception room. Turning, I pulled the catch on the spring lock, slammed the door and turned out the light. Then I walked into the private office.

There must have been that on my face which showed that I was on a mission which boded no good to the crooked shyster, an intentness of purpose which was apparent. He gave me one look, and then shrivelled down in his chair, cowering, his rat-like nose twitching, his yellow teeth showing.

I folded my arms and glared at him.

"Where's the girl?"

He lowered his gaze and shrugged his shoulders.

I advanced. Right then I was in no mood to put up with evasions. Something seemed to tell me that the girl was in danger, that every second counted, and I had no time to waste on polite formalities. That girl had grown to mean something to me. She had fitted in, uncomplaining, happy, willing, and she had saved me when I had walked into a trap there with Big Bill Ryan. As long as I was able to help that girl she could count on me. There had never been much said, but we understood each other, Jean Ellery and I. She had played the game with me, and I would play it with her.

"Atmore," I said, pausing impressively between the words, "I want to know where that girl is, and I mean to find out."

He ducked his hand, and I sprang, wrenched his shoulder, pulled him backward, crashed a chair to the floor, struck the gun up, kicked his wrist, smashed my fist in his face and sprawled him on the floor. He didn't get up. I was standing over him, and he crawled and cringed like a whipped cur.

"Miss Hare has her. Bill Ryan got her located through the number on a machine, and Hattie Hare went after her. She is a devil, that woman. She has the girl back at the Holton house."

I looked at his writhing face for a moment trying to determine if he was lying. I thought not. Big Ryan had undoubtedly traced that license number. That was but the work of a few minutes on the telephone with the proper party. He couldn't have gone after the girl himself because he had been at Dr. Drake's too soon afterward. On the other hand, he had gone to a public telephone because he had undoubtedly telephoned Dr. Drake and told him of his accident, probably warned him against me. From what the doctor had said, Ryan knew I was there, and he had dropped everything to come after me. What more natural than that he should have telephoned the cat-woman to go and get the girl.

I turned and strode toward the door.

"Listen, you rat," I snapped. "If you have lied to me, you'll die!"

His eyes rolled a bit, his mouth twitched, but he said nothing. I ran into the dark outer office, threw open the door, snapped the lock back on the entrance door, banged it and raced to the elevator. Then I turned and softly retraced my steps, slipped into the dark outer office, and tiptoed to the door of the private office. By opening it a crack I could see the lawyer huddled at his desk, frantically clicking the hook on the telephone.

In a minute he got central, snapped a number, waited and then gave his message in five words. "He's on his way out," he said, and hung up.

I only needed one guess. He was talking to the cat-woman. They had prepared a trap, had baited it with the girl, and were waiting for me to walk into it.

I went back into the hall, slipped down the elevator, went to my car and stepped on the starter. As I went I thought. Time was precious. Long years of being on my own resources had taught me to speed up my thinking processes. For years I had been a lone wolf, had earned the name of being the phantom crook, one who could slip through the fingers of the police. Then there had been a welcome vacation while I enjoyed immunity in California, but now all that was past. I was my own man, back in the thick of things. I had accomplished everything I had done previously by thinking fast, reaching quick decisions, and putting those decisions into instant execution. This night I made up my mind I would walk into the trap and steal the bait; whether I could walk out again depended upon my abilities. I would be matching my wits against those of the cat-woman, and she was no mean antagonist. Witness the manner in which she had learned that the girl had not been murdered, that I had convinced the girl of the woman's duplicity, had taken her in as a partner, the manner in which the cat-woman had known she could reach me through the girl, that I would pick on Atmore as being the weak link in the chain.

I stopped at a drug store long enough to read the paper I had taken from the book at Dr. Drake's house, and to telephone. I wanted to know all the cards I held in my hand before I called for a showdown.

The document was a strange one. It was nothing more nor less than a consent that the doctor should take an unborn baby and do with it as he wished. It was signed by the expectant mother. Apparently it was merely one of thousands of such documents which find their way into the hands of doctors. Yet I was certain it represented an important link in a strong chain. Upon the back of the document were three signatures. One of them was the signature of Hattie M. Hare. There were addresses, too, also telephone numbers. Beneath the three signatures were the words "nurses and witnesses."

I consulted the directory, got the number of H. F. Morton, and got him out of bed.

"This is Mr. Holton," I husked into the telephone. "Come to my house at once."

With the words I banged the receiver against the telephone a couple of times and hung up. Then I sprinted into the street, climbed into the machine, and was off.

I had no time to waste, and yet I was afraid the trap would be sprung before I could get the bait. It was late and a ring at the doorbell would have been a telltale sign. I parked the machine a block away, hit the backyards and approached the gloomy mass of shadows which marked the home of Arthur C. Holton, the oil magnate. I was in danger and knew it, knew also that the danger was becoming more imminent every minute.

I picked a pantry window. Some of the others looked more inviting, but I picked one which I would hardly have been expected to have chosen. There had already been a few minutes' delay. Seconds were precious. I knew the house well enough to take it almost at a run. When I have once been inside a place I can generally dope out the plan of the floors, and I always remember those plans.

In the front room there was just the flicker of a fire in the big fireplace. Above the tiles there glowed two spots of fire. I had been right in my surmise about the painting of the cat's head. The eyes had been tinted with luminous paint.

In the darkness there came a faint, dull, "click." It was a sound such as is made by a telephone bell when it gives merely the jump of an electrical contact, a sound which comes when a receiver has been removed from an extension line. With the sound I had out my flashlight and was searching for the telephone. If anyone was using an extension telephone in another part of the house I wanted to hear what was being said.

It took me a few seconds to locate the instrument, and then I slipped over to it and eased the receiver from the hook. It was the cat-woman who was talking:

"Yes, Arthur C. Holton's residence, and come right away. You know he threatened to return. Yes, I know it's Ed Jenkins. I tell you I saw his face. Yes, the phantom crook. Send two cars and come at once."

There was a muttered assent from the cop at the other end of the line, and then the click of two receivers. Mine made a third.

So that was the game, was it? In some way she had known when I entered the place. I fully credited those luminous, cat-eyes of hers with being able to see in the dark. She had laid a trap for me, baited it with the girl, and now she had summoned the police. Oh well, I had been in worse difficulties before.

I took the carpeted stairway on the balls of my feet, taking the stairs two at a time. There was a long corridor above from which there opened numerous bedrooms. I saw a flutter of pink at one end of the hall, a mere flash of woman's draperies. I made for that point, and I went at top speed. If my surmise was correct I had no time to spare, not so much as the tick of a watch.

The door was closed and I flung it open, standing not upon ceremony or formalities. I was racing with death.

Within the room was a dull light, a reflected, diffused light which came from the corridor, around a corner, against the half-open door, and into the room. There was a bed and a white figure was stretched upon the bed, a figure which was struggling in the first panic of a sudden awakening. When I had flung the door open it had crashed against the wall, rebounded so that it was half closed, and then remained shivering on its hinges, catching and reflecting the light from the hall.

In that semi-darkness the cat-woman showed as a flutter of flowing silk. She moved with the darting quickness of a cat springing on its prey. She had turned her head as I crashed into the room, and her eyes, catching the light from the hall, glowed a pale, baleful green, a green of hate, of tigerish intensity of rage.

Quick as she was, I was quicker. As the light caught the flicker of cold steel I flung her to one side, slammed her against the wall. She was thin, lithe, supple, but the warm flesh of her which met my hands through the thin veil of sheer silk was as hard as wire springs. She recoiled from the wall, poised lightly on her feet, gave me a flicker of the light from those cat-eyes once more, and then fluttered from the room, her silks flapping in the breeze of her progress. Two hands shot from the bed and grasped me by the shoulders, great, hairy hands with clutching fingers.

"Jenkins! Ed Jenkins!" exclaimed a voice.

I shook him off and raced for the door. From the street below came the sound of sliding tires, the noise of feet hurrying on cement, pounding on gravel. Someone dashed up the front steps and pounded on the door, rang frantically at the bell. The police had arrived, excited police who bungled the job of surrounding the house.

There was yet time. I had been in tighter pinches. I could take the back stairs, shoot from the back door and try the alley. There would probably be the flash of firearms, the whine of lead through the night air, but there would also be the element of surprise, the stupidity of the police, the flat-footed slowness of getting into action. I had experienced it all before.

In one leap I made the back stairs and started to rush down. The front door flew open and there came the shrill note of a police whistle. I gathered my muscles for the next flying leap, and then stopped, caught almost in midair.

I had thought of the girl!

Everything that had happened had fitted in with my theory of the case, and in that split fraction of a second I knew I was right. Some flash of inner intuition, some telepathic insight converted a working hypothesis, a bare theory, into an absolute certainty. In that instant I knew the motive of the cat-woman, knew the reason she had rushed from that other room. Jean Ellery had been used by her to bait the trap for Ed Jenkins, but she had had another use, had served another purpose. She was diabolically clever, that cat-woman, and Jean Ellery was to die.

I thought of the girl, of her charm, her ready acceptance of life as the working partner of a crook, and I paused in mid flight, turned a rapid flip almost in the air and was running madly down the corridor, toward the police.

There are times when the mind speeds up and thoughts become flashes of instantaneous conceptions, when one lives ages in the space of seconds. All of the thoughts which had pieced together the real solution of the mystery, the explanation of the actions of the cat-woman had come to me while I was poised, balanced for a leap on the stairs. My decision to return had been automatic, instantaneous. I could not leave Jean Ellery in danger.

The door into which the cat-woman had plunged was slightly ajar. Through it could be seen the gleam of light, a flicker of motion. I was almost too late as I hurtled through that door, my outstretched arm sweeping the descending hand of the cat-woman to one side.

Upon the bed, bound, gagged, her helpless eyes staring into the infuriated face of the cat-woman, facing death with calm courage, watching the descent of the knife itself, was the form of Jean Ellery. My hand had caught the downthrust of the knife just in time.

The cat-woman staggered back, spitting vile oaths, lips curling, eyes flashing, her words sounding like the explosive spats of an angry cat. The knife had clattered to the floor and lay at my very feet. The green-handled dagger, the jade-hilted knife which had been taken from my apartment. At that instant a shadow blotted the light from the hallway and a voice shouted:

"Hands up, Ed Jenkins!"

The cat-woman gave an exclamation of relief.

"Thank God, officer, you came in the nick of time!"

There was the shuffling of many feet; peering faces, gleaming sheilds, glinting pistols, and I found myself grabbed by many hands, handcuffs snapped about my wrists, cold steel revolvers thrust against my neck. I was pushed, jostled, slammed, pulled, dragged down the stairs and into the library.

The cat-woman followed, cajoling the officers, commenting on their bravery, their efficiency, spitting epithets at me.

And then H. F. Morton walked into the open door, took in the situation with one glance of his steely eyes, deposited his hat and gloves on a chair, walked to the great table, took a seat behind it and peered over the tops of his glasses at the officers, at the cat-woman, at myself.

The policemen jostled me toward the open front door.

The lawyer held up a restraining hand.

"Just a minute," he said, and there was that in the booming authority of the voice which held the men, stopped them in mid-action.

"What is this?" he asked, and, with the words, dropped his hands to the table and began to drum regularly, rhythmically, "rummpy-tum-tum; rummpy-tum-tum; rummpy-tum-tumpty-tum-tumpty-tum-tum."

"Aw g'wan," muttered one of the officers as he pulled me forward.

"Shut up, you fool. He's the mayor's personal attorney!" whispered another, his hands dragging me back, holding me against those who would have taken me from the house.

The word ran through the group like wildfire. There were the hoarse sibilants of many whispers, and then attentive silence.

"'Tis Ed Jenkins, sor," remarked one of the policemen, one who seemed to be in charge of the squad. "The Phantom Crook, sor, caught in this house from which he kidnapped the girl an' stole the necklace, an' 'twas murder he was after tryin' to commit this time."

The lawyer's gray eyes rested on my face.

"If you want to talk, Jenkins, talk now."

I nodded.

"The girl, Jean Ellery. She is the daughter of Arthur C. Holton."

The fingers stopped their drumming and gripped the table.

"What?"

I nodded. "It was supposed that his child was a boy, a boy who died shortly after birth. As a matter of fact, the child was a girl, a girl who lived, who is known as Jean Ellery. A crooked doctor stood for the substitution, being paid a cash fee. A nurse originated the scheme, Miss Hattie M. Hare. The boy could never be traced. His future was placed in the doctor's hands before birth and when coincidence played into the hands of this nurse she used all her unscrupulous knowledge, all her cunning. The girl was to be brought up to look upon the nurse as her aunt, her only living relative. At the proper time the whole thing was to be exposed, but the doctor was to be the one who was to take the blame. Hattie M. Hare was to have her connection with the scheme kept secret.

"But the doctor found out the scheme to make him the goat. He had in his possession a paper signed by the nurse, a paper which would have foiled the whole plan. He used this paper as a basis for regular blackmail.

"It was intended to get this paper, to bring out the girl as the real heir, to have her participate in a trust fund which had been declared for the child of Arthur C. Holton, to have her inherit all the vast fortune of the oil magnate;—and to remember her aunt Hattie M. Hare as one of her close and dear relatives, to have her pay handsomely for the so-called detectives and lawyers who were to 'unearth' the fraud, to restore her to her place, to her estate.

"And then there came another development, Arthur C. Holton became infatuated with the arch-conspirator, Hattie M. Hare. He proposed marriage, allowed himself to be prevailed upon to make a will in her favor, to make a policy of life insurance to her.

"The girl ceased to be an asset, but became a menace. She must be removed. Also Arthur C. Holton must die that Miss Hattie M. Hare might succeed in his estate without delay. But there was a stumbling block, the paper which was signed by Hattie M. Hare, the paper which might be connected with the substitution of children, which would brand her as a criminal, which would be fatal if used in connection with the testimony of the doctor.

"Doctor Drake demanded money for his silence and for that paper. He demanded his money in cash, in a large sum. The woman, working with fiendish cunning, decided to use me as a cat's-paw to raise the money and to also eliminate the girl from her path as well as to apparently murder the man who stood between her and his wealth. I was to be enveigled into apparently stealing a necklace worth much money, a necklace which was to be insured, and the insurance payable to Miss Hare; I was to be tricked into kidnapping a girl who would be murdered; I was to be persuaded to make threats against Mr. Holton, and then I was to become the apparent murderer of the oil magnate. My dagger was to be found sticking in his breast. In such manner would Miss Hare bring about the death of the man who had made her the beneficiary under his will, buy the silence of the doctor who knew her for a criminal, remove the only heir of the blood, and make me stand all the blame, finally delivering me into the hands of the law.

"There is proof. I have the signed statement in my pocket. Doctor Drake will talk. Harry Atmore will confess. . . . There she goes. Stop her!"

The cat-woman had seen that her play was ended. She had realized that she was at the end of her rope, that I held the evidence in my possession, that the bound and gagged girl upstairs would testify against her. She had dashed from the room while the stupefied police had held me and stared at her with goggle eyes.

Openmouthed they watched her flight, no one making any attempt to take after her, eight or ten holding me in their clumsy hands while the cat-woman, the arch criminal of them all dashed out into the night.

H. F. Morton looked at me and smiled.

"Police efficiency, Jenkins," he said.

Then he faced the officers. "Turn him loose."

The officers shifted uneasily. The man in charge drew himself up stiffly and saluted. "He is a noted criminal with a price on his head, the very devil of a crook, sor."

Morton drummed steadily on the desk.

"What charge have you against him?"

The officer grunted.

"Stealin' Mr. Holton's necklace, an' breakin' into his house, sor."

"Those charges are withdrawn," came from the rear of the room in deep, firm tones.

I turned to see Arthur C. Holton. He had dressed and joined the group. I did not even know when he had entered the room, how much he had heard. By his side, her eyes starry, stood Jean Ellery, and there were gleaming gems of moisture on her cheeks.

The policeman grunted.

"For kidnappin' the young lady an' holdin' her. If she stayed against her will 'twas abductin', an' she wouldn't have stayed with a crook of her own accord, not without communicatin' with her folks."

That was a poser. I could hear Jean suck in

her breath to speak the words that would have freed me but would have damned her in society forever; but she had not the chance.

Before I could even beat her to it, before my confession would have spared her name and sent me to the penitentiary, H. F. Morton's shrewd mind had grasped all the angles of the situation, and he beat us all to it.

"You are wrong. The girl was not kidnapped. Jenkins never saw her before."

The policeman grinned broadly.

"Then would yez mind tellin' me where she was while all this hue an' cry was bein' raised, while everyone was searchin' for her?"

Morton smiled politely, urbanely.

"Not at all, officer. She was at my house, as the guest of my wife. Feeling that her interests were being jeopardized and that her life was in danger, I had her stay incognito in my own home."

There was tense, thick silence.

The girl gasped. The clock ticked. There was the thick, heavy breathing of the big-bodied policemen.

"Rummy-tum-tum; rummy-tum-tum; rum-iddy, tumptidy, tumpy tum-tum," drummed the lawyer. "Officer, turn that man loose. Take off those handcuffs. Take . . . off . . . those . . . handcuffs . . . I . . . say. You haven't a thing against him in California."

As one in a daze, the officer fitted his key to the handcuffs, the police fell back, and I stood a free man.

"Good night," said the lawyer pointedly, his steely eyes glittering into those of the officers.

Shamefacedly, the officers trooped from the room.

Jean threw herself into my arms.

"Ed, you came back because of me! You risked your life to save mine, to see that a wrong was righted, to see that I was restored to my father! Ed, dear, you are a man in a million."

I patted her shoulder.

"You were a good pal, Jean, and I saw you through," I said. "Now you must forget about it. The daughter of a prominent millionaire has no business knowing a crook."

Arthur Holton advanced, hand outstretched.

"I was hypnotized, fooled, taken in by an adventuress and worse. I can hardly think clearly, the events of the past few minutes have been so swift, but this much I do know. I can never repay you for what you have done, Ed Jenkins. I will see that your name is cleared of every charge against you in every state, that you are a free man, that you are restored to citizenship, and that you have the right to live," and here he glanced at Jean: "You will stay with us as my guest?"

I shook my head. It was all right for them to feel grateful, to get a bit sloppy now that the grandstand play had been made, but they'd probably feel different about it by morning.

"I think I'll be on my way," I said, and started for the door.

"Ed!" It was the girl's cry, a cry which was as sharp, as stabbing as a quick pain at the heart. *"Ed, you're not leaving!"*

By way of answer I stumbled forward. Hell, was it possible that the difficulty with that threshold was that there was a mist in my eyes? Was Ed Jenkins, the phantom crook, known and feared by the police of a dozen states, becoming an old woman?

Two soft arms flashed about my neck, a swift kiss planted itself on my cheek, warm lips whispered in my ear.

I shook myself free, and stumbled out into the darkness. She was nothing but a kid, the daughter of a millionaire oil magnate. I was a crook. Nothing but hurt to her could come to any further acquaintance. It had gone too far already.

I jumped to one side, doubled around the house, away from the street lights, hugging the shadow which lay near the wall. From within the room, through the half-open window there came a steady, throbbing, thrumming sound: "Rummy-tum-tum; rummy-tum-tum; rummy-tum-tummy; tum-tummy-tum-tum."

H. F. Morton was thinking.

Rogue: The Patent Leather Kid

The Kid Stacks a Deck

ERLE STANLEY GARDNER

AS WAS TRUE of so many of the characters created by Erle Stanley Gardner (1889–1970), Dan Sellers, known as the Patent Leather Kid, works on both sides of the law. Much like another Gardner character, Sidney Zoom, Sellers hates injustice and will put himself at great risk to right wrongs. This generally involves going up against powerful gangsters and performing illegal acts, inevitably forcing the Kid to elude two antagonists: a gang of crooks and the police.

The Patent Leather Kid is an elegant, cultivated crook, hiding his identity with a mask, gloves, and shoes all made out of black patent leather. In reality, he is a wealthy socialite who appears to be a parvenu, dabbling at one thing or another, but he is an enemy of the underworld and devotes his life to battling it. The Depression was an era that spawned the rise of gangsters and the Kid chose to abandon his comfortable life to serve an unsuspecting public, however nefarious his methods might be. He has a bodyguard, Bill Brakey, to help out when the going gets tough.

The stories follow a formula, first featuring Sellers at his club chatting with other members. When he learns of a particularly egregious example of injustice, he leaves the club and his identity as an idle millionaire to don his costume. His nemesis is Inspector Brame, who has no luck in catching the Kid and so loathes him, going so far as to take no action when he learns of a gangster's plot to kill him.

"The Kid Stacks a Deck" was originally published in the March 28, 1932, issue of *Detective Fiction Weekly*; it was first collected in *The Exploits of the Patent Leather Kid* (Norfolk, Virginia, Crippen & Landru, 2010).

THE KID STACKS A DECK

Erle Stanley Gardner

DAN SELLER noticed the dummies in the window of the jewelry store because he made it his business to notice everything which was out of the ordinary. And this window display was certainly unique enough.

To the uninitiated, it would seem that a fortune in jewels was separated from the avaricious grasp of a cosmopolitan public only by a sheet of plate glass.

But the eye of Dan Seller, steel gray, coldly appraising, was not an uninitiated eye. He stared for some ten seconds, and, at the end of that time, knew that the majority of the stones were clever imitations.

The window of the big store was made to represent the interior of a drawing room. There were four people at a table playing bridge. A rather sissified looking young man, clad in the very latest of fashion in evening clothes, balanced a cup of tea upon the arm of a chair.

Another stiffly conventional figure leaned against a mantel, match in one waxen hand, cigarette in the other. Over in a corner a woman was extending a welcoming hand to another woman, both of whom glittered with jewels. The effect was impressive to the average spectator.

The men were introduced apparently for the effect of contrast, since they showed no jewelry beyond the conventional shirt studs, cuff links, and elaborate wrist watches. But the women were beautifully gowned, and the lights of the windows were thrown back in myriad sparkling reflections from the diamonds that occupied every point of vantage.

The display was a distinct departure from conventional jewelers' windows, and marked the opening gun of a new merchandising policy on the part of Hawkins & Grebe.

The display attracted a small crowd. Dan Seller had no doubt, but what it would also attract the attention of crooks. He filed away both facts for future use, and strolled toward his club.

Dan Seller was a man of mystery so far as his associates were concerned, and he was greeted with varying degrees of cordiality by the little group of members who were discussing the latest news bulletins.

Pope, the hard bitten explorer of the tropical jungles was there, taking a brief rest between expeditions. He gripped Seller's hand with a cordial clasp. He liked Seller, and didn't care who knew it.

Renfore, the banker, was more conservative. He knew that Seller maintained an active account which ran into large figures, but he had never been able to ascertain just what investments Seller made, and that fact nettled him. He bowed, did not shake hands.

Hawkins, part owner of the jewelry store, nodded and smiled. He knew Seller as a good customer. Inspector Phil Brame let his eyes get that coldly penetrating stare with which he customarily regarded every one about whom he was not quite certain. He knew Seller, and liked the man, but he could never entirely overlook those mysterious disappearances.

For to all of these men, Dan Seller was a mystery.

He was wealthy. Of that there could be no doubt. He was reserved, yet friendly. He was likeable. He was well posted. Outwardly he was an idler. Yet that failed to explain his character. There was a certain hard fitness about the man which made him seem as crisply active as Bill Pope, the jungle explorer.

Both in body and in mind he was hard, and fit. Yet he seemed to idle his time away. He laughed at life, strolled in and strolled out, was always interested in people and in things, always posted on recent developments. Yet he never played cards, never mentioned losses or gains in the stock market, never complained of business conditions.

And, occasionally, he disappeared.

At such times, he vanished utterly. Even Riggs, his valet, could give no information as to the whereabouts of his master. Twice there had been important matters at the club which had necessitated getting in touch with Dan Seller, and upon each of those occasions Seller had been where no one had been able to locate him. On the second occasion, Inspector Phil Brame, himself, had undertaken to locate Seller.

The inspector had ascertained that Seller had left the club, headed toward a charity bazaar for which he held a ticket. Seller had never arrived at that bazaar. Nor had he been heard from for a week.

At the expiration of that week he had appeared once more at the club, smiling, debonair, affable. Questioned as to his whereabouts, he had left no doubt whatever that he considered the affair purely a private matter.

Because of the fact that Dan Seller lived at the club, maintained a suite of magnificent rooms, sumptuously furnished, his comings and goings were within the knowledge of several members and his mysterious disappearances were bound to excite comment.

But Dan Seller lived his own life, talked interestingly upon many subjects, seemed always familiar with the latest book, deprecated all attempts to inquire into his personal life, and yet remained popular.

That he was of the finest stock, without a blemish upon his record, was evidenced by the fact that he had been admitted to the club at all. And, after all, a man's private life was his own.

Hawkins puffed upon his cigar after Seller joined the little group, and then continued with a discussion of the subject which had evidently been been the subject of the conversation before Seller had arrived.

"My partner couldn't see it at first," said Hawkins, assuming that air of a man who can say "I-told-you-so." "But I kept after him, and finally he gave in. The day has passed when old fashioned merchandising methods are going to pay for overhead. It's an age of keener competition, a more sound appreciation of values. It's time for an innovation in the jewelry trade.

"Look at our own case. Since we put in that window display we've sold exactly three hundred per cent as much merchandise. People pause to look at the display because it's unusual. The woman who pauses with her husband or father sees something that looks attractive. She wants to buy one like it. That's the way clothes are sold. Why not jewelry?"

He paused for an answer.

There was none.

Dan Seller drawled a comment.

"Your observation about keen competition

is interesting," he said. "How does it affect the crooks, Inspector?"

Inspector Brame started, flashed his hard eyes upon the younger man.

"Huh?" he said.

"I was wondering," said Dan Seller, "if crooks weren't feeling the depression, and turning to more efficient methods. I wondered, for instance, if they'd overlook the challenge of that unique window display."

Inspector Brame cleared his throat importantly.

"The police," he said, "can also become more efficient, as the necessity arises."

Hawkins added a comment.

"And don't think for a minute that we didn't take some pretty elaborate precautions before we decided on such spectacular advertising," he said. "We've got things fixed so that it's a physical impossibility for a crook to enter our store and get away with anything!"

Dan Seller's voice showed tolerant amusement.

"Really?" he drawled.

"Yes, really!" snapped Hawkins.

Dan Seller yawned, patted his lips with four polite fingers.

"Impossible," he said, "is rather a big word."

And he walked away.

Behind him, four pair of eyes regarded him with varying expressions. In each pair of eyes was a certain wonderment. In one was amusement, in at least one the dawning of a suspicion.

Inspector Brame was a hard man, and no respecter of persons.

II

Dan Seller, his overcoat turned up, felt hat pulled down, left the club, turned into the gusts of the windy night.

Apparently, he was just taking a walk.

He strolled for half a mile, leaning against the rush of the raw wind. A cruising cab solicited his patronage. Dan Seller climbed in. He went to one of the largest and most fashionable of the transient hotels, where hundreds of visitors checked in and checked out every day.

He secured a room under the name of Rodney Stone, was shown to his room, gave certain claim checks to the hotel porter. Half an hour later his light suitcases and hand trunks had arrived. They had been claimed under the checks from the baggage storage company.

To all appearances Dan Seller, masquerading as Rodney Stone, was merely a business man whose occupation necessitated frequent business trips. He had the poise of a seasoned traveller; the complete boredom of hotel life which characterizes one who is much on the road.

It was after midnight when Rodney Stone stepped from his room. He left the hotel by a back stairway and service entrance. He slipped unobtrusively into an apartment hotel which was within two doors of the transient hotel, and the transformation was complete.

The minute Dan Seller stepped into the Maplewood Hotel he became a different and very definite personality altogether. The boy at the desk nodded to him. The girl at the telephone gave him a smile.

Dan Seller was Dan Seller, the millionaire clubman, man about town no longer. He had become The Patent Leather Kid, and he had a definite niche in the underworld.

"You been away, Kid," said the elevator boy.

Dan Seller nodded.

Here, in this new world, every one called him "Kid." There was nothing disrespectful about it. It was a mark of honor, a badge of respect. The very voice of the elevator boy was deferential.

"Have a good trip?" asked the elevator boy as he shot The Kid up to the penthouse apartment.

"So, so," said Seller.

He took a key from his pocket, and, in so doing, opened his coat, disclosing that he was attired in evening clothes, that his shirt bosom sparkled with diamond studs. His shoes were patent leather.

He entered his apartment. The telephone was ringing as he closed the door behind him.

He answered it at once. The voice of the girl at the switchboard reached his ears.

"Kid, I didn't want to tell you before the gang down here, but there's been a woman trying to reach you for the last two days. She says it's life and death. She's left a number. Says to call it and ask for Kate. What'll I do?"

Dan Seller squinted his eyes in thought for a moment.

"Give me the connection," he said.

"Okay," the girl answered.

There sounded the whir of dialed numbers, then the noise made by a ringing of the telephone bell at the other end of the line. Then a man's voice.

"Kate there?" asked The Kid, making his voice sound casual.

"Who's speaking?"

"The Prince of Wales," said The Kid, "and don't wait too long to think it over because these transatlantic calls run into money."

He heard the man's voice, more distant this time.

"Is Kate here?"

Then a woman's voice, sounding just audible.

"I'll take the call for her. I'm a friend of hers."

The banging noise was made by steps coming over a wooden floor, Seller decided. Then a woman's voice said "Hello!" That voice was filled with suspense and excitement.

"The Kid speaking," said Dan Seller.

The woman's voice came to his ears now, low, vibrant, confidential, as though she was holding her mouth close to the transmitter.

"Listen, I've got to see you. Where, when, how? Quick!"

Dan Seller spoke without hesitation.

"Go to the Ship Café. Get a private room. Leave word with the head waiter that you're not to be disturbed, and that if anybody asks him for the number of Kate's room he's to tell that person the number of the private dining room. G'bye."

And The Kid hung up.

He was slightly irritated. This call undoubtedly was of grave import in the life of the young woman who had left her number. That much was apparent from the anguish of her voice, the tremulous words with which the message had been conveyed. But Dan Seller had not wished to waste time keeping after-midnight appointments with strange young women who thought their errands were of life and death. He had been interested in studying the possibilities of the new window display at Hawkins & Grebe's Jewelry Store.

However, Dan Seller, in his new character of The Patent Leather Kid, was always on the lookout for adventure, and anything sufficiently out of the usual called him with an irresistible attraction.

He took a taxi to the Ship Café.

He knew the head waiter, the manager, most of the waiters. He entered by a back door, slipped into a curtained room and rang a bell.

Within a matter of minutes the head waiter answered that summons.

"Hello, Kid!"

"Hello, Jack!"

"What can I do for you tonight, Kid?"

"A moll, coming in soon. She'll give the name of Kate and ask for a room. I want to look her over . . ."

"She's here already. Been here ten minutes. In room nineteen," said the head waiter.

The Kid whistled.

"That," he said, "is fast work. It looks almost as though . . ."

"As though what?" asked the head waiter, interested.

"As though the party had rather expected I'd pick this joint as the place for a meeting," vouchsafed The Kid. "Get me another room, Jack. Got one adjoining?"

"Nope. They're occupied. Give you sixteen."

"Okay."

"Want to let the broad know you're in?"

"Nix."

"Okay, Chief. How's tricks? You been away, ain't you?"

"Just on a business trip, Jack. I'm going on up. You stall the moll along, and send me a waiter into sixteen."

"Okay."

Dan Seller went to room sixteen, drew the curtain. Three minutes later a deferential waiter appeared with a menu, a glass of water, knives, forks and spoons, napkins, butter.

"Two?" he asked. And then started to set two places at the table without waiting for an answer.

"The order comes when I ring," said Dan Seller.

"Yes, sir."

The waiter glided from the room. Dan Seller picked up the water, the butter, the napkins, knives and forks. He threw one of the napkins over his arm, giving himself the appearance of a professional waiter, bowed his head slightly, and stepped into the corridor.

It was but a few feet to room nineteen.

He pushed aside the door and curtain, entered the room.

The girl who was seated at the table looked up with a face that was flushed, eyes that were starry, lips that were half parted. She saw the figure of a man, slightly stooped, bearing knives, forks, water, butter. The face underwent a rapid change of expression. She frowned.

"I'm served already. I'm waiting." Dan Seller straightened and met her eyes.

The eyes were brown. The lids were slightly reddened, as though she had been weeping. The face was young. So much of the figure as was visible across the table showed that she was attractive. A silken leg protruded from beneath the folds of the table cloth and the view was generous and enjoyable.

Both hands were in sight.

Dan Seller set the water and butter on the table, dumped the silverware into a pile, kicked the door shut with his heel, and let his hard gray eyes bore into those of the girl.

"Keep your hands in sight," he said.

She gasped.

The Patent Leather Kid gripped the table with his hands, swung it to one side. The girl remained motionless, frightened, staring.

Without the concealment of the table, the significance of the shapely limb which had been protruding from beneath the cloth became apparent. She was seated, skirts elevated sufficiently far to be out of the way of her snatching hand when it should drop to the butt of the pearl-handled automatic which nestled within the rolled top of the silk hose.

The Patent Leather Kid regarded the weapon.

"So that's the game, eh?"

She flushed as the concealment of the table vanished, but was mindful of the admonition to keep her hands elevated.

"No," she rasped, "that's not it. I just had that gun in case—"

"In case what?" asked Dan Seller.

"In case something happened."

"Well," said Seller, "it's happened."

And he leaned forward, possessed himself of the gun.

"Now," he said, "you can lower your hands."

She grasped at the hem of her skirt, pulled it down, raised her eyes.

"You're The Kid?"

"Yes," said Seller. "What's the lay?"

She shrugged her shoulders.

"Nothing now, except that I'm going for a ride. I was sent to frame you. I didn't want to. They gave me my choice between putting the finger on you or getting framed for a rap. I was to put you on the spot. Now I've ranked the job and they'll rub me out."

Dan Seller drew up a chair, sat down.

"Who will?"

"Beppo the Greek, of course. He's sore at you over that Carmichael job. Him and his mob are out to get you."

Dan Seller frowned.

"Beppo the Greek is becoming a source of annoyance. Would your safety be insured if you could tell him exactly where The Kid will be within exactly sixty minutes?"

She nodded.

"Sure. If it was a place where they could give him the works. That's what I was sent for."

The Patent Leather Kid lit a cigarette. He regarded the glowing end of it speculatively. Then he smiled.

"Okay, sister," he said. "I'm not The Kid. I'm the man he sent. The Kid ain't fool enough to walk into a trap like this. But he's fool enough to trust *me*, and I've got it in for him on a personal matter. The Kid is going to be knocking over Hawkins & Grebe's Jewelry Store in exactly sixty minutes. He's working on the joint now. Now that tip ain't for the bulls. It's just a private tip for Beppo the Greek. Do you get me?"

Her eyes studied his face.

"If that's on the level it means an out for me," she said.

"It's on the level," said The Patent Leather Kid, and extracted the shells from the automatic, skidded it along the floor to a corner of the room, grinned at her, and opened the door.

"Tell Beppo the Greek I'm expecting a cut," he said. "There's something I want, a favor. I'll ask for it when The Kid's rubbed out. You can hand it to him as the play came up, The Kid was wise. He sent me. I've got a score to settle. I'm putting him on the spot, not for the bulls, but for the mob. G'bye."

And Dan Seller banged the door shut, sprinted down the corridor and vanished into dining room sixteen.

Five seconds later he heard rapid steps walking past the curtained doorway of his dining room. Two minutes later the headwaiter sent him word that the mysterious woman in number nineteen had left quite hurriedly.

III

Dan Seller used a pair of long-nosed pliers to disconnect the wire which led from the barred window. That wire was one of the newer types of burglar alarms. A certain amount of current must flow through it regularly in order to keep the alarm inactive. Let that wire be cut, or the current short-circuited at any point and the alarm would ring.

Dan Seller performed a very difficult operation with those long-nosed pliers of his, and, when he had finished, the current was flowing just as it had been, yet the barred window offered no resistance to entrance save in the bars.

Those bars were speedily cut through. Dan Seller slid through the opening, dropped to the floor of the interior.

Apparently this interior was what would have been expected in the rear of a jewelry store. But The Patent Leather Kid knew that modern science has baited many clever traps for the criminal, and he governed himself accordingly.

In this game of matching his wits with the law, The Patent Leather Kid found his most fascinating recreation. He gambled with life and liberty, and enjoyed the game.

He dared not use a flashlight. He knew that delicate cells of selenium were advantageously placed so that the slightest change in the amount of light which impinged upon them would cause a change in electric current over a wire, would, in turn, ring an alarm at the headquarters of the detective agency which safeguarded the jewelry store.

The Kid knew that there would be some arrangement by which the early daylight would not set off this alarm. He started out to explore.

He finally found his lead in a narrow channel through which reflected rays from an electric sign were directed against an opposite wall. The principle was the same, only shadow instead of light served to give the alarm.

The Kid found a piece of ground glass, held that in front of his flashlight so that there was a generally diffused flow of light with no sharp pencil of brilliant illumination. And, as he glided in front of the selenium cells, he held the ground glass and the flashlight in such a manner that he cast no perceptible shadow as he made the passage, the diffused light taking the place of the reflected light which came from the sign.

The vault represented a more difficult problem. It had been cunningly constructed. But the burglar alarm was antiquated. The Kid found that within fifteen seconds of the time he started to work on the vault, and the burglar alarm was utterly valueless within ten seconds after it had been located.

When it came to the combination, The Kid had an invention of his own. It was a device by which an electric current was sent through the mechanism of the lock, the dials slowly twirled. Whenever there was the slightest interruption in that current, the slightest jar within the safe, that fact was communicated via the electric current to the ears of The Kid.

It took him fifteen minutes to get the door of the vault open and to inspect the contents.

The Patent Leather Kid was not in the least interested in the glittering array of gems which shone from the interior. He had learned long ago to restrain any natural cupidity which he might have.

He searched patiently and thoroughly, with gloved fingers going through the stock, searching, segregating, choosing. At length he selected three things, a wrist watch studded with diamonds, a necklace of pearls, and a pendant of platinum and diamonds with blood red rubies flanking either side.

When he had selected these things he looked at his wrist watch.

He found that he still had time to do that which he wished to do.

He moved more boldly toward the wrapping department of the big establishment. One does not customarily safeguard the package department of a store with the same elaborate protection given to jewels.

The Patent Leather Kid found a typewriter, and he addressed shipping labels to the individuals to whom he had determined to present the articles. He wrapped them securely, weighed them on scales which he found in the shipping department, and even went so far as to stamp them with postage stamps taken from the stamp drawer of the jewelry concern.

When he had done these things, Dan Seller, chuckling, went to a rear window on the second story of the building and surveyed the darkened shadows of the alleyway.

He found that the darkness impeded his vision, so he made one more requisition upon the stock of the jewelry store, a handsome and expensive pair of night glasses.

He focused these, raised them to his eyes, and contemplated the shadows.

The result was doubly gratifying.

He could see the form of a man crouching in the dark blob of shadow at the corner of a fence. This man was holding something in his hands. It looked like a snub-nosed telescope, supported on a three-legged stand.

The Patent Leather Kid chuckled.

A machine gun was held on the barred window, waiting for him to emerge. He swung the glasses in the other direction, wondering if the other corner would disclose another enemy.

His quest was rewarded.

The man who was partially concealed behind a packing case held an automatic in either hand, and those automatics were resting upon the wood of the packing case, ready for instant action.

Beyond doubt the mob of Beppo the Greek had acted upon the tip the young woman had relayed to them, had ascertained that the barred window of the jewelry store had been tampered with, and had ensconced themselves.

They wanted The Patent Leather Kid, and they wanted him badly enough for his own sake. But how much more of a prize would he be when he had emerged from the jewelry store, laden with valuables which only he could have obtained.

For the uncanny skill of The Patent Leather Kid was only too well known in crook circles. He was one man who could walk unscathed through a maze of burglar alarms which would have balked any other member of the profession. And he could open safes that defied the efforts of the most thorough-going and ruthless crooks.

So Beppo the Greek would win a double victory with the death of The Kid.

Dan Seller strolled back to the front of the store, picked up the wires of the burglar alarm in front of the safe, and deliberately pressed the two ends together.

Nothing happened so far as he was concerned.

He merely saw the naked ends of two wires come in contact.

But Dan Seller knew that plenty was happening in other sections of the city. The company which sold the burglary insurance and safeguarded the protective apparatus would have a watchman on duty constantly. That watchman would detect a certain red light which flashed on at the moment those wires came in contact. And a bell would ring in harsh clamor.

That light would remain on until an adjustment made at the other end of the wire put it out.

Seller looked at his wrist watch.

The watchman would just about be getting the police on the wire now. Now the riot cars would be roaring out of the nearest precinct station, packed with grim men, armed with sawed off shotguns.

Dan Seller walked to the front of the store, peered out through the plate glass show window, keeping himself concealed behind an ornamental screen.

There was no chance for escape. A touring car, side curtains concealing the interior, was parked at the corner. A man stood, leaning against a mail box, on the other side of the street.

The Patent Leather Kid chuckled.

He took the ornamental screen in his hands, his finger tips holding each side, raising it gently, just the merest fraction of an inch from the floor. Then he started shuffling toward the window, moving nearer and nearer.

When he had placed the screen in just the right position, he deposited it on the floor, straightened, turned, and walked once more to the back of the establishment. He dropped his wrapped, addressed, and stamped packages in the mailing chute. They would, he knew, be shipped out as a matter of course in the morning. In the meantime there was nothing incriminating upon him save certain electrical equipment.

He had technically violated the law in that he had broken and entered. But he had removed nothing, not directly. The very employees of the store would do that in the morning when they took the packages and sent them to the post office.

The Patent Leather Kid looked at his watch, smiled, walked back to his place of concealment behind the screen, waited. He had less than a minute to wait.

IV

A big machine skidded around the corner. Men debouched from it, started toward the store. At that instant the touring car started into motion. The man who had been lounging near the mail box, turned, waved a hand at the touring car, started to run toward it.

A man called a sharp command.

The touring car spat forth a vicious shot. The man jumped behind the mail box. His gun barked. The touring car roared into speed.

At the same moment there came the sound of a shot from the rear of the store. Then a police whistle trilled its warning sound. A machine gun sputtered into a *rat-a-tat-tat.* A police sawed off shotgun bellowed—twice. There were no further sounds from the machine gun.

From the front of the store the action swept to the corner. The police officer who had crouched behind the mail box, emptied his gun as the car lurched into the turn at the corner.

But there were other officers scattered along the sidewalk. And the big police car was roaring in pursuit. The touring car vomited a belching hail of death. Little tongues of stabbing flame darted from the cracks in the side curtains of the car.

Then a police bullet found the left rear tire as the car was midway in the turn.

It faltered, swung.

The driver flung his weight against the wheel. A shotgun bellowed, and the driver went limp. The car swung, toppled at the curb, skidded up and over, went sideways across the strip of sidewalk.

Plate glass crashed. Woodwork splintered. Metal screamed as it was wrenched apart. Then there was an instant of comparative silence.

Footsteps beat the pavement.

Men were running toward the car. Pedestrians ran screaming from the scene of the conflict. Men were rushing from the back of the store to the front. Flashlights gleaming here and there took in the confusion of the interior, the open safe, the littered contents.

But Dan Seller, masquerading as The Patent Leather Kid, was nowhere in evidence. He had vanished as into the thin air.

Sounds of battle continued to punctuate the silence of the night. Police whistles were blowing constantly. Sirens wailed in the distance, screamed as they swept nearer. The tide of battle swung through the dark alleys, and then became silent.

An ambulance came with clanging bell. Officers established a cordon and pushed the curious back, out of the active zone. And the crowd gathered with swift rapidity. There were people clothed in pajamas and slippers, with bathrobes or overcoats thrown over their night garments. There were men and women dressed in evening clothes with that overly dignified bearing which characterizes persons who are trying to impress the world with their sobriety.

The crowd became thicker until a squad of officers started pushing through it, dispersing the people, sending them to their homes. The ambulance carried away inert bodies of reddened flesh. The broken doors and windows of the jewelry store were sealed and guarded. Peace and order once more held sway.

Dan Seller lounged in the club, smoking a black cigar, watching the afternoon shadows climb slowly up the walls of the buildings on the opposite side of the street.

All about him men were discussing the robbery of the jewelry store. The subject of conversation had been in the air all afternoon, but it had been given fresh impetus by the arrival of Commissioner Brame. The Commissioner was discussing the affair with Hawkins, senior partner of the firm of Hawkins & Grebe, and neither party to the conversation seemed in a very agreeable humor.

Dan Seller managed to unobtrusively join the little group.

"Congratulations, Commissioner. You seem to have rounded up a pretty tough gang of crooks. Quite a wonderful record I'd say. Do you know, I happened along just as the shooting was at its height, and had an excellent view until the police started dispersing the crowd. I told them I was a friend of yours, but they sent me on about my business just the same."

The Commissioner glared.

"Very proper for them to do so!" he rasped. "Too damned much interference from bystanders cost us the biggest crook of them all."

"What," exclaimed The Patent Leather Kid, in mock surprise, "do you mean to tell me some one slipped through the cordon of police you threw about the place?"

"Huh," said the Commissioner, "that ain't half of it. He just made monkeys out of the bunch of us. We got the straight tip from a stoolie. It was The Patent Leather Kid that did that job at the jewelry store. Beppo's mob wasn't in on it at all.

"They just had a grudge against The Kid, and they were scattered around, ready to give The Kid the works when he should come out with the haul. When we swooped down and caught them by surprise they naturally showed fight. But The Patent Leather Kid got away, and I'd have given five years of my life to have had my mitts on him and eliminated that thorn in the flesh."

Dan Seller raised his eyebrow.

"Why, Commissioner, you surprise me! The

man has done you a service. He has enabled you to cover your department with distinction, show the very efficient police protection you are giving the community, and he's wiped out the Beppo gang! He seems to me to be a public benefactor. But how did he escape?"

Commissioner Brame became apoplectic.

"Benefactor!" he stormed. "Know what he did? Damn him! He took some of the best of the haul, all of it that's been checked as missing, in fact, and mailed it to the wife and myself as presents.

"Put me in a deuced embarrassing predicament. I had the devil's own time explaining to the wife that she had to send it back. A wrist watch and a necklace! Damn it! And as for escaping, you tell me, and I'll tell you. He just vanished into thin air!"

Dan Seller frowned, then struck his palm with his clenched fist.

"By Jove," he said, turning to Hawkins. "How many men were in the window dummies you displayed, Hawkins?"

The jeweler grunted a brief answer.

"Four," he said.

"That," said Seller, "explains it all. When I first reached the store I noticed the window display. The cops were just breaking in, pushing the people this way and that. There was a lot of confusion. And I noticed the fact that there were five men in the window display, five dummies, sitting motionless, staring straight ahead. And I was impressed by the fact that there were five men and but four women. And I happened to notice the shoes on the man who sat in the corner, near the screen. They were patent leather, and . . ."

Commissioner Brame made a noise that sounded like the noise made by a man who is choking over a glass of water.

Hawkins stared dourly at Dan Seller.

"Well," he snapped, "I wish I had that diamond pendant back. It's still missing."

Dan Seller smiled.

For the diamond pendant had also been one of the packages which had gone forward by mail. But that package had been addressed directly to the wife of Commissioner Brame.

He fancied there would be some further explanations in order in the family of Commissioner Brame one of these days.

And it was bad enough as it was. Brame was pacing the floor, cynosure of several amused eyes.

"Dummy, eh? Posed as a dummy, eh? Right under my nose! When the papers get hold of this! . . . Damn that rascal! I'll get him one of these days! And when I do . . . !"

Dan Seller made a deprecatory shrug of his shoulders.

"Well," he said, "I'll toddle along for a stroll in the park. Better watch the blood pressure, Commissioner. And, by the way, Hawkins, you said it was impossible for any one to rob your store. I told you at the time that 'impossible' was a pretty big word. I wish I'd had the foresight to place a small wager on the affair. Oh, well, better luck next time! And, in the meantime, the enemies of Beppo the Greek must be chuckling. I rather fancy the underworld will be doing some speculating—it won't hurt the prestige of The Patent Leather Kid. Well, so long, old grouch faces!"

And he was gone.

The Theft from the Empty Room

EDWARD D. HOCH

WITH THE PASSING of Edward Dentinger Hoch (1930–2008), the pure detective story lost its most inventive and prolific practitioner of the past half century. While never hailed as a great stylist, Hoch presented old-fashioned puzzles in clear, no-nonsense prose that rarely took a false step and consistently proved satisfying in most of his approximately nine hundred stories. He was named a Grand Master by Mystery Writers of America in 2001.

Born in Rochester, New York, Hoch (pronounced "hoke") attended the University of Rochester before serving in the army (1950–1952), then worked in advertising while writing on the side. When sales became sufficiently frequent, he became a full-time fiction writer in 1968, producing stories for all of the major digest-sized magazines such as *Ellery Queen's Mystery Magazine*, *Alfred Hitchcock's Mystery Magazine*, *The Saint*, and *Mike Shayne Mystery Magazine*. Hoch wanted to create a series character specifically for *EQMM*, and he came up with the professional thief Nick Velvet (whose original name was Nicholas Velvetta), his attempt to create an American counterpart to the hugely successful adventures in books and films of James Bond. The character quickly changed because Hoch didn't like the idea of his protagonist being a woman-chasing killer; Velvet remained faithful to his longtime girlfriend, Gloria Merchant, whom he met while he was burgling her apartment and who had no idea that he was a thief until 1979. The first Nick Velvet story, "The Theft of the Clouded Tiger," was published in the September 1966 issue of *EQMM*. Two major elements in the stories have made them among Hoch's most popular work: first, since Velvet will not steal anything of intrinsic value, there is the mystery of why someone would pay him twenty thousand dollars (fifty thousand in later stories) to steal something, and, second, the near impossibility of executing the theft itself (which involved stealing such items as a spider web, the water from a swimming pool, a baseball team, and a sea serpent).

"The Theft from the Empty Room" was first published in the September 1972 issue of *Ellery Queen's Mystery Magazine*; it was first collected in *The Thefts of Nick Velvet* (New York, Mysterious Press, 1978).

THE THEFT FROM THE EMPTY ROOM

Edward D. Hoch

NICK VELVET sat stiffly on the straight-backed hospital chair, facing the man in the bed opposite him. He had to admit that Roger Surman looked sick, with sunken cheeks and eyes, and a sallow complexion that gave him the appearance of a beached and blotchy whale. He was a huge man who had trouble getting around even in the best of condition. Now, laid low with a serious liver complaint, Nick wondered if he'd ever be able to leave the bed.

"They're going to cut through this blubber in the morning," he told Nick. "I've got a bet with the doctor that they don't have a scalpel long enough to even reach my liver." He chuckled to himself and then seemed about to drift into sleep.

"You wanted to see me," Nick said hastily, trying to focus the sick man's attention.

"That's right. Wanted to see you. Always told you if I needed a job done I'd call on you." He tried to lift his head. "Is the nurse around?"

"No. We're alone."

"Good. Now, you charge twenty thousand—that right?"

Nick nodded. "But only for unusual thefts. No money, jewels, art treasures—nothing like that."

"Believe me, this is nothing like that. I'd guess it's one of the most unusual jobs you've ever had."

"What do you want stolen?" Nick asked as the man's head bobbed again.

"First let me tell you where it is. You know my brother, Vincent?"

"The importer? I've heard of him."

"It's at his country home. The place is closed now for the winter, so you won't have any trouble with guards or guests. There are a few window alarms, but nothing fancy."

"You want me to steal something from your brother?"

"Exactly. You'll find it in a storeroom around the back of the house. It adjoins the kitchen, but has its own outside door. Steal what you find in the storeroom and I'll pay you twenty thousand."

"Seems simple enough," Nick said. "Just what will I find there?"

The sick eyes seemed to twinkle for an instant. "Something only you could steal for me, Velvet. I was out there myself a few days ago, but the burglar alarms were too much for me. With all this fat to cart around, and feeling as bad as I did, I couldn't get in. I knew I had to hire a professional, so I thought of you at once. What I want you to steal is—"

The nurse bustled in and interrupted him. "Now, now, Mr. Surman, we mustn't tire ourselves! The operation is at seven in the morning." She turned to Nick. "You must go now."

"Velvet," Roger Surman called. "Wait. Here's a picture of the rear of the house. It's this doorway, at the end of the driveway. Look it over and then I'll tell you—"

Nick slipped the photo into his pocket. The nurse was firmly urging him out and there was no chance for further conversation without being overheard. Nick sighed and left the room. The assignment sounded easy enough, although he didn't yet know what he'd been hired to steal.

In the morning Nick drove out to the country home of Vincent Surman. It was a gloomy November day—more a day for a funeral than an operation—and he wondered how Surman was progressing in surgery. Nick had known him off and on for ten years, mainly through the yacht club where Nick and Gloria often sailed in the summer months. Surman was wealthy, fat, and lonely. His wife had long ago divorced him and gone off to the West Indies with a slim handsome Jamaican, leaving Surman with little in life except his trucking business and his passion for food and drink.

Surman's brother, Vincent, was the glamorous member of the family, maintaining a twelve-room city house in addition to the country home. His wife Simone was the answer to every bachelor's dream, and his importing business provided enough income to keep her constantly one of New York's best-dressed women. In every way Vincent was the celebrity success, while Roger was the plodding fat boy grown old and lonely. Still, Roger's trucking business could not be dismissed lightly—not when his blue-and-white trucks could be seen on nearly every expressway.

Nick parked just off the highway and walked up the long curving driveway to Vincent Surman's country home. The place seemed closed and deserted, as Roger had said, but when Nick neared it he could see the wired windows and doors. The alarm system appeared to be functioning, though it wouldn't stop him for long.

Following Roger's directions and referring to the marked photograph, he walked along the driveway to where it ended at the rear of the house. There, next to the kitchen door, was the storeroom door that Surman had indicated. Both the door and the single window were locked, but at the moment Nick was mainly anxious to see what the room contained—what he'd been hired to steal for $20,000.

He looked in the window and saw a room about 20 feet long and 14 feet wide, with an inside door leading to the kitchen.

The room, with its painted red walls and white ceiling and wooden floor, was empty. Completely empty.

There was nothing in it for Nick Velvet to steal.

Nick drove to a pay telephone a mile down the road and phoned the hospital. They could tell him only that Roger Surman was in the recovery room following his operation and certainly could not talk to anyone or receive visitors for the rest of the day.

Nick sighed and hung up. He stood for a moment biting his lower lip, then walked back to the car. For the present there was no talking to Surman for a clue to the puzzle. Nick would have to work it out himself.

He drove back to the country home and parked. As he saw it, there were only two possibilities: either the object to be stolen had been removed since Roger saw it a few days earlier, or it was still there. If it had been removed, Nick must locate it. If it was still in the room, there was only one place it could be—on the same wall as the single window and therefore out of his line of vision from the outside.

Working carefully, Nick managed to bypass the alarm system and open the storeroom door.

He stood just inside, letting his eyes glide across every inch of the room's walls and floor and ceiling. The wall with the window was as blank as the others. There were not even any nail holes to indicate that a picture might have once hung there.

And as Nick's eyes traveled across the room he realized something else: nothing, and no one, had been in this room for at least several weeks—a layer of dust covered the floor from wall to wall, and the dust was undisturbed. Not a mark, not a footprint. Nothing.

And yet Surman had told Nick he was there only a few days ago, trying to enter the room and steal something he knew to be in it—something he obviously was able to see through the window.

But what was it?

"Please raise your hands," a voice said suddenly from behind him. "I have a gun."

Nick turned slowly in the doorway, raising his hands above his head. He faced a short dark-haired girl in riding costume and boots, who held a double-barreled shotgun pointed at his stomach. He cursed himself for not having heard her approach. "Put that thing away," he said harshly, indignation in his voice. "I'm no thief."

But the shotgun stayed where it was. "You could have fooled me," she drawled, her voice reflecting a mixture of southern and eastern origins. "Suppose you identify yourself."

"I'm a real-estate salesman. Nicholas Realty—here's my card."

"Careful with the hands!"

"But I told you—I'm not a thief."

She sighed and lowered the shotgun. "All right, but no tricks."

He handed her one of the business cards he carried for just such emergencies. "Are you the owner of this property, Miss?"

She tucked the card into the waistband of her riding pants. "It's Mrs., and my husband is the owner. I'm Simone Surman."

He allowed himself to relax a bit as she stowed the shotgun in the crook of her arm, pointed away from him. "Of course! I should have recognized you from the pictures in the paper. You're always on the best-dressed list."

"We're talking about you, Mr. Nicholas, not me. I find you here by an open door that should be locked, and you tell me you're a realtor. Do they always carry lock picks these days?"

He chuckled, turning on his best salesman's charms. "Hardly, Mrs. Surman. A client expressed interest in your place, so I drove out to look it over. I found the door open, just like this, but you can see I only took a step inside."

"That's still trespassing."

"Then I apologize. If I'd known you were in the neighborhood I certainly would have contacted you first. My understanding was that the house had been closed down for the winter."

"That's correct. I was riding by, on my way to the stables, and saw your car on the highway. I decided to investigate."

"You always carry a shotgun?"

"It was in the car—part of my husband's hunting equipment."

"You handle it well."

"I can use it." She gestured toward the house. "As long as you're here, would you like to see the inside?"

"Very much. I gather this room is for storage?"

She glanced in at the empty room. "Yes. It hasn't been used in some time. I wonder why the door was open and unlocked." She looked at the alarm wires, but didn't seem to realize they'd been tampered with. "Come around to the front."

The house was indeed something to see, fully furnished and in a Colonial style that included a huge brick oven in the kitchen. Nick took it all in, making appropriate real-estate comments, and they finally ended up back at the door to the storeroom.

"What used to be in here?" Nick asked. "Odd that it's empty when the rest of the house is so completely furnished."

"Oh, wood for the kitchen stove, supplies, things like that. I told you it hadn't been used in some time."

Nick nodded and made a note on his pad. "Am I to understand that the house would be for sale, if the price was right?"

"I'm sure Vincent wouldn't consider anything under a hundred thousand. There's a great deal of land that goes with the house."

They talked some more, and Simone Surman walked Nick back to his car. He promised to call her husband with an offer in a few days. As he drove away he could see her watching him. He had no doubt that she believed his story, but he also knew she'd have the alarm repaired by the following day.

The news at the hospital was not good. Roger Surman had suffered post-operative complications, and it might be days before he was allowed visitors. Nick left the place in a state of mild depression, with visions of his fee blowing away like an autumn leaf.

He had never before been confronted with just such a problem. Hired to steal something unnamed from a room that proved to be completely empty, he had no way of getting back to his client for further information. If he waited till Roger was out of danger and able to talk again, he would probably jeopardize the entire job, because Vincent Surman and his wife would grow increasingly suspicious when no real estate offer was forthcoming during the next few days.

Perhaps, Nick decided, he should visit Roger Surman's home. He might find some clue there as to what the fat man wanted him to steal. He drove out along the river for several miles, until he reached a small but obviously expensive ranch home where Roger had lived alone for the past several years.

Starting with the garage, he easily opened the lock with his tool kit. The car inside was a late-model limousine with only a few thousand miles on it. Nick looked it over and then went to work on the trunk compartment. There was always the possibility, however remote, that Roger had succeeded in his own theft attempt, but for some reason had not told Nick the truth. But the trunk yielded only a spare tire, a jack, a half-empty sack of fertilizer, and a can of red paint. The spotless interior of the car held a week-old copy of *The New York Times*, a little hand vacuum cleaner for the upholstery, and an electronic device whose button, when pressed, opened or closed the automatic garage door. Unless Nick was willing to believe that the fertilizer had been the object of the theft, there was nothing in the car to help him.

He tried the house next, entering through the inside garage door, and found a neat kitchen with a study beyond. It was obvious that Roger Surman employed a housekeeper to clean the place—no bachelor on his own would have kept it so spotless. He went quickly through the papers in the desk but found nothing of value. A financial report on Surman Travelers showed that it had been a bad year for the trucking company. There were a number of insured losses, and Nick wondered if Roger might be getting back some of his lost income through false claims.

He dug further, seeking some mention of Roger's brother, some hint of what the empty room might have contained. There were a few letters, a dinner invitation from Simone Surman, and finally a recent bill from a private detective agency in New York City. After another hour of searching, Nick concluded that the private detective was his only lead.

He drove down to Manhattan early the next morning, parking in one of the ramps off Sixth Avenue. The Altamont Agency was not Nick's idea of a typical private eye's office, with its sleek girl secretaries, chrome-trimmed desks, and wide tinted windows overlooking Rockefeller Center. But Felix Altamont fitted the setting. He was a slick, smooth-talking little man who met Nick in a cork-lined conference room because a client was waiting in his office.

"You must realize I'm a busy man, Mr. Velvet. I can only give you a few moments. Is it about a case?"

"It is. I believe you did some work for Roger Surman."

Altamont nodded his balding head.

"What sort of work was it?"

The detective leaned back in his chair. "You know I can't discuss a client's case, Mr. Velvet."

Nick glanced around at the expensive trappings. "Could you at least tell me what sort of cases you take? Divorce work doesn't pay for this kind of layout."

"Quite correct. As a matter of fact, we do not accept divorce cases. The Altamont Agency deals exclusively in industrial crimes—embezzlement, hijacking, industrial espionage, that sort of thing."

Nick nodded. "Then the investigation you conducted for Roger Surman was in one of those fields."

Felix Altamont looked pained. "I'm not free to answer that, Mr. Velvet."

Nick cleared his throat, ready for his final bluff. "It so happens that I'm in Roger Surman's employ myself. He hired me to try and clamp a lid on his large insurance losses. The company's threatening to cancel his policy."

"Then you know about the hijackings. Why come to me with your questions?"

"Certainly I know about the hijacking of Surman trucks, but with my employer in the hospital I thought you could fill me in on the details."

"Surman's hospitalized?"

"He's recovering from a liver operation. Now let's stop sparring and get down to business. What was hijacked from his trucks?"

Altamont resisted a few moments longer, then sighed and answered the question. "Various things. A shipment of machine tools one month, a load of textiles the next. The most recent hijacking was a consignment of tobacco leaves three weeks ago."

"In the south?"

"No, up here. Shade-grown tobacco from Connecticut. No crop in the nation brings as high a price per acre. Very valuable stuff for hijackers."

Nick nodded. "Why did you drop the investigation?"

"Who said I dropped it?"

"If you'd been successful, Surman wouldn't need me."

The private detective was silent for a moment, then said, "I told you we don't touch divorce cases."

Nick frowned, then brightened immediately. "His sister-in-law, Simone."

"Exactly. Roger Surman seems intent on pinning the hijackings on his brother, apparently for the sole purpose of causing a divorce. He's a lonely man, Mr. Velvet. He'll give you nothing but trouble."

"I'll take my chances," Nick said. "Thanks for the information."

When Nick arrived at the hospital late that afternoon he was intercepted by a brawny thick-haired man who bore more than a passing resemblance to Roger Surman.

"You're Velvet, aren't you?" the man challenged.

"Correct. And you must be Vincent Surman."

"I am. You're working for my brother."

"News travels fast."

"You were at my country house yesterday, snooping around. My wife caught you at it. This morning you were in New York, talking to that detective my brother hired."

"So Altamont's on your side now."

"Everyone's on my side if I pay them enough. I retain the Altamont Agency to do periodic security checks for my importing company. Naturally he phoned me after you left his office. His description of you matched the one Simone had already given me."

"I hope it was flattering."

"I'm not joking, Velvet. My brother is a sick man, mentally as well as physically. Anything you undertake on his behalf could well land you in jail."

"That's true," Nick agreed with a smile.

"Whatever he's paying you, I'll double it."

"My work for him is just about finished. As soon as he's well enough to have visitors I'll be collecting my fee."

"And just what was your work?"

"It's a confidential matter."

Vincent Surman tightened his lips, studying Nick. "Very well," he said, and walked on to the door.

Nick watched him head for the hospital parking lot. Then he went up to the information desk and asked for the doctor in charge of Roger Surman's case. The doctor, a bustling young man whose white coat trailed behind him, appeared ten minutes later, and his news was encouraging.

"Mr. Surman had a good night. He's past the worst of it now. I think you'll be able to see him for a few minutes tomorrow."

Nick left the hospital and went back to his car. It was working out just fine now—the money was as good as in the bank. He drove out the country road to Vincent Surman's place, and this time he took the car into the driveway, around back, and out of sight from the road.

Working quickly and quietly, Nick bypassed the alarm and opened the storeroom door once more. This time he knew what he was after. On his way to the hospital he'd stopped to pick up the can of red paint from the trunk of Roger's car. He had it with him now, as he stepped across the threshold into the empty room. He stood for a moment staring at the red walls, and then got to work.

It had occurred to him during the drive back from New York that there might be a connection between the can of red paint in Roger Surman's trunk and the red walls of the empty room. Roger had driven the car to the country house a few days before his operation to attempt the robbery himself. If the paint on the walls had been Roger's target—the paint itself—he could have replaced stolen paint with fresh red paint from the can.

Nick had stolen strange things in his time, and taking the paint from the walls of a room struck him as only a little unusual. The paint could cover any number of valuable things. He'd read once of a room that had been papered with hundred-dollar bills from a bank holdup, then carefully covered over with wallpaper. Perhaps something like that had been done here, and then a final layer of red paint applied.

He got to work carefully scraping the paint, anxious to see what was underneath; but almost at once he was disappointed. There was no wallpaper under the paint—nothing but plaster showed through.

He paused to consider, then turned to the paint can he'd brought along. Prying off the lid, he saw his mistake at once. The red in the can was much brighter than the red on the walls—it was an entirely different shade. He inspected the can more closely and saw that it was marine paint—obviously destined for Roger Surman's boat. Its presence in Roger's trunk had been merely an annoying coincidence.

Before Nick had time to curse his bad luck he heard a car on the driveway. He left the room, closing the door behind him, and had almost reached his own car when two men appeared around the corner of the house. The nearer of the two held a snub-nosed revolver pointed at Nick's chest.

"Hold it right there, mister! You're coming with us."

Nick sighed and raised his hands. He could tell by their hard icy eyes that they couldn't be talked out of it as easily as Simone Surman had been. "All right," he said. "Where to?"

"Into our car. Vincent Surman has a few more questions for you."

Prodded by the gun, Nick offered no resistance. He climbed into the back seat with one of the men beside him, but the car continued to sit there. Presently the second man returned from the house. "He's on his way over. Says to keep him here."

They waited another twenty minutes in silence, until at last Surman's car turned into the driveway. Simone was with him, bundled in a fur coat against the chill of the autumn afternoon.

"The gun wasn't necessary," Nick said, climbing out of the car to greet them.

"I thought it might be," Vincent Surman replied. "I had you tailed from the hospital.

You're a thief, Velvet. I've done some checking on you. Roger hired you to steal something from me, didn't he?"

"Look around for yourself. Is anything missing?"

"Come along—we'll look."

With the two gunmen staying close, Nick had little choice. He followed Vincent and Simone around to the storeroom door. "This is where I found him the first time," she told her husband, and sneezing suddenly, she pulled the fur coat more tightly around her.

"He was back here when we found him too," the gunman confirmed.

Vincent unlocked the storeroom door.

The walls stared back at them blankly. Vincent Surman inspected the place where the paint had been scraped, but found nothing else. He stepped outside and walked around, his eyes scanning the back of the house. "What are you after, Velvet?"

"What is there to take? The room's empty."

"Perhaps he's after something in the kitchen," Simone suggested.

Vincent ignored her suggestion, reluctant to leave the rear of the house. Finally, after another pause, he said to Nick, "All right. We'll look through the rest of the house."

An hour later, after they'd convinced themselves that nothing was missing, and after the gunmen had thoroughly searched Nick and his car, Vincent was convinced that nothing had been taken. "What's the paint for?" he asked Nick.

"My boat."

The dark-haired importer sighed and turned away. "Roger is a madman. You must realize that. He'd like nothing better than to break up my marriage to Simone by accusing me of some crime. Altamont was hired to prove I was hijacking Roger's trucks and selling the goods through my import business. He hoped Simone would quarrel with me about it and then leave me."

Nick motioned toward the gunmen. "These two goons could pass for hijackers any day." One man started for him, but Vincent barked an order. Simone's eyes widened, as if she were seeing her husband's employees for the first time.

"You don't need to hold them back," Nick said.

This time the nearer man sprang at him and Nick's fist connected with his jaw. The second man had his gun out again, but before he could bring it up Simone grabbed his arm.

"Simone!" Vincent shouted. "Stay out of this!"

She turned on her husband, her eyes flashing. "I never knew you used hoods, Vincent! Maybe Roger knows what he's talking about! Maybe you really are trying to ruin him by hijacking his trucks."

"Shut up!"

Nick backed away, his eyes still on the two hoods. "I'll be leaving now," he said. "You two can fight it out."

Nobody tried to stop him. As he swung his car around the others in the driveway he could see Vincent Surman still arguing with his wife.

The next morning Roger Surman was sitting up in bed, just finishing a meager breakfast, when Nick entered the hospital room. He glanced at the paper bag Nick was carrying and then at his face. "I'm certainly glad to see you, Velvet. Sorry I didn't have a chance to tell you what I wanted stolen."

"You didn't have to tell me," Nick said with a grin. "After a couple of false starts I figured it out."

"You mean you got it?"

"Yes, I've got it. I had a few run-ins with your brother and his wife along the way, but I got the job done last night."

"How did you know? How *could* you know?"

"I talked to your detective, Altamont, and learned about the hijackings. Once I started thinking about it—the country place, the driveway leading to the storeroom—my reasoning must have followed yours quite closely. Vincent's hired hijackers were bringing the loot there and leaving it in the storeroom for transfer to his own importing company trucks."

The fat man moved uncomfortably under his blanket. "Exactly. I tried to tell Simone, but she demanded proof."

"I think she's got it now. And I think you have too. It wasn't easy finding something to steal in an empty room—something that would be worth $20,000 to you. First, I considered the room itself, but you would have needed heavy equipment for that—and you told me you'd hoped to accomplish the theft yourself. That led me to your car, and I found the paint can in your trunk. Next, I almost stole the paint off the walls for you, until I ruled that out too. Finally, I remembered about the last shipment that was hijacked a few weeks ago. It consisted of bundles of valuable tobacco leaves, and certainly such a shipment would leave traces of its presence. Yesterday, out at the house, Simone walked into the storeroom and sneezed. Then I remembered something else I'd seen in your car."

Roger Surman nodded. "The little hand vacuum cleaner. I was going to use it if I got past the alarms."

Nick Velvet nodded and opened the paper bag he was still carrying. "I used it last night—to steal the dust from the floor of that empty room."

Villain: Bart Taylor

The Shill

STEPHEN MARLOWE

A PROLIFIC AUTHOR of popular fiction, especially science fiction and mysteries, Stephen Marlowe (1928–2008) was best known for his long series of novels about the international adventurer and private eye Chester Drum, beginning with *The Second Longest Night* (1955) and concluding a run of twenty exploits with *Drum Beat—Marianne* (1968).

The Drum character clearly owes a great deal to Mickey Spillane's very tough private detective, Mike Hammer. While most of Hammer's cases were set in New York City, the peripatetic Drum engaged in crime solving and espionage in such far-flung locales as Saudi Arabia, Yugoslavia, Berlin, India, South America, and Iceland. Commonly known as Chet, he was single, kept a bottle of booze in his office, and carried a gun that he wasn't afraid to use.

Born Milton Lesser in Brooklyn, New York, he legally changed his name to Stephen Marlowe in the 1950s, one of the many pseudonyms he employed over his long and productive career; other names were Adam Chase, Andrew Frazer, Darius John Granger, Jason Ridgway, C. H. Thames, and Stephen Wilder. He also was one of many authors who penned the later Ellery Queen novels, his titled *Dead Man's Tale* (1961). He collaborated on *Double in Trouble* (1959) with the very popular Richard S. Prather as Drum teamed up with Shell Scott, Prather's series P.I.

Marlowe was presented with The Eye, the lifetime achievement award given by the Private Eye Writers of America. He also won the Prix Gutenberg du Livre, a French literary award.

"The Shill" was originally published in *A Choice of Murders*, edited by Dorothy Salisbury Davis (New York, Scribner, 1958).

THE SHILL

Stephen Marlowe

EDDIE GAWKED AND GAWKED. The crowd came slowly but steadily. They didn't know they were watching Eddie gawk. That's what made a good shill, a professional shill.

He was, naturally, dressed like all the local thistle chins. He wore an old threadbare several years out of date glen plaid suit, double-breasted and rumpled-looking. He wore a dreary not quite white shirt open at the collar without a tie. And he gawked.

He had big round deep-set eyes set in patches of blue-black on either side of his long narrow bridged nose. His lower lip hung slack with innocent wonder. He had not shaved in twenty-four hours. He looked exactly as if he had just come, stiff and bone weary and in need of entertainment, off the assembly line of the tractor plant down the road at Twin Falls. He stared in big eyed open mouthed wonder at Bart Taylor, the talker for the sideshow, as Bart expostulated and cajoled, declaimed and promised the good-sized scuff of townsfolk who had been drawn consciously by Bart Taylor's talking and unconsciously by Eddie's gawking.

He was a magnificent shill and he knew it and Bart Taylor knew it and not only the people at the Worlds of Wonder sideshow knew it but all the folks from the other carnival tents as well, so that when business was slow they sometimes came over just to watch Eddie gawk and summon the crowd with his gawking and they knew, without having studied psychology, as Eddie knew, that there was something unscientifically magnetic about a splendid shill like Eddie.

They used to call Eddie the Judas Ram (cynically, because the thistle chins were being led to financial slaughter) and the Pied Piper (because the thistle chins followed like naive children the unheard music of his wondering eyes and gaping mouth). But all that was before Eddie fell in love with Alana the houri from Turkestan who did her dance of the veils at the Worlds of Wonder, Alana who was from Baltimore and whose real name was Maggie O'Hara and who, one fine night when she first joined the carnival at a small town outside of Houston, Texas, stole Eddie's heart completely and for all time. After that Eddie was so sad, his eyes so filled with longing, that they didn't call him anything and didn't talk to him much and just let him do his work, which was shilling.

From the beginning, Eddie didn't stand a chance. He was a shill. He was in love with Alana, who was pale, delicate, and beautiful, and everyone knew at once he was in love with her. In a week, all the men in the carnival were interested in Alana, whom nobody called Maggie. In a month, they all loved Alana, each in his own way, and each not because Alana had dunned them but because Eddie was a shill. It was as simple as that. Alana, however, for her own reasons remained aloof from all their advances. And the worst smitten of all was Bart Taylor, the talker and owner of Worlds of Wonder.

Now Bart finished his dunning and Eddie stepped up to the stand, shy and uncertain looking, to buy the first ticket. Bart took off his straw hat and wiped the sweat from the sweat band and sold Eddie a ticket. A good part of the scuff of thistle chins formed a line behind Eddie and bought tickets too. They always did.

Inside, Eddie watched the show dutifully, watched Fawzia the Fat Lady parade her mountains of flesh, watched Herko the Strong Man who actually had been a weight lifter, watched the trick mirror Turtle Girl, who came from Brooklyn but had lost her freshness in Coney Island and now was on the road, and the others, the Leopard Man and the Flame Swallower who could also crunch and apparently swallow discarded light bulbs and razor blades, Dame Misteria who was on loan from the Mitt camp down the midway to read fortunes at Worlds of Wonder and Sligo, a sweating red-faced escape artist who used trick handcuffs to do what Houdini had done with real ones.

But there was no Alana. Eddie waited eagerly for her act of the dancing veils, which was the finale of the show, but instead, the evening's organized entertainment concluded with Sligo. After that, the booths and stalls inside the enormous tent would remain in operation although the central stage was dark. The thistle chins, wandering about listlessly under the sagging canvas both because it was hot and because they too sensed something was missing from the show, had left the expected debris, peanut bags and soft drink bottles and crumpled sandwich wrappers, in the narrow aisles among the wooden folding chairs in front of the stage.

Eddie found Bart Taylor outside in his trailer, spilling the contents of his chamois pouch on a table and counting the take. "Two and a half bills," Bart said. "Not bad."

"How come Alana didn't dance?" Eddie wanted to know.

"Maybe she's sick or something."

"Didn't she tell you?"

"I haven't seen her," Bart Taylor said, stacking the bills and change in neat piles on the table in front of him. He was wearing a lightweight loud plaid jacket with high wide peaked lapels of a thinner material. One of the lapels was torn, a small jagged piece missing from it right under the wilted red carnation Bart Taylor wore. The carnation looked as if it had lost half its petals too.

"Well, I'll go over to her trailer," Eddie said.

"I wouldn't."

Eddie looked at him in surprise. "Any reason why not?"

"No," Bart said quickly. "Maybe she's sick and sleeping or something. You wouldn't want to disturb her."

"Well, I'll go and see."

A shovel and a pick-ax were under the table in Bart Taylor's trailer. Eddie hadn't seen them before. "Don't," Bart said, and stood up. His heavy shoe made a loud scraping sound against the shovel. He was a big man, much bigger than Eddie and sometimes when the carnival was on a real bloomer with no money coming in they all would horse around some like in a muscle camp, and Bart could even throw Herko the Strong Man, who had been a weight lifter.

"O.K.," Eddie said, but didn't mean it. He went outside and the air was very hot and laden with moisture. He looked up but couldn't see any stars. He wondered what was wrong with Bart Taylor, to act like that. He walked along the still crowded midway to the other group of trailers on the far side of the carnival, past the lead joint where the local puddle-jumpers were having a go at the ducks and candle flames and big swinging gong with .22 ammo, past the ball pitching stand where shelves of cheap slum were waiting for the winners, past the chandy who was fixing some of the wiring in the merry-go-round. For some reason, Eddie was frightened. He almost never sweated, no matter how hot it was. A shill looked too obviously enthusiastic if he sweated. But now he could feel the sweat beading his forehead and trickling down his sides from his armpits. He wasn't warm, though. He was very cold.

There was no light coming through the windows of Alana's trailer. The do not disturb sign was hanging from the door-knob. The noise from the midway was muted and far away, except for the explosive staccato from the lead joint. Eddie knocked on the aluminum door and called softly, "Alana? Alana, it's Eddie."

No answer. Eddie lit a cigaret, but it tasted like straw. His wet fingers discolored the paper. He threw the cigaret away and tried the door. It wasn't locked.

Inside, Eddie could see nothing in the darkness. His hand groped for the light switch. The generator was weak: the overhead light flickered pale yellow and made a faint sizzling sound.

Alana was there. Alana was sprawled on the floor, wearing her six filmy veils. In the yellow light, her long limbs were like gold under the veils. Eddie knelt by her side. He was crying softly before his knees touched the floor. Alana's eyes were opened but unseeing. Her face was bloated, the tongue protruding. From the neck down she was beautiful. From the neck up, it made Eddie sick to look at her.

She had been strangled.

He let his head fall on her breast. There was no heart beat. The body had not yet stiffened.

He stood up and lurched about the interior of the small trailer. He didn't know how long he remained there. He was sick on the floor of the trailer. He went back to the body finally. In her right hand Alana clutched a jagged strip of plaid cloth. Red carnation petals like drops of blood were strewn over the floor of the trailer.

"All right, Eddie," Bart Taylor said softly. "Don't move."

Eddie turned around slowly. He had not heard the door open. He looked at Bart Taylor, who held a gun in his hand, pointing it unwaveringly at Eddie.

"You killed her," Eddie said.

"*You* killed her," Bart Taylor said. "My word against yours. I own this show. Who are you, a nobody. A shill. My word against yours."

"Why did you do it?"

"She wouldn't look at me. I loved her. I said I would marry her, even. She hated me. I couldn't stand her hating me. But I didn't mean to kill her."

"What are you going to do?" Eddie said.

"Jeep's outside. Tools. We'll take her off a ways and bury her."

"Not me," Eddie said.

"I need help. You'll help me. A shill. A nobody. They all know how you were carrying a torch for her. You better help me."

"Your jacket," Eddie said. "The carnation. They'll know it was you."

"Not if we bury her."

"Not me," Eddie said again.

"It's late. There are maybe thirty, forty people left on the midway. We've got to chance it now. It looks like rain. Won't be able to do it in the rain. Let's get her out to the jeep now, Eddie."

"No," Eddie said. He wasn't crying now, but his eyes were red.

Bart came over to him. Eddie thought he was going to bend over the body, but instead he lashed out with the gun in his hand, raking the front sight across Eddie's cheek. Eddie fell down, just missing Alana's body.

"Get up," Bart said. "You'll do it. I swear I'll kill you if you don't."

Eddie sat there. Blood on his cheek. The light, yellow, buzzing. Bart towering over him, gigantic, menacing. Alana, dead. Dead.

"On your feet," Bart said. "Before it starts raining."

When Eddie stood up, Bart hit him again with the gun. Eddie would have fallen down again, but Bart held him under his arms. "You'll do it," Bart said. "I can't do it alone."

"O.K.," Eddie said. "I feel sick. I need some air."

"You'll get it in the jeep."

"No. Please. I couldn't help you. Like this. Air first. Outside. All right?"

Bart studied him, then nodded. "I'll be watching you," he said. "Don't try to run. I'll catch you. I have the gun. I'll kill you if I have to."

"I won't try to run," Eddie promised. He went outside slowly and stood in front of the trailer. He took long deep breaths and waited.

Eddie gawked at the trailer. It was like magic, they always said. It had nothing to do with seeing or smelling or any of the senses, not really. You didn't only gawk with your eyes. Not a professional shill. Not the best. You gawked with every straining minuteness of your body. And they came. The thistle chins. The townsfolk. Like iron filings and a magnet. They came slowly, not knowing why they had come, not knowing what power had summoned them. They came to gawk with you. They came, all right. You've been doing this for years. They always came.

You could sense them coming, Eddie thought. You didn't have to look. In fact, you shouldn't. Just gawk, at the trailer. Shuffling of feet behind you. A stir. Whispering. What am I doing here? Who is this guy?

Presently there were half a dozen of them. Then an even dozen. Drawn by Eddie, the magnificent shill.

There were too many of them for Bart to use his gun. They crowded around the trailer's only entrance. They waited there with Eddie. Unafraid now, but lonely, infinitely lonely, Eddie led them inside.

They found Bart Taylor trying to stuff carnation petals down his throat.

Rogue: Augustus Mandrell

The Dr. Sherrock Commission

FRANK McAULIFFE

A MODEST OUTPUT nonetheless garnered many devoted, almost cultish, fans for Frank McAuliffe (1926–1986), the author of four off-kilter books about Augustus Mandrell, the figure McAuliffe hints (with tongue pressed into his cheek) might be a real-life person and describes as "the most urbane killer in all the annals of hysterical crime." The Mystery Writers of America agreed and presented *For Murder I Charge More* (1971), the third book in the series, with an Edgar for best paperback original in 1972. Accepting the award, McAuliffe announced, "Ladies and gentlemen, you have impeccably good taste."

McAuliffe was one of eight children born to Irish immigrants in New York City, where he also married and had seven children. After moving to Ventura, California, he worked as a civilian technical writer for the navy while also writing fiction, mainly short stories, many of which were published in *Ellery Queen's Mystery Magazine*.

The first book in the Mandrell series, *Of All the Bloody Cheek* (1965), was written by hand as he sat in a station wagon outside a church while his wife took the children to Mass. The second volume of Mandrell's adventures was *Rather a Vicious Gentleman* (1968) and the last, published many years later from a long-lost manuscript, was the poorly conceived *Shoot the President, Are You Mad?* (2010), initially rejected by his publisher as inappropriate following the assassination of President Kennedy.

Incidentally, though Mandrell, the sole proprietor and only employee of Mandrell, Limited, is English and the author's style sounds like someone from the United Kingdom, McAuliffe never traveled outside the United States.

"The Dr. Sherrock Commission" was first published in *Of All the Bloody Cheek* (New York, Ballantine Books, 1965).

THE DR. SHERROCK COMMISSION

Frank McAuliffe

DR. SHERROCK is remembered by the firm of Mandrell, Limited, with unequivocal sentimentality. He put us on our feet, so to speak. Which is more than I can say for the service he extended to many of his patients.

Odd chap, this Sherrock. He was a medical doctor with a practice in Liverpool. His home, with its steel-shuttered windows, was located in the posh Clairemont section. Each day the doctor made his transit from home to office in the rear of a locked Rolls. The chauffeur of the Rolls, a barrel-shouldered young man named Ben Nett, carried beneath his left arm an ugly bit of iron manufactured in Belgium and containing within its contours seven steel-headed bullets.

Once the auto arrived at the building that housed the doctor's offices, it was driven down a ramp to an underground garage. Here the machine was parked in a wire-enclosed stall from which Sherrock stepped directly into an elevator that scheduled but two stops: the garage and the doctor's offices on the third floor.

And this strange regimen did not slacken with Sherrock's arrival at the office. He would not treat just anyone. Perhaps he had been less selective at one time, accepted patients purely on the criterion of their forfeiture of health. But in the period in which I knew the man he insisted that yours be an anatomy previously researched by his stethoscope before he would allow you the shelter of his office.

One would assume it financial folly for a doctor to so isolate himself from the community. Which M.D., I mean, survives without that one essential trapping of his practice—the patient? Not so. Sherrock sustained the vacuum and still remained the top yearly-income doctor in Liverpool. A feat, I am told, of no meager proportions, for the Liverpool of those days (about a year prior to the war) was a city glutted with medical men made notoriously tractable by starvation.

Sherrock prospered because he still retained a trusting core of old patients, his Clairemont neighbors for the most part—case histories he knew by memory—and their offspring.

What have we here, then? A snob who has discarded the ideals of his youth, the wistfully lofty tenets of his profession? No; there was more substance to Sherrock's withdrawal. During the several months prior to my acquaintance with the man, the doctor had been exposed to a series of odd adventures, an unsettling record of mayhem that prompted anything but a sense of security.

On June 19, for instance, Daisy Sherrock, the doctor's wife for eighteen years, encountered sudden escape from the balance of her life. On holiday in Wales the woman slipped, jumped, or was pushed from a promontory onto a covey of rocks bordering the Irish Sea. While it is true that the lady was renowned locally for her lack of beauty, it is doubtful that her extraordinary acrobatics improved her condition in any degree.

On December 26 of the same year (you will note that I am reluctant to wax specific regarding the identity of the year involved; I must refuse to do so for reasons that will remain my own)—anyway, on December 26 a Miss Sally Hickey received the following correspondence in the post: *If you go ahead and do it I'm going ahead and kill you and him.*

A rather irrelevant exhibition of faulty sentence structure, but noteworthy in this instance when you realize that Miss Sally Hickey was about to become the second Mrs. Sherrock. The doctor had announced their engagement on Christmas Day. Miss Hickey, a winsome slip of a girl, had, up until this time, known only that fame inherent in her occupation as a nurse in Dr. Sherrock's office. She was evidently a medical woman of precocious skill, for it was she (not the older, more experienced, nurses) whom the doctor kept alone with him in the office for those late-evening experiments that are so much a part of the life of the dedicated physician.

There was no further enlightenment from the letter writer. Perhaps he had exhausted his gift.

Then on February 13 (that birth date, historically, of beautiful women) of the new year, a rifle bullet splashed through the window of Dr. Sherrock's library. On February 19 a similar missile shattered the same window. These ballistic outrages commanded Dr. Sherrock's attention rather abruptly, for he chanced to be seated in the room on both occasions. All windows of the great house, except those of the servants' quarters, were shortly equipped with steel shutters.

Then on March 8, just three weeks prior to the wedding, Dr. Sherrock found himself face-to-face with the secret aggressor. On his way to the office in his Rolls, the doctor encountered a vintage saloon that forced his own machine from the roadway at high speed. The Rolls struck a stone wall that fortunately gave way to superior craftsmanship, and Sherrock went unharmed.

The doctor, for all his submersion in the medical profession, was not a dense man. Upon sensing the bent of his enemy's animosity—having it rather flung in his face, actually—Sherrock exhibited an astute knowledge of the basic ingredients of survival. He, for example, did not entrust his deliverance to the abilities of the Liverpool police (a loutish lot). Instead, following the roadway impertinence, he hired for himself the chauffeur with the automatic pistol, the Mr. Ben Nett previously mentioned.

In fact, the durable Mr. Nett became so much the constant companion of Dr. Sherrock and the doctor's fiancée in the ensuing weeks that when the day of the wedding finally arrived, a certain degree of good-natured joshing befell young Nett. The alcoholic mouths of the wedding guests speculated with Ben on the sleeping accommodations being provided for the trembling bride.

"What'll it be, lad? Three in a bed? Ho-ho-ho-ho."

"How many loaded guns will the poor lass find facing her tonight? Eh? Ho-ho . . ."

Ahhh, when will Englishmen ever learn that dignity is the least resident in the brandy bottle?

The wedding went off as planned, but I understand the honeymoon trip to Italy was postponed until less hostile times. That is, postponed until the police, or somebody, should apprehend Mr. Michael Bell.

It had been suspected all along that the caretaker of Dr. Sherrock's misfortune was one Michael Bell. After all, hadn't it been Michael Bell who had injected into the demise of the first Mrs. Sherrock the fascinating rumor of possible "foul play"? Hadn't it been Michael, a brash immigrant from Belfast, who had gone about the pubs in Clairemont muttering his dark, vulgar conclusions regarding ". . . me sister's accident—*if* you'll call that an accident . . ." immediately following the burial of the first Mrs. Sherrock? Yes, Michael was the brooding brother of the matron who had enjoyed the flamboyant swim in the Irish Sea. He was Dr. Sherrock's brother-in-law.

Michael had also been the frequent escort of Miss Sally Hickey prior to her engagement to Dr. Sherrock. Michael it was who had taken the vivacious young nurse about the sights of Liverpool on those evenings when she was not enmeshed in after-hours research with the good doctor.

Thus it must have seemed to poor Mr. Bell that his whole world was being unraveled before his eyes, and all of the yarn ending in the hands of the physician. Sister gone . . . lady friend gone.

As I said, Dr. Sherrock and the Liverpool police suspected that Michael was the secret tormentor. But it was not until the day of the automobile rowdyism that they knew for certain. Sherrock swore that he had seen the contorted face of Michael behind the wheel of the offending machine. The authorities of course took after the lad with laudable vindictiveness. But Mr. Bell proved worthy of their zeal. He eluded the pack, and was still, two months following the Sherrock-Hickey nuptials, at large. More power to you, lad.

Mrs. Sherrock (née Hickey), poor lass, came to despise Michael Bell with a fervor equal to that expressed by her doctor-husband. The young waif had indentured herself to the god Matrimony, and she was eager to test the residual benefits thereof—to wit, her new buying power. But instead, she found herself a prisoner in the steel-shuttered house. On the assumption that Mr. Bell had been rather in earnest when he threatened to kill both Sally and the doctor, the Liverpool police and Sherrock himself insisted that Sally remain confined.

The situation was at this flux when the talents of Mandrell, Limited, were solicited.

Despite the obvious impediments in the case, I accepted the Commission. My decision was considerably influenced by the hints of pending bankruptcy tended me by my creditors. As I deposited the advance fee to my account, my banker of the day, a Mr. Lovejoy, remarked, "Ah, it does my heart good to see so young a firm as your own finally making its way, Mr. Mandrell. Afraid there for a while we were going to lose you. So many bankruptcy decisions being brought on these days, eh? Although you young fellows shouldn't be believing all those things you read in the press about the commercial houses. We are certainly not the 'smugly solvent' lot you hear about from those Bolshevik crybabies. No, indeed . . . Ah, Mr. Mandrell, our dossier on Mandrell, Limited, appears somewhat delinquent. We do not have your exact activity listed. What is Mandrell, Limited, in?"

"Why, I suppose hunting describes it best," I murmured.

"Hunting? You mean big-game hunting? Buena macubula and all that?"

"Yes, big-game hunting," I said.

"My, my. That doesn't sound any too broad-based, reliable, or . . . ah . . . economy-attached, if I may say so." (Followed by a positive geyser of derogatory clichés.) "Can you tell me, is our Mr. FitzHunt aware of Mandrell, Limited's corporate structure?"

You suet-voiced popinjay. You no longer have Mandrell, Limited, beneath your pound-sterling thumb; the loan is up to date. So now you would impose this false insecurity to our negotiations. Bondage me with fear. Not on your life, sir. Mandrell, Limited, now has teeth.

"I would appreciate it, Mr. Lovejoy," I said, "if you would summon the necessary articulation to correctly pronounce my name. It is Man-DRELL. Not Man-DRILL. A minor distinction, to be sure, yet one the zoologists of the world have seen fit to emblazon with significance."

"Oh, I say, I hadn't meant to . . . well now, back to our analysis of Mandrell, Limited's growth potential. You see—"

"Good day, Mr. Lovejoy. You will find my checks in the post."

I moved on from my bank—yes, indeed, "my" bank—to a sleazy building in Blackpool. To the eternally suspicious gentlemen encountered therein I handed over the sum of nineteen pounds. They in turn grudgingly parted with an Afghan rug which they had been holding but which belonged to me.

"Nineteen pounds. That's not one-tenth the worth of this thing," I was informed by a Mr. Grimes of Customs.

"Not one-fiftieth," I corrected him. "But you see it is damaged here, the two holes? So the full import duty could hardly be assessed."

"Not if I'd been in charge . . . Here, those look to be bullet holes!"

"Yes, they certainly do. Good day, sir."

At this period in my life I was admittedly a bit dotty on the subject of fine rugs. An affectation, probably, that has not survived my maturity. On this occasion, however, I found myself particularly indebted to Dr. Sherrock. Had it not been for the advance monies from the Sherrock Commission, I fear I would have been driven to some desperate act in order to retrieve the Afghan rug from the customhouse.

These, then, were the fruits of my labor. Let us pursue now the labor itself. The Dr. Sherrock Commission.

In order that you may not be misled, let me point out that it was not Dr. Sherrock who negotiated the Dr. Sherrock Commission with Mandrell, Limited. That would have been somewhat incongruous, as you shall see.

My major concern, following my acceptance of the Commission, consisted of arranging a face-to-face meeting with the harried doctor. The meeting, of necessity, had to be within a format that Sherrock's schedule, with its bristling aura of defensive security, firmly did not allow.

As a first maneuver I motored up to Liverpool and presented myself at Sherrock's offices. With my arm supported by a dramatic, blood-spotted sling, I supplicated at the desk of the nurse-receptionist for emergency help. Through lips made blubbery by pain, I demanded that the talents of Dr. Sherrock should immediately be brought to bear on my tortured arm. I was informed that a Dr. O'Shaughnessy, a colleague of Sherrock's, would honor my affliction. "Dr. Sherrock is not available."

"You are not understand, Lady Nurse," I sniveled. "I am Igor Kaminski. Great pianist. Greatest since Gaultflegal. The critics, some say greater than Gaultflegal. I? I must be neutral. . . . I am trapped here, Liverpool, this stupid city, by the concert. I am let nobody, nobody, touch-a these lovely hands except Sher-rook."

I held out for the nurse's attention my injured paw. The fingers of the hand were so grotesquely intertwisted that I would be lucky were I ever again to zip my trousers with same, much less play the piano. The ring finger itself was split fully in half all the way to the second joint. The collection of malformed digits that she viewed was of course of my own manufacture. Mostly a block of plaster of Paris sculpted to my needs and carefully tinted to an over-all yellowish purple, except for the areas of bruised red where two of the fingernails hung by a thread of cuticle. Rather overdone, actually, but the thing passed for a ruptured hand if only because there was nothing else it could possibly have been.

"This Dr. Sher-rook, I am heard of him," I said. "He is must fix me. I must play tonight."

"Dr. O'Shaughnessy will see you, if you care to wait," the nurse said, staring coldly at my affliction. "We do not treat non-English patients, as a rule. Dr. Sherrock's orders. But in this case, since you are in the Arts, perhaps . . ."

I carried on a bit more, banging about Dr. O'Shaughnessy's office and screeching that none but "Dr. Sher-rook himself" should examine my hand, but to no avail. O'Shaughnessy and another white-smocked gentleman eventually prescribed massive home rest for me and flung me from the building. It would serve you right, you medical swine, should Igor Kaminski elect to never play again. How, I ask you, sirs, are you to explain my absence at the next Buckingham Palace command performance?

Thus, in my first move to complete the Sherrock Commission I gained little but a growing respect for the good doctor's hunger for privacy. I returned to London, taking with me the abused but talented hand of Igor Kaminski, and sat brooding at my desk in this bit of an office I had acquired just off Bristol Square. The Dr. Sherrock Commission represented the first substantial Commission in the short history of Mandrell, Limited. It had to be brought off with ringing virtuosity. The firm's reputation would be built on nothing less.

Following a full day of contemplation, I had all but decided that if I were to retain my infant business, and my Afghan rug, I would be forced to risk the temper of the doctor's armed chauffeur, Mr. Ben Nett. I would intercept Sherrock during his daily home-to-office ride. Then, lo! before I had time to act on this somewhat dangerous decision, the correct strategy came suddenly to me on the winds of Fortune. Fortunate for me, that is. A bit on the awkward side for the third party involved, a gentleman named John Austin.

Austin was an incumbent M.P. from Liverpool, Labour man. He had, according to the shocked report in *The Times*, been struck down by an auto on a street of his own district while returning home from an electioneering rally. The offending machine—described by a witness as an old Bentley, color red, if you can imagine such a thing—had sped off without pausing to ascertain even the extent of the M.P.'s injury; which, upon his removal to St. Malachy's Hospital, proved to be grievous.

The key, the very key to my dilemma, served up by the voting stock—slack, blind cattle—of Liverpool!

I immediately flew north and presented myself at old, gray St. Malachy's to involve myself in the succor being tended Mr. Austin. To the hospital authorities, I was a doctor engaged by the Labour Party. To the politicians on the scene, I was present on behalf of the Austin family. And to the family, I was a member of the hospital staff. It was all rather simple. Most of the people I encountered during my three days of medical duty, even the members of the M.P.'s family, appeared more concerned with the political ramifications surrounding the incident than the ministrations being accorded the near-deceased.

An ugly theory had invaded the affair. It was indignantly whispered, through filed teeth, that the Tories had done in poor M.P. Austin, had paid the driver of the red Bentley to obliterate their opposition, an expediency well in keeping with Liverpool political tradition. A very serious game down there.

On two occasions during my medical tour I was able to achieve the sickroom unescorted and spend a few minutes alone with the patient. Following the first of these visits, I looked in on the superintendent of the hospital and informed him that his famous charge had regained coherence for a few seconds during my visit and had voiced a request.

"He wants a particular doctor called in for further consultations," I told the super. "A Dr. Sherrock. I've heard of Sherrock but, unfortunately, do not know him personally."

"I know Dr. Sherrock," the super said. "I'm afraid he'll not come to the hospital. He lives under . . . well, some rather peculiar pressures."

I shrugged. "Just as well. The patient evidently has enormous faith in him; but, after all, Sherrock is no more than an M.D., possessing God knows what degree of competence."

"Dr. Sherrock is the highest caliber of physician," the super told me coldly. The super didn't like me. He didn't like my splayfooted stride, my paunchy, hunched posture, my stained school tie, or my grimy, fingerprint-crusted eyeglasses. He, in particular, did not enjoy the cloud of bad breath that hung about me like a cape (in reality a bit of pungent cheese smeared on the upper arms and neck). I was not at all the super's conception of the doctor one summoned to minister to a Member of Parliament. Which is not surprising, since the disguise I have described was inspired not by a doctor but by a banker, my Mr. Lovejoy.

"If Mr. Austin has so much faith in Dr. Sherrock," the super told me, "I will personally make every effort to bring Sherrock here. Are you, sir, so in command of your profession that you can deny the therapeutic effect such a visit might have?" Quackery on high. Nothing as ineffectual as medical attention was going to keep Austin from dying, and the super well knew it.

I did not leave the invitation of Dr. Sherrock to the super's influence alone. After maneuvering my second visit to the sickroom, I reported to the Labour Party people and the dying man's family that the M.P. had amazed me by a miraculous rally to consciousness. "He badly wants this Dr. Sherrock brought in," I informed them. "And I will venture only this diagnosis myself. As a humble medical scientist, I'd say that without Sherrock the M.P.'s chances are wholly dependent upon the whimsey of the supernatural. Which, at best, is . . . well, erratic."

I also mentioned that I had reported the patient's request to the superintendent of the hospital and that, while the man had promised action, I thought I had detected a bit of foot-dragging. "Does anyone . . . er . . . happen to know the super's political affiliations?" I asked slyly.

Ah, there are few spurs so sharp as the sudden knowledge that one is being made the victim of a conspiracy. My listeners exploded into activity. Poor Dr. Sherrock. He found his carefully erected isolation abruptly besieged from several impressive quarters. Entreaties to abandon his security shield for a trip to St. Malachy's rang upon him from people he could hardly ignore, from empire-level government people, from the medical hierarchy, and from his own insular neighbors in Clairemont. The doctor capitulated in twelve hours.

The routine was snapped. Instead of motoring home from his office that evening, Sherrock was chauffeured to St. Malachy's, protesting all the way that he did not know and had never met M.P. Austin. "Strange are the ways of modern medical science," the super soothed him.

I of course made it my business to be on hand when Sherrock arrived at the hospital, and I graciously agreed to attempt once more to rouse the unconscious patient. I insisted, however, that only Sherrock and myself should be present in the sickroom. There was grudging compliance.

Once in Austin's room, door locked behind us, blinds drawn, I guided Sherrock to the respirator tank in which Austin lay, living tenuously on the mechanical ability of his windowed boiler (or iron lung, as I believe the Americans affectionately call it). Dr. Sherrock stared down at the pallid face of the M.P. for a few seconds, then said crossly, "Never met him. And shouldn't care to either, I might add. Labour man, isn't he?"

"I doubt that introductions will ever be necessary, Doctor," I said, reaching into my black satchel, "I have something here you must digest, sir. Somewhat bitter I'm afraid . . ."

"Wha—"

I expended the time necessary to place the snout of my pistol against his smock directly in line with his heart. Accuracy was essential in this instance, for the silencer on my weapon was effective for but one shot, really, and Sherrock was already frisking about somewhat. The one discharge proved sufficient. Sherrock was deceased before I caught his body and lowered it to the tile floor.

I removed my gloves, washed my hands in the small lavatory (they generally perspire a bit); then I left the room. Prior to my departure I of course disconnected from its wall socket the electric plug that ensured the functioning of Mr. Austin's respirator.

In the outer room I encountered the M.P.'s family, a couple of Labour Party officials, and the super and a few of his staff. Dabbing at my eyes with a soiled handkerchief, I blubbered, "He's making every effort . . . Dr. Sherrock . . . Such skill . . . His hands, not a tremor . . . He requests that he be left alone with the patient until he summons you. . . . The finest physician I . . ."

My breath opened a passageway through the crowded room as I made for the corridor door. I paused by the door only long enough to unsettle the lush widow Austin by pressing on her an unwholesome leer, for no reason that I can recall now other than my possibly being a bit nervous by this time. Then I left St. Malachy's and Liverpool.

I received the balance of my fee in the Dr. Sherrock Commission a week later in my office off Bristol Square. The late doctor's chauffeur, the cleft-chinned and void-eyed Ben Nett, carried the crisp pound notes to my hand. He brought also my client, the widow Sherrock, née Hickey.

Sally was on her way to seclusion in Italy for the period of her bereavement. Mr. Nett had graciously consented to share her grief. They were utilizing the same steamship tickets, I believe, that had been held in abeyance from the doctor and Sally's postponed honeymoon.

We concluded our business; Sally made several fatuous but well-intentioned remarks regarding my Afghan; then they left. I have met Sally a few times over the years since that day, but Mr. Ben Nett I saw once more only, in Switzerland, just prior to his unhappy accident.

On the day following the payment of the fee, I returned to Liverpool and released my auto from its hiding place. I drove the sad machine to a local automotive shop and contracted repairs. As I turned to exit from the shop, I discovered the manager studying the dented front end of the red Bentley with an apprehensive eye of cocked suspicion. "Don't get many red ones, we don't," he observed nervously. "You say you'll be back to fetch it this afternoon?"

Out with it, mealymouth. What are you trying to say? I of course assured this idiot that I would return; then I left him and his uncharitable speculation.

The Bentley, I might mention, had been purchased and licensed under the name Lovejoy—a gesture of sorts to my banker. That I would never be allowed to reclaim the machine was not so staggering a loss as you might assume. The Tory people had been most generous and had budgeted into my fee the purchase price of the auto.

Thus: the Dr. Sherrock Commission. Actually, the Second Dr. Sherrock Commission. I can never be certain, I guess, but it did appear to me at the last moment there, as my finger enjoined the trigger, that recognition had floated to the surface of Dr. Sherrock's eyes. That he remembered me from our previous association. The matter of the first Mrs. Sherrock.

In Round Figures

ERLE STANLEY GARDNER

LESTER LEITH is only one of a huge number of series characters created by the indefatigable Erle Stanley Gardner (1889–1970). The most famous of his crime fighters was Perry Mason, but there also were a number of novels featuring district attorney Doug Selby and a long series about Bertha Cool and Donald Lam, produced under his A. A. Fair pseudonym. But most of Gardner's pulp characters were criminals, including Ed Jenkins (the Phantom Crook), the sinister Patent Leather Kid, the thieving Paul Pry, and Senor Arnaz de Lobo, a professional soldier of fortune and revolutionary.

It is Leith, however, who was the "hero" of the second greatest number of Gardner's crook stories, appearing in more than seventy novelettes (trailing only Ed Jenkins, "the Phantom Crook," who appeared in seventy-three), all written for the pulps. Leith approached his thievery from a slightly different angle, working as both a detective and as a Robin Hood figure of a kind that was very popular in the Depression era. He stole from the rich, but only those who were themselves crooks, and he unfailingly gave the money to charities—after taking a twenty percent "recovery" fee.

Debonair, quick-witted, and wealthy, he enjoyed the perks of his fortune, checking the newspapers in the comfort of his penthouse apartment for new burglaries and robberies to solve, and from which he could reclaim the stolen treasures.

He has a valet, Beaver, nicknamed "Scuttle" by Leith, who is a secret plant of Sergeant Arthur Ackley. Leith, of course, is aware that his manservant is an undercover operative, using that knowledge to plant misinformation to frustrate the policeman again and again.

"In Round Figures" was originally published in the August 23, 1930, issue of *Detective Fiction Weekly*; it was first collected in *The Amazing Adventures of Lester Leith* (New York, The Dial Press, 1980).

IN ROUND FIGURES

Erle Stanley Gardner

LESTER LEITH rolled over in bed and grinned at the ceiling. In the lazy flexing of his well-oiled muscles there was something of the litheness of a stretching panther.

The electric clock on the dresser marked the hour of ten-thirty.

Leith stretched forth a silk-sheathed arm and rang for his valet. Almost instantly a door swung upon silent hinges and a huge form made an awkward bow.

"You rang, sir?"

"My bath, Scuttle."

"Yes, sir."

The door closed as silently as it had opened. But the square-shouldered valet had oozed into the room between the opening and closing of the door. On ponderous tiptoes he set about the tasks of the morning. The bath water roared into the great tub. The clothes closet disclosed an assortment of expensive clothes, from which the heavy hands of the servant picked suitable garments.

Propped up in bed, smoking a cigarette, Lester Leith regarded the man through lazy-lidded eyes.

"Scuttle, you remind me of something, but I can't quite place what it is. Do you suppose you could help?"

The coal-black eyes of the valet glinted into smoldering fires of antagonism. He half-turned his head so that Lester Leith might not surprise the expression of enmity on his face.

"No, sir. I've reminded you of so much, sir. First it was of a reincarnated pirate, and you disregarded my real name to call me Scuttle. Then—"

Leith held up a well manicured hand. "I have it, Scuttle!"

"Yes, sir?"

"A locomotive, Scuttle; a big, black, shiny, powerful locomotive, but running on rubber tires."

"On rubber tires!"

"Quite right, Scuttle. It's the way you have of oozing about the room."

The man straightened. The broad shoulders snapped back. For a quick half-instant the sweeping black mustache bristled with aggressiveness. Then the servant sighed.

"Yes, sir. Very good, sir. The bath is to be just a little warmer than lukewarm, sir?"

"Quite."

The valet used the pretext to ease his huge body into the bathroom. He closed the door, turned, straightened, and the air of servility evaporated from his personality. His black, beady eyes glittered defiance. His hamlike hand knotted into a fist. For seconds he stood quivering with rage.

Lester Leith, lying back on the bunched pillows, chuckled softly and blew a smoke ring at the ceiling. It was as though he took a fiendish delight in flicking this man on the raw.

The valet took a deep breath, regained control of himself, shut off the bath and oozed into the bedroom.

"The bath is ready, sir."

Lester Leith yawned, stretched, paused with one pajamaed leg thrust over the edge of the bed.

"Scuttle, how long's it been since we checked the crime clippings?"

A look of eagerness flashed over the heavy face of the giant servant.

"Some time, sir. There have been several interesting crimes recently."

"Crimes the police haven't been able to solve?"

"Yes, sir."

"And you think I'd be interested?"

"I know it, sir."

"Why?"

"Because of the very valuable loot which the police haven't been able to trace yet."

"Tut, tut, Scuttle, how often must I tell you that my interest in crime is purely academic? That's why I never make personal investigations. I only study the reports published in the newspapers. Scuttle, get out the clippings and I'll glance over them."

And Leith slipped from his pajamas and into the lukewarm tub while the valet opened a drawer and thumbed out an assortment of newspaper clippings dealing with various unsolved crimes. By the time Leith had rubbed himself into a glow, attired himself in faultless flannels, and poured coffee from the electric percolator, the valet had arranged the crime clippings and took up a recital in a husky monotone.

"There was the affair of Mrs. Maybern's diamonds, sir. Missing."

"Robbery?"

"Yes, sir; she had been at a night club, dancing with one of the most attractive . . ."

"Pass it, Scuttle. It's probably blackmail."

"Very well, sir. How about the Greenwell murder?"

"Motive, Scuttle?"

"Robbery and, perhaps, revenge."

"Pass it, Scuttle. Is there, by any chance, a crime with a dash of imagination, with a touch of the bizarre, Scuttle?"

The heavy thumb of the police spy ran through the clippings.

"There's one, sir, but it's a cold trail."

"Tut, tut, Scuttle. You mustn't get the idea I'm seeking to trail these criminals. My interest is purely academic. Let's have the cold trail."

"The Demarest reception, sir."

"Mrs. De Lee Demarest?"

"The same, sir."

"Her reception was quite an affair, Scuttle. Seems to me we received an elaborately engraved invitation, did we not? The body of the invitation was engraved, the name scrolled in by hand. Rather on the ornate side."

"Yes, sir. And you perhaps remember reading of what happened, sir? The gems, the cash, all looted clean—the most carefully planned robbery in the past five years, sir."

Lester Leith poured himself a fresh cup of coffee, creamed and sugared it, lit a fresh cigarette, and sat back in the chair. There was a flickering gleam of real interest in his eyes.

"I never read the newspapers, Scuttle. You should know that. The crime news is all that interests me, and I have you to clip that. But a robbery of that nature interests me. It's a wonder our zealous friend Sergeant Ackley didn't suspect me of the job. Being a society robbery, I presume his first thoughts would be of me. And I suppose the robbers were attired in evening clothes, Scuttle?"

Scuttle, the police spy, refrained from telling Leith that he had been suspected of having a hand in that affair, that all that prevented a severe grueling at headquarters was that the police spies could account for every minute of Leith's time on the day in question.

"No, sir, they were not in evening clothes. In fact, it's quite a story."

"Tell it to me, Scuttle."

"It began with a Mrs. Pensonboy Forster—"

"What a ponderous name, Scuttle! She sounds like a mountain of respectability. One feels instantly that one should know Mrs. Pensonboy Forster, yet I don't remember having heard of her."

"Yes, sir," agreed the valet. "That's the very point. It was the name that enabled her to get into the reception."

"Tell me, Scuttle, was she fat?"

"Was she fat? Why, the woman was a mountain! She weighed three hundred and fifty pounds if she weighed an ounce. And she had a cold, fishy eye that sent chills through everyone she looked at."

Lester Leith pushed back the empty coffee cup, blew a smoke ring.

"Scuttle, I am going to like this case. Tell me more."

"Well, sir, you remember the elaborate invitations. They were printed by Garland. That is, the engraving was done by him. The names were lettered in by some artist that Mrs. De Lee Demarest secured. I understand he charged two thousand dollars."

"Never mind the charge, Scuttle. Mrs. Demarest has plenty of money. Give me the facts."

"Well, sir, the invitations were most distinctive. Each guest had one, and the invitation was in the form of a card, to be presented at the entrance. This Mrs. Pensonboy Forster drove up in a magnificent car, was assisted to the ground, sailed up the stairs, and presented an invitation. The police have it now, sir. It seems to be most regular in form, but the lettering of the name shows little distinctive mannerisms which prove it was not done by the artist engaged by Mrs. Demarest."

"In other words, Scuttle, the invitation was a forgery."

"Precisely so, sir. But the woman who presented it was so substantial, so portly, so—er—so fat, sir, that she was admitted without too close a scrutiny of the invitation."

"But how could a three-hundred-and-fifty-pound woman pull a holdup and get away with it? Her escape, Scuttle, would be quite a problem, even for a resourceful brain."

"She fainted, sir."

"Fainted!"

"Yes, sir. And, of course, there's the key to the whole scheme."

"What are you talking about?"

"The fat woman fainted, and fell downstairs, from the top to the very bottom, sir."

Lester Leith sighed. "What then?"

"Well, sir, you see the reception was in the nature of an announcement party. The daughter of Mrs. Demarest had been married in Europe, and the marriage was kept secret. There was quite a romance."

Lester Leith sighed again, patiently.

The valet flushed.

"It all fits together, if you'll just listen, sir. The marriage was performed in Europe. It was announced at the reception, given in honor of the husband. And there were presents displayed, sir. They were grouped in one of the front rooms and two detectives were employed to watch them. And, of course, the guests wore plenty of gems, sir.

"Therefore, when the woman fainted and fell downstairs, she fell right into the front room where the detectives were guarding the presents. They tried to lift her onto a couch, sir . . . but three hundred and fifty pounds! They just couldn't do it. She was a mountain of flesh, and she groaned frightfully.

"Then there was the clanging of an ambulance gong. Of course, everyone thought one of the other guests had summoned the ambulance, sir. It came to the curb with a big sign on the side: *Proctor & Peabody—Emergency Ambulance.* You know the type of car, sir. But on this one the sign was so big it was almost an advertisement."

Lester Leith nodded.

"They carried this fat woman away in the ambulance, Scuttle?"

The valet shook his head.

"Three stretcher bearers, all clad in white, came into the room. They tried to lift the woman and failed, and they sent out for the driver."

"Then what?"

"Then it happened, sir. The guests were all bunched together. The detectives were bending over the woman, trying to get her on the stretcher. The ambulance men were at very strategic positions. Then the woman sat upright and conked the detectives on the bean!"

"Conked, Scuttle?"

"Yes, sir. That is, tapped them with a heavy object. In this case it was the barrel of a gun. The detectives went to the mat, sir, and the woman swung the business end of the gun toward the guests. The ambulance men got guns out and herded the guests against the wall. They piled all the jewelry and cash on the stretcher, took the most expensive of the gifts, piled them on the stretcher, loaded the stretcher in the ambulance and all drove away."

Lester Leith sighed, a long drawn sigh of utter satisfaction.

"Scuttle, it is perfect!"

"Yes, sir. The loot was worth two hundred thousand—perhaps more."

Lester Leith nodded. "Yes, indeed, Scuttle. It would be. Of course, the success of the whole scheme depended on the fat woman. They couldn't lift her. They couldn't do a thing with her. And a fat woman who has fainted is such an awkward thing to handle. A gentleman is supposed to scoop the delicate form of a lady into iron-muscled arms and convey her to a couch. But in this case it would take a block and tackle."

The valet nodded.

"Yes, indeed, Scuttle. It was artistic. I presume they telephoned the police at once, Scuttle?"

"Yes, sir, and that's the peculiar part of it, sir. You see the ambulance was distinctive. It couldn't have escaped discovery, sir. It had the sign painted right on its side—a very large sign, almost distastefully large. The police realized at once that the ambulance was the point they should concentrate on. They dispatched police cars to form a cordon about the district; but no ambulance left the district. That's why the police feel certain the ambulance drove into a nearby garage."

Lester Leith nodded. "The police, of course, telephoned Proctor & Peabody—to find out if an ambulance had been stolen?"

"Naturally."

"And found out that none had. The ambulance was a complete imitation all the way through. Right?"

"How did you guess that, sir?"

"Simple, Scuttle. It's as simple as the solution to the whole affair. The police simply failed to see the obvious thing, Scuttle."

The valet teetered back and forth on his large feet.

"You mean to say you have deduced a solution to the crime—that is, a knowledge of the identity of the parties who are guilty—from a mere recital of the facts?"

Leith shrugged his shoulders.

"Let us say, a tentative solution, Scuttle. Now, for instance, the social secretary of Mrs. Demarest?"

"Was instantly suspected of complicity, sir. She was taken to headquarters and grilled. It appears that she had been very careless with the engraved invitations. She'd shown them to several people in advance of mailing, although she had been instructed not to do so. And the list of engraved invitations sent out and those remaining in her hands didn't tally. There were two unaccounted for. She *said* she had spilled ink on them and destroyed them, but didn't tell Mrs. Demarest. She got the artist to fix new ones."

Leith nodded again.

"You think it's the social secretary who's guilty?" asked the undercover man. "The police do. They've let her out, but they're shadowing her."

Lester Leith pursed his lips, blew a smoke ring, traced its perimeter with a well-manicured forefinger.

"Tell me, Scuttle. This social secretary. Is she very thin, perhaps?"

"No, sir. She's rather inclined to beauty of figure, sir. She has wonderful curves, and her eyes are quite expressive. She's the sort of a girl the newspapers like to photograph. Her name is Louise Huntington. There's her picture, sir."

Lester Leith stared at the newspaper picture of a beautiful girl. The face was smiling, happy. The well-turned limbs were crossed in such a manner as to show a tantalizing expanse of silken hose.

"Taken before the accusation?"

"So I believe, sir. I understand she was all broken up over the affair. She seems to think she'll never be able to get another position."

"Mrs. Demarest discharged her?"

"Of course, sir. She would, you know."

"Yes, indeed, Scuttle, *she* would."

"Was there anything else about the crime you wished to know, sir?"

Lester Leith did not answer for several minutes. He blew a succession of smoke rings.

"No," he said, at length, "nothing else," and then he chuckled.

"Something amuses you, sir?"

"Yes, Scuttle."

"May I ask what it is, sir?"

"Yes, indeed. I was thinking how perfectly ludicrous you would seem teaching a fat woman how to faint."

The valet's mouth opened and closed several times before his tongue got traction on the words that he sought to utter.

"*Me!* Teaching a fat woman how to faint! Good lord, sir, what an idea!"

"It *is* an idea, isn't it, Scuttle? Do you know, I think I should get a deep mattress to place on the floor. Then I'd have her fall over there in the corner."

"But . . . but . . . sir . . . I don't understand. Who is this fat woman, and where do we get her?"

"Ah, Scuttle, there you've placed your finger upon the point I wished to discuss. We advertise for her, of course. I would suggest a more mature woman, one who is about forty years of age, Scuttle. Experience has taught me that women of that age have adjusted themselves to the wear and tear of life. In short, Scuttle, such a woman would be much more likely to wear tights."

"Wear tights, sir!"

"Precisely. I would suggest green tights particularly if you are able to get a blonde. The advertisement should be worded something like this:

> "*WANTED:* Fair, Fat, and Forty. Good-Natured Woman Who Weighs at Least Three Hundred and Fifty Pounds. Should Know Something About Horses."

"Know something about horses! Have you gone stark, raving crazy, sir?"

"I think not, Scuttle. Evidently you have failed to consider certain elements of the Demarest robbery."

"Yes, sir. Such as?"

"Such as the fact that a woman who weighs three hundred and fifty pounds and deliberately falls downstairs, knowing in advance she won't be hurt, must have had some circus or stage training. Then, when you add the fact that she is rather handy with a gun . . . well, Scuttle, the answer is obvious. She has probably done work with a Wild West show."

"I'm not sure I follow you, sir."

"She fainted and fell, Scuttle. Yet they all knew—that is, those on the inside of the scheme—that she wouldn't be hurt."

"How do you reason that, sir?"

"Because the conking of the detectives was an important part of the scheme. The reasonable time to conk them was when they were bending over to assist the lady to a stretcher, and the person who could most effectively start the conking process was the woman herself."

The police spy stroked his mustache with what was intended to be a thoughtfully meditative gesture. But his washboarded forehead and twisted lips gave evidence of deep perplexity.

"And you want to put in an advertisement, get a fat woman?"

"Precisely."

"Because you think the same woman might answer the ad?"

Lester Leith shrugged his shoulders.

The valet pressed the point.

"Yet that's why you mentioned horses. A circus woman would know horses. You must admit that."

Lester Leith smiled. "Skip along, Scuttle, and insert that want ad. We should start getting replies almost at once."

"But what's the idea of teaching her how to faint?"

"That, Scuttle, is one of the things I must keep absolutely secret. It's between the lady and myself."

"But you don't even know who she is yet . . . Is it that you want to see from the way she acts if she's accustomed to faint? Is that it? A trap?"

Lester Leith glanced at his watch.

"Do you know, Scuttle, there are times when your reasoning powers absolutely surprise me?"

The valet flushed. "Is that so, sir?"

"Absolutely," remarked Lester Leith in a tone of finality. "And, may I add, Scuttle, that this is not one of those times."

Scuttle inserted the ad, but not until he had made an appointment with Sergeant Ackley. Scuttle, known as Beaver on the force, walked from the newspaper offices to find the sergeant, parked in his official red roadster, waiting for him.

"Well, Beaver, you got him working on that Demarest affair. That's fine! We'll tail along and let him lead us to the culprits, if he solves the crime. And then we'll nab both him and them. If he misses fire, nothing will be lost."

Beaver grunted.

"I got him started all right; but no one knows where he'll finish. He gets my goat with his Scuttling me this and his Scuttling me that."

"There, there, Beaver," soothed Ackley. "It won't be but a short time more and then we'll have the goods on him. When we do, you can start in working him over. I promise you fifteen minutes alone in the cell with him. If he resists an officer that'll just be too bad."

"There won't be enough left of him to arraign in court."

Ackley nodded.

"Now tell me about the set-up," he said, fitting a cigar to his lips with that perfect precision which characterizes a man who is about to enjoy some very welcome information.

"Well, I did just as you told me. When he called for the crime clippings I spoke of a couple of things I knew he wouldn't be interested in, then I pulled that Demarest affair and he fell for it right away. He's got an idea that's very logical, too.

"He says the fat woman had to be a tumbler from a circus, probably a Wild West show, and he pointed out reasons that are ironclad. Then he wants me to insert an ad for a fat woman of about the age of this Mrs. Pensonboy Forster. He says I've got to teach her how to faint."

Sergeant Ackley's lips snapped the cigar to an abrupt angle.

"Teach her how to faint!" he exclaimed through clenched teeth. "What does he want to do that for?"

The undercover man assumed an air of sophisticated wisdom.

"Tut, tut, Sergeant. It's simple."

Sergeant Ackley's big hand ripped the cigar from his mouth. He hurled it to the pavement with such force that the wrapper cracked into fragments.

"Where do you get that tut-tut stuff? And what gave you the idea you can drool over me with that air of superiority Leith puts on? Have you been battin' around him so long you think you're one of those masterminds? Because, if you have, I'll bust you so flat you'll make wrapping for a picnic sandwich, you bull-necked, fat-headed, cinder-eyed—"

Beaver made haste to mollify the sergeant.

"No, no. I didn't mean it that way. You got your nerves worked up. What I meant to say was that I've put two and two together from workin' with him so long. Gimme a chance to explain, will you?"

The sergeant took another cigar from his pocket.

"Well, get busy," he growled. "You tut-tut me again and you'll go back to pavements."

"Yes, Sergeant, but remember I've lived with that drawling stuff so long I can't help using some of it. It's unconscious . . . but let's look at the case. I gotta be gettin' back. He'll have more fool things for me to do.

"You see, he figures that one of the fat women who answers his ad will be either someone who has had circus experience, or, perhaps, the very one who pulled the faint on the Demarest job."

Sergeant Ackley's lip curled.

"What a boob you are, Beaver. It ain't nothing like that at all. In the first place, they made a good haul on the Demarest job. The woman who pulled that stunt is sittin' pretty right now. She's out of the picture, and as for finding anybody who'd know her and squeal, that's foolish. If any of the profesh knew her they'd have tipped us off by this time.

"No. It's something else, something deeper. I have an idea he's going to lift the idea and train this fat dame to pull the same stunt for him. It's just the sort of a stunt he'd have thought up. Wonder is that he didn't. Maybe he was back of it all the time."

The spy shook his head. "I'll keep you posted. But it's some funny scheme. Remember, he don't ever rob anybody except thieves. I wish to thunder he'd tip his hand just once! Too bad he smelled out that dictograph we had planted—makes it hard for me to report. But I'll keep you in touch with the situation. How about planting a woman to answer his ad?"

"No. There ain't a woman in the department who could answer the description. All of our lures are the vamping type."

Lester Leith was up early the next morning to receive applications for the position mentioned in his want ad. There were six of them, no more. Some of them were, perhaps, in the three-hundred-pound class, but there were only two who seemed to come anywhere near three hundred and fifty pounds.

Leith made his selection with a judgment that was almost intuitive. He jabbed his forefinger at a woman who stood in a corner.

"Name?"

"Sadie Crane."

"Come in," he said.

The woman was about forty. She weighed well into the three hundreds, yet there was about her a certain feminine attraction. Her figure was wadded with fat, yet gave the suggestion of curves. Her eyes were bright. Her flabby lips twisted in a perpetual smile.

"Side show?" she asked, as soon as she had entered the room where Lester Leith indicated a specially constructed armchair.

The police spy, hovering near the doorway, listened intently.

"Not exactly a side show. You've been in one?"

"Sure. When I started putting on fat I dieted for a while. After I passed two hundred pounds I decided I'd better go the other way and make some money out of it. So I made up for lost time on the sweets . . . and here I am. Been in side shows from Keokuk to breakfast and back."

"Married?"

She shook her head. A tender light came in her eyes. "Widow. I married the Human Skeleton out of Selig's Super Shows. He was at Denver. Poor Jim, he caught cold the second week we'd been married, and he went quick."

Lester Leith bowed his head gravely, silent comment upon the match-like man who had been the love of this mountain of flesh.

"You'd wear tights?"

"No."

Lester Leith gravely regarded the tip of a smoldering cigarette.

"Perhaps your modesty—"

"Modesty, heck!" she interrupted. "It ain't

modesty. I've showed my figure from Maine to California, from Mexico to Canada, and I've showed more skin area than any other woman in the world. I'll wear some professional clothes I've got, a jacket and shorts. That's the way I used to sit in the side shows. That's the way I'm willing to work."

Lester Leith nodded.

"That is reasonable. The salary will be twenty-five dollars a day. You will have to learn how to faint."

The fat woman leaned over and looked at Leith earnestly. "What the devil are you talking about?"

"Fainting. You'll have to learn to drop over to one side, or flat on your back in a faint. You'll have to learn to take the fall without hurting yourself. We'll have mattresses and sofa pillows to break the fall at first. Later on we'll gradually take them away and you can fall on the floor."

She sighed. "Living around a side show for fifteen years, I've naturally seen lots of freaks—but you're a new type."

"But you're willing?"

"Sure, I'm willing. Only I don't want to take any exercise that's going to get rid of any fat. This fat is my stock in trade. At my present weight I'm an attraction. If I should drop a hundred pounds or so I wouldn't be anything but a fat mommer."

Lester Leith motioned to the valet.

"Will you please explain to the other applicants that their services are not wanted, Scuttle? And you'd better get their names and addresses. That will make them feel better. Tell them the position is temporarily filled."

The valet nodded, took pencil and paper, and oozed through the door.

Lester Leith glanced significantly at the grinning fat girl who reclined in the specially constructed chair.

"You can keep your mouth shut?"

"Like a clam."

"Now is a good time to begin."

"From now on, Mr. Leith, you don't hear anything out of me except clam-talk."

Leith reached for a checkbook. "I will advance your salary for the first week." He wrote and signed a check.

"You'll be expected to be available at all times. And I'd prefer to have you keep off the streets. So I've arranged to rent the adjoining apartment. It's all furnished, ready for you to move in. Your living expenses are, of course, to be paid by me."

The fat hand folded along the tinted oblong of paper. The twinkling eyes regarded the figures.

"Two hundred and fifty bucks!"

Lester Leith nodded. "I like round figures."

She caught the point, stretched out her legs and let her eyes drift over her form.

"When that guy with the mustache comes back, get him to give me a pull, and I'll get out of this chair an' go look the apartment over. Better order two quarts of whipping cream and lots of candy. I drink pure cream. Seems to agree with my stomach. The candy I eat for a pick-up. A fat person has lots of body to keep fed."

The door opened. The valet appeared with a list of addresses.

"Got them all, Scuttle?"

"All five of them, sir."

"Pass them over. And you might help Mrs. Crane out of the chair."

The undercover man approached the chair, heaved and tugged. Slowly the inertia of the thickly folded flesh was overcome and the woman got her thick legs under the fat body. Her eyes and lips were smiling.

"Cheer up, big boy, you're goin' to have lots of this to do."

"Show Mrs. Crane into the adjoining apartment, Scuttle—and arrange to have half a gallon of whipping cream delivered every day. And order a twenty-five-pound case of assorted chocolates."

"Yes, sir."

"And then I'll want a social secretary, Scuttle. I think I'll go into the side-show business—not in a commercial way, but as a social activity."

"That'll be great," beamed Sadie Crane.

"Gimme a week an' I can put on twenty pounds. It'll seem good to get back into the game. You goin' to get a human skeleton?"

"Perhaps. Have you any suggestions?"

"I'd like to help pick 'm. Poor Jim was sort of sandy complexioned. If you could find another like him—"

Lester Leith nodded. "You shall have the sole selection."

The woman waddled slowly from the room.

The valet escorted her to the corridor. As he closed the door and indicated her apartment entrance, he leaned forward and lowered his voice.

"Find out just what he wanted?"

The fat woman's lips mouthed a succession of words, but no sound came from the throat.

The police spy puckered his forehead.

"Huh?" he said.

The puffy lips again went through the motions of speaking—silent words that conveyed no intelligence.

"What's the idea?" he asked.

She gurgled a laugh that rippled the folds of her loose garments.

"Clam-talk," she said.

And with ponderous dignity she opened the door of the apartment and side-swayed herself through the entrance.

Lester Leith, stretched before the wide open windows, listened to the distant voice of the city as it droned through the hot afternoon.

"I think, Scuttle, that we'll give Miss Louise Huntington a position. I regard her discharge as being rather an unwarranted act on the part of Mrs. De Lee Demarest. The salary, Scuttle, will be twice her former one. I have asked her to call, in a telegram which I dispatched in your absence."

The valet gulped.

"Think she can tell you anything about the robbery?"

Lester Leith regarded the man with cold eyes.

"I should hardly ask her, Scuttle. There's a knock at the door. You might answer it. I believe Miss Huntington is answering the telegram in person."

The police spy regarded his employer with smoldering eyes.

"You've got some clue on that Demarest affair. I believe that slick mind of yours has doped out a solution. You're just sittin' back an' laughin' at the police, and getting ready to hijack the swag—"

"The door, Scuttle!"

The big valet caught himself, gulped, turned, and pussyfooted to the outer door.

"Mr. Lester Leith?" asked a remarkably sweet voice.

Lester Leith himself came to the entrance hall and greeted the young woman.

"Miss Huntington?"

"Yes. I received your telegram. I'd like a position most awfully right now, but it's only fair to tell you the police are hounding my footsteps. There was even a shadow following me here."

She was beautiful, both of face and figure, but there was a sad-eyed expression to the face which spoke of recent worries.

Lester Leith smiled. "Please sit down. A police shadow is rather annoying, but not the least bit of an impediment to such activities as you'd have in my employ. Tell me, do you know anything about side shows?"

"Side shows?"

"Yes."

"My gracious! No!"

"That's fine. I always like a social secretary to start with no preconceived notions. Have you, perhaps, a good memory for names?"

"Yes, sir."

"Could you recall the names of the invited guests to Mrs. De Lee Demarest's reception?"

"I think so."

"That will be fine. I'd like to have engraved announcements of the side show sent to the same list of names—and there'll be some cards to have printed. *Fattest Human in the World.* And *Skelo, the Human Match.* You understand, Miss

Huntington, that the side show would be educational, but quite entertaining. And then I'd want to exhibit the most perfectly matched diamond necklace in the city."

The late social secretary of Mrs. De Lee Demarest regarded Lester Leith with eyes that were pools of suspicion.

"Are you trying to kid me?"

"No. I am serious."

"Is this job on the level?"

"You are to be the sole judge of that. I shall give you a week's salary in advance. You may quit at any time."

The girl settled back in the chair and crossed her knees in the position in which the newspaper photographer had snapped her. She was beautiful, judged by any standards, and something about Lester Leith's tone caused the sadness of her eyes to vanish into a twinkle of humor.

"If you're on the up-and-up I'm going to like this job," she said. "Maybe, after you get to know me better, you'll tell me what it's about."

Leith nodded gravely.

"I am telling you now. I think the Garland Printery will do excellent work on the invitations."

The police spy bent forward, his eyes lighting up.

"The same company that engraved the Demarest invitations!" he blurted.

"The same, Scuttle. Miss Huntington, does the Garland Printery do hand lettering as well as printing and engraving?"

The girl was studying his eyes with eyes that were singularly searching.

"So I understand."

"Very well. You might get in touch with Mr. Garland. You placed your order with him personally in the Demarest affair?"

She nodded assent.

"Your salary is twice what it was in your former position. I'd like to have you take one of the vacant apartments in this building, so you'll be available. I have already made arrangements with the owner. The rent is paid. It's only necessary to select your apartment."

Her voice was tonelessly level.

"There'll be only one key?"

Lester Leith smiled. "At the end of a week you may know me better."

The puzzled eyes swept his face.

"That still won't be very well—a side show, a human skeleton, a fat woman, the most perfectly matched diamond necklace in the city—are you crazy?"

And then something in the lazy drawl of Lester Leith's voice and in the idea of a side show brought laughter to the lips of the girl.

"I think," she said at length, "I'm beginning to get the idea."

A hot week of dreary monotony passed.

Sadie Crane, attired in vivid silk shorts and a scanty jacket, practiced fainting. She did it with perspiring good nature, the valet looking on, tugging at her arms as she arose from each fall.

Double mattresses were placed in the corner to cushion her falls. The eager eyes of the valet followed her every motion.

Louise Huntington tapped at a typewriter, addressing envelopes. Lester Leith came and went, his comings marked by casual comments of appreciation, his goings marked by police surveillance.

The police found out nothing. The strange routine of the apartment proceeded uninterrupted. The human skeleton, picked by Mrs. Crane, flitted in and out, surveying the tumbling performance with mournful eyes. He spent his evenings squiring the fat woman. Between the two was a fast friendship. He was a chronic pessimist. The woman preserved the unruffled calm of a jovial disposition and an indestructible optimism.

The mattresses became dented with deep furrows where the falling body banged itself a dozen times an hour. The face of the valet became haggard. His surreptitious reports to Sergeant Ackley were interspersed with querulous complaint.

The woman achieved skill at falling sidewise, rolling on her back, straightening her muscles and becoming rigid, an immovable mountain of flesh.

"Will you tell me why you're doing that?" asked Arthur Spinner, the human skeleton.

She turned toward him a flushed face on which the sweat had left shining streaks. The clacking of the typewriter in the corner abruptly ceased, proof of the interest of Miss Huntington in the question. Scuttle paused with a handkerchief halfway to his forehead, his ears attuned for the reply.

The fleshy throat convulsed with muscular effort. The smiling fat lips mouthed a silent reply.

"More clam-talk!" rasped the human skeleton.

Sadie Crane laughed. The tapping fingers of the social secretary once more sought the keys, and Scuttle groaned.

It was at that moment that Lester Leith inserted his latchkey, entered the apartment, and surveyed the strange assortment of humanity. His eyes were glinting. In his right hand he carried a black bag.

"Ladeez and gentllllemen!" he intoned. "Step forward and observe the most perfectly matched diamond necklace in the city. Note the purity and fire of the stones. Note the wonderful workmanship of the clasp. Observe one hundred thousand dollars in scintillating, sparkling, coruscating gleams of imprisoned fire!"

The two freaks crowded forward. The police spy raised himself so that his coal-black eyes could gaze over the heads of the others. Louise Huntington regarded the opened bag with open mouth and wide eyes.

The black bag lay wide open. White cotton backed a necklace which seemed to snatch pure fires from the air and send them out in glittering brilliance.

It was Louise Huntington who broke the silence.

"I'm quitting my job," she said.

Lester Leith arched his eyebrows.

"Personal reasons, or anything that might be remedied by an increase in salary?"

"Personal. If anything should happen to that necklace, I'd go to jail for the rest of my life. The police suspect me of one robbery already—and, of course, there's the added fact that you're as mad as a March hare."

Leith indicated an inner room where he had fitted up a combined den and study.

"Perhaps," he said gravely, "the time has come for us to talk," and he led the girl into the room, and closed the door.

There ensued nothing save the rumble of cautious tones. Scuttle's ear, plastered against the doorknob, heard nothing. Yet the effect of that conversation was magical.

The girl came from the room, smiling, vivacious. She went back to her typewriter with eager fingers. From time to time she glanced at Lester Leith as he busied himself with hat, coat, and stick. The moment Leith slammed the corridor doors, the valet pounced upon the typewriting girl.

"What . . ."

She kept her fingers busy on the machine. Her smiling lips parted in a most tantalizing manner, and then she began to form words which carried no sound.

The valet scowled in anger.

"Clam-talk," said the girl, and lowered her eyes to the work in the machine.

The rippling laugh that floated across the room came from Sadie Crane, the "fattest woman in the world."

Two days later the valet spy took it upon himself to question Lester Leith.

"The fat woman faints almost perfectly. I've eliminated the mattress, sir, and she makes—er—perfect landings."

"Very good, Scuttle."

"And what, may I ask, sir, is holding up our—er—circus side show?"

Lester regarded him with judicial gravity, then lowered his voice.

"Scuttle, can you keep a secret?"

"Yes, sir."

"Promise?"

"On my word of honor, sir."

"Very well, Scuttle, I am waiting for another ambulance robbery."

"Another ambulance robbery!"

"Precisely. You see, Scuttle, if my theory is correct, there will be another robbery within a few days in which an ambulance will figure. The ambulance will bear a large sign painted upon it, identifying it with Proctor & Peabody. It will make the ambulance so distinctive that it will seem impossible for it to vanish.

"Acting upon that theory, the police will comb the neighborhood in a house-to-house, garage-to-garage canvass. And that's all the good their search will do. The ambulance will have vanished as completely as though it had never existed."

"And then?"

"Then, Scuttle, we'll have our circus side show."

And Lester Leith, possessing himself of a polished cane, hat, and gloves, strolled out for an afternoon constitutional in the park.

The valet, after taking due precautions against being followed, oozed to a drugstore, telephoned Sergeant Ackley, and arranged for an appointment in an out-of-the-way parking station. Here he crawled into the red roadster and unburdened himself of many conjectures, reports, surmises, and facts.

Sergeant Ackley mouthed a cigar with a tempo which gradually increased until he whipped a damp newspaper from the rear of the car. "Haven't seen the *Record*, have you, Beaver?"

"No, why?"

Sergeant Ackley handed it over. Across the top of the front page was a screaming headline.

Phantom Ambulance Again Figures in Crime.

"Good gosh!" ejaculated the spy. "How did he dope that out?"

Sergeant Ackley's eyes were narrowed. He spoke with the manner of one who weighs his words carefully.

"He's smarter than the devil, Beaver—there's no getting around that. From the very first time you told him about the Demarest robbery he knew the answer. You can gamble on that. He wouldn't have tied up all that money in the preparation he's making if he hadn't been certain.

"Every time he's worked on a case, he's been able to get something from the newspaper clippings that the police missed completely. I've tried to figure out what it could be this time, but it beats me."

Beaver grunted.

"Well, I've still got the original clippings. I'll sit up tonight and study 'em. And I'll study the account of this last robbery in the *Record.* Maybe I can find out what he had in his mind."

"Think you're brighter than I am, eh, Beaver?"

"No. It ain't that. It's just that I thought maybe—"

"Well, forget it. I've covered that ground thoroughly. But we'll do one thing. We'll start shadowing this guy as though he was studded with diamonds in platinum settings. Eventually he'll lead us to the chaps we want. Then, maybe, we'll hook them for robbery and him for hijacking."

Beaver nodded slowly.

"And there's just a chance I can pump some information out of him. He's been acting sort of confidential lately. Gimme that paper and I'm going to be the one to break the news to him. That'll give me a break. He'll see those headlines, an' maybe he'll talk."

Scuttle was sitting facing the door when Lester Leith returned, and he thrust the folded paper forward before Leith had even deposited his hat and stick.

"There you are, sir."

"Where am I, Scuttle?"

"Right there on the front page. The mysterious ambulance figures in another robbery. This time it was shorter, quicker action. They got away with a bag from a bank messenger. The traffic police were notified by a prearranged signal. But the ambulance disappeared. The police have narrowed it down to a district of not more than forty square blocks. They're making an intensive search of that district."

Lester Leith took the paper from his valet, crumpled it into a ball and tossed it, unread, into the black cavern of the cold fireplace.

"Well, gang, we're ready to start."

"But aren't you interested in the account of the ambulance, sir?"

Leith shook his head.

"Scuttle, cover both depots, find out every train that leaves after ten o'clock this evening and before eleven thirty. Get me a drawing room on each one of those trains where such accommodations are available. You might mention when you get the tickets that they are for a woman whose weight is somewhat above the average. Scuttle, I want no slip-up in the reservations."

The valet's eyes glinted with the light that comes into a cat's eyes when the cat hears the faint sound of motion just back of a mouse hole.

"Yes, sir. Where shall I get the tickets to, sir?"

"Any place, Scuttle, just so it's at least four hundred miles away. Pick out various cities, depending upon the direction in which the train's going."

"Yes, sir, but there might be fifteen or twenty such trains, sir. It's the time when most of the crack trains leave."

"I would estimate the number at somewhere around that figure, Scuttle. Please get me a drawing room on each one of the trains."

The valet sighed. "Yes, sir."

"And at precisely nine-two tonight I shall have an errand for you to do, a most important errand."

"Yes, sir?"

"I shall want you to take these diamonds, the best matched necklace in the city, and show them to an artist in order to have a black and white drawing made. I shall want you to take Mrs. Crane with you. I shall want Mrs. Crane to have a suitcase all packed, ready to travel."

Sadie Crane regarded him for a minute with a puzzled frown. But she said no word.

The valet fairly oozed eagerness.

"Yes, sir. Your instructions will be obeyed to the letter. At nine-two, sir? May I ask why you fix that particular minute?"

Lester Leith lit a cigarette, blew a smoke ring.

"Because, Scuttle, that happens to be the exact time I wish you to be at the place I am going to send you."

And Lester Leith walked into his den, stretched himself out in an easy chair, and sent spiraling clouds of blue smoke drifting upward from the end of his cigarette. His eyes followed those twisting spirals of smoke with deep concentration.

Only Louise Huntington, the social secretary, showed no concern or excitement. Her face did not even change expression.

The valet took advantage of the first opportunity to get a telephone. In a guarded tone he apprised Sergeant Ackley of the latest developments.

"What's this fat woman look like?" asked Ackley. "If she's going to make a trip we'd better be ready to tail her."

The undercover man chuckled.

"She tips the beam at three hundred and fifty. If you can't find that sort of a woman in a drawing room on a train, one of us is crazy."

"Can that line of chatter," snapped Sergeant Ackley, "and remember you're making an official report. We won't try to tail you. You just go wherever he sends you, but contact the office as soon as you can reach a telephone, and keep us posted. Better rush back now—he'll be giving that fat dame secret instructions."

Scuttle laughed again, louder, more jubilantly.

"Sarge, I've got my rod, and I've got my bracelets. If that lump of tallow can pull anything on me you can start me back to the pavements tomorrow."

It was precisely seventeen minutes after nine o'clock in the evening. Three faces bent over a glittering necklace of diamonds. There was the heavy face of Scuttle, the valet; the jovial, good-natured face of Sadie Crane, the professional fat woman. And, in addition, there was the sharp, keenly thoughtful face of Stanley Garland, sole owner and proprietor of the Garland Printery.

"Well," said Garland, "what's he want done?"

"A black and white drawing," replied Scuttle.

Garland laughed. "I am an engraver. I have been a sign painter. I have done some art work. But will you tell me why any man should think an artist needed a real diamond necklace to copy from? If there is anything that is sketched entirely different from life it is a diamond. After all, my friends, art is mimicry. And when it comes to sketching light, one must use symbols. And a diamond is imprisoned light."

And Stanley Garland stood back and snapped his bony fingers, twisted the little cluster of waxed hairs that adhered to his upper lip, and gazed at his two visitors with obvious superiority.

Scuttle shrugged his heavy shoulders.

"I'm obeyin' orders. He said to take the necklace to you an' get a receipt. He said for the woman to take a few things and put them in a suitcase and be ready to travel. She's taking the ten o'clock Flyer.

"Now if you can put any of that stuff together and make sense out of it you can do more than I can. But the wages I get every month come from this chap, Leith, and when he says do something I do it."

Stanley Garland bristled.

"But I am an artist! I do unique illustrations for place cards. And I take orders from no one. I execute commissions, yes! But orders, *NO!*"

The fat woman placed a round hand upon the shoulder of the irate printer.

"Aw, be a sport! Give him a break."

"And a receipt for the diamonds," reminded Scuttle.

Stanley Garland looked at the diamonds once more.

"Where did he get them? I have heard about this perfectly matched necklace. I did the engraving for the invitations to his side show. But I have heard nothing of the history of this necklace. Who owns it? Where did it come from? What jeweler matched it? Was it purchased or borrowed?"

The undercover man stared gloomily.

"Now, brother, you're askin' real questions. We've had fifty men trying to find out the same thing for ten days, and they haven't uncovered a thing."

"Humph!" said Stanley Garland.

Sadie Crane waddled her impatient bulk across the office that had been fitted up at one end of the printing establishment. She carried her suitcase in her left hand—a suitcase packed under specific instructions from Lester Leith. It contained her professional costume—the jacket and the silk shorts—nothing else.

She walked to the door that opened into the printery—a door that opened inward. She put the suitcase down on the printery side of this door. Beyond gleamed the polished metal of huge presses, the dim perspective of the darkened printery.

Lester Leith had given her a sketch of the floor plan of the establishment. He seemed perfectly familiar with every detail. How Lester Leith had known these things she did not ask. She understood, generally, that Stanley Garland had a uniform method of impressing customers who called in the evening to consult with him upon important assignments. He had the lighting of the office just so, the dim perspective of the printery showing just so, behind the open door, and he always snapped his fingers and twisted his mustache and proclaimed he was an artist.

Lester Leith had advised her of all these things in detail. It was, of course, possible that he had secured the information from Louise Huntington, who had brought several orders to the office of the printery.

Now Stanley Garland made an exclamation of impatience.

"Take back the diamonds. I will tell him when I see him how foolish he is to send such a model. But you can tell him that, having once seen them, Stanley Garland can make a perfect . . ."

He broke off. There was the sound of a knob upon the outer door, turning very softly, very slowly.

The undercover man shot out a guarding hand to the diamonds.

The outer door swung slowly open.

The white face of Louise Huntington appeared in the crack. Scuttle recognized her, and the hand that had been at his hip relaxed slightly. But the hand that had held the diamond necklace remained in place.

"Hello, dearie!" said roly-poly Sadie Crane.

The girl acknowledged the salutation with a nod.

"Well," snapped Garland, "come in—if you're coming in."

"Are you alone?" asked Scuttle, suspiciously.

She nodded her head, came in, and kicked the door shut behind her. Then her right arm, coming slowly up, disclosed the glint of businesslike, blue steel.

"Those diamonds," she said, "are stolen. Put up your hands!"

Sheer surprise held the figures in that room motionless.

"Stolen!" exclaimed Scuttle.

The girl nodded down the barrel of the shaking gun.

"Don't point that gun this way. You might let it go off," said Scuttle, moving toward her.

"P-p-put up your hands!" said the girl. "I shall shoot!"

"Nonsense!" snapped Scuttle and took the gun from the quivering hand. "You fool! You might have killed somebody."

The girl flung herself against his shoulder and began to sob.

"No, no. I couldn't have. The gun wasn't loaded!"

The undercover man snapped back the breech of the weapon, laughed, and tossed it on the table.

"She's right. It wasn't loaded."

Stanley Garland regarded the valet with speculative eyes.

"You are brave, my friend. You advanced in the face of a threatening weapon in the hands of a hysterical woman."

"Bosh!" disclaimed Scuttle. "I've had experience with 'em. She wouldn't have shot, even if the gun had been loaded, but she might have jiggled her hand so bad the trigger got pulled. That was the danger."

"Nevertheless, it was brave."

Scuttle turned to the girl.

"Come on, Louise, kick through. What was the big idea?"

The girl sobbed, straightened, dried her eyes.

"Well, thank God, that's over with," she said.

Scuttle let his beady eyes bore into hers.

"Look here, you didn't think that necklace was stolen at all. You had orders from Lester Leith, now, didn't you?"

The girl hesitated, gulped, and nodded.

"Yes, I did. He told me to take this empty gun, come here and hold you up, on the pretext that the gems were stolen and that I thought you were all accomplices. Then I was to get the gems and go back into the printery . . . and then comes the funny part . . . I was to throw the stones out of the window and hide in the printery until Sergeant Ackley came."

Scuttle stiffened with astonishment.

"Sergeant Ackley!"

"Yes, I was to telephone him just before I came in here, telling him what I was to do. But I wasn't to tell anyone what I had done with the gems. I was to let them search me, and search the printery. I think Mr. Leith wanted Ackley to think the stones were hidden somewhere in the printery, and that I was a thief. I guess he wanted a search made."

Scuttle sat down in a chair.

"I've seen that goof pull some fool schemes, but this is the worst of the lot. You telephoned Ackley?"

"Yes, of course."

"He said he'd be here in fifteen minutes."

Sadie Crane glanced at a huge watch that was strapped around her fat wrist.

"I gotta be goin'. I gotta catch that train."

"You got a cab waiting?" asked Louise.

The fat woman nodded. "A special cab with a wide door, dearie."

"I saw it outside," said the girl in a toneless voice.

"What I don't understand . . ." began Scuttle, and stopped as a cold circle of metal touched his neck.

He rolled his eyes backward, saw the snapping orbs of Stanley Garland, the thin lips, the shrewd features.

"You are a brave man," said Garland, "and I do not take chances with you. Get them up, quickly! And this gun *is* loaded!"

The undercover man read the expression in those snapping eyes, and his hands shot up in the air, instantly, and without hesitation.

The exploring hands of Stanley Garland fished in Scuttle's hip pockets, found the service revolver, the handcuffs.

"Ah!" he purred, "a trap, perhaps. You are a special officer, eh? Well, my special officer, we shall give you a taste of your own medicine. How would you like to feel the bite of your own handcuffs, eh?"

And the printer clicked the handcuffs on Scuttle's wrists. Then he turned to the women—the beautiful social secretary, whose sobs had dried as though by magic, and the professional fat woman who regarded the whole proceeding with bubbling good nature.

"Stay where you are," he said. "A move and you will be dead."

And he scooped up the necklace which had been described as the most perfectly matched diamond necklace in the city, and darted through the door into the printery. He slammed that door shut, and there was the click of a bolt.

Scuttle regarded his handcuffed wrists in impotent fury.

"Well, of all things!" said Louise Huntington. "Now what do you think of that?"

Sadie Crane looked at her watch.

"I gotta make that train, an' I got to have my shorts an' my jacket. I promised him I would, an' he's been just like a brother to me! And now that sneaky-eyed cuss has gone and locked the door on my suitcase!"

Suddenly the roar of a revolver sounded from the printery. A call for help. That call was in the unmistakable voice of Lester Leith.

Then came the sounds of a struggle, of articles turning over with a crash. Type, piles of paper, chairs, tables, marble slabs, crashed to the floor. Then—silence.

"If you could just lean against that door right," suggested Scuttle to the three-hundred-and-fifty-pound woman, "I have an idea I could kick the lock and—"

He never finished. The bolt shot back and Lester Leith appeared on the threshold. His clothes were torn. His collar was ripped off. There was dust on his expensive evening suit. His hat was gone.

"What's all this?" he asked.

Scuttle regarded him with black, accusing eyes.

"That's what I want to know."

Lester Leith slumped in a chair. For once his calm control of himself and the situation seemed to have slipped from his grasp.

"I thought Garland was guilty of those Demarest and other ambulance robberies. I got Louise to pretend those gems were stolen, thinking Garland might fall into my trap when he heard the police were coming. I felt I could hide in the printery, watch him as he escaped, and that he might direct me to the hiding place of the Demarest loot.

"It worked like a charm, but when I tried to arrest him, he fought with the skill of a professional. And he had an extra gun on him. I took one away. He had another."

"Mine," admitted Scuttle.

Lester Leith regarded him reproachfully.

"Scuttle, I'm surprised. You shouldn't go around armed. That was where my plans went awry. He had that extra gun. I escaped being shot by a miracle—but, Sadie, you *must* get that train!"

She nodded.

"But my suitcase was locked up in the other room."

"Get it," said Lester Leith, "and get started! If you miss the train, my whole side show will be ruined."

The fat woman waddled toward the printery door.

"Did you really telephone Ackley?" asked Scuttle of Louise Huntington.

She shook her head.

"That was just the story I was to tell."

Scuttle washboarded his forehead.

"This is all too deep for me. But I'll get him right now."

He awkwardly worked the telephone, and got Sergeant Ackley on the wire. While he was talking with the sergeant, Sadie Crane waddled out of the room, her face streaming perspiration with the effort for speed.

Her heavy steps sounded on the short flight of stairs outside the door. Then there was the grinding of gears and her cab rolled away.

It was at that moment Scuttle finished his conversation and dropped the receiver back on the hook.

"There's more to this than appears on the surface," he said, fastening his coal-black eyes on Leith. "Ackley says he had you tailed and you slipped the shadow."

Leith nodded ruefully. He took a cigarette from the torn pocket of his dinner jacket and put it to his lips.

"Admitted, Scuttle. This is one time I made the mistake of actually trying to solve a crime riddle instead of taking only an academic interest in it. Is Sergeant Ackley coming?"

"Right now," snapped the undercover man.

"I'll tell him all about it when he gets here," said Lester Leith. "I'm all out of breath now."

It was but a matter of minutes before the wailing siren of the police car outside was followed by rapid steps, and Sergeant Ackley at the head of a determined knot of blue-coated men, thrust his way into the room.

"What's going on here?" he asked.

Beaver, the undercover agent, winked warningly at his superior.

"Take off these handcuffs and I'll tell my story first," he said.

Sergeant Ackley fitted a key to the cuffs, clicked them open.

"Shoot," he said.

Beaver, still keeping in the character of Scuttle, the valet, told his story; told it from the standpoint of a puzzled servant who didn't know what it was all about, but wanted the police to know the facts.

When he had finished, Sergeant Ackley turned to the social secretary.

"Now you."

The girl hesitated.

"Tell the truth, Louise," said Lester Leith.

"All of it?" she asked.

"All of it," said Lester Leith.

"Well, it started after I got my employment at Mr. Leith's place. Things just didn't seem right, and I was going to quit. Then Mr. Leith told me I was under suspicion in connection with the Demarest affair—which I knew already, of course. And he thought he knew who was really guilty.

"He told me if I would do just as he instructed he felt confident he could trap the criminal into exposing his guilt. Naturally, I agreed to remain on and follow his orders.

"Then, tonight, Mr. Leith told me to take an empty gun, go here and try to hold up Scuttle, telling him the necklace was stolen. He said Scuttle would take the gun away from me, and that I was to be sure and tell him I had notified you to come here and that the circumstances of your coming were such that you'd search the place.

"If Scuttle didn't take the gun away from me, I was to take the diamond necklace, run into the printery, and toss the stones out of the window."

Sergeant Ackley frowned.

Scuttle interposed a comment.

"Lester Leith, of course," he said significantly, "being concealed in the printery all the time. When it reached that stage he'd have interfered."

"I didn't know anything about that," said the girl.

Sergeant Ackley nodded his approval.

"Good point, Scuttle. I was just about to make it myself when you interrupted."

The sergeant turned to Lester Leith.

"And now we'll hear your story. It looks very much as though you'd finally stubbed your toe, my supercilious friend."

Leith raised a hand in a gesture of deprecation.

"Tut, tut, my dear sergeant, you *must* learn not to jump at conclusions. Wait until you hear my story. The law requires that a man shall have a hearing before being judged guilty, you know."

"You'll have your chance, fast enough," said Sergeant Ackley, "and just remember that anything you say can be used against you."

Lester Leith nodded, made some shift to straighten his torn and rumpled garments.

"You'll pardon my appearance, Sergeant?"

"Oh, most certainly," said the Sergeant, with an exaggerated air of nicety.

Lester Leith lit a fresh cigarette.

"Thank you, Sergeant. You see, I was interested in the Demarest affair. Of course you know of my penchant for studying the newspaper accounts of crime. And the newspaper clippings of the Demarest robbery pointed to what was, at least to my mind, an obvious clue."

Sergeant Ackley hitched well forward in his chair.

"Yes, I thought so. What was the clue?"

"The ambulance, Sergeant. You see, the ambulance figured as an integral part of the scheme. It had the words *Proctor & Peabody* painted on it, and everyone agreed that those words were painted quite prominently, too prominently to be in good taste.

"Now Proctor & Peabody run a line of ambulances and of hearses. It is impossible that a car could have their name lettered on it and escape detection. After the Demarest affair the roads were blocked within a given district and all cars within that district subjected to close scrutiny. Yet the ambulance vanished. Now I had a theory about that, but I couldn't be absolutely certain. I determined to wait for a short time and see if the ambulance wasn't used again. It was such a good idea and it worked so easily in the Demarest robbery that I felt certain the criminals would use it again.

"You know the answer. It was used, and most effectively. Once more the ambulance vanished from the face of the earth. But by that time I was certain of my theory.

"You see, the invitation presented by Mrs. Pensonboy Forster when she secured admission to the Demarest affair was forged. The engraving was forged perfectly, but the art work—the hand lettering of each guest's name, added later to the engraved invitation—the lettering showed discrepancies.

"You suspected the social secretary because the forgery of the engraving was so perfect that you felt the invitations must have been left where they would be accessible to the forger. But you overlooked the fact that the lettering was not so faithfully copied.

"Therefore, I came to the conclusion that the person who forged the invitation for Mrs. Pensonboy Forster had had access to the blank engraved invitation, but not to the *completed* invitation. Yet he was an artist or he wouldn't have drawn in the name as cleverly as he did.

"And the ambulance affair also pointed to an artist. You see, Sergeant, an ambulance legitimately bearing the name of *Proctor & Peabody*, displayed quite prominently, could never have escaped detection. But a sign painter–artist could easily have lettered the name on flexible curtains which could have been adjusted to a specially-made delivery truck, and made it look like an ambulance.

"The curtains could be snapped on, and the truck changed into an ambulance. They could instantly have been taken off, and the 'ambulance' would revert to a commercial truck.

"That suggested a business establishment with a light delivery truck. It suggested a criminal with access to engraving facilities, with access to the Demarest invitations. It suggested a criminal who was also an artist and a sign painter.

"You see, now, Sergeant, how the finger of suspicion pointed to Stanley Garland. He had but to fill in an extra, blank invitation with some of his own hand lettering, and his accomplice was passed into the Demarest reception. The rest was easy. His accomplices could be men who were actually employed in the printery. They changed the truck into an ambulance, looted the place, changed the ambulance back into a truck, and went through the police cordon with no difficulty whatever. The police recognized the truck with the sign of the Garland Printery upon it, and raised not so much as a question."

Sergeant Ackley heaved a great sigh.

"It sounds reasonable," he admitted, "and yet it's so obvious, why didn't we think of that? Go on."

The clubman shrugged his shoulders.

"The rest was easy, Sergeant, too easy. I secured some kunzite made into a necklace. That stone has almost as much fire as a diamond. Against white cotton it will fool anyone who is not an expert. By a process of suggestion I made everyone think it was a very valuable diamond necklace. Then I had my valet bring it to Garland.

"I knew he would be tempted. So I arranged to speed up the affair a bit. I had Louise Huntington come in with an empty gun and claim the necklace was stolen, that she had the police on the way. And I primed her with a story to tell, after Scuttle had taken the gun away from her, that would appeal to the ears of Garland alone.

"It was a story that sounded foolish unless its object had been to make the police enter the place to search the printery. Of course, Garland saw the scheme immediately. He thought I was onto him, and that the police were on the way. He had to get away rapidly and take what loot he could with him, so he decided he might as well take this well-matched diamond necklace too.

"I, of course, was waiting in the printery, watching and listening, and I was armed. I waited until Garland had come into the place, had rushed to his secret hiding place, had given unmistakable proof of his guilt, and then I tried to arrest him.

"I made him throw up his hands. And then, when I had taken his gun away from him, he surprised me. He had a second weapon on him, one that, it now appears, he had taken away from my valet.

"He surprised me with that weapon. We struggled. He overpowered me and made his escape with the kunzite necklace and the cream of the loot from the Demarest affair. But I have no doubt he had to leave a lot of his plunder. We might look, Sergeant?"

The sergeant was on his feet. "Come on, men. Take Leith with us. See that he has no chance to escape. I'm not entirely satisfied yet."

They entered the printery, found a light switch, flooded the shop with light, and, instantly, the correctness of Leith's reasoning was disclosed.

There was a secret panel in the wall. Inside it was a motley collection. There were rolled curtains of some fabrikoid material which were arranged with snaps to be fastened onto the side of a car. They bore in big letters *Proctor & Peabody.* There were gems, quantities of gold settings, and some coin. There remained none of the better class of stones or any of the currency. It appeared as though someone had scooped out about as much as could conveniently be carried.

Sergeant Ackley surveyed the secret hiding place, checked through the plunder which remained.

"It's the stolen stuff all right," he admitted. "There's around fifty thousand dollars of bulky stuff here. The man must have escaped with around two hundred thousand dollars, in round figures, if we count both the currency and the stones together."

Leith nodded.

"Too bad he got away," he said.

Sergeant Ackley looked at the clubman long

and earnestly. He stroked the angle of his jaw with a spade-like thumbnail, and the gray stubble gave forth little rasping noises.

"If your plan had worked, you'd have had him cornered here in the printery," he said.

Lester Leith nodded.

"And he'd have had about two hundred thousand dollars on him. And you two men would have been here alone."

Leith shrugged his shoulders. "Until I could have summoned the police, of course."

"Of course!" echoed Sergeant Ackley, and there was no attempt to disguise the sarcasm of his voice. "And we have been on your trail for a year as a hijacker. Now suppose you had made the arrest and then signified to Garland that he could escape if he left the loot behind. And then suppose you had ruffled yourself all up and claimed you'd been in a struggle, *and* told the same story you now tell. You'd be just two hundred thousand dollars to the good."

Lester Leith smiled faintly. "You wouldn't accuse me of a crime in the presence of witnesses unless you had some ground for the accusation."

"Certainly," agreed the officer, his voice still dripping sarcasm. "I wouldn't think of it for a moment. I was only mentioning that if the circumstances had been different, and if you had told the same story you now tell, the circumstances would appear the same as we now have them.

"Under the circumstances, I think I'll make a complete search of your person, Leith, and I'll have my men go through this printery with a fine-tooth comb, looking for a concealed package somewhere."

"Certainly," said Leith, repeating the word and tone of the officer. "I would like you to do that so I would be relieved of any suspicion."

They searched him, and they found nothing. They searched the printery and they found nothing, and then there came a wild exclamation from the undercover man.

"Good God! The fat girl! She took the Flyer!"

Ackley frowned at him.

"Spill it, quick!"

"And her suitcase was in the printery! If she'd set it down there, and then Garland had locked the door and gone to his hiding place, and Leith had hijacked the stolen gems from him, and simply put them in the fat girl's suitcase, and the fat girl had gone to the train, she wouldn't have ever suspected the contents of the suitcase until . . ."

Sergeant Ackley gave a bellow of inarticulate rage.

"Get to the telephone! The idea of letting anything like that go on under your nose!"

"I was handcuffed," reminded Scuttle.

"Seems to me," remarked Lester Leith, "that, for a valet, you show a most official and officious type of mind. I'm afraid you might instill a suspicion into the head of our dear but overzealous sergeant."

"Suspicion, hell!" yelled Ackley. "It's a certainty. Here, let me at that telephone."

He grabbed the instrument and began to throw out a dragnet. The Flyer left at ten o'clock. He assigned men to cover the depot, the gatemen, the taxicabs, and soon the reports began to filter in.

The telephone announced that special officers, covering the train, had reported a very fat woman who had held a ticket to a drawing room. She was carrying a suitcase, and the suitcase was constantly in her hand. She had been escorted aboard the train with difficulty, the suitcase with her. She had almost jammed in the door of the drawing room. It had taken assistance to get her in.

Sergeant Ackley got into immediate action. He ordered the arrest of the woman at a suburban stop where the Flyer was scheduled to make its last stop for through passengers.

Lester Leith gazed at him reproachfully.

"If you arrest that woman you will be responsible for a grave injustice and subject yourself to a suit for false arrest," he said.

"You admit you purchased the ticket on which she's traveling?" asked Ackley, his eye on Scuttle.

Lester Leith clamped his lips shut.

"You have accused me of a crime. I could

explain this whole affair in a few words. As it is, I shall say nothing until I have counsel present. But I want the witnesses to remember that I warned you against arresting this woman."

Sergeant Ackley's only comment was a sneer of triumph.

"You came so close to getting away with it, no wonder you're sore. If I hadn't thought of that fat woman, you'd have pulled one of the slickest jobs of all time."

Ten minutes passed. The telephone shrilled its summons. A report came in from the suburban town. They had caught the train, arrested the woman, taken her from the drawing room. The suitcase she carried had been opened. It contained a green silk jacket and some shorts, rather a skimpy costume for a fat woman in a side show.

Ackley chewed a cigar meditatively.

"Have men stay on the train and search every inch of the drawing room. Bring the woman to the central station. I'll meet you there."

He turned and glowered about him.

"This party's going to adjourn," he said.

They went to the central station. After an hour a police car arrived with an angry fat woman. She was taken to a cell. Sergeant Ackley gave her a third degree. The woman told a straightforward story. She had never seen Lester Leith but twice in her life—once when she went to his office in response to a want ad, once when he had called upon her with a suitcase and a railroad reservation and employed her to take the suitcase on the train to the destination of the ticket.

She refused to admit she had been previously employed by Leith, or that his valet had taught her to fall in a faint; she denied ever having been in a side show.

Ackley called in Beaver to confront her.

It needed but a glance at the goggle eyes of the undercover man to give Ackley his answer.

"That's not the one. I never saw her before . . . Yes I did, too. She was one of the unsuccessful applicants for the job Sadie Crane got."

Ackley's jaw sagged.

"Then . . . she doesn't even look like the other?"

"No. This one is blonde. The other was brunette. This one has black eyes, the other had hazel eyes. They're both fat—that's all."

"And because I didn't ask for a description I presume I'll be on the carpet," groaned Ackley.

They went back to the room where Lester Leith was being held.

"Where's Sadie Crane?" rasped Ackley.

Leith blew a cloud of smoke in a lazy spiral.

"I'm sure I wouldn't tell you."

Beaver spoke up again.

"He had fifteen drawing-room reservations on night trains. Maybe she went on one of those other reservations."

Ackley exploded into action.

"Beaver, you have the most infuriating habit of withholding important information!" he yelled, and got busy once more on the telephone.

Investigation disclosed a startling fact. Five of Leith's drawing-room reservations had been filled. Each one with a woman of astonishingly ample proportions, each woman with a suitcase which never left her hand.

It was a stupendous job to intercept each train and interview each woman, search each suitcase—chartered airplanes, long-distance telephone calls, emergency stop signals on various railroads . . .

By morning several facts were apparent.

The railroad systems out of the city had been badly confused by a wholesale stopping of limited trains at various points en route. Five fat women had been taken from trains to automobiles. They were all yelling vehement threats of lawsuits. Five suitcases had been confiscated. Each suitcase contained exactly the same thing—a pair of green trunks and a jacket.

Sergeant Ackley finally threw up his hands in disgust.

He had disrupted railroads, irritated powerful officials. He had done it all on a suspicion alone, and he had subjected himself to several suits by irate fat women who, as Lester Leith pointed out, were more inconvenienced at being jammed into police automobiles than were thin women.

Also, as Lester Leith managed to point out, Ackley had done virtually nothing toward apprehending the man, Garland, who had escaped; nor had he acted diligently in rounding up Garland's accomplices.

By the time Ackley had turned his attention to that angle of the case, the accomplices had vanished. There remained for him nothing but the glory of having solved the Demarest robbery, and he took unto himself every bit of that glory.

Three days later Ackley received a hurried call from Beaver.

"The apartment where Sadie Crane lived is occupied. No one knows who's in it, but the milkman delivers three quarts of whipping cream every day."

Sergeant Ackley gripped the receiver until the skin over his knuckles was pale. "I'm coming right over," he said.

"Leith is in his apartment," cautioned Beaver.

"Keep him there," roared Ackley, and slammed down the telephone.

He made record time to Leith's apartment house.

A hammering on the door of the apartment where Sadie Crane had lived was answered by a thin wisp of a man.

"Who are you?" demanded Ackley.

"I'm Spinner."

"What are you doing here?"

"I married Sadie Crane."

"Where's your wife now?"

"In the sitting room, the last I saw of her."

"Here?"

"Yes, sir."

Sergeant Ackley picked the thin little man up bodily by the coat collar, set him to one side, and strode into the apartment.

He came to a spacious room, in the center of which, sitting in a specially made armchair, cheerfully knitting, was a mountain of flesh.

"You Sadie Crane?" he yelled.

She shook her head.

"Who are you, then?"

"Sadie Crane Spinner. I married Arthur Spinner yesterday."

Sergeant Ackley took a deep breath, controlled the outburst that quivered on his lips.

"You were at the Garland Printery the night Scuttle was there?"

"Oh, yes."

"You were to take the Flyer?"

"Yes, indeed."

"At the request of Lester Leith?"

"Yes. He wanted me to take a suitcase with my things in it and put on a performance in some suburban town."

"But you changed your plans at the last minute?"

"Oh, yes. You see, when I left the printery to take a cab to the depot, the cabbie had a note that had just been delivered. It was from Leith telling me not to catch the train. He'd changed his mind. He said to take the suitcase up to his apartment and leave it there and go back to my apartment and wait until I heard from him. So I did it. It suited me—I don't like to ride on trains. The berths ain't big enough."

Sergeant Ackley's eyes were bulging.

"You came here, and have been here all the time?"

"Certainly. Then I got married and had to give up the idea of traveling. I've got to take care of Arthur."

"And your suitcase? What became of it?"

"Oh, Mr. Leith brought it back here the next morning. He said he'd changed his plans."

Sergeant Ackley fitted the mental picture puzzle together.

"What was in the suitcase when he returned it?"

"My trunks and jacket."

"Nothing else?"

"Nothing else."

"What are you doing now?"

"On my honeymoon. Times are good. Lester Leith employed me at twenty-five dollars a day as a human elephant, my husband at the same figure as a walking skeleton. When his side show blew up he gave us a month's pay in lieu of notice; and the apartment's rented until the middle of the month and the rent paid. So we're staying on here."

"Well," remarked Sergeant Ackley, "I'm a cock-eyed—"

The woman nodded cheerfully.

Sergeant Ackley strode into the apartment of Lester Leith. Scuttle let him in, flashed him a look of inquiry.

Ackley walked to the chair where Lester Leith was blowing spirals of cigarette smoke.

"Pretty clever, sending a woman to the only place I'd never look for her—*right back to her own apartment.* I covered every train, arrested five fat women who were false alarms, covered every hotel and rooming house—and here she was all the time!"

Lester Leith shrugged.

"Of course. That's where she *would* be if I were innocent of the crime you accused me of. But you thought I was guilty, so you looked in all the wrong places."

Sergeant Ackley's hands clenched.

"And you had only to take the loot from Garland, slip it in Sadie Crane's suitcase, have her take it out of the printery for you, then come to *this* apartment—take it out right under our noses—and you cleaned up two hundred thousand dollars!"

Lester Leith coughed deprecatingly. "You wouldn't want to accuse me of a crime without proof."

"Two—hundred—thousand—dollars!"

Leith traced the perimeter of a smoke ring with his forefinger.

"And even if you had proof, you couldn't convict me of any crime."

"Why not?"

"Because any package which *might* have contained any loot would have also had my kunzite necklace mingled with it, and it's no crime to recover your own stolen property. If any other property should have happened to be mingled with it, that would come under the legal head of commingled personal property."

Sergeant Ackley scraped his jaw with his thumbnail.

"I'll—be—"

"You will if you use profanity," interrupted Lester Leith.

But Sergeant Ackley had already stormed to the door . . .

Rogue: Paul Pry

The Racket Buster

ERLE STANLEY GARDNER

IN THE DECADE that Erle Stanley Gardner (1889–1970) wrote for the pulps (averaging nearly four thousand words a day), he created three dozen series characters, some that had long careers with numerous capers, some a little less, such as Ken Corning, a tough attorney who morphed into Perry Mason after six stories; Major Copley Brane, a "freelance diplomat"; Bob Larkin, an adventurer and accomplished juggler whose only weapon was a pool cue; El Paisano, who could see in the dark; Sidney Zoom, a millionaire con man who prowled the city streets with his vicious police dog; and Speed Dash, the "Human Fly," who gained his superhuman strength by crushing a raw potato in one hand every morning.

Paul Pry, who appeared in twenty-seven stories, is another of Gardner's crook protagonists. Much like Gardner's Lester Leith, Pry keeps an eye on other thieves and figures out how to acquire their ill-gotten gains, frequently calling on the police to (unwittingly) help him. He has befriended "Mugs" Magoo, a one-armed former cop, pulling him out of the gutter, and forms a kind of partnership with him—which turns out to be useful when he comes up against serious gangsters. Pry's most despised victim, and one he confronts in more than one adventure, is Big Front Gilvray, whose real name is Benjamin Franklin. Pry has taken offense that so great a name has been corrupted by the gangster.

"The Racket Buster" was originally published in the November 1930 issue of *Gang World Magazine*; it was first collected in *The Adventures of Paul Pry* (New York, Mysterious Press, 1990).

THE RACKET BUSTER

Erle Stanley Gardner

PAUL PRY lounged in well-dressed ease on a corner in the congested business district. From time to time he received provocative glances from passing women. But the eyes of Paul Pry were fastened upon the huddled figure of "Mugs" Magoo.

Mugs Magoo had earned his nickname years before when he had been the camera-eye man for one of the police administrations. A political shake-up forced him out. An accident took off his right arm at the shoulder. Booze had done the rest.

Paul Pry had found Mugs Magoo selling pencils on the street, had taken a liking to the man, learned his history, and reached a working arrangement to their mutual advantage. For Paul Pry was an opportunist of the highest degree of skill and efficiency. Even the closest observer would have failed to observe any connection between the slender, debonaire young man on one corner and the huddled figure of the crippled pencil-seller on the other. Yet between the two passed the flowing stream of human traffic, and that stream was instantly checked by Mugs Magoo, who knew every denizen of the underworld.

A young woman, modestly attired, strikingly beautiful, gazed with dazed eyes at the snarl of traffic. Her clothes proclaimed her as coming from the country. Her air of innocent unsophistication fitted nicely with the round-eyed wonder of her expression.

Mugs Magoo dropped the hat containing his stock of pencils some two inches, and seeing Mugs's signal, Paul Pry knew that the woman was a dip or pickpocket.

His keen eyes flashed over her in swift appraisal, then darted back to Mugs Magoo, and Mugs knew that his employer was not interested.

A short, well-tailored man strutted past, shoulders back, chin up. His face was a little pasty. His manner held a little too much assurance.

Mugs Magoo let his glassy eyes flicker once over the man's features, then the hand which held the hat raised and swept in a half circle. Paul Pry interpreted the signal to mean that the man was a gangster and a killer, a gun for a mob, and a top-notcher in his profession.

But Paul Pry's eyes did not even give the gangster a second glance. He was waiting for some choice tidbit to drift into his net.

Half an hour passed without any interchange of signals. Mugs Magoo, crouched against the wall of a bank building, sold a few pencils, mumbled a few words of thanks as coins clinked into his hat, and surveyed the passing pedestrians with glassy eyes that never missed a face.

A thin, dour individual with ratty, suspicious eyes, pattered his way along the sidewalk with quick, nervous strides. Mugs Magoo's gestures meant that the man was the pay-off for a gang of big rum-runners.

Paul Pry shook his head.

Another fifteen minutes and a man who might have been a banker paused on the corner, almost directly between Mugs Magoo and Paul Pry. Paul Pry moved abruptly to get the signals Mugs was making.

The man was slightly inclined to be fat. He was about forty-five. His cheeks were clean-shaven and massaged to pinkness. His motions were slow, weighted with the dignity of one who has accustomed himself to command. About him was none of the nervousness of a man who is forced to blast a living by the sheer force of his personality. Here was the calm assurance of one who reaps the crops others have sown. Serene, complacent, dignified, the big man with the broad chest and well-fitted waistcoat watched the flow of traffic with eyes that might have been concentrated rather upon some large financial problem than upon the composite rush of city traffic.

Mugs Magoo nodded his head, moved his hat in a circle, then shook it slightly. Paul Pry raised a hand to his hat, gave a flip to the cane which he held in his right hand, and sauntered a few steps toward the curb.

Properly interpreted, those signals meant that Mugs Magoo had recognized the dignified individual as the scout of a powerful mob, and that the mob in question was the one headed by "Big Front" Gilvray.

And Mugs Magoo had not needed Pry's answering signal to apprize him that his duties for the day were over. For it went without saying that any of the activities of Big Front Gilvray's gang would be of absorbing interest to Paul Pry. Ever since Paul Pry had found that Gilvray was far too clever to let the police pin anything on him, and that the initials B. F. reputed in the underworld to stand for Big Front, really stood for Benjamin Franklin, Paul Pry had cultivated Gilvray as a pet aversion.

Mugs Magoo gathered up his pencils, put them in a voluminous pocket, scooped the few silver coins from his hat, got to his feet, and walked away.

The portly man continued to stand in dignified meditation, his eyes fixed upon the door of the Sixth Merchants & Traders National Bank. For anything that appeared in his face or figure to the contrary, he might have been a Wall Street banker, turning over in his mind the advisability of purchasing a controlling interest in the institution. Certainly no ordinary detective would ever have placed him as a gangster, scouting out information of value to his mob.

Five minutes passed. The gangster looked at his watch, and there was something impressive in the very motion of his well-manicured hand as he took the timepiece from his waistcoat pocket.

Two more minutes. There was the rumble of heavy wheels sounding a base note deeper than the whining tires of the lighter traffic. An armored truck rumbled to a stop before the side entrance of the bank.

Instantly special police cleared the space between door and truck. The end doors of the truck were opened. Two men with heavy revolvers bulging from shiny holsters stood at watchful attention. Employees of the bank trundled out two hand trucks loaded with small, but heavy, wooden boxes.

The boxes were checked, and flung into the armored truck. One of the armed men signed a paper. The steel doors clanged shut. The armed men entered the truck through another door which, in turn, clanged shut. Then there was the grating sound of bars sliding across steel. The special police walked back into the bank. The truck rumbled out into the stream of traffic, a rolling fortress, laden with wealth, impregnable.

The men inside had sub-machine guns, and were encased in bullet-proof steel. Little slits gave them opportunity to fire in any direction. Bullet-proof glass furnished their vision of the entire four points of the compass. There would be a special police escort waiting to receive the shipment at its destination. In the meantime, thousands of dollars worth of gold was being moved safely and efficiently through the streets of the city.

The sides of the truck bore a sign, printed in the small letters of a firm that deals with conservative institutions in a conservative manner. "Bankers' Bonded Transportation Co."

Paul Pry inspected the sign with eyes that were slitted in concentrated thought. The truck turned a corner and was lost to sight. The gangster took a notebook from his pocket, took out his watch, and made a notation, apparently of the exact time.

Paul Pry managed to get a look at the face of the gangster. It was wreathed in a smile of satisfaction.

In impressive dignity, the man walked away, and Paul Pry followed him.

He walked for two blocks, and then approached the curb. Almost instantly a huge, shiny machine drew up beside him. The car was driven by a slight individual whose skin was a dead white, whose eyes were pin-pointed, but steady. In the rear of the car sat a large man whose flashing eyes were as keen as darting rapiers. Bushy brows covered those eyes as thunderheads cover the first flashes of lightning from a coming storm.

This was Big Front Gilvray. He might have been a United States senator, or a big corporation lawyer. He was, in fact, a crook, and a leader among crooks. The police had never pinned anything definite upon Big Front Gilvray.

The man Paul Pry had been following stepped into the car, and muttered something to Gilvray. To prove it, he produced the leather-backed notebook in which he had made a pencil entry at the exact time the armored truck had received its cargo of gold.

The information was not so satisfactory to Gilvray as it had been to the man Pry had shadowed. Gilvray's brows puckered together, his eyes filmed for a moment in thought. Then he shook his head slowly, judicially, in the manner of a judge who is refusing to act upon insufficient evidence. The car purred out from the curb.

Paul Pry hailed a taxicab. Through the congested traffic he managed to keep close to the car. In the more open stretches of through boulevard he dropped some distance behind. But the big car rolled along at a rate of speed that was carefully timed to be within the law. Big Front Gilvray did not believe in allowing the police to get anything on him, even a petty traffic violation.

In the end, Paul Pry could have secured the same information from a telephone book that he paid a taxi driver seven dollars and five cents to secure. For the big, shiny automobile was piloted directly to a suburban house where B. F. Gilvray was living.

Paul Pry knew that house was listed in the telephone directory, that there would be a name plate to the side of the door containing the words "Benjamin F. Gilvray."

Big Front Gilvray had given up his city apartment and moved into the suburbs. The house was set back somewhat from the street and was rather pretentious. There was a sweep of graveled drive, a huge garage, a struggling hedge, some ornamental trees, and a well-kept lawn.

Paul Pry looked the place over, shrugged his shoulders, and had the cab drive him back to the city.

Paul Pry's apartment was in the center of the most congested district he could find. He liked the feel that he was in the midst of things, surrounded by thousands of humans. He had only to raise his window and the noises of traffic would roll into the apartment. Or, if traffic were momentarily silenced, there would sound the shuffle, shuffle, shuffle of countless feet, plodding along the sidewalk.

Mugs Magoo was in the apartment, a bottle of whiskey at his elbow, a half emptied glass in his hand. He looked up with glassy eyes as Paul Pry entered.

"Find out anything, chief?"

"Not a thing, Mugs. The man you pointed out seemed to have gone to some trouble to find out exactly when an armored truck left the Sixth Merchants & Traders National."

"He would."

"Meaning?"

"That guy was Sam Pringle. He's one of Gilvray's best men. He got an engineer's education, and he believes in being thorough. When that bird writes down a seven it means a seven. It don't mean six and a half, or about seven, or seven an' a tenth. It means seven." And Mugs Magoo drained the rest of the whiskey in his glass.

His tone was slightly thick. His eyes were watery underneath their film, and he talked with a loquacity which he reserved for occasions of alcoholic stimulation. But Paul Pry accepted this as a part of the man's character. Mugs had cultivated the habit through too many years to put it lightly aside.

"What," asked Paul Pry, "do you know of the Bankers' Bonded Transportation Company?"

"A sweet graft. The illegal crooks built it up for the legal crooks. They have to ship gold back and forth every once in a while, now that they have lots of branch banks, and payrolls and all that sort of thing. The crooks went at it too heavy and almost killed the goose that was layin' the golden egg. A bunch of bankers got together and bought some armored trucks. They're lulus. No chance of cracking one of those things short of using a ton of dynamite. Then they bonded every employee, and got an insurance company to insure every cargo. Now the bank is responsible until the cargo gets aboard the truck. After that the bank don't have nothin' to worry about."

Mugs poured himself another drink and then continued: "In some cities the banks own their own trucks. Here, it's all done through this company. You watch 'em loading. You'll see a string of officers guarding the sidewalks. But the minute the last sack of gold bangs down on the floor of the trucks and the driver signs a receipt, the bank pulls in its cops. If there should be a hold-up the next second the bank officers would just yawn. They're covered by insurance, and bonds and guarantees. They should worry."

Paul Pry nodded, slowly, thoughtfully. "And why should the Gilvray outfit be so interested in the time the armored trucks make their appearance? Do you suppose they contemplate staging a hold-up just as the gold hits the sidewalk? Perhaps having a regular slaughter with machine guns?"

Mugs Magoo shook his head emphatically.

"Not those babies. They go in for technique. They pull their jobs like clockwork. I'm tellin' you the department ain't ever got a thing on Big Front. They know lots, but they can't prove a thing. That's how slick he is."

Mugs Magoo reached for his glass of whiskey.

"Don't get crocked," warned Paul Pry.

"Son, there ain't enough whiskey left in the world to crock me."

"Lots of fellows have wrestled with old John Barleycorn, Mugs."

"Yeah. I ain't wrestlin'. I'm gettin' ready to take the count whenever he slips over the kayo. But what the hell's left in life for a guy with one arm and no job?"

"Maybe you could get on the force somewhere."

"Not now. They keep too accurate records."

And because the talk had made Mugs Magoo blue, he tossed off the entire glass at a gulp, and refilled it.

Paul Pry crossed to the north wall of his apartment. Here were drums, all sorts of drums. There were huge war drums, Indian ceremonial drums, snare drums, cannibal tom-toms. Paul Pry selected his favorite drum as a violinist might select a favored instrument.

It was an Indian rain drum of the Hopi tribe. It was made from a hollowed log of cottonwood, the wood burnt to proper temper and resonance. It was covered with skin, laced with rawhide thongs. The stick was made of juniper, wadded with a ball of cloth.

Paul Pry sat in a chair and boomed forth a few solemn sound-throbs from the interior of the instrument.

"Get that note of haunting resonance, Mugs. Doesn't it arouse some savage instinct in your dormant memory cells? You can hear the pound of naked feet on the floor of a dance rock, get the suggestion of flickering camp fires, steady stars, twining bodies, dancing perhaps with rattlesnakes clasped in their teeth."

Boom—boom—boom—boom!

The drum gave forth regular cadences of weird sounds—sounds that entered the blood stream and heightened the pulse in the ears. Paul Pry's face took on an expression of savage delight. This was the manner in which he prepared himself for intellectual concentration.

But Mugs Magoo merely drank whiskey and let his bleary eyes remain fixed on a spot in the carpet.

Slowly the tempo changed. The booming of the drum became more somber. Gradually it faded into faint cadences of thrumming sound, then died away altogether. Paul Pry was in a rapt state of concentration.

Mugs Magoo poured himself another drink.

Fifteen minutes passed and became a half hour, and then Paul Pry chuckled. The chuckle rasped upon the silence of the room as a sound of utter incongruity.

Mugs Magoo cocked an eyebrow.

"Got somethin'?"

"I rather think I have, Mugs. Do you know, I have an idea I had better purchase a car."

"Another one?"

"Another one. And I think I'd better register it in the name of B. F. Gilvray at 7823 Maplewood Drive."

"Then he'd own it."

"Certainly."

"But you'd be paying for it."

"Right again. But I've always wanted to make Gilvray a present."

And Paul Pry, continuing to chuckle, arose, hung up the ceremonial drum, and reached for his stick, which contained a sword of finest steel, his hat, and gloves.

"The bottle, Mugs, will have to do you for the rest of the day," he said, and went out.

Mr. Philip Borgley, first vice president of the Sixth Merchants & Traders National, regarded the dapper individual who smiled at him with such urbane assurance, and then consulted the slip of pasteboard which was held between his fingers.

"Mr. Paul Pry, eh?"

Paul Pry continued to smile.

The banker squirmed about in his chair and frowned. He did not encourage smiles during interviews. The great god of money must be approached in a spirit of proper reverence. And Philip Borgley wished to impress upon his customers that he was the priest of the great god.

"You do not have an account here?" There was almost accusation in the question.

"No," remarked Paul Pry, and the smile became slightly more pronounced.

"Ah," observed Borgley in a tone which had shattered the hopes of many a supplicant before the throne of wealth.

But the smile upon Paul Pry's face remained.

"Well?" snapped the banker.

"The bank, I believe, has a standing reward for the recovery of stolen money?"

"Yes. In the event any is stolen."

"Ah, yes. And does the bank, perhaps, offer any rewards for crime prevention?"

"No, sir. It does not. And may I suggest that if idle curiosity prompted you to seek this interview it had best be terminated." Banker Borgley got to his feet.

Paul Pry poked at the toe of his well-fitting shoe with the tip of his cane. "How interesting. The bank will pay to recover the spoils of crime after the crime had been committed, but it will do nothing to prevent the commission of the crime."

The banker moved toward the mahogany gate

that swung in the marble partition which walled off the lower part of his office.

"The reason is simple," he said, curtly. "To reward the prevention of crime would merely make it possible for some gang to plan an abortive crime, then send some slick representative here to shake us down for not committing the crime they themselves had planned."

There was no attempt to disguise the suspicion in his voice.

"I'm sorry," said Paul Pry. "I guess, under those circumstances, I'll have to let the crime go through and collect a reward for recovery."

Philip Borgley hesitated, and it was apparent from his manner that he was debating whether or not he should call the police.

Paul Pry leaned forward.

"Mr. Borgley, I am about to make a confession."

"Ah!" snapped the banker, and returned to his chair.

Paul Pry lowered his voice until it was hardly above a whisper. "Will you treat my admission in confidence?"

"No. I accept confidences only from depositors."

"Sorry," Paul Pry said.

"You were about to make a confession?"

"Yes. I'm going to tell it to you. But it's a secret. I've never admitted it before."

"Well?"

"I'm an opportunist."

The banker straightened and his face darkened.

"Are you, by any chance, trying to play a practical joke, or are you just trying to act smart?"

"Neither. I called to warn you of a theft of rather a large sum of money which is due to take place within the next few days. I am, however, an opportunist. I live, Mr. Borgley, by my wits, and my information is never imparted gratuitously."

"I see," said the banker, his voice heavy with sarcasm. "And let me point out to you, Mr. Pry, that this bank doesn't temporize with crooks. This bank is well guarded, and the guards are instructed to shoot to kill. This bank is wired with the last word in burglar alarms. This bank is protected by devices which I do not care to discuss in detail. If any crook can rob us of any of this money he is welcome to it. And if any crook tries it, this bank will send that crook to the penitentiary. So now you understand. Have I made myself clear?"

Paul Pry yawned and got to his feet.

"I would say about twenty percent would be about right. Let us say two hundred dollars on every thousand you lose. That, of course, is for recovery. I would offer to prevent the crime for a mere ten percent."

Banker Borgley quivered with rage.

"Get out," he yelled.

Paul Pry smiled as he strolled leisurely through the mahogany gate.

"By the way," he said, "I feel quite sure your disposition is such that you would be most unpopular. I understand your best friends won't mention it. I am mentioning it because I am not your best friend. Good morning!"

The banker jabbed a finger on a button. An emergency alarm sounded and an officer came on the run.

"Show this gentleman out!" yelled the banker.

Paul Pry bowed his thanks. "Don't mention it. So good of you," he drawled.

The officer grasped Paul Pry's arm, just above the elbow, and instantly the smile vanished from Paul Pry's face. He turned to the banker.

"Are your orders that I should be ejected? Do you suggest that this officer lay his hands upon me?"

And something in the cold tone brought Borgley to a realization of lawsuits and assault actions.

"No, no," he said, hastily, and the officer dropped his hand from Paul Pry's arm.

"The price," said Paul Pry, "will be two hundred and fifty dollars for each thousand recovered. Good morning."

Truck number three of the Bankers' Bonded Transportation Company lumbered out of the garage where the trucks were stored. The driver had a series of yellow sheets in his pocket, a route list of places where calls were to be made and valuable shipments picked up.

It was a hot day, and the truck was empty. There was not five cent's worth of loot in the entire machine, and the guards were naturally enjoying the currents of air which came through the open windows. Later on, when the truck would become a rolling treasure chest, the guards would have to crouch within the hot steel tank, windows rolled up, suspicious eyes scrutinizing the surrounding traffic, perspiration smearing oily skins in a perpetual slime.

Now both driver and guard were relaxed, taking life easy. Their work had become mere routine to them. The contents of the boxes they carried meant nothing more to them than do the contents of packing cases to the drivers of department store trucks.

They were ten blocks from the garage, rolling down the boulevard with the steady speed of controlled momentum. There came a moment when there was no other traffic in sight.

The light car which flashed from the side street and disregarded the arterial stop, crashed against the curb, skidded, and sideswiped the big armored truck.

There was the sound of a splintering crash. The driver of the truck clamped his foot on the brake pedal. He had lost a little paint from the sides of the steel car. The flivver was wrecked. Its driver was jumping up and down, gesticulating.

"What the devil do you mean hogging the road? I'll have you arrested. I'll—"

The truck driver unwound himself from behind the wheel of the armored car and jumped to the ground.

"Sa-a-ay," he snarled. "How do you get that way?"

The man who had driven the light car moved his left with the trained precision of a professional fighter. The function of that left was to measure the distance, hold the outthrust jaw of the truck driver steady. It was the flashing right which crossed to the button of the jaw and did the damage.

"Hey, you!" yelled a startled guard, and jumped out of the truck. "You're in the wrong. What the devil are you trying to do? I'm an officer, and—"

He didn't finish the sentence. A black, shiny car slid smoothly to a stop.

"I saw it," said a man and jumped to the ground. "It was the truck's fault."

"What in hell—" yelled the infuriated guard.

The truck guard stopped. The gun that bored into his middle was held in a steady hand, and the eyes of the man who held it were aglitter with businesslike efficiency.

"Get into that car and be damned quick about it, both of you," said the man, as he swung his gun to cover the two astonished guards.

At that moment the door opened and two men stepped out. The guards' jaws sagged with astonishment, for these men were attired in an exact replica of their own clothing. There were the olive drab shirts with the insignia of the Bankers' Bonded Transportation Company; the identical caps with their shields, the belted trousers with their holstered weapons dangling from belts, the puttees, the polished shoes.

They never fully recovered from their gasps of surprise, for a tap with a slungshot collapsed them both like a sack of meal. Men moved with studied efficiency, and the two unconscious guards were in the shiny automobile before the first of an oncoming procession of cars came abreast of the scene of the accident.

Out of the little cluster of traffic two or three cars stopped. The drivers of these cars saw nothing unusual. The uniformed men who stood by the side of the truck were gravely exchanging license numbers with the driver of the demolished light car who was very, very meek.

The shiny sedan with drawn side curtains purred away. The meek man accepted a lift with a passing motorist. The armored truck rumbled away, and only the stolen flivver was left by the curb to mark the first step in the efficient plans of Big Front Gilvray.

From there on, it was smooth sailing. The Sixth Merchants & Traders National had some rather heavy gold shipments to make, and had telephoned its order for the truck to be at the door at a certain time.

The truck arrived, on time to the minute. The side door popped open, and special officers patrolled the sidewalk. Passing pedestrians gawked at the sight of the heavy boxes thudded to the floor of the armored car. The special officers watched the faces of the pedestrians with vigilance. The truck driver yawned as he signed the receipt for the given number of boxes.

The bank was rather casual in the matter. The drivers were bonded, the contents of the truck insured. The shipment had been safely transferred into the hands of the Bankers' Bonded Transportation Company. There was nothing to worry about. It was mere routine.

The guard slammed the door shut. The driver crawled in behind the wheel, and the truck rumbled away into traffic.

The truck was next seen abandoned by the curb in a residential district. Residents had noticed certain boxes being transferred to a delivery truck. They could give little additional information. The ones who made the transfer had worn conventional uniforms, and the residents had not been overly curious—at first.

The captured guards were released two hours later. They were groggy, mortified, enraged, and they had aching heads. They were able to give only a vague description of the men who had engineered the capture of the truck, and the police knew that these men, unmasked as they were, were crooks imported especially for this one job.

They were at a standstill, but they hesitated to admit it. They made a great show of getting fingerprints from the armored car, but they might as well have saved their time.

Philip Borgley immediately reported his interview with Paul Pry, and insisted that Pry must be one of the robbers. The police laughed. They had crossed the trail of Paul Pry before. That young man was just what he claimed to be—an opportunist. He had solved several crimes, and in every event had collected a reward. The total of those rewards amounted to a tidy income.

But the police had investigated Paul Pry from one side to the other. His methods were shrouded in mystery. His technique was baffling. But he was not in league with any criminal.

All of which called Paul Pry to the attention of the directors of the bank who were in session.

At about that time the bank's counsel delivered his opinion. The Bankers' Bonded Transportation Company was not responsible for the loss. They had never sent a truck to the bank, had never signed for the shipment. The theft of the truck had been completed before it called at the bank. Therefore, the bank had voluntarily delivered its shipment of gold to two crooks.

The directors promptly announced a reward for the recovery of the stolen gold. But gold is hard to identify and easy to divide. It looked very much as though the bank was about to make a rather large entry in red ink upon its books of account.

Paul Pry knew of the reward within half an hour of the time it was announced. He telephoned the bank to verify the report, and then sauntered to the parking station which was around the corner from his apartment.

He had sufficient information to lay before the police to secure a search warrant for the residence of Benjamin F. Gilvray, and doubtless recover the missing coin. But Paul Pry had no intention of killing the goose that laid his golden eggs. Big Front Gilvray had indirectly furnished Paul Pry with a very nice income during the past few months.

At the parking station, Paul Pry surrendered a ticket and had delivered to him a new, shiny automobile. This automobile was registered in the name of Benjamin F. Gilvray, 7823 Maplewood Drive, although the information would have come as a distinct shock to Benjamin F. Gilvray.

Paul Pry drove the new car to a point well out of traffic, parked it, and switched to a red roadster which was registered in his own name. He drove this roadster to a point about a block and a half from the residence at 7823 Maplewood Drive, and parked it. Then he called a taxicab and returned to the place where he had parked the new automobile he had registered in the name of the arch-gangster.

In a deserted side street, Pry stopped the car, opened the tool box, and took out a big hammer. With this hammer he started operations on the left front fender.

When he had finished, the car presented a striking appearance. The shiny newness of its factory finish was marred by a left front fender which was as battered as a wad of discarded tinfoil. The paint had been chipped off. The fender had been rubbed against a telephone pole and dented in countless places.

By this time it was the dusk of early evening, and Paul Pry blithely piloted his new car out into the boulevard.

At a side street where there was a little traffic, yet enough potential danger to warrant an automatic signal, Paul parked the car and awaited his opportunity.

A traffic officer stood just under the automatic signal box on the southwest corner, peering sharply at such machines as passed. He was there to arrest violators, the theory being that the amount thus received in fines would more than offset his salary.

When Paul Pry considered the moment opportune, he eased his car away from the curb. The street was deserted as far as he could see in both directions. The traffic signal was againt him.

The rest was absurdly simple.

With the bewildered stupidity of a new driver, he slowly drove the car out into the middle of the intersection and brought it to a stop only when the whistle of the officer on duty had blown its third imperative summons.

The position in which the car had stopped was such that Paul had an uninterrupted view up and down both streets. He was, in fact, almost in the exact center of the intersection.

The traffic officer, striding purposefully and irately to the left side of the machine, took due note of the crumpled fender and the new finish of the car. His voice held that tone of patient weariness with which mothers address wayward children after waywardness has become a habit.

"I suppose you're blind and can't see, and deaf and can't hear. You didn't know there was a traffic signal, nor hear me yelling for you to stop."

Paul Pry drew himself up with dignity.

"You," he said, slowly and distinctly, "can go to hell. I am B. F. Gilvray, Benjamin Franklin Gilvray."

The officer, his ears attuned to expectation of humble excuses, and half-inclined to be charitable with the driver of a new car, recoiled as though he had been struck. His face darkened, and the air of patient sarcasm slipped from him.

"You half-pint of a lounge lizard! You start talking to me like that and I'll push your nose so hard it'll stick wrong side out the back of your head. Who the bloody hell do you think you're talking to?"

And he thrust his rage-mottled face over the edge of the front door and glowered at Paul Pry.

Pry made no answer, none whatever.

For a full five seconds the officer glowered, hoping that the culprit would give him an excuse to use sufficient force to make an arrest on the charge of resisting an officer. But Paul Pry remained immobile.

The officer snorted and went to the front of the machine. He took down the license number, strode majestically back to the car and jerked open the left front door.

"Got your fender smashed. Did that just recently, didn't yuh?"

"That, my man, is none of your business."

The officer's hand shot into the car, clutched the collar of Paul Pry's coat, and Paul Pry came violently out from behind the steering wheel.

"Sa-a-ay, you've got lots to learn, you have. Get out your driving license and be quick about it. You're going to take a drive to headquarters. That's where you're going!"

And, still holding Paul Pry by the collar, he reached in his free hand and ripped out the registration certificate.

There was no traffic up either street. The intersection showed no approaching headlights. There were no pedestrians. Paul Pry had carefully chosen his corner and his time. Abruptly he changed from a passive but impudent citizen in the hands of the law, to a bundle of steel muscles, and wire-hard sinews.

"Crack!" the impact of his fist on the side of the officer's head sounded like a muffled pistol shot.

The officer staggered back, rage, surprise, and pain on his features. Paul Pry snapped his left home with that degree of accurate precision in timing which denotes the trained fighter.

The blow seemed almost unhurried, so perfectly timed was it, so gracefully were the arm and shoulder swung behind the punch. But the officer went down like a sack of meal, the registration certificate still clutched in his left hand.

Paul Pry got into the automobile, slipped in the clutch and purred down the street, turned on the next through boulevard and drove directly in front of the residence of Big Front Gilvray, where he parked the automobile.

Then he strolled across the street, sat down in the shadow of a hedge, and smoked a cigarette.

The house of Big Front Gilvray showed as a gloomy and silent pile of darkness. There was no sign of light from the windows, no sound of occupancy from within. The house was shrouded in watchful silence. But it was a tense silence. One sensed that perhaps there might be a cautious face, pressed against the glass of an upper window, surveying the street—that other faces at the four corners of the house might be cautiously inspecting the night.

It was a full half hour before Paul heard the wail of a siren, the sound of a clanging gong. The street reflected the rays of a red spotlight. The police were going to make something of a ritual of it. They had brought the patrol wagon with them.

Paul Pry walked down the street to the place where he had left his roadster, got in, started the motor, and warmed up the engine. Then he switched off the ignition the better to hear any sounds that the night had to offer.

The wagon drew up to the big residence with something of a flourish.

"Here we are, boys!" yelled someone. "Lookit the car! It's the kind Bill said, and the front fender's caved."

Another voice growled, "Drag him out."

The police car discharged figures who moved with grim determination up the walk to the house. The front steps boomed the noise of their authoritative feet into the night, and there came the sound of nightsticks beating a tattoo upon wooden panels.

But the door didn't open immediately.

The house gave forth signs of muffled activity. Then a porch light clicked on, and Big Front Gilvray stood in the doorway, his frame blocking out the soft glow from a lighted hallway.

Big Front lived true to his name. He put on a bold front. Behind him there were men armed with machine guns, determined to sell their lives as dearly as possible; but these men were out of sight, hidden where their guns could sweep hallways and staircases with the most deadly angle of fire.

Paul Pry heard Gilvray's booming voice.

"What in hell is the meaning of this outrage?"

It was Gilvray's code to be impressive, always to keep the other man on the defensive.

The only answer to the question was a counter question from one of the officers.

"Are you Benjamin F. Gilvray of 7823 Maplewood Drive?"

"I am. And I want to know—"

What Big Front Gilvray wanted to know was drowned in the sound made by a heavy fist impacting soft flesh. There followed the scuffle of feet, the thud of blows. After an interval someone said, "You're under arrest," and a knot of struggling figures threshed their way toward the patrol wagon.

There was the clanging of a bell, the wail of a siren, the roar of an exhaust, and the patrol wagon was on its way. From within could be seen moving figures, silhouetted against the lighted ribbon of roadway.

Big Front Gilvray was resisting arrest and the figures were doing their stuff.

Paul Pry started the motor on his car and slipped to the side street. From this position he could command a view of the alley entrance from the garages, also of the graveled driveway.

Lights blazed on in the house, then were subdued. Doors banged. There was the sound of running steps. A car shot out of one of the garages, skidded at the turn into the side street, and roared into the night. It was filled with men.

A truck followed. There were two men in the driver's seat. The cargo of the truck was covered with canvas. It was not particularly bulky.

Paul Pry followed the red light of the truck.

He kept well to the rear, yet, with the flexibility of his powerful roadster, was able to command the situation. The truck could not get away. Paul Pry drove without headlights and was invisible to the occupants of the truck.

The chase led for nearly a mile, and then the truck turned into a public garage. Paul Pry drove around the block and piloted his red roadster into the same garage.

The truck of the gangsters was parked at one end of the place and a sleepy-eyed attendant came forward with a ticket. His eyes were swollen with sleep, and he sucked in a prodigious yawn as he stretched his hands high above his head.

"I'd better park it," said Paul Pry. "The reverse is sticking a little."

The man in the dirty overalls yawned again and sleepily pushed a ticket into the crack over the hinges of the hood. That ticket was numbered, a string of black figures on a red background. The other half of the ticket, bearing a duplicate number, he thrust into Paul Pry's hand.

"Right next to the truck?" asked Paul casually, and didn't wait for an answer.

He drove the car down the dimly lit aisle of the garage, backed it into the first vacant stall to the side of the truck, switched off motor and lights, and got out.

It was, perhaps, significant that he got out of the car on the side that was nearest the truck, and that his hand rested against the hood of the powerful truck as he walked between the stalls.

In the dim light of the place, the sleepy-eyed attendant had no idea that Paul Pry was switching squares of pasteboard, that the red ticket which had been thrust into the hood of the roadster now adorned the truck, and that the truck ticket was transferred to the roadster.

Paul Pry had hardly intended to play the game in just that manner. He felt certain the gangsters, alarmed over the arrest of Big Front Gilvray, would transfer the treasure cargo, but he had hardly counted upon the audacious move by which they sought to insure safety for themselves.

It was simple. The very simplicity of it was its best protection. They felt the police might be on their trail. Therefore the thing to do was to place the stolen cargo where it would never be found. What more simple solution than to treat the boxes of gold as just an ordinary truck cargo, park the truck for the night, and make no further move until they heard from Gilvray.

If the police had the goods on Gilvray, the gangsters could take the truck's cargo, transfer it to fast touring cars and leave the city. If it was a false alarm, the gold was removed from the house which might be searched on general principles. If the police had complete information and knew the emergency headquarters the gang had established, a raid would reveal no incriminating evidence.

Paul Pry, however, was an opportunist. He had intended only to make certain that the gold was collected in one place, and then notify the police of that hiding place and claim the reward. As it was, he had an opportunity to make a much more spectacular recovery of the treasure, and leave the gang intact—an organization of desperate criminals, ready to commit other crimes upon which Pry might capitalize.

So it happened that when Pry left the garage he had with him a square of pasteboard containing a number, and, upon that truck with its illegal cargo, was a duplicate ticket containing the same number.

Paul Pry chuckled to himself as he walked out into the night.

He telephoned Sergeant Mahoney at headquarters.

"Pry talking, Sergeant. There's a reward out for the recovery of the gold that was slicked from the Sixth Merchants & Traders National?"

"I'll say there is. You haven't got a lead on it, have you?"

"Yeah. What say you drive out to the corner of Vermont and Harrison? I'll meet you there with the gold. You take the credit for the recovery and keep my name out of it. We split the reward fifty-fifty."

The sergeant cleared his throat.

"I'd like to do that all right, Pry. But it happens you've figured in two or three rewards lately. How come you get the dope so easily?"

Paul Pry laughed. "Trade secret, Sergeant. Why?"

"Well, you know, someone might claim you were pulling the crimes in order to get the rewards."

"Don't be silly, Sergeant. If I'd taken the risk of pulling this job I wouldn't surrender the coin for a fraction of its value. These boxes don't contain jewels. They contain gold coin and currency. I could take the stuff out and spend it—if I didn't want to turn it back. But if you think it might make trouble, we'll just forget it and I won't back the shipment and you can go ahead and work on the case in your own way."

"No, no, Pry! I was just thinking out loud. You're right. The corner of Harrison and Vermont? I'll be here in twenty minutes."

Paul Pry hung up the telephone, then rang his apartment. Mugs Magoo answered the ring.

"You drunk, Mugs?"

"No."

"Sober?"

"No."

"All right. Get a cab and pick up a pair of overalls and a cap, also a jumper. Get a leather coat if you can't get a jumper. Bring them to me in a rush. You'll find me at a drug store out on Vermont, near a Hundred and Tenth Street. Make it snappy."

And Paul Pry settled himself comfortably in the drug store, picked up a magazine, purchased a package of cigarettes and prepared to enjoy himself.

It took Mugs Magoo half an hour to bring the things. Paul Pry changed in the taxicab and arrived at the garage with clothes that were soiled and grimy. A little tobacco in his eyes gave them a reddened inflamed appearance.

He was cursing when the sleepy-eyed attendant, dozing in a chair tilted back against the office wall, extended a mechanical hand.

"That damned truck. Can you beat it? I don't any more than get to sleep when the boss rings up and tells the wife I've got to take that load down to the warehouse tonight, pick up a helper and start on another trip."

The attendant looked at Paul Pry with a puzzled frown.

"You the one that brought in that truck?"

Paul yawned and flipped him the red pasteboard.

"Uh huh," he said.

The attendant walked back to the truck, compared the numbers on the tickets, nodded.

"Your face looked familiar, but I thought—"

He didn't finish what he had thought.

Paul Pry got in the truck, switched on the ignition, got the motor roaring to life, turned on the headlights and drove to the street. Mugs Magoo in the taxicab, an automatic clutched in his left hand, guarded the rear. The treasure truck rumbled down the boulevard.

At the corner of Harrison, Sergeant Mahoney was parked in a police car. He shook hands with Paul Pry and ran to the canvas-covered cargo of the truck. A moment's examination convinced him.

"God, there should be a promotion in this!"

Paul Pry nodded.

"You drive the truck to headquarters. Claim you shook the information out of a stoolie. I'll drive your roadster to my apartment. You can have one of your men pick it up later. By the way, I've got a red roadster out at Magby's Garage, a mile or so down the street. I've lost my claim check for it. Wish you'd send a squad out there and tell the garage man it's a stolen car. You can leave it in front of my apartment when you pick up your car."

Sergeant Mahoney surveyed Paul Pry with eyes that were puckered to mere glinting slits.

"Did you switch tags and steal this truck, son?"

Paul Pry shook his head. "I can't very well answer that question."

"Afraid of something? You'd have police protection if you committed a technical robbery of a gangster truck."

Pry laughed. "No. There's a more personal reason than that."

"Which is?"

"That I don't want to kill the goose that's laying my golden eggs."

Sergeant Mahoney emitted a low whistle.

"Golden eggs is right! But you're monkeying with dynamite, son. You'll be pushin' up daisies if you play that game."

"Possibly," agreed Paul Pry. "But, after all, that's what makes the game more interesting. And it's something that's entirely between me and—"

"And who?" asked the officer eagerly.

"And a gentleman to whom I have presented a new car," said Paul Pry. With which cryptic remark, he walked toward the police roadster.

"Take good care of that truck, and good night, Sergeant. Let me know about your promotion."

The sergeant was clambering into the driver's seat of the truck as Paul Pry stepped on the starter of the police roadster. In the morning another consignment of golden eggs would find its way to him—one half of the reward money posted by the bank for a loss which it might have prevented.

Rogue: Kek Huuygens

Sweet Music

ROBERT L. FISH

AS HE TELLS IT in the introduction to *Kek Huuygens, Smuggler* (1976), Robert Lloyd Fish (1912–1981) was living in Rio de Janeiro, working as a civil engineer and trying to work on his golf game when a friend told him of a man who had legally—well, *almost* legally—smuggled five million dollars into the United States from Belgium. Fish was already writing Sherlock Holmes parodies featuring Schlock Holmes and detective novels about Jose da Silva, a Brazilian police detective, but he thought this story was too good to ignore, so he went on to write several clever stories and a novel, *The Hochmann Miniatures* (1967), about Huuygens, who was born in Poland, had a Dutch name, and carried a valid American passport.

During his career, Fish wrote more than thirty novels, won three Edgar Awards (for *The Fugitive*, the best first novel of 1962; for *Bullitt*, the best motion picture of 1969, based on his novel *Mute Witness*, published under his Robert L. Pike pseudonym; and for "The Moonlight Gardener," the best short story of 1971), was elected president of the Mystery Writers of America, and left the legacy of the Robert L. Fish Memorial Award, sponsored by his estate, that has given an annual award since 1984 for the best first short story by an American author as selected by MWA.

"Sweet Music" was originally published as a complete story within the novel *The Hochmann Miniatures* (New York, New American Library, 1967). It was first collected in *Kek Huuygens, Smuggler* (New York, Mysterious Press, 1976).

SWEET MUSIC

Robert L. Fish

THE MONTH WAS SEPTEMBER, the place was Paris, and the weather was hot.

Claude Devereaux, one of the large and overworked staff of customs inspectors at the incoming-passenger section of Orly airport, tilted his stiff-brimmed cap back from his sweating forehead, leaned over to scrawl an indecipherable chalkmark on the suitcase before him, and then straightened up, wondering what imbecile had designed the uniform he wore, and if the idiot had ever suffered its heavy weight on a hot day. He nodded absently to the murmured thank you of the released passenger and turned to his next customer, automatically accepting the passport thrust at him, wondering if there might still be time after his shift to stop for a *bière* before going home. Probably not, he thought with a sigh, and brought his attention back to business.

He noted the name in the green booklet idly, and was about to ask for declaration forms, when he suddenly stiffened, the oppressive heat—and even the beer—instantly forgotten. The bulletins on the particular name he was staring at filled a large portion of his special-instruction book. His eyes slid across the page to the smiling, rather carefree photograph pasted beside the neat signature, and then raised slowly and wonderingly to study the person across the counter.

He saw a man he judged to be in his early or middle thirties, a bit above medium height, well dressed in the latest and most expensive fashion of the *boulevardier*, with broad shoulders that seemed just a trifle out of proportion with his otherwise slim and athletic body. The thick, curly hair, a bit tousled by a rather bumpy ride over the Alps, was already lightly touched with gray; it gave a certain romantic air to the strong, clean-shaven face below. Mercurial eyebrows slanted abruptly over gray eyes that, the official was sure, undoubtedly proved very attractive to women. He came to himself with a start; at the moment those gray eyes were beginning to dissipate their patience under the other's blatant inspection. Claude Devereaux suspected—quite rightly—that those soft eyes could become quite cold and hard if the circumstances warranted. He bent forward with a diffident smile, lowering his voice.

"M'sieu Huuygens . . ."

The man before him nodded gravely. "Yes?"

"I am afraid . . ."

"Afraid of what?" Kek Huuygens asked curiously.

The official raised his shoulders, smiling in a slightly embarassed manner, although the glint in his eyes was anything but disconcerted.

"Afraid that I must ask you to step into the chief inspector's office," he said smoothly, and immediately raised his palms, negating any personal responsibility. "Those are our instructions, m'sieu."

"*Merde!* A nuisance!" The gray eyes studied the official thoughtfully a moment, as if attempting to judge the potential venality of the other. "I don't suppose there is any other solution?"

"M'sieu?"

"No, I suppose not." The notion was dismissed with an impatient shake of the head. "Each and every time I come through French customs! Ridiculous!" He shrugged. "Well, I suppose if one must, one must."

"Exactly," Devereaux agreed politely. What a story to tell his wife! No less a scoundrel than the famous Kek Huuygens himself had come through his station in customs, and had actually tried to bribe him! Well, not exactly to bribe him, but there had been an expression in those gray eyes for a moment that clearly indicated . . . The inspector dismissed the thought instantly. If his wife thought for one minute that he had turned down a bribe, she would never let him hear the end of it. Better just tell her . . . He paused. Better say nothing at all, he thought sourly, feeling somehow deprived of something, and then became aware that he was being addressed. He came to attention at once. "M'sieu?"

"The chief inspector's office? If you recall?"

"Ah, yes! If m'sieu will just follow me . . ."

"And about my luggage?"

"Your luggage?" Claude Devereaux looked along the now vacant wooden counter, instantly brought from his dream, immediately on the alert. The bulletins had been most definite about this one! Watch him! Watch him constantly! Watch his every move! His eyes returned to the man before him suspiciously.

"You mean your briefcase? Or is there more?"

"It's all I have, but it's still my luggage." Kek suddenly smiled at the other confidingly, willing to let bygones be bygones, accepting the fact that the inspector was merely doing his job. "I prefer to travel light, you know. A toothbrush, a clean pair of socks, a fresh shirt . . ." He looked about easily, as if searching out a safe spot where no careless porter might inadvertently pick up the briefcase and deposit it unbidden at the taxi-rank, or where someone with less honest intent might not steal it. "If I might leave it someplace out of the way . . ."

The official glanced at the high-vaulted ceiling with small attempt to hide his amusement, and then looked down again. Really, there had to be some way he could tell this story to his wife, or at least to his girl friend! It was just too delicious! He shook his head pityingly.

"I'm afraid, m'sieu, that your briefcase must go with you to the chief inspector's office." He brightened falsely. "In fact, I'll even carry it for you."

"You're very kind," Huuygens murmured, and followed along.

Charles Dumas, chief inspector of the Orly section, looked up from his cluttered desk at the entrance of the two men, leaned back in his chair with resignation, and audibly sighed. Today, obviously, he should have stayed home, or, better yet, gone to the club. The small office was baking in the unusual heat of the morning; the small fan droning in one corner was doing so without either enthusiasm or effectiveness; he was beginning to get a headache from the tiny print which somehow seemed to be the only font size available to the printing office, and now this! He accepted the proffered passport in silence, indicated with the merest motion of his head where he wished the briefcase deposited, and dismissed Inspector Devereaux with the tiniest lifting of his eyebrows. Even these efforts seemed to exhaust him; he waited until the disappointed inspector had reluctantly closed the door behind him, and then riffled through the pages of the passport. He paused at the fresh immigration stamp and then looked up with a faint grimace.

"M'sieu Huuygens. . . ."

Kek seated himself on the one wooden chair

the small office offered its guests, wriggled it a bit to make sure it was secure, and then looked up, studying the other's face. He leaned back, crossing his legs, and shook his head.

"Really, Inspector," he said a bit plaintively, "I fail to understand the expression on your face. It appears to me if anyone has reason to be aggrieved, it's me. This business of a personal interview each time I come through customs . . ."

"Please." A pudgy hand came up wearily, interrupting. The chief inspector sighed and studied the passport almost as if he had never seen one before. "So you've been traveling again?"

"Obviously."

"To Switzerland this time, I see." The dark eyes came up from the booklet, inscrutable. "A rather short trip, was it not?"

Kek tilted his chair back against the wall, crossing his arms, resigning himself to the inevitable catechism. "Just a weekend."

"On business?"

"To avoid the heat of Paris for a few days, if you must know."

"I see. . . ." The chief inspector sighed again. "And I also see that you have nothing to declare. But, then, you seldom do."

The chair eased down softly. Huuygens considered the inspector quietly for several seconds, and then nodded as if seeing the logic of the other's position.

"All right," he said agreeably. "If you people are sincerely interested in a soiled shirt and an old pair of socks, I'll be happy to declare them. What's the duty on a used toothbrush?" He suddenly grinned. "Not used as often as the advertisements suggest, but used."

"I'm quite sure you are as familiar with the duty schedule as anyone in my department," Inspector Dumas said quietly, and reached for the briefcase, drawing it closer. "May I?"

Without awaiting a reply he undid the straps, pressed the latch, and began drawing the contents out upon the table. He pushed the soiled clothing to one side, opened the shaving kit and studied it a moment, placed it at his elbow, and then reached further into the depths of the briefcase.

"Ah?" His voice was the essence of politeness itself. "And just what might this be?"

"Exactly what it looks like," Kek said, in the tone one uses to explain an obvious verity to a child. "A box of chocolates."

The chief inspector turned the package in his hands idly, admiring the patterned wrapping embossed in gold with the name of the shop, and the rather gaudy display of ribbon bent into an ornate bow. "A box of chocolates . . ." His eyebrows raised in exaggerated curiosity. "Which you somehow feel does not require declaring?"

Huuygens cast his eyes heavenward as if in secret amusement. "Good heavens, Inspector! A box of candy I faithfully promised as a gift to a lady, worth all of twenty Swiss francs!" He shrugged elaborately and came to his feet with a faint smile. "Well, all right. It's silly, I assure you, but if you wish it declared, I'll declare it. May I have my form back, please?"

The briefest of smiles crossed Inspector Dumas's lips, and then was withdrawn as quickly as it had come. He waved a hand languidly. "Please be seated again, M'sieu Huuygens. I'm afraid it is far from being all that simple."

Huuygens stared at him a moment and then sank back in his chair. "Are you trying to tell me something, Inspector?"

The inspector's smile returned, broader this time, remaining. "I'm trying to tell you I believe I am beginning to become interested in these chocolates, m'sieu." His hand remained on the box; his voice was suave. "If I'm not mistaken, m'sieu, while you were in Switzerland yesterday—to avoid the heat of Paris, as you say—you visted the offices of Ankli and Company. The diamond merchants. Did you not?"

Kek's voice was more curious than perturbed. "And just how did you know that?"

The chief inspector shrugged. "All visitors to diamond merchants are reported, M'sieu Huuygens." He sounded slightly disappointed. "I should have thought you would have known."

Huuygens smiled at him. "To be honest, Inspector, it never even occurred to me. I simply went there because M'sieu Ankli is an old friend of mine. We share an interest in—" his smile broadened "—pretty things. In any event, it was purely a personal visit."

"I'm sure. Probably," the inspector suggested innocently, "since you were merely avoiding the heat of Paris, you found his offices to be air-conditioned, which undoubtedly helped you serve the purpose of your trip." He picked the box up again, turning it over, studying it closer. "Suchard's, I see. A very fine brand. And from the famous Bonbon Mart of Zurich, too. I know the place. Excellent." His eyes came up, unfathomable. "Caramels?"

"Creams, if you must know," Huuygens said, and sighed.

"Oh? I prefer caramels, myself. Both, of course, are equally fattening. I hope the lady realizes that," the inspector added, and began to slip the ribbon over one corner of the box.

"Now, really!" Huuygens leaned forward, holding up a hand. "The lady in question has nothing to fear from fat, Inspector. Or from slimness, either. However, I rather think she would prefer to receive her chocolates with the minimum of fingerprints, if you don't mind."

"My personal opinion," said Inspector Dumas, sounding honest for the first time, "is that she will never see these chocolates," and he folded back the foil-lined wrapper and began to lift the cover of the box.

Kek frowned at him. "I still have the feeling you're trying to tell me something."

"I am," said the inspector succinctly, and placed the cover to one side. He raised the protective bit of embossed tissue covering the contents, stared into the box, and then shook his head in mock horror. "My, my!"

"Now what's the matter?"

"I'm rather surprised that a house as reputable as the Bonbon Mart would permit chocolates to leave their premises in this condition." Dumas looked up. "You say your lady friend prefers her chocolates without fingerprints? I'm afraid you should have explained that to the clerk who put these up. . . ."

Huuygens snorted. "With your permission, Inspector, now you are just being ridiculous! Those are chocolates, and nothing more. Creams!" he added, as if the exact designation might somehow return the other to sanity. "And exactly the way they left the store." He studied the inspector's face curiously. "How can I convince you?"

"I'm not the one who has to be convinced," said the chief inspector. He continued to study the contents of the box a moment more, nodding to himself, and then with a sigh at the foibles of mankind, he replaced the tissue and the cover. "I'm afraid it's our laboratory which requires conviction. And that's where these chocolates are going." His eyes came up, steady. "Together, I might add, with your shaving kit."

"My shaving kit?"

"Tubes, you know," said the inspector apologetically. "Jars and things . . ."

"You're quite sure, of course," Kek said with a touch of sarcasm, "that the shaving kit isn't going to one of your sons? And the chocolates to your wife?"

Inspector Dumas grinned at him. "Those chocolates to my wife? I'd fear for her teeth. Which," he added, his grin fading slightly, "have already cost me a fortune."

Huuygens sighed. "I only have one question, Inspector. To whom do I send a bill for the value of a practically new shaving kit? Plus, of course, twenty Swiss francs?"

"If you honestly want my opinion," said the inspector, appearing to have considered the question fairly, "I would suggest you charge it up to profit and loss. After all, once our laboratory is through with its investigation, the cost to m'sieu may be considerably higher." His voice hardened perceptibly. "And may I add that it would be wise for you not to leave the city until our report is in."

Huuygens shook his head hopelessly. "I don't believe you appreciate the position you're putting me in, Inspector. Extremely embarrassing. How do I prove to the lady that I did not forget her? That I actually did buy her a box of Swiss chocolates, only to lose them to—if you'll pardon me—the muttonheaded bureaucracy of the French customs?" His voice became sarcastic. "What am I supposed to use for proof? The wrapper?"

"Now that's not a bad idea," said the chief inspector approvingly, and grinned at the other's discomfiture. "It has the name of the shop on it, and if you wish, I'll even stamp it with the date as further proof." He checked the briefcase to make sure it was unlined, running his fingers along the seams at the bottom, and then folded the ornate wrapper, stuffing it into the empty space, and shoving the soiled laundry on top of it. He unfolded his stout five-foot-seven and came to his feet, his smile completely gone, his voice once more official. "And now, m'sieu, I'm afraid I must ask you to submit to a personal search."

Huuygens rose with a hopeless shrug. He ran his hand through his already tousled hair and studied the inspector's face. "I don't suppose it would do much good to inform you that I consider a personal search an indignity?"

"I'm afraid not," said the inspector. "And now, m'sieu . . ."

"And not only an indignity, but one which becomes boring when it is repeated each time I come through customs?"

"If I might offer a solution," Inspector Dumas suggested, with a brief return to humor, "it would be for m'sieu to control his wanderlust. In this fashion, of course, the entire problem of customs would be eliminated."

"We are not amused." Huuygens shook his head. "Admit one thing, Inspector. Admit that this treatment is unfair in my case—you've never once found me in violation of the law. Nor has anyone else."

"Not yet," the chief inspector conceded softly. "But one day we shall." His eyes went to the box of chocolates and then returned a bit smugly. "This—unfair treatment, as you put it—is the penalty one must pay for becoming famous among smugglers as a man who continually manages to outwit us poor *crétins* of customs inspectors. Or so, at least, we hear . . ."

His smile disappeared, wiped out as by a huge hand. He became quite businesslike, suddenly aware that time was passing, and of the further fact that—important as M'sieu Huuygens might be—other, lesser, smugglers might even now be requiring his attention.

"And now, m'sieu—your coat first, please. If I may?"

"Just don't wrinkle it," Huuygens requested, and began to remove his jacket.

Jimmy Lewis, by his own account the greatest roving reporter his New York newspaper maintained in Paris—a statement difficult to dispute, since he was the only one—leaned against one corner of a news kiosk in the main concourse of Orly airport, glancing through a magazine devoted in the main to pictures of bosomy girls and ads for Lonely Hearts clubs. He was a beanpole of a young man, with sandy hair and eyes that were surprisingly innocent considering some of the things he had looked upon in his life, including the magazine he had in his hand at the moment. He towered over the hurrying crowd that swept past him; the ever-present camera and raincoat slung over his shoulder were as much a uniform for him as the butcher jacket and cap were for the kiosk attendant who was eyeing him malevolently.

Jimmy finished studying the last of the revealing photographs of mammary exaggeration, and idly raised his eyes in time to see Kek Huuygens emerge from the escalator leading from the customs section below, moving purposefully in the direction of the taxi-rank. It was impossible not to recognize that stride; Huuygens always walked with his wide shoulders thrust forward, as if he were pushing his way through a blocking crowd. With an exclamation of surprised delight, Jimmy dropped the magazine on the rack and took a loping course calculated to intercept the other somewhere in the vicinity of the lower-level restaurant. The kiosk attendant retrieved the magazine, muttering something indubitably Gallic and undoubtedly impolite; he seemed to feel that people should either pay for magazines, or at least have the decency to return them to their proper stall.

Jimmy caught up with his quarry, shifted the load on his shoulder expertly, and grinned down genially.

"Hi, Kek. How've you been?"

Huuygens looked up; his preoccupied expression changed to a smile. "Hello, Jimmy. As a matter of fact, I've been better." He noted the raincoat and camera. "Are you coming or going?"

"Coming," Jimmy said, and tilted his head vaguely toward the concourse. "I was down at Marseilles on another wild goose chase. Why my editor has such a thing for missing persons, I'll never know. I could have been covering the tennis matches, or at least staying home with my feet on the windowsill. Or on my neighbor, a gorgeous dame, who looks like she'd make a great footrest." He grinned. "Right now I'm waiting for them to either bring my luggage out or admit frankly they lost it." A thought occurred to him. "How about a drink? I'll drive you home afterward, if I ever find my stuff."

Huuygens checked his watch and then nodded. "All right. I'd love one. I've got to make a phone call first, but I'll meet you in the bar."

"Fair enough. But let's make it the bar upstairs. Too many women in this one."

The mercurial eyebrows raised. "And what's wrong with women?"

"They cadge drinks," Jimmy informed him in solemn tones, and turned away, moving toward the staircase, grinning with pleasure. Huuygens was not only an old friend, he was also one of Jimmy Lewis's favorite people. Their habit of running into each other at odd times and strange places intrigued them both; and in the past some of Kek's exploits had furnished him with good copy, mainly because Huuygens trusted the other to keep information to himself when requested.

Jimmy mounted the steps two at a time, pushed through the door, and found an empty table that was protected from the vaulted concourse below by draped curtains that lined the windows of the room. He pushed aside the heavy cloth, staring down a moment, and then allowed the folds to fall back as a waiter approached.

By the time Huuygens joined him, two drinks were already waiting on the table. Kek dropped his briefcase onto a third chair already accommodating the camera and raincoat, and sank down, reaching for his glass. He raised it in the brief gesture of a toast and then drank deeply. There was a satisfied smile on his face as he replaced the glass on the table.

"Ah! That's much better."

Jimmy studied him with less sympathy than curiosity. "Have the big, bad men downstairs in customs been giving my little boy Kek a bad time again?"

Huuygens nodded solemnly, but his eyes were twinkling. "They have."

"I see." Jimmy twisted his glass idly, and then raised his eyes. "And would you like to tell Daddy all about it?"

"Not yet," Kek said calmly, and raised his glass once again.

Jimmy was far from ready to concede defeat; he had had to wheedle stories from Huuygens before. "Do you mean not yet meaning never? Or not yet like the girl in 'The Young Man On The Flying Trapeze'?"

"The girl in the what?" Huuygens stared at him.

"I keep forgetting you weren't born in America," Jimmy said, shaking his head. "This girl I refer to was in a song. The exact line goes something like this: da-dum, tum-tum, da-dum, something, something, and then ends up: 'But, gee, folks, I loved her, I offered my name; I said I'd forgive and forget—She rustled her bustle and then without shame, she said, Maybe later, not yet.' "

Huuygens laughed. "A hussy."

"Definitely," Jimmy agreed equably. "Indubitably. Meaning without a shadow of doubt."

He studied his friend. "Well? Which not yet is it? Maybe later, or never?"

Huuygens appeared to think about it. "Maybe later, I think. When the proper time comes."

"Good. Or anyway, better than never." Jimmy finished his drink and dragged aside the thick curtain, peering down. His eyes lit up. "I do believe they've finally decided to give up the loot. There's a blonde down there I saw on the plane, and the dear, sweet thing is laden with luggage. On the offhand chance that they aren't just handing out suitcases to beautiful blondes, I think I ought to go down and get mine." He set his glass aside. "Unless you'd like another?"

"No. I'll continue my drinking at home. I'm expecting a guest who's usually thirsty."

"Ah. Tough luck. Well, in that case I'll pick up my bag and meet you in the parking lot. You know my car." Jimmy smiled brightly. "To show you I'm not angry, I'll even let you pay for the drinks. You can call it taxi fare to your apartment on your income tax."

"Thank you endlessly," Kek said politely. He grinned at the other and raised his hand for the waiter.

In the parking lot Jimmy tossed his bag, camera, and raincoat into the rear of his battered Volkswagen, and somehow managed to squeeze himself behind the wheel while Kek got in the other side and pulled the door shut. Jimmy released the clutch with his normal exuberance and they roared from the drive, turning into the traffic heading for the city. Kek kept his heels pressed tightly against the floorboard; Jimmy had a tendency to brake at frequent and inexplicable times.

He swooped around a truck laden with lumber, passed between two motorcycles racing with each other, and turned to Kek, grinning cheerfully. "Hey? Did you see my new camera?"

Kek refused to take his eyes from the road. "I didn't notice."

"It's a beauty. I finally got a decent Graphic Super Speed 45 from the skinflints in the New York office. It used to take two porters to carry the ancient monster I had."

"Oh?"

"Yeah. And a lovely camera it is, too."

"Why? Did you get some good pictures in Marseilles?"

"Sure. Of the town in general plus a couple of good shots of the docks." Jimmy grinned. "I get sent off on these idiotic assignments and I'm supposed to cable back something that sounds like I know what I'm doing. Which is usually difficult."

"Why?"

"Because, my friend, assignment cables cost money, so my dear editor tries to economize. Net result: confusion. Half the time I have no clue of what they want me to do. However, by also cabling some decent pictures, and filing enough 'alleged's'—and keeping my fingers crossed—I manage to keep the brass from adding me to the unemployed."

Kek smiled. "You mean your editor is that easily satisfied?"

"Who? My editor?" Jimmy stared at his passenger as if he were mad; traffic zipped by as his attention was diverted. He looked back to the road just in time to neatly avoid a head-on collision with a three-wheeled *camionette.* "I said I managed to avoid being fired. My dear editor wouldn't be satisfied with an exclusive scoop on the secret formula for *Beaujolais de Texas.*"

"Whatever that is."

Jimmy grinned. "In the bars I patronize, it's the name given to Coca-Cola." He suddenly braked, swung into the Avenue de Neuilly, and jammed down on the accelerator, all, seemingly, in the same motion. "And in case you want to know the reason for this long dissertation, I'll tell you. I need some news."

Kek glanced at him. "Why tell me?"

"Because things happen to you, my friend. Or you make them happen." He spun the wheel without slackening speed; they shot around the Porte Maillot, nearly hitting an old man on a bicycle. Jimmy selected the Allée des Fortifications and raced on. His eyes came around again. "How about breaking down and giving me something I can use?"

Huuygens smiled. "I'll think about it."

"I wish you would," Jimmy said, and sighed. "I like Paris, and I'd hate to be transferred." He thought a moment. "Or fired." He swung into the Avenue du Maréchal Favolle, cut between a station wagon and a speeding car, and slammed on his brakes, slewing to a squealing halt before Kek's apartment. *"Voila, m'sieu."*

Kek climbed out and retrieved his briefcase, then leaned in at the window. "Jimmy," he said thoughtfully, "have you ever throught of doing a piece on the dangerous driving here in Paris?"

Jimmy shook his head. "I know French drivers are the worst in the world," he said sincerely, "but you'd never convince my editor. He lives in Jersey." He raised a hand. "Well, ta-ta. And don't forget I need some news."

"I won't," Huuygens promised. He watched Jimmy shoot into traffic, narrowly missing an irate cabdriver, and then turned with a smile into his apartment building.

His smile disappeared as soon as he entered the cab of the elevator, the little old man who operated the lift opened his mouth to greet him, but one look at the rigid features and he closed it again. Kek left the elevator at his floor, unlocked his apartment door, and closed it behind him. He dropped his briefcase on a chair and crossed the dim room to the balcony, throwing open the doors there, stepping out.

The view overlooking the Bois de Boulogne was lovely, with the stained tile roofs and their multiple searching fingers of chimney pots lost in the shimmering haze of distance beyond the green cover of the forest. The scented breeze brought with it the sharp, impatient blare of automobile horns, mixed with the delighted screams of playing children, and the admonishing cries of their exasperated nursemaids. He looked down. Below the balcony in the shadow of the tall apartment building, a small sidewalk cafe served as an oasis for the weary stroller; the colorful umbrellas, seen from above, gave it the appearance of a fanciful garden planted with careless geometry beside the river of asphalt that flowed past.

Paris! he thought, leaning on the filigree railing. A sardonic grin crossed his lips. Where else in the world could I enjoy noisy automobile horns or screaming children? Or rides with drivers like Jimmy Lewis? Or the personal attention of every customs inspector in town? The thought made him grimace; he glanced at his watch and straightened up. Anita was due in a very few minutes, and she was almost never late.

He came back into the apartment, closing the balcony doors behind him softly, as if reluctant to separate himself from the pleasant and uncomplicated life below, and then crossed to the bar in one corner of the elegant room. Two glasses were taken down from a shelf, inspected, and then meticulously wiped: his day-maid—poor, pretty soul—didn't consider cleanliness to be a part of housekeeping. He bent and removed an ice tray from the refrigerator hidden beneath the bar sink, placed the cubes in a small silver bucket for readiness, and then took down a bottle of Argentinian brandy for himself and English gin for the lady. And wouldn't his friends be shocked to see him drink Argentinian brandy in France! Oh, well—they just didn't know. They also didn't know the advantages of having friends in the import trade, he thought with a grin, and was just reaching for the Seltzer bottle when the doorbell rang. He wiped his hands on a towel, hung it back in place, and walked to the door, swinging it wide in welcome.

"Hello, Anita."

"Kek! Darling!" The young lady facing him was smiling in unalloyed delight. "How have you been?"

She came up on tiptoe to meet his height, presenting her lips half-parted, her blonde hair a delicate swirl that hid her beautiful face, her wonderful figure outstretched. Kek embraced her warmly, holding her tightly, feeling her full curves cushion against him, smelling the rich fragrance of her perfume, and enjoying the titillation of his senses fully. Behind them, in the foyer, there was a romantic sigh from the elderly elevator operator peering through a crack in the lift door, a sharp click as the doors were finally and reluctantly closed, and then the grinding whine of cable against drum as the elevator cab began to descend. Kek pulled away from the embrace, grinning broadly.

"Very good, Anita."

Anita made the motion of a curtsy. "Thank you, sir." She walked quite matter-of-factly into the apartment, fanning herself with one hand. "What a day! I'm dying of thirst!" Her blonde head tipped toward the door in curiosity. "I love these greetings, Kek—and I wish you loved them half as much—but, really! When you called me today, I couldn't imagine why you wanted me to put on such a show just for the benefit of the elevator operator."

"Because he's new," Kek said.

"You mean, you want to break him in properly?"

Kek laughed. "No. Because I'm sure he's being paid by the police to keep an eye on me." He moved back of the bar, busying himself with their drinks.

Anita seated herself on a barstool with a swirl of skirt that momentarily displayed long and beautiful legs, set her purse on another, and then reached for the cigarette box. She took one and lit it with a tiny lighter, blowing smoke, and then proceeded to remove tobacco from her tongue with the tip of her fingernail. This normal ritual attended to, she looked at him archly.

"And if he is being paid by the police, what of it? And why the necessity of a mad love scene in front of him? What are they after you for? Celibacy?"

Kek laughed again and handed her her drink. They clinked glasses, smiled at each other in true affection, and then tasted their drinks. Kek nodded in appreciation of the heady body of the brandy, and shook his head.

"No," he said quietly. "It's simply that they're expecting me to have a visit from a lovely lady today, and you're that lady."

"Wonderful! I like being your lovely lady. Only—" Anita took a sip of her drink and set it down "—it would be nice if you didn't have to be pressured by the police into asking to kiss me."

Kek grinned. "They only think they pressured me. Actually, they don't even think that."

"Whatever that means," Anita said, and looked at him pensively as a further thought struck her. "And just why did the police expect you to have a visit from a lovely lady today?"

"Because I told the customs that I had brought her some chocolates from Switzerland, and naturally . . ."

Anita shook her head disconsolately. "You make less and less sense as you go on, but I suppose I should be used to it by now. And anyway, I'd forgive you almost anything for chocolates. What kind are they?"

"They aren't, I'm afraid," Kek said ruefully. "Or if they still are, by this time they've been so mauled, pinched, poked at, X-rayed, and generally examined with the fabled efficiency of the police laboratory, that I doubt if anyone would want to eat them." He grinned and raised his eyes heavenward. "And may Allah give them sticky fingers for their nasty suspicions!"

"Amen," Anita said devoutly, and set her glass down firmly. "And speaking of nasty suspicions, who were you bringing those chocolates back for? Which lovely lady? Because I'm sure it wasn't me."

Huuygens's eyes twinkled. "Jealous?"

"Very." Her violet eyes stared into his seriously.

"Well," Kek said slowly, his big hand twisting his glass on the bar to form a series of damp circles, "in this case you needn't be. Because while I didn't realize it at the time, it seems I was actually bringing them back for a certain Inspector Dumas. Who, believe me, is certainly no lovely lady."

"And why were you bringing them back for this Inspector Dumas?"

"Because he searched me so nicely," Kek explained gravely. "Today he was even more careful than usual. Not one single tickle."

"Kek Huuygens, you are impossible!" Anita shook her head in exasperation and then immediately brought a hand up to check her coiffure. She saw the expression in Kek's eyes her gesture had triggered, and suddenly grinned. It was a gamin grin that made her look even younger than her twenty-five years. "Well, at least highly improbable. Are you going to tell me what this is all about, or aren't you?"

"I've been trying to tell you," Kek said with exaggerated patience. "You simply refuse to understand. I returned from Switzerland today, as you know, and the customs searched me, became suspicious of my chocolates—which I had brought as a gift for a lovely lady—and took them away."

"And I'm the lovely lady you brought them for."

"Right."

"I see." Anita nodded. "And you therefore immediately called me up and asked me to come over and kiss you publicly for the benefit of the elevator operator, just so I could be told that my chocolates were taken in customs. Is that it?"

"To a large extent—"

"But not entirely." Anita crushed out her cigarette, finished her drink, and set down her glass, eyeing him carefully. "What else did you want this lovely lady to do? Because I'm sure it's more than that."

"It is." Kek finished his drink and set it aside with an air of finality. "I want you to make a delivery for me."

"A delivery? From your trip today?" He nodded; she frowned at him uncertainly. "But you said they searched you."

"Oh, they did that, all right."

"So they took away the chocolates," the girl said, in a tone that indicated she didn't know whether to be disappointed or not. It seemed to her odd, from the story she had just heard, that Kek was not more subdued. "You seem to be taking it rather lightly."

"One learns to be philosophical about these things," Kek said, and smiled faintly. "Besides, the shaving kit was an old one, and the twenty Swiss francs, as the Inspector said, can be charged up to profit and loss. Or, rather, added to my expense account which, plus my fee, will be ten thousand dollars. Ask the man for a check, will you?"

The girl stared at him. "But you said—!"

"I said they took away the chocolates," Kek said gently. "They left me the wrapper. In fact, they practically forced it upon me." He reached into his briefcase and withdrew the garish paper. "Between the foil and the outer wrapper is the last known page of a particular Bach Cantata, original, in the hand of the master, and worth a great deal of money. Tell the man with a little heat, not too much, the foil and paper come away quite easily. The adhesives chosen were carefully selected; they'll do the manuscript no harm."

The girl looked at him in amazement.

"Kek, you are fantastic! And just what would have happened if the customs had kept the wrapper? Or thrown it in the wastebasket? I suppose then you would have had to go out and rob a garbage truck!"

Kek grinned at his associate affectionately.

"Not exactly rob one," he said. "I've spent quite a bit of time cultivating the driver who hauls away the trash. Fortunately," he added, patting the wrapper, "we shall not require his services, because I'd much rather spend the time with you. . . ."

THE MODERNS

Villain: Martin Ehrengraf

The Ehrengraf Experience

LAWRENCE BLOCK

OF THE MANY SERIES CHARACTERS created by Lawrence Block (1938–), perhaps the least well-known is Martin Ehrengraf, the lawyer who appears in only a dozen short stories but makes a lasting impression. Eight of the stories were collected in *Ehrengraf for the Defense* (1994); the complete stories were published as *Defender of the Innocent* (2014).

He is a fussy, meticulous little man who has never lost a case, mainly because most of his clients never have to go to trial. His mantra is "All my clients are innocent. That's what makes my work so gratifying. That and the fees, of course." He knows perfectly well that few, if any, of his clients are innocent, but his position is if they are not found guilty then, de facto, they are innocent.

Ehrengraf is strongly reminiscent in style to Randolph Mason, the superb character created by Melville Davisson Post. When the first Ehrengraf story was submitted to Frederic Dannay (half of the Ellery Queen writing team and the founder of the eponymous magazine), he pointed out that Mason clearly was the inspiration, but Block admitted that he'd never heard of the nineteenth-century lawyer. Still, there is no denying that both criminal defense attorneys employ a methodology that has no boundaries to how far they will go to protect their clients.

Block is one of the most honored mystery writers of all time; a small sampling of his awards include the Grand Master Award by the Mystery Writers of America, four Edgars, four Shamus awards, the Japanese Maltese Falcon (twice), and the Nero Wolfe award. He was proclaimed a Grand Maitre du Roman Noir in France, and is a past president of the Mystery Writers of America and the Private Eye Writers of America.

"The Ehrengraf Experience" was originally published in the August 1978 issue of *Ellery Queen's Mystery Magazine*; it was first collected in Block's *The Collected Mystery Stories* (London, Orion, 1999).

THE EHRENGRAF EXPERIENCE

Lawrence Block

"INNOCENCE," said Martin Ehrengraf. "There's the problem in a nutshell."

"Innocence is a problem?"

The little lawyer glanced around the prison cell, then turned to regard his client. "Precisely," he said. "If you weren't innocent you wouldn't be here."

"Oh, really?" Grantham Beale smiled, and while it was hardly worthy of inclusion in a toothpaste commercial, it was the first smile he'd managed since his conviction on first-degree murder charges just two weeks and four days earlier. "Then you're saying that innocent men go to prison while guilty men walk free. Is that what you're saying?"

"It happens that way more than you might care to believe," Ehrengraf said softly. "But no, it is not what I am saying."

"Oh?"

"I am not contrasting innocence and guilt, Mr. Beale. I know you are innocent of murder. That is almost beside the point. All clients of Martin Ehrengraf are innocent of the crimes of which they are charged, and this innocence always emerges in due course. Indeed, this is more than a presumption on my part. It is the manner in which I make my living. I set high fees, Mr. Beale, but I collect them only when my innocent clients emerge with their innocence a matter of public record. If my client goes to prison I collect nothing whatsoever, not even whatever expenses I incur on his behalf. So my clients are always innocent, Mr. Beale, just as you are innocent, in the sense that they are not guilty."

"Then why is my innocence a problem?"

"Ah, *your* innocence." Martin Ehrengraf smoothed the ends of his neatly trimmed mustache. His thin lips drew back in a smile, but the smile did not reach his deeply set dark eyes. He was, Grantham Beale noted, a superbly well-dressed little man, almost a dandy. He wore a Dartmouth green blazer with pearl buttons over a cream shirt with a tab collar. His slacks were flannel, modishly cuffed and pleated and the identical color of the shirt. His silk tie was a darker green than his jacket and sported a design in silver and bronze thread below the knot, a lion battling a unicorn. His cufflinks matched his pearl blazer buttons. On his aristocratically small feet he wore highly polished seamless cordovan loafers, unadorned with tassels or braid, quite simple and quite elegant. Almost a dandy, Beale thought, but from what he'd heard the man had the skills to carry it off. He wasn't all front. He was said to get results.

"*Your* innocence," Ehrengraf said again. "Your innocence is not merely the innocence that is the opposite of guilt. It is the innocence that is the opposite of experience. Do you know Blake, Mr. Beale?"

"Blake?"

"William Blake, the poet. You wouldn't know him personally, of course. He's been dead for over a century. He wrote two groups of poems early in his career, *Songs of Innocence* and *Songs of Experience.* Each poem in the one book had a counterpart in the other. 'Tyger, tyger, burning bright, In the forests of the night, What immortal hand or eye Could frame thy fearful symmetry?' Perhaps that poem is familiar to you, Mr. Beale."

"I think I studied it in school."

"It's not unlikely. Well, you don't need a poetry lesson from me, sir, not in these depressing surroundings. Let me move a little more directly to the point. Innocence versus experience, Mr. Beale. You found yourself accused of a murder, sir, and you knew only that you had not committed it. And, being innocent not only of the murder itself but in Blake's sense of the word, you simply engaged a competent attorney and assumed things would work themselves out in short order. We live in an enlightened democracy, Mr. Beale, and we grow up knowing that courts exist to free the innocent and punish the guilty, that no one gets away with murder."

"And that's all nonsense, eh?" Grantham Beale smiled his second smile since hearing the jury's verdict. If nothing else, he thought, the spiffy little lawyer improved a man's spirits.

"I wouldn't call it nonsense," Ehrengraf said. "But after all is said and done, you're in prison and the real murderer is not."

"Walker Murchison."

"I beg your pardon?"

"The real murderer," Beale said. "I'm in prison and Walker Gladstone Murchison is free."

"Precisely. Because it is not enough to be guiltless, Mr. Beale. One must also be able to convince a jury of one's guiltlessness. In short, had you been less innocent and more experienced, you could have taken steps early on to assure you would not find yourself in your present condition right now."

"And what could I have done?"

"What you *have* done, at long last," said Martin Ehrengraf. "You could have called me immediately."

"Albert Speldron," Ehrengraf said. "The murder victim, shot three times in the heart at close range. The murder weapon was an unregistered handgun, a thirty-eight-caliber revolver. It was subsequently located in the spare tire well of your automobile."

"It wasn't my gun. I never saw it in my life until the police showed it to me."

"Of course you didn't," Ehrengraf said soothingly. "To continue. Albert Speldron was a loan shark. Not, however, the sort of gruff-voiced neckless thug who lends ten or twenty dollars at a time to longshoremen and factory hands and breaks their legs with a baseball bat if they're late paying the vig."

"Paying the what?"

"Ah, sweet innocence," Ehrengraf said. "The vig. Short for vigorish. It's a term used by the criminal element to describe the ongoing interest payments which a debtor must make to maintain his status."

"I never heard the term," Beale said, "but I paid it well enough. I paid Speldron a thousand dollars a week and that didn't touch the principal."

"And you had borrowed how much?"

"Fifty thousand dollars."

"The jury apparently considered that a satisfactory motive for murder."

"Well, that's crazy," Beale said. "Why on earth would I want to kill Speldron? I didn't hate the man. He'd done me a service by lending me that money. I had a chance to buy a valuable stamp collection. That's my business, I buy and sell stamps, and I had an opportunity to get hold of an extraordinary collection, mostly U.S. and British Empire but a really exceptional lot of early German States as well, and there were also—well, before I get carried away, are you interested in stamps at all?"

"Only when I've a letter to mail."

"Oh. Well, this was a fine collection, let me say that much and leave it at that. The seller had to have all cash and the transaction had to go unrecorded. Taxes, you understand."

"Indeed I do. The system of taxation makes criminals of us all."

"I don't really think of it as criminal," Beale said.

"Few people do. But go on, sir."

"What more is there to say? I had to raise fifty thousand dollars on the quiet to close the deal on this fine lot of stamps. By dealing with Speldron, I was able to borrow the money without filling out a lot of forms or giving him anything but my word. I was quite confident I would triple my money by the time I broke up the collection and sold it in job lots to a variety of dealers and collectors. I'll probably take in a total of fifty thousand out of the U.S. issues alone, and I know a buyer who will salivate when he gets a look at the German States issues."

"So it didn't bother you to pay Speldron his thousand a week."

"Not a bit. I figured to have half the stamps sold within a couple of months, and the first thing I'd do would be to repay the fifty thousand dollars principal and close out the loan. I'd have paid eight or ten thousand dollars in interest, say, but what's that compared to a profit of fifty or a hundred thousand dollars? Speldron was doing me a favor and I appreciated it. Oh, he was doing himself a favor too, two percent interest per week didn't put him in the hardship category, but it was just good business for both of us, no question about it."

"You've dealt with him before?"

"Maybe a dozen times over the years. I've borrowed sums ranging between ten and seventy thousand dollars. I never heard the interest payments called vigorish before, but I always paid them promptly. And no one ever threatened to break my legs. We did business together, Speldron and I. And it always worked out very well for both of us."

"The prosecution argued that by killing Speldron you erased your debt to him. That's certainly a motive a jury can understand, Mr. Beale. In a world where men are commonly killed for the price of a bottle of whiskey, fifty thousand dollars does seem enough to kill a man over."

"But I'd be crazy to kill for that sum. I'm not a pauper. If I was having trouble paying Speldron all I had to do was sell the stamps."

"Suppose you had trouble selling them."

"Then I could have liquidated other merchandise from my stock. I could have mortgaged my home. Why, I could have raised enough on the house to pay Speldron off three times over. That car they found the gun in, that's an Antonelli Scorpion. The car alone is worth half of what I owed Speldron."

"Indeed," Martin Ehrengraf said. "But this Walker Murchison. How does he come into the picture?"

"He killed Speldron."

"How do we know this, Mr. Beale?"

Beale got to his feet. He'd been sitting on his iron cot, leaving the cell's one chair for the lawyer. Now he stood up, stretched and walked to the rear of the cell. For a moment he stood regarding some graffito on the cell wall. Then he turned and looked at Ehrengraf.

"Speldron and Murchison were partners," he said. "I only dealt with Speldron because he was the only one who dealt in unsecured loans. And Murchison had an insurance business in which Speldron did not participate. Their joint ventures included real estate, investments, and other activities where large sums of money moved around quickly with few records kept of exactly what took place."

"Shady operations," Ehrengraf said.

"For the most part. Not always illegal, not *entirely* illegal, but, yes, I like your word. Shady."

"So they were partners, and it is not unheard of for one to kill one's partner. To dissolve a partnership by the most direct means available, as it were. But why this partnership? Why should Murchison kill Speldron?"

Beale shrugged. "Money," he suggested. "With all that cash floating around, you can bet Murchison made out handsomely on Speldron's death. I'll bet he put a lot more than fifty thousand unrecorded dollars into his pocket."

"That's your only reason for suspecting him?"

Beale shook his head. "The partnership had a secretary," he said. "Her name's Felicia. Young, long dark hair, flashing dark eyes, a body like a magazine centerfold and a face like a Chanel ad. Both of the partners were sleeping with her."

"Perhaps this was not a source of enmity."

"But it was. Murchison's married to her."

"Ah."

"But there's an important reason why I know it was Murchison who killed Speldron." Beale stepped forward, stood over the seated attorney. "The gun was found in the boot of my car," he said. "Wrapped in a filthy towel and stuffed in the spare tire well. There were no fingerprints on the gun and it wasn't registered to me but there it was in my car."

"The Antonelli Scorpion?"

"Yes. What of it?"

"No matter."

Beale frowned momentarily, then drew a breath and plunged onward. "It was put there to frame me," he said.

"So it would seem."

"It had to be put there by somebody who knew I owed Speldron money. Somebody with inside information. The two of them were partners. I met Murchison any number of times when I went to the office to pay the interest, or vigorish as you called it. Why do they call it that?"

"I've no idea."

"Murchison knew I owed money. And Murchison and I never liked each other."

"Why?"

"We just didn't get along. The reason's not important. And there's more, I'm not just grasping at straws. It was Murchison who suggested I might have killed Speldron. A lot of men owed Speldron money and there were probably several of them who were in much stickier shape financially than I, but Murchison told the police I'd had a loud and bitter argument with Speldron two days before he was killed!"

"And had you?"

"*No!* Why, I never in my life argued with Speldron."

"Interesting." The little lawyer raised his hand to his mustache, smoothing its tips delicately. His nails were manicured, Grantham Beale noted, and was there colorless nail polish on them? No, he observed, there was not. The little man might be something of a dandy but he was evidently not a fop.

"Did you indeed meet with Mr. Speldron on the day in question?"

"Yes, as a matter of fact I did. I made the interest payment and we exchanged pleasantries. There was nothing anyone could mistake for an argument."

"Ah."

"And even if there had been, Murchison wouldn't have known about it. He wasn't even in the office."

"Still more interesting," Ehrengraf said thoughtfully.

"It certainly is. But how can you possibly prove that he murdered his partner and framed me for it? You can't trap him into confessing, can you?"

"Murderers do confess."

"Not Murchison. You could try tracing the gun to him, I suppose, but the police tried to trace it to me and found they couldn't trace it at all. I just don't see—"

"Mr. Beale."

"Yes?"

"Why don't you sit down, Mr. Beale. Here, take this chair, I'm sure it's more comfortable than the edge of the bed. I'll stand for a moment. Mr. Beale, do you have a dollar?"

"They don't let us have money in here."

"Then take this. It's a dollar which I'm lending to you." The lawyer's dark eyes glinted. "No interest, Mr. Beale. A personal loan, not a business transaction. Now, sir, please give me the dollar which I've just lent to you."

"Give it to you?"

"That's right. Thank you. You have retained me, Mr. Beale, to look after your interests. The day you are released unconditionally from this prison you will owe me a fee of ninety thousand dollars. The fee will be all inclusive. Any expenses will be mine to bear. Should I fail to secure your release you will owe me nothing."

"But—"

"Is that agreeable, sir?"

"But what are you going to do? Engage detectives? File an appeal? Try to get the case reopened?"

"When a man engages to save your life, Mr. Beale, do you require that he first outline his plans for you?"

"No, but—"

"Ninety thousand dollars. Payable only if I succeed. Are the terms agreeable?"

"Yes, but—"

"Mr. Beale, when next we meet you will owe me ninety thousand dollars, plus whatever emotional gratitude comes naturally to you. Until then, sir, you owe me one dollar." The thin lips curled in a shadowy smile. "'The cut worm forgives the plow,' Mr. Beale. William Blake, *The Marriage of Heaven and Hell.* 'The cut worm forgives the plow.' You might think about that, sir, until we meet again."

The second meeting of Martin Ehrengraf and Grantham Beale took place five weeks and four days later. On this occasion the lawyer wore a navy two-button suit with a subtle vertical stripe. His shoes were highly polished black wing tips, his shirt a pale blue broadcloth with contrasting white collar and cuffs. His necktie bore a half-inch wide stripe of royal blue flanked by two narrower strips, one gold and the other a rather bright green, all on a navy field.

And this time Ehrengraf's client was also rather nicely turned out, although his tweed jacket and baggy flannels were hardly a match for the lawyer's suit. But Beale's dress was a great improvement over the shapeless gray prison garb he had worn previously, just as his office, a room filled with jumbled books and boxes, a desk covered with books and albums and stamps in and out of glassine envelopes, two worn leather chairs and a matching sagging sofa—just as all of this comfortable disarray was a vast improvement over the spartan prison cell which had been the site of their earlier meeting.

Beale, seated behind his desk, gazed thoughtfully at Ehrengraf, who stood ramrod straight, one hand on the desk top, the other at his side. "Ninety thousand dollars," Beale said levelly. "You must admit that's a bit rich, Mr. Ehrengraf."

"We agreed on the price."

"No argument. We did agree, and I'm a firm believer in the sanctity of verbal agreements. But it was my understanding that your fee would be payable if my liberty came about as a result of your efforts."

"You are free today."

"I am indeed, and I'll be free tomorrow, but I can't see how it was any of your doing."

"Ah," Ehrengraf said. His face bore an expression of infinite disappointment, a disappointment felt not so much with this particular client as with the entire human race. "You feel I did nothing for you."

"I wouldn't say that. Perhaps you were taking steps to file an appeal. Perhaps you engaged detectives or did some detective work of your own. Perhaps in due course you would have found a way to get me out of prison, but in the meantime the unexpected happened and your services turned out to be unnecessary."

"The unexpected happened?"

"Well, who could have possibly anticipated it?" Beale shook his head in wonder. "Just think of it. Murchison went and got an attack of conscience. The bounder didn't have enough of a conscience to step forward and admit what he'd done, but he got to wondering what would happen if he died suddenly and I had to go on serving a life sentence for a crime he had committed. He wouldn't do anything to jeopardize his liberty while he lived but he wanted to be able to make amends if and when he died."

"Yes."

"So he prepared a letter," Beale went on. "Typed out a long letter explaining just why he had wanted his partner dead and how the unregistered gun had actually belonged to Speldron in the first place, and how he'd shot him and wrapped the gun in a towel and planted it in my car. Then he'd made up a story about my having had a fight with Albert Speldron, and of course that got the police looking in my direction, and the next thing I knew I was in jail. I saw the letter Murchison wrote. The police let me look at it. He went into complete detail."

"Considerate of him."

"And then he did the usual thing. Gave the letter to a lawyer with instructions that it be kept in his safe and opened only in the event of his death." Beale found a pair of stamp tongs in the clutter atop his desk, used them to lift a stamp, frowned at it for a moment, then set it down and looked directly at Martin Ehrengraf. "Do you suppose he had a premonition? For God's sake, Murchison was a young man, his health was good, and why should he anticipate dying? Maybe he did have a premonition."

"I doubt it."

"Then it's certainly a remarkable coincidence. A matter of weeks after turning this letter over to a lawyer, Murchison lost control of his car on a curve. Smashed right through the guard rail, plunged a couple of hundred feet, exploded on impact. I don't suppose the man knew what had happened to him."

"I suspect you're right."

"He was always a safe driver," Beale mused. "Perhaps he'd been drinking."

"Perhaps."

"And if he hadn't been decent enough to write that letter, I might be spending the rest of my life behind bars."

"How fortunate for you things turned out as they did."

"Exactly," said Beale. "And so, although I truly appreciate what you've done on my behalf, whatever that may be, and although I don't doubt you could have secured my liberty in due course, although I'm sure I don't know how you might have managed it, nevertheless as far as your fee is concerned—"

"Mr. Beale."

"Yes?"

"Do you really believe that a detestable troll like W. G. Murchison would take pains to arrange for your liberty in the event of his death?"

"Well, perhaps I misjudged the man. Perhaps—"

"Murchison *hated* you, Mr. Beale. If he found he was dying his one source of satisfaction would have been the knowledge that you were in prison for a crime you hadn't committed. I told you that you were an innocent, Mr. Beale, and a few weeks in prison has not dented or dulled your innocence. You actually think Murchison wrote that note."

"You mean he didn't?"

"It was typed upon a machine in his office," the lawyer said. "His own stationery was used, and the signature at the bottom is one many an expert would swear is Murchison's own."

"But he didn't write it?"

"Of course not." Martin Ehrengraf's hands hovered in the air before him. They might have been poised over an invisible typewriter or they might merely be looming as the talons of a bird of prey.

Grantham Beale stared at the little lawyer's hands in fascination. "*You* typed that letter," he said.

Ehrengraf shrugged.

"You—but Murchison left it with a lawyer!"

"The lawyer was not one Murchison had used in the past. Murchison evidently selected a stranger from the Yellow Pages, as far as one can determine, and made contact with him over the telephone, explaining what he wanted the man to do for him. He then mailed the letter along with a postal money order to cover the attorney's fee and a covering note confirming the telephone conversation. It seems he did not use his own name in his discussions with his lawyer, and he signed an alias to his covering note and to the money order as well. The signature he wrote, though, does seem to be in his own handwriting."

Ehrengraf paused, and his right hand went to finger the knot of his necktie. This particular tie, rather more colorful than his usual choice, was that of the Caedmon Society of Oxford University, an organization to which Martin Ehrengraf did not belong. The tie was a souvenir of an earlier case and he tended to wear it on particularly happy occasions, moments of personal triumph.

"Murchison left careful instructions," he went on. "He would call the lawyer every Thursday, merely repeating the alias he had used. If ever a Thursday passed without a call, and if there was no call on Friday either, the lawyer was to open the letter and follow its instructions. For four Thursdays in a row the lawyer received a phone call, presumably from Murchison."

"Presumably," Beale said heavily.

"Indeed. On the Tuesday following the fourth Thursday, Murchison's car went off a cliff and he was killed instantly. The lawyer read of Walker Murchison's death but had no idea that was his client's true identity. Then Thursday came and went without a call, and when there was no telephone call Friday either, why the lawyer opened the letter and went forthwith to the police." Ehrengraf spread his hands, smiled broadly. "The rest," he said, "you know as well as I."

"Great Scott," Beale said.

"Now if you honestly feel I've done nothing to earn my money—"

"I'll have to liquidate some stock," Beale said. "It won't be a problem and there shouldn't be much time involved. I'll bring a check to your office in a week. Say ten days at the outside. Unless you'd prefer cash?"

"A check will be fine, Mr. Beale. So long as it's a good check." And he smiled his lips to show he was joking.

The smile chilled Beale.

A week later Grantham Beale remembered that smile when he passed a check across Martin Ehrengraf's heroically disorganized desk. "A *good* check," he said. "I'd never give *you* a bad check, Mr. Ehrengraf. You typed that letter, you made all those phone calls, you forged Murchison's false name to the money order, and then when the opportunity presented itself you sent his car hurtling off the cliff with him in it."

"One believes what one wishes," Ehrengraf said quietly.

"I've been thinking about all of this all week long. Murchison framed me for a murder he committed, then paid for the crime himself and liberated me in the process without knowing what he was doing. 'The cut worm forgives the plow.'"

"Indeed."

"Meaning that the end justifies the means."

"Is that what Blake meant by that line? I've long wondered."

"The end justifies the means. I'm innocent, and now I'm free, and Murchison's guilty, and now he's dead, and you've got the money, but that's all right, because I made out fine on those stamps, and of course I don't have to repay Speldron, poor man, because death did cancel that particular debt, and—"

"Mr. Beale."

"Yes?"

"I don't know if I should tell you this, but I fear I must. You are more of an innocent than you realize. You've paid me handsomely for my services, as indeed we agreed that you would, and I think perhaps I'll offer you a lagniappe in the form of some experience to offset your colossal innocence. I'll begin with some advice. Do not, under any circumstances, resume your affair with Felicia Murchison."

Beale stared.

"You should have told me that was why you and Murchison didn't get along," Ehrengraf said gently. "I had to discover it for myself. No matter. More to the point, one should not share a pillow with a woman who has so little regard for one as to frame one for murder. Mrs. Murchison—"

"Felicia framed me?"

"Of course, Mr. Beale. Mrs. Murchison had nothing against you. It was sufficient that she had nothing *for* you. She murdered Mr. Speldron, you see, for reasons which need hardly concern us. Then having done so she needed someone to be cast as the murderer.

"Her husband could hardly have told the police about your purported argument with Speldron. He wasn't around at the time. He didn't know the two of you had met, and if he went out on a limb and told them, and then you had an alibi for the time in question, why he'd wind up looking silly, wouldn't he? But *Mrs.* Murchison knew you'd met with Speldron, and she told her husband the two of you argued, and so he told the police in perfectly good faith what she had told him, and then they went and found the murder gun in your very own Antonelli Scorpion. A stunning automobile, incidentally, and it's to your credit to own such a vehicle, Mr. Beale."

"Felicia killed Speldron."

"Yes."

"And framed me."

"Yes."

"But—why did you frame Murchison?"

"Did you expect me to try to convince the powers that be that *she* did it? And had pangs of conscience and left a letter with a lawyer? Women don't leave letters with lawyers, Mr. Beale, anymore than they have consciences. One must deal with the materials at hand."

"But—"

"And the woman is young, with long dark hair, flashing dark eyes, a body like a magazine centerfold and a face like a Chanel ad. She's also an excellent typist and most cooperative in any number of ways which we needn't discuss at the moment. Mr. Beale, would you like me to get you a glass of water?"

"I'm all right."

"I'm sure you'll be all right, Mr. Beale. I'm sure you will. Mr. Beale, I'm going to make a suggestion. I think you should seriously consider marrying and settling down. I think you'd be much happier that way. You're an innocent, Mr. Beale, and you've had the Ehrengraf Experience now, and it's rendered you considerably more experienced than you were, but your innocence is not the sort to be readily vanquished. Give the widow Murchison and all her tribe a wide berth, Mr. Beale. They're not for you. Find yourself an old-fashioned girl and lead a proper old-fashioned life. Buy and sell stamps. Cultivate a garden. Raise terriers. The West Highland White might be a good breed for you but that's your decision, certainly. Mr. Beale? Are you *sure* you won't have a glass of water?"

"I'm all right."

"Quite. I'll leave you with another thought of Blake's, Mr. Beale. 'Lilies that fester smell worse than weeds.' That's also from *The Marriage of Heaven and Hell*, another of what he calls Proverbs of Hell, and perhaps someday you'll be able to interpret it for me. I never quite know for sure what Blake's getting at, Mr. Beale, but his things do have a nice sound to them, don't they? Innocence and experience, Mr. Beale. That's the ticket, isn't it? Innocence and experience."

Villain: Quarry

Quarry's Luck

MAX ALLAN COLLINS

QUARRY (no first name) is a laconic hit man who appears in thirteen books, beginning with *Quarry* (also published as *The Broker*) in 1976, every one of which is highly readable and less predictable than one might expect of a series of adventures about a man hired to kill people.

After he returns from the Vietnam War, Quarry finds his wife has been cheating on him. When he locates the guy, tinkering under his car, Quarry kicks the jack out, crushing him. Unhappy and largely unemployable, Quarry is hired by a man known only as the Broker to be a contract killer. He is careful, methodical, and conscience-free, regarding the hits as nothing more than jobs. "A paid assassin isn't a killer, really," he says. "He's a weapon. Someone has already decided someone else is going to die, before the paid assassin is even in the picture, let alone on the scene. A paid assassin is no more a killer than a nine millimeter automatic or a bludgeon."

Although in a successful series, Quarry is not the best-known character created by the versatile Max Allan Collins (1948–), an honor that falls to Nate Heller, a Chicago private eye whose cases were mainly set in the 1930s and 1940s. Many involve famous people of the era, including Al Capone, Frank Nitta, and Eliot Ness in the first book, *True Detective* (1983), as well as such famous cases as the kidnapping of Charles and Anne Lindbergh's baby in *Stolen Away* (1991), the disappearance of Amelia Earhart in *Flying Blind* (1998), and the Black Dahlia murder in *Angel in Black* (2001).

Collins is also the author of the graphic novel *Road to Perdition* (1998), the basis for the 2002 Tom Hanks film; numerous movie and television tie-in novels; and the Dick Tracy comic strip after Chester Gould retired. He coauthored many books and stories with Mickey Spillane, completing works that were left unfinished when Spillane died.

"Quarry's Luck" was originally published in *Blue Motel* (Stone Mountain, Georgia, White Wolf, 1994); it was first collected in *Quarry's Greatest Hits* (Unity, Maine, Five Star, 2003).

QUARRY'S LUCK

Max Allan Collins

ONCE UPON A TIME, I killed people for a living.

Now, as I sit in my living quarters looking out at Sylvan Lake, its gently rippling gray-blue surface alive with sunlight, the scent and sight of pines soothing me, I seldom think of those years. With the exception of the occasional memoirs I've penned, I have never been very reflective. What's done is done. What's over is over.

But occasionally someone or something I see stirs a memory. In the summer, when Sylvan Lodge (of which I've been manager for several years now) is hopping with guests, I now and then see a cute blue-eyed blond college girl, and I think of Linda, my late wife. I'd retired from the contract murder profession, lounging on a cottage on a lake not unlike this one, when my past had come looking for me and Linda became a casualty.

What I'd learned from that was two things: the past is not something disconnected from the present—you can't write off old debts or old enemies (whereas, oddly, friends you can completely forget); and not to enter into long-term relationships.

Linda hadn't been a very smart human being, but she was pleasant company and she loved me, and I wouldn't want to cause somebody like her to die again. You know—an innocent.

After all, when I was taking contracts through the man I knew as the Broker, I was dispatching the guilty. I had no idea what these people were guilty of, but it stood to reason that they were guilty of something, or somebody wouldn't have decided they should be dead.

A paid assassin isn't a killer, really. He's a weapon. Someone has already decided someone else is going to die, before the paid assassin is even in the picture, let alone on the scene. A paid assassin is no more a killer than a nine millimeter automatic or a bludgeon. Somebody has to pick up a weapon, to use it.

Anyway, that was my rationalization back in the seventies, when I was a human weapon for hire. I never took pleasure from the job—just money. And when the time came, I got out of it.

So, a few years ago, after Linda's death, and after I killed the fuckers responsible, I did not allow myself to get pulled back into that profession. I was too old, too tired, my reflexes were not all that good. A friend I ran into, by chance, needed my only other expertise—I had operated a small resort in Wisconsin with Linda—and I now manage Sylvan Lodge.

Something I saw recently—something quite outrageous really, even considering that I have in my time witnessed human behavior of the vilest sort—stirred a distant memory.

The indoor swimming pool with hot tub is a short jog across the road from my two-room apartment in the central lodge building (don't feel sorry for me: it's a bedroom and spacious living room with kitchenette, plus two baths, with a deck looking out on my storybook view of the lake). We close the pool room at ten P.M., and sometimes I take the keys over and open the place up for a solitary midnight swim.

I was doing that—actually, I'd finished my swim and was letting the hot tub's jet streams have at my chronically sore lower back—when somebody came knocking at the glass doors.

It was a male figure—portly—and a female figure—slender, shapely, both wrapped in towels. That was all I could see of them through the glass; the lights were off outside.

Sighing, I climbed out of the hot tub, wrapped a towel around myself, and unlocked the glass door and slid it open just enough to deal with these two.

"We want a swim!" the man said. He was probably fifty-five, with a booze-mottled face and a brown toupee that squatted on his round head like a slumbering gopher.

Next to him, the blonde of twenty-something, with huge blue eyes and huge big boobs (her towel, thankfully, was tied around her waist), stood almost behind the man. She looked meek. Even embarrassed.

"Mr. Davis," I said, cordial enough, "it's after hours."

"Fuck that! *You're* in here, aren't you?"

"I'm the manager. I sneak a little time in for myself, after closing, after the guests have had their fun."

He put his hand on my bare chest. "Well, *we're* guests, and *we* want to have some fun, too!"

His breath was ninety proof.

I removed his hand. Bending the fingers back a little in the process.

He winced, and started to say something, but I said, "I'm sorry. It's the lodge policy. My apologies to you and your wife."

Bloodshot eyes widened in the face, and he began to say something, but stopped short. He tucked his tail between his legs (and his towel), and took the girl by the arm, roughly, saying, "Come on, baby. We don't need this horseshit."

The blonde looked back at me and gave me a crinkly little chagrined grin, and I smiled back at her, locked the glass door, and climbed back in the hot tub to cool off.

"Asshole," I said. It echoed in the high-ceilinged steamy room. "Fucking asshole!" I said louder, just because I could, and the echo was enjoyable.

He hadn't tucked towel 'tween his legs because I'd bent his fingers back: he'd done it because I mentioned his wife, who we both knew the little blond bimbo wasn't.

That was because (and here's the outrageous part) he'd been here last month—to this very same resort—with another very attractive blonde, but one about forty, maybe forty-five, who was indeed, and in fact, his lawful wedded wife.

We had guys who came to Sylvan Lodge with their families; we had guys who came with just their wives; and we had guys who came with what used to be called in olden times their mistresses. But we seldom had a son of a bitch so fucking bold as to bring his wife one week, and his mistress the next, to the same goddamn motel, which is what Sylvan Lodge, after all, let's face it, is a glorified version of.

As I enjoyed the jet stream on my low back, I smiled and then frowned, as the memory stirred . . . Christ, I'd forgotten about that! You'd think that Sylvan Lodge itself would've jogged my memory. But it hadn't.

Even though the memory in question was of one of my earliest jobs, which took place at a resort not terribly unlike this one. . . .

We met off Interstate 80, at a truck stop outside of the Quad Cities. It was late—almost midnight—a hot, muggy June night; my black T-shirt was sticking to me. My blue jeans, too.

The Broker had taken a booth in back; the restaurant wasn't particularly busy, except for an area designated for truckers. But it had the war-zone look of a rush hour just past; it was a blindingly white but not terribly clean-looking place and the jukebox—wailing "I Shot the Sheriff" at the moment—combated the clatter of dishes being bused.

Sitting with the Broker was an oval-faced, bright-eyed kid of about twenty-three (which at the time was about my age, too) who wore a Doobie Brothers T-shirt and had shoulder-length brown hair. Mine was cut short—not soldier-cut, but businessman short.

"Quarry," the Broker said, in his melodious baritone; he gestured with an open hand. "How good to see you. Sit down." His smile was faint under the wispy mustache, but there was a fatherly air to his manner.

He was trying to look casual in a yellow Ban-Lon shirt and golf slacks; he had white, styled hair and a long face that managed to look both fleshy and largely unlined. He was a solid-looking man, fairly tall—he looked like a captain of industry, which he was in a way. I took him for fifty, but that was just a guess.

"This is Adam," the Broker said.

"How are you doin', man?" Adam said, and grinned, and half-rose; he seemed a little nervous, and in the process—before I'd even had a chance to decide whether to take the hand he offered or not—overturned a salt shaker, which sent him into a minor tizzy.

"Damn!" Adam said, forgetting about the handshake. "I hate fuckin' bad luck!" He tossed some salt over either shoulder, then grinned at me and said, "I'm afraid I'm one superstitious motherfucker."

"Well, you know what Stevie Wonder says," I said.

He squinted. "No, what?"

Sucker.

"Nothing," I said, sliding in.

A twentyish waitress with a nice shape, a hair net and two pounds of acne took my order, which was for a Coke; the Broker already had coffee and the kid a bottle of Mountain Dew and a glass.

When she went away, I said, "Well, Broker. Got some work for me? I drove hundreds of miles in a fucking gas shortage, so you sure as shit better have."

Adam seemed a little stunned to hear the Broker spoken to so disrespectfully, but the Broker was used to my attitude and merely smiled and patted the air with a benedictory palm.

"I wouldn't waste your time otherwise, Quarry. This will pay handsomely. Ten thousand for the two of you."

Five grand was good money; three was pretty standard. Money was worth more then. You could buy a Snickers bar for ten cents. Or was it fifteen? I forget.

But I was still a little irritated.

"The two of us?" I said. "Adam, here, isn't my better half on this one, is he?"

"Yes, he is," the Broker said. He had his hands folded now, prayerfully. His baritone was calming. Or was meant to be.

Adam was frowning, playing nervously with a silver skull ring on the little finger of his left hand. "I don't like your fuckin' attitude, man. . . ."

The way he tried to work menace into his voice would have been amusing if I'd given a shit.

"I don't like your fuckin' hippie hair," I said.

"What?" He leaned forward, furious, and knocked his water glass over; it spun on its side and fell off my edge of the booth and we heard it shatter. A few eyes looked our way.

Adam's tiny bright eyes were wide. "Fuck," he said.

"Seven years bad luck, dipshit," I said.

"That's just mirrors!"

"I think it's any kind of glass. Isn't that right, Broker?"

The Broker was frowning a little. "Quarry . . ." He sounded so disappointed in me.

"Hair like that attracts attention," I said.

"You go in for a hit, you got to be the invisible man."

"These days everybody wears their hair like this," the kid said defensively.

"In Greenwich Village, maybe. But in America, if you want to disappear, you look like a businessman or a college student."

That made him laugh. "You ever see a college student lately, asshole?"

"I mean the kind who belongs to a fraternity. You want to go around killing people, you need to look clean-cut."

Adam's mouth had dropped open; he had crooked lower teeth. He pointed at me with a thumb and turned to look at Broker, indignant. "Is this guy for real?"

"Yes, indeed," the Broker said. "He's also the best active agent I have."

By "active," Broker meant (in his own personal jargon) that I was the half of a hit team that took out the target; the "passive" half was the lookout person, the back-up.

"And he's right," the Broker said, "about your hair."

"Far as that's concerned," I said, "we look pretty goddamn conspicuous right here—me looking collegiate, you looking like the prez of a country club, and junior here like a roadshow Mick Jagger."

Adam looked half bewildered, half outraged.

"You may have a point," the Broker allowed me.

"On the other hand," I said, "people probably think we're fags waiting for a fourth."

"You're unbelievable," Adam said, shaking his greasy Beatle mop. "I don't want to work with this son of a bitch."

"Stay calm," the Broker said. "I'm not proposing a partnership, not unless this should happen to work out beyond all of our wildest expectations."

"I tend to agree with Adam, here," I said. "We're not made for each other."

"The question is," the Broker said, "are you made for ten thousand dollars?"

Adam and I thought about that.

"I have a job that needs to go down, very soon," he said, "and very quickly. You're the only two men available right now. And I know neither of you wants to disappoint me."

Half of ten grand did sound good to me. I had a lake-front lot in Wisconsin where I could put up this nifty little A-frame prefab, if I could put a few more thousand together. . . .

"I'm in," I said, "if he cuts his hair."

The Broker looked at Adam, who scowled and nodded.

"You're both going to like this," the Broker said, sitting forward, withdrawing a travel brochure from his back pocket.

"A resort?" I asked.

"Near Chicago. A wooded area. There's a man-made lake, two indoor swimming pools and one outdoor, an 'old town' gift shop area, several restaurants, bowling alley, tennis courts, horseback riding . . ."

"If they have archery," I said, "maybe we could arrange a little accident."

That made the Broker chuckle. "You're not far off the mark. We need either an accident, or a robbery. It's an insurance situation."

Broker would tell us no more than that: part of his function was to shield the client from us, and us from the client, for that matter. He was sort of a combination agent and buffer; he could tell us only this much: the target was going down so that someone could collect insurance. The double indemnity kind that comes from accidental death, and of course getting killed by thieves counts in that regard.

"This is him," Broker said, carefully showing us a photograph of a thin, handsome, tanned man of possibly sixty with black hair that was probably dyed; he wore dark sunglasses and tennis togs and had an arm around a dark-haired woman of about forty, a tanned slim busty woman also in dark glasses and tennis togs.

"Who's the babe?" Adam said.

"The wife," the Broker said.

The client.

"The client?" Adam asked.

"I didn't say that," Broker said edgily, "and

you mustn't ask stupid questions. Your target is this man—Baxter Bennedict."

"I hope his wife isn't named Bunny," I said.

The Broker chuckled again, but Adam didn't see the joke.

"Close. Her name is Bernice, actually."

I groaned. "One more 'B' and I'll kill 'em *both*—for free."

The Broker took out a silver cigarette case. "Actually, that's going to be one of the . . . delicate aspects of this job."

"How so?" I asked.

He offered me a cigarette from the case and I waved it off; he offered one to Adam, and he took it.

The Broker said, "They'll be on vacation. Together, at the Wistful Wagon Lodge. She's not to be harmed. You must wait and watch until you can get him alone."

"And then make it look like an accident," I said.

"Or a robbery. Correct." The Broker struck a match, lighted his cigarette. He tried to light Adam's, but Adam gestured no, frantically.

"Two on a match," he said. Then got a lighter out and lit himself up.

"Two on a match?" I asked.

"Haven't you ever heard that?" the kid asked, almost wild-eyed. "Two on a match. It's unlucky!"

"*Three* on a match is unlucky," I said.

Adam squinted at me. "Are you superstitious, too?"

I looked hard at Broker, who merely shrugged.

"I gotta pee," the kid said suddenly, and had the Broker let him slide out. Standing, he wasn't very big: probably five seven. Skinny. His jeans were tattered.

When we were alone, I said, "What are you doing, hooking me up with that dumb-ass jerk?"

"Give him a chance. He was in Vietnam. Like you. He's not completely inexperienced."

"Most of the guys I knew in Vietnam were stoned twenty-four hours a day. That's not what I'm looking for in a partner."

"He's just a little green. You'll season him."

"I'll ice him if he fucks up. Understood?"

The Broker shrugged. "Understood."

When Adam came back, Broker let him in and said, "The hardest part is, you have a window of only four days."

"That's bad," I said, frowning. "I like to maintain a surveillance, get a pattern down. . . ."

Broker shrugged again. "It's a different situation. They're on vacation. They won't have much of a pattern."

"Great."

Now the Broker frowned. "Why in hell do you think it pays so well? Think of it as hazardous duty pay."

Adam sneered and said, "What's the matter, Quarry? Didn't you never take no fuckin' risks?"

"I think I'm about to," I said.

"It'll go well," the Broker said.

"Knock on wood," the kid said, and rapped on the table.

"That's formica," I said.

The Wistful Wagon Lodge sprawled out over numerous wooded acres, just off the outskirts of Wistful Vista, Illinois. According to the Broker's brochure, back in the late '40s, the hamlet had taken the name of Fibber McGee and Molly's fictional hometown, for purposes of attracting tourists; apparently one of the secondary stars of the radio show had been born nearby. This marketing ploy had been just in time for television making radio passe, and the little farm community's only remaining sign of having at all successfully tapped into the tourist trade was the Wistful Wagon Lodge itself.

A cobblestone drive wound through the scattering of log cabins, and several larger buildings—including the main lodge where the check-in and restaurants were—were similarly rustic structures, but of gray weathered wood. Trees clustered everywhere, turning warm sunlight into cool pools of shade; wood-burned signs showed the way to this building or that path, and decorative wagon wheels, often with flower beds in and around them, were scattered about as if some long-ago pioneer mishap had been beautified by nature and time. Of course that wasn't the case: this was the hokey hand of man.

We arrived separately, Adam and I, each having reserved rooms in advance, each paying cash up front upon registration; no credit cards. We each had log-cabin cottages, not terribly close to one another.

As the back-up and surveillance man, Adam went in early. The target and his wife were taking a long weekend—arriving Thursday, leaving Monday. I didn't arrive until Saturday morning.

I went to Adam's cabin and knocked, but got no answer. Which just meant he was trailing Mr. and Mrs. Target around the grounds. After I dropped my stuff off at my own cabin, I wandered, trying to get the general layout of the place, checking out the lodge itself, where about half of the rooms were, as well as two restaurants. Everything had a pine smell, which was partially the many trees, and partially Pinesol. Wistful Wagon was Hollywood rustic—there was a dated quality about it, from the cowboy/cowgirl attire of the waiters and waitresses in the Wistful Chuckwagon Cafe to the wood-and-leather furnishings to the barnwood-framed Remington prints.

I got myself some lunch and traded smiles with a giggly tableful of college girls who were on a weekend scouting expedition of their own. *Good*, I thought. *If I can connect with one of them tonight, that'll provide nice cover.*

As I was finishing up, my cowgirl waitress, a curly-haired blonde pushing thirty who was pretty cute herself, said, "Looks like you might get lucky tonight."

She was re-filling my coffee cup.

"With them or with you?" I asked.

She had big washed-out blue eyes and heavy eye make-up, more '60s than '70s. She was wearing a 1950s style cowboy hat cinched under her chin. "I'm not supposed to fraternize with the guests."

"How did you know I was a fraternity man?"

She laughed a little; her chin crinkled. Her face was kind of round and she was a little pudgy, nicely so in the bosom.

"Wild stab," she said. "Anyway, there's an open dance in the ballroom. Of the Wagontrain Dining Room? Country swing band. You'll like it."

"You inviting me?"

"No," she said; she narrowed her eyes and cocked her head, her expression one of mild scolding. "Those little girls'll be there, and plenty of others. You won't have any trouble finding what you want."

"I bet I will."

"Why's that?"

"I was hoping for a girl wearing cowboy boots like yours."

"Oh, there'll be girls in cowboys boots there tonight."

"I meant, just cowboy boots."

She laughed at that, shook her head; under her Dale Evans hat, her blonde curls bounced off her shoulders.

She went away and let me finish my coffee, and I smiled at the college girls some more, but when I paid for my check, at the register, it was my plump little cowgirl again.

"I work late tonight," she said.

"How late?"

"I get off at midnight," she said.

"That's only the first time," I said.

"First time what?"

"That you'll get off tonight."

She liked that. Times were different, then. The only way you could die from fucking was if a husband or boyfriend caught you at it. She told me where to meet her, later.

I strolled back up a winding path to my cabin. A few groups of college girls and college guys, not paired off together yet, were buzzing around; some couples in their twenties up into their sixties were walking, often hand-in-hand, around the sun-dappled, lushly shaded grounds. The sound of a gentle breeze in the trees made a faint shimmering music. Getting laid here was no trick.

I got my swim trunks on and grabbed a towel and headed for the nearest pool, which was the outdoor one. That's where I found Adam.

He did look like a college frat rat, with his shorter hair; his skinny pale body reddening, he was sitting in a deck chair, sipping a Coke, in sunglasses and racing trunks, chatting with a couple of bikinied college cuties, also in sunglasses.

"Bill?" I said.

"Jim?" he said, taking off his sunglasses to get a better look at me. He grinned, extended his hand. I took it, shook it, as he stood. "I haven't seen you since spring break!"

We'd agreed to be old high-school buddies from Peoria who had gone to separate colleges; I was attending the University of Iowa, he was at Michigan. We avoided using Illinois schools because Illinois kids were who we'd most likely run into here.

Adam introduced me to the girls—I don't remember their names, but one was a busty brunette Veronica, the other a flat-chested blond Betty. The sound of splashing and running screaming kids—though this was a couples hideaway, there was a share of families here, as well—kept the conversation to a blessed minimum. The girls were nursing majors. We were engineering majors. We all liked Credence Clearwater. We all hoped Nixon would get the book thrown at him. We were all going to the dance tonight.

Across the way, Baxter Bennedict was sitting in a deck chair under an umbrella reading *Jaws*. Every page or so, he'd sip his martini; every ten pages or so, he'd wave a waitress in cowgirl vest and white plastic hot pants over for another one. His wife was swimming, her dark arms cutting the water like knives. It seemed methodical, an exercise work-out in the midst of a pool filled with water babies of various ages.

When she pulled herself out of the water, her suit a stark, startling white against her almost burned black skin, she revealed a slender, rather tall figure; tight ass, high, full breasts. Her rather lined leathery face was the only tip-off to her age, and that had the blessing of a model's beauty to get it by.

She pulled off a white swim cap and unfurled a mane of dark, blond-tipped hair. Toweling herself off, she bent to kiss her husband on the cheek, but he only scowled at her. She stretched out on her colorful beach towel beside him, to further blacken herself.

"Oooo," said Veronica. "What's that ring?"

"That's my lucky ring," Adam said.

That fucking skull ring of his! Had he been dumb enough to wear that? Yes.

"Bought that at a Grateful Dead concert, didn't you, Bill?" I asked.

"Uh, yeah," he said.

"Ick," said Betty. "I don't like the Dead. Their hair is greasy. They're so . . . druggie."

"Drugs aren't so bad," Veronica said boldly, thrusting out her admirably thrustworthy bosom.

"Bill and I had our wild days back in high school," I said. "You shoulda seen our hair—down to our asses, right Bill?"

"Right."

"But we don't do that anymore," I said. "Kinda put that behind us."

"Well I for one don't approve of drugs," Betty said.

"Don't blame you," I said.

"Except for grass, of course," she said.

"Of course."

"And coke. Scientific studies prove coke isn't bad for you."

"Well, you're in nursing," I said. "You'd know."

We made informal dates with the girls for the dance, and I wandered off with "Bill" to his cabin.

"The skull ring was a nice touch," I said.

He frowned at me. "Fuck you—it's my lucky ring!"

A black gardener on a rider mower rumbled by us.

"Now we're really in trouble," I said.

He looked genuinely concerned. "What do you mean?"

"A black cat crossed our path."

In Adam's cabin, I sat on the brown, fake-leather sofa while he sat on the nubby yellow bedspread and spread his hands.

"They actually do have a sorta pattern," he said, "vacation or not."

Adam had arrived on Wednesday; the Bennedicts had arrived Thursday around two P.M., which was check-in time.

"They drink and swim all afternoon," Adam said, "and they go dining and dancing—and drinking—in the evening."

"What about mornings?"

"Tennis. He doesn't start drinking till lunch."

"Doesn't she drink?"

"Not as much. He's an asshole. We're doing the world a favor, here."

"How do you mean?"

He shrugged; he looked very different in his short hair. "He's kind of abusive. He don't yell at her, but just looking at them, you can see him glaring at her all the time, real ugly. Saying things that hurt her."

"She doesn't stand up to him?"

He shook his head, no. "They're very one-sided arguments. He either sits there and ignores her or he's giving her foul looks and it looks like he's chewing her out or something."

"Sounds like a sweet guy."

"After the drinking and dining and dancing, they head to the bar. Both nights so far, she's gone off to bed around eleven and he's stayed and shut the joint down."

"Good. That means he's alone when he walks back to their cabin."

Adam nodded. "But this place is crawlin' with people."

"Not at two in the morning. Most of these people are sleeping or fucking by then."

"Maybe so. He's got a fancy watch, some heavy gold jewelry."

"Well that's very good. Now we got ourselves a motive."

"But *she's* the one with jewels." He whistled. "You should see the rocks hanging off that dame."

"Well, we aren't interested in those."

"What about the stuff you steal off him? Just toss it somewhere?"

"Hell, no! Broker'll have it fenced for us. A little extra dough for our trouble."

He grinned. "Great. This is easy money. Vacation with pay."

"Don't ever think that . . . don't ever let your guard down."

"I know that," he said defensively.

"It's unlucky to think that way," I said, and knocked on wood. Real wood.

We met up with Betty and Veronica at the dance; I took Betty because Adam was into knockers and Veronica had them. Betty was pleasant company, but I wasn't listening to her babble. I was keeping an eye on the Bennedicts, who were seated at a corner table under a Buffalo head.

He really was an asshole. You could tell, by the way he sneered at her and spit sentences out at her, that he'd spent a lifetime—or at least a marriage—making her miserable. His hatred for her was something you could see as well as sense, like steam over asphalt. She was taking it placidly. Cool as Cher while Sonny prattled on.

But I had a hunch she usually took it more personally. Right now she could be placid: she knew the son of a bitch was going to die this weekend.

"Did you ever do Lauderdale?" Betty was saying. "I got *so* drunk there. . . ."

The band was playing "Crazy" and a decent girl singer was doing a respectable Patsy Cline. What a great song.

I said, "I won a chug-a-lug contest at Boonie's in '72."

Betty was impressed. "Were you even in college then?"

"No. I had a hell of a fake I.D., though."

"Bitchen!"

Around eleven, the band took a break and we walked the girls to their cabins, hand in hand, like high school sweethearts. Gas lanterns on poles scorched the night orangely; a half-moon threw some silvery light on us, too. Adam disappeared around the side of the cabin with Veronica and I stood and watched Betty beam at me and rock girlishly on her heels. She smelled of perfume and beer, which mingled with the scent of pines; it was more pleasant than it sounds.

She was making with the dimples. "You're so nice."

"Well thanks."

"And I'm a good judge of character."

"I bet you are."

Then she put her arms around me and pressed her slim frame to me and put her tongue half-way down my throat.

She pulled herself away and smiled coquetishly and said, "That's all you get tonight. See you tomorrow."

As if on cue, Veronica appeared with her lipstick mussed up and her sweater askew.

"Good night, boys," Veronica said, and they slipped inside, giggling like the school girls they were.

"Fuck," Adam said, scowling. "All I got was a little bare tit."

"Not so little."

"I thought I was gonna get laid."

I shrugged. "Instead you got screwed."

We walked. We passed a cabin that was getting some remodeling and repairs; I'd noticed it earlier. A ladder was leaned up against the side, for some re-roofing. Adam made a wide circle around the ladder. I walked under it just to watch him squirm.

When I fell back in step with him, he said, "You gonna do the hit tonight?"

"No."

"Bar closes at midnight on Sundays. Gonna do it then?"

"Yes."

He sighed. "Good."

We walked, and it was the place where one path went toward my cabin, and another toward his.

"Well," he said, "maybe I'll get lucky tomorrow night."

"No pick-ups the night of the hit. I need back-up more than either of us needs an alibi, or an easy fuck, either."

"Oh. Of course. You're right. Sorry. 'Night."

" 'Night, Bill."

Then I went back and picked up the waitress cowgirl and took her to my cabin; she had some dope in her purse, and I smoked a little with her, just to be nice, and apologized for not having a rubber, and she said, Don't sweat it, pardner, I'm on the pill, and she rode me in her cowboy boots until my dick said yahoo.

The next morning I had breakfast in the cafe with Adam and he seemed preoccupied as I ate my scrambled eggs and bacon, and he poked at his French toast.

"Bill," I said. "What's wrong?"

"I'm worried."

"What about?"

We were seated in a rough-wood booth and had plenty of privacy; we kept our voices down. Our conversation, after all, wasn't really proper breakfast conversation.

"I don't think you should hit him like that."

"Like what?"

He frowned. "On his way back to his cabin after the bar closes."

"Oh? Why?"

"He might not be drunk enough. Bar closes early Sunday night, remember? "

"Jesus," I said. "The fucker starts drinking at noon. What more do you want?"

"But there could be people around."

"At midnight?"

"It's a resort. People get romantic at resorts. Moonlight strolls . . ."

"You got a better idea?"

He nodded. "Do it in his room. Take the wife's jewels and it's a robbery got out of hand. In and out. No fuss, no muss."

"Are you high? What about the wife?"

"She won't be there."

"What are you talking about?"

He started gesturing, earnestly. "She gets worried about him, see. It's midnight, and she goes looking for him. While she's gone, he gets back, flops on the bed, you come in, bing bang boom."

I just looked at him. "Are you psychic now? How do we know she'll do that?"

He swallowed; took a nibble at a forkful of

syrup-dripping French toast. Smiled kind of nervously.

"She told me so," he said.

We were walking now. The sun was filtering through the trees and birds were chirping and the sounds of children laughing wafted through the air.

"Are you fucking nuts? Making contact with the client?"

"Quarry—she contacted me! I swear!"

"Then *she's* fucking nuts. Jesus!" I sat on a bench by a flower bed. "It's off. I'm calling the Broker. It's over."

"Listen to me! Listen. She was waiting for me at my cabin last night. After we struck out with the college girls? She was fuckin' waitin' for me! She told me she knew who I was."

"How did she know that?"

"She said she saw me watching them. She figured it out. She guessed."

"And, of course, you confirmed her suspicions."

He swallowed. "Yeah."

"You dumb-ass dickhead. Who said it first?"

"Who said what first?"

"Who mentioned 'killing.' Who mentioned 'murder.' "

His cheek twitched. "Well . . . me, I guess. She kept saying she knew why I was here. And then she said, I'm why you're here. I hired you."

"And you copped to it. God. I'm on the next bus."

"Quarry! Listen . . . this is better this way. This is much better."

"What did she do, fuck you?"

He blanched; looked at his feet.

"Oh God," I said. "You did get lucky last night. Fuck. You fucked the client. Did you tell her there were two of us?"

"No."

"She's seen us together."

"I told her you're just a guy I latched onto here to look less conspicuous."

"Did she buy it?"

"Why shouldn't she? I say we scrap Plan A and move to Plan B. It's better."

"Plan B being . . . ?"

"Quarry, she's going to leave the door unlocked. She'll wait for him to get back from the bar, and when he's asleep, she'll unlock the door, go out and pretend to be looking for him, and come back and find him dead, and her jewels gone. Help-police-I-been-robbed-my-husband's-been-shot. You know."

"She's being pretty fucking helpful, you ask me."

His face clenched like a fist. "The bastard has beat her for years. And he's got a girl friend a third his age. He's been threatening to divorce her, and since they signed a pre-marital agreement, she gets jackshit, if they divorce. The bastard."

"Quite a sob story."

"I told you: we're doing the world a favor. And now she's doing us one. Why shoot him right out in the open, when we can walk in his room and do it? You got to stick this out, Quarry. Shit, man, it's five grand apiece, and change!"

I thought about it.

"Quarry?"

I'd been thinking a long time.

"Okay," I said. "Give her the high sign. We'll do it her way."

The Bar W Bar was a cozy rustic room decorated with framed photos of movie cowboys from Ken Maynard to John Wayne, from Audie Murphy to the Man with No Name. On a brown mock-leather stool up at the bar, Baxter Bennedict sat, a thin handsome drunk in a pale blue polyester sportcoat and pale yellow Ban-Lon sportshirt, gulping martinis and telling anyone who'd listen his sad story.

I didn't sit near enough to be part of the conversation, but I could hear him.

"Milking me fucking dry," he was saying. "You'd think with sixteen goddamn locations, I'd be sitting pretty. I was the first guy in the Chicago area to offer a paint job under thirty dollars—$29.95! That's a good fucking deal—isn't it?"

The bartender—a young fellow in a buckskin vest, polishing a glass—nodded sympathetically.

"Now this competition. Killing me. What the fuck kind of paint job can you get for $19.99? Will you answer me that one? And now that bitch has the nerve . . ."

Now he was muttering. The bartender began to move away, but Baxter started in again.

"She wants me to sell! My life's work. Started from nothing. And she wants me to sell! Pitiful fucking money they offered. Pitiful . . ."

"Last call, Mr. Bennedict," the bartender said. Then he repeated it, louder, without the "Mr. Bennedict." The place was only moderately busy. A few couples. A solitary drinker or two. The Wistful Wagon Lodge had emptied out, largely, this afternoon—even Betty and Veronica were gone. Sunday. People had to go to work tomorrow. Except, of course, for those who owned their own businesses, like Baxter here.

Or had unusual professions, like mine.

I waited until the slender figure had stumbled half-way home before I approached him. No one was around. The nearest cabin was dark.

"Mr. Bennedict," I said.

"Yeah?" He turned, trying to focus his bleary eyes.

"I couldn't help but hear what you said. I think I have a solution for your problems."

"Yeah?" He grinned. "And what the hell would that be?"

He walked, on the unsteadiest of legs, up to me.

I showed him the nine millimeter with its bulky sound suppresser. It probably looked like a ray gun to him.

"Fuck! What is this, a fucking hold-up?"

"Yes. Keep your voice down or it'll turn into a fucking homicide. Got me?"

That turned him sober. "Got you. What do you want?"

"What do you think? Your watch and your rings."

He smirked disgustedly and removed them; handed them over.

"Now your sports coat."

"My what?"

"Your sports coat. I just can't get enough polyester."

He snorted a laugh. "You're out of your gourd, pal."

He slipped off the sports coat and handed it out toward me with two fingers; he was weaving a little, smirking drunkenly.

I took the coat with my left hand, and the silenced nine millimeter went *thup thup thup*; three small, brilliant blossoms of red appeared on his light yellow Ban-Lon. He was dead before he had time to think about it.

I dragged his body behind a clump of trees and left him there, his worries behind him.

I watched from behind a tree as Bernice Bennedict slipped out of their cabin; she was wearing a dark halter top and dark slacks that almost blended with her burnt-black skin, making a wraith of her. She had a big white handbag on a shoulder strap. She was so dark the white bag seemed to float in space as she headed toward the lodge.

Only she stopped and found her own tree to duck behind. I smiled to myself.

Then, wearing the pale blue polyester sports coat, I entered their cabin, through the door she'd left open. The room was completely dark but for some minor filtering in of light through curtained windows. I quickly arranged some pillows under sheets and covers, to create the impression of a person in the bed.

And I called Adam's cabin.

"Hey, Bill," I said. "It's Jim."

His voice was breathless. "Is it done?"

"No. I got cornered coming out of the bar by that waitress I was out with last night. She latched onto me—she's in my john."

"What, are you in your room?"

"Yeah. I saw Bennedict leave the bar at midnight, and his wife passed us, heading for the lodge, just minutes ago. You've got a clear shot at him."

"What? Me? I'm the fucking lookout!"

"Tonight's the night and we go to Plan C."

"I didn't know there *was* a Plan C."

"Listen, asshole—it was you who wanted to switch plans. You've got a piece, don't you?"

"Of course . . ."

"Well, you're elected. Go!"

And I hung up.

I stood in the doorway of the bathroom, which faced the bed. I sure as hell didn't turn any lights on, although my left hand hovered by the switch. The nine millimeter with the silencer was heavy in my right hand. But I didn't mind.

Adam came in quickly and didn't do too bad a job of it: four silenced slugs. He should have checked the body—it never occurred to him he'd just slaughtered a bunch of pillows—but if somebody had been in that bed, they'd have been dead.

He went to the dresser where he knew the jewels would be, and was picking up the jewelry box when the door opened and she came in, the little revolver already in her hand.

Before she could fire, I turned on the bathroom light and said, "If I don't hear the gun hit the floor immediately, you're fucking dead."

She was just a black shape, except for the white handbag; but I saw the flash of silver as the gun bounced to the carpeted floor.

"What . . . ?" Adam was saying. It was too dark to see any expression, but he was obviously as confused as he was spooked.

"Shut the door, lady," I said, "and turn on the lights."

She did.

She really was a beautiful woman, or had been, dark eyes and scarlet-painted mouth in that finely carved model's face, but it was just a leathery mask to me.

"What . . ." Adam said. He looked shocked as hell, which made sense; the gun was in his waistband, the jewelry box in his hands.

"You didn't know there were two of us, did you, Mrs. Bennedict?"

She was sneering faintly; she shook her head, no.

"You see, kid," I told Adam, "she wanted her husband hit, but she wanted the hitman dead, too. Cleaner. Tidier. Right?"

"Fuck you," she said.

"I'm not much for sloppy seconds, thanks. Bet you got a nice legal license for that little purse pea-shooter of yours, don't you? Perfect protection for when you stumble in on an intruder who's just killed your loving husband. Who *is* dead, by the way. Somebody'll run across him in the morning, probably."

"You bitch!" Adam said. He raised his own gun, which was a .38 Browning with a homemade suppresser.

"Don't you know it's bad luck to kill a woman?" I said.

She was frozen, one eye twitching.

Adam was trembling. He swallowed; nodded. "Okay," he said, lowering the gun. "Okay."

"Go," I told him.

She stepped aside as he slipped out the door, shutting it behind him.

"Thank you," she said, and I shot her twice in the chest.

I slipped the bulky silenced automatic in my waistband; grabbed the jewel box off the dresser.

"I make my own luck," I told her, but she didn't hear me, as I stepped over her.

I never worked with Adam again. I think he was disturbed, when he read the papers and realized I'd iced the woman after all. Maybe he got out of the business. Or maybe he wound up dead in a ditch, his lucky skull ring still on his little finger. Broker never said, and I was never interested enough to ask.

Now, years later, lounging in the hot tub at Sylvan Lodge, I look back on my actions and wonder how I could have ever have been so young, and so rash.

Killing the woman was understandable. She'd double-crossed us; she would've killed us both without batting a false lash.

But sleeping with that cowgirl waitress, on the job. Smoking dope. Not using a rubber.

I was really pushing my luck that time.

Villain: Mr. Smith

The Partnership

DAVID MORRELL

BORN IN KITCHENER, ONTARIO, David Morrell (1943–) was still a teenager when he decided to become an author. He was inspired by the *Route 66* television scripts written by Sterling Silliphant and encouraged by Philip Young (also known as the science fiction writer William Tenn), the Hemingway scholar at Penn State University, where Morrell eventually received his B.A., M.A., and Ph.D. In 1970, he took a job as an English professor at the University of Iowa, and produced his initial novel, *First Blood*, two years later.

Reviewers described *First Blood* (1972) as "the father of the modern adventure novel." It introduced the world to Rambo, who has gone on to become one of the most famous fictional characters in the world, largely through the movies that starred Sylvester Stallone. John Rambo (the famous name came from a variety of apple said to have been planted by Johnny Appleseed) is a Vietnam War vet, a troubled, violent, former Green Beret warrior trained in survival, hand-to-hand combat and other special martial skills; he was loosely based on World War II hero Audie Murphy. The film series began with *First Blood* (1982), and has continued with *Rambo: First Blood Part II* (1985), *Rambo III* (1988), and *Rambo* (2008).

Morrell has enjoyed numerous other bestsellers in various genres of his novels, including four volumes in the series that began with *The Brotherhood of the Rose* (1984), which became a popular TV miniseries starring Robert Mitchum in 1989; four volumes about the notorious Thomas De Quincey, set in the middle of the nineteenth century; stand-alone international thrillers; comic books; nonfiction; and highly popular horror fiction, notably *Creepers* (2005), which won the Bram Stoker Award from the Horror Writers Association. He is also the cofounder of the International Thriller Writers Association.

"The Partnership" was originally published in the May 27, 1981, issue of *Alfred Hitchcock's Mystery Magazine.*

THE PARTNERSHIP

David Morrell

SURE, IT WAS COLD-BLOODED, but there didn't seem another way. MacKenzie had spent months considering alternatives. He'd tried to buy his partner out but Dolan had refused.

Well, not exactly. Dolan's first response had simply been to laugh and say, "I wouldn't let you have the satisfaction." When MacKenzie kept insisting, Dolan's next response was, "Sure I'll let you buy me out. It only takes a million dollars."

Dolan might as well have wanted ten. MacKenzie couldn't raise a million, even half a million or a quarter—and he knew Dolan knew that.

It was typical. MacKenzie couldn't say "Good morning" without Dolan's disagreeing. If MacKenzie bought a car, Dolan bought a bigger, more expensive one and, just to rub it in, bragged about the deal he got. If MacKenzie took his wife and children on vacation to Bermuda, Dolan told him that Bermuda wasn't anything compared to Mazatlan, where Dolan had taken his wife and kids.

The two men argued constantly. They favored different football teams. Their taste in food was wildly different—mutton versus corned beef. When MacKenzie took up golf, Dolan suddenly was playing tennis, pointing out that golf was just a game while tennis was good exercise. But Dolan, even with his so-called exercise, was overweight. MacKenzie, on the other hand, was trim, but Dolan always made remarks about the hairpiece MacKenzie wore.

It was impossible—a Scotsman trying to maintain a business with an Irishman. MacKenzie should have known their relationship would never work. At the start, they had been rival builders, each attempting to outbid the other for construction jobs and losing money in the process. So they'd formed a partnership. Together they were more successful than they had been independently. Trying to outdo each other, one would think of ways to turn a greater profit and the other would feel challenged to be twice as clever. They cut costs by mixing too much gravel with the concrete, by installing low-grade pipes and sub-spec insulation. They kept special books for Uncle Sam.

MacKenzie-Dolan Enterprises. The two of them were enterprising, all right, but they couldn't bear to talk to one another. They had tried to solve that problem by dividing the work so that MacKenzie ran the office and let Dolan go out troubleshooting.

For a time that did the trick. But they still had to meet to make decisions and though they were seeing each other less, they seemed to save their tension up and aggravate each other more when they met.

To make things worse, their wives became good friends. The women were constantly organizing barbecues and swimming parties. The men tried not to argue at these get-togethers. When they did, they heard about it from their wives.

"I hate the guy," MacKenzie would tell his wife after a party. "He bugs me at the office and he made me sick tonight."

"You just listen to me, Bob—Vickie Dolan is my friend and I won't have your childish antics breaking up our friendship. I'll sleep on the couch tonight."

So both men braced themselves while their wives exchanged recipes.

What finally caused the big trouble was when Dolan started making threats.

"I wonder what the government would do if they knew about your special way of keeping books."

"What about the sub-spec plumbing and the extra gravel in the concrete?" MacKenzie had replied. "You're responsible for that, Dolan."

"But that's not a criminal offense—the judge would simply fine me," Dolan answered. "The IRS is quite a different kettle. If they knew you were keeping separate books, they'd lock you in a dungeon where I'd never have to see your ugly puss again."

MacKenzie stared at Dolan and decided there was no other choice. He'd tried to do the right thing, but his partner wouldn't sell. There wasn't any way around it. This was self-defense.

The man was waiting at the monkey cage, a tall, thin, friendly-looking fellow, young and blond. He wore a tailored light-blue jogging suit and he was eating peanuts.

At the water fountain, bending down to drink, MacKenzie glanced around. The zoo was crowded. It was noon on a sunny weekday, and people on their lunch breaks sat on benches munching sandwiches or strolled among the cages. There were children, mothers, old folks playing checkers. He heard tinny music from an organ grinder, muffled conversations, strident chattering and chirping. He was satisfied that no one was paying any attention to him, so he wiped water from his mouth and walked over.

"Mr. Smith?" he said.

The young man didn't turn—he just chewed another peanut—and MacKenzie was afraid he'd spoken to the wrong man. After all, the zoo was crowded and there were other men in jogging suits. Besides, no matter what the papers said, it wasn't easy finding someone who would do this kind of work. MacKenzie had spent several evenings haunting low-life bars before getting a lead. Once someone thought he was a cop and threatened to break both his legs. But hundred-dollar bills had eventually paid off and at last he'd arranged this meeting on a pay phone. But the man, apparently afraid of a trap, either had not arrived for the appointment or was playing possum.

As MacKenzie moved to leave, the young blond fellow turned to him. "Just a second, Bob," he said.

MacKenzie blinked. "Your name is Smith?"

"Just call me John." The young man's smile was brilliant. He was holding out the bag. "You want a peanut?"

"No, I don't think so—"

"Go on and have a peanut, Bob." The young man gestured with the bag.

MacKenzie took a peanut. He ate it, but he didn't taste it.

"That's right, relax, live a little. You don't mind if I call you Bob?"

"I don't care what you call me as long as we get this matter settled. You're not quite what I expected."

The young man nodded. "You were counting on George Raft and instead you got Troy Donohue. I know it's disappointing." He was frowning sympathetically. "But nothing's what it seems today. Would you believe I was a business major? But with the recession I couldn't get a job in management, so I'm doing this."

"You mean you're not experienced?"

"Take it easy, Bob. I didn't say that. I can handle my end. Don't you fret about a thing. You see these monkeys? Just watch this." He threw some peanuts. All the monkeys scrambled, fighting for them.

"See—they're just like us, Bob. We're all scrambling for the peanuts."

"Well, I'm sure that's very symbolic—"

"All right, you're impatient. I'm just trying to be sociable." He sighed. "No one takes the time any more. So what's your problem, Bob?"

"My business partner."

"Is he stealing from the kitty?"

"No."

"He's fooling with your wife then?"

"No."

The young man nodded. "I understand."

"You do?"

"Of course. It's very simple. What I call the marriage syndrome."

"What?"

"It's like you're married to your partner, but you hate him and he won't agree to get divorced."

"Why, that's incredible!"

"Excuse me?"

"You're right. That's it."

The young man shrugged and threw a peanut. "Bob, I've seen it all. My specialty is human nature. So you don't care how I do it?"

"Just as long as it's—"

"An accident. Precisely. You recall my price when we discussed this on the phone?"

"Two thousand dollars."

"Half now, half later. Did you bring the money?"

"It's in my pocket."

"Don't give it to me yet. Go over and put the envelope inside that waste container. In a moment I'll walk over and stuff this empty bag in. When I leave I'll take the envelope."

"His name is Patrick Dolan."

"The particulars are with the money?"

"As you asked."

"Then don't worry. I'll be in touch."

"Hey, wait a minute. Afterward, I don't have any guarantee that—"

"Blackmail? You're afraid I'll extort you? Bob, I'm surprised at you! That wouldn't be good business!"

Dolan walked out of the hardware store. The afternoon was glaring hot. He wiped his brow and squinted. There was someone in his pickup truck, a young guy eating corn chips. Blond, good-looking, in a jogging suit.

He stalked across the parking lot, reached the truck, and yanked open the door. "Hey, buddy, this is my truck you're—"

The young man turned. His smile was disarming. "Hi there, Pat. You want some corn chips?"

Dolan's mouth hung open. Sweat was trickling from his forehead. "What?"

"The way you're sweating, you need salt. Have some corn chips."

Dolan's jaw went rigid. "Out!"

"Excuse me?"

"Get out before I throw you out."

The young man sighed. Tugging down the zipper on his sweatshirt, he revealed the big revolver bulging from a shoulder holster.

Dolan's stomach lurched. He blanched and stumbled backward, gaping.

"What the—?"

"Just relax," the young man said.

"Look, buddy, all I've got is twenty dollars."

"You don't understand. Climb on up here and we'll talk a little."

Dolan glanced around in panic. No one seemed to notice him. He wondered if he ought to run.

"Don't try to run, Pat."

Relieved of that decision, Dolan quickly climbed inside the truck. He ate the corn chips the blond offered a second time but he couldn't taste the salt. His shirt was sticking to the back of the seat. All he could think of was the bulging object underneath the jogging suit.

"Here's the thing," the young man told him. "I'm supposed to kill you."

Dolan sat up so hard he bumped his head against the ceiling. *"What?"*

"Your partner hired me. For two thousand dollars."

"If this is a joke—"

"It's business, Pat. He paid a thousand down. You want to see it?"

"But that's crazy!"

"I wish you hadn't said that." The young man reached inside his sweatshirt.

"No, wait a minute! I didn't mean that!"

"I only want to show the note your partner gave me. Here. You'll recognize his handwriting."

Dolan glared down at the note. "It's my name and address."

"And your physical description and your habits. See, he wants your death to seem like an accident."

Dolan finally accepted this wasn't any joke. His stomach burned with sudden rage. "That dirty—"

"Temper, Pat."

"He wants to buy me out—but I won't let him have the satisfaction!"

"I understand. It's like the two of you are married and you want to make him suffer."

"You're damn right I want to make him suffer! I've put up with him for twenty years! So now he figures he can have me killed and take the business for himself? That sneaky, rotten—"

"Bob, I've got bad news for you."

MacKenzie almost spilled his Scotch. He turned. The young man had come up beside him without warning and was eating popcorn at the bar.

"Don't tell me you botched the job!" MacKenzie's eyes went wide with horror. He glanced quickly around as if expecting to be arrested.

"Bob, I never even got the chance to start." The young man picked at something in his teeth.

"My God, what happened?"

"Nearly broke a tooth. These kernels aren't all popped."

"I meant with Dolan!"

"Keep your voice down, Bob. I know you meant with him. No one cares if someone else breaks a tooth. They only care about themselves. Do you believe in competition?"

"What?"

"Do you support free enterprise, the thing that made this country great?"

MacKenzie felt his knees go weak. He clutched the bar and nodded weakly.

"Then you'll understand. When I went to see your partner—"

"Oh, my God, you *told* him!"

"Bob, I couldn't simply kill him and not let him have a chance to make a bid. That wouldn't be fair."

MacKenzie started trembling. "Bid? What kind of bid?"

"Don't get excited, Bob. We figured he could pay me not to kill him. But you'd just send someone else. So what we finally decided was that he'd pay me to come back and kill you. He offered double—two grand now and two when you were shoveled under."

"He can't do that!"

"But he did, Bob. Don't go simple on me now. You should have seen his face. I mean to tell you, he was angry."

"You accepted what *I* offered! You agreed to take *my* contract!"

"A verbal contract isn't binding. Anyhow, you're in a seller's market. What I'm selling is worth more now."

"You're a crook!"

The young man's face looked pained. "I'm sorry you feel that way."

"No, wait. Don't leave. I didn't mean it."

"Bob, you hurt my feelings."

"I apologize. I don't know what I'm saying. Every time I think about that guy—"

"I understand, Bob. You're forgiven."

"Pat, you'll never guess what Bob did."

At the railing, Dolan shuddered. He was watching as the horses thundered toward the finish line. He turned. The young man stood beside him, chewing on a hot dog.

"You don't mean you told him?"

"Pat, I had to. Fair is fair. He offered double our agreement. Four grand now, four later."

"And you've come to me to raise the price?"

"They're at the stretch!" the track announcer shouted.

"It's inflation, Pat. It's killing us." The young man wiped some mustard from his lips.

"You think I'm stupid?" Dolan asked.

The young man frowned.

"That I'm a moron?" Dolan said.

"Excuse me, Pat?"

"If I pay more, you'll go to him and *he'll* pay more. Then you'll come back to me and *I'll* pay more. Forget it! I'm not paying!"

"Fine with me, Pat. Nice to see you."

"Wait a minute!"

"Is something wrong?"

"Of course there's something wrong! You're going to kill me!"

"Well, the choice is up to you."

"The winner is number three, Big Trouble—" the track announcer shouted.

Horses rumbled by, their jockeys standing up to slow them. Dust was drifting.

"Damn it, yes. I'll pay you," Dolan muttered. "But do it this time! I can't sleep. I'm losing weight. I've got an ulcer."

"Pat, the race is over. Did you have a bet?"

"On number six to win."

"A nag, Pat. She came in last. If you had asked me, I'd have told you number three."

"You'll never guess what Pat did, Bob."

MacKenzie stiffened. Dolan stopped beside him, looked around and sighed, then sat down on the park bench. "So you figured you'd have me killed," Dolan said.

MacKenzie's face was gaunt. "You weren't above the same temptation yourself."

Dolan shrugged. "Self-defense."

"I should sit back while you sic the IRS on me?"

"That was just a joke."

"Some joke. It's costing me a fortune."

"It's costing me too."

"We've got a problem."

"I've been thinking," Dolan said. "The only answer I can see—"

"—is for both of us to kill him."

"Only way."

"He'll bleed us dry."

"But if we pay someone else to kill him, the new guy might try something cute too."

"We'll do it together. That way you can't point the blame at me."

"Or vice versa."

"What's the matter? Don't you trust me?"

They were glaring at each other.

"Hi there, Bob. How are you, Pat?"

The young man smiled from behind their files. He was munching a taco as he went through their records.

"What the hell is this now?" MacKenzie said.

"He claimed you expected him," the secretary said.

"Just shut the door," Dolan told her.

"Hey, fellas, your records really are a mess. This skimping on the concrete. And this sub-spec insulation. I don't know, guys—we've got lots of work ahead of us."

A drop of taco sauce fell on a file folder.

"Us?"

"Well, sure—we're partners now."

"We're *what*?"

"I took the money you gave me and invested it."

"In what?"

"Insurance. You remember how I said I was

a business major? Well, I decided this sideline doesn't suit me, so I went to see a specialist. The things a graduate is forced to do to get a job these days!"

"A specialist?"

"A hit man. If the two of you decide to have me killed, you'll be killed as well."

MacKenzie's chest began to stab. Dolan's ulcer started burning.

"So we're partners. Here, I even had some cards made up."

He handed one across to each of them. MACKENZIE–DOLAN–SMITH, it read. And at the bottom: CONTRACTORS.

Blackburn Sins

BRADLEY DENTON

IT IS TRICKY to define Jimmy Blackburn as a villain. Yes, he does kill people with disquieting regularity but, then, they really do deserve it. Bradley Denton (1958–) has essentially given his character carte blanche to eliminate bad people from the face of the Earth—and who among us hasn't wanted to do the same? True, we haven't actually done it but, then, we're not fictional characters.

Denton was raised in rural Kansas before attending the University of Kansas, receiving a B.A. degree in astronomy and an M.A. in English, then moved to Austin, Texas. Virtually all of his work has been in the fantasy and science fiction genres. Even *Blackburn* (1993), his single foray into book-length crime fiction, has elements of dark fantasy, being nominated for a Bram Stoker Award by the Horror Writers Association. Generally described as a novel, it is, in fact, a collection of connected short stories. Denton has admitted that he has found the nature of his character to be disturbing. "Basically," Denton said, "what I'm doing is taking a character who is more or less a normal human being but gets pushed in one direction just a little too far and does what I think any one of us could do under those circumstances."

Although not prolific, with only eight books to his credit in the thirty years since *Wrack and Roll* (1986), his first book, was published, Denton has received more than his share of honors, including for *The Calvin Coolidge Home for Dead Comedians and A Conflagration Artist* (1994), which won the World Fantasy Award for Best Collection, and *Buddy Holly Is Alive and Well on Ganymede* (1991), which won the John W. Campbell Memorial Award for Best Science Fiction Novel.

"Blackburn Sins" was first published in *Blackburn* (New York, St. Martin's Press, 1993).

BLACKBURN SINS

Bradley Denton

THE DEADBOLT WASN'T SET, so Blackburn broke into the apartment with a six-inch metal ruler. A lamp was on inside. He scanned the living room, but wasn't interested in the TV or stereo. This was a second-story apartment with outside stairs, so he couldn't take anything big. The VCR was small enough, but he decided against it anyway. He wasn't proud that he had turned to thievery, so he preferred to steal only those things that were of no use or pleasure to their owners. But that rule tended to limit him to class rings and junk, so he didn't always stick to it.

He didn't bother with the kitchen. Apartment dwellers didn't own silver. He pulled his folded duffel bag from his coat and stepped into the hallway that led to the bedroom. Bedrooms were good for jewelry. Houston pawn shops paid cash for gold chains and silver earrings.

The bedroom door opened, and a man stepped out. Blackburn froze.

The man closed the door behind him. He was tall. His face and most of his body were shadowed. His right hand was empty, but Blackburn couldn't see his left. It might be holding a weapon.

"What are you doing here?" the man asked. His voice was of moderate pitch. He didn't sound upset.

Blackburn was confused. He had watched this building for three days, noting the occupants of each apartment and their schedules. This unit's occupant was a woman who had left for her night shift at Whataburger twenty minutes ago. He was sure that she lived alone. The man at the end of the hall should not exist.

"Don't be afraid," the man said. "I just want to know why you're here."

Blackburn took two steps backward. His Colt Python was in its pouch in his coat, but he couldn't reach for it without dropping the duffel bag from his right hand. Then it would take two or three seconds to reach into the left side of his coat, open the Velcro flap, and pull out the pistol. If the shadowed man had a gun or knife, Blackburn might be dead before getting off a shot. So his best option was to leave, but he had to do it without turning his back.

"Tell me why you're here," the shadowed man said, "and I won't hurt you. But if you don't stand still, I will."

Blackburn stopped. "I was going to steal things," he said, "but I'm not going to now."

"What things were you going to steal?"

"Jewelry. Rings, necklaces. Maybe a musical instrument, like an old trumpet or an out-of-tune guitar."

"Why out of tune?" the shadowed man asked.

"A guitar that's in tune is in use," Blackburn said. "I don't like to steal things people use."

The shadowed man gave a short chuckle, almost a grunt. "A burglar with a moral code," he said. "But people use jewelry too, you know."

"It just hangs there," Blackburn said. "It's stupid."

"In your opinion."

Blackburn started to relax his grip on the duffel bag. He had decided to try for the Python. "Yes," he said. "In my opinion."

"And that's the only opinion that counts."

"Yes." The duffel began to slip from Blackburn's fingers.

"Don't reach for your pistol, Musician," the shadowed man said.

"I don't have a pistol."

"You have a lump in your coat. It's big, but the wrong shape for an automatic. I'm guessing a three fifty-seven. A forty-four would be awfully heavy."

Blackburn tightened his grip on the duffel bag again. "All right. I won't reach for it."

"Good. If you did, I'd have to kill you. And that would be a shame, because I agree with you. Your opinion is the only one that matters. *My* opinion is the only one that matters too."

"That's a contradiction," Blackburn said.

"Why? You create your world, I create mine. Contradictions only exist for people who aren't bright enough to do that. When they come up against someone who is, it's matter and antimatter. Know what I mean?"

"Yes."

"I knew you would," the shadowed man said. "I'm going to come toward you now so we can see each other. I'll move slowly, and you won't move at all. All right?"

"All right."

A smell of deodorant soap preceded the man as he stepped from the shadows. He had long dark hair, shot through with gray. It was pulled back from his face. His skin was sallow, his eyes a greenish brown. He was wearing a hooded black pullover sweatshirt, black sweatpants, and gray running shoes. His left hand held a small paper bag. There was no visible weapon.

Blackburn dropped his duffel and brought out the Python. He cocked it and pointed it at the man's face.

The man stopped. "You agreed not to move," he said.

"I lied."

"That doesn't seem consistent with a moral code."

"I've created my own world," Blackburn said. "In here, it's moral." He stepped backward.

"You don't have to leave empty-handed," the man said. He shook the paper bag, and its contents clinked. "See, I'm a burglar too. I don't know that I'm as moral as you, but I'm willing to split the take."

Blackburn paused. He eyed the paper bag. "I was watching this place. How'd you get in?"

"Through a window in the bathroom. On the back side of the building."

"Someone might see your ladder."

The man shook his head. "I climbed the wall. Plenty of space between the bricks." He turned the paper bag upside down. Rings, necklaces, and earrings fell to the carpet. "This has to be fifty-fifty, so don't cheat."

"Why let me have any of it?" Blackburn asked.

The man knelt on the floor and bent over the tangle of jewelry. His ponytail hung down over his shoulder. "So you won't turn me in." He looked up and smiled. "And so if we're caught, I can plea-bargain the punishment over your way."

Blackburn replaced the Python in its pouch. "I'll take that class ring."

The man flicked it toward him. "You can call me Roy-Boy."

"I don't need to call you anything," Blackburn said, squatting to pick up the ring. "I won't be seeing you again."

"The best laid plans, Musician."

"I'm not a musician."

"In your world, maybe not. In mine, you play electric guitar. You want to sound like Hendrix, but you're too white and you don't do enough drugs."

Blackburn said nothing. He took the ring and three gold chains, then picked up his duffel bag and left. He crossed the street and hid behind a dumpster to watch the apartment building. He wanted to see if Roy-Boy left too.

A few minutes later Roy-Boy appeared under a streetlight and looked across at the dumpster. He pointed his right finger and waggled his thumb to mimic a pistol. Then he walked away.

Blackburn waited until Roy-Boy was out of sight before walking the four blocks to his Plymouth Duster. The back of his neck tingled. He looked in all directions, but saw no one. He thought he smelled deodorant soap, but decided it was his clothes. Maybe he had used too much detergent.

Two nights later, on Friday, Blackburn stuffed his pockets with cash and drove to The Hoot, a bar near the Rice University campus. His coat felt light without the Python, which he had hidden in his closet. He wouldn't need a gun tonight. His goal was to seduce one of the college girls he had met at The Hoot the week before, preferably the thin brunette who was a flute player in the marching band. The last time he'd had sex had been behind a barbecue pit at a Labor Day picnic, and here it was almost Christmas. He was afraid the top of his head might blow off.

The Hoot was crowded. It smelled of moist flesh and beer, and throbbed with canned rock 'n' roll. The flute player was there. Blackburn went to her and made the comment that the Rice football team could have had more success the previous weekend had it used the band's woodwind section in place of its defensive line. The flute player laughed. She remembered him and called him Alan, the name he was using now. Her name was Heather. It seemed to Blackburn that at least half of the twenty-year-old women in the world were named Heather, but he didn't tell her that. He liked her. She had a fine sense of humor. It had been her idea, she said, for the Marching Owl Band to cover their uniforms with black plastic trash bags and lie down on the football field at halftime to simulate an oil slick.

Heather was a steady drinker, and Blackburn felt obliged to match her. After half an hour he had to excuse himself for a few minutes. When he came out of the men's room, he saw that someone had taken his place at the bar and was leaning close to Heather. Blackburn couldn't see this person's head, but he could tell from the way the jeans fit across the hips that it was a male.

Heather saw Blackburn and waved. "Hey!" she called. "Everything come out okay?"

The man beside her raised his head, and Blackburn saw that it was Roy-Boy.

Roy-Boy smiled as Blackburn approached. "Musician," he said. His ponytail was wet. It glistened in the neon glow.

Heather looked from Blackburn to Roy-Boy. "You guys know each other?"

"We're in the same business," Roy-Boy said. He turned on his bar stool so that his knee touched Heather's thigh.

Blackburn's teeth clenched. The sharp scent of Roy-Boy's deodorant soap was cutting through the other smells.

"Really?" Heather said. "What do you do?"

"We sell discount merchandise," Roy-Boy said. "We're competitors, actually."

Heather looked concerned. "Does that mean you don't like each other?"

"No," Roy-Boy said. "In fact, we can help each other."

"I'm thinking of getting into another line of work," Blackburn said. But if he stopped stealing, he would have to take a job at yet another fast-food restaurant. It was the only legal work he was qualified to do. He had fried burgers or chicken, or stuffed burritos, in every city he had ever stayed in more than a few days. He was sick of it.

"I'd be sorry if you did that, Alan," Roy-Boy said.

Blackburn looked at Heather. "Did you tell him my name?" He realized after he said it that it sounded like an accusation. The beer had made him stupid.

"No," Heather said, frowning. "Why would I? You know each other, right?"

"We've never exchanged names," Roy-Boy told her, "but I got curious and asked around about him. Has he told you he's a guitar player? He plays a left-handed Telecaster."

Heather's frown vanished. "You in a band?" she asked Blackburn.

"No," he said. "I mean, not right now."

"He was in three bands at once when he lived in Austin," Roy-Boy said. "He even played with Stevie Ray a couple of times."

Heather was gazing at Blackburn. "Why'd you quit?"

"No money in it," he said.

Roy-Boy got off the bar stool. "That reminds me," he said. "I have some work to catch up on." He dropped a five-dollar bill on the bar. "Next round's on me."

"Oh, that's sweet," Heather said.

"Yeah," Blackburn said.

Roy-Boy clapped Blackburn on the shoulder. "Happy to do it," he said. "Us old guys got to stick together." He headed for the door.

Blackburn imagined making Roy-Boy eat his own eyes.

"Bye, Steve!" Heather called. Then she grinned at Blackburn. "How old are you, anyway?"

Blackburn sat down on the empty stool. It was warm from Roy-Boy, so he stood up again.

"Twenty-seven," he said. "How about you?"

Heather raised her beer mug. "Twenty-one, of course. You don't think I'd come into a bar if I wasn't, do you?"

"Guess not."

"I'd love to hear you play sometime."

Blackburn's tongue tasted like soap. "I don't have a guitar now," he said.

Heather shrugged. "Okay, I'll play for you instead. You like flute music?"

"You bet," Blackburn sai
neck tingled, and he turned.

Roy-Boy was standing ou
through the cluster of neon s
window. He pointed his finger
waggled his thumb.

"So, you want to have another
asked. "Or would you like to hear

Blackburn turned back to he
said.

They stood to leave. Roy-Boy
the window. Blackburn left the five
the bar.

In the morning Blackburn awoke wi
rump against his belly. Since the enc
riage, it was rare that he spent an
with a woman, and even rarer that h
pen at his place. But as he and Heath
The Hoot, she had said that her apa
off-limits for sex because her roon
a born-again Christian. So they ha
to put off the flute recital, and Black
taken Heather to his studio crackerb
Heights. After a few hours they had fall
together.

He slid out of bed and went into t
room. He didn't flush, because he didn't
wake Heather. When he came out, he s
she had rolled onto her back. Her mou
open, and strands of her hair were stuck
face. She wasn't a beauty, as Dolores had
but she was fun. Blackburn didn't rem
ever having laughed in bed before.

He dressed and went out. His plan w
bring Heather a surprise for breakfast. L
night, she had told him a story about a Ric
ternity that had been getting noise compl
from the sorority next door. One morning
sorority women had received a box of do
from the fraternity, along with a note saying t
the donuts were the men's response to the co
plaints. The women had eaten the donuts
breakfast and then had received another delive
from the fraternity. It was a photograph of

enty-two men in their dining room, each one ked except for the donut on his penis. Heather ought the story was hilarious, so Blackburn nted to have a box of donuts waiting for her hen she awoke.

The sun had risen, but the air had the sting of winter night. Blackburn hadn't thought Houston ever got so cold. He breathed deep, and the hill cut into his throat. When he exhaled, his reath was white. He hurried across the parking ot to the Duster, hoping it would start. Its windows were opaque with frost. Blackburn didn't have an ice scraper, but maybe the defroster would do. He unlocked the driver's door and got nside, letting the door slam shut after him. The nterior smelled of deodorant soap.

Roy-Boy was sitting in the passenger seat. He was wearing the black sweatsuit again. The sweatshirt's hood was up over his head, and his hands were inside the pouch.

"Morning, Musician," he said, peering out from the hood. "Happy Pearl Harbor Day."

Blackburn was annoyed. "Get out," he said, "and don't come near me again. If you do, you won't do anything else."

"Now, come on," Roy-Boy said. "You're a moral guy, and I haven't done anything to you. You wouldn't whack me for looking at you wrong, would you?"

"You broke into my car," Blackburn said. "In Texas, it's legal to shoot people who break into your car."

"But I didn't break in. This door was unlocked."

"Doesn't matter. You didn't have my permission to enter. So I can shoot you."

"But you don't have your gun."

"I can get it."

Roy-Boy took his hands from his sweatshirt pouch. His right hand held a .22-caliber revolver. "You can try," he said.

Blackburn saw that the .22 was a cheap piece of crap. But at this range, it could kill him just as dead as a .357.

"What do you want?" he asked.

"Right now, to get warm," Roy-Boy said. "Then I want to talk a little. Let's drive, and crank the heater."

Blackburn put the key into the ignition. The Duster whined for a while, then started. The engine sputtered, and the car shook.

"Sounds like ice in the fuel line," Roy-Boy said. "Put a can of Heet in the tank. If you can find it in this city." He opened his door. "Hang on and I'll scrape your windows." He got out, leaving the door open.

Blackburn considered trying to run him over, but decided against it. A bullet might make it through the windshield. So he waited while Roy-Boy scraped. Roy-Boy's scraper was a long, pointed shard of glass with white cloth tape wrapped around one end. Roy-Boy had pulled it from his sweatshirt pouch. He was scraping with his left hand. His right hand, with the pistol, was in the pouch. Blackburn could see the muzzle straining against the fabric. It was pointing at him.

When the windows were clear, Roy-Boy got back inside and closed the door. He licked ice crystals from the glass shard, then replaced it in his pouch and looked at Blackburn. "What're you waiting for?" he asked. He pulled out the .22.

Blackburn drove onto the street and headed for I-10. He would wait for his chance. It would come. It always did.

"So, how was she?" Roy-Boy asked as the Duster entered the freeway.

"Fine."

"I'm glad. I was afraid I'd ruined things for you at The Hoot, so I tried to fix them before I left. Guess I did. What're you gonna do with her now?"

Blackburn glanced at him. "What do you mean?"

"Are you gonna fuck her again, kill her, or what?"

"Why would I kill her?"

"Because you're a killer, boy. That's what you do, right?"

Blackburn's neck tingled. "What makes you think so?"

Roy-Boy leaned close. When he spoke, his breath was hot on Blackburn's face.

"Takes one to know one," he said.

Blackburn flinched away, bumping his head on the window.

Roy-Boy returned to his previous position. "Don't worry," he said. "I promise not to stick my tongue in your ear or bite through your cheek." He pointed outside. "You just passed a Day-Lite Donut store. If you take the next exit you can cut back to it."

Blackburn stared at him.

"Watch the road," Roy-Boy said.

Blackburn took the next exit. He parked at the donut shop, then put his keys into his coat pocket and clenched his fist. Two keys jutted out between his knuckles. He watched Roy-Boy.

Roy-Boy smiled. "You want to kill me now. You're hoping I won't notice your hand in your pocket."

"You seem to know me pretty well," Blackburn said.

"Oh, yeah. I know you, Musician." Roy-Boy put his pistol into his sweatshirt pouch, then held up his empty hands. "So I also know that if you think about it, you'll decide not to kill me after all. I pulled a gun on you, but only because you pulled a gun on *me* Wednesday night. I figure we're even."

That made some sense to Blackburn, but it only went so far. "How did you know I was going for donuts?"

"Well, I was shooting the shit with Heather last night," Roy-Boy said. "You know, at The Hoot, while you were in the can. She was telling me about this donut gag some frat pulled. Then you came out this morning with a shit-eating grin on your face, so I thought: donuts. A dozen glazed be okay?" He got out of the car and went into the shop.

Blackburn waited. There was no point in leaving. Roy-Boy knew where he lived.

Roy-Boy returned with a white cardboard box. "I got a few extras," he said, exhaling steam as he entered the car. "Some jelly and some creme. Want one?"

"No."

Roy-Boy opened the box and took out a filled donut. Chocolate creme oozed when he bit into it. He gestured at the Duster's ignition switch. "Don't let me hold you back," he said around a mouthful of pastry. "We can talk while you drive."

"I'd like to sit here awhile," Blackburn said. "If that's all right."

"Sure," Roy-Boy said. He reached up and pushed his sweatshirt hood from his head. "I'm warm now. I just thought you might want to get home to your three fifty-seven. Why'd you take it out of your coat, anyway? Were you afraid Heather might feel it when she hugged you? Or did you shoot her and then leave it in her hand to make it look like suicide?"

"I wouldn't kill a woman."

Roy-Boy's eyebrows rose. "How come? Haven't you run across any who deserved it?"

Blackburn thought of Dolores. "It's just a rule I have."

Roy-Boy shook his head. "Sexist," he said.

"Maybe. But a man's got to have his rules."

Roy-Boy stuffed the rest of the chocolate-creme donut into his mouth. "Yeah," he said, his voice muffled. "If you say so."

"Have *you* ever killed a woman?" Blackburn asked. His fist tightened around his keys. The windows had fogged. No one could see in.

"No," Roy-Boy said, chewing. His eyes were steady, fixed on Blackburn's. "In fact, I've never killed anyone. But I'm still a killer, because I'd do it if I had to. If it was me or him. Or her."

"Why'd you think I killed Heather?"

"I didn't. I just thought it was a possibility. See, she's got a rep for screwing guys over. Narking on them, taking their money, leaving teeth marks, shit like that. I figured if she did it to you, you'd fix her." Roy-Boy swallowed. "But I was unaware of your rule."

Blackburn didn't know whether to believe what Roy-Boy said about Heather. He sounded like he was telling the truth, but some people were good at that. And Heather didn't seem like the kind of woman who would screw over a lover.

On the other hand, Dolores hadn't seemed like that kind either.

"Any other probing questions before you decide whether to poke holes in me with your car keys?" Roy-Boy asked.

"One," Blackburn said. "Why are you bugging me?"

Roy-Boy grinned. There were chocolate smears on his teeth. "Am I bugging you? That's not my intention. I just think we can help each other, like we did Wednesday. I take half, you take half. See, if we hit places together we'll have less chance of trouble, because we'll both be watching for it. And we could carry the big stuff. You see the advantages?"

"Yes."

Roy-Boy held out his hand. "Then it's a partnership."

"No. I can see the advantages, but I don't want them."

Roy-Boy lowered his hand. "Why not? Because you don't want to take 'things people use'? Man, people use everything. They just don't *need* all of it. If it'll make your moral code happy, then I promise we won't steal any insulin kits or dialysis machines. But a TV set ought to be fair game."

"My moral code doesn't have anything to do with it," Blackburn said. "The problem is that I'm leaving town." It wasn't really a lie. He hadn't been planning to leave, but he hadn't been planning to stay either.

Roy-Boy looked surprised. "How come?"

"I never stay anywhere more than a few months." That was most often because he had no choice, but Roy-Boy didn't need to know that. "And I've been here since August, so another week and I'm gone. By Christmas for sure."

"Where to?"

"Don't know yet."

Roy-Boy looked away and sighed. "Ain't that the way it goes. I find a partner with morals, and he's no sooner found than lost." He opened the door and got out, leaving the box of donuts on the seat. "No hard feelings, though, hey?"

Blackburn said nothing.

"You don't still want to kill me, do you?" Roy-Boy asked. His hand went into his sweatshirt pouch.

"No," Blackburn said.

Roy-Boy stooped and peered in at him. "You should grow your hair into a ponytail," he said. "All of the great statesman-philosophers had ponytails. Thomas Jefferson, for example, who philosophized about independence and freedom, and owned slaves. What a great world *he* created." Roy-Boy straightened. "Have a good trip, Musician, and enjoy the donuts. I'm gonna get some more for myself. See, I only have one testicle, so I have to eat twice as much as most men in order to manufacture enough jism for my needs." He turned and walked toward the donut shop.

Blackburn leaned over to pull the door shut, then wiped the fog from the windshield and watched Roy-Boy enter the shop. He still had the feeling that he should kill Roy-Boy, but he couldn't think of a good reason why. All Roy-Boy had done was pester him. That might have been enough to warrant death, had it cost Blackburn anything, but it had cost him nothing but a little time. And now he had a free box of donuts, which pushed Roy-Boy's behavior even further into a gray area.

He started the Duster. No matter what he felt, he would not kill someone for behavior that fell into a gray area. He required a clear reason. If he started killing people without such reasons, he would be in violation of his own ethics. It was bad enough that he had become a burglar. A man had to have his rules.

On the way home, he stopped at a convenience store and bought a can of Heet, which he poured into the Duster's tank. Then he drove to his apartment and carried the box of donuts inside. Heather was in the bathroom with the door shut.

When she emerged, Blackburn was lying on the bed wearing nothing but a donut. Heather stayed two more hours, then said she had to get home to study for finals. Blackburn was going to drive her, but the Duster refused to start. So Heather took a cab. After she had gone, Blackburn realized that he didn't have her phone number or address. He might be able to find her at The Hoot again, but he wasn't sure that he should. He liked her a lot, and he knew what that could lead to.

Blackburn was still in Houston the next Friday evening, watching a three-story apartment building in Bellaire. He had decided to leave the city by Christmas, but he needed traveling money. He had also decided that he had to stop breaking into houses and apartments, even if it meant working in fast food again. If he found some worthwhile items tonight, this would be his last day as a burglar.

He had not returned to The Hoot to look for Heather, and she had not come by his apartment to look for him. That was all right. They'd had twelve good hours together, which was twelve more than he'd had with most people, and he had the sense to leave well enough alone. It didn't feel good, but good feelings had nothing to do with good sense.

The sun had set, and lights in some of the apartments had come on. Blackburn, sitting across the street in the Duster, noted the number of cars in the building's lot and the number of apartments that were lit. He compared these numbers to those he had counted at other times since midafternoon, when he had started watching. He had been careful—sometimes driving by, sometimes parking a few blocks away and walking, and now parked under a broken streetlight—but he hadn't observed this building for two or three entire days, as was his habit. He had figured that some of the residents would have already left for Christmas vacations, and their apartments would be easy to spot. He had been right. Two apartments on the top floor were staying dark, as were three on the second floor, and one on the first. Two other apartments had lights that had been on since he'd started watching, and he didn't think anyone was home. He would wait a few more hours to be sure. He could turn on the radio now and then to keep from getting bored.

He was listening to a ZZ Top song when the back of his neck tingled. He looked around and saw a man standing under a streetlight in front of the apartment building. The man was wearing a black sweatsuit, and his hair was pulled back in a ponytail. He was pointing at Blackburn and waggling his thumb. It was Roy-Boy.

Blackburn turned off the radio. He gave Roy-Boy a violent sidearm wave, trying to tell him to go away. But Roy-Boy stayed put, still pointing. Someone would drive by and notice him before long. Blackburn changed his wave to a "come here" gesture, then unzipped his coat and reached inside. He opened the Velcro flap over the Python's pouch.

Roy-Boy jogged across the street, his ponytail bouncing. He had put his hands into his sweatshirt pouch, so Blackburn had to take his own hand out of his coat to let him into the car. The smell of deodorant soap was even stronger than before. Blackburn wondered what Roy-Boy was trying to cover up.

"Evening, Musician," Roy-Boy said. "Happy Friday the thirteenth."

"I was here first," Blackburn said.

Roy-Boy shook his head. "I've been watching that building since last Saturday. It's mine." He grinned. His teeth looked as if they were still stained with chocolate creme from the week before. "Unless you want to share. Two of the apartments on the top floor are rented by college students who've taken off for winter break. I've heard their stereos, and they sound expensive. They probably have VCRs and Sony Trinitrons too. We could clean 'em both in fifteen minutes, hit my fence in the morning, and be done."

"I don't use fences," Blackburn said. "They're crooks. And I already told you I'm not interested in teamwork. If you've been planning on this place for a week, you can have it. I'll leave."

Roy-Boy gave his gruntlike chuckle. "But don't you see, Musician? That won't work now. If you take off with nothing, I'll be afraid that you'll call the cops on me. So in self-defense, I'll make a call of my own after I've done the job. I'll describe you and your car, and when the cops ask the neighbors, some of them'll remember seeing you hanging around. And we've got the same situation in reverse if you stay and I go. One or both of us gets screwed. You know where that leaves us?"

Blackburn was keeping his eyes on Roy-Boy's, but his right hand was creeping back into his coat. He didn't want to shoot Roy-Boy while they were inside the Duster, but he would if he had to.

"Where?" he asked.

"MAD," Roy-Boy said. "As in mutual assured destruction." His right hand came out of the sweatshirt pouch with the .22. He pointed it at Blackburn's face.

Blackburn froze with his hand on the Python's butt.

"This is how I see it," Roy-Boy said. "I have the advantage, but I'd have to waste you instantly, with one shot, or suffer retaliation. In other words, although you might be mortally wounded, you could still do me with your superior weapon. So our only choices are to work together or be destroyed. You feel like being destroyed?"

"No," Blackburn said. He saw Roy-Boy's point. "I'll work with you this one time, but I can't promise anything else. I still want to leave town."

Roy-Boy nodded. "Fair enough. We've achieved diplomatic relations. Now comes the disarmament phase. Take out your pistol, slow. You can point it at me if you want, but I'll be watching your hand. If the fingers start to flex, I'll shoot. MAD, get it?"

Blackburn pulled out the Python and held it so that it pointed down at his own crotch.

"Careful or you'll wind up like me," Roy-Boy said. "A one-ball wonder. Of course, mine's the size of an orange."

"Mine aren't. I'd just as soon keep them both."

"Then put your gun on the seat between us. I'll do the same. Our hands should touch, so we'll each know if the other doesn't let go of his weapon. This is known as the verification phase." Roy-Boy turned his pistol so that it pointed downward. "Begin now."

They moved as slow as sloths. The pistols clicked together on the vinyl seat. The men's hands touched. Blackburn waited until he felt Roy-Boy's hand begin to rise, and then he lifted his own hand as well.

"So far so good," Roy-Boy said. "Where's your tote bag?"

"Under the seat."

Roy-Boy clucked his tongue. "I can't have you reaching under there. We'll have to find a grocery sack or something in the apartment. That acceptable to you?"

"I suppose so."

"In that case," Roy-Boy said, "we can get out of the car. Doors open at the same time."

"We can't leave the guns on the seat," Blackburn said. "Someone'll see them."

"No, they won't. Once we're outside, take off your coat and throw it back inside to cover them. That'll also assure me that you aren't packing another piece."

"What's to assure me that *you* aren't?"

"Good point. Okay, as you take off your coat, I'll take off my sweatshirt. The pants too, if you want. I'm just wearing shorts and a T-shirt underneath."

Blackburn took his keys from the ignition. "All right," he said. "Lock your door on the way out." He and Roy-Boy opened the doors and got out. Blackburn took off his coat while watching Roy-Boy pull off his sweatshirt on the other side of the car. It was like a weird dance. Cars going by on the street illuminated the performance with their headlights. Roy-Boy's face went from light to dark to light again, and then disappeared as the sweatshirt came up over his head. But even while Roy-Boy's head was inside the sweatshirt, the eyes were visible through the neck opening. They didn't blink.

Blackburn tossed his coat into the car, covering the pistols. Roy-Boy tossed his sweatshirt in on top of the coat. Then they closed the doors. The Duster shuddered.

"What's in your shirt pocket?" Roy-Boy asked.

"Penlight."

"Okay. It's a tool of the trade, so keep it. Now put your keys away, and we can meet at the rear bumper. It'll be our Geneva."

Blackburn put his keys into a jeans pocket, and he and Roy-Boy walked behind the car. Blackburn was wearing a long-sleeved shirt, but he was cold. He crossed his arms for warmth. Roy-Boy's gray T-shirt was cut off at the midriff, but he seemed comfortable. His bare arms swung at his sides. When the two men met at the bumper, Roy-Boy held out his right hand. Blackburn kept his arms crossed.

"Pants," he said.

Roy-Boy shucked off his sweatpants and turned around to show Blackburn that he was unarmed. His legs were pale and hairless. They looked shaved.

"That's enough," Blackburn said, suppressing revulsion.

Roy-Boy pulled his sweatpants back on, then held out his hand again. "Ratify our treaty," he said, "and I won't ask you to take off your pants too. I'll believe that your moral code won't allow you to hide a second weapon from me. That ruler in your back pocket I'll let go, since it's a tool of the trade too."

They shook hands. Roy-Boy's was dry and cold. He held on too long. Blackburn pulled free.

Roy-Boy looked across the street at the apartment building. "Top floor, second unit," he said. It was one of the apartments that had stayed dark. "Two bedrooms. Its collegiate occupants have gone home to Daddy for Jesus's birthday and left all their shit behind."

"Jewelry first," Blackburn said. "Then I'll help you carry one big thing, and that's all. Once I'm out, I'm not going back in. And my car's not for hire to haul freight. You have a vehicle?"

"Yeah. That black Toyota in the lot. Yesterday its former owner rode away in a car with snow skis on top. So it's mine now."

Blackburn couldn't object. He had stolen cars himself, and didn't think he was in any position to cast a stone.

Blackburn and Roy-Boy crossed the street and climbed the stairs that zigzagged up the face of the building. It was almost midnight, but TVs and stereos were turned up loud in some of the lighted apartments. Blackburn was glad. Two burglars would make more noise than one, but the ambient sound might cover it. And every apartment's drapes were closed, so none of the residents would see them.

They reached the top balcony and apartment 302. "You're the front-door specialist," Roy-Boy whispered.

Blackburn tried the knob. The door had a half inch of play. As at his last burglary, the deadbolt hadn't been set. People who didn't set their deadbolts were asking to be robbed. He reached into his back pocket and pulled out the metal ruler. In a few seconds the door popped open, and Blackburn and Roy-Boy went inside.

Blackburn took the penlight from his shirt pocket and turned it on. The pale circle of light revealed that the apartment was well furnished. A thick carpet muffled the men's footsteps.

"Ooh, lookee here," Roy-Boy said. "A Sony Trinitron. Tell you what—I have great night vision, so I don't need the light. I'll unhook the TV cable and look around in here, and you see what you can find in the other rooms."

Blackburn couldn't think of a reason against the plan, so he went into the blue-tiled kitchen and took a black plastic trash bag from a roll under the sink. Then he stepped into the hall. Here the penlight revealed four doors, two on each side. The first door on the right was open, and he saw more blue tile. The bathroom. He opened the door across from it and found a linen closet stacked with towels. It smelled like a department store, so he leaned inside and breathed deep. It wasn't a smell he was crazy about, but it cleared his head of Roy-Boy's deodorant-soap stink.

He continued down the hall and opened the next door on the right. This was a small bedroom, as clean as a church. There was a brass cross on the wall and stuffed animals on the dresser. The window was open, and Blackburn's neck tingled from the cold. White curtains puffed out over the narrow bed. The bed had a white coverlet with a design of pink and blue flowers.

A jewelry box on the dresser contained only a small silver cross on a chain. It was worth maybe thirty dollars at a pawn shop, but Blackburn left it. He himself had given up on Jesus while still a child, having seen more evidence of sin than of salvation, but he didn't want to mess with someone else's devotion. He found nothing else of value in the room, so he started back into the hall. Then he paused in the doorway.

The window was open. Even the screen was open. But no one was home.

He looked at the closed door across the hall and turned off his penlight. Then he stepped across, dropping the trash bag, and turned the doorknob. He moved to one side as the door swung inward, and caught a whiff of rust and vanilla. He stood against the wall and listened for a few seconds, but heard only Roy-Boy rummaging in the living room and the dull thumping of a stereo in another apartment.

Then he looked around the doorjamb. Except for the gray square of a curtained window, the room was black. He turned the penlight back on and saw the soles of two bare feet suspended between wooden bars. The toes pointed down. He shifted the penlight and saw that the wooden bars were at the foot of a bed.

A nude woman lay on the bed face-down, spread-eagled, her wrists and ankles tied to the bedposts with electrical cords. She was bleeding from cuts on her back, buttocks, and thighs. Strands of her brunette hair were stuck to her neck and shoulders. Her legs moved a little, pulling at their cords with no strength.

Blackburn sucked in a breath, then entered the room and closed the door. He dropped his penlight, found the wall switch, and turned on the ceiling light. He began to tremble. What he had smelled was blood and semen, and sugared pastry. There was a white cardboard box on the floor, and half-eaten donuts on the floor and the bed.

He stepped closer and saw a long shard of glass on the bed between the woman's knees. One end of the shard was wrapped in white cloth tape. The glass and the tape were smeared with blood.

On the woman's back, in thin red lines, were the words HI MUSICIAN.

Blackburn went to the head of the bed on the left side and knelt on the floor. The woman's wrists were tied so that her arms angled upward. Her face was in her pillow. Even this close, he couldn't hear her breathing. But he saw her back moving. There were teeth marks on her shoulders.

He lifted her head and turned her face toward him. The face was Heather's. Her eyes opened, and they widened as she recognized him. Her mouth was covered with duct tape. He pulled the tape away and then saw that a donut had been stuffed into her mouth. She tried to cough it out, but couldn't.

Blackburn lowered her head to the pillow and dug out the donut with his fingers. The smell was thick and sweet. His trembling became violent. He tried to untie the cord around Heather's left wrist, but his fingers were clumsy and numb. He was worthless, useless, a sissy, a pussy. Little Jimmy, dropping his pants and grabbing the rim of the wheel well. He could hear the fiberglass rod cutting the air. Its hiss became a scream, and it bit into his flesh. His skin caught fire.

Then his hands spasmed, and his fingers sank in. It wasn't the rim of a wheel well. It was the edge of a mattress.

He wasn't little Jimmy anymore. He had learned better. He had no father, no mother, no sister, no friends. His only trust was in himself. He could see not only what was, but what should be. He was Blackburn.

And Blackburn always knew what to do, and how to do it.

He tried the cord again. Heather's left wrist came free, and her arm fell to the bed. Her fingernails scratched his face on the way down. The pain was sharp and pure. His trembling stopped.

"Nasty," a voice said. "But maybe she didn't mean it."

Blackburn looked up. The bedroom door was open, and Roy-Boy was standing in the doorway. He was holding a small silver pistol. He gave his chuckle, his piglike grunt.

"Look what somebody left behind the TV," he said. "A twenty-five-caliber semiautomatic. Who woulda thought?"

Blackburn stood. "This is what comes of committing a sin of omission," he said.

Roy-Boy's expression became quizzical. "Omission of what?"

"Your death," Blackburn said. "I could see its place in the pattern of my world, but I left it out because I didn't understand why it needed to be there. Now I see that the reason was obvious. Maybe even to you. Do you know why I should have killed you?"

"Beats me," Roy-Boy said. "But now you can make up for it with a surrogate. I was grooming her for myself, but when I saw you watching the place, I decided to save her for you. See, you need to become aware of the superiority of *my* world, and to do that you've got to live in it a while. In your world you've got your stud attitude, and she's got her bouncy little ass . . . but when you try to pull that shit on me, it's a different story. I'm Thomas Jefferson, and you're slaves."

Blackburn took a step toward him. "So command me."

"Stop," Roy-Boy said. He pointed the pistol at Blackburn's face. "And pick up my ice scraper."

Blackburn stopped. He was at the foot of the bed, four feet from Roy-Boy. He reached down between Heather's knees and picked up the glass shard.

"Now cut her," Roy-Boy said. "Anywhere you like. But cut deep, or I'll shoot you."

"You'll shoot me anyway."

"No, I won't. I promise. I'm a moral guy too."

Blackburn gripped the taped end of the shard with both hands. The sharp end was pointed up.

"Why should I have killed you?" Blackburn asked again.

"Maybe because I threaten your masculinity," Roy-Boy said. "So stick the glass between her butt cheeks. That should make you feel like a stud again."

Blackburn placed the point of the shard under his own chin and began to push upward. It hurt, but like Heather's fingernails on his face, the pain was pure, cleansing. He thought again of Dad's fiberglass rod. No matter how much he had hated it, it had contributed to his creation. This new pain reminded him of that truth.

Roy-Boy grimaced. "Not *you*, Musician," he said. He took a step toward Blackburn and pointed the silver pistol at Heather. "*Her.* Just turn around and—"

Blackburn thrust his fists out and down, cutting his chin, and slashed Roy-Boy's right wrist.

Roy-Boy shrieked. He swung his pistol toward Blackburn again.

But Blackburn was already lunging. He sank his teeth into Roy-Boy's slashed wrist. With his left hand he grabbed the silver pistol and tried to yank it away. With his right hand he used the shard to rip and stab. Roy-Boy stumbled backward. He was screaming things that might have been words, but Blackburn didn't listen to them. The only voice he listened to now was his own, the voice that told him what needed to be done.

They fell to the floor in the hall. Blackburn kept his teeth clamped and his left hand on the pistol, but concentrated on driving the shard into Roy-Boy's eyes, throat, belly, and groin. The odor of soap was overwhelmed by stronger smells. Before long the pistol came free.

Blackburn rolled off Roy-Boy and squatted beside him. He threw the shard into the living room. Then he looked down at what remained of Roy-Boy's face.

"You'd like to believe you're evil," Blackburn said. "But you're only stupid. Anyone who's done it seriously knows there's only one good way to kill: a bullet to the head. Of course, with the smaller calibers, it might take more than one." He placed the muzzle of the silver pistol against Roy-Boy's forehead. "Do you know the answer to my question yet?"

One of Roy-Boy's hands flopped aimlessly.

"It's simple," Blackburn said.

He cocked the pistol.

"*Because I felt like it.*"

He squeezed the trigger until the gun was empty.

Blackburn dropped the pistol on Roy-Boy's chest and stood. He was dizzy for a moment and steadied himself against the wall, leaving a handprint. He was a mess. There had been a lot of blood some of the other times, but never this much. He wanted to brush his teeth and take a shower. He wanted to scrub and burn incense until Roy-Boy's stink was gone.

On the floor, the carcass twitched. Its ponytail had come loose, and the hair was spread out like a fan on the trash bag Blackburn had dropped. The plastic was keeping most of the hair off the wet carpet. Blackburn thought of taking the scalp, then rejected the idea. He didn't want a trophy. He wasn't proud of the way things had gone with Roy-Boy.

He heard a noise in the bedroom and turned to look. Heather was up on her knees. She had managed to free her right wrist and was now trying to loosen the cords around her ankles. She wasn't having any success. She was unsteady, swaying.

Blackburn went to her. "I can do that," he said.

She looked up at him and tried to say something, or to scream. All that came out was a moan.

Blackburn wiped his hands on his shirt. It didn't help. His shirt was wet. "This is mostly his," he said.

Heather looked away as Blackburn untied the cords around her ankles. When she was free, he tried to help her up, but she pulled away and got off the bed on the other side. She stumbled into the hall.

Blackburn pulled the top sheet from the bed. The apartment was cold, and he thought Heather should cover herself. He went into the hall and saw her step over Roy-Boy's body. She didn't seem to notice it. He followed her into the kitchen and turned on the light. Then he draped the sheet over her shoulders, and she didn't even glance at him.

He saw that she was no longer the Heather who had slept with him, and he knew that he was responsible. For the first time in his life, he was horrified at himself. Not for what he had done, but for what he had failed to do. In that failure, he had become an accessory to torture and rape. Killing was not always murder, and stealing was not always a crime . . . but torture and rape were absolutes.

Heather lifted the receiver from a wall telephone and pushed 911. Blackburn heard the dispatcher answer the call, but Heather didn't put the receiver to her ear. She stared at it as if trying to figure out why it was making noise.

"Let me," Blackburn said. He reached for the receiver.

Heather jerked it away, then hit him in the face with it.

His eyes filled with tears. The receiver had struck his nose hard. "Let me talk to them," he said. "You're hurt. You need to go to the hospital."

Heather dropped the receiver and yanked the telephone from its wall jack. The sheet fell away, and Blackburn saw the red lines that her wounds had left on it.

She swung the telephone and hit his head. Then she hit him again, and again. The telephone clanged, and the receiver bounced on its cord, thunking against the floor.

Blackburn backed up against the refrigerator and then stood there, letting Heather hit him. He should never have begun stealing for a living. That moral slip had led to the next one, and that in turn had led to this. So he would take his punishment. It was the only punishment he had ever received that made sense.

"I'm sorry," he told Heather. She had become a blur. "I'm sorry, I'm sorry."

The telephone clanged. Heather began to grunt with each clang, and then to shout. There were no words. Only the voice of her rage.

Blackburn heard it and knew it was just. He slid to the floor. The tiles were like cool water against his cheek.

And so the State of Texas took him, and healed his face, and charged him with rape and murder. He let the rape charge stand. Murder, however, he could not accept. He had killed, but he had never committed murder. This went double in the case of Roy-Boy.

His court-appointed attorney said that this was not a suitable defense.

Homicide investigators from across the nation came to Houston to question Blackburn, but he was only able to help two of them. Most of the others were trying to track down serial killers of women, and Blackburn had nothing to tell them about that sort of thing—except to say that there were a lot of bastards out there, and he should know, having killed a number of them.

Then the State of Texas charged him with murder again.

He was told that on the night that he and Roy-Boy had met, there had been a woman in the bedroom from which Roy-Boy had emerged. Blackburn had not known of her existence because she had been sick in bed for a week. She had been the sister of the apartment's other occupant, the woman who worked the night shift at Whataburger.

The sick woman had been tortured, raped, and killed.

And since Blackburn admitted that he had been in her apartment on the night of her death, he was accused of the crime.

Blackburn was astonished. "I've never killed a woman," he told his interrogators.

"Yet you've confessed to raping a woman," one of them said.

Blackburn shook his head. "No. What I confessed to was *responsibility* for that rape. And I won't let you use that as grounds to blame me for something else." He turned to his attorney. "You have to make them see my point."

"What point is that?" an interrogator asked.

Blackburn looked at him.

"One sin," he said, "is more than enough."

Villain: Peter Macklin

The Black Spot

LOREN D. ESTLEMAN

BOTH VERSATILE AND PROLIFIC, Loren D. Estleman (1952–) began his writing career as a journalist but soon turned to fiction and became one of the most significant mystery writers to emerge in the 1970s, while also producing Western novels of such distinction that he was given the Owen Wister Award for Lifetime Contributions to Western Literature, the highest honor given by the Western Writers of America. Other awards include the Eye, the lifetime achievement award of the Private Eye Writers of America, from which he has also received four Shamus Awards, an Edgar nomination from the Mystery Writers of America, a nomination for a National Book Award, and nearly twenty additional honors.

Among his more than seventy published books, it is Estleman's series about Detroit private eye Amos Walker for which he is best known. Beginning with *Motor City Blue* (1980), this hard-boiled series has been praised by fans as diverse as Harlan Coben, Steve Forbes, John D. MacDonald, John Lescroart, and the Amazing Kreskin. Fans are equally enthusiastic about the wise-cracking P.I. and Estleman's depiction of his much-loved but decaying Detroit, where "the American Dream stalled and sat rusting in the rain." His next most successful series character is Peter Macklin, a professional hit man whose victims are worse than he is. The five Macklin novels are *Kill Zone* (1984), *Roses Are Dead* (1985), *Any Man's Death* (1986), *Something Borrowed, Something Black* (2002), and *Little Black Dress* (2005).

"The Black Spot" was first published in the March/April 2015 issue of *Ellery Queen's Mystery Magazine*; it was first collected in *Desperate Detroit and Stories of Other Dire Places* (Blue Ash, Ohio, Tyrus Books, 2016).

THE BLACK SPOT

Loren D. Estleman

THEY SAID LEO DORFMAN had forgotten more about the law than most lawyers ever knew.

A couple of his clients, currently serving as guests of the federal government, agreed.

He'd been eighty for as long as Peter Macklin could remember, a stopped clock now in semi-retirement, working out of his Redford Township dining room in one of the three-piece suits he continued to wear every day. Mrs. Dorfman, brown and wrinkled in a woven sun hat, sleeveless blouse, and yellow shorts, knelt in her flower garden outside. Macklin glanced at her from his seat opposite the lawyer's at the round table.

"Don't worry about Lyla," Dorfman said. "She can't hear herself fart."

But Macklin kept his voice low. "Laurie's divorcing me."

"I'm sorry. Being a criminal attorney, I can't help you. But I can recommend some good divorce men."

"I'm going to settle. I can't afford to have experts performing archaeology on the source of my finances."

"That's wise. Do you have a figure in mind?"

"Half a million should do it. Another hundred for incidentals."

"Have that much?"

"No. That's why I'm here. I need to work."

"What about your legitimate business?"

"I should have sold out ten years ago. No one goes to camera stores any more. Any prospects?"

"I may have something, but you won't like it."

"A name?"

"Sal Malavaggio."

Macklin didn't like it.

"I didn't know he was out," he said.

"He's in a halfway house in the Irish Hills. Next week he'll be back in Detroit. One of his people called. I said I didn't have those contacts any more. I thought you were out of it."

Macklin said nothing. He never wasted time on regrets.

The lawyer said, "Your timing couldn't be better—if you want the job. He wants six guys dead, and he wants it fast. I know you like groundwork, but you'll have to scramble on this one. I think we can get him up to a hundred a pop."

"I need a hundred up front."

"I don't know if he'll agree to that."

"He will. This isn't a job for Costco."

Since he'd moved out of the house in Toledo, Peter Macklin was renting a house in Pontiac, thirty miles northwest of Detroit. When he got back from Redford, he switched on the TV for company. Somebody had blown up something in the Middle East. It seemed to be a big deal.

He wasn't thrilled about working for Salvatore Malavaggio. The man was as Sicilian as they came—his family tree didn't branch—and had done fifteen years on a RICO rap he might have beaten if he'd gone into Witness Protection; but he was an old-school Omerta man, buried so deep in the foundations of the Mafia he flossed his teeth with a garrote.

Macklin had thought to leave that all behind many years ago. After his first divorce he'd gone independent, demanding that prospective clients come up with income tax forms and bank statements detailing everything they owned, which was what he charged for committing murder. This policy weeded out the frivolous. It was amazing how many people were willing to take a vow of poverty just to tip someone the black spot.

Then he'd met Laurie, a beautiful, intelligent woman half his age, and retired on his legitimate investments; but eventually the truth of his past had come out, and that was the end of that.

Now here he was, in his forties, separated, forced to fall back on the only skill he had to survive.

When the FedEx package arrived he took out a small rounded rectangle of plastic.

"Expect it," Dorfman had said. "It's a burn phone, anonymous and untraceable. Throw it in the river when you're through with it. The money will be electronically deposited in the following banks, first the advance, then an additional payment each time you score; nine thousand in each account, so it won't be reported to the IRS. My ten percent comes off the top."

A series of names and account numbers followed, all prearranged for just such a situation. Macklin had written them all down. "We don't meet face-to-face after today. Wait for instructions by text."

No room for bargaining on the fee. Leo Dorfman was the only lawyer in the country who'd go near the case. It had made him a millionaire many times over, but the other side of the coin was he'd installed a remote starter in his car in case of detonation.

The first text came in ten minutes after Macklin finished charging the phone. Something buzzed, he pressed a key, and looked at the screen. It provided a name, address, vital statistics, and a photo. A second text informed him that ninety thousand dollars had been deposited in his name, spread out among ten separate accounts. It was really amazing what technology had done for crime.

Nikolai Kobolov lived in Bloomfield Village, where a house smaller than 5,000 square feet was considered a starter. When the Berlin Wall fell and the KGB temporarily lost interest in the Russian Mafia, he'd emigrated to the U.S. and invested his Swiss bank accounts in the insurance business, selling protection to expatriate Communists from their enemies, and occasionally from his own people, who respected such things as Molotov cocktails.

He hung his bullet-shaped body in good tailoring and in the wintertime wore a long belted overcoat and a fur hat, like Omar Sharif in *Doctor Zhivago.* He was part Ukrainian, descended from Cossacks.

When he left his house, riding in the back of a stretch Lincoln driven by a chauffeur in livery, two cars followed, one containing four men licensed to carry firearms in defense of his life. Two FBI agents rode in the other. It was almost four o'clock, the time appointed for his daily shaving. He liked a clean head.

The shop downtown, which called itself a salon, was all glistening glass, chrome, and tile. He took a seat in his customary chair while his bodyguards read newspapers in the waiting area and the two FBI men sat in their car outside. A man Kobolov didn't recognize covered him in crisp white linen. He wore a white jacket fastened at one shoulder with buttons.

"Where's Fred?" the customer asked.

"Sick today."

He shook a thick finger at the man. "No nicks. I'm going out with a young lady tonight."

"Yes, sir." The barber removed a towel from the warmer and wrapped it turbanlike around Kobolov's head. The Russian sighed, lulled into a doze, as always, by the heat. He barely shuddered when the ice pick entered the top of his spinal column. The bodyguards were still reading when the barber went out through the back room.

Sanders Quotient was a third-round draft choice for the Detroit Lions, but he'd been drummed out of the league for unsportsmanlike conduct. He'd sued on the basis of discrimination; however, the NAACP had refused him use of its counsel. He'd invested the proceeds from his first year's contract in one of the biggest drug operations in the Midwest, dealing in cocaine and heroin. Some of it was too strong for the clientele, who'd died of OD.

He lived in an original Frank Lloyd Wright house in St. Clair Shores. The open plan, and the unobstructed view through big windows, appealed to him.

He had no bodyguards. At thirty-five, in excellent condition, he could take care of himself. If that was overoptimistic, he had two DEA agents watching his house in eight-hour shifts, hoping to catch him in an illegal transaction.

He got up around 2:00 A.M., leaving a fine young woman in his round bed, to crack open a bottle of imported beer. In the kitchen, he heard a thump coming from his deck.

On the way through the rec room he selected a Glock nine from the rack and went to the sliding glass door to investigate. Gripping the weapon tightly and hugging the wall, he reached for the lock. It was open. He always made sure everything was sealed tight before bed.

He was turning from the door, pistol in hand, when his head exploded.

The coroner assigned cause of death to a blow that caved in his skull, pieces of which clung by blood and gray matter to a blackjack, discarded without fingerprints.

Zev Issachar controlled most of the illegal gambling between Chicago and the East Coast. At seventy-two, he was retired, but there wasn't an underground casino or unsanctioned high-stakes poker game that didn't pay him tribute. He'd changed his name legally from Howard Needleman before applying for residency in Israel to avoid arrest. Tel Aviv had turned him down.

He was awaiting trial for violation of the laws of interstate commerce. It was a rap he could beat, but he considered the electronic ankle tether humiliating, and it aggravated his arthritis.

On Saturday, he boarded a van belonging to the Justice Department, bound from his modest home in Highland Park to synagogue, in the company of two U.S. deputy marshals. Inside the temple, as his manacles were being removed, a man dressed as a Hassidim shot him three times in the chest before vanishing into the crowd waiting for the inner doors to open. Zev died instantly. The marshals gave chase, but found only a coat, hat, wig, and false whiskers in a pile by the fire exit.

"I thought we'd moved beyond all this after nine-eleven."

Inspector Deborah Stonesmith commanded the Detroit Major Crimes Unit, which was helping to coordinate the efforts of the three major homicide divisions involved. She was a tall, handsome black woman with reddish hair, dressed conservatively in tweeds. The only touch of femininity in her office at 1300 Beaubien, Detroit Police Headquarters, was a spray of peonies in a vase on her desk.

"That's just it." Wes Crider, a homicide lieutenant, lifted a shoulder and let it drop. "These mobsters think we're too busy looking for Islamic Fascists to bother with them."

"They never heard of multitasking? If this is the Russian Mafia taking on the black Mafia, or the Jewish Mafia taking on either of the others, it's a turf war. Targeting all three makes it something else."

"A synagogue, yet; a place of worship. Is nothing sacred?"

"As opposed to plain murder? Who else we got?"

Crider took out a notebook with scraps of ragged paper sticking out of the edges at every angle, like Grandma's cookbook. "Kim Park? Got all the massage parlors nailed down; prostitution, with a little shiatsu on the side. Korean Cosa Nostra."

"He's a maybe. What about Sal Malavaggio? He's a sitting duck in that halfway house. Security there's to keep them in, not others out."

"He's strictly a Mustache Pete. Those Sicilians went out with Pet Rocks."

"Let's put a car out front, just in case. Who else?"

Flip, flip. "Vittorio Bandolero, runs the best restaurant in Mexicantown. Smuggles illegals into the country. Last time his people thought they were being tailed, they machine-gunned the carload."

"Next."

"Jebediah Colt: Jeb the Reb, on the street. Dixie Mafia, Stolen Goods Division. Fences everything from bellybutton rings to catalytic converters."

Stonesmith smiled. "I've seen his file. Sweetbreads in his freezer is what he's got for brains. What else?"

"That's the kit. All the Mafias: Russian, black, Jewish, Asian, Mexican, Dixie, and the Sicilian original. You know, if they'd just trademarked the name—"

"They'd be Microsoft."

"*Sí*, I understand. I, too, would exit the driver's seat of a truck when a helicopter flew overhead; however, I might have waited until a searchlight came on, just to make sure it wasn't a traffic vehicle from a radio station."

Vittorio Bandolero hung up and scowled at the man seated across the desk. They were in the back room of the Mexicantown restaurant whose income he reported to the federal government for taxation purposes. "I am losing patience with Immigration. Not all of my people have the slightest interest in overthrowing the government. I merely want *muchachos* who can fry a tortilla and cut the occasional throat. Is that too much to ask?"

Bandolero's *segundo*, a small man with scars on both cheeks and black hair swept back from his temples—longer than those on top, like the fenders of a 1949 Mercury—moved his shoulders, paring his nails with a switchblade. "There are people to grease, *jefe*. We should meet with them."

"*Dónde?*"

"The Alamo; ten o'clock, so I am told."

The Alamo Motel stood on East Jefferson facing the river, a dump that rented rooms by the hour. Bandolero knocked at the door he'd been directed to. It opened at the pressure of his fist. He stepped inside.

Something swooped, tightened around his throat. He couldn't get his hands under it. He thrashed, crooked his elbows, made no contact. His tongue slid out of his mouth just before he lost consciousness.

The first officer on the scene reported a deceased male, apparently strangled to death with nylon fishline.

Deborah Stonesmith stood over the body of Vittorio Bandolero, dragged into a sitting position against the wall of the motel room. The fishline was embedded two inches into his neck.

"No more Mr. Nice Guy," she said. "Someone's moving in."

Lieutenant Crider said, "We need to open a tip line. An army of hit men can't go unnoticed for long."

"So it's an army."

"We got us an ice pick, a bludgeon, a gun, and a garrote. Heavy-lifters specialize. Nobody uses this much variety."

"One does," she said, smoothing her tweed skirt. "I thought he was dead, or moved—or hoped so; but wishful thinking never got nobody nothing but thinking wishful."

Kim Park had come to the U.S. with a dollar eighty-seven in his pocket; also three hundred thousand dollars in Krugerrands in the false bottom of his suitcase, belonging to a Detroit politician who died before taking delivery. Park had invested this windfall in a string of massage parlors. He found America truly to be the Land of Opportunity.

The girls were skilled. What did it matter if their trained hands were joined by their bodies, so long as they split the tips with the management? But then an undercover cop had found a girl willing to testify that she'd been sold into slavery by her parents. She'd managed to stumble into a number of Dumpsters between Detroit and Flint: her torso here, a leg there, and her head and hands who knew where. A man couldn't be held responsible for the bad choices of all his employees.

In any case, Kim Park never went anywhere without a train of vice officers making note of where he stopped and whom he spoke to. It pleased him to think of them stuck in their cars while he took a steam in one of his own places in Detroit.

He'd just poured a dipper of water over the heated rocks when the door opened, stirring the thick vapor. He grinned, expecting a half-naked Korean girl ready to escort him to the table. His head was still wearing the grin when it rolled out of the steam room, cut off with a hunting knife found in a towel hamper, its handle wiped clean.

———

Sal Malavaggio selected a cigar from the humidor on his desk, rustled it next to his ear, dropped it back into the box, and shut the lid. "Remind me to order fresh cigars. *I* kept better than these did."

"Way ahead of you," Miriam Brewster said. "A colleague in Key West has a standing order of Montecristos. Two boxes on the way."

Malavaggio, short and stout, with a glossy head of dyed-black hair, had chosen Brewster out of vanity; she was an inch shorter than he was, and fatter yet in a tailored suit. But she had turned out to be a double blessing as one of the country's foremost Constitutional scholars.

"Tell me again about overturning RICO." He settled himself in the upholstered leather chair, taking in the comforts of home for the first time in fifteen years.

She sat facing the desk and crossed her chubby legs. "It will take years, and maybe a change or two on the Supreme Court, but anyone can tell you it's a jump-wire around the Bill of Rights. The government couldn't get your people legally, so it crooked the system. In a way it was a victory for you."

"Yeah. That brought me comfort in stir, while them animals took over the works. Russian Mafia, black Mafia, Jewish Mafia, Asian Mafia. They couldn't even come up with a name of their own. But I'm changing that."

He looked at his Rolex, lifted a remote off the desk, and snapped it at the new flatscreen TV mounted on the wall opposite. A local reporter stood in front of one of Kim Park's rub-a-dub parlors, chattering breathlessly as morgue attendants carried a body bag on a stretcher out the door. "Trouble with whacking a chink," Malavaggio said, "an hour later you want to whack another one."

"I didn't hear that." Brewster's lips were tight. "Be patient, Sal, I beg you. What good's winning our point when you're doing life for murder?"

"What murder's that, Counselor? I was

checking out of the halfway house when some *feccia* made that improvement in Jackie Chan's looks. Same place I was when the Russky bought it, and the porch monkey and the Hebe. Sounds like the start of a joke, don't it? They go into a bar?"

"Sure, Sal. You're clean."

"Cleaning house," he said. "When I'm through, everybody'll know there's only one Mafia."

Colt's Ponies sold campers, travel trailers, and motor homes from four locations in the Detroit metropolitan area. The business provided an income Jebediah Colt could declare on his taxes and a neat bit of camouflage: Who'd look for a trailer containing hot transmissions on a trailer lot?

He'd declared his independence at fourteen, when he cold-cocked his father with a meat hammer, stole a car, and drove north to assemble Mustangs at Ford River Rouge. He was fired for stealing tools and parts, but by then he'd put enough away to open his own full-time business at twenty. He dealt in jewelry, rare coins, copper plumbing, and genuine factory auto parts, all stolen.

He hadn't much overhead. All you needed was a roof, preferably one with wheels; that way, when you got the tip a raid was coming, all you had to do was hitch up and move to another lot. Now he owned a fleet of Mustangs he hadn't had a thing to do with in the manufacture and a house in Grosse Pointe, down the street from the Ford family itself.

"Mr. Colt? Deborah Stonesmith. I'm an inspector with the Detroit Police Department." The tall black woman who'd rung his doorbell showed him a shield.

"You got a warrant?"

"I'm not here to arrest you. I assume you've heard about the recent gangland killings."

He grinned his baggy grin, scratched the tattoo on his upper left arm. "No shit, you're here to *protect* me?"

"We've got a car on this block, an early response team in radio contact, and a man on each side of the house. I'm going to ask you to stay in tonight. Since this business started, no more than two nights have passed between killings. This is the third since Kim Park's."

His smile vanished. "That pimp? What's the connection?"

"We think someone's out to eliminate the competition in organized crime in the area. You and Salvatore Malavaggio are the only honchos left. My lieutenant is at Sal's place in Birmingham, explaining these same arrangements."

"Well, I'm expecting delivery of an Airstream at my lot in Belleville, straight from the factory. I like to be there when something new comes in."

"You can inspect your swag another time, Jeb. Either that, or we'll send a car to follow you; for your own safety, of course."

Macklin spotted the early response van first thing. The panels advertised a diaper service, a stork in a messenger's cap with a little bundle of joy strung from its beak. There wasn't a playset or a bicycle or anything else on the block that indicated a resident young enough to have small children. He drove past, located the unmarked car containing two plainclothesmen drinking Starbucks across the street from Colt's house, and saw flashlight beams prowling the grounds.

A big-box department store stood near downtown, connected with a service station. He bought a two-gallon gasoline can, put in a quart from the pump, stashed it in his trunk, and entered the store. In the liquor section he put a liter bottle of inexpensive wine into his basket. Browsing in entertainment, he came upon a James Brown retrospective on CD and a cheap player. He bought them at the front counter, along with a package of batteries and a disposable lighter from the impulse rack.

The restrooms were located inside the foyer. Finding the men's room empty, he unscrewed the cap from the wine bottle and dumped the contents down the sink. In the parking lot he opened his trunk, the lid blocking the view from the security camera mounted on a light pole, filled the bottle with gasoline, replaced the cap, wrapped it in an old shirt he used for a rag, tucked the bundle under his arm inside his jacket, slammed the trunk, got into the car, and drove away.

Three blocks from Jebediah Colt's house, a FOR SALE sign stood in the yard of a brick split-level on a corner. The inside was dark except for a tiny steady red light.

There were no security cameras visible. He walked up to the front door and rang the bell; a househunter, hoping to catch someone at home. When no one answered after the second ring, he produced the CD player from under his coat, placed it on the doorstep, and switched it on, turning up the volume until James Brown's lyrics were distorted beyond comprehension. He returned to the car, moving quickly now, drove around the corner, opened the gasoline-filled bottle, spilled a little onto a piece he'd torn off the old shirt, stuffed the rag into the neck, and lit it with the disposable lighter. When it was burning, he opened the driver's window and slung the bottle at the nearest window. The security alarm went off shrilly.

The bottle exploded with a whump and the flame spread. He drove away at a respectable speed, hearing the Godfather of Soul screaming at the top of his lungs from the direction of the burning house.

Police on stakeout might ignore a house fire, expecting local units and the fire department to take care of it; but someone screaming in the flames was another story. The early response team reported the hysterical noises over the radio, and within five minutes Jeb "the Reb" Colt was a man alone.

The sirens started up with a whoop, loud enough to make him jump up from in front of the NASCAR channel and draw aside his front curtains. The noises were fading away. He got his nunchuks from the drawer, turned off the lights to avoid being framed in the doorway, and stepped onto his front porch.

He saw an orange glow three blocks away and lights going on in his neighbors' houses. Shrugging, he swung the chuks together in his fist and turned to go inside. Someone stood between him and the doorway. The heel of a hand swept up, driving bone splinters from his nose into his brain.

Miriam Brewster switched off the flatscreen and turned to Malavaggio, leaning back in his desk chair with his pudgy hands folded across his broad stomach and his lids drifted nearly shut. He looked like a toad. "I don't suppose you know anything about this."

"The arson? Insurance job, probably. Guy can't keep up his mortgage, he torches the place for case dough."

"I mean Jeb Colt."

"One cracker more or less don't mean much to the world."

"You must have squirreled away plenty before you went to prison. Six hits in ten days, all professionally done. That doesn't come cheap, even on double-coupon days."

"Even so, I arranged a discount. Why pay for finished work? What's he going to repossess?"

She made him stop before sharing any details.

Macklin had several ways of knowing when someone had entered his house when he was gone. Whoever it was, cop or killer, had stumbled on the one least subtle, forgetting which lights he'd left on and which he'd turned off. He didn't even have to stop his car. The windows told him everything.

In the crowded parking lot of a cineplex, he used his burn phone one last time to call Leo Dorfman.

"How'd he know where I live?" he asked.

The lawyer didn't ask who. "I never told him; but his outfit's got its thumbs in lots of places, why not realty agencies?"

"I need to have been somewhere else when most of those packages were delivered."

"Most, or all?"

"All would look like planning. I can tell 'em I went to the movies for the others."

"Okay."

The parking lot exit passed over an ornamental bridge leading to the highway. Macklin threw the phone out the window into the swift little stream.

Dorfman would take care of the cops; if it was cops. If it was a killer, all he had to do was cut off the source of income.

Salvatore Malavaggio snipped the end off a crisp Montecristo, got it going with a platinum lighter, and blew a smoke ring at the acoustical ceiling in his home office. It had been a good first week out of stir. The Russian, the black, the Jew, the Mexican, the chink, and the hillbilly were gone, leaving a void only an experienced don could fill. His former associates would know the truth. There would be some resistance, but he'd struck too fast and too deep not to have put the fear of Sal into them all. Even Miriam, as cold-blooded a dame as he'd known, had looked at him with new respect after the mug shots of all six rivals appeared on the TV report capping recent events.

There was only one Mafia. There was no room in it for Slavs, coloreds, kikes, greasers, chinks, or inbred morons. Those outsiders only got such big ideas when the Sicilians became careless and gave incriminating orders direct to unreliable street soldiers instead of going through buffers. Malavaggio had used Dorfman, never laying eyes on this Macklin, who was familiar by reputation. The law, too, would know what happened, but it could never prove a connection, no matter what the chump said when he was arrested.

Which was how they'd done things in the old country. *Omerta* was for equals only.

From now on, if you couldn't point at that island off the toe of the boot and name the birthplace of every one of your ancestors, you're just the guy we send out for coffee. *Napolitano?* Ha! *Calabrese?* As if! *Sola Siciliana, per sempre.*

Something clinked in the next room: Miriam, setting down the latest of who knew how many glasses of his best grappa. He hoped she wasn't turning into a lush. She needed all her senses to get the Supreme Court to act and return *La Cosa Nostra* to its days of glory.

And he'd saved himself a hundred grand.

Something stirred in the connecting doorway.

"Counselor? Thought you went home."

"She did. I waited to make sure she didn't come back for something she forgot."

Malavaggio didn't recognize the man coming in carrying a revolver. They'd never met face-to-face.

Rogue: Leo Skorzeny

Car Trouble

JAS. R. PETRIN

JAMES ROBERT (JIM) PETRIN (1947–) ranks among the most popular and prolific writers of recent years to appear in *Alfred Hitchcock Mystery Magazine*, where his first story, "The Smile," appeared in 1985. Since that time he has contributed more than seventy stories to the publication.

He does find time to write for other magazines and for anthologies, for which he has written a broad range of crime fiction. Much of his work has been produced for audio books and television films. Petrin's stories have been shortlisted for numerous awards and he has won several others, most notably the Arthur Ellis Award (the Canadian equivalent of the Edgar) for Best Short Crime Fiction on two occasions.

Although many of his stories are stand-alone tales of crime and mystery, often with a humorous undertone, one of Petrin's most popular series characters is Leo Skorzeny, known to his friends (and others) as "Skig." He is a Shylock, a moneylender at usurious rates, who is so tough that no one dares to fail to pay him what he's owed. There is a bit of softness to him, however, that puts him into the rogue category rather than filling the role of villain.

Born in Saskatchewan, Petrin now lives with his wife, Colleen, at Mavillette Beach, on the Gulf of Maine, in southwest Nova Scotia.

"Car Trouble" was originally published in the December 2007 issue of *Alfred Hitchcock Mystery Magazine*.

CAR TROUBLE

Jas. R. Petrin

"THIS TIME," Skig said, "tell you what. Try not to make it stand up at the back, some kind of antenna sticking outta my head."

"It's just the way your hair goes, dear. Nothing I can do. You should be glad to have hair on the top of your head. Some men your age are ready for a comb-over."

"When I'm ready for it, shoot me."

Every month they exchanged this banter. Leo Skorzeny sitting on a straight-back chair in Eva Kohl's kitchen, a sheet around him, snippets of his stiff, iron-gray hair on the floor. Eva, retired from hairdressing maybe ten, twelve years now, click-clicking away with her scissors.

"Tell me about that new car you're buying," Skig said. He shifted his weight, trying to ease the pain in his gut.

She laughed. Took a playful snip at the empty air.

"Not buying—leasing. The way they explained it to me, Mr. Skorzeny, it's cheaper."

"Smaller payments."

"That's right."

"That don't mean it's cheaper. The long run."

"For me it is. It really is. The salesman told me I'm perfect for a lease. I put on hardly any mileage—mostly just shopping."

"You bargain down the suggested retail?"

"The what?" She stopped snipping, puzzled.

"The price."

"No. I thought I explained. I'm not buying, I'm leasing."

Skig closed his eyes, held them shut a second, opened them.

"You got a good trade?"

The snipping started again. "My old car still runs well. They're giving me two thousand dollars for it."

"Your old car's like new. Why not keep driving it?"

"It isn't all that good. And I feel like a change. Anyway, I've made up my mind. I'm signing the papers this afternoon." She ran the trimmer over his neck, cold steel humming against his skin, then handed him a fan-shaped hand mirror. She held a second mirror behind his head, left, then right. "How's that?"

"Perfect," Leo said, "as always. That's why I come to you."

"Don't kid. You come here because I'm cheap. And I'm only just down the street from you."

Before he left, Skig got the name of her dealership.

He trudged heavily back along the sidewalk, one hand under his billowing sports coat to brace the pain there low in his gut. He would get his car out of the garage, head down to the quack's office, and collect the bad news sure to be waiting for him. All those tests last week. The quacks liked to tell him how lucky he was, that he should be dead by now. Yeah, right. How lucky could you get?

Skig lived in an old made-over filling station, bought years ago as an investment. He'd converted the office area to a few livable rooms after Jeanette died—couldn't stay in the house and didn't know why. Or maybe he did. Sensing her presence there was still too much for him, and at other times it was just too empty.

He crossed the large graveled lot, his front yard, fumbled a key out, and heaved open the repair bay door, all blistering paint: no power assist on this baby, built before the friggin' flood. He backed the Crown Vic into the lot, got out, and hauled the big door down, locked it, then eased back in behind the wheel. He rolled off along Railway Avenue at a sedate five clicks under the limit, windows open to blow the stink off. The Crown Vic still reeked after running off the jetty into the harbor one time, but Skig had no interest in replacing it. Why bother if you were one church service shy of a planting, the way he saw it.

The clock on the dash said two fifteen. Time enough for that one small matter before he had to be at his appointment.

He found the lot on Robie, not a first-rate dealership, but not too scuzzy a place. The showroom supported a colossal roof-mounted sign that said HAPPY DAN DUCHEK'S AUTO WORLD, with two sculpted Ds each the size of a grand piano. Another, smaller, sign said WE'RE NOT HAPPY UNTIL YOU ARE! "Right," Skig muttered as he turned in. He rolled slowly between two rows of gleaming new cars. Bigger than it looked from the street. There was even a detailing shop at the back for well-heeled car enthusiasts, Happy Dan covering all the angles. Skig saw movement in the next row over. An extremely pretty young woman, dressed for the office, talking heatedly with her hands to a young man in sagging-butt pants who stared back at her with lifeless eyes.

"Don't argue with that one, dear," Skig cautioned her under his breath, looking for a place to park. Something familiar about the guy.

He found Happy Dan in the manager's office. Shiny hair. Smile on him like it was wired there. Dan had just unwrapped a tuna sub on his desk and was holding out a coffee mug to the extremely pretty young woman Skig had seen a moment ago. She must have nipped inside while he was parking, now in the process of pouring Dan a fill of seriously black joe from a steaming Pyrex pot. Dan didn't look too happy with her. The guy with the sagging pants was nowhere in sight.

As he stepped into the room, Happy Dan met Skig's gaze, his open face brightening in cheery lines. "Good afternoon, sir. Welcome. Time for a new car?" He showed even white teeth.

"Name's Leo Skorzeny," Skig said flatly. "You heard of me?"

Happy Dan raked his memory. Concentrated. Then something clicked and his smile wilted. He set his mug down. "Yes, I've heard of you."

"We need to talk."

Leo then stared at the extremely pretty young woman until she took the hint and stalked out of the room, carafe in hand, trailing an aroma of burnt coffee.

Happy Dan edged around a filing cabinet and took up a defensive position behind his desk.

"We were trading stories about vacation resorts," Happy Dan said, with a nervous stab at affability. Silk tie. Gel in his hair like it was spooned on. "You see, I just got back from Aruba, and—"

"What I really come to see you about was the

hose job you're planning to do on a nice old lady, Mrs. Eva Kohl, supposed to come in here later today an' sign some papers."

"Mr. Skorzeny, we don't—"

"Sit down," Skig said.

Happy Dan looked uncertain for a second, then sat. Skig lowered himself into the visitors' chair. Jeez, his gut hurt.

"The lady's a friend of mine. I want her treated right."

"Mr. Skorzeny, I assure you—"

Skig's shoulders moved, his big hands on the heavy desk, trapping Happy Dan against the wall. Dan's jaw sagged. Disbelief on his face.

Skig said, "There's not a car salesman alive wouldn't hose a woman like that, unless he's a saint, and you got no halo floatin' over your head." He watched Happy Dan turn purple. "Here's what you do. You come down fifteen hundred on the MSRP—cash-back covers that—an' you give her three, not two, for the trade, which is more what it's worth. That's forty-five hunnerd, good for ninety bucks off the monthly payment, an' you still do okay. An' don't suck it all up with some BS prepping fees, like you polished the mirrors or something, or I'll be back here for more negotiating. You getting all this?"

Sweat droplets gleamed along the hairline of Dan's spiffy do. He managed a bob of his head. Skig held him there a few more seconds, scrutinizing the Aruban tan for signs of perfidy. Satisfied that there were none, he yanked the desk back and heaved himself to his feet.

"An' make sure she gets the free gap insurance the leasing company likes you to forget about," Skig said, not looking back, moving on out the door.

The clinic's parking lot was jammed as usual, the waiting room packed with distressed humanity. But there had been a cancellation, and Skig's name came up quickly. Shown to a room the size of a large closet, he waited until the quack breezed in. Not his usual quack. A specialist. Like most specialists, this guy had the charm of a forensic pathologist.

"Just tell me," Skig said, "am I still gonna die?"

The quack hunched over a child-sized table, briskly flipping through some arcane-looking charts. "We're all going to die, Mr. Skorzeny."

A pathologist *and* a philosopher. Skig crossed his brawny arms above his thick belly, waiting to hear the bad news.

Finally the quack glanced up. Jeez, he was young. How much could a kid this age know about diseases of the colon? Plenty, judging by the framed degrees, diplomas, and certificates tacked to the wall. But Skig wasn't impressed. Paper was paper.

"The tests were inconclusive," the quack said.

"What!"

"The tests were inconclusive. We'll have to run them again."

"Somebody screwed up, you mean."

"There's no need for acrimony."

"There's a need for something. You think it's happy days goin' through all that?"

"You're overwrought."

"No, I'm *under*wrought. When I get overwrought, you'll know it."

The quack was unintimidated. That impressed Skig. With cool detachment, the young man insisted Skig leave another sample for the lab. The Styrofoam container looked just like the kind the Greek at the corner sold his chili burgers in.

When Skig got home, there was company waiting. An unmarked car with two watchful dicks in it, parked in the front yard where the gas pumps used to be. In his younger years he might have cruised on by, circled the block, gave some thought as to how he would handle things. Now he just rolled in and stopped right beside them. What were they after? Someone to shoot? Pick me, Skig thought.

They got out of their car slowly and purposefully, an air of menace hovering about them. Something they learned at the academy: how to get out of your vehicle with an air of menace. Skig got out too. As he straightened, the pain darted inside him like the tip of a cork puller he'd ingested by accident somehow, and he steadied himself.

The dicks were focused, professionally intense. The older one moved in. He was going to fat, wore an old loose-fitting suit, and showed salt-and-pepper hair around his ears. The one who'd been driving was younger, tall and lanky, and dressed like he was going to a job interview.

"You guys collecting for underprivileged cops?" Leo said. "I gave at the office," thinking of the container he had left with the quack. He brushed past the dicks, jangling his keys, and unlocked the repair bay door. When he heaved it up he thought his stomach would bust open and dump some major organ right there on the ground. He swayed.

"Mr. Skorzeny?" the fat one said.

"You know it."

"Are you all right?"

"Top shelf. Right up there with the chips and cheesies."

The dick studied him, taking his measure.

"We've got a few questions. Think we could go inside?"

"No."

The dick held his gaze. Then he shrugged. "Suit yourself." He took a pen and notebook out of his pocket, flipped pages, glanced up again. "You know a man named Dwight Keevis?"

"No."

"Owns a car dealership. Also goes by the name of Dan Duchek. Happy Dan."

"Oh, that Dwight Keevis."

"Then you do know him."

"No."

The dick pinched the bridge of his nose. "All right. Let's go about this another way. An employee says you dropped by to see Mr. Keevis earlier today, unannounced. You didn't come to buy a car, and you weren't very friendly. We'd like to know what you talked about."

"You asked if I knew the guy. I don't." Skig looked the two dicks over again. A mulish-looking couple of plugs. Stubborn as dirt. Better give them something. The truth was best. "I did stop by about a car. I been told I should trade up."

Behind the fat dick, the lanky one stooped over the window of the Vic. He made a sour face. "That might be a plan. This one stinks."

"Funny," Skig said, "it smelt good till you showed up."

The lanky dick's face tightened, and the older one reined him in with his eyes. Then the older one turned back to Skig.

"The employee claims you threatened Mr. Keevis when you left his office today."

"Is that what this is about? I said an unkind word to somebody?" Skig remembered the extremely pretty young woman, the acid look on her puss as she trip-trapped out of the room.

"Well," the dick said, "whether you did or you didn't, Mr. Keevis now happens to be dead. Died of gunshot wounds at the QE Emergency"—he glanced at his watch—"going on two hours ago."

"You don't tell me."

"I do tell you. And after what the employee said, and seeing as you're not exactly a stranger to us—"

"Got a sheet on you like the Yellow Pages," the lanky dick put in with venom.

"—we thought," the older dick continued, determined to finish, "that it might be a good idea to come by and hear what you had to say about it."

"An' you did. An' I answered you," Skig said. "So take off."

"You won't get far with that attitude."

"I only need to get through that door to my bottle of scotch. You want to arrest me because some rip-off artist stopped a long overdue slug, go ahead. But my doctor may have something to say about that. And my lawyer will cut you off at the knees."

Skig got back in the Vic, dropped it in gear, and let the fast idle roll the smelly old car inside.

In the gloom of the kitchen, he rinsed a glass in the sink, rattled some ice into it, and topped it up with Teacher's. He pushed the news about Happy Dan around in his head. Not all that surprising. Probably tried to screw the wrong sap, that's all. The sap got wise, dug his howitzer out of a shoebox, and returned to the lot, bent on revising the terms of their understanding. The fat monthly payment and, oh yeah, a little something else.

Skig glanced at the clock. Solly Sweetmore was late. If he didn't show, Skig would have to go to him, give him a slap or two to get his attention.

He sat down in his ratty recliner—collapsed into it, was more like it. Switched on the TV, jabbed the mute button, took a quick slug from his glass. The liquor did what it was supposed to do, burned for a moment, then mellowed him, but it didn't help his gut. He shook out two of the big fat brown capsules the quack had slipped him—samples, he'd said, take one before eating—and washed them down with a swallow of booze.

Then he closed his eyes.

When he opened them again, there were shadows in the room, the afternoon sun dying fast behind the fly-specked window over the sink. The light from the silent television winked and gamboled on the walls.

A TV news lady was doing a location shot. The background looked vaguely familiar. Skig frowned as two giant double Ds reared up on the screen—Dan Duchek's rip-off center. It was an earlier tape, sunlight beating down in the background where a bagged stiff was being rolled out on a gurney. He poked the mute button. The TV lady, brushing a sweep of lustrous hair out of her eyes, said, ". . . all police would reveal was that the owner of this downtown dealership was shot dead in his office by an unidentified assailant." Skig wondered if Dan still wore his grin. "CTV has learned that at least one person has been taken into custody . . ." The canned shot changed. And to Skig the monologue faded as a jerky camera lens zoomed in on a gray-haired woman being bundled into a police patrol car. The woman looked dazed. It was Eva Kohl.

"Ah jeez," Skig said.

He made a call to his lawyer Saul Getz, then rolled down to the cop shop in the Vic. Saul was there waiting for him. A thin man with patient eyes, he was thoughtfully stroking his trim, white goatee.

"You talk to her?" Skig asked.

"Yeah, I talked to her. They didn't arrest her. That woman wouldn't shoot a pop-gun at a plastic monkey to win a coconut."

"You got that right. You pry her loose?"

"Oh sure. She's an unhappy lady, though. Forensics impounded her car. Seems Happy Dan was about to drive it into the shop when the shooter stepped in and popped him. Two hits, one miss. Quite a mess." He smiled. "She's feisty. She says if the police take people's cars away, then they ought to provide loaners. I sent her home in a cab."

Skig said, "They recover the gun?"

"No. But they think it belonged to the victim. He kept a Smith in the desk, according to an employee, and the cops can't find it anywhere."

That helpful employee again. "Anything else?"

"One slug was recovered in pretty good shape. Went into the headrest. When they find the gun they'll do their ballistics thing, and that'll be it."

"They think."

"They're pretty sure. One of the techs took a quick look. He said it ought to be a slam dunk, far as the gun is concerned."

"Meantime, Eva doesn't get her car back."

"Oh, it gets worse. When I showed up and started speaking for her, the detectives figured out the connection pretty quick. I mean, from me to you, then Eva. They brightened a little.

The younger one grinned and said maybe they'd bring her back in for more questioning."

"They're outta their minds."

"They seem a little miffed at you, Leo. Did you yank their chains or something?"

He told them how he had been at the lot for a few minutes and how the fat cop and the thin cop had stopped by and braced him later.

"Buying a new car, Skig? Hey, that's a plan."

"Don't start. I was there at the lot just before the guy got it, an' because I'm me, they made a little too much of it." Skig eyeballed a policeman stepping by them in the hall. "I ran them off."

Saul stroked his goatee, thinking. "No, there's more to it. They got that witness. That employee. We don't know what she saw, or what she says she saw. She could be fingering you *and* your friend." He puffed his cheeks out, gave his head a shake. "Did you rub her the wrong way too?" When Skig didn't answer, he added, "Why would she finger a nice old doll like that?"

"I dunno," Leo said, "but I'm gonna find out."

He had just caught a glimpse of the extremely pretty young woman being ushered out of an interview room down the hall.

The sun had gone down fast. Wisps of pink-bellied clouds lingered way out low over the Arm.

Skig sat in the Crown Vic with the blower on and the windows all the way down. The car smelled especially rank today. The sludge at the bottom of the harbor wasn't violets, that was a fact. But minutes later the night breeze was buffeting through the car again, as he trailed the extremely pretty young woman's taillights down Gottingen Street. She drove fast. She tailgated. She yapped into her cell nonstop.

She drove out to Clayton Park, sped north on Dunbrack, then turned in at a block of apartments that sprawled above the slope to the basin. Shot down the ramp into the underground parking with the phone still glued to her head. Skig found a slot outside in the visitors' lot, angled so that he could watch for an apartment light to go on. He knew he had about a fifty percent chance, and his number came up. Tenth floor, northwest corner.

"Bang," Skig said.

He kept waiting. Imagined the cell phone burning. Minutes later, headlights lit the Vic from behind, a car coming up fast, flashing by him into the visitors' lot, subwoofer pumping out some irritating hip-hop crap. Nice car. A yellow Audi.

"Boom," Skig said.

Skig knew the vehicle. He'd seen it around. A car like that, you might as well have a neon sign over your head jabbing blinking arrows at you. And seeing it here now, Skig suddenly realized who the kid at the car lot had been, the one with the eyes.

The name he went by was Caesar DeLuca. His real tag? Probably not. He was Filipino. Smart with the ladies. Though what young women saw in guys who looked like extras from *Night of the Living Dead*, Skig had never been able to figure out. And DeLuca was mean. He liked to hurt people. It wasn't just an unavoidable part of doing business with him, he enjoyed it. Beyond that, Skig didn't know much about the guy and didn't want to. He couldn't care less what turned DeLuca's crank, but that would change fast if the guy had his rat's nose buried in this business somehow.

DeLuca swaggered from his car to the building, gold chains, body ink, and attitude. Skig considered the setup so far.

A car dealer shot dead. In his proximity, four people: a gentle unassuming older lady, the extremely pretty young woman, and rat boy here, Caesar DeLuca. And himself. Which of these was most likely to have had something to do with it? Since the cops apparently didn't know about DeLuca, Skig was number one on the list. But he had an alibi with the quack. The cops had probably discovered that. Which left the girl—and the older lady, of course, according to Fatty and Skinny. They had sherlocked it out.

Of course, they hadn't seen DeLuca nosing around the car lot earlier, but on the other hand they didn't seem too interested in finding out about him either. Had they asked Skig if he'd seen anybody else there? No. Had the girl volunteered the information? Skig didn't think so.

Upstairs, the window darkened. Somebody had pulled the drapes. After about half an hour, DeLuca sauntered out of the building and squealed away in his thumping pimp mobile. Skig eased out of the old Vic, locked the door, and followed a tenant and his fuzzy white dog in through the front entrance.

The apartment door on the tenth floor had a spray of dried flowers on it and a ceramic plaque that said RUSSELL. The girl pulled open her door and stared at him.

"Name's Leo Skorzeny, Ms. Russell," Skig said. "Remember me?"

Her face paled in alarm, she started to close the door, and he put his foot in the way.

"Tired of talking about what happened to your boss today?"

That stopped her. She hesitated, found that hissy look somewhere inside herself, then stood back and let him in. She waggled her fingers at a chair and flounced down on the sofa, one leg tucked up, lips clamped together tight. Skig didn't like the idea of fighting his way back out of the overstuffed bucket she had consigned him to, so he dragged a kitchen chair out of the ell and sat down gingerly on it. Jeez.

She shot a meaningful look at a table clock, something modern in plastic and glass. "You've got five minutes." She had a harsh voice. He hadn't been expecting that.

"I'll take it. I can use all the time I can get, according to my proctologist."

"Are you trying to be crude?"

"I'm trying to be accurate. You were pretty accurate yourself when you put those holes in your boss."

She brought one foot down hard on the rug, shoving forward at him. "Don't you *dare* imply I had anything to do with that!"

"I'm not implying it. I'm saying it. You shot him, all right, you or your boyfriend did. An' when you couldn't frame me, you had to settle for the old lady."

She jumped to her feet. "Get out!"

"I could do that. An' I could head back down to Gottingen Street and lay it all out for the dicks."

She stood there breathing, dainty nostrils flaring, considering her options. Then she plumped down on the sofa again and gnawed at her lip. He knew he was on the right track then.

"Fine," she said. "Let's hear your delusional idea."

"I got two, three of 'em," Skig said, ignoring the dramatics. "I been thinking down there in the car. First one is, you were cozy with Happy Dan, shining his cars for him, only somethin' went wrong. He took off to Aruba without you, had a good time in the sun, an' when he got back you tore a strip off of him."

She gave a short, barking laugh.

"That's insane. You don't know anything. What makes you think I wasn't with him?"

"Where's your tan?"

It stopped her. But just for a moment.

"Dwight was married. He flew down there with his wife. He couldn't have taken me along if he'd wanted to."

"Oh, there's ways. But we'll put that on hold. Here's delusion number two, coming at it from the other side. The guy was hitting on you, you finally lost it with him, an' you pegged him."

"Oh puh-lease!" She made her eyes go round. "Why would I do that? I could have walked away if what you're saying is true. Do you think I'm out of my mind?"

Skig looked at her. She was struggling. A pretty bundle of raw nerves curled up there on the couch.

"No," he said, "I don't think that. I think

your boyfriend's got a loose connection someplace. What's his part? He came to your rescue?"

"My boyfriend? Now what are you talking about?"

"The little weasel I just saw scuttling out of here."

She rolled her eyes again. "I don't even *have* a boyfriend. Nobody left here."

"He was in this building."

"It's a big place."

"Yeah," Skig said. He wasn't ready to mention he'd seen the two of them arguing earlier under the big double Ds at Happy's place. "Where can I find him?"

She studied Skig a moment. Worked on that lip again. She really didn't want to get going on DeLuca, that was obvious, and suddenly a miracle occurred. Her face turned all sweetness and light. Just like that.

"Look, we can be friends, you know."

"Sure."

"You don't think I'm cute?"

"Puppies are cute. So are Kewpie dolls. You're in there somewhere, I guess."

She threw her drink at him, the glass tumbling past his ear, splatting against the heavy drapes, then falling to the rug, miraculously unbroken. The drapes hadn't fared so well, a broad stain running down them. A few drops darkened Leo's sleeve.

He got up painfully. "Nice to have met you, Ms. Russell."

Two things he'd gotten out of this. Number one, she was scared of the cops. Number two, she was protecting rat boy.

Skig opened his eyes next morning and wondered where the hell he was. Found he was stretched flat out in his recliner. Last night after taking three of the big fat free samples, he had tumbled into Never-Never Land as if someone had batted him with a jack handle. He yanked the chair lever, sat up, and explored his side with his stubby fingers.

Not too bad this morning. The pain was still there, but it was biding its time. Sometimes it did that. Went away to a seminar on how to really rip a guy's innards apart, then came back and practiced on him. The respite would be short.

He showered, ran his razor over his face, and went out the door without bothering to eat. He stopped at a drive-through for a coffee, double milk, no sugar, which he drank in the Vic at the edge of the lot. There was a contest on. Win a TV. Coffee cups had the good news hidden on them. A kid rooting through the trash can by the doors for a winning cup glanced up as Skig held his out the window. He edged over suspiciously and took it from him. "Jeez, mister. Don't you want to win a plasma TV?" Skig started up the Vic. "I already got a TV. I could prob'ly use the plasma, though."

Skig drove to the recycling depot out past Lakeside. A big Loadmaster trash truck was grunting up to the dock, spewing diesel fumes, and a bunch of cars stood around, engines idling while people hauled out bags filled with beer cans, newspapers—bags filled with bags, for crying out loud—to get their four or five bucks. Save the ozone layer. He found Solly Sweetmore in his upstairs office under the corrugated sheet-metal roof.

Skig was overweight. He needed to drop forty pounds. But Solly had such a colossal gut on him he had to straighten his arms to reach his desk. His face, tracked with broken blood vessels, showed alarm when he saw who his visitor was. He set down the can of Coke he was nursing.

"You were supposed to drop by yesterday," Skig said, wincing. The pain was back. The steep stairs killed him.

"I know, Leo, I know." The trashman leaned away from his desk, moving his hands around. "I just got busy. This place is a nuthouse. You can see—"

"Fine with me, Solly," Skig said, "you want

to pay another day's juice. Go for it. Only next time tell me, okay? That's what the phone is for."

"About that, Skig, listen—"

"No, you listen. This is how things get outta hand. You keep taking more time, more time, you run outta time pretty fast. Then I got to lean on you. I don't like that, Solly."

"I know. I should've phoned you, Skig, but listen—"

A gaunt man in a knit cap interrupted, thrusting his small balding head in the door. "That compactor crapped out again, boss, the old green one, so maybe—"

Solly surged up and screamed at him. "Will you get outta my face?" He threw his pop at the man, the half filled can smashing into the door-frame, cola fizzing and splattering over a calendar and running down the cheap paneling in streams. The head withdrew.

"Lots of people throwing drinks these days," Skig said, shaking his head. "People need to relax." He tapped the book in his breast pocket. "Six-five, Solly, plus another half a point for today. Pay me now an' that's an end to it."

"But I got other bills."

"Not like mine you don't."

Solly threw his head back and let out an anguished moan. Then he jerked open a cash-box. Counted the six-five out right there on the desk.

"An' the half a point, don't forget," Skig said. Then he held up his hand. "Or maybe this'll work." He leaned in. "You know a guy named Caesar DeLuca? Drives a car like a birthday cake?" Warily, Solly nodded. Skig said, "Tell me about him."

Solly looked even more stressed out, if that was possible.

"What's to tell? I see him on Argyle there, Hollis Street, sometimes down at the casino. He's trouble."

"What kind of trouble?"

When Skig drove away fifteen minutes later, he had his money, and more information on Caesar DeLuca than he needed. The kid was also in the car business. He and Happy Dan had that in common. He did custom work, prime merchandise only, a certain kind of car, a special customer. He got an order, shopped around till he filled it. Then—this part Solly was shaky on—he delivered the wheels out in Sackville, a guy with a long-haul business there. It got loaded on a semi, other stuff packed around it, and a day later it was in New York or Montreal, on its way to the special client.

Skig had said to Solly, "Rat boy. Where does he live?"

"I dunno. Nobody knows. He keeps that to himself."

"This merchandise. Always a special order?"

"Prob'ly not. He wouldn't walk away from something."

Skig thought a minute. "Get a message to him. There's an old Vette, one a them Sting Rays, been parking on the street all night behind the Armories. You don't know why. But you seen it there, an' you want a spotting fee."

Solly had shaken his fleshy face. "Jeez, I dunno, Leo."

"Just do it." Skig shifted his weight. "Do it an' we'll call it square on the point."

"Fine. But I don't like it," Solly said. "I'm telling you that guy is a crazy man."

Back home, Skig dialed Saul Getz. "They pick her up? Eva Kohl?"

"No, of course not. What case have they got? But they're thinking about it."

"Why?"

"Something about her being a suicide risk."

"They're full of it."

"I'm with you. She doesn't look the type. A little bewildered maybe, but who wouldn't be?"

"Whatever happened to a free country?"

"Things are relative, Leo."

"Things are crap. Listen, do what you can for her. They pull her in, I want you there with her."

"Leo, this is costing you. It's adding up fast."

"Just do it. An' don't bring me into it. She thinks she owes me, that's bad for a friendship. It changes things."

"Yeah, well, she is starting to wonder."

"Just be there for her. Say you're court appointed or something. Make somethin' up, you're a lawyer, for cryin' out loud."

"Fine, but I've got to bill you."

"So cheer up." Skig winced. The pain was back. "One more thing. I need to borrow your Vette."

There was dead silence. Then Saul started breathing again.

"You *what*?"

"I know it's your toy, you only drive it to church on Sunday, but tonight I want you to park it behind the Armories, take a cab home, an' forget about it."

"You're not serious."

"Anything happens to it, I'll pay the shot. You know I'm good for it."

There was a short pause. Then Saul said, "You're up to something."

"Go see Mrs. Kohl."

Skig spent the rest of the day at the clinic. The lousy tests all over again. When he got home that evening he felt as if he was a sample of something himself. He ate beans, cold out of the can, and washed them down with scotch, both food items totally forbidden to him. To hell with it. Then he set his alarm clock—the blender plugged into the timed outlet on the stove—and fell into his recliner. He dreamed Fatty and Skinny, dressed like surgeons, were stooping over him, making a large incision in his belly and smiling about it.

The alarm was howling in the kitchen, the empty blender dancing around on the metal stovetop like it was going to explode. Midnight.

He limped out the door.

He parked one street over from the Armories where through the gap of a vacant lot he could eyeball Saul's money-pit Vette—a '65 fastback, Nassau Blue. Tilted the Vic's power seat back until only his eyes showed above the dash.

He dozed a few times, and then something woke him. The clock read one fifteen. A tow truck was backing toward Saul's ride. It stopped and rat boy got out, gold chains flashing under the sodium streetlamp. He held something down low at his side that looked for a second like a long-barreled handgun. It was a cordless drill with a foot-long bit in it. Rat boy put the bit to the fiberglass fender and sank a hole into the Vette's engine compartment. An old trick. Drain the battery. That way the alarm wouldn't sound unless there was a backup.

There wasn't. Something to mention to Saul. The guy hooked up the Vette and dragged it away. Elapsed time, three minutes. Skig readjusted his seat and took off after him.

Rat boy would have places to store his cars, places where he could keep them out of sight for a while. Rented garages here and there, probably. After a ten minute drive out to Spryfield, the tow truck halted before an old swayback shed. The kid was good with the boom and the winch, and the Vette was tucked out of sight in no time.

The rat dropped off the truck—another darkened house a few blocks south—hopped in the Audi, and beat it out of town along Purcell's Cove Road, stereo thumping all the way, a good night's work behind him. Skig gave him room, not wanting to spook him. Maybe too much room. He came over a hill near Herring Cove, overshot the place, and had to double back. Good thing he'd been watching the drives on either side, and caught a flash of brake lights and yellow paint.

The rat appeared to be doing all right for himself. It was a modern chalet in bleached cedar, overlooking the ocean. In need of some TLC but pretty fine all the same. Skig took the Vic back up the hill to a market gardener's he'd spotted, parked in the darkened lot by the greenhouse, got out, and walked back. A short stroll, no more than two hundred yards or so, but on a steep incline. His gut wasn't happy about it.

Partway up the drive to the house, Skig stopped. There were two cars here. The Audi and, in front of it, the car he had followed from the cop-shop the previous night. He grunted. It was the car of the extremely pretty young woman.

"No boyfriend, huh?" Skig said.

He heard voices.

The house stood on a brutally unaccommodating chunk of granite, cantilevered over the cliff face to provide a picture-perfect view of the sea. A wide deck embraced it. In the quiet gaps when the surf wasn't pounding, voices drifted from the seaward side.

Skig climbed three broad steps to the deck. Against the house were some sturdy-looking loungers, a plastic cooler filled with ice and beer. Skig helped himself to a beer and sat down on a bench. He pressed the cold can to his side. From here he could make out the voices better.

". . . I brought the beer like you told me, but I didn't think you'd be here this soon," the girl's voice said.

"I told you two, two thirty."

"Yes, but you're never early."

"What's the late-breaking news, it couldn't wait till tomorrow?"

A wave heaved in. "A man came to see me."

"What man?"

"The man I told the cops about—you know who I mean."

"The guy who threatened your boss?"

"Yes."

"So what did he want?"

"He accused me of killing Dwight."

Another pause in the conversation. The guy deliberating. Down below the house a big wave thundered in. Skig could smell the salt.

"Lemme guess. He thinks he can blackmail you."

"No. That's the funny thing. He just made these crazy accusations, then left. I thought about it all day and finally decided I'd better tell you about it."

"This happened yesterday?"

"Yeah. In the evening. Just after you left." She hesitated. "I think . . ." Her voice trailed off.

"You think what?"

"I think he knows something about you. I mean, he asked me where he could find you, and—Stop that! You're hurting me!"

"You waited all this time to tell me?"

"Let go of me!"

There was a scuffle, a muffled slap.

Skig swished his beer around, took another swallow. Then he got up. He walked around to the front of the house and saw him there, rat boy, staring down at the girl. She was crouched on the deck against the railing, one hand to the side of her face.

The guy must have seen her eyes move. He spun around in surprise.

"Name's Leo Skorzeny," Skig said. "You heard of *me*?"

"Where the hell'd you come from?"

"You heard of me?"

"Yeah, I hearda you. Some kinda shy. You heard of me?"

"Yeah. Some kinda rat." Skig looked at the girl. There was a red welt blossoming along one side of her face. Her nose was bleeding. His eyes moved back to the rat, and he shook his head. "What's the matter with you?"

The dead eyes narrowed, and Skig followed their quick shift to a pile of split wood near the door. A weapon on this guy's mind. A hatchet, maybe.

"Don't even think it," Skig said, "'less you want to wear the thing. Walk around with it stickin' outta you, some kinda new body piercing."

"You talk tough."

"It's the mileage," Skig said. "Want to hear what I got?" He finished the beer and set the can down carefully on the railing. "One part of Happy's business, he had that detailing place out back of the lot. The way I figure it, somebody goes through the records there, they can find out who owns what in town. All the good stuff. The best rides. Cars you don't see on the street too much. Practically a catalogue to a guy like you."

"So what."

"You come onto Ms. Russell here so you can get your nose in those records." The girl was getting to her feet. Dawning realization on her face, eyes jumping from Skig to rat boy. "Pretty soon, Happy Dan's customers lose a car or two. Maybe a string of them. Happy Dan is scratching his head. Then one day he finds you goin' through his records, your rat's nose twitching, an' he calls you on it. Or no, more likely the girl's doin' it. He threatens to call the cops. You can't have that."

The dead eyes didn't waver.

"There's some shouting. Some more threats. He has to step out to start processing the old lady's trade, an' the girl calls you up, panicking. You panic too. She tells you where the gun is, or she told you about it before. You're back in a minute, an' you use it to make those big holes in the guy."

The rat edged closer to the woodpile. A car started out back of the house. Skig looked for the girl again, but she was gone. He shrugged.

"What you gonna do? I think the girl figures it out. She remembers me sorting out her boss, an' she's thinking—some nutty idea in her head—that she can put the jacket on me. It's a long shot, but it's all you got. An' it turns out I got an alibi. Then there's the gun. You screwed that up too. Not likely I'd pop somebody with their own gun. Not my style. An' bein' a thief it's really tough for you to give up a perfectly good Smith. I bet you still got it. The gun ties you to it."

By this time DeLuca had sidled halfway across the deck, and now he dived for the open door. Skig moved to block him. He saw what DeLuca was reaching for—not the woodpile but something else, his hand thrusting into the room and coming out with the gun. It must have been on the kitchen counter.

Skig brought the heel of his fist down on the rat's arm so hard he heard something pop and rat boy screamed. The gun clattered over the boards. The rat's bony knee came up, and a huge pain shot through Skig's belly. Skig reeled backward, left hand clenched in the rat's shirt, pulling the rat with him as the knee came up again. A wave of nausea. Skig was going down. He grabbed handfuls of the rat's baggy pants with both fists and heaved, putting his shoulders into it. The jolt hammered all the way up his spine when his butt struck the deck, and he sat there a moment, dazed, chunky legs splayed out, hand pressed to his side. There was one good thing though. Rat boy was gone. A flying header over the railing, sixty feet down to rocks and pounding surf.

Boom.

After a bit, Skig got up and put the gun back on the kitchen counter, careful how he touched it.

"You gonna be all right?" Skig asked Mrs. Kohl.

"I'll be just fine, Mr. Skorzeny. Go ahead to your doctor's appointment."

"He can wait. I'm more worried about you. Somethin' happens, who's gonna cut my hair?"

Skig helped her settle into her glider rocker. She smiled up at him.

"That Mr. Getz is an awfully nice man. He's helped me a lot. I was relieved when he told me the police figured out who killed Mr. Duchek. He was a nice man too." Then she frowned. "Mr. Getz isn't very happy with you, though. Something about a car?"

"Could be."

"Cars are an awful lot of trouble."

"They are for some people."

"I'm going out again tomorrow to see if I can lease one."

Skig was silent a moment, then said, "You want some company this time?"

A bright laugh. "You're afraid I'll get cheated. Men have an easier time of it at car lots than women do, is that it?"

"Lemme think about that one," Skig said.

Keller on the Spot

LAWRENCE BLOCK

OKAY, KELLER IS A PROFESSIONAL HIT MAN, killing people that he's paid to eliminate, which leads one to think he's a black-hearted sociopath. His stock doesn't rise when we watch him get to know many of his targets, become friendly with them, and still coldly pull the trigger. On the other hand, he seems otherwise fairly normal, a man with a hobby (stamp collecting) who is easygoing, laid back, and friendly. He does not torture anyone, nor does he take any particular pleasure in killing his victims, though he does allow that "some people need killing."

Keller's creator, Lawrence Block (1938–) has produced such series characters as Matthew Scudder, an alcoholic ex-cop who accidentally shot and killed a little girl and now functions as an unofficial private eye, doing favors for friends; Bernie Rhodenbarr, a professional burglar and bookseller; Evan Tanner, a spy with a disorder that prevents him from sleeping—ever; Martin Ehrengraf, an amoral lawyer who charges a fortune but wins every case, no matter what it takes; and Chip Harrison, a teenager who thinks of little besides sex but works for Leo Haig, a private detective modeled after Nero Wolfe.

The Keller stories began in the pages of *Playboy* and proved so popular that a series of books followed; disguised as episodic novels, many of the murderous incidents had previously appeared as short stories. The first of the five Keller books was titled, perhaps not surprisingly, *Hit Man* (1998); it was followed by *Hit List* (2000), *Hit Parade* (2006), *Hit and Run* (2008), and *Hit Me* (2013).

"Keller on the Spot" was originally published in the November 1997 issue of *Playboy*; it was first collected in *Hit Man* (New York, William Morrow, 1998).

KELLER ON THE SPOT

Lawrence Block

KELLER, drink in hand, agreed with the woman in the pink dress that it was a lovely evening. He threaded his way through a crowd of young marrieds on what he supposed you would call the patio. A waitress passed carrying a tray of drinks in stemmed glasses and he traded in his own for a fresh one. He sipped as he walked along, wondering what he was drinking. Some sort of vodka sour, he decided, and decided as well that he didn't need to narrow it down any further than that. He figured he'd have this one and one more, but he could have ten more if he wanted, because he wasn't working tonight. He could relax and cut back and have a good time.

Well, almost. He couldn't relax completely, couldn't cut back altogether. Because, while this might not be work, neither was it entirely recreational. The garden party this evening was a heaven-sent opportunity for reconnaissance, and he would use it to get a close look at his quarry. He had been handed a picture in the old man's study back in White Plains, and he had brought that picture with him to Dallas, but even the best photo wasn't the same as a glimpse of the fellow in the flesh, and in his native habitat.

And a lush habitat it was. Keller hadn't been inside the house yet, but it was clearly immense, a sprawling multilevel affair of innumerable large rooms. The grounds sprawled as well, covering an acre or two, with enough plants and shrubbery to stock an arboretum. Keller didn't know anything about flowers, but five minutes in a garden like this one had him thinking he ought to know more about the subject. Maybe they had evening classes at Hunter or NYU, maybe they'd take you on field trips to the Brooklyn Botanical Gardens. Maybe his life would be richer if he knew the names of the flowers, and whether they were annuals or perennials, and whatever else there was to know about them. Their soil requirements, say, and what bug killer to spray on their leaves, or what fertilizer to spread at their roots.

He walked along a brick path, smiling at this stranger, nodding at that one, and wound up standing alongside the swimming pool. Some twelve or fifteen people sat at poolside tables, talking and drinking, the volume of their conversation rising as they drank. In the enormous pool, a young boy swam back and forth, back and forth.

Keller felt a curious kinship with the kid. He was standing instead of swimming, but he felt as distant as the kid from everybody else around.

There were two parties going on, he decided. There was the hearty social whirl of everybody else, and there was the solitude he felt in the midst of it all, identical to the solitude of the swimming boy.

Huge pool. The boy was swimming its width, but that dimension was still greater than the length of your typical backyard pool. Keller didn't know whether this was an Olympic pool, he wasn't quite sure how big that would have to be, but he figured you could just call it enormous and let it go at that.

Ages ago he'd heard about some college-boy stunt, filling a swimming pool with Jell-O, and he'd wondered how many little boxes of the gelatin dessert it would have required, and how the college boys could have afforded it. It would cost a fortune, he decided, to fill *this* pool with Jell-O—but if you could afford the pool in the first place, he supposed the Jell-O would be the least of your worries.

There were cut flowers on all the tables, and the blooms looked like ones Keller had seen in the garden. It stood to reason. If you grew all these flowers, you wouldn't have to order from the florist. You could cut your own.

What good would it do, he wondered, to know the names of all the shrubs and flowers? Wouldn't it just leave you wanting to dig in the soil and grow your own? And he didn't want to get into all that, for God's sake. His apartment was all he needed or wanted, and it was no place for a garden. He hadn't even tried growing an avocado pit there, and he didn't intend to. He was the only living thing in the apartment, and that was the way he wanted to keep it. The day that changed was the day he'd call the exterminator.

So maybe he'd just forget about evening classes at Hunter, and field trips to Brooklyn. If he wanted to get close to nature he could walk in Central Park, and if he didn't know the names of the flowers he would just hold off on introducing himself to them. And if—

Where was the kid?

The boy, the swimmer. Keller's companion in solitude. Where the hell did he go?

The pool was empty, its surface still. Keller saw a ripple toward the far end, saw a brace of bubbles break the surface.

He didn't react without thinking. That was how he'd always heard that sort of thing described, but that wasn't what happened, because the thoughts were there, loud and clear. *He's down there. He's in trouble. He's drowning.* And, echoing in his head in a voice that might have been Dot's, sour with exasperation: *Keller, for Christ's sake, do something!*

He set his glass on a table, shucked his coat, kicked off his shoes, dropped his pants and stepped out of them. Ages ago he'd earned a Red Cross lifesaving certificate, and the first thing they taught you was to strip before you hit the water. The six or seven seconds you spent peeling off your clothes would be repaid many times over in quickness and mobility.

But the strip show did not go unnoticed. Everybody at poolside had a comment, one more hilarious than the next. He barely heard them. In no time at all he was down to his underwear, and then he was out of range of their cleverness, hitting the water's surface in a flat racing dive, churning the water till he reached the spot where he'd seen the bubbles, then diving, eyes wide, barely noticing the burn of the chlorine.

Searching for the boy. Groping, searching, then finding him, reaching to grab hold of him. And pushing off against the bottom, lungs bursting, racing to reach the surface.

People were saying things to Keller, thanking him, congratulating him, but it wasn't really registering. A man clapped him on the back, a woman handed him a glass of brandy. He heard the word "hero" and realized that people were saying it all over the place, and applying it to him.

Hell of a note.

Keller sipped the brandy. It gave him heartburn, which assured him of its quality; good cognac always gave him heartburn. He turned to look at the boy. He was just a little fellow, twelve or thirteen years old, his hair lightened and his skin lightly bronzed by the summer sun. He was sitting up now, Keller saw, and looking none the worse for his near-death experience.

"Timothy," a woman said, "this is the man who saved your life. Do you have something to say to him?"

"Thanks," Timothy said, predictably.

"Is that all you have to say, young man?"

"It's enough," Keller said, and smiled. To the boy he said, "There's something I've always wondered. Did your whole life actually flash before your eyes?"

Timothy shook his head. "I got this cramp," he said, "and it was like my whole body turned into one big knot, and there wasn't anything I could do to untie it. And I didn't even think about drowning. I was just fighting the cramp, 'cause it hurt, and just about the next thing I knew I was up here coughing and puking up water." He made a face. "I must have swallowed half the pool. All I have to do is think about it and I can taste vomit and chlorine."

"Timothy," the woman said, and rolled her eyes.

"Something to be said for plain speech," an older man said. He had a mane of white hair and a pair of prominent white eyebrows, and his eyes were a vivid blue. He was holding a glass of brandy in one hand and a bottle in the other, and he reached with the bottle to fill Keller's glass to the brim. "'Claret for boys, port for men,'" he said, "'but he who would be a hero must drink brandy.' That's Samuel Johnson, although I may have gotten a word wrong."

The young woman patted his hand. "If you did, Daddy, I'm sure you just improved Mr. Johnson's wording."

"Dr. Johnson," he said, "and one could hardly do that. Improve the man's wording, that is. 'Being in a ship is being in a jail, with the chance of being drowned.' He said that as well, and I defy anyone to comment more trenchantly on the experience, or to say it better." He beamed at Keller. "I owe you more than a glass of brandy and a well-turned Johnsonian phrase. This little rascal whose life you've saved is my grandson, and the apple—nay, sir, the very nectarine—of my eye. And we'd have all stood around drinking and laughing while he drowned. You observed, and you acted, and God bless you for it."

What did you say to that? Keller wondered. *It was nothing? Well, shucks?* There had to be an apt phrase, and maybe Samuel Johnson could have found it, but he couldn't. So he said nothing, and just tried not to look po-faced.

"I don't even know your name," the white-haired man went on. "That's not remarkable in and of itself. I don't know half the people here, and I'm content to remain in my ignorance. But I ought to know your name, wouldn't you agree?"

Keller might have picked a name out of the air, but the one that leaped to mind was Boswell, and he couldn't say that to a man who quoted Samuel Johnson. So he supplied the name he'd traveled under, the one he'd signed when he checked into the hotel, the one on the driver's license and credit cards in his wallet.

"It's Michael Soderholm," he said, "and I can't even tell you the name of the fellow who brought me here. We met over drinks in the hotel bar and he said he was going to a party and it would be perfectly all right if I came along. I felt a little funny about it, but—"

"Please," the man said. "You can't possibly propose to apologize for your presence here. It's kept my grandson from a watery if chlorinated grave. And I've just told you I don't know half my guests, but that doesn't make them any the less welcome." He took a deep drink of his brandy and topped up both glasses. "Michael Soderholm," he said. "Swedish?"

"A mixture of everything," Keller said, improvising. "My great-grandfather Soderholm came over from Sweden, but my other ancestors came from all over Europe, plus I'm something like a sixteenth American Indian."

"Oh? Which tribe?"

"Cherokee," Keller said, thinking of the jazz tune.

"I'm an eighth Comanche," the man said. "So I'm afraid we're not tribal bloodbrothers. The rest's British Isles, a mix of Scots and Irish and English. Old Texas stock. But you're not Texan yourself."

"No."

"Well, it can't be helped, as the saying goes. Unless you decide to move here, and who's to say that you won't? It's a fine place for a man to live."

"Daddy thinks everybody should love Texas the way he does," the woman said.

"Everybody should," her father said. "The only thing wrong with Texans is we're a long-winded lot. Look at the time it's taking me to introduce myself! Mr. Soderholm, Mr. Michael Soderholm, my name's Garrity, Wallace Penrose Garrity, and I'm your grateful host this evening."

No kidding, thought Keller.

The party, lifesaving and all, took place on Saturday night. The next day Keller sat in his hotel room and watched the Cowboys beat the Vikings with a field goal in the last three minutes of double overtime. The game had seesawed back and forth, with interceptions and runbacks, and the announcers kept telling each other what a great game it was.

Keller supposed they were right. It had all the ingredients, and it wasn't the players' fault that he himself was entirely unmoved by their performance. He could watch sports, and often did, but he almost never got caught up in it. He had occasionally wondered if his work might have something to do with it. On one level, when your job involved dealing regularly with life and death, how could you care if some overpaid steroid abuser had a touchdown run called back? And, on another level, you saw unorthodox solutions to a team's problems on the field. When Emmitt Smith kept crashing through the Minnesota line, Keller found himself wondering why they didn't deputize someone to shoot the son of a bitch in the back of the neck, right below his star-covered helmet.

Still, it was better than watching golf, say, which in turn had to be better than playing golf. And he couldn't get out and work, because there was nothing for him to do. Last night's reconnaissance mission had been both better and worse than he could have hoped, and what was he supposed to do now, park his rented Ford across the street from the Garrity mansion and clock the comings and goings?

No need for that. He could bide his time, just so he got there in time for Sunday dinner.

"Some more potatoes, Mr. Soderholm?"

"They're delicious," Keller said. "But I'm full. Really."

"And we can't keep calling you Mr. Soderholm," Garrity said. "I've only held off this long for not knowing whether you prefer Mike or Michael."

"Mike's fine," Keller said.

"Then Mike it is. And I'm Wally, Mike, or W. P., though there are those who call me 'The Walrus.'"

Timmy laughed, and clapped both hands over his mouth.

"Though never to his face," said the woman who'd offered Keller more potatoes. She was Ellen Garrity, Timmy's aunt and Garrity's daughter-in-law, and Keller was now instructed to call her Ellie. Her husband, a big-shouldered fellow who seemed to be smiling bravely through the heartbreak of male-pattern baldness, was Garrity's son Hank.

Keller remembered Timothy's mother from the night before, but hadn't got her name at the time, or her relationship to Garrity. She was Rhonda Sue Butler, as it turned out, and everybody called her Rhonda Sue, except for her husband, who called her Ronnie. His name was Doak Butler, and he looked like a college jock who'd been too light for pro ball, although he now seemed to be closing the gap.

Hank and Ellie, Doak and Rhonda Sue. And, at the far end of the table, Vanessa, who was married to Wally but who was clearly not the mother of Hank or Rhonda Sue, or anyone else. Keller supposed you could describe her as Wally's trophy wife, a sign of his success. She was young, no older than Wally's kids, and she looked to be well bred and elegant, and she even had the good grace to hide the boredom Keller was sure she felt.

And that was the lot of them. Wally and Vanessa, Hank and Ellen, Doak and Rhonda Sue. And Timothy, who he was assured had been swimming that very afternoon, the aquatic equivalent of getting right back on the horse. He'd had no cramps this time, but he'd had an attentive eye kept on him throughout.

Seven of them, then. And Keller . . . also known as Mike.

"So you're here on business," Wally said. "And stuck here over the weekend, which is the worst part of a business trip, as far as I'm concerned. More trouble than it's worth to fly back to Chicago?"

The two of them were in Wally's den, a fine room paneled in knotty pecan and trimmed out in red leather, with Western doo-dads on the walls—here a branding iron, there a longhorn skull. Keller had accepted a brandy and declined a cigar, and the aroma of Wally's Havana was giving him second thoughts. Keller didn't smoke, but from the smell of it the cigar wasn't a mere matter of smoking. It was more along the lines of a religious experience.

"Seemed that way," Keller said. He'd supplied Chicago as Michael Soderholm's home base, though Soderholm's license placed him in Southern California. "By the time I fly there and back . . ."

"You've spent your weekend on airplanes. Well, it's our good fortune you decided to stay. Now what I'd like to do is find a way to make it your good fortune as well."

"You've already done that," Keller told him. "I crashed a great party last night and actually got to feel like a hero for a few minutes. And tonight I sit down to a fine dinner with nice people and get to top it off with a glass of outstanding brandy."

The heartburn told him how outstanding it was.

"What I had in mind," Wally said smoothly, "was to get you to work for me."

Whom did he want him to kill? Keller almost blurted out the question until he remembered that Garrity didn't know what he did for a living.

"You won't say who you work for," Garrity went on.

"I can't."

"Because the job's hush-hush for now. Well, I can respect that, and from the hints you've dropped I gather you're here scouting out something in the way of mergers and acquisitions."

"That's close."

"And I'm sure it's well paid, and you must like the work or I don't think you'd stay with it. So what do I have to do to get you to switch horses and come work for me? I'll tell you one thing—Chicago's a real nice place, but nobody who ever moved from there to Big D went around with a sour face about it. I don't know you well yet, but I can tell you're our kind of people and Dallas'll be your kind of town. And I don't know what they're paying you, but I suspect I can top it, and offer you a stake in a growing company with all sorts of attractive possibilities."

Keller listened, nodded judiciously, sipped a little brandy. It was amazing, he thought, the way things came along when you weren't looking for them. It was straight out of Horatio Alger, for God's sake—Ragged Dick stops the runaway horse and saves the daughter of the captain of industry, and the next thing you know he's president of IBM with rising expectations.

"Maybe I'll have that cigar after all," he said.

"Now, come on, Keller," Dot said. "You know the rules. I can't tell you that."

"It's sort of important," he said.

"One of the things the client buys," she said, "is confidentiality. That's what he wants and it's what we provide. Even if the agent in place—"

"The agent in place?"

"That's you," she said. "You're the agent, and Dallas is the place. Even if you get caught red-handed, the confidentiality of the client remains uncompromised. And do you know why?"

"Because the agent in place knows how to keep mum."

"Mum's the word," she agreed, "and there's no question you're the strong silent type, but even if your lip loosens you can't sink a ship if you don't know when it's sailing."

Keller thought that over. "You lost me," he said.

"Yeah, it came out a little abstruse, didn't it? Point is you can't tell what you don't know, Keller, which is why the agent doesn't get to know the client's name."

"Dot," he said, trying to sound injured. "Dot, how long have you known me?"

"Ages, Keller. Many lifetimes."

"Many lifetimes?"

"We were in Atlantis together. Look, I know nobody's going to catch you red-handed, and I know you wouldn't blab if they did. But *I* can't tell what *I* don't know."

"Oh."

"Right. I think the spies call it a double cut-out. The client made arrangements with somebody we know, and that person called us. But he didn't give us the client's name, and why should he? And, come to think of it, Keller, why do you have to know, anyway?"

He had his answer ready. "It might not be a single," he said.

"Oh?"

"The target's always got people around him," he said, "and the best way to do it might be a sort of group plan, if you follow me."

"Two for the price of one."

"Or three or four," he said. "But if one of those innocent bystanders turned out to be the client, it might make things a little awkward."

"Well, I can see where we might have trouble collecting the final payment."

"If we knew for a fact that the client was fishing for trout in Montana," he said, "it's no problem. But if he's here in Dallas—"

"It would help to know his name." She sighed. "Give me an hour or two, huh? Then call me back."

If he knew who the client was, the client could have an accident.

It would have to be an artful accident too. It would have to look good not only to the police but to whoever was aware of the client's own intentions. The local go-between, the helpful fellow who'd hooked up the client to the old man in White Plains, and thus to Keller, could be expected to cast a cold eye on any suspicious death. So it would have to be a damn good accident, but Keller had managed a few of those in his day. It took a little planning, but it wasn't brain surgery. You just figured out a method and took your best shot.

It might take some doing. If, as he rather hoped, the client was some business rival in Houston or Denver or San Diego, he'd have to slip off to that city without anyone noting his absence. Then, having induced a quick attack of accidental death, he'd fly back to Dallas and hang around until someone called him off the case. He'd need different ID for Houston or Denver or San Diego—it wouldn't do to overexpose Michael Soderholm—and he'd need to mask his actions from all concerned—Garrity, his homicidal rival, and, perhaps most important, Dot and the old man.

All told, it was a great deal more complicated (if easier to stomach) than the alternative.

Which was to carry out the assignment professionally and kill Wallace Penrose Garrity the first good chance he got.

And he really didn't want to do that. He'd

eaten at the man's table, he'd drunk the man's brandy, he'd smoked the man's cigars. He'd been offered not merely a job but a well-paid executive position with a future, and, later that night, light-headed from alcohol and nicotine, he'd had fantasies of taking Wally up on it.

Hell, why not? He could live out his days as Michael Soderholm, doing whatever unspecified tasks Garrity was hiring him to perform. He probably lacked the requisite experience, but how hard could it be to pick up the skills he needed as he went along? Whatever he had to do, it would be easier than flying from town to town killing people. He could learn on the job. He could pull it off.

The fantasy had about as much substance as a dream, and, like a dream, it was gone when he awoke the next morning. No one would put him on the payroll without some sort of background check, and the most cursory scan would knock him out of the box. Michael Soderholm had no more substance than the fake ID in his wallet.

Even if he somehow finessed a background check, even if the old man in White Plains let him walk out of one life and into another, he knew he couldn't really make it work. He already had a life. Misshapen though it was, it fit him like a glove.

Other lives made tempting fantasies. Running a print shop in Roseburg, Oregon, living in a cute little house with a mansard roof—it was something to tease yourself with while you went on being the person you had no choice but to be. This latest fantasy was just more of the same.

He went out for a sandwich and a cup of coffee. He got back in his car and drove around for a while. Then he found a pay phone and called White Plains.

"Do a single," Dot said.

"How's that?"

"No added extras, no free dividends. Just do what they signed on for."

"Because the client's here in town," he said. "Well, I could work around that if I knew his name. I could make sure he was out of it."

"Forget it," Dot said. "The client wants a long and happy life for everybody but the designated vic. Maybe the DV's close associates are near and dear to the client. That's just a guess, but all that really matters is that nobody else gets hurt. Capeesh?"

"'Capeesh?'"

"It's Italian, it means—"

"I know what it means. It just sounded odd from your lips, that's all. But yes, I understand." He took a breath. "Whole thing may take a little time," he said.

"Then here comes the good news," she said. "Time's not of the essence. They don't care how long it takes, just so you get it right."

"I understand W. P. offered you a job," Vanessa said. "I know he hopes you'll take him up on it."

"I think he was just being generous," Keller told her. "I was in the right place at the right time, and he'd like to do me a favor, but I don't think he really expects me to come to work for him."

"He'd like it if you did," she said, "or he never would have made the offer. He'd have just given you money, or a car, or something like that. And as far as what he expects, well, W. P. generally expects to get whatever he wants. Because that's the way things usually work out."

And had she been saving up her pennies to get things to work out a little differently? You had to wonder. Was she truly under Garrity's spell, in awe of his power, as she seemed to be? Or was she only in it for the money, and was there a sharp edge of irony under her worshipful remarks?

Hard to say. Hard to tell about any of them. Was Hank the loyal son he appeared to be, content to live in the old man's shadow and take what got tossed his way? Or was he secretly resentful and ambitious?

What about the son-in-law, Doak? On the surface, he looked to be delighted with the aftermath of his college football career—his work for his father-in-law consisted largely of playing golf with business associates and drinking with them afterward. But did he seethe inside, sure he was fit for greater things?

How about Hank's wife, Ellie? She struck Keller as an unlikely Lady Macbeth. Keller could fabricate scenarios in which she or Rhonda Sue had a reason for wanting Wally dead, but they were the sort of thing you dreamed up while watching reruns of *Dallas* and trying to guess who shot J.R. Maybe one of their marriages was in trouble. Maybe Garrity had put the moves on his daughter-in-law, or maybe a little too much brandy had led him into his daughter's bedroom now and then. Maybe Doak or Hank was playing footsie with Vanessa. Maybe . . .

Pointless to speculate, he decided. You could go around and around like that and it didn't get you anywhere. Even if he managed to dope out which of them was the client, then what? Having saved young Timothy, and thus feeling obligated to spare his doting grandfather, what was he going to do? Kill the boy's father? Or mother or aunt or uncle?

Of course he could just go home. He could even explain the situation to the old man. Nobody loved it when you took yourself off a contract for personal reasons, but it wasn't something they could talk you out of, either. If you made a habit of that sort of thing, well, that was different, but that wasn't the case with Keller. He was a solid pro. Quirky perhaps, even whimsical, but a pro all the way. You told him what to do and he did it.

So, if he had a personal reason to bow out, you honored it. You let him come home and sit on the porch and drink iced tea with Dot.

And you picked up the phone and sent somebody else to Dallas.

Because either way the job was going to be done. If a hit man had a change of heart, it would be followed in short order by a change of hit man. If Keller didn't pull the trigger, somebody else would.

His mistake, Keller thought savagely, was to jump in the goddam pool in the first place. All he'd had to do was look the other way and let the little bastard drown. A few days later he could have taken Garrity out, possibly making it look like suicide, a natural consequence of despondency over the boy's tragic accident.

But no, he thought, glaring at himself in the mirror. No, you had to go and get involved. You had to be a hero, for God's sake. Had to strip down to your skivvies and prove you deserved that junior lifesaving certificate the Red Cross gave you all those years ago.

He wondered whatever happened to that certificate.

It was gone, of course, like everything he'd ever owned in his childhood and youth. Gone like his high school diploma, like his Boy Scout merit badge sash, like his stamp collection and his sack of marbles and his stack of baseball cards. He didn't mind that these things were gone, didn't waste time wishing he had them any more than he wanted those years back.

But he wondered what physically became of them. The lifesaving certificate, for instance. Someone might have thrown out his baseball cards, or sold his stamp collection to a dealer. A certificate, though, wasn't something you threw out, nor was it something anyone else would want.

Maybe it was buried in a landfill, or in a stack of paper ephemera in the back of some thrift shop. Maybe some pack rat had rescued it, and maybe it was now part of an extensive collection of junior lifesaving certificates, housed in an album and cherished as living history, the pride and joy of a collector ten times as quirky and whimsical as Keller could ever dream of being.

He wondered how he felt about that. His certificate, his small achievement, living on in some eccentric's collection. On the one hand, it was a kind of immortality, wasn't it? On the other hand, well, whose certificate was it, anyway? He'd been the one to earn it, breaking the instructor's choke hold, spinning him and grabbing him in a cross-chest carry, towing the big lug to the side of the pool. It was his accomplishment and it had his name on it, so didn't it belong on his own wall or nowhere?

All in all, he couldn't say he felt strongly

either way. The certificate, when all was said and done, was only a piece of paper. What was important was the skill itself, and what was truly remarkable was that he'd retained it.

Because of it, Timothy Butler was alive and well. Which was all well and good for the boy, and a great big headache for Keller.

Later, sitting with a cup of coffee, Keller thought some more about Wallace Penrose Garrity, a man who increasingly seemed to have not an enemy in the world.

Suppose Keller had let the kid drown. Suppose he just plain hadn't noticed the boy's disappearance beneath the water, just as everyone else had failed to notice it. Garrity would have been despondent. It was his party, his pool, his failure to provide supervision. He'd probably have blamed himself for the boy's death.

When Keller took him out, it would have been the kindest thing he could have done for him.

He caught the waiter's eye and signaled for more coffee. He'd just given himself something to think about.

"Mike," Garrity said, coming toward him with a hand outstretched. "Sorry to keep you waiting. Had a phone call from a fellow with a hankering to buy a little five-acre lot of mine on the south edge of town. Thing is, I don't want to sell it to him."

"I see."

"But there's ten acres on the other side of town I'd be perfectly happy to sell to him, but he'll only want it if he thinks of it himself. So that left me on the phone longer than I would have liked. Now what would you say to a glass of brandy?"

"Maybe a small one."

Garrity led the way to the den, poured drinks for both of them. "You should have come earlier," he said. "In time for dinner. I hope you know you don't need an invitation. There'll always be a place for you at our table."

"Well," Keller said.

"I know you can't talk about it," Garrity said, "but I hope your project here in town is shaping up nicely."

"Slow but sure," Keller said.

"Some things can't be hurried," Garrity allowed, and sipped brandy, and winced. If Keller hadn't been looking for it, he might have missed the shadow that crossed his host's face.

Gently he said, "Is the pain bad, Wally?"

"How's that, Mike?"

Keller put his glass on the table. "I spoke to Dr. Jacklin," he said. "I know what you're going through."

"That son of a bitch," Garrity said, "was supposed to keep his mouth shut."

"Well, he thought it was all right to talk to me," Keller said. "He thought I was Dr. Edward Fishman from the Mayo Clinic."

"Calling for a consultation."

"Something like that."

"I did go to Mayo," Garrity said, "but they didn't need to call Harold Jacklin to double-check their results. They just confirmed his diagnosis and told me not to buy any long-playing records." He looked to one side. "They said they couldn't say for sure how much time I had left, but that the pain would be manageable for a while. And then it wouldn't."

"I see."

"And I'd have all my faculties for a while," he said. "And then I wouldn't."

Keller didn't say anything.

"Well, hell," Garrity said. "A man wants to take the bull by the horns, doesn't he? I decided I'd go out for a walk with a shotgun and have a little hunting accident. Or I'd be cleaning a handgun here at my desk and have it go off. But it turned out I just couldn't tolerate the idea of killing myself. Don't know why, can't explain it, but that seems to be the way I'm made."

He picked up his glass and looked at the brandy. "Funny how we hang on to life," he said. "Something else Sam Johnson said, said there wasn't a week of his life he'd voluntarily live through again. I've had more good times than bad, Mike, and even the bad times haven't been that godawful, but I think I know what he was getting at. I wouldn't want to repeat any of it, but that doesn't mean there's a minute of it I'd have been willing to miss. I don't want to miss whatever's coming next, either, and I don't guess Dr. Johnson did either. That's what keeps us going, isn't it? Wanting to find out what's around the next bend in the river."

"I guess so."

"I thought that would make the end easier to face," he said. "Not knowing when it was coming, or how or where. And I recalled that years ago a fellow told me to let him know if I ever needed to have somebody killed. 'You just let me know,' he said, and I laughed, and that was the last said on the subject. A month or so ago I looked up his number and called him, and he gave me another number to call."

"And you put out a contract."

"Is that the expression? Then that's what I did."

"Suicide by proxy," Keller said.

"And I guess you're holding my proxy," Garrity said, and drank some brandy. "You know, the thought flashed across my mind that first night, talking with you after you pulled my grandson out of the pool. I got this little glimmer, but I told myself I was being ridiculous. A hired killer doesn't turn up and save somebody's life."

"It's out of character," Keller agreed.

"Besides, what would you be doing at the party in the first place? Wouldn't you stay out of sight and wait until you could get me alone?"

"If I'd been thinking straight," Keller said. "I told myself it wouldn't hurt to have a look around. And this joker from the hotel bar assured me I had nothing to worry about. 'Half the town'll be at Wally's tonight,' he said."

"Half the town was. You wouldn't have tried anything that night, would you?"

"God, no."

"I remember thinking, I hope he's not here. I hope it's not tonight. Because I was enjoying the party and I didn't want to miss anything. But you *were* there, and a good thing, wasn't it?"

"Yes."

"Saved the boy from drowning. According to the Chinese, you save somebody's life, you're responsible for him for the rest of *your* life. Because you've interfered with the natural order of things. That make sense to you?"

"Not really."

"Or me either. You can't beat them for whipping up a meal or laundering a shirt, but they've got some queer ideas on other subjects. Of course they'd probably say the same for some of my notions."

"Probably."

Garrity looked at his glass. "You called my doctor," he said. "Must have been to confirm a suspicion you already had. What tipped you off? Is it starting to show in my face, or the way I move around?"

Keller shook his head. "I couldn't find anybody else with a motive," he said, "or a grudge against you. You were the only one left. And then I remembered seeing you wince once or twice, and try to hide it. I barely noticed it at the time, but then I started to think about it."

"I thought it would be easier than doing it myself," Garrity said. "I thought I'd just let a professional take me by surprise. I'd be like an old bull elk on a hillside, never expecting the bullet that takes him out in his prime."

"It makes sense."

"No, it doesn't. Because the elk didn't arrange for the hunter to be there. Far as the elk knows, he's all alone there. He's not wondering every damn day if today's the day. He's not bracing himself, trying to sense the crosshairs centering on his shoulder."

"I never thought of that."

"Neither did I," said Garrity. "Or I never would have called that fellow in the first place. Mike, what the hell are you doing here tonight? Don't tell me you came over to kill me."

"I came to tell you I can't."

"Because we've come to know each other."

Keller nodded.

"I grew up on a farm," Garrity said. "One of those vanishing family farms you hear about, and of course it's vanished, and I say good riddance. But we raised our own beef and pork, you know, and we kept a milk cow and a flock of laying hens. And we never named the animals we were going to wind up eating. The milk cow had a name, but not the bull calf she dropped. The breeder sow's name was Elsie, but we never named her piglets."

"Makes sense," Keller said.

"I guess it doesn't take a Chinaman to see how you can't kill me once you've hauled Timmy out of the drink. Let alone after you've sat at my table and smoked my cigars. Reminds me, you care for a cigar?"

"No, thank you."

"Well, where do we go from here, Mike? I have to say I'm relieved. I feel like I've been bracing myself for a bullet for weeks now. All of a sudden I've got a new lease on life. I'd say this calls for a drink except we're already having one, and you've scarcely touched yours."

"There is one thing," Keller said.

He left the den while Garrity made his phone call. Timothy was in the living room, puzzling over a chessboard. Keller played a game with him and lost badly. "Can't win 'em all," he said, and tipped over his king.

"I was going to checkmate you," the boy said. "In a few more moves."

"I could see it coming," Keller told him.

He went back to the den. Garrity was selecting a cigar from his humidor. "Sit down," he said. "I'm fixing to smoke one of these things. If you won't kill me, maybe it will."

"You never know."

"I made the call, Mike, and it's all taken care of. Be a while before the word filters up and down the chain of command, but sooner or later they'll call you up and tell you the client changed his mind. He paid in full and called off the job."

They talked some, then sat a while in silence. At length Keller said he ought to get going. "I should be at my hotel," he said, "in case they call."

"Be a couple of days, won't it?"

"Probably," he said, "but you never know. If everyone involved makes a phone call right away, the word could get to me in a couple of hours."

"Calling you off, telling you to come home. Be glad to get home, I bet."

"It's nice here," he said, "but yes, I'll be glad to get home."

"Wherever it is, they say there's no place like it." Garrity leaned back, then allowed himself to wince at the pain that came over him. "If it never hurts worse than this," he said, "then I can stand it. But of course it will get worse. And I'll decide I can stand *that*, and then it'll get worse again."

There was nothing to say to that.

"I guess I'll know when it's time to do something," Garrity said. "And who knows? Maybe my heart'll cut out on me out of the blue. Or I'll get hit by a bus, or I don't know what. Struck by lightning?"

"It could happen."

"Anything can happen," Garrity agreed. He got to his feet. "Mike," he said, "I guess we won't be seeing any more of each other, and I have to say I'm a little bit sorry about that. I've truly enjoyed our time together."

"So have I, Wally."

"I wondered, you know, what he'd be like. The man they'd send to do this kind of work. I don't know what I expected, but you're not it."

He stuck out his hand, and Keller gripped it. "Take care," Garrity said. "Be well, Mike."

Back at his hotel, Keller took a hot bath and got a good night's sleep. In the morning he went out for breakfast, and when he got back there was a message at the desk for him: *Mr. Soderholm—please call your office.*

He called from a pay phone, even though it didn't matter, and he was careful not to overreact when Dot told him to come home, the mission was aborted.

"You told me I had all the time in the world," he said. "If I'd known the guy was in such a rush—"

"Keller," she said, "it's a good thing you waited. What he did, he changed his mind."

"He changed his mind?"

"It used to be a woman's prerogative," Dot said, "but now we've got equality between the sexes, so that means anyone can do it. It works out fine because we're getting paid in full. So kick the dust of Texas off your feet and come on home."

"I'll do that," he said, "but I may hang out here for a few more days."

"Oh?"

"Or even a week," he said. "It's a pretty nice town."

"Don't tell me you're itching to move there, Keller. We've been through this before."

"Nothing like that," he said, "but there's this girl I met."

"Oh, Keller."

"Well, she's nice," he said. "And if I'm off the job there's no reason not to have a date or two with her, is there?"

"As long as you don't decide to move in."

"She's not that nice," he said, and Dot laughed and told him not to change.

He hung up and drove around and found a movie he'd been meaning to see. The next morning he packed and checked out of his hotel.

He drove across town and got a room on the motel strip, paying cash for four nights in advance and registering as J. D. Smith from Los Angeles.

There was no girl he'd met, no girl he wanted to meet. But it wasn't time to go home yet.

He had unfinished business, and four days should give him time to do it. Time for Wallace Garrity to get used to the idea of not feeling those imaginary crosshairs on his shoulder blades.

But not so much time that the pain would be too much to bear.

And, sometime in those four days, Keller would give him a gift. If he could, he'd make it look natural—a heart attack, say, or an accident. In any event it would be swift and without warning, and as close as he could make it to painless.

And it would be unexpected. Garrity would never see it coming.

Keller frowned, trying to figure out how he would manage it. It would be a lot trickier than the task that had drawn him to town originally, but he'd brought it on himself. Getting involved, fishing the boy out of the pool. He'd interfered with the natural order of things. He was under an obligation.

It was the least he could do.

Boudin Noir

R. T. LAWTON

AFTER WORKING AS AN UNDERCOVER AGENT for the DEA for twenty-five years, Robert Thomas Lawton (1943–) devoted himself to writing mystery short stories in five different series, producing more than a hundred tales for *Alfred Hitchcock's Mystery Magazine*, *Easyriders*, *Outlaw Biker*, and other magazines and anthologies.

One series of historical mysteries features an Armenian trader who solves crimes set in a dangerous region of tsarist Russia, one is set in the France of Louis the XIV with the despicable leader (self-proclaimed "king") of the criminal underworld of Paris, and another sequence of stories features the Twin Brothers Bail Bond firm, which accepts only special clients who must put up very high-value collateral that may not be entirely legal. Oddly, its clients seem unusually accident prone and seldom claim their goods.

On his use of initials for his byline, the author tells this story: "Being named after both grandfathers, the R. stands for Robert and the T. stands for Thomas. I started going by my initials decades ago while working with state and local drug task forces and every outfit had their own radio call numbers which was too confusing, so we used first names for radio call signs. But we had too many Roberts and Bobs. The case agent would come on the radio to say the bad guy was leaving the house and for Bob to follow him. At that point, all the surveillance cars would leave. So, I became R.T."

"Boudin Noir" was first published in the December 2009 issue of *Alfred Hitchcock's Mystery Magazine*.

BOUDIN NOIR

R. T. Lawton

I HAD LOVED Josette ever since she first showed me how to pick a fat merchant's pocket on the busy streets of Paris. And no doubt she would have loved me in return, had it not been for that damned Chevalier, the one we called Remy. He was a thief, a trickster, and a well dressed popinjay, who had no right to deprive me of her affections. No matter that she was nineteen at the time, and I a mere several years younger. Someday, I swore, I would make an end to Remy for having robbed me of my dreams. I would find a way to turn the tables on this fallen son of nobility and see how he liked it. Then my sleep would be much more at ease. Or at least without his constant interruptions.

"Boy, you're wanted."

Ah, that voice again. The very devil himself calls me from my slumbers. No doubt he has new torments to inflict upon my young life. I thought to pretend sleep longer, but that never seemed to work. Better to answer and get it over with.

"Leave me alone. It's barely morning."

"Morning? The sun's past midday. Get up."

I soon felt the toe of Remy's leather boot prodding through a ragged hole in my shirt, nudging several of my bare ribs as he continued with his tirade.

"King Jules requests your presence."

King Jules, he says, as if this second devil in my life were the anointed ruler of France and all its holdings. Even the least of us knew this so-called king was nothing more than a base-born tyrant who had seen fit to crown himself with a lofty title. At most, he ruled our motley underworld of thieves, beggars, counterfeiters, and trollops, and did it through fear of his personal wrath. That, and his grim bodyguard of muggers and dark-faced assassins used to enforce his every dictate. All souls within his grasp paid tithes out of their hard earned coins that each managed, by one means or another, to separate from the unwary citizens of Paris. It seemed the compass of Jules's fiefdom stretched from the old Roman ruins atop the Buttes Chaumont down to the River Seine, on across the bridges and deep into the shadowed backstreets of Paris. Even so, Jules was no king of royal blood like our young Louis the XIV, our *Roi Soleil*, our true Sun King.

To avoid another nudge in the ribs, I opened one eye and glared at Remy, but my tormentor was not one to be put off that easily.

"What, I wonder," he mused aloud, "could Jules possibly want with an orphan pickpocket? Especially one who is so . . ."

"I pay my share at tithing time," I quickly interrupted, "just like all the rest."

". . . so incompetent," he finished. "One who barely graduated from Mother Margaux's School for Orphan Pickpockets. I suspect that Mother threw you out rather than suffer further embarrassment from your lack of talent."

"I can pick a pocket as well as any other."

The Chevalier rubbed his chin. "The fact that you believe so troubles me."

He shook his head slowly, then stepped out through the open doorway of our hovel, a simple structure consisting of nothing more than three remnant walls of a small storeroom in one of the villa's outbuildings. A scrap of oiled canvas stretched overhead served to keep out rain and some of the wind. Just beyond the rubble doorway, the Chevalier paused long enough to give parting words.

"Tarry at your own peril, boy. Jules does not brook delays of his grandiose schemes, and it seems you are to have some involvement in his latest one." Then he turned and started off.

"I'm not afraid of Jules," I retorted as I threw a rock at the Chevalier's back, but that meddling popinjay was already beyond my range. He had no idea how lucky he was. Bah, enough of him.

Now that I was fully awake, with no chance of returning to sleep, hunger pains gnawed at my belly. Pushing myself up into a sitting position, I scrounged through a leather pouch kept tied at my waist. Tucked somewhere in this bag, among all the other small objects of value to me, was a wrapped length of blood sausage recently liberated from a common laborer who had obviously intended it as part of yesterday's noon meal. Had the man been more vigilant of his possessions, no doubt it would still be his. Of course, in thinking back on the incident, the lingering scent on the man's lunch basket should have warned me that my victim spent his days toiling in the endless sewers of Paris. I had been better served to have found a victim with a less fragrant job and a more decent lunch.

Preparing now to break my morning fast, I almost bit deeply into this meat delicacy when its slightly off aroma tickled my nostrils. I held the sausage closer to my nose and sniffed. That one quick whiff warned I had waited too long in this autumn heat. The meat was slowly turning. Still, I was hungry and my next meal could be a ways off. I sniffed again. No, not good at all. My appetite fled. Wrapping the blood sausage back in its scrap of cloth, I returned the package to my leather pouch. If nothing else, I'd find a way to slip the tainted sausage into the Chevalier's evening soup and let him be sick for a couple of days. It would serve him right for all the trouble he dealt me.

Still scheming on ways to even the score against Remy, I made my way to the enclosed yard where Jules usually held his private court. And there his majesty lounged upon his throne, a high-backed wooden chair that had seen grander times. Its cushioned seat of once-rich fabric was now threadbare and faded. Stuffing poked awkwardly out of rents in the cloth. Yet, Jules sat with his left leg resting over one arm of this declining chair as if the whole world were his. A wine goblet dangled from the fingers of his right hand.

"I am here as requested," I blurted out with small attempt to restrain my sarcasm. My resulting bow was much exaggerated.

Jules's eyes went narrow. He appeared to study me closely. I feared I'd gone too far this time, but then his face gradually creased in a smile, and I assumed I was safe after all. I grinned back.

"It was good of you to come so quickly," said Jules. "I have a very important job for you."

An important job. Ah yes, if no one else, Jules had a true appreciation for my light-finger talents.

"What would you have me do?"

Jules motioned me closer and lowered his voice. "I have it on good notice that the Abbess of the Benedictine Convent currently has a purse of gold coins in her possession."

"I see," I replied, but I really had no idea as to what he had in mind, other than he desired to somehow separate the Abbess from her gold and I was to play a part in this separation.

"The Abbess," he continued, "has business matters to attend in the city. As such, she will walk along a certain street this afternoon. In doing so, she is always careful to let few men, other than the Monastery Door Keeper, get close to her person."

Jules paused and appeared to have a weighty decision working on his mind. "What I need is a young boy, someone with a look of innocence, but one who has the proper skills to relieve her of her purse." He spread his hands as if to embrace me. "Without her knowledge, of course."

There came a long moment of silence between us. His eyes gazed into mine with a look of expectancy.

Oh.

Suddenly I realized this was my chance to prove myself to all in our little community. I moved quickly into the void. "I will not fail you."

Jules smiled again, but I must admit such contortions of his facial muscles always seemed to give a wolfish cast to his countenance. I was tempted to remark to him on this aspect of his appearance, but he can sometimes be touchy about the slightest comment, and I had no wish to lose the prospect of earning a few gold coins.

"I know you won't fail me," he replied, "and as your payment for this job, you may keep one fourth of all you acquire from the Abbess."

"One half is a better amount," I bargained.

Jules raised his right hand, palm forward, and curled his fingers. Immediately Sallambier, a hulk of a man, appeared out of a nearby nook and stepped to the right of Jules's throne. The hulk's mangled nose had the appearance of having once collided with the sharp edge of a paving brick. It was said that Sallambier had afterward lost his sense of smell. No matter to me, he was merely one more of King Jules's killers. I had no business with this man.

"One third to you for your services," concluded Jules as he watched for my reaction, "and no more."

Standing silently at Jules's side, Sallambier removed a long knife from the leather belt at his waist, using its pitted blade to slice chunks off a large red apple held in his other hand, and then stuffing those chunks into his maw of a mouth. No emotions showed on his pockmarked face, but his eyes seemed to linger on the vicinity of my bare throat.

Ha. The meaning of that look came quite clear to me. Even I knew that further bargaining on my part was obviously at an end.

"Done," I said, figuring I had already gotten more than I had hoped for when the day began.

"We are agreed then. Sallambier will take you to a place of advantage along the Abbess's route. All you need do is acquire her purse and bring it to me."

"And then we'll divide the coins?"

"Of course."

I waited to see if there was more, but my audience with King Jules was evidently over. Although I did notice him occasionally wrinkling his nose and glancing about as if something faint were in the wind.

Sallambier grabbed my elbow and led me onto the dirt path winding down from the Buttes Chamont and on past ancient stone quarries in the lower land. These open pits and underground tunnels from Roman times were now used as refuse pits by the citizens of Paris. A place for garbage and human outcasts. A hiding place for deserters from the army. I pulled my elbow free of Sallambier's grasp and fell into step behind him. Twice, he looked back over his shoulder to be sure I still followed.

After a long walk, we crossed a stone bridge over the Seine and passed by the great chains which would be stretched across the road by the nightwatch when curfew fell. Moving deeper into the city, where we were mostly ignored by the throngs of farmers, wives, and tradesmen going about their daily business, we made our way to a house near the building where the Abbess had business to conduct. Here, we waited in a doorway shadowed from the sun by the building's overhanging second story. Citizens crowded the street, parting once for a drover moving a few sheep to market, and once for a line of chained convicts being prodded along by stern-faced bailiffs. We averted our faces from the convicts lest one call out in recognition and ruin our scheme. Their passing gave a flutter to my stomach.

Hours dragged by. Gradually, I became bored and found myself nodding off in the autumn heat, when Sallambier suddenly reached over and flicked my ear with his thick index finger.

I started to yelp in protest but caught the warning in his face. He pointed at the doors to the building across the street. My gaze went to the Abbess and her Door Keeper descending upon the paving stones and proceeding in our direction. We waited until they passed. Then quickly, we stepped out of our doorway and moved into position, me behind the stout Abbess, while my newly appointed warden, the hulk with the mangled nose, edged closer to the elderly Door Keeper.

"Now," whispered Sallambier in his grating voice which seemed seldom used.

"In a minute," I muttered back.

I took a breath and prepared to steel myself.

"Now," he whispered again.

"Not yet," I murmured.

All would have gone well in the next couple of minutes, except Sallambier shoved me forward before I was truly ready. My right hand was barely reaching for the purse at her waist when his abrupt push from behind caused my left forearm to crash into her plump right hip.

She squawked in disgust and whirled in my direction.

My right hand had already lightly encircled her purse, but her sudden turn toward me drew the purse strings taut against her belt, and she felt the tugging at her waist. She quickly seized my right hand with both of hers, holding on with all the fervor of a drowning woman. And then she filled her lungs and screamed.

That high pitch split my eardrums.

Farmers and housewives, all the passing citizens of Paris, stopped their activities to see what was causing such a commotion.

I struggled to get free.

The Door Keeper rushed in to help his employer, but someone in the crowd jostled the old man, knocking him to the street. That's when I saw Sallambier stepping forward to politely assist the Keeper up from the paving stones, brushing him off and apologizing for any mishap. Several times, the old man tried to break away from Sallambier's helpful grasp, but he only succeeded in barely brushing the left shoulder of his Abbess with his outstretched fingertips.

At this new touch to her person, the Abbess paused in surprise, swiveled her head away from me, and drew in another deep breath.

I didn't wait for the second shriek. Taking advantage of this distraction, I wrenched my hand loose from the Abbess's clutch. Somehow, in all the turmoil, she managed to maintain hold on her precious purse still tied to her belt. No matter that, I ran for my very life, all the way to the Buttes Chamont.

At last, safely back at the ruined villa, I ducked into our hovel and collapsed on my bed, panting for breath. Sweat coursed down my heated face.

What to do now? I had escaped one trouble and was left confronting another. What could I tell King Jules? I'd obviously failed him. No purse to split two ways, even if my share was only to be a third. Of course, had I gotten the purse as planned, I could have lightened its contents a little before giving it to Jules for the agreed upon dividing. No chance of that now.

This whole mess of me being caught in the act was obviously all Sallambier's fault, but since his intervention with the Door Keeper allowed me to escape from the Abbess, I needed to be careful laying any blame on him. He might take it wrong, plus I obviously knew who Jules would then side with. No, no, I'd have to come up with a very good story for Jules, a believable one.

Two hours later, I was still polishing the details of my excuse and wondering if maybe it might just be best to hide out in the quarries for several days, when someone quietly entered the hovel.

"You were lucky to get away."

I quickly recognized the Chevalier's voice behind me and tried not to flinch.

"That's because Sallambier kept the Door Keeper from getting at me," I muttered. "Otherwise, I'd been locked up in the prison for sure."

"So, that gargoyle-faced assassin is now your hero?" inquired Remy in his know-it-all way.

"I didn't say I liked him, only that he helped me out of a predicament. Unlike some who pretend to be my friend and then act otherwise when trouble comes."

"Oh, he definitely helped you."

I detected a faint hint of sarcasm.

"How would you know?"

Remy sat down at the far end of my bedding and faced me.

"I was curious as to Jules's sudden interest in your pickpocket abilities, so I followed you and Jules's assassin into the city."

"I didn't see you there."

"Then you can say I did my job well. In any case, I watched Sallambier deliberately push you into the Abbess."

"His timing was bad," I freely admitted, but then I paused to consider Remy's statement. This was a good turn for me, now I had the Chevalier as a witness to verify my excuse to Jules.

I continued with my narrative. "But then you also saw Sallambier help me by detaining the Door Keeper."

"No, boy, the assassin did just as Jules no doubt instructed him to do."

"How so? Jules gave no such instructions to the man in my presence."

"I'm sure he didn't, but when Sallambier helped the Door Keeper up from the street and dusted off his clothing, he was actually busy making wax impressions of keys hanging from the Keeper's waist. You, my little friend, were supposed to be caught, a diversion to allow Sallambier to do as Jules intended. If necessary, you were expendable."

"What?"

"Exactly, so I contemplated what purpose Jules would have for keys to the Benedictine Monastery."

My feelings were still wrapped up in the betrayal of being taken for a fool. However, the Chevalier's words did explain why the Abbess's purse had felt lighter than Jules had led me to believe. That meant Jules had lied. He didn't really believe in my stealing talents. Oh, he and that mangled-nose monstrosity of his were going to pay for their trickery just as soon as I found a means for revenge. But in the meantime, I couldn't help being curious about the keys.

"And what did you decide about his purpose?" I inquired.

Remy gave me that arrogant smile of his. If he only knew how much I hated that look of having superior knowledge.

"The Door Keeper always carries at least two main keys on his person, one for the monastery itself, while the second key is rumored to fit the staircase door leading down from the interior of the Val-de-Grâce Church."

"Stairs descending beneath the church?" This was new. I crossed myself. "You mean, down into the eternal fires for heretics and sinners?" For good measure, I made the sign a second time.

Remy laughed.

"There are some who would call it a staircase leading to sin, but most, like me, consider it merely to be a source of very worldly pleasure."

I was confused. "What's on the other end of this staircase?"

"Do you not listen to gossip in the marketplace, boy? Perhaps you are too young and it is a matter of history now."

The Chevalier could be exasperating at times like these.

"Just tell me."

"Very well. After our Sun King was born, his previously barren mother promised the Benedictine nuns that she would build them a church as thanks. But there was a problem."

"What kind of problem?"

"When the original architect, François Mansart, started the foundation for Val-de-Grâce, he found a great emptiness beneath the ground."

"An emptiness like the pits of Hell?" I tried again.

"No, this emptiness was one of the network of tunnels from the old Roman stone quarries. What better place for the Benedictine monks to store their alcoholic beverage of brandy, sugar, and aromatic herbs? Thus, the monks built a staircase from the church down to the tunnel. That second key supposedly fits the door that goes down. It's my guess that Jules plans to steal the Benedictine liquor after Sallambier finds where it's hidden."

I nodded my head in understanding, but had no idea yet how to use this information to my own advantage.

Remy stood up to leave. To me, he seemed in a hurry.

"Where are you going?"

"To keep an eye on Sallambier while he makes his false keys from the wax molds. When he is almost finished, I will go before him and hide in the church to see if I am correct in my assumptions."

I rose from my bed and headed for the door.

"I'll go too."

Remy blocked my way and sternly shook his head.

"No, boy, you've gotten yourself in enough trouble for today. You stay here, and away from Jules."

I sat back down and played the role of reluctant, but obedient. Let Remy think what he would. For my part, the reluctance was real.

With a further warning to stay away, the Chevalier left me.

Of course I waited until he was out of sight. If he only knew that never would I force myself to be obedient to his demands. He had no claim on me.

My feet soon found the dirt path leading to the Valley of Grace. In my reasoning, if I went to Val-de-Grâce Church now, then I would be well hidden before either Sallambier or Remy arrived. And, since one must feed his stomach as well as his soul, I managed en route to acquire an unguarded crust of bread, two shriveled carrots, and a chunk of fairly fragrant cheese for my supper. By the time their shrill-voiced owner finished arguing with her husband, I doubted he would have much appetite for them anyway.

At the church, the door stood partly open with no one in sight, either outside or inside. Now the problem was to find a hiding place, one that Remy would not be likely to use for himself. As for Sallambier, he was probably busy making himself a key for the staircase door. He would come when the church was locked up and empty, assuming they locked the huge front doors at night. My knowledge of this and other facts about the actual workings of the church were sadly lacking. I felt a twinge of remorse in not having come here more often for the good of my soul, my very salvation. But, after my bread and cheese were gone, that feeling soon left me alone.

At the sound of leather scuffing on stone, I glanced hurriedly around. Someone was coming and I still had no good hiding place. I dived to the floor and crawled forward under one of the heavy wooden pews used by the rich folk. Incoming footsteps continued down the aisle. There was a pause, and then I heard the wood creak in a pew somewhere in front of my hiding place. A sinner no doubt, clicking his rosary and come to seek redemption. However, by the way this one kept sniffing loudly, I assumed he also had a bad cold and was praying for better health. For the time he took on his knees, his sins must have been many. Before his list of concerns with the Almighty had been completed, I nodded off into sleep on the stone floor.

I might have slept through until Morning Mass, but a cool chill on my backside and the grating squeak of opening and then closing door hinges brought me awake. Except for the flickering of candles set in rows along the walls, the light inside had a dim grayness to it. Still, it was good enough for me to watch the worn leather boots of a man as he proceeded down the aisle and across in front of the altar without a single drop to his knee as someone once told me you are supposed to do in a place like this. He then proceeded over to a door in the vestibule behind the altar.

This had to be Sallambier. I poked my head over the wooden pew and peeked, but the man had already unlocked the door and descended. As a precaution, I waited to see if anyone else followed. There was no other movement in the church. Remy's plans must have gone awry, else he was somehow already in front of me down the staircase.

The partially open door beckoned.

With great stealth, I left my hiding place and crept to the top of the stairwell. From down in the tunnel came soft sounds and the yellow glow of a torch disappearing along a stone corridor. It was either hurry, or be left behind in eternal darkness. My feet flew down the stairs.

Having reached the cellar floor, I hurried forward to the first branching out of the tunnel. It was dark to my front and dark to the right. I pressed against the left wall and peered around that corner. The man with the torch had stopped at another intersection and was using a piece of chalk to mark one of the walls. After he finished, I waited while he continued walking straight ahead. Before I could follow, he returned to the intersection and erased the previous chalk mark he'd made. Then he turned and drew a white arrow on a different wall.

Ah, I told myself, he must have run into a dead end in the tunnel. This time, when the man started off in a new direction, I let him get farther out of sight before I stepped out to follow.

I only got three steps.

A large hand covered my mouth, stifling any attempt to cry out. I tried to bite the fingers of that hand, but then another strong hand grabbed me by the scruff of the neck and lifted me off my feet. At my ear, I heard a whispered voice.

"Be quiet and I'll put you down."

I tried to nod my head in compliance, but my entire body was suspended by the neck and I'm not sure anything above that point could move.

"I told you to stay behind," continued the voice.

The ground felt good to be beneath my feet again. I rotated my neck to get the kinks out.

"Jules owes me for this afternoon's purse stealing," I retorted, "and this may be my only chance to collect my coins, one way or another."

"You didn't actually get the purse," countered Remy in a whisper.

"That was Sallambier's fault. You yourself saw him push me, and since an agreement is an agreement, Jules owes me. I won't let him cheat me."

Remy gave a grunt of exasperation, then we stood there in silence.

"Sallambier is leaving us behind," I said at last.

The Chevalier turned the setting on a bull's-eye lantern at his feet, and a single narrow ray of white pierced the tunnel's dark.

"Don't worry, boy, Sallambier will probably run into several filled tunnel shafts and other dead ends before he locates the monk's cache of Benedictine. We don't want to be too close in case he doubles back and finds us instead."

"He's marking the walls with chalk so he knows which corridors he's already searched," I volunteered.

"That's good to remember," Remy replied. "Now stay behind me." He picked up the lantern and set off down the tunnel.

To my right, I distinctly heard the skittering of little rat claws on the stone floor and thus made sure I did not linger far behind the Chevalier.

"Stay farther back," muttered Remy, "you're stepping on my heels."

Occasionally, we passed by iron torch brackets mounted on the walls. All brackets stood empty, but on the ceiling above them were soot and black scorch marks from previous torches over the years. At other twists and turns, we passed chiseled inscriptions in a foreign language.

"Those are Roman writings," remarked the Chevalier.

Twice we came upon stone engravings, and these seemed to interest the Chevalier the most. At these, he whispered to me tales of ancient gods, emperors, the history of a long ago civilization.

Bah, what did I care? I was here to collect what was owed to me. The next time Remy started one of his lectures on history and old literature, I went off on my own. After all, I could see the glow of Sallambier's torch reflected far down the corridor and it hadn't seemed to move for some time now. Maybe he had found the Benedictine cellar. I would go see.

Advancing noiselessly down the tunnel, I at last came to the doorway where Sallambier's torch, now set into an iron bracket, lit the roughly chiseled room beyond. I peered carefully around the edge of the stone entrance. Only a bare side wall was in view. I'd have to move over farther in order to see what was in this room.

Two steps sideways and my vision caught the rounded top of a wooden cask. Another step and I could see several barrels and casks stacked against the back wall. We'd found it. And then my view was suddenly blocked.

Sallambier.

Even in his surprise at seeing me, his reactions were faster than mine. For the second time this night, I was grabbed by the neck and lifted off the ground, only this time it was by the throat instead of the nape.

"I had wondered where you disappeared to after your escape from the Abbess," Sallambier grated in that raspy voice of his.

He carried me deeper into the Benedictine cellar. Then his eyes noticed the small leather pouch swinging from my belt, a place where most citizens kept money or other valuables. He turned to cast more light from the torch onto my person.

"What did you bring me?"

When he drew his knife I thought I was dead, but he merely sliced through the leather thongs on my pouch. It dropped to the floor. His fingers tightened on my throat as he bent over to retrieve the bag. I began drifting into unconsciousness, but I first remembered Sallambier stuffing my leather pouch into a pocket of his jerkin. It was later that the sudden slamming of my hindquarters onto the stone floor jolted me partially awake.

"I told you to stay behind me," growled Remy. His voice came to me through a fog.

At the moment, my brain had feathers in it and my throat too sore to reply. All I could do was stare at Sallambier's body stretched out at my feet as if he were sleeping. However, upon seeing the growing lump on the side of Sallambier's head, I was fairly sure that if the gargoyle were sleeping, then he'd had some assistance in the matter from Remy.

A strong hand grasped my shoulder.

"We'll have to move him to another part of the tunnels. You grab his feet."

I wanted to protest my condition, but soon found myself struggling with a pair of familiar looking worn boots. As much as my end of the hulk weighed, Sallambier must have stuffed himself with food during all his waking hours. In the end, I have no idea which part of the labyrinth we stashed his sleeping form in, nor where Remy left me while he cleaned up any evidence of our passing. I do remember Remy coming back with a canvas bag over his shoulder. His way was lighted by the bull's-eye lantern, and the extinguished torch was under his arm. He also paused at each turning of the tunnels to erase any white chalk marks.

At the top of the stairs, the Chevalier locked the staircase door behind us. We slunk out of thechurch like thieves in the night and headed home.

Remy quickly roused Josette from her slumbers. For a celebration is how he termed it. For my part, I didn't know what we had to celebrate. I had no coins for my efforts, and I vaguely remembered Remy tossing Sallambier's key to the staircase door into one of the garbage pits on our way back to the villa. No cache of holy liquor for us to sell to tavern keepers on the back streets. When I'd inquired about the key, Remy replied, "No gentleman steals from the church."

I could have believed him better, except for the clinking of glass bottles in the canvas bag he carried on his shoulder. Sure enough, to help us celebrate, Remy dragged a couple of bottles of Benedictine out of the bag and opened the tops. I reminded him about his statement concerning not stealing from the church.

"Stealing, my boy?" He laughed loud. "No, no, these few bottles are merely payment which I'm sure the monks, had they known, would have gladly given me for rescuing their entire Benedictine cellar from the greed of King Jules."

As I grew older, I was beginning to realize how full-grown people rationalized their behavior based upon their desires of the moment. The only distinction among them being that different persons used varying degrees of ethics in their decision making, whether it was King Jules or the King of France. Still in my youth, I didn't have this problem yet, but it meant I'd have to keep a closer eye on the Chevalier in future dealings. As for Jules, I'd left his chief assassin lost in the long twisting tunnels of the Roman quarries. That would serve as partial payment for Jules's debt to me. Remy was another matter.

And then I remembered. My leather pouch. I reached desperately for my belt.

"What are you doing so in such a frantic manner?" inquired Remy. "You act as if you had lost something."

"My pouch," I exclaimed. "It contained all my valuables."

"What could a poor pickpocket like you possibly have of value?"

"I had a length of blood sausage," I retorted before I recalled what I was going to use it for.

Remy laughed.

"*Boudin noir?* In these hot autumn days? You're lucky you didn't eat it. Even the ancient Greeks knew this dark pudding became poisonous if it set in the heat too long. It's pig's blood, cereal, and seasonings stuffed into the intestines of an animal. Better you forgo this delicacy until cooler weather."

Well, that did explain the lingering odor it had. But since Sallambier now had the blood sausage in his possession, that meant I'd not be able to slip it into Remy's evening soup and get some measure of revenge on him.

Then I pictured Sallambier and his constant appetite. When he awoke in the dark and spent hours trying to feel his way out of the stone labyrinth, he would no doubt be hungry. And when he rooted through my leather pouch stuffed into his jerkin, he would recognize the feel of a length of sausage.

At least I wouldn't have to worry about making amends to Sallambier and his pitted blade one dark night. No, years from now some Benedictine monk off course in the tunnels below Val-de-Grâce Church would probably find no more than rat-gnawed bones, a rusted knife, and some tattered clothes.

I was sure that the Chevalier wondered why the sudden smile on my face, but as I saw the situation, it was one down and two devils to go. I had all the time in the world to get even.

Rogue: Bernie Rhodenbarr

Like a Thief in the Night

LAWRENCE BLOCK

MANY MYSTERY WRITERS have been described as prolific, but few have been as versatile and as accomplished as Lawrence Block (1938–), who has produced more than a hundred full-length books and countless short stories and articles, many on the art of writing. While most authors are happy to create one series character that is popular enough to engage a wide readership, Block has somehow managed to give literary birth to a half dozen, the *second* most successful (after his iconic private eye Matthew Scudder) being Bernie Rhodenbarr, a reasonably successful burglar and a slightly less successful bookseller.

Bernie owns the nice little bookshop called Barnegat Book on the border of New York City's Greenwich Village on East Eleventh Street, between Broadway and University Place, not far from New York University. He is a mild-mannered fellow given to good-humored quips and observations about life's foibles. He enjoys his bookshop but also enjoys breaking into people's homes and stealing. Admittedly, he has been pressured into it for altruistic reasons on more than one occasion, but there's no denying he's proud of his skill. His bad luck is that on too many occasions he comes across murder as frequently as he does treasures.

His best friend is a lesbian dog groomer, Carolyn Kaiser, with whom he often shares a nice dinner and a bottle of wine. The first book in the series, *Burglars Can't Be Choosers* (1977), served as the basis for a dreadful film titled *Burglar* (1987) that starred Whoopi Goldberg as Bernie (I could not make this up) and Bobcat Goldthwait as Carl Hefler, her whacky dog groomer best friend.

"Like a Thief in the Night" was originally published in the May 1983 issue of *Cosmopolitan*; it was first collected in Block's *Sometimes They Bite* (New York, Arbor House, 1983).

LIKE A THIEF IN THE NIGHT

Lawrence Block

AT 11:30 the television anchorman counseled her to stay tuned for the late show, a vintage Hitchcock film starring Cary Grant. For a moment she was tempted. Then she crossed the room and switched off the set.

There was a last cup of coffee in the pot. She poured it and stood at the window with it, a tall and slender woman, attractive, dressed in the suit and silk blouse she'd worn that day at the office. A woman who could look at once efficient and elegant, and who stood now sipping black coffee from a bone-china cup and gazing south and west.

Her apartment was on the twenty-second floor of a building located at the corner of Lexington Avenue and Seventy-sixth Street, and her vista was quite spectacular. A midtown skyscraper blocked her view of the building where Tavistock Corp. did its business, but she fancied she could see right through it with x-ray vision.

The cleaning crew would be finishing up now, she knew, returning their mops and buckets to the cupboards and changing into street clothes, preparing to go off-shift at midnight. They would leave a couple of lights on in Tavistock's seventeenth floor suite as well as elsewhere throughout the building. And the halls would remain lighted, and here and there in the building someone would be working all night, and—

She liked Hitchcock movies, especially the early ones, and she was in love with Cary Grant. But she also liked good clothes and bone-china cups and the view from her apartment and the comfortable, well-appointed apartment itself. And so she rinsed the cup in the sink and put on a coat and took the elevator to the lobby, where the florid-faced doorman made a great show of hailing her a cab.

There would be other nights, and other movies.

The taxi dropped her in front of an office building in the West Thirties. She pushed through the revolving door and her footsteps on the marble floor sounded impossibly loud to her. The security guard, seated at a small table by the bank of elevators, looked up from his magazine at her approach. She said, "Hello, Eddie," and gave him a quick smile.

"Hey, how ya doin'," he said, and she bent to sign herself in as his attention returned to his magazine. In the appropriate spaces she scribbled *Elaine Halder, Tavistock, 1704,* and, after a glance at her watch, *12:15.*

She got into a waiting elevator and the doors closed without a sound. She'd be alone up there, she thought. She'd glanced at the record sheet while signing it, and no one had signed in for Tavistock or any other office on seventeen.

Well, she wouldn't be long.

When the elevator doors opened she stepped out and stood for a moment in the corridor, getting her bearings. She took a key from her purse and stared at it for a moment as if it were an artifact from some unfamiliar civilization. Then she turned and began walking the length of the freshly mopped corridor, hearing nothing but the echo of her boisterous footsteps.

1704. An oak door, a square of frosted glass, unmarked but for the suite number and the name of the company. She took another thoughtful glance at the key before fitting it carefully into the lock.

It turned easily. She pushed the door inward and stepped inside, letting the door swing shut behind her.

And gasped.

There was a man not a dozen yards from her.

"Hello," he said.

He was standing beside a rosewood-topped desk, the center drawer of which was open, and there was a spark in his eyes and a tentative smile on his lips. He was wearing a gray suit patterned in a windowpane check. His shirt collar was buttoned down, his narrow tie neatly knotted. He was two or three years older than she, she supposed, and perhaps that many inches taller.

Her hand was pressed to her breast, as if to still a pounding heart. But her heart wasn't really pounding. She managed a smile. "You startled me," she said. "I didn't know anyone would be here."

"We're even."

"I beg your pardon?"

"I wasn't expecting company."

He had nice white even teeth, she noticed. She was apt to notice teeth. And he had an open and friendly face, which was also something she was inclined to notice, and why was she suddenly thinking of Cary Grant? The movie she hadn't seen, of course, that plus this Hollywood meet-cute opening, with the two of them encountering each other unexpectedly in this silent tomb of an office, and—

And he was wearing rubber gloves.

Her face must have registered something because he frowned, puzzled. Then he raised his hands and flexed his fingers. "Oh, these," he said. "Would it help if I spoke of an eczema brought on by exposure to the night air?"

"There's a lot of that going around."

"I knew you'd understand."

"You're a prowler."

"The word has the nastiest connotations," he objected. "One imagines a lot of lurking in shrubbery. There's no shrubbery here beyond the odd rubber plant and I wouldn't lurk in it if there were."

"A thief, then."

"A thief, yes. More specifically, a burglar. I might have stripped the gloves off when you stuck your key in the lock but I'd been so busy listening to your footsteps and hoping they'd lead to another office that I quite forgot I was wearing these things. Not that it would have made much difference. Another minute and you'd have realized that you've never set eyes on me before, and at that point you'd have wondered what I was doing here."

"What *are* you doing here?"

"My kid brother needs an operation."

"I thought that might be it. Surgery for his eczema."

He nodded. "Without it he'll never play the trumpet again. May I be permitted an observation?"

"I don't see why not."

"I observe that you're afraid of me."

"And here I thought I was doing such a super job of hiding it."

"You were, but I'm an incredibly perceptive human being. You're afraid I'll do something violent, that he who is capable of theft is equally capable of mayhem."

"Are you?"

"Not even in fantasy. I'm your basic pacifist. When I was a kid my favorite book was *Ferdinand the Bull.*"

"I remember him. He didn't want to fight. He just wanted to smell the flowers."

"Can you blame him?" He smiled again, and the adverb that came to her was *disarmingly.* More like Alan Alda than Cary Grant, she decided. Well, that was all right. There was nothing wrong with Alan Alda.

"*You're* afraid of *me*," she said suddenly.

"How'd you figure that? A slight quiver in the old upper lip?"

"No. It just came to me. But why? What could I do to you?"

"You could call the, uh, cops."

"I wouldn't do that."

"And I wouldn't hurt you."

"I know you wouldn't."

"Well," he said, and sighed theatrically. "Aren't you glad we got all that out of the way?"

She was, rather. It was good to know that neither of them had anything to fear from the other. As if in recognition of this change in their relationship she took off her coat and hung it on the pipe rack, where a checked topcoat was already hanging. His, she assumed. How readily he made himself at home!

She turned to find he was making himself further at home, rummaging deliberately in the drawers of the desk. What cheek, she thought, and felt herself beginning to smile.

She asked him what he was doing.

"Foraging," he said, then drew himself up sharply. "This isn't your desk, is it?"

"No."

"Thank heaven for that."

"What were you looking for, anyway?"

He thought for a moment, then shook his head. "Nope," he said. "You'd think I could come up with a decent story but I can't. I'm looking for something to steal."

"Nothing specific?"

"I like to keep an open mind. I didn't come here to cart off the IBM Selectrics. But you'd be surprised how many people leave cash in their desks."

"And you just take what you find?"

He hung his head. "I know," he said. "It's a moral failing. You don't have to tell me."

"Do people really leave cash in an unlocked desk drawer?"

"Sometimes. And sometimes they lock the drawers, but that doesn't make them all that much harder to open."

"You can pick locks?"

"A limited and eccentric talent," he allowed, "but it's all I know."

"How did you get in here? I suppose you picked the office lock."

"Hardly a great challenge."

"But how did you get past Eddie?"

"Eddie? Oh, you must be talking about the chap in the lobby. He's not quite as formidable as the Berlin Wall, you know. I got here around eight. They tend to be less suspicious at an earlier hour. I scrawled a name on the sheet and walked on by. Then I found an empty office that they'd already finished cleaning and curled up on the couch for a nap."

"You're kidding."

"Have I ever lied to you in the past? The cleaning crew leaves at midnight. At about that time I let myself out of Mr. Higginbotham's office—that's where I've taken to napping, he's a patent attorney with the most comfortable old leather couch. And then I make my rounds."

She looked at him. "You've come to this building before."

"I stop by every little once in a while."

"You make it sound like a vending machine route."

"There are similarities, aren't there? I never looked at it that way."

"And then you make your rounds. You break into offices—"

"I never break anything. Let's say I let myself into offices."

"And you steal money from desks—"

"Also jewelry, when I run across it. Anything valuable and portable. Sometimes there's a safe. That saves a lot of looking around. You know right away that's where they keep the good stuff."

"And you can open safes?"

"Not every safe," he said modestly, "and not every single time, but—" he switched to a Cockney accent "—I has the touch, mum."

"And then what do you do? Wait until morning to leave?"

"What for? I'm well-dressed. I look respectable. Besides, security guards are posted to keep unauthorized persons out of a building, not to prevent them from leaving. It might be different if I tried rolling a Xerox machine through the lobby, but I don't steal anything that won't fit in my pockets or my attaché case. And I don't wear my rubber gloves when I saunter past the guard. That wouldn't do."

"I don't suppose it would. What do I call you?"

"'That damned burglar,' I suppose. That's what everybody calls me. But you"—he extended a rubber-covered forefinger—"you may call me Bernie."

"Bernie the Burglar."

"And what shall I call you?"

"Elaine'll do."

"Elaine," he said. "Elaine, Elaine. Not Elaine Halder, by any chance?"

"How did you—?"

"Elaine Halder," he said. "And that explains what brings you to these offices in the middle of the night. You look startled. I can't imagine why. 'You know my methods, Watson.' What's the matter?"

"Nothing."

"Don't be frightened, for God's sake. Knowing your name doesn't give me mystical powers over your destiny. I just have a good memory and your name stuck in it." He crooked a thumb at a closed door on the far side of the room. "I've already been in the boss's office. I saw your note on his desk. I'm afraid I'll have to admit I read it. I'm a snoop. It's a serious character defect, I know."

"Like larceny."

"Something along those lines. Let's see now. Elaine Halder leaves the office, having placed on her boss's desk a letter of resignation. Elaine Halder returns in the small hours of the morning. A subtle pattern begins to emerge, my dear."

"Oh?"

"Of course. You've had second thoughts and you want to retrieve the letter before himself gets a chance to read it. Not a bad idea, given some of the choice things you had to say about him. Just let me open up for you, all right? I'm the tidy type and I locked up after I was through in there."

"Did you find anything to steal?"

"Eighty-five bucks and a pair of gold cuff links." He bent over the lock, probing its innards with a splinter of spring steel. "Nothing to write home about, but every little bit helps. I'm sure you have a key that fits this door—you had to in order to leave the resignation in the first place, didn't you? But how many chances do I get to show off? Not that a lock like this one presents much of a challenge, not to the nimble digits of Bernie the Burglar, and—ah, *there* we are!"

"Extraordinary."

"It's so seldom I have an audience."

He stood aside, held the door for her. On the threshold she was struck by the notion that there would be a dead body in the private office. George Tavistock himself, slumped over his desk with the figured hilt of a letter opener protruding from his back.

But of course there was no such thing. The office was devoid of clutter, let alone corpses, nor was there any sign that it had been lately burglarized.

A single sheet of paper lay on top of the desk

blotter. She walked over, picked it up. Her eyes scanned its half dozen sentences as if she were reading them for the first time, then dropped to the elaborately styled signature, a far cry from the loose scrawl with which she'd signed the register in the lobby.

She read the note through again, then put it back where it had been.

"Not changing your mind again?"

She shook her head. "I never changed it in the first place. That's not why I came back here tonight."

"You couldn't have dropped in just for the pleasure of my company."

"I might have, if I'd known you were going to be here. No, I came back because—" She paused, drew a deliberate breath. "You might say I wanted to clean out my desk."

"Didn't you already do that? Isn't your desk right across there? The one with your name plate on it? Forward of me, I know, but I already had a peek, and the drawers bore a striking resemblance to the cupboard of one Ms. Hubbard."

"You went through my desk."

He spread his hands apologetically. "I meant nothing personal," he said. "At the time, I didn't even know you."

"That's a point."

"And searching an empty desk isn't that great a violation of privacy, is it? Nothing to be seen beyond paper clips and rubber bands and the odd felt-tipped pen. So if you've come to clean out that lot—"

"I meant it metaphorically," she explained. "There are things in this office that belong to me. Projects I worked on that I ought to have copies of to show to prospective employers."

"And won't Mr. Tavistock see to it that you get copies?"

She laughed sharply. "You don't know the man," she said.

"And thank God for that. I couldn't rob someone I knew."

"He would think I intended to divulge corporate secrets to the competition. The minute he reads my letter of resignation I'll be persona non grata in this office. I probably won't even be able to get into the building. I didn't even realize any of this until I'd gotten home tonight, and I didn't really know what to do, and then—"

"Then you decided to try a little burglary."

"Hardly that."

"Oh?"

"I have a key."

"And I have a cunning little piece of spring steel, and they both perform the signal function of admitting us where we have no right to be."

"But I work here!"

"Worked."

"My resignation hasn't been accepted yet. I'm still an employee."

"Technically. Still, you've come like a thief in the night. You may have signed in downstairs and let yourself in with a key, and you're not wearing gloves or padding around in crepe-soled shoes, but we're not all that different, you and I, are we?"

She set her jaw. "I have a right to the fruits of my labor," she said.

"And so have I, and heaven help the person whose property rights get in our way."

She walked around him to the three-drawer filing cabinet to the right of Tavistock's desk. It was locked.

She turned, but Bernie was already at her elbow. "Allow me," he said, and in no time at all he had tickled the locking mechanism and was drawing the top drawer open.

"Thank you," she said.

"Oh, don't thank me," he said. "Professional courtesy. No thanks required."

She was busy for the next thirty minutes, selecting documents from the filing cabinet and from Tavistock's desk, as well as a few items from the unlocked cabinets in the outer office. She ran everything through the Xerox copier and replaced the originals where she'd found them. While she was doing all this, her burglar friend worked his way through the office's remaining desks. He was in no evident hurry, and it struck her that he was deliberately dawdling so as not to finish before her.

Now and then she would look up from what she was doing to observe him at his work. Once she caught him looking at her, and when their eyes met he winked and smiled, and she felt her cheeks burning.

He was attractive, certainly. And unquestionably likable, and in no way intimidating. Nor did he come across like a criminal. His speech was that of an educated person, he had an eye for clothes, his manners were impeccable—

What on earth was she thinking of?

By the time she had finished she had an inch-thick sheaf of paper in a manila file folder. She slipped her coat on, tucked the folder under her arm.

"You're certainly neat," he said. "A place for everything and everything right back in its place. I like that."

"Well, you're that way yourself, aren't you? You even take the trouble to lock up after yourself."

"It's not that much trouble. And there's a point to it. If one doesn't leave a mess, sometimes it takes them weeks to realize they've been robbed. The longer it takes, the less chance anybody'll figure out whodunit."

"And here I thought you were just naturally neat."

"As it happens I am, but it's a professional asset. Of course your neatness has much the same purpose, doesn't it? They'll never know you've been here tonight, especially since you haven't actually taken anything away with you. Just copies."

"That's right."

"Speaking of which, would you care to put them in my attaché case? So that you aren't noticed leaving the building with them in hand? I'll grant you the chap downstairs wouldn't notice an earthquake if it registered less than seven-point-four on the Richter scale, but it's that seemingly pointless attention to detail that enables me to persist in my chosen occupation instead of making license plates and sewing mail sacks as a guest of the governor. Are you ready, Elaine? Or would you like to take one last look around for auld lang syne?"

"I've had my last look around. And I'm not much on auld lang syne."

He held the door for her, switched off the overhead lights, drew the door shut. While she locked it with her key he stripped off his rubber gloves and put them in the attaché case where her papers reposed. Then, side by side, they walked the length of the corridor to the elevator. Her footsteps echoed. His, cushioned by his crepe soles, were quite soundless.

Hers stopped, too, when they reached the elevator, and they waited in silence. They had met, she thought, as thieves in the night, and now they were going to pass like ships in the night.

The elevator came, floated them down to the lobby. The lobby guard looked up at them, neither recognition nor interest showing in his eyes. She said, "Hi, Eddie. Everything going all right?"

"Hey, how ya doin'," he said.

There were only three entries below hers on the register sheet, three persons who'd arrived after her. She signed herself out, listing the time after a glance at her watch: 1:56. She'd been upstairs for better than an hour and a half.

Outside, the wind had an edge to it. She turned to him, glanced at his attaché case, suddenly remembered the first schoolboy who'd carried her books. She could surely have carried her own books, just as she could have safely carried the folder of papers past Eagle-eye Eddie.

Still, it was not unpleasant to have one's books carried.

"Well," she began, "I'd better take my papers, and—"

"Where are you headed?"

"Seventy-sixth Street."

"East or west?"

"East. But—"

"We'll share a cab," he said. "Compliments

of petty cash." And he was at the curb, a hand raised, and a cab appeared as if conjured up and then he was holding the door for her.

She got in.

"Seventy-sixth," he told the driver. "And what?"

"Lexington," she said.

"Lexington," he said.

Her mind raced during the taxi ride. It was all over the place and she couldn't keep up with it. She felt in turn like a schoolgirl, like a damsel in peril, like Grace Kelly in a Hitchcock film. When the cab reached her corner she indicated her building, and he leaned forward to relay the information to the driver.

"Would you like to come up for coffee?"

The line had run through her mind like a mantra in the course of the ride. Yet she couldn't believe she was actually speaking the words.

"Yes," he said. "I'd like that."

She steeled herself as they approached her doorman, but the man was discretion personified. He didn't even greet her by name, merely holding the door for her and her escort and wishing them a good night. Upstairs, she thought of demanding that Bernie open her door without the keys, but decided she didn't want any demonstrations just then of her essential vulnerability. She unlocked the several locks herself.

"I'll make coffee," she said. "Or would you just as soon have a drink?"

"Sounds good."

"Scotch? Or cognac?"

"Cognac."

While she was pouring the drinks he walked around her living room, looking at the pictures on the walls and the books on the shelves. Guests did this sort of thing all the time, but this particular guest was a criminal, after all, and so she imagined him taking a burglar's inventory of her possessions. That Chagall aquatint he was studying—she'd paid five hundred for it at auction and it was probably worth close to three times that by now.

Surely he'd have better luck foraging in her apartment than in a suite of deserted offices.

Surely he'd realize as much himself.

She handed him his brandy. "To criminal enterprise," he said, and she raised her glass in response.

"I'll give you those papers. Before I forget."

"All right."

He opened the attaché case, handed them over. She placed the folder on the LaVerne coffee table and carried her brandy across to the window. The deep carpet muffled her footsteps as effectively as if she'd been wearing crepe-soled shoes.

You have nothing to be afraid of, she told herself. *And you're not afraid, and—*

"An impressive view," he said, close behind her.

"Yes."

"You could see your office from here. If that building weren't in the way."

"I was thinking that earlier."

"Beautiful," he said, softly, and then his arms were encircling her from behind and his lips were on the nape of her neck.

"'Elaine the fair, Elaine the lovable,'" he quoted. "'Elaine, the lily maid of Astolat.'" His lips nuzzled her ear. "But you must hear that all the time."

She smiled. "Oh, not so often," she said. "Less often than you'd think."

The sky was just growing light when he left. She lay alone for a few minutes, then went to lock up after him.

And laughed aloud when she found that he'd locked up after himself, without a key.

It was late but she didn't think she'd ever been less tired. She put up a fresh pot of coffee, poured a cup when it was ready and sat at the kitchen table reading through the papers she'd taken from the office. She wouldn't have had half of them without Bernie's assistance, she realized. She could never have opened the file cabinet in Tavistock's office.

"Elaine the fair, Elaine the lovable. Elaine, the lily maid of Astolat."

She smiled.

A few minutes after nine, when she was sure Jennings Colliard would be at his desk, she dialed his private number.

"It's Andrea," she told him. "I succeeded beyond our wildest dreams. I've got copies of Tavistock's complete marketing plan for fall and winter, along with a couple of dozen test and survey reports and a lot of other documents you'll want a chance to analyze. And I put all the originals back where they came from, so nobody at Tavistock'll ever know what happened."

"Remarkable."

"I thought you'd approve. Having a key to their office helped, and knowing the doorman's name didn't hurt any. Oh, and I also have some news that's worth knowing. I don't know if George Tavistock is in his office yet, but if so he's reading a letter of resignation even as we speak. The Lily Maid of Astolat has had it."

"What are you talking about, Andrea?"

"Elaine Halder. She cleaned out her desk and left him a note saying bye-bye. I thought you'd like to be the first kid on your block to know that."

"And of course you're right."

"I'd come in now but I'm exhausted. Do you want to send a messenger over?"

"Right away. And you get some sleep."

"I intend to."

"You've done spectacularly well, Andrea. There will be something extra in your stocking."

"I thought there might be," she said.

She hung up the phone and stood once again at the window, looking out at the city, reviewing the night's events. It had been quite perfect, she decided, and if there was the slightest flaw it was that she'd missed the Cary Grant movie.

But it would be on again soon. They ran it frequently. People evidently liked that sort of thing.

Rogue: Dortmunder

Too Many Crooks

DONALD E. WESTLAKE

WHEN WRITERS OF HUMOROUS CRIME fiction are judged, it is inevitable that they will be compared to Donald Edwin Westlake (1933–2008), inarguably the most consistently funny producer of laughs in the history of mystery fiction.

In *Two Much* (1975), the protagonist pretends to be twins in order to marry both twin heiresses; *God Save the Mark* (1967), winner of the Edgar for best novel, tells of the many people who try to cheat a man who wins a fortune; in *Jimmy the Kid* (1974), a gang tries to get rid of a monster child it kidnapped (much like O. Henry's "The Ransom of Red Chief"); in *Dancing Aztecs* (1976), a large cast of criminals compete to learn which of sixteen statues is the real treasure. But it is with *The Hot Rock* (1970) that Westlake assured immortality, producing the first book about John Dortmunder, a mastermind thief for whom everything goes wrong—through no fault of his own. In the debut novel, he and his gang are hired to steal a priceless gem, and then are forced to steal it again. And again. They even have to break *into* prison. It was memorably released on film in 1972, starring Robert Redford and with a screenplay by William Goldman.

Westlake produced about a hundred books, both under his own name and as Richard Stark (very tough crime novels about Parker, a remorseless professional criminal); Tucker Coe (highly sensitive, Ross Macdonald–inspired novels about disgraced ex-cop Mitch Tobin); Curt Clark (science fiction); Alan Marshall (early soft-core sex stories); Samuel Holt (about an ex-actor named Samuel Holt, now so typecast from a popular television series that he can't find work and turns to solving crimes), Timothy J. Culver (political thriller); Judson Jack Carmichael (a complex caper); and several others.

More than twenty of his books have been adapted for feature films, and he won an Edgar for writing the screenplay for *The Grifters* (1990), for which he was also nominated for an Academy Award. The Mystery Writers of America named him a Grand Master in 1993.

"Too Many Crooks" was originally published in the August 1989 issue of *Playboy*; it was first collected in *Horse Laugh and Other Stories* (Helsinki, Finland, Eurographica, 1990). It won the Edgar for best short story in 1990.

TOO MANY CROOKS

Donald E. Westlake

DID YOU HEAR SOMETHING?" Dortmunder whispered.

"The wind," Kelp said.

Dortmunder twisted around in his seated position and deliberately shone the flashlight in the kneeling Kelp's eyes. "What wind? We're in a tunnel."

"There's underground rivers," Kelp said, squinting, "so maybe there's underground winds. Are you through the wall there?"

"Two more whacks," Dortmunder told him. Relenting, he aimed the flashlight past Kelp back down the empty tunnel, a meandering, messy gullet, most of it less than three feet in diameter, wriggling its way through rocks and rubble and ancient middens, traversing 40 tough feet from the rear of the basement of the out-of-business shoe store to the wall of the bank on the corner. According to the maps Dortmunder had gotten from the water department by claiming to be with the sewer department, and the maps he'd gotten from the sewer department by claiming to be with the water department, just the other side of this wall was the bank's main vault. Two more whacks and this large, irregular square of concrete that Dortmunder and Kelp had been scoring and scratching at for some time now would at last fall away onto the floor inside, and there would be the vault.

Dortmunder gave it a whack.

Dortmunder gave it another whack.

The block of concrete fell onto the floor of the vault. "Oh, thank God," somebody said.

What? Reluctant but unable to stop himself, Dortmunder dropped sledge and flashlight and leaned his head through the hole in the wall and looked around.

It was the vault, all right. And it was full of people.

A man in a suit stuck his hand out and grabbed Dortmunder's and shook it while pulling him through the hole and on into the vault. "Great work, Officer," he said. "The robbers are outside."

Dortmunder had thought he and Kelp were the robbers. "They are?"

A round-faced woman in pants and a Buster Brown collar said, "Five of them. With machine guns."

"Machine guns," Dortmunder said.

A delivery kid wearing a mustache and an apron and carrying a flat cardboard carton containing four coffees, two decafs and a tea said, "We all hostages, mon. I gonna get fired."

"How many of you are there?" the man in the suit asked, looking past Dortmunder at Kelp's nervously smiling face.

"Just the two," Dortmunder said, and watched helplessly as willing hands dragged Kelp through the hole and set him on his feet in the vault. It was really very full of hostages.

"I'm Kearney," the man in the suit said. "I'm the bank manager, and I can't tell you how glad I am to see you."

Which was the first time any bank manager had said *that* to Dortmunder, who said, "Uh-huh, uh-huh," and nodded, and then said, "I'm, uh, Officer Diddums, and this is Officer, uh, Kelly."

Kearney, the bank manager, frowned. "Diddums, did you say?"

Dortmunder was furious with himself. Why did I call myself Diddums? Well, I didn't know I was going to need an alias inside a bank vault, did I? Aloud, he said, "Uh-huh. Diddums. It's Welsh."

"Ah," said Kearney. Then he frowned again and said, "You people aren't even armed."

"Well, no," Dortmunder said. "We're the, uh, the hostage-rescue team; we don't want any shots fired, increase the risk for you, uh, civilians."

"Very shrewd," Kearney agreed.

Kelp, his eyes kind of glassy and his smile kind of fixed, said, "Well, folks, maybe we should leave here now, single file, just make your way in an orderly fashion through—"

"They're coming!" hissed a stylish woman over by the vault door.

Everybody moved. It was amazing; everybody shifted at once. Some people moved to hide the new hole in the wall, some people moved to get farther away from the vault door and some people moved to get behind Dortmunder, who suddenly found himself the nearest person in the vault to that big, round, heavy metal door, which was easing massively and silently open.

It stopped halfway, and three men came in. They wore black ski masks and black leather jackets and black work pants and black shoes. They carried Uzi submachine guns at high port. Their eyes looked cold and hard, and their hands fidgeted on the metal of the guns, and their feet danced nervously, even when they were standing still. They looked as though anything at all might make them overreact.

"Shut up!" one of them yelled, though nobody'd been talking. He glared around at his guests and said, "Gotta have somebody to stand out front, see can the cops be trusted." His eye, as Dortmunder had known it would, lit on Dortmunder. "You," he said.

"Uh-huh," Dortmunder said.

"What's your name?"

Everybody in the vault had already heard him say it, so what choice did he have? "Diddums," Dortmunder said.

The robber glared at Dortmunder through his ski mask. "Diddums?"

"It's Welsh," Dortmunder explained.

"Ah," the robber said, and nodded. He gestured with the Uzi. "Outside, Diddums."

Dortmunder stepped forward, glancing back over his shoulder at all the people looking at him, knowing every goddamn one of them was glad he wasn't him—even Kelp, back there pretending to be four feet tall—and then Dortmunder stepped through the vault door, surrounded by all those nervous maniacs with machine guns, and went with them down a corridor flanked by desks and through a doorway to the main part of the bank, which was a mess.

The time at the moment, as the clock high on the wide wall confirmed, was 5:15 in the afternoon. Everybody who worked at the bank should have gone home by now; that was the theory Dortmunder had been operating from. What must have happened was, just before closing time at three o'clock (Dortmunder and Kelp being already then in the tunnel, working hard, knowing nothing of events on the surface of the planet), these gaudy showboats had come into the bank waving their machine guns around.

And not just waving them, either. Lines of ragged punctures had been drawn across the walls and the Lucite upper panel of the tellers' counter, like connect-the-dot puzzles. Wastebaskets and a potted Ficus had been overturned, but fortunately, there were no bodies lying around; none Dortmunder could see, anyway. The big plate-glass front windows had been shot out, and two more of the black-clad robbers were crouched down, one behind the OUR LOW LOAN RATES poster and the other behind the OUR HIGH IRA RATES poster, staring out at the street, from which came the sound of somebody talking loudly but indistinctly through a bullhorn.

So what must have happened, they'd come in just before three, waving their guns, figuring a quick in and out, and some brownnose employee looking for advancement triggered the alarm, and now they had a stalemate hostage situation on their hands; and, of course, everybody in the world by now has seen *Dog Day Afternoon* and therefore knows that if the police get the drop on a robber in circumstances such as these circumstances right here, they'll immediately shoot him dead, so now hostage negotiation is trickier than ever. This isn't what I had in mind when I came to the bank, Dortmunder thought.

The boss robber prodded him along with the barrel of his Uzi, saying, "What's your first name, Diddums?"

Please don't say Dan, Dortmunder begged himself. Please, please, somehow, anyhow, manage not to say Dan. His mouth opened, "John," he heard himself say, his brain having turned desperately in this emergency to that last resort, the truth, and he got weak-kneed with relief.

"OK, John, don't faint on me," the robber said. "This is very simple what you got to do here. The cops say they want to talk, just talk, nobody gets hurt. Fine. So you're gonna step out in front of the bank and see do the cops shoot you."

"Ah," Dortmunder said.

"No time like the present, huh, John?" the robber said, and poked him with the Uzi again.

"That kind of hurts," Dortmunder said.

"I apologize," the robber said, hard-eyed. "Out."

One of the other robbers, eyes red with strain inside the black ski mask, leaned close to Dortmunder and yelled, "You wanna shot in the foot first? You wanna *crawl* out there?"

"I'm going," Dortmunder told him. "See? Here I go."

The first robber, the comparatively calm one, said, "You go as far as the sidewalk, that's all. You take one step off the curb, we blow your head off."

"Got it," Dortmunder assured him, and crunched across broken glass to the sagging-open door and looked out. Across the street was parked a line of buses, police cars, police trucks, all in blue and white with red gumdrops on top, and behind them moved a seething mass of armed cops. "Uh," Dortmunder said. Turning back to the comparatively calm robber, he said, "You wouldn't happen to have a white flag or anything like that, would you?"

The robber pressed the point of the Uzi to Dortmunder's side. "Out," he said.

"Right," Dortmunder said. He faced front, put his hands way up in the air and stepped outside.

What a *lot* of attention he got. From behind all those blue-and-whites on the other side of the street, tense faces stared. On the rooftops of the red-brick tenements, in this neighborhood deep in the residential heart of Queens, sharpshooters began to familiarize themselves through their telescopic sights with the contours of Dortmunder's furrowed brow. To left and right, the ends of the block were sealed off with buses parked nose to tailpipe, past which ambulances and jumpy white-coated medics could be seen. Everywhere, rifles and pistols jittered in nervous fingers. Adrenaline ran in the gutters.

"I'm not with *them*!" Dortmunder shouted, edging across the sidewalk, arms upraised, hoping this announcement wouldn't upset the other bunch of armed hysterics behind him. For all he knew, they had a problem with rejection.

However, nothing happened behind him, and what happened out front was that a bullhorn appeared, resting on a police-car roof, and roared at him, *"You a hostage?"*

"I sure am!" yelled Dortmunder.

"What's your name?"

Oh, not again, thought Dortmunder, but there was nothing for it. "Diddums," he said.

"What?"

"Diddums!"

A brief pause: *"Diddums?"*

"It's Welsh!"

"Ah."

There was a little pause while whoever was operating the bullhorn conferred with his compatriots, and then the bullhorn said, *"What's the situation in there?"*

What kind of question was that? "Well, uh," Dortmunder said, and remembered to speak more loudly, and called, "kind of tense, actually."

"Any of the hostages been harmed?"

"Uh-uh. No. Definitely not. This is a . . . this is a . . . nonviolent confrontation." Dortmunder fervently hoped to establish that idea in everybody's mind, particularly if he were going to be out here in the middle much longer.

"Any change in the situation?"

Change? "Well," Dortmunder answered, "I haven't been in there that long, but it seems like—"

"Not that long? What's the matter with you, Diddums? You've been in that bank over two hours now!"

"Oh, yeah!" Forgetting, Dortmunder lowered his arms and stepped forward to the curb. "That's right!" he called. "Two hours! *More* than two hours! Been in there a long time!"

"Step out here away from the bank!"

Dortmunder looked down and saw his toes hanging ten over the edge of the curb. Stepping back at a brisk pace, he called, "I'm not supposed to do that!"

"Listen, Diddums, I've got a lot of tense men and women over here. I'm telling you, step away from the bank!"

"The fellas inside," Dortmunder explained, "they don't want me to step off the curb. They said they'd, uh, well, they just don't want me to do it."

"Psst! Hey, Diddums!"

Dortmunder paid no attention to the voice calling from behind him. He was concentrating too hard on what was happening right now out front. Also, he wasn't that used to the new name yet.

"Diddums!"

"Maybe you better put your hands up again."

"Oh, yeah!" Dortmunder's arms shot up like pistons blowing through an engine block. "There they are!"

"Diddums, goddamn it, do I have to *shoot* you to get you to pay attention?"

Arms dropping, Dortmunder spun around. "Sorry! I wasn't—I was—Here I am!"

"Get those goddamn hands up!"

Dortmunder turned sideways, arms up so high his sides hurt. Peering sidelong to his right, he called to the crowd across the street, "Sirs, they're talking to me inside now." Then he peered sidelong to his left, saw the comparatively calm robber crouched beside the broken doorframe and looking less calm than before, and he said, "Here I am."

"We're gonna give them our demands now," the robber said. "Through you."

"That's fine," Dortmunder said. "That's great. Only, you know, how come you don't do it on the phone? I mean, the way it's normally—"

The red-eyed robber, heedless of exposure to the sharpshooters across the street, shouldered furiously past the comparatively calm robber, who tried to restrain him as he yelled at Dortmunder, "You're rubbing it in, are ya? OK, I made a mistake! I got excited and I shot up the switchboard! You want me to get excited again?"

"No, no!" Dortmunder cried, trying to hold his hands straight up in the air and defensively in front of his body at the same time. "I forgot! I just forgot!"

The other robbers all clustered around to grab the red-eyed robber, who seemed to be trying to point his Uzi in Dortmunder's direction as he yelled, "I did it in front of everybody! I humiliated myself in front of everybody! And now you're making fun of me!"

"I *forgot*! I'm sorry!"

"You can't forget that! Nobody's ever gonna forget that!"

The three remaining robbers dragged the red-eyed robber back away from the doorway, talking to him, trying to soothe him, leaving Dortmunder and the comparatively calm robber to continue their conversation. "I'm sorry," Dortmunder said. "I just forgot. I've been kind of distracted lately. Recently."

"You're playing with fire here, Diddums," the robber said. "Now tell them they're gonna get our demands."

Dortmunder nodded, and turned his head the other way, and yelled, "They're gonna tell you their demands now. I mean, *I*'m gonna tell you their demands. *Their* demands. Not *my* demands. *Their* de—"

"*We're willing to listen, Diddums, only so long as none of the hostages get hurt.*"

"That's good!" Dortmunder agreed, and turned his head the other way to tell the robber, "That's reasonable, you know, that's sensible, that's a very good thing they're saying."

"Shut up," the robber said.

"Right," Dortmunder said.

The robber said, "First, we want the riflemen off the roofs."

"Oh, so do I," Dortmunder told him, and turned to shout, "They want the riflemen off the roofs!"

"*What else?*"

"What else?"

"And we want them to unblock that end of the street, the—what is it?—the north end."

Dortmunder frowned straight ahead at the buses blocking the intersection. "Isn't that east?" he asked.

"Whatever it is," the robber said, getting impatient. "That end down there to the left."

"OK." Dortmunder turned his head and yelled, "They want you to unblock the east end of the street!" Since his hands were way up in the sky somewhere, he pointed with his chin.

"*Isn't that north?*"

"I knew it was," the robber said.

"Yeah, I guess so," Dortmunder called. "That end down there to the left."

"*The right, you mean.*"

"Yeah, that's right. Your right, my left. *Their* left."

"*What else?*"

Dortmunder sighed, and turned his head. "What else?"

The robber glared at him. "I can *hear* the bullhorn, Diddums. I can *hear* him say 'What else?' You don't have to repeat everything he says. No more translations."

"Right," Dortmunder said. "Gotcha. No more translations."

"We'll want a car," the robber told him. "A station wagon. We're gonna take three hostages with us, so we want a big station wagon. And nobody follows us."

"Gee," Dortmunder said dubiously, "are you sure?"

The robber stared. "Am I *sure*?"

"Well, you know what they'll do," Dortmunder told him, lowering his voice so the other team across the street couldn't hear him. "What they do in these situations, they fix a little radio transmitter under the car, so then they don't have to *follow* you, exactly, but they know where you are."

Impatient again, the robber said, "So you'll tell them not to do that. No radio transmitters, or we kill the hostages."

"Well, I suppose," Dortmunder said doubtfully.

"What's wrong *now*?" the robber demanded. "You're too goddamn *picky*, Diddums; you're just the messenger here. You think you know my job better than I do?"

I know I do, Dortmunder thought, but it didn't seem a judicious thing to say aloud, so instead, he explained, "I just want things to go smooth, that's all. I just don't want bloodshed. And I was thinking, the New York City police, you know, well, they've got helicopters."

"Damn," the robber said. He crouched low to the littered floor, behind the broken doorframe, and brooded about his situation. Then he looked up at Dortmunder and said, "OK, Diddums, you're so smart. What *should* we do?"

Dortmunder blinked. "You want *me* to figure out your getaway?"

"Put yourself in our position," the robber suggested. "Think about it."

Dortmunder nodded. Hands in the air, he gazed at the blocked intersection and put himself in the robbers' position. "Hoo, boy," he said. "You're in a real mess."

"We *know* that, Diddums."

"Well," Dortmunder said, "I tell you what maybe you could do. You make them give you one of those buses they've got down there blocking the street. They give you one of those buses right now, then you know they haven't had time to put anything cute in it, like time-release tear-gas grenades or anyth—"

"Oh, my God," the robber said. His black ski mask seemed to have paled slightly.

"Then you take *all* the hostages," Dortmunder told him. "Everybody goes in the bus, and one of you people drives, and you go somewhere real crowded, like Times Square, say, and then you stop and make all the hostages get out and run."

"Yeah?" the robber said. "What good does that do us?"

"Well," Dortmunder said, "you drop the ski masks and the leather jackets and the guns, and *you* run, too. Twenty, thirty people all running away from the bus in different directions, in the middle of Times Square in rush hour, everybody losing themselves in the crowd. It might work."

"Jeez, it might," the robber said. "OK, go ahead and—What?"

"What?" Dortmunder echoed. He strained to look leftward, past the vertical column of his left arm. The boss robber was in excited conversation with one of his pals; not the red-eyed maniac, a different one. The boss robber shook his head and said, "Damn!" Then he looked up at Dortmunder. "Come back in here, Diddums," he said.

Dortmunder said, "But don't you want me to—"

"Come back in here!"

"Oh," Dortmunder said. "Uh, I better tell them over there that I'm gonna move."

"Make it fast," the robber told him. "Don't mess with me, Diddums. I'm in a bad mood right now."

"OK." Turning his head the other way, hating it that his back was toward this bad-mooded robber for even a second, Dortmunder called, "They want me to go back into the bank now. Just for a minute." Hands still up, he edged sideways across the sidewalk and through the gaping doorway, where the robbers laid hands on him and flung him back deeper into the bank.

He nearly lost his balance but saved himself against the sideways-lying pot of the tipped-over Ficus. When he turned around, all five of the robbers were lined up looking at him, their expressions intent, focused, almost hungry, like a row of cats looking in a fish-store window. "Uh," Dortmunder said.

"He's it now," one of the robbers said.

Another robber said, "But *they* don't know it."

A third robber said, "They will soon."

"They'll know it when nobody gets on the bus," the boss robber said, and shook his head at Dortmunder. "Sorry, Diddums. Your idea doesn't work anymore."

Dortmunder had to keep reminding himself that he wasn't actually *part* of this string. "How come?" he asked.

Disgusted, one of the other robbers said, "The rest of the hostages got away, that's how come."

Wide-eyed, Dortmunder spoke without thinking: "The tunnel!"

All of a sudden, it got very quiet in the bank. The robbers were now looking at him like cats looking at a fish with no window in the way. "The tunnel?" repeated the boss robber slowly. "You *know* about the tunnel?"

"Well, kind of," Dortmunder admitted. "I mean, the guys digging it, they got there just before you came and took me away."

"And you never mentioned it."

"Well," Dortmunder said, very uncomfortable, "I didn't feel like I should."

The red-eyed maniac lunged forward, waving that submachine gun again, yelling, "*You're* the guy with the tunnel! It's your tunnel!" And he pointed the shaking barrel of the Uzi at Dortmunder's nose.

"Easy, easy!" the boss robber yelled. "This is our only hostage; don't use him up!"

The red-eyed maniac reluctantly lowered the Uzi, but he turned to the others and announced, "*Nobody's* gonna forget when I shot up the switchboard. Nobody's *ever* gonna forget that. He wasn't *here*!"

All of the robbers thought that over. Meantime, Dortmunder was thinking about his own position. He might be a hostage, but he wasn't your normal hostage, because he was also a guy who had just dug a tunnel to a bank vault, and there were maybe 30 eyeball witnesses who could identify him. So it wasn't enough to get away from these bank robbers; he was also going to have to get away from the police. Several thousand police.

So did that mean he was locked to these second-rate smash-and-grabbers? Was his own future really dependent on *their* getting out of this hole? Bad news, if true. Left to their own devices, these people couldn't escape from a merry-go-round.

Dortmunder sighed. "OK," he said. "The first thing we have to do is—"

"We?" the boss robber said. "Since when are you in this?"

"Since you dragged me in," Dortmunder told him. "And the first thing we have to do is—"

The red-eyed maniac lunged at him again with the Uzi, shouting, "Don't you tell us what to do! We know what to do!"

"I'm your only hostage," Dortmunder reminded him. "Don't use me up. Also, now that I've seen you people in action, I'm your only hope of getting out of here. So this time, listen to me. The first thing we have to do is close and lock the vault door."

One of the robbers gave a scornful laugh. "The hostages are *gone*," he said. "Didn't you hear that part? Lock the vault door after the hostages are gone. Isn't that some kind of old saying?" And he laughed and laughed.

Dortmunder looked at him. "It's a two-way tunnel," he said quietly.

The robbers stared at him. Then they all turned and ran toward the back of the bank. They *all* did.

They're too excitable for this line of work, Dortmunder thought as he walked briskly toward the front of the bank. *Clang* went the vault door, far behind him, and Dortmunder stepped through the broken doorway and out again to the sidewalk, remembering to stick his arms straight up in the air as he did.

"Hi!" he yelled, sticking his face well out, displaying it for all the sharpshooters to get a really *good* look at. "Hi, it's me again! Diddums! Welsh!"

"Diddums!" screamed an enraged voice from deep within the bank. "Come back here!"

Oh, no. Ignoring that, moving steadily but without panic, arms up, face forward, eyes wide, Dortmunder angled leftward across the sidewalk, shouting, "I'm coming out again! And I'm *escaping*!" And he dropped his arms, tucked his elbows in and ran hell for leather toward those blocking buses.

Gunfire encouraged him: a sudden burst behind him of *ddrrritt, ddrrritt*, and then *kopp-kopp-kopp*, and then a whole symphony of *fooms* and *thug-thugs* and *padapows.* Dortmunder's toes, turning into high-tension steel springs, kept him bounding through the air like the Wright brothers' first airplane, swooping and plunging down the middle of the street, that wall of buses getting closer and closer.

"Here! In here!" Uniformed cops appeared on both sidewalks, waving to him, offering sanctuary in the forms of open doorways and police vehicles to crouch behind, but Dortmunder was *escaping.* From everything.

The buses. He launched himself through the air, hit the blacktop hard and rolled under the nearest bus. Roll, roll, roll, hitting his head and elbows and knees and ears and nose and various other parts of his body against any number of hard, dirty objects, and then he was past the bus and on his feet, staggering, staring at a lot of goggle-eyed medics hanging around beside their ambulances, who just stood there and gawked back.

Dortmunder turned left. *Medics* weren't going to chase him, their franchise didn't include healthy bodies running down the street. The cops couldn't chase him until they'd moved their buses out of the way. Dortmunder took off like the last of the dodoes, flapping his arms, wishing he knew how to fly.

The out-of-business shoe store, the other terminus of the tunnel, passed on his left. The getaway car they'd parked in front of it was long gone, of course. Dortmunder kept thudding on, on, on.

Three blocks later, a gypsy cab committed a crime by picking him up even though he hadn't phoned the dispatcher first; in the city of New York, only licensed medallion taxis are permitted to pick up customers who hail them on the street. Dortmunder, panting like a Saint Bernard on the lumpy back seat, decided not to turn the guy in.

His faithful companion May came out of the living room when Dortmunder opened the front door of his apartment and stepped into his hall. "*There* you are!" she said. "Thank goodness. It's all over the radio *and* the television."

"I may never leave the house again," Dortmunder told her. "If Andy Kelp ever calls, says he's got this great job, easy, piece of cake, I'll just tell him I've retired."

"Andy's here," May said. "In the living room. You want a beer?"

"Yes," Dortmunder said simply.

May went away to the kitchen and Dortmunder limped into the living room, where Kelp was seated on the sofa holding a can of beer and looking happy. On the coffee table in front of him was a mountain of money.

Dortmunder stared. "What's *that*?"

Kelp grinned and shook his head. "It's been too long since we scored, John," he said. "You don't even recognize the stuff anymore. This is money."

"But—From the vault? How?"

"After you were taken away by those other guys—they were caught, by the way," Kelp interrupted himself, "without loss of life—anyway, I told everybody in the vault there, the way to keep the money safe from the robbers was we'd all carry it out with us. So we did. And then I decided what we should do is put it all in the trunk of my unmarked police car in front of the shoe store, so I could drive it to the precinct for safekeeping while they all went home to rest from their ordeal."

Dortmunder looked at his friend. He said, "You got the hostages to carry the money from the vault."

"And put it in our car," Kelp said. "Yeah, that's what I did."

May came in and handed Dortmunder a beer. He drank deep, and Kelp said, "They're looking for you, of course. Under that other name."

May said, "That's the one thing I don't understand. Diddums?"

"It's Welsh," Dortmunder told her. Then he smiled upon the mountain of money on the coffee table. "It's not a bad name," he decided. "I may keep it."

PERMISSIONS ACKNOWLEDGMENTS

Lawrence Block. "The Ehrengraf Experience" by Lawrence Block, copyright © 1978 by Lawrence Block. Originally published in *Ellery Queen's Mystery Magazine* (August 1978). Reprinted by permission of the author.

Lawrence Block. "Keller on the Spot" by Lawrence Block, copyright © 1997 by Lawrence Block. Originally published in *Playboy* (November 1997). Reprinted by permission of the author.

Lawrence Block. "Like a Thief in the Night" by Lawrence Block, copyright © 1983 by Lawrence Block. Originally published in *Cosmopolitan* (May 1983). Reprinted by permission of the author.

Everett Rhodes Castle. "The Colonel Gives a Party" by Everett Rhodes Castle, copyright © 1943 by Everett Rhodes Castle. Renewed. Originally published in *The Saturday Evening Post* (May 8, 1943). Reprinted by permission of Christopher G. Castle on behalf of the estate of Everett Rhodes Castle.

Leslie Charteris. "The Damsel in Distress" by Leslie Charteris, copyright © 2014 Interfund (London) Ltd. Excerpt from *The Saint Intervenes* (a.k.a. *Boodle*) by Leslie Charteris, reprinted under a license arrangement originating with Amazon Publishing, www.apub.com.

Max Allan Collins. "Quarry's Luck" by Max Allan Collins, copyright © 1994 by Max Allan Collins. Originally published in *Blue Motel* (White Wolf, 1994). Reprinted by permission of the author.

Richard Connell. "The Most Dangerous Game" by Richard Connell, copyright © 1924 by Richard Connell; copyright renewed © 1952 by Louise Fox Connell. Used by permission of Brandt & Hochman Literary Agents, Inc. All rights reserved.

Bradley Denton. "Blackburn Sins" by Bradley Denton, copyright © 1993 by Bradley Denton. Originally published in *Blackburn* (St. Martin's, 1993). Reprinted by permission of the author.

George Fielding Eliot. "The Copper Bowl" by George Fielding Eliot, copyright © 1928 by *Weird Tales*. Renewed. First published in *Weird Tales* (December 1928). Reprinted by permission of Weird Tales, Ltd.

Paul Ernst. "Horror Insured" by Paul Ernst, copyright © 1936 by *Weird Tales*. Renewed. First published in *Weird Tales* (January 1936). Reprinted by permission of Weird Tales, Ltd.

Loren D. Estleman. "The Black Spot" by Loren D. Estleman, copyright © 2015 by Loren D. Estleman. Originally published in *Ellery Queen's Mystery Magazine* (March/April 2015). Reprinted by permission of the author.

Bruno Fischer. "We Are All Dead" by Bruno Fischer, copyright © 1955 by Bruno Fischer. Originally published in *Manhunt* (January 1955). Reprinted by permission of Nora Kisch on behalf of the Estate of Bruno Fischer.

Robert L. Fish. "Sweet Music" by Robert L. Fish, copyright © 1967 by Robert L. Fish. Originally published in *The Hochmann Miniatures* (New American Library, 1967). Reprinted by permission of MysteriousPress.com.

Erle Stanley Gardner. "The Kid Stacks a Deck" by Erle Stanley Gardner, copyright © 1932 by Erle Stanley Gardner; copyright renewed © 1959 by Erle Stanley Gardner. Originally published in *Detective Fiction Weekly* (March 28, 1932). Reprinted by permission of Queen Literary Agency, Inc., on behalf of the Erle Stanley Gardner Trust.

Erle Stanley Gardner. "The Racket Buster" by Erle Stanley Gardner, copyright © 1930 by Erle Stanley Gardner; copyright renewed © 1957 by Erle Stanley Gardner. Originally published in *Gang World* (November 1930). Reprinted by permission of Queen Literary Agency, Inc., on behalf of the Erle Stanley Gardner Trust.

Erle Stanley Gardner. "The Cat-Woman" by Erle Stanley Gardner, copyright © 1927 by Erle Stanley Gardner; copyright renewed © 1954 by Erle Stanley Gardner. Originally published in *Black Mask* (February 1927). Reprinted by permission of Queen Literary Agency, Inc., on behalf of the Erle Stanley Gardner Trust.

Erle Stanley Gardner. "In Round Figures" by Erle Stanley Gardner, copyright © 1930 by Erle Stanley Gardner; copyright renewed © 1957 by Erle Stanley Gardner. Originally published in *Detective Fiction Weekly* (August 23, 1930). Reprinted by permission of Queen Literary Agency, Inc., on behalf of the Erle Stanley Gardner Trust.

Edward D. Hoch. "The Theft from the Empty Room" by Edward D. Hoch, copyright © 1972 by Edward D. Hoch. Originally published in *Ellery Queen's Mystery Magazine* (September 1972). Reprinted by permission of Patricia M. Hoch.

William Irish. "After-Dinner Story" by Cornell Woolrich writing as William Irish, copyright © 1938 by Cornell Woolrich; copyright renewed © 1966 by Claire Woolrich Memorial Scholarship Fund. Reprinted by permission of JP Morgan Chase Bank as Trustee for the Claire Woolrich Memorial Scholarship Fund.

Gerald Kersh. "Karmesin and the Big Flea" by Gerald Kersh, copyright © 1938 by Gerald Kersh. Originally published in *Courier* (Winter 1938/1939). Reprinted by permission of New World Publishing.

Donald E. Keyhoe. "The Mystery of the Golden Skull" by Donald E. Keyhoe, copyright © 2016 Steeger Properties, LLC. Originally published in *Dr. Yen Sin* (July/August 1936). Reprinted by permission of Steeger Properties, LLC. All rights reserved.

R. T. Lawton. "Boudin Noir" by R. T. Lawton, copyright © 2009 by R.T. Lawton. Originally published in *Alfred Hitchcock's Mystery Magazine* (December 2009). Reprinted by permission of the author.

Stephen Marlowe. "The Shill" by Stephen Marlowe, copyright © 1958 by Stephen Marlowe. Originally published in *A Choice of Murders*, edited by Dorothy Salisbury Davis (Scribner, 1958). Reprinted by permission of Ann Marlowe.